DEATH'S COLLECTOR

DARK LANDS

BILL MCCURRY

BOOKS BY BILL MCCURRY

DEATH-CURSED WIZARD SERIES

Novels

Death's Collector

Death's Baby Sister

Death's Collector: Sorcerers Dark and Light

Death's Collector: Void Walker

Death's Collector: Sword Hand

Death's Collector: Dark Lands

Novellas

Wee Piggies of Radiant Might

For Caryl:
A lot of coffee under the bridge, my friend.

ONE

If they gave out brass medals for bad decisions, mine would drag me to the bottom of the ocean. My wife used to smile and tell me that, so it seemed harsh that one of my decisions ended in her death. When somebody you love dies, you know that your decision was bad.

When the gods went to war, I believed that a big slice of the killing would be my fault. My wise friends patted my shoulder and rolled their eyes behind me, and they whispered about my ego being the size of a bull's hanging parts. It was all terribly dignified in the way that certain people can insult you so much it's clear that they love you.

It didn't matter whether they loved me. They didn't grasp how wrong they were, and they haven't grasped it yet.

As the war began, I stood before one of the universe's great, incomprehensible powers. He had caught me being inattentive, and he bitched at me with such force that my ears and eyes were bleeding.

Why was I suffering this indignity? I had recently found myself close to dying. I had decided to live, and the universe creates suffering for the living. The universe doesn't give a damn about dignity, though. Dignity is a human invention.

The great, incomprehensible power that was bellowing and threatening me stood on the other side of a melting, smoking blue forest. Crazily, that didn't worry me as much as the little white birds that flew out of the vast black hole in the sky, shitting rubies and sapphires. I noted all these phenomena as if I were making a list of outrages to complain about later, or to repair when I had time.

I faced all of that as a sorcerer should: with false objectivity, some real disdain, and a facial expression that I hoped would appear detached. Then I made the mistake of glancing above the trees again, and I remembered that I did not want to know that what I saw was possible.

"Well?" The deep, crushing word battered me, and I staggered backward.

I lifted my gaze to the speaker's furnace-bright eyes, which forced me to observe his whole self, with apelike legs, a lizard-skinned human body, and a hawk-shaped head, displaying the least wholesome aspects of each creature. The monster's name was Gek, and his glare fell on me from a height of nearly three hundred feet.

I stood tall to answer him, but when I opened my mouth, only empty breath came out.

Gek lowered his already rumbling voice. "Do you understand me?"

"Well . . . probably not, Mighty . . ." I trailed off with my eyebrows raised.

"I do not have a title, and I need no compliments. Don't waste my time by telling me I'm wise or saying that my feathers are pretty." Gek lifted his head the way someone does when they really do want compliments but say they don't. His other name was Cheg-Cheg, Dark Annihilator of the Void and Vicinity. Anybody with a name like that had an ego that would take a regiment of soft-handed women to massage.

I almost succeeded in smiling. "I don't believe I understood you, Gek. I thought I heard you say that you want me to kill the Father of the Gods."

"No, that's ridiculous," Gek said, continuing to drool acid in streams onto the forest. "I don't expect you to kill Krak. That's impossible."

I waited for some sign of laughter on Gek's inhuman maw.

"You're going to assassinate him. Or rather, you will make sure that he is assassinated, which is almost the same thing."

I stared at Gek with my mouth open for a time that would have been embarrassing if I had been able to care what anybody thought of me just then.

"Well, you'll figure it out." Gek stretched his immense, knobby fingers. Each ebony claw stuck out from a fingertip as far as a man was tall.

I glanced down at Ella. She sat curled tight in the tall, purple grass, holding her head and weeping like a little girl whose dog had bitten her to the bone. I wished I could sit down and cry too.

Taking a breath so huge it hurt, I said, "Gek, why do you want Krak dead?"

The monster leaned forward and turned his head to examine me with one eye. "Don't you want him dead?"

I considered that for a second and then nodded.

"Don't worry about my motives then. You're my servant. Go kill who I say to kill."

I had agreed to become Gek's servant before I saw him sprout into a great, horrifying monster. I swallowed and said, "Now that I see your true self, Gek, you should let me change my mind about this servitude business."

Gek began descending as if he were walking down steps set into the ground. His head disappeared behind the forest. A few seconds later, he came out of the trees as a regular person of human size, paying no attention to the great barrelsful of acid that had drooled from his titanic mouth a minute before. He strolled toward me with a slight limp, helped by a cane.

Non-monstrous Gek was tall and thin, with blue-black hair and a beak nose, and he wore a green silk suit with high, black boots. He stopped three feet from me and said, "No. You can't change your mind."

To keep myself from cringing or running, I knelt to wipe Ella's cheeks and murmur that everything was fine. Then I said, "Gek, send Ella back home. She couldn't have known about any of this shit."

"No."

"You dog-knocking bastard!" I froze. The insult had just hurtled out of my mouth, and now I felt cold all over as I waited for Gek to destroy us.

Gek chuckled. "As I said, I like surly servants. No, I won't send her back. You can leave her here if you like. She will starve if she's not eaten by herds of tiny carnivores first. I have seen people die that way. It looks distressing."

I sighed. "You really can't kill Krak yourself? Seriously?"

"I prefer not to, and before that vein in your forehead ruptures, you're not going to kill him, either. You are unfit to assassinate the Father of the Gods."

After a moment of silence, I asked, "Why am I not fit?" I heard myself say that and marveled that I could criticize Gek for having a big ego.

"You've been broken too many times. And you're too old. Had we been discussing this ten years ago . . ." Gek shrugged.

"I don't understand what you expect me to do then!"

"You will protect the assassin. You will escort her and hand her the weapon."

"Who is her?" I asked.

"Your companion, Pil."

"What? She's not even grown!" I shouted.

Gek's lips twitched upward. "But she is. Traveling with you has prepared her for this murder. You have trained her for it. And be honest, do you think the God of War named her the Knife because she cuts her meat in nice squares?"

"Gek, why do you think I can even get her there, wherever *there* is?" I swallowed. "I have a shitty record of keeping the girls in my care alive."

"You can succeed now. I doubt that even you need to kill more than two little girls before you learn how not to do it."

I reached for my sword. "Damn you! You sticky, hobbling rooster!"

"That's better," Gek said. I found that my hand bounced away whenever it got close to my sword. "As I said, she's not a little girl. If you want her to die, go ahead and treat her like a child. Oh, I don't need to tell you not to mention any of this to Pil."

"Of course not," I lied. I had already been thinking about where to find her when we got back to the castle.

Gek smiled at me, the bastard.

I burst out, "Damn it! Just . . . damn it to my father's right fist! Why do you want all this? Pil and I are probably going to get killed, so what will it hurt for us to know?"

Gek gazed at me for a few seconds. "The gods are making war on us. If we lose, it will be a tragedy for the Void Walkers."

"Oh. Well, a tragedy would be a bad thing, for sure."

"It would be worse for mankind. The gods already treat you like pots full of jam to scrape out as fast as possible and toss on the ground. Does that sound accurate?"

"I suppose. Even a little poetic," I said.

"Well, it's not accurate!" Gek shouted.

Even though Gek wasn't three hundred feet tall anymore, I found myself lying on my back, tasting blood.

Gek limped up to stand over me. "It is inaccurate because the gods do not scrape you out as fast as possible. They could do it a lot faster. They could bring mankind to such a state of primitive coarseness you would gaze upon a stone-tipped spear as a wonder to be revered. Bib, only we can defeat the gods. We can defeat them only if the final battle begins with Krak's death. Only you can ensure that Krak dies that day."

I stared up at Gek, using my sleeve to wipe blood off my nose. "Bullshit. That is operatic bullshit built around a fact or two." It was a reckless and stupid thing to say, but I couldn't help it.

Gek smiled. "Six facts. You should question them all. I recommend that you do so while you run, because you're already being pursued."

"I suppose I should get going then," I said as I stood. I hadn't

5

given up on escaping this situation or cheating my way out of it, but I couldn't do that with Gek there watching me and suspecting treachery.

"I will send you back to the Denz Lands." Gek tapped his stick against the ground as he said it. "Once there, you should begin traveling immediately."

"Which direction?"

"At this point, it doesn't matter. Just don't stand still."

Before I drew another breath, I was standing beside my bed in the Denz Lands, inside the dim, chilly castle called the Eastern Gateway. I was naked, just as I had been when Gek took me away minutes ago.

Ella was standing beside the far wall, looking around with her blond hair falling into her eyes. She was wearing a long, blue cloak that suited her tall form. Blinking, she said, "That's odd. How did I get here beside the wall? And whose cloak is this?"

"We shouldn't have drunk that fourth bottle of wine, darling. I can't remember much after dinner, but you said you liked the cloak. Can you remember anything?"

Pulling at the cloak's ties, Ella examined the room. "No, I cannot. Bib, why is there an enormous ham under that table?"

That ham had been Ella's sword before Gek transformed it. Even when she had been disarmed, Ella had tried to bash in Gek's skull with the ham.

"I stored that there in case we ran short of food." I grabbed my trousers from the back of a tall chair.

Ella rolled her eyes, but she didn't seem fearful. Gek must have removed her memory of seeing his monstrous form. I wished he had removed my memory of that too.

I chatted with Ella while we dressed, and I considered how to send her away or leave her behind. Maybe Pil and I had to go fight the gods and die, although I wasn't giving up on finding a way around that. But Ella didn't have to go at all.

Ella smiled. "Come collect your weapon so we can practice in the yard." She glanced around the room. "I feel like hitting something, and you are something. Have you seen my sword?"

"No," I said, maybe a little too fast.

"Ah, so you have seen it! Did you take it away for Desh to enchant? No? For Pil to sharpen?" She grinned the way my sister would have when contemplating new jewelry.

"No. It's probably under the bed." I pointed. "I do need to talk with Pil, though, about a different thing."

"Bib! You're twitching like a sticky-fingered boy who stole a slice of cake."

"No, I just need to talk to her about sorcery," I said. "The gods. All those things you hate. You should come along with me—I'll explain everything! It's fascinating once you get past the immolations and sacrificing lambs and such. Very technical."

Ella made a face. "It's nothing dangerous, is it? If it's dangerous, I will accompany you."

"Nothing out of the ordinary," I said. I felt a wild urge to tell her it was nothing worse than murdering the Father of the Gods, but I smiled to push down that urge.

"Very well. I shall be in the training yard when you wish to find me. I almost defeated the guard captain yesterday, and I believe I have determined his secret." Ella kissed me and yanked open a cupboard to poke through it.

I marched down the hallway, intending to ride away as soon as I collected Pil. At least Ella would be safe, whatever happened.

When we had arrived five weeks ago, Desh and Pil had found a cramped storeroom on the ground floor and taken it over. Quite a few people now knew that the two sorcerers were busy in there enchanting crowns, building carriages that fly, and forging swords that burn with fire. It unnerved some people, but others found it novel and charming. I didn't know what Desh was really creating, but I felt sure it was not charming. It was more likely to be devious and destructive. Pil was a quick study, but she had only worked up to enchantments that were useful and nasty.

Pil answered the door when I knocked. The young woman normally wore her black hair braided out of the way, but now it hung tangled halfway down her back. She used a grimy hand with two black bruised fingernails to push a lock back from her face. The other hand propped a heavy hammer over her shoulder.

Pil had a striking smile that I had seen distract even unfriendly people. Instead of smiling at me, she barked, "What do you want? Can it wait?"

"No, it really can't."

She opened the door wider and jerked her head for me to come inside. "Desh will be back in a few minutes, and you'll need to leave then, so hurry up. I mean, don't meander and tell stories about the old days." She scowled, and I wondered what I had done to aggravate her.

I told Pil all about Gek and the assassinations, or I intended to. My first word became a sneeze instead. Excusing myself, I tried again but sneezed louder. I ran at the problem, pushing to get enough words out before Gek picked me up by the nose and slammed me into the walls, metaphorically.

A sneezing fit that left my eyes sore overcame me. Pil was holding out a rag that wasn't too dirty. Then she watched me with her head cocked.

I needed another tactic, and since I couldn't say anything about Gek or assassinations, I prepared to lie without shame. "Pil, I need a favor from you. It's a big one, and I'm relying on your help."

Pil held up a hand. "Bib, I'm sorry I was so rude to you, because I'm not mad at you. Well, really, I'm angry about you, or about me and you, and I've avoided this for as long as I can."

"Well, let's just avoid—"

"No, hush, I'm not done!" Pil grabbed a curved piece of metal off the workbench. "Do you remember this?"

"Sure, you found it in the Dark Lands. It's one part of a trident. You called it a 'dent, which I thought was kind of charming."

Pil shook the 'dent toward my face. "This is the broken weapon of a dead god, and do you know what it does? Nothing! All my enchanting has made it so magical it does not do a single darn thing!"

I waited, not sure what to say. I didn't want to get in the middle of another sorcerer's business, but Pil was throwing hers at me with both hands.

"This thing should be able to make people's bones turn to water," Pil snapped. "Or create a lake in the desert or make fifty people weep themselves unconscious."

"None of that sounds entertaining, or even useful except in limited circumstances."

Pil's eyes widened, and I stepped back in case she swung that hammer at me. Instead, she slumped as the air eased out of her. "That's not the point, Bib. Powerful sorcerers don't give charming names like 'dent to god-weapons. That's what I've concluded. What does that say about me?"

"That's a rather foolish way to think." I stepped toward Pil but reversed myself when she raised the hammer.

"That's my point! You try to protect me, so I'm leaving. Really, I'm not that angry at you, or not too much. It's just that when I leave, that will probably be the last time I ever see you, because you're old, and I'm inexperienced, and the world is pretty good at killing sorcerers. Hell, I guess I am angry! That's why I'm acting like a bitch, and I'm leaving tomorrow."

I stared at her and considered all that. I didn't quite know what Gek had in mind for Pil, but if she rode away on her own, I wouldn't be able to protect her. I skimmed right over the fact that she was leaving for that very reason.

It shouldn't take more than an hour to change her mind. I said, "I understand. You should leave, and I'd like a favor before you go. Ride with me this afternoon—"

"No! No more rides or errands or favors. I'm ready to go, and if I get distracted, it may take me another year to break free, so don't ask."

"All right." I smiled and hoped it looked sincere. "I won't stop you. Hell, I'll kick your ass until you go away. Just let me ride with you the first day or two. I have some things to teach you that we've never talked about."

I didn't even blink at the lies I was telling her. I had started to fear she'd be dead in a few hours if she went away alone.

"You're lying." Pil gritted her teeth.

"That hurts."

"Maybe, but you're not denying it. Ella told me how to tell when you're lying."

That stopped me. I thought back on quite a few lies I had told Ella in the past six months. I had told them for good, noble reasons. Hadn't I? I swallowed and then opened my mouth to lie about having lied. Desh shoved open the door, interrupting me. He strode in and glanced at me without slowing down. "Good, you're here!" He grabbed his sword, which was propped in a corner.

Muddled shouting came from the hallway.

"Something's happening at the throne room," Desh said over his shoulder as he rushed into the hallway. "It doesn't sound like something good."

I poked my head out and saw Desh running down the hallway, followed by our profane friend, Stan, whose tall, purple hat flopped with every step. Pil pushed past me and chased them, holding her bare sword. The 'dent was shoved into her belt.

"Shit!" I had lost control of events from the moment Pil opened the door. I couldn't have done worse if I had sat in the hall drinking wine and pitching rocks into the room without looking. I liked King Moris and wouldn't mind helping him, but if I had to hack him apart to keep Pil alive, that would be fine.

I ran after Pil, cursing every third step.

TWO

Off in the corner of the throne room, I shoved my sword into the knobby bastard of an imp, and he laughed at me the whole time I was killing him. I laughed back in his face, as if that would hurt his feelings. He giggled and farted divine air before all ten feet of him fell, dragging me down too. Death didn't mean a damn thing to his kind. By dawn, the gods would make him whole again, but not the thirteen men he had just torn up like paper. They weren't useful to gods and would stay ripped apart forever.

I stood and yanked my sword from the imp's chest while glancing around the enormous throne room. All the imps I had fought in the past had been hulking monsters. These, too, were so massive that their corpses lay in lakes of blood, as if they had been fountains of gore rather than the gods' mystical thugs.

The imps had appeared out of nothing and brought four dozen soldiers with them for a jolly assassination, or maybe a kidnapping. Pil, Desh, and I joined the fight late since we had to run through a good part of the castle to get there. By the time we killed the last imp, twenty surviving assassins were still carving their way toward the king, who was protected by only ten men. Weapons clashed, and the stone walls hurled the sound back at us. More guards were trick-ling in like beer from a near-empty keg.

Pil was now racing to save King Moris, but she slipped and slid on her belly across the bloody floor. She dropped her sword, which clattered away. Nobody bent to help her. I didn't pause to help, either, since killing our enemies would protect her life better than offering her a hand up.

Every invading soldier wore the same uniform, but only one hadn't drawn his weapon. I peered at this notable young man, who was tall and slim, and saw him slip something from a white pouch. Two seconds later, every king's guard dropped his weapon with a sound like glass breaking against the stone floor. A few invading soldiers lost their swords too. They cursed and glared at the man with the pouch.

"Sorry!" the man called out. "That one was my fault!"

I saw shards of sword blades strewn across the floor. The man had to be a sorcerer, a Binder creating hell and destruction with bones, carvings, and wads of unlikely crap he had enchanted. I changed direction toward him.

Some soldier pointed and warned the sorcerer I was coming. I promised myself I'd kill that man later, a promise I might forget to keep. The sorcerer spun to face me, reaching into a yellow cloth pouch. Some guard was yelling for everybody to fall back and protect the king.

The throne room was a looming stone box big enough to hold a market fair, and I had slain that jovial imp a fair distance from the throne. I was still sprinting toward the sorcerer when he pointed at me and rubbed a dirty-looking bit of cloth across his palm. It was hardly a terrifying act.

My feet lost all purchase on the floor, and I sprawled. I didn't slide as far as Pil had, but when I put a foot down to stand, it slipped right out from under me. The soles of my boots had become as slick as butter.

The sorcerer dropped the rag and smiled, displaying fine teeth, before he reached into a brown leather pouch. I was twenty feet away, but he advanced on me a couple of steps. Maybe his next attack would involve a stick, or a magical biscuit, or a virgin's earlobe, and he had to be closer before he could turn my heart to jelly.

I pushed up to my knees, pulled out my knife, and threw it at the man. It wasn't the most awkward stance for throwing. That would have been lying on my chest facing the other way. But it was tolerably challenging, so it gratified me to see the knife impale the lanky sorcerer's left forearm as he raised it to protect his throat.

The sorcerer's enchanted doodad flew out of his hand. It appeared to be a mummified mouse, but I never saw it again to confirm that. The man didn't cry out or even clutch his wounded arm. He reached for a canvas pouch, but he paused and peered at me when I made a show of fumbling with my sword. I also swayed a little but felt that dropping my weapon might be too obvious.

Once I steadied my sword, I rushed toward the sorcerer. I was not rushing too fast since I was walking on my knees, swinging my arms hard like a five-year-old.

The sorcerer made a mistake then. He should have backed away, pulled out another devastating mouse corpse, or whatever else he had with him, and destroyed me from a distance. Instead, he came at me with his sword.

An old man huffing along on his knees must not have terrified the sorcerer. The knife I had thrown might have been luck. Killing me by hand would conserve magical energy, which was always desirable for a sorcerer. And the man moved with the grace of a trained swordsman, so his tactic should succeed.

The sorcerer thrust at my heart, a solid attack that wasn't fancy except for his splendid form. I parried and thrust hard into his knee. When he yelped and tried to recover, I stabbed him just below the breastbone. He shuddered but didn't fall.

When fighting sorcerers, it is poor practice not to kill them right away in the most thorough manner possible. That can be grueling since sorcerers possess somewhat greater resilience than other people. The effort is worthwhile, because even a dying sorcerer can kill or cause immense harm. Hell, a naked, dying sorcerer is a respectable threat.

Still on my knees, I stretched up and sliced the sorcerer's throat. Blood sprayed from this fellow whose name I had never known.

Some god seized my spirit and stretched it straight up through the top of my head. A divine and cruel being was bringing me to the trading place. That was where sorcerers give up the things they love most in exchange for power that will make them suffer and die young.

As I left my body, I felt Pil grab on. It was a thing that sorcerers could do if they're quick and canny. I wished she hadn't done it. She probably wanted to protect me, but there wasn't a single way she could do that. There were plenty of ways for her to accidentally invite trouble from the gods, though.

Time could be perplexing in the Gods' Realm. The journey seemed to take a couple of seconds. However, while trading with gods, no time at all passes in the world of man. That resulted in occasional awkwardness with comrades in arms or spouses who might not understand such nuances.

I glanced around the trading place as well as I could without moving my head. Heat crushed me, and standing under the sun was like being punched. I ignored the forest and the flowers, even though they usually interested me. I didn't even pay close attention to the god inhabiting the marble gazebo, eager to take away every precious thing I was willing to give.

I found myself staring right at the sorcerer I had just killed. He looked fine, not bloody or even disheveled. He must have called on the gods a bare moment before his death and then convinced them to summon me.

From behind me, Pil called out, "Bib, are you all right?" Her voice sounded confident and even a bit offended.

I couldn't simply speak to Pil or to the sorcerer. I was supposed to be blind and deaf to everything here unless the gods intended me to perceive it. However, I could indeed see and hear everything the gods wanted to keep from me. I didn't know why, and the gods didn't even know I could do it. I preferred they not find out.

I also preferred they not find out that we planned to assassinate their father.

So, I pretended that Pil and the sorcerer didn't exist in this place. Instead, I announced, "Mighty Harik, you have summoned me with your lips, which are drier and more repugnant than lips fashioned from the private areas of many venomous reptiles. In fact, how do you convince your wife to kiss you? The Goddess of Life must be repelled."

Harik stepped out from the gazebo depths between two marble benches suitable for the asses of the gods. His black robe and hair stood out stark against his blandly perfect face. "I am the God of Death, and I am concerned with matters more profound than kissing. I leave that to Effla, Goddess of Love."

Two ragged imps like the ones we had killed in the throne room shuffled out and stood to Harik's left, one step behind him. I had never before seen Harik with bodyguards.

Harik continued, "However, that does bring us to your offense, Murderer. It is an offense against Effla."

"I offend a lot of people," I said. "Whatever I did to offend her, I volunteer to do it twice to you."

"You stole Effla's property. You have murdered the Gosling here."

"That's right, you took me away!" the sorcerer said in a high-pitched, almost sweet voice. It seemed odd for such a tall man.

"I am sorry about that, Gosling, but you came attacking me, and with imps along to harvest the arms and legs. So, I'm not too sorry."

Gosling snorted. "Of course you're not. You shouldn't be. It's the way sorcery works. We might be enemies today and allies tomorrow. Or we could have been."

I said, "That's mighty damn open-minded of you there, Gosling. I like speaking with a man of subtle thought. But let's keep any regrets in the sack for a minute. Harik, why are you screwing around with King Moris? He's an inoffensive old walrus. Why do you care if he exists, let alone send your toad-belly-dragging hooligans after him? Gosling, I don't mean offense by that."

The sorcerer grunted.

Harik paused. "We need not explain ourselves to you, Murderer." Then Harik whispered over his shoulder, "That's especially true with certain actions that he is too Void-sucking ignorant to contemplate."

"Hush, Harik." I recognized the Goddess of Love's whispered voice. "Don't distress yourself, dear. You won't be able to enjoy every little bit of the party tonight."

My spine shivered when I heard Effla's voice. In an instant, I wanted her so much that every other woman I had known seemed as coarse as a filthy wad of hair stuck to a goat's hind parts.

Effla whispered, "Besides, better opportunities have popped up." Her voice slowed to a breathy tease. "We could hurt the Murderer a delicious amount. Couldn't we?"

Harik whispered, "Hurt him? I would applaud that. But you just attempted to kill him and failed, as I predicted. Do you think I haven't tried? Do you want to bring the curse on yourself? Must I distract you with well-oiled demigods every hour?"

"It's lovely of you to offer," she whispered. "Watch me, dear brother." Effla slunk out of the shadows, her unblemished mahogany skin as smooth as gossamer, caressed by a silk gown in every simmering shade of red. Her blonde hair was disarrayed in such an enchanting manner that I wondered whether she had a team of demigods working to keep it that way at all times.

My legs trembled. Before I closed my eyes, I saw two imps follow her and stand to her right.

"Oh, Gosling!" Effla called out. "You have come for your final trade before death, a challenge that few sorcerers rise to meet. Congratulations, my darling! Let me be clear. You cannot save your own life, no matter what you ask for or receive."

If Gosling couldn't help himself out of his trouble, what did he want? I almost threw that out as an open question before I remembered that the gods might not intend for me to hear that part of the conversation. Seeing and hearing like a god could be exhausting.

"Wait!" Pil shouted randomly. "I want to make an offer first!"

Harik sighed. "Murderer, control your little friend."

I said, "Pil, please don't. It's my problem."

"Your problem is that everything is always your problem, and you won't let anybody else help you with your stupid problems!" Pil took a deep breath. "At your age, you can't keep having all these adventures by yourself. You're going to adventure yourself to death."

Harik frowned at Pil. "Silence! Knife, if you do that again, I will hollow you out and float you like a buoy, and Lutigan can be damned if he doesn't like it. If you want to stay, you must be quiet and respectful."

"Fine," Pil muttered, sounding like a teenage girl, which she was.

Effla rolled her eyes and whispered, "Just send her back."

Harik sniffed. "She's a weapon. We can better influence her if she's here."

"Are we done?" Gosling said. "Does anybody want to sing now or talk about life back on the farm? I want one-tenth of one square of power. In exchange, I will use the last decision of my life to hurt the Murderer."

Now it made sense. At the end of his trade, Gosling would be required to give the gods a year of his life, or ten years of other people's lives. He was about to give them ten years of my life. I had already lost ten years in just this way, and I might not have many more to lose.

Effla and Harik were nodding at each other. Effla said, "Done!"

Harik flourished the sleeve of his robe. "Now, for your fee. How do you wish to pay? With your own life, or with the lives of others?"

"Others," Gosling said. "Take all the years from the Murderer."

And there it was. Another ten years had been ripped off the end of my life. It wouldn't age me now, but I'd die twenty years sooner than my allotted lifespan—if I died a natural death. Of course, the chances of that were damn thin.

"To be sure I understand," Harik said, smiling, "you want all thirty years taken from the Murderer? Correct?"

"Yes." Gosling nodded.

"Hold on!" I shouted. "What happened to ten years? The last time I was here, you taxed us ignorant sorcerers ten years of life for each trade. What happened to that, you ass-biting lump of damnation?"

"Conditions are always shifting with the whims and eddies of the Void . . ." Effla offered a shrug so languorous I almost fell to my knees. "This is the new arrangement."

"No, wait!" I bellowed. Both gods flinched away from the sound of my voice and then stared at one another. In a calmer tone, I said, "Wait. This means that a total of forty years will be taken away from me. And I'm already over forty years old, so . . . when you send me back, will I fall over dead?"

"You might," Harik said.

"You're the God of Death!" I shouted. Both gods peered at me, and I lowered my voice. "You're the God of Death. Don't you know?"

Effla whispered, "Is he doing that thing with his voice on purpose? He shouldn't be able to. Is he an oddity, like a three-headed sheep?"

"I don't like it," Harik whispered in a drawl.

"Really?" Effla whispered and then sneered. "I am astounded. You don't like it. One of the deep mysteries of existence has been revealed, for we now understand that Harik doesn't like it. The Murderer is yours, so this is your fault! Assuming this is anything besides a coincidence, and I don't commit to the notion that it is!"

Harik hauled back, and I thought he would hit his sister. Instead, he punched the imp next to her on the side of the head. The hulking creature flew as if hit with a tree trunk, tumbled over a marble bench, and plunged to the gazebo's lowest level. It didn't move.

I wondered if I could get away while they were fighting, but Harik would just reach out and summon me again.

Effla had jumped out of the way with immense grace. Now she seized a thick, marble bench that must have weighed four hundred pounds. She hurled it at the imp beside Harik, and the creature didn't even flinch. The bench slammed into the monster's jaw and kept going, taking the imp's head with it as the body thumped onto the floor.

"You'll pay!" Harik whispered. "You'll pay for everything!" He bounded to Effla's remaining imp and kicked it in the side. The imp made a noise like a barn door collapsing and flopped over. Harik stuck out his chin at Effla.

Effla grabbed another bench and waggled it at Harik like it was a serving platter. She grinned and whispered, "Ah, brother, you are the most predictable of creatures. But I enjoy anticipating what you will do." She dropped the bench with a slam, and the two embraced.

It was a long embrace. I felt uncomfortable, but I couldn't turn away. I closed my eyes and said, "Harik? Effla? Are you still there? Can I go now?"

"No!" Harik said. "Just wait there."

Effla whispered, "All right, let's run through this. We can't kill him unless we want to be cursed. So, we're not killing him, not at all. He just happens to be among those whose lifespans we have chosen not to know."

Harik nodded. "He and the other twelve. Did I say that I don't like this?"

"Pish, we are not at fault. Even though the fee is thirty years, we can't know with certainty that it will kill him. We're just following the rules we set for everybody. Well, for thirteen people. If he plops down on his bottom dead when he gets back, that's not our fault. No one could reasonably say we killed him, so no curse." Effla smiled.

I closed my eyes again so I wouldn't run over and beg her to make love to me until I died.

Harik whispered, "I do not feel confident about avoiding the curse in this fashion. We cannot fool the laws of existence. Krak's hairy chin, we can't even fool ourselves. Wait—I think the Murderer twitched. Do you suppose he's listening to us?"

Both gods examined me with disturbing intensity.

"Never mind," Effla whispered. "He's too dim to understand anything he hears."

Harik nodded and spoke out, "Diversions of far grander signifi-cance await us, so we—"

"No!" Pil burst in. "Whatever you're doing, just no." She took a deep breath. "Take the thirty years from me. That much time will kill him, but I'm young."

"Hah!" Gosling laughed.

Pil lifted her chin. "At least take half the years from me!"

Harik said, "Knife, that is entirely enough out of you. And you too, Murderer. Goodbye."

I didn't even have time for a ripe insult before he flung me back into the world of man.

I returned to the throne room at the precise moment I left. As Gosling toppled over, I waited to die, breathless and still on my knees. I was so distracted that a boy could have walked up and killed me using a bent spoon.

But I didn't die.

Still on my knees, I turned toward Pil, who had finished sliding across the floor and then gotten to her feet. She was blinking at me. Her lips were trembling, and I could see the pulse in her neck.

A soldier who ought to have been attacking the king turned away from the assault for no reason I have ever been able to understand. It put him right behind Pil. I shouted at her, but she just stared at me. I reached for my knife to throw it, but all I had was an empty sheath.

The soldier swung his sword and struck Pil on the back of the neck. She fell straight down with all her limbs slack, settling in an untidy pile. Her blood welled out into the generous bloody pool already spreading across the king's floor.

THREE

A sorcerer rarely achieves his ends through an overwhelming onslaught of mercy.

When I first met Pil, I decided to kill her. She was a sorcerer who had tried to swindle me, had cursed at me, and had pressed a knife against tender parts of my body. I ought to have killed her, and I could have convinced a blind mule to agree and cheer me on while I did it.

I let Pil live instead, but not because I gave much of a damn about her. I had just seen too many girls die and found I couldn't kill another one just then, even if it meant she'd creep up with a big rock and smash me as I slept.

In the months since I spared her, Pil had twice betrayed me, once with a knife aimed at my groin. I damn near died both times, and I must have been a softhearted boob for not murdering her right then.

I didn't murder her, though, and in between betrayals, Pil had risked herself over and over to help me. Hell, she had just offered thirty years of her life to save mine. Pil was my disrespectful, dangerous, unpredictable friend, and I didn't mind. That was one more friend than most sorcerers had.

After Pil fell wounded in King Moris's throne room, I crawled to my feet and fell right back down when my boots slipped like jelly on glass. I cursed, implying that Krak's manhood would fit in an eggshell, as I half crawled, half slid across the bloody floor toward her.

The soldier who had cut Pil's neck glanced at me, smirked, and ran to rejoin the attack on the king. I promised myself I would kill him later, and I didn't intend to forget that promise.

Lying with her legs bent under her and one arm wrenched aside, Pil looked dead. The inch-deep sword wound across the back of her neck made it likely. I pulled a green band of magical energy out of the air to explore her neck and head.

Pil was alive but couldn't last more than a minute, maybe no more than seconds. Her wound was so tricky that a minute probably wouldn't be enough for me to save her. Three minutes might not be enough. I pulled another green band and got to work anyway.

I flinched when light burst from the ceiling and blinded me. I almost fumbled my work away but held steady. The light was the kind of thing Desh might do when outnumbered. If he and Stan had held their eyes shut, then they could cut down a lot of blind and bumbling attackers.

None of that would help Pil. I felt sick when she stopped breathing, but after ten seconds, she took a shallow breath. I tried to work faster without screwing up too much. Another ten seconds, and she hadn't yet breathed again.

Some god dragged my spirit upward. I tried to roar a curse on the brief trip to the trading arena, but it was like yelling with my head underwater.

I had been bargaining in the Gods' Realm less than a minute ago, and gods rarely called sorcerers again right after a trade. In fact, sometimes they would reject any contact for months. I felt damn suspicious about this.

I was still cursing when I popped out into the trading place, shouting, ". . . shaggy-assed crotch goiters down through eternity!" I stopped talking. Out of all the principles I had learned while trading with the gods, only one was invariably true: getting angry makes everything worse. I imagined taking a deep breath.

I hadn't expected the weather in the Gods' Realm to change in less than a minute, but now dense rain drove straight down. I could hardly see past the edge of my muddy spot. "Mighty Harik, did you forget about some horrible disease you wanted to afflict me with? Want to fill my stomach with scorpions and lye? For the sake of Krak, don't read to me from one of your plays. That would be true pain."

"What wit, Murderer. I almost regret that you will certainly die soon. Never mind about that, for the day is filled with great moment. I am prepared to aid you." Through the rain I saw a dark outline at the center of the gazebo, and I assumed it was Harik.

I paused. "So, you . . . are prepared to aid me." I loaded the words up with all the sarcasm I could gather.

Harik seemed immune to my mocking. "Indeed, aid you. You and the Knife are experiencing great difficulty just now. I can provide vital assistance in exchange for specific future consideration."

"So, you'll help a little with my immediate misfortune, but only if I agree to face some catastrophe later."

"Catastrophe. I find that rather hyperbolic."

I had recently come to understand that the gods' greatest bargaining advantage wasn't their power or their knowledge. They simply understood time better than men did. A man will always value today more than any number of future days, because who knows what may happen by then?

So, men were always in a damn rush about everything. The immortal gods were not, and it pleased the gods to help a sorcerer today for a stiff fee, knowing that whatever the shortsighted sorcerer asked for would likely destroy him in a few years.

It did me no good to understand this, because my problem with time was of the immediate sort. Pil needed more of it, or she'd die.

I said, "Harik, you dank, perverted ghost of your former lovers' dismay, I have nothing important to do just now. What do you have in mind?"

"You cannot save the Knife without more time."

That was certainly true, so I said, "Maybe."

Harik sniffed. "For my side of the bargain, I will extend her life by half a minute. If you cannot save her with that assistance, you are truly as worthless as everyone says."

"Wait, why would you even make an offer to help me?" I asked.

"Think, Murderer. Will this extend your life?"

"Not unless Pil learns to make people live forever."

"This will not keep you alive. It is not helpful to your well-being. It might even harm you. Do you agree?"

I paused, wishing I could risk a big sigh. "I want an hour, not a shitty little half a minute."

Harik paused. "Rather than circling one another like mating rhinos, I will lay out what I offer and what I want. If you do not wish to accept, you may go back and watch the Knife die. Don't even bother to bargain—this is what we are doing. I will extend the Knife's existence for as long as you can hold your breath. If you cannot save her, that is your own failure."

I said, "Before I answer, I'd like to call you a bitter, greasy patch of red spots on the butt of creation. Now, I might agree to these terms depending on what you want."

"Excellent. We shall discuss the murders you owe me."

"I don't have anything to say about that." I owed Harik a certain number of killings, and only he knew what that number was. I had already decided that I couldn't murder enough people in one lifetime to satisfy the God of Death. I would be indebted to him until I died, or maybe longer.

Harik said, "Then you may listen to me speak. I have become concerned that you will renege on our arrangement by inconsiderately dying in a premature fashion. Perhaps by tomorrow or in a few days. That is unacceptable, so I am calling in your debt." Harik paused, and I realized he was waiting for me to say something.

"What does that mean, you clump of toad guts?"

"Toad guts? Truly, your wits are dispersing. Never mind. You must finish slaying the number of people I require, and you must do it by the fifth sunset from now."

"Ah." My heart started beating in my ears. "How many killings is that?"

"Fah! You remember the terms of our deal. You may not know the number."

I almost glared at him. "No! That's an unreasonable and lousy thing to do! It breaks the spirit of our bargain."

Harik leaped out of the gazebo and emerged from the rain like a diving hawk. His sandaled toes landed touching the muddy patch where I stood. "Murderer, I decide what is proper. I could demand that the debt be paid at any time for no further consideration. That's a well-accepted practice in commerce and in divine bargaining. The other parts of our deal remain in force, including the condition that you shall not know how many people you must kill to retire the debt." He leaned toward me. "I am offering you compensation, which is an act of incomprehensible generosity on my part."

"Mighty Harik, Your Magnificence, whose glance wipes out armies and whose breath destroys nations . . ." Some toadying couldn't hurt at that point. "I will be better able to succeed if I know how many people to kill. Having five months instead of five days would help too."

Harik smiled. "You have had forty years taken from the span of your life. I do not think you have five more months to live."

"But—"

"Don't believe me to be heartless," Harik said. "I offer a bonus if you kill the requisite number of people within five days. I will restore the forty years of life that I have taken from you. You will find yourself unburdened!"

"Just like that? You'll wipe out all my debts?"

"Must you question everything? If I offered to make you emperor of the world, you would ask whether the royal undergarments were scratchy. No, you agreed to this obligation years ago. Now you must accept the consequences, good and bad, which were entirely foreseeable by any person who does not drink as much as you. Meet your commitment by the fifth sunset, and you may not know how many you must murder. Fail and suffer, or succeed and be rewarded."

Harik was staring at me from a few feet away. I tried not to close my eyes or even blink much. This bargain was the only way I could think of to save Pil, and Harik was right: I probably didn't have much life remaining.

Maybe I could avoid killing a bunch of people unnecessarily by ignoring Harik's goal. "Mighty Harik, what happens if the fifth sunset arrives, and I still owe you deaths?"

"I offer you a choice," Harik said. "For each murder still outstanding, I will take the life of a person I choose. It might be you, but not before I take every person you care about."

"To hell with that shit."

"Very well, here is an alternative. You will commit now that if any killings remain undone at the fifth sunset, even one, you will surrender your life. You agree to this freely and of your own will. It will be no one's responsibility but yours."

That was the way out. If I made this deal, maybe I could save Pil. And if I just accepted that I would die in five days, I wouldn't need to kill every stranger who wandered past as I tried to meet an unknown quota. It wouldn't be that much of a sacrifice for me. I might only have five days left anyway.

I asked myself whether I could give up my life for a parcel of strangers. Some of them would be evil or at least fairly bad, so they probably deserved death. But sparing the rest didn't quite sound like something I would do.

"I agree, Harik," I said without thinking any more about it.

He didn't jump around and clap, but I got the sense he wanted to. Hell, if I gave up my life willingly, he'd probably be a hero among the gods. Harik said, "Fine. When you return, don't forget to take a deep breath." He tossed me back into my body with force, but not enough to send me skidding.

I was still blind, but my hands were on Pil's neck. I drew a great breath and kept working. The sounds of fighting were slackening around me.

Over the next minute, I made good progress. Pil was breathing, although not well. My eyes began seeing shapes as they recovered from the blindness.

Then somebody tripped over me and landed hard on my back. Most of the breath flew out of my lungs, and my hands were yanked off Pil's neck. I fumbled away the power I had been using to help her.

I wanted to curse and bellow, but instead I locked my throat tight. Just a bit of the great breath I had taken was still inside me, and I held it in to give me more seconds to help Pil. Grimacing, I pulled another green band. Harik must have known that some idiot would fall on me. He had made me pay a harsh price to save Pil, all the time knowing that something would happen to kill her anyway.

My lungs started burning as I went on putting Pil back together one shred at a time. My vision fully returned, but I didn't look away from her.

Ella touched my shoulder. "Bib, I am so sorry. Can you save her?"

I shrugged and kept working, not bothering to wonder when Ella had arrived. I clenched my teeth, as if that would help hold in the air. My own neck felt like a red-hot blade was being pushed in from the back as I pulled some of Pil's pain into me.

A king's guard ran up and stood over me. "The king is dying! Come save him!"

I shook my head and kept working. My eyesight was fading from lack of breath.

The guard shouted, "You have to come! He's the king! This girl can wait!"

"Stand away," Ella said.

Stan shouted from across the room, "Leave off, you greasy butt muffin!"

More guards came to stand around me. One of them yelled "Sorcerer! Come here now!" while two more hauled me upright. Ella knocked one down. I found that my boots had stopped being slick, so I kicked the other's shin hard. Then the air flew out of my lungs.

Two more guards grabbed my arms. Ten seconds later, both of them lay on the bloody floor, shaking their heads. But Pil lay on the floor too, not moving. I couldn't see her breathe.

When I tried to kneel back down to help Pil, three more guards came for me, yelling about the king. I grabbed my sword and stabbed one in the heart, even though I felt as if my head were being cut off from the back. I could sense my sword wanting these goddamn guards to be dead, and I wanted the same thing twice as much. I knocked the next guard down and thrust my sword through his right eye before he raised his head.

Over the next few minutes, I cut down guards until none were standing. Every time I tried to get back to Pil, some guard got in my way. At the end, Pil was lying flat in the blood, with Ella bent down shaking her head.

Three guards still lived, wounded and helpless. I walked from one to the next, thrusting my blade into their hearts as they lay there. Then I stood staring at nothing with my sword dangling in my hand.

Somebody grabbed my arm from behind. I threw them aside and had my sword halfway to their throat when I saw it was Ella. "Bib, we must move, and quickly! Desh and Stan cannot hold the doors."

"Get Pil," I muttered. "I don't want to leave her behind."

"What do you mean? We won't leave her, but I fear she cannot walk."

"Of course she—"

I whipped around and saw Pil lying on her side, looking paler than any of the white-skinned Denzmen I had just killed. She gazed at me for a moment and might have smiled a little. Then her eyes closed.

I blinked around at the room. "Ella, which way should we run?"

Ella was a superior leader, and she must have already worked out our next move, and maybe the five after that. She pointed. "Warp that large door shut. Then bring Stan along to meet us at the small door." She picked up Pil, who was lithe and no great burden for a strong woman like Ella.

"What then?" In truth, my neck hurt so much I wasn't thinking beyond the next thing that had to be done.

"Then we'll escape," Ella said. "I will guard your left side. You will kill every armed man you see until we reach freedom."

FOUR

Ella told me to kill every armed man between us and escape, which meant she had a lunatic regard for my fighting prowess. It aggravated me a little. Or maybe she had merely wanted me to feel a bit of optimism before we were killed. That would be awfully kind of her as well as defeatist. Such a combination of concern and futility pissed me off.

There was just no way for her to win with me.

I thought magic might save us, at least for a while, but my creativity lagged. I called for Harik anyway in case the sight of his condescending face inspired me, but the God of Death did not answer. Maybe he hated me too much to bear talking to me for a third time in less than ten minutes.

Ella nodded at me and then unbarred the smaller door, which opened like a split artery with guards rushing through. Some yelled threats, some snarled, and some roared for the hell of it, but each man screamed or went silent when I cut him down.

By the time the guards stopped running in to get killed, I had created a considerable pile of the bloody dead and the begging wounded. I sprang out into a pale stone hallway with lamps all down the walls burning enough oil to buy a small tavern. Eight guards were hanging back, fierce enough to shake their weapons but too timid or wise to trot into my slaughterhouse.

Their caution didn't save them.

"Clear the hallway!" Ella shouted, bounding up beside me.

"All right, dear." I frowned because I sounded like my father when my mother told him to paint or mend something.

I lunged at the guards, and three didn't retreat. Soon, two of them lay dead and the third was on his knees, weeping over his ruined hand like a boy whose wooden sword had split. I could have killed that man and should have, really, but I ignored him and pushed on. It was crazy, but I kept thinking about my father. If he were here, he wouldn't understand a single thing that was happening except for my letting that fellow live.

Thinking that way was a fine and moral way to get killed.

I shoved the next guard to the floor before I twisted and killed another. Then someone behind me shrieked like a pony being slaughtered. Like a fool, I glanced back. The man I had spared lay curled on the floor with his un-mangled arm severed at the elbow. The dead hand lay on the floor clutching a big knife.

Ella shook blood off her sword and pointed down the hallway. "The enemy is there! Don't be soft! This one nearly killed you!"

Before I pushed on, I glimpsed Desh following us, with Stan behind him carrying Pil. Ella caught up with me on my left side.

I rushed ahead and killed another man. He gave me a shallow cut on the thigh first, but I forced the others to back away faster. "We'll just kill everybody in the castle, right?" I yelled at Ella. A couple of men hesitated at that.

Ella's laugh sounded harsh. "It may not be necessary! I hope to spare some children. And the dogs, of course."

I sprinted thirty feet to force the guards farther back. One man lagged, but he dodged my sword, as deft as a king's champion. I faked a slash and kicked him in the knee so hard it sounded like splitting lumber. He staggered, and I sliced both his forearms deeply with one cut. This son of a bitch wouldn't be trying to stab me in the back.

"Help!" Stan squawked, and I glanced around. Guards were

now chasing us up the hallway from the throne room. Ella dropped back, but before she got there, the entire hallway behind us collapsed. It buried the guards in a mass of sand that rolled on toward us like a wave.

"Go! Go! Go!" Desh bellowed, waving something in his hand and backing up fast. He bumped into Stan, and they both sprawled. Pil grunted when Stan dropped her. Then sand overwhelmed Desh entirely before covering both Stan and Pil to the waist.

Ella pointed at Stan as she jumped past him. "Dig out and help me!"

I had looked at them for only a moment, but when I turned back, the hallway ahead seemed full, like a big stone sausage packed with angry men. I dragged in a breath and charged, screaming profanity and leaving the rescue to Ella.

When I thrust my blade into the next man, I felt a brush of pleasure, the same pleasure I usually felt when I killed, but simpler. It felt clean and certain. In that moment, it seemed silly that I had ever dithered over whether to kill somebody or to leave them alive. If experience meant anything, my judgment on the subject was superior, if not profound.

Those were peculiar feelings, but a mass of guards was preparing to overwhelm me, so I didn't wait for them. I rushed on, thrusting into hearts and bellies, slicing throats and wrists. I parried and dodged but never blocked. It would have wasted a moment I could use to take somebody's life.

Soon, guards began shoving backward against their comrades, trying to get away from me. I killed them as they cowered, and I killed them from behind when they tried to run. Some men rolled or crawled away from me when I wounded them. I killed every one of those I could reach.

When at last I saw the end of the hallway, I was breathing so hard my shoulders were pumping up and down. Our passage slammed into another one, so I could only turn left or right there. The few guards who had run fast enough to live turned right when they reached the intersection.

"Bib!" Desh shouted, and then he coughed while my heart tapped a dozen times. "Go right!"

I yelled, "Glad you're alive, but are you sure?"

"Damn it to Fingit, yes, I'm sure! I know my way out!"

I blinked. When I had been imprisoned here, Desh had always gotten in and out of the castle unnoticed. The passage to the right looked empty now, so I trotted down it, gasping. Ella ran up behind me, while Stan half dragged Pil along. She was holding her left arm tight against her body. I heard Desh bang into a wall and curse.

"Desh!" I yelled, still gasping but not as hard.

"What?"

"Are you really sure about this?"

I didn't hear him answer, maybe because of my little coughing fit.

After we had all turned and were trotting along, I heard an enormous slopping sound, as if someone were pouring batter for a cake as big as a house. Two men screamed but were cut off by sticky, bubbling noises.

"That's a rough job, but it works," Desh said. "Now run!"

I sprinted down the hallway for ten seconds. Then I hurried along for most of a minute, gasping but pushing on. After that, I trotted for a respectable time, swearing that I would stab myself in the head if I was reduced to an embarrassed jog.

We met two more guards along the way. Ella jumped ahead and disabled one. I killed him as he leaned against the wall, but that blocked Ella from engaging the second guard.

"Move!" Ella screamed.

The guard had every right to think he was about to kill me, since I was a panting, off-balance old man. But as he thrust, I twisted onto one foot, let his sword slip past, leaned, and thrust straight into his heart. It all happened so fast it surprised even me.

"Fine," Ella said, squeezing my shoulder. "I'll trot behind you and watch."

I turned toward the wall and threw up.

Ella stepped past me to guard the passageway ahead of us while I heaved. "Step back, ladies! He's all mine."

At an intersection, I saw several more guards running toward us from our left. Desh flung something shiny their direction, and it shattered, tinkling against the floor. The guards skidded to a stop, yelling curses and asking each other where that damn wall had come from. I could see them slapping the empty air and pushing against nothing.

Desh soon passed me, and he called out, "Here!"

I stopped and put my hands on my knees, but for just a few seconds. I wanted to be standing up straight when I died from embarrassment.

Desh pricked his finger and wrote his name on the wall in blood. Then he leaned his forehead against the wall and whispered something. The bloody name faded, and Desh stood back while smiling at the wall.

Nothing happened, and after ten seconds, Desh stopped smiling. He whispered to the wall again and gave it a couple of nice pats with his palm. Still nothing happened. Desh spat some vexed words under his breath and even kicked the wall hard enough to make him wince.

My breath had returned faster than I expected. "Should we sing to it, Desh? I'm a poor singer, but enthusiastic."

"No!" Desh said. "Don't dance around or draw a picture, either! You . . . just don't try to help."

Pil joined Desh and sagged against the wall while they whispered together for most of a minute. Then Desh sighed and hung his head. He pricked his finger again and wrote his name in blood. He pricked the same finger on the other hand before writing "Limnad" on the wall beside his name. This time, the forehead-pressing and the whispering made a section of the stone wall swing in with a swish like a regular door.

We shuffled into a bare stone chamber. The five of us would fit if we pressed in nearly tight enough to have intimate relations. Desh entered last, bringing one of the lamps from the hallway. As he closed the door, I leaned back against a wall to press my searing neck against the cool stone. It was merely the pain I had earned by healing Pil's neck. I wasn't damaged, and the feeling would fade over a few hours or at most a day. I grinned a little because I had done a generous thing and would be entitled to bitch about how much I was suffering.

Ella said, "I am, I admit, mystified by this attack. Moris had enemies, but with supernatural aid?"

Stan poked at me with his free hand. "Bib did it. I don't know what he did, but he did it. Ow!"

Two of Stan's nasty fingers had been broken saving Desh, and Pil was tying them together using one hand and her teeth. "You be quiet." She yanked the binding tight, and he yelped again.

"I didn't do nothing wrong! I carried you and your sword and your damn lead-soled boots here to safety, and now you torture me."

Pil raised an eyebrow and glanced around. "This is safety?"

Desh lifted the lamp. "Quiet! Someone will hear you. At this moment, it doesn't matter why they attacked and killed poor old Moris."

"It matters," Pil said, patting Stan's fingers before she pushed hair off her sweaty forehead. "They came to kill Bib."

Everybody fell quiet and stared at me for several seconds.

"Told you," Stan said.

Desh said, "Everybody wants to kill Bib, sure, but these weren't gamblers or angry husbands." His lips turned up.

I considered arguing with him but just shook my head and then wished I hadn't.

"Not husbands," Pil said. "These were Effla's handpicked killers, complete with sorcerers and demons."

Had Pil been eavesdropping on Effla and Harik along with me?

Ella grabbed my hand and squeezed hard. "If that was so, why did they not descend on him in a pack? Why waste even a moment threatening the king? Or you, Pil?"

Pil let her mouth hang open for a second. "I don't know. That part doesn't make sense. I don't really know." She shrugged and winced.

If Pil had been listening to Effla, she would have known the answer to that question. Some god might be dosing her with half-truths about me.

Ella said, "Why then? Why do they want to kill him?"

I said, "Same reasons as anybody else, probably. Pil, show me your arm."

"You'll have to come get it. I haven't been able to move it since I woke up."

"Shit!" I crawled over to kneel beside Pil while holding my neck stiff and pulled a band to find out where I had screwed up putting her back together. When Desh started talking, I snapped, "Hush! Do you want me to break her on both sides? You figure out where we're going and leave me alone."

Ella and Desh began murmuring together. Stan leaned back and closed his eyes. Pil whispered, "They deserve to know. They're your friends."

"They do? Deserve to know what?" I muttered. "Just what do you know that you think they ought to know?"

She snorted. "Good effort. Try to fool me some more. See what happens."

"Don't pretend to be some wise woman. Giving up thirty years of your life for a raspy old cob like me is the most foolish offer I've ever heard."

"I was just throwing confusion into the situation," she said. "They weren't going to say yes to that, but you should pretend that I offered up half my life and be really grateful to me. I want the best horse. When we get horses, promise me the best one."

"Does that mean you're not striking off on your own yet?"

"I . . . well, I'd be an idiot to run away by myself while the whole Denz army is looking for us."

"Then sure, you get the best horse. Now be still." Effla had tried to kill me but ended up helping me keep Pil around. It was the kind of shit the gods liked to perpetrate on men, so for Effla it must have been an embarrassing failure. Probably. Maybe.

I murmured, "Pil, am I smart enough to say whether a god has failed or succeeded at something?"

Pil snorted. "If you have to ask the question . . ."

"Keep reminding me that I'm not that smart, all right?"

"Thanks, Bib. While you're giving me presents, I'd like a wealthy prince who doesn't stink too much and knows what a spoon is for."

I ignored that and focused on Pil's neck. I used more magical power to pick my way through bits of Pil's neck than I should, but conditions in the stuffy, dim room were poor. At some point, everybody stopped talking, although Stan snored like he was sucking a lizard up the back of his throat. At last, Pil's hand twitched and made a fist. She grabbed my arm with it and laughed. "Thanks, Bib!" She made a soft neighing sound.

I sighed. "Desh? Is there a plan?"

"Perhaps. How close does a horse need to be for you to call it?"

"I doubt that I could get one in here with us."

He nodded as if I'd given him a serious answer and then waited. Maybe Desh did need to know some details about my abilities so we could escape, but I sure as hell didn't want him to know the limits of my power. He might choose to kill me someday. I said, "They don't always have to be in view for me to call them."

Desh clenched his teeth. "I'm trying to save us. How far out of view can the horse be?" He glanced at Pil. She had a fine notion of my limits in this area, if she chose to reveal them.

Pil shook her head. "I never paid much attention. It's just boring old horse stuff." That was a big damn lie. Pil paid attention to everything.

"Distance depends on many factors," I said, trying to imitate the most disastrously dull sorcery teacher I could remember.

Ella put her hand on my shoulder. "If your only means of saving my life was to call a horse from absolutely the greatest possible distance, how far would that be?"

"Oh, hell," I said. "Fine. If conditions are good and time isn't a factor, that is, if I have huge buckets of time to spare, I could reach as far as forty miles." I shrugged.

"Shit." Stan grunted. "If you can fetch them that far, we ought to find a nice tavern for us to wait in until they come. Something with drinks and a few chairs."

Desh rolled his eyes. "Bib, that simplifies things. I'll bet it's expensive, though." He handed me a small leather bottle. I knew it held a sizable amount of magical power that would be mine to use once I opened it.

"Thank you, Desh! I'll do kind and generous works with this."

"I expect you to." Desh handed Pil the lantern and reached out a hand to Stan, who was still reclining. "Up. I need to open that door your butt is against."

"What door?" Stan scrambled up as if he'd been sitting on a scorpion. "I might have got stabbed in the back, what with you letting me rest myself against a door. Desh, I thought we was brothers."

Desh put his hands on the wall and didn't answer. Stan had sort of adopted Desh when the sorcerer was young and green. Now Desh was cold and powerful, but Stan acted as if nothing had changed.

Desh pushed and winced when we heard the grinding clink of stone hitting other stone. All of us jumped in to help, and we managed to shove a foot-wide opening in the wall.

"Good thing Ralt's not here," Stan said. "His tubby ass would be stuck in this place for the rest of time."

Desh said, "Bib, hunt for horses, and start now if you think it will take time. In half an hour, we'll burst out of the ground near a farm on the north side of the castle." He squeezed through the gap and yelped before I heard him hit the ground. "Damn it!" he said.

Ella drew the sword that she had taken from a soldier. "Do you need help?"

"No, I tripped. Be careful of this body lying against the doorway. He's not fresh, so whatever killed him probably left a long time ago. Stay back a moment. All right, shine that lamp in."

I followed Desh through. The corpse had been a man, and rats had chewed him well. Bits of his clothes had likely made some warm rat nests, and the rodents had even made away with his hat and a glove. I said, "He died without much of an estate. His sword has rusted and wasn't worth a damn before. Why was he in your tunnel, Desh?"

The young sorcerer shrugged and reached for the lamp. "It's not my tunnel. I found it like this. That is my magically sealed hidden door, though. This man may not have expected to find that down here."

"I wonder who he was?" Pil asked.

"Maybe he was sneaking through here to go bump naughties with the queen," Stan said. "You know, some handsome boy who charms women and then snogs them. Or if not the queen, then her fancy friends. It happens all the time."

Desh shook his head and walked off down the low, narrow passageway.

I sensed plenty of horses in stables, in the castle yard, and out among the farms, but it took me a while to locate some that were saddled and also unattended. I found five and whipped out five yellow bands to convince them that plenty of delicious food would be found in a particular quiet spot that Desh had described to me.

We walked through that tunnel for more than twenty minutes before Desh halted at a blank stone wall with a ladder leaning against it. Desh looked back and held his finger to his lips before he climbed the ladder and shoved up against the stone ceiling. The stone slid aside, letting a couple of bucketsful of dirt and grass fall on us.

Desh hopped up the ladder and through the hole. I climbed up right after him into nice, concealing darkness, as I had expected. Though I hadn't expected to be surrounded by firelight, feisty music, and dancing people. The music faded as I stepped out of Ella's way and looked around at the partygoers. They were murmuring and pointing at us.

I waved. "Hello, it's a beautiful night for a party! Is somebody getting married? We brought a gift."

A tall woman muttered, "Demons from out of the ground . . ."

"Stay away, demon!" an older girl shouted before she picked up a rock.

"Call the guard! Help!" yelled a clean-shaven man.

I snapped, "Damn! Krak smash it with both his balls!"

The merrymakers got into a rhythm. "Guard! Demons! Call the guard! Help!"

I drew my sword but hesitated since I didn't really need to kill any of these people. Besides, I might kill the bride, and that would be rude behavior in anybody's way of thinking.

The horses were standing two hundred paces away, waiting for what I had promised would be the best meal of their lives. I shouted "This way!" and sprinted toward the deeper darkness. I knocked down three people before I ran clear of the party, trusting that Ella and the others were following me.

Once free and in the darkness, I slowed a bit to adjust course.

Pil snarled as Stan helped her along. "Go! Don't slow down, go faster!"

Her young ears had heard the hoofbeats before my old ones had. At least four horses were approaching us at a gallop. I didn't know whether they were guards, but I did know something else for sure. After today, anybody we met in the Denz Lands would be pleased to see us dead.

I ran faster. I also pulled a yellow band and held it. I might need it to convince the pursuing horses to throw their riders and kick them until they run away.

FIVE

I blame the gods for a lot of things I dislike, or that dislike me. That's a common failing among sorcerers because gods treat us like talking chickens who will stop laying eggs one day and be good to eat.

It's easy to hate the gods because they are hateful. They offer sorcerers the chance to perform miracles if we give up what we cherish or do things we despise, and a sorcerer who lives long enough will give up everything that makes him human. The gods will take all the eggs, and then they'll watch the sorcerer lose interest in life and in doing the things that keep humans alive.

Most days, all of that seems true to me, but when I'm ripping drunk in some tavern and about to whip a parcel of singing idiots, the odd wave of honesty might hit me. The gods are not to blame for anything that has happened to me. I freely decided to trade with them. I agreed, out loud with my own mouth, to everything I did for power and all that was done to me.

However, the gods had begun demanding that sorcerers give up years of life along with each bargain. Most of us would not choose to cut short our own lives. Instead, we'd take years from other people, which was allowed. The victims would usually not be sorcerers, would never have talked to a god, and would never have agreed to any of this crap.

The gods, especially that pinch-butt weasel Harik, must have smiled at the notion of demanding years of life from everybody in this way. However, their godly wisdom was too self-involved to understand that they had actually declared war on the entire world of man.

The gods wouldn't have feared Desh, Ella, and the rest of us too much. Riding our asses off across the grassland, we resembled terrified rabbits more than warriors. Our most direct path for escaping the Denz Lands lay north. That path also wound along three days of mountain trails that were perfect for ambushes. If Moris's men overtook us, all they had to do was climb up above, kick a few rocks, and watch us die.

So, we rode hard toward that trail with soldiers chasing us through the darkness. We led them long enough to establish that we were headed north—straight north and not any other direction, a fact that even the thickest soldier could understand. Then I convinced the pursuers' horses to create pandemonium. Kicking and biting abounded, and some mounts decided to gallop away with no encouragement from me. We left the clamor behind and curved west.

The immense Summer Marsh ran along most of the Denz Lands' northern border. It froze hard in winter, when people crossed it as easily as they'd walk out to gather eggs. Once it thawed in late spring, few who walked far into the marsh ever came out.

Summer travelers who didn't care to die in swamp water could leave the Denz Lands by one of two mountain passes. We had already considered the one in the east and said to hell with it. The other pass, two days' ride to the west, might not have been much better, to be truthful. I had never seen it. But we had the whole width and breadth of the kingdom to lose ourselves in while we traveled. Moris's sons and their soldiers would need to search every road, barn, and clump of trees to find us.

It didn't seem that Gek cared which direction Pil and I traveled anyway.

At sunrise, our shadows stretched ahead to the horizon, and if we could have ridden on those shadows, we would have crossed the kingdom in a moment. We urged our horses through the tall grass of late summer, although for most of the world, a Denz summer wouldn't feel hot, or even too warm. This was the far south, where ice was more common than flowers. I couldn't see much of the sky through the puffed clouds, and without sunshine, we might feel chilly today.

"Woods ahead!" I shouted, pointing at some trees that would shelter us as we rested our mounts. Ella waved to show that she had heard me, and I angled toward the lone stand of timber.

The range of evergreens was bigger than I had thought, a couple of hundred acres in size. We rode in past the tree line before dismounting.

"I wish we'd find some water," Desh said. Nobody ever packed for a long journey just to wander around in the castle hallways, so we had fled without provisions, bedrolls, packs, cloaks, or spare anything of any kind.

"The horses need water more than we do," I said.

Somebody behind me shrieked, "What?" Every horse spooked, and Desh's galloped away. I drew my sword as I spun.

Ella was staring at Pil and looked as if she'd been whacked on the head with a cookpot. Pil was looking down and fiddling with her sleeve.

Ella made a greased turn, and her eyes met mine. I couldn't read them, but they looked sunken, even though she'd been fine a few minutes earlier. She stalked toward me, halfway drawing her sword as she came before shoving it back into the scabbard. Grabbing me by the collar with both hands, she yelled, "Thirty years?"

I realized I should have told Ella about my imminent death, or at least mentioned it before Pil could. "I'm sorry I didn't say anything, darling, but we've been struggling for our lives."

"Did you know of this when we were trapped in Desh's little room?"

I swallowed. "Yes."

"We weren't struggling for our lives at that very moment, were

BILL McCURRY

we? You had time to whisper this knowledge to Pil but not to me?" She shook me by the collar to emphasize her point.

"I see the misunderstanding." I nodded and hoped it made me look wise and trustworthy. "I didn't tell Pil. She was there when it happened."

"That's true," Pil said, "I was there. I tried to fix it, but . . ." She looked at the ground again.

Ella released my collar and grabbed my hand, growling, "Sheathe your sword."

I sheathed the weapon, and she led me away.

"Wait! Where are you taking him?" Stan shouted.

"Hush!" Pil said.

"Oh, I see." I glanced back and saw Stan grin like a gap-toothed hyena. "Be careful out in them trees! I've set my willy loose in just about every sort of terrain there is on this earth. You might not imagine so, but these trees are perilous. You're damn near sure to get pine needles in places you don't want 'em."

Sometime later I lay beside Ella on too many of those lousy pine needles. "It's cold. Are you cold?"

"Yes." She grabbed the back of my hair when I moved. "No! You may not sit up yet. You are forbidden."

"Well . . . I know thirty years sounds bad, but I've been in danger ever since you've known me. I might have died any minute that whole time. This isn't all that different."

Ella sighed. "It's different to me."

"Ah. I don't know how to make it better, darling."

She frowned. "I wish I could have children."

"I thought you decided you were done with all that."

"No, I wish I could have *your* children."

I think there's only one possible response to a statement like that. "I do too."

Ella sat up and smiled at me. "Hand me my shirt."

I passed the soft, blue garment to her and then stood up. "Are you all right?"

"Certainly. I do not intend to weep and shiver about all this. We face too many threats to allow such preoccupation." She patted my

44

shoulder as if I were a stablehand who had done a good job. "I must adjust to the idea that you are dead—as if you have already died."

"I guess that's smart," I said slowly.

She pulled me close and kissed me a long time. "I may not be good at it immediately."

Ella and I hurried back to the others. The realization crept upon me that we had been foolish to give our pursuers this much time to catch up. No one seemed angry at us, though. Pil waved at us through the trees, smiling her astonishing smile. Desh had recovered his horse. Stan leered at us and nodded approval, but he kept quiet.

Pil met us and said to Ella, "I promise that it's not over for Bib. If a god can take those years away from him, then a god can give them back, and we know how to get things from gods. I'm not giving up."

Standing behind Pil, Desh gave her a wry look and shook his head.

I said, "Pil, I don't think that's likely."

"You shut up!" Pil snipped. "This is between Ella and me."

We cantered our horses around the edge of the little forest and traveled west, staying away from roads when we could and avoiding towns. We would need to stop somewhere to provision ourselves, and our best choice would be some small village around sunset. We'd buy what we could and ride on during the night.

The stands of forest became more frequent and larger. We weren't always able to stay off roads unless we wanted to weave through a fair stretch of trees. We continued to skirt any towns, although we had to cross some farmers' fields. Sweating men and women looked up from their crops to watch us pass.

At midafternoon, as we rode down a rutted path that cut through dense evergreen woods, I drew rein and held up a hand. "I see two riders far ahead. I can't make out more than that."

"It ain't fair. I don't see shit," Stan whined.

Pil said, "Oh, let him have his pearly eyesight. He's as deaf as a rock."

That was an exaggeration, but my hearing had faded to poorer than average. "They're riding this direction, but I doubt they're soldiers hunting us. After the massacre at the castle, the army won't chase us in patrols smaller than twenty men, and half of them with bows."

"I miss my bow," Pil said. "Maybe we'll fight some soldiers, and I can take a bow from one of them."

Stan spoke up: "After we cut all their heads off?"

Pil hesitated. "Of course."

We rode on toward the two horsemen, who weren't pushing their mounts. One seemed twice the size of the other, and I started feeling queasy as the distance closed. At one hundred paces, I halted; the strange riders did the same.

"I recognize the big one," I said.

"It's Cael," Ella said through gritted teeth. "I know how he sits a horse. You said he was trapped in the Dark Lands."

"I last saw him there guarding a gate to other worlds. I guess if you can guard a gate, then you can hop through it whenever you want to."

Cael and I had not been back-slapping chums when I last saw him. I had needed to pass through that gate, and Cael was bound to kill anybody who tried. He was a phenomenal warrior, and I did not in any way deserve to defeat him. I only managed it through magic, and we about killed each other.

After I defeated him, I had intended to let him die. He was as dangerous as an avalanche and in times past had been so cheerful that I wanted to smash out his fine smile. But the Dark Lands had turned him into a sad man who was maybe a little crazy. I felt I had to save him even if I was just preserving him to suffer some more.

No good thing had ever happened in the Dark Lands, or so I'd been told by a helpful stranger. My time there had not made me believe that was a tearing great lie.

"Perhaps we can ignore him," Ella said. "Or ride around him through the woods."

Ella did not care for Cael, and she had once tried to burn him alive. I didn't believe they would begin hacking away just because they saw each other's faces again, at least not before engaging in some discussion and insults.

I didn't wish to avoid Cael, mainly because I wanted to know why he was here on the same road as me. I did not believe in coincidence. It was a way of saying I'm too lazy to figure things out, so I'll give the problem a fancy name and blame the universe for my ignorance. Cael was here for a reason.

SIX

My voice bounced off the trees when I bellowed, "I hope you're not here to fight, Cael! My neck still hurts from last time!"

Cael shouted, "No, I'm not. I'm bringing a message! And a bribe!"

Pil whispered, "Desh, do you have some magic that will do something like turn his bones into broomsticks? Just in case." Cael had once nearly slain Pil too.

"No," Desh whispered. "I can cause him blinding pain." He frowned. "That won't distract Cael for more than a couple of seconds, but they might be critical."

"Cael!" I yelled. "How did you know to find me here?"

"A mutual acquaintance told me where you'd be."

I was aware of only four beings who knew both Cael and me. One was human—Ella. The others weren't from around these parts. "Who is he?"

"He limps like a three-legged dog."

That would be Gek. "That's puzzling. I guess we ought to talk then," I shouted. I kicked my horse into a trot, and Cael did the same, along with his smaller companion. As we drew closer, I realized that although Cael was larger than his crony, he didn't dwarf her. He seemed enormous only because he was riding a beast of a black horse, the one he had owned in the Dark Lands.

The mare stood taller than any riding horse I had ever seen, and I remembered that she had been superbly trained for combat. The creature kept turning her head to look at me, and I got the sense she recognized me.

A tall girl rode with Cael on an unexceptional gelding. I put her to be fourteen or fifteen with a strong jaw and wide forehead. Her dark hair was braided long, just as Pil wore her black hair. The young lady looked familiar, but I couldn't place her.

I whispered, "Pil, is that your sister? Or a cousin?"

Pil shook her head. "I don't have a sister, and my cousins are all shaped like squares—strong but not tall."

The girl wore a sword on her belt next to two knives, with another knife in a sheath on her chest. A short bow and a long lance were strapped to her saddle. She was toting enough weapons for three men.

We halted close enough to converse without strain. Cael said, "Yita, this is Bib, and that's Ella. Both of them have nearly killed me. I saw the rest of you in the Dark Lands, but I never learned your names. I apologize for not being able to introduce you. Everyone, this is Yita the Survivor."

Yita examined me from my hat to my horse's hooves. "I expected more."

"I haven't had my afternoon nap," I said.

"Hurry up and take it. You look as if you'll fall over dead any time."

For a second, I wondered if Yita was a future-teller. Then I decided she was just rude as hell.

Yita turned to Ella. "You're a little more imposing. It's in the eyes. You were dumb to fight Cael, though."

Ella paused. "Yita, that's a very wise observation. I am pleased to meet you."

I introduced Pil, Desh, and Stan. Cael nodded while Yita scrutinized them.

Yita pointed at Pil. "Are you from Hep? No, you're too pretty to be from Hep. I like your braid, though."

"Thank you," Pil said. "I'm from the Lake Countries. Where are you from?"

Yita cocked her head and squinted. "I'm from Hep. We just talked about that. I'm surprised you had to ask."

I pushed down the urge to knock Yita off her horse and kick dirt on her. "Now that we're all suspicious acquaintances, what's this message, Cael?"

"It would have been better if you stayed near that castle. Ridden away from it, but not far. Why didn't you?"

I turned to Desh. "I told you we should stay close! If we had, we could have failed to do whatever stupid thing Cael wants us to do. We'd be dead and covered by a bunch of dirt. You wanted to be alive. Selfish oaf."

Desh raised his eyebrows but grinned.

Cael looked sour but then gazed upward. "Let's see, what did Gek say? He said, 'Bib, the attack on that king was obviously a trap to kill you, so you should have called for more wine, ridden out for a picnic, and let the old fart-bag die.' It's mere luck that you survived. That part's from me."

"Was that the entirety of the message?" Ella asked.

"No, he wasn't specific. Gek was raging a little. Essentially, he wants you to travel north and cross the Summer Marsh."

It was clear now that I was facing two problems. First, I didn't want to say anything to Cael that revealed I was working for Gek. The gods might be listening, and then they might say to hell with the curse and crush me out of existence. Second, I wasn't just going to accept that Cael was the mouthpiece of Gek.

I decided to deny I knew Gek, squeeze out everything Cael knew, tell him nothing, and leave him behind on this road. "Cael, I don't know much about this Gek. I think I met him once. Is he promising to grant you the power of flight so that you're not eaten or sucked under to drown in the marsh?"

"He didn't say anything about it." Cael rubbed his chin. "He isn't known for providing detail, though. He expects his people to exercise initiative."

"I'm not—" I paused when I remembered that I was technically Gek's servant. I was one of Gek's people more than anybody else there except for Cael. "I'm nobody's servant," I added without much force.

Cael gave me the masterpiece of a smile I remembered from when he was still pleased with life. "Bib, I've had a little more time to consider this, so here's what I think we should do and why. Go north. I can guide us through the marsh by an unknown path."

"And then?" Desh asked.

"You know about the war, right? You're a sorcerer. You know things," Cael said.

"Do you mean the war between . . ." I let the question dangle.

He nodded. "The war between the gods and Gek."

It wouldn't do to act too ignorant. "Ah, that war. Isn't Gek a Void Walker? So, the gods are at war with the Void Walkers?"

"No, the war is between the gods and Gek. By himself. Or rather, Cheg-Cheg by himself."

"Well, that's as confusing as a three-headed goat." Sweat jumped out on my skin as I remembered Cheg-Cheg's gargantuan, realm-spanning self. It was easy to accept that Cheg-Cheg could fight the gods by himself. It was harder to accept that he could win, especially if he had to depend on Pil and I to kill gods for him.

I went on: "Cael, what do you really know about Gek? Why does he want me to do whatever he wants me to do? Are you sure he has the right person?"

"Why do you keep asking questions about this?" Yita asked. "I think you're scared."

I bowed to her from the saddle. "To my most profound depths, yes."

She blinked at me. "I'm scared too. You just have to pretend you're not. That's what I do. Sometimes I cry after the fight's over, but that's all right because my enemies are dead."

"I'll try that," I said.

Cael said, "Bib, you should come north with me. There's a weapon that can kill a god if he's in the Dark Lands." He gave me a hard look.

I definitely didn't want to act as if we were interested in killing gods, so I yawned. "Why would you want to kill a god? What have the gods done to you? That's a hard story to believe, anyway. What kind of weapon is it supposed to be?"

"Well, I don't know precisely, but I can find it."

"I just bet you can."

Cael scowled at me.

I gazed at the forest on one side of us and then the other. "Cael, I'm not your servant. Everything you've said today could be a bunch of damn lies. If this Gek wants me to hop on my butt across the swamp, he can come here and ask for my help. I'd probably ignore him, though."

Yita spoke up to ask, "Bib, do you hate the gods?"

"Most of the time," I said. It would sound suspicious if I said anything else.

"I hate the gods too. This is how we will kill them and be free."

"Kill them? That's impossible. Enjoy your time in the marshes, Yita."

Yita glanced at Cael. "Bribe?"

Cael nodded and dismounted. "Bib, if you come north, I will give you my horse. She is the finest horse in any realm, and I believe you can tell that by looking at her." Cael held out the reins.

I was tempted. I believed the horse to be a creature from beyond the normal world. She was standing motionless with all her slabs of muscle relaxed. Not even her ears twitched. "What's her name?"

"Gea."

"I beg your pardon?" Pil said.

Cael repeated, "Gea. G. E. A." None of us spoke while Cael chuckled. "Why is this so hard for you, eh? Say it slowly. Gay. Uh."

I mouthed the word, almost forgot it again, and said it out loud four times before it was solid in my thoughts. I had never before run across a name that tried to make people forget it once it was spoken.

Gea would be a difficult creature to bind unless the sorcerer had plenty of time to prepare.

Ella and the others were mumbling the name with furrowed brows and trying to recall it. This removed any doubt that Gea was a supernatural creature.

I chewed my lip and thought about it. "I am sensible of your generosity, Cael, but no."

"Well, shit," Cael said. "I'm afraid that the rest of my bribe may not entice you to an agreement. I also came here to put Yita in your care."

"What? Why?"

"You and Ella are the only people I know who understand anything about raising girls." He lifted his hands. "You're a heartless dog of a killer, but I don't think you're heartless enough to turn her away. She needs someone."

I didn't consider the request seriously, but a question rose in my mind. "Before I answer you, why is she called the Survivor?"

"Yita's father and all his men were slain. Only she lived."

Glancing at Yita, I said, "I'm sorry. That's a hard thing."

Yita didn't answer.

Instead, Cael said, "I think so too, even though I'm the one who killed them. So, you can see why she might not be fully comfortable with me."

The thought of children ran through my mind, and I glanced at Ella. I couldn't help myself. But she was staring at the ground.

After a long pause, Yita lowered her voice, almost reaching a growl. "I didn't think you'd want me. Well, you're a liar and a . . . drunkard. I don't want you, either!" She pointed her finger at me like it was a poisoned knife. "I'd rather live with hogs!"

She sounded just like my daughter, Manon, who had perfected the role of frustrating smartass. Yita turned her horse and rode a hundred feet away. I couldn't be sure, but I thought she might be crying.

Cael drew his sword. "I have no choice but to challenge you, Bib."

"Again?" I shouted. "It's the third time! Fingit's ripe farts, there's got to be something else we can do. Are you a good dancer?"

My horse reared and neighed, and so did every other horse except for Gea. When I got my mount controlled, I saw three ten-foot-tall imps, the gods' hooligans, standing beside two portals that hung like windows in the empty air. Horsemen began cantering out of both portals, each held open by imp arms with muscles upon muscles. The third imp leaped toward me like a murderous jackrabbit bigger than a bull.

My mount was too terrified to be useful, so I slid off and thrust my sword at the flop-eared, bloody-jawed imp when it landed. My blade slipped off its knotty hide. Cael attacked it a moment later with about the same success. Gea kicked the imp's knee, and it sounded as if she could have split an iron-bound door. I don't think the imp noticed.

The quasi-divine monster reached out and snatched Cael around both shoulders with one enormous hand. In a birdlike trill, it said, "Gimme, you turd-machine!" With the other hand, it grabbed Cael's left forearm and broke it in the middle.

Cael shouted in pain but aimed a thrust at the imp's huge, flat nostrils. The creature shook its head and knocked the sword aside. I put all my strength into thrusting up under the creature's ribs, and Desh's enchanted sword pierced its hide. I shoved again and slid the blade into the monster's heart.

But at the same moment, the imp twisted Cael's wrist as if it were pulling a weed, tearing Cael's forearm in two. Cael thrashed and screamed as he threw back his head. As the creature fell dying, it tossed Cael's hand and wrist to one of the riders.

Another imp let one of the portals slide shut and leaped sixty feet toward me. It glared and warbled, "You crusty asshole." Before I could thrust at this imp, it snatched the dead one with a single hand and jumped back to the remaining portal. Seconds later, all three imps had passed through, and the portal dissolved with a pop.

About thirty horsemen who had ridden in through the portals were organizing into troops. One of them, a broad-shouldered, bald man with a long, black beard, rode a short distance toward us. He was carrying three swords that I could see—one in his hand and two on his back, their hilts sticking up over his shoulders.

The swordsman pointed his blade at me and bellowed over Cael's groaning, "Do not follow me, Bib! I'm having a hard enough time keeping you alive as it is!"

The horsemen wheeled and galloped away north. None of us rode after them, unless my mount's random sidestepping and bucking counted as pursuit.

Generally, I felt sorry for men who strapped on more swords than they could use at once. Strutting around like a human weapons rack wouldn't help a man prevail in combat, although it did sometimes boost his confidence. Also, he probably had a tiny dick, or believed that he did. My opinion on this matter was another reason why the God of War hated me, since he carried fourteen swords wherever he went.

I named this bald man Teeny and decided he wasn't trying to save me, no matter what he said. Teeny was mocking me, and I intended to watch him eat dirt and die.

I set about convincing Teeny's horses to toss all their riders and stomp holes in their pretty green costumes. Then he'd think twice about throwing around orders. I began pulling yellow bands of energy and flinging them out toward the horsemen. The range was increasing fast, so I pulled bands and used up power even faster.

A minute later, the horses should have been biting and stomping their riders, but nothing like that happened. The horses didn't even slow down. I knew I had their attention. I could feel it. They just didn't care. Maybe some powerful sorcerer was shoving my suggestions aside as if they were idle hints, and that thought disturbed me quite a lot.

Ella and the others were quieting our horses and gathering them. Yita was kneeling beside Cael, trying to stop the bleeding. I looked again and saw she was crying quiet tears as she worked. It seemed odd to cry over somebody who had killed her father.

I glared at the green-clad horsemen as they dwindled, making away with Cael's hand. Those bastards could suck rotten pork in hell, especially Teeny. Keeping me alive? That was a burning lie if ever one was uttered, and I knew lies as well as any person alive.

I silently promised to kill Teeny and every one of his disgusting ass-polishers. And I would keep that promise—as long as I didn't pitch over dead first.

SEVEN

Few sorcerers begin training younger than age ten. Even fewer wait until they're past age twelve. By that time, uncontrolled sorcery would have destroyed them, probably their families, and maybe everybody in their town.

Training ends at sixteen, no matter when the trainee started. Without exception, sixteen is the age when sorcerers are tossed out, having more or less learned what they need to survive on their own.

About one in four of the new children is murdered by their teachers during the first week. History shows that kids who can't learn to suppress their magic in the first few days never will, and they are too dangerous to let live.

I hated the first week of training because I was an awful student, and every night I thought I'd be killed in my bed. I survived, though, and I enjoyed training after that, although my teachers didn't enjoy my sarcastic mouth.

I think almost any child would like to learn how to be a special person with fantastic powers. I had a fine time. It beat fishing all to hell. Not many children die in the years after that first week. Almost every surviving child enjoys their fifteenth birthday while in training.

Three months after that birthday, more than half of them are dead.

Age fifteen is when young sorcerers begin trading with gods, and that's when they undo themselves. They give away too much in exchange for power, or they use magic when they could do something else. Some spend power on foolish or dangerous things, and some fail to spit in a god's eye, so they get beaten apart by bad trades.

The deadliest error is spending power because the sorcerer wants to, not because he needs to. It's an awful thing for a sorcerer to magically help somebody just because he loves them. Love feels limitless, so his need to help them because of love becomes limitless too. But only so many parts of a sorcerer can be traded away before he's gone.

Every sorcerer learns this rule if he lives through training. But I've never met a sorcerer who didn't ignore it sometimes, and I include myself in that.

Fortunately, I didn't love Cael a single goddamn bit. I healed his wound. I felt no obligation to restore his arm. Having a one-handed Cael around wouldn't hurt me, and his unmatched fighting skills might diminish to the point where I could match them, should that be required.

Desh watched me heal Cael for five minutes. Then he said, "Cael, I might go north with you. It sounds interesting, and maybe there's something to be learned. But I'm not sure Bib will go."

I whipped around. "North? You couldn't prevent from going there if you chained me to a whorehouse." That sort of popped out, but it was the right thing to say. "I need to kill enough people to drown a village in bodies, and killing those green-frocked, horse-riding pissants will be a good start. There will probably be plenty of other people to kill along the way."

I didn't really intend to slay all the people it would take to cover up a village. But if I claimed that was why I was going north, any gods listening would probably accept that reasoning. It sounded like the kind of bloody destruction I have often engaged in. The gods wouldn't suspect me of plotting against them, nor of letting Gek order me to go places for him.

Since I was going north now, I claimed ownership of Gea. I busied myself adjusting the stirrups to mount my wonderful new horse.

"Bib, what's happened?" Desh murmured. "Why do you need to kill more people now?" He hesitated but didn't ask the next question.

"Don't inquire about my goddamn business!" I said without looking at him. "You know better. Maybe you're the swinging bull of all sorcerers now, but I can whip you if you need it." I yanked the left stirrup. "Hell, I always need to kill people, you know that. I need it more than sleep or warm socks. I was speaking a little too enthusiastically is all."

After about ten seconds, I heard Desh walk away. When I glanced back, he and Ella had their heads together.

"Shit!" I whispered. I didn't need them getting in my way by trying to protect me.

Pil walked up and laid her hand on my shoulder. "Thank you, Bib."

"You're welcome. For what?"

"Thank you for adjusting my stirrups. They look just about right, maybe a little bit long, but I can fix that."

I'm sure my face looked blank and stupid. Then I closed my eyes and waited for her to say it.

"You agreed that I'd get the best horse," she said. "You would have to argue all day to convince me that Gea isn't the best one."

"That's not particularly reasonable, Pil. When we agreed on that, I didn't know I'd be getting some kind of magic horse."

Pil let her hand drop. "Sure, Bib, I understand, I know you're a liar, and I guess that's all right. It's just a surprise when you lie to me the way you do to other people."

Five minutes later, I was checking the cinch on the mare Pil had been riding. This mare was my horse now. Pil had robbed me of Gea using guilt as if it were a sword, and I had already given my strong gelding to Cael. At least my new mount didn't mind whispered profanities.

When Pil mounted, she had to scale Gea's side as if the horse were an oak tree. Cael stared at Pil, raised his eyebrows at me, and then stared at Pil some more when I kept my face straight.

"Bib," Cael whispered, "the possibility is quite real that Gea will throw the girl and crush her."

I had been thinking the same thing. Pil was a fine rider now and had improved a lot in the past weeks, but she still lacked experience. I shook my head. "Pil's a sorcerer. I have no business telling her what to do. Now, I assume that you can find these sons of bitches who took your arm, right? You said you can find paths and weapons, so you must be able to find your own damn arm."

In the past, I had seen Cael's white face go to pink when he was embarrassed, but now he turned the shade of a nearly ripe tomato. "I think so. I was given a means of finding certain things."

I waited a few seconds. "What is this 'means'? Fetch it out and ask it to help us."

"It's a glove."

I waited for more. He glanced at his stump. My mouth fell open.

"Yes, that glove!" he said. "And I can guess exactly why those men want it."

"Damn it, Cael! Couldn't you have kept it in a sack or something?"

"I couldn't have predicted that a brutal emissary of the gods would rip my arm in half! Would you have guessed that could happen? Or would you have been wearing it to keep it safe, just the way I did? Damn you for a smug, condemning hypocrite!"

Ella trotted over to us. "Gentlemen, is everything well? If so, I suggest you behave accordingly. If not, I suggest you behave yourselves anyway."

Cael gave her a strained smile. "I may have saved us, at least a bit." He reached into a pouch and pulled out a piece of gray wool.

Ella reached for it. "A . . . worm warmer?"

"A little finger to a glove," Cael said. "The last two knuckles."

He flexed the little finger on his remaining hand. "I cut it off the glove—just in case."

"That was almost clever," I said.

Cael huffed. "I am an—"

"I know, you're an architect, historian, warrior, hero of pure-thinking people everywhere, master of the spinet . . ." I trailed off as I watched his face age ten years in ten seconds. "Well . . . how does the silly thing work, anyway?"

Cael cleared his throat. "You wear it, think about what you want to find, and point it around in various directions. When you're pointing the right way, the glove squeezes your hand."

"Or squeezes your finger," I said. "Let's try it. Think about how to get your hand back."

Ella pushed the glove-finger onto Cael's real finger. He pointed his pinkie in all directions and then sighed. "Nothing."

Ella put the glove-finger on her own pinkie finger and repeated what Cael had done, with the same unhappy result. She tried the other hand, then passed it to me. I soon joined them in their complete lack of success.

"I'll hold on to it," Cael said. "Maybe it will work when we get closer."

At last, all of us had made ready, and we mounted. I led us north at a hard pace. We were twenty minutes behind Teeny and his men, and if they had any sort of problem or delay, we were likely to overtake them. We could figure out what to do with them at that point.

Teeny's thirty horses tore up a wide space of ground, even on the road, which was soft. I had no trouble following along. He didn't stay away from towns, though, so we were forced to ride straight through townships or risk losing the track.

Sunset arrived, and I blinked at it. I had killed thirteen men since my agreement with Harik, and I doubted that those murders had cut down my debt in a noticeable way. Unless I killed far more people soon, I would die four sunsets from now. I decided not to tell Ella. She had been pissed off about my losing thirty years from my life. If I told her about the sunsets, I might not need to wait for the fifth one to die.

We still faced the problem of provisions. Without supplies, we would have to travel hungry, thirsty, and cold for an uncertain length of time. That would be hard enough on the grassland, but if we crossed the wet, chilly marsh, it could be fatal.

Slowing enough to speak about it, we agreed that buying supplies would cost us a dear amount of time.

"It would be better to send someone ahead, wouldn't it?" Pil asked. "They could buy everything we need and have it waiting, and then everybody could just load up in a couple of minutes before we ride away."

"And they could buy a wagon of beer and some of them soft beds that fly from place to place, then light wherever you want to plop down your head," Stan said. "We could get some of those while we're getting things that can't possibly be got and doing what can't be done!"

Pil smiled at the ex-soldier. "Do you want some meat pasties, Stan?"

"Sure, and I want my mam to bake 'em."

Pil kicked her horse, and Gea leaped ahead. Soon the animal was outpacing us at a drumming gallop, which impressed me. Ten seconds later, Gea hit her stride and stunned me. She wasn't twice as fast as a speedy horse, but she was respectably close to it. I blinked to be sure I was seeing clearly. I assumed that Pil would halt at the next town and shake the tradesmen into action. I had seen her face down generals and monarchs. A baker or two would be no challenge.

As I watched Pil ride away, it struck me that maybe she really was better suited to killing gods than I was. My job was to escort her, which I had forgotten until that moment. Letting her go off alone was the stupidest thing I could have done. I cursed at my poor old mare.

"You think it's her." I hadn't heard Cael walk his horse up beside me. "That's why you gave her Gea. You think she's the one who will kill—"

"Kill every bit of fun we could be having on this trip," I cut in, giving Cael what I hoped was a hard and significant look.

"I'm shocked that your ego can stand being pushed into the secondary role, Bib. I guess you've grown."

"I don't mind sitting back and letting Pil choose the campfire songs." I raised my voice and glanced at the sky as I said, "No matter who is listening!"

Looking up, Cael nodded and sighed. "You're wrong, Bib. Yita will be . . . choosing the songs. Even the hardest and oldest ones of all. She was born to do it. I was told it by the, um, limping music master."

I leaned in the saddle and pointed at Cael. "I don't care if the farting harpist told you everything, you're full of shit! And this is a stupid conversation!" I clucked my horse into a trot.

"We're all here for Yita!" Cael called after me. "Accept it."

I ignored the gut-flopping, arrogant bastard. I also hoped that he was right.

EIGHT

Twilight was settling thick when we topped a rise and saw a small town at the bottom of a gentle slope. It lay on the other side of a steep-banked river, too steep for horses to manage. A wooden bridge, just wide enough for a wagon, crossed the river in an eighty-foot span.

The town did not appear ready to settle in for a quiet evening. One wooden building was afire, or at least smoldering well. Several people stood on the bridge and more had gathered across the river from us. Barrels, furniture, and crates had been stacked on the bridge to make a barricade.

"That's a blasted pack of unfriendly people right there," Stan said. "I may not be the smartest one here. Hell, I may be too stupid to spit sand compared to you sorcerers and fine heroes, but I'm clever enough not to prance down into the middle of all that."

"I have to agree with Stan," Desh said.

"I do as well," Ella added. "There must be another place to cross."

"Does anybody see Pil?" I asked, scanning the town.

No one answered me.

I said, "Do you just want to assume she's all right? No? Then we're going down there. I don't know why we're talking about doing anything else." Without looking around, I clucked and trotted my mare down toward the bridge. My companions clopped along behind me.

Two Denz soldiers stood on the bridge, and one of them carried a torch. Thirty men of various ages, not soldiers, had gathered on the town side carrying a half dozen more torches and a selection of long, pointy farming tools. A soldier stood ahead of them facing us. A fourth soldier was stationed beside the smoldering house with a torch and a bucket ready.

I halted before I reached the bridge and opened my mouth to say something clever, persuasive, and threatening. I stopped, though, when I got a good look at one of the soldiers on the bridge.

He was tall and powerfully built, but trim and relaxed. His sword hung at a spot on his belt that made for a smooth draw, and his face was strong but not harsh. Few men looked truly at ease wearing a helmet, but this man gave the impression he was comfortable in his and would rather wear it than go bareheaded.

One couldn't look at this fellow without thinking, "Finest soldier in the kingdom."

I held up a hand. "Good evening, Captain, I am Zim the hound trainer. It looks as if you have difficulty here, and I don't wish to add to it. I'm done teaching the southern lords' hounds to rend flesh on command or curl up around cold babies, as the situation demands, and I am in search of the next rich man in need. Oh, we're following a young woman too, our cook. She was riding a black horse and may have purchased food. Have you seen her?"

I glanced at my companions behind me.

With eyes pulled wide, Yita murmured, "I don't think he said a single thing that was true."

"Shh," Cael muttered. "That's his way. I don't know why, but it seems to work out."

The fine soldier raised one hand. "I'm Corporal Frutt," he said in a mild tone. "I may have seen her. Was her horse taller than a house? Do you train horses too? If you trained hers, then well done. What a jump."

65

I sat back to think about that.

Corporal Frutt went on, rubbing his classically carved chin: "My dog needs training. Bounder keeps peeing on my pillow. How long would it take to train him out of that? I can pay, but you have to do it quickly."

I asked, "So you won't be here for long?"

The other soldier on the bridge hissed and shook his torch before snarling, "Training dogs not to piss ain't in our orders, is it, *Corporal?*" He said "corporal" as if the word had been vomited into the gutter.

Frutt waved a lazy hand at the man. "Will it take long, Master Zim?"

"Lead me to this beast, Corporal!"

"Oh, no," Frutt said. "Do you think I'm foolish? I won't take you to Bounder. I'll call him here so you can see how good his training is already." The man whistled.

The soldier beside Frutt shook his head. "Our orders are to capture assassins, aren't they? Not to screw around with dogs who've got fig-all respect for spineless owners! Right?"

"You're right, you're right," Frutt said. "This shouldn't take long, though. How often do you find a real hound trainer?"

The soldier acted as if he was muttering, but I could hear him fifty feet away. "You still ain't found one, you knob."

A knee-high, fuzzy brown dog shoved through a gap in the barricade, ran to Frutt, and began jumping up against the corporal's legs.

"Get down. Sit," Frutt said in a voice that wouldn't intimidate a duckling. He beckoned me. "Come on and see what you can do!"

The soldier across the bridge called out, "What? Again?"

The man beside Frutt yelled back, "What do you think?" He turned to Frutt. "Corporal . . ."

Frutt didn't look at the man. "Just wait, Ben, just a minute. Master Zim, you see my problem. Please help me."

I had dismounted, and Stan was holding my horse's reins. I could pull a yellow band and stop the dog from pissing on any pillow in the kingdom. I could make him jump as if bits of chicken hung in the air, crawl on his belly, and howl in key. But I didn't want to spend the power.

I petted Bounder, made friends, told him who was boss, and trained him to sit in about two minutes. "You try it, Corporal. Louder. Yes, but lower your voice. Good."

The dog sat. Frutt didn't clap his hands, but he made the motion. "That's amazing! What about the peeing?"

"It shouldn't be a problem," I said. "Take me to the sleeping place in question. Oh, my friends might want to purchase some things from the people of this town."

"That's enough!" shouted Ben, the soldier beside Frutt. "Mordie! Fire it!"

The man beside the smoldering house tossed the bucket's contents on it, and the flames jumped higher than the roof. Ben was swinging his sword at me, so I dodged, kicked him in the shin, drew my sword, and thrust it through the man's neck.

Frutt had grabbed Bounder and fallen back out of the way against the bridge railing.

I started heaving the pieces of barricade out of the way, and a few seconds later, Ella joined me. The closest soldier across the bridge was charging us and shouting for the townspeople to do the same. They followed him with an eagerness that surprised me, but then Moris had been a well-liked king.

While I was wrestling a barrel over the railing, Yita raced in and hurdled the remaining barricade. She drove toward the soldier and the villagers behind him. I dropped the barrel to help her, since she was outnumbered about thirty to one. Cael joined in, two steps behind me.

Yita charged straight at the soldier. As he swung, she dodged aside and sliced partway through his leg at the knee. Then she came up and beheaded him from behind with power that surprised me. It was as smooth as any killing I had seen in a long time. Without pausing, she yelled and ran toward the townspeople with blood trailing off her sword. They slowed almost to a stop.

Behind me, Ella screamed and then shouted a curse filthier than any I had uttered in weeks. I glanced back and by the growing blaze saw an arrow in her arm.

Desh shouted an obvious "Arrows!" while unwrapping the sling from where he always wore it around his waist, as tidy as an ugly belt. I finished clearing the barricade and helped Stan lead the horses across. Ella stomped over the bridge behind me, cursing with every step.

The townspeople edged away from Yita and then scattered. Maybe they wondered if the smallest of us was such a demon, what must the rest of us be like? Or maybe she was just scary as hell. Once the townspeople had fled, Yita ran back to help clear the barricade. Cael ran along the riverbank to kill the soldier at the burning house.

Desh had killed three bowmen who must have been waiting for strangers, hidden across the river from the town and ready to attack when signaled. Two others escaped Desh's fury to ride away east, so we could expect a visit from the rest of the Denz army soon.

As we organized ourselves at the edge of town, Pil and Gea appeared from the darkness between two buildings. "Fantastic diversion, everybody! I robbed them of everything we need."

"What if they had killed us all? Eh?" Stan whined. "How much good would your thieving have done then? You could have attacked them from behind if you really wanted to help. Poor Mistress Ella might still have both her arms. Or, well, you know what I mean."

"I knew you'd be safe," Pil said. "Nothing really bad can happen while you're with us, Stan."

Stan threw his purple hat on the ground. "Don't say that! You're tempting fate to kill me first! For a sorcerer, you don't know shit!"

Cael pointed at Pil and murmured to Desh, "Why does that ugly man hate her?"

Desh said, "Stan? It's about what you'd expect. He used to be in love with her."

Cael nodded.

I had decided to destroy the wooden bridge, hoping to slow down however many hundreds of soldiers were probably riding this way. I counted heads and realized Yita was missing.

"Where's Yita?" I shouted, and a moment later saw her walking off the bridge with Frutt. The corporal was still holding his dog, which had an arrow sticking straight out of its side. Yita led him over.

Frutt cocked his head at me, his mouth and eyes drooping like an old dog's. "Help," he said. When he dropped to his knees, I saw that the arrow had gone all the way through the dog and into Frutt's body.

NINE

If I didn't give a shit about Cael, then I didn't give a fragment of a shit about Corporal Frutt. Sadly, his dog was already dead, and Frutt might be soon, but at that moment, I couldn't think of any creature more useless to us than the corporal.

"Don't pull out the arrow," Ella told Yita, ignoring the fact that her own arm had an arrow sticking through it. Ella shook her head at me. "I can wait. Were it required that I have something shoved all the way through me, I could not ask for better than this."

Yita said, "Bib, heal this man. I saw you heal Cael, so I know you can save this man." She was helping the corporal sit down. Then she put one hand on his shoulder as if Frutt belonged to her.

I was examining the bridge, figuring out how to wreck it while expending as little power as possible. "Sure, Yita, maybe I could help him. But I will not. If I save him now, maybe I won't have the power to save your life tomorrow, and if you don't stop making ignorant suggestions, maybe I won't save you anyway."

The river's current was lazy, so I couldn't count on it to do much of the demolition work. That was inconvenient.

Yita looked back and forth among everybody there except Frutt, who sat with his head sagging forward. She asked in a low voice, "Do all of you feel this way about people who can't help you?"

"Great question!" I said, still examining the bridge. "Which of you wants to risk all our lives for this boob who can't help us?"

Cael cleared his throat. "If we can save him, we should. It's the right thing to do. I used to do the right thing sometimes."

"Anybody else think it's the right thing?" I asked, preparing to tear the bridge all to hell.

Ella agreed with Cael. Stan didn't quite agree, but he thought we were being too hard on Frutt just because he was a shitty soldier, which probably wasn't his fault. Pil argued both sides for a moment and then shut up. Desh watched everybody and waited.

I pulled a dozen blue bands and rotted the wooden bridge at critical places. The structure collapsed as if an avalanche had fallen on it.

As I worked, I said, "You are all correct: saving him is what decent people would do. Well, we're still not doing it, so stop yammering about it."

The yammering continued anyway.

Yita pushed her way past Ella to face me. "You're a very bad person, even worse than Cael said you were. Maybe somebody won't save you tomorrow. I don't think I'd sleep for a year if I let someone die like this. Is saving power worth more than a man's life?"

"Hell yes, sometimes," I said. "Anyway, you don't know what I gave up for this power, so you have no business judging what I do with it. Well, we can't keep standing here making philosophical statements and watching him bleed." I reached for my knife and remembered that it was gone—maybe still in the throne room stuck through a dead sorcerer's arm. "Desh, let me borrow your knife."

Yita drew her knife. "Here, use mine."

Ella frowned. "Why are you helping if you don't want him killed?"

Yita said, "Bib is going to be stubborn and cruel, and I can't help that. But I can help make sure that man doesn't suffer anymore. That's worth loaning a sharp knife to a cruel thug."

I smiled and took Yita's knife, but Desh said, "Wait!"

I raised my voice. "What is it, Desh? Just because I took her knife and not yours, that doesn't mean I like her better than I like you."

Pil turned away, and Cael watched me, his foot tapping. Frutt coughed a little with his eyes closed.

Desh said, "I know what was given up for some of your power, because I passed it on to you."

I thought back to the little leather bottles full of power that Desh had given me over the years. "Huh. I had sort of assumed you gave me that power to use as I pleased. Although you have sometimes made gentlemanly suggestions."

"I did give it freely, Bib. I would never dictate how you use magic. I might observe ways you could employ the power that I have given you happily and at no cost. Right now, I observe that it might be useful to heal this fancy, floppy soldier—useful in ways we don't yet see."

Yita's knife was in my hand, ready to end Frutt's life. I could do with another killing to pay down my debt to Harik, but I hesitated. "Desh, do you have some specific knowledge about the corporal here?"

Frutt raised his head, wheezed once, and dropped his head forward again.

Desh sighed. "No. In fact, he will probably never help us. He might even hurt us. I don't know, and you don't either."

I shifted my grip on the knife, and a ripple of disappointment surprised me. I had been working hard to kill Frutt. Why wasn't he dead yet? "Don't confuse things, Desh. The man is useless to us and about to die."

Yita said, "You only care about people you can use! Everybody else can go drown in the river. Nobody's life is worth a spit but yours!"

I stood up with the vague notion of threatening the girl. "I haven't been saying that! Well, I guess maybe I have, a little bit. Maybe he's not harmful, but . . ." I glanced at Ella and Desh. Neither of them looked encouraging. "Shit! I'm tired of arguing about it! Take your knife back." I took a steady breath as I handed the blade to the girl. I didn't want any approval from her, and she didn't offer any. "He has to wait until I've helped Ella!"

I examined Ella's arm with her standing. It was as simple as any arrow wound as I had ever seen. I decided to remove the arrow and bind the wound without using any magic.

"Horses are coming," Pil said a couple of minutes later.

I didn't even listen for the hoofbeats. Instead, I rushed to finish with Ella. Then I knelt beside Frutt and hurried to explore his damage. The wound would kill him unless he got help, but I could pull him out of danger without much trouble.

As I worked, I finally noticed the hoofbeats, shouts across the river, and answering shouts from the town.

Ella leaned over my shoulder. "Bib, hurry up!"

"You wanted me to do this," I muttered, but I became aware that the townspeople were pointing us out to the soldiers, and they were calling out Frutt for cowardice, treason, and witchcraft. Then two torches were tossed from a house to land near us. Arrows began falling.

"All right, good enough!" Standing, I left Frutt seated but awake. I ran away from the river into the darkness of the town, huffing around the pain below my breastbone while Cael and Yita followed me. The others had collected our horses farther inside the town. I mounted and counted heads as well as I could in the moonless night. "Ready?"

I heard shouts of agreement, and I led us north out of town at a gallop. We had lost the better part of an hour.

I halted frequently to make sure we were still following the track that Teeny's horses had left. We lost the trail several times, but I picked it up again. Once the moon rose, the track became easier to follow, so we made better time despite occasionally walking the horses to rest them.

At last, not long after midnight, we halted for an hour. Stan and Pil passed around food and beer, with Stan cackling the whole time. I realized we had one head too many.

"What in the name of Krak's big toes is he doing here?" I

pointed at Frutt, who was lying back on the grass with a roll clamped in his teeth.

"They would have hanged him as a traitor if we left him," Yita said. "It would have made your healing nothing but a waste. You should thank me."

"Is he riding double with you?" I asked.

Yita nodded.

"He isn't slowing us down any," Desh said. "We can leave him the first safe place we find. I sense that generosity will help us."

"The same way you sensed that your escape tunnel would come up in the middle of the biggest wedding of the year?" I sneered.

"Yes," Desh said. "We popped right out of the earth and ran. It shocked the guests. What direction do you suppose they told the guards to look? Every different direction, including up and down. I bet it gave us a two-hour head start."

"Fine, I don't care! Just keep him out of the way." I tore off some bread with my teeth.

Yita spoke up: "Now would be a good time to finish healing him."

I stared at her. "Do you think about these things before you say them?"

"Yes."

"Can you round out that answer? Will you, I mean?"

Yita nodded. "The conditions are right. We're resting, Frutt is still alive, and you haven't gotten yourself killed yet, although you might soon, so we shouldn't wait." Yita took a deep breath. "Earlier you said you'd kill him, but you didn't, so deep down you must not have wanted to."

I hadn't admitted it to myself, but she was right. "You are full of five kinds of shit!"

Yita gazed at me as if nothing I could say would matter to her.

"Well, a lot of shit!" I glanced at Cael, who shrugged. I sat down beside Frutt, told him to keep quiet, and finished healing him. I walked away from that with a nice nail of pain in my chest.

We resumed travel before dawn, although we still had to halt once in a while to search for the track. I figured that Teeny was increasing his lead, and I snapped at everybody who talked to me.

Dawn arrived to show the trail clearly. Although we and our horses had been running on little sleep over the past two days, we pushed hard. Now was the time to catch up.

Just before midmorning, the tracks stopped. They didn't disappear in water or on rock. The horses hadn't ridden single file or doubled back. The tracks ended in unmarred earth and grass, as if Teeny's force had been plucked out of the world. Maybe it had, since that's how it had arrived on the trail, but I wasn't willing to stipulate that without investigating.

We rode expanding circles to examine the area but found no tracks. After half an hour of failure, I sat on the unmarred ground, contemplated, and cursed.

Desh stood over me. "Either the horses were changed, or the ground was changed."

I nodded. "Assume it's the ground. Changing the horses would be a cast-iron bitch. So, if it's the ground, either it was physically changed, or its appearance was changed."

"Or it was moved," Pil added.

"Or it was moved." Desh pulled a piece of quartz out of a pouch and stared at the ground through it. "I don't think the appearance was changed."

"Physically changed or physically moved then?" Pil asked. "Changing is easier than relocating."

"And cheaper." I pulled a green band to explore the grass and found nothing odd. Well, some sorcerer had slapped my hand and taken Teeny's horses away from me. I piled five more bands on. Grass stalks all across the area had been broken and then mended.

"They were changed," I said. "The grass was repaired by a Caller who's stronger and smarter than me. Maybe a better lover too, I don't know."

Desh kicked at the grass as if it were doing something bad to us, which I guess it was. "Damn it. We're facing some strong sorcerers."

"Umm . . ." Pil said.

"What is it?" Desh asked.

"Never mind."

"Speak!" I said. "I mean, speak, please. Don't be quiet for fear of looking like a goddamn idiot. Lots of sorcerers die because of that."

"Are we looking at a pent?"

A full ten seconds of silence followed.

Desh said, "I see Bib has been teaching you things. A pent? That's an enormous leap. The evidence is almost nonexistent."

A pent was made up of five cooperating sorcerers, which was uncommon since most sorcerers couldn't cooperate well enough to serve supper without bloodshed. Each sorcerer had a different type of power.

One of the five, the leader, was the center of the pent and held the four corners together. A logical person would notice right away that a center and four corners make a square, or at least a rectangle, whereas "pent" is short for pentagon, which has five corners. That leaves an empty corner.

Some sorcerers in the past preferred "pent" because a square has four corners and four is an unfortunate number, whereas five is a strong number. Also, since magical power was measured in squares, using "square" for both things was confusing as hell.

Opposing sorcerers argued that calling something a pentagon would not make one of the corners disappear, no more than calling an elephant a loaf of bread would make its tusks disappear. Reality was not to be flouted, so sit down and shut up about it.

After forty years of the bitterest war in the history of sorcery, the "pent" side won.

The pent's benefit was that magic cost much less than normal for the corners. An astounding amount less.

Being so efficient, the corners could use magic cautiously and go for a long time using little power. Sadly, sorcery and caution do not always go together. Instead of being careful, corners tended to burn normal amounts of power to wield amazing, powerful magic. If they didn't blow themselves up doing that, they soon poured on extra power to produce tremendous, shattering magic, then lost control and obliterated themselves, even though they had sworn they wouldn't be so foolish.

Forming a pent was an ass-whipping, but it continued to exist until one of the members decided to leave or was killed.

"Let's put the idea of a pent aside until we have more evidence," I said. "If I was our enemy, once I hid my trail, I would change direction."

Cael spoke up. "Maybe I'm not supposed to eavesdrop on sorcerers, but we should try the magic glove's finger again." He pulled out the scrap of wool. Since I had no better ideas, I jammed it onto Cael's pinkie for him. Cael trained his little finger on all points of the compass.

"Maybe you should chant," Pil said. "I hear it works better if you chant." She turned away and held her breath against laughing.

"Nothing," Cael said after a minute. "Cutting this finger off the glove was useless."

"Maybe it needs to be higher, Cael," Desh said.

"Really? Are you going to laugh at me too?"

"I'm serious."

I said, "Desh is an expert on magical objects and what makes them work. I'd say he's a genius on the matter." I scanned around, but the flat terrain was treeless.

Without a word, Cael mounted his horse and pointed all the way around him with his pinkie. He shook his head.

"How about a taller horse?" Pil suggested, holding out her hand and nodding toward Gea.

Cael waved her hand away. "I can do it."

"Like hell you will! She's my horse now, and I don't want her to get confused about that." Pil took the finger from Cael, mounted Gea, and eased her pinkie around the compass like she was shoving it through honey. "Damn it!"

Desh said, "Don't get down yet, Pil. Are you sure you didn't feel it squeezing even a little? Or feel anything at all? I got the sense that something was happening." He turned to me. "Bib, you're skinny. Climb on Pil's shoulders and try it from up there."

"Oh, hell! What about Yita? She's lighter than me!"

Desh said, "Yita, I don't intend this as an insult, but I don't know you and I don't trust you."

"I'm not insulted," she said. "That's one of the smartest things I've heard any of you say."

Desh nodded at Yita before turning to me.

I almost accused Desh of playing a joke on me, but he looked as grim as a shipwreck. I climbed and wobbled my way onto Pil's shoulders, donned the finger, and started pointing. Ten seconds later, the wool gave my pinkie the gentlest of squeezes as I pointed it northwest.

Desh had been watching my face. "Was that it?"

I gritted my teeth. "I refuse to ride like this."

I didn't try to ride on Pil's shoulders, but I did ride double and hang on behind her. We halted every fifteen minutes or so for me to climb up Pil as if I were scaling a mast and then sitting at the mast-head. I corrected our course if necessary and climbed back down, cursing Cael, Desh, Teeny, Pil, and Gea. Pil laughed as I worked to climb without hurting her, and she asked about my age and health an improbable number of times.

During one of these pauses, Frutt asked Ella, "Are all three of them sorcerers?"

"Yes," Ella said, pointing at Desh, Pil, and me.

"Oh. I've never seen a sorcerer. I guess I thought they were made up, like unicorns." Frutt watched Pil atop her horse with me balancing on her shoulders, pointing my little finger in different directions while cursing under my breath. "Is this the kind of thing sorcerers do?"

Ella nodded slowly. "Yes. I would consider this typical."

TEN

An hour after the pinkie finger gymnastics, we found Teeny's track again, and we followed it straight north into the afternoon. As the day became warmer, clouds began forming, first drifting toward us and then blooming right overhead. The wind freshened, and the air softened with the chance of rain.

"I hate goddamn riding wet!" Stan shouted as we rode. "Plasters my groin to the saddle." He stared at me. "Somebody that can change the weather ought to do something."

"It feels good!" Pil yelled. "Wish I could unbraid my hair."

That kicked off a meandering argument about the weather.

I angled to ride next to Desh.

He glanced at me. "Well?"

"I don't sense anything wrong," I said. "I don't sense anything not wrong, either. This weather is sort of . . . blank, I'd say."

Within a few seconds, the wind swung to blow into our faces and stiffened so much that grass stalks began flying through the air.

I drew rein and shouted, "Dismount!"

"You'll put us on foot?" Desh yelled. "We might need to run away."

"Do you plan to run away from the wind? If your horse is that fast, sell it and buy a castle. Stan! Hold the horses!"

"Over there!" Cael yelled. "They just appeared, like they grew out of the ground." He pointed into the wind at six men on foot a hundred paces away. Their horses were gathered a fair distance behind them.

"They're wearing green," I said, shading my eyes.

Desh was unwrapping his sling, and Pil was stringing a bow she had taken from one of the dead soldiers back at the bridge. Four arrows flew toward us from the strangers, but they fell short. Each one exploded when it landed in the tall grass, throwing fist-size balls of fire in all directions.

Frutt had drawn his sword and was shaking it at our enemy, but when the arrows exploded, he backed away, lowering his weapon. Whatever he did for the rest of the fight, he did it from behind me.

The wind stirred the little fires into clusters of whipping flames.

"No! We did that to the Hill People," Pil said. "It's not right for these dinks to do it to us!"

Cael and Yita charged the men, jumping through the burning grass as they ran. Ella raised her eyebrows at me.

"Let them go," I said.

I had already tried pushing back against the wind, but it was like lifting a bear with my tongue. Either the other Caller was using an obscene amount of power, or he was getting power at a discount— maybe as part of a pent. I couldn't beat him with brute force, so I'd have to bewilder him. Cael and Yita would hold his attention while I did other things.

I turned to Pil. "Aim at the ones not shooting at us."

Her mouth opened, but then she nodded.

Desh was already digging in a pouch with a small grin on his face.

I pulled a white band and tossed it into the sky. Then I hurled three yellow bands out beyond the enemy. I almost chuckled but shook my head. I threw yet another white band to push harder but uselessly against the wind. The Caller pushed back at me with such force it hurt my arms.

Finally, I threw five more white bands beyond the Caller to use for purposes I expected him not to like too damn much.

The grass fire had become a sheet of flame sweeping toward us. Pil fired an arrow, which bent in midair and fell to the ground. Cael and Yita continued running with their weapons raised.

"Ella, attack their flank!" I yelled. She was a fine general, but this was a sorcery fight. She didn't know a damn thing about it, so she followed my order in an instant by running at an angle toward the enemy.

Desh held two small rocks over his head and banged them together while shouting, "Asshole!" I heard his voice echo in front of him, then echo again farther away. The echo became twice as loud every time it jumped out another ten or twenty paces. It staggered Cael and Yita when it overtook them.

The immense, echoing "Asshole!" that reached our enemies threw them all down into the grass.

During that distraction, I threw another white band into the sky and squeezed it to draw rain. Maybe the other Caller hadn't thought to prevent that, or maybe he was stunned on the ground. Maybe he just couldn't keep track of too many things at once.

I rattled the yellow bands I had flung out past the enemy. The creatures out there grew passionate and ravenous.

By the time the Caller and his men gained their feet, Desh was poking around in another pouch. Pil fired again. This arrow didn't bend, but it twisted into pieces and wobbled aside. The Caller's archers fired, but none of them hit us.

Cael and Yita were nearing the enemy when suddenly her sword bent in the middle. A moment later, they both pitched forward onto the ground. I could hear Cael cursing. I had suspected that we were facing not just a Caller but also a Bender, who could reshape a person's boots and link them. It was the sorcery equivalent of tying a classmate's shoes together.

My rain was thinning out the flames. Maybe out of frustration, the Caller pushed more power into his wind. I used a small amount of power to pull a small wind toward me from behind him. His tremendous wind sucked my breeze along with it and made a prodigious gale blow from behind him. Hundreds of small rodents and large insects had climbed up in the grass looking for the food I had promised them, and the blast hurled them like missiles against our enemy's backs. The men staggered forward, covering their heads.

Desh lifted a tiny wooden carving of a ship over his head. I never found out what devastation that would have produced because the ship bent into the shape of a small penis, which I assumed was an insult from the Bender.

The sorcerers and bowmen ran for their horses. The beasts were bucking and stomping, which must have made mounting difficult. Ella reached them while this was happening and fell on the green-clad men from the side. She cut down two archers as they covered the retreat.

"Smarmy, dawdling bastard!" Desh snapped as he examined the wooden penis in his hand.

The fires were almost out, and the wind was dying away fast. The rodents were angry, but it had been an emergency.

I turned to Desh. "Asshole?"

He pitched the penis into the grass. "It has a good sound for an echo—the right vowels, syllables, and accents. I could have said hash bowl, but asshole is a little stronger, and I think it's more poetic."

I grinned. "Well, it wasn't pretty, but it was a victory."

"Um," Stan said from behind me, "maybe so, but not as much, I guess."

I turned and saw him with an arrow through his wrist. His face was white, and he was sweating. "I'm sorry," he said. "Damn arrow sent me spinning." He shrugged and waved his good hand toward where our horses ought to be—but weren't.

I spotted the horses leaving at a frantic gallop and whipped a yellow band after them. I may as well have thrown my hat and spit. The Caller had convinced them of some damn thing so terrifying that they might not pay attention to me for hours.

Only Gea had stood her ground. Now she was twisting her head from side to side examining us all. I had never been mocked by a horse, but Gea mocked me then, and she mocked everybody else too. I didn't know what kind of supernatural warrior heroes she was accustomed to serving, but we were not measuring up.

I hadn't killed a single soul in that fight. My third sunset was just a few hours away, and without horses, I might not get out of this damn kingdom before the fifth sunset arrived.

ELEVEN

Ella had attacked two of the soldiers in green, but only one of them survived. He'd be dead by sunset because the sword wound in his side wouldn't stop bleeding. Since Teeny's sorcerers had ridden off and left us on foot, our only strategic move was to interrogate this man, hoping that something he said would turn our weaknesses into strengths and make us feel better about things in general.

"I'll torture him," Yita muttered out of the prisoner's hearing.

I raised an eyebrow at her. Nobody else looked inclined to believe her, either.

"I will! Although I don't want to," she said. "He must know he's dying, and Bib wouldn't heal a bunch of smashed-up orphans, so all we can threaten him with is pain. We're his enemies. He can't expect us to be nice to him."

Cael nodded. "It's logical."

Pil burst out, "Maybe it's logical in the Crazy Lands of Hep and wherever Cael is from, but it's not here!" She hesitated and glanced at Desh. "Is it?"

Before Desh answered, Ella said, "How much can he know?

He's not an officer. We might gain nothing in exchange for causing him great pain."

I said, "Let me try something. If it doesn't work, you can torture what's left of him."

I brought Stan over to the prisoner, who was lying flat on the grass. He was a fit young man, apart from his mortal wound, with short black hair, tanned skin, and pale blue eyes. He was sweating and wincing but making no sounds.

I said, "Young man, what's your name?"

"Sam," he said in a controlled whisper.

"Sam, I want you to watch this. Watch closely. It may be the most important thing you see all year."

Stan and I sat. I removed the arrow from Stan's wrist while he hooted and squirmed. Off to the side, I saw Frutt turn away and throw up. Then I healed Stan's wound.

"Do you see, Sam? Now he has a better wrist than he had when he was a boy. Do you understand what I can do?"

Sam nodded.

"Do you know that you're dying?"

He nodded again.

"If you answer all my questions—all of them—truthfully, then I will heal you and you can go free. Before you agree, I must warn you about something: I'm a sorcerer, as you saw. I don't already know what you'll tell me. Otherwise, why would I ask? But if you tell me something that's not true, I will know that for sure. That is a fact you can chisel on your tomb. If you lie to me, I will let that girl torture you. In her country, she is the king's torturer, raised to have great imagination and no conscience."

Sam was looking back and forth between Yita and me, but he didn't seem to think we were worth wasting another syllable on.

Yita stretched to her full height and put on a face that was tolerably scary.

Sam glanced away from her, smiling. "I'll answer you, sir, but what's your name?"

"My name is Martel." I didn't think about the name before it slipped out. I realized that Sam reminded me of Prince Martel of Bellhalt—now King Martel. He had been a smart boy, but a little too serious.

Sam the soldier nodded.

I said, "All right, where are you from, who's leading you, and what do you want with my friend's glove?"

I expected a robust profession of ignorance, but Sam surprised me.

"I'm from the Kingdom of Balibuc. Our leader is King Famm, and the glove will lead us to a weapon."

Keeping my face straight, I digested all that. Balibuc lay on the far northern coast of the Northern Kingdoms. It was about as far away from the Denz Lands as one could get without drowning. I had met people from Balibuc in the past, but just a tiny handful.

The land of Sam's birth was a curious thing to learn, but when he mentioned King Famm, that was all I could think about. "Sam, do you mean that Famm is your king, or that he is here in the Denz Lands with you?"

"Both."

I had heard a dozen different stories about King Famm. He was said to have never gone to war for conquest, but three kings had tried to conquer him. He defeated all three on the battlefield and chased them all the way to their throne rooms. There, Famm personally hanged each king so that his body dangled directly over his throne.

After the third time that happened, kings stopped trying to conquer Balibuc. That was the story, at least.

Other stories said Famm possessed a whole barrelful of virtues. He was invincible in single combat, was loved by his people, had fathered nine children, wrote poetry, could play any musical instrument, fed orphans out of his personal wealth, and wept when the humblest of his subjects suffered.

The stories were outrageous, of course. But if one one-hundredth of them was true, I wouldn't be fit to lick the ground clean behind him wherever he walked.

I nodded. "King Famm, eh? What's his favorite musical instrument?" I tried not to grin.

Sam didn't blink. "I've never seen him pick up an instrument he couldn't play."

My face must have looked skeptical.

"Not right away, maybe. He might sound like a dying goose for an hour or so, but then . . ." Sam winced and turned red as he pressed his wound with one hand.

I needed to hurry up my interrogation, or the boy would die in the middle of an answer. I couldn't resist asking the next question, though. "Why does old Famm carry three swords? Does he fight with one in his teeth? Or is he compensating for his deficiencies?"

Sam surprised me by giving a little smile. "Some people get confused about that. They're not his swords. They belonged to his sons, who died defending the kingdom."

I put that aside to think about later. "Why is Famm working for the gods?"

Sam furrowed his brow. "The gods are at war with some demons who killed our people and burned our cities. So, now we fight the demons alongside the gods."

"All right. What is this weapon?"

"I don't know," Sam said before stopping to wince again. "I can't imagine such a thing, but it's supposed to be able to kill a god. We have to get it before the demons do."

"Why don't the gods just get it themselves?"

"I don't know that, either."

"Where is it?" I asked. "How far?"

Sam sighed and shook his head.

"I guess it's the glove's job to know that, huh?" I said.

Sam nodded and then squirmed, groaning a little.

"He'll die," Pil whispered. "Save him. You promised."

I ignored her. "Tell me about these sorcerers traveling with you."

"One's all right," Sam said. "The others are assholes."

"How many others?"

"Um. Four others. Seems like too many to me. A lot, at least."

If there were five sorcerers, most likely they were a pent. I leaned close to Sam's face. "Which god is Famm taking his orders from?"

I didn't expect an answer. Why would a king share that kind of information with one of his soldiers?

Sam whispered, "Fingit."

"Hurry! He's dying!" Yita said as she poked my shoulder.

Without looking at her, I said "No, he's not. He hasn't asked my permission to die. Sam, why in the name of the gods' eleven crotches would your king say he was keeping me alive?"

"Fingit wants you to live," Sam whispered.

That was as far as I thought I could push him. I pulled a green band and began healing Sam's wound.

I had recently heard Fingit agree with the other gods that I should be dead, but he was slightly less of an awful villain than the others. He and I had gossiped, and he told a good joke. I couldn't imagine Fingit caring about me, but he might not jump over a six-rail fence to kick me.

Also, Fingit was the one who learned about the curse that was keeping the gods from stomping me like a loose board. Could he have just made it up to keep me alive? Did he expect me to help them fight Gek?

That led me to another question. Famm was helping the gods because the Void Walkers had wiped out a bunch of his people. But why would Gek do something stupid like that? What reason did he have for pissing off Famm and giving the gods an ally?

Once I finished healing Sam, I had a load of questions that he couldn't answer, and a slab of pain shoved into my side. If I wanted to go anyplace in the next few hours, I would be limping there.

The dry, scratchy grass looked as soft as a feather cushion to me, but I shoved myself upright instead of plopping down onto it. "Go on home, Sam. It'll be a hike to get back there."

Stretching his side, Sam smiled. "Thank you. You should go home too. The king has been asked to let you live, but that's not the most important thing for him, Bib."

I started to ask how he knew my real name, but he beat me to it.

"The king hides nothing from us. Almost nothing. He told us we were fighting you." Sam turned and trudged away north.

Ella squeezed my hand and nodded toward Pil, who was mounted on Gea. "Sweetheart, you must ride to find our horses and bring them back. I'm sorry, you cannot rest yet. We will continue on foot until you return with our mounts."

"Well . . . I can't think of a better plan," I said. "Give me a hand up, Pil."

Pil helped me drag myself and the piercing pain in my side up behind her. She didn't make any chuckling comments about my age, either.

Yita scrambled up Gea and planted herself behind me.

I was so surprised I just watched her do it. "What do you think you're up to?"

"The two of you cannot go by yourselves."

Cael snapped, "Effla and Trutch! Yita, get down!"

Instead of leaping back off the horse, Yita said, "Two is a very bad number. Three people can be successful."

"You're not going without me, and I don't have a horse!" Cael folded his arms.

Yita said, "Don't talk foolishness! It's not like you at all to say stupid things. You couldn't go with us anyway. Four is a worse number than two!"

Pil grinned. "Even if you had a horse, Cael, you couldn't keep up."

I said, "This is as entertaining as my wife's mother, but it's time to go." I elbowed Yita to knock her off, but she scrambled aside and escaped me. Well, I had been slowed by the pain from healing Sam. I tried again. She slipped away, hanging from the saddle by one hand before popping back up.

Cael started laughing.

I attempted to dislodge the girl three more times and failed every time.

Everybody was laughing now but me.

I shouted, "Damn it, Cael, can't you do something besides giggle like a lunatic? She's your responsibility!"

Still chuckling, Cael reached for Yita and grabbed an ankle. The girl seized me as an anchor, swung her other leg over, and kicked Cael in the face. He let go and stepped away, holding a bleeding lip.

I laughed at him and pointed.

"That's enough!" Cael yelled, pushing up his sleeves.

"Hold on, you big hero," I said. "How many people do you figure can whip you and me at the same time? It's not my decision, but I think you should let her go wherever she wants before she cripples us both."

Yita grabbed me tight, but since none of my ribs broke, I concluded she was hugging me. I didn't want Yita's help, but I did want to observe her more closely since Cael had said she was supposed to kill Krak.

Cael leaned in and growled, "I don't want her to end up like Manon!"

"Me neither. You were planning to put her in my care, so you couldn't have been too worried."

Cael turned pink.

I said, "All you can do is your best, Cael. Are you going to fight her, or are you going to help her fight?"

Cael flapped his hand at us and then turned away.

Gea leaped into a run. I wasn't sure that Pil commanded her to do it.

After a few minutes, Yita yelled into my ear, "Where is your wife?"

"What?"

"You mentioned your wife's mother. Where is your wife?"

I turned my head toward the girl. "She's dead, years ago."

"How did she die?"

"Not that it's a damn bit of your business, but I broke her heart when I let our daughter die." I knew that wasn't entirely accurate, but sometimes I still felt that way. Yita shut up, so I figured stretching the truth had been worthwhile.

Several minutes later, Yita asked, "How did Manon end up? And who is he?"

Without pausing, I said, "Manon was my other daughter. *She* ended up dead because I stabbed her."

That made Yita stop talking for a good long while. At last, she said, "That must be terrible. No wonder you became such a cruel, awful murderer."

I tried to say something sarcastic, but I couldn't quite get it out.

TWELVE

We followed the broad trail our horses left behind. They had run northeast but soon veered dead north—the same heading as Famm and his little army of sorcerers.

"Ladies, I don't think we're going to find the horses running around loose. That Caller has gathered them in, and Famm's men will ride them at a gallop all the way to the Northern Kingdoms."

Pil was silent for a short time. "I can't think of any reason why you'd be wrong about that. What should we do?"

"I guess we could surrender to Famm and become his subjects," I said. "But let's make that our second choice. How about we sneak in and steal them while everybody's sleeping?"

"No," Pil said. "We're pretty, but we're not stealthy, and I don't think any of us could successfully sneak out of bed. Can we ambush them, or bribe them, or throw a party? Come on, get creative."

"What's our advantage?" I asked. "What do we have that Famm can't match? And that he'd never suspect?"

Yita said, "I doubt that anyone else in the world has a horse like this."

Pil patted Gea's neck.

Gea could travel almost twice as fast as Famm's horses. A little magic could make that advantage decisive. Desh had been obsessed with light and fire lately, and he had taught Pil a couple of things.

Pil and I babbled ridiculous ideas, and Yita threw in a couple of unexpectedly insightful ones. Pil pulled out a knife and a small block of wood, and she began whittling, relying on Gea's smooth gait to save herself from lopping off a finger.

"I can make fire for you, if you have something to burn," Pil said, "but you'd better be satisfied with something the size of a big campfire, because you won't be turning our enemies to ash."

I grumbled, "It's better than throwing horse turds at them. Our goal is the horses, clear? Theirs and ours both. We'll never get them unless we disable the Caller first." I pointed in the direction of the far-off enemy as if the Caller were over there waving at us. "We'd be better off killing him. That would break the pent. If Gea gets a chance to kick the man's head off, she should take it."

"What can I do?" Yita sounded as bouncy as if she were helping plan a party.

Pil called back, "I bet there will be jobs for everybody, so we'll figure it out when we get there."

Just before sunset, I spotted Famm's thirty men and forty horses, still riding north. We jumped down to walk. I had no trouble since my side had just about recovered. I could barely see the mass of men and horses, and one of Famm's men would need fantastic eyesight to spot us, a single horse with three people on foot.

I gazed at the coming sunset as we walked. If I didn't begin killing in a diligent fashion, I would die in three more sunsets. If I did kill like a maniac and retire Harik's debt, he had promised to restore the forty years that he had taken from me. I shouldn't believe him, of course, but I found myself yearning to live more than I thought I would.

I said, "Don't kill any of these people if you can keep from it."

"You are offering them mercy?" Yita asked.

"No, I want to kill them myself." That ended the conversation for a while.

We matched the enemy's pace and trailed them. Famm didn't

seem to be in a furious hurry. Of course, he had the glove and all our horses. He could afford to spare his mounts a bit.

Before long, only stars lit the plains. I had hoped Famm would break to rest for a few hours before moonrise. His men and horses had been traveling hard. The King of Balibuc rewarded me by doing exactly what I wanted him to do.

History has taught me to exercise care whenever somebody does exactly what I want them to do. History has taught me that, but sometimes I forget.

Our plan couldn't be called simple, but it wasn't rash. At least we started off together and wouldn't mistime the attack. We approached the camp in darkness from the side where Famm kept his horses. His men had spread out under a big, half-dead oak tree on the other side of the camp from us.

I held up a wooden cylinder Pil had carved, then whispered, "I'll mark the Caller. Pil, you kill him. Yita, once hell has broken out down there, you set loose the horses. Ready?"

Pil grinned and raised her left hand to show that she was gripping the 'dent.

I leaned forward and peered. "You fixed it? What's it going to do?"

"Wait a minute, and I'll show you."

"All right, then. Go!"

Pil pointed a wooden doodad at the big tree and caused fire to burst from the deadest limb. The fire wasn't hot enough to do much damage, but I had already weakened the limb. Just as the flames appeared, I hit the limb with so much rot that it fell right off the tree with a massive crack, trailing bits of dead, flaming wood.

I shouted "Burner!" and held my breath until somebody else took up the warning. Within seconds, men were yanking off their clothes. Some shouted and stomped around, calling the half-naked soldiers idiots. Others shuffled about, and I heard weapons drawn, even though marking a target was impossible in that darkness.

"Scoot!" I hissed at Yita.

I had counted on Famm's men knowing what a Burner could do since they were traveling with one. Somebody was shouting curses at men who had their trousers off. That made me giggle, which is undignified in a sorcerer, but nobody heard me. I could just make out Yita in the starlight as she sprinted for the horses. Pil and Gea would be running a curve to take them right through the camp.

I watched the camp for a moment before following Yita toward the horses. On the way, I saw the outline of a running sentry who must have been watching his comrades in the camp go insane. Something moved behind him, and I made out Yita looking toward me, jumping up and down, and pointing at the man. I stabbed him in such a rush that he never raised his sword.

Gea thundered across the camp, and I doubt any of the shocked soldiers got a clear look at her. Pil flung four freshly carved spheres in both directions as she passed. They landed with a fine boom and set the grass afire for six feet around like healthy campfires.

A moment later, two of the fires were doused as if a thousand weight of sand had dropped onto each. Pil shouted "Shit!" as she and Gea galloped back into the night.

I had three jobs now and not much time for them. The first was to locate the Caller. I had taken pains to remember the man after he mystically slapped me around like a dead fish. He was a short, thin fellow who moved like he was bouncing everyplace he went.

I spotted the man by the remaining firelight and watched him while I pulled yellow bands to get our horses' attention. By the time I hurled my fifth band, the Caller was staring right at me, never mind that I was still in darkness.

Before the Caller could do anything annoying, I encouraged the tall, tough grass near him to grab at his feet and ankles. He took a step and nearly fell. Then he looked back and forth between the grass and me before focusing my direction and ignoring the grass.

Gea's hoofbeats were growing louder again. I broke Pil's wooden cylinder in my hand while pointing at the Caller. The man's shirt lit up with a glow that was visible even over the fires.

The Caller had begun plucking the horses' attention away from me like I was a baby sorcerer. When his shirt lit up, he hesitated. Gea charged back into the camp. The Caller tried to run, but his feet were tangled in grass. I sensed him throwing a band, probably to distract Gea. It must have been disappointing when Gea ignored him.

Gea reared, and the Caller raised his arms to protect his head from the horse's supernatural hooves. A hoof struck, and the Caller crumpled.

Gea galloped away again, her hooves pounding like a rockslide. Once she charged into the darkness, the hoofbeats stopped. It was as if Gea had halted and was waiting for the soldiers to come get their asses—and all their other parts—kicked. A few soldiers, some without shirts or trousers, ran to follow Gea out of camp. King Famm was bellowing for everybody to stop acting like goddamn blind sheep.

Yita had scrambled through the herd and cut most of the horses' hobbles. I finished snatching their attention. It brought my level of magical energy sadly low, but this would all have been for naught if we didn't get the horses. I worked at convincing the beasts to follow Gea.

The horses already wanted to follow the fittest, strongest leader around, so convincing them to follow Gea wasn't hard. In fact, I feared it was too simple, and I might accidentally convince the horses to follow Gea around until they died. I tried to ease them into the idea of following.

Pil and her horse arrived from around the edge of the camp, pacing at a smooth, quiet gait. I mounted another horse and waved in Pil's direction. Yita mounted a horse not far away, and we joined the blanket of horseflesh following Gea south. Now King Famm was without horses. I bet he wouldn't like it too damn much.

A few seconds later, I saw Yita fall off the side of her horse, along with her saddle. My saddle slipped off too. Famm's Breaker must have disintegrated the cinches. I clung to the horse's mane, let the saddle go, and rode bareback.

I turned to go back for Yita, but my horse fell out from under me. The beast neighed in fear as we slapped against the bottom of a pit, and the horse rolled over my left leg, breaking it. Pain marched up my leg from the break, but I was lucky he hadn't rolled all the way over me.

Shaking my head, I saw I was at the bottom of a wide hole probably too deep to crawl out of, even with two legs. The horse was struggling and frightened but seemed whole. The saddle was gone, and the horse had lost his bridle too, as well as his blanket. My clothes, belt, scabbard, and boots were likewise missing. I would have bet that the horse's iron shoes had disappeared too. The Breaker must not have been able to pin me down, so he picked out a big area in my direction and obliterated every nonliving thing in it, an impressive feat of brute force.

The only thing that hadn't disappeared was the sword Desh had enchanted for me. It had never been harmed by any kind of magic. I scooted over to hide the sword beneath my body.

The glow of torches approached, and five men leaned their heads over the edge of the hole to gaze at me. "Very fine aim, Kyle," King Famm said in a profound, bass voice.

A head nodded.

Another man said in a small voice, "Thad may die."

Famm said, "And you want this man punished?"

"No, I want to use him!" Small Voice said.

Famm cleared his throat. "Maybe. I could try to exchange him for our horses, but it seems a little like horse thievery that could go on between us all year. Right, Bib?"

"I'd say the chance of that is zero, King Famm." I sniffed. "The odds are better that one of us will be dead by morning. And despite our circumstances, don't be too damn sure that you'll be the one still alive."

Small Voice laughed quietly.

Kyle snapped at me: "Remember that you speak to a king, you nasty Ir-man. Be respectful."

I said, "Sorry, Your Majesty. I've heard good things about you. I'll be sure to send your body home with all three of your dead sons' swords. Maybe one of your daughters can ride around the kingdom with them."

Nobody spoke. Then Famm said, "You almost made me angry. I can see why Fingit wants you to live."

"Oh, Fingit." I waved that away. "I owe him money. Otherwise, he wouldn't give a shit whether I live or turn into a horse apple." I snapped my fingers. "Your Majesty, I invite you into my lovely hole. And thank you, young Kyle, for creating it."

Famm stared at me for five seconds before looking over his shoulder. "All right, bring him out."

When I sat up, grabbed my sword, and killed the first soldier who climbed down, Famm may have thought it was luck. After I killed the pair that scrambled down next, he looked worried.

"Send them down three or four at a time!" I laughed. "I can't lay around here all night."

Famm and his men walked away. A few minutes later, he returned with more men. "Bib, I could kill you with arrows, but . . . well, you don't have to say thanks."

The soldiers started throwing firewood down at me. They threw hard. Maybe the men I killed had been popular or owed a lot of people money. I covered my head and endured it for a minute before I got across the idea that I was giving up.

Pain spiked in my leg as the soldiers pulled me out of the hole, but that wasn't the most aggravating thing. Now the earliest I'd be able to kill Famm would be after breakfast.

THIRTEEN

King Famm's men dumped my naked self on the grass in the middle of his camp. Two of them pressed sword points against my body, one at my throat and one over my heart. Two more seized my hands.

Small Voice spoke to me, almost chatting. "No magic, all right? Not even to heal yourself. The instant you swirl a finger, these men will pin you to the earth. I'm sorry, I didn't need to be that aggressive. They'll kill you, unless you can kill all four of them at the same time. I don't think you can, but maybe. Danis will stand over there ready to pile a hundred pounds of dirt on your head if you stir."

It was too dark to see the speaker's features well, but he had long hair. From the ground, he seemed tall but thin. His voice sounded young, but then almost all sorcerers were youthful. I wondered where Yita was, and I hoped she had escaped to run for help. Pil hadn't turned back for us, and she had been right not to.

Spitting a little blood, I worked my sore jaw. The soldiers had chucked enough firewood to turn me into a carpet of scrapes and bruises, but nothing was broken except my leg. I said, "I'll behave. I know that these four fellows can watch me like this forever without moving or getting distracted, so I have no hope. I surrender."

Small Voice snickered and then cleared his throat. "I guess we should lop off your hands, but I'd rather not. It's a risk, but . . . I hate to do something we can't easily undo."

"A wise policy. I subscribe to it myself." I imagined how Ella would snort at that, knowing I'd be tickled to murder every one of these fellows. A girl shrieked someplace behind me. I knew it was Yita. She couldn't have screamed with any more terror and pain if her eyes were being cut out.

Small Voice ran in the direction of the screams.

I shouted, "Leave her be! Whatever you do to her, I'll do three times to you!"

The screaming went on with no words and hardly a pause for breath. Men were yelling at Yita and at each other. I heard the crack of somebody being slapped hard. After a pause, Yita went back to shrieking like she was damned. I didn't think her screams could get any more horrible, but they did.

Men shouted and cursed. I was one of them.

At last, the screaming came closer. Two men pushed Yita to the ground near me. She stopped mid-scream and said "Thank you" in a calm voice.

One of the soldiers pointed at me and yelled at her, "See? He's fit as an anvil! We ain't beating him or raping him to death, and he's got all his teeth still!"

Yita's knees, ankles, and wrists had been bound, but somebody had thrown a long shirt on her first. She rolled faceup and smiled at the soldier. "Well, I guess you're not a demon baby murderer after all. Sorry. You're just a child-beating thug."

The soldier walked away. "Bitch! Hole-rolling bitch!"

Yita twisted to catch my eye and whispered, "It will be all right. It's a good thing I came with you."

In the faded firelight, I saw blood running down the side of her head. I asked, "Are you hurt?"

Yita grinned. "Oh, no, not at all."

Small Voice and Kyle stepped over, and Small Voice squatted beside Yita. "Don't do that anymore." He turned to Kyle. "Are you sure she's not a sorcerer?"

"I checked twice. There's no sign."

Yita made a face. "Bib, he came so close that I thought he'd kiss me."

Kyle huffed away.

Small Voice said, "Girl, I don't like to kill children, but it's been done. Be quiet now. Quiet as a dead mouse."

Yita said, "Oh, I'll shut up if—"

I jumped in: "So, you're the middle part of this sorcery pent, eh? I mean, Danis is just a lackey standing over there like a shovel with legs, Kyle is off disintegrating other men's trousers to get a look at their bits, your Caller is busy dying, and your fourth has wandered off into the darkness to be awfully mysterious."

I heard a smile in the man's voice. "Yeah, I'm the middle. You're wrong about the others. They are brave, clever sorcerers. But I understand how you feel."

"Brave meaning too stupid to duck, and clever meaning they can follow simple orders most of the time. What's your name, Center?"

"Ace."

I blinked a couple of times.

"I know, right?" he said.

It was a brave name, even reckless. The letters were the first, third, and fifth, which were some of the strongest numbers of all. Also, the name had three letters in it, which made it even more powerful. But the letters also added up to nine. That was one of the unluckiest of all numbers—three squared. It was bold.

It was a name of greatness or tragedy with nothing in between. Ace must have clanked when he swaggered.

I said, "Your fourth corner is a Binder."

"Why would you think that?"

"He's not a Burner, or I'd be burned up by now. So, he's the Binder and you're the Burner." I almost nodded but held back in case the soldiers with swords should panic and kill me, fearing I would magically pull their faces out through their assholes.

Ace nodded, about as concerned as if I had caught him taking a second biscuit. "Yeah, that's us. Not for long though if Thad dies.

From getting kicked by a horse." He shook his head. "What a mundane death."

Obviously, Ace hadn't clearly seen Gea if he thought anything about that kick was mundane. I could understand that. Not many of us were prepared to recognize a supernatural horse when we saw one.

King Famm appeared out of the darkness, broad and bareheaded. I couldn't tell anything more because the fires had died away at last. The king clapped Ace on the shoulder like an old friend.

Ace said, "He's contained for now, Your Majesty, but that can't last. I didn't think he could be as devious as he's said to be, but I might have been wrong. I suggest you decide soon what to do about him."

Famm didn't move, but his thumping bass voice said, "Check on Thad for me, won't you?" After Ace walked off, Famm said, "Bib, why are you serving those demons and fighting against the gods?"

"Have you ever talked to a god?" I asked.

"Yes, I have."

I raised an eyebrow.

Famm smiled. "Fingit speaks to me in the darkness. He . . . he likes dirty stories."

That sounded like Fingit, and it surprised me. I had never heard of anyone besides sorcerers talking with the gods. I pushed on. "Have you seen a god?"

Famm's shoulders moved as if he might chuckle. "No."

"I have," I said. "Have you ever seen or spoken to a Void Walker? A demon?"

Hesitating, Famm said, "No."

"Then I beat you three out of four, Your Majesty. Maybe I have better information about this situation than you."

"You may have better information but still make a poorer decision," Famm said. "I know that the gods can be harsh and even unfair. Most of my life, I had no use for them. But they have helped mankind—sure, for a price. Everything has a price, and I know that sorcerers pay it. The rest of us should be grateful for that.

"But the demons only bring wreckage and slaughter," Famm added. "They brought horror, and I have to protect my people from that."

"Let me guess what your deal with the gods is," I said. "You will throw yourself and your best men into this war as the gods' allies. In exchange, the gods will defeat or maybe wipe out these 'demons' to prevent them from hurting you in the future."

"That's essentially correct," Famm said.

"Fantastic," I said. "Did the gods promise to restore your cities?"

"Well, no."

"Bring your people back to life? After all, they're gods."

After a breath, Famm said, "No, and I didn't think to ask."

"Did they give you any assurance that they won't throw you smack into the worst part of the battle to be killed?"

Famm's voice dropped even lower. "Not that either."

"All that sounds typical of the gods. Now consider something. Just consider it. What if it was the gods who ravaged your kingdom, and they just told you that the Void Walkers did it?"

Famm took half a step toward me. "That is not true! It's outrageous!"

"Maybe, but it would be a simple way to recruit you."

"Why go to all that trouble to make me their ally? Why me specifically?"

I stopped myself from shrugging. "You can answer that better than I can. The fact is you are now their ally. What do they get from that?"

Famm didn't answer.

"Your Majesty, let me tell you how the gods work. They like pain and irony, the more the better. So, first they wreck your kingdom and feed on your pain. Then they blame it all on their enemy so that you become their ally. That's a taste of irony right there.

"But let's add to that. The gods got you to join up without any effort to rebuild cities or raise dead people. All they had to do was promise that the attacks would stop. Well, since the gods did the ravaging in the first place, they can simply choose to ravage no more! That costs them nothing."

"But—"

"I'm not done. If you survive whatever repulsive task the gods give you, they will then throw you into the fiercest battle to die so they can enjoy your deaths and collect your lives. In the end, they will have paid nothing and gotten everything they wanted. You'll have lost everything. That is how the gods work, King Famm. I'm surprised your sorcerer didn't inform you. When you trade with the gods, there are no good deals."

Famm stepped back and paced until I thought maybe I had harmed his ability to think. At last, he stopped beside me. "You are devious. I think you're too dangerous to live. I'll ask Fingit for permission to kill you." He strode away as if he could split forests and crush castles as he walked.

If I had been able to shake Famm's confidence, maybe he would have made peace with us and let us alone. He might even have shared the actual glove so we wouldn't be working with one awkward little finger. I didn't know whether Famm was really a hero king, but he was too stubborn, and maybe too unimaginative, for me to convince.

I broke down and called for Fingit. If I could plead my case fast enough to beat out that noble lummox Famm, I might help my situation. However, Fingit didn't answer. He failed to answer so entirely that I couldn't sense him or even the trading place.

The moon rose just after midnight, and more soldiers came to replace the ones guarding me. My broken leg had begun to throb, but I suspected it was a simple break.

Ace walked up soon. "You pissed off the king something fierce. Nobody has been able to reach Fingit, but as soon as we do, you'll be dead within a minute. Sorry about that."

"I hate to tempt fate," I said, "but if you knew how many times I've heard that I'd be dead within a minute . . ."

He chuckled. "My guess would probably be on the low side. I might be able to help you or help us all, really. The king could change his mind if you save Thad's life. Maybe."

Yita shook her head at me.

I said, "I'm not sure that keeping him alive—and your sorcery pent unbroken—will help my friends much."

"If you save him, you might still be alive when your friends get here. Then we can trade you for our horses. Everybody will be alive, everybody will have horses, and we'll go back to an even footing for killing each other."

"How do we know we can trust you?" Yita asked.

Ace cocked his head at her. "I guess you can't know, but trust this—when His Majesty walks over here, Bib is going to die."

I said, "How do you know you can trust me? I might put my hands on Thad, kill him, and tell you he died of his wounds."

Ace crossed his arms. "You're right. If he dies, we'll kill you the next second without asking why he succumbed. But if things are hopeless for you anyway, you might as well kill Thad. No, I guess we shouldn't risk it. Too bad."

"Will the king guarantee that if I save Thad, we won't be killed?"

"Well . . . maybe. I'll see."

"Only if I can heal my leg first," I said.

Now that the moon was up, I could tell that Ace's cheeks were long, almost like a set of vertical lines. He gazed at me for a few seconds. "I understand. Thad's injury is severe. You won't be able to heal yourself after you're done with him. Krak, you probably won't be conscious. Let me see." He walked away.

Five minutes later, Famm watched from a distance as I healed myself. Four blades pressed against my body the whole time. Famm said, "Bib, if you twitch in a way I don't like, you'll have so many holes we'll be able to strain soup through you."

I smiled to acknowledge his threat. Healing the Caller was foolish of me, but now that I had two good legs, my prospects had improved quite a bit. Once I recovered from healing Thad, I'd find some chance to kill a couple of men, grab Yita, and run away. Then I could follow behind Famm and his boys, killing a lazy one here and there before slipping away again.

With luck, I could kill most of them by the next sunset and drive the rest frantic. That probably wouldn't satisfy Harik's debt, but at least I'd be doing something constructive about it.

The Caller's head wound was deep and chilling to look at. He probably should already have been dead, but over the next thirty minutes, I repaired all the damage. My own head grew a searing pain as I worked, and then I lost vision in my right eye. I vomited twice before I finished, and by the end, I was fully blind. I may have been deaf too—I didn't hear anything before I fell over and passed out.

I woke up in dimness, and I saw light on the eastern horizon. My head hurt but felt stable, so I sat up. Both my eyes went blind again, and I puked before falling backward. Ace was saying something, but I passed out again before I understood it.

The next time, I woke in morning light. I didn't feel awful, so I rolled onto my side and eased up to sit. In moments, three sword points were pressed against my body. While I slept, somebody had dressed me fully except for my bare feet.

"Breakfast?" Ace asked, holding out some kind of dried meat and rough bread.

I shook my head. "You just want to see me throw up again."

He wrinkled his nose. "It didn't exactly make me swoon the first three times, so no. Thad seems well, as rowdy as ever. Thank you. When we first caught you, I was thinking that if Thad died, we might ask you to join the pent in his place."

I started laughing.

Ace waved a hand. "I know! That seems like years ago now, when I was an innocent lad and had never heard your corrupting words. Both you and Thad can walk now, so His Majesty will lead us north on foot soon. We expect your people to catch up later today, or at least tomorrow. Maybe your friends will think you're worth forty horses. I don't believe it myself, but you might have hidden qualities." He winked and turned away.

I had always thought that to hold a pent together a sorcerer had to be stern, masterful, and unyielding. Ace seemed to do it with pleasant talk, an occasional laugh, and a talent for doing favors.

Yita appeared, fully dressed. Now her legs were free, but her hands were still bound. She said to the soldiers, "You're doing your duty, so we will try not to kill you when we escape."

Two of the soldiers laughed at her.

"Maybe I'll kill you after all," she said.

A few minutes later, soldiers began yelling and pointing weapons out past the edge of camp. I craned my neck and saw Desh standing by himself, unarmed, a double stone's throw away from the camp's edge. All the horses, both Famm's and ours, wandered around grazing far behind Desh. Gea stood with the herd, and Pil sat mounted on her.

Famm and his officers silenced the soldiers. The king called out, "Who are you, sir? Are you here to trade?"

"I am Desh, King Famm. What are you offering?"

Two of the sorcerers, Kyle and Danis, started whispering to each other.

I shouted, "Desh, these sorcerers have heard of you! They look scared!"

"Quiet!" Famm snapped.

I kept going. "If you promise not to turn them into piles of toenails, they might surrender!"

Famm wheeled toward me, his jaw tight. "Be silent! You are frivolous and speaking out of turn—"

Desh shouted, "He's a pain in the butt, isn't he, Your Majesty? But if you keep him, every one of you will be dead by this time tomorrow. I'll take him and the girl away to save your lives, and I'll return your horses, but only if you give me the glove."

"Hah!" the king boomed like an enormous drum. "Bring my horses, and you can have this insolent viper along with the girl, but that's all!"

"Half the glove," Desh said.

"What? Are you trying to be amusing?"

"No. Your Majesty, you want the horses. Give me Bib and Yita, unharmed, and half the glove. It will leave you with an entire half!"

Famm started walking toward Desh and shouted, "This is moronic, but I bet you're not a moron. What do you really want?"

"I want the whole glove. I apologize, I thought that was clear."

Ace and twenty soldiers were running to catch up with the king. The soldiers guarding me didn't, so I couldn't break free. Yita quietly showed me the ropes on her wrists. They were now loose, and she was holding them to hide that fact.

I heard Ace say, "You might not want to push him, Your Majesty. I've heard that the sorcerer Desh is a reasonable man."

Still stalking toward Desh, Famm answered in a calm voice, "He's not behaving reasonably."

"Reasonable until he cooks your bones inside you."

Desh wasn't backing away. I glanced around, hoping one of my guards would get caught up in the drama. If Yita attacked them barehanded, they would probably kill her. They might make a mistake and kill me too.

Famm shook his head. "I know this sorcerer's type. He thinks he's a great power. He has to be shown that he's not." Famm drew one of his sons' swords.

Ace turned back toward his sorcerers and made three gestures over his head. I assumed they were hand signals calling for some preplanned, sorcerous kick in the groin.

A brilliant shaft of light flashed from Desh's left hand, which was pointed at the ground in front of him. He swept it ahead of him in an arc for just a heartbeat before the light disappeared.

The light shook me, but I wasn't blinded. Desh had cut an eighty-foot-long, twenty-foot-deep trench in the king's path. The grass all around it was on fire, and smoke was rising from the seared dirt walls.

Desh raised a small object over his head and called out through the smoke, "We don't have to be rude. Do we, Your Majesty?"

King Famm coughed and backed away. "No, we don't, Desh the sorcerer." It sounded as if the king was smiling.

Desh smiled too. "Good! Maybe asking for the whole glove was unreasonable. I'll accept the thumb and two fingers. You choose which two."

Famm sheathed his sword. The men around me relaxed their blades a bit, as if I also had agreed not to kill them and their king.

I heard a distant whistle and carefully twisted my head to look past Desh. Gea was galloping toward us, and the entire herd was chasing her like enormous, sweaty puppies following their mother. Pil whistled again, pointing north with great emphasis.

Soon, I heard hoofbeats to the north, behind me. I tried to count them, but there were too many—anywhere between a hundred and a thousand.

"Let me see," I said to my guards. "Come on, let me turn around."

"Uh," the oldest guard answered, and he lowered his sword a bit. I turned, ready to kill or maim my guards and then escape. Yita grabbed one man's wrist and twisted him to the ground. She wrenched his elbow with a *snap* and took his sword.

Three other guards surrounded her, but they were distracted by three columns of horsemen approaching from a quarter mile away. Although the columns were only two horses wide, each could have contained twenty, fifty, or even a hundred men. The robust cloud of dust trailing them looked to me like something that three or four hundred horses might produce.

"Everybody, stop!" I shouted. "Yita, wait! You can kill them in a minute! Look over there!"

Yita skipped away from a soldier's sword. Then they both stopped and stared north along with me.

I turned back around to look for Desh. He was swinging up behind Pil. Gea then carried them away south at a hard gallop, followed by her equine admirers.

I didn't feel deserted. Desh hadn't become one of the greatest sorcerers in the world by letting hundreds of strange riders capture him.

Famm walked past me toward the approaching horsemen. "Let Bib relax, men," he rumbled. "He's as deep in this as we are. Unless those are more of their friends." He glanced back at me.

I shook my head. "No, but I intend to make friends with them if there's any way that doesn't leave me forever damaged."

That was a lie, of course. This had to be part of the Denz army, so I didn't want to make friends. Our beliefs were too different. The Denz soldiers believed they would soon kill me or take me to be executed. I believed that four hundred men had arrived so I could kill them, just when I needed them most.

Fulfilling Harik's debt didn't seem as impossible as it had a few minutes ago.

FOURTEEN

The riders coming to visit us were not part of the regular Denz army after all. Instead of blue uniforms, they wore a muddy reddish brown. Also, they carried no banners, something that any Royal Army commander would find intolerable.

"Who are they?" Famm glanced at Ace and then at me.

I shaded my eyes. "Probably not bandits. They're well-disciplined riders. And you'd have a hell of a time stealing enough crap to keep that many bandits happy."

Famm grunted. "Ace, do you have any more incisive thoughts than that?"

"I wish I knew more about these lands, Your Majesty. I don't know a thing that can help you."

I said, "Since matters are so unclear, we might be in combat here in a minute or two. I'll be more useful with my sword." Famm had hung my scabbarded sword from his belt. Now the ferocious dumpling-head carried four swords. If I had tried that, I'd have tripped and broken an arm, but Famm didn't seem hindered.

"Do you mean this breathtaking weapon?" the king asked, pointing at my sword. "No, you might turn around and slice my head off with it. Maybe you want to get even now. I haven't been a kind host to you, after all."

Once Famm turned away, Yita grabbed my arm and leaned in, murmuring, "We must escape and return to Cael, not fiddle with this bald king! I have to kill—"

I elbowed her in the stomach, and the air flew out of her. She stepped back, gulping for breath and raising the sword she had stolen.

"I'm sorry, Yita. I turned without realizing you were so close. You probably don't know that in these lands it's awful luck to talk about who you intend to kill." I glanced toward the sky. "Your victim or his friends might be listening."

Yita nodded at me. Then she thrust at my heart and almost put a few inches of steel in it. I jumped back and slapped the blade aside with my left hand. As she withdrew, she cut that hand deep enough for blood to drip on the ground.

One thrust seemed all that Yita could manage while she was empty of air. She pointed the sword at me and sucked for wind.

"Stop that!" Ace yelled. Yita's sword bent in the middle a moment later, and two soldiers grabbed her arms. "You may have plenty of people to fight in a minute. Can't you wait?"

Yita nodded again.

"Stop nodding!" Ace snapped.

"All right!" Yita squeaked. She nodded again, glaring contempt at the sorcerer.

Ace clenched his fists for a moment and then sighed. He told his soldiers, "Let her go, but watch her."

I raised my bloody, dripping hand toward Yita and put my finger to my lips. She sneered at me, which was fine. As long as she despised me, she wouldn't try to chat with me about killing gods.

Yita was right, though: we shouldn't be farting around with King Famm. She had a charge, and if she was so keen to kill the Father of the Gods, why couldn't Pil and I forget all this, go off, and get drunk?

Thad, the Caller I had healed, edged closer to me as we watched the strange riders approach to almost within shouting distance. "You helped me, Bib, so if we have a chance before we break free, I'll mend your hand."

"Thank you, that's thoughtful," I said, wondering how Famm intended to break free with no horses.

Kyle, the Breaker, was standing nearby. "That's crazy, Thad. There's generous, and there's stupid. This man's people gave you that wound, or his horse did."

"Oh." Thad blinked at me. "Right. To hell with you and your hand." He bounced away to join the king, and Kyle joined him with smooth, lazy strides.

It didn't surprise me, or even disappoint me.

Presently, I could make out faces among the oncoming riders. I could also see that three of the men in front had wounds that were bandaged but had bled through. Their uniforms were actually red, but bloodstains had mottled the clothing to brown.

"Damn," one of Famm's soldiers muttered. "I don't know where they been, but they lost."

"Maybe," Famm said. He smiled at the soldier as if the young man had been offering a formal military assessment. Then the king went back to examining the horsemen, who had nearly reached us.

The center column halted beyond the edge of the camp and began shedding riders to both sides, making a wall in front of us. The other columns rode around us on two sides, and I saw that the total number of riders was closer to three hundred than four hundred. They were leading about fifty horses with empty saddles.

Once they had nearly surrounded us, all the newcomers halted. One of them, a big, white-skinned man with a black beard to his chest, shouted, "You goddamn took long enough to get here! Where are the rest?"

I whispered to Famm, "Don't even ask if I know what the hell he's talking about, because I don't."

"Me neither," Ace said.

The king scowled and then yelled, "I'm afraid you have confused us with someone else!"

Riders all around the circle began talking to one another. Within seconds, a few shouting arguments arose. The long-bearded man who had talked to Famm was yelling orders to the riders near him. Quite a few others, probably officers, began quieting the men around them.

When the horsemen had more or less settled down, Long Beard called out, "Who are you then? And why are you here if it's not to help us, weasel dick?"

"I am Famm, King of Balibuc, and I'm fulfilling an oath made to the gods."

"Right." The man scratched his beard as if a woodchuck might be hiding in it. "I'm Zak, King of the Flying Twat Whorehouse. I guess I'm here to save your lives, although they're probably not worth a bucketful of snot."

Zak pointed at an older man a hundred feet from him. "Get them mounted and do it damn fast!"

The gray-haired rider nodded and began passing orders to the men near him. Then he rode toward Famm. "Gather in your boys, King of Whatever. The men we lost back there left enough horses to carry you, so come on. We're not throwing you a feast, mind you. But since you're here, I won't spit on the idea of having a few more swords alongside us tonight." He turned to ride away.

"Wait!" Famm said. "Who are you at war with? The Denzmen?"

"Hah! We *are* Denzmen!" the soldier called over his shoulder.

"Wait!" Famm shouted.

Gray Hair trotted away without looking back, but he made a nasty gesture.

Soldiers began arriving with mounts for us. The one who brought mine had a bandage covering half his head, and his skin was so pale I could almost see through it. He handed me the reins and slurred his words as he said, "Be grateful, foreigner. You're not fit to ride his horse."

I said to Famm, who wasn't far from me, "Clearly somebody bad is charging around in this country. You ought to give me my sword now."

"No. I don't trust you. Nothing you can say will change that, since I don't trust anything you say."

"But you've been asking my opinion about things."

"That's so I'll know what's not true."

I cursed under my breath and mounted my horse, a black mare with a narrow chest. She probably had poor wind. If I had to run, I'd be unlikely to escape.

We formed up, joining the Denzmen's column. King Famm's Bender, Danis, was riding next to me. I said to him, "I haven't found out much. What about you?"

The short, bent man shook his head. "Nothing that answers my main question, which is why Ace and the king haven't already killed you."

The rest of the morning riding next to Danis was not convivial. We traveled west across shallow hills studded with clusters of evergreen timber until we stopped for a short break at midday. Yita dismounted and stretched, trying to ignore me and give me mean looks at the same time.

I stole a small pot off Danis's saddle and walked around as if I was looking for water. By watching and listening to the soldiers, I learned several things.

The men were afraid to be away from their city, and they were even more afraid of the dark.

Some insisted that help was coming. More argued there was no hope.

A lot of men sat staring at the ground, or their boots, or a tree.

A few men sat and cried. Nobody poked fun at them or bothered them about it.

I handed the pot to a puzzled Danis on my way to find Ace. "Something horrible is going on, Ace, but I can't tell what."

He nodded. "Rood told me that something comes out of the great marsh and attacks them every night, but he wouldn't say what. Or he couldn't say."

"Who is Rood?"

"The gray-haired officer. The one who flipped us the dog as he rode away. The attacks have been happening for a week. Our hosts keep sending off for help, but nobody has come yet."

I didn't know what to say to that, so I didn't say anything.

"We're in the Duchy of Cadellan, which is part of the Denz Kingdom. The duke has run away, or maybe he's gone mad, or killed himself. There are a lot of rumors, but he's no help now, people agree on that."

"Damn, you learned just about everything," I said.

"People like me." He shrugged. "They don't know any better."

I snorted. "I can only add one thing. Some soldiers are crying, and the others aren't making fun of them."

Ace breathed, "Krak's great knobs."

I said, "In fact, the others look like they wish they could cry too."

Ace looked at the ground and shook his head.

I healed my hand in the remaining minutes of the break. It would have healed on its own in a couple of weeks, but I'd almost certainly need to fight with it before then.

We remounted and continued west. Danis ignored me for a while, then he suddenly asked whether I was scared. I said I was, and he said he was scared too. He started talking, and by midafternoon, I had heard his entire life story, including that he and his pregnant wife planned to name their kid Val, no matter whether it was a boy or a girl.

It had been hard to concentrate on the latter parts of Danis's tale. The towns we passed were mostly deserted, and one was smoldering. We saw nobody working the fields, although the livestock appeared healthy. In one larger town, the graveyard held a lot of fresh graves along with a fair number of new holes waiting for occupants. The crumpled bodies scattered around might have been gravediggers, or mourners, or people hunting for a safe place.

The largest two towns weren't deserted. Residents hurried around boarding up windows and doors—most had been boarded before. They also prepared barricades for the doors they couldn't close. When Danis had finished explaining his existence up to the present moment, he said, "We should run. Ride back south until our horses buckle."

"You should suggest that to your king," I said. "I'd go talk to him with you, but I'm farting a lot and might offend him."

116

Danis frowned and rode on beside me in silence.

Duke Cadellan's stronghold stood atop the highest point I had seen since the Eastern Gateway. It topped at about fifty feet above the surrounding plains, so the duke and his ancestors couldn't have counted on elevation to be much of a defense.

However, somebody in the past had built a dark, stone castle with thirty-foot walls, a fine crop of defensive towers, and an impressive gatehouse. It surprised me to see that the ponderous, wooden gate had been broken apart. The open gateway was blocked by wagons loaded with crates. A great pile of barrels, furniture, and lumber was stacked just inside the gateway for building up barricades.

I saw that pile from outside the gatehouse while I was awaiting a good opportunity for Yita and I to escape, kill people, or both. Men were leading their horses into the castle yard. Hundreds of soldiers trudged and carried things in all directions, most of them dragging along like men already dead. A good chance to break free would come along soon.

The soldier named Rood pushed his way through the horseflesh toward King Famm. I shoved myself in that direction so I wouldn't spend the rest of the afternoon in ignorance.

Rood was saying, "It's a matter of prioritization, damn it. There are areas of defense. Those who can't fight, such as children and the aged, stay inside the keep. It is the place of last defense, so those of greatest skill and importance are stationed there."

I asked, "Greatest fighting skill? Or the greatest skill at drinking and whoring and cheating the poor?"

Rood glared at me.

"I may qualify!" I said.

Ignoring me, Rood said, "The most loyal soldiers and retainers guard the castle yard as the primary defense."

I could see where this was headed.

"The all-important secondary defense is stationed outside the walls with great freedom to maneuver and support one another."

"Really?" Famm sneered.

"Yes." Rood glanced up but couldn't hold the king's eyes.

"Where will you be?" Famm asked.

"I'll be in the castle yard," Rood said.

"Uh-huh."

Rood leaned forward. "Look, think about it. Your importance to the nobles determines how many walls you get to stand behind. The ones toting around the most velvet over their skins get to be in the keep. Us loyal ones who've been serving for years are put in the yard behind the walls. Strangers or those who've acted like asses stay outside the wall. I'd say I'm sorry, but I'm not."

Famm stepped toward Rood, and the older man backed up. The king grated, "You brought us here to die for you then."

"No, we didn't. If you had been out on those plains alone tonight, you'd have been overrun and beaten to death. Now that you're here, you know what's coming and you have allies."

"Wait," Famm said. "Nobody attacked us last night."

"Ah, but the attacks spread out farther every night. They'd have gotten you tonight for certain."

I tried not to react as I thought about Ella and the others. They would be following us, unless every horse died and all their legs were broken. I had to help them somehow. I at least had to warn them about whatever this was that nobody would describe.

I raised a fist. "What the hell is coming here? Tell us. You people hold on to facts like they were candy in your mouth."

Rood sighed. "Some kind of demons that look like your dead parents and dead children. They come out of the swamp at sunset, and in the name of Krak's flaming asshole, I wish I knew why. It's been six nights since it started."

If dead people were involved, Harik was likely doing this. I couldn't imagine why, though. Big acts of destruction weren't his way. He liked to savor every bit of pain.

Rood continued: "They run faster than any man, and they're stronger too. But they look and sound just like your family. They can say anything . . ." Rood shook his head. "They'll beat you to death. They hit like mallets. You've got to cut them apart to stop them—arms, legs, and head. If you set one on fire, the damn thing keeps coming like a fireball made just for you. And they talk to you."

Tears had started dripping down Rood's cheeks. "I killed my parents and my little boy six times already." He paused for a while, and we waited. He said, "They talk to you while you're killing them, and even after, and they'll beg you the whole time not to do it. And even if you kill them tonight, they come again tomorrow. Yours will come straight for you and nobody else." He walked away without saying anything more.

FIFTEEN

After Rood finished demoralizing us to the point of terror and then walked away, I turned to King Famm. His face was so pale it looked gray. I might not have looked much better. Yita turned away with her head down.

Famm said, "Ace, we need to protect the sorcerers so you can fight these demons with magic." He pointed at the slope. "We'll form a curved line right out there with the sorcerers in the pocket and plenty of room for us to retreat toward the wall. We'll need a reserve. Maybe four men. You get the sorcerers ready—it's not long until sunset."

"I have a thought," I said. "Pair everybody. When one man's family comes for him, his partner will fight them, and vice versa. Less likely you'll have to kill somebody you love."

The king closed his eyes for a few seconds. "Good idea. Ace, tell Bekke I want him."

"Is there somebody for you to pair with, King?" I knew there wasn't. I had already counted.

"No, but I don't need anybody," he said.

"Join Yita and me."

Famm glanced at me as if I'd suggested we open a tavern together. "That's not going to work."

"It will," I said. "Be honest, do you think you can kill your sons? I don't think I can kill my daughters." I had already proven that was a lie. "My power is low, and your Caller is a lot more powerful than I am, may he eat sand in hell. You don't need me as a sorcerer."

Famm sighed, and I thought I might have him convinced. He asked, "Can you fight when you're not sitting on your butt at the bottom of a hole?"

"Sure. Not quite as well, but not bad."

He snorted. "Not beside me, but you can fight."

Famm reached for one of his swords.

"No. My sword," I said. "I don't guarantee we'll live if I have it, but our chances are better."

He hesitated. "Maybe I should fight with it if it's such a world-beater."

I shook my head. "It's enchanted for only me to wield. Besides, do you want to fight demons with a sword you've never even swung? And are you sure I'm not luring you into using a blade that will blow up in your hand?"

Famm glanced at Ace, who said, "All of his objections could be true. Or none of them."

"Dammit, when we get home, I'm getting a new sorcerer!" He took a few moments to remove my scabbard from his belt and pass it to me.

"Thank you," I said. "Now I need to prepare myself, mentally and spiritually."

Famm grunted as I walked away.

Standing beside the wall, I whispered, "Gek! Hey, Gek, come grace me with your plover-faced presence." Sweat ran down my forehead and sides as I made smartass comments to a legendary monster.

A few seconds later, Gek, in the form of a small brown bird, landed on my shoulder.

I said, "Don't get mixed up and land on me sometime when you're a monster that weighs a million pounds."

"This isn't helpful," Gek said. "You shouldn't have come here. If you don't start making better decisions, I'll have to get another servant."

"Then I'll be free!"

"Then you'll be dead. When servants become stupid and useless, I kill them to warn the others. Be stupid and useless on your own time when I am finished with you."

"I understand and will do my best to comply. But I need a favor. Please warn Desh and the others about the monsters that are coming. Even better, save them. Even better than that, save all of us! It couldn't be hard to turn these monsters into lily pads or golden anvils."

"It wouldn't be hard, but it does not serve my purposes," Gek snipped. "Survive this, and then leave here."

"To go where?"

His voice was tight. "North into the marsh."

I raised my eyebrows and stared at the bird on my shoulder. "Really? Where the monsters come from?"

"You do not understand the complexities. Go north, and everything will be clear."

"You could make it all clear right now. It would only take a couple of minutes."

Gek shook his bird head.

I said, "I know, it does not serve your purposes. Will you help Desh and the others?"

"I might. Ella is there, and you're less difficult when you're in love. As soon as this battle finishes, ride away from here, north into the marsh. Promise to do that. If you promise, I will save them and tell them where to find you. Not because I care, but because it serves my purposes."

"I promise to make every effort."

Gek was silent.

"I sense, Gek, that you're about to threaten to kill some fantastic number of people to compel my obedience. However, if you do that, then I will never kill anybody for you, not Krak, not even Krak's barber. We should not be using threats against one another."

"Very well, I shall not threaten you in the future," Gek said. "After the battle, go north."

I nodded. "Save my companions, tell them where to find me."

Gek nodded and flew away.

Famm positioned us as the sun was setting, and we waited. This was the fourth sunset since Harik had called in my debt, and my progress in paying it off had been pathetic. A shot of panic went through me as I thought about that snake Harik killing me, but I pushed the feeling down.

Yita didn't object to fighting beside me, which I found surprising. She said, "You are an evil man, and I do not trust or like you, but . . . please kill the demon that looks like my mother. I don't know whether I can."

"Point her out, and I will," I said as solemnly as I could. "What about your father?"

"Oh. Him. I'll cut off his head right after I cut off his balls."

Soon, a five-foot-tall earthen berm raised up from the ground in front of us and all the way down the upper edge of the slope. A rattling boom sounded from the other side of it. I peeked over the berm and saw a trench running along that side, twenty feet wide and twelve feet deep.

By the time it reached full dark on that moonless night, nothing had yet come to attack us. A bit past midnight, the moon rose and outlined the landscape in chalk, but still no demon families came. I called out, "Maybe they're taking the night off. I won't criticize them if they do."

Famm, who was close by, grunted, "Quiet."

Yita shifted her grip on her sword.

I hadn't offered to partner with Famm because I liked the man. He had to be the best fighter around, though, or close to it. Also, his sorcerers would do everything possible to protect him. If I were standing right beside him, his loyal subjects might keep me alive by mistake. I tried to set up as close to Famm as possible.

Light hadn't quite touched the sky when men on the slope below us began chattering and pointing. Famm's sorcerers hadn't protected the unlucky men down there with berms and ditches. I gazed beyond them and spotted dozens of man-size creatures running toward us, upright but faster than a cantering horse. I scanned in all directions in case this was a diversion, but it didn't seem to be.

The first creatures reached the base of the slope. Five of them, two adults and three children, pounced on a soldier who swung his sword in a wild arc. They smashed him to the ground and pounded him for ten seconds. Then they retreated, leaving something I could recognize as a body, but it was an effort. The attackers ran back toward the marsh with the little girl dragging one of the soldier's legs behind her.

"Gorlana protect us," Yita muttered.

"Not unless you bribe her," I said, rubbing a palm on my trousers. "Remember, we have to dismember them." Yita nodded and shifted her feet. Now I had to shout over the screaming that came from lower on the slope.

A few seconds later, Yita pointed with her sword and yelled, "My mother! And father!" In the moonlight I spotted two people running toward us, neat and clothed. I'd have thought they were out for a pleasant evening if they hadn't been silent and charging us almost as fast as a horse. Yita backed away from the berm but didn't look fearful. I realized she was baiting them. I shifted so I could take them from the side when they went after her.

Yita's father leaped but slammed against the berm. He tumbled into the ditch shouting, "Help me, Bit!"

Yita's mother jumped the trench and scrambled over the berm, calling Yita's name. She was a tall young woman with long braided hair. Her dress was fine and crisp, as if she had just stepped out for the day.

I lunged and swung but didn't quite hack off the creature's leg. It crumpled under her, though. Yita's mother crawled toward her, weeping like her heart was breaking.

I cut at Yita's mother again. The creatures were strong and fast but not agile. The mother saw me and tried to pivot, but I cut her other leg out from under her at the knee. She fell, begging Yita to protect her from me, until I stepped in and cut off her head. I likely couldn't have done such damage in one blow with a regular weapon, and I silently thanked Desh for the sword he'd given me.

The severed head of Yita's mother kept talking, saying how much she loved Yita and begging for her help. The girl was backing away, her eyes huge.

"Don't look!" I yelled. Then I swung hard and cut the creature's head in half.

A second later, Yita shouted "Watch out!" as her father climbed out of the ditch and over the berm. He was on me almost before I could move, so I thrust my sword straight through his chest. He swung his fist at my head, but he hit my shoulder when I ducked. Something in my shoulder crunched, and my sword arm went numb.

I was in no way capable of switching hands, pulling my sword free, and decapitating the creature using my left hand all in one movement, but that's what I did. I gave the sword all the credit.

Yita had closed in to begin hacking off her father's arms and legs while I finished doing the same for her mother. I heard dirt crunching behind me and fell to the ground, crazily wondering why there was no blood on the dirt. Something man-size flew over my head. From off to my side, my mother aimed a stone-crushing kick at my ribs, but I rolled away from it.

Gray and wrinkled, my mother stepped toward me holding out both arms. "I'm sorry!" she said, and she sounded like she really was. Something in me clenched when Yita swung and sliced off her head. Then she hacked away one of her own mother's hands that had grabbed her ankle. Yita limped toward me, and in the moonlight, I could see the bruised finger marks pressed into her flesh.

I rolled to my feet and ducked as my father threw a familiar punch at me. He looked just the way he had the last time I saw him, when he took me away for training. He must have died soon after. Now he said "I shouldn't have let you go" as he swung with his other hand. I swung left-handed to cut that arm off at the elbow and back down in an arc to hack off his leg. As he hit the ground, I sliced off his head with no regret.

My daughters hadn't come, so I helped Yita make sure all the creatures around us were dismembered. The shouts and wailing were fading down on the hillside and behind us in the castle yard. The enemy must have breached the gate again.

I heard my daughter Manon first. Well, she had always known she was right about everything and wanted to make sure people knew it. Then I heard Bett, who hadn't cared who was right, but she cared about everything else. Now both of them called out that they loved me and cried because I wouldn't help them, and they reminded me about a lot of promises I had broken.

When I looked down at them in the ditch, they got nearly hysterical with loving and needing to be loved. I knelt on top of the berm and clenched my teeth against answering them. I knew these weren't my girls, and that kept me from jumping down to hug them. It didn't keep me from talking to them after a few minutes had crumbled my willpower. Part of me realized that they were saying everything I wanted them to say, but I didn't care about that.

Light was showing in the sky when Yita limped up beside me. She was crying as she shook my arm. "Bib, stop it. They're not real."

"Of course they're not!" I asked Bett if she had seen her mother.

Yita hugged my arm with both of hers. "We need to finish them."

My muscles snapped as tight as if I were being branded.

Patting my arm, Yita said, "I'll do it."

"I'll let you."

Yita led me away from the trench, and we sat down to heal her leg. When I was finished, I said, "I should be the one to finish them. If you go down there alone and get killed, Cael will drag me up a mountain and throw me off."

Part of me wondered whether I could find some way to save them, although the rest of me knew that was crazy.

Famm came and led us back to the trench. He stared down into it before examining my face. His own face looked like hell, stretched and dirty with sunken eyes and clean lines running down his cheeks.

He said, "Bib, don't climb down there. You shouldn't have to kill your own child. I have a plan."

"Of course. You without a plan is like a turkey without a wattle." I guess I should have thanked him, but I couldn't.

I watched my not-daughters in the ditch and tried hard not to answer when they called to me. Soon, the sorcerer Danis raised two big mounds of earth over the girls, covering them up. Famm climbed down and held one of his sons' swords ready. Then Danis pulled away enough dirt so that only the girls' heads stuck out. They started screaming.

I ran away.

Yita found me a few minutes later as I was healing my shoulder. "Thank you." She said it as if it was something embarrassing.

I nodded. "Yita, you're a fine choice to kill whoever you plan to kill, and I hope never to hear you speak about it again, whatever it is, and that it will stay secret. Do you understand?"

She squinted at me. "No, I don't."

I sighed. "I'm talking the way Pil talks. Maybe I'm spending too much time around her. Yita, don't speak about what you plan to do. There are good reasons for that. You're the right one to do it, though. I'll tell our mutual friends. I'll help you all I can."

Yita smiled. "Good! It's about time! I didn't see how anybody could be as selfish, deceitful, and foolish as you seemed to be. Maybe I was not entirely right about you."

I smiled at the girl. She couldn't know that I planned to make sure she and Cael would be the ones facing Krak, not Pil and me. With luck, Pil and I could be close enough to the murder to satisfy Gek, but far enough away to survive. Maybe we could critique the fight and enjoy a beverage.

SIXTEEN

Famm's men had suffered in the attack. He began with nearly thirty men, but only thirteen—five sorcerers and eight soldiers—survived until the next morning. Before the sun was well up, the survivors borrowed shovels and began digging graves.

A few of the thirteen survivors had been badly wounded. I did not offer to heal them. Famm had his own Caller, who could heal better than me and eat soup at the same time.

Maybe one in ten of the locals had perished. Since these attacks had been going on for a week, those who had survived to this point were a sturdy bunch. Quite a few appeared to be stunned or exhausted, though.

The graying soldier, Rood, walked out of the castle yard and stopped when he saw us. "I shouldn't be surprised. You look like the type who lives through things when better folks get killed. It was a damn bloody night. Besides those killed, figure another two or three will give up and cut their own throats sometime today." He scanned the slope and sighed. "I'll eat a toad if there's not room for you behind the walls at sunset."

"You're just waiting for them to come?" Famm asked. "You're

128

already dead then. They'll finish you tonight, or tomorrow, or next week, because you've decided to embrace death like a five-bit whore."

Without much anger, Rood said, "Bite my dog's dick, King Plumpbottom. You don't know a god-cursed, raging thing about it."

"I know that today we'll trail these demons back to their lairs and destroy them." Famm gazed around at his men. They straightened, and a couple nodded.

Rood said, "That's wonderful. Our whole duchy is too busy drooling and picking our asses to have thought up something like that. It's a good thing you arrived to tell us what we ought to do! The only little smidge of a thing wrong with your plan is that we tried it on the second, third, and fourth days! Everybody we sent disappeared!" By now, Rood was shaking and screaming at the king. "You got any sharp ideas about how to get out of that marsh once you go in after monsters, Your Goddamn Majesty?"

"I didn't mean to offend you," Famm said quietly.

Rood sighed. "You didn't hurt my feelings a bit. There isn't enough left of me to offend." He wandered away while Famm was asking him a question about the marsh.

I leaned toward Famm. "I wouldn't recommend trailing these creatures back home. I don't know if they're clever, but they are supernatural. Walking the same path as them is a fine way to have your parts rearranged or hidden in obscure parts of the world."

"What do you recommend we do?"

"I plan to wait for my friends, give you your horses, and ride out of here before the next horrible thing happens." I didn't add that I also intended to watch for an opportunity to kill Famm and the rest of his men. They had mutilated Cael, so that was in their favor. But they had attacked us twice, broken my leg, and pounded me with firewood.

But worst of all, Famm killed my daughters. It didn't matter that they weren't really my daughters—he did it as a favor to me—and that blaming him was crazy. He killed them, and I couldn't stop thinking about it.

I had given up on the idea of killing Cadellan's soldiers, though.

The people around there had enough trouble without my murdering them.

"You intend to let these people die unaided?" Famm glared at me as if the furniture in my house was made out of starving children strapped tightly together.

"You can go save them in the name of the gods, I suppose," I said.

Famm nodded. "Yes, I could. We could, if you had a speck of decency."

"Wait," I said. "How do you know that the gods aren't the ones making this happen?"

Famm stopped, his mouth halfway open.

I went on: "The gods aren't always nice. In fact, they're hardly ever nice. The people around here may have offended the shit out of the gods, who are now punishing them. Saving these people could be the most unholy thing you could possibly accomplish."

I had hoped to piss him off, but Famm smiled at me. "You are devious and wicked. I need a man like you in my service. If we live, I intend to offer you an earldom to serve me by doing the cruel, dishonorable things that a king must have done."

"If I don't get a better offer by then, I promise to consider yours with the gravity it deserves."

Famm said, "My offer only stands if you stay here and help me save these people."

Before I answered, I heard Desh shouting my name.

I waved at him, and he limped up the slope leading three horses. A big patch of skin had been scraped off the side of his face. He pointed at Stan, Yita, and Frutt several hundred feet away watching a big herd of horses. Frutt's right arm appeared bound to his body. I didn't see Cael.

I asked, "How is everybody, Desh?"

"Alive but battered. If we hadn't gotten your warning, I don't think that would be true." Desh winked at me, gave the king an even look, and said, "Hello, Teeny."

Famm stood taller. "What did you say?"

This wasn't an advantageous time to start murdering people, so

I jumped in. "Desh, this is King Famm of Balibuc. Your Majesty, this is Desh the sorcerer."

After a moment of staring, both men gave slow nods and hunched like bulls about to charge.

I stepped between them. "Famm is the mightiest king in the world, Desh. And Your Majesty, Desh is the most powerful sorcerer alive. Don't fight. There's glory aplenty for everybody."

Desh relaxed his shoulders and said in a mild tone, "Famm, we brought your horses back, all safe and well. I don't know why, but the dead rellies don't seem to care about animals."

"What was that word?" Famm asked.

"Ah . . ." Desh rubbed his eyes. "Pil called them 'dead rellies,' which is a horrible name, but nobody has come up with a better one. Anyway, if you're willing to give up the joy of Bib's company, you may send some of your people down to get your horses." He pointed toward the herd.

By this time, all five of the sorcerers in Famm's pent had gathered behind the king, examining Desh as if he might turn into a pile of gold.

I glared at Ace, Danis, and the others. "What is it? Desh likes women, and he likes them blue, so don't pester him."

Ace ignored me and gave Desh a friendly nod. "The way you burned a hole in the earth was a clever feat, Desh. When you're done here, if you wouldn't mind, we'd like to talk. Share ideas."

Desh squinted one eye. "Mm. I don't know. I still might have to kill you, so sharing ideas is probably foolish. Sorry."

I exhaled and let my hand drift toward my sword, ready to move. Desh had, by himself, just threatened a sorcery pent that had kicked my ass twice. He didn't look worried, but he had to be counting on me to help if things started getting burned up and disintegrated.

However, Ace and his band nodded and smiled as if Desh had said he couldn't join them for drinks right now but would later on.

Desh turned back to King Famm and me. "I know where the dead rellies come from. In case we want to do something about them."

Ella, Cael, and Pil arrived in time to hear that. Ella said, "We can save these people, at least those who have not already been slain."

Cael didn't speak, but he stood beside Ella and nodded. Pil didn't speak, either, but she looked away.

I raised my eyebrows at Desh but didn't ask where his knowledge came from.

He gave me an astonishing smile. "It's northwest in the marsh, and I know someone who is good with water."

Desh's lover, Limnad, was a river spirit, but she had abandoned him months ago. It sounded as if they had reconciled, and that pleased me. Because of his bargains with the gods, Desh couldn't be happy. But he could be a lot less sad.

Desh's idea shocked me, though. He knew better than anybody how desperate a fight against the supernatural could be, yet here he was suggesting we attack dozens or maybe hundreds of such beings.

When Desh mentioned his stupid idea, I had thought that Famm might get enthused, maybe laugh or rub his hands together. Instead, his deep voice evened and slowed, as if he were working on a hard problem. "That's fine. Thank you, Desh. Will you be ready to depart soon?"

"Wait!" I said. "Remember that we don't know why this is happening. If the gods sent this curse, then stopping it would be like whacking the gods with something nasty. I don't think we should risk it. These things happen for a reason."

"Bib, what are you talking about?" Desh asked.

Ella grinned. "Who are you? How can you be Bib if you say something as foolish as 'These things happen for a reason'? I can think of no words less likely to come from Bib's mouth."

I had pushed my objections a little too far, and of course there had been no reason for it. If Desh was right, these dead rellies were in the marsh. Gek wanted me to ride to that same marsh—maybe not quite the same direction, but the same marsh. I could follow Gek's command and also ride toward these rellies at the same time. I didn't think we could wipe out a poorly understood supernatural threat, even with eight sorcerers. But if the task seemed too challenging, that was what running away was for. Besides, the next sunset would be my fifth and probably last.

Harik wanted human lives. Supernatural deaths did not apply toward retiring my debt to him. He had clarified that matter years ago. Pausing to fight otherworldly forces would almost certainly prevent me from crossing the marsh, finding a lot of people there who deserved to be dead, and then murdering them all before sunset.

I could kill Famm and his men, of course. I felt no doubt that I could put them in a spot where they would die. But I would be shocked beyond comprehension if a mere fourteen murders paid off Harik.

The smart move was running from this fight to find deserving victims beyond the marsh. I would need to employ a shocking amount of magic to kill a great number of people so fast. Maybe Desh would give me a few of those wooden bottles if I was vague about why I needed them.

Ella embraced me, and I felt the tightness in her shoulders relax. She pulled away and whispered, "I'm happy I caught up before you rode away to save these wretched people. And I'm proud of you."

I saw in Ella's face that she would not be running away from anything. And I sure as hell wasn't leaving her behind.

"Even if we die?" I asked.

She looked around. Most of the residents trudged across the slope as if they were dragging sleds stacked with bricks. The rest sat on the ground with their heads dangling. Ella said, "Can you think of a nobler cause for which to risk your life?"

"No, I guess I can't." I was not given to acts of nobility, but I couldn't look at her and say to hell with these people. "It's a damned noble thing to stay here, and it tickles me to die tonight."

I hadn't meant to say that, but there it was. A cold, deep lake grew inside me as I accepted it all. It scared me, but the fear was edged with relief.

I glanced around and realized that everyone was still staring at me all narrow-eyed and tense. "Hell, I'm sorry, I was making a bad joke."

Everybody relaxed. Bad jokes were expected from me. It hit me that I could say damn near anything and explain it away as a bad joke, but I'd probably feel cheap and cowardly to hide my intentions that way. If I was going to insult somebody, I wanted to insult the shit out of them. "Desh, where exactly do we find these rellies?"

"Northwest, about ten miles deep in the marsh. I can lead us there."

All right, Gek wanted me to go north. Northwest for the first ten miles was probably close enough. For a legendary, realm-spanning monstrosity, he had always seemed reasonable.

I scanned the area. Five of Famm's men were picking their horses out of the herd. Yita and Pil were leading our mounts toward us. Famm would be abandoning a lot of horses, but that wasn't my problem. We needed to check provisions, but we should still have plenty. "Ella, what do you think? Will we be ready to go in half an hour?"

"Yes, that sounds right," she said.

"I agree," Famm said. "We'll muster here and ride to destroy these creatures, which I am certain were not sent by the gods."

We had gathered to talk in a ring about fifteen feet across. Now three of those feet sank into the ground, or rather a circle three feet wide did. A few seconds later, Gek climbed out of the hole, dusting off his green silk suit and not looking much like a bird. The hole filled in behind him. He limped two steps toward me, jutted his long, beak-nosed face, and thrust his walking stick toward my eye. "This was not what you promised."

Everybody except Ella had backed away from Gek, babbling ridiculous statements and pointless questions.

"I don't see it that way, Gek," I said. "You told me to go north to the marsh. The marsh is north, and I will ride to it. Simple."

Gek raised his voice, deliberate and round. "You did not promise to travel northwest. We agreed that you would ride north. I kept my part of the agreement. I do not often deign to make agreements."

"Northwest is also north, in the technical sense." I was starting to breathe fast.

"There is a profound difference that is beyond your understanding."

"I see," I said, my voice shaking. "If I knew the nature of the difference, maybe—"

"Quiet!" Gek boomed. I glanced and saw people hundreds of paces away jerk to look at us. Gek shook his head, setting his long, blue-black hair swinging. "I will not threaten you, for you desired that I should not, and I agreed." He scribed a circle on the ground with his stick. The dirt dropped away to form a hole, and Gek climbed down into it. Once he had disappeared, the hole filled in with earth. Every tuft of grass looked undisturbed.

Famm sneered at me. "So that's the demon you serve? He's more gopher than demon."

"I hope so." I had never seen Gek this angry.

Ella grabbed my arm and turned me to her. "What's going to happen?" she whispered.

"Maybe nothing at all."

Something exploded in the castle yard, sending a curtain of loose dirt and boulders bigger than horse carts high into the air. Screaming people might have been crushed when the mighty debris fell, but none came down near us. I looked around for Gek, and I knew I'd have to look up high.

Gek had put on his other body, which was ten times taller than the castle walls and known to make the gods quite uncomfortable. Cheg-Cheg, Dark Annihilator of the Void and Vicinity, whose heart was the blackest thing in existence, now stared at me. His voice slammed against my body. "This is not a threat, Bib. Let's be clear on that."

Each of Cheg-Cheg's hands was an insane, sinewed catastrophe with claws as long as a man was tall. He twisted to obliterate one of the stone wall's defensive towers with his hand, hurling stones that crushed running people below. As long as he was already twisting, he went ahead and dragged his hand through a second tower. He managed a third tower with the same blow, and even though he had to stretch a bit to reach it, I had the crazy feeling that he was pleased.

Some people were screaming, and some were running. King Famm was doing both. Ella had fallen and pressed her face into the grass, moaning.

I shouted, "I apologize, Gek! I wouldn't—"

"You need not apologize, Bib, my fine servant." Cheg-Cheg bent and snatched up a double handful of oxen from a pen in the yard. While he was down there, waterfalls of drool ran from his mouth and began eating into the earth. He brought eight oxen up and poured the beasts into his maw as they lowed in terror.

I ran toward the gatehouse, although I didn't know why or what I would do if I got there alive.

Cheg-Cheg rumbled, "You may go where you wish, Bib, even if it disappoints me." He reached down, seized the two wagons standing beside the gate, and crushed them with one hand. Lumber was raining when I got to the gatehouse, so I stayed under cover. Cheg-Cheg flung what was left of the wagons at three men fleeing toward me, and I ducked away. When I looked back into the yard, the men were nothing but lumpy smears.

I forced myself into the castle yard. "Gek, please stop! I'll go whatever direction you want!"

"You want me to stop this? Why? This has nothing to do with you." Cheg-Cheg smashed his open hand through the keep wall and dragged out a fistful of struggling people. He pulled back his arm to throw.

"No!" I screamed.

"Yes." He hurled the shrieking people out toward the hills.

I ran back out of the yard. When I lost sight of those people, they were still in the air.

Cheg-Cheg bent to meet my eye. "Bib, if you force yourself to be honest, you will admit that you won't need to save these people once they're all dead. Will you?" He turned and raised his foot, which looked like an enormous metal boot covered in spikes and blades. "They will all be dead within minutes. Then you'll be free to do something else. Maybe ride north."

When he stomped on the keep, it smashed apart as if he had

stomped a cake. Stones, furniture, and people flew. I was almost killed by a hurtling footstool.

Then I ran.

Outside the castle, Desh was holding our horses, which seemed bored by everything that was happening. Desh himself was breathing deep, and his eyes were strained, but otherwise he looked in control. Cael was facing away from the castle and shaking his head. Stan was pacing back and forth, yelling curses at nothing.

Yita and Pil were clinging to one another. Pil was trying to push her body between Yita and the monster until Gea trotted up to join them. A moment later, they were mounting. Frutt was galloping his horse away, and he had already made it a quarter mile toward the marsh.

I got Ella on her feet and helped her up onto a horse before I mounted. "Follow me!" I yelled over the crashing, rumbling, and screaming. I shouted "Desh!" and pointed at Cael. He nodded and ran leading the horses. On the way, he kicked Cael, who looked around and then followed.

"I'll be done in here soon," Cheg-Cheg called out. Then he raised his voice in a singsong, "Anybody who doesn't want to be mashed to dust should be gone before then!"

The immense blast of his voice threw down every person I could see. Some of the horses stared around at us with puzzled looks.

We all crawled to our feet and remounted. Desh gathered Stan, and we galloped away north. We happened to be following Frutt, but that didn't matter to me. If Cheg-Cheg threw the whole gatehouse and crushed Frutt, I wouldn't care.

The sounds of annihilation faded. I led us as straight north as I could.

I had come to think of Gek as a rational being I could manage and hoodwink. The people of Cadellan were paying for my stupidity now.

Well, most likely I wouldn't have to worry about these sorts of things after sunset today, unless I could cross the marsh fast and find a shocking number of people to kill. The odds of that seemed poor, but not impossible.

I saw King Famm and his men waving from two hundred paces to our left, and we halted. Famm bellowed, "This beast is what you serve, Bib? Damn you for a traitor to mankind!"

I shouted, "Does this mean you do not want me to work for you anymore?"

"Go to hell! Do not follow me!" Famm answered. "If I see you again, I will kill you!"

"Come over and kill me now!"

Famm waved a nasty gesture at me and wheeled his horse. His men followed him northwest.

"Should we follow them?" Cael asked.

"No! By all of Weldt's members, no," I said. "We go straight north to the marsh! Do you want to doom fifty orphanages to be demolished?"

"I say we should go home. If we had one," Stan said. "Nobody said we'd fight monsters bigger than mountains. It ain't right."

"We shall reach home eventually, Stan," Ella said, her voice shaking.

"Just in time to get buried there. Ain't this all a pocket full of piss!"

Nobody told him he was wrong.

Yita was mounted behind Pil on Gea, and she was leaning against Pil's back. Pale and sweating, she quavered, "Cael. Was that thing the thing we're serving?"

Cael hesitated. "The great powers can be difficult to understand. Matters are often more complicated than they seem."

"Sometimes they're exactly what they seem to be." Pil reached back and patted Yita's hand. "Here, Gea brought a horse for you." A fine black mare had been following Gea since we left the castle wreckage."

"I . . . can I ride with you for a while?"

"Of course you can."

Desh whispered to me, "Yita has never stood before an enraged god."

I raised an eyebrow at him. "You weren't scared today?"

"I puked twice."

"This is all sweet as a damn plum cake!" Stan said. "But what about the glove? Ain't we here because of some flippin' glove?"

I forced myself to smile around at everybody. "Let's not worry about that for now. We have a beautiful marsh to race across. On the other side, we'll dig out the finger again."

SEVENTEEN

I have spent more time running away from things than I have running toward them. Cheg-Cheg was the most horrible thing I had run away from so far, but I began my long series of retreats by fleeing from the people of my homeland. They hated me because I dared to help them but wouldn't use sorcery to make their lives perfect. Since then, I have been chased by criminals, guards, wild animals, pissed-off sorcerers, bartenders, and the feeling that I could have handled things a lot better.

Running toward things challenged me more since I had to know what I wanted before I could run toward it. I had a family for a few years, and I generally understood then what I wanted, although my wife often thought what I wanted was bad for me. Before I married, I just wandered around raising hell and looking for money. After my family was gone, I wandered from murder to murder, and it didn't matter where I went as long the place had people who looked to me as if they ought to be killed.

In the past couple of years, ever since Ella gave my life a kick in the ass, I had spent a shocking amount of time running toward places and chasing people. I engaged in those pursuits in order to do things, and even if they were nasty things I hated, they sometimes turned out to be worth doing.

Ella aggravated me into giving a damn, and I will always love her for that no matter what.

We overtook Corporal Frutt at the first boggy ground where his horse had thrown him. Half of his body still dripped water, and if his ears had been floppier, he'd have looked a handsome but unhappy dog. He even howled when he saw us, waving both hands over his head.

The rest of us dismounted before we reached the marshy grass. Rampaging Cheg-Cheg was twenty minutes behind us.

I said, "Desh, crossing this marsh will be easier with a bit of supernatural help. Do you think Limnad would agree to guide us across?"

"I don't know," Desh said.

After a few seconds, I asked, "How can we find out?"

Desh pointed back toward the castle being destroyed and shouted, "We can start by telling me what the hell all that was!"

Cael stepped up beside me. "It was a monster, a terrible beast. One of the worst." Even though Cael served Gek, his description of Gek's awfulness sounded convincing. "We're lucky to be alive, and if we don't escape, it may kill us yet." He held out the woolen pinkie to Desh. "Put this on me. Please."

Desh stared at Cael for a moment before turning toward me, still pointing. "If you don't explain all this, I will not only leave Limnad undisturbed, but I'll ride off this minute and pretend I never knew you."

I smiled at Desh while I thought. The gods couldn't see anything near Gek, and he couldn't spy on anything near them. Gek had explained that to me, and based on what the gods didn't talk about, it seemed to be true.

Considering only what we had said and done while away from Gek, it didn't seem that we had given away our idiotic plan to kill Krak. But if I described all our plans, problems, and dreams to Desh now, some god might be paying attention.

"I can't fully explain it just yet, Desh. It's a surprise." I glanced at the sky, but he just kept staring at me. I added, "You never know when the person you want to surprise may be listening."

Desh stepped back, shaded his eyes, and turned all the way around, as lazy as a weathervane. Then he crossed his arms. "I don't see anybody. Bib, that was a legendary being back there!"

"Wait!" I held up both hands.

Pil jumped forward to stand beside Desh. "Wait for what? What aren't you telling us, Bib, and you'd better sound convincing! Desh isn't the only one who can ride away as if you're a bad-smelling hole in the ground."

Desh kept going: "That was the Dark Annihilator. I've read about him. Yes, I have studied, even if I'm not formally schooled. Why is he here? And why did he chat with you in the middle of all his annihilating as if you tormented dogs together as boys? If you don't answer, I will mount up and leave this minute."

I laughed too loud and then glanced around. "Just give me a minute! And I never tormented a dog!"

All right, Desh was blabbing about Cheg-Cheg but might not have given us away yet. Maybe no god was listening just then. Gods didn't listen to everything all the time, I knew that. They did pay close attention to what sorcerers were doing, though. Well, maybe they heard all kinds of people say the words "Dark Annihilator," so it wouldn't be out of the ordinary to hear them.

I shook the stupid look off my face. "Desh, we shouldn't be too certain about the identity of anybody we meet in the middle of some chaotic happening. As it is, we might have missed some details."

Pil yelled, "Bib, it was bigger—"

I cut her off. "Bigger than I expected too, but other people"—I made a show of glancing at the sky—"wouldn't have been able to experience it the way we could. They might have looked right at it but not recognized it. I've seen such things happen before."

Desh examined my face.

I said, "We may actually have seen a Dark Baker, or a Big Fiddler, or a Round Crusher and been mistaken about the whole thing, right? We've all been drinking too much this morning and could have imagined any damn thing at all. Still, certain other people wouldn't have had the opportunity to see, would they?"

Pil gasped and stepped back, her mouth hanging open. She understood. I doubted that she was more intuitive than Desh, but she knew me better and understood my blathering.

Desh glanced at her and then deliberately said to me, "So . . . who knows what we saw? It could have been anything big. But other people, say those high up in the castle"—he glanced up—"couldn't have seen what we saw." He raised his eyebrows, and I nodded. Desh went on: "But why would that be important?"

I smiled again. "If we were planning to oh, play a mean trick on those people in the castle, we wouldn't want them to see or hear us planning, would we?"

Desh slapped his hands over his eyes, turned, and trotted thirty feet away from me.

"Desh . . ." I didn't know what to say.

"Are you all right?" Pil asked.

Stan ran over and put a hand on Desh's shoulder. "What in the ass of a rat-poke bastard? Is sorcery melting your eyes out? Did you see something ugly?"

Desh patted Stan's hand and walked back to me. He was pale, his forehead was drawn, and his eyes were shut. "I'm sorry, Bib. I was ignorant, which is a flimsy defense, especially since I might still have done it, even if I'd known better."

"What do you mean, Desh?" I asked.

With a blank face, Desh said, "I made a bargain with Harik. He's allowed to see through my eyes three separate times."

I took a calming breath. "When did you make this deal?"

"Two weeks ago. He can see what I see, but he can't hear what I hear."

If Harik had been watching when Gek and I talked during all that devastation, he wouldn't need to hear in order to grasp that we're plotting something. Although it would be crazy to mention "Harik" and "omniscience" in the same conversation, he was brutally cunning.

Ella asked, "Desh, what induced you to make such a bargain?"

Desh whispered something too soft for me to hear.

Two seconds later, Gea neighed. Limnad stepped out from behind the horse, unclothed, with water dripping from her blue skin and long blue hair. She rushed like a stream to Desh and embraced him.

She must have taken enormous care. Being a river spirit, Limnad was strong enough to tear Desh apart in a few seconds, along with the rest of us too if she decided that would amuse her. I thought well of Limnad and trusted her more than not, but I never felt certain that I knew what might amuse her next.

Desh and Limnad kissed for a time that seemed long to somebody who has had forty years peeled off the end of his life. Afterward, still embracing, Limnad lay her head on his shoulder and sighed as if out of all the places in the world, that was the best place she could be. The few drops of water still falling from her hair slowed and then stopped in midair.

Although Desh clung to Limnad, he seemed awkward.

"What's wrong?" Limnad asked.

Desh relaxed. "Nothing at all."

I wasn't sure I could have relaxed in his place. A few weeks ago, Limnad had told Desh his spirit was repugnant, and she wasn't sure how she could bear to talk with him again. She flat out stated that she could never again love him. Desh must have bargained with Harik to make Limnad love him once more. I had no doubt she would destroy him if she ever found out.

Whenever sneaky things are done for love, they are almost always discovered. In the same fashion, when surreptitious dealings are introduced into magic, they are always discovered in the end. When Desh decided to do both at once, he guaranteed that Limnad would find out.

I made a note for myself to be far away when that happened.

Desh eased away from Limnad but held her hands. "We plan to cross this swamp. Would you please help us?"

"Of course!" Limnad giggled. She swirled around our group, unbraiding Pil's hair in a second before she wove Ella's hair into a nest of narrow braids all tangled together. She passed Frutt without looking at him, but he found he was holding a head-size ball of mud. Limnad kissed Gea on the nose and turned Cael's shirt inside out before giving Stan a deep kiss that knocked him on his ass. Limnad grinned at Desh but then stopped in front of Yita.

Limnad slapped her palm against Yita's chest. The girl pulled away with a horrified glare, but Limnad followed to keep her hand pressed against Yita. Both Desh and Pil lurched forward when Yita reached for her sword, but Limnad snatched it out of the scabbard.

The river spirit drifted back, her feet not touching the ground. "Desh, can I keep her?"

Desh's brow creased. "I wish you wouldn't. I think she'd be sad."

Spirits were keen on collecting singular things, such as the man with the longest nose in the world, or a flower from an extinct bush. I asked, "What's special about her? Is she a queen in disguise?"

Almost too fast to follow, Limnad grabbed Yita in an embrace, whispering and stroking the back of her hair. Yita struggled for a moment and then relaxed.

Stan looked side to side and started blushing.

Desh raised his voice. "Don't fight, Yita! Limnad, please tell us what's happening."

Limnad let go, and Yita fell to her knees, her eyes wide. Then the spirit put the sword in Yita's hand and gazed with hard eyes at the rest of us. "Don't fight her, and don't say mean things to her. Don't even say them when she can't hear. In fact, you should give her some presents. Pretty clothes or a poisoned knife. Something . . . comforting. She ought to have that." She turned to Yita. "I won't cry unless you go first."

Yita stood up and stared at Limnad with her mouth open. The river spirit turned and ignored the girl as if she didn't exist.

Pil rushed to Yita, but the girl stood and pushed her away. "It's nothing. She's crazy."

Limnad leaned toward Desh and said in a whisper that everybody could hear, "I haven't gone mad, so don't worry about that."

Desh said, "Limnad! What's happening here? Is it dangerous?"

The spirit frowned and took a deep breath before whispering, "Being specific could be bad luck, but I'll say that there are lots of ways to hurt somebody that doesn't leave a mark. She knows what most of them are."

Yita made a choking sound and ran off into the marsh with Pil chasing her and Stan close behind.

Limnad paid no attention to the pursuit. Instead, she rushed to circle me twice. "Bib! You're almost dead! You have been a terribly careless sorcerer. I was angry at you, but I can't remember why, so I guess you didn't do anything awful. Do you want me to wait? I can sit here with you while you die." Limnad jerked her head at Ella. "I'll bet she thinks there are a hundred things more important than that. Eighty of them involve men paying her money."

Ella normally would have insulted Limnad in return, but now she simply stared at me.

I found that my fingernails were digging into my palms. "Thank you, Limnad, you are kind. Do you mean you can see that I'll die within the next few hours?"

"You might," Limnad said, examining my left fist. "It can't be too long, not over a year. Probably less, but maybe more! That's how good a friend I am. I'll sit here with you for maybe more than a year so I can watch you die. If I'm watching, then you won't die by yourself. Somebody will be here, and I'll be somebody for you!"

I opened my mouth a couple of times.

Limnad lowered her voice and leaned toward my ear. "It will be good practice for the day I must watch Desh die." When she stepped back, tears were running fast down her cheeks.

I said, "Limnad, your offer is generous, and I would admire it if you attended my death." The words slipped out, and I hoped I hadn't just told the universe I would be fine with Limnad killing me. "I think I'll keep moving for a while beforehand, though. I might find an interesting animal to look at or see another pretty river before the end."

Spinning back to Desh, Limnad asked, "Which way do you want to go?"

Desh pointed. "North."

"You'll get muddy. Don't get mad at me later if you don't like it!" She scowled. "Especially Ella, that whiner."

146

Ella gritted her teeth.

"You're free, Frutt!" I called out. "I guess you always were. Now we're free of you."

"Please don't leave me here!" Frutt cried, going up on his toes as if we might pick him up. "I can help you in the woods. Or the swamp. I know what the poisonous plants look like."

"Me too," I said, turning my back to follow Desh and Limnad.

"They still think I'm a traitor! They'll hang me!"

"You are a traitor! They should hang you. Maybe I'll hang you!"

Yita caught up to trudge beside me. "Let him come, Bib, at least through the marsh. He can make a new life in the north."

"He's as white as Cael's ass!"

Cael straightened. "I won't stand for such an insult!"

"Then sit on your pasty ass!" I said, then pointed at Frutt. "The northerners won't take him in, and then he'll starve or be eaten by wolves."

"I'll take that chance!" Frutt said.

Desh stopped and faced us. "I don't care whether we let him come or we cut off his head, as long as we're quiet about it."

"Fine, he can come." I shook my head, ready to pretend Frutt didn't exist.

Cael said, "Bib, what makes you think it's up to you?"

I reached for my sword. If I had to die this afternoon, killing Cael wouldn't be my worst choice for a final act.

"Boys," Pil said, grasping my arm.

Yita got between Cael and me. "Cael, let's move over there where the ground's less . . . murky."

Cael shook his head at me but let Yita push him thirty feet out where he could walk parallel to me, glare, and say things under his breath.

EIGHTEEN

The ground grew soggier as we walked, and within a hundred paces, the marsh came up to my ankles at every step. I glanced ahead at Limnad, hoping that she'd do something soon to help us move faster, but not so fast we'd be sucked down to join a thousand years' worth of inattentive men and wildlife.

I didn't see Limnad do anything obvious, but in an instant, the grassy ground became no more than moist. We picked up the pace, and everybody sounded pleased except for Stan, who predicted that all the water had gone someplace we'd regret later.

We hiked at a good speed for several minutes, with Desh and Limnad leading and Pil with Gea at the rear. However, the ground gradually became wetter and stickier again. Just as I was thinking I might gently mention that to Limnad, the ground under us dried out once more, becoming squishy under the grass but no impediment to walking.

We traveled that way for about an hour. At first, I thought we'd parade across the marsh as if it were the Great Empire Road. But at last, the grass died away to tufts, exposing uneven slabs of mud. We had to cross low places, and while the ground wasn't covered in water, it was muddy slop.

"Limnad," I said, "I don't mean to appear unmindful of your assistance, but we are struggling a bit through this sticky mud. Is there any help for it?"

The river spirit glanced over her shoulder. "I could pull every bit of water from around you. If I do, the ground will have no water in it. The air won't either and will probably hurt you to breathe. Or water might accidentally be removed from your body! If you end up with a withered leg or something, I will apologize, of course. Bib, if you are that anxious to cross the marsh quickly, I will remove all the water for you. It would be easy!"

"No, thank you, Limnad," Desh said. "We don't mind a little mud, as long as we're not swallowed by swamp water."

The morning had been fair and almost hot, but clouds began sliding in from the west, high and wispy at first. I watched the western sky and soon spotted thunderheads forming as they sailed toward us.

I stomped and slid my way up to join Desh and Limnad, shaking clumps of mud off my boots. Pil arrived just behind me. I said, "I don't think those clouds are natural."

"I'm glad you're here to tell us that." Pil raised an eyebrow and pointed at the arriving sheet of dark clouds whipping in above the thunderheads.

"Oh, some sorcerer is doing that," Limnad said. "It's terribly annoying. I should go kill him."

"Wait!" Desh and I yelled at the same time. Desh said, "Please don't do that. We know those people, and there are five sorcerers with them. They also have men with swords and bows." Limnad had great strength and powerful magic, but her body was fragile.

Limnad smiled at Desh and squeezed his hand.

I said, "Can you do those nasty water-removing things to them? Choke them and wither their bits?"

"Yes! But I need to be close to them."

"How close?" Pil asked.

"Standing beside them would be good." Limnad frowned that direction.

"Don't do that either then," Desh said. "Do you have any ideas?"

Limnad bit her lip as she examined the sky. "That storm can make a lot of rain, but I can protect you, even for days. No rain or flooding will hurt you while I'm here."

"I don't think they have anything so subtle in mind," I said. "They'll cook us with lightning and drink to our damnation."

Limnad's face dropped like a child who'd been told she can't have something. "Then I can't help you at all!" She grabbed Desh in one arm and me in the other. "We should leave." She carried us behind a swamp tree.

The water spirit took a step, and the world rushed past in a crazy river of color, wind, and smells. I closed my eyes to hold down my breakfast. I knew that Limnad was traveling miles with every step. She had carried us this way before.

Desh said, "Limnad, please take us back to the others!"

"But I'm taking you across the marsh. Sort of across. Isn't that where you want to go?"

I wondered how many miles we had traveled. It had to have been at least a dozen.

"Here we are!" Limnad dropped us and pecked Desh on the cheek. "That beautiful marsh is behind us."

Looking back, I saw a dim, misty swampland, far more challenging for men on foot than the other side had been.

"Please take us back, Limnad," Desh said.

"Why? You and Bib are the only important ones, although Bib will die soon. I suppose I should have brought someone else, but I feel sentimental."

I had been scanning the horizon. To the east stood a thick woodland with sunlight falling in shafts through the trees. To the north a brush-studded grassland sloped down to what might be a river valley. To the west, black clouds swirled over grassland, which died to dull gray between us and a broad city. It was built around a great tower, and looking at the place hurt my eyes.

Desh pointed at the city. "Let's not go there."

Limnad made a face. "Right, just ignore it. Let's go to the Elbow River." Limnad pointed at the river valley and jumped up and down. "There are otters!"

"First, please tell me about that city," I said.

Limnad sighed. "It's a regular old city. The people who lived there made She Who Must Not Be Named angry, which was a stupid thing to do. I'll bet they wished they hadn't!"

Desh said, "I've never heard of this place. What's it called?"

"Oh, it's not allowed to have a name. Isn't that boring? But think, a city full of people being punished. There should be more places like that."

I asked, "How long has it been this way?"

"Three-hundred and seventy-one years, four months, and one day. I remember the day it happened. Three heroes tried to cross my river that morning. They hardly knew any riddles at all."

I peered at the city again and then looked away, rubbing my eyes. "Three hundred years? All those people are dead now."

Limnad nodded. "Yes. Well, sort of. I want to see the otters!"

Desh lay a hand on Limnad's arm. "Please, please take us back to the others. They need our help."

"Fine." Limnad pouted and picked us up. She stepped off south, and I closed my eyes. Less than a minute later, she said, "You can open your eyes now, you infant." She dropped us, and I followed her around a tree to find the others.

The wind had risen almost to a gale, and the clouds were as angry as any I had ever seen.

"Where did you go?" Yita shouted.

Ella yelled, "They went carousing with that man-drowning whore!"

Limnad was circling the muddy area we occupied. Although Ella was standing perfectly still, she slipped and fell on her butt in the mud. "You're as clumsy as a sinking rowboat," Limnad said with a smirk.

Our open space was thirty paces across and mostly flat, with a broad, six-foot-deep ditch running through it. Limnad stopped.

"You should spread out. You're perching here like stupid turtles on a log!" She raced away, but not east toward Famm and his sorcerers.

My hair stood up as I felt the lightning build in the ground, ready to leap up to meet the bolt from the clouds. "Everybody, get away from that tree! No steel weapons! Damn it, don't get in that ditch—there's water in the bottom!" I bellowed.

As the lightning built further, I pulled two white bands and shoved the base of the lightning bolt out to a tree in the marsh water. The light and thunder stunned me for a second. Although the bolt didn't hit us, my body felt like it was sizzling.

Thad the Caller had far more power to draw on than I did, so I couldn't protect us this way for long. Pil was firing arrows, which couldn't possibly reach Famm's men. Desh was kneeling in the mud, tying together some complicated mess of string and cloth.

Another lightning bolt built, and I shoved it away from us, not as far as the first time. Yita staggered, and Cael stopped cursing for a couple of seconds. Ella crouched beside me, as if being one foot shorter would save her. Stan lay flat in the mud next to Frutt.

"Desh, I need more power," I yelled. Without looking up, he tossed a small, wooden bottle to me. I broke the seal and felt power rushing out, ready for me to use.

As the next lightning stroke built, Cael shouted, "Attackers from behind!"

Two imps lumbered out through portals. I saw some sunny place through them. Looking around, the imps stepped aside to let two more imps come through. Harik must have been watching through Desh's eyes after all, and now his soldiers were coming to kill us. I almost drew a weapon, but the lightning's charge surged under us. I decided not to get electrocuted and left my sword in its scabbard.

I pushed the lightning bolt so that it struck at the portals, dangerously close to Cael and Yita. The lightning smashed the four imps. It also sent Cael and Yita flying. They lay on the mud, shaking their heads and smoking.

One of the burned imps staggered to its feet. I snarled and risked drawing my sword. Before I could step toward the monster,

Desh pitched a small, glowing ball that flew into the imp's mouth. Then a brilliant light exploded inside the imp's skull. The creature swayed and thumped to the ground not far from Cael with smoke billowing from every hole in its skull.

Two more imps trotted through the portals.

"Everybody, back!" Desh shouted.

Pil and Ella grabbed Cael while Frutt grabbed Yita, and they hauled the dazed pair on their butts away from the portals. Stan moved up to protect Desh from the imps, which wasn't necessary since both monsters ran straight toward me.

I backed away, drawing the imps with me. Desh threw something up in the air, and it flew away. As I retreated from the portals, both imps slipped and fell on their bellies.

Pil laughed and dropped whatever she had used to knock down the imps. She drew her sword and rushed toward the closest one. The monster flailed its arm into Pil and clipped her leg with one finger. I heard the leg snap like a dry limb. Gea reared and slammed a hoof onto the imp's skull right between its floppy ears, but the hoof bounced off.

The two imps lay in front of me, and one was almost up on its knees. Then two more imps trotted through the portals just as I sensed the next lightning bolt building. Ella ran toward me, leaving Cael and Yita dazed and guarded by the mighty Corporal Frutt. I hoped that Desh was about to save us all.

"Goddamn it!" Desh shouted. "Damn it to your mother's eyes!"

That did not sound like salvation. I pulled two white bands with my left hand as I thrust my blade through the closest imp's forehead. The imp went slack, but my blade got stuck.

When the two newest imps arrived, they paused to glance at all the dead imps scattered on the mud. The lightning came, and I edged it away from us to blast those imps that had considerately halted.

Harik had sent eight imps after me so far. I didn't need to wonder now about whether he really wanted me dead.

The remaining imp jumped at me from its knees, swinging both arms. I skittered back as Stan swung hard at the creature's skull. Stan's sword broke in half. "You goat-puke asshole!" Stan shouted as he turned and ran.

Panting, I dragged my sword free of the dead imp's skull, turned, and swung. The monster was cursing at Stan and looking away from me. All sorcerers knew that imps, being the gods' servants, were damned hard to kill and impossible to dismember. So, it surprised me when I cut the thing's head right off. I stared at the head. Pil was leaning against Desh, and they, too, stared at the head as it rolled across the clearing.

We turned back to the portals, but no more imps came through. The next lightning bolt started building. My breath was beginning to settle, and I yelled, "I can't keep doing this forever. He's too strong."

"You're right," Desh said. "I tried to stop them——"

The lightning bolt came, and I pushed it out into the marsh. I couldn't shove it to a truly safe distance, though. The blast knocked me to the ground and nearly blinded me.

I heard Limnad say, "I can't stop these sorcerers who have penises like minnows. Like the penises minnows have. I'm sorry." I blinked for a second and saw cuts on her arms and chest that shone blue with her blood. Her shoulder had taken an awful puncture.

Desh and I glanced at the portals at the same time. From my knees I almost didn't catch the next lightning strike. It landed close and knocked down everyone except Gea.

"The next one may be on top of us," I gasped.

Cael was up but a little groggy. "I'll go through first. I've been there before."

"Where?" Yita yelled.

Cael jogged through the right-hand portal before anyone could stop him.

"Lightning's coming. Everybody who's going should go now!" I swallowed.

Stan followed Cael through the right-hand portal. Yita half dragged Pil through with her. Ella, Frutt, Limnad, and Gea were running toward the other portal. Desh and I charged through two different portals at the same time.

I stumbled when I passed through the portal, almost falling to my knees in a broad, bright valley of nothing but dusty rocks. The rocks ran from the size of my thumb to as large as a wagon, and just about all the possible shades of rock were represented.

The valley was dry and severe. I glanced around, grateful that at least we weren't in the Gods' Realm. Then I felt the yellow sunlight as warm as a blanket and as rich as cream—something you can feel, taste, and wrap yourself in. I had felt it dozens of times but still almost wept. I knew that all the good things I feared I had thrown away in my life were still right there in front of me. I didn't know how I could have doubted it.

Cael's eyes were closed, and Pil was sniffling. Everybody else, even Desh, was openly crying since they had never before felt the sun in the Home of the Gods.

Desh wiped his cheeks. "Where is Limnad?"

"Where's Gea?" Pil asked. "And Frutt?"

I looked around but didn't see them. "The portals must have closed before they made it through." I thought about what we had left Limnad and the others to face, and a chill marched over me despite the sun.

A long row of rough, wooden houses stood halfway up the slope with their doors open. No living creature was in sight.

"Eight houses," Pil said.

Cael nodded. "That makes sense. Eight imps came to destroy us."

"Are you saying we're in the Gods' Realm?" Yita whispered, glancing up and down the valley.

"We are," I mumbled. I was hardly paying attention to her.

She glanced around some more. "It's less impressive than I expected."

"Gods' Realm. Well, shit," Stan said as if he'd broken a boot-lace. I had thought he might be hysterical, but he just sighed. "How do we get home then? Do any of you clever sorcerers have a plan for solving this whale turd of a problem?"

I matched his sigh. "Stan, getting home isn't the problem. The problem is that the God of Death is on his way here right now to collect us in person."

NINETEEN

The gods had never allowed me to see their home except for the tiny bit where they traded with sorcerers. So, except for the profoundly moving sun, the Gods' Realm disappointed Yita and me both. I had imagined forests, fields, and vistas beautiful enough to stun a human being. I had seen the gods' white marble gazebo in the trading arena, and I had assumed that gods lived in white marble palaces of surpassing grandeur. Even the gods' servants must live in greater opulence than the richest king in the world of man. That's what I expected.

What I got was a rocky valley with some shoddy wooden huts.

A bit later, probably a few seconds, Pil yelled, "Bib, wake up! Why are you staring at those rocks?"

I closed my eyes. There was something mysterious and powerful about the rocks around us.

"They're rocks of the gods!" I yelled. "Don't concentrate on them!"

Everybody except Cael looked at me as if I had lost my mind. Then they all looked down at the rocks.

"I said don't!"

They stared at the rocks, gradually stiffened, and stood still.

Cael shook his head. Well, he had been dragged here by an imp years ago. He must already know about the rocks. He began shaking people out of their trance.

When everybody had been revived, Cael looked out at the horizon. "Don't stare at the rocks. Let me explain."

"To hell with that!" I said. "Harik must have been watching his imps fight us, so he also saw us flee here through the portals. He wants me, so you run. You may be able to escape."

"How?" Stan yelled. "Where are we? Escape to flippin' where?"

I said, "Just run up that slope and over it so that nobody in this valley can see you. I don't have any advice after that. But hurry!"

"I'm not leaving," Ella said.

"Me neither," said Pil, who was leaning on Ella.

I snarled. "Fine, I can't stop you. Anybody who wants to live another few minutes should take off now."

"Wait." Desh held up both hands. "I can hide us. I think. Everybody, climb on top of that crappy house."

None of us hesitated, which I suppose was a measure of how much we believed Desh when he said he'd do something.

I only glanced at the closest house to get the dimensions and a few details. I didn't want to be mesmerized by one of the crappy wooden huts of the gods. It was thirty feet square and ten feet high, which must have been a cozy fit for an imp. It was made of well-joined lumber with a flat roof, and a variety of objects hung on ropes from the eaves: carvings of animals and people, rotting human limbs, bunches of flowers in various stages of freshness, jewelry with some shockingly large gemstones, and two struggling live squirrels.

I climbed onto Cael's shoulders to reach the roof and then started hauling people up. Ella boosted Pil by her good leg while I dragged the young woman onto the rooftop. Pil groaned but didn't cry out.

"Lie down flat!" Desh said. He held out an oval onyx medallion on a heavy gold chain. "Everybody, grab the chain and don't let go. Lie still! Don't move at all!"

We all grabbed on without hesitating. Then we glanced around at one another. Cael whispered, "I think you had better explain this."

"Why are you whispering?" Desh asked.

"It . . ." Cael shrugged. "It just seemed as if I should whisper."

"That's odd. Does anybody else feel like you have to whisper?" None of us did.

Desh said, "Huh. A fluke, I guess. Do you still have to whisper, Cael?"

Cael stared at Desh. "No."

This interrogation seemed to me like a horrid waste of the little time we had, but I assumed Desh had a reason for it.

"All right," Desh said. "But don't move! Don't twitch, and I'll explain. When I agreed that Harik could see through my eyes, I decided it might be good if I could hide from him. So, I made this medallion."

After a moment, Pil said, "Will it cover us all if we just hold on?"

"Maybe. I hope so."

I snapped, "Do you even know if the damn thing works?"

"Can you think of any way I could have tested it?"

Nobody said anything.

Desh sniffed. "I'd like to remind you that we're stranded in the Gods' Realm. Anything we do is an act of desperation. When this is over, I don't expect you to apologize. But it would be nice."

Rocks flew as Harik's sandals smashed onto the valley floor. He seemed to drop right out of the sky. I didn't know whether Harik could fly or just leap great distances. For any purpose I cared about, it didn't matter.

"Murderer!" Harik roared. "I know that you fled to this place. You are too pathetic to have run far." He raced out of my view, but I heard him hurry up the slope behind me. After twenty beats of my terrified heart, he rushed back across the valley and up the far slope faster than any man could run. He scanned in all directions for a bit and then frowned. From where he stood, he could look right down at us on the house's roof, and I felt him staring straight at me.

As Harik paced back down to the valley floor, I glimpsed a

sword in his hand for just a moment. I closed my eyes and blinked a few times, gathering some details between blinks. The blade was made of white metal, and black smoke drifted off it. Then the sword and the smoke all vanished.

Harik spoke in smooth but short tones. "Murderer, you have little time to live. I see no way in which you can pay your debt to me in time, and you shall die by natural means before long, anyway. If you surrender yourself to me, I will allow your fellow trespassers to leave unharmed."

Moving only his eyes, Desh looked at me. I shifted my gaze left and right as fast as I could, hoping Desh would understand that I was shaking my head. Once Harik started killing, he would kill us all no matter what he promised.

Harik paced along the valley floor, and his sword materialized again. The black smoke wafted off the blade like fog rising off ice, and it dissolved ten feet in the air. Then the sword disappeared again.

"Murderer, are you still here?" Harik called out. He walked up to the house on one end of the row. A hollow "Hello?" told me he had walked into that house, or at least poked his head in. "You cannot hide. You must know that."

That house was smashed apart as if a boulder had landed on it, throwing timber in all directions. A sizable board landed between Ella and me before bouncing off the roof.

Ten seconds later, the second house was blasted apart in just the same way. Our hiding place was only three more houses down the row from the one Harik had just destroyed.

After all the debris had settled, Harik called out, "I intend to keep destroying houses. You are not the cleverest of beings, Murderer, so if you are unable to discern the pattern in that, ask your friend the Nub to explain it to you. He's a fairly smart fellow, except when he's in love."

Harik demolished the third house. A flying board as long as my arm slammed down onto Yita's leg, but she didn't squeak or move.

I couldn't think of a curse nasty enough for the situation. Letting go of the necklace, I pushed back, scrambled, and dropped off the roof. Walking toward the valley floor, I shouted, "I've been here the entire time, Harik! Do gods lose their eyesight after a certain number of wicked, petty acts? Or are you just stupid as hell?"

Harik strode around the corner of the fourth house. "You are too insignificant for your death to give me pleasure, Murderer, but I anticipate a tinge of relief, as if you were a tiny itch." He swaggered toward me.

I didn't consider drawing a weapon. I knew that gods could be destroyed but not in their own realm. If I tried, Harik might do something worse than kill me.

Ella screamed from the top of the house and struggled against Desh and Cael, who were holding her back from jumping. She elbowed Desh in the face, but he didn't let go. Nobody seemed to be clinging to Desh's necklace anymore.

Harik paused and glanced at Ella with a little smile. "Yes, you have brought your surly concubine along, the receptacle for the urges that you pass off as love. I shall kill her next."

"You promised to let them go free, Mighty Harik."

"No, I didn't." He smirked. "And you can't prove that I did." Harik laughed but didn't strike to slay me yet.

"Ah, we miscommunicated," I said. "To clarify, you promised to let them go free, you soggy bag of entrails torn from unclean creatures. And you're a dick."

"Excellently done, Murderer. It whets my desire to end your life." He stepped toward me.

"How's the war going?" I asked.

"Hah!" The sword appeared in Harik's hand as he swung.

I threw myself backward with no hope of dodging him. He would have cut me in two except that I stumbled on a rock and fell on my ass. The sword whipped over me, and the point of his blade only nicked the tip of my left little finger. I rolled backward and onto my feet, but my left arm had withered to nothing except bone and sinew covered by skin.

Harik frowned. "Murderer, that was recalcitrant in the extreme. Hold still, or I shall punish you. You may think you understand torture, but you are mistaken. I can tear off your arms and legs an inch at a time, hang you up, and then open you so that your viscera fall out and your entrails dangle. You will suffer through it all and continue to experience agony until I say that you may die. I might not allow it for an exceedingly long time. Millenia mean nothing to me."

I forced myself to keep breathing. "Gek thinks the war is going well, at least in his view. He and I chat about it fairly often."

Harik hesitated. "Why does he think that?"

"Because you don't know about his surprise attacks."

The God of Death stepped forward and thrust his sword of death at me, stopping a fraction away from my chest. "Tell me about these surprise attacks."

"I wish I knew the details, especially since I'm supposed to be involved. Gek wants me to scout and lead an army and get killed, I imagine. He's a dick too. But he hasn't confided in me about the details yet." I smiled. "Once he does, I'll be in a fine position to tell you all about it. I don't owe Gek anything. He forced me into servitude."

"Is that what you're doing for him?" Harik glanced upward for a moment. "No, this is a ridiculous ploy. If I release you, then you will betray me before you are well out of sight."

"I promise I won't."

Harik raised an eyebrow at me.

I nodded. "That sounded hollow, even to me. How about this? If I betray you, then you can do the entrail thing to me. I won't resist."

"It doesn't matter whether you resist. I can torture you in any manner I choose without your consent."

Ella shouted, "I will serve as hostage, Harik! If you let Bib live, I pledge with my life that he will do as he promises."

"You sure as hell will not!" I yelled.

"Hush!" Harik said. "Very well, Murderer, you will bring word to me of all Gek's plans and progress. If you fail in that, I will destroy this blonde woman, perhaps using the 'entrail thing,' as you call it. This bargain shall remain in force until the conclusion of the war, and no longer."

"No. Leave her alone. Go ahead and kill me."

"Murderer, she has already made her offer!" Harik grinned. "If you fail to support her in it, then she forfeits and I will destroy her out of hand."

"Damn you for the father of five ass-leaking donkeys!"

"Is that a yes?" Harik asked.

"I may agree, but this agreement won't last until the end of the war. It will only extend for a week. Maybe the war will be over by then anyway."

"I think not," Harik said. "The war might not be concluded so quickly. Let us say a month rather than a week."

"Shit. All right."

"You are now my agent in the enemy's camp," Harik said.

"Yes." I nodded. "By the way, to be your agent for a month, you'll have to give me at least that long to pay off my debt, not this five sunsets bullshit." I managed not to laugh.

Harik grinned. "Oh, you are still required to complete your killings within five sunsets. I will kill you should you fail, but I need not take your life immediately. I might wait for, say, a month to pass. Or an hour. It depends upon how useful you prove yourself to be."

The air went out of me. I had been about to congratulate myself on being the cleverest fellow around. "Damn you, Harik! You putrid spew of a thousand goats! May venomous spiders lay eggs in all your tender places! May their millions of spawn bite you until your skin falls off!" I took a breath and tried to smile. "For the sake of our past work together, how about another three sunsets?"

"Since you asked in such a charming fashion . . . no."

"One sunset?"

Harik shook his head and smiled.

"Shit! What are you going to tell your father about all this?"

"Everything, of course."

"Oh, so you plan to keep it a secret from everybody then."

Harik didn't answer but narrowed his eyes. That meant he wouldn't be telling the rest of the gods anything about this.

I growled, "This has been a regular jubilee, Your Magnificence. If you'll point us to the way out of here, I'll start spying."

Harik frowned. "Exiting the Gods' Realm is not a simple matter."

"Just whip open a portal for us."

Before he could answer, Krak's titanic voice echoed from far away, "Harik! Come here, boy!"

The God of Death's eyes widened. His sword disappeared, and he pointed vaguely down the valley. "To leave . . . go that way. Ask around and don't kill anyone."

Krak bellowed, "Harik! Now! Don't make me come over there!"

Before I could call him a bad name, Harik jumped lightly to the top of the house, grabbed Ella around the waist, and leaped away into the sky. He left behind a trail of Ella's curses.

"You piss-crusted bastard!" I shouted. That made me feel a tiny bit better. It didn't make Harik bring Ella back, though.

TWENTY

Pil hissed as I probed her broken leg before starting to heal it. "You're hurting her!" Yita snapped. She was holding Pil's hand. I didn't know why, but the two seemed as close as sisters now.

"Oh, this isn't much," I said as I pulled a green band. I was too busy worrying about Ella to say anything else.

Pil examined my face. "Tell Yita why this isn't much."

"What?" I glanced at Yita. "Oh, I made Pil listen to me sing once. That's real pain."

"That isn't funny!" Yita said.

Pil almost smiled. "Bib's not funny, but he thinks he is, so it's a little funny. Ella says it's his way of protecting himself, because the people who stay around in spite of his lousy humor are the ones who love him, and everybody else can go screw themselves."

I stared at Pil. "That's not true. That's the opposite of true."

"See? Not funny," Pil said as she sighed.

Yita squeezed Pil's hand with both of hers. "I don't think he's funny, either."

"Let's just do this in respectful silence," I said. "I might heal your damn leg wrong so that your knee points backward."

Pil nodded at Yita and whispered, "Not funny."

We were unlikely to snatch Ella from Harik's mountain fortress, or enchanted island, or wherever the son of a bitch lived. We'd be forced to pretend to go along with him until we found a way to steal her back.

Carrying Pil and her broken leg along would slow us, so we paused to heal her. I didn't like how the break looked anyway and feared it would turn into a worse injury. Once I finished with Pil, I tried to heal my withered arm. The limb just hung off my shoulder no matter what I tried, but I could feel it tingle a bit, so I decided to give it some time.

Cael led us down the valley. "Remember, don't stare at the rocks."

"What else shouldn't we stare at?" Stan whined. "The dirt? The air?"

"Maybe. It's hard to predict what will affect us and what won't. It would be best if we try not to look at anything for more than a second or two."

Stan muttered, "You can stare at my asshole for a second or two, you washed-out flounder."

With my leg hurting from healing Pil, I limped along behind, grunting and sweating. I kept my eyes moving but even so gathered a solid image of the land around us. The valley soon flattened until the rocks curved away like a road headed down a slope. Ahead of us lay a narrow band of deep, even grass more vibrant than any I had ever seen. Beyond that stood a grove of widely spaced, short trees. Their leaves were silver and orange. Snowy mountains stood tall and sharp in the distance. The breeze was blowing toward us and smelled like cinnamon.

"Which way?" I asked.

Cael smirked. "Where do you want to go?"

"Well, home."

Cael said, "Bib, do you know how to get there? I don't. If I had known, I would have come right back after that imp brought me here."

"I guess any direction's as good as another when we don't know

166

a blessed thing," I said. "I'm tired of hobbling on rocks, though, so let's go toward those trees."

Yita said, "Cael, did you kill the imp who brought you here? You should have killed him."

"No, I never had the chance. And imps aren't male or female. Say 'it' when you speak about one."

"Can we find it? What was its name?" she asked.

"No, I won't say the name. I don't want to risk calling it here."

Yita scowled. "It sounds like you're afraid. I'll help you kill it, and I believe Pil will help too. I wouldn't count on these others."

"I admit that I fear it a little," Cael said. "But I've learned that vengeance is like tying yourself to a bear. I have put that imp out of my mind, and you should too."

Yita grunted, gazed down at the grass, and looked right back up.

Just then, Pil stopped. As Cael walked past her, he poked her shoulder and said, "Don't stare at the trees." Pil shook her head and followed him.

I noticed that the trees were planted in rows like an orchard. I saw figures walking around under them.

"Let's run off the other direction," Stan said. "Every one of them might be a god!"

Desh said, "On the other hand, these may be the people who will help us escape."

"One of us should scout them," I said. "I guess I'm the most expendable, having not so long to live."

"Hah," Pil said. "You're not going alone."

"I'm going with you, Pil," Yita said.

"I will not allow Yita out of my sight again," Cael said.

After a pause, Stan said, "Screw this! I'm staying here. If it's safe, come back and tell me."

As we marched toward the trees, Desh said, "Bib, you're not limping."

I stopped and probed my leg. "That was as quick as a snake. The pain's gone in less than half an hour."

"Maybe magic is stronger here in the God's Realm," Pil said. "Everybody, pay attention if you do any magic. This could be the kind of knowledge that Desh can write down in a book and hide under his pillow so he can smile when he dreams of being the wisest sorcerer in the world."

Desh clenched his fists and glared at Pil. "You're going to mock me after all the knowledge I've shared with you?"

"That wasn't mocking," Pil said quietly. "It was gentle teasing. I do it to Bib all the time."

Desh stomped past us toward the trees without saying anything.

Pil looked at me with big eyes and raised eyebrows, but I didn't have any answers for her. Desh was in a complicated romantic situation and liable to be touchy.

It took me some time to gather the full picture while not looking at any one thing for more than a second. Ten people were moving around among the nearest trees, gazing up at bright fruit on the branches. Nine of them wore rags that a corpse would reject as unstylish. The tenth wore a crimson shirt with yellow trousers under a full purple cloak, and she carried a glowing sack. As I watched, she reached up to catch a piece of golden fruit that fell from a limb. Then she dropped it into the sack.

"I wonder whether anything good can happen if we talk to her," Desh said.

Before I could give an opinion, the woman turned and shouted at us, "Slaves! Don't pretend that you don't hear me! Where are you supposed to be?"

A bent woman wearing some torn cloth that hardly covered her pointed at a tree and spoke up. "That one's ripe, Excellency."

"Quiet!" the fancy woman yelled. She took three steps and backhanded the woman, who flew twenty feet, slammed into a tree trunk, and lay still. The colorful, violent woman growled at the limp person loud enough for us to hear. "Don't talk to me again without asking permission!"

Pushing past Desh, I ambled toward the woman with my head down. I drew my sword and held it reversed, still clasping the grip but with the blade pointed away from her. I let it dangle awkwardly, as if I had never touched a sword in my life. It might fool her. I decided she was a demigod, which meant she was arrogant as hell, if I knew anything about demigods. I knew a fair amount since I had killed four.

I put a quaver in my voice. "Please, Excellency, may I bring this to you?"

"Come here!"

Trudging and looking at the ground, I approached to within ten feet of her before I stopped and waited.

She said, "Open your mealy face and speak! And look at me!"

When I looked at her face, I hesitated. She was stunning, among the most beautiful women I had ever seen, with fair skin, auburn hair, and an oval face. I glanced down and said, "Excellency, I found this weapon in the rocks."

I held the sword up but didn't extend my arm.

The demigod said, "That's interesting. Give it here." She stepped forward and reached for it.

With my sword still reversed, I lunged and slashed her throat deep enough to kill a person, although maybe not enough to kill a semidivine being. Wide-eyed and gagging, she reached for my sword. I knocked her arm down with my other hand just far enough to swing again. Using all my strength, I swept her head off her neck. Her body swayed and fell straight to the ground.

As I gazed down at the demigod's body, I realized something about my sword. I knew that Desh had enchanted it to want things to be "really, really dead." Now I decided what that meant. The more powerful the enemy, the more readily the sword could kill it.

"Desh, can I kill a god with this sword?"

"No. That's a stupid thing to say."

I pointed at the expired demigod. "When you enchanted it, would you have said I could kill a demigod with it?"

He sighed. "No, I wouldn't have. I also wouldn't have claimed it was impossible. Killing a god with it is impossible. Bib, I know you. You came up with this idea, so you're going to think it's true, because nothing you think can possibly be wrong, can it? Well, you're wrong about this. Leave it alone."

I nodded but didn't say anything.

"Bib, your arm," Cael said.

I glanced down and then felt of my left arm. It wasn't withered anymore. In fact, it seemed almost as well and strong as my right. "Well, I could feel something happening when I tried to heal it. I guess it was slow to get started. And then damn quick to finish for some reason."

"Has anything like this ever happened before?" Pil asked.

I shook my head.

"That's interesting. I'd like to see it again," Desh said.

"Do you want me to find Harik and ask him to cut my finger again? Is that what you're saying?"

"Of course not. You're certain to get yourself stabbed soon. That ought to be enough. I'll watch then."

"Sure. I give you leave." Now that we were done fighting, I saw that golden apples hung from the trees. I felt myself blinking and leaning forward, so I shook myself before looking away.

Three of the nine slaves had run away when they saw me kill the demigod. I checked the poor woman who had been knocked into a tree. I expected that she'd be dead, and she was. Cael and Yita gathered the remaining five slaves at the edge of the orchard. Pil and Stan were examining the glowing sack. I imagine it was hard to tell much when they couldn't look at it for more than one second at a time.

I waved at the five people in rags—four men and one woman. None of them waved back. Only two of them even looked at me. "Hello. Everybody who wants to go back to the world of man, stand over by that tree."

All five walked to the tree.

"That's just fine. All right, anybody who knows how to get back to the world of man, raise your hand."

Three men walked away from the tree back to where they had first been standing. The two who remained were a scarred, bent woman and a graying Hill Man. The Hill Man raised his hand, which was missing his two smallest fingers. He had a square face, a fringe of white beard, and eyes so pale they looked silver.

"Wonderful," I said. "My name is Bib."

"My name is Gerapai," the Hill Man said. "You should know that I am immortal."

"Do you mean you're a god?" Cael asked.

Gerapai stared at Cael.

"Introduce yourself," I whispered.

"Fine, I'm Cael."

"No, I am not a god. But I cannot be killed. Probably." Gerapai hesitated. "I am almost certain."

"Why is that so?" I asked.

"I have been here a long time. All who were here when I came are dead, and the ones after them are dead, and the ones after them have died too. I must be immortal. It is logic."

Like all Hill People, Gerapai was small. Cael, who weighed at least twice as much as the old Hill Man, jumped forward and knocked him to the ground. He clamped one hand on Gerapai's neck and squeezed his throat shut. The Hill Man kicked and struggled but couldn't break free. Yita shouted and dragged at Cael's arm but couldn't pull him loose. Pil and Stan, who had fought Hill People in the past, weren't so quick to save this one.

At last, Cael released Gerapai and stood. The Hill Man sat up and coughed for a while before nodding to Cael. "I am not immortal, after all. You have done a big favor for me. I might have done a reckless thing and died because I was not immortal. Thank you." He held up a hand, and Cael helped him to his feet.

Gerapai rubbed his neck for a few moments while looking at the other slave. "Lily, are you ready to go home, or do you want to die here?"

She grunted and stared around. I saw she was blind in one eye. She snatched the glowing sack out of Pil's hands, then held the sack open as she squatted and peed in it.

Gerapai watched her. "The gods will not eat golden apples defiled by the hand of a slave. Maybe they will like those apples better."

Lily stood and faced Gerapai. "I'm ready to go home now, you vicious, heartless son of a bitch."

"Shit, I miss my mates," Stan said. "Ever since I come with you people, it's been gods, and burning cities, and wars, and dragons, and all kinds of other vile crap. Ain't no chance of a clean death with you lot. And look at them!" He jerked his chin at Gerapai and Lily. "I never have seen such useless and homely companions!" He rubbed his upper lip with the back of his hand. "And . . . well, I'll think of some more later!"

Desh said, "Stan, if things look ugly, I'll stab you in the heart."

"Yeah, you may promise that . . ." He spit on the grass.

Gerapai had been watching Stan and Desh argue. "Is the time for sadness and spitting ended? Do you want to leave the Place of Tears and Death now?"

"Yes, fine," I said. "Lead us home."

Gerapai walked ten steps through the orchard with a powerful stride, but then he slowed. "This will be dangerous, and I am not immortal anymore. I am afraid, and I am ashamed of it."

"We will keep you from harm," Cael said. "What's so dangerous ahead of us?"

Gerapai picked up the pace again. "There are monsters. Worse than the black cows. Canyons full of flying spears. And lava. And a god may see us. Then we will be dead because the gods cannot be killed."

"Bib killed that demigod," Yita said.

"He should not feel special," Gerapai said. "During the war, demigods fell like snowflakes. Gods did not."

"Wait!" Desh yelped, and he grabbed the Hill Man's arm. "You were here during the last war?"

"Yes."

"What happened?" Desh asked.

Gerapai blinked several times. "There is a lot to say about that."

"How did it start?" I asked.

"Do you want to know how it began, or how it started?"

"Which one came first?" Desh asked.

I added, "And tell this story while we're walking."

Gerapai lifted his chin and stared away from me, not speaking a word.

Desh said, "Please tell us, Gerapai. Ignore Bib. Your knowledge may save us all."

"That is true." Gerapai nodded. "I will be generous and share my wisdom. To speak from the beginning, this may not all be true. I will tell it, and you can decide the true parts."

"Shit!" I muttered.

"No, it may help us!" Pil said. "Be patient. Please go ahead, Gerapai."

"It begins with the goddess Sakaj taking a bath——"

I knocked the Hill Man to the ground and slapped a hand over his mouth, but the damage was done. Sakaj, the insane Goddess of the Unknowable, always arrived when her name was spoken, and her arrival brought murder and destruction on a godlike scale.

We had all drawn our weapons and were trying to look in every direction at once. It was the absolute definition of futility.

TWENTY-ONE

Holding my sword ready, I knelt over the Hill Man and waited for the goddess Sakaj to appear and destroy us all. My heart tapped fast for the first half-minute. The slave Lily was weeping with her back to me. Pil, Cael, and the others had armed themselves and were scanning every direction, as if Sakaj were a sandstorm that would appear over the horizon.

I was pressing my hand over Gerapai's mouth, but that didn't improve my mobility. Besides, was there anything else he could say that would invite even more destruction? I glanced down at him and saw bored, brown eyes. He sighed and gave a slow roll of his eyeballs.

I heard Lily cackling, not crying, so I set Gerapai free. She crossed her arms and stared around at us. "I have never seen such a lot of flit-willows act so asshole-gaping scared of getting killed by a god. Happens every day around here. Don't imagine you're special or anything."

The Hill Man said, "In this place, Sakaj does not come when you say her name. Sakaj, Sakaj, Sakaj. See? She only does it in our world. Here she would have to run around like a dog while the other gods made people call her name for fun."

"I apologize then," I told him. "But you can understand my concern."

Gerapai resumed walking through the orchard. "Sakaj was bathing in the Dim Lands when she was visited—"

Desh broke in. "What are the Dim Lands?"

Gerapai took a breath. "I see that this story will take a long time. The Dim Lands are where the gods go when they elevate."

"What is—" Pil started, but Gerapai cut her off by clapping his hands.

"No! Do not chirp like baby birds. Listen. If you stab a god in the head, he does not die. If Krak drops a mountain on a god, he does not die. The god elevates and arrives in the Dim Lands. The next morning, he is reborn."

Desh, Pil, and I gaped at one another. We had never heard anything like this.

The Hill Man ignored us. "Cheg-Cheg killed Sakaj on the final day of the war. Not the last war. The one before that."

"How many wars have there been?" Yita asked.

"I do not know."

"How long have you lived here?" she said. "It seems lazy not to have learned such an important thing."

Gerapai said, "Yes. I have worked hard for many years and not been killed by the gods because I am so lazy. I was working too hard to count all the wars that you might want to know about someday."

Lily tried to trip Yita, but the girl skipped out of the way.

Cael pointed behind us. "Yita, go back and get Stan. He looked at the grass and was stunned."

Gerapai said, "Leave him behind. Listen, there have been a lot of wars. Cheg-Cheg came to Sakaj in the Dim Lands and tricked her into doing a thing that kept magic out of our world. That was the beginning."

"So that's what happened!" Desh said. "That's why magic stopped working back home."

"Be sure to write that down," Pil said in a sharp tone. Desh frowned.

"Mankind was better off after magic was gone," I said.

Gerapai said, "The gods were not. They got weak and crazy. Slaves were happier, though. Then Cheg-Cheg came back to kill all the gods. We laughed, even if he killed us too."

"But he didn't kill them," I said, starting to worry at what I was hearing.

"No, the gods got strong again. They poked a hole into our world, and a traitor called the Murderer helped them make the hole bigger and bigger. He should be thrown into a fire. Every child should be taught to curse him."

"Yes, he sounds bad." I nodded, trying not to look guilty.

"The gods went to an evil place called the Dark Lands, and they fought Cheg-Cheg there until he went away. That was the last war."

Cael said, "A new war will be starting soon. We'll all see it. Or be in it."

Gerapai shook his head. "I want to go home. I do not want to know the story of the next war."

Lily patted him on the shoulder. "You won't get to go home. And I don't care about it as long as there aren't any more goddamn golden apples."

We hiked for another few minutes. Yita went back and got Stan again. I looked too long at the grassland and slowed almost to a stop before Pil poked me in the ribs.

Then Gerapai said, "These trees are the Grove of Righteous Captivation."

Pil nodded. "All right."

Gerapai added, "I do not know what that name means. Do you?"

Lily snarled, "No, they don't, because it doesn't mean anything, you ball-dragging idiot! Shut up about it!"

"Desh, you should write that down anyway," Pil said, glaring at the balding sorcerer.

Gerapai didn't answer Lily or seem upset. He trekked on without talking.

"Lily is right," I said. "It sounds like one of the grand, useless names the gods give things. I imagine they ran out of names that made sense about a million years ago."

176

The Hill Man didn't seem upset about that, either, but he said, "That is disappointing. What about the Valley of Redolent Passion? Brem's Tavern of Crisp Unction? Krak's Sage and Lustrous Jar?"

"Stop it!" Lily screamed.

Yita grabbed the old woman. "Be quiet! Curse him if you want to, but whisper!"

Gerapai ignored Lily, but he did start whispering. "The Peaks of Audacious Grinding? The Falls of Hope and Loss? The Arrows of Incisive Disregard? The Loincloth of—"

"Wait!" Desh said. "Go back. The Falls of what?"

Pil cleared her throat. "The Falls of Hope and Loss. Desh, I told you to start writing things down. Do you want me to tell you what you said at breakfast? How about breakfast nine days ago?" Pil wasn't joking. I had never known her to forget anything.

Desh let his head drop forward. "Fine. Pil, I'm sorry I got mad at you."

"Are you sorry for being a touchy old fart?" Pil asked. I almost snorted, since Desh was no more than six or seven years older than her.

He nodded. "Sure, for that too. But I think Fingit mentioned those Falls of Hope and Loss once."

"Right," I said, "he told me he loved them. They made him philosophical or something like that. We should avoid them in case he's in a pensive mood today. Where are these falls?"

Gerapai and Lily glanced at one another and pointed behind us.

"You're worrying about nothing then," Yita said.

Pil snapped, "Get down!"

We all dropped to the grass. Lily and Gerapai were the first ones to hit the ground.

Desh pointed at a figure running through the trees, so far off it was hardly visible. He whispered, "What is that?"

"Does it matter?" Cael asked, staring that direction. "No creature in this realm means us well."

"Shut up! It's an imp!" Lily whispered.

Stan punched Cael's boot and whispered, "Hell, don't stare at it long enough to draw a picture! You might freeze up and drool!"

"Don't worry, imps don't come from the Gods' Realm," Cael whispered. "Nobody falls into a reverie because they looked at an imp's scabby face."

Pressed flat against the ground, Lily whispered, "They can stomp you to death, though. Shut up. Don't move."

With my head hardly raised, I watched the imp cross in front of us at least a quarter of a mile away. I had known imps to cover ground with brutal speed, and this one showed I hadn't been imagining it.

When the imp was out of sight, Gerapai dragged himself to his feet. I hadn't before noticed how scrawny he was. His ribs stood out like sticks. He said, "That monster is hunting for you, Ir-man. You killed Pabluet, who was the daughter of Chira."

Lily muttered, "Who's a randy, hooting cow of terror."

"A literal cow?" Yita asked.

Pil patted Yita's shoulder and shook her head.

"Bib, Chira wants to torture you," Gerapai said. "She owns a lot of imps. They all like torture."

"Lead us home then," I said.

Gerapai glanced left and right.

"You told us you know the way back!" Yita said.

"Yes. There is a way. I know it."

"Balls and marbles!" Stan snapped. "Lies! The lying little dick of a sand rat lied to us!"

Gerapai glanced down but then lifted his chin. "Calling me names will not get you home faster."

"Where are the rest of your Hill People friends?" Stan shook his fist at Gerapai. "Up ahead in them trees waiting to gouge out our damn guts? We were crazy to trust you!"

Stan pulled a knife and reached for Gerapai with his other hand. Maybe he planned to kill the emaciated wretch, or maybe he thought to scare him. Stan did not think about the fact that even if Gerapai was old, he was still a Hill Man, trained to kill since he could walk.

Gerapai grabbed Stan's arm and used it as a lever to lift the ex-soldier up on his toes and then slam him to the grass on his back.

The air whooshed out of Stan as Gerapai knelt and crushed Stan's windpipe with one punch.

"He was very rude," Gerapai said as he stood and ignored Stan's gagging.

I didn't pay attention to the curses and furor because I was busy pulling a green band to save Stan's life. I did tell myself that I couldn't judge the Hill Man harshly. Stan had attacked him holding a weapon. I had killed a hell of a lot of people for doing the same thing to me, or for things not as bad.

By the time I helped Stan to his feet, my throat was squeezed tight by a band of pain.

Stan said, "I'm sorry, Bib. Thanks for not letting me die croaking on the ground there."

I told Stan to be more careful in the future, or at least I meant to. All that came out of my mouth was a breathy squeak.

Pil whispered, "Bib can't talk."

Cael's head whipped around. "He cannot speak at all?"

I shook my head.

"He can't talk." Pil smiled. "Krak has heard my prayers and made Bib without speech, although I guess Krak doesn't like us much now, but that's all right because Bib can't talk!"

"Should we do something to celebrate?" Yita asked.

I nodded and kept nodding, waiting for them to get done with it all.

Cael said, "We shouldn't mock his impairment. We could mock many other things about him." His lips were quivering as he tried not to smile.

"Stop it!" Stan said. "We're forgetting to thank Krak that he can't sing, either."

I turned to Lily and Gerapai, who were watching us with narrowed eyes, as if it would all make sense once they squinted the right way.

I crossed my arms and waited for everybody to joke and laugh themselves out. They got done in less than a minute.

"Gerapai, which way?" Cael asked. "Do not try to tell me you can't lead us to the path home. I can be much, much ruder than Stan."

If Gerapai was having doubts, he didn't show them. He adjusted our course to the right, and soon we left the stupid god-named grove. We walked onto an expanse as flat as a pond, covered in knee-high silvery grass. The blades were soft and thin, and walking through them was easy.

I kept my eyes moving and didn't stare at any one thing, although it was a challenge.

A couple of hundred paces into the grassland, Cael stopped. "We're walking downhill."

"We are not!" Stan said. "There ain't a blister or a bobble on the ground in sight. It's all even."

"Cael is a great warrior," Yita said. "I would accept his word over that of a man who foolishly invited his own death just twenty minutes ago."

I had closed my eyes and taken a dozen steps before I felt it. Cael was correct—the whole grassland was tilted just a hair, as if somebody had cut a finger's width off two legs of a table. If we had been giant apples, we'd have been rolling across that plain.

I slapped Cael on the shoulder, nodded, and made everybody watch me tilt my flat hand in a deliberate fashion. Cael and I rarely agreed on anything, so our combined opinion was persuasive.

However, nobody made a convincing suggestion as to what the tilted terrain meant. After a minute of discussion, we marched on without changing direction. It seemed unimportant to even consider changing course, although some bit of me thought that was odd. So, establishing the slope of the ground had been an exercise in mere curiosity.

The divine sun dropped toward afternoon as we trudged through grass that smelled sweet and minty at the same time. When the scent hit us, we all staggered and Pil fell to her knees. Cael told us to think about things that smelled bad—ripe privies, unwashed sailors, and angry skunks. It took a couple of minutes, but we managed to keep moving without too much stumbling.

Twice, Lily spotted imps in the distance even before I saw them.

I figured that her razor-keen sense of survival counted for more than my sharp eyesight.

Without thinking, I asked Lily a question about the first imp. My voice had returned, and the pain was gone. I had healed Stan just twenty minutes earlier and recovered from it a lot faster than I expected.

About midafternoon, Gerapai walked right into a wide, fast-moving stream and stood there, thigh-deep in the water, gazing around with a blank look. I didn't laugh because I hadn't seen the stream before he walked into it, either. Once I was made aware that it existed, I could look straight through the clear water to the stony streambed. It seemed as if somebody had dug a trench in the plains and filled it with cold water and bright fish.

Judging by the sun, when the bird crapped on my arm and startled me, we had all been staring at the stream for less than half an hour. I shook everybody awake. Gerapai was still standing in the stream, looking uncertain.

"Should we follow you across, Gerapai? We'll wait to see whether you survive, of course." I tried to say it as a joke, but I think all of us were shaken.

Without speaking or hesitating, the Hill Man climbed back out of the water and walked upstream along the bank. Pil shrugged at me, and we all followed.

Within the next thirty seconds, the grass grew shorter and brighter and the stream broadened. It felt like the act of walking changed the land around us and ahead of us. On both sides of the stream, silver-leafed trees as gnarled as old women emerged. It took a great act of will to avoid staring at any one thing, but we all seemed to be getting better at it.

A couple of hundred steps went by before the trees had spread to cover us and most of the stream. Deer, squirrels, and other animals wandered or raced around, sometimes drinking from the stream within twenty feet of us. None of them seemed to think we were worth running from, or even looking at.

Pil said, "Stop! Listen."

I turned my head and heard the merest rumble, then I frowned at Pil and Desh. They slowly shook their heads, and Desh shrugged. I drew my sword, but it felt unusually heavy. "Well, we know what's behind us. Who wants to go back?"

Everybody said we should turn around.

"Good!" I sheathed my sword.

We continued walking toward the rumbling sound, not turning around at all, even though that's what we intended. I knew we were doing it, but somehow it didn't bother me. Everybody followed along without complaining.

Not a minute later, a waterfall materialized in front us. Somewhere up above, it was divided into two columns of water that plunged into the stream, although at some time when I wasn't looking, it had grown wide enough to be called a river.

The falls plunged in front of a black stone cliff, shiny with water. I stared up and swallowed. The cliff seemed to disappear into the sky.

This time, I felt myself slowing down, as I couldn't drag my gaze away from the waterfall. "Shit." I felt it, but I couldn't stop myself.

Lily came around waking us all, mostly with hard kicks to the shin.

Cael shaded his eyes with his remaining hand to block out the view every couple of seconds. He murmured, "If I were commissioned to build something called the Falls of Hope and Loss, it would look exactly like this. And appear like magic out of nothing at all. Gerapai, I thought you were going take us away from this place!"

Gerapai closed his eyes. "I tried to go someplace else. In the Home of the Gods, sometimes if you try to stay away from a place, the place will make sure you find it."

"That's an oversimplification," came a voice echoing from above us. "I could show you the math."

I recognized the voice and cringed. "Hello, Mighty Fingit. I'm sorry to intrude on your meditations. We'll just go."

Fingit plunged down from someplace high on the cliff and landed on a ledge not far above us. I expected him to slam like a boulder, but he landed as if he were stepping off a curb.

The Blacksmith of the Gods pushed back his red hair with one great, sinewed hand. Like most of his brothers, he was so ideally handsome that I found him boring to look at. When I glanced at Pil, she was staring away from Fingit with her head down. Yita, red-faced and panting, stood gaping at the god. Hell, if I'd been drawn to men, maybe I'd have been gaping too.

Fingit knelt with such dexterity he avoided exposing anything private under his red robe. "Sorcerers—this is surprising. Knife and Nub, you have followed the Murderer to your death. That's a shame since you have both belonged to me at one time."

"How do you know he didn't follow me?" Desh asked.

Fingit lowered his brows and smirked. "What are the three of you doing here?"

I glanced at Desh, Cael, and Stan, hoping for inspiration. They were a dry hole. I whispered Pil's name to ask her for ideas. She looked around, and when she glimpsed Fingit, her face went slack. Now both she and Yita had been bludgeoned by Fingit's beauty.

Turning to Gerapai and Lily, they surprised me with raw expressions of horror and rage. They must have hated Fingit a lot. Then I realized that Fingit had told them I was the Murderer—the traitor who should be burned alive while children cursed me.

I smiled at them. "It's a complicated story . . ."

Lily and Gerapai threw themselves at me with fists, claws, and teeth.

TWENTY-TWO

I have long told people that I've been paying off Harik by murdering folks who deserve to die. However, I'm still honest enough with myself to admit I've killed quite a few people who only deserved it if measured by a damn harsh standard. I killed some other people only because they attacked me, and death was a sure way to make certain they didn't do it again. I killed some who didn't need to die, and there was no way to make that sound better.

But I had never killed two starving old slaves, and I hadn't come to the Home of the Gods to start. Gerapai swung his fist and popped my cheek. Then when he tried to kick me, I flung him to the ground. Lily went right for my eyes. I stepped aside and yanked her past me, where she fell to her knees.

"See, around here you are the traitorous Murderer," Fingit said with a little smile. "Everybody wants to kill you. Why are you here? Wait." He pointed at Lily, who had jumped to her feet. "Slaves! Stop that!"

Lily and Gerapai were taking another run at me, but they stopped so short they stumbled.

Fingit nodded. "Good. That was terribly annoying. So, Murderer, why are you here?"

I said, "Mighty Fingit, I was chased here by that cross-eyed fart bubble, Harik. I am searching out the way home right now, not that I despise the gods' hospitality."

"Hm. You do belong to Harik. Maybe I should wait for him to find you and kill you. Or maybe I should call for him so he can do it now."

I said the first thing I thought of. "I'm his spy now. He might not want me dead."

Fingit stood. "You're his spy? Who are you spying on?"

"Everybody. Not you, of course, Your Magnificence."

Fingit dropped down off the little cliff and picked me up by one arm. "Don't bother with the *magnificence* crap. What did Harik say? What words did he use?"

Dangling, I gave Fingit a serious look. "Harik said, 'You are now my agent,' and then I said, 'What are you going to tell your father about this?' and he said, 'Everything, of course,' and then I said, 'So, you plan to keep it a secret from everybody.' And he didn't answer me on that."

Fingit dropped me. "That son of the Black Drifting Whores! I've been wondering."

I backed away from him and didn't say anything.

After a few seconds, Fingit turned to me, his eyes bright. "You know that Harik will betray you. His tongue is a fountain of lies."

I squinted.

"Yeah, that was a bit too much," Fingit said. "He's a liar, but now you're my spy."

"Who am I spying on?"

"Harik! Who else?"

I almost said, "What about the war with Gek?" but I stopped myself. I could spy on Gek for Harik and also spy on Harik for Fingit at the same time. If it would keep me alive a bit longer, I'd count the hairs on Krak's butt and report that back too.

"Of course, Mighty Fingit," I said. "I'll spy for you."

Fingit laid a hand on my shoulder, and it felt as if he'd bruised me. "I know I don't have to warn you not to betray me."

I smiled. "Of course you don't."

"And I don't need to threaten you."

I shook my head, worried about where this was going.

"I don't need to because you know that of all the gods, I'm the only one that keeps his word."

"Ah."

Fingit said, "Oh, I still take every advantage I can get, and while I'm telling the truth, there's a universe of things I won't reveal. And I can outwait any sorcerer ever born. But I keep my word."

And the hell of it was that he did keep his word. At least I didn't know of any time he had broken it. The other gods broke their promises like twigs underfoot. I wondered occasionally if Fingit was all god, or if some human was hiding in his ancestry.

The god continued, "I'll protect you from Harik—but not anybody else—until you leave this realm, as long as you don't do anything to hurt the gods. But if you act against us—if you even sing a deprecating song—I will hold you down while Harik peels you away to nothing, one tiny strip at a time. I am not exaggerating. I've seen him do it. So, I don't have to warn you, do I?"

"No, Mighty Fingit, you don't."

"All right, call for me when you have something to report about Harik. Now, go away. You've defiled the Falls with your human feet and gasses. It'll take a week to air out."

"Fingit, since I'm spying for you now, will you make King Famm stop trying to kill me?"

"What do you mean?"

"Tell Famm he should go back to protecting me instead of trying to kill me."

Fingit tilted his head. "Who is King Famm? Is he a sorcerer?"

"No, but sorcerers work for him. He's the King of Balibuc—"

The god raised a hand. "Stop. I don't care about kings. I wouldn't let a king wipe my sandals. And I have never told any human they can't kill you, Murderer. I'd have slept better if one of them had killed you. But no, somebody is playing a joke on you."

I blinked at Fingit. Was King Famm lying to me? Or was he being fooled by another god?

Fingit glanced from Desh to Pil to me. "All right. Go! Now!"

Cael and Stan collected the still-smitten Yita and Pil, and then we trotted back downstream. Before long the grass grew tall, the trees disappeared, and the river became a stream again. Since we had come this way, I found it easier to keep my eyes where they should be.

I glanced back and saw no sign that a wall or a waterfall had ever existed.

Soon, Gerapai and Lily stopped. She pointed at me. "We don't walk with any damn traitors!"

"That's fine," I said, still walking. "Goodbye. Say hello to the imps looking for escaped slaves."

"You do not know where to go!" Gerapai yelled.

"I don't think it matters," Yita said. "You were trying to stay away from the waterfall, and that didn't work out so well."

Cael shook his head and reached into a pouch with damn good dexterity for a man with one hand. I placed the little woolen finger on Cael's pinkie.

"It's likely not to work in this realm," Desh said.

"That way." Cael pointed downstream.

For half an hour, the short grass on either side of us had been pocked with plump, wide-spaced, knee-high bushes. Their waxy leaves were dark, and their blood-red flowers were as delicate as silk. The bushes had dwindled in the past few minutes, leaving us as conspicuous as possible, unless we were on fire.

Desh bit his lip. "Guess I was wrong. But wait, let's stop for a minute."

"It's a poor spot for a meal," I said.

"It will be worth it, I think. Keep watch."

For the next ten minutes, Desh sat on the ground with his eyes closed, weaving blades of grass into little rings. Then he rubbed each ring with something wet that he poured onto his finger from a small wooden bottle. At last, he got up and handed a ring to each of us.

"Hold it in your hand," he said. "It should allow you a few more seconds before whatever you're looking at pounds you into a stupor."

Pil examined hers. "Desh, I admit that you're better than every other sorcerer around, but I don't see how you could make this work, especially in just a few minutes. I don't care whether you used oil, or blood, or tears, or the snot of a hippo."

Desh held up the wooden bottle. "Bib killed her. I just collected the blood."

Yita groaned and tried to shake the blood off her hand.

Desh went on: "If you want power in the Gods' Realm, use a god's blood, or a demigod's. That's as close as I could get since Bib didn't slice off Harik's arm or head for us."

"Thank you, Desh," I said. "Although I'd rather we not go out of our way to test these."

We walked on downstream as the shadows lengthened. The slaves followed along, grumbling as they glared at the back of my head.

By late in the day, the stream had dwindled to a small creek that wove between shallow, rolling hills. Usually, waterways got larger as they flowed downstream, but not this one. I didn't know where the water had gone, and I guessed it didn't matter. We had left the deer and squirrels behind. Now a few birds flew high above us, and jumping lizards as big as jackrabbits leaped out of the grass now and then.

Cael led us over a gentle rise and stopped. "Sheep."

About a hundred of the little white creatures grazed in the tall grass a good distance away from us. I didn't scrutinize them, no matter what Desh said about his little grass rings. I had seen sheep before, and I doubted that even witnessing divine sheep would be momentous.

"I guess they'll run," Desh said, walking onward. "Unless they're the Mighty Sheep of the Gods."

"Are there such sheep?" Yita asked with wide eyes.

Desh shrugged and turned away from her, smiling.

Cael stepped between Yita and Desh. "He is trying to be clever. Don't let him distract you."

"That wasn't very nice, Desh," Pil said.

"Stop!" Yita snapped. "Cael, stop trying to protect me! If I'm going to . . . do what I have to do, I should take care of myself. So shut up about it!"

I examined Yita's face and saw that she was scared but trying to hide it. Well, murdering Krak was a task that would shake anybody.

Pil put an arm around the girl, who was just a few years younger. "Yita, what do you have to do? Maybe we can do it together."

Cael glared at me. "You haven't told her?"

"Well . . ." I shrugged.

Yita pushed away from Pil. "It doesn't matter! You're as bad as Cael! I'm not your baby sister, you know. Just stay out of it!"

"Stay out of what?" Pil asked. She turned to me. "Bib, what didn't you tell me?"

Cael reached out to Yita, but she knocked his hand away. "Stop it!" she yelled, and I heard the fear in her voice. She had seen two gods today and had probably never seen one before. It may have daunted her.

When Yita yelled at Cael, the flock ran away from the noise. They didn't go far, but that wasn't what I noticed. The creatures were running on hooves, like horses.

"What the hell?" I glanced back at Gerapai and Lily, but they looked away from me. I scrutinized the animals from a distance for a few seconds. "They're little horses."

"That's cute, but we have more important things to talk about," Pil snapped. "Don't we, Bib?"

Lily cleared her throat. "This is our way home."

"Really?" I examined the horses again. They all looked a bit chubby. "I don't see how. Even Yita is too big to ride one of these baby horses."

"They are not infants," Gerapai said. "Unicorns grow only this big."

We all stared at the animals for a few seconds before jerking and looking around at the sky for a bit.

Pil spoke. "You're kidding. This is a joke, isn't it?"

"They are not humorous creatures," Gerapai said. "They are not from the Home of the Gods, either. You can look at them."

"No. No, I don't think this is right," Desh said. "The writings about unicorns all agree. They exist in the form of white horses—of normal size or larger. They are graceful, strong, magical as all get out, and have one horn on their forehead. Some stories say they can only be seen by virgins." He glanced at Stan and me, then frowned.

"These are unicorns, you snot-eating moron!" Lily sneered. "You don't ride 'em! You make friends with 'em."

Gerapai added, "Then they will take us back to our world. It is said they can do that." He scowled as if daring me to question him.

Cael stared at the ground for a moment. "I don't know whether anything you say is correct, but I believe we cannot pass up this chance." He walked three steps toward the little herd and then glanced over his shoulder at us. "A virgin. Are you positive, Desh?"

"Practically." Desh nodded hard, as if making up the fact he didn't feel too certain about it.

Cael tapped his foot. "I may not be the best choice."

"I'll go," Yita said as she shouldered past Cael.

"No!" Cael caught her with his one hand. "It's too dangerous. What if they all turn and attack you?"

"I don't see any horns." Yita scowled. "I'll be fine. Stop worrying."

Cael put one hand on her arm to stop her. "Let me go with you!"

"I said stop worrying!" Yita shook him off and snarled, "You're worse than my father."

Cael flinched as if she had slapped him, but he drew his sword a moment later and held it out to her. "At least take this. I defended the gate in the Dark Lands with it—along with another sword that Bib broke. That doesn't matter. It will protect you."

Yita stared at the ground for a few breaths before smiling at Cael and taking the sword. "Thank you." She turned back toward the herd.

Pil called out, "I'll come with you! It will be fine!"

Stan gaped at her.

Pil raised an eyebrow as she walked past him.

The young women eased toward the herd. Pil hung back as Yita picked out one of the unicorns to befriend. I had edged closer and could see that the creature had a three-inch-long nub, maybe of bone, in the middle of its forehead.

After a long, breathless time, Yita reached out and touched the unicorn on the nose. The little beast reared and smacked her on the chest with both hooves. None of the other unicorns joined in, which was fortunate since the angry unicorn went straight into tromping on whatever parts of Yita it could catch. With Pil's help, Yita scrambled up and made a safe retreat.

Yita had a swelling bruise on her forehead, and she dabbed at a scrape that went across her chin. One of her lower front teeth was broken off.

I shook my head at her. "Just be glad they weren't shod with iron horseshoes."

"I do not want to hear any jokes!" she snapped as her face bloomed deep red. "And I don't want to hear anyone question my virginity!"

"I don't want to hear it, either," Cael growled.

I held up both hands. "Hell, Cael, nobody's insulting your cub. I couldn't give less of a damn what she does or doesn't decide to do, as long as she's the one deciding. I don't know what to do about these unicorns, though."

With a furrowed brow, Stan said, "We tried to stay away from that damn waterfall, didn't we? And we ran right into the middle of it. That doesn't make a sliver of sense. It's all backward."

Desh said over his shoulder, "It's the Home of the Gods, Stan. You can't expect everything to make sense to us. Don't worry too much."

I stood in front of Yita and asked, "Are you badly hurt?" I reached out to touch the wounds on her face.

Yita twisted her head away from me. "No, I am not all that injured. Worry about somebody else."

"Oh, shit," Pil breathed.

I spun to see Stan marching toward the unicorn herd as if he were headed for the tavern.

"Come back!" I yelled at him.

"No!" Desh said. "This isn't the stupidest thing he's ever done."

Stan stopped a few paces from the herd, pointed at a unicorn, and started talking. I couldn't hear him, but at least he wasn't trampled by four hundred little hooves. After most of a minute, Stan jerked his head, kissed the air a couple of times, and walked back toward us. One of the unicorns followed him like a big, pudgy dog.

Stan knelt and scratched the unicorn's ear when he got back. "If these critters don't care for virgins, well, whatever the opposite of a virgin is, I guess I'm it."

The unicorn's pure white coat was long and curly. Her mane and tail were just as white but untangled, as if somebody had just combed them. Her eyes were deep blue. She examined me with one eye, not blinking at all.

Stan put his arm around the creature as if she were a sack of grain that he could carry away. Then he squinted around at us as he patted the unicorn's forehead and bump of a horn. "Well, we got her attention. What now?"

"What now, Gerapai?" I asked without looking away from Stan and his new friend.

"What is the unicorn's name?" Gerapai asked.

"I don't think you need to know that." Stan scowled at the Hill Man. "Somebody might try to enchant her and make her do tricks, jump over pits of fire, crap like that."

Gerapai nodded. "Then make it take us home."

Stan tilted his head. "That ain't too damn polite. At least you could say please."

Cael leaned toward the supernatural beast. "Unicorn, please take us home."

"Hell, she doesn't understand you." Stan frowned at Cael as if he were a toddler staggering through a room full of tables.

"Because I don't speak her language?" Cael asked.

"No, because you're a gloomy, arrogant son of a bitch." Stan gave the unicorn a grin that had horrified a lot of sensitive people. "Please, Sweetie, why don't you take us back to the place we came from? I'd appreciate it. I know you don't like these other gankers much, but would you bring 'em along? I expect one of them to save my life pretty soon."

The unicorn tossed her head.

"Hell, don't be like that! There's demons and gods and shit hunting us right now. They might fall out of the damn sky and stick a hundred spears in me any minute."

The unicorn tossed her head again and gave a delicate whinny.

Stan sighed. "But he's Lord Bib!"

Stan's unicorn didn't move.

"Bib, she hates you all to bits," Stan said. "Did you ever kick a unicorn or cook one for supper, something like that?"

"No, I don't remember such a thing. Why does she hate me?"

I couldn't tell that the unicorn even moved, but I guess Stan understood her.

"It's your sword. I couldn't exactly understand why, but if you toss it on the ground, then we can go."

I clenched my jaw. "That's not going to happen."

Stan rubbed his face. "I hate to leave you here, Bib, but I'd hate worse to get mashed to death by gods while they were mashing you. Can you come up with any good ideas to change her mind in the next thirty seconds or so?"

"Get down!" Lily snapped.

We all dropped, but too late. Two distant figures turned toward us.

Pil stood back up. "I'm not going to lie here on the dirt and die like a worm!"

"Pil, you go with Stan and the unicorn," I said. "Desh, you go too. Save yourselves." I glanced at Cael and Yita but didn't recommend that they try to save their lives.

The imps were bounding toward us. I knew that imps cleared sixty or seventy feet with each leap. They would be on us in less than a minute.

"Go!" I yelled.

Nobody went, mainly because the unicorn didn't take anybody away. She stood beside Stan, nuzzling his leg.

"Really?" Stan asked his unicorn friend. "Really?"

"What is really real, Stan?" Desh was digging in a pouch for objects, glancing at each one before shaking his head and dropping it back in.

"Bib, she says——"

Cael cut him off, holding his sword low. "Prepare yourselves now!"

Stan said, "Bib, give me your sword!"

I pointed at the imp and said, "What? No, I . . . no." It wasn't my most eloquent moment. The imps jumped more than a hundred feet and landed with a shivering thump not far from us.

The broad, ten-foot-tall imp twittered in its tiny voice, "Smash me in the balls with a boulder! If I had any balls. You're still a damned disappointment."

"Dark?" Cael stepped back from the creature that had hauled him out of our world to become the gods' slave. Now Cael's face grew pink, and he bared his teeth.

Dark scratched its crude, barrel-shaped belly, using a hand veined with sinew and muscle. It shook its head, and its dog ears flopped back and forth while it smiled at Cael with a perfect human mouth. "What are you doing crawling around loose, kitty? I'll put you back in your cage where you belong. Or maybe I'll kill the shit out of you."

Cael trembled but didn't charge.

The imp warbled a laugh. "Murderer, I see you brought two more girls for me to play with. I'll just put them in the cage with your smartass daughter and ring the three of them like bells twice a day."

I had found peace with Manon's death. I had finally come to carry her in a quiet place inside me, a place apart from the life I had gone on living without her. When I found my sword buried a foot deep in Dark's groin, I couldn't remember how it got there.

Dark warbled almost too high for me to hear. He didn't sound like he was in much pain, or even offended.

TWENTY-THREE

I twisted my sword and hauled on it, but the blade was stuck tight in the imp's groin. I had to let go and fall to the ground to avoid having all my bones broken when Dark, the imp, swung its crushing hand. Before it could stomp me, Cael cut at the imp's knee. The blade slipped off as if Cael had swung a blunt stick.

Dark glanced at the sword sticking out of its crotch and trilled, "Bastard! I'll tear off everything you've got between your legs!"

I rolled away and jumped to my feet. I still didn't have a knife, but it would have been as deadly as a stick of butter anyway. When I saw Pil run toward the monster, I shouted, "Pil! Stay back!" In the past, I had seen Dark kill a man by slapping him.

Desh raised something tiny over his head. Five spikes flew from his hand and smacked into the other imp's enormous left eye. They bounced off, but the imp stopped and shook its head.

Cael roared at Dark. On the other side of the beast, Pil buried her sharp, enchanted knife halfway to the hilt in the back of Dark's leg. Yita raced in behind Pil as the imp turned toward her, and she swung, slashing the imp's forearm. Black blood splashed from the wound. I remembered that Cael had loaned Yita his enchanted sword from the Dark Lands.

Yita's blow had distracted Dark, and he missed Pil's head so closely that the air ruffled her bangs. While Dark was occupied, I charged at its groin and grabbed my sword. Nobody snickered, but I wouldn't have been surprised if they had.

I twisted my sword again and yanked it free. Dark raised both fists to drive me into the dirt. Before I could dodge, the unicorn knocked me down as she ran past and curved away to the other imp. She slammed her horn-nub against the imp's shin. The monster whistled and staggered back.

"Hey! Unicorn! Stop that!" Dark warbled. "I'll tell Chira."

I realized that since Chira was the Goddess of Forests, the unicorn might belong to her.

The unicorn wheeled toward me, reared, and smashed both forehooves against my sword hand, which went numb. A second later, Stan grabbed the sword away from me and ran, shouting, "Let's go! Follow me!"

Desh held out the severed beak of a bird. The ground under both imps opened, and they fell into the hole up to their chests. The ground closed with a snap on them. Dark produced a string of tiny but vile profanity. The ground opened for another bite, but Dark jumped out of the hole toward us.

I backed away and glanced behind me. The unicorn was opening a portal, and Stan was waving us on. Pil, holding her knife, fell back to join me, while Cael and Yita slowed down Dark.

"Don't you try dragging your asses out of here!" Dark said in a sharp trill. "You don't want to see how much worse it'll be for you. I'll be wearing your eyeballs on a bracelet!"

Yita swung at Dark's knee but missed. The imp raised its hand to crush her head and probably the rest of her. I jumped forward one step and then stared at my empty sword hand. Cael shoved Yita aside, and Dark's hand glanced off Cael's shoulder instead. I heard bones snap, and he fell to one knee.

As she stumbled from the shove, Yita shouted for Cael to get up. I ran to grab the man, but before I got there, Dark stomped on him. Cael sounded like a bundle of sticks cracking.

Yita screamed, but Pil seized her from behind before she could charge the imp. I snagged Yita's arm, which was fortunate since I doubt Pil could have dragged the girl away by herself.

I shouted, "He's dead!" I wasn't sure Yita could hear me over her screams. "We have to go!"

The unicorn jumped through the portal first, followed by Stan. Gerapai and Lily shoved their way through next, and then Desh stepped through. Last of all, Pil and I hauled Yita through just a few feet ahead of Dark. The portal snapped shut in the imp's face.

As I stepped backward through the portal, I felt a moment of panic. No time passes in the world of man while one is in the Gods' Realm. If we returned to the spot we departed from, we were now a few seconds away from being killed by lightning.

But the portal had not delivered us to the same spot. We stood on a solid space surrounded by marsh, but we were far from the place where Famm's men had been throwing lightning on us. Now mere flecks of lightning shone in the distance rather than on top of our heads, and I couldn't hear thunder. I figured that Famm was more than a dozen miles away.

Lily fell on the wet dirt, and I thought she'd been wounded. When she curled up on her side and started shaking, I became pretty damn sure she was hurt or maybe sick. Then she began laughing from a place deep in her belly, and she kicked her feet like a little girl.

Gerapai stood over her with no expression. "I said you could get home. You may say you are sorry for all the bad things you said to me."

Lily just laughed harder and waved one muddy hand at the Hill Man.

Yita sat on the muddy ground with her arms around her knees, staring straight ahead. She growled, "It's my fault. I should have given him the sword back!" She glared at me. "I should have made you heal his other arm!" Pil sat with Yita holding her hand.

A portal opened right in the middle of us, and Dark stepped through.

"Krak's great ass!" Stan shouted.

Dark grinned. "I'm going to make you eat each other, and I'll eat what's left!"

Another portal opened under the imp, and he fell through. Both portals closed.

Dark ran out of a portal fifty feet away just as it opened. I hardly saw him before another portal opened in front of him and he skidded through it, cursing. Again, the portals closed.

The unicorn had to be opening and closing portals to screw with Dark. I glanced around and froze, my mouth open. Stan's unicorn was now a tall and lustrous white creature in the shape of a horse, with gleaming hooves and a straight horn as long as my forearm.

Yet another portal opened, and Dark leaped out of it in an arc that would carry him eighty feet. A second portal opened eighty feet away, angled like a net.

Dark flapped his arms once before he hung his head. "I'm so damn stupid." He plunged through the portal, which disappeared.

We waited a few damp minutes listening to marsh creatures struggle and die before deciding that Dark had given up.

"Where are Gea and Limnad?" Pil stared across the misty swamp around us and the wide, slick tree trunks that rose into the dimness. The far-off lightning flashes marked where we had left Limnad and Gea, at least a dozen miles away. "They must have survived, right?" Pil didn't sound too certain about that.

Desh said, "If anybody could survive being blasted by a constant, malevolent lightning storm, it would be them."

"We can barely help ourselves," I said. "I think we have to let Limnad and Gea find us."

"And Frutt," Pil added.

I said, "I feel sure Limnad is smart enough to feed him to a crocodile."

"Hush!" Pil whispered. "Yita wants him to live, so let's do our best."

"Why?" Desh asked. "Frutt's almost sure to die if he stays with us. Does she hate him? Or is she in love with him?"

"He is pretty," I whispered. "But the girl's as sentimental as a cobblestone."

Pil stuck out her jaw. "You don't know a damn thing. Not a single damn thing. She told me in Hep they make their children kill each other, for years and years, until the best ones are left. They learn not to like anybody."

Desh was nodding. "I see. And if they have to kill someone they like or love . . . well, maybe Frutt looks like someone she once loved."

I whispered, "Or maybe she's a rude girl who makes poor decisions about people."

Pil slapped my face hard. The crack made everybody look. Even the unicorn turned her head to watch us. Pil snarled, "You are a mean old bastard. I don't know why I keep forgetting that." She stomped back to Yita, slipping twice in the mud but catching herself.

"She's a keen observer," I muttered to Desh.

"Yes, she is," he said. "But you're going to have to try harder to drive her off. Hurry up about it. She cares too much about you. She needs to get away from you, otherwise she'll be ruined. If I had stayed, you would have ruined me."

I nodded. I wasn't somebody for a young sorcerer to learn from. Desh was right, but it made me feel old. Well, if I didn't kill a boatload of people by sunset tonight, it wouldn't matter.

"We need a plan," Desh announced, gazing around the dim marsh.

Stan said, "Sweetie and I plan to not get sucked down in the damn swamp."

"Sweetie?" Pil asked.

"We plan not to get burned up by sorcerers, or smashed apart by imps, or get cut in a thousand pieces by gods, or get leeches in our goddamn ass cracks, neither!" Stan turned away and began whispering to the unicorn.

"Will the two of you help us avoid those things too, Stan?" I asked.

"Maybe. Some," Stan said. "Not if you carry that sword, Bib, not then."

"But you can carry it?" I asked.

"Right. I promise not to fling it in some bog or sell it, if you're worried."

"I'm not."

"You trust me?" Stan asked, smiling.

"Of course I do," I said.

His smile disappeared. "Doesn't sound like the Bib I know. It's unsettling."

"Well . . . I figured your new friend would encourage you not to do anything wicked."

Stan turned away and grumbled something before whispering to the unicorn again.

Desh murmured, "We ought to trust him. He's had a hundred chances to rob us or betray us, but he hasn't."

"Stan, will you trade swords with me so at least I'm armed?" I asked.

Stan shook his head. "She ain't worried about this sword in particular. She's worried about you running around here with a sword. Mainly she doesn't like you. Now, she'll take us on a path out of here, but it's as crooked as my first wife's daddy."

"Going north?" Desh asked.

Stan nodded but didn't answer.

We walked away from the little dry mound we'd been waiting on. The unicorn led us due south.

Sweetie did as she promised, though. Her path wound and doubled. It crossed stretches of water I would have sworn must be fifty feet deep but only came to our knees. By midafternoon, we had walked seven miles to travel three miles north.

Every moment that brought us closer to sunset shoved me further into despondency.

Sweaty and dragging, we reached a clearing that Stan declared would be a good resting spot—someplace imps couldn't find us—so we sat to wait for a bit and eat. We carried plenty of food, but we had already drunk a great amount of our water. The marsh air was thick, warm, and still.

We put no effort into posting guard. If we were attacked by

something a unicorn couldn't sense, we might as well lie with our bellies in the air and welcome death.

The clearing lay three miles' walk from the edge of the marsh, and if we pushed, then we might get there before sunset. As I ate, I imagined seeing a thousand traitors and child-beaters standing just outside the swamp when I stepped out, all prepared to be slain. It was a foolish image, but I kept coming back to it and imagining how best to kill them with an onslaught of magic.

Pil walked over to sit down facing me, grabbed a stale bun out of my hand, and took a bite. She glared, daring me to say something about it. Once she swallowed, she said, "Krak, huh?"

I whipped my ahead around as if the Father of the Gods might be standing there listening.

"Yita told me."

"I wish Yita would have waited until we're someplace safe to talk," I said.

"Why? The gods are already trying to kill us," Pil said. "Are they going to try harder if they know we're planning all this? I mean, maybe they would, but do you think Krak is afraid of us, or afraid of me? We're awfully darn pathetic. If you knew that a bug wanted to kill you, would you get out four extra shoes to stomp him, in addition to the two you're wearing?"

I stared at the muddy ground. Could I have been scurrying around like a mouse with a bit of bread, afraid of being stomped, when the house's owners didn't care what my insignificant self was doing? "Maybe you're right. Let's talk about it then. But at least let's not use names anymore, all right? I didn't tell you because—"

She cut me off. "I know why you didn't tell me. It's because you think you always know the right thing. If you care enough to think about it, that is. You decided it would be better for me not to know, and I guess I should feel good that you cared enough to think about it. Can . . . the Big Moose be killed?"

"I doubt it."

"Why are we doing this then?"

I said, "I owe . . . the Mighty Pigeon a killing."

After a second, she said, "That's it? Default and let's go someplace warm and nice, and by that, I mean anyplace not like here."

"That's easy to suggest," I said. "The Pigeon has a long reach. I doubt there's anywhere we could go to escape him."

"All right, if you owe the Mighty Pigeon a killing, why am I involved? I have better things to do than follow you around doing stupid stuff."

I smiled, even though I didn't feel like it. "I know you do. I wish you could go do them today. But the Pigeon has decided I'm too old and torn up for this task. He wants you, a sorcerer in her prime. And he believes he can get you."

"That's stupid!" she said. "You could kill me four times before I stood up, so I don't think the old Pigeon sounds too smart. I bet you could fool him into letting you out of this obligation."

I looked over my shoulder. I couldn't help it. "You might not want to disparage the Pigeon too hard after the way he ripped apart that castle in the . . . the Roost." I winced. "He said he planned to kill every person in the duchy, and I imagine he did it."

Pil's face had been getting whiter as I reminded her about Cheg-Cheg the Dark Annihilator. A sense of invulnerability was a bad trait for anybody, but it was an insanely horrible trait in a sorcerer. Pil rarely seemed burdened with it. But she was young, and every young person possesses a certain amount of irrational invincibility. I hoped that hers had just been shattered.

Pil whispered, "What are we going to do?"

"We kill the Big Moose!" I winked at Pil to say that was the stupidest statement I had ever uttered.

Pil said slowly, "How do we go about doing that?"

"There's a weapon that will—" I froze and then jumped to my feet. "Desh! Cael was carrying the pinkie finger! It's still lying on the ground in the Home of the Gods!"

TWENTY-FOUR

I was still babbling about the glove's missing pinkie finger when Limnad walked out from behind a tree. All her wounds had healed. She held Corporal Frutt clamped under her left arm, and he was hanging like an empty sack.

Limnad said, "What's wrong with Bib? He shouldn't spend the last few days of his life acting crazy." She hurried to Desh, dropping Frutt on the muddy ground with a thud. He moaned but didn't move.

Limnad embraced Desh but sounded frustrated. "I couldn't find you! Did you cast some magic spell to hide—" She saw the unicorn and jerked, one of the few times I had seen Limnad ungraceful. She breathed, "Ooh."

"She saved us!" Stan said. "Worth more than a thousand sorcerers!"

The water spirit eased toward the unicorn as slowly as an old, sluggish stream. The unicorn stood still, flipping its tail. When Limnad was a few feet away, she suddenly whirled around the creature on all sides, including over its back and under its belly. The unicorn stiffened and snorted, but Limnad returned to stand beside Desh before the unicorn could move.

"Pretty!" Limnad said. "I want to keep it!"

The unicorn neighed, pawed the ground, and lowered her head to threaten Limnad with her horn.

"Feisty!" Limnad squealed.

"She ain't no puppy dog or singing birdy you can stick in a cage!" Stan shouted.

Limnad smiled at Stan and nodded. "Look, Desh, he's devoted to her. Let's keep them both. It would be mean to separate them."

Desh said, "Limnad, we may not want to capture and imprison a unicorn."

"Oh, I'll release them before they die." Limnad waved a careless hand.

"But something this beautiful should be free," Desh said. "You don't want to keep her by force, do you?" He swallowed.

Limnad paused to examine Desh's face, a line between her brows. "I suppose not." She sighed and then smiled back at Stan and his unicorn friend. "You're the only unicorn I've ever seen. But I won't keep you. Because it's wrong, I guess." She shrugged.

The unicorn raised her head and backed away from Limnad, staring.

Pil spoke up: "Limnad, where's Gea? Is she all right, or does she need help, and if she does need help, can you take me to her?"

Still looking the unicorn over from a distance, Limnad said, "She's not hurt! But she can't run across the water, the poor thing, so she won't catch us for a while. All of you should start walking again, even though you walk so slowly it hurts my eyes. You don't want to be sloshing about in the marsh after dark."

We started gathering up our supplies. I noticed Gerapai and Lily watching Limnad.

I told them, "Don't be afraid of Limnad. As long as you're polite, and as long as you're not beautiful or something she's never seen before, she's unlikely to hurt you." I winced a little, but it was hard to tell them not to be afraid of something that could pull out their kidneys and stick them on their heads like ears.

"We're not afraid." Lily sounded almost bored.

"No," Gerapai added. "We have seen the God of War read

poetry for three hours balancing a bull on his head. Nymphs fed him cups of ambrosia between stanzas."

I shrugged and continued packing.

We hiked at a much faster pace now that Limnad removed water from our path, and we traveled north with few detours. I trotted and even ran at times, ignoring everybody who told me to slow down. However, I slipped in the mud so much that I never pulled far ahead.

I heard Desh and Pil, discussing what to do now that the glove's pinkie couldn't guide us. Pil suggested we go find Gek and ask for instructions. Desh said that if we were going to follow Gek's orders and act like idiots, we might as well act like raving idiots and try to take the glove from King Famm.

Late in the afternoon, I slipped and fell in the mud. Yita grunted as she trudged past me staring at the ground. I stood, wiping off mud and sweat, and I called out, "Stan, did you bring anything to drink?"

He paused, then said in a guilty voice, "No."

"Come on, share a little."

"Hell no! You haven't even bought the hankies you promised me and Ralt all that time ago when we was about to get killed south of Crossoak. You've had most of two years to make good! You're not trustworthy, Bib."

I nodded. "I guess it was easier to call me 'Lord Bib' before you spent so much time around me."

"Shut up!" Yita shouted. "Stop moping about hankies and your hurt feelings! Cael was better than any of us, and we all just let him die!"

I looked away and kept walking, pretending to examine the swamp trees. Yita probably didn't know what a cruel terror Cael had been in his youth, worse than I ever imagined being. If I told her, that might shock the grief out of her. Probably not, though. It was more likely she'd try to cut out my heart. She needed to calm down soon, because she was in no state to go around attacking gods.

Now that Cael was gone, somebody needed to protect, guide, and manipulate Yita. I decided right then to take on that task. If I helped Yita undertake Krak's murder, then Pil would be free of the job. She could escape before people in the Dark Lands started getting cut down and blasted apart in the ways gods dealt with their unruly inferiors.

I ignored the fact that at sunset I'd be giving my life to Harik and wouldn't be able to do any of those things. It felt better to plan what I'd be doing, even if what I'd be doing was reckless and stupid and I'd never do it anyway. The contradiction didn't bother me too much.

I turned back toward Yita but found Frutt catching up to walk beside her. She ignored him, but he took a deep breath.

"Excuse me. Excuse me, I'm sorry to be a bother, but I was wondering whether . . ." Frutt trailed off, and Yita gave him no encouragement. He cleared his throat. "Wondering whether Ella has gone ahead, maybe? Clearing a trail? I'm a little worried about her."

Yita clenched her teeth, staring straight ahead. "Bib threw her away. He gave her to a god as a hostage."

Corporal Frutt faltered and glanced at me before looking away. "He what?"

Yita glared at the corporal. "He handed her over to an eternally damned being without a fight! He didn't even say goodbye! He's hardly mentioned her since, so I guess he doesn't care if she's tortured, or—" Yita swallowed and snapped her head to look forward again. "That's what love means to the pathetic people in these pathetic lands."

I sighed. Although Ella had volunteered to be Harik's hostage, Yita's telling of the story contained a fair amount of truth.

Frutt wheeled and stomped toward me. I hadn't appreciated that he was half a head taller than me with impressive shoulders and thick arms. He swerved and paced along beside me, outside of kicking range. "Go back and get her! Go right now! You were wrong to leave her, and you must fix it!"

"Really? I must, eh?"

"Yes! If you love her, protect her! If you don't, well, protect her anyway. I'd go, but I don't know the way, and I'm a coward."

I grinned. "It sounds like maybe you love her."

"That doesn't matter!" Frutt snapped. "She'd never love me. But I want you to think about how things will be tomorrow, or a month from now, when you're done pretending to be a noble hero—"

"I never pretended that."

"Just shut up! Pretending to be a noble hero, or a hound trainer, and when all the killing's over, will Ella be dead like poor little Bounder? He'd still be alive if you hadn't walked onto that bridge, so go save Ella right now!"

I turned on Frutt and growled, "You don't know a goddamn thing about Ella and me. Mind your own business and mind it from over there!" I reached to draw my sword, which wasn't there. My glare must have been threatening enough because he scrambled away from me.

On the other side of me, Desh murmured, "Do you think that was necessary?"

"Yes!"

Desh smiled. "Because you can't untangle the true from the false in what he said? And what Yita said? And what everybody except that frog over there has said or will probably say to you?"

"You ripe squirt!" I snapped. "You don't . . ." I trailed off and then glanced around. "Hell, why is everybody telling me things I don't want to hear?"

"It makes you think, doesn't it?" Desh said.

"Oh, it's a disappointing day for Bib," Limnad said, reaching around Desh to pat my shoulder. "You kind of stink too. And you have more gray hair than yesterday."

"Somebody's doing this to me," I muttered, glancing around. "Some sorcerer made a bargain for this to happen. Ace and his band of tongue-warts!" I looked around for Pil, but she was busy consoling Yita.

I sped up to a trot again and daydreamed about abandoning every damn one of them. I could walk away and spend the time I had left drinking my way from here to the ocean. That depressed me, so I started daydreaming about all the rash and satisfying things I'd do after I paid my debt to Harik at the very last minute.

The mud opened up and sucked me into the ground to my waist. At first, I thought I had walked into a bog of some kind. But everybody was yelling, and a quick scan showed that every other person had been swallowed to the waist like me. Only Limnad and the unicorn remained free.

"Oh, be still!" a woman shouted from someplace ahead of us. "The next loudmouth who talks will be sucked a hundred feet into the earth!"

Limnad hissed and signaled us to stop.

The woman continued, "River spirit, it's bad enough that you crossed my marsh without asking permission. It's worse that you did it twice. It's unimaginable that you didn't bring me a present either time. But the worst outrage of all is bringing these people and their repugnant digestive processes."

Limnad rushed out onto the water with her feet just touching the surface. "I apologize, Spirit of the Summer Marsh! I didn't mean any kind of disrespect. We are fleeing from some men who are even worse than these people here. Although most of these really are bearable. Two of them are sweet company sometimes."

A woman-shaped spirit rose out of the water not thirty paces away. Like Limnad, she was unclothed and ideally beautiful, but this spirit had moss-green skin and brown hair. Her face was hard, and she made a languid turn to gaze at each of us. When she reached the unicorn, a smile melted her harsh expression, but the hardness came right back when she looked at Limnad.

"Fleeing? That's not much of an excuse, and it doesn't change a thing, Spirit of the Blue River. How will you make it up to me?"

Limnad pointed at Frutt. "He's pretty. You can have him!"

Frutt's shout turned into a squeak when Pil punched his shoulder.

The marsh spirit said, "If he's so wonderful, why don't you make him your lover? Hm?"

"Bleh." Limnad made a face. She pointed at Desh and me. "You can't have these two, but do you see any others you like?"

"No. They're awful, and they stink."

Limnad nodded. "You noticed that from all the way over there?

If you let us pass, I'll bring you back four beautiful presents by sunset tomorrow."

The Marsh Spirit's eyes opened wide. "Really? You're so generous and honest! You would never fool me by running away and not bringing back my damn presents!" The spirit frowned. "What else do you have?"

Limnad glanced at Desh and then at me, her brows raised. She was far away from her home river. The marsh spirit would be strong here in her home, and Limnad couldn't win a fight with her. Unfortunately, I had no smart ideas to give her.

The marsh spirit approached Limnad with a languorous glide. She leaned forward to examine Limnad and then Desh, who was half-buried beside her. "This is your lover? I'll take him."

I almost argued, but since I didn't care to be buried in a hundred feet of mud, I shut up.

Limnad argued for us. "That's a creative suggestion. I would clap my hands and sing about how wonderful it is, but if you took him, it would break my heart."

Something yanked me down into the earth, and I couldn't kick my way loose. I couldn't breathe, either. I struggled, but soon my straining turned into jerking and then trembling. All at once, I was above ground again, still buried to my waist and coughing, just like everybody else.

"Please don't do that again!" Limnad cried.

"All right, I won't." The spirit sniffed.

Pil disappeared into the ground.

"I mean I won't do them all at once," the spirit added.

Pil popped back up just as Lily was swallowed by the mud. Then Desh was sucked down, and after a few seconds, Frutt was pulled down just as Lily reappeared.

The marsh spirit nodded. "If I tied a bell onto each of them, I could play music, at least until they died."

"Please stop!" Limnad cried. "I know I did a wrong thing, but please stop this! Punish me!"

All of us bobbed out of the earth like baby ducks, spitting, coughing, and in some cases vomiting.

"Punish you? Why would I do that? Maybe I'm being unfair to demand your lover like this," the marsh spirit said. "You may earn the chance to keep him."

"A riddle contest?" Limnad sounded hopeful.

"Are you river spirits still asking riddles? That's cute. No, deadly combat. Not between us, if that's what you're thinking. No, your lover will fight, and if he wins, you can keep him. If he loses, I'll take him if he's still alive."

"Isn't that a little like . . . well, a little like something barbaric humans would do?" Limnad asked.

"He is a barbaric human, so it's proper. I need a champion."

I didn't know whether to look down or raise my hand. I ended up staring at the spirit like a stunned rabbit.

The marsh spirit pointed at me. "You'll do. You look stupid, so you're probably tough." The ground spit me two feet in the air, and I landed ready to run or fight. The same thing happened to Desh simultaneously. Neither of us had a fleck of mud on us.

The marsh spirit pointed at the unicorn. "You be still. I can break off that horn and jam it in some nasty places if I want to." She pointed at Desh. "Now, I expect you boys to fight hard. If you don't give it your best, I'll use those trees over there as masts, tie everybody's guts up as rigging, and use your skin for sails. You can fight now."

"I don't have my weapon!" I said.

"Fine, all right. Give him his weapon."

I nodded at Stan. He hesitated before pulling my sword out of his belt. It was coated with mud. He shook it, which didn't help at all, before he tossed it to me.

Desh and I stared at each other. People had sometimes speculated, just for fun, about which of us would win if we fought. Whenever somebody asked my opinion, I said Desh was the most powerful sorcerer in the world, so shut up about it. I had heard Desh say that if I decided to kill him, he may as well sit down and wait for it because he didn't want to be buried in a sweaty shirt.

We kept on staring at one another.

The spirit said, "I guess you think this is impressive, that you're intimidating and unsettling each other. Stop it. Fight now."

Desh eased his hand toward his belt for some entertaining trinket made of bark, or iron shavings, or a pig's tongue. At the same time, I brought my sword up on guard. But then we both came to a halt.

"By Gorlana's sweet cleavage, fight!" the spirit shouted, hurting my ears.

Lily shrieked but just for a second. When I looked, my stomach clenched. Lily's upper body still stuck out of the ground, but her head had fallen forward. Her sides were soaked with blood. Lily's ribs had been removed and poked into the ground to make a circle around her, like a grisly picket fence.

"I am merciful and made an example of the oldest, most useless of you," the marsh spirit said. "But if I don't see fighting right now, every one of you will look like that!"

I ran toward Desh. It would be simple for one of us to die in the next few seconds.

Bucketfuls of mud flew up from the ground into my face. I rolled forward through the wall of mud, blinking and holding my sword out to my side, ready to slash.

When I came up, I swung low for Desh's legs, but he had scooted out of range. As I followed with a lunge, I saw him throw a walnut at my feet. A spray of limbs as thick as my arm shot out of the ground like a fountain.

The limbs could have killed me if one had caught me under the jaw or below my breastbone, but I shifted to my right. One of them still slammed into my left armpit and dislocated my shoulder.

That made me mad.

Instead of lunging again, I ran toward Desh as fast as I could. My shoulder screamed with every step. He raised his right hand to fry me like a chicken, or make my balls fall off, or something else bad. I whipped a slice across his forearm, cutting the tendon. His hand opened and something made of metal fell out of it.

I recovered in an instant and thrust toward Desh's heart. I could already taste his death and was sick at how excited I felt. At the last moment, I twisted and thrust deep into his shoulder instead. That was his opening to beat me, and I hoped he wouldn't kill me while he was at it.

A brilliant flash stunned me and knocked me on my ass. I was blinded and had dropped my sword. My dislocated shoulder hurt like snorting lye, and my thighs hurt a little too. I held both hands up in surrender. Hopefully, the spirit would accept this as a victory for Desh.

Pil was shouting and calling Desh a lot of foul names. That was curious since she rarely used profanity. I hoped she wouldn't make the marsh spirit mad.

Somebody grabbed my hand. I supposed it was Desh, since he said, "I'm sorry. You could have killed me, but you didn't. I'm sorry for this."

My vision was coming back from the flash. Desh had blood on his shirt and neck, and his eyes were tight. I said, "Hell, Desh, I admit I'm conceited, but I don't mind getting whipped by the best sorcerer in the world. Help me up and buy me a beer sometime."

Desh hesitated. He didn't often look uncertain, but he looked dubious as hell now. "Just be ready." He helped me sit up.

Both my legs had been burned off at the upper thigh. "Look at that," I said. I pushed down a wave of panic. Although it would require a big parcel of power, I should be able to heal these wounds. That suppressed the panic, which was good since my seared stumps looked appalling. The panic didn't come back, but physical shock arrived, and I would have fallen over sideways if Desh hadn't eased me back to lie down.

Stan was throwing a spare shirt over my chest and called out, "Somebody raise his legs—oh, hell."

The stumps hadn't particularly hurt when I didn't know about them. Now pain was starting to climb up my thighs. Now I could smell burning flesh. Why hadn't I smelled it sooner? I looked around for my legs, but they seemed to have turned into piles of ash.

I laughed, a little too loud. "You damn near did fry me like a chicken and remove my balls too."

"I did, and I'm sorry about it." Desh frowned.

"You don't have to say that anymore. Your apology will be an understood thing between us, and I'll hold it over your head forever."

Limnad poked her head over Desh's shoulder. "Bib, the unicorn won't let you ride her, so you'll have to heal yourself before we can leave here. But the spirit of this place is letting us leave. Isn't that wonderful? You know, you're very good at getting crippled. We should take advantage of that skill more often."

"Blue River Spirit!" the marsh spirit called out. "I need to tell you one thing before you leave. Not long ago, you thought your lover was repulsive. You left him."

"No, I didn't! That's silly!"

Desh held still and kept silent.

The marsh spirit said, "But you did. And he, like the cheating, nasty sorcerer he is, made a deal with the gods."

"No, he didn't," Limnad said with much less strength.

"The gods made you love him again. If he did that to you, how much could he really love you?"

Limnad turned to Desh, but he didn't say or do anything. After a moment, she whisked away across the marsh.

The Spirit of the Summer Marsh sank into the water, watching Limnad with a sly smile.

TWENTY-FIVE

A lot of things happened while we waited in the marsh the rest of the day. I healed Desh, and then he went off by himself to enchant a variety of weeds and bugs, or maybe it was gold figurines and rubies as big as my thumbnail. Desh also gave me some more power to apologize for cutting off half my body.

I restored both my legs during an eight-hour groaning and sweating ordeal. Pil stayed with me, making jokes and insulting me to keep me focused through the pain and slapping me awake whenever I faded during the last hour.

Frutt helped Gerapai bury Lily as well as they were able, which was not too damn well. They had no tools, and once they dug down ten inches, water filled up their hole in seconds. Afterward, Frutt looked at me with disgust and fear, so Gerapai must have explained that I was a horrible, traitorous waste of human skin.

Gea arrived sometime during my healing. I wouldn't have noticed except that Pil ran off to help Stan keep Gea and the unicorn from killing one another. Pil came back red-faced, panting, and complaining about wild magical creatures with no more self-control than a goose.

A lot of things occurred that day, but one didn't happen: Limnad did not come back.

Once I had two legs again, I dropped off and slept until morning. While I was asleep, I gave up my life to Harik. I felt a bit surprised that I even woke up, but I told myself I'd better get more accustomed to knowing that the breath I was taking might be my last one.

Gea had navigated the marsh on her own without drowning. The unicorn was still sulking and turning her hindquarters to Gea, so Pil asked the horse to lead us out of the swamp. I don't guess she would have refused unless she wanted to stay and eat swamp grass for the rest of her existence. She guided us through the slow, grimy, tortuous miles to the north edge of the marshland by midafternoon.

When we reached drier land, we didn't throw a party right away. Desh and I crept out onto the sloping grassland to scout for King Famm. He had been behind us, but events had delayed us in an awful fashion.

"Why do you think we might see him?" Desh murmured. "We don't have the glove, or horses, or much food, or any beer, so Famm doesn't need a single thing we have."

"That's true," I said.

"If he's smart, he'll hurry on past us to wherever the glove points him."

"Also true," I said. "He is liable to surprise us and do something foolish, though. Such errors aren't uncommon. We'll just watch for them."

"You'll watch for them," Desh said. "I'm leaving. This was always your task, not mine. I have other things to do."

I examined the young man's face. I had grown so accustomed to there being no happiness there, I hadn't noticed how forlorn it had become. "Well, thank you for coming this far. I hope things turn out well for you, Desh. If we live through this and you need help, send for me."

Yita surprised me by begging Desh not to go, but he just shook his head. Stan and Pil said they understood why he had to leave. Stan even said he'd been expecting it. None of it seemed to matter to Desh. He waved once and strode away east without a word.

"Inscrutable," Pil said. "Desh has that mastered."

"What's out that direction?" Yita asked, pointing after Desh.

Stan coughed and said, "The Blue River, where naked blue spirits live, and that's where the boy's going to get all torn apart and made to eat his own eyeballs. The eyeball-eating will come first."

We all watched Desh for a minute. Then I said, "Now for our next steps."

I jumped when Stan shouted, "No!" A moment later, the unicorn trotted away through a portal that opened and shut. He started cursing in what was a quiet tone for him.

Pil immediately wrapped her hand in Gea's mane. I didn't know whether she was trying to hold her or go with her if she left.

Another portal opened, and the unicorn walked back in through it. Stan smiled as if Sweetie had been dead and come back to life.

I glanced back and forth between Stan and Pil. "Are we done with all that? Yes?"

"Sure," Stan said, running his fingers through the unicorn's mane. "Sweetie just had to tell the others she ain't coming back."

The unicorn pawed the ground and shook her head, but Stan didn't notice over his grinning and cackling.

I closed my eyes and sighed. "We have plans to make."

"I plan to go with Gerapai," Frutt said. "He's leaving for his homeland."

"If I take you to the Hill Lands, you will be killed," Gerapai said.

"Then I'll stop someplace before we get there. Someplace with good soil. I grew squash and peppers behind the barracks. And a few roses."

"That sounds better for you than soldiering," Yita said. "It sounds a whole lot better than where we're going."

"Bib . . ." Frutt stared at me.

"Yes? Speak!"

"What's so important about all these gods and demons?" Frutt asked in a rush. "Why do you do all these things for them? Why don't you go home too?"

"I don't do things for them!" I said. "Well, I guess I do, sort of. Once you fall in with gods and demons, it's hard to fall back out."

"You're not a god or a demon, are you?" he asked.

Pil said, "There have been a lot of arguments about that."

I ignored her. "No, I'm not."

"Maybe . . ." Frutt shrugged. "You ought to do things for people sometime, since you're one of them."

"Hell, I can hardly stand people!" I snarled.

Nobody disagreed. Frutt looked away.

After a few seconds of silence, Pil said, "Bib, I found a—"

I cut her off. "Yita, will you come with me on our special murderous task?"

She glared and said, "I'll come with you, but you're not Cael."

"That's true. He was a better man than me on almost every count. But he didn't stay alive, and I did. His many fine qualities are useless to us now."

I turned to Pil and paused. She wasn't actually Gek's servant. As long as I brought Yita along on the murdering party, why couldn't Pil just go home?

"Pil, will you take Gea and Stan and his unicorn home, or at least someplace where not so many things are trying to kill you? Gerapai and Frutt, I believe the closest town is to the northeast. Here are a few coins to help you along."

Pil said, "Bib, this is my murderous task too. I'm coming with you."

"No need. Yita will handle it, probably better than you and I could working together. You are relieved of duty."

Pil crossed her arms. "Tell me this: where are you going?"

I grinned. "Oh, the Dark Lands, probably."

"How do you think you'll get there?"

I waved that question away. "Hell, I've blundered into the damn place twice already! I'd probably have to work hard to stay out."

Pil rolled her eyes. "What about the mighty weapon Cael was crowing about?"

"We'll pick it up on the way. Can you loan me a knife?" I patted the empty sheath on my belt.

"No!" Pil stepped toward me. "And how will you find this weapon, huh? Trip on it in the dark?"

I smiled. "I'll ask King Famm to give me the glove. Then I'll cut out his liver when he says no."

"Bib! Famm and his sorcerers will kill you both!" Pil shook her head the way my mother had when I was too foolish for words.

"They won't kill us." I smiled at Yita. "Famm thought Yita and I were his prisoners, but we were two hours away from killing every damn one of them. Right, Yita?"

Yita scowled at me, but her voice was steady. "That's true. Pil, you saved all their lives when you caught up with us. So, go home. You'll just be in our way."

I'm not sure what Yita thought Pil would say, but she probably didn't expect Pil to point and laugh.

Yita started turning red. "I mean it! Go!"

"Right now?" Pil chuckled. "Can't I even eat supper first? Oh, never mind. Bib, Famm has already passed us, hasn't he?"

I shrugged.

Pil gave me a doubting squint. "They have unless half of them broke their ankles in the mud. Maybe you can trail them, but how can you catch them? Gea is coming with me, and I bet that touchy unicorn is coming with Stan."

I had no answers that didn't involve Famm losing his mind or Krak granting us the power of flight.

Pil held something up close to my face. "Look what I found."

I peered. "It's a string."

"Two strings." Pil smiled as if she'd found a pitcher full of gold. "They were in my pouch where I held the pinkie finger when you climbed up on my shoulders." She waved the threads. "These came off the woolen finger."

I examined her face. "Can you do anything with them?"

Pil's grin disappeared. "Maybe. I'd need power, and I don't have much."

"We should wait," I said. "Who knows what might happen in our favor?"

"We might fall farther behind, Bib." Pil shook her head like my mother again.

Yita said, "Pil, if it's that easy, go on and get the power!"

"It's not like picking up rocks off the road!" I said. "Dammit, Pil, will you give up thirty years of your life for this?"

Pil closed her eyes for a few seconds. "Yita doesn't know what she's talking about, and she's still right." She smiled at the younger girl.

Corporal Frutt dropped straight to the ground like a sack of straw. Gerapai and Yita knelt beside him.

Yita jumped up and stared at Pil. "He died! Dead. For no reason. He just fell down!"

While Stan trotted over to confirm the death, Pil grabbed my arm and stared at me, her face white. She whispered, "I didn't mean to."

"You gave away thirty years of his life?" I whispered.

"No! Twenty-four from me, four from Yita, and two from Frutt. But he was so young! I didn't think he'd die!" She exhaled and sniffed a couple of times. "I have to tell. Who do I have to tell?"

"You told me," I whispered. "I guess his normal span of years wasn't too long. Don't tell anybody else."

"What are you two whispering about over there?" Stan asked, walking toward us.

"What to do next," I said. "We didn't want to be disrespectful toward poor Corporal Frutt while we bitched at each other about it. Pil has a way to point us in the right direction. She'll do that, and then the two of you will go off someplace safe."

"I'm not going anywhere safe," Pil said. "I don't even know a place like that."

While Pil worked on the threads, Stan and Gerapai dug a sadly shallow grave with knives. We laid Frutt in it and covered him with the healthy black soil. White clouds peppered the clear afternoon sky.

I said, "It's a pretty place. The marsh, a forest, and this grassland all meet here."

"He told me the name of every plant we walked past," Gerapai said. "He wanted to know what my people call them." He turned his back to the grave.

In under half an hour, Pil announced that she was done. I figured she would weave the threads into a grass bracelet or necklace. Instead, she placed it under the skin of her forefinger, wrapped around the first knuckle.

"Dammit, Pil! All we know about this is that it comes from a glove that points to a god-pounding terrible weapon! You don't put something like that inside your body!"

"You're not a Binder, and you don't know what I would or wouldn't do," Pil snipped. She held her finger up as if it were a dagger and smiled. "We're not going to lose this! And you won't be able to use it unless you bring me with you!"

I growled, "I could cut off your finger."

She squeezed my arm. "You and Yita can ride with me on Gea. Stan can ride his white monster and keep her at a reasonable distance."

Stan grumbled under his breath.

I looked around for Gerapai, but he must have walked away while we were arguing about fingers and horseflesh. I couldn't spot him anywhere, so he had probably disappeared into the forest.

Pil's finger guided us west, pointing through a part of the marsh that bellied out from the rest. We rode in a curve around that marshland, which was beginning to seem familiar. The grassland sloped toward what looked like a river valley.

"Ouch!" Pil yelled. "Lutigan burn it twice!"

I leaned my head to look over Pil's shoulder and saw the cursed city that Limnad had pointed out to Desh and me. Within seconds, my eyes burned and pressure built in my head. "Go around! Go a different way!"

"Go around?" Pil said. "I guess you don't want that weapon then, since my finger says it's in that city."

TWENTY-SIX

Dragons really existed once. A cheerful young sorcerer showed me a stuffed dragon's head not long after she murdered a nasty, even younger sorcerer and stole his collection of magical curiosities. The dragon's head was as big as a pony, with a mouth full of teeth longer than my hand. It also had a scaly ruff around its neck and four stubby, curved horns behind its forehead.

The dragons were all killed centuries ago. My teachers said so, and I knew they wouldn't lie to me. Over the next twenty years, I found that my teachers had lied like sweaty thieves about a mort of things. I hadn't seen a dragon yet, but I didn't mock the possibility.

As Gea galloped toward the cursed city and I hung on behind Pil, I didn't spot any dragons. But in the past couple of days, we had fought monsters that looked like our families, lied our asses off to escape two gods, decapitated a nasty demigod, made friends with a unicorn, and almost killed each other because a spirit of mud and dirty water told us to.

After all that, I figured the next logical thing would be a dragon landing in front of us. My eyes throbbed and watered from trying to watch the city, so I shouted at Pil, "Do you see any dragons?"

"What?"

"Or anything else that might eat us?"

"What? No. What are you talking about?"

"Never mind, I'll yell a couple of times if I see one." I set myself to watch for any kind of danger, including dragons.

The unicorn ran just as fast as Gea, and neither seem bothered by this odd magic that hurt our eyes. With normal horses, I doubt we could have approached the city directly. We might have ridden all day at angles or in circles without ever reaching the place. But on these mounts, I figured we'd reach the city in twenty minutes and then do some clever, bold thing that I hadn't yet thought of.

Yet before we had covered half that distance, I saw a lonely cloud lying on the ground ahead and to our right. As we overtook it, I spotted men marching into the cloud, which lay between them and the city.

"It's Famm!" Pil shouted.

I nodded. "Right. Old Thad is raising fog and moving it along to protect their eyes from the city. That's clever for a bouncy, little beaver-faced son of a bitch. The conditions are all wrong for fog, though. I bet he's spending enough power to grow a forest. Let's ride in a curve around them to keep the range . . . Shit, they've seen us!"

Gea wheeled away from Famm's men, but a mound of earth rose in front of her. The black horse climbed halfway up and leaped the rest of the way over. Once we had passed, I glanced back and saw the unicorn spring all the way over the mound, landing as lightly as a sparrow.

I pulled two white bands and flung them toward Famm just as one of his bowmen fired. The range was impossibly far. While the arrow was in the air, Gea's saddle disappeared out from under us. It was an unimaginative tactic by the Breaker, but it was so common because it worked so well. If he tried the same trick with the unicorn, he must have been disappointed to find she had no saddle to disintegrate.

Pil grabbed Gea's mane to hold on but dropped whatever object she had pulled from her pouch. I clung to Pil and twisted bands to raise a small wind. Just then the arrow arrived. The unicorn writhed out of the way like a fish. Yita fell off to one side, whirling her arms for balance. The arrow struck Stan's arm, and he shouted a filthy curse.

I pushed the wind toward the fog. Thad shoved back against me with plenty of power to overwhelm me. But he had to maintain the fog too, and I had seen that he didn't manage well with more than one task at a time. I pulled three more bands and strained against the man.

The archer fired again, this time in my direction, just as a portal opened in front of Stan and the unicorn. She and Stan galloped through it, and they emerged from a portal that opened behind the archer. The unicorn speared the man from back to front and carried him for two hundred feet. Then she tossed the body aside and galloped away through another portal that snapped open and then closed.

"Krak!" Pil shouted, pointing at the unicorn brutality. "Lutigan's left hand!"

I didn't have a chance to swear along with her. When the unicorn attacked, Thad's pressure against the wind almost disappeared, and the fog began blowing away. The archer must have been one of the sorcerers, and when he died, the sorcery pent was broken.

The dead man's arrow arrived. I tried to warp the shaft but failed, which meant it was a magical arrow, and it plunged into Gea's side. She neighed and pitched over, throwing both Pil and me off as she fell.

A portal opened near us, and the unicorn trotted out next to Yita so she could mount. Holding his arm, Stan shouted, "The same damn wrist! Why do the gods hate me? Well, I guess I know, but Krak! Two arrows in the same damn wrist twice in the same damn week!"

I ignored Stan and approached Gea. The horse was lying on her side, heaving and blowing, but otherwise still. "Pil, what are Famm's men doing?" I leaned over Gea.

"Nothing except for running around crying and waving their

hands. Sorry, that wasn't funny. We're pretty far away from them, and they must be shocked by the unicorn assault, and besides, they have other things to worry about now that they don't have mist protecting their eyeballs."

"I'd commiserate with the bastards except I hope every one of them dies of a dripping disease. Gea, I'll help you if you let me."

The horse stayed quiet and only quivered when I removed the arrow, which was buried almost to the fletching not far from her heart. The fact that she was a magical being might have saved her. I healed Gea, gaining a deep pain in my side.

When I turned away from the horse, I found Stan right behind me, holding out his wounded wrist like a boy wanting a splinter pulled from his finger. I healed him as well. That, and calling the wind had brought my reserves of power awfully low.

"Famm's men look disorganized still," Yita said. "They might be shocked. I think I would be."

Stan grunted, "Shocked. That's good. I hope they stay that way until winter."

Gea climbed back to her feet, and we mounted. She and the unicorn carried us toward the city at a gallop, and I tried to keep my eyes pointed away from the place. Traveling through the Gods' Realm had been good practice for that. As we rode closer, I saw a broad river resting at the edge of the city. Just then, as if a soap bubble had popped, the pain from looking at the place vanished.

From my angle, the city was broad enough across for thirty blocks of buildings or houses. If it was just as deep, as many as five thousand people might have lived there once. I saw no walls or other defenses, although most structures were built of stone. The dark stone blocks were partly stained as if watery whitewash had been poured down from the roofs. Few buildings reached more than three stories, but a wide tower stood two hundred feet tall in the center of the city.

I couldn't see anything moving in the streets, but it was late in the day. All the buildings except the tower lay in shadow.

"Pil, does your finger still say we should go into that city?"

"Yes," she answered, unusually curt. "Right in the middle."

"Don't you wish you'd gone home when I told you to?"

"Yes, so shut up about it."

"There's a bridge," I said. "Let's start there."

I spotted something moving on the tower and almost decided it was a dragon wrapped around the structure. But the movement was merely small, worn-out banners fluttering here and there. Then I realized they weren't banners. They were bodies clad in torn, flapping clothes.

And not just clothes waved. What looked like entrails dangled and swung. A couple of arms on the verge of falling off swung as well. I closed my eyes, wishing my eyesight was poorer.

I made myself look again and saw that the bodies were moving and straining. Their heads twisted, and they struggled to reach behind themselves, I supposed to pull themselves free of the tower wall.

With no warning, Gea halted a minute's walk from the bridge. Pil and I almost fell.

Stan announced, "Sweetie is done with all this shit. She says that's a bad place over there. Hell, I didn't need no fine, mystical beast to tell me that. Look at it!" Stan jumped to the ground.

Pil slid down from Gea's back. "Bib, come on."

As soon as my feet touched the dirt, Gea bolted back toward the marsh. The unicorn opened a portal, trotted through, and closed it behind her.

"Well . . . shit," Yita said.

"No, it's fine," Pil said. "They wouldn't have been able to come with us in the tower."

"Who said we're going there?" Stan shouted. "And I'll tell you, Sweetie could go anywhere she wanted, even the inside of a beer barrel!"

"Well, she didn't want to go with us," I said.

"That ought to tell you something!" Stan said. "I'm becoming suspicious of this whole venture."

Pil said, "Go on home if you want to, Stan. We won't think ill of you."

"You won't think I'm a coward, you mean! I ain't no damn

coward, and I ain't afraid to die. But I am afraid of dying in a place like this. Maybe it's fine for sorcerers, but it's not right for real people. Look at them sad bastards!" Stan pointed at the bodies wriggling on the tower wall. "While you're drinking tea with gods and making magic socks, that'll be me!"

"Stan, you're right," I said. "Go home if you want and live a regular, happy life. I promise none of us will think anything bad about you. Go if you want to."

"Really?"

I nodded.

"You mean it?"

"Yes!"

Stan folded his arms. "You don't care if I stay or go." His lower lip twitched, but he didn't pout. "To hell with you then. I'll show you. I'm staying."

I nodded, fearing that I'd set him off again no matter what I said.

"If you two have made up and kissed, let's hurry on," Yita said. "Famm may be right behind us."

Pil said, "I wish we could wait and not walk into that city at twilight."

Yita grimaced. "As I said, Famm may be right behind us."

The four of us trotted to the bridge, which had weathered badly and had no railing. The river was only two hundred feet wide, and the bridge crossed it in a shallow arc. I began striding across, my head up as if somebody in the city were throwing a party for me.

As we reached the top of the bridge, Stan said, "Be quiet! I hear something!"

We all paused and could hear soft moaning from beneath the bridge. I looked over the side but saw nothing except the river sliding past.

Pil gasped. "It's the bridge," she said with a tremor.

I stared at my feet and realized I was walking on somebody's back. The entire bridge was paved with moaning bodies tied together.

We sprinted the rest of the way across the bridge of dead

people, or mostly dead people, I wasn't sure about that. The bridge emptied onto a road about sixty feet wide that might have been one of the main thoroughfares in the city. I didn't see anything moving, living or dead, except for the bodies on the tower fifteen blocks ahead of us.

Pil checked her finger again. "Straight for the tower."

I couldn't think of anything useful to say, so I drew my sword and swaggered toward the tower. I didn't know whether zeal would give us an advantage, but it didn't cost much. The others followed me, maybe with a bit less arrogance.

On the second block, I saw a rustle of something moving behind a window. I pointed at it.

A moment later, Stan said, "This side too."

"Do you think we can clear the buildings before we keep going?" Yita asked.

"We might as well knock down each building as we pass," I said. "I think that would be just as easy. Let's stop for a moment, though. Pil, do you have any useful magic for us?"

"Maybe." She poked around in a narrow, red pouch.

I debated spending the power to gather some storm clouds. The road to the tower looked awfully damn long, so I went ahead and pulled two white bands. Using so little power, a storm might take twenty minutes or more to gather. We couldn't idle there gossiping in the street until clouds showed up, so we pushed on.

On the third block, I saw two faces peep out of a doorway. They looked rough and weathered gray, with no more expression than a stump. Pil and Stan watched the other side of the street and reported that three figures over there were gazing at us with bright eyes. One of them was armless.

I looked back when we entered the fourth block. Through the dimness, I made out a dozen creatures walking behind us. The tower stood eleven blocks ahead.

"I hope you got better ideas than hitting them with swords," Stan said. "They don't seem to care how many arms or legs they've had cut off."

Another dozen creatures waited along the side of the street on the fourth block. One leaned against a wall because he had lost a leg. Another had taken a brutal wound that almost chopped her head in two. She blinked at me with her one eye and didn't seem concerned.

By the fifth block, more than twenty of these beings had gathered behind us and were closing with us at a trot. Except for the ones missing limbs, they seemed as active and lively as any living person. Ten more edged toward us from the buildings on that block, and I saw another twenty or thirty appear from the gathering darkness ahead of us.

We were not going to make it to the sixth block without fighting.

Pil threw something onto the road. It shattered like glass and threw weak light around us. Since it was shining from the ground, it cast shadows upward. The effect would have been more disturbing, but since long-dead, cursed creatures were running to kill us, I hardly noticed which way shadows pointed.

One of the figures ran at Pil, and she threw something else at the ground in front of her. The creature jerked to a halt, struggling to lift its feet, which seemed glued to the ground. A second being charged her and got caught too. Pil dodged a third before cutting his arm, severing the limb like it was a sausage. He swiped at her with his remaining arm, and she threw herself aside. These enemies didn't seem to hesitate over anything as simple as losing an arm or a leg.

I heard Stan cursing the creatures and Yita insulting Stan behind me. The storm was a long way from gathering. I jumped out and cut off a monster's leg at the knee. Could we cripple enough of them so they couldn't outrun us?

The next figure hurled herself at me. I stabbed her in the heart and stepped out of the way. She threw her head back for a moment and then collapsed.

Every one of the creatures stopped in place, staring at us.

"What the hell?" I said.

"Shh!" Yita said. "You'll break the spell. Can we sneak past them?"

The figure closest to me stood up straight. Looking at me, he pointed at himself, opened his mouth, and croaked. He tried again and said in a raspy voice, "Me too. Kill me too."

I peered at the being. He pointed one of his remaining fingers at his chest, so I stabbed him in the heart too. He convulsed, fell to the street, and lay still.

On all sides, the creatures walked toward me, their chests pushed forward. Stan thrust his blade into one's heart. When he withdrew, the being stared down at her chest and shook her head.

Pil said, "It looks like they can only be killed by a sword that wants things to be really, really dead."

The enormity of it hit me. Hundreds or thousands of these people had been living a tortured semi-life for centuries. Thanks to Desh's enchantment, my sword could end that for them.

Yita said, "I can see you thinking it, Bib, but you should also think about this: if you save these poor creatures, they won't be here to stop Famm when he arrives. If you leave them the way they are, Famm will never catch us."

Stan said, "That sounds smart, but . . ." He shook his head and whistled.

Pil said, "Bib, you can't leave them like this."

For a few seconds, I considered abandoning them. I could leave the world's most horrible booby trap for Famm. But what Sakaj had done to them was an insult to life and an insult to death too. "Let's start by destroying the ones on the bridge. And then destroying the bridge. At least that will slow Famm down."

Gek, in the form of a small bird, landed on my shoulder. "You must not pause to dispatch these creatures."

I stopped breathing, and my heartbeat pounded in my ears. To cover up my terror, I thrust my sword into the hearts of two residents before I answered him without too much shaking. "I was hoping you'd show up, Gek. If you just kill them all, I won't have to stop here. You're fantastic at killing. I saw it back in Cadellan." I swallowed hard but reminded myself that Harik had already killed me, even if he hadn't quite finished the job. I destroyed three more cursed people.

"Who are you talking to?" Yita asked. I glanced at Bird-Gek and rolled my eyes.

Gek chirped, "I do not care about these entities, nor should you. Gather them at the tower on the pretext of killing them there, stab a few, and enter the tower while the rest are waiting."

"Won't they be pissed when I come back out of the tower?" I killed another one and started walking toward the bridge.

Gek said, "I will deal with that problem. And you're going the wrong way!"

"If you're upset about the delay, kill them all. You can do that with one waggle of your omnificent claw." I grinned at Bird-Gek. I was both terrified of him and angry at him, and for the moment, anger was winning. "Or bring them back to life, whole and healthy! I'll have no reason to stay then. You can do that, right?"

"If I wished it to be so, it would present no challenge," Gek said.

My mouth hung open. "Well, that's a damn lie!" When Gek didn't respond, I said, "I know a lie when I hear one spoken, and that one rattled windows a thousand miles from here."

"That is not the point. I have given you a charge."

"When I walked in here, how did you expect me to survive and get to the tower if I wasn't going to help these people?"

"Help a few and be about your business!" Gek said in an irritated tweet.

I started stabbing residents as I passed them. "Kill these people or revive them, Gek—those should be two of the easiest things in the world for you. Do it, and I'll hurry on down the trail, or into the tower, I guess." I stopped. "Is it possible you're unable to kill them or revive them? That you can't break the curse? Because She Who Must Not Be Named has bigger balls than you? At least she did three hundred years ago. How close am I to the truth?"

"This is pointless," Gek said. "Go ahead and try to climb the tower without my help. You and your young women are not my only weapon."

Bird-Gek flew off into the night.

TWENTY-SEVEN

Over the past three hundred-odd years, most of the city's inhabitants had already flung themselves into the river, or so the survivors told us. The most articulate of the remaining citizens was called Sepp and spoke on everyone's behalf. She once had a name of her own but couldn't remember it. I called her Sepp because that was my mother's name and I had found myself thinking about her lately.

By hurling themselves into the river, Sepp's people had hoped to drown, or perhaps be carried far enough away from the cursed place by the current so they could die. Maybe they had been right, but I doubted it. When somebody is punished by Sakaj, they shouldn't expect to find peace so easily. I didn't offer that opinion to Sepp, though. Although her face had almost no expression, I could tell she agreed with my pessimism but hoped she was wrong.

I started killing people at the bridge. After I had slain everyone who'd been part of the bridge, I stared at the structure for a few minutes. I needed to destroy it, but that might require more power than I had left.

I raised my spirit and called for Harik. He answered without delay, and I found him alone in the trading arena. It was daytime, but black ash fell so thickly that I couldn't see the sun. Piles of it came up to my ankles, and nothing could be seen apart from the gazebo, although that was perfectly clear.

"Trouble with your volcanoes?" I asked. Then I froze. I couldn't believe what I had just said.

Harik hissed. "I suspected that you could see us, as well as everything else here. At last, you give yourself away."

I stared right at him. "I've been able to do it for a long time. You must feel awfully foolish."

"Now that I know, it doesn't matter at all. Let's discuss other things."

I hadn't been prepared for him not to care. "Ah . . . don't you want to know how I did it?" Actually, I hoped he would tell me, since I had no idea.

"Keep your secret, Murderer. It could not possibly matter less. I find that I can endure your tricks and paltry humor because today you are annoying Sakaj beyond reason. It is well that you haven't long to live. She is preparing curses for you worse than those suffered by the wretches you are releasing."

I felt a little disoriented by Harik's unconcern, but I rallied. "Wonderful. I thought she and I wouldn't have a chance to sit and gossip before the end."

Harik gave an oily grin. "Also, do compliment the Nub on his shining craftsmanship. I would not have believed that your sword could cut through Sakaj's curse. Astonishing, and I have felt astonishment fewer than a dozen times in the past century."

"Desh has always been a handy fellow," I said.

"And I suspect a less aggravating swordsmith than Fingit, that maundering bore."

I forced a smile. "Since we're chatting like farmers over the fence, could I trade for a bit of power, Your Magnificence? By way of a thank-you for brightening your day?"

Harik stepped forward, sweeping his black robe aside. "What a ridiculous suggestion. It crushes the mote of joy that I might have experienced over these events. Power—is that why you are here?"

I stood a little straighter and lied, "I'm here to report!"

Harik lifted an eyebrow. "Go on."

"Gek is in a thrashing great hurry over things, so whatever's going to happen will happen soon."

"Is that all?" Harik sighed.

"He said that he has other weapons besides me. I don't even know why he's calling me a weapon, but whatever he intends me to do can be done by somebody else." I waited.

"Well, who?" Harik snapped.

Leaning forward, I said, "I believe it's King Famm, although I don't have absolute proof."

"Who is this King Famm?"

"Oh, he's a hero king. Invincible, terribly wise, everything you'd expect. Fantastic beard. Carries three swords, which is mighty unconventional if you ask me."

"What does Gek expect this king to do?"

I shrugged. "I don't even know what he expects me to do. But Famm is a dangerous, clever, legendary figure that could kick the gods' plans right in the butt if he kicks at the right time. You should probably destroy him before he gets a chance."

"Hm. I'll consider that," Harik said.

I almost explained again how much Famm needed to be dead, but I feared pushing too hard. "That's my full report, Mighty Harik."

"Then we are done. Do not continue to beg for power. I find it distasteful."

"Right. Oh, I intend to kill a lot of people here in this city today, Harik. I mean a really astounding number. It would probably have been enough to retire my debt to you, although I can't be sure without knowing what the final number was . . ."

Harik didn't hesitate. "You are aware that you were not allowed to know the number ahead of time. Since you didn't accomplish the killings, I see no reason why you should know what the number was." His smile was as large as I'd ever seen it.

"I could kill everyone in this city with the right incentive, Your

Magnificence. Hundreds of people, or even thousands, killed in your name."

Harik snorted. "You intend to slay them no matter what. I need offer you no incentive." As he said this, Harik rubbed his hands together. I didn't know why he'd do such an obvious thing if he remembered I was watching him.

Well, sometimes gods failed to remember that existence didn't worship them, or at least that existence didn't always do as it was told. Maybe Harik was so used to my blindness here that habit had taken over. I eased around so I wouldn't be looking straight at him and give away that I could see him—again.

I said, "Oh well. Maybe I just won't kill them. I'll leave them alive."

"No, no, you are a horrible, nasty killer, but your villainy does not extend to the suffering of innocents."

"Maybe today it does, Harik. I'm sure you already have all the lives you need, especially since you're getting mine pretty soon. Let's just bypass these. I'm sure that would please your sister. It would be as if you had given her a gift."

Harik showed his teeth but sounded calm. "There is no need to torture these creatures any further. As for providing enjoyment to Sakaj, I do not see why you would find that appealing. After all, she abused you and your daughter abominably."

I held my face still. "That's all past. These folks are cursed and fairly well dried out, but I can pass by without showing them mercy. Don't doubt me on it. But if Your Magnificence were to give me a few more sunsets to pay my debt, then I would kill them all for you."

"And apply them to the balance? I shall offer nothing of the sort."

It had been a desperate stroke. The chances of Harik granting me even more time were remote. But he sounded greedy for the lives of the city's residents, and I might need power before he finally decided to take me.

"I'll kill them in exchange for five squares," I said. "Of course, all of them will count against my debt, but only if you decide to give me more time."

"It does not matter whether these killings count against a hypothetical debt that no longer exists," Harik said, staring at the floor and rubbing his chin. He jerked and glared at me before assuming an erect, dignified pose.

"You forgot that I could see you! Well then, what about my offer? Five squares, and I'll kill them all for you—and the killings count if my debt is reinstated."

Harik inclined his head and gave me a condescending smile. "Oh, I've grown weary of looking at you. I suppose I shall destroy you now."

I froze and couldn't breathe while he scrutinized me.

He said, "Very well. You may have one square when every one of these awful, desiccated entities has been destroyed in my name— you may not overlook even one. And each one that you kill will be accepted against your debt, should it ever be revived."

"I would say that an offer of five squares sounds better."

"You have already made that offer, Murderer. Don't be tiresome. Due to my embarrassing generosity, I offer two squares."

"Oh?" I hoped I was judging Harik's greed correctly. He had a war to fight, and I guessed he'd need whatever gods got when they traded with sorcerers. "Let's say six squares," I said.

"What? You realize that you have already granted me leave to destroy you on a whim, correct? Is this the time for ridiculous games?"

"It might be the best possible time, Mighty Harik, so I now propose that you offer me seven squares. Otherwise, I won't kill a single one of them. I may even heal a few."

"No!" Harik snapped. "Consider this. By agreeing to my terms, you can eliminate thirty years from the end of that fuzzy king's life. Who knows, perhaps he shall expire on the spot. Do you wish to forego such an opportunity along with, oh, three squares?"

I hesitated. I couldn't know what would be happening in the next few days. Between Gek, Harik, Krak, Fingit, Sakaj, King Famm, and any imps or spirits that wanted to pile on, this promised to be an invigorating time. Without power, I would likely get invigorated to death, which would leave Ella the prisoner of this infected, decomposing udder of a god.

No other god would trade with me since Harik already owned my life. Gek had never shown any interest in helping me along the magical line. Maybe that was another thing he couldn't do. Desh was gone along with his little wooden bottles. Harik was my only source of power.

That put me in a lousy position, so I attacked. "Harik, you moldy bucket of excretions, I want eight squares."

Harik sat down on a bench and crossed his legs at the ankles. "Your offer is sad and petty. You may have three squares in exchange for all these lives."

"My offer is magnificent and gives you exactly what you want!" I said. "You'll get mighty benefit from all these killings. I can sense it. Considering that, this deal is worth nine squares instead of eight."

"That's preposterous! To hell with offering you three squares. You can have two squares, and only if you beg!"

"Harik, while I'm here in the Gods' Realm, no time passes at home. But it certainly does pass here. How long until the war commences? I'd say my offer looks better every minute."

"Do not be childish, you squirming nit!"

I put my hand over my heart. "Stop it, Harik, you'll hurt my feelings. Ten squares, and listen to me. You are bargaining with a dead man, unless you decide to change that. You can't win by taking away things I care about. They're already gone. And you can't tempt me by offering things I won't live to have."

Harik let his head hang for an instant before straightening up and glancing at me. "Very well, I agree to provide ten squares. In exchange, you will ensure that every one of the crusty inhabitants of that cursed city are killed in my name, missing none. Due to my mercy and benevolence, every one of them that you kill shall be applied to your debt, should I ever lose my mind and reinstate it. Does that satisfy you?"

"It does, Mighty Harik."

"By the Unnamed Mother's fourth finger, Sakaj cannot plunge you into appalling, hopeless agony too soon for me. I would do it myself, but actually torturing my own sorcerers reflects poorly on my leadership."

"What?"

"My ability to lead the sorcerers in my care. I'm known to excel at it."

I didn't know what to say to that. I didn't even know how to think about it. I stared at him for a while that seemed long. "Mighty Harik, it's not that I don't trust you—it's that I don't trust you one damn bit. Let me confirm this. All of these cursed people I destroy will count toward my debt to you."

Harik grinned. "And see that every one of them dies."

"And you will provide me ten squares. Now. Not when all of them are destroyed."

His grin disappeared. "Three now and seven when it is done."

That seemed like the most advantageous deal I might get. "All right. Harik, you don't look as happy as you did a few seconds ago."

"Oh? This bargain does not distress me overmuch, Murderer. If I seemed pensive, it was because I was contemplating your dead children sitting inside your hollowed-out self, sailing you like a boat on the ocean while you scream. Something like that. Sakaj is better at these sorts of shenanigans than I, damn her."

"That's just . . ." I closed my eyes and looked down, squeezing the bridge of my nose. "Maybe we men were created by some gods, and maybe they care about what they created, but you are not one of them, you whirling baboon's whang."

Harik jumped up. "Have care for how you speak to me!"

"I will. A whirling, oozing, spotty, sad little baboon's whang."

Harik scowled and muttered, "You'll be dead soon."

"How many times have you said those words, Your Magnificence?"

He ignored that. "How do you wish to pay—"

"Take all thirty years from King Famm."

I pushed myself down from the trading place. I found myself still staring at the bridge, and I began figuring out how to destroy it using the smallest possible amount of power. Maybe I would have ten squares, which was a fortune in power, but that was no call to become sloppy.

"Bib," came a voice from behind me.

I turned to find Desh standing almost at my shoulder. Limnad waited stiffly ten feet behind him. I hadn't ever seen either of their faces look so tight and solemn.

I said, "You two have come to a horrible place, but I'm happy to see you here. That's not nice of me, I guess."

Limnad said, "That doesn't matter, Bib, you're never nice. I don't care about that. I'm here to watch you die. Desh believes I owe you that, and when he explained it, I decided he was right."

"I appreciate that, Limnad, but you can go if you want to."

"No! You have behaved terribly sometimes! But one time, you healed me when I would have died, which isn't that important, and you brought back my birthright, which I would never have seen again, and that was destroying me." She glanced away. "I can never love Desh again, but I remember how much I loved him, and you brought him to me."

Not sure what to say, I mumbled, "Well, I'm glad, and I'm happy you've forgiven Desh."

Limnad turned her head slowly toward Desh. Her face was as hard as a sheet of iron with her eyes burning through it. I wanted to back away. "I didn't forgive him. I thought you would need him." She turned back to me and smiled like she was explaining a painting or a toy she had made. "I think he'll die before you, and you'll die soon anyway. So, it's really not so much helping you as it is killing him in some ironic way."

Desh blinked, but otherwise his relaxed face didn't react.

Limnad said, "Bib, I need to tend my river this autumn, or at least by winter, so please try to hurry up about dying. Why were you staring at that bridge with all the dead people tied to it?"

"I was deciding how to destroy it."

"Oh." She waved a careless hand. "Well, go off and do something else. You look skinny, so go eat." She put both hands on my shoulders and leaned toward me. "I don't expect you to starve yourself to death. You'll do something dashing and stupid like you've done a hundred times, but I guess this time you'll die. Who knows why? Do you want me to feed you to my fish when you're dead? Some of them are blue!"

I was wondering how to answer any of that when I heard rumbling. A thirty-foot-high wall of water charged down the river with unfathomable force, and it battered the bridge to pieces.

As I watched timber and bodies float downstream, I said, "Thank you, Limnad. That was helpful." Then I muttered, "I didn't need any power to accomplish that, I guess."

"What did you say?" Desh asked.

I shook my head. "Thank you for coming back, Desh. I know you didn't have to. We're liable not to live through this, though."

"Then we won't inconvenience Limnad by making her wait around."

I snorted. "I guess not. I ought to stop acting dramatic about it, eh?"

"That would make you better company. Oh, here." Desh handed me five little wooden bottles full of power. "That's all I have left. You'll probably need them more than I will, and I might not be there when you do."

Staring at the bottles in my hands, I realized that my deal with Harik hadn't been necessary at all. It seemed like a reasonable deal anyway, maybe even a good one. I had to kill the people of this city, but I was going to do that anyway to set them free. Harik would probably never reinstate my debt. But if he did, then today I'd pay it down by hundreds of lives, or even thousands.

I had made far worse bargains. Maybe Harik had been distracted, or maybe he had let me run free a bit because he already owned my life.

I missed the next couple of things Desh said. He was waving his hand at me. "Bib! I said you should hold on to these bottles in case Pil needs a couple. All right?"

"Give them to her yourself."

Desh shook his head. "She'll be where you are. She is the one doing this stupid thing we're here for, right?"

"Oh, no," I said. "Yita has signed up for that task. My job is to get Yita there. I'm counting on you to keep Pil away from that party."

Desh stared at me. "Bib, maybe the gods are correct about you not being very bright. Pil will be where you are. Count on it. Unless you want me to burn off both her legs."

TWENTY-EIGHT

Sepp gathered her people around the tower in a terrific mass that spread down every nearby street. It was just after full dark, and the moon had lifted above the buildings to throw enough light that we didn't smack into walls as we walked. I would normally have found the sight of so many gaunt, often-dismembered beings chilling, especially by moonlight. Now they just seemed grim and even sad.

Limnad helped us bring down the people from the tower walls, and she scoured all the city's cellars and buildings so that none of the residents was left out. That was lucky, since a few had lost both their legs and wouldn't have reached the tower anytime soon.

At last, I raised my sword and thrust at the nearest man's chest, but my blade halted a finger's width from his ripped, rotting shirt. I thrust again and then tried from various angles, but I couldn't so much as nick him.

"Are you cursed?" Stan asked me. "Or maybe the sword's cursed. I know what, it's that poor, dusty bugger there that's cursed. Look at him—sure he's cursed, and the curse slopped over on you."

"I think the most likely answer is that Bib has been cursed," Desh said.

"I agree, but why do you think that?" Yita asked.

Desh said, "Probably for the same reason as you." He pointed at the half-dead man I couldn't kill the rest of the way. "Who would want to lay a new curse with no warning on this specific man here? What has he done today that he hasn't been doing for three hundred years? Likewise, the odds are poor that someone would want to curse the sword itself. It does what it was made to do. It's a constant. If you drop eggs on the floor, it's not the floor's fault they break."

I stepped back when Desh turned toward me. "Who would want to curse Bib? Who has he offended, or widowed, or maimed, or lied to? The list is lengthy."

None of this made sense to me. Harik wanted these people dead, so why would he be causing problems? Who else would want to interfere? Sakaj? Probably, but she was catastrophe inside a nightmare. I set that possibility aside for a moment. Gek? Did he want me to ignore these people and trot right into the tower without any more farting around? I whispered, "Gek! Come here and explain this shit!" I took a breath. "I mean, please."

While I waited for Gek to land on my shoulder, I closed my eyes and reviewed every word spoken in Harik's presence, both by him and by me. Soon my shoulders sagged.

Harik had offered me power if I made sure every resident was killed. Also, any resident I killed would count against my debt, so it seemed like a decent deal.

But like a careless baby sorcerer, I forgot to get Harik to promise that I'd be allowed to kill the residents. Now the tricky, death-dripping bastard was preventing me from killing them with my own hand. That might be called unfair, but the gods wouldn't give a thimbleful of spit for an ocean of fairness.

I still had to make sure all the residents were killed. That meant somebody besides me had to kill them.

So, as it turned out, my deal sucked. It wasn't among the worst I had ever made, though. At least I'd get power, and we'd set the city's people free. "That wily, old pot full of grease and deceit!" I snarled.

"Grease and what? I think I'd better write that down," Pil said, winking.

"It's Harik. He's doing this. I think somebody else will have to kill them."

After a pause, Desh reached out with care for my sword. "Here, Bib, I'll do it."

Desh tried, but he couldn't kill the city's fine residents, either. No matter how he thrust, the sword wouldn't quite reach his victim. Desh lowered the sword and looked offended. Stan cackled that Desh must have been jumping out of married women's beds and ignoring beggars while they starved right there in front of him.

"Yes, of course. You caught me." Desh smiled a little. "I still don't think it's the sword, though."

Yita said, "Here," beckoning as if she were reaching for a broom. She took my sword and made the thrust, but something held the blade away.

Stan tried next but had no better luck. He handed my sword to Pil, who swallowed hard but thrust into the heart of the closest man. He shivered and collapsed.

Pil glanced around at the hundreds of near-dead citizens, then looked at me with round eyes. "No. I'm not going to." She backed away from me but bumped into the closest waiting residents. "Bib, I can't do this."

"You'll be helping them, Pil."

"I know that!" she snapped. "I know! But I can't kill all these people who are just standing still, waiting for me to do it, and for sure I can't do it to so many. It feels . . . worse than murder, although that's crazy now that I think about it, but it still feels that way."

"It's not murder, and it's the right thing to do," I said, patting her shoulder. "Out of all us cutthroats, I expect you to be the first one in there when it's time to do the right thing. But I understand. Even if it's right, you don't know what killing all these souls will do to you."

"I do know." She scowled as she examined my face like I was a crippled horse.

I nodded slowly. "I guess you're right, Pil. You don't want to be like me. I don't blame you, and I don't want it for you. But either you take on this burden now, or you leave these people to suffer for some more centuries. You're a sorcerer, and sometimes that leads you to a choice like this."

"Leads me to it?" Pil sneered. "As if it just happened, like a leaf falling, as if you were standing idly nearby when Harik made the deal? No, Bib, you went to the gods and made this bargain!"

Pil grabbed the sword away from me, spun, and stabbed a woman, who shivered and collapsed. "I almost wish that was you!" she yelled at me and then killed eight more people as they pushed toward her to be stabbed. Pil glared at me in between each one.

After twenty-five killings, I turned away. Pil shouted, "Don't you turn around! You watch every time! You count them!"

Pil cursed every time she thrust the sword for most of an hour. Nearly half of those curses were for me. She stopped after the 107th killing, faced me, and said in a quiet voice, "I know I shouldn't blame you. Yes, you made the deal, but I'm choosing to do this. It's like any other hard choice, and I've made a lot of them. It's no different."

I stepped toward her, but she didn't lower the sword. "Pil, it's different."

Pil waved me away and killed the next woman with a smooth, easy motion. I sort of wished she was still calling me a son of a bitch.

I realized then that my deal with Harik had been appalling. I had felt like a damn clever fellow for outwitting him. I had been deceitful and suspicious, but the God of Death had rolled me like a barrel.

For the next thirty murders, while the city's residents carried away the dead, Pil worked hard, as calm and steady as a blacksmith at his anvil. She got shaky for the next twelve killings, and I thought she might throw down the sword.

But then Pil steadied and went back to relaxed killing, agile as she stepped aside when the dead fell. Her face was calm, almost blank. She went on that way for 172 murders, changing hands whenever her arm got tired.

When Pil came to the first child, she froze. Then she broke down and cried for ten minutes while Yita held her. Standing and wiping her face, she grabbed my arm to pull me aside and whisper, "Harik won't talk to me, and neither will Lutigan. Go back to Harik and make a new deal so you can do this. You won't mind, you like to kill. I'll pay whatever it costs."

I called for Harik, but he refused me. "I'm sorry, Pil."

"I tried all the other gods! You try!"

After a minute of effort, I shook my head. "They won't answer."

Pil sighed and trudged back to the crowd. She stabbed the little boy in the heart without hesitating and moved to the next killing without watching him hit the ground.

Over the next two hours, Pil killed 244 of the city's cursed residents. She switched hands every few minutes, but she never slowed down. The palms of her hands got raw and then bloody as the skin wore away. Her face went hard, and she killed in a steady rhythm. After half an hour, I saw tears on her cheeks, but her expression didn't soften.

Yita said to me, "I don't know why she's crying so much for these people. They want to die."

I heard Stan off to the side muttering, "She ain't crying for them."

By the time Pil had been freeing these people for three hours, she had killed 565 in all. She had begun panting and sweating, and she paused twice for a few minutes to lean on the sword. The next time she stopped, she rested on one knee with her head down until her breathing eased. I knelt to heal her hands and saw that she had stopped crying. But half an hour later, she dropped to her knees and then lay flat on the street with her ribs working like bellows.

Pil had slain 752 people so far. Looking around, I saw what looked like just as many still waiting to be killed, and I feared that Pil couldn't go on. I knelt beside her, and she turned on her side away from me. Then she surprised me by rolling to her feet, raising the sword, and regarding me without too much interest.

Once the predawn sky lightened and we could see better, Pil kept her eyes closed as much as she could, looking only when she made the thrust. That didn't last too long, though—just eighty-seven killings. By then, she paused more often, and she grunted or cried out each time she stabbed somebody.

After the 880th death, Pil turned and walked away shaking her head. She pushed through the crowd of people waiting to die. I thought about going after her, but Yita stopped me. She followed instead, but Pil shoved her way back out of the crowd just as Yita reached it.

Pil nodded to me with her jaw clenched as she walked past. After leaning on the sword for a while, she killed 489 people over the next three hours without pausing. Finally, she came to Sepp, who was the last of her people and Pil's 1,369th victim. Pil stabbed Sepp in the heart, threw the sword at me so hard she cut my arm, and dropped to sit on the ground with her head bent.

I walked over to Pil, but she mumbled "Go away" without looking up.

Stan hesitated and then said, "At least they were dry. There'd be a lake of blood if you killed that many regular folks."

Pil didn't show that she had heard him, and she ignored every other person who came near.

Desh whispered to me, "We should have chased her away weeks ago. Now it's too late."

"She's not ruined!" I whispered.

"No, but she thinks she is."

Over the next fifteen minutes, everybody but Pil and me prepared to enter the tower. Pil sat on the street, hiding her face from the hundreds of dead bodies lying on the streets around her. I watched her in case she asked for help, or collapsed, or tried to do something crazy like stab herself in the heart.

Pil didn't do any of those things. After a little while, Desh told me, "We're ready to go."

"Does Pil look ready?"

Desh chewed his lip. "No."

"Then we're not ready to go."

Pil sat up with a jerk. Her enchanted knife seemed to appear in her hand. I rushed over to grab it from her, but she laid it on the ground. Without looking up, she said, "What are you going to do? Stand over me forever? Take away every knife I ever own?"

"I might."

She ignored me and pulled a whetstone out of a pouch. Bending forward, she began sharpening the blade of her knife, which was already sharper than any other blade I'd ever seen.

I whispered to Desh and Stan, "Should we worry?"

"Yes," Stan said.

I stared at him.

"Oh, about her?" He shrugged. "Might as well worry about her while we're worrying about everything else."

Pil must've heard us, but she didn't make any smartass comments.

"Leave her alone," Desh said. "She's busy enchanting her knife."

"It's already enchanted all to hell!" I said.

Desh frowned. "I guess that's not enchanted enough for her. She may know things now that she wouldn't have thought of yesterday."

"I guess she's a better weapon for Lutigan now, the red-assed son of a bitch!"

Desh nodded. "You've done him a favor. Maybe he'll send you a cake."

I had to walk away.

After a few more minutes, Pil stood. I looked for the knife, but it wasn't in her hand, in a sheath, on the ground, or anyplace else I could see.

I said, "Pil, why don't you sleep awhile? We can wait."

Without answering me or meeting anybody's eyes, Pil walked toward the tower's tall doorway. Normally, her smile was remarkable, but now her face looked as if it had never smiled and never would. When Stan saw her face, he looked away.

One of the nine-foot-tall tower doors was rotting and hung off its hinges. The other had been carried away someplace or possibly had been disintegrated in some magical fight. Pil shook off Yita's hand and walked through the doorway without hesitating. She stared straight ahead, not watching out for deadfalls, or bears, or hundred-foot-long dragons.

I ran and caught her. "From here on, I'm going first. I'm not arguing about it, either."

Pil shrugged and looked away.

"Damn it, if you plan to get yourself killed, at least say goodbye first and tell us who should get your stuff!"

Pil said, "If you're going to lead, go ahead."

I took four steps and then stopped. "I don't know which way to go. Pil, what does your finger say?"

"It says I ought to lead."

"I could cut it off and put it on a stick to watch it spin and point around at things. That would work just as well."

I had hoped to get a grin, but I got a hard, tired stare. Pil pointed her finger in various directions and then said, "Straight up."

A big, dim chamber lay beyond an open door on the tower's ground level. My instincts said to search it before climbing the stairs, but I hesitated.

"Go on up," Desh said. "I'll make sure nothing bad is waiting to come up the stairs behind us. I'll be along." He nodded at Stan, who drew his sword.

Stan trudged after Desh, muttering with every step. Limnad watched Desh until he walked through the doorway, and then she glided after him.

I climbed the stone stairway that curved against the inside of the tower wall. Small, square windows were set into the thick wall, letting daylight shine through. Pil followed me up, with Yita right behind her.

We halfway circled the tower before reaching a large landing. A shabby, wooden door stood open, letting me peer a few feet into a darkened room toward the center of the tower.

"Still upward," Pil said.

As I put a foot on the next step, a clattering noise came from the room. A woman's voice said, "Bother!"

Walking over to stand beside the doorway, I listened but heard no more sounds or voices. "Come out!" I shouted. "Let's talk! We don't want to be bad guests."

Nobody answered or emerged from the room.

Yita said, "If someone's inside that room, why didn't Limnad find them last night?"

I hissed. I didn't like my answers to Yita's question. They involved mystical events or creatures waiting to surprise us. Or possibly Limnad was only here for vengeance and was betraying us to some enemy. That thought sickened me. All of that seemed a bit too complicated for a first answer, though. "Maybe there's a really well-hidden closet."

Yita gaped at me and then rolled her eyes.

Desh hadn't caught up, and that did worry me a little. I stepped back to peer down the stairs and considered calling out to him.

"No!" Yita shouted.

When I turned, Pil was walking into the darkened room. Before I reached the doorway, I heard a body fall to the floor.

TWENTY-NINE

When I followed Pil through the doorway, the room beyond it went from dim to softly lit. Seven silver lanterns hung on the walls. Pil lay in front of me on one end of a red rug that covered most of the space, which was the size of a sitting room. I didn't pause to find out whether she was breathing. I'd do that after I killed whoever had attacked her. I scanned the room to figure out just how many I needed to kill.

A robust, dark-haired woman in a plum-colored dress was kneeling amid some broken crockery near a side table. She was using a handkerchief to sop up a patch of liquid soaking into the rug. "Please hand me one of those towels." Without looking up, she pointed at a stack of towels on a small, square table near me.

Yita rushed into the room behind me, stopped, and blinked at the situation. Then she fell to the rug like a baby bird, unconscious.

"Stop that!" I shouted at the woman. "And wake them up!"

"I wish I could, but they are doing it to themselves." The woman stood and smiled at me. A large black stone that seemed to throb hung from a silver chain around her neck, and that was her only jewelry. Her eyes crinkled as she dabbed at her hands with the soaked handkerchief. "Do please bring me a towel. Why don't you bring one for yourself and help?"

She seemed unarmed. I stared around the room, looking for a good reason to kill her. Two cream-colored stuffed chairs sat on each side of a modest round table in the middle of the rug. A silver tray of food and two pewter mugs lay atop the lace tablecloth.

"Please stay for a moment, Bib. I need to chat with you. You may leave anytime you wish." She pointed with the wet handkerchief at the open door behind me.

I spun and stuck my head out to shout for Desh. The open door turned out to be an image placed on a solid wall, and I smacked my head against it hard. Holding my forehead with one hand, I stepped toward the woman and threatened her with my blade.

"Yes, you're correct, I lied to you. I should be ashamed, and I am. Beer?" She lifted one of the two surviving pitchers off the side table. "I have ginger cakes too."

People who eat food offered by magical creatures often end up as slaves owned by magical creatures. "I don't think so. I guarantee I'm not the sort of slave that will let you rest easy. Now let us go." I raised my sword again.

"Please don't kill me. It would be a tragedy for you as well as for me. How will you leave this room when I am dead?" She carried the pitcher to the table, raising her other hand to exclaim, "Ginger cakes and mince pies cannot sustain you for terribly long!"

"I guess I'll die then. But I won't die first."

She poured what looked like beer into both mugs and then sat in one of the chairs before glancing at my sword. "Will you use that weapon to make me really, really dead? There's a great deal to say, so please join me. You needn't drink or eat anything." She winked. "Not even my delicious ginger cakes."

"Stop it," I said. "Somehow you know that my mother made ginger cakes, but I see through you, so stop."

The woman grinned. "So, you know that I knew about your mother's cakes. And I knew you would know. Before we go mad over who knew what when, let us mind what's important. I put chocolate buttons on the ginger cakes."

"Be quiet! I'll find a way out of here, but I won't kill you until I do. In the meantime, wake up my friends!" I turned back to the not-door and slapped it with the palm of my hand, which didn't help, but I felt better.

The woman said, "My name is Marseline Drothus. My children found that difficult to say."

I snarled, "They probably still hate you."

She chuckled. "I am occasionally called Mara. By the way, Gek and Krak are brothers."

I slowly turned. "What?"

"I am sorry, I told you another lie. Void Walkers do not have relatives as you would understand them."

I leaned toward Mara and lowered my voice. "Do you want to die? I've killed people for a hell of a lot less than you've done so far."

"I know you have. If Void Walkers had brothers, that is what Krak and Gek would be."

"Hah! Krak's a god, not a Void Walker."

"You had never seen the Falls of Hope and Loss until two days ago, Bib. Are you certain you know everything that can be known about the Father of the Gods?"

I examined the woman's face. It was oval-shaped, with a wide mouth, a slight double chin, and pale blue eyes. I had assumed she was about fifty, but she could have just as easily been half that. "Why do you want me to know such a fact? I remind you that you've lied to me twice, so I have no reason to believe your stories."

"You can learn something even from lies, don't you think? Please sit."

"No thank you. I'll only listen to your chatter if you wake up those girls."

Both Yita and Pil sat up. Pil rubbed her knee. Yita asked her, "What happened to us?"

Mara stood and carried the silver tray to them. Over her shoulder, she said, "Gek and Krak were brothers just the way these ladies are sisters. Although the boys were a bit rowdier, I am given to understand. Ladies, please do sit." She pointed at two straight-backed chairs beside another small table. I hadn't noticed any of that furniture.

"Go ahead and sit," I told them.

Pil scowled. "We don't need your permission." Yita and Pil sat on the chairs and began poking at the sweets on the tray.

"Don't touch that!" I said.

Yita frowned. "She said we don't need your permission!" She selected a hefty biscuit and hurled it at my head. It was a fine throw, and I had to duck.

Mara perched on the edge of her chair with her back as straight as a signpost. I became aware of how much I was slouching. She looked at me earnestly as she said, "Do you think you can get them there alive?"

"What are you talking about?" I picked up the mug by reflex and put it back down.

"Can you deliver them safely so that they may kill Krak?"

I sat up straight but a little stiff. "That sounds crazy. Do you have an affliction? You're talking nonsense."

Mara gave me a little smile. "No one can hear us in this place. Can you protect these women until they assassinate the Father of the Gods as the opening stroke in Gek's war of vengeance, a conflict arising from Gek's defeat and maiming during the last war? Have I provided enough detail now?"

"Tolerably so." Without thinking about it, I drank from the mug. Then I squinted at the woman with one eye, wondering why my mistrust had disappeared for a moment. "I provisionally accept that you are not as crazy as a frog on fire. Why do you want to educate me?"

"I don't mean to be dismissive, but you were not my first choice. Yet you do tend to be underestimated by those with less discernment. As for why . . . please let me return to that in a moment."

She paused, and I realized she was waiting for my permission to come back to that point later. "Sure, your beer is good." I paused. "Maybe it's too good in a turn-you-into-an-enchanted slave kind of way."

Mara smiled and said, "Do you have difficulty with your relatives?"

"I doubt I have any that are still living. So, not a bit."

"Please be prepared to recall that statement. The gods believe that men are stupid little grubby hypocrites. Why do you suppose the gods do not destroy mankind?"

I had been wondering why Pil and Yita were so quiet. The words "destroy mankind" should have gotten some reaction from them. But when I glanced over, I saw them in their chairs, eating and drinking as if sitting by themselves in a garden. I glared at Mara. "Do you intend to give me useful knowledge, or just ask a bunch of questions?"

"Indulge me, please. More beer?" She raised the pitcher.

I hesitated before holding out my mug. After she filled it, I set it on the table and pushed it away. "The gods need power for some reason, and they get it when they trade with sorcerers."

"Yes! It's all about power. The universe creates suffering for the living. And a living creature often creates its own suffering."

"Sure, but now you're just making pretentious statements to sound philosophical."

"You would think so, wouldn't you?" Mara's smile wrinkled her nose. "But be honest. Haven't you often created your own pain? Exceedingly often? To an embarrassing extent?"

"All right, yes!" I didn't see where Mara was going with this trail of bullshit.

"In fact, the gods encourage you to do it. They have made bargains that required you to plunge yourself into suffering, correct?"

"Yes, goddamn it, we all know that!"

"When you and a god trade, they reap power from your pain, and they deliver a small amount of power back to you. It's the most charming of arrangements for the god, don't you think?"

I exhaled and muttered something about it sounding far-fetched.

"Can you think of a simpler explanation?"

"Wait! Wait!" I waved the empty mug I was holding, and I stared at it. I didn't remember picking it up or draining it.

Mara cleared her throat.

I set down the mug. "There's something wrong with all this, apart from the haunted beer mugs. What is this 'pain being the same as power' bullshit? Come on, why would gods get power in exchange for my pain?" I set down the mug with a thump.

Mara smiled and blinked back a couple of tears as if she was suffering right along with mankind. "Bib, the universe arranges for the living to suffer. I assure you that the universe is not flippant about such things, and in this matter, the gods are the universe's representatives. Come, has any god ever engaged you to do anything besides suffer? Have they?"

I shook my head. Right now, the universe was engaging me to both suffer and look stupid.

Mara said, "The gods set an exchange rate many centuries ago. Power from sorcerers in exchange for power returned by gods. Do you want to guess what it is? The rate is quite arbitrary."

I snorted. "Fine, let me think. The gods are a greedy, conceited bunch who think they're entitled to every good thing. I'd say twenty to one—in their favor. No, fifty to one."

"The exchange rate is one thousand to one. Men go through anguish to create power, and the gods keep all but one one-thousandth of it."

I couldn't think of anything to say to that.

Mara sipped from her mug. "On the other hand, Void Walkers do not trade for power. They gather useful power by moving through the Void. You may wish to think of them as whales that feed as they move through the ocean."

"That sounds nicer, I guess."

"Also less lucrative," Mara added. "So, they arranged to place parts of themselves inside sorcerers. When a sorcerer receives usable power, a portion is first collected by the Void Walker."

"Huh. How much?"

"The Void Walker takes nine-tenths," Mara said, wincing on behalf of all sorcerers.

After a moment, I shouted, "What?"

The silver tray clattered to the floor as Pil and Yita jumped up.

I yelled, "I get one ten-thousandth of the power I sweat and suffer to produce? Why did you tell me this? So that I'd be extra motivated to kill Krak?"

"Not at all," Mara said. "You have been pulled into this war, and you cannot escape. I feel you should know where your people stand in this conflict."

"We stand nowhere! We're a bug under the gods' boots with the Void Walkers jumping up and down on the gods' shoulders!"

"It is unfortunate, but better that you should have no illusions. This is the first war between gods and Void Walkers in which men will play a part. But then this is the first war that will be fought in the Dark Lands."

"Where gods can be destroyed," I said. "And Void Walkers too, I guess."

"You're correct. All past wars were fought in places where death was not permanent for gods. They weren't even aware that the Dark Lands existed. Not even Krak knew. Someone did an excellent job of keeping it a secret." Mara smiled and twisted a strand of hair behind her ear.

"How could you have done that? I met people in the Dark Lands. Bixell the bridge guardian for one. And Hurd, our guide. Hell, Cael was there, and then he left!"

"None of them entered the Dark Lands before it was discovered, except for Bixell. And the guardian of the bridge was fated never to leave the Dark Lands. Well, fated is an ambiguously fraught term."

I thought back to how despondent Bixell had been when I refused to take over as guardian. I had taken away his chance to escape. "Somebody found the place, though. Were you caught napping? What happened?"

Mara frowned. "Sakaj found it, the twit. That's not fair. She is a smart girl, but not entirely sane. I would like to blame her mother, but Fingit turned out to be a fine boy. He may be the best of the lot."

"Fingit and I used to—"

Holding up a hand, Mara cut me off. "I would of course enjoy hearing about your drunken, prurient exploits with Fingit, but the young ladies appear restive."

Pil and Yita had sat back down, but they were whispering and fidgeting.

Mara turned in her chair to face me head-on. "I shall tell you a thing that few beings understand: gods and Void Walkers exist in a much weaker state while in the Dark Lands. They are more fragile and do not possess all their powers. Men are stronger than normal, comparatively. Sorcery might be more powerful as well, but that has not been demonstrated."

I found myself peering at the ceiling, and Mara might have been reading my mind. She said, "Did you truly believe that you could kill three demigods at once? You did that in the Dark Lands. They were weakened and you strengthened."

"Well, that's a hell of a disappointment."

"Do not discount yourself. Even in the Dark Lands, any god is far more powerful than any man. Perhaps you will feel better with another mug of beer. Listen to me. No god nor Void Walker will want to fight a real threat in the Dark Lands. Concern over being destroyed would prevent it. Yet they might not withdraw if facing men, whom they disdain. Gek is clever to send you and your allies against Krak. Only men could come near killing him."

I nodded my head too long, then realized there was nothing to nod about. "That's something to think over."

"Think this over," Mara said. "You shall almost certainly fail. I would say you have one chance in one hundred of even touching Krak. Perhaps he will be weaker in the Dark Lands, but he will still be Krak."

"What about this god-smashing weapon we're looking for?"

Mara shrugged. "That might help. Or perhaps it will be a hindrance. I ask that you not take the chance. Lie to Gek. Lie to Fingit. Lie to anyone and everyone else to whom you have made promises. There is no need for anyone on either side to be sent to oblivion. There is no call for mankind to risk quietus."

"That seems like questionable advice. Gek promised not to

257

threaten me. He didn't promise not to smash me flat with no warning."

"I may be able to influence Gek's thinking so that he does not smash you flat. I state it as a possibility, not a certainty. Balance that possibility against the assured demise of you and these young ladies should you attempt to kill, or harm, or even denigrate Krak."

I leaned back to get a better look at the woman. She seemed to care about everybody, with the possible exception of me. "Who are you?"

"Oh, I clean up in the Dark Lands. I'd rather not be hip-deep in bodies and dead gods the morning after the battle. You can help me with that, can't you?"

"I promise to think it over. Hard."

Mara jumped up and before I could move, she kissed the top of my head. "That's wonderful! I may see you in the Dark Lands. Probably not. I hate wars! Oh, which god hates you the most?"

"Lutigan."

"Don't you find that odd? I do." She nodded. "Take some ginger cakes with you."

The silver tray filled with cakes and pies had reappeared on the table. I took two cakes for the girls and said, "Thank you, Unnamed Mother."

The Unnamed Mother of All Existence was a grandiose name, but since most of the gods called her Mom, she could be forgiven. Only Sakaj and Fingit, the two youngest, had been born to a different being. Fingit had told me that his parentage was something that the Unnamed Mother had not suffered quietly at the time, and she could still stir up a storm about it. I felt I had enough clues to guess her real identity, and I wouldn't be surprised to meet any being in the Dark Lands, legendary or puny.

Mara smiled big enough to dimple, raised the hem of her skirt, and stuck out one foot. "Do you like my shoes?"

Ella had tried and failed to teach me the importance of noticing shoes. Mara's shoes matched her dress and had an impressive number of straps. I couldn't tell whether that made them worth a damn, but clearly she liked them.

"They're beautiful," I said.

"Thank you! They're a gift from an admirer."

I took a step toward the door but paused. "If I'm going to fight in this war, I'd like to know why the hell it's happening. You're pretty persuasive. Can't you talk them all into going home?"

Mara sighed. "I'll try to explain it concisely. Krak began his existence as a Void Walker, but he learned to create things of permanence. No other Void Walker could do that, nor did they wish to."

"But I've seen them turn people into fruit and swords into wriggling piglets."

"Void Walkers transform, but they do not create. Krak created his own realm. None of the Void Walkers were pleased, but no one loved Krak more than did Gek, so no one endured so great a wound as Gek."

I nodded. "I see. So Gek went to war to wipe out Krak and the gods."

"You do not see with perfect clarity. Since no god nor Void Walker could be permanently destroyed in any of their realms, the wars were at first punitive. You may consider them the equivalent of kicking over your sibling's sandcastle. Indeed, after the first few hundred battles, the entire conflict became little more than an exceedingly harsh game without rules. Although they would not have admitted such a thing, everyone involved came to enjoy and anticipate the hostilities. Eternity is long.

"The Dark Lands changed everything. When your enemy can destroy you forever, you must destroy him first. That is how Gek and Krak see it."

I stared at the floor, thinking about the only important question.

Mara asked, "Do you now understand why I cannot convince everyone to go home?"

"Did Krak create us? Mankind?"

The Unnamed Mother of All Existence stepped back, her eyes wide. "If that were so, every man would resemble him, and every woman would possess an abundant bosom that challenges gravity."

THIRTY

Every sorcerer deals with at least one god. Not too many meet a Void Walker, but I have talked to a couple who said they had. Maybe they weren't lying.

I read one account by a woman who said she met the Unnamed Mother of All Existence, a title that was obviously fanciful. That had happened four centuries ago, if it indeed happened at all. Whenever I thought about that, I assumed that at least a few people must have encountered the Unnamed Mother over the years.

I didn't know of anybody except me who had met gods, Void Walkers, and the Mother. If I could arrange to meet the Black Drifting Whores of the Universe, I would have encountered all the legendary powers known to exist. I suspected that the Black Drifting Whores' title was as capricious as that of the Unnamed Mother, but nobody knew. Maybe I'd ask them when I met them.

I didn't understand why any of them considered me worth noticing. Sure, Gek resided in my head. Maybe toting around such a mighty being made me worth talking to, but I doubted it. No god had ever said I was special. They almost always treated me as if I was shit on their nice kitchen floor. The Unnamed Mother had offered me cake and been polite. But the nicest thing she said was that I wasn't her first choice and that others might not be as smart as her when it came to looking past my faults.

None of it made sense. I had lived a long time and I was pretty. That didn't make me fit to be part of realm-defining events. Before I walked out of Mara's sitting room, I decided that in a cross-realm sense, I must be standing in a place that everybody wanted to have or to use, and I was too stubborn and ignorant to get out of the way.

I adopted that as my working explanation.

If that was true, though, why didn't the first one of those mighty beings who came along stomp me to the consistency of slush? I had no answer to that and had no great hopes of finding one.

I found Desh on his hands and knees, rubbing the stone floor with his palm, when I walked through the door Mara opened for us. Nobody else was on the landing. He looked around and then jumped to his feet.

"Where did you run away to?" he asked through clenched teeth. "Limnad wanted to tear this tower into a pile of stone blocks to find you."

"I'm sorry, Desh, we got lost." I stopped with my mouth open. I meant to say we learned all about the war and the universe from Mara, which is what we called the Unnamed Mother because we were now drinking buddies. "We got lost" is what came out of my mouth.

Desh stared, waiting until I said something else.

I tried again. "We got really lost." I turned to Pil and Yita, who were squinting as if I said mice had carried us away.

Pil pushed me aside and said, "We were so lost. It was terrible." She stared at me with eyes as big as plums.

Yita bit her lip and nodded to Pil and me. "They got lost. I just followed them." She clamped her hand over her mouth.

Desh sighed. "All right. Can you write down the real answer?"

I said, "Yes! I'll write down everything about getting lost, and how it made us feel, and what songs we sang to keep our spirits up. I'm sorry, Desh, I can't help it."

Desh pulled out a pencil from a pouch and pointed at the stone wall. I wrote, *I've never gotten lost before.*

Desh took the pencil out of my hand. "Never mind." He shouted up the stairs, "I found them! Well, they're back at least."

From upstairs Stan shouted, "Come on up then, Desh! Don't make us walk down there and then walk all the way back up. That would be inconsiderate, which isn't like you."

Desh led us up the narrow, curving stairway past one landing. He stopped at the next where Stan was leaning against the wall watching for us. Limnad rushed down to us from the next level.

I figured that in another two or three levels, we'd be halfway up the tower.

"Bib!" Limnad cried loud enough to hurt my ears. "Don't leave again!"

"I apologize, Limnad."

"You might die without me there to watch it!"

"I understand." I had long ago learned that Limnad didn't mean ill when she said such things. It was just her way of being alive.

"The next two floors are abandoned," the spirit said. "There's some broken furniture. Before it was smashed, it was prettier than the chairs Desh made, but not as durable. Or as enchanted. And there are rotted rugs and candles made out of pig fat! And some skeletons."

"Why didn't you mention the skeletons first?" Yita crossed her arms. "Anybody ought to know that's the most important thing when we're fighting our way up a tower!"

Limnad said, "They weren't walking around! And who is fighting up a tower? I haven't seen fighting!" She turned to Stan. "Have you seen fighting?"

"Not so far." He grunted. "The day ain't over."

I said, "All right. I'm glad they aren't walking or even dancing. Let's go up."

Limnad led us up the stairs with me just behind her. Stan guarded our rear. At the next landing, Limnad pointed at an open door and said, "Nothing interesting, unless you think a kingdom of mice is intriguing."

"An actual kingdom?" Yita asked.

Limnad stopped to look back past me at Yita. "No, not with crowns and that sort of thing. Just a lot of mice."

"Be specific," Yita whispered. "Ow! Pil, stop!"

"Then you stop," Pil muttered.

An open door stood on the next landing. I followed Limnad inside. Sunlight wove into the space through the doorway and through three window-like openings in the ceiling. Desh examined one. "That's awfully clever. They're open all the way to the outside to bring in some light and air. I believe they run under the stairs to the outside. Whoever built this tower was an excellent engineer."

"Cael would have liked to see it," Yita said. It sounded as if she might be tearing up. Pil ignored her to examine a jumble of wooden sticks and cloth in one corner.

Limnad screamed.

I drew my sword, and everybody else did the same, despite the fact that there was nothing around to cut.

"I'll kill you!" Limnad yelled. "I'll build a cage of your bones and keep your heart in it!"

"Somebody's binding her!" Desh shouted.

This was dire news. A sorcerer could give a bound spirit five commands before the spirit was set free, and those commands could be anything. Limnad was without doubt capable of ripping us all apart in a few seconds. We might have only fifteen or twenty seconds before the binding process finished and the ripping started.

Desh was running toward Limnad. "Where are they?"

Although she couldn't move, Limnad turned her eyes toward the wall opposite the door. "I'll tear out your eyeballs!" Limnad screamed. "I'll put your testicles in the sockets! Then I'll kill you!"

Desh snatched something out of a red cloth pouch, and he hurled it at the wall. Nothing happened.

"Damn it!" Desh screamed.

The entire wall turned to sloppy mud and collapsed to the floor in a mound one foot high. The room on the other side looked about the same as ours, except that it was full of King Famm, his four sorcerers, and his eight soldiers. We all paused to stare at each other.

Famm and I charged one another at the same time. Six of his soldiers were right behind him, while Yita and Stan followed me. A couple of his men had bows, but firing arrows in this crowded space would be a ticklish business.

I saw little to no hope that I could figure out which sorcerer was binding Limnad, and I had no hope of stopping him. My hope was that Desh and Pil would handle that. If they had a doodad that would make our enemies' guts fall out through their assholes, that would be nice too.

I dodged to Famm's left and sliced a soldier's throat, then swung back at Famm's head with the same movement. Not bothering to block, he ducked my blade and cut at my waist. I rolled away, but he sliced me across my ribs.

Stan thrust at Famm from the other side to give me a moment to reach my feet. I thrust at Famm to let Stan turn back to face the men attacking him. Famm parried my thrust and riposted. I could have rushed him, but a man of Famm's skill would probably transfix me. I retreated instead.

I hoped that Desh and Pil had a real sledgehammer of an attack coming, because they hadn't done a damn thing yet. Yita shouted, and I was vaguely aware that she was killing men on that side like they were chickens.

After feinting high and feinting low, I struck Famm's throat with a thrust. He was throwing himself backward, and I wasn't sure whether I had scratched him or killed him. Either way, he ended up lying on his back. I preferred not to run up and allow him to cut off my foot, so I paused. I would wait until he was halfway up and off balance.

Pil skipped aside and aimed her knife at one of the sorcerers. She hurled the enchanted blade and struck the man in the middle of his chest. The knife didn't embed itself in the man. Instead, it punched through him in a cloud of blood and went on to plunge into the chest of another sorcerer behind him.

Limnad stopped cursing and started laughing so loud it hurt to hear. Pil had just killed whoever had been trying to bind the spirit.

Famm was halfway up, but I didn't lunge to stab him. Within a few seconds, Limnad would tear him and all his men into chunks small enough to fit in a beer pitcher.

I hadn't noticed that a long pile of wooden boards and sticks had been placed along the base of the wall on King Famm's side. That was because it had been covered by mud when the wall came down. I felt Thad the Caller reach out to that pile. I didn't know what kind of nastiness he was planning, but I spent half a square right quick and whipped out a big red band. I slapped it down on the pile to push against anything Thad might do to it.

A moment later, the pile of wood exploded, blasting us with splinters. I landed on my back. Before I could sit up, flames erupted from my clothes. I rolled to smother the flames, knowing it was too late. But before I felt pain, I was slammed with what felt like a lake of water. It smothered the fire, and I silently thanked Limnad for being a water spirit.

I rolled to my feet and swayed just in time to see Desh on his knees pointing something upward. The ceiling between Famm and us collapsed. As the stone blocks fell, I saw Famm and his surviving men struggling to stand in a great pool of water a foot deep. Then falling stones separated the rooms with a wall that must have been eight feet thick at the base.

Still on his knees, Desh reached into a pouch, hesitated, and then reached into a different one. He threw a chunk of glass at the fallen stones, and it shattered.

I gasped. "We'd better move."

Desh stood and blew out a breath. "Don't bother. When they look for us, the charm will make them think we're two hundred feet from our true position in a random direction."

"All right, I won't bother."

I heard Pil crying out and turned to find her with a moderate-size splinter embedded in her left eye. She was rolling from side to side, trying to hold her eye and at the same time trying not to touch it.

Pil's skin was blistered like a bad sunburn near where her clothes had touched her, but no worse. I saw that my burns looked the same as hers, and the burned-off nubs of eight or ten splinters were sticking out of my arms, legs, and chest. None of them felt too deep.

I grabbed her hand. "I'll help you. Try to hold still." If I hadn't slowed down Thad's explosion, the splinter would likely have been driven all the way through Pil's eye and killed her. I used one hand to grip hers and used the other to examine her eye. "Now you've been through a real, desperate, spitting-distance sorcery battle, darling. We used to have them all the time in the old days."

"Bib!" Desh shouted.

"In a minute," I said.

"Bib!" Desh sounded panicked.

I gave Pil's hand to Yita and ran across the room. Desh knelt by Limnad, who lay on the floor. Her chest and shoulders were covered with her blue-toned blood. An arrow had struck her between her throat and the center of her chest. She was hardly breathing.

"You've saved her before." Desh didn't sound hopeful.

I laid my hands on Limnad's forehead and beside the wound. Like all spirits, she was astoundingly strong and fast. She was also easily harmed but resilient. If I could keep her alive for even a short time, she might recover on her own.

"Limnad, wake up!" I called out as if she was fifty feet away.

Desh was holding her hand. "Limnad, don't leave," he murmured.

Limnad stopped breathing. I couldn't sense any life inside her body.

"I'm sorry, Desh, she's gone."

Desh didn't move. "I convinced her to come here."

I didn't have anything to say to that. Then I felt Desh's spirit leave his body for a visit to the gods. I grabbed on.

THIRTY-ONE

T he air in the gods' trading arena was clear and fresh enough to drink. I could have counted the green and purple leaves of the forest if I had wanted to do something so pointless. On the other side of us, the great expanse of flowers had always seemed to run to the horizon. I could only see a corner without turning my head, but I wondered whether I could see the far edge today if I looked.

Out of habit, I hadn't gazed around or made comments when I arrived. So, I only saw a few of the field's blooms turn, catch the divine sun's light, and reflect it onto the gazebo.

I sometimes forgot what it meant to be a god. Now Sakaj and Fingit let the rich sun of the Gods' Realm wash over them, and they grew at least a foot taller while I watched without looking straight at them. The power of it battered me. I closed my eyes and panted while at the same time trying not to pant. The habit of hiding my ability to see them was hard to break.

Sakaj threw back her shoulders, making her low-cut black gown slide across her breast. I glanced, which was an appalling mistake. She did not manifest a shockingly enormous bosom like Gorlana and Chira did. She claimed not to care about bosoms, clothing, jewelry, or any adornment.

The Goddess of the Unknowable was as beautiful as a razor—cold, murderous, and perfect. The sight of her could stun the words and breath right out of most men. It knocked the breath out of me, and I didn't have to worry about panting anymore.

Before I closed my eyes again, I saw Sakaj raise both arms toward the sun. She whispered, "Today we destroy Cheg-Cheg and all his works!" Such drama sounded strange in a whisper, and it hit me that she must not know I could hear her.

Fingit had raised his arms too, but now they came halfway back down. He whispered, "He's a Void Walker. They don't have works. They literally don't build anything. You'll have to settle for destroying his army."

"Shut up!" Sakaj spun to face her brother. "You whine about every detail, you pedantic infant!"

Fingit gazed off into the sky as he whispered, "Can an infant be pedantic? It seems unlikely."

"Be quiet!" Sakaj whispered, taking a step toward her younger brother.

I couldn't imagine Fingit and Sakaj behaving this way if they knew I was watching and listening. But I also couldn't imagine that Harik wouldn't have run and told every other god about my ability to see them.

Desh couldn't see the gods, though, unless he had created some dandy new magical bauble to allow it. He said, "Sakaj, are you there?"

"I can't even explain how disappointed I am in you, Nub!" Sakaj scolded Desh like an exasperated mother. "I wanted those people to stay where they were. They were wicked and deserved to be there! But you didn't just allow them to escape. You helped the six-times-damned Murderer as he did it!"

The goddess turned to me and used a much less motherly tone. "And you, Murderer! Your arrogance is unbelievable. You undid my work, pretending to be wiser than me. And don't blame it on the Knife—she killed them all to save you as much as to save them!

Does she know that you used her as you'd use a rag to wipe your ass?"

Desh was looking around blindly. "Bib? You're here?"

I said, "Be careful, Mighty Sakaj. You sound less like my sweet little Aunt Salli and more like a drunken, crotch-scratching dockworker." I didn't think she'd kill me while my life belonged to Harik. My thinking that wouldn't keep me alive, though.

Sakaj said, "I suspect there will be something left behind when Harik has finished with you. I will discover how much pain that something can feel before it passes out. Several hundred such efforts will be required before we achieve a reliable understanding of the matter." Sakaj settled herself on a bench. The move was both airy and throbbing with power.

"I'm always prepared to expand our knowledge, you reeking bucket of whorish insanity."

Sakaj glanced at Fingit and whispered, "Not bad."

Fingit shrugged and sat on another bench. Although sunlight still drenched the gazebo, the gods had returned to their normal height.

Desh said, "Mighty Sakaj, I come to trade."

"Yes, I know what you want." Sakaj picked imaginary lint off her gown.

"I offer—"

I cut him off. "Hold on, Desh. I didn't hear what you want." I knew quite well what he wanted, but he had almost violated one of the main rules I had taught him: let the gods make the first offer. It was one of the few real advantages a sorcerer could achieve.

"You already know, Bib," Desh said evenly. "And I know why you stopped me. This is how I intend to proceed. Now, Sakaj, if you allow Limnad to live, unharmed and whole, I will declare your open-ended debt paid. You won't have to give me power anymore."

Sakaj jumped up and raised both fists but didn't make a sound. She smiled at the ceiling of the gazebo. Fingit watched her with a crooked grin. After a few seconds, Sakaj sniffed. "Debt? That thing? I told my doorman to handle that. I hardly ever think about it anymore. Maybe if you offered something worthwhile in addition to the debt?"

I said, "Or, if the debt is so insignificant, you can just take it off the table, Desh. It doesn't seem like it'll help you in these negotiations."

"I didn't say it's worthless!" Sakaj said, leaning forward. "It would be like a grace note to our deal, whatever it ends up being. In fact, it should be part of any bargain, for the sake of . . . sentimentality." Sakaj winced as she said the word, and Fingit laughed silently.

"In fond remembrance of all the good times you had together?" I asked. "Did you have any of those, Desh?"

"Murderer, be quiet!" Sakaj shouted.

"Yes, Your Magnificence."

Desh said, "What else do you want, Sakaj?"

She paused.

Fingit whispered, "Is there anything you want besides that?"

Sakaj shook her head.

"Then take the offer!"

"How would it look if I don't bargain?" she whispered, her teeth showing.

Desh said, "Mighty Sakaj, is there anything else you want?"

"Speak when you're spoken to." She sounded eerily like my mother. "I suggest two things. I can make the spirit love you again, knowing that you'll be found out and lose her sooner or later."

"No thank you. What else?"

"You will never speak to her again," Sakaj said. "The words will refuse to come out of your mouth."

He didn't hesitate. "That—"

I jumped in and bellowed, "Desh! Wait!"

Desh bellowed back at me, "Krak's nose! Why?"

I bit my lip and then said, "All she wants is the open-ended debt. She's just screwing with you on the other stuff."

Desh said, "That's a guess. You can't know that."

"I can know that. Because I can see her and hear her."

Both gods sat up like hounds spotting a squirrel. I didn't know which of them flung me out of the trading place, but they did it so hard I fell and skidded when I returned to our world.

Desh was still sitting beside Limnad. Since no time passed with the gods, we both returned to the moment we left.

Limnad sat up, still covered with blood but with no arrow in her chest. "That was strange. I never fall down. Did one of you trip me? And . . . was I bleeding?"

I said, "It's a strange story." I stopped when Desh, from behind Limnad, shook his head at me. "I'll have to tell it when I pluck out all the splinters around here."

"Fine, I'm not hurt a bit, so go look at somebody else. And take Desh with you. And after you help everybody, take him someplace dangerous where it's easy to get killed, or at least maimed." She scowled at Desh, who didn't react.

I ran back to Pil, who was lying on her back moaning.

Yita held both of Pil's hands. "She's trying to pull it out herself."

I leaned down beside her ear and said, "Hold as still as you can. It'll be over in a minute." She held still, and I eased the splinter out of her left eye, making sure no bits of wood had been left behind. In less than a minute, Pil was breathing easier.

Nobody else looked to be in danger of dying, so I healed Pil's eye first. Although wounds to the eyeball itself aren't painful, the splinter had gone all the way through to some places that hurt a lot. My eye was hurting like a son of a bitch after healing her.

After that, I dealt with the splinter wounds on her body, which would only be dangerous if I left bits of wood behind. Then I went down the line, healing Yita, Stan, Desh, and then myself. Locating the damage was easy since all of us had our clothes burned off. Limnad was equally unclothed but needed no help with tiny wounds like these.

At the end of it all, I felt as though I'd been stung by a hundred hornets, although some of them had been lackadaisical about it. It was far from the worst I had felt after healing so many people. Only my eye truly bothered me, but I didn't intend to dawdle because of that. We had already spent too much time in this room.

Desh pulled me aside before I could bitch about sitting around waiting for Famm to come execute us. "Thank you, Bib. I didn't know you could see and hear the gods. I'd like to know how that was done, if you'll tell it sometime."

"I have no notion at all. Sorry."

He shrugged. "Seeing and hearing them must have been an unparalleled advantage when bargaining. You gave it up to help Limnad and me. I'll always be grateful."

"It wasn't too great a sacrifice, Desh. Harik already knew, so all the gods will know before long. Fingit and She Who Must Not Be Named must have been off drinking someplace and missed the word. No need to be grateful about it."

"But I am."

"No, if you want to be grateful about something, be glad I didn't stab you in the liver seven times after you burned off my legs. I've killed men for pointing a sword at me, yet here you are walking around."

Desh looked down and smiled.

"So, you lost the power She Who Must Not Be Named gave you every day, but you still have the curse to never know happiness?"

"Yes, that's the way it worked out. In the end, the gods always win."

I didn't have the right to comment on that after my recent disastrous bargain with Harik. "Desh, why won't you tell Limnad what you did to save her?"

He shook his head.

"She ought to know."

"I've treated her badly and gotten her killed. I shouldn't use tricks and magic to make her love me."

"Is that all? What you did wasn't a trick," I said.

"Maybe, but she shouldn't know about it anyway."

I frowned at the floor and sighed. "Well, to hell with that shit." I called out, "Limnad! You were killed in the fight, just as dead as you can get. Desh went to the gods and gave up his greatest gift as a sorcerer. Without it, he's just another hand waver like me. He did it to bring you back, and now he's standing there with his head up his ass and not telling you. I'm telling you for him. Go on now and fight, or kiss, or write a damn poem about it. I wash my hands of this whole mess."

Everybody in the room stared at me.

I said, "If we're climbing this tower, let's go."

Limnad and Desh were staring at each other when I passed them.

I walked in front. I was known to be lucky, my eyesight was exceptional, and I was the most expendable person since I was the next best thing to dead already. I climbed the stairs holding my sword. When Ace burned our clothes away, he also burned our belts, boots, and most everything else. The fire had been doused before it could destroy metal things, such as Stan's sword. Anything that was enchanted survived too. Magic didn't often affect enchanted objects unless the magic was overwhelmingly strong. Pil and Desh had seen this sort of thing before, so they had prepared by enchanting all their pouches and belts to resist fire.

A door stood at the first landing we reached. Yita and I found nothing when we investigated, so I kept climbing. When I looked back at the landing, I saw Desh and Limnad talking close together with great emphasis and lots of hand motions. I hoped that Desh wouldn't at last provoke Limnad into killing him, but at this point, it was out of my hands.

An empty room stood at the second landing. Pil said, "There's another stairway in this tower, isn't there? That's how Famm caught us. He's probably ahead of us now."

"You were a little slow to figure that out," I said without looking back. "Pil, don't let all the pain distract you too much."

"Uh-huh."

I tapped my cheek. "I don't just mean the pain of getting skewered in the eyeball."

"I know what you mean. I won't." Her shoulders fell, then she leaned closer to me and said, "This is how you live, isn't it? With all this death inside you."

Glancing at her as I walked, I said, "This didn't have to happen to you, Pil. You shouldn't even be here. I wanted you to go home, and I didn't want all this killing for you."

Pil jerked to a stop and shouted, "I didn't want it either, you bastard!"

Yita stomped up and put herself between us. "Yell louder. The monsters can't hear you. Famm can't, either." She pointed at Pil. "He's just stupid, but you should know better!"

When I reached the next landing, I turned to face everyone. "We're more than halfway up the tower. Does anyone want to say something before we push to the top? I don't plan to halt again."

Stan spit on the floor. "What kind of thing are we hunting for again?"

"We don't know." Pil bit her lip.

I added, "It's some kind of weapon that slays the mighty and protects orphans, but I don't know what it looks like." I shrugged.

"How does it slay the mighty?" Stan swung his sword in the air. "Do you whack the mighty on the head with it? Put it in the mighty's beer?"

"I don't know that, either." I tried not to grin.

"Why the hell do we want the thing then?" Stan whined. "Let's get out of here and go someplace civilized with beer and whores. I've got no feud with gods."

I said over my shoulder, "Desh, will you explain it to him again?" I glanced back and saw Limnad embracing Desh. "I guess I'll do it."

Some force threw me against the slanted ceiling over the stair-way. I tumbled up the ceiling as if it were a ramp. When I rolled onto the flat space over the next landing, I managed to stop myself. A moment later, Pil rolled into me, followed by Yita, Desh, and Stan. Limnad did not come with them. I would have been shocked if the graceful, unworldly creature had done something so mundane as to fall on the ceiling and tumble along.

I lay on the ceiling as if it were the floor. "Something feels strange."

"Then get your hand out of your trousers," Stan said.

Despite everything, I couldn't help smiling.

Pil rubbed her palms along the stones under her. "Whatever's holding us on the ceiling is strong magic, probably stronger than any human could conjure. I can't feel anything specific, though. Desh, can you?"

Desh was staring back the way we came. "Do you see Limnad?"

"I seen my ass and my armpit when I got crunched up here," Stan grumbled. "My idea about hauling away to civilized places sounds like a fine plan now, doesn't it?"

We each tested the ceiling by standing up. None of us smashed our skulls falling back to the floor.

"Limnad!" Desh yelled.

Yita hissed at Desh. "Lutigan's left toe, will you keep quiet?"

Desh spun and pointed his sword at Yita's face. "You don't know anything! You're an infant. What could you know?"

I expected Yita to try disarming him or to say something rude. Instead, she lowered her sword and backed away. "Maybe you don't know some things, either." Her face looked tired. Hell, we were all tired.

"Hey!" Pil was poking her arm up to the shoulder in a window. "Where's the light coming from? I only see dirt through here."

I realized that the landing above us was glowing bright enough to see by. I jumped over to where Pil was exploring the window, edged her out of the way, and pulled a white band to explore things. A few seconds later, I snarled, "Shit! Damn it to my father's crusty pipe! We're in the Dark Lands!"

Stan moaned, "It's too late then. We'll die here, and I'll never see my wife again."

Pil and I glanced at Stan but didn't ask any questions.

"The first thing to do is get down from the ceiling," Yita said.

"Limnad!" Desh called out as he walked on the ceiling to check down the stairway for her.

Pil caught her breath. "No!"

"What is it?" I asked. "That bastard Famm?"

"No, it's not him." She examined the floor over our heads with her mouth open. "We're not climbing a tower in our world."

I pointed at a darkened window. "I already said we're in the Dark Lands! Keep up. Remember what I told you about pain."

She ignored that. "We're not climbing up a tower, Bib. We're in

275

the Dark Lands, descending through a hole in the earth, a hole with rooms and stairways."

"What are you blabbering about?" Yita said. "How do you feel? Does your eye hurt?"

"No, think about it this way. The tower brought us to the Dark Lands. When it got here, it turned upside down and buried itself in the earth. We're not standing on the ceiling. It used to be the ceiling. Now it's the floor."

I couldn't think of anything to say, so I whistled.

Yita put a hand on Pil's shoulder. "What are you saying? That the top of the tower is now the bottom of a hole?"

"Right. This hole, and I think the bottom, is where we're going." Pil pointed her finger at what had become the floor.

THIRTY-TWO

I believed Pil when she said the tower had become a hole, or a pit, or a well, or something else deep in the earth where men ought not be. I also believed that I shouldn't have been down there, as it reminded me of an unpleasant year underground in which I had no hands with which to wipe my ass. And Pil's theory explained the strange feeling I had while lying on the ceiling.

I said, "Do we climb out of this place back to light and freedom, or do we descend to the bottom of this horrible well?"

"Don't strain yourself hiding how you feel about it," Stan said.

After a pause, Pil asked, "Why do you say it's a well?"

That was the kind of question Desh would have asked, such as why people named things the way they did, or what made them think they had to do an unusual thing. Now he sat with his back against the wall, not looking at us or anything else.

I said, "Calling it a well sounds friendlier than calling it a pit or a burrow. We could call it a gap in the earth, but I'd rather not."

Yita said, "A particularly deep depression."

"We're wasting time." Pil scowled at me.

"You're not. I'm confident I know where the awfulness is in this situation." I pointed down. "You and Desh can find a way home, and Stan too. Yita and I will take over the doing of stupid things."

Stan jumped to his feet, grinning like a feral chicken with a few teeth.

Pil said, "What if you get to the bottom and there are seven doors? Without my finger, how will you know which one to open?"

"He's clever," Stan said. "Hell, he's Lord Bib! Wave goodbye and let's go." He tossed his head toward the ramp upward.

"It's all right. You can go back," Yita said. "I'll insult Bib for you."

I said, "Pil, go! Stan can go to his wife and Desh can find Limnad. You can get away from this shit and find a regular life."

Pil sort of laughed as if I had said the least funny thing she'd ever heard. "Bib, you and I came here, and I'm staying until one of us is dead. Probably you, but I wouldn't count on that."

I couldn't think of anything to say, so I stood and began walking down the ramp that was once the ceiling.

"Shit!" Stan yelled.

"You can go back," Desh said as he passed Stan. "We keep telling you that."

"Hell no! I hate the damn Dark Lands. I don't want to walk around up there by myself."

When I glanced back, I saw Stan, just as naked as the rest of us, trailing along with his sword in his hand. It had been charred but not so much that it wouldn't kill people.

We tramped down seven more levels. At each landing, we passed a doorway set against what was now the ceiling, and we didn't stop to explore them. I had begun to feel that we should hustle to the bottom of the well, finish whatever drastic business waited for us there, and go find out what was happening on the surface.

The ramp below our feet ended at a flat landing. A plain old wooden door stood in front of us, and I opened it without having a philosophical debate.

The air inside the room smelled like wet dirt and stone, but I didn't see any water. It was softly lit from the ceiling in a circle one hundred feet across. Pale stone walls curved around the glowing circle, or the top ten feet of them did. The bottom ten feet of the walls had been dug away into darkness, creating an overhang that might have been fifty feet deep or a thousand.

I noticed those details in passing because the room was lined with an army of statues, although it had hundreds of stone people and animals instead of soldiers. They stood in well-separated groups of a dozen or more all the way around the room, and they ran to all sizes. I spotted a group of five dancing children, all one foot tall. Off to my right stood a life-size walrus. Across the room was a sleeping rabbit that was eight feet tall at the ear tips.

"You can touch them, but don't abuse them. I mean don't break them or anything like that," said an echoing voice from the recess across the way. A middle-aged, wiry man walked out wearing trousers and a shirt so dusty I couldn't tell what color they were. He pointed at a life-size statue of a cloaked man with a sword. "You can name that one if you want to. The others already have names."

Yita said, "Name him Cael."

"He's now named Cael." The man smiled for a second and stretched his back while looking me over. "I didn't think I'd see you. I didn't think I'd see so much of you, either, by which I mean your bare butt."

I said, "We didn't know what to wear, so we said to hell with it."

"I'd give you some trousers or a long shirt, but . . ." He gazed around and shrugged.

Desh and the others had come in behind Yita. The man waved them inside.

I said, "What do you mean that you didn't expect to see me?"

"I hear things. You should have been dead ten times in the last six months. I didn't expect a smashed corpse to drag itself in here. Maybe you hate Lutigan, but maybe you should be thanking him." His voice stopped echoing as he walked toward us, but it was deep, clear, and loud.

"Lutigan? I haven't even seen him lately. And I don't exactly hate him."

He barked a laugh. "Everybody hates him. His wives leave him, his children run away, and Krak trusts him like he'd trust a viper."

"Why should I thank him?"

Before the man could answer, King Famm crept into the light from the recess off to my left. I held my sword down, ready to charge him.

The man nodded at Famm. "You, I expected to see. Come on in. I don't make people stand outside just because they aren't family."

He beckoned to Famm and then to me too. "Both of you bring your friends inside and come here. They can perch over there. I haven't fed Macks today, but he couldn't eat more than three of them." He pointed at a long bench carved like a writhing snake.

"I admire your artwork," Pil said.

"It passes the time." He didn't sound too impressed by his work as he walked toward the center of the room. The light showed me his face, which was strong and blunt. His right eye was icy blue. His left was smooth, solid gold.

The man said, "My name's Apen." He stood about my height and was thin like me too. "Before we start all this crap, we should agree on something."

King Famm boomed, "There's nothing that this demon-sucker and I could agree on!"

"I agree!" I grinned and said, "I'm sorry. He's likely to be correct."

Apen glanced at Macks, the snake-bench, and squinted his blue eye. No one had taken a step that direction. He raised his already loud voice. "Nobody said this would be easy or pleasant, and I mean not easy for you. This is better than a ball with pretty girls for me." He glanced at Ace, who was standing at King Famm's shoulder. "All the people who refused my hospitality in the past got turned into these statues."

"Including the rhino?" Pil asked, pointing at a four-foot-tall statue.

"Cobbie? She was my wife. She used to be prettier. I want to be clear that I didn't turn my other visitors into statues using magic or anything. I normally stabbed them to death and carved the statue after."

"All right," Pil said, taking a step back. "Thanks for making that clear."

Apen said, "You're welcome. Feel free to ask any more questions. We don't get a lot of pretty girls down here."

"Do you mean there's someone else here?" Famm asked, gripping his sword.

"Just Cobbie and me and our stiff friends. Now, we've got to agree on one thing: I can whip the whole bunch of you. You'll all die here. Your friends will always wonder what ever happened to you."

Ace pushed forward. King Famm held him back, saying, "You'd be smart not to threaten me."

"That sounds a lot like *you* are threatening *me*," Apen said. "We're getting nowhere if we threaten each other all day. King, you can't get what you're looking for without my help. You neither, sorcerer." He nodded at me and then raised his voice: "Everybody but these two rat-baggers, get over there and sit! And mix yourselves up! I'm coming over there in three minutes to inspect you."

After looking at King Famm for permission, his men straggled to the benches. Desh and the others followed, and they all sat in one group rather than two clumps.

Apen walked closer, wearing a sword I hadn't noticed before. He said, "I may have made a joke or two, but this isn't a joke. Evidently you want something, or you wouldn't be at the bottom of this hole in the damned Dark Lands. 'Damned' is not a curse—it's a literal description. What do you want? I don't care who talks first."

Famm bent his head. "I shouldn't have acted like an ass earlier."

I said, "That's not really an apology."

"It's not an insult, so I say I'm ahead." Apen grinned.

Ignoring me, Famm said, "I want the weapon that can kill a god."

I raised my hand. "Me too."

Apen nodded at Famm. "That's a clear answer but not too complete. You could want it for a lot of things. Maybe you need to chase away some dogs."

I said, "I want to kill a god. I guess 'want' may be an exaggeration. I plan to kill a god. I don't expect I'll enjoy it much."

Famm said, "I intend to give the weapon to the gods so that no gods will be killed, especially by this scrawny criminal." He pointed at me.

"I see," Apen said. "King, once you give this deadly thing-a-honky to the gods, what do you think will happen? I'll tell you. They'll start killing each other with it, and you'll have a bunch of dead gods. If you think they won't do it, you've never eaten dinner with them."

"Perhaps that's true," Famm said. "But once I deliver the weapon, the matter is out of my hands."

"So, if the gods want to kill each other off, that's just fine, huh? That's some loyalty. I hope I never have a minion like you." Apen smiled. "King, why do you really want the weapon?"

Famm stuck out his jaw. "If I give it to the gods, they will protect my kingdom."

I asked, "Did they say they'd do that? I mean, did they say those words?"

"Yes!" Famm shouted at me. "Words very much like that."

Apen winced. "Ooh, that's not good. What about you, sorcerer? Why do you want to kill a god? They're not so bad if you can overlook the rudeness, debauchery, and careless destruction."

"Actually, I can appreciate those things," I said. "A Void Walker made me his servant. It's a complicated story. He has commanded me to kill a god, and if I don't, he'll kill me, along with half the world of man."

"Interesting. Why doesn't he just kill all of mankind so the gods won't have sorcerers or worshippers? That would poke the gods in the eye really hard, wouldn't it? I mean, killing all the humans couldn't be that much more challenging than killing half of them. Something about your complicated story stinks."

I knew that Gek and his kind were powerful, and they often talked about killing vast numbers of people. I had never seen them do it, though, and I didn't feel like asking Gek to demonstrate. Maybe he talked about it but couldn't do it. Maybe he couldn't do a lot of things. He couldn't break Sakaj's curse, but Desh's sword had sliced right through it.

Why were the gods terrified of Gek, though? I stood up straighter as I stopped breathing. Had any god actually told me that Gek petrified them? The Unnamed Mother said that the wars had become like a game to him and the gods. Maybe the gods weren't all that afraid of him.

"You can answer me now," Apen said.

"I just want to save myself," I said. "Well, and my companions."

"And why are you even this Void Walker's servant?"

Slowly I said, "Because I wanted to save myself and my companions."

"Interesting, by which I mean I've heard it so often it's boring. 'I did it to save myself.' That helps me decide."

"What does that mean?" Famm said. "What have you decided?"

"King, you trusted the gods, but I guess you meant well. Sorcerer, you trusted the Void Walkers, but I guess you were saving yourself. Being stupid is better than being stupid and selfish. I wish I could tell both of you to get the hell out of here and get girlfriends, but I can't."

My stomach dropped.

Apen clapped his hands together, and the sound echoed so loudly I could feel it in my jaw. "Sorcerer, you're just too awful to contemplate. I'm sorry to say that to family, but it's that way." He turned to Famm. "King, you are mighty awful, but I can stand to think about you for a few seconds at a time. Really, boys, it was closer than it sounds."

Apen reached up and pulled the golden eye out of his socket before tossing it to King Famm. "I won't warn you about putting your eye out with that weapon. You'll have to replace your own eye with it if you want to use it."

"I shall not be using it," Famm said.

"I'll bet." Apen smirked before turning to me. "Sorcerer, I wish I could make this up to you. You seem like a nice fellow to go drinking with. King! Did I say you could go yet? You can stand there another two minutes!"

"Wait!" I shouted. "What the hell is all this? The gods are lying. The Void Walkers are lying too. How do we know you're not lying? Maybe that's just a chunk of gold with your eyeball fluids on it."

Apen smiled at me. "Maybe there's hope for you yet. Stupid and selfish, but also suspicious, which makes up for a lot. All right, two things. Toss it here." He held out his hand to Famm.

Famm put the ball behind his back.

"Don't be that way," Apen said. "Give it here."

"Now that I have it, I will only surrender it to a god."

Apen pointed at the palm of his outstretched hand. "You don't learn very fast, do you? How do you know I'm not a god?"

Famm glanced side to side. "If you are, why would you give me the weapon?"

"I was testing you. You're doing lousy, by the way."

I pointed at Apen. "This is the god Lutigan! I've seen him many times."

"He doesn't sound like Lutigan," Ace said. "And how could you have seen Lutigan?"

Apen said, "I'm in disguise, but the sorcerer saw through it. I can vouch for the fact that he has seen me more than once. I wouldn't say many times, though."

King Famm waited.

"Throw me the damn god-destroyer!" Apen snapped. "I'll give it right back. After all, I gave it to you in the first place, and that's pretty darn fair in my book."

Famm tossed the gold ball to Apen, who stuck it back in his face. He turned toward a group of statues, which twisted and then melted into pools. The wall behind them was melted and dripping too.

"Does that obliterate your doubts?" Apen pulled out the ball again.

I said, "Hey! Stupid, selfish, and also suspicious here! Doesn't that make me more worthy? And I'm family!" I didn't know why Apen had been saying that, but I'd trade on it if I could.

"Sorry, sorcerer, I promised." He threw the ball back to Famm. "And no fighting in the well! Go outside if you're going to kill each other. You can all go now. Use separate doors."

Famm and his men charged their door. Pil, Stan, and the others did the same to our door.

I stayed where I was. "Apen . . . Lutigan?"

Apen guffawed. "Nice try."

"Fine, you said there were two things. The first is that the ball is a powerful weapon. I'm convinced. What's the second?"

"Oh! Lutigan is my father."

I took a deep breath, relaxing to rush him if he reached for his sword. "I've killed a few of your brothers."

"I know! It puzzled me why you'd do that, until we met. You don't know, or if you do it's buried pretty damn deep. About one hundred fifty years ago, my daddy screwed your great-great-great-great grandmother."

"What?"

"There's not enough of him in you to matter. Or it doesn't matter much, anyway. You do kind of remind me of him when he's been drinking and isn't itching to wipe out some inoffensive people who have a shitty army. That may have something to do with all the hatred and vengeance between you. Kids, huh?"

"Bullshit! I'm not his nasty little descendant. Why are you saying this?"

"The Unnamed Mother told me, and she's astonishingly well-informed."

I said, "But I don't have any powers. I can't even walk straight after riding all day."

"I'd be surprised if you did have powers. But you are family. Our family hates and betrays each other all day long, but we're still family."

"Apen, why are you down here?"

"Exiled. Dad likes to exile his kids when they do things he doesn't care for. He exiled the shit out of Memweck, didn't he? I would have been killed in the Void a thousand years ago if Grandma hadn't brought me here to guard whatever she thinks is important this week."

I shook my head. "Apen, I could ask questions for a month, but I have to chase down Famm, kill him, and pull the weapon out of his face. He won't last an hour before he breaks down and convinces himself he must insert it into his eye socket—for the good of everybody. Thanks for telling me that Gek is lying and not that fearsome."

Apen stared. "I didn't say that. Did you hear me say that?"

I shook my head.

"The gods are all terror-stricken by him, except for Krak, who's just afraid in the regular way. Gek is probably the most horrifying and destructive being in existence."

"Oh. I guess I misunderstood. Uh . . . I wish you had given me the golden eyeball."

"I couldn't. Famm will cause less death with it than you would. Why don't you let him go? Fewer will die, except for him. He'll be the first one killed. Wait until the war's over and pick it up off the ground someplace."

"Sorry. Staying is the smart thing to do, but I have to be true to myself—stupid, selfish, and suspicious."

THIRTY-THREE

D uring the war between the Empire and the Hill People, I chose to fight my way up a horrendous number of steps. I also embarrassed myself when I couldn't do it in a lively way. I could make it up the steps and kill people at the same time, but not without a lot of panting and sweating.

My part in the war ended when I came to the Eastern Gateway, and later I discovered the war's outcome through rumor. One story said that the empress and her army had retreated from the capital and would mount a counterattack soon. Another held that the Hill People overran the capital and tortured everybody to death, including the empress, and they then went on merrily burning the rest of the Empire to ash.

Everybody agreed that the Hill People had invaded with at least half a million fighters, and more likely a million. I found no witnesses who had seen an army of that size. Maybe some of the empress's soldiers survived to talk about the ocean of Hill People. However, I had seen no more than two thousand Hill People at any one time, and they had appeared to feel that was sufficient to take and destroy the capital of the world's greatest empire.

After I escaped the war and arrived at the Eastern Gateway, I

287

spent a certain number of days lying around in bed with Ella. Once those lazy days had passed, I spent the next week climbing to the top of the keep several times a day, cursing my age at every landing. But before long, I was running up those steps ten times every morning. I borrowed a sword twice as heavy as mine and sparred with two guards at a time for a couple of hours before the midday meal. I rode horses all afternoon, but that was for pleasure.

Those weeks of activity taught me two things. First, exerting myself so much during the day made me not as much fun at night, but Ella didn't complain.

Second, my lack of wind may not have been due entirely to my age. Years of sitting on my ass getting drunk in taverns probably contributed.

I climbed out of Apen's lair and ran up the steep ramp, all two hundred feet to the surface. Famm had a head start, and we wouldn't overtake him by strolling around to admire the awful scenery. My pains from healing our people had begun fading, and the climb left me breathing deep but not out of breath. I felt a little smug.

Yita was waiting for me at the surface. After one look, she said, "You've let yourself get soft. Cael could have run right to the top while singing songs." Then she loped away across the tall black grass. Over her shoulder she yelled, "Try to keep up!"

I didn't indulge in a sharp reply. I would probably need that breath, because she was some sort of champion among her people, with the conditioning that implied. She also had fifteen-year-old lungs.

The Dark Lands hadn't changed in any way that would suggest they needed a different name. The cool, black grass still stretched between wide-spaced gray trees, and it still flowed over the shallow hills. The black sky held no sun or moon. Stars of all colors were smeared across it, some of them racing along.

I saw a big lake several miles away. It was black and as untroubled as glass. I realized I had never felt a breeze in the Dark Lands, but even without any wind, the place always felt chilly.

Yita led me toward the lake, and we ran barefoot. I could see

Desh, Pil, and Stan far ahead of us. I could just make out King Famm, even farther ahead.

"Hurry! We'll never catch them!" Yita called back as she pulled away from me.

I did not push myself faster. Every one of the people up ahead was younger than me. Why chase them on foot like a fool when I could do something really stupid? The war was about to begin, and I didn't have many prospects for a future life. This was the time for risks.

"Mighty Fingit, I come to report," I said, lifting my spirit toward the gods' trading place.

Lightning showed Fingit, the gazebo, and me in a one-second flare. Thunder chased it an instant later, tremendous and staggering. I saw fire in the forest where the bolt had struck. I could have jogged to it in a minute. On the other side of me, the endless field was charred and smoking. All the flowers had been obliterated.

A lightning storm crashed close by, and more bolts flashed in the distance without pause. I couldn't see outside the trading arena, but the sky glowed red from fires in all directions.

Fingit was leaning against a marble column, tapping his fingers. "Krak likes to rouse the troops by displaying his unfathomable might." He blinked when more lightning crashed in the forest. "Watching your home destroyed is great for morale, don't you think? Before you answer, only disloyal idiots who want to have their parts seared off would imply that it isn't great for morale." Fingit sighed.

"I guess he knows what he's doing," I said.

"Mm. All right, if you have a report, then report."

"Mighty Fingit, I'd like to ask a question. The answer will let me organize my report in the best way for the circumstances."

Fingit leaned forward. "Don't try your vague sorcery garbage with me."

I assumed that meant I should go ahead. "Why did Harik wait to tell you and Sakaj that I can see you?"

"You should be telling me that!"

"Well, Mighty Fingit—"

Fingit cut me off. "Screw this 'mighty' business—it bores me to no end. Just say what you're here to say." His eyes flicked down. "And while you're at it, you tell me why you think he did it."

Long experience told me that when Fingit avoided a direct answer, he was usually hiding something. The gods often seemed unaware of habits that showed they were lying. But at other times, they used such behaviors on purpose when trying to fool an overconfident sorcerer. I figured to hell with it. I'd throw out my best guesses and act like I knew everything. "Harik never did tell you about my sight. And he didn't explain why."

Fingit paused. "No, he didn't."

Encouraged, I fired right back. "Because you haven't even seen him! I bet nobody has."

Nodding, Fingit said, "Don't get too impressed by your own cleverness."

"Here's my report. Harik gave me ten squares to make sure all those wretches in Sakaj's cursed city were killed in his name."

"In his name?"

"Right," I said. "And he arranged things so that Pil had to kill them."

Fingit turned and paced across the gazebo. "Krak and the Void hump it forever!"

I continued, "All right, Harik has disappeared, probably to do something everybody would find nasty. But whatever he got by trading with me couldn't have been too much, right?" If Mara had been truthful about trades and power, then Harik had gotten one hundred thousand squares from our trade. I didn't know how many volcanoes a god could raise with that.

"I don't know what you mean." Fingit shook his head but seemed distracted. "Why do you think gods get anything in these bargains? That's fiction. We just do it for fun."

"Ah. I apologize for my impertinent assumption."

I debated pushing my luck with Fingit. If I needed an ally among the gods, he was my best chance. However, he'd have to know that I wasn't just another ignorant sorcerer waddling around to be bled dry. He needed to know that I had dealt with the great powers.

I opened my mouth to mention I'd seen Mara and said, "Breakfast was delicious this morning." I shook my head.

"What? Is this some deranged bargaining tactic?"

It didn't surprise me that I still couldn't talk about the Unnamed Mother, but I had hoped I could. Well, I could be indirect. "Of course you do all this for fun, Fingit. Yesterday I wagered the Nub one thousand to one that trading with sorcerers was a mere lark."

Fingit narrowed his eyes and leaned toward me.

"That's right, one thousand to one. And our hypothetical Harik *does not* get a load of hypothetical power by taking years of life from thousands of people. It's a jolly romp for no reason."

Fingit hurtled out of the gazebo, slammed me to the ground, and grabbed my neck. I knew his hands were big, but I hadn't appreciated how enormous they really were. He growled, "Where did you hear this? Who else have you told?"

Through my coughing and squeaking, I said, "I haven't told anybody else!"

"Bullshit!" Fingit squeezed my neck.

I tried to say Mara's name. "Sausages!"

Fingit didn't ease his grip even a fraction. "What are you babbling about?"

"Beautiful shoes! The buttered toast . . ." I obviously wasn't allowed to say *mother*. "The older feminine entity that . . . you fell out of would love some shoes like that too."

Fingit eased off a smidge and narrowed his eyes. "Would love some buttered toast?"

"No!" I glared. "Beautiful. Shoes. A gift from all the older kids, but not that bitch Sakaj."

It was a horrid little batch of clues, but Fingit was said to be the smartest of the gods. Now he said slowly, "The Unnamed Mother told you?"

"Yes!" I squeaked. "Mara!" When Fingit guessed I was talking about Mara, that must have cracked the charm that kept me from talking about her.

BILL MCCURRY

"Damn it!" he yelled. "Shit on it with every ass in the realm!" Fingit released me and stood, but he didn't leap back into the gazebo. He paced on the grass just outside the patch of dirt that the gods kept sorcerers in, like an arcane goat pen. "I thought you and the Knife killed those amusing cursed people without any prompting. It sounds like the kind of merciful thing she'd do."

"Thing that she'd do? What about me?"

Fingit glanced at me with one eyebrow raised. "The same way you're known for building orphanages all across the land? How many people did the Knife kill after your trade?"

"I counted one thousand three hundred sixty-nine."

Fingit stared down as he paced for half a minute. When he stopped, his face looked as if he'd just heard somebody was coming to chop off his favorite arm. "Harik got almost three million squares. May the Void suck off that bastard's face. And his godhood. I need to tell Krak, but he's already in the Dark Lands. I'll send a messenger. He'll want to question you, Murderer. Hey . . . I bet you're in the Dark Lands too, aren't you? You're there right this minute. Aren't you? I can't see you, but you're there, as sure as anvils are heavy."

I didn't see any point in lying about it. If I said I wasn't in the Dark Lands, where would I tell him I was? I didn't know of any other place where the gods couldn't see across realms. "Yes, I'm in the Dark Lands."

Fingit clenched his teeth. "Good. Come to the lake that's five miles north of the portal and six miles west of the ridge."

"Um, how do I tell which way is north?" I asked.

"You just . . . never mind, just go to the lake and look for the Unquenchable Host of Sterling Perspective."

"Of course."

Fingit relaxed and grinned. "Great name for an army, right?"

"Sure. I need one thing, Fingit. I'm chasing down that villain, King Famm. The one who lies about talking to you."

Fingit yelled, "Who is this King Famm? He sounds like a creep."

"Maybe he's working for Harik and trying to blame things on you."

292

"I can't concentrate on crap like this and fight a war at the same time. Trutch's armor needs to be adjusted, and the flame on Weldt's sword keeps going out! You go destroy this Famm jerk."

"To do that, I—"

"But don't get killed doing it, not until Krak's done talking to you. Hunt down this king and stab him from every direction, including upward."

"I need help catching him," I said. "He has a big head start. I need you to move me so that I'm in front of him."

Fingit crossed his arms. "All right. What are you willing to offer?"

"But my report was so helpful, I thought you might . . ." I gave him my most charming smile.

"Be realistic, Murderer. I have a war to fight, and I may have to fight Harik too. I need all the power I can get."

"I ask that you make the first offer, at least."

"Fine. In exchange for giving you the power to move yourself no more than, say, half a mile, I want you to kill the Knife."

I jerked. "That's a bold bargaining position, Fingit. In exchange for moving myself as much as two miles, I promise to wear no clothes for the next day."

"That's just awful and sad," Fingit said. "You get the power to move up to a mile, you're naked for a day, and you kill the next two people you run across who are also naked."

I tried not to react. "How about this? I can move myself up to a mile and a half, and I'll kill King Famm in your name."

Fingit rolled his eyes. "You already intend to do that."

"All right, I'll capture the bald, posturing toad."

"Maybe," Fingit said. "It might be useful to question that liar myself. I'll agree if we stipulate that once you capture him, you'll bring him to me."

I didn't feel quite ready to run over to the spot where Krak was mustering his army. So, I hoped Fingit wouldn't be disappointed if I didn't deliver the king right away. Fingit should have set me a schedule if time was important to him.

I piddled with considerations of time as I ignored the real question. The deal seemed reasonable. So where was the misery hidden? I examined the terms and couldn't find the flaw that would rise up and make me pray for death. I examined it again while Fingit waited. Patience must have been a highly refined quality in immortal beings.

"Fingit, I agree."

"Then it's a bargain, Murderer. You'll be able to move yourself up to a mile and a half in an instant. Remember, don't get killed before Krak talks to you. If a battle looks uncertain, withdraw."

"I will, Fingit. I hope we talk again."

"Why? You are no more than an ant to grind under my sandal. You are dust beneath my notice." Fingit smiled. "Still, try not to get yourself murdered."

Fingit threw me back into my body hard enough to stagger me. Maybe he was reminding me who was the god and who was the sorcerer. I shouted, "Yita! Yita, wait!" I wanted to explain why I was about to disappear and where I'd be going. But she didn't look back.

"Yita! I'm about to leave and jump ahead of Famm! Wait a few seconds!"

Yita still didn't look back or slow down, although she waved a dismissive hand back at me.

To hell with her. When she showed up, I could explain things while I pointed at Famm trussed up on the grass.

I saw that Famm's force wasn't running directly toward the closest part of the lake. They must've known where the gods were concentrating their forces. I picked out a spot that was a long sprint ahead of Famm and slightly between him and the lake. Then I told myself to go there.

I appeared just about where I intended, which was a victory. I had feared I might go some different direction, or a hundred miles away, or a mile into the sky or under the earth. I arrived on what looked like the correct grass, celebrated for an instant, and plunged feetfirst into marsh water over my head.

THIRTY-FOUR

I have done a world of foolish things in my life. A fair number of them could be called stupid. But until I chased Famm through the Dark Lands, I had never traded with a god for the power to dunk myself in nasty, supernaturally malevolent swamp water. The profound depth of my idiocy dispirited me for a few seconds.

My feet couldn't touch the bottom. I couldn't see the surface, either, but it couldn't be too far up. I started swimming and realized I was holding my sword. I couldn't sheath it because my naked self had no sheath or even a belt.

I ended up working hard not to swim in a damn circle. But the surface was only a few feet above me. Maybe some part of my situation wasn't stupid after all.

Floating vegetation blocked my view and hid King Famm from me. I searched for my mortal enemy by trying to fling my upper body out of the muck like a porpoise over and over.

That might have been the stupidest moment of my life.

After a short period of floundering and cursing, I felt dirt under my feet. The water became shallower as I eased forward, and at last I poked the top half of my head above the tangled, drifting grass.

King Famm was exactly where I thought he would be, so I crept on through the water and weeds. Famm would be surprised as hell when I leaped at him from out of the evil marsh itself.

One of the soldiers pointed my direction and shouted. Another fired an arrow. I dodged by pushing to my right, slipping on the muddy bottom, writhing in the hope that I could still dodge, and flopping face-first into the water. I sank three feet. A quarter of a second later, the arrow drove into my back just above the shoulder blade.

That was my new stupidest moment.

I lifted my head just high enough to be blinded by the beautiful masses of floating weeds. Cursing hard enough to shatter bricks, I reached behind myself to explore the wound. I couldn't grasp the arrow with either hand.

Drifting for a couple of seconds, I admitted that right now I could be a lazy fisherman living in a town with a well-stocked bar. I could have a friendly dog and a bunch of children who hated me.

My deal with Fingit had seemed so reasonable. He was a good fellow, as far as gods were concerned.

I got angry and rushed Famm. Five feet of water will prevent any man from effectively charging his enemies. It's even more of a challenge with an arrow sticking out of your back, but I did my best. I focused on figuring out what Thad the Caller intended to do to me. He might try to use the weeds and vines to drag me under and drown me, but I was carrying an embarrassingly huge amount of power. Harik had sold it to me, and Pil had paid for it. Even wounded, I should be able to overwhelm any magical feat that Caller tossed at me.

Ace the Burner shocked me all to hell when he created a ferocious blaze in the arrow embedded in my back. Of course, the arrow was wet, but I might as well have tossed a cup of water into a fireplace. On a normally dry day, the arrow would burn up in ten minutes or so with a nice little flame. Ace took all the heat he would have received from those ten minutes and released it in three seconds.

I fell forward into the water and floated, motionless. Part of me wondered how bad it was. The burns didn't hurt. Those are the worst kind.

The most important thing was exploring my wounds. That seemed wise to me. I had forgotten that I was floating facedown in the water. When I started sucking the evil, Dark Lands swamp water, instinct flopped me over like the world's least graceful walrus.

My face rolled to the surface and into a clump of damp, floating swamp grass. Some of it poked up my nose. A blade sticking in my ear felt like it must be rotting.

That became the stupidest moment of my life.

I thought about my arrogance in trying to impress Fingit, acting like I was someone to take seriously. *Look at me! I've dealt with the great powers! Everybody's getting scones, so give me one too!* I floated and cursed my unfathomable idiocy.

But by the time I passed out, I was making new plans.

I woke up lying on my belly in dry, black grass. The burns still didn't hurt much, but the arrow wound in my shoulder hurt like a rod of fire all by itself.

Desh was kneeling beside my head. "Nice that you're awake. I thought I'd have to start slapping you."

"How far ahead is Famm?" I croaked.

From behind Desh, Pil said, "Too far."

"You can't be sure," I said. "You don't know everything."

Pil turned and walked away.

I raised my voice as much as I could, which wasn't much. "That's a cheap way to win an argument!"

"Bib, you need to heal yourself right the hell now," Desh said. "I'm using something to keep you alert, but it won't last much longer. I'm afraid that if you take too long, you'll become delirious, not be able to heal yourself at all, and die."

"Hell, I can't die yet. I have plans. You'll be amazed when you see." I thought I might not be making total sense, so I focused on my back. "I once grew you two new eyeballs, Desh, so I imagine I can handle a little burn or two."

Ace had done a fine job of cooking me. The burns were deep and ran from the top of my head to the middle of my back and along both arms. Desh was right to be worried about them killing me. I could reach a fair amount of that area, which made healing an easier and less costly proposition than it might have been. I spent extra power to heal the spots I couldn't reach.

I made a mistake in healing myself. I would like to have blamed the general situation, or my struggles working with such wounds, or the fact that Desh was standing so close and breathing all my air. But it was my mistake, and that was fine because I was the one who suffered for it.

I should have dealt with my shoulder wound first and then the burns. My current, awful burns were just about painless. But once I healed them, the residual pain was agonizing. I sweated and clenched while Desh cut the arrowhead out of me.

Passing out when I finished would've been nice. I didn't pass out, though, which is more proof that Krak and his children do not love us. At least they didn't love me.

The pain of those tortures didn't come close to the agony from those healed burns I didn't have any more. I couldn't explain why. I strained, groaned, cursed heroically, wept, and called for my mother for a time that seemed exceedingly long. Desh told me afterward that the entire panorama of anguish lasted over nine hours. I declared that to be a long goddamn time.

By the time I could sit up again, I was referring to the ordeal as "getting burned up." Pil had sat beside me for all nine hours, holding my hand and wiping sweat off my face. After it was all over, she stood close enough to ask whether I needed anything, an optimistic question since we had nothing.

However, the third time I described my experience as "getting all burned up," Pil shook her head and walked away, muttering something about "pompous twat."

Yita handed me a water jug. "There's almost none left, so just wet your lips."

"You have clothes!"

She brushed the filthy shoulder of the uniform shirt she wore. "Pil killed one of the soldiers, so I took his."

"I approve." I handed her the jug. "Those garments must have great utility, and I can hardly see the blood. Where did Famm go?"

Yita pointed toward the lake. "He traveled right over this marsh."

I peered at the surface. "How?"

"Magic," Pil growled as she stalked back into the conversation.

Desh said, "I think Famm used the god-killing eyeball to clear a path, and the water filled in behind him."

Pil said, "I don't see how we can follow Famm to the lake. We probably shouldn't now, even if the gods are there. We need food and water. We need a new plan, if we ever had one in the first place."

I smiled at Pil. "Not long ago, you'd have said all that without pausing for breath."

She roared "Well, I didn't this time!" before stomping away.

We all watched her go.

I said, "Do you think I should—"

"Hell no!" Stan cut me off. "And people call me the dumb one."

As if nobody had gotten mad, Yita said, "Pil's right, and Bib, you look dumb for pretending she's not. She ought to be leader, not you."

"Am I leader?" I looked around. "Why am I leader? I'm a terrible leader. Desh?"

He shrugged. "I abstain from making observations. For now."

"I am not the leader! But it's my job to get Yita—yes, you—to the proper spot for the divine death blow." I stood for dramatic effect, swayed, and fell to my knees. "We'll start on that soon."

Desh sat down not far from me. He waved everybody else over, even Pil, until all of us were sitting in a small circle. "This isn't the time to joke. Bib, why are we doing this? Really, what are we trying to accomplish here?"

I said, "Well, since the gods can't eavesdrop on us here in the Dark Lands, I'll say it right out. We're here so Yita can assassinate Krak."

"I thought that was a joke," Stan muttered.

Pil sighed, and Yita looked down, but not before I saw that her eyes were bigger than her fists.

"I admit it sounds like a joke, but it's not," I said. "I'm helping her, so the rest of you should go on home."

Stan grated, "That would fulfill my heart's fondest goddamn wish, but how do we get there?"

"Let's wait on that," Desh said. "Are you chasing us away, Bib? Would you feel all right if we stay?"

"Of course, I would admire having any one of you along to accomplish acts formerly thought impossible."

Desh scratched his balding head. "All right. You say you're off to stomp Krak like he was a mouse in your cupboard. I want to know why."

Pil glared damnation at me as she reached across to press my hand between both of hers. "Because Bib's a slave. More—" She choked. "More than once." She snarled like a dog that's been kicked, dropped my hand, and sat up tall. A tear dripped from one eye.

Desh and I glanced at each other. If Pil was becoming unbalanced, we all had a big problem. An insane sorcerer could kill all her enemies for miles around. She might also kill all her friends, all the people she didn't care about, and all the animals, both woodland and barnyard. The trees and grass couldn't take survival for granted.

Pil met our eyes and shook her head, whispering, "Not yet." I figured she was asking us not to kill her while we sat there, at least not yet.

Desh nodded to her before saying, "Bib, I want to understand everything before I decide whether to follow Stan home. I don't think that 'killing Krak' is the entire story. Not enough, anyway."

"I know for an ass-kicking, goddamn fact that it's not enough!" Stan said.

Without looking up, Yita said, "It's what I was born to do, and it's why Cael brought me to you. Bib's right. Go home if you want to."

Pil blinked at Yita a few times.

I held up a hand. "I admit there's more to it. Gek wants to

conquer the gods, which would be bad for Krak and his children. Then they might not be such cast-iron, spiked, rolling bitches to deal with."

"So, we're fighting for Gek?" Pil asked.

"No, not really," I said.

"Then we're just fighting to hurt the gods?" Desh asked.

"Not that, either," I said. "Look, the gods are hurting us more and more. Mankind, I mean. If the gods win this war, they'll keep doing it and then hurt us even worse. Gek doesn't care about us. If he wins, he'll weaken the gods. Then they won't be able to treat us like shit, or not as much."

"And this all depends on killing Krak?" Pil asked.

"Well, that's the one thing Gek has asked for over and over." I stared around at them. "Look, to hell with the gods and the Void Walkers. We're fighting for ourselves."

Yita was still looking at the ground, but her voice was steady. "I'm going no matter what anybody says."

"I'll come," Pil said.

I smiled. "Thank you for trusting me."

Pil sneered. "I don't. I don't trust you or like you or believe in the things that you say are right. I'm so angry at you all the time I can hardly keep from throwing rocks at you."

"Then why?" I murmured.

"I can't tell what's right. It's—" She shrugged. "You may not be right. But at least you're persistent."

I waited.

"Aren't you going to make a dumb joke?" Pil asked.

"No." I shook my head. I wasn't surprised she hated me after everything that had happened. It surprised me that she felt ambiguous at all.

Desh said, "I'm going too. That's four of us. Stan?"

"Oh, hell! I hate this place!" Stan walked away. "There's not a single flippin' thing to kick here if a man's disgusted. It's not enough that we suffer back home. The gods made these lands so they could watch us suffer in the dark and the cold." He stomped back toward us. "Where the hell are we going this time?"

THIRTY-FIVE

S quishing through the soggy grass, we hustled around the marsh that lay between Famm and us. Pil, Desh, and I spent that time elaborating on my plans. We soon agreed that only one plan gave us a real chance of success.

First, we would capture King Famm and take the god-killing eyeball away from him.

Then Yita and I would pass through the gods' army to the rear. Since Fingit wanted me to bring Famm as a captive, we'd use that as an invitation.

While I entertained Fingit, Yita would wander around in the most inoffensive manner possible, keeping her eyelid slammed shut over the god-killing eyeball I would insert into her.

Once Yita found Krak, she would melt him into an omniscient puddle. Somebody on Gek's side would declare victory. It wouldn't be Yita or me, since we'd be killed at once, or maybe tortured for eternity.

While it was a fine plan, we admitted that most of its parts would probably fail. Famm may well have already gone home, never to be captured by us. Even if he hadn't fled, I didn't expect him to stand under a conspicuous tree to get whacked on the head. Also, he probably wouldn't have the eyeball. He'd been tasked with making sure nobody could use it against the gods. If that had been my task, I would have popped that thing out of my face and given it to the first god who walked past.

That led to our backup plan.

Fingit also wanted me to report to Krak about Harik, so we'd get in that way.

Once I had an audience with Krak, I would describe Harik's actions in enough detail to paint a repulsive landscape of his perfidy.

While that was going on, Yita would wander around carrying a basin or basket of fruit, seemingly on a mission, but she would actually be searching for the god-destroying eyeball.

Once Yita found the eyeball, she would shove it into her eye socket, which I would have prepared beforehand.

Then I would hold Krak down while she destroyed him.

The last part of the plan sounded a bit unlikely. That's because the entire plan was unlikely to succeed.

That led to the crazy plan.

I had come to believe that the more powerful a being was, the better my sword could kill it. Well, nobody was more powerful than Krak.

First, we would ask Gek to mount an attack on the gods. Nothing too big. Ten thousand men or so.

While that distracted the gods and their army, Yita and I would sneak behind the gods' lines, hiding ourselves with magic that Desh and Pil would provide.

Then we'd find Krak. Yita would stab the Father of the Gods in the back using my sword, while I held off the rest of the divine army if necessary, probably armed with a handy stick.

Both of us expected to be killed a few seconds later. In fact, we hoped for it. If we weren't, that meant the gods had captured us. I didn't know how long gods could keep people alive to torture, and I didn't want to think about it.

I took Yita aside as we walked. "Do you still want to do this? You know there's no chance to live through it."

The girl looked pale as she pushed a stray hair back off her brow, but her voice was hard. "I am here to do this. I don't know why it has to be done, but that doesn't matter."

"It does matter. I'm sorry that I can't talk about why it needs to be done, but it's important."

"Don't you want to give up and run?" she asked.

"I don't guess so. If I'm not killed here, I'll just go back home, drink too much, insult everybody, and make Ella mad for a few days before I die. Maybe a few months. Hell, it's worth destroying the Father of the Gods just to avoid all that."

Yita grabbed my arm, stopped me, and then hugged me hard. "Thank you for going with me. You're not all that much worse than Cael."

"I'll tell Desh to carve that on my tomb, if he survives and I have a tomb."

I almost asked Yita again if she was sure she didn't want to withdraw. A young person like her didn't have to go die, although plenty did in wars less exotic than this one. If Yita wanted, I bet I could find a way to send her home or to someplace she'd like better. Desh would do it if I couldn't.

But I didn't ask. Yita's purpose had always seemed clearer than anybody's, and it wasn't my place to stand in the way of great and foolish acts. I decided not to send her home, and I regret that decision more than anything else I did in the Dark Lands.

I pushed the pace on the chance that Famm had chosen to nap and rest his feet on the way to the lake. Halfway around, we reached the base of a ridge about a hundred feet tall and more than half a mile long. It was the highest point I had ever seen in the Dark Lands. The idea of climbing it flashed to mind, but at this point, I didn't want anything to delay us. The gods were only a few miles away, and I felt ready to end this fight.

A few minutes later, a voice far ahead of us shouted, "Hey! Dang it, hey! I'm talking to you! You, Bib the sorcerer, don't act like you never seen me before!"

"Hurd?" I yelled back.

Hurd was short, blocky, and broad with long arms and a head

like a ball. I didn't know what realm he was born in, but I had met him on my last trip through the Dark Lands.

I waved at him and shouted, "We don't have time to wait!"

"You can darn well wait five seconds! You ain't too good to spare an old friend one word, are you? Or maybe you don't want me for a friend. You'll feel sad over that, I promise you!" He had covered half the distance between us and waved some big sacks over his head.

Everybody else was drifting toward Hurd, so I gave up trying to keep us moving.

As Hurd drew close, he tossed a sack to Pil, a sack to Stan, and another to Desh.

"Beer!" Stan yelped.

Desh began handing out loaves of bread and packets of meat. Pil reached into her large, heavy bag and pulled out a boot.

Except for slurping and swallowing, I heard no sounds for the next couple of minutes. I was as greedy for food as anybody.

Hurd asked, "You done gumming your food? Not yet? Who wants to tell me what's been happening?"

Yita bubbled, "The tower turned upside down, and there was a sorcery fight!"

"Yita!" I held up a hand. "Hurd, you tell us what's been happening."

With a tremor in his voice, Hurd said, "That hurts me. It's like you don't trust me, even with the food and such I brought you. Don't tell me you wasn't hungry! This little girl is nothing but a bone."

I nodded. "Thank you for the food, thank you for the beer, thank you for the clothes, what the hell are you doing here? Beside slowing us down? Is there a trap up there?" I nodded toward the lake.

Hurd leaned back. "Well, yes, there's traps, but the gods have set 'em. Not me. I brung you all this because Gek told me you'd need it. He's getting fit for battle, otherwise he might have come himself. Or he might not. You're so dang rude, Bib, maybe that's why he didn't want to come."

Yita poked my arm. "We can spare a minute. Don't be mean. He brought us food!"

Pil grinned as she held up a tough, warm shirt and pulled it on.

I said, "Yita, I know that he brought all these things. But Hurd, I can feel that something's happening, so we don't have time to wait. We're walking out of here as soon as we're all shod. Whatever you have to say, speak it now."

Hurd pointed behind him at the ridge. "There's a hundred fifty thousand troops on the other side, anxious to hurry out and destroy some gods."

"Won't the gods just retreat? Leave the Dark Lands?" Desh asked.

"Gek is taking care of that. Once his scouts bring word that you've killed Krak, the army will come stomp the gods flatter than melted butter."

Pil asked, "What if Yita doesn't kill Krak?"

Hurd glanced at Yita with a slow nod. "Then the army will set off when you two are dead, Bib."

I gazed toward the lake. "Anything else?"

Hurd scowled. "The gods know you're on the way, and they know you're loyal to . . . well, maybe not loyal to Gek, but serving him."

"How the hell do they know that? Who told them?"

"That nasty stain, King Famm did it. What other warriors are running around here too noble for their own good? Now that Cael's dead, I mean?" Hurd turned to Yita. "Of course, Famm ain't a tenth of the man Cael was."

Yita beamed at the creature.

"Gek has scouts," Hurd added. "They know what Famm told the gods. That lousy king Famm is hurrying this way right now like his ass was on fire. I guess the gods told him something he didn't like too much, so the rat's ass run away from them."

"Famm has deserted the gods?" Pil asked.

"Like a fart in the wind. He's a weasel in a bunch of lions."

"Farting weasel?" Pil smirked.

"Desh, what do you think?" I asked.

He chewed his lip. "If Famm told the gods about the eyeball, then they know we intend to kill a god."

"That's what I was thinking. Shit!"

Desh grinned. "But Famm doesn't know we're going after Krak, so everything should be easy, right?"

"Again, shit." I turned to Hurd. "I apologize for acting so rudely, Hurd. Thank you. We don't have any more time to gossip about the riffraff, but I do need——"

"Wait!" Desh interrupted. "If Famm's a weasel in a bunch of lions, who are the lions?"

Hurd stood silent, his eyes flicking between Desh and me. "I might shouldn't have said that."

I took a step toward Hurd.

He stepped back with his hands raised. "All I can tell you is that Gek paid mind to four men. I never heard him talk about one unless he talked about the others too. And before you ask, they was you, Famm, Cael, and Bixell, and I shouldn't have said that much."

"Who's Bixell?" Yita asked.

Stan said, "A great, huge ganker, lives in the Dark Lands, kind of whiny."

Bixell was also the guardian of bridges here and had been for an appalling number of years. As I understood it, he didn't age while in the Dark Lands. He believed I should take his place so he could sample the pleasures of the flesh in some less dreary realm.

Did Hurd slip and blunder into telling me this? Or did he slip on purpose? I said, "That's mighty damn interesting, so let's forget about it until the war's over. Hurd, let me ask a favor. Tell Gek to mount diversion, ten thousand men or so." I glanced at Desh. "In two hours?"

Desh nodded. "If Famm told the gods about your allegiance to Gek, he killed any chance you'll be invited into the gods' camp. We're down to the crazy plan."

"Two hours, Hurd," I said.

"Wait!" Pil said. "Why not four hours? Or six? Nobody's pushing us. Let's take a breath to be a little careful."

"No," I said. "This is the time to charge, not tiptoe into battle."

307

"One meal doesn't make up for days of suffering!" Pil glanced at Yita.

"We're not waiting, and we're not slowing down!" I shouted. "Everybody except Yita and me will be part of the diversion, unless you choose to withdraw from the field."

I stared around, but nobody moved to leave. "All right. From now on, if somebody has to fall out, we'll leave them behind. If somebody goes chasing butterflies, they can chase butterflies all the way home! Pil, I've been in dozens more battles than you. Real battles, not just killing people while they stood there."

Pil's jaw fell open, and she grunted as if I had kicked her in the stomach. I hated to hurt her, but I didn't have time to argue about being careful when we needed to be closing with the enemy and destroying him.

I snapped, "Everybody fall in and keep up!" Pil had to have been glaring at me with molten hatred, so I made myself not look at her. We left Hurd behind as I led us toward the lake at a fast march.

Stan brought up the rear, saying, "Desh, when did Bib forget he's a lousy leader? Should we even listen to him here in this war with demons and that crazy goddamn sky?"

I didn't hear Desh's answer, but Stan snorted a laugh.

About ten minutes passed before Stan yelled, "Hey! Come back here!"

I craned my neck and saw that Yita had dropped back behind us. She was sneaking up behind an imp that was sitting cross-legged. Somehow, I had overlooked it, and she had drawn her sword. I sprinted back toward her with my own sword drawn, but several facts came together to shock me, causing me to slow to a trot.

The imp was Dark, and it didn't seem to be aware of Yita. Also, the creature was glowing with a soft light.

Looking at its lap, Dark warbled, "What the hell? Are you trying to screw me?"

At my elbow, Desh asked, "Is it really here?"

Yita thrust her sword into the base of the imp's skull, but it passed through as if Dark was empty air.

"I guess maybe not," Desh said. "Who's it talking to?"

"It's talking to me," I said. "Or it was me, over a year ago. Everybody, stay back!"

"To hell with you!" Pil said, running past me.

I grabbed her and turned my head to save my nose from her elbow. "Wait! The thing's not really here!"

Yita cut at the imp's neck, but the blade slipped right through.

"See? Not here!" I pointed at Dark as it held up a small book and shook it. Pil stopped struggling, but I held on to her. "This has happened before, the first time we met Dark. Well, none of you were there. Maybe we shouldn't interrupt whatever this is. There could be repercussions."

Yita had walked around to stand in front of Dark, who was still glowing.

The imp looked straight at her, leaned forward, and squinted. "Well, I didn't expect that. Who is she? Who are you, girl? Did you kill your husband in his sleep? That would be pretty damn convenient for me."

I said, "I'm so stupid! I knew Yita looked familiar. She's the girl who chased away Dark."

Yita sneered as she looked Dark up and down.

"Talk, bitch! I asked you questions."

Pil shouted, "Yita, come back here!"

The girl ignored her.

Dark reached out to grab Yita, but its hand went through her. "Nothing but pictures. I'm not thrilled so far, Murderer."

Desh turned to stare questions at me.

"It's following what happened before," I said.

While Yita watched, Dark leaned closer and cocked its head. Then it leaned back and scooted away on its butt.

"What happened before?" Desh asked.

"She'll chase it away in a minute."

"Away?" Pil asked. Then she yelled in my face, "Away where?"

The imp dropped the book and jumped up before shuffling back a few feet.

I said, "She chased it away through a portal."

"Portal to where?" Desh asked, stepping toward Yita and Dark.

The realization hit me like a club. "I don't know where. Yita! Come back here!"

Yita strode toward Dark. The imp turned and ran like hell away from us with Yita a step behind. Dark swept an arm in front of itself without slowing down and pulled open an imp-size portal. It ran through the hole but didn't disappear. Instead, it stopped glowing. Yita followed Dark through the hole but didn't seem to change.

Yita thrust Cael's enchanted sword, piercing Dark's back but missing its heart. She withdrew and skipped away while the imp was spinning around.

All of us ran toward Yita now, shouting warnings, advice, and nonsense. Yita was standing right between us and Dark.

Desh ran a step ahead of us, pointing some tiny piece of metal like it was a sword.

"Move! Move!" Pil shouted, pulling the 'dent from her belt. She flung the curved piece of enchanted metal, and it flew spinning in an arc around Desh and Yita. It slammed into the side of the imp's head and bounced off. Dark didn't seem to notice.

Pil roared as she dug in a pouch.

Dark tried to whack Yita with both hands, but she stayed out of range. Before the creature could wind up for another smash, she charged in and thrust her sword up into Dark's nasty heart. She twisted the blade, pulled it free, and retreated fast.

Dark swayed on its feet, and Yita stopped thirty feet away to watch Cael's murderer die. I ran toward her, intending to drag her away and yell at her for doing something so stupid as stopping to watch an enemy die.

Instead of falling, Dark leaped at Yita. She scrambled out of Dark's reach and kept going. The monster landed on its knees, skidded in the soft grass, and stretched out to smack Yita against the ground as she ran.

Pil screamed, and I think Stan did too. Desh pointed his metal device at the imp while I stabbed it through the head, twice. It was dead already and probably had been since the moment it slapped Yita.

Pil and Stan lifted Dark's enormous hand off Yita, and I hurried so I could heal her. Dark had hit her when it was just about dead, and I hoped that had diminished its power.

When I saw Stan on his hands and knees crying like an infant, I knew that Yita was gone. Pil sat next to the body holding the girl's hand, the one that still looked like a human hand. Yita must have raised her other hand by instinct, and Dark crushed it, along with her arm, shoulder, and everything below them down to her legs.

I saw all that had been done to Yita and looked away. I didn't need to see it again. She had been dead before the imp finished its death-shudder. Somehow, her head and face had hardly been touched.

Stan was still weeping as if Yita had been his own child. Pil had hardy moved. She didn't seem upset. In fact, she looked calm. That concerned me more than if she'd been shrieking. I knelt close beside her.

Pil gazed at me. "Bib, when something horrible happens because of you, do you know what Ella always says?"

"No."

"You didn't mean for it to happen. You didn't set out to make something horrible happen. It just happened. And it wouldn't have happened without you."

"I'm sorry, Pil."

"No, you're not. Not too much, anyway. You've kept things from us, manipulated us, flat-out lied, and I guess I should expect all of that. You didn't hide it."

"No, I didn't."

Pil smiled. "So, when I die because of these things you've done or didn't do, it's my fault, not yours. I'm doing stupid, reckless things, but nobody forced me to do them."

I didn't know what to say, so I kept my damn mouth shut.

Pil gritted her teeth and pointed at Yita's body. "But she didn't know what a duplicitous reptile you are, so none of that applies to her. You led her to this death because you wouldn't wait two more fucking hours. Cael was an iron fencepost that walked like a man, but he would never have failed Yita this way. Don't you have anything to say?"

I shook my head. At that point, any syllable that came out of my mouth would make things worse for me.

Pil stood and lifted Yita's sword. "I guess I'll be killing Krak now that Yita's dead."

"You don't have to—"

Pil cut me off. "If you tell me to go home, I will ram this sword down your throat all the way to the hilt. Desh, help Stan! We need to be on the march in one minute. The diversion will happen in . . . what? An hour and a half?"

Desh said, "You may want to allow two minutes before we set off."

When I turned, I saw Ella walking toward us across the black grass. She looked healthy and well-kempt, and I ran toward her. I had expected Harik's dungeons to be more brutal, but I wasn't going to complain.

Ella smiled at me and waved as she trotted to meet me. In a few moments, she'd find out that I failed Yita and killed her. Ella knew every horrible thing about me, but she still loved me. It was precious. Hell, nothing in my life was as valuable as that.

At least I thought she'd still love me.

Ella trotted to meet me, calling out, "Bib! Gek rescued me and sent me here . . ." She stopped before she reached me, staring at Yita's mangled corpse. "What happened to that poor child?"

Pil pointed at me. "He did it." She walked away to help Stan get up.

Ella stared at my face and then embraced me.

When Ella appeared, I had seen her and nothing else. After glancing to see Pil's accusation, I looked back at Ella and saw the dark, nine-foot-tall, wasp-waisted shape of Bixell striding up behind her.

THIRTY-SIX

"The diversion troops are overtaking us," Bixell said three feet from my ear. His voice sounded like the clanging of bells, but I could understand every word. "Bib, the force consists of eleven thousand troops and three sorcerers. Did you hear me?"

I stopped kissing Ella long enough to say, "I heard you! I plan to spend one more minute kissing before we continue the march, and I don't want to waste it on you!"

Bixell backed away. "Yes, I'm sorry. I've forgotten what it's like to love someone."

Ella and I resumed kissing. A few seconds later, I heard Pil say, "That's all right, Bixell. You can't be in love with me, but I'll be your friend." I glanced and saw her hugging the huge warrior around the waist. Her head didn't come up to his chest, and he held his black eight-foot-long sword aside so it wouldn't touch her. Bixell whispered something that sounded like tiny bells.

Ella and I let each other go, holding hands until the last possible moment before I walked over to Bixell and stared. He patted Pil's back, and she left without looking at me.

Bixell said, "We will gather one mile from the gods and from there commence the attack. That will happen 'about an hour from now. I promise it. I will lead you to the assembly point." He drummed his finger on his leg. "Bib, how do you intend to perform this astonishing murder?"

"Simple. Pil and I will make our way over there behind the gods. Then she'll destroy Krak while I watch."

Bixell's face was shadowed within his helmet, and his skin was dark. I watched it pale to gray. "Is that really the plan?"

"Not all of it. We'll improvise the rest along the way."

Pil and Ella both said, "Bib!"

I said, "All right, we have more than that planned, Bixell, but it's better that you don't know. Our chances will improve if we knock King Famm on the head and steal everything he owns. Do you know where he is? Can we intercept him on the way to the assembly point?"

Bixell nodded. "We can if we move quickly."

"Then go. Your legs are longer than my body, but I'll keep up."

As Bixell strode away toward the lake, I grabbed Ella in a quick embrace. "Thank you for escaping and for being alive."

"I did not escape. I told you, Gek rescued me."

"Well, remind me to knit him a codpiece. I love you."

"You'd better."

Within the first twenty minutes of chasing after Bixell and his everlasting stride, I thanked each of the steps I had climbed at the Eastern Gateway. Even though I was fit, I still was panting and sweating by the time the tall warrior halted.

Bixell pointed. "Famm is over there—"

"I see him." The king and Ace were hard to make out in the black-and-gray terrain, but I recognized them by the way they moved.

Bixell clanged, "Let me parlay with him. You needn't kill the man. He's no longer our enemy."

"Maybe," I said. "But we have each chewed the other up something fierce. If he wants to finish the fight and get killed, I won't deny him."

"I should go," Bixell insisted.

I said, "His friend is a Burner."

"You should go." Bixell slapped my shoulder.

Although I wanted Famm and Ace to trust me, I didn't trust them worth a damn. I took off every stitch of clothing and handed it all to Ella. Then I strode toward the king, holding my sword over my head.

I stopped at an easy shouting distance. Famm and Ace looked filthy, beaten up, and exhausted, about like me. I yelled, "I'd like to talk."

"Talk from there!" Famm said. "I don't trust you, and I won't trust anything you say."

"Your Majesty, if I wanted to kill you, fifteen seconds from now you'd both be dead, although I admit I'd be a little singed. But I don't want to kill you. I never did until you decided to hate me."

That was an appalling lie. I had wanted to murder Famm almost from the moment I saw him, and I still did. But that desire meant little compared to the realm-shaking events around us.

"Threatening to kill me won't cause me to trust you more!" Famm shouted.

I sighed. "I'll say three things. Then I will leave my sword here and come meet you unarmed. That'll give you an even chance of surviving should our conversation go poorly. You don't need to agree. I'm just going to keep talking.

"First, you weren't conversing with Fingit all this time. It was some other god who won't confess now. Second, I was right when I told you that the gods would take everything and put you in the most deadly, hopeless spot imaginable. That's why you left them."

The king gave a slow nod.

"Now that you know both of those things are true, you should believe that the thing I'm about to say is true. I intend to kill some of those divine sons of bitches, but I need the golden eyeball that's in your skull to do it."

I stuck my sword into the ground and walked over to Ace and the king. They didn't force me to kill either one of them, which I realized was a mixed victory. If I had killed them both, I could have enjoyed the murders and still taken the eyeball. I didn't want to change tactics at that point, though.

Famm lowered his sword. "What do you propose?"

"Let me take the eyeball. That's all. We'll be done."

"What will you give in return?"

"Oh, come on!" I snapped. "You got the damned thing for free. You found it at the bottom of a hole. That's technically true, and you know it."

Ace said, "Your Majesty, don't bargain with Bib. He'll have the deed to half your kingdom, and he'll marry your eldest daughter. You'll have to put up with him at every holiday dinner."

"Do not jest," Famm growled.

"I'm sorry, Your Majesty."

I said, "The king has no sense of humor, huh? Is it better when he's drunk?"

"You're not helping much." Ace glared at me, but the corner of his mouth was trying to turn up. "What I mean, Your Majesty, is that it's impossible for you to outbargain him. He has too much experience. Maybe I could do it, but I'm not sure I should."

I almost started calling Famm nasty names to move things along. His eyes looked uncertain, and that probably felt unfamiliar to him. But a thought struck me first. "How many years, Ace?"

"What do you mean?"

"I had to pay thirty last time."

Ace turned his eyes down. "Forty."

"What are you talking about?" Famm snapped.

I ignored him. "It'll be fifty before long, then sixty, and who knows? What's stopping the gods from charging a hundred, or a thousand? You'll make one deal, and twenty bystanders will drop dead."

Ace said, "You know, I've been wondering the same thing."

"The gods have declared war on the world of man," I said.

"And Gek is fighting that war for us," Ace murmured.

Famm bellowed, "Tell me what this bullshit is all about!"

"It's about survival, King Famm," I said. "A couple of us are about to take the gods by stealth, and a big attack will cover our approach. Give me the eyeball. Then join the diversion. If Gek is fighting the war for us, at least you can help."

Ace bent his head. "Your Majesty, I'm joining up with Bib."

Famm stared at me, his mouth open. "Damn you! Somehow you stole Ace from me!"

Five minutes later, I had my clothes back on and the golden eyeball in a cloth pouch. I also enjoyed a round ache in my left eye. I had taken the god-killing eyeball from Famm mercifully with magic instead of efficiently with a sharp pop.

I followed Bixell at a trot, Ace ran beside me, and Famm followed, grumbling without letup. If Gek really had been watching Cael, Bixell, Famm, and me, all three survivors could now be killed by a single runaway oxcart.

The assembled soldiers came into view to our right, and Bixell angled to meet them. He called back, "If somebody hadn't stopped to reminisce with passing royalty, we would have arrived ahead of the troops. By somebody, I mean Bib."

An object dove out of the sky onto the nearest soldiers, who were still a couple hundred paces to our right. That created a bit of furor in the ranks until several more of the things came down like hawks but more massive. A couple dozen soldiers screamed, jumped around, and ran. Six creatures had fallen and attacked. Four zoomed back into the sky, climbing faster than a bird.

"That's unfortunate," Bixell said as he held his sword ready and kept jogging.

"A lot of things could be unfortunate, such as an ex-wife dropping on you," I said.

The tall man snorted.

"Don't laugh about being assaulted by your relatives."

"Very well, you judge then. Which is more unfortunate? A former relative or flying scorpions the size of small dogs?"

After a pause, Desh asked, "Is that hypothetical?"

Bixell pointed his sword at four objects dropping almost straight down at us.

Pil hurled her knife and struck one, which began tumbling. She stepped aside as it smacked into the ground. At the same time, Desh threw something sparkly at another scorpion. It jerked and fluttered, then flew away toward the lake in untidy spirals.

Bixell and I swung at the same time. I sliced one in half as it fell, while Bixell's sword smashed the last one into bits that spattered in all directions, including on us.

"Damned untidy for a mystical bridge guardian," I said, bending to examine the creature I had cut in two. It had been a squat, red scorpion as long as my forearm, with stubby wings and an extra-long tail. "How dangerous?"

Scanning the sky, Bixell clinked, "If you had been stung, you wouldn't have had time to say your farewells. Not even one."

"Watch out!" Pil shouted, pointing to our left.

An imp was bounding toward us, about two jumps away.

Pil ran toward it holding her knife, which was in her hand again.

"Come back!" I yelled, following her. It was a foolish thing to say to another sorcerer, but I dreaded losing Pil the way we lost Yita, who had been far more dangerous than Pil with hand weapons. Ella was also shouting "Come back!" from behind me. I didn't know whether she was talking to Pil, me, or both of us.

When Pil threw her knife, I felt a little despair. Only a magic weapon could pierce an imp's hide, and even then, it required a powerful, well-placed thrust. Also, Pil threw the damned knife at the ground, not the imp.

The imp landed, and Pil's knife arrived an instant later. It sliced halfway through the creature's ankle, and the imp crumpled. It slid toward us, flailing. I sprinted to jump on its shoulder and then thrust my sword through its head.

"That was a good, sneaky throw," I said.

Stan said, "I don't guess we need to find your magical-as-a-specter's-dick knife, do we, Pil?"

Pil smiled at him and shrugged. "Don't worry yourself about it."

Bixell cleared his throat, which sounded like several out-of-tune bells rung together. "We must keep running. It's not yet time to paint the marks of victory on our breasts and buttocks."

"No, I guarantee it's not that time," I said, following him.

Bixell laughed. "Bib. So gullible! He's like a child, isn't he?"

THIRTY-SEVEN

We joined up with the main body of soldiers a few minutes after we killed that imp. A wild-haired, thick-bodied sorcerer named Harbinger was in command of the entire force.

I had never seen people like these. The shortest women stood about my height while most men topped me by a head or more. They all wore long tunics and kilts in a clash of colors. Most of the people were lighter skinned than me and had fair hair.

Pil, Desh, Ace, and I conferred with Harbinger and his fellow sorcerers. One was a slender, striking woman named Certain. The other was a red-faced boy not much older than sixteen, and he was named Follow. We all spoke through Harbinger, who interpreted.

Harbinger said, "We live far north of you, across the ocean. We never knew you existed until Gek told us." Harbinger snarled, "The gods worked hard to keep us apart."

Desh asked, "How did you learn to speak our language?"

"Gek brought men to teach us." Harbinger nodded at Ace. "They looked like you."

"That figures," Ace said. "Our kingdom must be closest to you. Did our people volunteer to go teach you?"

"No, they were prisoners," Certain said. "Maybe it was wrong to take them, but the war is too big for us to argue about things like that."

Ace frowned but nodded. "When I left, the gods made us give up forty years of people's lives with every trade."

Harbinger conferred with his colleagues. Then he said through the interpreter, "It was fifty years for us, but the gods stopped at that number months ago. After that, they began also requiring arms and legs. The most they got to was five. Just before I left, they started requiring children's lives—two children."

Everybody was silent for a bit while that sank in.

Follow said, "Many sorcerers killed themselves when they discovered they must choose children to die."

I said, "That was better for the gods. It caused just as much pain, but they didn't have to deliver on the power they promised."

Pil examined Harbinger and his fellow sorcerers. "So, I guess you three didn't kill yourselves."

Harbinger, Certain, and Follow all looked down or looked away.

I could have asked how many children they had condemned, but that wouldn't have helped the situation one damn bit. Instead, I said, "May the gods suck rancid clams until the ass-end of time."

The interpreter shook his head. "I know all of those words, but I can't translate them into a phrase that means anything."

"Death to the gods," I said.

We all nodded and said, "Death to the gods," each in our own language.

I said, "Desh, Ace, and our other companions will stay behind to fight alongside you."

"That is fine. We need them." Harbinger nodded at Pil and me. "Thank you for attacking the gods. We know it means you will die."

I grinned. "Hell, we'll all probably die." Everybody got a good laugh out of that.

As we walked away from our allies, Desh pointed at Pil and me. "I need to talk with the two of you."

"Not everybody?" I looked back at Ella and saw she had her arm around Stan's shoulders. Yita's death had hurt him worse than

I ever would have expected, although in Ella's opinion, he was mainly missing his own children, who were about Yita's age. Now he stood nodding along with whatever Ella was telling him. He had taken Yita's enchanted sword, and nobody had argued against it. It would keep him alive much better than that old piece of steel he'd been swinging.

"Not everybody. Sorry, Ace," Desh said.

"That's fine," Ace said. "I can guess what you want to talk about. I'm not interested in heroics." He ambled off to where Famm was pacing back and forth. I wasn't sure whether the king had ever stopped cursing.

Desh said, "Bib, I'm grateful to you. You set me on this life of—"

I cut him off. "Stop there. You may start crying, and I'll have to ruin this beautiful moment by kicking you."

"All right, here's something you'll find pretty damn sentimental." Desh reached into a soft, white leather pouch and pulled out two golden bracelets, which he handed to Pil and me. "This is the summit of my work with light. Invisibility. I don't mean that 'make people decide not to look at you' crap. This is real bending of light. Once you put it on, it will last for about three hours. But don't take it off! If you do, it will never work again."

"I figured you'd have something like this," I said.

"It's wonderful how you express awe at my accomplishment. Never mind." Desh began pulling rings off his fingers and tossing them to Pil and me. "Here, you may need these more than I will. Pil, you already have some rings of your own, but here are two more for you. This black ring glows when you ask for light. It's not bright enough for reading, but you can see by it. You should keep one thing in mind: while it's glowing, you'll have a toothache that would make an elephant puke."

Pil nodded. "I understand."

"Now this other ring lets you walk across mud, water, or things like that. You have to sing the whole time, and the more liquid the substance, the louder you have to sing."

"Thank you, Desh." Pil smiled. "It's as if you're my friend, even though you're another sorcerer, so we know that's impossible." She winked and held one of the rings up for a better look.

"Why the toothaches and the singing?" I asked.

Desh's mouth tightened. "Flaws and drawbacks make something cheaper to create. It takes less time too. I don't have until the end of the universe to make these things, you know."

"I know that now." Until then, I had never appreciated how bizarre and masochistic Binder magic could be. I scrutinized my palmful of rings and wondered what I'd have to suffer to use them.

Desh said, "Bib, this gold ring makes you warm when it's cold, and this silver one keeps you dry up to the knees."

"That's it? I don't have to drag my privates on the ground or anything?"

"Go ahead if you really want to." Desh shrugged. "This tarnished ring makes dogs and wolves like you. I admit that may not be of much use in the Dark Lands, but who knows? This copper ring makes everything taste like warm bread, no matter how disgusting it is. The last ring here lets you break stone with one punch. It only works once, and after you hit the stone, your hand will feel as if you just punched, well, punched a big rock. You'll probably break some fingers, but the stone will shatter."

I flexed my fingers. "Thank you, Desh."

"I'm not done." Desh was pulling necklaces off over his head. He handed a silver chain to Pil. "If you're hit by lightning, this will save you. It will knock you out for about a day, though."

I said, "That sounds inconvenient."

"More inconvenient than lying on the ground dead?" Desh shook his head. "This one here will prevent anybody from hearing you for a short while. You just have to think about using it."

"How short awhile?" I asked.

Desh shrugged. "It could be ten seconds, or it could be up to one hundred seconds."

"That's quite a spread."

"It's an order of magnitude," Pil said in a tone that implied I should have known that. "That's common in Binder magic."

Desh went on: "It only works once, so don't squander it."

I opened my mouth to ask why it only worked once, but Desh cut me off. "Come on, be a little grateful. Pil's not complaining. She knows I could be giving her a necklace of grass joined together with snot."

Pil chuckled.

I said, "Sorry. I'll be good."

"Bib, here's one for you that sort of balances things." Desh handed me a smooth silver chain. "It improves your hearing, since you're as deaf as an old stick."

"Nice. Thank—"

"Wait." He held up a chain of rusty iron links. "This is my favorite one. It lets you move through the earth like a gopher for—"

"Ten to one hundred seconds?"

"One to ten seconds," Desh said.

I grinned. "This is your favorite one?"

"Seriously. You can activate it just by thinking about it, and you can do that once every three minutes. Pretty much forever. It can be enormously useful."

"Thank you, Desh. I'm grateful, truly."

"Hurry up!" Bixell called out. "We're attacking in two minutes."

"Two more," Desh said in a hurry. "Pil, this amulet will save you from death by suffocation, just in case Krak tries to smother you in his armpit. The last one is this crappy-looking copper strand . . ." He hesitated. "If you are mortally wounded, you can strike one last blow before you die. Probably."

"You're joking," I said.

"It may not work, but I'm not joking."

"Will it work if your head's cut off?" Pil asked.

"Maybe." Desh didn't sound confident.

I asked, "Does using the eyeball count as one last blow? If not, Krak could cut off Pil's head and she could hold her head up like a melon and still attack with the eyeball over and over."

"I don't know all the details, I admit that!" Desh snapped. "Nobody has volunteered to be mortally wounded so that I could test it. Look at it this way. If it works, that's a plus. If it doesn't, you'll be dead and won't care."

Pil nodded. "Thank you, Desh. Even if you are another sorcerer, you know that I love you." Pil hugged him and said something sentimental about meeting again, which was nonsense. Then she turned away without looking at me.

I walked off, muttering, "Damn. She'll have to talk to me sometime, even if it's just to say move so she can fall down on a clean spot to die."

Ella squeezed my arm. "She only treats you in this fashion because she loves you too. Not in that way, of course. But this is how you behave when someone you love disappoints you and hurts you."

"That explains a lot about your behavior toward me over the years, I guess."

She grinned. "It was a factor."

I put on Desh's rings and dropped the necklaces over my head. The noise staggered me. I almost fell to my knees. I pulled off the necklaces and threw them on the ground. The avalanche of sound stopped.

"What is the matter?" Ella asked, grabbing my arm with two hands.

I yelled, "Desh!"

As he ran to us, Desh said, "I should have warned you. Decide how far away you want to hear. You may have been hearing everything within a quarter mile."

"Damn right you should have warned me!"

"You'll accustom yourself to it. I really am sorry." As he turned away, I saw him grin.

I slipped on the necklaces, and it felt as if the noise would crush my head. When I concentrated on hearing within one hundred feet, the astounding crash of noise became a disturbing wave of sound. I pushed it to fifty feet, focused through the noise, and easily heard King Famm thirty feet away muttering to Ace about how much he hated me.

"Ella! Say something!"

"What do you wish me to say?"

I had been ready for her voice to batter me, but she sounded normal. "I have no idea how this thing works."

I heard rumbling from underneath us a moment later, so I wasn't shocked when the ground beneath Ella swirled and became a four-foot-wide hole in the earth. I reached, caught her hand, and pulled her out of the hole. A few seconds later, the grass spun back up to fill the opening.

Bixell said, "Oh, that will disappoint Gek."

I snarled, "Why did Gek try to take her, you ding-dong son of a bitch?"

"He thought you would feel better knowing that she's safe. He was going to send her back to your world."

I yelled, "That Dark Annihilating Twat should have asked her! And why now? At this moment?"

"Well, it seemed to be the right time, so I gave the word."

Ella ran up and kicked Bixell on the shin. He flinched.

I shouted, "Word? What kind of word? Oh, I don't care—just don't try it again. Damn it, Bixell, think about how it would have been if I hadn't pulled Ella back. I love her, and we wouldn't have had a chance to say goodbye or hug or anything! It wouldn't matter to my dead and rotting ass, but Ella might care about those things!"

"Or I might not," Ella said coldly as she frowned and then looked away from me.

I winced. "I shouldn't have said dead and rotting ass, should I?"

"My apologies to you both," Bixell said. "I didn't think about it that way. I don't—"

"Right, you don't remember what it's like to smooch your giant honey in whatever realm you come from," I said.

I turned away from Bixell and embraced Ella one last time. "I'll tell you the truth, darling, which may shock you. You allowed me to love you, even when it must have seemed like the most foolish thing in the world to you. And you loved me, even when that made no sense, either. I will miss that more than anything else."

Then Ella said about the same things to me, but they sounded better when she said them, even though she was crying.

Drums began beating all the way down the line of soldiers.

"There it is! That's the signal!" Bixell joined the men moving forward but then turned back toward me. "Goodbye, Bib! I don't love you, but do you want to hug or something anyway?" He laughed and ran on toward the gods' army before I could call him a nasty name.

THIRTY-EIGHT

Pil and I cut away from the main body of troops, slipping Desh's bracelets on as we left. I confirmed that hers worked when she disappeared beside me as if I had been hallucinating her. A soldier out of formation ran straight into my back and demanded to know what dripping bull's ass had gotten in his way and where the bull's ass had gone.

"That was fun to watch," Pil said.

"It sure was," Desh said from someplace behind us.

Pil and I glanced back, although we didn't stop jogging. Desh seemed to be no more visible than we were.

I took a deep breath. "Desh, why are you here? And you'd better not say to watch us assassinate Krak."

"I'm coming to watch you assassinate Krak. It will be the most momentous event in centuries, or even millennia. Even if you fail, it will be a historic happening. The whole thing should be chronicled."

"Chronicled?" Pil asked in a voice full of sarcasm.

"By me," Desh added. "I won't get in your way. I might even help." When we paused, Desh went on: "Look, I gave you all kinds of useful magic. That should give me some rights, shouldn't it?"

"You did give us some twitchy but probably useful trinkets," I

327

said, realizing that I couldn't argue him out of it. I understood that he didn't care about chronicling a damn thing. He was spouting that historical bullshit to hide the fact that he was coming along to protect us and probably die with us.

I heard the smile in Desh's voice. "Besides, do you want to go to the trouble of forcing me to stay behind?"

Sighing, I said, "You can stay as long as your chronicle makes me sound brave and handsome. Even beautiful. Hold here for a second, you two. It looks like the soldiers will reach the gods' force in about fifteen minutes." In fact, the formation was already skirmishing with the enemy. A few imps and what may have been a couple of demigods were tearing holes in the formations.

"Why are we waiting then?" Pil snapped.

I said, "Let's be sure we agree on where we're headed. We'll strike the lakeshore by that enormous bent tree. Then we'll follow the shore in behind the gods' lines. So—"

"Pil, why are you so angry at Bib?" Desh asked. "I guess this is a bad time to ask, but I likely won't be able to ask later."

"I'm not angry." She sounded like a little girl saying she hadn't broken a pitcher.

"That's all right. There's always a good reason for people to be mad at me." I tried to make it sound like a joke but did a poor job.

Pil acted as if Desh and I hadn't said anything. "Fine, ten minutes to the lake and then along the shore for who knows how long to find Krak. I've thought about this!"

"How will we keep from losing each other while we're running invisible?"

Pil hesitated. "I haven't thought about that." I could imagine her chewing her lip. "We can hold our belts between us. Of course, two disembodied belts bouncing along in the Dark Lands might look suspicious. And our pants would fall down."

"Just hold out your hand," Desh said. After ten seconds of fumbling around, he grabbed my hand. "Don't let go."

Just then a beam of impossibly searing light flashed out from the gods' lines and swept across the near edge of the battlefield. When it disappeared, at least fifty men no longer existed, and my eyes throbbed to the back of my skull.

I said, "That's Krak. Normally, he'd have killed a thousand, but they say he's puny in the Dark Lands. We'll find him by that beacon. Lucky."

"I didn't expect so much luck." Pil cleared her throat. "Bib, are you scared?"

"Hell yes, I'm scared!"

"Well . . . I'm not." Her voice was shaking. "You're such a baby."

The three of us ran down the gentle slope toward the black lake, holding hands like three children at the village fair. The gods' front rank seemed to be a loose collection of charging, bounding imps surrounded by scurrying, man-shaped creatures. I spotted what might have been a unicorn among them. The second rank was probably the demigods. They looked like men and women, but glowing weapons were scattered among them.

Darkness shrouded the third rank, so I couldn't see any details. However, Krak's beams of light emerged from that rank, so the gods themselves had to be there.

During the next few minutes, two groups of scorpions flew over us and an imp loped across our path only fifty paces away. None of them seemed to notice us. Our soldiers made a lot of noise—ferocious roaring rather than agonized screaming. Krak obliterated men with light three more times, but I wasn't looking right at it.

Halfway to the lakeshore, I pulled Pil and Desh to a halt. "Now. Sit on the grass, Pil. This next bit will make killing Krak seem like warm blankets and pie."

Pil plopped onto the grass and leaned back. "Crap! Who thought of this eyeball-as-a-weapon business? Krak? I hope it was Krak so he can say he's sorry before I kill him." She was babbling but stopped when I placed my thumbs above and below her eye.

Pil's body went stiff, and she groaned, but she held still as I removed her left eye. I healed her as I went, which I hoped would ease her pain. My left eye already hurt from witnessing Krak's searing light. Now I acquired some additional throbbing around that eye.

Compared to removing Pil's real eye, pressing the golden sphere into her eye socket was a holiday. When I finished, I probed the skin near her eye and felt tears, so I pressed my hand to her cheek. "That wasn't so bad, right? It'll make a good story back home."

She choked. "Hah! It was as easy as . . . hell, don't ever do that again, Bib!"

I sat back on my heels and grinned. "It's supposed to hurt, sorcerer. It makes you grumpy, the better to kill gods."

Desh started to chuckle and then cleared his throat.

The sounds of battle increased, at least twice as loud in a few seconds. Rank after rank of soldiers were charging into the gods' front lines, and all the men in each rank perished soon after they reached the front. But the men in each rank of Harbinger's men pushed forward, and they gained agonizing ground before they died.

Pil, Desh, and I resumed running. The smells of blood and burning flesh floated over us from the battle. Off to the right, I saw twenty men kill an imp, with human bodies flying as the imp threw them off before it was killed. Some sorcerer engulfed another imp in flames. I wondered whether Ace had done that. That imp charged toward the back ranks, flailing its arms. A demigod killed it, and the creature's body lay burning.

Within sight of the shoreline, I felt the ground tremble. A moment later, something with an absurd number of teeth jumped up at me from under the grass. It was the size and shape of a keg of nails with a circle of teeth on the top. Invisibility hadn't protected us from it, nor from four of its friends. They probably felt our footsteps as we passed.

I dropped Desh's hand as I drew my sword, rolled away, and hacked one creature halfway through the body. I heard Pil scream a foul word as I kicked another creature over. I thrust deep into it because I didn't know where it carried its vital organs.

I spun around toward Pil's voice. A monster stood behind her, wobbling like a barrel on its end. From the noises, I guessed that

Desh, still invisible, was ramming his sword straight down the monster's throat. Pil lay twisted on the grass, leaning against a dead creature while stabbing another one as it chewed its way up her left arm. Before I could reach her, the beast shuddered and went still.

Panting, Pil said, "The nasty thing ate my bracelet."

"That's not all he ate, is it?" I knelt over her. Her left arm was gone to the elbow. Her right leg had been eaten to mid-calf.

Before I could pull a band to heal her, Pil dropped her knife and grabbed my arm. "No! I can't be invisible now. My bracelet has been taken off."

I lifted my eyebrows. "Yes, in the most profound way possible. It won't work even if we cut it out of that squatty collection of saw blades."

Pil pushed my arm away. "So, you're the killer now, and if you heal me, it will hurt you." She panted some more but didn't faint. "You can't ask the Father of the Gods to hold still while you limp up and kill him."

"We're not going to leave you here bleeding to death!" Desh pulled off his belt to make a tourniquet.

I glanced around to see whether anybody or anything had heard Pil scream.

"Just go. I have a charm to stop the bleeding," Pil said, shivering.

"Sure you do," Desh said. "I have a cast-iron helmet that keeps a man hard in the bedchamber. Lay your head back so we can get some blood up there."

"I do so have a charm to stop blood!" Pil said without much conviction.

"You're in shock, so you're not stopping anything." I grabbed her remaining hand to slip on the ring that keeps you warm. "Desh will stop the bleeding, and I'll close the wounds. I won't do anything more because I don't want to listen to you bitch about it in the after-life that probably doesn't exist."

"Stop it!" Pil tried to slap me but missed because she only had one hand and I was still invisible. "Bib, don't waste healing on me. Something will find me here soon and kill me. If you fail because you stopped to help me, I'll . . ." She took a deep breath and relaxed a tiny bit. "I can't think of what I'll do, but it will be awful." Tears were running down her face, probably from the pain.

"You're right about every single thing," I said. "As usual. Now keep still and please don't kill me with that knife that you're holding but that I can't see."

Pil closed her eyes and stopped cursing me before I finished closing her arm wound. She hissed and grumbled most of the time I was working on her leg. When a sorcerer is healing, sometimes a wound can throb with a sharp pain for him. My leg and arm had begun doing that.

"Almost finished," I murmured.

"You're a bastard."

"That's objectively untrue. You'd know that if you ever met my mother. Now I'm about to make you hate me even more."

"Lutigan's baby teeth," she breathed. "I forgot that you need the eye."

"I'd spare you if I could," I said. "Before we do this, I need to tell you something important."

"Probably a bunch of lies."

"I'll say this anyway and you can judge whether I'm lying." I took a deep breath. "Pil, it's better that I'm taking over. I should do this murder instead of you."

"Oh? Do you want to cut off my other arm?"

I grabbed her collar with both hands. "Young woman, look right here into the place where my eyes are supposed to be. You're not full of death. You are filled to the top with anger, and you're pretty full of pain, although you can't admit it."

"No. I killed all those people." She shook her head hard.

"You helped them. If we could live longer, you'd see it eventually."

"No, I don't think so," she muttered.

I let her go. "Oh, you see that I'm right. I'm always right, and just you remember that. Pil, you will never want to kill somebody just because they're alive, so you're not full of death. It pleases me greatly that you aren't." I patted her shoulder. "I'm your friend. Lean back now so I can pull out your eyeball."

Three minutes and some harsh groaning later, I held the golden ball in my hand. "Now I get to have all the fun you had."

Removing my own eye was worse than I thought it would be. During the event, I whispered, "Pil . . . thank you for not cutting my throat when I did this to you."

Putting in the golden eyeball wasn't as bad. I don't know why, but I thought I'd be able to see with the new eye and maybe even have some kind of magical sight. But I couldn't see at all with that chunk of gold, no matter how magical it was.

When I had finished that little ordeal, I said, "Now, give me the amulets Desh gave you. And Desh, give me any more good ones you planned to give Pil. It's my mission now. The amulets are mine. Pil, you can have the rusty gopher one."

"What about the rings?" she asked.

I waved a hand before remembering I was invisible. "To heck with them. That dirt monster probably ate the best ones, which I don't think were too good to start with. Well, Desh, what do you intend to do? Come watch historic shit and probably die? Help Pil get back to Gek's army and probably die? Wait it out here and definitely die?"

"What do you advise?" he asked.

"To hell with waiting. And even if I'm not killed trying to wipe out Krak, I have only months or days to live when we get home. Pil's entire life is waiting for her. There's only one right choice, and you could make it even while drunk being stomped by thugs in an alley."

Desh shook his head. "I hate it when you're ambiguous like this. All right, I'll help Pil get back to Gek's army—and to Ella and Stan."

I said, "Desh . . . I'm sorry. When you came to Crossoak, I should have sent you home."

He smiled. "I'm responsible for everything that happened to me."

"Almost," I said. I knelt down next to Pil. "I'm sorry, I should have been more of a bastard so you'd leave."

Pil squinted. "I don't know what to say to that."

"Good. You've been my most patient friend."

She stared. "Most patient?"

"That says a hell of a lot, doesn't it?" I kissed her forehead and limped on toward the lake.

The battle reached its most violent and horrible point about the time I arrived at the shore. Hundreds of men were struggling and dying. I could hear them better than I could see them, but I spotted men driving well into the demigods. I saw at least a hundred men work together to overwhelm one of them. When those men had been massacred, the demigod didn't get up.

Gorlana, the Goddess of Mercy, anchored the gods' right flank, so I passed behind her forces first. She had planted herself behind her demigods, breathtaking in her sparkling blue armor. With no helmet to hide her long, blonde hair, she directed her forces to slaughter men by pointing with her mace, which was longer than she was tall.

None of Gorlana's personal army was guarding the lakeshore. If one hundred of our soldiers had been able to attack from out of the lake, they could have assaulted her unopposed and lived an extra minute or even two before being torn apart. But if a thousand men had done it, they might have survived to raise weapons against the goddess. They might even have killed her.

Still invisible, I dragged my throbbing leg past Gorlana's position and moved on to the area occupied by Chira, the Goddess of the Forests. While Gorlana stood back and commanded like a general, Chira fought as hard as her troops. Wearing holly-green armor, she relentlessly fired her bow, a weapon that was known to have never missed. She shouted orders to her imps and demigods in between shots. The fighters of her household chanted battle cries in unison.

Chira had posted three imps on the lakeshore to guard her rear. I paused, considering ways to sneak past them. Imps were not bright, but they weren't hopelessly stupid, either. Some, like Dark, were brutally clever. The idea of invisibility wouldn't puzzle them for long.

I pulled a white band to investigate the area, but I dropped it fast when I found that Krak was just beyond Chira's position. I didn't know whether he could sense my magic brushing over him, but the possibility shook me.

I searched more cautiously and considered various options. I could swim around the imps, but what if they saw an empty hole swimming through the water? Could I get the imps pissed off and fight each other? That shabby tactic was old when my great-grand-father was chasing girls.

How about sneaking through? The theory was good, but what if they started moving around for some reason, like being relieved of duty? I could be caught in the middle of them with no ability to control anything except my own little feet.

At last, I pulled a couple of green bands and whipped them far out onto the lake. Soon, a few lake weeds poked up above the surface and waved around slowly. I pulled a couple more bands, added a few weeds, and encouraged them to move faster.

"What the kidney-spitting hell is that?" the shortest imp said, pointing at the weeds.

"Could be a deadly trick," the thick one said. "You go find out."

"Why me? I cooked breakfast!"

The third imp, with a broken ear, said, "Breakfast tasted like dragon ass after the dragon puked in its own asshole, that's why! Go!"

Shorty clamped his teeth shut and swam toward the weeds. As it swam, I threw five more bands. When Shorty arrived, one hundred weeds slipped around the beast's body and pulled it under the surface.

"Hey! Where'd Silvereyes go?" Broken Ear yelled, running to the water's edge.

"Silvy is just screwing around," Thick said. "You watch. Just screwing around."

The two imps watched.

I had never imagined that imps had names so melodious as Silvereyes. It was nice to learn something more before I died. Silvereyes was still struggling hard twenty feet under the surface, so I kept adding vines until the imp was cocooned and not struggling so much.

"I don't like this," Broken Ear said.

"Just screwing around!" Thick brayed with his hands on his hips. "Silvy'll show up in ten minutes, and we'll laugh about the whole thing."

"No, no, and by your shiny groin, no! You go see."

"Eat your own ass end!" Thick yelled.

Broken Ear pointed. "Go! Now!"

"Damn you! Too stupid to pull your ear out of the fire." Thick waded out into the lake.

With Broken Ear busy watching Thick swim away, I sneaked past the imps at an aggressive limp and moved on down the shore. I drew my sword, even though I didn't expect I'd be able to use it for anything.

Krak himself stood fifty paces on down the line, wearing white armor so bright I could hardly bear to look at him. His white hair hung tousled to his shoulders, and he had both hands on his hips. He was scanning the battlefield.

My entire body went stiff. I tried to pull a band to determine what sort of defensive magic I had been caught in. Neither of my hands could move, not even the tiniest wiggle of a finger. I calmed my breathing and blinked my eyes a few times. I swallowed.

Krak raised his hand, and I closed my eyes. The beam of light he hurled shone through my eyelids. I shook my head before opening them again and then realized what was happening. Krak didn't have defensive magic as most people might understand it. When I looked at him, his unfathomable presence had petrified me.

I had never seen Krak before other than in the trading arena, which must make his presence more bearable to piffling beings like me. How bad would it have been if he had turned his gaze on me?

I drew another deep breath and was able to move.

Eleven demigods were arrayed in front of Krak. I almost froze again when I saw Sakaj, Goddess of the Unknowable, twenty paces beyond Krak in shimmering armor that shifted from color to color. Like Krak, she was surveying the battle. With a start, I realized that the sounds of fighting had begun to fade.

Krak boomed, "If the bastards can't fight any harder than this, we can stay here to the end!"

Sakaj flipped back her night-black hair. "Why did Cheg-Cheg attack us with men? It makes no sense at all."

"Maybe he's lost his damned mind! After you and I whacked off his foot, I'll bet the strain has left the hideous old thug demented." He and Sakaj both laughed.

"Perhaps he'll leave us alone now, Father."

"Maybe," Krak said. "It may not be done until one of us is dead. Damn shame."

I activated the amulet that prevented people from hearing me, and I hoped it worked on gods. I approached Krak from behind at the stealthiest limp I could manage. When I was thirty feet away, I released the god-killing eyeball's power with just a thought.

Krak began warping, liquifying, and oozing downward. My breath caught. The demigods beyond him started melting too, and they became bubbling lumps within seconds.

I took a step back to watch the Father of the Gods die. I saw that the eyeball had melted all of Krak's white armor until it slid into a puddle around his unharmed feet. Krak's legendarily muscular self was now naked and not melted a bit. He stared around with his mouth open, as if somebody had dared to tickle his bottom with a torch of terrible and unyielding flame.

"What the hell?" Krak grunted.

I realized that I had made the same mistake Yita made. I had stopped to watch my enemy die. Except that he didn't die.

Before I could think about it, I staggered toward Krak and thrust my sword at his chest. It was a perfect blow, and the blade pushed twelve inches into that mighty chest, piercing his heart.

Krak stared at his chest and then right at me. "You little turd." He yanked my sword out of his chest, and it shattered into thousands of tiny shards. His other massive hand shot out and grabbed me by the neck. "Murderer? Is that you?"

Krak patted my arms, legs, and body as if he were searching for a weapon. When he came to Desh's invisibility bracelet, Krak laughed in the cruelest way I could imagine. He used his thumb and forefinger to pinch off my left hand at the wrist.

I screamed.

The Father of the Gods shook me like a doll. "You presumptuous bit of repugnance! You tried to kill me! You are mine now, Murderer. The battle's over, so I can devote my full attention to you."

THIRTY-NINE

I first encountered Krak when I was a young sorcerer hardly out of training. My teachers had warned me never to do even the tiniest thing that might anger him. In fact, I should hope to never hear his voice. If I stumbled into his presence sometime, I was to make a quick excuse and leave once he gave me permission.

If Krak did not permit me to run away screaming, in no case should I say anything that I thought was clever. I was to speak when spoken to and hope I didn't need to speak at all.

I asked my teachers why I should follow all these rules about this particular god, even if he was extra powerful. During my studies, I had already dealt with three gods, so by then I knew everything. One of my teachers explained that talking to Krak was like dancing on the rim of a volcano.

I nodded but wasn't convinced.

One day a few years later, I found myself waiting in the trading arena, listening to Gorlana and Trutch shout at each other about something they wanted me to do. They suddenly went silent. Trutch stopped talking right in the middle of a word.

Something vibrated in my hearing, a profound note almost too low to perceive. The sound started in my left ear and flowed across to my right. It reminded me of the great whales that would pass beside my father's fishing boat, full of mysterious power. I imagined that this noise felt like one of those whales if it was ten times bigger, twenty times cleverer, and infinitely greater in malice.

The sound faded to my right until I could hardly hear it. I hesitated but couldn't help myself. "Mighty Gorlana, do you think Father Krak would be interested in solving this dilemma?"

The noise rushed back toward me and then filled my ears as if I were being swallowed. I forced myself to appear calm. That worked as well as forcing myself to throw a ship across a lake. At last, the sound moved off to my right, steady and relentless, until it faded away.

I am now convinced that Krak was passing through the trading arena. If so, he was probably cursing those goddesses and me hard enough to pulverize marble. How could I have heard him? I have learned to see as the gods see, and if that's because I'm one one-thousandth part god, maybe I could feel Krak vibrate as the gods feel Krak vibrate.

Also, a few seconds after the noise ceased, Gorlana flung me back into my body, and no god would answer me for the next five months. I consider that compelling evidence.

In the Dark Lands, after I got caught failing to assassinate Krak, he lifted me with one fist clenched in my shirt front. He hadn't grown four feet in two seconds to grab me around the waist as he might have done in the Gods' Realm. I focused on that happy fact since it would probably be the best thing I would experience before my death.

Krak tossed out an echoing, malevolent laugh. "It would be just like you to try some pissant sorcerer magic on me, Murderer. Let's not tempt you now." The bastard had already pinched off my left hand. Now he grabbed my right. I screamed as he twisted with divine might to tear off that hand. He dislocated my elbow and shoulder along the way.

My head hung and my ribs heaved.

"I'm aware that you can do magic with your toes, which makes you the chimpanzee of the sorcerer world." Krak smiled and tore off both my feet at the ankles, one after the other.

I screamed until Krak asked in a calm tone, "What in the name of the Void's nasty corners is that thing in your eye?" I shook my head frantically. "Sakaj, do you know what it is?"

"I do not, Father Krak." Sakaj's voice was as mesmerizing as ever, but I hardly noticed.

"Fingit, what about you?" Krak swung me toward Fingit and turned me sideways so that my left eye was easy to examine.

"No, Father," Fingit said. "I've never seen anything like it." Fingit's voice was tense. He probably didn't want Krak to know that I'd been spying for him.

"Huh." Krak lifted me so that my face was a foot from his. "Well, you two are the only gods with any thoughts beyond screwing and drinking, so I guess it's a mystery. Whatever it is, we can't have the Murderer turning demigods into goo, can we?"

I babbled, "No, it's nothing at all, nothing."

Krak stuck a finger into my eye socket and removed the golden eyeball with a pop. I howled like a dog.

"Where did you get this melty thing, eh?" Krak asked.

After groaning and sweating for a bit, I said, "Bottom of a big hole in the Dark Lands. Father Krak."

"That's interesting. I'll have to go there after I chase Gek's ass out of this realm. Or kill him, I guess."

Lutigan had arrived at some point and was standing beside Krak. "The Murderer tried to kill Father?"

Somebody said yes.

"And he actually struck a blow? Twice?" Lutigan rubbed his knobby jaw. "It would be easier to believe if you said he knocked Mount Humility across the realm with his penis."

"Don't sound so impressed!" Krak bellowed. "What the Murderer has done is unequivocally bad! Quite bad indeed. Here, Lutigan, hold the little butt chunk."

Through the pain, I felt myself passed across to Lutigan like a platter of holiday ham and laid out on the ground.

"Who are you working for, Murderer?" Krak asked. "Tell me

now, and I'll have Lutigan impale you with one of his swords. The pain will cease. Speak."

I tried to think clearly. I settled for being able to think at all. Harik had wanted me to spy on the other gods, and Fingit had said the God of Death was missing. I glanced around and didn't spot Harik among the half dozen gods who had gathered. I licked my lips and said, "Harik."

"Damn it and damn him!" Krak shouted in a voice that I could feel in the ground. "What did he say?"

Fingit was glancing between Krak and me.

I croaked, "He wanted me to spy on you. Then kill you at the start of the battle."

"Shit." Krak stared at the ground and looked truly old for a second. He grumbled, "I hate that. Harik went over to Gek. He was always an aggravating, disobedient tit, but now he's a traitor, and I have to kill him." Krak looked up and rubbed his hands together with a smile. "Can't be helped!" He glowered at the other gods. "All of you listen and listen hard! Traitors get killed. Really killed. Dark Lands killed."

Krak heaved me up above his head. "Let's see what other parts you don't need anymore."

"What about killing me with the sword?" I asked.

The Father of the Gods showed me his perfect teeth from two feet away. "You really are stupid, aren't you?"

A woman shouted, "They're coming again!" Trutch, the Goddess of Life, charged into the ring of gods wearing brilliant yellow armor that was almost as hard to look at as Krak's now-melted armor. "Another wave is coming fast, for men, that is. They simply appeared on the field two miles away."

"Gek. That clever, grunting hog. Hiding his army with magic." Krak pointed toward the front line using the fist that still held me. I swung like an old pillow and wept. "How many are there?"

"Sixty thousand." Trutch paused while Krak stared at her. "Well . . . maybe only fifty-five thousand."

Krak ground his teeth but then stood straight and defiant. "We shall defeat Gek and his pathetic collection of puny men! We are the gods! None match us in might or majesty!" He raised both arms in a sign of victory with me still dangling from one of his hands. "I order an immediate strategic withdrawal back to the Gods' Realm where we will position our forces to crush Gek by surprise—at a later time."

The gods rushed to agree in relieved voices.

Krak lifted me and shook me a little. "I have more to concern myself with than you, Murderer. That's too bad. You have been as annoying as a grain of sand somewhere in my nether parts. I wish I had a few free centuries in which to torture you, but . . ." He shrugged. "Really, you're dumb but less than completely pathetic and nasty, as sorcerers go."

I wheezed, "Father Krak, I am part god. A tiny part, but . . ."

"Really? Part god? Sure you are."

Krak slammed me against the ground. I felt bones shatter and organs burst inside me for a moment. I tried to scream but couldn't push out any air. Then my entire body below the neck went numb —I expect from a broken neck. Krak was already striding away.

Desh's amulet would allow me to strike one more blow after a mortal wound. I couldn't die until I struck that blow. Well, these wounds were about as mortal as one gets, but I would never strike another blow, not even with magic.

Did that mean I would live forever now as a carpet of smashed and crunchy flesh? Desh's magic couldn't be that strong. Maybe it would fade in a year to let me die. Or in ten years. Or maybe in a thousand.

Perhaps I'd only live until my body rotted. I mouthed the words "Thanks a lot, Desh" with my broken jaw and teeth. My tongue seemed whole. I could think, so my head must have taken the least damage. After all, Krak had been hanging on to my shirt at the neck.

Krak paced back to me and knelt down. "I'm sorry, Murderer. That was thoughtless. Blink if you're still alive."

Malevolence inspired me. If Krak came close enough, I could try to bite him. I didn't blink.

Krak leaned down further. "Blink, boy! Blink!"

I held still to bait him.

He grumbled, "Damn it to my hairy toes." His mouth twisted like he smelled something bad.

I thought Krak was about to stand up, so I blinked.

Jumping to his feet, Krak shouted, "Aha!" He turned his head and yelled, "Weldt, you owe me fifty unicorn steaks!"

Krak's hairy toes were a foot away from me. I snapped my teeth toward him, but I guess I was too far away for the magic to consider that a real attack.

"Krak!" one of the gods shouted, probably Casserak.

The Father of the Gods glared at somebody down the lakeshore.

"I mean, *Father* Krak. We can't go home!"

"Stop babbling, you selfish little squeaker!" Krak growled. "That's nonsense. Of course we can go home." High above me, Krak held still for five seconds. Then he closed his eyes and strained as if he were having a bowel movement. That lasted for half a minute or so before Krak's breath exploded out of him. He snarled around at his children with his head low like a feral dog.

Most of the gods started apologizing for allowing bad things to happen, or for not fixing them, or for just being unworthy.

"Quiet!" Krak bellowed. "Everybody, command your defenses. Lutigan, get ready to counterattack. Sakaj and Fingit, you figure out what in the name of your mother's harsh spine is going on with this business about not going home. Is Gek doing it? Is that little turd Harik responsible? Find out and kill whoever needs to be killed to make it stop!"

Krak spun back toward Gek's army and may have stepped on me, although I couldn't tell for sure with my one fluttering eye. "And keep the trash off the beach!" he shouted. Krak grabbed me and hurled me into the lake.

The murky water felt cold on my face. Since my body couldn't hold air, I began sinking. I wondered which of Desh's charms was saving me from drowning. The one that kept me from being smothered in Krak's armpit? Or the one that kept me alive after a mortal wound? It didn't matter, but the question occupied my mind. I might need a lot of questions to occupy my mind over the next thousand years.

My face struck the soft lakebed and my head settled as thick soil pushed up my nose. I strained with my lips and tongue to turn my head and free some of that dirt. I had begun to make progress when the lakebed started rumbling. Some unknown tons of shifting soil slid onto me from above and kept sliding for a good while.

I was buried, but Desh had taken the first step to save me. He had given me the perfect charm for this situation. It would allow me to move through the earth like a gopher, I could make it work just by thinking about it, and it never wore out. It was ideal.

Too bad I gave it to Pil before I ran off to kill Krak.

FORTY

I have never accepted bad things without a fight, even when I deserved them. When I did deserve them, I fought especially hard. Throughout my life, from boy to old killer, I have dreaded being unable to fight back.

When I realized I had been buried, helpless in a Dark Lands mystical lake and that I might be there for years or centuries, I prepared myself for panic and shock. Those feelings didn't come, though. Instead, I felt calm and quiet. My whole life I had struggled against everything and everybody, and no more struggle was possible.

Whatever evil I had done, it was too late to make up for it, and I couldn't do any more of it. No matter what good I had done or love I had given, now it was beyond my ability to screw it up.

Maybe being buried in the lake wasn't going to be so bad. It felt a little like being rewarded in that afterlife the gods insisted was real. Although I was now buried in a destroyed body, so long as I could relax, then it would be a reward. I suppose that said something about how I lived my life.

I let those thoughts float along for a while before I realized that I had been striving for this a long time. Not smashed and buried, exactly. Accomplishing something and finding an end. I had come close more than once. It was clear now that agreeing to kill Krak had been stupid as hell, and I had known it. I embraced death to accomplish something that might have been good, although now I doubted it.

The important thing was this: Nobody who has killed the way I have killed deserves any kind of reward. So, even if being buried in a lake did nothing other than relax my mind, I had come out ahead on rewards.

This was what I thought about while I was buried.

Soon after the slow-motion avalanche ended, I heard whispering. Mostly I wanted to rest, but the part of me that likes to kill and raise hell got excited. Maybe Desh, and Pil, and Ella were searching for me. If they were, I needed to signal them.

After hard thought, my best plan for signaling was to dig through the soil with my jaw until I created a visible depression in the lakebed above me. Realistically, that would take several years or maybe dozens. My teeth would wear away long before I finished.

My other plans were worse.

I listened hard, hoping to make out the whispering. Suddenly I heard every damn sound on the lakeshore and beyond, an enormous assault of noise. I'd have flinched and cursed if either had been possible. When I thought about quieting things down, the noise pulled back in to just beyond the shore.

I listened for a few more minutes and realized that Desh wasn't looking for me. Neither was Ella, Pil, Stan, Bixell, Stan's unicorn, nor Yita from beyond the veil of death. They must have thought I was dead, and they were 99 percent correct.

I relaxed and accepted the calmness again, although I kept listening to the beach. Maybe I would hear the gods weeping and cursing themselves for being mean to sorcerers, just before Gek killed them.

My mind drifted until I heard Krak bellowing from a distance. All I needed to do was try harder to hear him, and then his voice was clear.

"What about the front rank?" Krak was asking.

Lutigan's voice said, "Nine-tenths of the imps are dead. All the bulgers are either dead or run off."

"Damn them!" Krak snapped. "I'll throw them off a thousand-foot cliff onto a million pissed-off serpents!"

"They don't mean a flame-farting thing now," Lutigan said. "Thirty thousand troops are pushing into the demigods all down the line. The damned men are killing too many. They can trade a hundred of theirs for one of ours."

"We'd kill them all in ten minutes if we were in the world of man," Chira said. "Father, you could do it by yourself in eleven minutes."

"Well, we're not in the world of man, are we?" Sakaj said. "We must conquer in the realm in which we find ourselves."

"That's very wise," Fingit said. "So wise I'll sit at your feet so you can teach me until my butt falls off! Arrogant bitch!"

"Impotent weakling!" Sakaj sneered.

"That's enough," Krak said quietly. Everybody stopped talking. Even the sound of battle faded for a couple of seconds. "How is Gorlana?"

"Holding her guts in with one hand," Chira said. "I won't say she was asking for it, but she's the only one wounded so far."

Krak said, "Has anyone seen Harik?"

There was silence.

"Lutigan, will your counterattack succeed?" Krak asked.

"Yes. We'll split them apart, surround them, and defeat them in detail. I'll make sure we kill them all."

"That's it then?" Fingit said. "With his army gone, we can stay safe here until Cheg-Cheg leaves our realm. Once he's no longer blocking us, we'll make a triumphant return—"

Krak cut in. "You can ease up on the 'triumphant return' shit. We all know what this was."

After a long space of silence, Lutigan asked, "What if Cheg-Cheg has another thirty thousand troops hidden someplace? Hell, he could have a hundred thousand."

"If he does, that could be the end," Sakaj said. "We'll all be dead. Except for Harik, may an ocean of lava flow up his penis.

Father, you should have let me kill him the first time we came here."

"To hell with regrets!" Krak boomed. "We fight like gods! If we must die, we'll die like gods! If we fail, Gek will kill us, destroy our works, and obliterate all that we have touched, but even then, we still have . . ." Krak sighed.

"A shining span of glory," Fingit said.

"Good enough," Krak said.

Lutigan said, "Father, are you sure the Murderer is dead?"

"Why do you keep asking about the Void-blowing, red-rimmed Murderer?" Krak shouted. "I crushed him entirely! When I crush things, they are crushed beyond belief. Do you disagree?"

"Of course not! It's just that he succeeded in striking you. Something is wrong with that."

"Forget him. He was crushed, and anything left over was drowned."

The gods must have rushed off to fight then. I couldn't hear them even when I tried to listen farther away.

My mind drifted as I considered what the gods said. There was a lot of talk about fighting, and there were some interesting insults. It sounded as if the gods might lose and be destroyed, which would show that the universe loves us at least a little bit.

I kept coming back to one thing Krak said. Gek would obliterate everything the gods had touched. Well, the gods had touched sorcerers, who had touched the entire world of man.

I had come to doubt that Gek could wipe out vast numbers of people the way he claimed. But did he need to? Even if he could only destroy extremely large numbers of people, that could be enough. He and all his Void Walker friends could spend a year or two on the job and kill every wriggly human that existed. I wouldn't bet it was impossible.

Too bad I was no longer concerned with such things. I had struck my blow—twice—and now I was done.

Of course, my attacks had failed. Or maybe they hadn't. From my vantage down under the bottom of the lake, it seemed that Harbinger and his men had died as a diversion to help me kill Krak, but Gek didn't plan for me to succeed. Hell, he sent me to kill Krak with a weapon that couldn't hurt Krak. I was probably supposed to get myself loudly killed as a diversion for Gek's main attack of sixty thousand men.

In that light, my mission had succeeded, but to hell with that. I didn't so much mind being a diversion, but I'd sure as hell like to know it. That son of a bitch Gek had tricked me into it.

And my mission succeeded in doing what? Was I helping Gek destroy the gods, do some shitty Void Walker victory dance, and trot on down to kill every person in the world of man?

I had struck my blow and was done, but that was like drinking one round and going home. Well, maybe it was more like drinking one round, getting stabbed in the chest, and falling off your chair.

Analogies were a good way to convince anybody of anything.

It sounded stupid coming from somebody smashed nearly to death and then trapped under the earth and the water, but what had I really done? Murder a lot of people, do a thing or two to help a few folks, and then die. And I didn't even goddamn help them in the end!

As legacies go, that sucked. I didn't give a gold-plated dog's ass about legacies, but I'd rather not have one unfit to blow my nose on.

In my heart, I was no longer Gek's servant, but he didn't have to know that. I'd call on him for help. I wondered whether he'd breathe water as a little bird or show up as a little fish. Or maybe a little duck or a turtle. My mind was drifting, so I focused.

I mouthed the word "Gek." He didn't answer. I felt he must be able to hear my thoughts, even if I couldn't make sounds. He was a goddamn Void Walker. I called him again, over and over for a long time, but he never answered.

I blinked twice and realized my mind had been drifting. I had been calling Gek. Well, if Gek didn't care to talk, I'd be forced to call on a god. There was only one choice. All the gods seemed to be trapped in the Dark Lands except for Harik. He might be carousing at home in the Gods' Realm while Gek murdered all his kin. I'm not sure anybody who knew Harik would doubt that.

My jaw was stiff, but I worked it to mouth, "I'm calling you,

Mighty Harik. Answer my plea." No answer. "I am ready to deal, Your Magnificence, and I'm highly motivated to trade." Still no answer. "If you can hear me, stomp your left foot twice."

Harik either couldn't hear me or didn't care to help me. I called on Fingit to test the theory that gods couldn't hear us in the Dark Lands. I may as well have been trying to shout across the ocean.

Since I was on my own, I took stock of my resources. I could move my jaws, tongue, and eyelids. I could wiggle my ears a bit and flare my nostrils. I could move my one eyeball, which didn't sound as if it would prove decisive, but I added it to the list.

My first goal would be restoring one of my hands. Even buried, that hand should be able to pull enough power to heal myself back from the point of death. I might need my other hand along the way. Everything would be crude since I couldn't actually touch with my hand the places I was healing.

I thought carefully about when to heal my neck. I needed to heal it before I could use my arms. But my pulverized body would be shockingly painful. I might be in too much pain to do anything. My broken neck was all that kept the pain away. It was a tricky problem, but not my first one in this endeavor.

I had never tried to do magic using my tongue before, but why wouldn't it be possible?

Maybe it was possible, but the next half hour showed that it was impossible for me. I finally gave up on employing my tongue to fling bands of sorcerous energy. I tried all the other moving surfaces on my head. I couldn't make any of them work, either.

That was so discouraging that I tried to contact Gek and Harik again, but they still ignored me. I took a chance and called for Lutigan, since he seemed to care whether I was alive. He didn't answer, either.

I considered what else I could control. I could swallow, sort of. Ten minutes of that produced nothing useful, which didn't surprise me. I couldn't move my brain, but at least it was something I could control. Fifteen minutes into my brain efforts, I tried to pull energy, and something pulled back.

I had never once, in my long career as a sorcerer, thought it might be possible to use magic without some physical motion. Then again, I had been a sorcerer for over twenty years before I realized I could use magic with my feet. My teachers had never mentioned non-wiggly magic as a real possibility, although people joked about it.

But I had never seen a god wiggle their fingers before they used magic to fling another god across the gazebo or make it rain sausages. They just stood there and made it happen. Was my itty-bitty speck of god blood making this possible?

I set all my questions aside for now. If I lived through the next couple of days, I could investigate the mysteries of brain magic. When I told Desh about this new mystery to explore, he would act like I had given him a puppy.

My plan changed. Who needed to restore a hand when I already had a brain?

I used my mind to heal the wounds and broken places in my body as well as I could, which wasn't too damn well. Then I healed my neck. The pain made my eye roll, but it was bearable.

Once my whole body could feel again, I discovered something exciting. My body from the shoulders up, including my arms, was buried, but the rest of me wasn't. Suddenly all kinds of things became possible. I lay half-drifting for a good long while and plotted. It was long enough for some of my pains from healing to fade.

I got my badly healed legs under me and pushed using the raw stumps of my ankles, hoping to pull my head and arms out of the lakebed. I pushed some more and shifted to different angles, but they wouldn't come free. I mouthed curses for a while and listened to the ferocious sounds of battle.

No weeds or other plants were sturdy enough to dig me out. As for animals, the lake was empty. I wasn't going to suck myself out with a tornado or blast free with lightning, even if I could do such feats in the crazy Dark Lands sky. No amount of healing would pull me out of the lakebed.

With a shock, I realized I'd have to save myself using the opposite energy. I used my mind to pull blue bands and began rotting off my left arm. It wasn't quite that simple. I killed the flesh at the top of my arm until I couldn't stand any more pain. Then I healed the shoulder-most side as much as I could without closing the gap I was creating. Then I would create some more rotting pain to go along with the pain from the healing I had just done.

It took a hell of a long time to remove my left arm this way. The battle noises had died away, but I heard the gods making plans for the next wave. I got my legs under me again and pushed. This time, my head and arm pulled free, scraping through the soil. I passed out and drifted underwater.

When I woke up, a good amount of the pain had disappeared. Instead of swimming ashore, I floated in the lake and healed myself —first my right hand, then my feet, and then all the bones and organs that I'd given a poor healing job the first time. At the end, I was missing a left arm and a left eye. I still had quite a bit of pain, as well as a profound disgust for Gek, the gods, the lake, the entire Dark Lands, and for myself too, as long as I was being disgusted with things.

I waded out of the lake a few hundred paces down the beach from the gods. I'm sure I looked like some dripping dead thing rising from the black water to commit evil acts, and maybe that's exactly what I was.

The sounds of battle were rising again, but my first task was to find Pil and Desh. I had abandoned them for what turned out to be a stupid reason. Helping them, if they were alive, came first. Everything and everybody else could sit down, shut up, and wait.

FORTY-ONE

I swaggered away from the lake in the Dark Lands, searching for Pil and Desh. I pretended I was swaggering to show I was aggressive and confident. Actually, I was so damn tired I couldn't move any faster.

My strategy for finding my friends consisted of searching for the last place I had seen them and then sort of hunting around. The Dark Lands didn't have many landmarks other than trees. Most of them looked the same, but a peculiar bent tree stood near the lakeshore. I calculated a triangle in a few seconds using the tree and my location, and I set a distant point as my goal.

If I was correct, I had left Desh and Pil somewhere along the line I was staring down, so I swaggered my ass along. I hoped that none of those leg-eating keg monsters found me, since I was unarmed.

Half an hour later, I admitted that my math had been poor, or else Pil, Desh, and the five dead keg monsters had been carried away by wicked Dark Lands pigeons. I began walking in circles. My body was done with swaggering. Along about the third circle, I heard a faint noise. It was a far-off click, softer than a whisper. I concentrated on listening to it, and Desh's charm pushed my hearing far out. Somebody was yelling, so I urged myself to jog that direction.

Within minutes, the voice sounded like Pil. Soon after that, I saw two dots through the clear air. One tiny, waving figure stopped shouting and grew into Pil while Desh supported her. I ran to them since Pil had only one working leg, waving harder although I had only one working arm.

"How did you know I was out there?" I asked as Pil hugged me one-handed and Desh whacked me on the back.

"I heard you," Pil said.

"Bullshit."

Pil said, "Desh isn't the only one who can make charms to improve your hearing. Why do you think I'm always the first one to hear things?"

"Did you kill Krak?" Desh asked. "If you did, why are you still alive?"

"I didn't," I said. "It's too complicated to explain right now."

Both Pil and Desh looked as if they'd been rolled in dirt for a week. Black soil had been ground into their faces, hair, and clothes, so their smiles looked bright even in the dimness.

"Why are you two so filthy?" I asked.

Pil said, "Oh, I burrowed us into the ground so we could hide. That gopher amulet you left with us probably saved our lives."

I looked down so she couldn't see me smile. Despite everything, she sounded enthusiastic—a bit the way she'd sounded before all her killings.

"Here, sit down," I said. "I'll heal your foot."

"Do you have enough power?" Desh asked in a doubtful tone.

"I have been using quite a bit, but I had ten squares from Harik and five more from you. I have more than twelve left."

Pil whistled.

I handed Desh the five unopened wooden bottles of power he had given me. He grinned, handed two back, passed two more to Pil, and kept one for himself.

"Bib, healing me will take time." Pil pushed my hand away.

I said, "It would take a hell of a lot more time to wait for you while you jump along on one foot. And we're sure as spit not going to carry you back home. And don't even open your mouth to suggest leaving you behind. I've done enough of that."

Pil smiled again. "All right, if that's the way you feel about it." She held out the stump of her leg, and I started the work of restoring it from mid-calf down.

I was halfway done with Pil's leg when I heard Harik's voice. "Murderer!"

He sounded close, so I stood and glanced around. The god was a quarter mile away and stalking toward me. His black robe billowed even though there was no wind. Harik was accompanied by three beings with fanciful clothing and glowing weapons. I had to assume they were demigods.

I glanced at Pil and Desh. They looked pale underneath the dirt. We had no chance to outrun Harik and his repugnant spawn.

Swallowing, I yelled, "Mighty Harik, how did you find me?"

"I am the God of Death! None may veil themselves from me. Also, if you wish to remain concealed, ask your friends not to scream your name for five minutes."

"Excellent advice, Your Magnificence. I am ready to report on the gods' situation! To summarize, their situation is shitty."

"I do not require your disordered observations in order to know that." Harik kept walking toward me, implacable as an avalanche. The demigods, all three of them female, flanked him. I pushed out my chest and walked toward the God of Death while showing that my hand was empty.

Desh murmured from behind my shoulder, "I'm with you."

Rising to her knees, Pil called after me, "Bib! Don't go far!"

I slowed down. "Harik, what's this war about? I don't understand. What do you get out of all the hell and uproar, anyway?"

He smiled. "I shall be Monarch of the Gods."

"All the gods will be dead. It'll get mighty lonely on your throne. Boring too."

"New gods can be created. It has been done before. Do you think that all of the gods you know have been gods from the beginning like me?" Harik came close enough that I could fling a stone at him, had that been at all helpful.

The idea of new gods was a fascinating sliver of information. I started pulling yellow bands, not that I expected to find anything that would help us. I just didn't want to give up. Harik glanced at my fingers, looking amused.

"Harik, maybe your daughters here can be made into goddesses." I pointed at the especially beautiful one with powerful shoulders under her black-and-red armor. "She can be the Goddess of Adultery and Other Shameful Behavior. This other one here can be Goddess of That Nasty Spot Downhill from the Privy." I waved hello at her, a tall, blonde woman in a bright pink robe, with intelligent eyes and a clenched jaw. "And this one . . ." I pointed at the dark-skinned one in golden armor that somehow made her look like a wolf. "She can be the Goddess of Walking behind Harik and Cleaning Up the Shit He Breaks. I bet you repopulate the Gods' Realm before lunchtime."

The blonde demigod raised her spear and charged toward me. Since she was a supernatural being and I was a weaponless, one-armed man, she was due a certain amount of confidence.

"Here." Desh held out his sword without looking at me.

"Enchanted?" I asked as I took it.

"Enough for this."

I thought back to the day I had barely survived my battle with the demigod, Memweck. Now this demigod thrust two rapid, deadly strikes, and I guided both past me. Either would have ended my life. She hesitated a smidge before the next strike. I'm not sure what she expected me to do then. She clearly didn't expect me to dodge her next attack, rush in, fake a swing at her hand, and thrust my sword into her chest. Her eyes popped open right before I halfway decapitated her.

Stepping back, I handed Desh his sword as I watched the body fall.

Harik frowned. "Ladies, I suppose I should have warned you about him."

I laughed. "Harik, you puling, pasty-ass halfwit, Gek will kill you before you think about making a single new god. He doesn't want gods around making the universe into an orgy of tidiness and repetition."

"Oh, now you understand the designs of the great powers, do you?" Harik sneered. "You have always been pompous and offensive. Now you have become grasping and repellant."

Every conversation with Harik reaches a critical point. Perhaps the preliminary blather reveals something he wants. Otherwise, you either shoot for a graceful exit, or you attack him with everything you have and hope something useful falls out. There in the Dark Lands no retreat was possible, and I had no damn clue what he wanted. All I could do was attack.

"Speaking of great powers," I said, "your mother said she's disappointed that you turned out so pretentious and unmanly. Mara does still love her little boy, though."

I had hoped that barb would anger Harik so that he'd make a mistake. Instead, he *hmphed* and glanced at his remaining demigod daughters. "Bring the Murderer to me and kill the other two."

I reached out for Desh to hand me his sword again. That's when portals opened on either side of Harik, vomiting imps at us.

"Crap!" Desh spat as he tossed the sword at me. He dug in a pouch while yelling, "Don't get in front of me!"

I didn't answer him. Both demigods were advancing on me, not hurrying a bit. They angled to trap me from both sides. But before they attacked, an immensely brilliant flash of light exploded from Desh's direction.

The demigods hadn't expected that flash, but I sure as hell had. I lunged left and mangled Golden Wolf's sword hand, then spun and thrust through Black Armor's face. Black Armor fell straight down, already dead. Golden Wolf turned to run just as another flash of light ripped the sky behind me. That made her flinch. I stabbed her in the back and beheaded her from behind.

Two more shots of intense light came one after the other. Pil bellowed, "Bib! Here!"

I skipped back toward Desh to guard him. Three imps were

charging toward him, but when I moved up, he yelled at me to stay back.

Pil flung what appeared to be a rock into the closest portal, and it smashed like a pane of glass. "Bib! Help me to the other one!" she shouted.

Another blast of light slapped me. I glanced back at the three imps that had been about to overrun Desh. I saw only six burned-off, glowing imp legs on the ground.

I had done away with the demigods. If Desh could control the imps and Pil could close the portals, we would still all die when Harik decided to draw his sword and cut us in two. All this heroism and dirty fighting would have been for nothing.

Harik looked unhurt by Desh's blazing attacks. He had stepped back to a better spot for witnessing our destruction, watching everything with an oily smirk. I had thought that my disgust for him couldn't grow any larger, but it did then. If I were the God of Death, I would sure as hell show a little more class than this.

As I helped Pil stumble around behind Desh, I pulled one more yellow band, flung it out, and squeezed at what I had found.

Four of the keg-shaped, leg-eating creatures burst out of the ground at Harik's feet. A squatty one actually started chewing its way up the god's ankle. Scowling, Harik cursed and swatted at the monsters, trying to drive them away like they were overexcited puppies. More of the beasts boiled out of the ground, climbing on top of the ones at Harik's feet. One of them clamped on to Harik's left hand and gobbled it to the wrist.

Just as Pil destroyed the second portal, Harik began cursing and threatening me. I encouraged more of the chomping beasts to leap out of the earth as it broke open. They hadn't eaten the god up, but they were making a damn good effort, clamping onto him all over.

"Come on! Run!" Desh yelled. We hefted Pil between us and hurried past Harik toward Gek's army. Dozens of the keg monsters had engulfed Harik as if he were an ant mound. He fell over sideways as we passed him.

Desh and I ran as fast as we could while carrying Pil. I doubted these creatures could digest a god, and I didn't know how badly Harik was hurt, but I didn't want to dally regardless.

Half a minute later, Harik thundered from behind us, "Stop right there!"

We stopped. We turned. Harik's robe had been chewed away, and bloody gashes marked his entire body. He was using one hand to flail around with his sword. The blade was white, black smoke drifted off it, and any creature it touched shriveled as it fell to the ground. He used his other hand to scrape the beasts off his body and throw them out to easy slashing distance. Harik shouted, "That was awful and repulsive! Disrespectful! Just rude."

We didn't run. There was no place to go. We were mice.

Harik finished withering the keg monsters and laughed. "Do you know what's funny? Murderer? Nub? Knife? Do you know? Murderer, you called these nasty creatures to obliterate me. But now they're dead!" He raised his eyebrows. "Dead!" He rolled his eyes. "Oh, you are obtuse." Harik swept his hand in a circle over his head.

When the God of Death waved his hand, every one of the dead, withered keg monsters stood up.

"Rolling bastards!" I yelled. "I'm an idiot!" I had metaphorically handed the god a gigantic hammer for smashing us.

Pil took one step to run away and fell down. Maybe she had forgotten she'd lost a leg.

Desh started yanking things out of pouches with both hands. "Hide!"

At least fifty newly dead keg beasts ran toward us in a herd, teeth clacking.

"Hide where?" I yelled.

Pil knocked my feet out from under me, grabbed my hair, and shoved both our faces into the grass.

Light exploded above us, brighter and more piercing than any so far. It kept going, burst after burst, for seven or eight seconds. I started wondering how long it could go on. It faded for a moment but then blazed again, even brighter and sizzling without any pauses this time, for another fifteen seconds. Finally, it ceased, as if Desh had slammed a door.

I rolled to my feet almost into the mouth of a scorched, staggering keg beast. I jumped aside and killed the creature. Two more of them came at Desh, who was lying on the grass. I killed both of them too.

I didn't see Harik coming when he leaped to knock me down and planted his bare, uneaten foot on my chest. His sword seemed to disappear in his hand. I could hardly breathe as Harik brushed ash off his bare, muscled arm. "You have always possessed the ability to aggravate me, Murderer."

"Don't you mean . . . anger you? I'm Lutigan's . . . descendent, after all."

"Bah. A sickly ploy."

He was right; it was a puny effort to distract Harik, but I was running out of tools. I asked, "Don't you need to hurry . . . back to the Gods' Realm . . . to help Gek . . . keep the gods trapped?"

"He is managing that without me. I expect him to return here soon." Harik leaned over me, putting a little more weight on my chest. "There are a few things I want to say to you before you die. You are a nasty, eye-dripping piece of goat filth. May your groin become a brothel for frothing vermin. May your spirit collapse in putrefaction and your body curdle in blight. You are the false and hopeless ruin of your children's most cherished dreams. Do you understand me, Murderer?"

I nodded.

"Wondrous. Goodbye." A few seconds passed before Harik tilted his head. "Why aren't you dying? I own you. You should be vomiting up your stomach and liver right now." He furrowed his brow like a man whose stove suddenly makes things cold instead of hot.

"Oh!" I jerked my head up. "I think Krak said I belong to him. I guess . . . you can't just wish me dead anymore."

Harik sneered. "That merely affords you a few more seconds."

A knife hurtled past me, slicing into Harik's calf and spinning on.

Harik glared at Pil, shifted his feet, and turned toward her. It took most of his weight off my chest. He glowered and bared his teeth at Pil as his sword appeared in his hand.

An instant later, Pil's knife showed up in my palm. I swung it up and cut off Harik's thumb.

Harik's sword fell out of his thumbless hand. He called me a baboon's penis and bent to grab the weapon with his other hand.

I snatched the sword off the ground and plunged it through Harik's chest as he bent over. He reeled backward fifty feet with the sword sticking out of him before he pitched over and lay still.

I ran back to Pil, who was balancing on both knees.

"I'm fine," she said. "I'll check on Desh."

Grabbing her arm, I said, "Wait. We may not be done fighting."

I held Pil's knife, waiting for Harik to sit up, fly, or drop a house made of diamonds on us. A minute or so passed, and none of those things happened.

"Holy shit," I breathed. "Is Harik dead?"

"Go poke him," Pil said, now standing with a hand on my shoulder.

"I'm not going to poke him! I don't trust him. Here's your knife."

Pil grasped the knife. I tried to see where she put it but failed.

"I think he's trying to fool us," I said. "What do you think? Are you hiding some magic doodad that can tell whether somebody's alive? From all the way over here, I mean?"

Pil turned and stared at me. "Don't you think he can kill us from a lot farther away than this if he's faking?"

I took a deep breath and strolled over to Harik, ready to die any moment. He looked awful. His face was sunken, and his hands were bony. I had thrust the sword right through the center of his chest. The skin around the wound was white and puckered.

Pil asked, "Is he dead?"

"Yes." I was already running to help Desh, who lay face down on the black grass. He wasn't moving, and I pulled a green band as I ran. Dropping to my knees, I pressed my palm against Desh's back. I couldn't feel life in him, but that didn't mean anything. Even back home, I sometimes could be mistaken. Here in the damned Dark Lands, life was even more elusive.

Pil arrived, hopping on one foot, just as I rolled Desh onto his back. She made a strangling sound and then breathed, "Krak! Look at his hands . . ."

Desh's split and melted fingers were charred black and no longer looked like something that belonged on a human being. It was appalling but didn't concern me too much. Healing his hands wouldn't be a grueling task. I spun another band and lay my hand on his chest. Desh's shirt had burned away, and his hairless skin was brick red.

I searched for Desh's life, glancing at Pil, who had sat on the grass and pulled Desh's head into her lap. All of the young man's hair had been singed from his face and his balding head. His round cheeks were blistered. Pil bent her head down and started whispering into Desh's ear, the one that hadn't been burned off.

I found no life in Desh with the second band, either. I took a deep breath.

"Don't you stop!" Pil shouted. "If you stop, I'll never talk to you again!"

"I wasn't going to." I pulled three green bands, reconsidered, and pulled six more. I sent them spinning through Desh with one hand against his chest and the other on his forehead. I shouted, "Come on, Desh, you're a cruel, baby-kicking bastard for scaring us like this! Open your eyes! A duckling could do that, and you're a mighty sorcerer."

Pil yelled, "Desh, come back! Limnad is waiting for you!" Pil's face was wet with tears now.

We shouted encouragement and threats. After a minute, I felt a twitch, and I lifted my head.

Pil glanced from Desh to me and back. "What? What can I do?"

I kept searching for a minute, pulled more bands, and continued the hunt, but at last I realized that twitch had been my imagination. My mind knew how much I wanted Desh to live, and it was happy to provide me some delusion.

"Pil, he's gone."

"Damn it to hell!" she burst out. "He shouldn't have come with us, and I wish he hadn't, although if he hadn't, then I guess we'd be dead, and Harik wouldn't be dead at all. Shit! No good thing happens in the Dark Lands. I never really believed that until now." She hung her head and began crying harder.

I sat on the ground beside Pil and held her while she wept into my arm. I'm not too proud to admit that I cried for Desh too, and any bastard who wants to criticize can go choke on an imp's nuts.

After a time, we quieted down. I patted Desh's burned-red shoulder. "When I first met Desh, he had no clue what sorcery really was. Well, he faced down a god using sorcery today."

"I wish we could take him with us," Pil said, a few tears still sliding down. "I don't want to leave him in this horrible place."

"I don't think we have much choice, at least for now. But wait here a minute." I ignored Pil when she asked why. I rushed around gathering the dead and withered keg-monsters, stacking them in two piles on each side of Desh. Then I collected the demigods' glowing swords, and I lay one on Desh's breast, as if he could grip it with his ruined hands. I jammed the other two into the ground above his head. Finally, I severed all three demigods' heads and lined them up under Desh's feet.

Pil said, "That's . . . some monument. You know that Desh would laugh and tease us for laying all that crap around him."

"I know, but we're not doing it for him."

Pil nodded. "We're doing it for us. It makes us feel better, I guess."

"To hell with that! We're doing it so that anybody who wanders by will look at Desh with the appropriate awe and fear. They should be terrified that he'll sit up and start lopping off heads." I helped Pil stand.

"Of course, that's why." Pil sniffed and cleared her throat.

"We'll come back for him if we can," I said. "Pil, if you get home and I don't, you have to tell Limnad."

Pil glanced at me with a worried look.

I trudged back to Harik's body and reached for the sword in his chest.

"Don't!" Pil shouted.

I pulled the sword out.

"I was going to say, 'Don't do that.'" Pil shook her head.

"I'm declaring Harik dead. Just as dead as Desh. Maybe more." I examined the sword in my hand.

"If Harik's not dead, I'm sure he'll be impressed by your declaration."

I said, "Now . . . Pil, how do I carry this blade? What's the secret?" The black smoke floating off it dissipated not far above my head. "I don't want to stick it in a scabbard and carry the thing around next to my crotch."

Pil glanced back at Desh before she turned to me. "Harik doesn't even have a scabbard. The sword's probably too dangerous for that."

I felt cold. "Pil, can you tell me what this sword does?"

"You know one thing it does."

"It kills gods."

She nodded. "Now you know everything I know about it. So, how to carry it—you probably noticed that I don't carry my knife in a sheath."

"That has caught my attention once or twice. Like now." I looked at her hand. I hadn't seen the knife there, but now she was holding it.

"I keep the knife in another realm, a tiny one. I bring it out when I want it, and I can bring it back to me through that realm." She waggled the knife in her hand. "Also, I didn't know it until today, but I can use the realm to put the knife someplace else—like your hand."

"You didn't know you could do that?" I asked. "What if you were wrong?"

Pil gave a lopsided grin, which disappeared when she glanced at Desh again. "Harik would have killed us both. Don't be such a baby about things." She hesitated, and her eyes looked strained. "Bib, I'm sorry I was so mean to you. Nobody's responsible for what I do but me."

"You don't need to apologize."

"I want to before you . . . while you're still alive," she said. "Do you forgive me?"

"It's not my place to forgive you or to judge you. But I'll go so far as saying that you're above average."

I kissed her head when she hugged me, and then she taught me how to find and use a distinct realm of my own for my sword. I had already begun to think of it as mine.

When Pil was seated and I had begun restoring her leg again, I said, "You should know that Gek isn't our friend. In fact, he wants to kill every human being, young and old. I guess he'll spare the dogs and cats, but he's still a son of a bitch."

Pil was quiet for a minute, then two. "I trust you on this, although I sure hate to, and I don't know what we're going to do about it. He has Ella, and Stan, plus Ace and maybe lots of other hostages. We can't kill Gek."

I raised an eyebrow. "We killed Harik."

"That's different! Harik couldn't grow taller than three trees on top of each other, or gush acid, or eat us both in one bite. If you try to stab him, he'll laugh while he's stomping us smaller than dust."

I said, "Maybe he can't grow to monster-size here in the Dark Lands. The gods seem a little wobbly, so maybe he is too."

"I guess . . ." She leaned her head forward and rubbed her forehead. "If you try to kill Gek, I'll go with you."

"We can't go yet. We need to make a deal with the gods first."

"Krak's nasty toes, why?"

"I want to make them be nice to us," I said.

Pil gaped at me. "Well of course. That's so stupid, it's brilliant."

"Good, you can—"

Pil cut me off. "No, I'm sorry. It's so stupid, it's stupid. You tried to kill Krak, so the gods will obliterate us the moment they see us."

"Maybe not." I patted her restored foot. "There you are. One nice, new foot. Sorry I can't replace the boot that monster ate off you. You can pay me back, though, by fetching me Harik's hand— the one that's still got a thumb."

Pil didn't hesitate. She jumped to her feet, trotted to Harik's body, and severed his hand using her sharp knife. She brought it back and handed it to me. "Bib, I hope you don't mind that I'm keeping Harik's thumb to use when I need it for some magical feat I haven't thought of yet."

I waved my hand before I thought about the fact that it was holding Harik's hand in it. "Keep his toes too, I don't care."

"I almost said I should keep a toe for Desh." She rubbed her eyes while glancing back at Desh's body.

"No time anyway," I said. "It sounds like the battle is in a lull. Let's nip over there and bargain with the gods. Since I only have one arm, I need you to hold Harik's hand over your head as our calling card."

Pil nodded. "Right. So stupid, it's stupid."

We marched side by side up the lakeshore to meet with the gods.

FORTY-TWO

Pil and I strode along the beach until we came within a hundred paces of the gods' position. A raspy-throated woman running toward us shouted, "Stop! You're my prisoner!" She held a long, curved blade over her head in a fine position to split my skull.

"Pil, wave Harik's hand harder," I murmured. Then I called out, "We surrender. Take us to Krak."

I could see the woman straighten and blink at me with her unbandaged eye. I figured her for a demigod, since she wore a silver waistcoat under a long, ocean-blue jacket, a crimson shirt, white trousers now bloodstained, and shiny black shoes. She was squat with long arms, so she made a memorable sight.

I said, "Is there a problem? Do you want us to fight back? We're unarmed, but I could throw mud at you."

"No . . ." she said.

"No to the mud, or no to the fighting back? You've got to be specific."

Most of the demigods I had met were stupid as hell. She fit right in.

368

"Wait right there! And no mud!" she yelled. Another demigod, a tall and handsome fellow, was charging up to join her. He moved well even though a bloody bandage was wrapped around his chest.

I decided not to aggravate them more than I had to. "Look!" I pointed at Harik's hand, which Pil was waving back and forth. "We killed the shit out of that traitor, Harik. Take us to Krak so we can tell the gods all about it. We're unarmed. You don't need to be scared of us."

The tall demigod who was running to join our little celebration swung a long, straight sword at my head. I grabbed Harik's sword out of its realm, cut this lanky thug's blade in two, and thrust into his thigh. He fell squealing, and suddenly his trousers hung loose when his leg withered.

"Stop crying, your leg probably won't stay withered forever." I pointed the blade at the other demigod, and she backed away. "Sorry, maybe we are just a little bit armed." Pil and I walked past her, and I put away my sword.

Thirty paces later, Chira and Lutigan ran toward us with their weapons drawn. Chira had a shocking, open wound on her neck, but she didn't seem to notice it. I couldn't tell whether Lutigan was wounded, but he was as blood-soaked as if he'd stood under a blood fountain all day. Both gods slid to a stop and stared at me, which I appreciated. There was no way I could defeat the God of War in single combat, and I damn well knew it.

Lutigan muttered to Chira, "I don't know how the Murderer is alive, or why, but somehow I knew that he was."

Chira rubbed her face. "Krak killed him. Krak smashed him and drowned him, but now he's strolling around here like it's an orgy with dancing. The Dark Lands really is a place of insanity."

Lutigan yelled, "Murderer, how come you're not dead?"

"Mighty Lutigan, when it came time to die, I said that I wouldn't goddamn go."

"Smartass," Chira said.

I nodded. "Maybe. But the Knife and I are the ones toting around Harik's hand."

Krak strode up behind Lutigan, followed by Fingit and Weldt. Krak's mouth and eyes opened wide for a moment, which almost looked comical since blood had run down his forehead and dried around his eyes and nose. Then he raised his chin, which was still nobler than any other chin in existence, growling, "Am I supposed to be impressed?"

"Not at all, Father Krak," I said.

"Gek saved you, didn't he?" Krak said. "Come over here so I can smell you. Come on, don't dawdle. I hate dawdlers!"

"Father Krak, I served Gek once, but I don't now. I've seen what the raw bastard plans to do. And no, he didn't save me."

I doubt that Krak actually grew taller, but he stood straighter. "Are you defying me, sorcerer? Defying me, just hours after you bloody tried to kill me? Lutigan, bring me some of his organs. Any three, I don't care."

Lutigan drew one of his swords.

I backed up fast and almost ran over Pil. "Wait! I want to help you get out of here and back home!"

Lutigan wasn't rushing to cut me apart. He took a couple of deliberate steps toward me while I backed away, scrambling like a terrified goose, if geese could scramble backward.

I shouted, "Father Krak! Gek thinks I'm serving him!"

"You probably are serving him!" Krak roared.

I shouted back, "He won't know I'm on your side! I can do something to hurt him! There's nothing I can do to hurt you now, so don't worry about that!"

Krak raised one hand. "Hold on a moment, Lutigan. Keep your sword ready. Murderer, what do you think you can do to help us?"

I hadn't thought out this part of my plan too carefully. "Gek sent me to kill you, so I'll go back and convince him you're dead."

Krak laughed. "Nobody would believe that you killed me."

"Nobody would believe that I survived your beating and lived to kill Harik, either."

Krak bared his teeth.

Fingit said, "Father, let's hear his plan." His words were garbled, and I saw a great, bloody wound on the side of his jaw.

Lutigan said, "I agree with Fingit, a fact which I find appalling. What's your plan, Murderer? You do have a plan, don't you?"

Pil jumped in. "Give us back the golden eyeball. That will convince Gek that we killed you, Father Krak, because if you were alive, you'd never let us leave with it. Then tear a sleeve off your robe and stain it with your mighty blood. Bib will wound me but not quite kill me, so we can credibly say I was hurt while escaping."

Krak scowled.

"Wait, I'm not done." Pil held up her hand, which was still holding Harik's hand, to interrupt the Father of the Gods. "All of that crap will help us convince Gek that you really are dead. He'll unblock your way home, planning for the surviving gods to go back to be ruled by Harik—"

"Stop there," Krak interrupted, nodding. "That may be the stupidest plan I have ever heard."

"Well . . . we're open to improvements," Pil said.

Krak said, "If you are cooperative and humble, I may allow you to help us a bit. Gek will never allow any gods to return home just because of something you say. And your efforts to convince Gek that I'm dead sound ridiculous. A child would be embarrassed to consider them."

I glanced at Pil. "Father Krak, what are you proposing?"

"Here's a thought," Krak said in a meditative way. "We last drove Gek away by cutting off his foot. This time, you'll drive him away by using Harik's sword to wither the other foot. Impaired and shamed, Gek will flee and stop blocking our return to the Gods' Realm."

"Can Harik's sword hurt him?" I asked.

"It can with my help." Krak's grin was nasty. "I will provide better evidence of my death than a fake eyeball and a bloody sleeve."

I glanced from Krak to Pil and back. "It can't be that simple."

Krak clenched his fists. "Sure, there are inconveniences, but nothing important. When you strike Gek, the sword will be destroyed. Gek may try to kill you too. You'll need to step fast, or he will succeed."

I said, "Father Krak, I may agree to do this, but I want something in exchange. These fees that gods charge sorcerers after a bargain—they have to stop. No more giving up thirty years of life after a bargain. No more paying with a child's life."

Krak shrugged. "If you are successful and we return to the Gods' Realm, that is acceptable. It was Harik's little scheme anyway."

I almost reminded Krak that he was the one who had allowed Harik to act like a terrorizing ass, but that wouldn't have helped things. "Thank you, Father Krak, and I want something else. The gods will stay out of the Dark Lands from now on. If nobody goes there, nobody can die the real, Dark Lands death."

Krak glanced at Fingit, who gave a little headshake. Staring at me with no expression, Krak said, "That's acceptable. We didn't want to come to the Dark Lands in the first place. Miserable place. If Gek agrees to stay out, I will agree."

"Thank you. One more thing. I want the exchange rate on power reduced from one thousand to one down to ten to one."

All the gods fell silent. At last, Krak said, "You must be insane. I would rather see every god dead and scattered across the Void."

"Is that a counteroffer, Father Krak?" I asked.

Krak shouted, "No, it's not a damned counteroffer, you malodorous smear of filth!" He took a step toward me with his fists clenched.

"I see," I said, trying not to piss myself. "Then is there a counteroffer you'd care to make?"

"Yes!" he thundered. "I offer to smash you flatter than worm shit and fling you into the ocean!"

I stared at him.

Krak pursed his lips. "I guess that didn't work out so well last time. Very well, I will lower the rate to eight hundred to one."

"I see. How about fifty to one?"

"No, not fifty to one! You are straining my patience!"

I sighed. "Thank you, Father Krak. Come on, Pil, let's go." We turned around and walked away from Krak along the lakeshore.

"Don't turn your back to me! Come here!" Krak said. "All right, seven-fifty to one."

Pil and I kept walking.

"Damn you! Six hundred to one."

I turned and strode back toward the Father of the Gods, smiling. "Thank you, Father Krak! How about one hundred to one?"

Krak's right hand opened a fraction, and a pinpoint of light escaped. My head pounded, but I ignored it. Krak snarled. "Five hundred to one, and that's the last thing I'll consider."

"Except maybe for two hundred to one?"

"No!" I could feel the force of Krak's bellowing in my bones. His hand started glowing as he scowled at me. He shouted, "No, not two hundred, not three hundred, not four hundred and damned ninety-nine! I mean five hundred to one, and that is the end! Beyond that point, entrails start flying!"

"Yes, Father Krak, five hundred to one it is!" I ducked my head.

Krak rushed over and grabbed my arm so fast I couldn't twitch. Then he spoke as if we were neighbors building a shed together. "Murderer, you won't be able to pierce Gek's skin, even with that sword you lifted from Harik's stinking corpse, unless I help you." He drew a knife that was quite a lot nicer than any knife I had ever seen, made a cut across his left wrist, and then made a cut across my right one.

My voice went up as I said, "Father Krak, what is this?"

"Quiet," he said in a mild tone. "You've come this far. Don't let your courage fail now." He pressed our wrists together so that our blood intermingled, and he chuckled. "When it comes time to share stories about the most interesting thing that's ever happened to you, you'll have everybody beat from now on."

When Krak let go of my arm, I found that the cut wasn't much deeper than a scratch. Then he shocked me by holding his own arm up against a tree and slicing off his left hand at the wrist. He sheathed his knife, picked up the hand, and held it out to me. "Show this to Gek. It ought to convince him that I'm dead. Well, I guess it would be better if you had my head, but this will have to do."

"Um, thank you, Father Krak."

"Hah. I suppose you do have a dash of the family blood in you. Not enough to mean anything. Now go strike down our enemy! And try not to embarrass us." He pointed across the battlefield and then dropped his arm as his face fell.

I peered that direction. Three or maybe four miles away the three-hundred-foot-tall form of Cheg-Cheg appeared, striding toward us.

"He's here! Hurry! Somebody, try to go back home!" Krak yelled.

Based on their less-than-divine babbling, I gathered that over the next thirty seconds every god tried to reach the Gods' Realm. Nobody made the trip.

Krak said, "Well, hell. That's an unwelcome development. Cheg-Cheg's here, and we're still trapped. Murderer, if Cheg-Cheg reaches us, he will kill us all, and that means we'll die forever. It won't take him too long to crush us worse than I crushed you. Don't screw around now. Go!"

I ran toward Cheg-Cheg, clutching Krak's severed hand. Pil ran right behind me. We faced about two thousand of Cheg-Cheg's troops advancing in front of him. I silently thanked those soldiers for being there. On his own, the monster could probably saunter to us in a couple of minutes, but those troops kept him from moving faster than a man could run.

Cheg-Cheg plucked a tree out of the earth and flung it toward us. It crashed onto the ground sixty feet to our left, showering us with dirt and small branches. The tree skipped on behind us like a stone on a pond.

Pil passed me, shouting with a wild note, "Gods! Gods protect us! Run faster!"

I ran faster, but I didn't answer her. I was too busy watching archers preparing to put dozens of holes in us as soon as we came into range.

I waved Krak's hand over my head as I ran and then laughed at myself for doing something so asinine.

"Murderer!" somebody yelled indistinctly off to my right. I looked and found Fingit pacing me.

He said, "Keep running! There's another choice! You can use Krak's power to heal Gek's missing foot."

I laughed. "Really? Hell, I'll just do that! Then Gek won't want to kill me!"

Fingit said, "Well, it may not work. And he may want to kill you even more."

"More?" I yelled. "What if it does work, though?"

"He may be grateful and give you a gift. But maybe he'll try harder than ever to kill you. He may look upon you as a traitor— which I guess you are."

I yelled, "Shit! Why should I even try healing him?"

"If you do, he and Krak may stop trying to kill each other. They'll go back to regular war where nobody dies. That would be a good outcome, right?"

I ran without commenting for a few moments.

Fingit added, "Or, maybe it's a bloodbath no matter what you do. Also, if you heal Gek, you'll never be able to heal anyone again."

"Screw that!"

"I know, that's pretty bad," Fingit said. "But once you're in the process of healing him, that's a great time to betray him. Pull out the sword, wither the other leg, and run like hell. It will destroy the sword, but you'll still be able to heal."

"Did you say that 'run like hell' is part of the plan?"

"I didn't say it was a perfect plan, or even good," Fingit said. "Well, that's all. Those arrows will be here in a minute."

"I hate you!"

"Good," Fingit said. "I'm a god. You're supposed to hate me. It's the proper relationship between sorcerers and gods." Fingit ran back toward the other gods.

Pil shouted, "We're not going to do any of that stuff, are we?"

"I don't know. It's so screwed up, we could probably try to do all of it."

"No! We run in, you stab, we run away. That's it. Right?" Pil yelled. "Right?"

I pointed. "Look! Arrows!"

I didn't know what I wanted to do, but I didn't want to say that to Pil. I didn't think I could lie to her now, either. So, I had never been more grateful to see dozens of deadly missiles flying toward me.

FORTY-THREE

ek's soldiers fired a storm of arrows at Pil and me. When she shouted, "Save yourself! I'm fine!" I felt no more urge to protect her. She was a sorcerer, not a duckling. If she wanted help, or applause, or somebody to laugh at her, she'd have to ask.

However, I ran right into a problem of mechanics. My five surviving fingers were busy hanging on to Krak's severed hand, and I didn't want to throw the thing on the ground. I had learned to do magic with my brain, of course, but my brain didn't have much practice. I didn't trust it to save me from twenty or thirty arrows coming my way.

I stuck the Father of the Gods' severed hand in my mouth and started pulling bands to rot arrow shafts.

One arrow scraped my elbow out of that first volley. I felt another fly in between my legs, but I had chomped down on Krak's hand in time to save myself. Pil looked to be in good shape except that she was staring at Cheg-Cheg with big eyes and a slack mouth.

I took Krak's hand out of my mouth and shouted "Pil! before stuffing the hand back in.

She glanced at me and nodded, staring straight ahead as she ran.

The next arrows were fired about twenty seconds later. Although Pil appeared to be doing nothing at all to defend herself, arrows curved away from her and even snapped in midair for no reason. I felt pleased that she was safe and perversely aggravated that she didn't seem to struggle. I mumbled curses around the hand while pulling bands like mad.

The archers didn't have time to fire again, so they fell back behind the front line, happy to let their foot-soldier friends stab us to death. I pulled Krak's hand out of my mouth and waved it like a battle standard.

Bixell's voice clanged at the soldiers in their own language so loudly my ears hurt. The soldiers halted, and Bixell pushed his way through the lines toward us. "Bib! It's very fine to see you alive. Some claimed that you had betrayed us. I was more optimistic and thought you must have been killed."

Pil and I trotted to meet Bixell, our chests heaving from the run. "Betray you?" I gasped. "You know me better than that. I'm a liar and a killer, not a betrayer. I'm bringing Gek some good news."

"No, within the hour, he will kill all the gods. That is the only good news he needs! Is that Krak's hand you're holding?"

I glanced at the hand. "How do you know it's Krak's hand? It could be anybody's."

Bixel laughed. "That's funny, Bib. I needed a chuckle. Anybody can see that's the hand of Krak. You should study more."

I stared at the hand. It looked like any old hand to me. "Sure. It's Krak's hand. I can't fool you."

Bixell peered. "Why are there tooth marks on it?"

I took a breath. "That's part of the news too. Everything's part of the news. I need to talk to Gek. Not to titanic, mountain-eating Cheg-Cheg, but regular-size Gek."

Shaking his head, Bixell motioned for us to follow. "You can ask him, but you shouldn't hope that he will change shape. The destruction of his eternal enemies is at hand. Changing now would be like putting your trousers on while making love."

Bixell led us through the lines of soldiers. Once behind the lines, I saw that Cheg-Cheg was still nearly a mile away. The next thing I saw was Ella smiling and grabbing me in a brutal hug.

"I thought you had news for Gek," Bixell said while I was kissing Ella.

I ignored him. "Ella, are you hurt?" The side of her head was covered with dried blood.

"It's not important." She sighed, leaning against me. "Famm and Ace are dead. We would all have perished but for them."

I hugged her. "Desh is dead too." Saying it felt like a punch in the stomach. I realized that I hadn't really believed he could die here.

Ella stared at me with wounded eyes, her mouth opening and closing like she would ask whether I was joking. Then she leaned her forehead against my shoulder and sobbed for a few breaths. Before I could say anything else, Ella stepped back, pale and rubbing her cheeks. "We can grieve when the battle is finished, right?"

"That's wise, I guess," I said. "Where's Stan?"

Ella sagged for a moment. "Stan is badly wounded."

I looked past her. "Where is he? I want to see him."

Bixell shouted, "Bib! Do you have news for Gek or not?"

"Of course I do. Pil, would you please tell Bixell how we came by this news? We can't leap into these things without context."

Pil smiled at Bixell, and even through all the grime, it was a moderately devastating smile. She took his arm, the one not holding a gory, eight-foot-long sword. "I'm happy to see you alive, my friend. I can tell that you've suffered." She patted his hand, and the big warrior's shoulders dropped as he let out a sigh.

I followed Ella at a run more than a quarter mile down the line and into the rear. We found Stan lying on his back with his purple hat wadded up under his head for a pillow. He held his blood-soaked stomach with both hands.

"How long?" I asked Ella.

"He's been lingering since the first attack."

Stan smiled at me, and I wondered whether he had lost another tooth. He croaked, "You ain't dead yet, Bib! It wouldn't have been right you getting your head or something whacked off before I was killed."

Ella had knelt to lay a dirty wet rag on his forehead.

Stan shook his head. "Bib still alive. The world ain't entirely horked up here in these Dark Lands after all, is it?"

"To hell with all this," I said. "You'll outlive me, Stan. Be still."

Stan's belly wound would have killed him soon, but I found it wouldn't be too hard to mend.

When I had been working on Stan's wound for a few minutes, Bixell tapped my shoulder. "Cheg-Cheg is here, but he won't alter his size for you. Whatever you have to tell him, do it now."

I glanced at Bixell and was surprised to see tears on his face. "I'll be there in two minutes."

"He's ready now," Bixell clinked. "No one keeps the Dark Annihilator waiting."

Behind and far above Bixell, Cheg-Cheg tilted his head and stared at me. The boom of his voice shook me to my guts. "I have no use for you now, Bib." He reached down with one clawed hand.

"Cheg-Cheg, I am about to tell you something you have never heard before, not once in your entire spooky existence. But I won't say it until I've healed this man. Hell, those gods over there are terrified. If you shouted 'Boo!' half of them would fall over dead. A few more minutes won't change that. And aren't you immortal? If an immortal being can't wait for two minutes, I'm not sure this existence is worthy of people like us."

I turned back to Stan, ready to be crushed into lumps or burned up with acid by Cheg-Cheg. When those things did not happen, Stan said, "Nobody around here has the nuggets on 'em to tell off old Beakface there but you. When we get back home, you and me'll stomp into every tavern we see and tell the pissing old drunks this story. They'll beg to buy us drinks!"

"You go ahead and save me a table, Stan." I met Ella's eyes.

"Bullshit!" Stan said. "You're just talking all miserable so people'll think you're mysterious and feel sorry for you. I seen you do it a dozen times. We've come this far, and we're going home soon. I can feel it."

"I can feel it too," I said, holding one hand across my belly pain from healing Stan. "All right, we'll be going home. I just have one thing to do first." I hesitated. "Oh, hell, I can spare another two minutes." I shifted over and healed Stan's teeth and gums. Afterward, he stared at me, holding his mouth. I had never seen him unable to get a word out.

I turned and held up Krak's hand so that Cheg-Cheg's eyes, hundreds of feet above me, could see it.

The monster reached down and snatched me between his finger and thumb. He squeezed the air out of me, and I wondered whether he had broken one or two of my ribs. I kept waving Krak's hand like an idiot, though.

"That hand does not mean Krak is dead," Cheg-Cheg said. The blast of sound was like being slapped. "That just means Krak will have trouble putting on his shoes."

I sagged inside. If Cheg-Cheg knew Krak was alive, he'd be too wary to let me walk up and stab his good leg. I had to convince the monster to let me heal him. Then I could either do it properly or betray him.

"I'm not saying that Krak's dead," I shouted, even though five seconds earlier that's exactly what I wanted Cheg-Cheg to think. "It means that he has given me some of his power."

"You haven't said anything that I have not heard before." Cheg-Cheg raised his other hand and pointed one of his claws straight at my face.

I rushed to say, "I came here to restore your lost foot, using the power I got from Krak."

"That's a ridiculous thing to say. Are you begging me to scratch off your head?"

"I'm not!" I yelled. "Krak didn't want me to heal you. He gave me the power for something else, but I came here to heal you with it."

Cheg-Cheg paused for a few seconds. "Why did he give you this power?"

"To make me more persuasive." I was lying my ass off now. "To convince you to let the gods go home."

381

"Ah. And you want to heal me instead. Why?"

"The same—to convince you to let the gods go home. But I figured healing you would be more persuasive than just talking to you."

Cheg-Cheg opened his beak, but I cut him off. "I also want you to stay out of the Dark Lands. The gods will stay out too, so nobody will have to worry about getting killed." The lies were flying around thick now, which made me nervous.

The monster paused. "Anything else?"

"Not really."

"I do not find any of that persuasive," he said. "There must be another reason for your behavior."

"Well, I am your servant."

"Then I command you to be silent and heal me now."

I winced. "Maybe I'm not quite that much of a servant anymore."

"Which is why you didn't kill Krak for me." I wasn't sure that Cheg-Cheg's beak could pout, but it came close.

"The weapon you armed me with didn't work! If it had, Krak would be draining away into the lake right now!"

"Complaints are the refuge of the weak." The Dark Annihilator Gek squeezed me again, and I gurgled.

I nodded and smiled, deciding right then that I would betray the smug bastard and wither his other leg. "That's fair. All right. The real reason is that if I can end the war, I'll look so good that Krak will reward me with power and gold and women." I glanced down at Ella, glad that she couldn't hear me.

Cheg-Cheg tilted his mythically enormous head. "I have heard that the gods think you're stupid. Perhaps you really are."

"But consider this!" I yelled. "How many more chances will you get to heal your foot? Krak has only one more hand." Technically, I wasn't lying. I just didn't mention that Krak gave me the power before he gave me the hand.

Cheg-Cheg clicked his beak. "If you restore my foot as it was, I promise to let the gods go home. I will then leave the Dark Lands.

But I do not promise that I will never return. I see you looking as if you cannot trust my word. Have I ever lied to you or cheated you?"

"Not as far as I know, you arrogant dimwit with genitals that flap like laundry." I nodded. "Put me down then. I need you to be a hell of a lot smaller than this."

Cheg-Cheg didn't object. He set me down near Ella and Stan. Then he scribed an enormous circle on the ground, which became a hole, and he walked down into it. A moment after the hole closed, a man-size hole opened and Gek climbed out.

I said, "Sit here on the ground with your legs stretched out."

"Very well. Please observe that I have taken a hostage to ensure your proper conduct."

I heard Ella cry out behind me. Gek had found or created a five-foot-tall tree stump, and Ella lay on top of it faceup with the stump in the middle of her back. Heavy-looking weights had been chained to her ankles and wrists, dangling so that none of them touched the ground. It looked painful as hell.

"Set her free!" I shouted.

"Hurry up with your work. That is the fastest way to set her free."

I was definitely going to betray this son of a bitch and wither the shit out of his leg, and maybe his crotch too, as soon as he was too distracted to turn me into a bucket of frogs.

Gek's false leg looked like a marvel of magical and physical construction. Desh would have loved to spend a week or two taking it apart. I set it aside and began mending Gek's ankle, and I had never seen a wound so resistant to healing. It seemed more like old, dead wood than flesh. Within a minute, I was sweating. Ella's cries and moans didn't help my concentration.

Just as I was making good progress and burning quite a bit of power, Ella's groans ended with the sound of a body hitting the ground. I glanced around and saw Stan helping Ella to her hands and knees. Every chain had been snapped. Pil stood thirty feet away from Ella, ignoring her and Stan so hard it was almost funny.

"I will just restore those chains," Gek said.

"If you do, I'll stop right now. You can tell I'm healing you, right? Should I stop?"

Gek sighed. "No. Continue. I will pay the closest attention to your work."

I didn't like to hear that, but at least Ella wasn't suffering. She was on her feet with Stan steadying her.

Over the next forty minutes, I rebuilt most of Gek's foot. The work became more and more grueling as I went. My own foot began throbbing, while the pain from healing Stan kept on cutting and burning. My hand shook, and sometimes I had to prop my wrist against my knee to steady it.

When the end was in view, Pil shouted, "Stop it! You'll kill them!"

I whipped around to see Stan and Ella standing stiff and stretched, like hides nailed to a barn. Their skulls stood out under their skin, and neither showed any sign that they knew what was happening.

I snarled at Gek, "Stop that! Let them go!"

Gek raised his eyebrows. "Me? I'm doing nothing. I thought you were draining them intentionally."

I didn't know how I was doing that to them, but I intended to stop. I let go of Gek's foot to stand, but he grabbed my wrist. If I had been chained to a stone building, it couldn't have been any harder to pull away.

Gek said, "You may not give up at this point. It is unacceptable."

"I have to save them!" I kept pulling.

"Do you even know how?"

"Well . . . do you?"

"Of course I do." Gek didn't move, but Ella and Stan dropped into holes that appeared in the ground under them. I met Ella's eyes for a second, and then she was gone. Gek said, "I returned them to the world of man. There they will soon recover. Now that I have saved your friends from your own predatory magic, you may thank me when you are at leisure."

"This is leisure enough, so thanks."

As I kept working, I decided that the best time to betray Gek would be the moment just before I finished healing him. If he was ever going to be distracted, that would be the time. Then with both legs crippled, Gek would withdraw into the Void. At least I hoped he would do that. I also hoped he wouldn't pause to destroy me first.

But even if Gek fled hopping like a toad into the Void, he and the gods would keep coming to the Dark Lands. The war would never end, and if Gek destroyed the gods, he'd mash out mankind next.

I stopped healing. "Before I finish this up, you have to promise not to come back to the Dark Lands."

"Oh, no," Gek said. "I already rejected that condition."

"Sure, but be honest. At the time, you didn't really think I could heal you. Now you know that I can. That should change things."

After a moment, Gek said, "If that's what you want, I agree. I won't come back to the Dark Lands. It is an unpleasant place in any event. I much prefer the Dim Lands."

"The what lands? Dim Lands?"

"It is unimportant. Finish your work."

I kept refashioning the foot, sweating even more. As I did, I started silently cursing my stupidity. Gek's promise to stay out of the Dark Lands meant nothing. He could just as well promise me a mechanical dog made of silver. That didn't mean I should start building a damn kennel.

It was one more reason to betray the eternal asshole and drive him out of the Dark Lands.

Soon, I was so close to being done I could feel my ability to heal fading. I mentally reached out to Harik's sword to be sure I could strike with it instantly.

In that moment, a pure, sharp yearning to kill slammed through me, as exact and hard as a cold chisel. I felt certain I could use the sword to kill Gek, not just cripple him, and that would be one way to keep the titanic bastard out of the Dark Lands.

I would need absolute surprise. I'd only have that when Gek was fully healed and marveling that he could tiptoe and dance again.

I didn't think about it. I felt it was right. So, I finished restoring

Gek's foot. My ability to call healing magic faded to nothing. I said, "Stand up, Gek. Stomp around and give the foot a try."

As Gek stood, I stepped around him for the one stroke that would fix everything.

I stopped dead. I was trying to solve eons of divine bullshit with one thrust. That was how I had tried to fix things a hundred times, and it never solved a single goddamn thing, not in the end.

Ella and Pil had both told me: I never meant to ruin things. I just did it.

I realized all of that in less than two seconds. Gek was taking his third step. He dropped his walking stick and stood taller. I could still kill him.

If I did, the next-toughest Void Walker would take over. He'd fight the war and come after me for murdering Gek. He'd hunt down and torture Ella and Pil. We couldn't hide from a being that walks from realm to realm the way I'd walk to the privy.

But what would happen if I let Gek live? I would look like a merciful goddamn hero, wouldn't I? Not that I cared about that, but it wouldn't be awful.

And without my acting entirely like an asshole, it would screw nearly everybody in some way. No one would get all that they wanted, but at least they wouldn't die. They wouldn't if they just stayed out of the damned Dark Lands.

This solution was brilliant. I was brilliant.

Pil grabbed my arm with her remaining hand. She leaned close to whisper, "Nice job, but don't you need to stab something?" She glanced at Gek's leg and nodded.

I shook my head. "No. I'm too wise now."

Pil stared as if I'd said I was too full of lead shavings and dog butts.

I patted her hand and called out to Gek, "You're leaving the Dark Lands and never coming back, right?"

"Correct." Over the next minute, Gek and every soldier disappeared into the ground, each in his own hole. Bixell had already disappeared someplace.

Pil helped me limp back down to the lake, where we found not a single god anywhere.

"We may be the only ones left in the Dark Lands." I paused to shake my throbbing foot.

"Maybe," Pil said. "Except for Apen, Mara, and any monsters that want to eat us. Perhaps Bixell."

"You remember Mara?"

Pil squinted one eye at me. "Why wouldn't I?"

I shook my head.

Pil slapped my shoulder. "Lie down and sleep, Bib. You've had a challenging day, probably extra challenging because, well, I'm sure it's difficult to be so wise. Are you wise because you're so old?" She grinned and pointed at the ground. "Take a nap. I'll wake you up in time for you to watch the monsters bite off your legs."

"While I'm sleeping, figure out how to get us home." I curled up and fell asleep as soon as my head hit the torn, muddy Dark Lands grass.

FORTY-FOUR

I woke up when somebody kicked my boot. Pil said, "Come on, Bib, stand up. You'll want to appreciate this on your feet."

Blinking, I sat up, took a breath, and rolled to my feet. "Be respectful, or I won't . . ."

Fingit stood watching us as if we were piglets that might do something interesting. His jaw was healed, and his hands rested in the pockets of his pristine rust-colored robe.

I said, "Damn, Fingit, I never figured you for such courage. You're not a bit afraid of getting killed here in the Dark Lands, are you?"

The Blacksmith of the Gods gazed around at the horizon, his brow a bit wrinkled and his jaw set. "Not too much. War in the Dark Lands has made me reassess the definition of courage." He smiled so briefly that it hardly happened at all.

"I regret we can't offer you anything to drink," I said.

Pil added, "We could recite poetry."

"I should accept and force you to give me a few hundred stanzas of poetry," Fingit said. "Too bad we don't have time. I guess that's a lie. Since no one ages in the Dark Lands, we have time without limit. We're lucky that I hate poetry. Hold hands."

"I'm sorry?" I asked.

"I don't want you getting lost."

Holding hands challenged Pil and me for a second, since we each had only a right hand remaining. Then I found myself lying on a green marble floor under bright light. Pil lay next to me, clutching my hand as she cried like a lost little girl who had just found her mother.

I sat up and glanced around, disgusted. "Gods' Realm," I muttered to Pil.

"Why?" she asked, wiping her cheeks. "Fingit, why did you bring us . . ." She leaned forward, slowing down as she stared at the swirls in the marble.

"Here," I said, poking Pil's shoulder. She jerked and looked around. I went on: "Fingit, why did you bring us here?" We were in the center of a large marble pavilion with massive, dark wooden benches all around the edges. Forests and snowy mountains stood in the distance.

Krak's voice boomed, "I want to reward you, Murderer!"

"Oh. Even though I didn't kill Gek?"

Krak smiled, and he almost looked relieved. "I didn't want the towering cucumber dead if there was any way to keep him alive. As long as he stays in his place and doesn't try to kill us, I'm satisfied. If only he'll stay out of the Dark Lands, it should all be fine, eh?"

I squinted at the Father of the Gods, who appeared to have two perfect hands. "Right. If you want to reward me, then why did you bring her, Father Krak?" I jerked my chin at Pil.

"I want to reward her too! I admit that her reward will mainly consist of watching you be rewarded, but that should still be nice for her. She likes you well enough."

I dipped my head. "Thank you, Father Krak, but I don't want a reward."

"You don't even know what it is yet!"

"If it's not a trip home, you can bet I don't want it."

Krak leaned forward and lowered his voice. "It's restoring all your missing bits. Arms, eyes, and what have you."

"Oh. Well, if it's not that or a trip home, I don't want it."

"Wonderful. You make it damned hard to be nice to you, Murderer. This will require a couple of hours. Fingit, deal with it."

"I will, Father." Fingit motioned for us to follow him out into a meadow of soft, low grass and bright wildflowers. He handed us each a pair of silver spectacles. "These are called Fingit's Mordant Eye Lights. Put them on. They will save you from being mesmerized by every bug that walks past."

"Do we just stand around in this pasture?" Pil asked.

Fingit shrugged. "You can stroll about if you want to. Meet people. I'll come when we're ready for you."

We watched Fingit leave us. Gods probably didn't scurry much, but Fingit scooted right along. Pil and I wandered around talking about home. She picked some flowers and then panicked because they might be divine flowers that we were forbidden to pick. When nobody came to yell or throw lightning at us, we put it out of our minds.

I turned away from the flowers and found myself facing my daughters, Manon and Bett, just twenty feet away. Before I could move, they charged and threw themselves at me, laughing and babbling. I hugged them but couldn't get words out. They didn't seem to care. Both girls looked exactly the age they had been when they died.

I had never thought about the girls being in the Gods' Realm, but it made sense. Once I could speak again, I reminisced about little events from their lives with me. They filled in the gaps that I had left on purpose, and they poked me for having a lousy memory. It was as if I had found something precious that I had thrown away or torn apart, and I had no right to think I'd see it again.

After three hours, I touched my face. "Pil, my face hurts. Does your face hurt?"

"No, but of course yours hurts. I've never seen you smile without stopping for this long."

Sometime during the reunion, Fingit said, "This was a reward too, but if you don't want it . . ."

I laughed at him. "How long can they stay?"

"As long as you stay, they'll be here."

I listened to the girls tell me about all the things they had done while playing in that meadow, which was one of their favorite places. I put Fingit off when he came to fetch me for healing, and I made excuses two more times before I gave in, on the condition that the girls come with me. Pil had never met either girl, but she had been a girl a few years before, and they became acquainted fast.

Lutigan arrived just before sunset, which filled me with dread. But he invited us to one of his homes, which was kind even if the invitation sounded like a command. He was gruff and sometimes insulting, and at dinner he watched me in a creepy way.

The next morning, Lutigan plucked the spectacles off my face. "Maybe you don't need these. They look stupid anyway. Stare at that axe on the wall for a while."

I stared for maybe a minute and never became stunned.

"So much for that," Lutigan said, crushing the spectacles in his hand. "I guess we are related somehow."

"All right," I said.

"I end up killing most of my relatives."

"All right." I couldn't think of anything to say that might not be perilous.

Lutigan said, "Well, go someplace else." He marched away, muttering.

Fingit pointed us to the Gossamer Forest, which was an insipid name, but that wasn't surprising. It was named by gods. However, over the years, more than one god had told me that it was the most beautiful place in existence.

The woods were pretty but didn't seem exceptional to me. After an hour or so, I got the feeling that the forest was watching me in a kindly way. It led me to remember other forests and woods I thought beautiful. I realized that the forest was slowly changing around me, and I thought that was clever, finding what I loved and showing it to me.

But the forest that appeared then was unlike the place I had loved. Maybe I had been looking for this place without knowing it. Walking through it didn't wash away years of struggle and worry, but it washed them thinner.

None of us could describe the forest in any detail once we left. I could describe mine as dim and well-groomed. The girls had nothing to say, but they giggled off and on for hours.

I couldn't remember a time when I had felt so happy. Something was definitely wrong.

I found out what was wrong that evening when Krak summoned me. Fingit didn't bring me back to the marble pavilion. Instead, we mounted a golden chariot pulled by eight mystical lions. The chariot followed a silver-paved road up an immense, pale mountain. We reached a green-and-white granite palace twenty-three stories high, surrounded by extensive gardens and ponds.

Krak received us seated on a massive, raised chair. "Welcome to the Cottage of Rapturous Thought. I didn't want to make too much of this conversation by inviting you to one of my actual homes. We can speak more comfortably here." He waved, and imps in gold livery brought chairs.

Krak's smile seemed fierce and bright enough to burn down forests. Maybe it seemed that way because it really could. "I have a proposition, Murderer. How do you fancy being God of Death?"

My mind struggled for a few seconds. "I don't, Father Krak. First, I'm not a god, and second, it just sounds horrible."

Krak scowled and raised his voice. "Don't judge this hastily. Not many beings get offered immortal godhood, you know. Listen to me. First, you are already as intimate with death as any person I've ever seen, and in my case, I mean 'ever' literally. Second, you're already accustomed to dealing with gods and telling them to go eat a bug. You won't be intimidated. Third, you have a smidge of god in your ancestry, which will make the transition far easier. And fourth, a few of the other gods don't hate the idea. Fingit and Gorlana are almost optimistic."

I didn't want to do it. Some deft toadying was in order. "Father Krak, thank you for the offer and the honor. No man could want more. But I despise everything I know about the God of Death."

"You're thinking of Harik!" Krak waved both hands. "Once you're God of Death, you can arrange things however you like. Be nice if you want. Be merciful, like you were with Gek. Sometimes mercy is the best way to kick somebody in the nuts. You'll have fantastic leeway!"

"I don't want the rest of my life to be about death."

The Father of the Gods gazed at me with eternal eyes. "What makes you think that any of us can choose what the rest of our life will be about?"

I couldn't think of anything to say.

Krak threw his head back and laughed. "Refusing makes no sense at all! Why throw away the deep understanding of death you've gained? To do what? Farm turnips? You don't create a beautiful lamp, smash it, and try to make a miserable butter dish out of the pieces."

"Father Krak, I—"

Krak stood taller and bellowed, "The Unnamed Mother scrape it raw with a chain! You killed the God of Death! That right there is the universe pointing at you and saying that it's your turn!"

I tried not to sound as pissed off as I felt. "I just don't want to do it."

Krak said, "You adore having your daughters with you, correct? As God of Death, you would have them with you all the time. When the blonde woman you love dies, she will be with you too. So will the Knife upon her death. The Nub will be making an appearance soon. Your wife too! Anyone you wish."

He sold me for a moment. I almost said yes right then before I could think about it. Instead, I swallowed and asked a question I hadn't wanted to express out loud. "Are my daughters real?"

"Certainly, they are! Do they not seem so?"

"I don't know." I rubbed my eyes. "How long until you need my answer?"

"We want to move along quickly," Krak said. "Things can become awkward with no God of Death. There are benefits for you, though. Now that Harik's dead, your debt to him is canceled. So, too, with all those years of life you lost. You have those back now. Oh, I suppose I'll need an answer within thirty years."

It sounded generous, but really it was thirty years for Krak to wear me down.

I bowed my head and left him. Krak's rewards seemed lavish. Godhood was quite a gift, especially since I could manage things however I wanted. Maybe I was lacking courage.

The next morning, I asked Fingit to take us to the Falls of Hope and Loss. It was a short hike filled with butterfly chasing, flower picking, and hiding from each other behind trees.

Before we reached the falls, a short, chubby unicorn trotted through some bushes and stopped twenty feet from us, stamping and tossing its head. We waited, but it didn't come any closer.

Pil said, "I think it's Stan's unicorn."

"Sweetie?" I asked.

Pil nodded just as the girls decided it was time to chase unicorns. We finally calmed things down with only a small amount of crying, one skinned knee, and no tramplings.

Fingit led us on to the falls, and the unicorn followed.

The clear, sharp river at the bottom of the falls lay in a shallow valley. When we reached the rim of that valley, I stopped to appreciate the river, the falls rising into the clouds, and the far-off multicolored hills beyond. Bett and Manon stood on one side of me and Pil on the other. Manon wanted to know why I had stopped to look at some stupid river. Bett dragged at my hand, promising she just wanted to look at the unicorn and wouldn't try to touch it. The unicorn swished her tail and snuffed.

It was a perfect day in a perfect place, and perfection is no reward for creatures who can die. They yearn to live forever so that perfection never ends, or else they want to die this very moment so that perfection never ends. The only way to live in the Gods' Realm was to be immortal. Krak was offering me that.

I hadn't noticed the benches when we had visited the falls before. They were carved of pale, waxy wood without a single straight line. Some had been set close enough to the river for a chat with somebody dangling their feet in the most divine water of the Gods' Realm.

Krak had probably tasked Fingit with minding us, but I didn't care. I had quietly asked Fingit to help me if I needed it, and he had hinted he might. Now reclining on a bench, he said, "I don't suppose you'd like to know what the blasted hell has been going on, would you?"

I froze. "Is it something I'll want to know?"

"I guess so. Probably. Let's see, the last war ended like a rotten turd for everybody. Two gods died, and we lopped off Gek's foot. We knew the next war would be in the Dark Lands, and whoever lost might be wiped out."

I knew all of that but didn't want to give anything away to Fingit. I nodded with a polite smile.

Fingit snorted but then gritted his teeth. "I hate to speak badly of my fellow gods, but I must. We gathered power like mad in the run up to the war, but we're as organized as a drunken midnight dance on the village green. Meanwhile, Gek . . ." Fingit shook his head. "You know that King Famm bastard who said he talked to me so much? Actually, Gek was talking to Famm and impersonating me."

"What?" The word just jumped out of my mouth.

Fingit nodded. "Gek was manipulating everybody in sight. You, Cael, Famm, and this Bixell dolt. He fooled tens of thousands of men into joining his army. He probably had the other Void Walkers confused or cowed. And of course he turned Harik against us—not that corrupting Harik would have been harder than building a crooked table. And Gek trapped us in the Dark Lands for the battle."

"That's admirable diligence," I said. "It seems like a disjointed effort, though."

"It was blunt but not disjointed." Fingit sat forward. "He planned to throw heroes, armies, and traitorous gods at us until we were beaten down and as confused as magpies. Then his gigantic backside would walk across the battlefield and squash us."

"It was bold," I said.

Fingit laughed for a couple of seconds. "It almost worked too. It would have if you hadn't dealt with Gek for us. The gods owe you a debt. Krak's offering you the most astounding reward any man has gotten in thousands of years."

"And I appreciate it! I just need to think it over a little more."

"Krak isn't accustomed to his gifts being rejected."

I leaned my head back, closed my eyes, and listened to the waterfall.

Before I could fall asleep, Manon said, "Father . . ." She hesitated, which she almost never did. "Gorlana says that for years and years you were a sorcerer with no power. How did you ever find the Dark Lands and save the gods?"

I said, "That's a lengthy story, darling, too long to tell just now."

Fingit smiled. "No one is waiting for us. Come, I'll call for food."

"You're joking."

Bett squealed, "I'm not joking! I want to hear it if she hears it!"

Pil said, "Go on. I bet someone will bring wine."

I shook my head. "All right. If any of you feels your spirit being chased out of your body by boredom, throw up a hand . . . a good starting point is a backward snip of a village called Crossoak in the Kingdom of Glass. I had been guarding that inoffensive place full of unloving people for too long, and on the day I perched downhill from Crossoak Village, I had just about forgotten that love was a reason for doing things . . ."

The girls dangled their feet a lot during the next three days while I told the entire story, from Crossoak until now, not leaving out any acts, thoughts, or insults. I told it until I reached this day.

I gazed around for a couple of breaths. My once-lost daughters were sitting on each side of me, so I nudged each with an elbow. "Darlings, I've made you listen to this long, long, boring story while we sat here in the Home of the Gods. I hope this eternal bench and the holy dirt you sat on haven't put your butts to sleep."

Bett said, "I never slept even one second!"

"That's a good lie. It spares my feelings."

Manon added, "I know a lot of things I didn't know before. I forgive you for killing me."

My throat closed, so I nodded before patting their shoulders. "Your butts can rejoice anyway because the story ends here, this very instant."

∼

— PIL

Bib leaned back on the bench, and he squinted at Fingit, looking a little mean. "Why do you want me to replace Harik, anyway? What do you get out of it?"

Fingit had been lying on his back on another bench—there wasn't room on Bib's bench—and he sat up to look at Bib. "If you become the God of Death, you will fight alongside us in the war. You must know that it will continue, regardless of any promises to stay out of the Dark Lands. You can help us and protect mankind from Gek at the same time. Also, I hated Harik. He was such a pretentious squint. I think we can be friends, Bib."

"Are you friends with any of the other gods?"

"No."

"Have you ever been?"

Fingit pursed his lips, but he didn't lick them or anything. "I don't remember. Maybe you'd be the first."

Bib crossed his arms, so Bett grabbed on to one and started swinging on it. Bib patted her shoulder and said, "Fingit, please deliver a message to Krak for me. Send it to Gek too, if you can."

Fingit oozed off the bench, which I think meant he was uncomfortable, but what do I know about how gods feel? He said, "What message is that?"

"I'm entering the Dark Lands. I'm going there to stand guard and raise hell. Anybody who comes there should expect me to kill them. Anybody who has promised to stay out and breaks that promise should expect me to kill them and make it hurt. Once I get there, I will stay. Take it as a fact that I will be there waiting." He stared hard at Fingit. "I asked you to help me while I'm here. Will you take me to the Dark Lands?"

Fingit sighed. "I see what you're doing. If the gods don't enter the Dark Lands, we don't need to worry about dying—and mankind needn't worry about being destroyed, either. But you don't have to exile yourself there. We can find other means, so please change your mind and stay. It would please Krak and me too."

"And Sakaj?"

Fingit paused. "It would make Krak and me happy."

I thought Bib might grin or do some other "I don't give a shit" thing, but he didn't. He said, "I'd make a lousy God of Death, worse than Harik. I'll keep his sword, though. It'll look mighty stylish in the Dark Lands."

I watched Bib stand up and hitch his sword belt, something he did all the time, maybe a hundred times a day, and I don't think he ever knew it, and the girls didn't notice it now because they were crying. So, I bit my lip and didn't bawl.

Bib smiled at me. "Pil, Ella won't understand this. Hell, maybe I don't understand it, either. She shouldn't expect to see me again." His eyes were red and tearing up, but he didn't stop. "Tell her some things for me. Say I love her. And she knows that she hasn't changed me, but I did just happen to change a fair amount while she was around. I fought it, but she was a good influence."

I broke in. "If somebody was leaving forever and said these things to me, I'd write their name on a rock and throw turds at it every day. Bib, if you don't want to be the God of Death, just go home where you can say anything you want to Ella. Screw the Dark Lands."

Bib chuckled. "I'd like that. But if Ella were in my place, you know damn well that she would go to the Dark Lands. She's noble and unselfish and all that sort of thing. I can fake that for her. I don't know what else to say. Tell her I love her until she gets tired of hearing it and slaps you."

I glared at Bib for a couple of seconds but couldn't hold it.

Bib looked at the sky. "Pil, let me ask you another favor. I know it's stupid as hell, pure vanity, but would you remind a few people that some of these things happened? All this shit I told you these past days, but not the boring or stupid parts that make me look bad. If you remember any of it, that is."

I said, "Bib, I remember every word. I remember how you said them. I remember the look on your face when you spoke each one."

"You never forget a single flipping thing, I guess. Well, throw in some extra lies here and there, or nobody will believe it was really me. And tell a few falsehoods that make you look even more heroic."

"I will. You'll be so undeservingly worshipped that you'll be too embarrassed to ever come home." I stopped with my mouth open, and that did it. I turned away so he wouldn't see me crying, which is something he always said sorcerers don't do, although of course I had caught him at it a couple of times.

When I turned back, Bib was kneeling to hug and kiss the girls. Then he came to me, and I held out a pebble I had saved for him. "It's the only one in existence now, Bib, so don't waste it and don't swallow it. Hold it under your tongue while you cross into the Dark Lands. I didn't exactly make it for that, but if I'm right, it will give you the energy of a young man for a long while, and if I'm really, really right, it will last as long as you're there. I doubt that it will blow up in your mouth. Less than one percent chance."

"Why, thank you, Pil, that's kind." He hugged me and whispered, "I trust you to take care of the girls while you're here. You know, if they're real."

"I will." That trust meant a thousand times more than him saying he loved me or that he thought I was the smartest sorcerer to ever summon a toad.

Then it happened fast. Gods had to reach the Dark Lands by dying in the Gods' Realm, which wasn't true death. Bib turned to Fingit, who nodded, and then they drew knives and stabbed each other in the chest. Both crumpled to the grass and lay there, all bleeding and empty.

When I glanced back, I saw Bett and Manon come apart and blow away like smoke. Krak had been lying all along, telling Bib he could stay with his real daughters forever if only he agreed to become the God of Death. Now they were gone, and Bib was gone, and so was everybody but me, and I stared at the ground for a good while.

At last, I drew a deep breath and reminded myself that moping was undignified in a sorcerer, and Bib would tell me to cut it the hell out because it would embarrass him. The gods had given me new clothes, so I made sure all my pouches and weapons were secure. I pulled my knife from its hidden realm and examined it, even though it was always in perfect shape.

I walked up to the hairy, sour-smelling imp that had been lurking beside the river these past days, fetching and carrying for Fingit. It was nearly twice as tall as me, and its arms were thicker than my body.

The imp sniffed and said in a birdlike warble, "Don't leave any ass stains on the damn bench, girl. I'll make you lick them clean."

I looked at the creature as if it was the least interesting thing I had ever found on a muddy road. Then I lunged and sliced off its little finger before jumping away.

Shaking its bloody hand, the imp twittered, "Krak chew off your ears, bitch! Effla tear off your tits!" It stepped toward me but stopped when I pointed my knife at its belly. It tweeted, "Lousy rat-humping sorcerer!"

"Sorry about that." I smiled my sweetest smile and pointed downstream. "Be a nice fellow and fetch me my friend's unicorn. Right the hell now."

EPILOGUE

When I was a boy, I had dreams. Long before I showed the merest smidge of sorcery potential, I could not imagine that I'd grow up to be a fisherman. I sure as hell didn't envision living a brief, grubby life until I drowned, or broke my neck, or was stabbed to death lying beside some other man's wife, all of which were common ways to die in my village.

I would lie in bed thinking about leaving home once I finally discovered that I was secretly the son of a courageous, deposed prince, and how we'd wage a clever campaign to free his suffering kingdom. Since I had a miraculous, innate mastery of warfare and combat, I'd be his most important lieutenant.

After a suitable amount of defeat, torture, and escape, we would fight our way into the pretender's stronghold and confront him. When the treacherous bastard pulled a sneaky damn trick, and we were all about to die, I would come up with a shrewd, perilous move and kill the son of a bitch.

Someplace in there I would fall in love with a beautiful girl, but the details were vague. I was only seven or eight years old when this dreaming happened.

My father would rule as king for many years. When he died, I would become a powerful king, still young even though forty years must have passed. In the end, I would rule a vast realm with absolute but benevolent power. My people would be joyous and love me. There would be happiness forever, or at least until I died.

My real life led me to an existence in the Dark Lands. It was about the same as that of my boyhood imagination, except that the kingdom was a dread but pissant death realm. No people lived there, and if any showed up, I killed them. My power was the opposite of benevolent. It would indeed last forever, and I mean really forever since I didn't age, but there was not much happiness in the dank hills and the black lakes of the Dark Lands.

Other than those things, it was just like my boyhood dreams.

When I arrived in the Dark Lands and Fingit left me behind, I wondered how soon somebody would come to test me. I'd be outnumbered, so I had best make tactical preparations.

The gods never took less than a week to decide who was bringing the wine, so I felt I need not rush. However, the amount of time that elapsed before they tested me turned out to be five minutes.

Somebody in the Gods' Realm must have decided I was a meddling son of a bitch because six demigods arrived at a spot more than a mile away from me. I ran toward my enemies, happy that Pil's pebble had given me the endurance of my younger self.

The demigods didn't get any negotiations or threats from me. Every demigod I had ever met seemed to know with deep certainty that a single demigod could slaughter any number of men. I charged in and killed three who believed that. The rest didn't grow wary fast enough. They fell like water dripping from an icicle.

I cut off their heads but had no way to send them to Krak. I settled for stacking the heads near the place the invaders had entered, hoping to perplex future visitors.

An hour later, five more demigods arrived. The gods themselves were a randy bunch and had spawned what seemed like an endless number of demigods. The heads of these five joined the first six.

The next eight demigods arrived an hour after that and must have grown uncertain about their invincibility. The fight was brutal, and I took a bad wound in my left arm. But in the end, eight more heads joined the pile. I regretted that I could no longer heal.

The next dozen demigods showed up three hours later. I killed them in a running, forty-minute fight and suffered a batch of small wounds. Without Harik's sword of death, I would have perished for certain. I stacked these heads too. Most demigods wore extravagant headgear, and I made certain each head in the stack was correctly covered so their friends could identify them without confusion.

Sweating and bleeding, I waited for the next twenty, or fifty, or a hundred of those bastards to show up. A few hours later, eighteen demigods arrived. They looked at the thirty-one heads piled up and went home. Thirty-one was a strong number.

I didn't feel like performing any victory dances, however. After a short rest, I felt moderately recovered, apart from the wounds. I wandered up to the bridge across the gorge to look for Bixell. He normally stood guard there, blocking the bridge in the most imposing way.

I found him sitting against a pile of logs with his long legs crossed, scraping at something he held in his palm. Without looking at me, he said in a clang, "Screw you, asshole. If you wanted to come guard things, you should have taken over for me. Technically, this job is yours."

Sounding contrite, I said, "You're right, and I'm sorry. I found myself needing to guard in a different way."

"How would you know which ways there are to guard?" He still didn't look up. "When you've been here seven hundred years, then you can tell me about different ways to guard!"

"Well, I said I was sorry." I walked away, although I didn't know where I was going.

"Aren't you going to ask me any questions? By Cheg-Cheg's fifty-foot-long knob, you won't last twenty years."

"All right. Where's a good place to live?"

"Wherever you want. You won't get cold. It doesn't rain. You do not need to sleep, or even eat or drink for that matter. A home is not quite necessary, but if you don't have one, then after a few years you'll think people are looking at you all the time." He shrugged.

I nodded. "All right, thanks. What's the most important thing I need to know?"

"Take care of that." He pointed up at the mess of stars and star-like things in the black sky.

I remembered Cael talking about the Dark Lands' sky and how it stared at him every minute. He took pride that it hadn't made him insane. I thought about it for a while. "No sun. You can't tell what time it is."

"Good," Bixell clanked, standing up. "There are no sunrises. The stars do not move in any regular manner. You never become tired, so you can't count the days by how often you need to sleep. It's a problem. If you lose track of time, after a few years nothing will make sense to you. You'll walk into the lake and drown."

That got my attention. "We can drown?"

Bixell nodded. "You can be crushed, or cut up, or burned, or have your heart broken. But if it doesn't kill you, you'll heal. You're not one of the great powers, like Gek—they don't heal, as you well know. Here the greater you are, the more greatly screwed you are."

"I think I see."

"You'll be sure about that the first time you're surrounded by thirty pissed-off demigods." Bixell smirked.

"All right, thanks. How do you tell time then?"

"I make a mark on the wall whenever a week has passed. Whenever I think one has passed, I mean."

I stared at him. "That's how you do it? I'm sure the master clockmakers of Karre would be impressed."

Bixell scowled and crossed his long arms. "When you think of a better way, you can tell me. Or write it down so all future guardians can appreciate your wisdom with an intensity that is almost sexual."

"I didn't mean to offend you." I realized that making my only guide angry was foolish, and maybe I wasn't as entirely wise as I thought. I then proved that by asking another question. "If this is how you record time, how do you know you've been here seven hundred years?"

Bixell's face went from anger to despair in an instant. "I know because it feels like seven hundred years."

I reached up and almost patted his shoulder. "I'm sorry. I am thoughtless and rude today."

"Just today? Never mind. Here combat is nearly as important as time. Draw your sword."

I pulled my sword from its small realm, and it appeared in my hand.

Bixell smiled. "That is a terribly elegant draw. Can you teach me?"

"You have to be a sorcerer, sorry."

He shrugged. "Your sword is beautiful. You certainly have fine tools to work with." He drew a four-foot-long sword from a scabbard by the woodpile and held it one-handed. "Attack me."

"My sword is dangerous beyond belief," I warned.

"Come on."

I thrust at his chest. An instant later, my sword spun aside as he disarmed me. I retrieved it and feinted before slashing at his knees. He smacked my wrist with the flat of his blade, and my hand went numb.

Bixell bit his lip. "Oh dear. That's . . . oh dear." He shook his head. "Bib, you are execrably far below the standard. I'm busy just now, but come back later. To be truthful, I hate you a lot, but guardians have a reputation. I can't have you dying the first time you point your sword at somebody."

I thanked him and then wandered around the Dark Lands for a while until I found myself at the entrance to the Unnamed Mother's well. The stairway down was blocked by fallen stone and earth after thirty feet. I declared this place my home. Then I sat on a step not knowing what to do.

An eternity of this was going to feel mighty damn long.

I adopted Bixell's fine timekeeping method and marked the wall of my home whenever I felt sure a week had passed. I didn't miss sleeping too much. I had always felt that sleep just robbed me of part of my life. On the other hand, I remembered eating and drinking with great fondness. I guess it was good that I didn't need to do those things, since the Dark Lands contained nothing the least bit edible or drinkable.

I wondered whether the Unnamed Mother had changed me in these ways so I could survive in the Dark Lands. If so, I wished I could have dug down to her home to thank her and, while I was there, eat a couple dozen ginger cakes.

Bixell trained me regularly, insulting my skill the entire time. He often cut me "by accident" and even threw things at me when I was particularly slow. That did not make him the most abusive teacher I had ever trained with. After each session, he told me to go away and then ignored me.

When I had made twenty marks on my wall, I decided to survey the Dark Lands and understand them better. I had no plan or pattern of travel. I just wandered with no purpose, really. When I came across Desh's body, it shocked me.

I sat on the black grass beside Desh for a long time, more than a day I expect, thinking about him and everything that happened to me before the Dark Lands. I considered burying him. Maybe one of the keg monsters would try to eat his body, bite into a bag full of magical junk, and make a fantastic crater in the monster-shredding explosion that followed. Desh would have enjoyed that.

In the end, I did not bury Desh. I found a unique, curved tree on the ridge at the highest spot in the Dark Lands and carried him there. Then I hauled stones to the top of that damn ridge for days, building a cairn under the tree. The whole time I imagined him watching me with that little smile that said I was a dumbass.

Six marks later, I ran across Yita's crushed body. I carried her up the ridge and put her under her own cairn beside Desh's. For a while, I found that looking up at the cairns unsettled me, so I stayed away from the ridge.

At thirty-one marks on my wall, three demigods entered the realm, wandering around as if they had made a wrong turn on the way to the tavern. They didn't even look at the pile of heads. It was so unlikely that I thought this might be a deadly ruse. Hanging back, I listened to the loud, chatty, drunken bastards. They talked about how much the Dim Lands had changed, how it was no improvement, and why that bobbling piece of filth Huldah was making them wait.

They were so pathetic I wanted to talk to them rather than kill them. I even considered different ways to open the conversation. But soon I admitted they were demigods and technically superior beings who must be slain without hesitating.

The event made me realize I was a far more garrulous bastard than I had ever understood. I'm sure that everybody around me had known it. When I started paying attention, I found myself talking to trees sometimes.

I went to Bixell and asked, "How do you deal with having nobody to talk to?"

He clanked, "Don't think that you're going to come make small talk with me. I hate you a little less than I hate fungus of the crotch."

"I hate you too," I said. "That's a given. Who do you talk to? Do you have a straw effigy of Mrs. Bixell in a cave someplace?"

The big warrior shocked me by chuckling. "No, of course not. I don't talk to anybody."

"For seven hundred years? Really?"

"Yes." Bixell gave a loose nod. After a long pause, he said, "It helps to have a hobby. I understand that Apen carves some fine sculptures."

I leaned forward, trying to imagine how Bixell spent his time. "A hobby! What's your hobby?"

"Nothing special."

"I want to know. Seriously."

Grumbling, he reached into a pouch and pulled out a wooden carving of a pig. It was the size of my thumbnail and immensely detailed. I thought I could see the chin hairs.

"What fine work! Have you done others? I'd love to see them."

Without hesitating, Bixell gave me a tour of his cave in the gorge. It included his workshop and a nice library.

Bixell ran a hand across his books. "I collected them one volume at a time from people with inferior fighting skills. Only a few have significant bloodstains."

The rest of the sizable space displayed thousands of tiny carvings. I exclaimed over everything and wasn't faking my appreciation.

Outside the cave I saw a rough bed made from what looked like clothing of the people he had killed.

"Bixell, I thought you said we don't sleep."

Bixell sounded embarrassed. "Sometimes I do lie down and pretend to sleep."

I waited for him to explain that.

After a pause, he said, "I'd rather not do so on the ground like a cow."

At fifty-one marks, I sensed somebody else enter the Dark Lands at a different spot than that used by the demigods. I loped that direction and found about one hundred men already deployed, with fifty more in the process of arriving. They were the same type of folks who had served Gek in the battle against the gods. The Void Walkers were finally testing me.

This tactical situation was far different than fighting six overconfident, semidivine assholes. Not waiting, I charged into the formation and out the other side, killing as I went. Aided by Harik's sword, I slew about three dozen, and I hoped that the rest were stunned.

The men reorganized, but if they expected me to charge them again, they must also have believed in free beer. I allowed them to chase me along the ravine, nipping back to kill one or two whenever I could.

The Dark Lands were disorienting to newcomers, and I took advantage of that. I lured the men into a gap where they could attack me only two at a time. More than eighty of them died before they withdrew.

The survivors retreated to the place where they had entered the realm, and they stopped there. My best guess was that they were trying to go back home, but the Void Walkers would not bring them through.

Those men and women had no hope, really. They needed sleep, but I didn't. I forced them to stay awake until they were too exhausted to defend themselves. Before the next mark, I stacked 151 heads near the spot where the soldiers had entered.

When I returned home, I found the black mare Gea standing there. I almost danced.

Gea ignored my every attempt to become her friend. No tactic that I had ever used with any other horse worked. But she allowed me to mount and then carried me where I asked to go at stunning speed. I decided that she was allowing me to work with her, but she did not become friends with beings such as myself.

At the seventy-third mark, twenty-five demigods arrived and charged my direction. They might have killed me had it not been for Bixell's training and Gea's deadly service as a mount. In the end, I killed them and stacked their heads at the cost of ten wounds, but none threatened my life.

One mark later, the Void Walkers' soldiers arrived again. They must have decided that their first men weren't coming back. They sent 240 soldiers, and my wounds hadn't yet healed. But I defeated them in the same manner as I wiped out their friends before them, all without magic. I had preserved the nine squares I brought with me to the Dark Lands. I felt no thirst to kill these men. In fact, I wished they had stayed home, but they hadn't, so I took their lives in a professional fashion.

Those men had cut me several times, and two wounds were nasty. Even Gea was cut. The pace of the assaults was wearing me down, so I was not overjoyed when four hundred men arrived an hour later. However, they spent several thoughtful minutes admiring my stack of heads and the many scattered bodies. That allowed me time to position myself.

Gea and I led them on a three-day chase through the Dark Lands, which was a challenge since the Dark Lands weren't a large realm. We charged in and back out to slaughter some whenever they stopped paying close attention. We also showed them how splitting their force was the greatest of follies. They discovered that men who withdrew from the fight to rest would not live to return.

The soldiers' need to sleep undid them in the end, and soon I stacked all 791 heads. I was forced to start a whole new pile. Then I visited Bixell, who pointed out all the mistakes he had seen me make.

I had rested and recovered by the 121st mark, when I sensed an intruder arrive at a new place of entry five miles' ride around the lake. Gea carried me there at breathtaking speed, and I held my sword ready to attack. When we arrived, Gea stopped dead and I lowered my sword.

Ella stood smiling at me, surrounded by bags stuffed full.

I ran to Ella, grabbed her, and tripped over what turned out to be a sack full of books. Laughing, we ended up on the ground with Gea making disdainful snorts behind us. In the next minutes every being who wasn't a horse shed some tears.

We finally stood, but I didn't let go of Ella. I felt a crazy fear that whatever brought her would drag her away again. I managed to ask, "How did you get here?"

Ella held up a curved piece of metal, which I recognized as Pil's 'dent. "Pil explained this charm comprehensively, but I grasped only two facts. It is a broken tine from the trident of the god Madimal, who was slain in the Dark Lands. Also, Pil enchanted it so that one person may travel to the Dark Lands and then return."

I laughed. "Pil finally discovered what this thing was good for! But here is the critical question. How many trips can you make?" I didn't think Pil could afford to enchant the charm for more than a trip or two before it failed, unless she included some harsh penalties for the user.

"I do not understand. I can use it whenever I want." Ella said that as if it was impossible for the charm to work any other way.

I forced my face to stay calm. If the charm could be used at will and had no drawbacks for the user, I was stunned by how much Pil must have paid and sacrificed to enchant it.

But mainly I was happy. I grabbed Ella in a tighter embrace and said, "What's in all the sacks?"

"You have been here almost a year."

By my wall-mark calendar, I had been there over two years. Clearly, I was not good at guessing how long a week was.

"I did not know what you might need." Ella pulled out bread, a net full of apples, roast chicken, and rashers of bacon. Two bags held nothing but sacks of beer. She had also brought cloth, canvas, rope, two knives, a whetstone, and an assortment of small tools.

"I have no need for food or drink," I said. "But maybe I can still drink and eat if I want. Now's the time to find out." I grabbed a sack of beer from the closest bag and took two swallows. We waited a minute, and nothing bad happened. I took another drink. "This is great! Darling, if I didn't already love you, I would love you all to hell now!" I said, proving that I am the very spirit of romance.

We draped the sacks across disgruntled Gea's back and returned to my simple, admittedly squalid home. Ella examined it with a grim face but didn't criticize.

Ella knew me tolerably well, so she understood that I am an enjoyable companion for a few days, after which people want to stab me. Her intention was to spend four days with me and three days in the regular world each week. She didn't ask for my opinion on that. She described the plan the way she might describe the ocean: beyond the power of man to change.

Neither Ella nor I aged in the Dark Lands, but she did age on those days she spent in her world. Despite that, we figured that we could reasonably have fifty or sixty more years with one another. That seemed lavish since we had been minutes away from death during most of our life together.

I believed Ella was correct in her thinking about splitting her time, but I threatened to be a pain in the ass about it unless next time she brought a saw, woodworking tools, and a timepiece. I was about to become both the best and the worst furniture maker in the Dark Lands.

Demigods, being such mighty and condescending wads of conceit, always fought with magical weapons, and I collected those weapons after I killed their owners. I tossed the glowing hand weapons in a corner, but I found a nice bow that almost never missed and three arrows that would plunge all the way through their target every time, except for those times when they shattered in the archer's face. I found a useful shield too—the angrier I got, the harder it became.

Over time, I put together a nice armory, far better than Bixell's.

He said he didn't care, but really it irked him so much that he insulted me about everything except that.

Ella brought a timepiece for Bixell too, but we actually told time according to two measures. How many visits from strangers had I wiped out? And what awkward pieces of furniture had I made?

Gea and I massacred an average of four incursions each year. They varied in composition, size, timing, and apparent objective. Bixell helped me whenever invaders tried to cross a bridge. Men may as well have been ducklings for him to stomp. Demigods seemed to know better and stayed away from the bridges.

Not counting Ella's bed, the most notable pieces of furniture I built were two chairs so that we didn't have to sit our asses on stone steps, a nicer bookshelf for Bixell, and a bar with stools. Bixell often joined us at the only bar in the Dark Lands as we told stories and drank too much during the hours that our timepieces said were evening. Hurd even showed up on occasion once he somehow learned that we served alcohol. I could never tell when Hurd arrived. He appeared in the Dark Lands without notice and left the same way.

One morning about four years after Ella arrived, as we sat in our chairs eating breakfast, I asked her, "Could you bring more beer and fewer books when you come back next time?"

Ella patted my arm. "I should nag you about drinking, but you never seem to be inebriated."

"I'm cursed to never get drunk anymore. I think it's one of the most horrible curses, and I've been cursed quite a few times in my life."

Then I wandered off to struggle with the legs of an uneven table. Ella gathered her empty sacks, held up the 'dent, and disappeared with a sizzling sound.

Ella was supposed to return in three days, but she was late sometimes. She was still gone the next day, but that had happened once before. By the fifth day, I was worried. At the end of the week, I was so frantic I vibrated.

I searched for a way to follow her, but I had no means of returning to the world of man. Bixell was no help. He looked sad and shrugged. I stood at the top of the well and shouted to Mara for help, but she didn't answer, even though I finally called her quite a few profane names. I shouted for Hurd but didn't hope for much. Bixell said that Hurd only came when he wasn't called.

I couldn't follow Ella.

Twice I shouted questions about Ella to confused invaders who didn't speak my language. I killed them for their ignorance, although I would have killed them anyway.

Three times I captured demigods and promised they could live if they would find out where Ella was. Two said they would rather die than go home in shame, so I killed them. One agreed to help me. She returned to the Gods' Realm, and I never saw her again.

Bixell tried to cheer me up with jokes too simple even for a child to laugh at. He would sit with me in the evening, clearing his throat a lot and drumming his big fingers on the bar. I didn't care about training anymore.

One day Bixell said, "Bib, I think you have become as proficient with weapons as you can be, given the limitations with which you were born."

"All right," I said.

He waited a few minutes. "You have been sitting on that barstool for a long time, staring at nothing."

"That's all right too."

"We have drunk all the beer," he clinked. "Nothing will happen if you sit on that stool."

I ignored him, and he went away.

Ella never came back, and I never knew why.

The gods and the Void Walkers kept sending incursions now and then. The Void Walkers sent a pent of sorcerers. It proved a difficult fight, but I killed them just as I had killed sorcerers before. The burns took two months to heal and left a lot of impressive scars.

The Big Invasion was what I called it. The gods probably called it The Grinding Battle of Rumination or something. Two years after Ella left, fifty demigods arrived. At almost the same moment, one thousand men with sorcerers showed up.

I felt relieved. Until I saw all those invaders, I hadn't realized how goddamn angry I had been since Ella left.

I had never yet employed magic to defeat intruders in the Dark Lands, but that day I did not hesitate. Mists rose, trees fell, and lightning came out of the empty sky. I led four hundred men into the breeding ground of the limb-eating keg monsters. Not many men came out.

Bixell lured twenty demigods into attacking the bridge. I witnessed curses, cries, and spraying blood on the bridge before I galloped off toward a formation of soldiers.

After four hours of fighting, I still felt uncertain about whether we would win. By then, I couldn't hear anything from the bridge. I would already have bled to death from my wounds except for a magic shirt I had taken from a demigod months before. Blood couldn't escape from it, at least up to an unknown amount of blood. Beyond that point, it would fail as if it were a net.

After Gea and I had routed the soldiers, just fifteen demigods still lived. I turned to face them just as the goddess Chira appeared among them.

I wanted to stay far away from her, so I drew my bow and fired. The magic arrow exploded in my face, and blood ran to cover my left eye. I shook my head and nocked another arrow. Gea then decided that my plan to keep our distance was crap, and she charged. When I fired, I could tell that the arrow was flying toward the center of the goddess's chest and would punch her heart straight out of her body.

Chira stepped back and swatted the arrow out of the air with the palm of her hand. Then she laughed at me and raised her bow.

I called her a salty name as I dropped my bow and grabbed my shield off the saddle, all while Gea kept charging. A second later, Chira's arrow slammed into my shield. It felt as if somebody had hit me with a great stone block. Fifteen seconds after that, her next arrow struck the shield. It broke my arm before carrying the shield away.

I called my sword and focused on Chira, who was aiming an arrow at my chest. She fired, and I swung, cutting her arrow in two.

It fell apart as the shaft turned to ash, although the arrowhead thumped into my chest hard enough to leave an appalling bruise. I laughed until I saw that Chira was pointing and laughing at me. She nocked another arrow, still grinning.

Then Gea jumped over a demigod and fishtailed as Chira's next arrow struck her. Gea fell, sliding on her side. I jumped free and rolled, roaring at the pain in my broken arm. I threw myself flat, which was fortunate since Chira had begun swinging an awful-looking mace.

Lying on the ground, I stretched and nicked Chira's ankle with the point of my sword. She fell over sideways as her leg withered. I flopped like a fish to get closer and then thrust my sword an inch deep into the flesh under the goddess's armpit. Her whole body spasmed and went still as it petrified.

I dragged myself to my feet, ready to kill demigods until I died. They were running back toward the place of their arrival. I yelled curses, insulted them for not staying to die, and then fell straight down on my butt.

After panting for a couple of minutes, I dragged myself up and stumbled to where Gea lay on her side. I blinked at the wound and smiled at our first really good luck of the day. The arrow had flown through the fleshy part of her shoulder and torn a long, deep gash along the way, but nothing important was harmed.

Gea got to her feet about the same time I fell down again. I lay on the bloody grass, breathing deep and deciding to be ready for death, since there wasn't a damned thing I could do about it.

My resilience as a sorcerer probably kept me alive. Nothing I did contributed, since I slept lying on the battlefield for what felt like a long time. When I woke, Gea was gone, so I stumbled up to Bixell's bridge. I met no soldiers on the way. They all seemed to have died or fled.

Bixell didn't answer my call, and I feared to find him dead or badly hurt. But I didn't find him at all, just dozens and dozens of dead soldiers and demigods. Perhaps he had died, and his body drifted away like mist. Maybe he fled somehow, or maybe the

Unnamed Mother rewarded his service by sending him home. I hoped that last one was true.

Within a few weeks, I was mostly healed, except for my left eye. When the arrow burst, it blinded me on that side and peppered my face with scars. Despite that and the burns on the other side of my face, I was still the handsomest fellow in the Dark Lands. I wanted to joke that I was more scar than skin now, but there was nobody to laugh. Neither Bixell nor Gea ever came back.

I spent a few weeks gathering and stacking all the heads. I had built a rough cart to make things easier but had come to hate the task. It served a purpose, though. Also, it was something to do.

After the Big Invasion, the gods and Void Walkers stopped invading for a while. I supposed that the demigods and the troops seemed useless, and no more gods cared to risk being destroyed. No Void Walkers ever came through.

I spent months patrolling the Dark Lands. My anger had burned away, and I now could just guard the realm, which was the reason I had come there, after all. I walked across every part of the place, but that didn't seem quite adequate. During that time, demigods or men arrived now and then. They seemed to be scouting. They ran home when they saw me.

When I crossed the realm's highest ridge for the fifth or sixth time, right next to Desh's tree, I looked out and at last understood how much of the Dark Lands I could see from there. I could protect everything much better from that vantage, and it would be easier too. I decided that Desh's and Yita's cairns would be my home, and I stood watch there most of the day every day.

I must have made a good choice because almost nobody invaded while I was up there. Only three little groups of demigods came scouting, and two of the groups fled before I killed every one of them. There didn't seem much point in winding my timepiece, so I stopped. My guess is that except to fight I never came down from that ridge for over three years.

One day it struck me like a slap in the face that I was standing in the wrong spot. I hurried down to the bridge where Bixell had posted himself, and I spent my days on watch there. I moved into

Bixell's cave. I laid out and cleaned all our weapons, tidied up, and read a good number of his books. I reviewed all my training.

I wound Bixell's timepiece every day. The bridge felt like the right place to be for a long while. But after a time, standing in Bixell's spot made me nervous. Something had happened to Bixell there. At last, I understood that even though I hadn't seen what happened to Bixell, I was waiting in his spot now hoping the same thing would happen to me.

I moved back to my old home by the stairway where I had lived with Ella. I hoped that somebody would invade from someplace, but no one even came to scout, so I made furniture. Over the next year, I built a small table and a stool. That didn't seem like much, but it was good production since I spent most of every day in our bed pretending to sleep.

At last, I abandoned that home. I found an unremarkable old tree halfway between the gods' gateway and the Void Walkers' gateway, and I declared that was my new home. I kept careful count of days and hours by the timepiece, and each day I walked from one gateway to the other and back again for seventeen hours. Then I went home and sat on the ground until the next day.

For a long time, nobody showed up for me to kill or converse with. At one point, I counted up the time and found that I hadn't spoken a word in more than ten years.

After I had been in the Dark Lands a good while, twenty-two or maybe twenty-three years, I sensed somebody enter. It was the first time anybody had come in years, and they arrived in the spot Ella had used. I ran all the way there with my sword drawn. A woman who was not Ella stood in the middle of some loaded bags. I recognized her as Pil with her dark braid, although she was older, of course.

"Bib!" she yelled, running toward me and smiling. "I didn't know for sure that I could reach you since this thing has been in salt water for years, but I guess since the God of Deep Waters was . . ." She was holding her arms open but slowed to a stop when I began backing away. "I can see that you have suffered," she said quietly.

I stared at her. Maybe Bixell had wept when Pil said such a

thing, but not me. I opened my mouth, and at first no words came out. Then I croaked, "Where's Ella?"

Pil's face dropped. "I'm sorry, Bib. She died in a storm at sea. It was tragic, and no one could find the 'dent to come tell you since it was lost in the ocean with her." She stood still, watching me.

My breath stopped. The Dark Lands had stripped me down to just what I needed to watch for enemies and kill them. I thought I had accepted that I'd be there alone until I died, but I had been fooling myself. A hidden part of me had been imagining Ella was still there with me.

I walked a few steps away from Pil. I didn't want her to see my face as that hidden part of me withered too.

"Bib?" Pil said.

I waved her away from over my shoulder. I couldn't decide whether I was full of pain or just empty.

"I'm so sorry. I wish I could have saved her," Pil murmured. She walked up and patted my shoulder.

Grief shot through me, but it wasn't as harsh as I had expected. Ella had been gone a long time. I couldn't recall her face anymore, and I didn't remember how her voice sounded. I couldn't be sure which memories of her were real and which were just things I imagined. The pain didn't have a solid place to grab on to.

It confused me all to hell.

Pil walked around me, pushed my arms out of the way, and hugged me. I stood there a while, waiting for something to get better or get worse, but nothing changed. At last, I eased out of the hug and turned away. I think I was about to walk off and leave her, but it was hard to be sure of anything.

Some seconds later, I heard the sound of liquid being poured. I turned back to see Pil filling a mug with beer. That stopped me, and I blurted the first words that came to mind. "If the 'dent was lost, when did you find it? Or did you make another?"

Pil handed me the mug. "I searched off and on for years and searching under the ocean was challenging. You know, I should write a book on how to do it, I never thought of that before. I finally found the 'dent day before yesterday, and it took a day to gather supplies, so when you consider everything, I got here fairly fast."

I drained the mug. The beer tasted like liquid love from somebody who wants to kick your ass. "I can't get drunk anymore."

She looked at me as if I might say something else. After a long pause, she said, "Bib, it's been twenty-two years and a couple of months."

I considered it for a while. "That's not so long."

Pil laughed but stopped when I didn't laugh along with her.

I stared up at the bizarre sky for most of a minute, and she waited. "Your sense of time changes after the first ten years or so." A long couple of minutes passed, and I saw that Pil was watching me. I raised an eyebrow and said, "I'm not crazy."

My statement didn't seem to reassure her, so I tried to behave like a person with all their wits. "Sit down on my fine grass. I own all of it around here." While Pil poured more beer, she examined my scarred face and ruined eye, probably trying to decide how I'd take a friendly insult about my looks.

I thought fast and saved her. "Did you find a husband?"

She gave a sweet smile, almost as charming as the one I remembered. "I did! A tavern owner and a kind man, and we have two boys who are grown men now, but I'll always think of them as boys."

I nodded. "I bet you're a strict mother."

"They think I am. If only they knew how many people I've killed—they'd never talk back again."

After another silence, Pil asked, "Bib, what's happened here?"

She had caught me staring up at the sky. "The usual Dark Lands bullshit."

Pil watched me and seemed to expect more.

"I built a dresser."

After a long wait, she said, "That's all?"

"Well . . . I've collected one hundred seventeen magic weapons. Take your pick. Take some to your friends when you go home." I took a deep breath. "I don't have a right to ask this . . ."

"Go ahead and ask."

I nodded at the 'dent in her hand. "What did you pay to enchant that thing so a person can come here and go back?"

Pil frowned. "You're correct, you don't have a right. Well, I didn't have to kill anybody, if that's what you're wondering. Let's just say there were a number of nice things I would have had in my life, but the gods prevented them."

"Thank you, and . . ." I swallowed. "I hope Ella said thanks."

"I didn't do it for her. I did it for you."

"She should have thanked you anyway." I blinked a few times. "You've grown beautiful. If men don't tell you that, beat them with bricks."

Pil looked worried. With a jerk, she held out the curved 'dent. "Bib, take this and go home. To hell with the Dark Lands. You've done enough."

I thought I had accepted life in the Dark Lands, but this was the second time in five minutes something had blown that idea to hell. Looking at the 'dent, I started to feel that I had to get out of the Dark Lands or I wouldn't exist. I stared at the object in Pil's hand and almost reached for it.

Pil stretched her arm as if she was going to put the 'dent in my hand. "You don't have to go away forever. I'll stay a month, and then you come back a month. We can go back and forth."

"If there's an invasion, you'll be killed."

"You don't know that to be true. I could be ten times more powerful than you by now."

I reached behind my back and grabbed my belt to prevent myself from reaching for the 'dent. "Maybe, but if I go, aren't you afraid I'll strand you here?" I didn't smile as I said it.

"No. Not a bit. I trust you." She wiggled the magic object at me.

"Maybe I don't trust me."

"Bib! I don't think you're happy here!"

"I'm not unhappy. Well, that's a damn lie," I said. "But I don't trust happiness, anyway. People fawn over it too much."

"I just think that . . . after everything you've done, you deserve a better life than this."

I laughed hard, which shocked me. It felt strange, as if I was imitating an animal. "There are a lot of dead people who would disagree with you about what I deserve."

"You're not a good judge about what you deserve!"

I nodded. "Probably not. Come with me. I'll show you the least creepy spots in the Dark Lands. I should at least take you to visit Desh and Yita. Don't forget to bring the beer."

"That reminds me! Stan is retired and playing with his grand-children. I'm sure he'd say hello if he knew I'd be seeing you."

"I'm glad to hear he's well. When does your family expect you home for supper?"

"They don't."

"Hell, you shouldn't let them take you for granted. I have a sword over there that burns with green fire. It will keep admirable order at the supper table."

"I want it then! But not for that." She smiled like a girl with a new doll and then looked serious. "As I said, my boys are grown, and Garrgo died last summer."

"Garrgo?"

"My husband."

"You married a man named Garrgo?" I tried not to laugh. "I'm sorry." I put a hand over my mouth.

Pil's head had come up, and her teeth were clenched. "You should be sorry. You're being cruel."

I forced a straight face. "You're right, I really am sorry. I apolo-gize to the memory of your husband. And also to the memory of your mule named Garrgo!" I rocked back and forth laughing. I hadn't laughed in years.

Pil sighed. "So many of the things Ella said about you are clearer with twenty years of perspective. I'm staying here."

When she said Ella's name, that knocked the laughter out of me. When she said she was staying, my anger flashed. "Goddamn it, staying here is a stupid idea!" I glanced at the sky again and pointed at it. "Look at that crappy mess up there in the heavens. It takes a long time to make friends with it. Don't bother. Staying here is a terrible idea."

Pil poked the grass hard with two fingers. "Who made you Lord of the Dark Lands? Show me the crown. You don't get to decide where I live."

"Well . . . I suppose I don't."

She reached across and took both my scarred hands in hers. "Besides, you're not as old as you were twenty years ago."

ABOUT THE AUTHOR

Bill McCurry blends action, humor, and vivid characters in his dark fantasy novels. They are largely about the ridiculousness of being human, but with swords because swords are cool. Before being published, he wrote three novels that sucked like black holes, and he suggests that anyone who wants to write novels should write and finish some bad novels first. You learn a lot.

Bill was born in Fort Worth, Texas, where the West begins, the stockyards stink, and the old-money families run everything. He later moved to Dallas, where Democrats can get elected, Tom Landry is still loved, and the fourth leading cause of death is starvation while sitting on LBJ Freeway.

Although Dallas is a city that smells like credit cards and despair, Bill and his wife still live there with their five cats. He maintains that the maximum number of cats should actually be three, because if you have four, then one of them can always get behind you.

STAY IN TOUCH!

My newsletter often announces discounts on my books and other products—discounts only announced to newsletter subscribers. There are also bits of news (or previews) about what I'm working on, the lowdown on other authors I think are fun, and some of whatever I'm thinking about at the time. Sign up and try it out. You can unsubscribe at any time.

No spam.

I will never sell or give your information to anybody else.

Did I say **no spam**?

Sign up for the newsletter on my website using this link: https://bill-mccurry.com/index.php/newslettersignup.

- Bill

LEAVE A REVIEW

Please leave a review on the platform of your choice!

https://linktr.ee/reviewdarklands

CONNECT WITH THE AUTHOR

Bill-McCurry.com
Facebook.com/Bill.McCurry3
Twitter.com/BillMcCurry
Instagram.com/bfmccurry

PURCHASE OTHER BOOKS IN THIS SERIES

Shop at: https://tinyurl.com/billmccurrybooks

Made in the USA
Coppell, TX
13 November 2023

24164717R00243

Ancient Christian Gospels

Ancient Christian Gospels

Their History and Development

Helmut Koester

TRINITY PRESS INTERNATIONAL
Philadelphia

SCM PRESS LTD.
London

Third printing 1992

SCM Press Ltd
26–30 Tottenham Road
London N1 4BZ

Trinity Press International
3725 Chestnut Street
Philadelphia, Pa. 19104

Copyright © Helmut Koester 1990

British Library Cataloguing in Publication Data

Koester, Helmut
    Ancient Christian gospels.
    1. Bible. N. T. Gospels - Critical studies
    I. Title
    226.06

    ISBN 0-334-02459-5
    ISBN 0-334-02450-1 pbk

Library of Congress Cataloging-in-Publication Data

Koester, Helmut, 1926-
    Ancient Christian Gospels : their history and development / Helmut
Koester.
        p.   cm.
    Includes bibliographical references.
    ISBN 0-334-02459-5
    1. Bible. N.T. Gospels--Criticism, interpretation, etc.   2. Q
hypothesis (Synoptics criticism)   3. Apocryphal Gospels--Criticism,
interpretation, etc.   4. Gnostic literature--Relation to the New
Testament.   5. Bible. N.T. Gospels--Harmonies--History and
criticism.   I. Title.
BS2555.2.K64 1990
226'.06--dc20   90-34716
                                            CIP

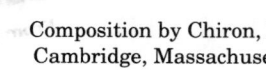

Composition by Chiron, Inc.
Cambridge, Massachusetts

À L'UNIVERSITÉ DE GENÈVE ET À SA FACULTÉ DE THÉOLOGIE
EN TÉMOIGNAGE DE GRATITUDE
POUR LA COLLATION DU DOCTORAT HONORIS CAUSA

Table of Contents

Acknowledgments

Quotations from the Bible are either my own translations or are adapted from the *Revised Standard Version* or the *New Revised Standard Version.*

Many quotations of sayings from the Synoptic Sayings Source are adapted from John Kloppenborg, *Q Parallels.*

English translations of apocryphal literature are taken from Hennecke-Schneemelcher-Wilson, *NT Apocrypha.* Nag Hammadi writings are quoted from Robinson, ed., *The Nag Hammadi Library in English,* or from the extant critical editions in Nag Hammadi Studies.

Quotations from ancient Greek, Roman, and Christian literature are usually adapted from the volumes of Loeb Classical Library.

The treatment of the *Secret Gospel of Mark* and the translation of the text are based upon the manuscript which I have submitted to Polebridge Press for its new edition of the New Testament Apocrypha.

Abbreviations

— *Ecl. Proph.*	— *Eclogae ex scripturis propheticis*
— *Exc. Theod.*	— *Excerpta ex Theodotou*
— *Strom.*	— *Stromateis*
1 Clem.	*1 Clement, Epistle of*
2 Clem.	*2 Clement, Epistle of*
CSCO	Corpus Scriptorum Christianorum Orientalium
CSSN	Corpus sacrae scripturae neerlandica medi aevi
Diogn.	*Diognetus, Epistle to*
Dial. Sav.	*Dialogue of the Savior* (NHC III,5)
Did.	*Didache (Teaching of the Twelve Apostles)*
Diog. L.	Diogenes Laërtius
Diss.	Dissertation (unpublished)
EHT.T	Europäische Hochschulschriften. Reihe 23: Theologie
EdF	Erträge der Forschung
ed(s).	edition, edited, editor(s)
EKK	Evangelisch-katholischer Kommentar zum Neuen Testament
Epiphanius	
— *Haer.*	*Panarion seu adversus lxxx haereses*
Epist. Apost.	*Epistula Apostolorum*
ET	English translation
et al.	et alii (and others)
EtB	Etudes Bibliques
EThL	*Ephemerides theologicae Lovaniensis*
ETR	*Etudes théologiques et religieuses*
EvTh	*Evangelische Theologie*
F&F	Foundations and Facets
FGNK	Forschungen zur Geschichte des neutestamentlichen Kanons
FKDG	Forschungen zur Kirchen- und Dogmengeschichte
FRLANT	Forschungen zur Religion and Literatur des Alten und Neuen Testaments
GBSNTS	Guides to Biblical Scholarship, New Testament Series
GCS	Die griechischen christlichen Schriftsteller
GGA	Göttingische Gelehrte Anzeigen
GLB	De Gruyter Lehrbuch
Gos. Egypt.	*Gospel of the Egyptians*
Gos. Pet.	*Gospel of Peter*

Gos. Thom.	*Gospel of Thomas* (NHC II,2)
Hist. eccl.	*Historia ecclesiae* (Eusebius's *Church History*)
HNT	Handbuch zum Neuen Testament
HNT.EB	Handbuch zum Neuen Testament, Ergänzungsband
HSem	Horae Semiticae
HTR	*Harvard Theological Review*
HTS	Harvard Theological Studies
Ibid.	Ibidem
IDBSup	*The Interpreter's Dictionary of the Bible, Supplementary Volume* (Nashville: Abingdon, 1976)
Ign. *Eph.*	Ignatius, *To the Ephesians*
— *Mg.*	— *To the Magnesians*
— *Trall.*	— *To the Trallians*
— *Rom.*	— *To the Romans*
— *Phld.*	— *To the Philadelphians*
— *Sm.*	— *To the Smyrnaeans*
— *Pol.*	— *To Polycarp*
inscr.	*inscriptio* (introductory phrase or sentence of a writing)
Irenaeus	
— *Adv. haer.*	*Adversus haereses*
JBL	*Journal of Biblical Literature*
JR	*Journal of Religion*
JTS	*Journal of Theological Studies*
Justin	
— *1 Apol.*	*First Apology*
— *Dial.*	*Dialogue with Trypho*
KAV	Kommentar zu den Apostolischen Vätern
KEK	Kritisch-exegetischer Kommentar über das Neue Testament
KlT	Kleine Texte für Vorlesungen und Übungen
LCL	Loeb Classical Library
LSJ	Liddell-Scott-Jones, *Greek-English Lexicon*
LXX	Septuaginta (= the Greek translation of the Old Testament)
MPG	*Migne, Patrologia Graeca*
MPL	*Migne, Patrologia Latina*
n(n).	note(s)
N.F.	Neue Folge (new series)

NHC	Nag Hammadi Corpus
NHS	Nag Hammadi Studies
Noct. Att.	*Noctes Atticae* (Aulus Gellius)
NovT	*Novum Testamentum*
NovTSup	Novum Testamentum Supplements
NT	New Testament
NTA	Neutestamentliche Abhandlungen
NTS	*New Testament Studies*
NumenSup	Supplements to Numen
OLZ	*Orientalische Literaturzeitung*
OrChr	*Oriens Christianus*
OrChrA	Orientalia Christiana Analecta
OT	Old Testament
𝔭	Papyrus of the New Testament
p(p).	page(s)
Pap. Eg. 2	*Papyrus Egerton 2*
Pap. Oxy.	*Papyrus Oxyrhynchus*
par(r).	(Synoptic) parallel(s)
PETSE	Papers of the Estonian Theological Society in Exile
Pol. *Phil.*	Polycarp, *To the Philippians*
Ps-Clem. Hom.	*Pseudo-Clementine Homilies*
PTS	Patristische Texte und Studien
Q	*Quelle: The Synoptic Sayings Source* (the chapter and verse numbers for Q are identical with those of the Gospel of Luke)
RAC	*Reallexikon für Antike und Christentum*
RB	*Revue Biblique*
RGG	*Die Religion in Geschichte und Gegenwart*
RThL	*Revue Théologique de Louvain*
RThPh	*Revue de Théologie et Philosophie*
SAQ	Sammlung ausgewählter kirchen- und dogmengeschichtlicher Quellenschriften
SBB	Stuttgarter Biblische Beiträge
SBLDS	Society of Biblical Literature Dissertation Series
SBLMS	Society of Biblical Literature Monograph Series
SBLTT	Society of Biblical Literature Texts and Translations
SBT	Studies in Biblical Theology
SC	Sources Chrétiennes

SHG	Subsidia hagiographica. Societé des Bollandistes
SHR	Studies in the History of Religions
SHW.PH	Sitzungsberichte der Heidelberger Akademie der Wissenschaften, Phil.-hist. Klasse
SJLA	Studies in Judaism in Late Antiquity
SNTS.MS	Society for New Testament Studies. Monograph Series
StD	Studies and Documents
StNT	Studien zum Neuen Testament
StTh	*Studia Theologica*
StUNT	Studien zur Umwelt des Neuen Testaments
sv. (svv.)	*sub verbo (verbis)* or *sub voce (vocis)*
TaS	Texts and Studies
Tatian, *Or.*	Tatian, *Oratio ad Graecos*
TDNT	*Theological Dictionary to the New Testament*
ThWAT	*Theologisches Wörterbuch zum Alten Testament*
ThLZ	*Theologische Literaturzeitung*
ThR	*Theologische Rundschau*
trans.	translated by
TRE	*Theologische Realenzyklopädie*
TU	Texte und Untersuchungen zur Geschichte der altchristlichen Literatur
VigChr	*Vigiliae Christianae*
VNAW	Verhandelingen [k.] nederlandse akademie van wetenschappen. Afdeling letterkunde
vol(s).	volume(s)
WdF	Wege der Forschung
WMANT	Wissenschaftliche Monographien zum Alten und Neuen Testament
vs., vss.	vers, verses
WuD	*Wort und Dienst*
WUNT	Wissenschaftliche Untersuchungen zum Neuen Testament
ZKG	*Zeitschrift für Kirchengeschichte*
ZNW	*Zeitschrift für die neutestamentliche Wissenschaft*

List of Short Titles

Aland, ed., *Die alten Übersetzungen*
   Kurt Aland, ed., *Die alten Übersetzungen des Neuen Testaments, die Kirchenväterzitate und Lektionare* (ANTT 5; Berlin: De Gruyter, 1972)

Aland, *Kurzgefaßte Liste*
   Kurt Aland, *Kurzgefaßte Liste der griechischen Handschriften des Neuen Testaments* (ANTF 1; Berlin: De Gruyter, 1963).

Aland, *Repetitorium*
   Kurt Aland, *Repetitorium der griechischen christlichen Papyri I: Biblische Papyri* (PTS 18; Berlin: De Gruyter, 1976).

Aland, *Synopsis*
   Kurt Aland, *Synopsis Quattuor Evangeliorum* (Stuttgart: Württembergische Bibelanstalt, 1963 and reprints).

Allison, "Pauline Epistles"
   Dale C. Allison, Jr., "The Pauline Epistles and the Synoptic Gospels: The Pattern of the Parallels" *NTS* 28 (1982) 1–32.

Attridge, "Greek Fragments"
   Harold W. Attridge, "The Greek Fragments," in Layton, ed., *Nag Hammadi Codex II,* 103–9.

Attridge, *Nag Hammadi Codex I*
   Harold W. Attridge, ed., *Nag Hammadi Codex I (The Jung Codex)* (2 vols.; NHS 22–23; Leiden: Brill, 1985).

Baarda, "2 Clement 12"
   Tjitze Baarda, "2 Clement 12 and the Sayings of Jesus," in Delobel, ed., *LOGIA,* 529–56.

Baarda, *Early Transmission*
   Tjitze Baarda, *Early Transmission of the Words of Jesus: Thomas, Tatian and the Text of the New Testament* (Amsterdam: Uitgiverij, 1983).

Baltzer, *Biographie*
   Klaus Baltzer, *Die Biographie der Propheten* (Neukirchen: Neukirchener Verlag, 1975).

Bauer, *Leben Jesu*
Walter Bauer, *Das Leben Jesu im Zeitalter der neutestamentlichen Apokryphen* (Tübingen: Mohr/Siebeck, 1909).

Bell and Skeat, *Unknown Gospel*
H. Idris Bell and T. C. Skeat, *Fragments of an Unknown Gospel and
Other Early Christian Papyri* (London: British Museum, 1935).

Bellinzoni, *Sayings in Justin Martyr*
Arthur Bellinzoni, *The Sayings of Jesus in the Writings of Justin Martyr*
(NovTSup 17; Leiden: Brill, 1967).

Best, "1 Peter"
Ernest Best, "1 Peter and the Gospel Tradition," *NTS* 16 (1969/70)
95–113.

Betz, *Essays*
Hans Dieter Betz, *Essays on the Sermon on the Mount* (Philadelphia:
Fortress, 1985).

Bornkamm-Barth-Held, *Tradition and Interpretation*
Günther Bornkamm, Gerhard Barth, and Heinz-Joachim Held, *Tradition and Interpretation in Matthew* (Philadelphia: Westminster, 1963)

Bovon, *Evangelium nach Lukas*
Francois Bovon, *Das Evangelium nach Lukas. 1. Teilband: Lk 1,1–9,50*
(EKK 3/1; Zürich: Benziger Verlag, and Neukirchen: Neukirchener
Verlag, 1989).

Bovon, "Synoptic Gospels"
Francois Bovon, "The Synoptic Gospels and the Noncanonical Acts of the
Apostles," *HTR* 81 (1988) 19–36.

Brown, *Birth of the Messiah*
Raymond E. Brown, *The Birth of the Messiah: A Commentary on the
Infancy Narratives of Matthew and Luke* (Garden City, NY: Doubleday,
1977).

Brown, *Gospel of John*
Raymond E. Brown, *The Gospel According to John* (2 vols.; AB 29–30;
Garden City, NJ: Doubleday, 1966–70).

Brown, "Thomas and John"
Raymond E. Brown, "The Gospel of Thomas and St. John's Gospel," NTS
9 (1962/63) 155–77.

Bultmann, *Gospel of John*
Rudolf Bultmann, *The Gospel of John: A Commentary* (Philadelphia:
Westminster, 1971).

Bultmann, *Synoptic Tradition*
Rudolf Bultmann, *The History of the Synoptic Tradition* (2d ed.; New
York: Harper & Row, 1968).

Bultmann, *Theology*
> Rudolf Bultmann, *Theology of the New Testament* (2 vols.; New York: Scribner's, 1951–1955).

Cameron, *Apocryphon of James*
> Ron Cameron, *Sayings Traditions in the Apocryphon of James* (HTS 34; Philadelphia: Fortress, 1984).

Cameron, *Other Gospels*
> Ron Cameron, *The Other Gospels: Non-Canonical Gospel Texts* (Philadelphia: Westminster, 1982).   ⋅

Cameron, *Parable and Interpretation*
> Ron Cameron, *Parable and Interpretation in the Gospel of Thomas* (F&F 2.2; Sonoma, CA: Polebridge Press, 1986).

von Campenhausen, *Ecclesiastical Authority*
> Hans von Campenhausen, *Ecclesiastical Authority and Spiritual Power* (Stanford, CA: Stanford University Press, 1969).

von Campenhausen, *Formation*
> Hans von Campenhausen, *The Formation of the Christian Bible* (Philadelphia: Fortress, 1972).

von Campenhausen, *Frühzeit*
> Hans von Campenhausen, *Aus der Frühzeit des Christentums: Studien zur Kirchengeschichte des ersten und zweiten Jahrhunderts* (Tübingen: Mohr/Siebeck, 1963).

Conzelmann, *1 Corinthians*
> Hans Conzelmann, *1 Corinthians: A Commentary on the First Epistle to the Corinthians* (Hermeneia; Philadelphia: Fortress, 1975).

Conzelmann, *Theology of St Luke*
> Hans Conzelmann, *The Theology of St Luke* (London: Faber, 1960).

Conzelmann and Lindemann, *Interpreting the NT*
> Hans Conzelmann and Andreas Lindemann, *Interpreting the New Testament: An Introduction to the Principles and Methods of N.T. Exegesis* (Peabody, MA: Hendrickson, 1988).

Crossan, *The Cross that Spoke*
> John Dominic Crossan, *The Cross that Spoke: The Origins of the Passion Narrative* (San Francisco: Harper & Row, 1988)

Crossan, *Four Other Gospels*
> John Dominic Crossan, *Four Other Gospels: Shadows on the Contours of Canon* (Minneapolis: Winston, 1985)

Crossan, *In Parable*
> John Dominic Crossan, *In Parable: The Challenge of the Historical Jesus* (New York: Harper & Row, 1973).

Daniels, *Egerton Gospel*
    Jon B. Daniels, *The Egerton Gospel: Its Place in Early Christianity*
    (Dissertation Claremont Graduate School, Claremont, CA: 1990).

Davies, *Paul and Rabbinic Judaism*
    W. D. Davies, *Paul and Rabbinic Judaism: Some Rabbinic Elements in
    Pauline Theology* (London: S.P.C.K., 1965).

Deissmann, *Light from the Ancient Near East*
    Adolf Deissmann, *Light from the Ancient Near East* (New York: Doran,
    1927).

Delobel, ed., *LOGIA*
    Joël Delobel, *LOGIA: Les paroles de Jésus — The Sayings of Jesus:
    Memorial Joseph Coppens* (BEThL 59; Leuven: Peeters, 1982).

Dibelius, "Jungfrauensohn"
    Martin Dibelius, "Jungfrauensohn und Krippenkind: Untersuchungen
    zur Geburtsgeschichte Jesu im Lukasevangelium," in idem, *Botschaft
    und Geschichte: Gesammelte Aufsätze,* vol. 1 (Tübingen: Mohr/Siebeck,
    1953) 1–78.

Dibelius-Greeven, *James*
    Martin Dibelius, *James: A Commentary on the Epistle of James,* rev. by
    Heinrich Greeven (Hermeneia, Philadelphia: Fortress, 1976).

Denker, *Petrusevangelium*
    Jürgen Denker, *Die theologiegeschichtliche Stellung des Petrusevan-
    geliums: Ein Beitrag zur Frühgeschichte des Doketismus* (EHS.T 36;
    Bern and Frankfurt: Lang, 1975).

Deppe, *Sayings of Jesus*
    Dean B. Deppe, *The Sayings of Jesus in the Epistle of James* (Disserta-
    tion Amsterdam, Free University, 1989).

Dodd, *Historical Tradition*
    C. H. Dodd, *Historical Tradition in the Fourth Gospel* (Cambridge: Cam-
    bridge University Press, 1963).

Dormeyer, *Evangelium als Gattung*
    Detlev Dormeyer, *Evangelium als literarische und theologische Gattung*
    (EdF 263; Darmstadt: Wissenschaftliche Buchgesellschaft, 1989).

Dormeyer and Frankemölle, "Evangelium als Begriff"
    Detlev Dormeyer and Hubert Frankemölle, "Evangelium als litera-
    rischer und als theologischer Begriff: Tendenzen und Aufgaben der
    Evangelienforschung im 20. Jahrhundert, mit einer Untersuchung des
    Markusevangeliums in seinem Verhältnis zur griechischen Biographie,"
    ANRW 2.25/2. 1541–1704.

Emmel [Koester, Pagels], *Nag Hammadi Codex III,5*
    Stephen Emmel, ed., with an introduction by Helmut Koester and Elaine
    Pagels, *Nag Hammadi Codex III,5: The Dialogue of the Savior* (NHS 26;
    Leiden: Brill, 1984).

Fallon and Cameron, "Forschungsbericht"
  Francis T. Fallon and Ron Cameron, "The Gospel of Thomas: A Forschungsbericht and Analysis," *ANRW* 2. 25/5, 4195–4251.

Foerster, *Gnosis*
  Werner Foerster, *Gnosis: A Selection of Gnostic Texts* (2 vols.; Oxford:
  Clarendon, 1972–74).

Frankemölle, *Evangelium: Forschungsbericht*
  Hubert Frankemölle, *Evangelium. Begriff und Gattung: Ein Forschungsbericht* (SBB 15; Stuttgart: Katholisches Bibelwerk, 1988).

Friedrich, "εὐαγγελίζομαι"
  Gerhard Friedrich, "εὐαγγελίζομαι, κτλ." *TDNT* 2 (1964) 707–37.

Furnish, *Theology and Ethics*
  Victor Paul Furnish, *Theology and Ethics in Paul* (Nashville: Abingdon,
  1968).

Gibson, ed., *The Commentaries of Isho^cdad*
  M. D. Gibson, ed., *The Commentaries of Isho^cdad of Merv* (HSem 5–7; 3
  vols.; Cambridge 1911)

Hengel, *Evangelienüberschriften*
  Martin Hengel, *Die Evangelienüberschriften* (SHW.PH 1984.3; Heidelberg: Winter, 1984).

Hennecke-Schneemelcher-Wilson, *NT Apocrypha*
  Edgar Hennecke, *New Testament Apocrypha* (2 vols.; 3d. ed. by Wilhelm
  Schneemelcher, trans. R. McL. Wilson; Philadelphia: Westminster,
  1963).

Hennecke-Schneemelcher, *NT Apokryphen I*
  Edgar Hennecke, *Neutestamentliche Apokryphen in deutscher Über-
  setzung*, vol. I: *Evangelien* (5th ed. by Wilhelm Schneemelcher;
  Tübingen: Siebeck/Mohr, 1987).

Hoffmann, *Studien*
  Paul Hoffmann, *Studien zur Theologie der Logienquelle* (NTA, N.F. 8; 3d
  ed.; Münster: Aschendorff, 1982).

Huck-Greeven, *Synopsis*
  Albert Huck, *Synopsis of the First Three Gospels* (13th ed. fundamentally
  revised by Heinrich Greeven; Tübingen: Mohr/Siebeck, 1981).

Jeremias, *Parables*
  Joachim Jeremias, *The Parables of Jesus* (rev. ed.; London: SCM, New
  York: Scribner's, 1963).

Jeremias, *Unknown Sayings*
  Joachim Jeremias, *Unknown Sayings of Jesus* (2d. ed.; London: S.P.C.K.,
  1964).

Kirchner, "Brief des Jakobus"
Dankwart Kirchner, "Brief des Jakobus," in Hennecke-Schneemelcher, *NT Apokryphen I,* 234–244.

Kloppenborg, *Formation of Q*
John S. Kloppenborg, *The Formation of Q: Trajectories in Ancient Wisdom Collections* (Studies in Antiquity and Christianity; Philadelphia: Fortress, 1987).

Kloppenborg, *Q Parallels*
John S. Kloppenborg, *Q Parallels: Synopsis, Critical Notes & Concordance* (F&F; Sonoma, CA: Polebridge Press, 1988).

Klostermann, *Apocrypha I*
Erich Klostermann, *Apocrypha I: Reste des Petrusevangeliums, der Petrusapokalypse und des Kerygma Petri* (KlT 3; 3d ed.; Berlin: De Gruyter, 1933).

Klostermann, *Apocrypha II*
Erich Klostermann, *Apocrypha II: Evangelien* (KlT 8; 3d ed.; Berlin: De Gruyter, 1929).

Köhler, *Rezeption des Matthäusevangeliums*
Wolf-Dietrich Köhler, *Die Rezeption des Matthäusevangeliums in der Zeit vor Irenäus* (WUNT 2/24; Tübingen: Mohr/Siebeck, 1986).

Koester, "Apocryphal and Canonical Gospels"
Helmut Koester, "Apocryphal and Canonical Gospels," *HTR* 73 (1980) 105–30.

Koester, "From Mark to Secret Mark"
Helmut Koester, "History and Development of Mark's Gospel: From Mark to Secret Mark and 'Canonical' Mark," in: Bruce C. Corley, ed., *Colloquy on New Testament Studies: A Time for Reappraisal and Fresh Approaches* (Macon, GA: Mercer University Press, 1983) 35–58.

Koester, "Gnostic Writings"
Helmut Koester, "Gnostic Writings as Witnesses for the Development of the Sayings Tradition," in: Bentley Layton, ed., *The Rediscovery of Gnosticism,* vol. 1: *The School of Valentinus* (NumenSup 41; Leiden: Brill, 1980) 239–61.

Koester, "ΓΝΩΜΑΙ ΔΙΑΦΟΡΟΙ"
Helmut Koester, "ΓΝΩΜΑΙ ΔΙΑΦΟΡΟΙ: The Origin and Nature of Diversification in the History of Early Christianity," in Robinson-Koester, *Trajectories,* 114–57.

Koester, *Introduction*
Helmut Koester, *Introduction to the New Testament* (2 vols.; New York, Berlin: De Gruyter, 1982).

Koester, "Kerygma to Gospel"
Helmut Koester, "From the Kerygma-Gospel to Written Gospels," *NTS* 35 (1989) 361–81.

Koester, "La tradition"
Helmut Koester, "La tradition apostolique et les origines du Gnosticisme," *RThPh* 119 (1987) 1–16.

Koester, *Synoptische Überlieferung*
Helmut Koester, *Synoptische Überlieferung bei den apostolischen Vätern* (TU 65; Berlin: Akademie-Verlag, 1957).

Kuhn, *Ältere Sammlungen*
Heinz-Wolfgang Kuhn, *Ältere Sammlungen im Markusevangelium* (StUNT 8; Göttingen: Vandenhoeck & Ruprecht, 1971).

Kümmel, *Das Neue Testament*
Werner Georg Kümmel, *Das Neue Testament: Geschichte der Erforschung seiner Probleme* (Orbis 3.1; Freiburg/München: Alber, 1958).

Layton, *Gnostic Scriptures*
Bentley Layton, *The Gnostic Scriptures: A New Translation with Annotations and Introductions* (Garden City, NY: Doubleday, 1987).

Layton, *Nag Hammadi Codex II*
Bentley Layton, ed., *Nag Hammadi Codex II,2–7 Together with XIII,2*, Brit. Lib. Or. 4926(1) and P. Oxy. 1, 654, 655* (NHS 20–21; Leiden: Brill, 1989).

Leloir, ed., *Saint Éphrem*
Louis Leloir, ed., *Saint Éphrem, Commentaire de l'évangile concordant, version arménienne* (CSCO 137 [text] and 145; Louvain: Peeters, 1953 & 1954).

Lipsius-Bonnet, *Acta Apostolorum Apocrypha*
Ricardus Albertus Lipsius and Maximilianus Bonnet, *Acta Apostolorum Apocrypha* (2 vols.; Leipzig: Mendelssohn, 1891–1898; reprint Darmstadt: Wissenschaftliche Buchgesellschaft, 1959).

Lührmann, *Redaktion*
Dieter Lührmann, *Die Redaktion der Logienquelle* (WMANT 33; Neukirchen: Neukirchener Verlag, 1969).

Lührmann, *Markusevangelium*
Dieter Lührmann, *Das Markusevangelium* (HNT 3; Tübingen: Mohr/Siebeck, 1987).

Lutz, *Matthew 1–7*
Ulrich Lutz, *Matthew 1–7: A Commentary* (Minneapolis: Augsburg, 1989).

Marxsen, *Markus*
Willi Marxsen, *Der Evangelist Markus* (FRLANT 67; Göttingen: Vandenhoeck & Ruprecht, 1956).

Massaux, *Influence de l'Évangile de Saint Matthieu*
Édouard Massaux, *Influence de l'Évangile de Saint Matthieu sur la littérature chrétienne avant Saint Irénée* (reprint; Leuven: Leuven University Press, 1986).

Mayeda, *Leben-Jesu-Fragment*
Goro Mayeda, *Das Leben-Jesu-Fragment Papyrus Egerton 2 und seine Stellung in der urchristlichen Literaturgeschichte* (Bern: Haupt, 1946).

McDonald, *Formation*
Lee Martin McDonald, *The Formation of the Christian Biblical Canon* (Nashville: Abingdon, 1988).

Metzger, *Text*
Bruce Metzger, *The Text of the New Testament* (Oxford: Clarendon, 1964).

Metzger, *Textual Commentary*
Bruce Metzger, *A Textual Commentary on the Greek New Testament* (New York: United Bible Society, 1971).

Neirynck, *Minor Agreements*
Frans Neirynck, *The Minor Agreements of Matthew and Luke against Mark* (BEThL 37; Louvain: Leuven University Press, 1974).

Nestle-Aland, *NT Graece*
Erwin Nestle, *Novum Testamentum Graece* (26th ed. by Kurt Aland et al.; Stuttgart: Deutsche Bibelstiftung, 1979 and later reprints).

Niederwimmer, *Didache*
Kurt Niederwimmer, *Die Didache* (KEK, KAV 1; Göttingen: Vandenhoeck & Ruprecht, 1988).

Pearson, "Earliest Christianity in Egypt"
Birger A. Pearson, "Earliest Christianity in Egypt: Some Observations," in idem and James E. Goehring, eds., *The Roots of Egyptian Christianity* (Studies in Antiquity and Christianity; Philadelphia: Fortress, 1986) 132–56.

Pesch, *Markusevangelium*
Rudolf Pesch, *Das Markusevangelium* (2 vols.; Herders Kommentar; Freiburg: Herder, 1977)

Petersen, *The Diatessaron and Ephrem Syrus*
William L. Petersen, *The Diatessaron and Ephrem Syrus as Sources of Romanos the Melodist* (CSCO 475; Leuven: Peeters, 1985).

Robinson, "Kerygma and History"
James M. Robinson, "Kerygma and History in the New Testament," in Robinson-Koester, *Trajectories,* 20–70.

Robinson, "LOGOI SOPHON"
James M. Robinson, "LOGOI SOPHON: On the Gattung of Q," in Robinson-Koester, *Trajectories,* 71–113.

Robinson, ed., *Nag Hammadi Library*
James M. Robinson, ed., *The Nag Hammadi Library in English* (3d completely rev. ed.; San Francisco: Harper & Row, 1988).

Robinson-Koester, *Trajectories*
    James M. Robinson and Helmut Koester, *Trajectories through Early Christianity* (Philadelphia: Fortress, 1971).

Rudolph, *Gnosis*
    Kurt Rudolph, *Gnosis: The Nature and History of an Ancient Religion* (Edinburgh: Clark, 1983).

Schmithals, *Einleitung*
    Walter Schmithals, *Einleitung in die drei ersten Evangelien* (GLB; Berlin: De Gruyter, 1985).

Schmithals, *Markus*
    Walther Schmithals, *Das Evangelium nach Markus* (Ökumenischer Taschenbuchkommentar zum NT 2/1; Gütersloh: Gütersloher Verlagshaus, 1979).

Schniewind, *Euangelion*
    Julius Schniewind, *Euangelion: Ursprung und erste Gestalt des Begriffs Evangelium* (BFChTh 13; Gütersloh: Bertelsmann, 1927; reprint: Wissenschaftliche Buchgesellschaft: Darmstadt, 1970).

Schoedel, *Ignatius*
    William R. Schoedel, *Ignatius of Antioch: A Commentary on the Letters of Ignatius of Antioch* (Hermeneia; Philadelphia: Fortress, 1985).

Schulz, *Spruchquelle*
    Siegfried Schulz, *Q: Die Spruchquelle der Evangelisten* (Zürich: Theologischer Verlag, 1972).

Morton Smith, *Clement of Alexandria*
    Morton Smith, *Clement of Alexandria and a Secret Gospel of Mark* (Cambridge, MA: Harvard University Press, 1973 [transcription, plates, and translation: pp. 445–54]).

Stendahl, *School of St. Matthew*
    Krister Stendahl, *The School of St. Matthew and Its Use of the Old Testament* (2d ed.; Philadelphia: Fortress, 1968).

Streeter, *Four Gospels*
    B. H. Streeter, *The Four Gospels: A Study of Origins* (London: Macmillan, 1924).

Stuhlmacher, ed., *Evangelium und Evangelien*
    Peter Stuhlmacher, ed., *Das Evangelium und die Evangelien* (WUNT 28; Tübingen: Mohr/Siebeck, 1983).

Stuhlmacher, *Das paulinische Evangelium*
    Peter Stuhlmacher, *Das paulinische Evangelium: I. Vorgeschichte* (FRLANT 95; Göttingen: Vandenhoeck & Ruprecht, 1968).

Throckmorton, *Gospel Parallels*
    Burton H. Throckmorton, *Gospel Parallels: A Synopsis of the First Three Gospels* (4th ed.; Nashville and New York: Nelson, 1979).

Vielhauer, *Geschichte*
Philipp Vielhauer, *Geschichte der frühchristlichen Literatur* (GLB; Berlin: De Gruyter, 1975).

Vogels, *Beiträge zur Geschichte des Diatessaron*
Heinrich Joseph Vogels, *Beiträge zur Geschichte des Diatessaron im Abendland* (NTA 8/1: Münster: Aschendorff, 1919).

Völker, *Quellen*
Walther Völker, *Quellen zur Geschichte der christlichen Gnosis* (SAQ 5; Tübingen: Mohr/Siebeck, 1932).

Wengst, *Didache*
Klaus Wengst, *Didache (Apostellehre), Zweiter Clemensbrief, Schrift an Diognet* (Schriften des Urchristentums 2; Darmstadt: Wissenschaftliche Buchgesellschaft, 1984).

Williams, "Apocryphon of James"
Francis E. Williams, ed., "The Apocryphon of James," in Harold W. Attridge, ed., *Nag Hammadi Codex I (The Jung Codex): Introductions, Texts, Translations, Notes* (NHS 22; Leiden: Brill, 1985) 13–53.

Wilson and MacRae, "Gospel According to Mary"
R. McL. Wilson and George W. MacRae, "The Gospel According to Mary," in Douglas M. Parrott, ed., *Nag Hammadi Codices V,2–5 and VI with Papyrus Berolinensis 8502, 1 and 4* (NHS 11; Leiden: Brill, 1979) 470.

Zahn, *Kanon*
Theodor Zahn, *Geschichte des neutestamentlichen Kanons* (2 vols.; Erlangen: Deichert, 1888–89).

Preface

Forty years ago, in the year 1950, when I visited my teacher Rudolf Bultmann at his house, Calvinstraße 14 in Marburg, he suggested that I write a dissertation on the "Gospels in the Second Century." At that time, rumors about the discovery of a *Gospel of Thomas* had not yet reached the peaceful University of Marburg. Some other apocryphal gospels were, of course, known, and my subsequent research involved me, among other things, in some frustrating study of the problem of the Jewish-Christian Gospels. But it was fortunate that a simple treatment of the "Synoptic Tradition in the Apostolic Fathers" was deemed satisfactory as a doctoral thesis and that I was thus freed from the much more ambitious aims of the thesis topic that my Doktorvater initially suggested.

However, I always felt that I should one day write a book on the gospels in the second century. My study of the gospel traditions in the Apostolic Fathers had brought me to the conclusion that gospel materials that were not dependent upon the canonical writings might indeed have survived well into the second century. But I was also aware of the prevailing opinion, which saw all apocryphal gospels as works that came into existence after the completion of the canonical writings. Attempts to discover in apocryphal materials pre-canonical traditions regularly met with severe criticism. That point of view still dominated the third edition of Edgar Hennecke's "Neutestamentliche Apokrypen," which was published by Wilhelm Schneemelcher in 1959, and which served as the basis for R. McL. Wilson's English translation of this work.[1]

The publication of the *Gospel of Thomas* in the year 1959 marks the beginning of a change. Equally important, however, was the redis-

---

[1] I was informed by the publisher Westminster/John Knox Press that an English translation of the new and thoroughly revised 5th German edition of this work, published in 1987, will be published presently.

covery of Walter Bauer's *Rechtgläubigkeit und Ketzerei im ältesten Christentum,* which had been published in 1934. The appearance of a second edition of this epochal work thirty years after its original publication and four years after the death of its author[1] as well as the publication of an English translation[2] signified a fundamental change in the climate of scholarship. It seemed as if almost two millennia of discrimination against those whom the Fathers of the church had labelled as "heretics" would come to an end. If these "heresies" were not simply secondary deviations from an already established orthodoxy, but resulted from developments in the Christian communities that occurred as early as the time of Paul's mission to the Gentiles, also their gospels could claim to be genuine continuations of the earliest stages of the formation of the traditions about Jesus of Nazareth.

What is put to the test is the "early-catholic" or "orthodox" tradition, which asserts the monopoly of the canonical gospel tradition. That there were Christians who disputed this assertion cannot be questioned. Later, in the second half of the second century, "catholic" and "heretical" Christians began to become more clearly distinguished from each other. However, the gospels discussed in this book belong to an earlier period in which these dividing lines had not yet been drawn. There were controversies, to be sure, and some of them are clearly visible as early as the the middle of the 1st century, that is, in the time of the apostle Paul. But the traditions about Jesus were shared to a large degree by all participants in these controversies. In his arguments against the heretics, the early 3d-century apologist Tertullian (*De proscriptione hereticorum*) insisted that the claims of the heretics were null and void and had to be ruled out of court because they could not prove that they existed in the very beginning. It is, however, not possible to substantiate this claim. The earliest gospel traditions and gospel writings contain the seeds of both, later heresy as well as later orthodoxy. For the description of the history and development of gospel literature in the earliest period of Christianity, the epithets "heretical" and "orthodox" are meaningless. Only dogmatic prejudice can assert that the canonical writings have an exclusive claim to apostolic origin and thus to historical priority. Whether my own reconstruction of the development of this literature is plausible, should be argued on historical and source-critical grounds.

The result of this new orientation was a shift in focus for the investigation of the apocryphal gospels. Those apocryphal writings, which

---

[1] Second edition by Georg Strecker (BHTh 10; Göttingen: Vandenhoeck & Ruprecht, 1964).

[2] *Orthodoxy and Heresy in Earliest Christianity* (Philadelphia: Fortress, 1971).

might yield insights into the earliest stages of the development of the gospel tradition, moved into the center of the scholarly debate, while the investigation of other extra-canonical writings, which were evidently dependent upon the gospels of the canon, however important and rewarding, had to take second place.

This book is the result of this shift. It includes extensive treatments of all those writings from which one might, in my judgment, learn more about the earliest stages of the history and development of gospel literature—a history that must have begun with smaller written collections of materials about Jesus and eventually resulted in the composition of a number of gospel writings, including so-called apocryphal gospels as well as the Gospels of the New Testament canon, John, Mark, Matthew, and Luke. This historical development culminated in the only partially successful attempt to create the one gospel for the church, that is, Tatian's *Diatessaron* (I thank Professor Petersen, one of the few experts of this ancient work, for contributing a chapter on the *Diatessaron,* which may well prove to be one of the most valuable parts of this book). As a consequence, I had to choose. The Synoptic Sayings Source (Q), the *Gospel of Thomas,* the *Dialogue of the Savior,* the *Unknown Gospel of Papyrus Egerton 2,* the *Apocryphon of James* and the *Gospel of Peter* seemed to have contributed to this first phase of the history of gospel literature and therefore had to be moved to center stage. But gospel writings that were dependent upon these earliest gospels and upon the Gospels of the New Testament canon, including such important writings as the Jewish-Christian Gospels, the *Epistula Apostolorum,* the *Gospel of Nicodemus* and many other non-canonical gospels and gospel fragments, had to take second place and are not included in this volume. Deo volente, some day I may be able to write a sequel to this book in which these later gospels will be discussed.

This book is the result of a still ongoing debate. I owe much to those who have expressed their disagreement with my view of these earliest non-canonical writings, and it is evident that the publication of this work will not end the controversy. I owe even more to the scholars, students, and friends, whose work has pointed into similar or analogous directions. It is perhaps appropriate, in this preface, to mention at least three friends who have been most helpful and influential on my way to the completion of this book. James M. Robinson of the Claremont Graduate School and Director of the Institute for Antiquity and Christianity in Claremont, California, to whom I am indebted for more than three decades of a shared path; François Bovon of the University of Geneva, Switzerland, who once dedicated a book to me as "le défenseur des Apocryphes"; Klaus Baltzer of the University of

Munich, Germany, whose wisdom and advice has accompanied my work throughout my career, beginning in 1954 when we both served as "assistants" of the Faculty of Theology at the University of Heidelberg.

But I also owe an apology to all those scholars whose work I failed to acknowledge. Whatever I have learned from others I have tried to indicate in every instance. I also noted in many cases my disagreements with the work of my colleagues. I have not listed what I thought was irrelevant, but I am sure that I have missed much that may very well be significant. But to achieve a complete coverage of all relevant literature became a task which I was unable to accomplish, especially with respect to the canonical Gospels. There are numerous questions that I consciously excluded. This book is not devoted to the age-old problem of the historical Jesus, nor can I claim to contribute to the more recent question of "the gospels as literature." My interest is the historical development of ancient traditions and writings, and I wish that those who want to discuss such important problems as the historical Jesus and the literary dimensions of gospel writing would pay more attention to the transmission of traditions about Jesus and to the process of the collection of materials in ancient books. If the social component of the development of these traditions is barely mentioned on the following pages, I would like to remind the reader that this will involve a thorough investigation of the relevant literary and archaeological data from the world of ancient Christianity—a work that we have scarcely even begun.

I am grateful that my student John Lanci read the manuscript and gave helpful advice in numerous instances. When I visited the University of Göttingen recently, Professor Gerd Lüdemann showed me some of the original photographs of the scholars of the "Religionsgeschichtliche Schule," of whom published pictures are well known. In several instances the originals pictured these scholars together with their wives—but their spouses had been cut out of the published photographs. My wife, Gisela Koester, has translated two theological books into German, and in the translator's preface she gives me credit for the typing of the manuscript. It is, therefore, fitting that I should express here my indebtedness to her for all her patient and helpful listening to the progress of my work and for her indulgence with respect to all sorts of things around the house that I should have done rather than working on this manuscript.

Lexington, Massachusetts
Friday, July 13, 1990

Helmut Koester

1
The Term "Gospel"

1.1 The Origin of the Term "Gospel" [1]

1.1.1 THE GREEK USAGE OF THE TERM

The English noun "gospel" is the translation of the Greek word εὐαγγέλιον (Latin *evangelium*). It is commonly understood to designate "good news" as the corresponding verb εὐαγγελίζεσθαι is normally translated "to proclaim good news" or "to preach (the) good news." Both the noun and the verb occur frequently in the New Testament and in other early Christian literature. However, in Greek literature outside of the Biblical and Christian writings both the noun and the verb are comparatively rare. The verb εὐαγγελίζεσθαι occurs for the first time in Greek literature in Aristophanes. It is used for bringing news about victories or other joyful events, but soon becomes synonymous with and stands for the bringing of any news, good or bad.[2] In classical Greek, the noun εὐαγγέλιον means "reward for good news" and, especially in the plural, "thankoffering for good news" (εὐαγγέλια θύειν). In the Roman imperial period, the noun was also used

---

[1] A discussion of the entire complex was presented by Peter Stuhlmacher, *Das paulinische Evangelium: I. Vorgeschichte* (FRLANT 95; Göttingen: Vandenhoeck & Ruprecht, 1968). The most recent extensive treatment was published by Detlev Dormeyer and Hubert Frankemölle, "Evangelium als literarischer und als theologischer Begriff: Tendenzen und Aufgaben der Evangelienforschung im 20. Jahrhundert, mit einer Untersuchung des Markusevangeliums in seinem Verhältnis zur griechischen Biographie," *ANRW* 2.25/2. 1541–1704.; see also Detlev Dormeyer, *Evangelium als literarische und theologische Gattung* (EdF 263; Darmstadt: Wissenschaftliche Buchgesellschaft, 1989). A critical discussion of the various positions in the scholarly debate can be found in Hubert Frankemölle, *Evangelium. Begriff und Gattung: Ein Forschungsbericht* (SBB 15; Stuttgart: Katholisches Bibelwerk 1988). See also Helmut Koester, "From the Kerygma-Gospel to Written Gospels," *NTS* 35 (1989) 361–81.

[2] Cf. Gerhard Friedrich, "εὐαγγελίζομαι, κτλ.," *TDNT* 2 (1964) 707–37; Stuhlmacher, *Das paulinische Evangelium*, 180–206.

to designate the good news itself.[1] Although the words are formed with the Greek prefix ευ- (= "good," "well") which gives terms composed in this way often a positive connotation, there is little reason to assume that the meaning "'good' news" was felt strongly in ordinary Greek usage. Rather, the noun normally means simply "news," "message" and particularly in Christian usage "preaching"; the verb should then be translated as "to bring a message," or "to preach." Other terms formed with the same prefix confirm this translation.[2]

1.1.2 THE USAGE OF THE TERM IN THE OLD TESTAMENT

The noun occurs only a few times in the Greek Old Testament (Septuagint).[3] It has no particular technical meaning and can be used for all sorts of messages.[4] More significant is the use of the verb εὐαγγελίζεσθαι which occurs several times in Deutero-Isaiah.[5] Εὐαγγελίζεσθαι occurs four times in Deutero-Isaiah, twice each in Isa 40:9 and 52:7. The context is theological: the proclamation of the message of the beginning of the rule of Yahweh and thus of the beginning of liberation and peace. It is used here to designate the message that announces the liberation of the people. This is even heightened in the use of the verb in Trito-Isaiah where the prophet describes his own mission as "to proclaim to the poor" (εὐαγγελίζεσθαι πτωχοῖς, Isa 61:1). This has certainly influenced the usage of the term in the New Testament. Isa

---

[1] This is not made clear in the article of Friedrich quoted above. For the use of the term in the Greco-Roman world see especially Julius Schniewind, *Euangelion: Ursprung und erste Gestalt des Begriffs Evangelium* (BFChTh 13; Gütersloh: Bertelsmann, 1927; reprint: Wissenschaftliche Buchgesellschaft: Darmstadt, 1970) 113–258.

[2] For the use of εὐχαριστία = "thanksgiving" in the NT, cf., e.g., 1 Cor 14:16; Eph 5:4; 1 Tm 2:1, 3, 4; Rev 4:9; 7:12. As a designation of the thanksgiving meal (= the Lord's Supper), cf. Ign. *Eph.* 13.1; *Phld.* 4; *Sm.* 7.1 (see Hans Conzelmann, "χάρις, εὐχαριστέω, κτλ." *TDNT* 9 [1974] 407–15). For the use of εὐλογία = "blessing" in the NT, cf. 1 Cor 10:16; Gal 3:14; Jas 3:10; Rev 5:12, 13; 7:12. In classical Greek, this term means "praise," "laudation" (cf. Hermann Wolfgang Beyer, "εὐλογέω, κτλ.," *TDNT* 2 [1964] 754–65). In its Christian usage, this term is entirely determined by the Hellenistic-Jewish language of worship and by the Septuagint where it occurs as a translation of ברכה.

[3] Εὐαγγέλιον occurs in the Septuagint only three times: 2 Kings 4:10; 18:22, 25, each time as the translation of בשרה. The feminine εὐαγγελία is used in 2 Kings 18:20, 27; 4 Kings 7:9 as a translation of the same Hebrew term. Except for 2 Kings 4:10, where it means "reward for good news," it must be translated in all instances as "news," "message."

[4] Since the Hebrew equivalent בשרה is used for "bad message" in at least one instance (1 Sam 4:17: the news of the defeat of Israel and of the death of the sons of Eli), one must assume that the term was neutral. See also the discussion and literature in O. Schilling, "בשׂר," *ThWAT* 1. 845–49.

[5] Each time as a translation for a Hebrew verb from the root בשׂר.

52:7 is quoted in Rom 10:15: "as it is written, 'how beautiful are the feet of those bringing good news'" (καθὼς γέγραπται· ὡς ὡραῖοι οἱ πόδες τῶν εὐαγγελιζομένων ἀγαθά). Matthew sees the proclamation of John the Baptist and of Jesus in terms of Isa 40:9 and 52:7. Luke 4:18 refers to Isa 61:1, cf. Luke 7:22 (= Matt 11:6). In both instances, however, the dependence upon the usage of the term in the Book of Isaiah is the product of secondary redaction of older materials.[1] There is no evidence that the earliest Christian use of εὐαγγέλιον and εὐαγγελίζεσθαι in its formative stage is in any way influenced by these prophetic passages from the Old Testament.[2] The assumption that the occurrence of the verb in Deutero-Isaiah is ultimately responsible for the widespread technical use of the noun in early Christianity is unwarranted. It must also be noted that in Isa 52:7 (which Paul quotes in Rom 10:15), the verb alone does not have the meaning "to bring good news"; rather, the meaning "good" is expressed in the object of the verb (ἀγαθά).

1.1.3 THE TERM IN THE IMPERIAL INSCRIPTIONS

More closely related to the early Christian usage of the term is the occurrence of εὐαγγέλιον in a number of inscriptions from the early Roman imperial period. Most of these inscriptions are related to the introduction of the Julian Calendar, that is, the calendar of Julius Caesar, which was generally introduced in the Roman world during the time of Augustus.[3] The inscription from Priene (9 BCE) is probably the most famous among these calendar inscriptions. It celebrates the benefactions which have come into the world through Augustus, whom divine providence has sent as a savior (σωτήρ) and who has brought the wars to an end and established an order of peace:

> ... and since the Caesar through his appearance (ἐπιφανεῖν) has exceeded the hopes of all former good messages (εὐαγγέλια), surpassing not only the benefactors who came before him, but also leaving no hope

---

[1] For a critical discussion of the assumption that already Jesus may have understood himself as the messenger of Deutero-Isaiah see Frankemölle, *Evangelium: Forschungsbericht,* 73–79; also idem, "Jesus als deutero-jesajanischer Freudenbote," Paper presented to the Forty-Third General Meeting of the SNTS in Cambridge, England, August 1988.

[2] Other allusions to Deutero- and Trito-Isaiah's use of εὐαγγελίζεσθαι are rare in the NT. Perhaps Acts 10:36; Eph 2:17 and 6:15 could be mentioned (see above on the use of these Isaiah passages in Matthew and Luke).

[3] On the use of εὐαγγέλιον for the announcement of the enthronement of the emperor see the materials in Friedrich, "εὐαγγέλιον," 721–25; Adolf Deissmann, *Light from the Ancient Near East* (New York: Doran, 1927) 366–67; Schniewind, *Euangelion,* 87–93; Stuhlmacher, *Das paulinische Evangelium,* 196–203.

that anyone in the future would surpass him, and since for the world the birthday of the god was the beginning of his good messages (Ἦρξεν δὲ τῷ κόσμῳ τὴν δι' αὐτόν (sc. τὸν Σεβαστὸν) εὐαγγελίων ἡ γενέθλιος ἡμέρα τοῦ θεοῦ) [may it therefore be decided that . . .].[1]

All these inscriptions result from the religio-political propaganda of Augustus in which the rule of peace, initiated by Augustus's victories and benefactions, is celebrated and proclaimed as the beginning of a new age. This usage of the term εὐαγγέλιον is new in the Greco-Roman world. It elevates this term and equips it with a particular dignity. Since the Christian usage of the term for its saving message begins only a few decades after the time of Augustus, it is most likely that the early Christian missionaries were influenced by the imperial propaganda in their employment of the word.[2] Also the Christian usage is eschatological, as the missionaries proclaim the beginning of a new age and call this proclamation their "gospel."

1.2 The Use of the Term "Gospel" in the Pauline Tradition

1.2.1 THE LETTERS OF PAUL

In the earliest Christian documents, i.e., the letters of the apostle Paul, the terms "gospel" (εὐαγγέλιον) and "to preach (the gospel)" (εὐαγγελίζεσθαι) are already well-established technical terms for the Christian message and its proclamation.[3] With this meaning, both the noun and the verb appear frequently in the Pauline writings.[4] Whether

---

[1] For the entire Greek text of the inscription see Wilhelm Dittenberger, *Orientis Graeci inscriptiones selectae* (2 vols.; Hildesheim: Olms, 1960) # 458, vol. 2, pp. 48–60. The text quoted above is found in lines 40–42. The Greek text of the portion of the inscription quoted above is conveniently reprinted with a brief commentary in Gerhard Pfohl, ed., *Griechische Inschriften als Zeugnisse des privaten und öffentlichen Lebens* (Tusculum; München: Heimeran, no year) 134–35.

[2] Most scholars are very hesitant to see a connection of the early-Christian use and the employment of the term in the imperial propaganda; e.g., Rudolf Bultmann, *Theology of the New Testament* (2 vols.; New York: Scribner's, 1951–1955) 1. 87; cf. the discussion in Frankemölle, *Evangelium: Forschungsbericht*, 80–88.

[3] It is very difficult to establish evidence for a pre-Pauline Christian usage of these terms, *pace* Stuhlmacher (*Das paulinische Evangelium*, 209–44) who discusses Rev 10:7; 14:6; Matt 11:5 (= Luke 7:22); Luke 4:18; Mark 1:14; and Matt 4:23; 9:35; 24:14; 16:13 as possible evidence for the use of εὐαγγέλιον and εὐαγγελίζεσθαι by the Palestinian church, possibly by Jesus himself. It is more probable that the Pauline use of the terms derives from the early Hellenistic church from which Paul derives such kerygmatic formulations, called "gospel," as 1 Thess 1:9–10 and 1 Cor 15:3–5; cf. Bultmann, *Theology*, 87–89.

[4] The noun εὐαγγέλιον occurs forty-eight times in the genuine Pauline letters. In twenty-six of these occurrences it is used absolute, without a following genitive; four-

Paul says "the gospel of God"[1] of which he is the apostle,[2] or "the gospel of Christ,"[3] he is always referring to one and the same gospel. Most frequently he uses the term without a genitive as a technical term for both the action of the proclamation and for the content of the message.[4] He presupposes that the content is understood and requires no further definition or explication. This use of the word in the absolute sense reflects a distinctively Christian development. While in pagan and Jewish literature the term designates any kind of message and therefore demanded further explanation of its content, in the early Christian usage the word refers exclusively to the one and only saving message of Christ.[5]

The verb εὐαγγελίζεσθαι, however, does not have quite the same exclusive technical meaning. In 1 Thess 3:6, Paul speaks of the arrival of Timothy "who brought the (good) message" (εὐαγγελισαμένου) of the Thessalonians' faith and love. Here the verb refers to some information that Paul received. But in 1 Cor 1:17 ("Christ did not send me to baptize, but to preach," εὐαγγελίζεσθαι) the verb clearly designates the Christian missionary's activity of proclamation.[6] However, other verbs are frequently used with the same meaning; cf. Phil 1:14–17 where "to say the word" (λόγον λαλεῖν), "to announce" (κηρύσσειν), and "to proclaim" (καταγγέλειν) are used side by side in the same context.[7]

---

teen times the genitive "of God" (τοῦ θεοῦ) or "of Christ" (τοῦ Χριστοῦ) follows. Τὸ εὐαγγέλιον ἡμῶν (1 Thess 1:5) means "the gospel that we preach." ἕτερον εὐαγγέλιον (2 Cor 11:4; Gal 1:6) is used in such a way that the implication is unmistakable: there is no such thing as "another gospel." The term has a somewhat different meaning in the phrase τὸ εὐαγγέλιον τῆς ἀκροβυστίας (Gal 2:7): it is the office of preaching to the uncircumcised, but not a different gospel that is preached to them. "My gospel" (τὸ εὐαγγέλιόν μου) in Rom 16:25 is certainly not Pauline; Rom 3:16, where the same phrase appears, may also be a later interpolation; cf. 2 Tim 2:8.

[1] τὸ εὐαγγέλιον τοῦ θεοῦ, 1 Thess 2:2, 8–9; 2 Cor 11:7.

[2] Rom 1:1; 15:16.

[3] τὸ εὐαγγέλιον τοῦ Χριστοῦ, Rom 15:19; 1 Cor 9,12; 2 Cor 12:12; etc.

[4] Rom 1:16; 1 Cor 4:15; 9:14; etc.

[5] On this technical usage of the term see Bultmann, *Theology*, 1. 87–88.

[6] The verb appears nineteen times in the genuine Pauline letters. It can be used in a technical sense insofar as it means not only "to announce," "to proclaim" (1 Cor 9:16, 18; Gal 1:16, 23; 4,13; 1 Thess 3:6), but also in the full sense "to preach the gospel" (Rom 1:15; 15:20; 1 Cor 1:17; 2 Cor 10:16; Gal 1:8–9). For emphasis, Paul can also say εὐαγγελίζεσθαι τὸ εὐαγγέλιον (2 Cor 11:7; cf. Gal 2:11; 1 Cor 15:1).

[7] Full equivalents of εὐαγγελίζεσθαι are κηρύσσειν ("to proclaim," Rom 10:8, 14, 15; 1 Cor 1:23; 9:27; 15:11; Gal 2:2), καταγγέλλειν ("to announce," 1 Cor 2:1; 9:14; 11:26; Phil 1:17–18), λαλεῖν ("to speak", Phil 1:14; 1 Thess 2:2, 4, 16). In the Acts of the Apostles, διαμαρτύρεσθαι appears frequently as the equivalent of εὐαγγελίζεσθαι (Acts 2:40; 8:25; 10:42; 18:5; 20:21, 24; 28:23).

In the letters of Paul, there is no fixed formulation for the content of the "gospel." But there are some passages in which Paul characterizes the content of the gospel with words that may be described as short kerygmatic or credal formulae. The earliest of these formulae appears in 1 Thess 1:9–10:

> How you turned from the idols to God in order to serve the true and living God, and to wait for his Son from heaven whom he raised from the dead, Jesus who delivers us from the wrath to come.

In 1 Cor 15:1–5 Paul reminds the Corinthians of the message that he had been proclaiming among them. The phrases used here seem to suggest a fixed formulation of the content of the gospel that was formally handed down like a piece of tradition:[1]

> The gospel
> that I preached to you (τὸ εὐαγγέλιον ὃ εὐαγγελισάμην ὑμῖν)
> which you received (ὃ καὶ παρελάβετε),
> in which you stand, by which you are also saved,
> with which word we preached (εὐαγγελισάμην) to you,
> ... because I handed it over (παρέδωκα) to you in the beginning what I
> also received (ὃ καὶ παρέλαβον),
>> that Christ died for us according to the scriptures,
>> that he was buried,
>> that he was raised on the third day according to the scriptures
>> and that he appeared to Cephas, then to the Twelve.

It is clear that Paul wants to emphasize that the gospel preached by him was not his own special gospel, but the common gospel of the entire enterprise of the Christian mission. Therefore, he emphasizes the "receiving" and "transmitting" of the gospel. This, however, does not imply that the "gospel" was a written document, nor can it be assumed that the formulation of the orally transmitted gospel was fixed and stable. Neither the formula quoted in 1 Corinthians 15, nor any other formulaic statement of the content of the gospel in Paul is ever repeated in the entire Pauline corpus. On the contrary, the heterogeneity of such formulae is striking. There are only a few central elements which appear repeatedly in these formulations, albeit in

---

[1] Of these verses, at least 1 Cor 15:3–5 can be considered part of a tradition that is introduced by a quotation formula containing terms that are analogous to the technical Pharisaic-Rabbinic terminology for the transmission of traditions. However, Paul apparently expanded the cited tradition, and he does not refer to any names in a chain of transmission which would guarantee its trustworthiness. On the whole question, see Klaus Wegenast, *Das Verständnis der Tradition bei Paulus und in den Deuteropaulinen* (WMANT 8; Neukirchen: Neukirchener Verlag, 1962) 57–70.

different combinations and in different assortments of terms. These elements are:

> Christ's suffering and death
> > his sacrifice "for us,"
> > his cross,
> > his being raised from the dead (or rising from the dead),
> > his appearances,
> > his coming again in the future.

1.2.2 THE LETTERS OF IGNATIUS

A further development in the history of these gospel formulae is visible in the letters of Ignatius of Antioch, written ca. 110 CE.[1] Here the "gospel" is still in general the preaching of Jesus Christ, and Ignatius never implies that he is speaking of a written text when he uses this term. But whenever the content of the gospel is quoted, the formulations—though still variable—become more fixed. Cross, death, and resurrection are more often mentioned together in formulaic expressions. In *Phld.* 8.1, Ignatius juxtaposes the gospel to the "archives," i.e., the Scriptures in which his opponents claim to possess the basis for Christian faith:

> But for me the archives are Jesus Christ, the inviolable archives are his cross and death and his resurrection and faith through him.[2]

Furthermore, additional topics supplement these formulations in Ignatius: Christ's birth through the virgin and his baptism. This expansion of the gospel formula is most clearly evident in *Eph.* 18.2:

> For our God, Jesus the Christ, was carried in the womb by Mary according to God's plan—of the seed of David and of the Holy Spirit—who was born and baptized that by his suffering he might purify the water.[3]

The origin of these additions, particularly the birth from Mary, belongs to the incipient anti-docetic controversy, that is, they are directed against a christology which denied the real humanity of Jesus. Igna-

---

[1] On the use of the term "gospel" in Ignatius's letters see Helmut Koester, *Synoptische Überlieferung bei den apostolischen Vätern* (TU 65; Berlin: Akademie-Verlag, 1957) 6–10; William R. Schoedel, *Ignatius of Antioch: A Commentary on the Letters of Ignatius of Antioch* (Hermeneia; Philadelphia: Fortress, 1985) on *Phld.* 8.2; 9.2.

[2] Other passages in which suffering or death and cross and resurrection appear together in formulaic language are Ign. *Eph.* 7.2; *Mg.* 11; *Trall.* 9.1; *Sm.* 5.3; 7.2; 12.2.

[3] See also *Eph.* 19.1 about the three mysteries that were hidden from the rulers of this age: the virginity of Mary, her giving birth, and the death of the Lord.

tius quotes a fully developed gospel formula in a clearly anti-docetic context in Trall. 9.1–2:

> Jesus Christ,
>   of the family of David, of Mary,
>   who was truly born,
>   both ate and drank,
>   was truly persecuted under Pontius Pilate,
>   was truly crucified and died . . . ,
>   who was also truly raised from the dead.[1]

But in spite of the evident tendency toward more comprehensive and possibly more stable formulation in Ignatius, the term "gospel" does not designate any fixed formula and it certainly does not refer to any written text enumerating the basic topics of Jesus' appearance.[2] It is rather the message of salvation in general of which the center is Christ's death and resurrection:

> . . . to pay attention to the prophets and in particular to the gospel, in which the passion is shown us and the resurrection accomplished. (*Sm.* 7.2)

> . . . the gospel has something distinctive: the coming of the Savior, our Lord Jesus Christ, his suffering and resurrection. (*Phld.* 9.2)

1.2.3 THE DEUTERO-PAULINE EPISTLES AND THE BOOK OF ACTS

The same use of the term "gospel" is found in the deutero-Pauline epistles of the New Testament. Eph 3:6 speaks of the fulfillment of the plan of salvation that the Gentiles should also be heirs of the promise "through the gospel"; cf. Eph 3:8: "(Paul) has been appointed to preach (εὐαγγελίζεσθαι) to the Gentiles the inexhaustible richness of Christ." In the later Pastoral Epistles, probably written in the first half of the 2d century CE, Paul's "gospel," that is, what he had once proclaimed,

---

[1] Traditional sentences and formulations are combined into a comprehensive credal statement—though in this form devised by Ignatius himself—in *Sm.* 1.1–2; see on this passage and on its traditional elements Schoedel, *Ignatius,* on *Sm.* 1.1–2.

[2] Gillis P:son Wetter (*Altchristliche Liturgien: Das christliche Mysterium* [FRLANT 30; Göttingen: Vandenhoeck & Ruprecht, 1921] 1. 121–22) understands εὐαγγέλιον in the letters of Ignatius as a central feature of the enactment of Christian cult, a text that represents the Christian myth of salvation so that its reading "creates life." Heinrich Schlier (*Religionsgeschichtliche Untersuchungen zu den Ignatiusbriefen* [BZNW 8; Gießen: Töpelmann, 1929] 165–66) has further elaborated this suggestion. However, there is no indication that Ignatius is actually quoting a text of any kind, nor is it evident that the wording of this gospel was fixed in any way; cf. Schoedel, *Ignatius,* especially on *Sm.* 1.1–2.

becomes the guarantee for the correct Christian proclamation; cf. 2 Tim 2:8:

> Remember Jesus Christ, risen from the dead, from the seed of David, according to my gospel (κατὰ τὸ εὐαγγέλιόν μου).

Also in the Acts of the Apostles, the term "gospel" designates Paul's message of salvation that is preached to the Gentiles (Acts 15:7; 20:24). In this respect, the terminology of Acts agrees with that of the Pauline tradition.[1]

In the entire realm of the Pauline mission and in literature that is dependent upon Paul and his letters, there is no evidence that the term "gospel" was in any way related to gospel writings or to any other form of written materials. At the beginning of the 2d century, the term still always designates the Christian missionary preaching and its message.[2]

1.3 The Term "Gospel" in the Gospels of the New Testament

1.3.1 THE PROBLEM

It was apparently in the Pauline communities where the technical use of the term "gospel" became established. All writings considered in the previous section are dependent upon, or related to, the Pauline churches and their traditions. The question arises whether the authors of the Gospels of the New Testament understood their writings as "gospels," and whether the established technical meaning of the term, "the proclaimed message about Christ's death and resurrection," had any effect on the conception and structure of their works.

The use of the noun "gospel" in the Gospels of the New Testament is puzzling. In the Gospel of John as well as in the Johannine Epistles, neither noun nor verb are ever used. The absence of those terms in the Johannine writings is only one among other pieces of evidence which prove that the beginnings of the Johannine community lay outside of the scope of the Pauline mission area. But the Synoptic Gospels—

---

[1] On the Lukan usage see below # 1.3.2.

[2] Rev 14:6 (". . . an angel who had an eternal gospel to be proclaimed to those who were living on earth") uses the term εὐαγγέλιον as a general, non-technical designation for a "message." The author is not influenced by the Pauline usage of the term. Also in Rev 10:7, ". . . as he has proclaimed (εὐηγγέλισεν) to his servants the prophets," demonstrates that the author of this book is not familiar with the technical usage of these terms as designation for the message of Christ's death and resurrection.

Matthew, Mark, and Luke—belong to this realm and are dependent upon it. And even here the use of the term "gospel" is by no means easy to understand. In fact, it remains somewhat enigmatic and, moreover, is very different in each of the three Synoptic Gospels.

1.3.2 LUKE

In the Lukan writings, the verb is used in both parts of the Lukan work, but the noun "gospel" only in the Book of Acts.[1] In both the Gospel of Luke and in the Acts of the Apostles the verb εὐαγγελίζεσθαι can simply mean "to announce" and thus refer to any kind of good message.[2] But in most instances, it is used to designate the Christian missionary proclamation. In many cases[3] th ϶ verb has no direct object. It either means simply "to preach," or the direct object is implied: "to preach the gospel." Sometimes the object of the verb is made explicit: "the rule of God" (Luke 4:43; 8:1; cf. 16:16; Acts 8:12), "Christ Jesus" (Acts 5:42; 8:35; 11:20), "the word (of the Lord)" (Acts 8:4; 15:35), "peace" (Acts 10:36), "the promises to the fathers fulfilled" (Acts 13:32), "Jesus and the resurrection" (Acts 17:18).

If Luke does not use the noun "gospel" in the first part of his work, he also does not conceive of this writing as a "gospel." On the contrary, in the prologue to his work (Luke 1:1–4), he speaks of others who have tried to compose a "narrative" (διήγησις) about the "events" (πράγματα) which have occurred among us. "Narrative" could possibly have been the title which scribes would have given to this work.[4]

1.3.2 MATTHEW

The absence of the noun in the Gospel of Luke seems odd because the Gospel of Mark, employed by Luke as a source, had used the noun "gospel" repeatedly. However, even Matthew reproduces only a few of the Markan occurrences of the term "gospel." On the other hand, Matthew uses the term several times in non-Markan contexts and, in two instances, adds the phrase "and he preached the gospel of the kingdom" to a Markan summary statement about the activity of Jesus.[5] These are clearly redactional Matthean passages. This raises

---

[1] It occurs only twice here: 15:7 and 20:24.

[2] Luke 1:19: 2:10; Acts 14:15.

[3] Luke 3:18; 4:18 (= Isa 61:1); 7:22; 9:6; 20:1; Acts 8:25, 40; 14:7, 21; 16:10.

[4] This has been suggested by Bovon, "The Synoptic Gospels and the Non-canonical Acts of the Apostles," *HTR* 81 (1988) 23. Bovon remarks that Matthew might have been called "Beginnings" (Γέννησις) or "Life" (Βίος), and Mark could have borne the title "Memoirs" (Ὑπομνήματα).

[5] καὶ κηρύσσων τὸ εὐαγγέλιον τῆς βασιλείας, Matt 4:23; 9:35; cf. Mark 1:39; 6:6.

the question of why the author of the Gospel of Matthew, who is quite familiar with the term "gospel," does not reproduce the term when it occurs in a number of Markan passages, which he had copied from his source. The following table shows the use of the term in the respective Markan and Matthean passages.

Mark[1]		Matthew	
1:1	beginning of the gospel of Jesus Christ		——— ———
1:15a	proclaiming the gospel of God	4:17a	he began to proclaim[2] ———
1:15b	and believe in the gospel	4:17b	———
8:35	on my behalf and of the gospel	16:25	on my behalf ———
10:29	on my behalf and on behalf of the gospel	19:29	on behalf of my name ———
13:10	the gospel must be proclaimed	24:14	this gospel of the kingdom will be proclaimed
14:9	wherever the gospel is proclaimed	26:13	wherever this gospel is proclaimed

The use of the term in Mark 13:10 and 14:9 (also in 16:15) corresponds to the conventional missionary terminology of the Pauline churches.[3] Matthew, however, in the two instances in which he reproduces passages from Mark in which the term "gospel" appears, adds the demonstrative "this" to the word "gospel" and, in the first instance, also the qualifying genitive "of the kingdom." Thus, he understands the passages in question as references to a more specific message. What message is meant, is not immediately clear in Matt 26:13.[4] The phrase "gospel of the kingdom" appears, independently of Mark, also

---

[1] There is a further occurrence of the term in the secondary longer ending of Mark: "Go into all the world and proclaim the gospel to every creature" (Mark 16:15).

[2] The term used here, both in Matthew and in Mark, is κηρύσσειν.

[3] However, Mark 13:10 interrupts the close connection between 13:9 and 13:11. Can 13:10 be considered a secondary intrusion into the text of Mark from the parallel in Matthew? Commentaries usually ask whether vs. 10 was inserted into an older tradition, either by Mark or in a pre-Markan stage of the text; cf. Rudolf Pesch, *Das Markusevangelium* (2 vols; Herder Kommentar; Freiburg: Herder, 1977) 2. 285; see also idem, *Naherwartungen* (Düsseldorf: Patmos, 1968) 129–31. On the term in Markan usage in general, see Willi Marxsen, *Der Evangelist Markus* (FRLANT 67; Göttingen: Vandenhoeck & Ruprecht, 1956) 77–92.

[4] All modern commentaries agree that "this gospel" in Matt 26:13 cannot refer to the book of Matthew's Gospel. The phrase is variously understood as the gospel of Christ, the proclamation of the passion of Jesus, or the announcement of the coming of the

in Matt 4:23 and 9:25. In these two passages (as well as in Matt 24:14) the meaning of this phrase is evident: it is the message that Jesus is preaching, that is, the message of the coming of the kingdom of heaven. It is Jesus' message as it already was the message of John the Baptist (compare Matt 4:17 with 3:2). But it is not the gospel about Jesus' death and resurrection. Matthew never uses the term "gospel" in this latter meaning, which is so common in the tradition of the Pauline churches. It is characteristic that the term "gospel" is also missing in the commissioning of the disciples at the end of Matthew's Gospel (Matt 28:18–20). The difference between Matt 28:18–20 and Mark 16:15 is striking. While in the (albeit secondary) ending of Mark, Jesus commands the disciples to go into all the world to proclaim the gospel, Matthew reports Jesus' mission command as a charge to the Eleven to make all the nations disciples, to baptize them, and to teach them to observe everything that he had taught. The very distinctive understanding of "gospel" in Matthew may be the reason for his omission of the term in many of the Markan passages.

1.3.4 MARK

The use of the term "gospel" in Mark raises several problems: (1) Does the term belong to the original text of Mark in the passages in which it occurs in the extant manuscripts? (2) What is the content of the "gospel" in Mark?

It is by no means evident that Matthew read the term in his text of Mark where it now appears in our Markan manuscripts. One is tempted to argue that the term had been inserted into a number of Markan passages by a later redactor. In Mark 8:35 and 10:29, the phrase "and for the sake of the gospel" (καὶ ἕνεκεν τοῦ εὐαγγελίου) is redundant after "for my sake" (ἕνεκεν ἐμοῦ), and it is indeed missing in the Matthean parallels (16:25; 19:29).[1] There is also no Matthean correspondence to the use of the term "gospel" in Mark 1:15 (= Matt 4:17).[2]

---

kingdom of the heavens; see on this problem Stuhlmacher (*Das paulinische Evangelium*, 241–43) who argues that these passages are Matthean formulations which presuppose the technical usage of the Pauline mission, but do not identify Matthew's writing with the "gospel."

[1] See the chart above in # 1.3.3.

[2] Marxsen (*Markus*, 81) argues that Matthew used Mark 1:15 also in Matt 4:23 and 9:35. See further on this question Helmut Koester, "History and Development of Mark's Gospel: From Mark to Secret Mark and 'Canonical' Mark," in: Bruce C. Corley, ed., *Colloquy on New Testament Studies: A Time for Reappraisal and Fresh Approaches* (Macon, GA: Mercer University Press, 1983) 43–44.

In three of these Markan passages (1:15b: 8:35; 10:29), the term "gospel" appears without a genitive designating its content. This use corresponds to the use of "gospel" as a technical term in the Pauline letters.[1] It is the gospel about Jesus' death and resurrection. In Mark, this "gospel" can even assume the same dignity that is accorded to Christ himself: "on behalf of Christ and the gospel" (Mark 8:35; 10:29). Belief in Christ is identical with belief in the gospel (Mark 1:15b).[2] "The gospel of God" in Mark 1:15a is, therefore, no other gospel than the one mentioned in other Markan passages in which the term "gospel" occurs, namely, the gospel of Christ's death and resurrection. That conclusion holds in spite of the somewhat odd consequence that Jesus here is the one who proclaims that gospel which has as its content his own death and resurrection.

That same gospel is referred to in Mark 1:1, in the incipit of the Markan writing: "Beginning of the gospel of Jesus Christ." It is quite possible that a later scribe added this phrase in order to indicate the point in his manuscript at which the text of another writing began: "Beginning of the gospel of Jesus Christ."[3] As the text stands, Mark 1:1 must be understood together with Mark 1:14–15. The term "gospel" in these two passages forms an inclusio which indicates that the Baptist's message of repentance belongs together with Jesus' announcement of the nearness of the kingdom which resumes the call for repentance.[4] Mark himself does not thereby designate his own

---

[1] Stuhlmacher (*Das paulinische Evangelium,* 234–38) argues for a close relationship between Mark's use of the term and the Pauline understanding of the content of the gospel.

[2] The expression πιστεύειν ἐν is peculiar and without parallel in the NT. However, it is hard to interpret this phrase in any other way than as an equivalent of the common πιστεύειν εἰς = "to believe in"; see Marxsen, *Markus,* 90. Marxsen also argues convincingly that the term εὐαγγέλιον always occurs in redactional materials and never in any traditions or sources used by Mark. The peculiar phrase of Mark 1:15 cannot be explained by recourse to an older Aramaic tradition used by Mark (against Pesch, *Markusevangelium,* 105). Detlev Dormeyer ("Die Kompositionsmetapher 'Evangelium Jesu Christi, des Sohnes Gottes,' Mk 1.1. Ihre theologische und literarische Aufgabe in der Jesus-Biographie des Markus," *NTS* 33 [1987] 254–55) explains the choice of the preposition ἐν as a deliberate Markan finesse by which Mark wants to indicate that the gospel preached by Jesus in 1:14–15 is not the entire gospel but only one of its ingredients (*Teilmenge*).

[3] Cf. Walther Schmithals, *Das Evangelium nach Markus* (Ökumenischer Taschenbuchkommentar zum NT 2/1; Gütersloh: Gütersloher Verlagshaus, 1979) 73–74.

[4] Dormeyer ("Die Kompositionsmetapher," 452–68) has tried to demonstrate that the "genitive-syntagma" ἀρχὴ τοῦ εὐαγγελίου can be reversed to "gospel of the beginnings" and thus become the title of a writing. This suggestion overlooks the fact that "gospel" in both passages refers to a message.

work as a "gospel."[1] Ancient writings either begin with a formal dedication describing the purpose of the book (like Luke-Acts) or with a
sentence marking the first subject treated. The latter is the case in
Mark 1:1, especially when this passage is seen as a pointer to Mark
1:14–15. It is not a cryptic phrase which mysteriously suggests to the
modern interpreter that the author somehow wanted to imply that his
work was a "gospel." Rather, the sentence of Mark 1:1 says that the
proclamation of Christ's resurrection and death began with the
preaching of repentance by John the Baptist and with Jesus' own call
for repentance. Thus there is no indication whatsoever that either
Mark or any of the authors of the Gospels of the New Testament
thought that "gospel" would be an appropriate title for the literature
they produced.

1.4 "Gospel" in the Apostolic Fathers

1.4.1 THE APOSTOLIC FATHERS AS WITNESSES FOR THE GOSPELS

Traditionally the writings of the so-called Apostolic Fathers have
been viewed as the earliest witnesses for the existence and use of written gospels.[2] Accordingly, their references to the "gospel" were understood as testimonies for the use of this term as a designation for gospel
writings. This view was challenged since the beginning of this century.[3] However, more recent publications have tried to reestablish the
position that at least the Gospel of Matthew has been widely used
in early Christian literature. In 1950, Édouard Massaux, in a
comprehensive investigation,[4] attempted to demonstrate once more
that Matthew was not only known but also used even in the earliest
writings among the Apostolic Fathers. More recently, Wolf-Dietrich

---

[1] Marxsen, *Markus,* 87–88.

[2] Most characteristic of this position is the very influential work of Theodor Zahn,
Geschichte des neutestamentlichen Kanons (2 vols.; Erlangen: Deichert, 1888–89)
1. 840, 916–41. Zahn even believed that Papias of Hierapolis, the second-century
bishop who argued strongly for the trustworthiness of the oral tradition, drew his "sayings of the Lord" from a written gospel.

[3] The first study to challenge this traditional view came from *The New Testament in
the Apostolic Fathers* by a Committee of the Oxford Society of Historical Theology
(Oxford, 1905). See further Koester, *Synoptische Überlieferung bei den Apostolischen
Vätern.*

[4] *Influence de l'Évangile de Saint Matthieu sur la littérature chrétienne avant Saint
Irénée* (reprint; BEThL 75; Leuven: Leuven University Press, 1986).

Köhler[1] has tried to come to a more differentiated judgment. He assesses each passage according to a graduated scale of the judgment about dependence which runs from "probable" (*wahrscheinlich*), "quite possible" (*gut möglich*), "at best theoretically possible" (*allenfalls theoretisch möglich*), to "rather improbable" (*eher unwahrscheinlich*). The result of Köhler's detailed, even if pedantic, investigation is that "in the overwhelming majority of the writings analyzed the use of the Gospel of Matthew is probable."[2] The question of the actual use of canonical Gospels in the New Testament, the Apostolic Fathers, and other early Christian writings will be discussed later and has to be judged on its own merits.[3] The concern here is with the problem of the employment of the term "gospel" as a designation of written documents. Even if it is possible that certain writers drew their gospel materials from written documents, this does not imply that they called such documents "gospels."

The occurrences of the term in the letters of Ignatius of Antioch have already been discussed above: Ignatius employs the term exclusively in the same way in which it had been used by Paul, that is, as a designation of the proclamation of Christ's death and resurrection.

1.4.2 THE FIRST EPISTLE OF CLEMENT AND
THE EPISTLE OF BARNABAS

In the First Epistle of Clement, the oldest writing in this group of the Apostolic Fathers, sent to Corinth from Rome in the year 96 CE, the term "gospel" means preaching in general: "as Paul wrote to you in the beginning of his preaching" (*1 Clem.* 47.2). The author did not know or use a written gospel. The quotations of sayings of Jesus in *1 Clem.* 13.2 and 46.8 are drawn from the oral tradition. This is borne out by their form and wording, which does not reveal any redactional features of a known gospel author, and by the quotation formula which appears in the past tense: "he said" (εἶπεν), that is, the Lord said when he was preaching and teaching.[4]

---

[1] *Die Rezeption des Matthäusevangeliums in der Zeit vor Irenäus* (WUNT 2/24; Tübingen: Mohr/Siebeck, 1986).
[2] Ibid., 520 (translation mine).
[3] For a discussion of the literature on this subject since the publication of Massaux's work and my own *Synoptische Überlieferung bei den Apostolischen Vätern* see Frans Neirynck, "Introduction à la réimpression," in the reprint of Massaux, *Influence de l'Évangile de Saint Matthieu*, pp. vii-xv.
[4] Koester, *Synoptische Überlieferung*, 6; see below # 2.1.4.3.

In the Epistle of Barnabas, probably written at the same time or a few decades later, the term "gospel" also refers to the oral proclamation: Jesus chose the apostles in order that they should proclaim his "message" (*Barn.* 5.9).[1]

1.4.3 THE DIDACHE

It is more difficult to determine the use of the word "gospel" in the *Teaching of the Twelve Apostles* (the so-called *Didache*). This writing may have been composed as early as the last decades of the 1st century CE or early in the 2d century, although some scholars prefer a date later in the 2d century. The *Didache* is a compilation of several older sources; some of these older components may have preserved the terminology of an earlier period.[2] On the other hand, redactional passages reveal the vocabulary of the later editor.

In *Did.* 8.2, the Lord's Prayer is introduced with the words: pray "as the Lord has commanded in his gospel" (ὡς ἐκέλευσεν ὁ κύριος ἐν τῷ εὐαγγελίῳ αὐτοῦ). The form and wording of the Lord's Prayer, as it is quoted in the *Didache,* is on the whole the same as that of the Gospel of Matthew (6:9–13). However, there are a few details in the *Didache* version which are more original than the parallel expressions in Matthew's version.[3] It is also most unlikely that a Christian writer would have to copy from any written source in order to quote the Lord's Prayer. Moreover, the verb in the quotation formula appears in the past tense, which makes it quite unlikely that "his (i.e., the Lord's) gospel" refers to a written document. The quotation formula is, therefore, best understood as a reference to the preaching of Jesus during his earthly ministry.[4]

---

[1] Ibid., 6; cf. also *Barn.* 8.3.

[2] J. M. Creed, "The Didache," *JTS* 39 (1937) 370–78; Jean Paul Audet, *La Didachè: Instructions des Apôtres* (EtB; Paris: Gabalda, 1958) 104–20; Audét argues for a composition in two stages. More recent discussions of the issue and of relevant literature can be found in Klaus Wengst, *Didache (Apostellehre), Zweiter Clemensbrief, Schrift an Diognet* (Schriften des Urchristentums 2; Darmstadt: Wissenschaftliche Buchgesellschaft, 1984) 18–32; and especially in Kurt Niederwimmer, *Die Didache* (KEK, KAV 1; Göttingen: Vandenhoeck & Ruprecht, 1988) 64–80. The latter commentary gives the best account of the compilation of the Didache, although Niederwimmer's date for the final redaction (early in the 2d century) cannot be substantiated by external evidence. See also Frankemölle, *Evangelium: Forschungsbericht,* 33–34.

[3] Koester, *Synoptische Überlieferung,* 103–9. Köhler (*Rezeption des Matthäusevangeliums,* 31–36) has no doubts with respect to the dependence of *Did.* 8.1–2 upon Matthew. Massaux (*Influence de L'Évangile de Saint Matthieu,* 616–18) also argues for such dependence. However, he assumes a date for the Didache after the middle of the 2d century, while Köhler (p. 30) would prefer an early date in the last decade of the 1st or the first decade of the 2d century.

[4] Niederwimmer (*Didache,* 170–73) denies a dependence upon the text of Matthew

In the next part of the *Didache,* which deals with instructions for church officers, the following formula occurs twice: "(do this) as you have it in the gospel" (ὡς ἔχετε ἐν τῷ εὐαγγελίῳ, *Did.* 15.3 and 15.4; cf. also 11.3). This suggests that there was a document in which the respective instructions were written down.[1] But nothing in the context of these references indicates the presence of materials which were derived from any known gospel writing. Moreover, even if the phrase refers to a written document —which is by no means necessary—it obviously stems from the hand of the later editor of the *Didache,* while the materials quoted in this context are derived from an older tradition.[2] Therefore, these passages cannot be used as evidence for an early use of the term "gospel" as a designation of a written document.

There is only one instance in which sayings quoted in the *Didache* are certainly drawn from written gospels: *Did.* 1.3–5. This passage is a compilation of sayings from the Sermon on the Mount, but with distinct features of harmonization of the texts of Matthew and Luke. It is an interpolation that must have been made after the middle of the 2d century[3] and cannot, therefore, be used as evidence for the original compiler's familiarity with written gospels.[4]

1.4.4 THE SECOND EPISTLE OF CLEMENT

By the middle of the 2d century CE some proof for the use of the term "gospel" as a designation of written documents begins to appear. The so-called Second Epistle of Clement which was written ca. 150 CE,

---

and demonstrates that the doxology is not indebted to Matthew's doxology, but to the tradition of prayers from which also the meal prayers in chaps. 9–10 are derived.

[1] Niederwimmer (*Didache,* 245) sees in *Did.* 15.3–4 references to a written gospel but leaves open whether the redactor refers to the Gospel of Matthew or to some other gospel that is no longer extant.

[2] There is no external evidence which would force a date of the final composition of the *Didache* before the end of the 2d century (*pace* Wengst, *Didache,* 61–63). To be sure, the materials used in this final composition are much older. But the general references to the "gospel" may stem from the hand of the final editor; cf. Niederwimmer (*Didache,* 168–69) who shows that the phrase in *Did.* 8.2 has been clumsily interpolated into older material and argues (pp. 214, 244) that all other references to the "gospel" reveal the hand of the final redactor.

[3] Bentley Layton, "The Sources, Date and Transmission of *Didache* 1.3b–2.2," *HTR* 61 (1968) 343–83.

[4] In order to maintain his hypothesis of the *Didache*'s dependence upon the Gospel of Matthew, Wengst (*Didache,* 18–20) is forced to admit that these verses are a later interpolation, using a harmonized gospel text. See also Niederwimmer, *Didache,* 93–100 (uncommitted report about the various solutions concerning the problem of this interpolation) and pp. 115–16 (an older traditional piece which was revised by the compiler of the work).

probably even later,[1] may reveal such a use, although the evidence is
somewhat ambiguous. *2 Clement* repeatedly quotes sayings of Jesus
which have parallels in the Synoptic Gospels. The verbs in the quotation formulae vary. Twice a saying is introduced by "the Lord said
(εἶπεν),"[2] but in other instances the present tense of the verb (λέγει) is
used in the quotation formula.[3] The present tense is customarily
employed for the introduction of quotations from Scripture or from any
written document. This would suggest that *2 Clement* quotes sayings
of Jesus from a written work. A confirmation could be found in *2 Clem.*
8.5 where a saying of Jesus is introduced with the words "because the
Lord says in the gospel" (λέγει γὰρ ὁ κύριος ἐν τῷ εὐαγγελίῳ). Is this a
reference to a book in which the Lord presently speaks to the church?
Several of the sayings of Jesus quoted in *2 Clement* indeed reveal
features which derive from the redactional activities of the authors of
Matthew and Luke.[4] On the other hand, only sayings of Jesus are
quoted in *2 Clement*. There is no indication that the author knew any
narrative materials. If he drew his sayings from a written document,
it was most likely a sayings collection which was in turn based upon
the Gospels of Matthew and Luke but also included some non-
canonical materials (cf. *2 Clem.* 12).[5] It must remain highly unlikely,
though by no means impossible, that such a sayings collection was
called a "gospel."

1.4.5 THE SHEPHERD OF HERMAS

There are numerous instances in which passages of the *Shepherd of
Hermas* seem to allude to phrases and stories of the Synoptic Gospels.[6]
Actual quotations, however, never occur. But that is simply part of the

---

[1] For the date of *2 Clement* see Wengst (*Didache,* 222–27): 130–150 CE. However,
since there is no external attestation for this writing before the end of the 2d century,
any date in the 2d century would be possible. The use of harmonized sayings based on
both Matthew and Luke with many similarities to the harmony used by Justin Martyr
and the use of apocryphal materials (see below, # 5.1.2–3) would argue for a date
around 150 or later; see Koester, *Synoptische Überlieferung,* 79–99. Martin Hengel
(*Die Evangelienüberschriften* [SHW.PH 1984.3; Heidelberg: Winter, 1984] 34: "einige
Jahrzehnte vor Justin") and especially Karl Paul Donfried (*The Setting of Second Clement in Early Christianity* [NovTSup 38; Leiden: Brill, 1974] 55–56) fail to give convincing arguments for an earlier date.

[2] εἶπεν ὁ κύριος, *2 Clem.* 4.5; 9.11.

[3] λέγει, *2 Clem.* 3.2; 5.2.

[4] Koester, *Synoptische Überlieferung,* 70–99; see below # 5.1.1–2.

[5] For further discussion of the quotations of sayings in *2 Clement* and their non-
canonical parallels see below # 5.1.3.

[6] For a collection and comparison of these passages with their synoptic parallels, see
Koester, *Synoptische Überlieferung,* 242–56.

particular way in which the author of this writing uses other sources and traditions. Though obviously dependent upon Scriptural passages and other traditional materials, the author rarely quotes a source.[1] It is therefore extremely difficult to determine whether the author is dependent on a particular writing or is drawing on oral tradition. Parallels to the Synoptic Gospels in the *Shepherd* show no peculiar features of the redactorial work of any of these gospels. Thus, dependence upon any of these gospels cannot be demonstrated, but neither can it be excluded.

The term "gospel" (εὐαγγέλιον) never occurs and the verb "to preach" (εὐαγγελίζεσθαι) is also missing. Thus we cannot know whether the author, if he indeed used written gospels, knew them under this designation. If an early date of ca. 100 CE can be assumed for the composition of this book,[2] it is unlikely anyway that the author would have known gospels under this title.

1.4.6 POLYCARP OF SMYRNA

The absence of the term "gospel" is equally noteworthy in the letter of bishop Polycarp of Smyrna to the Philippians. It is very likely that the major portion of the preserved letter is a writing that dates from the last decades of Polycarp's career,[3] which started at the time of Ignatius of Antioch at the beginning of the 2d century and ended with his martyrdom after the middle of that century, perhaps as late as the time of the emperor Marcus Aurelius, i.e., after 160 CE.[4] Polycarp's first letter, written at the time of Ignatius as a cover letter for sending copies of the letters of Ignatius, is preserved in chapters 13–14 of the extant document. But it is in the portions which belong to the later letter (chapters 1–12 and 15) that several quotations of gospel materials occur.

One of these quotations, Pol. *Phil.* 2.3a, is copied from the quotation of the sayings of Jesus in *1 Clem.* 13.1–2, including the quotation for-

---

[1] The only more explicit reference occurs in *Vis.* 2.3.4 where the author introduces a now lost apocryphal writing ("Eldad and Modad") with the formula "as it is written."

[2] It is tempting to identify the "Clement who will send the book to the foreign cities" (*Vis.* 2.4.3) with the the secretary of the Roman church to whom we owe *1 Clement*.

[3] The convincing thesis that the preserved letter is actually a composition of two different letters was proposed by P. N. Harrison, *Polycarp's Two Epistles to the Philippians* (Cambridge: Cambridge University Press, 1936). This thesis was endorsed by Hans von Campenhausen, *Polykarp von Smyrna und die Pastoralbriefe* (SBH.PH 1951.2; Heidelberg: Winter, 1951) 39–40, reprinted in idem, *Aus der Frühzeit des Christentums: Studien zur Kirchengeschichte des ersten und zweiten Jahrhunderts* (Tübingen: Mohr/Siebeck, 1963) 197–252.

[4] According to Eusebius, *Hist. eccl.* 3.14.10–15.1.

mula ("Remember what the Lord said when he was teaching"). However, while the quote in *1 Clem.* 13.2 had been drawn from the oral tradition, Polycarp, who knew the Gospels of Matthew and Luke, corrected the text in order to establish a more faithful agreement of Jesus' words with the wording of the written gospels from which he has also drawn his other gospel materials (*Phil.* 2.3b; 7.2; 12.3).[1] At the same time, it is remarkable that Polycarp never uses the term "gospel" for these documents and that the words of Jesus are still quoted as if they were sayings drawn from the oral tradition.

The term "gospel" appears several times in the report of Polycarp's martyrdom which was written shortly after the death of the famous bishop of Smyrna. A clear reference to a written gospel is the remark in the postscript which says "that his martyrdom happened according to the gospel of Christ" (κατὰ τὸ εὐαγγέλιον τοῦ Χριστοῦ γενόμενον, *Mart. Pol.* 19.2).[2] But neither this passage, nor the phrases which try to establish a correspondence between the martyrdom of Polycarp and the suffering of Jesus, as it is described in the Gospels of the New Testament, appear in the copy of the document that is preserved in Eusebius' *Church History*.[3] They belong to a later redaction of the story of Polycarp's martyrdom. The original report did not use the term "gospel" at all and does not show any signs of the use of written gospels in the description of the sufferings and death of the bishop of Smyrna.[4]

1.5 The Term "Gospel" in Gospels from the Nag Hammadi Library

1.5.1 THE GOSPEL OF THOMAS[5]

The manuscript of the *Gospel of Thomas* in Codex 2 of the Nag Hammadi Library does not use the term "gospel" in its text. The term occurs only in the colophon of a scribe or translator at the end of the writing: "The Gospel according to Thomas." The formulation "Gospel according to . . ." imitates the secondary titles of the canonical Gospels

---

[1] Cf. Koester, *Synoptische Überlieferung*, 114–20.

[2] Cf. also *Mart. Pol.* 4.2: ". . . for the gospel does not teach this" (ἐπειδὴ οὐχ οὕτως διδάσκει τὸ εὐαγγέλιον).

[3] *Hist. eccl.* 4.15.

[4] A critical analysis of the various layers of the report of Polycarp's martyrdom was presented by Hans von Campenhausen, *Bearbeitungen und Interpolationen des Polykarpmartyriums* (SBH.PH 1957; Heidelberg: Winter, 1957) 5–48; reprinted in idem, *Frühzeit*, 253–301.

[5] More information about the date, composition, and character of these gospels from the Nag Hammadi Library will be provided in later chapters.

which they received after their incorporation into the four-gospel canon of the New Testament. The writing itself, however, which may have been composed as early as the end of the 1st century, gives its title and the name of its author at the beginning:

> These are the secret sayings which the living Jesus spoke and which Didymus Judas Thomas wrote down. (NHC II 32,10–11)

This is the original incipit of the book. Thus the title of the book should be more appropriately "Thomas's Book of Secret Sayings." Whoever composed the book and wrote its incipit was certainly not aware of the possible designation of the work as a "gospel."

1.5.2 THE GOSPEL ACCORDING TO MARY

Also in this document from the Coptic Papyrus Berolinensis 8502 the title "[The] Gospel according to Mary" appears in the colophon of the scribe or translator, not in the document itself.[1] If there was a title in the incipit of the writing, it is now lost, because the first six pages of the Coptic manuscript are no longer extant, and the Greek fragment parallels only the last three pages of the Coptic version. However, the *Gospel according to Mary* uses the term "gospel" (εὐαγγέλιον) in its text:

> . . . he (Jesus) greeted them all, saying: ". . . For the Son of man is within you. Follow after him! Those who seek him will find him. Go then and preach the gospel of the kingdom. Do not lay down any other rules beyond what I appointed for you. . . ." (BG 8502 8,18–22)

> They wept greatly saying: "How shall we go to the Gentiles and preach the gospel of the kingdom of the Son of man?" (BG 8502 9,6–10)

> Levi answered and said to Peter: ". . . Rather, let us be ashamed and put on the perfect man and acquire him for ourselves as he commanded us, and preach the gospel, not laying down any other rule or other law beyond what the Savior said." (BG 8502 18,15–21)

The "gospel" is the message which the disciples have to proclaim. That it is twice designated as the "gospel of the kingdom" and that the command to preach the gospel is twice combined with the injunction not to

---

[1] The parallel, but very fragmentary, Greek version of the *Gospel According to Mary* in *P. Ryl. 463* has no title at the end of the writing; but it is possible that the missing lines at the end of the document were occupied by the title; cf. R. McL. Wilson and George W. MacRae, "The Gospel According to Mary," in Douglas M. Parrott, ed., *Nag Hammadi Codices V, 2–5 and VI with Papyrus Berolinensis 8502, 1 and 4* (NHS 11; Leiden: Brill, 1979) 470.

lay down any other rule, reveals a fixed technical terminology for the Christian proclamation.[1]

1.5.3 THE APOCRYPHON OF JAMES

Although this writing contains discussions of Jesus with his disciples and includes materials which belong to the tradition of Jesus' sayings, the term "gospel" does not appear.[2] A scribal colophon is missing. The document begins with a dual identification of its purpose. In the first, the writing is characterized as a letter from James to another person whose name is no longer legible (NHC I 1,1–7). The second speaks of "A Secret Book (= Apocryphon) that was revealed to me (i.e., James) and Peter by the Lord" (NHC I 1,10–12).[3]

1.5.4 THE DIALOGUE OF THE SAVIOR

The dialogues of Jesus (usually called "the Lord") with individually named disciples and the use of traditional sayings argue for the inclusion of this writing under the category of gospel literature. The title "Dialogue of the Savior" appears in the incipit (NHC III 120,1). A colophon is missing, and there are no other designations of the genre of the work or of its author. The term "gospel" never occurs.

1.5.5 THE GOSPEL OF TRUTH

This book may have been composed by the famous Gnostic teacher Valentinus, and must be dated in the middle of the 2d century. It is not a writing that belongs to the gospel literature; but it is a homily or meditation. It uses the term "gospel" in its incipit, from which it received its modern title, and twice more in the course of the writing:

> The gospel of truth is joy for those who have received from the Father of truth the grace of knowing him. . . . (NHC I 16,31–33)
>
> . . . in the name of the gospel is the proclamation of hope, being discovery for those who search for him. (NHC I 17,1–4)
>
> From this, the gospel of the one who is searched for, which was revealed to those who are perfect through the mercies of the Father, the hidden mystery, Jesus Christ, enlightened those who were in darkness through oblivion. (NHC I 18,11–19)

---

[1] This terminology is possibly related to or dependent upon the use of the same phrase in the Gospel of Matthew (see above # 1.3.2).

[2] The verb εὐαγγελίζεσθαι is used once with the meaning "to proclaim": "Blessed are they who have proclaimed the Son before his descent" (NHC I 14,37–39).

[3] For further discussion of the genre of this document see below # 3.1.2.

Although the author certainly knew and used written gospels, the term "gospel" in each instance designates the message of salvation. The *Gospel of Truth* is therefore an important 2d-century witness for the continuing use of the term "gospel" as a designation of the Christian proclamation.

1.5.6 OTHER INSTANCES OF THE USE OF THE TERM

In the Nag Hammadi library, "gospel" is used as a designation of a written source for the first time in the *Treatise on the Resurrection,* which must be dated at the end of the 2d century.[1] The reference is clearly to a written gospel, possibly to Mark 9:2–8:[2]

> For if you remember reading in the Gospel that Elijah appeared and Moses with him, do not think the resurrection is an illusion. (NHC I 48,7–11)

The author is also familiar with other writings of the New Testament, quotes a combination of Rom 8:17 and Eph 2:5–6 explicitly as said by "the Apostle" (NHC I 45,23–28), and alludes to other New Testament passages.[3]

The term "gospel" also appears in the scribal colophon of the *Gospel of Philip,* a Valentinian treatise from the end of the 2d century: "The Gospel according to Philip" (NHC II 86,18–19). Like the colophon of the *Gospel of Thomas,* the phrase seems to imitate the later designations of the canonical gospels. The genre and style of the work itself does not accord with any known gospel literature, although the author quotes a number of sayings of Jesus and refers to some narratives about him.

This brief survey of some books from the Nag Hammadi library demonstrates that the gospel writings preserved in this library never use the term "gospel" as designations for their own works. Various other titles ("Secret Sayings," "Secret Book") are used instead in the incipits of these gospels. On the other hand, whenever the term "gospel" appears in the earlier documents from this corpus, it either comes from the hand of a later scribe or translator or it designates the oral proclamation of the Christian message.

---

[1] See Malcolm L. Peel, "The Treatise on the Resurrection," in Harold W. Attridge, ed., *Nag Hammadi Codex I (The Jung Codex)* (2 vols.; NHS 22–23; Leiden: Brill, 1985) 1. 146.

[2] Ibid., 2. 192–94.

[3] Ibid., 1. 133; 2. 162–63.

1.6 Why Did Written Documents Come To Be Called "Gospels"?

1.6.1 THE WRITTEN GOSPEL AS KERYGMA

In the second half of the 2d century certain documents came to be called "gospels." But it is not evident why the term "gospel"—once the technical term for the early Christian missionary preaching—became the title for a particular type of literature. Explanations for this change have been closely associated with the attempt to define the special genre of the gospel literature. Most commonly accepted, in one form or another, is the thesis developed by Karl Ludwig Schmidt and Julius Schniewind. It states that the gospels, specifically the four Gospels of the New Testament canon, are representatives of a literary genre *sui generis* which cannot be related to other developments in the history of literature in antiquity.[1]

In a famous carefully argued essay published in the year 1923, Karl Ludwig Schmidt[2] presented a fundamental and incisive criticism of various attempts to understand the genre of the gospels in analogy to Greek biography or other literary genres from antiquity (e.g., Jewish apocalyptic literature). Schmidt referred to Franz Overbeck's distinction between Christian "primitive literature" (*Urliteratur*) and Patristic literature.[3] According to Overbeck, the Letters and Gospels of the New Testament belong to the former category because they owe their existence to the special circumstances and requirements of Christian beginnings. Writings of this genre could no longer be reproduced in the later period because these special circumstances no longer obtained. Patristic literature, on the other hand, belongs to the "high literature" (*Hochliteratur*) of antiquity because it is influenced by established literary genres of the ancient world and their critical standards. In addition to utilizing Overbeck's distinction between these two types of literature, Schmidt relied on the insights of the form-

---

[1] The modern discussion of the kerygma genre of the written gospel has been summarized by Frankemölle, *Evangelium: Forschungsbericht*, 4–16.

[2] "Die Stellung der Evangelien in der allgemeinen Literaturgeschichte," in H. Schmidt, ed., ΕΥΧΑΡΙΣΤΗΡΙΟΝ: *Studien zur Religion und Literatur des Alten und Neuen Testaments, Hermann Gunkel zum 60. Geburtstag . . . dargebracht* (FRLANT N.F. 19/2; Göttingen: Vandenhoeck & Ruprecht, 1923) 50–134.

[3] "Über die Anfänge der patristischen Literatur," *Historische Zeitschrift* 14 (1882) 417–72; reprinted in book form: Darmstadt: Wissenschaftliche Buchgesellschaft, 1954 and 1966. On the influence of Overbeck's essay on the view of the gospels in New Testament scholarship, see Dormeyer, *Evangelium als Gattung*, 48–58.

critical studies of Rudolf Bultmann[1] and Martin Dibelius,[2] as well as of his own work.[3] These publications had demonstrated that the Synoptic Gospels of the New Testament were primarily collections of materials which had been formed in the pre-literary, oral stages of their transmission in the early Christian communities. Therefore, Schmidt concluded, the genre of the gospels cannot be determined on the basis of a comparison with the products of literary culture. Rather, they must be understood as collections and publications of traditions in the form of "casual literature" (*Kleinliteratur*) according to the needs of a developing religious community.

A few years after the appearance of Karl Ludwig Schmidt's essay, Julius Schniewind published a now-noted review article of works on the Synoptic Gospels.[4] In this article, he proposed a further elaboration of Schmidt's arguments with respect to the use of the term "gospel" as a designation of a literary genre. Observing the close relationship in form and content between the Synoptic Gospels and the early Christian kerygma or creed, Schniewind concluded that the gospels constituted a special literary genre that had no parallels anywhere else:

> There can be no doubt: only because there was a kerygma, proclaiming a human being who lived "in the flesh" as "the Lord," is it possible to understand the origin of our gospels, including any forms of Christian literature that preceded them.[5]

Schniewind's explanation of the origins of this literature and of its designation as "gospel" has been widely accepted, together with Overbeck's distinction between Christian "primitive literature" (*Ur-literatur*) as a representative of casual literature or popular cultic writing, and Patristic literature, as representative of literary culture.[6] Vielhauer's judgment characterizes this view:

---

[1] *The History of the Synoptic Tradition* (2d ed.; New York: Harper & Row, 1968). The first German edition had been published two years before the appearance of Schmidt's essay: *Die Geschichte der synoptischen Tradition* (FRLANT 29; Göttingen: Vandenhoeck & Ruprecht, 1921).

[2] *From Tradition to Gospel* (New York: Scribner's, 1934). First German edition: *Die Formgeschichte des Evangeliums* (Tübingen: Mohr/Siebeck, 1919).

[3] Karl Ludwig Schmidt, *Der Rahmen der Geschichte Jesu* (Berlin: no publisher, 1919; reprint Darmstadt: Wissenschaftliche Buchgesellschaft, 1964, 1969).

[4] "Zur Synoptiker-Exegese," *ThR* N.F. 2 (1930) 129–89.

[5] Ibid., 183.

[6] Cf. Günther Bornkamm, "Evangelien, formgeschichtlich," *RGG* 2 (3d. ed.) 750. For a critical discussion of this "old consensus" and full bibliography, see M. J. Suggs, "Gospel, Genre," *IDBSup* 370–72.

The question of the literary character of the gospels and of their position within the context of the general history of literature must be answered, for the time being, in this way: the gospels do not reflect any of the genres of the contemporary Old Testament and Jewish or Greek literature; within the context of such literatures, the gospels are unique with respect to their literary character, and they do not have any predecessors or any successors.[1]

1.6.2 THE GENRE OF THE GOSPEL OF MARK: KERYGMA OR BIOGRAPHY?

The thesis of the kerygma structure of the written gospel has received support through the observation that the oldest of the gospels, the Gospel of Mark, is essentially a passion narrative with an extended introduction. Its primary purpose, therefore, was to present a narrative account of the individual topics of the Pauline kerygma which is quoted as "gospel" in 1 Cor 15:1–5. Whether or not this is in fact an appropriate description of the intent of Mark's writing, it remains to ask whether Mark and other writings of this character were called "gospels" for this very reason. And if the author of the Gospel of Mark was not aware of the kerygma structure of his writing, is it possible that Mark and other gospels were recognized later as deserving the designation "gospel" because of their close relationship to the Christian proclamation which the apostles had called "the gospel"?

One might even find a confirmation for this hypothesis in the observation that the written gospels grew in the same way in which the kerygmatic formulations were expanded. The kerygma, called "gospel" in the writings of Ignatius of Antioch, began with the virginity of Mary and the birth of Jesus,[2] just as the later Gospels of Matthew and Luke opened their accounts of the story of Jesus with narratives about the virginity of Mary and the birth of Christ.

However, our survey of the use of the term "gospel" has not turned up a single instance in which any such literature was designated with this title before the middle of the 2d century. Hengel[3] has recently tried to renew the thesis that the titles of the canonical Gospels, as they appear in the earliest manuscripts of ca. 200 CE, existed in the same form already at the beginning of the 2d century.[4] Hengel's claim

---

[1] *Geschichte der frühchristlichen Literatur* (GLB; Berlin: De Gruyter, 1975) 282.

[2] Ignatius *Trall.* 9:1–2; cf. *Eph.* 18.2: see above # 1.2.2.

[3] *Evangelienüberschriften*, passim.

[4] Dormeyer (*Evangelium als Gattung*, 17) discusses Hengel's thesis critically, but still gives too much credit to his arguments. Wilhelm Schneemelcher ("Einleitung," in Edgar Hennecke, *Neutestamentliche Apokryphen in deutscher Übersetzung*, vol. I: *Evangelien* [5th ed. by Wilhelm Schneemelcher; Tübingen: Mohr/Siebeck, 1987] 68)

that the canonical Gospels must have circulated from the very beginning under the name of specific authors may be correct.[1] But there is
no evidence whatsoever that their original book titles were identical
with the later "The Gospel according to ..." (τὸ εὐαγγέλιον κατά ...).
On the contrary, there is evidence in the Nag Hammadi Library that
these standard titles were later added by scribes to writings that had
different original titles. Moreover, the term "gospel" continues to be
used widely as a technical term designating the Christian proclamation.

In any case, the more recent discussion of the literary genre of the
gospels has reopened the question of the relationship of the genre,
especially the Gospel of Mark, to biography, however cautiously.[2]
With respect to Hellenistic models for the genre of biography, Albrecht
Dihle encouraged the attempts to understand the Gospels of the New
Testament as biographies, but warned that the search for adequate
models in Greco-Roman literature could be futile.[3] This warning
should not be overlooked. Detlev Dormeyer, who has pursued this
question vigorously in two publications,[4] has achieved a breakthrough
insofar as he takes his starting point not from Greco-Roman models of
biography but from Klaus Baltzer's work on the biography of the prophets.[5] Hellenistic biography is primarily interested in the character
of the philosopher or the poet whose "life" (βίος) is described; "conversion" is understood as a conversion to a philosophical life, a life of
"virtue" (ἀρετή). This interest is present even in the biographies of
military and political figures.[6] The biography of the prophet, however, is concerned with office and function; "conversion" here is the call

---

emphasizes that Hengel's thesis simply cannot be substantiated. See for the following
the useful summary by Schneemelcher, ibid., 67–68.

[1] It must be stated, however, that, except for the Papias fragments in Eusebius
Ecclesiastical History, there is no single instance of the mention of any gospel by the
name of its author before Theophilus of Antioch (ca. 170 CE); cf. Hans von Campenhausen, *The Formation of the Christian Bible* (Philadelphia: Fortress, 1972) 129.

[2] Most of the literature is treated in Dormeyer (and Frankemölle), "Evangelium als
Begriff," 1581–1634. For a comprehensive discussion of gospel and Greek biography
see Klaus Berger, "Hellenistische Gattungen im Neuen Testament," *ANRW* 2.25/2.
1231–45.

[3] Albrecht Dihle, "Die Evangelien und die griechische Biographie," in Peter Stuhlmacher, ed., *Das Evangelium und die Evangelien* (WUNT 28; Tübingen: Mohr/Siebeck,
1983) 383–411.

[4] Dormeyer (and Frankemölle), "Evangelium als Begriff," and idem, *Evangelium als
Gattung.*

[5] Klaus Baltzer, *Die Biographie der Propheten* (Neukirchen: Neukirchener Verlag,
1975).

[6] See Plutarch's *Parallel Lives* and Suetonius's *Lives of the Emperors.*

to the office, and even the personal sufferings of the prophet are part
of the exercise of the responsibilities of this office. Birth and death
are only the external framework. Even within such a framework the
emphasis is placed upon the individual stages of the official life. To
these belong, e.g., the installations into various offices. "Life" and
"office" are to a large extent identical in the presentation.[1]

It may be useful here to summarize some of the typical features of
the office biography which Klaus Baltzer highlights in his brief discussion of the Gospel of Mark:[2] Just like the authors of Old Testament
biographies, Mark is using various existing collections of older materials and traditions. In the design of the outline of his work he follows
essentially the framework of the "biography of the prophets." He
begins with Jesus' baptism (not with his birth), which is not described
as a public presentation of Jesus but as the personal call which also
pronounces the title of his office ("you are my beloved son," 1:11). The
following chapters describe in various episodes the typical features of
the conduct of office. In the story of his suffering and death, the primary concern is the legitimation of Jesus' office. That his official title
is indeed "Son of God" is confirmed by the statement of the centurion
(Mark 15:39) after this claim has been officially denied by the
Jerusalem authorities (Mark 14:61). The ending of the Gospel of Mark
(16:1–8) with its rejection of the veneration of the tomb of Jesus—this
would have been appropriate for a famous sage but not for one who
was holding a divine office—corresponds to the official character of the
biography.[3]

Baltzer's proposal has the advantage of presenting a unified genre
instead of searching for various and sundry biographical and other
motifs which would have influenced Mark to different degrees in
his attempt to design a framework for the story of Jesus. It may be
possible to improve upon Baltzer's suggestion by investigating Greco-

---

[1] Baltzer, *Biographie*, 20.

[2] Ibid., 185–89.

[3] Baltzer's suggestions have been elaborated with some modifications in the
interpretation of the Gospel of Mark by Dieter Lührmann, "Biographie des Gerechten
als Evangelium: Vorstellungen zu einem Markus-Kommentar," *Wort und Dienst* N.F. 14
(1977) 25–50, and idem, *Das Markusevangelium* (HNT 3; Tübingen: Mohr/Siebeck,
1987) 42–44 and passim. It is difficult to understand Dormeyer's hesitation with
respect to the acceptance of this model which he justifies with the remark that this
genre had come to an end with the exile (see his *Evangelium als Gattung*, 168–73).
The biography of Nehemiah and the biographical substratum of Deutero-Isaiah are certainly post-exilic. Moreover, the latter has strongly influenced the narrative of the
suffering righteous and his vindication in Jewish literature after the exile; cf. George
Nickelsburg, "The Genre and Function of the Markan Passion Narrative," *HTR* 73
(1980) 153–84.

Roman instances of office biography, such as the Roman *commentarius,* the autobiography of the Roman official, to which Dihle has pointed as an important analogy.[1]

That Mark should have combined the genre of the office biography with the concept of the "kerygma" as it appears under the term "gospel"—assuming that this term is a linguistic metaphor with a presupposed implicit meaning—would require the demonstration that Mark indeed knew that he was writing "a gospel." As has been shown above,[2] Mark 1:1 cannot bear this burden of proof. There is no justification whatsoever to speak of Mark's writing as an attempt to transform the oral "gospel" (= the Christian proclamation) into a literary document.[3]

There is indeed no evidence that the writers of the 2d century who first used the term "gospel" as a reference to a written source had any awareness of the kerygma-character of this literature. If the final redactor of the *Didache* is indeed referring to a written gospel, what he has in mind is not the kerygma that could be found in that gospel, but rules and regulations for the Christian community which were transmitted in such a writing under the authority of Jesus (as, e.g., Matthew 18).[4] What *2 Clement* calls "gospel" is a collection of sayings of Jesus, not the story of Jesus' birth, life, death, and resurrection.[5] Marcion and Justin Martyr come closer to such a kerygma concept of the written gospel; this will be discussed in the following chapter (# 1.7). But for most of the first two-thirds of the 2d century the best characterization of the meaning of the term "gospel" is that given by Hans von Campenhausen: "'The Gospel' to which appeal is normally made, remains an elastic concept, designating the preaching of Jesus as a whole in the form in which it lives on in church tradition. The normative significance of the Lord's words, which is the most important point, ... is not transferred to the documents which record them."[6]

1.6.3 THE GENRE OF THE GOSPEL SOURCES

The problem of the literary genre of the Gospel of Mark could possibly be solved as suggested above. However, this would only explain

---

[1] "Die Evangelien und die griechische Biographie," 407–11.

[2] See above the discussion of Mark's use of the term "gospel" (# 1.3.4).

[3] It is all nigh impossible to translate the German monstrosity *Verschriftlichung des mündlichen Evangeliums* (Dormeyer, passim) into an adequate English expression.

[4] *Did.* 8.2; 15.3, 4: see above # 1.4.3.

[5] *2 Clem.* 8.5; see above # 1.4.4.

[6] von Campenhausen, *Formation,* 129.

the genre of the gospel as it was designed by Mark and as it was further developed by the later gospel writers who wrote their works on the basis of Mark's framework, i.e., Matthew and Luke and the various gospels and gospel harmonies dependent upon these gospels. But any attempt to define the genre of the written gospel in this way will not be useful as a comprehensive definition of all gospel literature because it does not include either the sources of the canonical gospels or the extant apocryphal gospel literature. To date the entire discussion of the genre of the gospel has been exclusively concerned with the gospel writings of the New Testament canon, often only with the three Synoptic Gospels at the expense of the Gospel of John.[1]

The sources used by the canonical as well as the apocryphal gospels are writings which incorporate and develop older traditions about the words and the life of Jesus. Even the Gospel of Mark, the oldest of the canonical gospels, is not the oldest representative of gospel literature, but used written sources, and there can be no doubt about the use of written sources in the later gospels of the canon. However, these sources—except for a written passion narrative—have little or no relationship to the Pauline kerygma of the death and resurrection of Jesus, *pace* the genre of biography.

Among these older gospel writings are collections of sayings (Synoptic Sayings Source), a collection of parables (the source of Mark 4), catenae of miracle stories (employed by Mark and recognizable in the Semeia Source of the Gospel of John), books of apocalyptic prophecies (Mark 13 and Matthew 24–25), and legends about Jesus' birth (Matthew 1–2; Luke 1–2). Günther Bornkamm has correctly remarked that such collections are formed "according to genres and conventions which can be observed also in other popular, secular, and religious literatures."[2] The kerygma of cross and resurrection has had no influence whatsoever upon the formation of these literatures. Rather, their genre has been determined by theological and sociological motifs of a very different character, such as "sapiential invitation," "aretalogy," and "dialogue." Moreover, these and other factors have also had an influence upon the further development of the gospel form created by Mark as well as upon the writings which are commonly known as the apocryphal gospels. Schniewind's definition and subsequent attempts to define the genre of the gospel are not only inadequate, if one considers the genre of the sources used by the canonical

---

[1] That is especially true of the more recent German discussion of this topic. In all the works cited in the preceding footnotes, one looks in vain for the mention of a single apocryphal gospel, and even the Gospel of John is rarely used.

[2] "Evangelien, formgeschichtlich," *RGG* 2 (3d ed.) 750.

gospels; they are also entirely useless for defining the literary genres which have determined the form and content of the apocryphal gospels.[1]

1.7 From the Oral Tradition to the Written Gospel

1.7.1 AUTHORITIES IN THE EARLIEST PERIOD

In the first one and one-half centuries, "scripture," i.e., authoritative writing, comprised exclusively what was later called the Old Testament.[2] Any additional authority referred to in order to underline the legitimacy of the Christian message and the teaching of the church was present in a variety of traditions which were still undefined.[3] Sometimes these were transmitted orally, sometimes in written form. Such authority could be called "the sayings of the Lord," usually transmitted orally.[4] But even the quotations of Jesus' sayings in *2 Clement*, although drawn from a written source, are still introduced as words of the Lord,[5] just as Justin (*1 Apology* 15–17) introduces the teachings of the gospels as "what Jesus said" and not as quotations from a book.

The pronouncements of Christian prophets constituted another important authority. They could be transmitted orally or in written form. Prophets were not only concerned with predicting the future;[6] they often functioned as instructors and church leaders together with "teachers" (διδάσκαλοι).[7] Prophetic writings, too, claim authority for the regulation and the renewal of the life of the church; such instructions appear as substantial sections of the Revelation of John and the *Shepherd of Hermas*.

In other cases, early Christian authors refer to "the pronouncements of the apostles," although there seems to be no particular tradition that is connected with the authority of the apostles. *1 Clement* 44 relates the offices of the church to the apostles, but in very general

---

[1] This question will be discussed below (# 1.8).

[2] von Campenhausen, *Formation*, 21–61; idem, "Das Alte Testament als Bibel der Kirche vom Ausgang des Urchristentums bis zur Entstehung des Neuen Testaments," in idem, *Frühzeit*, 152–96; Lee Martin McDonald, *The Formation of the Christian Biblical Canon* (Nashville: Abingdon, 1988) 48–68.

[3] For the use of authority in the Pauline letters see Hans von Campenhausen, "Die Begründung kirchlicher Entscheidungen beim Apostel Paulus," in idem, *Frühzeit*, 30–80.

[4] Acts 20:35; *1 Clem.* 2.8; 13.1; 46.8; *Did.* 8.2.

[5] *2 Clem.* 3.2; 4.5; 5.2–4; 6.1; 8.5; 9.11; 12.2; cf. also Polycarp *Phil.* 2.3.

[6] E.g., Acts 11:28; 21:10–11; Rev 22:6–7.

[7] Cf. Acts 13:1; *Did.* 10.7; 11.7–13.7.

terms. In 2 Pet 3:2 the apostles appear as guarantors of the Lord's commandment:

> That you should remember the predictions of the prophets and the com-
> mandment of the Lord and Savior through your apostles (μνησθῆναι ...
> τῆς τῶν ἀποστόλων ὑμῶν ἐντολῆς τοῦ κυρίου καὶ σωτῆρος).

The formulation is typical of the general way in which one refers to apostolic authority, though 2 Peter may have been written as late as the middle of the 2d century. *Did. inscr.* "Teaching of the Lord through the Twelve Apostles" (διδαχὴ κυρίου διὰ τῶν δώδεκα ἀποστόλων) is difficult to date; it is possible that the title was added later. It is an attempt to give material substance to the hitherto undefined authority of the apostles.[1] This presentation of the authority of the apostles in writings for the instruction of the church is continued in the subsequent production of such books as the *Catholic Didascalia of the Twelve Apostles of the Savior* and the *Apostolic Constitutions*.[2]

Apostolic authority was claimed early for writings in which the sayings of Jesus were collected. The recourse to Thomas as apostolic authority for the *Gospel of Thomas* is most likely very old, as is the reference to Matthew as authority for the "sayings" in Papias of Hierapolis (see below). Still in the second half of the 2d century, the Valentinian Ptolemy in his letter to Flora says:

> If God permit, you will learn in the future about their origin and genera-
> tion, when you are accounted worthy of the apostolic tradition which we
> also have received by succession, because we can prove all our state-
> ments from the teaching of the Savior. (*Ptolemy to Flora* # 7.9)[3]

It seems that apostolic authority for the esoteric tradition of Jesus' pronouncements was especially favored by Gnostic writers.[4]

1.7.2 PAPIAS OF HIERAPOLIS

A closely related appeal to tradition is the citation of "the traditions of the elders." The oldest witness for the teaching authority of the "elders" or "presbyters" (πρεσβύτεροι) is bishop Papias of Hierapolis.[5] The

---

[1] On the entire question see Hans von Campenhausen, *Ecclesiastical Authority and Spiritual Power* (Stanford, CA: Stanford University Press, 1969).

[2] On the titles of these books see R. Hugh Conolly, *Didascalia Apostolorum* (Oxford: Clarendon, 1929) pp. xxvii–xxviii.

[3] ET by R. McL. Wilson in Werner Foerster, *Gnosis: A Selection of Gnostic Texts* (2 vols.; Oxford: Clarendon, 1972–74) 1. 161.

[4] Helmut Koester, "La tradition apostolique et les origines du Gnosticisme," *RThPh* 119 (1987) 1–16.

[5] The relevant fragments of his writings are quoted in Eusebius *Hist. eccl.* 3.39.3–4.

date for his writings is usually given as some time between 100 and 150 CE.[1] More abundant evidence for the presbyter traditions comes from Irenaeus and Clement of Alexandria at the end of the 2d century.[2]

Eusebius quotes the following from Papias's writing (Five Books of Interpretations of the Oracles of the Lord):

> And I shall not hesitate to append to the interpretations all that I ever learnt well from the presbyters and remember well (καλῶς ἐμνημόνευσα) . . .; but if ever anyone came who had followed the presbyters, I inquired into the words of the presbyters, what Andrew or Peter or Philip or Thomas or James or John or Matthew, or any other of the Lord's disciples had said, and what Aristion and the presbyter John, the Lord's disciples, were saying.[3]

What Papias says about Mark reflects the use of categories which are drawn from the oral tradition:

> And the presbyter used to say this: "Mark became Peter's interpreter and wrote accurately all that he remembered (ὅσα ἐμνημόνευσεν), not, indeed, in order everything said or done by the Lord (τὰ ὑπὸ τοῦ κυρίου ἢ λεχθέντα ἢ πραχθέντα), . . . Mark did nothing wrong in thus writing down single points as he remembered them (ὅσα ἀπεμνημόνευσεν).[4]

Papias says about Matthew that he composed "the sayings" (τὰ λόγια).[5] In neither statement does Papias use the term "gospel." Even in their written form, these traditions about Jesus and of Jesus' words do not carry any greater authority than that which was transmitted orally. The written gospels' authority is assured by the same technical terms which had been established for the oral tradition. At the same time, Papias shows that these written documents did not come without the names of apostolic authors or of men who had followed the apostles. These names, which already guaranteed the trustworthiness of the oral tradition, are now used to assure the faithfulness of the written documents. The titles of such writings may have been something like "The sayings of the Lord written by Matthew (in Hebrew[6])."

---

[1] It is notoriously difficult to give a more precise date to Papias' writings; see Johannes Munck, "Presbyters and Disciples of the Lord in Papias," *HTR* 52 (1959) 223–43. On Papias references to Matthew and Mark see von Campenhausen, *Formation,* 129–35.

[2] See Günther Bornkamm, "πρεσβύς κτλ.," *TDNT* 6 (1959) 670–80; von Campenhausen, *Ecclesiastical Authority,* 162–77.

[3] Eusebius *Hist. eccl.* 3.39.3–4. Translation by Kirsopp Lake in LCL.

[4] Eusebius *Hist. eccl.* 3.39.15. ET by Kirsopp Lake in LCL.

[5] Quoted in Eusebius *Hist. eccl.* 3.39.16.

[6] It is noteworthy that the incipit of the *Apocryphon of James* says that the book was

The term "remember" (μνημονεύειν/ἀπομνημονεύειν) was decisive for the trustworthiness of the oral tradition. It played an important role in the earliest quotation formulae for sayings of Jesus.[1] It appears not only in Papias with reference to the written tradition, but also in a parallel in the *Apocryphon of James,* a writing that can be dated to approximately the same time as Papias's writing:[2]

> ... the twelve disciples [were] all sitting together at the same time and remembering what the Savior had said to each one of them, whether in secret or openly, and [putting it] in books. (NHC I 2,7–15)

The terminology of "remembering" is deliberate and, as Vielhauer had already remarked about Papias,[3] it is part of the controversy with the Gnostics. Gnostic writers were composing their written documents on the basis of the claim that they remembered well from the apostles and from those who had followed them.[4] It was important that such books could claim to rest on legitimate memory and that they carried apostolic authority. However, there was no concern with the title that was given to a particular book. Nowhere is the title "gospel" used for such books.[5]

---

written "in the Hebrew alphabet." Papias's reference to Matthew writing in Hebrew may rest upon such a statement in the original incipit of the book. Thus Papias would not be a witness to the existence for a Semitic original, but would simply report that such a reference occured in the title of the book.

[1] Acts 20:35; *1 Clem.* 13.1–2; 46.7–8.

[2] A date early in the 2d century was originally proposed by Willem van Unnik, *Evangelien aus dem Nilsand* (New York: Scheffer, 1959) 93–101. Van Unnik's argument was that this writing contained gospel materials which are still dependent upon oral tradition. In spite of some criticism of this early date (see F. E. Williams, "The Apocryphon of James," in Attridge, ed., *Nag Hammadi Codex I*, 1.26–27), van Unnik's arguments have now been confirmed by Ron Cameron, *Sayings Traditions in the Apocryphon of James* (HTS 34; Philadelphia: Fortress, 1984) 91–124.

[3] Vielhauer, *Geschichte,* 762.

[4] On this entire question see Cameron, "Remembering the Words of Jesus," in his *Apocryphon of James,* 91–124.

[5] Hengel (*Evangelienüberschriften,* 8–18) argues that Papias already presupposes the title "Gospel according to ..." (Εὐαγγέλιον κατά ...) with the implied meaning that this is the *one* gospel according to Matthew, Mark, etc. But there is no evidence for this in the surviving Papias fragments, and it would be completely anachronistic. That the *one* gospel was extant in different writings, which were all called "gospels" and transmitted under apostolic names, became a problem only after Marcion (see below). For Papias, all emphasis lies upon the apostolic names no matter what title could be derived from the incipit of a particular book.

1.7.3 MARCION

Hans von Campenhausen[1] suggested that the impulse for a radical change came from the Christian scholar, church leader, and reformer Marcion. At about the time when Justin Martyr arrived in Rome, coming from Ephesus, and about a decade before the publication of Justin's *Apologies,* Marcion (who was a wealthy shipowner) also came to Rome from Sinope in Pontus. Like other Christians of his time, Marcion knew the authoritative Christian scripture (the "Old Testament") and the still undefined and mostly oral traditions of the apostles and of the elders; under the same authority also some writings with the words and deeds of Jesus were transmitted. But Marcion had studied the letters of the apostle Paul, and he had become deeply impressed with the Pauline thesis of Christ as the end of the law. Marcion understood this to imply a rejection of the law and the prophets, the scriptures of Israel. Marcion's protest against the use of these scriptures in the churches also entailed a protest against what he called the Judaizing falsifications of the traditions of the apostles. He thus attacked a universally recognized authority, i.e., traditions guaranteed by names of various apostles and accepted by all churches and by many Gnostic teachers.

Moreover, Marcion thought that even the Pauline writings themselves had been contaminated by Judaizing interpretations. What he deemed necessary for a reform of the church was the dismissal of the Jewish scriptures and a new critical edition of the letters of Paul, that is, written documents under the authority of the only apostle who had fought against the Judaizers. This newly edited Corpus Paulinum, consisting of ten letters (the Pastoral Epistles are missing), became the basis of Marcion's ecclesiastical reform.

In these letters, Marcion found references of Paul to "my gospel."[2] Because of his fundamental doubts regarding the oral tradition, he understood these as references to a written document called "gospel." He may have known more than one writing which contained the reports of Jesus' words and deeds. But it is no longer possible to determine with certainty whether he was acquainted with the Gospels of Matthew and John as well as with the Gospel of Luke. Even if he knew Matthew, it is obvious that the pervasive references in this Gospel to the prophecies of Israel would have made this writing an

---

[1] *Formation,* 147–63.

[2] The phrase τὸ εὐαγγέλιόν μου appears in Rom 2:16 (Rom 16:25 is part of a secondary addition to Paul's letter); τὸ εὐαγγέλιον ἡμῶν is found in 2 Cor 4:3; 1 Thess 1:5; 2 Thess 1:8; 2:14, but see also Gal 1:11. Since Marcion did not know the Pastoral Epistles, 2 Tim 2:8 is not relevant.

unlikely choice for Marcion. In any case, Marcion believed that it must have been Luke's writing to which Paul had been referring as "my/our gospel."[1] When he published his revised edition of the letters of Paul, he included a purified version of Luke's Gospel in the novel authoritative book which he propagated as the new scriptures that were designed to replace the old scriptures of Israel.

As we have seen, there is no evidence that anyone before Marcion had used the term "gospel" as a designation for a written document. But all reports about Marcion agree that he called his revised edition of Luke "gospel."[2] Marcion introduced this novel usage in conscious protest against the still undefined and mostly oral traditions to which the churches of his day referred as their dominical and apostolic authority. Thus Marcion's new ecclesiastical organization was not only the first Christian church with its own "scripture"; it also possessed for the first time a written document called "the gospel." Marcion was excommunicated from the Roman church in 144 CE. According to the witness of Justin Martyr,[3] Marcion's church had already established itself throughout the whole world at the time of the writing of Justin's *First Apology*, i.e., less than a decade after Marcion's excommunication. It had obviously become a powerful and well-organized movement in a brief period of time, and it constituted a veritable threat to all those Christian churches which continued to insist that theology and ecclesiastical organization had to be based upon the writings of Israel, the law and the prophets, the "Holy Scripture" of Christendom.

1.7.4 JUSTIN MARTYR AND MARCION

Justin Martyr composed his writings in the later years of the emperor Antoninus Pius (150 to 160 CE). We know that Justin was involved in the earliest phase of the Marcionite controversy, because he reports in a later writing that he had published a book against Marcion.[4] But because his "Anti-Marcion" and his "Syntagma Against all Heresies" are not preserved, we do not know the details of his argu-

---

[1] The choice of Luke is interesting, because this Gospel was certainly written later than the other canonical Gospels, and "at first its standing was strikingly inferior to that of Mark and, above all, of Matthew" (von Campenhausen, *Formation*, 128).

[2] Adolf von Harnack, *Marcion: Das Evangelium vom fremden Gott* (2d ed.; Leipzig: Hinrichs, 1924 [reprint Darmstadt: Wissenschaftliche Buchgesellschaft, 1960]) 184*; von Campenhausen, *Formation*, 155–56.

[3] On Justin about Marcion see *1 Apol.* 26.5–8; 58.1–2. Cf. Eusebius *Hist. eccl.* 4.11.10.

[4] On Justin against Marcion see *1 Apol.* 26.8 ("Syntagma Against All Heresies"); Irenaeus *Adv. haer.* 4.6.9; Eusebius *Hist. eccl.* 4.11.8 (Syntagma against Marcion).

ments. However, those writings of Justin which are preserved, his two *Apologies* and his *Dialogue with Trypho,* clearly show the effects of Marcion's challenge. Most noticeable in these writings is the complete suppression of Paul and his letters. While earlier writers, even in Rome, never hesitated to refer to Paul as their authority,[1] there is not a single quote from the Pauline Corpus in Justin's writings, nor is the apostle ever mentioned. On the other hand, his writings abound with quotations from the "Old Testament" (the Septuagint) and from the Gospels of Matthew and Luke.

A positive effect of Marcion's challenge in the writings of Justin Martyr is the adoption of the concept of a written gospel and the departure from the oral tradition. Justin agrees with Marcion: reliable traditions of the church must be preserved in written records. However, while Marcion emphasized the irreconcilable contradictions between the written gospel and the Jewish scripture, Justin linked the writings which he called "Memoirs of the Apostles" as tightly as possible to the law and the prophets. While Marcion revised the Gospel of Luke in an effort to eliminate all quotations and references to the law and the prophets, Justin did not hesitate to revise the texts of Matthew and Luke on several occasions in order to establish an even closer verbal agreement between the prophecies of the Greek Bible and the record of their fulfillment in the text of the gospels.[2]

1.7.5 JUSTIN'S "MEMOIRS OF THE APOSTLES"

That Justin saw the written gospels as a more reliable record of the words and deeds of Jesus and that he advertised them as replacement of the established, but less trustworthy oral traditions about Jesus is evident in his designation of the gospels as the "Memoirs of the Apostles" (ἀπομνημονεύματα τῶν ἀποστόλων), a designation he used in many instances referring to the Gospels of Matthew, Luke, and possibly Mark. The designation occurs twice in his *First Apology*:

---

[1] In addition to numerous allusions to Paul's letters, *1 Clement* contains several explicit references: *1 Clem.* 32.5–6 = Rom 1:29–32; *1 Clem.* 37.5 = 1 Cor 12:21–22; *1 Clem.* 47.1–3 = Phil 4:15; cf. *1 Clem.* 49.5 = 1 Cor 13:5. With respect to the debated question of the dependence of 1 Peter (also written in Rome) upon Paul see Francis Wright Beare, *The First Epistle of Peter* (3d ed.; Oxford: Blackwell, 1970) 28–29, 212–16 (cf. also the literature cited on p. 28, n. 1).

[2] Helmut Koester, *Septuaginta und Synoptischer Erzählungsstoff im Schriftbeweis Justins des Märtyrers* (Habilitationsschrift Heidelberg, 1956); see also my essay "The Text of the Synoptic Gospels in the Second Century," in William L. Petersen, ed., *Gospel Traditions in the Second Century: Origins, Recensions, Text, and Transmission* (Christianity and Judaism in Antiquity 3; Notre Dame: University of Notre Dame Press, 1989) 19–37. See further below # 5.2.

The apostles in the memoirs which have come from them, which are also called gospels, have transmitted that the Lord had commanded them as follows, "that Jesus had taken bread, etc." (*1 Apol.* 66.3)

And on the day which is named after the sun there is an assembly of all those who live in each city or village; and the memoirs of the apostles or the writings of the prophets are being read as long as it is allowable; when the reader has stopped, the leader will speak and give an admonition and an invitation to imitate all these good things. (*1 Apol.* 67.3–4)[1]

It is clear here that these "memoirs" are indeed gospel writings and that they are used liturgically as instructions for the sacrament and as texts for homilies.

All other occurrences of the term are found in *Dialogue* 99–107 where Justin systematically employs gospel materials for his interpretation of Psalm 22. In this context he uses the designation "Memoirs of the Apostles" thirteen times.[2] In each instance the materials quoted derive from written gospels, usually from Matthew and Luke, in one instance from Mark, and each time the term serves to quote, or to refer to, gospel materials which demonstrate that the prophecy of the Psalm has been fulfilled in the story of Jesus. The "Memoirs of the Apostles" are used as reliable historical records.

The term "Memoirs of the Apostles" has often been explained as a title designed by Justin in order to raise the gospels to the status of Greek memoirs of a philosopher. This suggestion was first made in 1857.[3] It has been repeated by most authors because the name seemed to be "well-chosen and very appropriate in order to give to the educated Greeks the right ideas about the character of the gospels."[4] However, the term is problematic with respect to its usage for philosophical memorabilia.[5] It was never used for a philosopher's memorabilia before the Second Sophistic in the 2d century CE. The primary older example for such "Memoirs" commonly cited is Xenophon's

---

[1] But cf. also *1 Apol.* 33.5: "As those who remembered (οἱ ἀπομνημονεύσαντες) everything about the savior Jesus Christ have taught" (a quote of Luke 1:31 follows).

[2] *Dial.* 100.4; 101.3; 102.5; 103.6, 8; 104.1; 105.1, 5, 6; 106.1, 3, 4; 107.1.

[3] E. Köpke, *Über die Gattung* ἀπομνημονεύματα *in der griechischen Literatur* (Programm der Ritterakademie zu Brandenburg, 1857).

[4] Zahn, *Kanon*, 1. 471.

[5] Klaus Berger ("Hellenistische Gattungen im Neuen Testament," *ANRW* 2.25/2 [1984] 1245–47) has discussed the use of this term in detail, but he does not pay sufficient attention to the time of its earliest occurrence. Berger defines the term Ἀπομνημονεύματα as personal remembrances about particular persons which are written down, whereas Ὑπομνήματα can report all sort of things, persons, and events as well as other matters. Cf. also Nils Hyldahl, "Hegesipps Hypomnemata," *StTh* 14 (1960) 70–113.

Memorabilia of Socrates. But this Latin title was not used for Xenophon's work in antiquity; it appears for the first time in the year 1569 in Johann Lenklau's edition of Xenophon. In Plutarch and in Diodorus Siculus, ἀπομνημόνευμα means an anecdote that is heard or written down.[1] The Latin equivalent of the Greek plural ἀπομνημονεύματα, *commentarii*, is first used for Xenophon's writing in Aulus Gellius [2d century CE] *Noct. Att.* 14.3.5 (*quod Xenophon, in libris quos dictorum atque factorum Socrates commentarios composuit*). The Greek term does not appear in Xenophon's writings, but only as a title of his work in later manuscripts: "First Book of Xenophon's Memoirs of Socrates" (Ξενοφῶντος Σωκράτους ἀπομνημονευμάτων βιβλίον πρῶτον), and in the pseudepigraphical letter # 18 of Xenophon from the time of the Second Sophistic: "But I am composing some memoirs of Socrates" (πεποίημαι δέ τινα ἀπομνημονεύματα Σωκράτους).[2] Xenophon himself uses the verb "to remember distinctly" (διαμνημονεύειν) once in this work: "I shall write that which I remember distinctly" (τούτων δὲ γράψω ὅποσα ἂν διαμνημονεύω, 1.3.1).

That Justin should have known the term ἀπομνημονεύματα from its occasional use in the Second Sophistic is possible, but not very likely. It is highly unlikely, however, that his choice of the term as a designation for the gospels was dependent upon this usage, and it is certainly not the case that Justin adopted the term in order to lend to the written gospels the rank of historical sources[3]—simply because ἀπομνημονεύματα did not have any such meaning at Justin's time.[4] On the other hand, the simple form of the verb "to remember" (μνημονεύειν) occurs frequently in the quotation formulae for orally transmitted sayings of Jesus.[5] The composite form of the verb "to remember" (ἀπομνημονεύειν) had been used by Papias of Hierapolis as a technical term for the transmission of oral materials about Jesus. If Justin's term "Memoirs of the Apostles" is derived from this usage, it designates the written gospels as the true recollections of the apostles, trustworthy

---

[1] Plutarch, *Cato maior* 9; Diodorus Siculus 1.14: "What is said in simple words briefly and clearly is for the one who speaks an ἀπόφθεγμα, for the one who has heard it an ἀπομνημόνευμα."

[2] Ed. Hercher, *Epist. Graec.*, 623; cf. also Diog. L. 4.2; 7.4, 36, 163.

[3] Dormeyer, *Evangelium als Gattung*, 15. *2 Apol.* 10 and 11 connect in no way the gospels as "memoirs" with Xenophon's *Memorabilia* of Socrates (*pace* Dormeyer, p. 15–16). Justin rather refers to a statement of Plato's *Apology* (24 b) about Socrates in *2 Apol.* 10.5, and to Xenophon's famous story about Herakles at the crossroads in *2 Apol.* 11.

[4] Trustworthy historical record would rather be designated by several other terms, such as ὑπομνήματα (= *commentarii*), συγγράμματα, see LSJ, *svv.*

[5] See above in the discussion of Papias of Hierapolis.

and accurate, and more reliable than any oral tradition which they
are destined to replace.[1]

Moreover, when Justin composed the interpretation of Psalm 22—
an earlier treatise that was later incorporated in his *Dialogue*[2]—it is
evident that he knew of the presbyter tradition quoted in Papias's
work. In *Dial.* 106.3 he refers to the "Memoirs of Peter" in the context
of a citation from Mark 3:16–17.[3] This reveals that Justin connected
the Gospel of Mark with Peter like the presbyter tradition that is
quoted in Papias.[4] That Justin, relying on Papias, coined the term
"Memoirs of the Apostles" with an anti-Gnostic intention, is quite possible, considering the use of the terminology of "remembering" in such
writings as the *Apocryphon of James*.[5] But what is of primary importance is the fact that the use of this term advertises the written gospels as replacement for the older oral traditions under apostolic
authority.

1.7.6 JUSTIN AND THE GOSPELS

Justin uses the term "gospel" only three times in his extant writings
which fill almost two hundred-forty pages in a modern edition of the
Greek text. Considering the large amount of quotations and references to gospel materials, this is surprizing:

> The apostles in the memoirs which have come from them, which are also
> called gospels (ἃ εὐαγγέλια καλεῖται), have transmitted that the Lord had
> commanded . . . (*1 Apol.* 66.3)

---

[1] The first to draw attention to this close relationship of Justin's term to Papias was
Richard Heard, "The ἀπομνημονεύματα in Papias, Justin, and Irenaeus," *NTS* 1
(1954–55) 122–29. Heard's thesis has been criticized by Nils Hyldahl, "Hegesipps
Hypomnemata," *StTh* 14 (1960) 70–113. However, Hyldahl does not appreciate the
differences between ὑπομνήματα, συγγράμματα, and ἀπομνημονεύματα, nor the fact that
the latter term occurs relatively late in Greek literature.

[2] Luise Abramowski, "Die 'Erinnerungen der Apostel' bei Justin," in Stuhlmacher,
ed., *Evangelium und Evangelien*, 341–53.

[3] All other references speak of memoirs of a plurality of apostles except for *Dial.*
106.3 where, after mentioning Peter, Justin speaks of "his memoirs." This is either a
specific reference to the Gospel of Mark, written by the amanuensis of Peter, or—less
likely—the text should be emended to "his (Jesus') apostles' memoirs." In any case,
since Justin continues to refer to a Markan passage (Mark 3:16–17, there are no parallels in Matthew and Luke), the reference to the presbyter tradition that connects Peter
with Mark may still be implied, even if the text must be emended.

[4] Abramowski, ibid., 353. However, this reliance on the presbyter tradition does not
prove that, in general, second-century authors preferred the oral tradition to written
documents; this is no longer true for Justin Martyr (*pace* E. F. Osborn, *Justin Martyr*
[BHTh 47; Tübingen: Mohr/Siebeck, 1973] 125–26).

[5] Abramowski, ibid., 352.

(Trypho said:) . . . I know that your commandments which are written in the so-called gospel (ἐν τῷ λεγομένῳ εὐαγγελίῳ) are so wonderful and so great that no human being can possibly fulfill them. (*Dial.* 10.2)

And in the gospel it is recorded that he (Jesus) said (ἐν τῷ εὐαγγελίῳ δὲ γέγραπται εἰπών), "Everything has been handed over to me by the Father . . ." (*Dial.* 100.1)

In each of these three passages in which the term occurs, it designates a written gospel. It is evident that "gospel" refers to the same literature that Justin otherwise calls "Memoirs of the Apostles." The use of the plural in *1 Apol.* 66.3 indicates that Justin knew of more than one written gospel. This is confirmed by the fact that Justin's quotations reflect the texts of the Gospels of Matthew and Luke and, at least in one instance, Mark. Moreover, he also quotes sayings which may derive from an apocryphal gospel.

These gospels, for Justin, possess the authority of written records. Although they are read in service of the church, they are not "Holy Scripture" (γραφή) like the law and the prophets. The latter are enhanced by the inspiration of the prophecies which they record,[1] but Justin never considers the "Gospels" or the "Memoirs of the Apostles" as inspired writings. While he regularly quotes the law and the prophets with the formula "it is written" (γέγραπται), he uses this term only rarely for the gospels. In the few instances where he does so, he combines this formula with other verbs. Introducing gospel quotations, the formula does not mean "it is written in Holy Scripture," but "it is recorded in a written document that Jesus said" (*Dial.* 100.1).[2]

The character of the gospels as historical records (rather than holy scripture) is underlined by the fact that Justin can occasionally refer to gospel materials as if they were written in secular records:

(About the dividing of Jesus garment at the crucifixion) . . . and that this happened you can learn from the acts which were recorded under Pilate (ἐκ τῶν ἐπὶ Ποντίου Πιλάτου γενομένων ἄκτων). (*1 Apol.* 35.9)

(About Jesus healing the sick and raising the dead) . . . that he has done these things, you can learn from the acts which were recorded under Pontius Pilate (ἐκ τῶν ἐπὶ Ποντίου Πιλάτου γενομένων ἄκτων). (*1 Apol.* 48.3)[3]

---

[1] *1 Apol.* 32. However, Justin does not ascribe the inspiration to the text of the Greek translation (Septuagint) or to the Hebrew text, but rather to the prophets themselves whose words were recorded in Hebrew and translated into Greek.

[2] "It is written" is used in connection with the quotation of materials from the "Memoirs of the Apostles" also in *Dial.* 103.6, 8; 104.1; 105.6; 106.3, 4; 107.1.

[3] It is possible that the same phrase should be added to the statement in *1 Apol.* 38.7: "That all these things were done to Christ by the Jews, you can learn."

(On Bethlehem as Jesus' place of birth) . . . as you can learn from the census lists which were recorded under Cyrenius (ἐκ τῶν ἀπογραφῶν τῶν γενομένων ἐπὶ τοῦ Κυρηνίου), your first governor in Judea. (*1 Apol.* 34.2)

These are the earliest references to Acts of Pilate in Christian literature. The next mention of Pilate writings is found in Tertullian (*Apologeticum* 21.24):

Pilate, who was already a Christian in his conscience, reported all these things about Christ (i.e., his life activity, cross, and resurrection) to Tiberius who was Caesar at that time.

While Tertullian may have known a letter of Pilate, a Christian forgery of the late 2d century (in its preserved form mistakenly addressed to Claudius),[1] it is unlikely that Justin knew any such document.[2] But the parallel references to the "Gospels," the "Memoirs of the Apostles," and official records show why Justin values the written gospels so highly: they are records which document the historical factuality of the events of the story of Jesus. As records of this nature the gospels are, indeed, the foundations of the truth of the Christian beliefs and they substantiate the validity of the Christian kerygma. That this is the case, in Justin's understanding of their function, is not related to the "kerygmatic" character of these writings. Rather, the gospels as records document the historical fulfillment of prophecy, and thus the truth of the Christian faith. The testimony of true divinity is the fulfillment of prophecy:

It is the work of God to announce something before it happens and then to demonstrate that it happened as it was predicted. (*1 Apol.* 12.10)

In a brilliant formulation, this principle occurs in Tertullian *Apologeticum* 20.3:

---

[1] Greek Text in the *Acts of Peter and Paul*, 41–42 (Ricardus Adalbertus Lipsius and Maximilianus Bonnet, *Acta Apostolorum Apocrypha* [2 vols.; Leipzig: Mendelssohn, 1991–1898; reprint: Darmstadt: Wissenschaftliche Buchgesellschaft, 1959] 1. 196–97). There is also a Latin version, preserved as an appendix to the *Gospel of Nicodemus,* and a somewhat different Syriac translation; see F. Scheidweiler, "The Gospel of Nikodemus, Acts of Pilate and Christ's Descent into Hell," in Edgar Hennecke, *New Testament Apocrypha* (2 vols.; 3d ed. by Wilhelm Schneemelcher, trans. R. McL. Wilson; Philadelphia: Westminster, 1963) 1. 444–84 (English translation of the letter on pp. 477–78).

[2] The preserved *Acts of Pilate* are a work of the 4th century, most likely produced by a Christian as a response to a pagan writing with this title which was circulated during the Diocletian persecution as anti-Christian propaganda. On the later *Acts of Pilate,* see Stephen Gero, "Apocryphal Gospels: A Survey of Textual and Literary Problems," *ANRW* 2.25/5 (1988) 3986–88.

testimonium divinitatis veritas divinationis ("The testimony of divinity is the truth of divination").

In direct antithesis to Marcion's use of the written gospel, Justin binds these gospels to the prophetic revelation of the Old Testament scriptures.

Justin Martyr, to be sure, knows expanded kerygmatic formulations, and he closely associates their topics with narrative materials which he draws from the Gospels of Matthew and Luke. As he prepares to present his scriptural proof for the truth of the Christian faith, he quotes an expanded kerygmatic formulation:

> In the books of the prophets we find that it was proclaimed beforehand that Jesus our Christ would appear, be born by a virgin, reach manhood, heal every disease and every sickness and raise the dead, that he would be despised and denied and crucified, and that he would die and be raised up and ascend into heaven, and that he is and will be called the Son of God, and that some people would be sent by him in every nation of humanity to proclaim that . . . (*Apol.* 31.7)

He then quotes prophecies from the law and the prophets which predict each of the topics of the Christian kerygma, and quotes the corresponding sections from the gospel narratives in order to demonstrate that each of the prophecies has found its exact fulfillment in the history of Jesus. But neither does Justin ever call the kerygma or creed of the church a "gospel," nor does he show any awareness of the kerygmatic structure of the gospel writings which he is using.

1.8 Apocryphal and Canonical Gospels

1.8.1 THE PREVAILING PREJUDICE

Schniewind's definition of the genre gospel which emphasizes the kerygma structure as the constitutive element has resulted in the assumption that only the canonical gospels qualify as genuine gospel literature. We have seen, however, that the term gospel as a designation of a certain type of literature came into use without any awareness that it was their peculiar literary genre that distinguished these writings from others. Therefore a great variety of writings of very different character eventually came to be called "gospels" toward the end of the 2d century, including so-called "apocryphal" gospels.

When the kerygma structure of the canonical gospels is used as the criterion for the definition of the genre, the apocryphal gospels appear

as inferior and as incompatible with this genre. Ancient and venerable prejudices—as old as the anti-heretical polemics of the Fathers
of the catholic church—were reinforced. Even in recent times, scholars have characterized the apocryphal gospels as secondary, derivative, speculative, and merely concerned with the edification and
entertainment of their readers, while the canonical gospels are routinely seen as original, historical, and replete with theological insight.
One can still read judgments like the following in modern scholarly
works:

> The Jewish-Christian Gospels are characterized by a grotesque appeal
> to vulgar taste and are obviously fictitious. The Gnostic Gospels are
> marked by an esoteric wisdom which renders Jesus' message and mis
> sion unintelligible save for the initiated few.[1]

In the third edition of *New Testament Apocrypha,* Wilhelm Schneemelcher[2] had suggested that the apocryphal gospels constitute a different
genre altogether, because the exalted Lord is speaking in these writings, communicating wisdom and life—as if mediation of wisdom and
life through the exalted Lord were alien to the Gospels of the New Testament! Schneemelcher distinguished two types of apocryphal gospels: (1) those connected with the Synoptic (or canonical) Gospels
which are designed to edify the reader (such as the *Gospel of Peter*)
and (2) those "allied with Gnosis" (to this group he assigns the *Gospel
of Thomas,* the *Dialogue of the Savior,* and many others). About the
latter he wrote:

> They are revelation writings the purpose of which is to convey the
> redeemer's words and therewith "knowledge" or "gnosis."[3]

1.8.2 CRITERIA FOR THE DEFINITION OF A "GOSPEL"

It is evident that criteria like "speculative rather than historical"
and "edificational rather than theological" cannot be used in order to
determine which writings should be included in a history of the

---

[1] Robert Spivey and D. Moody Smith, *Anatomy of the New Testament* (New York:
Macmillan, 1969) 173.

[2] Wilhelm Schneemelcher, "Introduction," in Hennecke-Schneemelcher-Wilson, *NT
Apocrypha,* 1. 80–84. In his revised "Einleitung" (pp. 71–72) in the 5th edition of *NT
Apokryphen,* Schneemelcher.has changed his judgment considerably and suggests that
the genre "gospel," even if defined narrowly, can be applied to some of the apocryphal
materials in so far as they consist of sayings and/or narrative materials related to
Jesus traditions.

[3] Hennecke-Schneemelcher-Wilson, *NT Apocrypha,* 1. 83. For further discussion of
such characterizations of apocryphal literature see my article, "Apocryphal and Canonical Gospels," *HTR* 73 (1980) 105–30.

development of gospel literature.

Moreover, any definition of the literary genre "gospel" on the basis of traditional classifications or theological observations is not helpful when one is faced with a rather complex and diversified corpus of literature.[1] Even for the canonical Gospels, taken by themselves, the establishment of one literary genre is not without problems. These four gospels have much in common. All four include sayings and narrative materials, and at least three of these gospels end with a passion narrative and stories about the appearances of Jesus after his resurrection.[2] But some of these common features are simply due to the fact that Matthew and Luke used the Gospel of Mark as their common source and employed a second common source for their sayings materials.

A closer scrutiny of the four canonical Gospels reveals that even here the theological definition of a gospel genre has its problems. The structure of the Gospel of Matthew is controlled by five major and a number of smaller speeches of Jesus into which the traditional sayings materials have been gathered; the passion narrative, i.e., the central piece of the "kerygma," is no longer a fundamental structural element of Matthew's Gospel. The same could be said about the Gospel of Luke, which presents the events of Jesus' life and ministry in the form of a biography of the divine man. Conversely, the Gospel of John, which is not dependent upon Mark like Matthew and Luke, is a writing of an entirely different character. It may resemble the Synoptic Gospels because of the use of a passion narrative; but its presentation of Jesus' miracles as divine epiphanies and its transformation of the sayings into revelation discourses hardly fits the definition of the genre of the gospel developed on the basis of the Gospel of Mark.

The application of such a genre definition becomes altogether impossible if one considers the sources used by the canonical gospels. The Synoptic Sayings Source, used by the Gospels of Matthew and Luke, was a collection of wisdom sayings and apocalyptic prophecies; it never contained a passion narrative. The catenae of miracle stories employed in the first part of the Mark's Gospel, the Semeia Source of the Fourth Gospel, a parable collection (Mark 4), the pamphlet of apocalyptic prophecies (Mark 13), and the legends about the birth of a divine child (Matthew 1–2; Luke 1–2)—all these are examples of

---

[1] Vielhauer (*Geschichte,* 256–57) rightly warns that any preconceived notion of the genre gospel, developed in the analysis of just one or two canonical gospels, is a dogmatic prejudice that does not do justice to the variety of writings which were indeed called "gospels" in the ancient church.

[2] Resurrection appearances are missing in the original text of the Gospel of Mark; only the secondary ending of this gospel relates such appearances.

sources and materials appearing in the gospels of the canon which hardly fit the genre of the kerygma gospel.

On the other hand, what characterizes some of these sources reappears in several of the apocryphal gospels. The *Gospel of Thomas* is a collection of prophetic and wisdom sayings. The *Dialogue of the Savior* preserves discourses and dialogues of Jesus with his disciples, which are closely related to those employed by the author of the Gospel of John. The *Infancy Gospel of Thomas* preserves legends about the divine child—a genre that has influenced the first two chapters of the Gospel of Luke. The *Proto-Gospel of James* tells about the virginity of Mary and of Jesus' birth by a virgin. Only the *Gospel of Peter*—at least in the form in which it is preserved—is constituted by a passion narrative and stories about the appearances of the risen Christ and thus is related to the kerygma of cross and resurrection. Whether or not any of these apocryphal gospels are dependent upon the Gospels of the New Testament canon, they represent, like the sources of the canonical gospels, literary genres which have parallels in other popular and religious literatures. Genres like "wisdom book," "dialogue," and "aretalogy" were employed when oral traditions about Jesus were assembled and composed in literary forms for the first time, and they continued to be influential in the development of later gospel literature. Compared with these written compositions of Jesus traditions, the Gospels of the New Testament appear as rather complex literary products in which such sources are blended together in various and distinctive ways.

On the basis of these observations one must establish a criterion by which it can be determined whether any extant writing from the early period of Christianity belongs to the corpus of gospel literature. This corpus should include all those writings which are constituted by the transmission, use, and interpretation of materials and traditions from and about Jesus of Nazareth. Obviously, such writings belong to different literary genres. Some of these writings may have preserved the genre which determined their character at the stage of their earliest composition. Others may have come into being through the conflation or combination of sources of different literary genres, or they may be later developments or interpretations of earlier compositions. Whether or not they are canonical, and regardless of their commitment to the kerygma of Christ's death and resurrection, all of them must be included in a consideration of the history and development of gospel literature.[1]

[1] For practical reasons I am excluding from this treatment some of the later gospels which show dependence upon the canonical gospel literature, including the Jewish-

This working hypothesis provides a criterion for the exclusion of a number of writings which may appear to be gospels, or which have traditionally been known as "gospels," or received this title in the colophon of a manuscript but are not related to or constituted by the continuing development of sources containing materials from or about Jesus of Nazareth.

1.8.3 WRITINGS WHICH ARE NOT TO BE COUNTED AS GOSPELS

The following writings will, therefore, not be treated in the context of this book:

The *Gospel of Philip* (NHC II,3), a collection of aphoristic theological reflections and comments, perhaps derived from a theological treatise.

The *Gospel of Truth* (NHC I,3), a meditation about the "true gospel," i.e., about the message of gnosis brought by Jesus which creates joy among those who hear it.

The *Gospel of the Egyptians,* also called *The Holy Book of the Great Invisible Spirit* (NHC III,2 and IV,2), a mythological description of the work of salvation which was accomplished by the Great Seth, the son of Adam.[1]

The *Sophia of Jesus Christ* (NHC III,4 and BG 8502,3), a secondary elaboration in the form of a dialogue of Jesus with his disciples of the philosophical religious writing *Eugnostos the Blessed* (NHC III,3 and V,1).

The *Apocryphon of John* (NHC II,1; III,1; IV,1; BG 8502,2), a Gnostic revelation discourse containing extensive interpretations of the first chapters of the Book of Genesis. It is probably of pre-Christian origin; its only Christian element is a secondary framework which presents the entire book as a revelation discourse given by Jesus to his disciple John.

The *Pistis Sophia* (Codex Askewianus) and the *Two Books of Jeu* (Codex Brucianus), as well as other Gnostic books containing revelation discourses and dialogues of Jesus with his disciples, whenever the pattern of discourse of Jesus with his disciples is employed as a secondary stylistic devise, while the materials presented in this form have little or no relationship to the traditions from or about Jesus.

It is, of course, not always possible to draw a clear line. The *Epistula Apostolorum,* for example, is in its external form a letter of the

---

Christian Gospels, the *Epistula Apostolorum,* and the *Gospel of Nicodemus.* I have also excluded a number of fragments.

[1] This writing must be distinguished from the *Gospel According to the Egyptians* which is known through quotations from Clement of Alexandria. It belongs to the genre of gospel literature, but will not be treated in this volume.

Twelve Apostles in which they report about Jesus' discourses with them after the resurrection. Gospel materials are clearly used, especially in the introduction—a brief narrative of Jesus' ministry—and in the report of the resurrection appearance. On the other hand, large parts of the discourses are composed of church order materials and of parenetical traditions. But the writing is relevant insofar as it represents a response, based on traditional gospel materials, to the speculative gnostic discourses of Jesus with his disciples in which a relationship to traditional gospel materials is not evident.

A number of other writings called "gospel," of which often only the name or a tiny fragment or a brief quotation are known, will also not appear in the following treatment of gospel literature.[1] It is often impossible to determine the character of these writings and to be certain that their content merits inclusion.

---

[1] For a listing and brief description of these see Hennecke-Schneemelcher-Wilson, *NT Apocrypha*, vol. 1, passim.

2

The Collection of the Sayings of Jesus

2.1 Sayings of Jesus in early Christian Writings

2.1.1 THE ATTESTATION OF THE ORAL TRADITION

During the last century scholars have critically analyzed the extant gospel writings in order to determine the sources and traditions which were used in their composition. The method employed in this endeavor, once called "literary criticism,"[1] is now commonly called "source criticism."[2] It has resulted in the hypothesis that a number of larger and smaller written documents were used by the authors of the four Gospels of the New Testament canon. These earliest written materials are in turn composed of smaller units which circulated orally during the first decades of the early Christian movement. The method by which the oral traditions about Jesus have been determined is called "form criticism" (*Formgeschichte*); it reveals the social and

---

[1] The older term "literary criticism" (*Literarkritik*) has more recently been used to designate the investigation of the literary structure of writings in their final form. Good introductions into this method are William A Beardslee, *Literary Criticism of the New Testament* (GBSNTS; Philadelphia: Fortress, 1970) and Norman R. Petersen, *Literary Criticism for New Testament Critics* (GBSNTS; Philadelphia: Fortress, 1978).

[2] There is a wealth of literature on the source criticism of the canonical gospels, mostly consisting of commentaries and monographs to individual gospels (see below on the treatment of the individual Gospels of the New Testament). The classic works on the source criticism of the Synoptic Gospels are Heinrich Julius Holtzmann, *Die synoptischen Evangelien: Ihr Ursprung und ihr geschichtlicher Charakter* (Leipzig: Engelmann, 1863); Julius Wellhausen, *Einleitung in die drei ersten Evangelien* (2d ed.; Berlin: Reimer, 1911); B. H. Streeter, *The Four Gospels: A Study of Origins* (first published London: Macmillan, 1924). Also see Martin Lehmann, *Synoptische Quellenanalyse und die Frage nach dem historischen Jesus* (BZNW 38; Berlin: De Gruyter, 1970). A comprehensive review can be found in Walter Schmithals, "Evangelien, Synoptische," *TRE* 10 (1982) 575–609.

religious function of oral traditions of and about Jesus in the early Christian community.[1]

The purpose of this chapter is to investigate the beginnings of the collection of sayings. The most natural and convenient point of departure for a discussion of the earliest formation of the gospel tradition would seem to be the life, teaching, work, and death and resurrection of Jesus of Nazareth. From here one could move on to a description of the traditions about Jesus, their growth and collection, and finally to the analysis of the extant gospel literature. To be sure, all traditions and writings which are the subject of this book are ultimately related to Jesus of Nazareth. But the collection of the oldest materials is not related directly to the life and ministry of Jesus of Nazareth.

The relationship of the earliest traditions about Jesus to the historical ministry of Jesus is complex. The earliest traditions do not give a mirror image of Jesus' ministry. The life of the community reflects the source of experience in a different way: the light that is received from its source is refracted into many colors as in a prism or in a rainbow. There are many colors close at hand instead of one unified brightness. In fact, one may see only one single color without realizing that its fount is a light of very different qualities. Our task here is not the reconstruction of the source but the description of the refracted light and of the way in which the many colors are finally composed to the various colorful (or sometimes monochrome) pictures which we call "gospels." Diversity rather than unity is the hallmark of the beginning of the traditions about Jesus.

Our story of the history and development of gospel literature, therefore, cannot start with Jesus of Nazareth but must try to determine the point at which the various and diverse traditions about Jesus begin to take form. However, the reconstruction of their formation and use is not exclusively dependent upon the internal evidence derived from the source-critical analysis of the gospels themselves, but can also rely upon some external evidence which is available in other early Christian writings, primarily the letters of Paul, which testify to

---

[1] The most important form-critical work remains Rudolf Bultmann, *The History of the Synoptic Tradition* (2d ed.; New York: Harper, 1968); cf. also idem and Karl Kundsin, *Form Criticism* (New York: Willet, Clark, 1934; reprint New York: Harper, 1962); furthermore the influential work of Martin Dibelius, *From Tradition to Gospel* (New York: Scribner's, 1934). For a brief introduction see Edgar V. McKnight, *What is Form Criticism?* (GBSNTS; Philadelphia: Fortress, 1969). An instructive collection of essays of various authors was published by Ferdinand Hahn, ed., *Zur Formgeschichte des Evangeliums* (WdF 81; Darmstadt: Wissenschaftliche Buchgesellschaft, 1985). See also the general survey with bibliography by Helmut Köster, "Formgeschichte/Formenkritik II. Neues Testament," *TRE* 11 (1983) 271–99.

the way in which Jesus' sayings and stories about Jesus were collected and used in the earliest period.

However, one immediately encounters a major difficulty. Whatever Jesus had preached did not become the content of the missionary proclamation of Paul, nor of the churches from which his proclamation took its origin, nor in other writings closely related to this missionary enterprise, i.e., most of the letters of the New Testament. The "gospel" of Paul and of the Pauline mission was the proclamation of an eschatological event: the death and resurrection of Jesus as the turning point of the ages. With this gospel, Paul proceeded to carry the missionary proclamation of the Christian community from Antioch into Asia Minor and Greece.

Antioch's church was founded within a few years after the death of Jesus by the Hellenists, Greek-speaking Jewish Christians, who had been forced to leave Jerusalem during the persecution in which Stephen was martyred. It is unlikely that any personal followers of Jesus were involved in the establishment of this church because they were still resident in Jerusalem many years thereafter (cf. Gal 1:18–19; 2:1–10). But there were contacts between the church in Antioch as well as other Gentile-Christian churches and the brothers and sisters who had remained in Jerusalem, culminating in the so-called Apostles' Council in Jerusalem (Gal 2:1–10). At this Council, the Jerusalem church was represented by Jesus' brother James and by Peter and John, all three from Galilee, while the Gentile mission from Antioch had sent its leaders Paul and Barnabas, both Greek-speaking Israelites from the diaspora, and Titus who was a converted Gentile. The credal formula quoted in 1 Cor 15:3–7 in which the "gospel" is defined as the death, burial, resurrection, and appearances of Christ makes it probable that this understanding of the gospel was shared not only by the church of Antioch from the very beginning, but also by others who are named in the citation of those to whom Jesus appeared (Peter and James). This is confirmed indirectly in Paul's report about the Apostles' Council (Gal 2:1–10). What Paul preached was never the subject of the controversy between Paul's Gentile mission and the church in Jerusalem. Jesus death and resurrection was the event upon which their common proclamation was based. Through the proclamation of this eschatological event the communities of believers became the new Israel. As new members were received into this community, they were baptized into the death of Jesus so they would share also in Jesus' resurrection (Rom 6:2–10). Looking back to the death of Jesus, they celebrated their common meals in anticipation of his return in glory (1 Cor

11:23–26).[1] What was debated was the admission of Gentiles into the community of the New Israel as well as the celebration of a common meal in which both circumcised Jews and uncircumcized Gentiles could participate together. The latter problem is evident in the conflict which arose in Antioch after Peter's move to that city, when the "people from James" came for a visit (Gal 2:11–14).

On the other hand, Paul and his fellow missionaries, like Barnabas, certainly had access to reports about Jesus' life and death and about his words and deeds. In fact, Paul reports that three years after his call he visited Peter in Jerusalem for two weeks during which stay he also saw James, though none of the other apostles (Gal 1:18). This visit can be dated as early as the year 35 CE, certainly not later than the year 38/39 CE. Moreover, Peter came to Antioch after the Council (Gal 2:11). There was no lack of opportunity for Paul and other missionaries to learn something about Jesus' words. And indeed the letters of Paul demonstrate that he was familiar with a tradition of Jesus' sayings, though they did not become part of the message that he and others proclaimed. However, we will soon discover that there were other Christians for whom the sayings of Jesus actually constituted the message of salvation upon which they based their faith.

2.1.2 JESUS' SAYINGS IN PAUL'S WRITINGS

Though explicit references to sayings of Jesus are relatively rare[2] in Paul's letters, they play a certain role in his arguments, especially

---

[1] This strictly eschatological understanding of the common meals appears everywhere in the earliest layers of the tradition, even outside of the circle of the Pauline churches; cf. Mark 14:35; Luke 22:16; *Didache* 9–10).

[2] The debate about the frequency of the use of, and allusions to, words of Jesus in Paul's letters cannot be repeated here. A critical and, for the time being, definitive review of the debate has been presented by Dale C. Allison, Jr., "The Pauline Epistles and the the Synoptic Gospels: The Pattern of the Parallels" *NTS* 28 (1982) 1–32.; see also James M. Robinson, "Early Collections of Jesus' Sayings," in Joël Delobel, ed., *LOGIA: Les Paroles de Jésus—The Sayings of Jesus: Mémorial Joseph Coppens* (BEThL 59; Leuven: Peeters, 1982) 392–93. In his zeal to discover traces of the original written gospel, Alfred Resch (*Der Paulinismus und die Logia Jesu* [TU NF 12; Leipzig: Hinrichs, 1904) found over one thousand references to the Synoptic Gospels in Paul (including the deutero-Pauline letters to the Ephesians and the Colossians and the Book of Acts). While there is general agreement that Resch vastly overstated his case, some scholars would still maintain "that it was the words of Jesus himself that formed Paul's primary source in his work as ethical διδάσκαλος" (W. D. Davies, *Paul and Rabbinic Judaism: Some Rabbinic Elements in Pauline Theology* [London: S.P.C.K., 1965] 136). For a critical assessment of this and similar positions see Allison's article quoted above; Victor Paul Furnish, *Theology and Ethics in Paul* (Nashville: Abingdon,1968) 51–64.

with respect to the order of the life of the Christian communities. There are six explicit references to sayings or traditions which derive from Jesus. All but one are references to church order materials:

1 Cor 7:10–11	Ruling against divorce	Mark 10:11–12 parr
1 Cor 7:25	No dominical command	
1 Cor 9:14	Support for apostles	Q/Luke 10:7
1 Cor 11:23–26	Institution of Lord's Supper	Mark 14:22–25 parr
1 Cor 14:37	Command concerning prophets	
1 Thess 4:15–17	Apocalyptic saying	

In addition to these, one can probably list as many as eight parallels in which Paul alludes to sayings of Jesus which are attested in the Synoptic Gospels:[1]

Rom 12:14	Blessing of the persecuted	Q/Luke 6:27
Rom 12:17; and	Not repaying evil with evil	Q/Luke 6:29
1 Thess 5:15		
Rom 13:7	Paying taxes to authorities	Mark 12:13–17 par
Rom 14:13	No stumbling block	Mark 9:42 par
Rom 14:14	Nothing is unclean	Mark 7:15 par
1 Thess 5:2	Thief in the night	Q/Luke 12:39
1 Thess 5:13	Peace among yourselves	Mark 9:50

One might add to these also the following:

| Rom 12:18 | Have peace with everyone | Mark 9:50[2] |
| Rom 14:10 | Do not judge | Q/Luke 6:37 |

Also in these allusions the predominance of church order materials is evident. 1 Thess 5:2, an apocalyptic saying, is the only exception.

With respect to these church order materials, two observations are relevant: (1) they are concentrated in certain sections of the Pauline writings (Romans 12–14; 1 Corinthians 7–14; 1 Thessalonians 5); (2) their synoptic parallels are either church-order materials of the Gospel of Mark or sayings of the Sermon on the Plain in Luke (= Q); only in one instance (1 Cor 9:14) the synoptic parallel is a Q saying

---

[1] This is the conclusion of Furnish's (*Theology and Ethics,* 55–67) discussion of W. D. Davies's (*Paul and Rabbinic Judaism*) listing of synoptic parallels in Paul. Furnish is right in arguing that all other parallels are due to common dependence upon biblical references, more general Jewish wisdom tradition, and shared proverbial materials.

[2] Charles H. Talbert ("Tradition and Redaction in Romans XII. 9–21," *NTS* 16 [1969/70] 87) mentions this verse as one of "at least four injunctions in this section (i.e., Rom 12:14–21) [which] appear to echo sayings attributed to Jesus in the existing gospel tradition." He also considers vs. 19a as an echo of Matt 5:44.

from a different context.[1] That Paul, on whatever occasion, quotes or alludes to sayings of Jesus at random is therefore very unlikely. Rather, Paul is dependent upon units of materials which have been established for the order of the communities and, moreover, have already been subject to discussion and interpretation. That Paul is familiar with such secondary interpretations which eventually found their way also into the Synoptic Gospels has been demonstrated by David Dungan in his investigation of the commands about divorce (1 Cor 7:10–11) and support for the apostles (1 Cor 9:14).[2] Paul is therefore an early witness for the development of certain units of church order materials under the authority of Jesus. These same units reappear later in the sayings collections used by Mark and by the Synoptic Sayings Source; in the latter, one of these units provided the basis for the Q collection used for the composition of Matthew's "Sermon on the Mount" (Matthew 5–7) and Luke's "Sermon on the Plain" (Luke 6:20–49).[3] Perhaps it can also be argued "that Paul knew some version of the missionary discourse."[4] However, in this respect the parallels are much less certain. That a collection of church order materials, incorporated into Mark's Gospel, was known to Paul is evident. But the extent and order of this composition of sayings is difficult to establish.[5]

Of the two apocalyptic sayings among the Synoptic Gospel materials in Paul, the first (1 Thess 4:15–17) is explicitly quoted by Paul as a saying of the Lord,[6] but there is no close synoptic parallel to this saying. With respect to its form, it is problematic as a saying of Jesus, because it speaks of Jesus in the third person (αὐτὸς ὁ κύριος ... καταβήσεται). There are, however, several elements in vs. 16 (the voice of

---

[1] The mission instructions of Mark 6:8–11 lack an explicit command about the support for the missionaries.

[2] David L. Dungan, *The Sayings of Jesus in the Churches of Paul: The Use of the Synoptic Tradition in the Regulation of Early Church Life* (Philadelphia: Fortress, 1971).

[3] See Allison, "Pauline Epistles," 11–12. Charles H. Talbert ("Tradition and Redaction in Romans XII. 9–21," *NTS* 16 [1969/70] 84–93) has tried to show that Paul used and revised an originally Semitic code; Talbert's argument is based on a critical evaluation of David Daube's thesis that Rom 12:9–19 reflects an originally Aramaic Christian ethical code; cf. David Daube, "Participle and Imperative in I Peter," Appended Note in Edward Gordon Selwyn, *The First Epistle of St. Peter* (2d ed. reprint; London: Macmillan, 1955) 467–88; idem, *The New Testament and Rabbinic Judaism* (London: Athlone, 1956) 90–97.

[4] Allison, "Pauline Epistles," 12–13.

[5] Allison (ibid., 13–15) argues for a pre-Markan collection of sayings incorporated in Mark 9:33–50. But one also has to account for the Pauline parallels to Mark 7:15; 10:11–12; 12:13–17, and possibly 14:22–25.

[6] Τοῦτο γὰρ ὑμῖν λέγομεν ἐν λόγῳ κυρίου (vs. 15).

the archangel, the trumpet of God) which have close parallels in traditional apocalyptic materials.[1] There is no question that Paul here quotes apocalyptic tradition. But it is not clear how firmly such tradition was designated as part of the tradition of the sayings of Jesus, because virtually the same tradition is quoted as a mystery saying (ἰδοὺ μυστήριον ὑμῖν λέγω) in 1 Cor 15:51–52 ("We shall not all fall asleep, but we shall all be changed . . . at the last trumpet . . ."). Such apocalyptic sayings are designated as "mysteries" also in 1 Cor 2:7 and Rom 11:25. As Mark 13 shows, such apocalyptic traditions were incorporated into the corpus of the sayings of Jesus. Considering the way in which they are used by Paul, this still seems to have been an ongoing process.

The other apocalyptic saying in Paul, "The day of the Lord is coming like a thief in the night" (1 Thess 5:2), appears in a traditional Jewish form. "Day of the Lord" is a standard designation of the final day of judgment that is frequently used since the time of the prophet Amos.[2] The same traditional statement is used in 2 Pet 3:10 and Rev 3:3 ("I shall come like a thief"; cf. Rev 16:15), and it has been expanded into the parable of the Thief transmitted by the Synoptic Sayings Source (Q/Luke 12:39–40). The latter form is clearly secondary. There is no indication in 1 Thess 5:2 that Paul knew this tradition as a saying of Jesus.

2.1.3 WISDOM IN CORINTH

There is most likely another collection of sayings of Jesus of a very different character which was known to Paul. The first chapters of Paul's First Letter to the Corinthians reveal that there were, at a very early date, believers who had a different perception of the central Christian message.[3] The terminology which Paul uses in 1 Corinthians 1–4 in his debate with the wisdom theology of the Corinthians is striking and has only few parallels elsewhere in the Pauline epistles:

"to keep secret" (ἀποκρύπτειν) 1 Cor 2:7,[4]

---

[1] See the materials cited in Beda Rigaux, *Saint Paul: Les Épitres aux Thessaloniciens* (EtB; Paris: Gabalda, 1956) 542–43.

[2] Materials in Rigaux, *Les Épitres aux Thessaloniciens*, 555–56.

[3] In the following I am repeating some of the arguments which I presented in my article, "Gnostic Writings as Witnesses for the Development of the Sayings Tradition," in: Bentley Layton, ed., *The Rediscovery of Gnosticism*, vol. 1: *The School of Valentinus* (NumenSup 41; Leiden: Brill, 1980) 239–61. See this article for further documentation.

[4] It appears only here in the genuine Pauline writings, but is used twice in deutero-Pauline epistles (Col 1:26; Eph 3:9).

"to hide" (κρύπτειν) 1 Cor 4:5,[1]
"to uncover" (ἀποκαλύπτειν) 1 Cor 2:10; 3:13,[2]
"to reveal" (φανεροῦν) 1 Cor 4:5,[3]
"childish," "immature" (νήπιος) 1 Cor 3:1.[4]

Most striking is the frequency of the terms "wise" (σοφός) and "wisdom" (σοφία). The former occurs ten times in these four chapters of 1 Corinthians,[5] but elsewhere in Paul only four times,[6] the latter is used sixteen times here,[7] but elsewhere only three times.[8]

This special terminology leads to a group of sayings of Jesus that has always been noted as distinctly different from other sayings which are preserved in the synoptic tradition:

Matt 11:25–26 = Luke 10:21
Matt 11:27 = Luke 10:22
Matt 13:16–17 = Luke 10:23–24.[9]

The first and the third in this group of sayings are alluded to in the context of 1 Corinthians 1–4, while there seems to be no reference to the second.[10] The most prominent of these sayings is the first (Matt 11:25–26 = Luke 10:21):[11]

---

[1] Used only here in this letter and sparingly elsewhere in Paul: Rom 1:19; 3:21; frequently in 2 Corinthians.

[2] In 1 Corinthians only here and in 14:30; elsewhere in Paul Rom 1:17, 18; 8:18; Gal 1:16; 3:23; Phil 3:15.

[3] Elsewhere in Paul Rom 1:19; 3:21 and frequently in 2 Corinthians.

[4] It is used once more in this letter (1 Cor 13:11) and in Rom 2:20; Gal 4:1, 3. The original reading in 1 Thess 2:7 is certainly ἤπιοι ("gentle"), not νήπιοι (pace Nestle-Aland).

[5] 1:19, 20, 25, 26, 27; 3:10, 18 (twice), 19, 20.

[6] 1 Cor 6:5; Rom 1:14, 22; 16:19 (Rom 16:27 is not Pauline).

[7] 1 Cor 1:17, 19, 20, 21 (twice), 22, 24, 30; 2:1, 4, 5, 6 (twice), 7, 13; 3:19.

[8] Rom 11:23; 1 Cor 12:8; 2 Cor 1:12. Quite striking are the frequent references to σοφία in some deutero-Pauline letters: Eph 1:8, 17; 3:10; Col 1:9, 28; 2:3, 23; 3:16; 4:3.

[9] Bultmann (Synoptic Tradition, 166) characterizes these sayings as belonging to a milieu that is completely different from the Aramaic environment which has produced almost all other sayings of the synoptic tradition.

[10] I shall discuss the second saying (Matt 11:27 = Luke 10:22) in the following chapter.

[11] The classical treatments of this passage are Adolf Harnack, The Sayings of Jesus (New York: Putnam's, 1908) 272–310, and Eduard Norden, Agnostos Theos (Stuttgart: Teubner, 1912; reprint Darmstadt: Wissenschaftliche Buchgesellschaft, 1956) 277–308. Most of the following observations have been anticipated by these two treatments. Harnack (p. 301) already pointed out the close relationship of Matt 11:25–26 and 1 Cor 1:19–21. Norden demonstrated that the formulaic (liturgical) language of this passage belongs to a tradition which spans the entire spectrum of religious language from the Wisdom of Solomon to the Hermetic literature. An attempt to illuminate the history-of-religions context of this passage was made by Thomas Arvedson, Das Mysterium

> I praise you, Father, Lord of heaven and earth,
> that you have hidden (ἔκρυψας) these things from the wise and clever
>   (σοφῶν καὶ συνετῶν)
> but have revealed (ἀπεκάλυψας) them to the unlearned (νηπίοις).

The hendiadys "the wise and the clever" (σοφοὶ καὶ συνετοί) appears nowhere else in the New Testament. But both terms occur in parallelism in 1 Cor 1:19 in a quote introduced by "it is written."[1] What Paul quotes here is the LXX text of Isa 29:14, "I will destroy the wisdom of the wise and the cleverness of the clever I will thwart" (ἀπολῶ τὴν σοφίαν τῶν σοφῶν καὶ τὴν σύνεσιν τῶν συνετῶν κρύψω).[2] However, also the term "unlearned" (νήπιος) of the saying Matt 11:25 par = Q/Luke 10:21), rarely used by Paul, appears in the context of Paul's discussion of wisdom in Corinth (1 Cor 3:1). In addition, there are several allusions to other sayings which speak about the contrast of hidden and revealed.

In 1 Cor 2:7 Paul speaks of "the hidden wisdom which God has predetermined before the ages." A close parallel appears in Matt 13:35:[3]

> I will utter what has been hidden since the foundation of the world.

This saying is introduced by "in order to fulfill what was said by the prophet." But the most likely scriptural reference is Ps 77:2 (LXX) that is only remotely related to this Matthean saying.[4] Other sayings actually parallel this passage more closely. The small sayings collection in Mark 4 contains a similar saying, Mark 4:22:

Christi: Eine Studie zu Mt 11:25–30 (Leipzig and Uppsala: 1937). For a review of previous discussions see A. M. Hunter, "Crux Criticorum—Matt. xi.25–30—A Reappraisal," *NTS* 8 (1961–62) 241–49. The relationship of this passage to wisdom theology has been discussed in detail by M. J. Suggs, *Wisdom, Christology, and Law in Matthew's Gospel* (Cambridge, MA: Harvard University Press, 1970) 71–108.

[1] On the relationship of the passage in 1 Cor 1:19 to the text of Isaiah see Hans Conzelmann, *1 Corinthians: A Commentary on the First Epistle to the Corinthians* (Hermeneia; Philadelphia: Fortress, 1975) 42, n. 21.

[2] Paul has ἀθετήσω instead of κρύψω. Also Justin Martyr *Dial.* 78.8 quotes Isa 29:13–14 with ἀθετήσω. This suggests that the change was not made by Paul, but that both Paul and Justin were dependent on a different version of the LXX, though the two medieval manuscripts of the LXX which also have ἀθετήσω (564 and 301) as well as Eusebius may have been influenced by 1 Cor 1:19.

[3] Harnack (*The Sayings of Jesus*) noticed this parallelism. But few scholars have followed Harnack's lead.

[4] On the question of the relationship of Matt 13:35 to its assumed source, Ps 77:2 (LXX), see Krister Stendahl, *The School of St. Matthew and its Use of the Old Testament* (2d ed.; Philadelphia: Fortress, 1968) 116: the sentence is quoted in a form "differing entirely from the LXX and the later Greek versions."

There is nothing hidden, except to be revealed;
nor anything secret that will not come to light.

This saying appears independently also in the *Gospel of Thomas* # 5:

Recognize what is in your sight,
and that which is hidden from you
    will become manifest to you.
For there is nothing hidden
    which will not become manifest,
and nothing covered
    will remain without being uncovered.

and # 6:

... for all things are plain in the sight of heaven.
For nothing hidden
    will not become manifest,
and nothing covered
    will remain without being uncovered.

The same contrast between hidden and revealed is employed in 1 Cor 4:5: "... the Lord who will illumine the hidden things of darkness and reveal the councils of the hearts." This is best explained as a commentary on the saying Mark 4:22 and the parallel saying preserved in the *Gospel of Thomas*.

To these evident relationships of Paul's language in these chapters of 1 Corinthians to this peculiar group of sayings must be added the occurrence of the strange "quotation from scripture" in 1 Cor 2:9:[1]

... what eye has not seen
and ear has not heard,
nor has it risen in the human heart,
what God has prepared for those who love him.

Whereas Paul introduces the passage by "as it is written," the *Gospel of Thomas* (# 17) quotes it as a saying of Jesus:

I shall give you what no eye has seen
and what no ear has heard,
and what no hand has touched,
and what has never occurred to the human mind.[2]

---

[1] Attention to this was drawn first by James M. Robinson, "Kerygma and History in the New Testament," in idem and Helmut Koester, *Trajectories through Early Christianity* (Philadelphia: Fortress, 1971) 42–43.

[2] Unless indicated otherwise, translations from writings of the Nag Hammadi Library follow James M. Robinson, *The Nag Hammadi Library in English* (3d completely rev. ed.; San Francisco: Harper & Row, 1988).

This saying is quoted frequently in Gnostic writings in this form.[1] Its source has never been determined with certainty.[2] But it has also made its way into the Synoptic Sayings Source in a somewhat altered form in which it appears in Matt 13:16–17 = Q/Luke 10:23–24:

> Blessed are the eyes that see what you see [and the ears that hear what you hear]. ... many prophets [and righteous men] have desired to see what you see and did not see it, and to hear what you hear and did not hear it.[3]

In Luke, this saying appears in the same context as the sayings discussed above (following upon Matt 11:25–27 = Luke 10:21–22), and it is likely that this is the context in which it also appeared in Q.[4] The first part of the saying (Matt 13:16 = Luke 10:23) parallels 1 Cor 2:9 and *Gos. Thom.* # 17 very closely. The second part (Matt 13:17 = Luke 10:24) appears to be a secondary elaboration which tries to set this saying into a framework of historical-biblical reference.[5]

There is another instance in which Paul reveals acquaintance with a saying that is preserved in Q. While the discussion in 1 Corinthians 1–4 is evidently concerned with wisdom theology, one wonders why Paul is introducing also the concern of "the Jews seeking signs" (1 Cor 1:22). James M. Robinson[6] has drawn attention to the fact that this

---

[1] For references to such quotes see Hans Conzelmann, *1 Corinthians,* 64. A fragment of the saying appears in *Dial. Sav.* # 57 (140, 1–4: "The Lord said [. . .] ask me about a saying [. . .] which eye has not seen, [nor] have I heard it except from you"). It is also used elsewhere in the writings of the Nag Hammadi Library; cf. *Pr. Paul A* 25–29.

[2] For a full discussion and literature see Conzelmann, *1 Corinthians,* 63–64. Origen (*In Matt.* 5.29 on Matt 27:9) ascribed the saying to the *Apocryphon of Elijah.* Eckard von Nordheim ("Das Zitat des Paulus in 1 Kor 2,9," *ZNW* 65 [1974] 12–20) has argued that the quote is drawn from the Jewish *Vorlage* of the Coptic Christian *Testament of Jacob.*

[3] The two bracketed phrases occur in Matthew only. But the first of these may be original to Q, whereas the second seems to be added by Matthew.

[4] Harnack (*Sayings of Jesus,* 135) assigned the saying to this Q context. Dieter Lührmann (*Die Redaktion der Logienquelle* [WMANT 33; Neukirchen: Neukirchener Verlag, 1969] 61) is undecided. John S. Kloppenborg (*The Formation of Q: Trajectories in Ancient Wisdom Traditions* [Studies in Antiquity and Christianity; Philadelphia: Fortress, 1987] 201–2) places the saying into the context of Q = Luke 9:57–62 + 10:2–16 + 10:21–24, but remarks: "The relation of Q 10:21–22, 23–24 to the rest of the discipleship/mission sermon is more difficult to determine."

[5] It is possible that this elaboration utilizes another saying like the one which is preserved in *Gos. Thom.* # 52:

> His disciples said to him, "Twenty-four prophets spoke in Israel, and all of them spoke in you." He said to them, "You have omitted the one living in your presence and have spoken (only) of the dead."

[6] "Kerygma and History," 42.

association of "signs," "kerygma," and "wisdom" occurs in only one
other place in early Christianity, namely in Q (Matt 12:38–42; Luke
11:29–32). Here the demand of the Jewish leaders for a "sign" is connected with Jonah's "kerygma" and Solomon's "wisdom."

Finally, in 1 Cor 4:8 there is an ironic reference of Paul to the
Corinthians as the ones who have already been satisfied, who have
already become rich, and who have become kings (ἐβασιλεύσατε)
without him. The verb "to be king" (βασιλεύειν) is used elsewhere in
1 Corinthians only of Christ (15:25).[1] This characterization of the
Corinthians is most likely an ironic rendering of a phrase from the
saying of *Gos. Thom.* # 2:[2]

> Let him who seeks continue seeking until he finds.
> When he finds, he will become astonished,
> When he becomes astonished, he will be king,
> and when he has become king, he will find rest.[3]

It must also be remembered that the democratization of the concept of
kingship genuinely belongs to Jewish wisdom language.[4]

The Corinthians insisted that revelation is communicated to them
through "wisdom." That most of the references to wisdom can be substantiated on the basis of wisdom literature has been demonstrated by
Ulrich Wilckens.[5] But this general statement can be made more
specific: wisdom sayings of Jesus must have been the vehicle on the
basis of which the Corinthians claimed to have received this salvation.
The various instances in which the language of these chapters reflects
known wisdom sayings cannot be accidental. A collection of such sayings must have been known to both Paul and the Corinthians.

[1] Otherwise Paul uses the verb of the believers in Rom 5:17–21. There the believers
rule on the basis of their having received grace, whereas in 1 Corinthians 4, those who
already are kings are asked whether they can boast of anything they have not received.

[2] Robinson, ("Kerygma and History," 43) suggests that Paul's critical description of
his opponents in this verse might recall the woes of the Sermon on the Plain (Luke
6:24–25). This is possible, but it would only explain the phrase, "You have already
become rich," not the reference to "having become kings."

[3] This translation follows the Greek text of the *Gospel of Thomas* = *Pap. Oxy.* 654,2
(. . . θαμβηθεὶς βασιλεύσῃ, καὶ βασιλεύσας ἀναπαήσεται). This text is confirmed by the
quotation in Clement of Alexandria, *Strom.* 5.14, # 96; in *Strom.* 2.9, # 43, Clement
ascribes this saying to the *Gospel According to the Hebrews.*

[4] See especially Wisdom's invitation in Prov 9:6 where some important manuscripts
read ἀπολείπετε ἀφροσύνην ἵνα εἰς τὸν αἰῶνα βασιλεύσητε ("leave behind foolishness so
that you may become kings forever"). Editors consider this as an intrusion from Sap
6:21 and prefer the reading ζήσεσθε. But even if the latter is the original reading, the
former reading may have circulated very early.

[5] *Weisheit und Torheit: Eine exegetisch-religionsgeschichtliche Untersuchung zu
1. Kor. 1 und 2* (BhTh 26; Tübingen: Mohr/Siebeck, 1959).

It is striking, however, that Paul never quotes any of these sayings directly. Rather, in one instance he quotes such a saying with the formula "as it is written" (1 Cor 2:9). In another instance he quotes a scriptural passage upon which such a wisdom saying is based (1 Cor 1:19 where Isa 29:14 is introduced by "it is written"). Paul does not use sayings as authority in a theological debate, neither here nor elsewhere.[1] Sayings of Jesus do not play a role in Paul's understanding of the event of salvation. But in this context, Paul not only alludes to the sayings which were evidently of crucial importance to his opponents, he also adopts their schema of revelation which speaks of the things that were formerly hidden, but have now been revealed.[2] This schema is characteristic of the Q sayings quoted above, though it is not really typical of the Synoptic Sayings Source as a whole.[3] In the genuine Pauline letters, it is used only in 1 Cor 2:6–16, while it occurs frequently in the deutero-Pauline letters[4] and also appears in the secondary ending of Romans (16:25–26).

For the Corinthian wisdom theology this revelation schema, of central importance for their understanding of salvation, is related to the sayings tradition by another element, namely, the recourse to the authority of certain persons: Paul, Apollos, Cephas, possibly Christ (1 Cor 1:12; 3:4–5, 22). This phenomenon is still one of the most puzzling conundrums of New Testament scholarship.[5] There are three elements which together call for an answer: (1) The Corinthians knew a number of sayings which they understood as the revelation of hidden wisdom and life-giving knowledge. (2) Paul explicitly rejects the suggestion that his calling had anything to do with baptism (1 Cor 1:15–17); the claim of belonging to a specific person may have been

---

[1] That Paul has no hesitation to use sayings from the synoptic tradition in debates concerning church order has been demonstrated in an investigation of 1 Corinthians 7 and 9 by David L. Dungan, *The Sayings of Jesus in the Churches of Paul: The Use of the Synoptic Tradition in the Regulation of Early Church Life* (Philadelphia: Fortress, 1971).

[2] See on this schema especially Dieter Lührmann, *Das Offenbarungsverständnis bei Paulus und in paulinischen Gemeinden* (WMANT 16; Neukirchen: Neukirchener Verlag, 1965) 124–33; Nils A. Dahl, "Form-critical Observations on Early Christian Preaching," in idem, *Jesus in the Memory of the Early Church* (Minneapolis: Augsburg, 1976) 31–36.

[3] Kloppenborg, *Formation of Q*, 197–99.

[4] Col 1:26–27; Eph 3:5–10; 2 Tim 1:9–10; Tit 1:2–3; cf. also 1 Pet 1:20. On the use of this revelation schema in 1 Cor 2:6–16 see Conzelmann, *1 Corinthians*, 57–60.

[5] As is well known, the literature on this problem is as immense as is the number of unsatisfactory suggestions for a solution. For a brief survey see Conzelmann, *1 Corinthians*, 33–34.

connected with the relationship of the initiate to his/her baptizer.[1]
(3) Papias, *The Gospel of Thomas, The Apocryphon of James,* and even
Ptolemy's *Letter to Flora* show that apostolic authority, appealed to
with the name of specific apostles, played a role in the transmission of
sayings of Jesus, especially in Gnostic circles.[2]

If all three observations are combined, one must conclude that Paul
faced a Corinthian faction in which believers claimed that baptism
was their initiation into the mystery of wisdom. They understood particular apostles as their mystagogues from whom they received sayings which revealed life-giving wisdom. The dual role of baptizing
mystagogue and guarantor of a tradition of wisdom sayings is quite
natural. Both the action and the sayings can be understood as μυστήριον. Paul's arguments against this understanding of salvation
become much clearer if they are understood against this background.
The well-attested reading μυστήριον, instead of μαρτύριον, in 1 Cor 2:1[3]
as well as Paul's reference to Christ's crucifixion as the "hidden mystery predetermined by God before the ages" (2:7) become understandable.[4] Nowhere else does Paul speak about the cross of Christ in such
terms.

Can the character of the collection of sayings used by the Corinthians be determined with more accuracy? It has already been said that
the Q sayings used here are not typical for this document. In fact, the
connections to Q material do not go beyond Q/Luke 10:21–24 (perhaps
also Q/Luke 11:29–32). The other sayings to which Paul alludes in
1 Corinthians 1–4 do not belong to Q: Matt 13:35; Mark 4:22; *Gos.
Thom.* ## 2, 5–6, and 17. The topic of the revelation of hidden wisdom,
at best marginal in Q, unites all the sayings to which Paul alludes in
this context. It will be seen that it is important for the sayings collections that have been used for the composition of the *Gospel of Thomas*
and which were also known in the Johannine tradition.

---

[1] Here and in the following note I must refer to my previous publications, simply
because this problem has concerned me for a long time. In a review of Ulrich Wilckens,
Weisheit und Torheit (BHTh 26; Tübingen: Mohr/Siebeck, 1959), which was published
in *Gnomon* 33 (1961) 590–95, I made the suggestion that the Corinthians understood
the apostolic authorities they referred to, possibly also Christ, as mystagogues who initiated them through baptism into the mystery of the new faith.

[2] This thesis was first put forward by von Campenhausen, *Formation.* I have
expanded this suggestion in my article "La tradition."

[3] Shunned by previous editions of Nestle's *NT Graece,* but now correctly adopted by
Aland in the 26th edition.

[4] Elsewhere in Paul the singular μυστήριον is used only of specific sayings (cf. 1 Cor
13:2; 15:51), never of the event of Christ's crucifixion or of the gospel as a whole. The
latter use appears for the first time in the Pauline corpus in Eph 3:3–4, 9; 6:19.

2.1.4 SAYINGS IN THE POST-APOSTOLIC WRITINGS

2.1.4.1 Acts and the Pastoral Epistles

There is comparatively little use of sayings of Jesus in the post-apostolic literature. Outside of the genuine Pauline letters, a saying of Jesus is quoted explicitly only once, in Acts 20:35:

> Remember the words of the Lord Jesus that he himself said, "To give is more blessed than to receive" (μακάριόν ἐστιν μᾶλλον διδόναι ἢ λαμβάνειν).

In the Book of Acts, Luke has occasionally used gospel materials,[1] but this saying is nowhere recorded in the known written gospels.[2] This "alleged word of the Lord is actually a Greek aphorism with a slight Christian touch, namely, the selection of μακάριον, "blessed," instead of ἥδιον, "more gladly."[3] *1 Clem.* 2.1 (ἥδιον διδόντες ἢ λαμβάνοντες) refers to the same aphorism in the more typically Greek form without indicating any relationship to the tradition of the sayings of Jesus. Luke introduces the saying with a formula that is characteristic for the quotation of sayings from the oral tradition (μνημονεύειν τῶν λόγων τοῦ κυρίου Ἰησοῦ ὅτι αὐτὸς εἶπεν).[4] It is evidently drawn from that tradition to which Luke still had access.

Use of sayings in the deutero-Pauline epistles cannot be demonstrated with certainty. If such sayings are used in Ephesians and Colossians, they are hidden in the parenetic sections of these letters, e.g., "Let no evil talk come out of your mouths" (Eph 4:29; cf. Mark 7:15; Matt 15:11).[5] Even the Pastoral Epistles, written in Asia Minor at a time when several written gospels were known there, show no desire to refer to sayings of Jesus and never appeal to them as authorities. Most remarkable is the instance of the regulation for payment to church officials in 1 Tim 5:17–18:

[1] Cf. Acts 6:14: "We have heard that he (Stephen) has said that Jesus the Nazorean will destroy this place." Luke uses the accusation against Jesus from Mark 14:58 (We have heard that he said, "I shall destroy this temple . . .") which he had omitted in his reproduction of the Markan passion narrative.
[2] There is a parallel in the *Didache* (1.5): "Blessed is he who gives according to the commandment."
[3] Hans Conzelmann, *The Acts of the Apostles: A Commentary on the Acts of the Apostles* (Hermeneia; Philadelphia: Fortress, 1987) 176; see ibid. for Greek parallels.
[4] See below on *1 Clem.* 13.
[5] Davies (*Paul and Rabbinic Judaism,* 139–40) lists eight passages in Colossians for which he assumes dependence upon sayings of Jesus. Although there are some verbal similarities, they are not sufficient to prove the actual employment of the tradition of sayings.

The presbyters who govern well as presiding officers should be deemed worthy of a double compensation, especially those who are engaged in speaking and teaching. For the scripture says, "You shall not muzzle an ox when it is treading out the grain," and "the worker is worthy of his wages."

The first of the two sayings is a scripture quotation (Deut 25:4), also used by Paul in 1 Cor 9:9; but it is debated whether the second quote is either a quote of Luke 10:7 as "scripture" or comes from a lost apocryphon that was accepted as scripture by the author of 1 Timothy.[1] In any case, it is surprizing that there is no appeal to the authority of Jesus.

2.1.4.2 The First Epistle of Peter

A more extensive use of sayings of Jesus appears in the First Epistle of Peter. However, in a critical review of assumptions about the use of sayings of Jesus in 1 Peter, Ernest Best has demonstrated that the case has been vastly overstated.[2] Only the following parallels remain as probable evidence for the use of sayings of Jesus in this New Testament letter:

1 Pet 4:14	Q/Luke 6:22
If you are reproached (ὀνειδίζεσθε) for the name of Christ, you are blessed.	Blessed are you when people hate you, and when they exclude you and and reproach (ὀνειδίσωσιν) you, and cast out your name as evil on account of the Son of man.

1 Pet 3:9	Q/Luke 6:28
Do not return evil for evil or insult for for insult, but on the contrary bless (εὐλογοῦντες) . . .	Bless (εὐλογεῖτε) those who curse you,

1 Pet 3:16

. . . that, when you are abused, those who revile (οἱ ἐπηρεάζοντες) your good behavior in Christ may be put to shame.	pray for those who revile (τῶν ἐπηρεα-ζόντων) you.[3]

---

[1] See Martin Dibelius and Hans Conzelmann, *The Pastoral Epistles* (Hermeneia; Philadelphia: Fortress, 1972) 78–79.

[2] Ernest Best, "1 Peter and the Gospel Tradition," *NTS* 16 (1969/70) 95–113.

[3] These are the only two passages in which the verb ἐπηρεάζειν appears in the NT and in the Apostolic Fathers. Cf. Best, "1 Peter," 106–7. Thus this is probably a use of the saying of Q/Luke 6:28, although the two reminiscences of this saying in 1 Peter are separated by several verses.

1 Pet 2:19–20	**Q/Luke 6:32–33**

For this deserves credit (τοῦτο γὰρ χάρις), if . . . one endures pain while suffering unjustly. For what credit is it (ποῖον γὰρ κλέος), if when you do wrong and are beaten for it you take it patiently? But if you do good (ἀγαθοποιοῦντες) and suffer for it and take it patiently, that is credit before God (τοῦτο χάρις παρὰ θεῷ).

If you love those who love you, what credit is that to you (ποία ὑμῖν χάρις ἐστίν)? For even sinners love those who love them. For if you also do good to those who do good to you (καὶ ἐὰν ἀγαθοποιῆτε τοὺς ἀγαθοποιοῦντας ὑμᾶς), what credit is that to you? (ποία ὑμῖν χάρις ἐστίν;).

1 Pet 3:14	**Matt 5:10**

But even if you suffer for righteousness sake (διὰ δικαιοσύνην), you are blessed (μακάριοι).

Blessed (μακάριοι) are those who suffer for righteousness sake (ἕνεκεν δικαιοσύνης).

1 Pet 2:12b	**Matt 5:16b**

Maintain good conduct among the Gentiles, so that in case they speak against you as wrongdoers, they may see your good deeds (ἐκ τῶν καλῶν ἔργων ἐποπτεύοντες) and glorify (δοξά-σωσιν) God (τὸν θεόν) on the day of visitation.

Let your light so shine before people that they may see your good works (ἴδωσιν ὑμῶν τὰ καλὰ ἔργα) and glorify (δοξάσωσιν) your Father who is in heaven (τὸν πατέρα ὑμῶν τὸν ἐν τοῖς οὐρανοῖς).

In the first three instances (1 Pet 4:14; 3:9 and 16; 2:19–20) the author of this Epistle uses material that belongs to the nucleus of the Q materials for the Sermon on the Plain/Sermon on the Mount (Q/Luke 6:22, 28, 32–33).[1] It is the same collection that also provided the sayings for Rom 12–14.

The other two uses of sayings of Jesus in 1 Peter (3:14; 2.12b) concern sayings of a typical Matthean character. Both Matt 5:10 and Matt 5:16b appear to be Matthean additions to the Q material that formed the basis for this section of the Sermon on the Mount. However, it is unlikely that these sayings are creations of the author of the Gospel of Matthew. Rather, they were already part of a Jewish-Christian document that Matthew used in chapters 5–7.[2] The makarism of those persecuted for righteousness' sake as well as the saying

---

[1] There are several other passages in 1 Peter for which dependence upon sayings of Jesus in Luke's Gospel has been assumed. For a listing and for arguments against this assumption see Best, "1 Peter," 103–8.

[2] See the several articles by Hans Dieter Betz, now collected in his *Essays on the Sermon on the Mount* (Philadelphia: Fortress, 1985).

about the visibility of the good works of the disciples[1] belong to this originally independent composition.[2] We must, therefore, conclude that 1 Peter had access to a collection of sayings that was related to or identical with Matthew's special Jewish-Christian source. Whether also the Q sayings used by 1 Peter came from this same source is difficult to determine because there is not enough extant verbal agreement with the text of either Matthew or Luke in the quotations as they appear in 1 Peter. A use of any of the Synoptic Gospels is not apparent.[3]

2.1.4.3 The First Epistle of Clement

1 Clement quotes sayings of Jesus twice, in 13.1–2 and in 46.8.[4] *1 Clem.* 13.1–2 introduces the quotation with the formula:

Especially remember the words of the Lord Jesus which he spoke when he was teaching gentleness and longsuffering; for he spoke thus (μάλιστα μνημνημένοι τῶν λόγων τοῦ κυρίου Ἰησοῦ . . . οὕτως γὰρ εἶπεν).

A similar formula is used in *1 Clem.* 46.7–8:

Remember the words of Jesus; for he said (μνήσθητε τῶν λόγων τοῦ κυρίου Ἰησοῦ, εἶπεν γάρ).

The use of the verb "to remember" (μνημονεύειν) as well as the aorist tense "he said" (εἶπεν) instead of the present "he/it says" (λέγει)—typical for quotations from Scripture—indicates that oral tradition is cited.[5]

The quotation in *1 Clem.* 13.2 consists of seven brief sentences of similar structure of which all but one have synoptic parallels:

---

[1] Betz (*Essays*, 5) calls this saying "a programmatic passage" of this document.

[2] Also Best ("1 Peter," 109) argues for this possibility. He observes that the term δικαιοσύνη and its cognates occur in contexts that "very often represent material which must have come to Matthew in the tradition peculiar to him. In fact, while the term δικαιοσύνη appears five times in the Sermon on the Mount (5:6, 10, 20; 6:1, 3), it is used only twice elsewhere in the Gospel of Matthew (3:15; 21:23)—both times in connection with John the Baptist.

[3] Best ("1 Peter," 99–102) has demonstrated that there is not a single instance in which the use of Mark or of Markan sayings materials can be assumed, nor does 1 Peter show any acquaintance with John or the Johannine tradition (Best, "1 Peter," 96–99).

[4] On these two quotations see Koester, *Synoptische Überlieferung*, 12–19; on the first of these quotations also Best, "1 Peter," 112–113.

[5] See above on the quotation formula in Acts 20:35. Closely related is the composite form of the verb "to remember" (ἀπομνημονεύειν) which is used in the Papias fragments, see above # 1.7.2. On the use of this formula in Polycarp of Smyrna's letter to the Philippians see Koester, *Synoptische Überlieferung*, 5.

1 Clem. 13.2	Matt 5:7

Be merciful that
    you may obtain mercy.
	Blessed are the merciful,
	    because they will obtain mercy

Matt 6:12

Forgive,
    that you may be forgiven.
	Forgive us our debts,
	    as also we have forgiven our
	       debtors.[1]

Q/Luke 6:31 (Matt 7:12)

As you do,
 	
    so shall it be done unto you.
	As you want that people
	    should do to you,
	do also to them.

Q/Luke 6:38a

As you give,
    so shall it be given to you.
	Give,
	    and it shall be given to you.

Q/Matt 7:2a (Luke 6:37a)

As you judge
    so shall you be judged.
As you are kind,
    so shall kindness be shown to you.
	By which criterion you judge,
	    you shall be judged.
	—————
	—————

Q/Matt 7:2b (Luke 6:38b)

With what measure you measure,
    it shall be measured to you.
	And in what measure you measure,
	    it shall be measured to you.

What *1 Clement* is quoting is a fixed small catechism. The seven[2] parallel well-balanced sentences reveal that it was formulated for oral transmission. Six of the seven sentences have synoptic parallels, and all these parallels appear in the Sermon on the Mount and/or Sermon on the Plain (Matthew 5–7 and Luke 6:20–49). However, the affinity to Matthew is striking, while there is very little that parallels anything in Luke or in the version of Q used by Luke. The first sentence is paralleled by one of the beatitudes added in Matthew's version of the Sermon, though probably preserved in a more original form in *1 Clem.* 13.2. The second sentence also has only a Matthean parallel in the fifth petition of the Lord's Prayer; however, the command of Mark 11:25 to forgive each other resembles the formulation in *1 Clem.* 13.2

---

[1] A close parallel appears in Mark 11:25 = Matt 6:14, "Forgive, if you have anything against anyone, so that your Father also, who is in heaven, may forgive your debts."

[2] The number "seven" is not accidental; see Betz, *Essays,* 23; the numbers eight (or seven) and ten express perfection.

more closely. The third sentence, the Golden Rule, shares the positive version[1] with both Matthew and Luke, but is formulated differently; since this proverb is so widespread in antiquity,[2] a particular source for its quotation is not required. The fourth sentence ("As you give . . .") has no parallel in Matthew. It is a free logion that Luke has inserted into Q/Luke 6:36–37a, 38b = Matt 5:48; 7:2. The parallel to the following sentence in *1 Clement* appears in the same cluster of Q sayings; however, its formulation resembles Matt 7:2a which has no parallel in Luke. To the same context belongs the Q parallel to the last sentence of *1 Clem.* 13.2 which shares with Matt 7:2b the simple form of the verb "to measure" (μετρηθήσεται) instead of Luke's (6: 38b) probably secondary composite form (ἀντιμετρηθήσεται). However, the parallels to Matt 7:2 a and b are separated by an insertion which has no parallel anywhere in the canonical gospels. An admonition to show kindness is incorporated in the parenetical section of Ephesians (γίνεσθε δὲ εἰς ἀλλήλους χρηστοί, 4:32), and the verb is used once by Paul in 1 Cor 13:4 (ἡ ἀγάπη . . . χρηστεύεται). Also the noun (χρηστότης) appears in parenetical usage.[3] Thus, it is easily understandable that such a parenetical sentence could be added to a catechism composed of sayings of Jesus.[4]

It is evident that this passage of *1 Clement* cannot be explained as a secondary composition based upon the canonical texts of Matthew and Luke (and possibly also Mark). But neither could one argue for direct dependence upon the Synoptic Sayings Source. These sayings belong to the same complex of logia which we encountered already in Romans 12–14 and in 1 Peter and, once more, there may be traces of the editing of Q materials upon which Matthew based his Sermon on the Mount. Since both 1 Peter and *1 Clement* were written in Rome at approximately the same time, it is quite possible that they are both witnesses to the existence in Rome of a sayings book that was identical with, or

---

[1] The negative version of the Golden Rule ("What you do not want to be done to you, also do not do to others") appears more often, also in Christian texts; cf. *Did.* 1.2b, Acts 15:29 Western text.

[2] Albrecht Dihle (*Die Goldene Regel: Eine Einführung in die Geschichte der antiken und frühchristlichen Vulgärethik* [Studienhefte zur Altertumswissenschaft 7; Göttingen: Vandenhoeck & Ruprecht, 1962]) presents an overview and a discussion of its usage.

[3] Gal 5:22; Col 3:12; *Diogn.* 10.4. Elsewhere the noun usually describes the attitude or action of God; cf. Rom 2:4; 11:22; 2 Cor 8:6; Eph 2:7; Tit 3:4; *2 Clem.* 15.5; 19.1; Ign. *Mg.* 10.1; *Sm.* 7.1; *Diogn.* 8.8; 9.1–2, 6.

[4] Massaux (*Influence de l'Évangile de Saint Matthieu*, 12–13) recognizes the special catechetical rythm of the passage, but argues for dependence upon the Sermon on the Mount. Köhler (*Rezeption des Matthäusevangeliums*, 67–71) judges dependence upon Matthew as "quite improbable."

related to, the Jewish-Christian writing which, as Hans Dieter Betz[1] has argued, was the source of Matthew 5–7. But *1 Clement* also knew sayings of Jesus which did not belong to this source. This is evident in the second quote of Jesus' sayings in this letter, *1 Clem.* 46.8, to which a synoptic parallel is found in Mark (9:42) as well as in Q (Luke 17:1–2). While Luke seems to have preserved the original wording of Q, Matt 18:6–7 conflated it with the Markan version:[2]

1 Clem. 46.8	Synoptic Parallels
Woe to that man (τῷ ἀνθρώπῳ)	τῷ ἀνθρώπῳ only in Matt 18:7
	Mark 14:21
	Woe to that man through whom the Son of man is handed over;
it were good for him, if he had not been born,	it were good for him, if that man had not been born.
than that he should offend one of my elect (ἐκλεκτῶν μου).	Mark 9:42: μικρῶν τούτων τῶν πιστευόντων = Matt 18:6 who adds εἰς ἐμέ.
It were better (κρεῖττον) for him	Matt: συμφέρει Mark: καλόν ἐστιν Luke 17:2: λυσιτελεῖ
that a millstone (μύλον)	Matt and Mark: μύλος ὀνικός. Luke 17:2: λίθος μυλικός.
be hung on him (περιτεθῆναι)	Matt: κρεμασθῇ. Mark and Luke: περίκειται.
and he be drowned (καταποντισθῆναι)	Matt: καταποντισθῇ. Mark: βέβληται. Luke: ἔριπτει.
in the sea (εἰς τὴν θάλασσαν)	Matt: ἐν τῷ πελάγει τῆς θαλάσσης. Mark and Luke: εἰς τὴν θάλασσαν.
than that he should turn aside one of my elect.	

Although the quote of *1 Clem.* 46.8 shares some terms with Matthew[3]

---

[1] See his *Essays,* passim.

[2] For a detailed comparison of the Greek texts see my *Synoptische Überlieferung,* 16–19.

[3] Köhler (*Rezeption des Matthäusevangeliums,* 62–64) finds in the appearance of the term καταποντίζομαι a strong reference for dependence upon Matthew, but assigns the quotation to the less probable category of "possible" dependence. Massaux (*Influence de l'Évangile de Saint Matthieu,* 24–27) argues for a combination of several gospel texts in this quotation.

in general and in its structure (Matthew reverses the sequence of the
woe and the sentence about offences), it is more closely related to the
Q version. Indeed, all terms used by the quote in *1 Clement* could
have been part of the original Q version. Peculiar is the parallel with
the woe in Mark 14:21. However, this Markan woe against the man
who hands over the Son of man is a secondary formulation for which
Mark may have used a saying like the introduction to Q/Luke 17:1–2.[1]
In any case, while *1 Clem.* 13.2 reflects sayings from one of the early
collections, which is also attested elsewhere, *1 Clem.* 46:8 may not
have been derived from a written source but from the free tradition of
sayings.

There may be several other passages in which *1 Clement* is dependent upon the synoptic sayings tradition. *1 Clem.* 24.4–5 recalls the
parable of the Sower (Mark 4:3–9):[2]

> Let us take the crops: how and in what way does the sowing take place?
> "The sower went forth" and cast each of the seeds into the ground, and
> parched and bare they fall on to the ground and perish; then from their
> decay the greatness of the providence of the Lord raises them up, and
> from one grain many more grow and bring forth fruit.

The sentence "The sower went forth" (ἐξῆλθεν ὁ σπείρων) agrees verbatim with the first sentence of the parable of the Sower in all three
synoptic versions (Mark 4:3 parr.) and in the *Gospel of Thomas* (# 9).[3]
However, *1 Clement* does not give any indication that he is quoting a
parable of Jesus but summarizes it, like the parable of the Vine in
chapter 23.4 and the story of the Phoenix in chapter 25, without any
reference to source or authority. The parable was certainly taken from
the tradition in which this as well as other parables of Jesus were
more generally known.

It is possible that there are other instances in which the formulation
of a particular passage or sentence is influenced by a saying of Jesus.
One could quote as such an instance *1 Clem.* 16.17:

> ... for if the Lord was thus humble-minded (ἐταπεινοφρόνησεν), what
> shall we do who have come through him under his yoke (ζυγός) of grace.

If there is indeed a recollection of Jesus' invitation to come under his
yoke (ζυγός), because he is gentle and humble (ταπεινός) in his heart

---

[1] Lührmann, *Markusevangelium*, 237.

[2] Massaux (*Influence de l'Évangile de Saint Matthieu*, 32) does not argue for a
dependence upon a written gospel, but assumes that *1 Clement* developed further the
image of the seed which he took from the early Christian literary tradition.

[3] Mark 4:3 and *Gos. Thom.* 9 begin the sentence with ἰδού.

(Matt 11:29), it must be remembered that this was a free saying circulating in the oral tradition, attested also in the *Gospel of Thomas* (# 90).[1]

2.1.4.4 The Epistle of James

Were the Epistle of James indeed written by Jesus' brother James, the numerous instances in this epistle which have words and phrases in common with sayings of Jesus could be explained as personal reminiscences of these sayings.[2] But scholarship has seriously challenged this assumption of authorship. Martin Dibelius, in his influential commentary which was first published in 1920,[3] has argued that the author's affinity with Jesus' sayings is due to the following three factors: (1) formal similarity, since both consist to a large degree of parenesis; (2) similarity of style (use of short, pointed imperatives and a fixed group of metaphors); (3) both share the same convictions (ethical rigorism, warnings against worldly attitudes, piety of the poor).[4] Even closer connections exist because a large portion of Jesus' sayings in the Synoptic Gospels consists of early Christian parenesis. Therefore, any writing that is made up primarily of parenesis, like the Epistle of James, is likely to include phrases and sentences which have parallels in these gospels.[5]

There are no explicit quotations of Jesus' sayings in James, and many of the assumed parallels, as Deppe has shown in his dissertation,[6] are simply due to similarities in wording, terminology, and/or

---

[1] It is typical for the methodological weakness of Köhler's approach that he points out that the "yoke of grace" is the "yoke of Jesus" and finds "great nearness to Matthew"; therefore, this "passage can be reconciled with the assumption of the dependence (of *1 Clement*) upon Matthew," although he admits that it cannot carry the burden of proof (*Rezeption des Matthäusevangeliums*, 60). Unfortunately, Köhler never considers seriously the existence of the oral tradition or of early collections of sayings.

[2] In German scholarship, this position has been most strongly defended by Gerhard Kittel, "Der geschichtliche Ort des Jakobusbriefes," *ZNW* 41 (1942) 71–105. The extent to which this explanation is still held today has been described recently by Dean B. Deppe, *The Sayings of Jesus in the Epistle of James* (Dissertation Amsterdam, Free University, 1989). James B. Adamson, in his commentary (*The Epistle of James* [New International Commentary to the New Testament; Grand Rapids: Eerdmans, 1976]) writes about the similarities between James's Epistle and the Canonical Gospels: "We ourselves believe that this is at least mainly due not merely to James's early sharing some of the oral and written evidence to which those Gospels sooner or later were indebted, but to his own personal witness of the life and teaching of Jesus."

[3] English translation: Martin Dibelius, *James: A Commentary on the Epistle of James*, rev. by Heinrich Greeven (Hermeneia, Philadelphia: Fortress, 1976).

[4] Dibelius-Greeven, *James*, 28.

[5] Ibid., 28–29.

[6] Deppe, *Sayings of Jesus;* see especially the summary on pp. 219–21. Deppe (pp. 237–50) also presents cogent arguments against the assumption of dependency in

content. Only eight instances remain in which one can assume the
use of the same tradition of a saying or a sentence of parenesis:

James	Synoptic Parallels
1:5	Q/Luke 11:9 (Matt 7:7)
But if someone among you lacks wisdom, let him ask from God—who gives to all without hesitation and without grumbling —and it will be given to him.	Ask, and it will be given to you, seek, and you will find, knock, and it will be opened to you.
4:2c–3	
. . . you do not have, because you do not ask; you ask and you do not receive, because you ask with the wrong motive. . .	
2:5	Q/Luke 6:20b (Matt 5:3)
Has Jesus not chosen those who are poor before the world[1] to be rich in faith and heirs of the kingdom which he has promised to those who love him?	Blessed are the poor (Matt adds: in spirit), for yours is the kingdom of God.
4:9	Q/Luke 6:21b (Matt 5:4)
Be wretched and mourn (πενθήσετε) and weep (κλαύσετε)! Let your laughter (γέλως) be turned to mourning (πένθος) and your joy to sorrow (ἡ χαρὰ εἰς κατήφειαν).	Blessed are those who weep (κλαίοντες) now, because you will laugh (γελάσετε).
4:10	Q/Luke 14:11 (Matt 23:12)
Humble yourself before the Lord, and he will exalt you (ταπεινώθητε ἐνώπιον κυρίου καὶ ὑψώσει ὑμᾶς).	Everyone who exalts himself will be humbled, and he who humbles himself will be exalted (πᾶς ὁ ὑψῶν ἑαυτὸν ταπεινωθήσεται, καὶ ὁ ταπεινῶν ἑαυτὸν ὑψωθήσεται).

"The Twenty-five Most Frequently Mentioned Parallels."

[1] This translation presupposes the text πτωχοὶ τῷ κόσμῳ ($\mathfrak{p}^{74}$ ℵ A B C) rather than
"the poor in the world" (πτωχοὶ ἐν τῷ κόσμῳ, some minuscules) or "the poor of the world"
(πτωχοὶ τοῦ κόσμου, most manuscripts); see the discussion in Dibelius-Greeven, *James*,
137.

5:1	Luke 6:24–25
Come, you rich (οἱ πλούσιοι), weep (κλαύσετε) and wail (ὀλολύζοντες) at the miseries which are coming upon you.	Woe to you, the rich (τοῖς πλουσίοις), for you have received your consolation. Woe to you who are full now, for you shall go hungry. Woe to you who laugh (οἱ γελῶντες) now, for you shall weep and mourn (πενθήσετε καὶ κλαύσετε).

5:2–3a	Q/Matt 6:20 (Luke 12:33b)
Your wealth has rotted (σέσηπεν) and your garments are moth-eaten (σητόβρωτα), your gold and silver has rusted (κατίωται) and their rust will devour your flesh like fire	Lay up for yourselves treasures in heaven where neither moth nor rust corrode (οὔτε σὴς οὔτε βρῶσις ἀφανίζει) and where thieves do not dig through and steal. (Luke has only this last phrase.)

5:12	Matt 5:34–37
Above all, my brothers and sisters, do not swear (μὴ ὀμνύετε), either by heaven or by earth,	But I say to you not to swear at all (μὴ ὀμόσαι ὅλως), either by heaven, because it is the throne of God, or by earth, because it is the footstool of his feet,
nor with any other oath.	or by Jerusalem, because it is the city of the great king; nor shall you swear by your head, because you cannot make a single hair white or black.
Let your yes be yes and your no be no (ἤτω δὲ ὑμῶν τὸ ναὶ ναὶ καὶ τὸ οὒ οὔ), so that you may not fall under condemnation.	Let what you say be "Yes, yes" and "No, no." Everything beyond this is from evil.

Jas 1:5 and 4:2c–3 have a parallel in a Q saying and it is certainly an expansion of the saying about prayer and faith. However, this saying of Jesus is so widespread in early Christianity[1] that a reference to a specific source is not warranted. The reference to God who gives "without grumbling" may reflect an older Jewish saying about giving rather than a saying of Jesus.[2]

The designation of the poor as the heirs of the kingdom in Jas 2:5 seems to echo the respective beatitude of the Q version of the Sermon

---

[1] See also John 16:23–24; *Gos. Thom.* 92, 94. See the discussion in Deppe, *Sayings of Jesus,* 68–70.

[2] Dibelius, *James,* 79.

on the Mount/Sermon on the Plain, without the typical Matthean interpolation "in spirit" (τῷ πνεύματι). However, nothing indicates that the author was referring to a specific beatitude of Jesus; rather, he simply states a principle of the traditional piety of the poor.[1]

Also Jas 4:9 exhibits some verbal similarities to a beatitude from the same context (Luke 6:21, following upon the blessing of the poor, Luke 6:20b). Yet, the meaning is quite different: instead of a blessing, one reads a call for repentance. In Jas 4:10 another allusion to a Q saying (Q/Luke 14:11) follows. The basic statement of Luke 14:11 is changed into an imperative and incorporated into the sequence of sayings calling for repentance; this entire sequence (vss. 7–10) may have been formulated in the parenetic tradition and was appropriated by James as a unit.[2] Thus, neither 4:9 nor 4:10 reveal a direct acquaintance of the author with Q.

Materials from the tradition of the pious poor in Jas 5:1–3 show close resemblances to several sayings from the synoptic tradition. The closest parallel to Jas 5:1 appears in special Lukan materials, the woes against the rich of Luke. In both cases, the style is prophetic, though only Luke has formulated the threats against the rich as "woes" in order to establish a formal contrast to the preceding beatitudes (Luke 6:20–23). Luke has interpolated these woes into his Q materials; they are drawn from the same tradition which has also informed James' piety of the poor. The following sentences (Jas 5:2–3a) have a parallel in the Q saying of Matt 6:20 and Luke 12:33b, but in this instance they show a closer resemblance to the Matthean version (Matt 6:20); an even closer parallel is provided by *1 Enoch* 97.8–10. Also here the terminology is not new; it had already become well established in several descriptions of the perishability of wealth in Jewish writings.[3]

In Jas 5:12 there can be no question that James is quoting the same injunction that Matthew used in the third antithesis of the Sermon on the Mount. James has preserved an earlier form.[4] The reasons given for not swearing by heaven, earth, and Jerusalem seem to be secondary explanations,[5] and the injunction against swearing by one's own head is apparently a later expansion.[6] Moreover, James's "Let your

---

[1] Dibelius-Greeven, *James,* Introduction, chap. 6, pp. 39–45.

[2] Ibid., 208.

[3] Ibid., 236.

[4] For the following see the detailed analysis and comparison of the two passages by Georg Strecker, "Die Antithesen des Bergpredigt," *ZNW* 69 (1978) 56–63.

[5] Strecker ("Antithesen der Bergpredigt," 60–61) points out that these expansions rest upon the LXX text of Isa 66:1 and Ps 47:3.

[6] Bultmann (*Synoptic Tradition,* 135) points out that "the first three examples, swearing by heaven, by the earth, and by Jerusalem, reject such oaths for being encroachments upon the sphere of God's majesty," whereas the last example, swearing

yes be yes" recommends truthfulness in speech, whereas Matthew's "Let what you say be 'Yes, yes'" seems to be a substitute oath formula.[1] In the conclusion, the threat of judgment against untruthfulness in James's version was replaced in Matthew by a condemnation of any affirmation which goes beyond this substitute oath formula.[2] Jas 5:12 is certainly not dependent upon Matthew, but draws the saying from the parenetical tradition. It is difficult to say whether this tradition knew the injunction as a saying of Jesus. This is possible, although a quotation formula is not used.[3]

The comparison of similar sentences and materials in the Epistle of James and in the Synoptic Gospels does not reveal the use of any particular collections of sayings, but rests upon James's use of parenetic traditions which also provided materials to these gospels and/or their sources. It is quite possible that some of these sayings and injunctions were known to James as sayings of Jesus.

2.2 The Gospel of Thomas[4]

2.2.1 DISCOVERY AND ATTESTATION

A Coptic translation of the *Gospel of Thomas* was first identified in Cairo in the year 1948 in one of the codices of the Nag Hammadi Library which had been found in upper Egypt near Chenoboskion in the fall of 1945.[5] In the spring of 1948, when eleven of the original thir-

---

by one's head, "makes swearing ridiculous." Bultmann wonders whether the first three examples are later additions. That, however, is unlikely, unless one wants to argue that James is dependent upon Matthew.

[1] For the discussion of this question see Deppe, *Sayings of Jesus,* 136–40. "The teaching no longer says what one ought to *be* (i.e., truthful), but rather what one should *say* if one had to make an affirmation" (Dibelius-Greeven, *James,* 251).

[2] Strecker ("Antithesen der Bergpredigt") 57–58 shows that Matthew's last clause reveals typically Matthean language.

[3] Dibelius-Greeven (*James,* 251) considers this the only instance in which one can safely assume that the author of this epistle is indeed using a saying of Jesus. See also the discussion in Deppe, *Sayings of Jesus.*

[4] The best general presentation of the *Gospel of Thomas* with extensive bibliographies was published by Francis T. Fallon and Ron Cameron, "The Gospel of Thomas: A Forschungsbericht and Analysis," *ANRW* 2.25/5, 4195–4251.

[5] The best critical account of the story of the discovery is James M. Robinson, "The Discovery of the Nag Hammadi Codices," *BA* 42 (1979) 206–24. For a brief description see James M. Robinson, "Introduction," in idem, ed., *The Nag Hammadi Library,* 22–26; John Dominic Crossan, *Four Other Gospels: Shadows on the Contours of Canon* (Winston: Minneapolis, 1985) 15–23. The first lengthy and sometimes mystifying account was published by Jean Doresse, *Les livres secrets des Gnostiques d'Égypte*

teen codices of the Nag Hammadi Library were still in the hands of the Cairo antiquities dealer, Phokion Tano, Jean Doresse was retained to photograph some of the manuscripts and to prepare an inventory of the tractates. At the end of the second tractate of Codex II, Doresse read the words inscribed in titular fashion in the middle of the page: ΠΕΥΑΓΓΕΛΙΟΝ ΠΚΑΤΑ ΘΩΜΑC ("The Gospel According to Thomas").[1] In 1957, Pahor Labib, the director of the Coptic Museum in Cairo, published a series of photographs of leaves from the new codices, among them the pages from Codex II containing the *Gospel of Thomas*.[2] Within a year, Jean Doresse published a French translation,[3] and the East-German scholar Johannes Leipoldt published a German translation of the *Gospel of Thomas*.[4] The Coptic text was published a year later with French, German, and English translations.[5]

It soon became apparent[6] that some parts of the *Gospel of Thomas* had indeed been known for many decades: three Greek papyri with sayings of Jesus, all three written ca. 200 CE, had been found in Oxyrhynchus in Egypt in the years 1897, 1903, and 1904 respectively.[7] These papyri are actually portions of the Greek original of the Coptic *Gospel of Thomas. Pap. Oxy. 1* preserves the Greek original of *Gos. Thom.* 28–33, *Pap. Oxy. 654* the first seven sayings, and *Pap. Oxy. 655* sayings 37–40 of this gospel.[8] The discovery of the full Coptic text

---

(Paris: Librairie Plon, 1958; fully revised ET: *The Secret Books of the Egyptian Gnostics* (New York: Viking, 1960) 116–36.

[1] Doresse, *Secret Books,* 120.

[2] *Coptic Gnostic Papyri in the Coptic Museum of Old Cairo.* Vol. I (Cairo: Government Press [Antiquities Department], 1956).

[3] *Secret Books,* 333–83.

[4] "Ein neues Evangelium: Das Koptische Thomasevangelium übersetzt und besprochen," *ThLZ* 83 (1958) cols. 481–496; reprinted in Johannes Leipoldt and Hans-Martin Schenke, *Koptisch-gnostische Schriften aus den Papyrus-Codices von Nag Hamadi* (ThF 20; Hamburg-Bergstedt: Reich and Evangelischer Verlag, 1959).

[5] A. Guillaumont. H.-Ch. Puech, G. Quispel, W. Till and Yassah 'Abd al Masih, eds., *The Gospel According to Thomas: Coptic Text Established and Translated* (Leiden: Brill, 1959); a reduced reprint of the editio princeps of 1959 with English translation was published recently: San Francisco: Harper & Row, 1984.

[6] Doresse (*Secret Books,* 227) ascribes this discovery to the French scholar H.-Ph. Puech.

[7] They were published by B. P. Grenfell and A. S. Hunt, ΛΟΓΙΑ ΙΗΣΟΥ: *Sayings of Our Lord* (Egypt Exploration Fund; London: Frowde, 1897); idem, *New Sayings of Jesus and Fragment of a Lost Gospel from Oxyrhynchus* (Egypt Exploration Fund; London: Frowde, 1904); idem, *The Oxyrhynchus Papyri, Part IV* (London: Egypt Exploration Fund, 1904) 1–28.

[8] For the relationship of the Greek fragments to the Coptic text see Fallon and Cameron, "Forschungsbericht," 4201–4.

made it possible to reconstruct the entire Greek text of these fragmentary papyri.[1] The definitive publication of the Coptic text and the reconstructed Greek fragments, together with translations and introductions, are now available in a volume of Nag Hammadi Studies edited by Bentley Layton.[2]

The three Oxyrhynchus Papyri had been widely discussed in the first decades of this century and valued highly by some scholars as possibly original sayings of Jesus;[3] but it was not clear whether these three papyri belonged to any particular gospel. No doubt all three Oxyrhynchus fragments are part of the Greek text of the *Gospel of Thomas*. Yet they are not portions of one single manuscript and they do not necessarily represent the Greek text from which the Coptic translation was made. Yet they do not derive from the Coptic text, but are independent developments of the Greek original underlying the Coptic translation.[4] Thus the *Gospel of Thomas* is well attested as a Greek gospel writing that circulated widely during the 2d century. The attestation is just as strong as that for the canonical gospels.[5]

That is affirmed by the early testimonies to this gospel. The earliest reference to the *Gospel of Thomas* appears in Hippolytus *Refutatio* 5.7.20 (222–235 CE in Rome):[6]

---

[1] The first reconstruction of the very fragmentary Greek texts was published by Joseph A. Fitzmyer, "The Oxyrhynchus Logoi of Jesus and the Coptic Gospel According to Thomas," now in idem, *Essays on the Semitic Background of the New Testament* (London: Chapman, 1971) 355–433; corrections were presented by Robert A. Kraft, "Oxyrhynchus Papyrus 655 Reconsidered," *HTR* 54 (1961) 253–62. A new edition of these Greek texts by Harold W. Attridge is now available in Bentley Layton, ed., *Nag Hammadi Codex II, 2–7* (see the following note).

[2] "The Gospel According to Thomas," in Bentley Layton, ed., *Nag Hammadi Codex II, 2–7 Together with XIII, 2*, Brit. Lib. Or. 4926(1) and P. Oxy. 1, 654, 655* (NHS 20–21; Leiden: Brill, 1989) 38–130: "Introduction" by Helmut Koester, "Critical Edition" by Bentley Layton, "Translation" by Thomas O. Lambdin, "Appendix: The Greek Fragments" by Harold W. Attridge. An earlier edition with French translation and commentary was published in the same series by Jacque-E. Ménard, *L'Évangile selon Thomas* (NHS 5; Leiden: Brill, 1975). Numerous translations have appeared during the last three decades. Good English translations are most conveniently available in Ron Cameron, *The Other Gospels: Non-Canonical Gospel Texts* (Philadelphia: Westminster, 1982) 23–37; Bentley Layton, *The Gnostic Scriptures: A New Translation with Annotations and Introductions* (Garden City, NY: Doubleday, 1987) 376–99. Thomas O. Lambdin's translation is also available in Robinson, ed., *Nag Hammadi Library*, 126–38. For a survey of publications of the text, translations, and basic research tools see Fallon and Cameron, "Forschungsbericht," 4197–4201.

[3] The respective literature is listed in Hennecke-Schneemelcher-Wilson, *NT Apocrypha*, 1. 99 and 105.

[4] Attridge, "The Greek Fragments," in Layton, ed., *Nag Hammadi Codex II*, 99.

[5] See my article, "Apocryphal and Canonical Gospels," 107–12.

[6] The references to the *Gospel of Thomas* are assembled by Harold W. Attridge, "The Greek Fragments," in Layton, ed., *Nag Hammadi Codex II*, 103–9. For a discussion of

(The Naassenes) speak . . . of a nature which is both hidden and revealed at the same time and which they call the thought-for kingdom of heaven which is in a human being. They transmit a tradition concerning this in the Gospel entitled "According to Thomas," which states expressly, "The one who seeks me will find me in children of seven years and older; for there, hidden in the fourteenth aeon, I am revealed."[1]

The second early attestation comes from the Alexandrian theologian Origen *Hom. in Luc.* 1 (233 CE):

> For there circulates also the Gospel according to Thomas and the Gospel according to Matthias and many others.[2]

The *Gospel of Thomas* was also used and valued highly by Mani. This is mentioned by several Church Fathers who claim that the Manichaean gospel was actually written by one of Mani's disciples named Thomas. However, Augustine refers in this context to the phrase "he will never experience death" which echoes the first saying of the *Gospel of Thomas*.[3]

2.2.2 JUDAS THOMAS

The traditions that the apostle Thomas was the missionary to India are as old as the end of the 2d century.[4] The *Acts of Thomas*, written in eastern Syria at the beginning of the 3d century, reports the mission of the apostle Thomas to the court of King Gundaphoros (chapter 17), thus locating the activity of Thomas in North India. However, in chapters 3 and 4, the *Acts of Thomas* depict Thomas as embarking on a

---

the testimonies see also Fallon and Cameron, "Forschungsbericht," 4204.

[1] The phrase "a little child of seven" appears in saying 5 of the Coptic *Gospel of Thomas*.

[2] Later writers who also refer to these two gospels are apparently dependent upon Origen: Eusebius *Hist. eccl.* 3.25.6; Jerome *Comm. in Matt.* Prologue; Ambrose *Expositio evangelii Lucae* 1.2. See further, Attridge, "Greek Fragments," passim.

[3] *Contra epistula fundamenti* 11. See also Cyril of Jerusalem *Catechesis* 4.36; 6.31. The *Decretum Gelasanium* (5th century) lists among the heretical books "A Gospel attributed to Thomas which the Manichaean use."

[4] A survey of the relevant information can be found in A. F. J. Klijn, *The Acts of Thomas: Introduction, Text, Commentary* (NovTSup 5; Leiden: Brill, 1962) 27–29. For a discussion of the Thomas tradition and Thomas writings see Crossan, *Four Other Gospels*, 23–26. Curiously, one old piece of information about India (Eusebius *Hist. eccl.* 5.10.3) connects Indian Christianity with Bartholomew:

> Pantaenus (Alexandrian teacher of Origen) . . . went to the Indians, and the tradition is that he found there that among some of those there who had known Christ the Gospel according to Matthew had preceded his coming; for Bartholomew, one of the apostles, had preached to them and had left them the writing of Matthew in Hebrew letters, which was preserved until the time mentioned.

sea voyage to India; apparently the editor of this part of the book wanted to connect the mission of Thomas with South India.

All traditions agree that the authority of the apostle Thomas and the area of his mission must be located in the East, i.e., in eastern Syria, specifically in Edessa (upper Mesopotamia), and in India. In the *Acts of Thomas,* the apostle's name is "Judas who is also called Thomas" ('Ιούδας ὁ καὶ Θωμᾶς) and in chapter 1 he is introduced as "Judas Thomas who is also called Didymus" ('Ιούδας Θωμᾶς ὁ καὶ Δίδυμος).[1] This triple designation agrees with the form of the name as it appears in the original title of the *Gospel of Thomas:*

> These are the secret sayings which the living Jesus spoke and which Didymus Judas Thomas wrote down.[2]

Who was Didymus Judas Thomas? Thomas appears in the lists of the "Twelve," or the "Twelve Apostles," in Matthew 10:3; Mark 3:18; Luke 6:15; and Acts 1:13. But none of these books say anything about him. However, in the Gospel of John, Thomas is mentioned several times, twice as asking a question (11:16 and 14:5) and then in the story of the "Unbelieving Thomas" (20:24–28), finally in the list of seven disciples in John 21:2. In three of these passages the phrase "who was also called Didymus" is added. In John 14:22 the Syriac translation reads "Thomas" instead of "Judas, not the Iscarioth"; obviously the translator connected the name Judas with Thomas, which corresponds to the tradition of the Syrian church. This is also reflected in the Abgar Legend about the mission in Edessa where the apostle is introduced as "Judas who is also called Thomas."[3]

"Thomas" is not a proper name but a transcription of the Aramaic word for "twin," and the Greek word "Didymus" also means "twin." The Syrian tradition as well as the *Gospel of Thomas* have preserved his given name: Judas. There are several persons with this name mentioned in the New Testament: (1) Judas Iscarioth who betrayed Jesus; (2) "Judas, the son of Jacob," listed as one of the apostles together with Thomas (Luke 6:16 = Acts 1:13; thus these were two different persons); (3) "Judas," the brother of Jesus (Mark 6:3 = Matthew 13:55). The New Testament writing known as the "Epistle of Jude" introduces as its author "Judas the brother of James" (= the brother of Jesus).

(ET Kirsopp Lake, LCL).

[1] Lipsius-Bonnet, *Acta Apostolorum Apocrypha,* 2.100, lines 4–5. The Syriac text reads instead "Judas Thomas, the Apostle."

[2] This is the reading of the Coptic text. The Greek text of *Pap. Oxy. 1* reads [. . . 'Ιούδα ὁ] καὶ Θωμᾶ.

[3] Eusebius *Hist. eccl.* 1.13.11.

"Judas, the Twin, brother of Jesus" is the representative of an independent tradition of the Eastern Church.

Eventually, in the *Acts of Thomas,* he became the twin-brother of Jesus.[1] In the *Gospel of Thomas* there is a connection between James the Righteous (i.e., Jesus' brother), who is designated as the leader of the church (*Gos. Thom.* 12), and (Judas) Thomas as the apostle who knows the secret wisdom (*Gos. Thom.* 13); but no family relationship between Jesus, James, and Thomas is established. Thomas is important because he guarantees the reliability of the wisdom sayings, not because of his family ties to Jesus. Yet the significance of Thomas for the Eastern Church argues for an east-Syrian origin of the Gospel of Thomas.

2.2.3 CHARACTER AND GENRE

The designation "The Gospel of Thomas" was added later at the end of the document by the scribe who copied it. The incipit designates the writing as a "Book of Secret Sayings." Normally each saying is introduced by "Jesus said." The sayings are not embedded into a narrative framework, although occasionally the disciples are introduced as asking questions. There are no references to the story of Jesus, no mention of his birth, life, death, and resurrection; rather Jesus is simply designated as "the Living One."

The author was certainly not trying to compose a "gospel" of the type that is known from the Gospels of the New Testament. Just stringing sayings together into a written document is a mode of composition that was well known from wisdom books, like the Book of Proverbs from the Hebrew Bible, or the *Wisdom of Ben Sirah* and the *Wisdom of Solomon,* which are preserved among the so-called Old Testament Apocrypha. There are also early Christian examples for this type of literature. Most scholars believe that both Matthew and Luke used as a common source a collection of Jesus' sayings, known as the Synoptic Sayings Source (see below # 2.3). The Epistle of James in the New Testament is such a wisdom book, and also the first six chapters of the early Christian manual known as the *Didache* or *Teaching of the Twelve Apostles.*

The sayings of the *Gospel of Thomas* consist for the most part of aphorisms, proverbs, wisdom sayings, parables, prophetic sayings about the "Kingdom of the Father," and community rules.[2] "Wisdom"

---

[1] This also the case in the *Book of Thomas (the Contender)* (NHC II, 7) where Jesus address this apostle as "My brother" and as "my twin and true companion."

[2] For a listing of examples of the types of sayings in the *Gospel of Thomas* see Helmut Koester, "One Jesus and Four Primitive Gospels," in Robinson-Koester, *Trajectories,* 168–87; Fallon and Cameron, "Forschungsbericht," 4205–13.

is the theme of this writing. As in the *Wisdom of Solomon,* wisdom
sayings express the truth about God and about the essence of the
human self. They speak about human nature and destiny and, by
extension, about the nature of the world and the proper relationship to
the world in which people dwell. The wisdom sayings of the *Gospel of
Thomas,* like other Jewish and Christian sayings collections of this
type, contain sayings that reveal what is fundamental about people
and their behavior. Still other sayings point to the tenuous nature of a
human being's sojourn in the world. Such wisdom sayings, as well as
many others, have parallels in the canonical gospels. Thus such sayings and the orientation they reveal are by no means unique to Thomas. They are typical of the early Christian sayings tradition to which
Thomas, together with Matthew, Mark, and Luke, was heir.

What is most puzzling about the composition of sayings in this wisdom book is the arrangement and order of the sayings. There is seemingly no rhyme or reason for the odd sequence in which the sayings
occur in the *Gospel of Thomas.* Moreover, in one instance, the Greek
and Coptic texts differ in the order of sayings. *Pap. Oxy. 1* combines
30 and 77b of the Coptic text. Several attempts have been made to
find the author's compositional principle,[1] none of them convincing.
Some principles of order can be discovered in smaller sections. *Gos.
Thom.* 62–65 brings a sequence of parables introduced by a saying that
points to the mystery character of these parables. Another group of
parables, each introduced by "The kingdom is like . . . ," appears in the
final section of the book in ## 96, 97, 98, 107, 109. However, in this
case other materials have been inserted after the first three and
between the last two of these parables. Thus this is not an order established by the author of this gospel, but it reflects the use of a written
source in which materials of a certain type had been grouped together.
In other instances one can observe catchword associations of two or
more sayings, e.g., ## 2 and 3 are obviously associated through the
catchword "to be king" and "kingdom." ## 25 and 26 both speak about
"your brother" and use the word "eye," though each time with a different metaphorical meaning. ## 31, 32, 33, and 35 may have been
brought together through the catchwords "village," "city," "housetops,"
"house," though the connection to the last is obscured by the insertion
of an unrelated proverb (# 34). Also in this instance, such a compositional principle is more likely a feature of the author's source.

The writer of the *Gospel of Thomas* is, in fact, not an author who
deliberately composed his book according to a general master plan. He
is rather a collector and compiler who used a number of smaller units

---

[1] They are surveyed by Fallon and Cameron, "Forschungsbericht," 4205–8.

of collected sayings, some perhaps available in written form, and composed them randomly. He shows no desire to express his own understanding of these sayings through the manner of composition. This can be explained by considering the hermeneutic principles employed for the interpretation of sayings: each saying has meaning in itself. In some instances, the author expresses that in the form of additional phrases. *Gos. Thom.* 16, for example, quotes three traditional sayings (= Q/Luke 12: 51, 52 and 53) and then adds "and they will stand as a single one." # 78 quotes Q/Luke 7:24–25 and adds "and they are unable to discern the truth." We shall see in the further development of this tradition of sayings that the next step is the composition of dialogues which explore the deeper meaning of just one or two sayings, sometimes drawing additional sayings into the dialogue, but rarely making any attempts to bring the sayings into any rational order and sequence.[1]

The author's own understanding of traditional sayings is also expressed in the way in which he adds sayings of a different character to the collection. A number of wisdom sayings go beyond the commonplace understanding of what is wise and what is unwise in human life. They speak of divine Wisdom who invites human beings to follow her in order to find the true life here in this world and in the hereafter. Some of these Thomas sayings have parallels in the Gospels of the New Testament, for example, the famous saying in which Jesus speaks with the voice of heavenly Wisdom, inviting people to take up his yoke:

Gos. Thom. 90	Matt 11:28–30
Come unto me, for my yoke is easy and my lordship is mild, and you will find repose for yourselves.	Come to me, all who labor and are heavy laden, and I will give you rest. Take my yoke upon you and learn from me; for I am gentle and lowly in heart, and you will find rest for your souls. For my yoke is easy, and my burden is light.

It is necessary, therefore, to recognize the moment in which the words of Jesus are heard; this is expressed in a number of eschatological and prophetic sayings, for example:

His disciples said to him, "When will the repose of the dead come about, and when will the new world come?" He said to them, "What you look forward to has already come, but you do not recognize it." (*Gos. Thom.* 51)

---

[1] See below on the *Dialogue of the Savior* and on the discourses and dialogues of the Gospel of John.

His disciples said to him. "Twenty-four prophets spoke in Israel, and all of them spoke of you." He said to them, "You have omitted the one living in your presence, and have spoken (only) of the dead." (*Gos. Thom.* 52)

Such eschatological sayings have parallels in the canonical Gospels, especially sayings and parables which emphasize the contrast between the old and the new and which speak about the coming of the kingdom.

The coming of the kingdom is not dated to a future time, but is clearly understood as an event of the present time. However, this radicalization of the eschatological expectation is not without parallel in the canonical Gospels, as a comparison of *Gos. Thom.* 113 with its parallel demonstrates:

Gos. Thom. 113	Lk 17:20–21
His disciples said to him, "When will the kingdom come?" Jesus said, "It will not come by looking for it. It will not be a matter of saying, 'here it is,' or 'there it is'. Rather, the kingdom of the Father is spread out upon the earth, and people do not see it."	Being asked by the Pharisees when the kingdom of God was coming, he answered them, "The kingdom of God is not coming with signs to be observed; nor will they say, 'Lo, here it is!' or 'There!' for behold, the kingdom of God is in the midst of you."

However, Thomas sees this coming of the kingdom primarily as an event that takes place as the disciples gain a new understanding of themselves:

Jesus said, "If those who lead you say to you, 'See, the kingdom is in the sky,' then the birds of the sky will precede you. If they say to you, 'It is in the sea,' then the fish will precede you. Rather the kingdom is inside of you, and it is outside of you. When you come to know yourselves, then you will be known, and you will realize that it is you who are the sons of the living Father. But if you will not know yourselves, you dwell in poverty and it is you who are that poverty." (*Gos. Thom.* 3)

To the sayings of this type, one must add those which seem to express Gnostic themes and reveal a more radical concept of secret knowledge. They speak of hidden truths about human existence, heavenly origins, separation from the world, and liberation of the soul from the body (see below). This has prompted some scholars to date the *Gospel of Thomas* later in the 2d century CE. However, it has become more and more evident that the rise of Gnosticism must be dated earlier than the 2d century and that it cannot be viewed as a relatively late Christian phenomenon. Among the tractates discovered at Nag Hammadi, one finds a number of texts which unfold a rich legacy of Jewish Gnosticism which likely predates the beginnings of Christianity.[1] Thus Thomas's religious perspective, even if it is "Gnostic," may have been right at home in the 1st century. In order to determine the date of the *Gospel of Thomas* relative to other early gospel traditions and writings, it is necessary to investigate the relationship of its sayings to the sayings of the canonical gospels and their sources.

2.2.4 THE GOSPEL OF THOMAS AND THE SYNOPTIC TRADITION

2.2.4.1 Thomas and the Canonical Gospels

As soon as the full text of this gospel had been recovered, it became clear that it was a book of sayings of Jesus of which many had parallels in the Gospels of Matthew, Mark, Luke, and John. Just as after the discovery of the Oxyrhynchus Papyri, scholars immediately set out to compare the sayings of the new Coptic *Gospel of Thomas* with their parallels in the canonical gospels. Scholarly opinion was divided from the very beginning. While few hailed the *Gospel of Thomas* as a collection of sayings containing the pure and unsullied words of Jesus, some interpreters believed that it represented an early tradition of sayings which was independent of the canon of the New Testament. On the other hand, many scholars saw in this gospel a heretical fabrication, a Gnostic interpretation of the teachings of Jesus, using sayings which were drawn from the the canonical gospels. The latter alternative was endorsed soon after the initial publication by a large number of authors, among them such respected scholars as Robert M. Grant of the University of Chicago,[2] and in Germany Professor Ernst Haenchen of the University of Münster.[3] The first exponents of the view that the *Gospel of Thomas* was an independent witness for the tradition of the sayings of Jesus were the Dutch scholar Gilles Quispel,[4] the Elsassian

---

[1] The most comprehensive treatment of this question can be found in Kurt Rudolph, *Gnosis: The Nature and History of an Ancient Religion* (Edinburgh: Clark, 1983); see especially pp. 275–294.

[2] "Notes on the Gospel of Thomas," *VigChr* 13 (1959) 170–180; Grant followed this article with a book coauthored with David Noel Freedman, *The Secret Sayings of Jesus* (Garden City, NY: Doubleday, 1960).

[3] In his critical survey of the first publications on the *Gospel of Thomas:* "Literatur zum Thomasevangelium," *ThR* 27 N.F. (1961/62) 147–178, 306–338; and in his translation and commentary: *Die Botschaft des Thomas-Evangeliums* (Berlin: Töpelmann, 1961).

[4] "The Gospel of Thomas and the New Testament," *VigChr* 11 (1957) 189–207. Quispel has defended and further elaborated his hypothesis in a number of subsequent articles which were published in subsequent issues of the same journal: 12 (1958) 181–96; 13 (1959) 87–117; 14 (1960) 204–15; 16 (1962) 121–53; 18 (1964) 226–35; see also idem in *NTS* 5 (1958/59) 276–90; *NTS* 12 (1965/66) 371–82.

Patristic scholar Oscar Cullmann,[1] and in England, Hugh Montefiore.[2] Those who assume that the *Gospel of Thomas* is dependent upon the Gospels of the New Testament[3] have not been able to show that there is any concrete and consistent pattern of Thomas's dependence upon one particular gospels' version of the tradition of the sayings.[4] There is also no trace of the narrative framework into which the sayings are often embedded in the Gospels of the canon. Moreover, a number of studies have shown that in many cases a saying or parable, as it appears in the *Gospel of Thomas,* is preserved in a form that is more original than any of its canonical parallels. This means that the tradition of sayings of Jesus preserved in the *Gospel of Thomas* pre-dates the canonical Gospels[5] and rules out the possibility of a dependence

[1] "Das Thomasevangelium und die Frage nach dem Alter der in ihm enthaltenen Tradition," *ThLZ* 85 (1960) 321–334; ET in *Interpretation* 16 (1962) 418–38.

[2] "A Comparison of the Parables of the Gospel According to Thomas and the Synoptic Gospels," *NTS* 7 (1960/61) 220–248; republished in idem and H. E. W. Turner, *Thomas and the Evangelists* (SBT 35; London: SCM, 1962).

[3] In addition to the literature quoted above, see Wolfgang Schrage, *Das Verhältnis des Thomas-Evangeliums zur synoptischen Tradition und zu den koptischen Evangelienübersetzungen* (BZNW 29; Berlin: De Gruyter, 1964); with respect to Schrage's thesis of a dependence of the *Gospel of Thomas* upon the Coptic translation of the Synoptic Gospels see John Sieber, "A Redactional Analysis of the Synoptic Gospels with Regard to the Sources of the Gospel of Thomas" (Ph.D. diss., Claremont Graduate School); cf. also the important review of Schrage by R. McL. Wilson, *VigChr* 20 (1966) 118–123. Arguments for a dependence of the *Gospel of Thomas* upon the canonical Gospels have also been advanced by Jacque-E. Ménard, *L'Évangile selon Thomas* (NHS 5; Leiden Brill, 1975); idem, "La tradition synoptique et l'Évangile selon Thomas," in F. Paschke, ed., *Überlieferungsgeschichtliche Untersuchungen* (TU 125; Berlin: Akademie-Verlag, 1981) 411–26; B. Dehandshutter, "L'Évangile selon Thomas: témoin d'une tradition prélucanienne?" in: Frans Neirynck, ed., *L'Évangile de Luc* (BEThL 32; Gembloux: Duculot, 1973) 287–97; idem, "L'Évangile de Thomas comme collection des paroles de Jésus," in Delobel, ed., *LOGIA*, 507–15; J.-M. Sevrin, "L'Évangile selon Thomas: Paroles de Jésus et révélation gnostique," *RThL* 8 (1977) 265–92.

[4] Failure to demonstrate any consistency of dependence is again evident in the recent article of Klyne R. Snodgrass, "The Gospel of Thomas: A Secondary Gospel," *Second Century* 7 (1989–90) 19–38. Snodgrass completely ridicules with rhetorical questions all hypotheses about the development of the sayings tradition, and then procedes to show that the *Gospel of Thomas* has certain words and phrases in common with all four canonical Gospels. Without a theory about the pre-canonical history of the tradition, it is no wonder that dependence upon the canonical Gospels is the only possible answer. Nothing can be learned here. See the more balanced assessment and methodologically better informed essay by Charles W. Hedrick, "Thomas and the Synoptics: Aiming at a Consensus," *Second Century* 7 (1989–90) 39–56.

[5] This does not exclude intrusion of canonical sayings at a later stage of the Thomas tradition. That this tradition was not fixed, even in its written form, has correctly been emphasized by Kenneth V. Neller, "Diversity in the Gospel of Thomas," *Second Century* 7 (1989–90) 1–18. This had been stated well already by R. McL. Wilson in his review of Schrage (*Das Verhältnis des Thomas-Evangeliums zur synoptischen Tradition*) in

upon any of these Gospels.[1]

2.2.4.2 Thomas and the Synoptic Sayings Source (Q)[2]

One of the most striking features of the *Gospel of Thomas* is its silence on the matter of Jesus' death and resurrection—the keystone of Paul's missionary proclamation. But Thomas is not alone in this silence. The Synoptic Sayings Source (Q), used by Matthew and Luke, also does not consider Jesus' death a part of the Christian message. And it likewise is not interested in stories and reports about the resurrection and subsequent appearances of the risen Lord. The *Gospel of Thomas* and Q challenge the assumption that the early church was unanimous in making Jesus' death and resurrection the fulcrum of Christian faith. Both documents presuppose that Jesus' significance lay in his words, and in his words alone.

Another striking feature of the *Gospel of Thomas* is an almost total absence of christological titles, such as "Christ/Messiah," "Lord," and "Son of man." With respect to the latter title, the *Gospel of Thomas*

VigChr 20 (1966) 121: "Indeed the possibility that some logia were only added in the Coptic tradition is not to be excluded; but the direct copying of certain sayings word for word from a Coptic version of our Gospels would prove nothing for the collection as a whole—the Oxyrhynchus fragments show that some part at least was current in Greek, and moreover that this Greek version already had a manuscript tradition behind it."

[1] For a general review see Helmut Koester, "Introduction [to the Gospel of Thomas]," in Layton, ed., *Nag Hammadi Codex II*, 1. 40–43. Some of the studies which have argued for the independence of Thomas and its tradition include R. McL. Wilson, *Studies in the Gospel of Thomas* (London: Mowbray, 1960); Gilles Quispel, "Gnosis and the New Sayings of Jesus," *Eranos Jahrbuch* 38 (1969) 261–96; Robinson-Koester, *Trajectories*; J.-D. Kaestli, "L'évangile de Thomas: Son importance pour l'étude des paroles de Jésus et du gnosticisme chrétien," *Études Théologiques et Religieuses* 54 (1979) 375–96; S. L. Davis, *The Gospel of Thomas and Christian Wisdom* (New York: Seabury, 1983); John Dominic Crossan, *Four Other Gospels: Shadows on the Contours of Canon* (Winston: Minneapolis, 1985) 35–37; Layton, *Gnostic Scriptures*; now also Beate Blatz, "Das koptische Thomasevangelium," in Hennecke-Schneemelcher, *NT Apokryphen I*, 96. C. M. Tuckett (*Nag Hammadi and the Gospel Tradition* [Edinburgh: Clark, 1986]) does not deal specifically with the *Gospel of Thomas* but is open to the possibility of an independent preservation of gospel materials in this writing (see pp. 6–9). Stephen J. Patterson, has presented a detailed investigation of this question in his doctoral dissertation (Claremont Graduate School, 1988) which will be published in the near future. For this chapter of my book, I owe much to this dissertation and to the contributions of Stephen J. Patterson to our essay, "The Gospel of Thomas: Does it Contain Authentic Sayings of Jesus?" *Bible Review* 6/2 (1990) 28–39.

[2] The entire material that can be assigned to this collection of sayings is now well presented, both in the original Greek text and in an English translation, by John S. Kloppenborg, *Q Parallels: Synopsis, Critical Notes & Concordance* (F&F; Sonoma, CA: Polebridge Press, 1988).

and Q part company: In Q, the title "Son of man" plays a significant role as a designation of Jesus as the one who will appear from heaven at the end of the time: "As the lightning flashes and lights up the sky, so will the Son of man be in his day" (Luke 17:24). Similar statements about the Son of man also appear in the so-called Synoptic Apocalypse (Mark 13 and Matthew 24–25). But in recent studies, Dieter Lührmann[1] and, following him, John S. Kloppenborg,[2] have demonstrated that Q was composed in two successive stages and that the understanding of Jesus as the future Son of man was not yet present in the earlier stage of its composition. The sayings which speak about the coming of the Son of man for the final judgment and the addition of the title Son of man to older sayings[3] belong to the second stage of this document which originally presented Jesus as a teacher of wisdom and as a prophet who announced in his words the presence of the kingdom.

It is exactly with respect to the material that belongs to the earlier stage of Q, written probably within ten or twenty years of Jesus' death, that we find parallels in the *Gospel of Thomas*. Of the seventy-nine sayings of Thomas with Synoptic Gospel parallels, forty-six have parallels in Q, but the typical apocalyptic perspective of the later redaction of Q does not appear in any of these sayings. Rather, they are non-apocalyptic wisdom sayings, proverbs, prophetic sayings, parables, and community rules, as the following listing demonstrates.[4]

Q AND THOMAS
(*Q = also transmitted in Mark; Q/Matt = only in Matthew, but from Q)

Q / Luke	Thomas	Type of Saying	Title / Beginning
Q 6:20	# 54	prophetic saying	Blessed are the poor
Q 6:21	# 69b	prophetic saying	Blessed are the hungry
Q 6:22	# 68	prophetic saying	Blessed when hated
Q/Matt 5:8,10	# 69a	prophetic saying	Blessed the persecuted
Q 6:31	# 6	proverb	Golden Rule
Q 6:34a	# 95	wisdom saying	Lending at interest
Q 6:39	# 34	proverb	Blind leading the blind

---

[1] *Redaktion der Logienquelle.*

[2] *Formation of Q.*

[3] Cf. below the comparison of Gos. Thom. 68 and Luke 6:22.

[4] For the comparison of sayings in the synoptic and the apocryphal traditions, a useful synopsis of sayings in English translation has been published by John Dominic Crossan, *Sayings Parallels: A Workbook for the Jesus Tradition* (F&F; Philadelphia: Fortress, 1986).

Q 6:41–42	# 26	proverb	Speck in brother's eye
Q 6:43	# 43	proverb	Love tree, hate fruit
Q 6:44b–45	# 45	proverb	No figs from thorns
Q 7:24–25	# 78	wisdom saying	Why come into the desert
Q 7:28	# 46	prophetic saying	Superior to John
Q 9:58	# 86	wisdom saying	Foxes have holes
Q 10:2	# 72	community rule	The harvest is great
Q 10:8–9	# 14b	community rule	Eat what is before you
Q 10:22a	# 61b	wisdom saying	Given from the Father
Q 10:23–24	# 17	wisdom saying	What eye has not seen
Q 11:9–10	# 92, 94	wisdom saying	Seek and find
Q 11:27–28	# 79a	prophetic saying	Blessed the womb
*Q 11:33	# 33b	wisdom saying	Lamp under a bushel
Q 11:34–35a	# 24	wisdom saying	Eye lamp of the body
Q 11:39–40	# 89	community rule	Wash outside of the cup
Q 11:52	# 39	prophetic saying	Keys of knowledge
*Q 12:2	# 5, 6	wisdom saying	Hidden and revealed
Q 12:3	# 33a	prophetic saying	Preach from housetops
*Q 12:10	# 44	community rule	Blasphemy against Spirit
Q 12:13–14	# 73	community rule	Divide the possessions
Q 12:16–21[1]	# 63	parable	Rich fool
Q 12:22–31[2]	# 36[3]	wisdom saying	On cares
Q 12:33	# 76b	wisdom saying	Treasure in heaven
?Q 12:35	# 21c	wisdom saying	Guard against world
Q 12:39	# 21b, 103	parable	Thief in the night
Q 12:49	# 10	prophetic saying	Fire upon the earth
Q 12:51–53	# 16	prophetic saying	Peace on the earth?
Q 12:56	# 91	prophetic saying	Read face of sky & earth
*Q 13:18–19	# 20	parable	Mustard Seed
Q 13:20–21	# 96	parable	Leaven
Q 14:16–24	# 64	parable	Great banquet
Q 14:26	# 55a, 101	community rule	. . . hate his father

[1] There are no Matthean parallels to Luke 12:13–14 and 16–21. A majority of scholars hesitate to assign this and the following pericope to Q. However, there are good reasons for the inclusion: in style and wording, this section is closely related to the following Q section (12:22–46); see Kloppenborg, *Formation of Q*, 215; idem, *Q Parallels*, 128.

[2] Only parallels to vss. 22, 27a, and 31(?) are present in the Greek version of *Gos. Thom.* 36; see also the following note.

[3] The text of the Greek version in *Pap. Oxy.* 655 is much longer than the Coptic version of *Gos. Thom.* 36 ("Do not be concerned from morning until evening and from evening until morning what you will wear"); see Attridge, "Greek Fragments," 121–22 and 127.

*Q 14:27	# 55b	community rule	. . . take up his cross
Q 15:3–7	# 107	parable	Lost sheep
Q 16:13	# 47	proverb	Serving two masters
*Q 17:6	# 48	community rule	"Tree" move away
Q 17:20–21[1]	# 113	prophetic saying	Kingdom is among you
Q 17:34	# 61a	prophetic saying	Two will rest on a bed
*Q 19:26	# 41	prophetic saying	Who has will be given

Parallels in Thomas are especially frequent in sections of Q which became the basis of the Lukan Sermon on the Plain (Luke 6:20–49) and the Matthean Sermon on the Mount (Matthew 5–7). To Q/Luke 6:20–49, there are parallels to verses 20, 21, 22, 31,[2] 34, 39, 41–42, 43, 44b–45. To these sayings, which the *Gospel of Thomas* shares with Luke 6, one must add two sayings which occur in different contexts in Luke but belong to Matthew's "Sermon on the Mount" (*Gos. Thom.* 92, cf. 94, and 47a), and at least one Q saying preserved in Matthew only (Matt 5:8, 10). It is also striking that all apparent Lukan additions to Q are missing in the *Gospel of Thomas:* the curses against the rich (Luke 6:24–26)[3] and the Lukan additions to the saying about lending out money (6:34b–35).

In a number of instances Thomas has clearly preserved a more original form of the saying.

Gos. Thom. 68	Q/Luke 6:22
Blessed are you when you are hated and persecuted, and no place will be found, wherever you have been persecuted.	Blessed are you when people hate you, and when they exclude you and reproach you, and cast out your name as evil, on account of the Son of man.

The phrase "and cast out your name as evil on account of the Son of man" is certainly Lukan; it is missing in the parallel passage Matt 5:11. Moreover, the reference to persecution has disappeared in the Lukan redaction of this saying, but is preserved in Matt 5:11.

---

[1] Luke 17:20–21 is not included in Q by most scholars (see Kloppenborg, *Q Parallels,* 188). But the occurrence of the close parallel in *Gos. Thom.* 113 (see also *Gos. Thom.* 3) should prompt a reconsideration of this question.

[2] It is not certain whether this saying of the *Gospel of Thomas* is actually a parallel to the Q saying of Luke 6:31, the Golden Rule. One would have to translate *Gos. Thom.* 6 as follows: "Do not lie and do (to others) what you hate (to be done to you)."

[3] However, Lührmann (*Redaktion,* 105) assigns the curses to a later form of Q used only by Luke. Kloppenborg (*Formation of Q,* 172) states that "the close parallelism between the Lukan woes and beatitudes excludes the possibility that the woes circulated independently of 6:20–23b," but argues, at the same time, against Schürmann who defends the view that the woes are pre-Lukan; for an overview of the divided scholarly opinion see Kloppenborg, *Q Parallels,* 26.

Gos. Thom. 95	Q/Luke 6:34
If you have money, do not lend it at interest, but give [it] to one from whom you will not get back.	If you lend to those from whom you expect repayment, what credit is that to you? Even sinners lend to sinners to receive as much again.

The ending of Luke 6:34 ("Even sinners lend to sinners . . .") is a secondary addition in analogy to the ending of the preceding saying Luke 6:33 ("Even sinners do that"). Matt 5:42 reads, "Give to the one who asks you, and do not refuse one who wants to borrow from you." This may have preserved the wording of the original saying better than Luke 6:34, and Thomas's version can be best explained as a development of this form.

Gos. Thom. 47a-b	Q/Matt 6:24/Luke 16:13
It is impossible for a man to mount two horses or to stretch two bows. And it is impossible for a servant to serve two masters; otherwise he will honor the one and treat the other contemptuously.	No servant can serve two masters; for either he will hate the one and love the other or he will be loyal to the one and despise the other. You cannot serve God and mammon.

Most scholars would argue that "servant" in Luke 16:13 is a later addition, while Matthew's "no one" is an accurate reproduction of the text of Q. However, the version of *Gos. Thom.* 47a-b stays completely within the limits of natural expansion of a popular proverb by prefixing the analogous examples of mounting two horses or stretching two bows. Thomas's version, at the same time, shows no sign of the unnecessary duplication "hate the one and love the other" and of the secondary application of the proverb (serving God and mammon).[1] Both of these appear already in Q; thus *Gos. Thom.* 47b presents the form that this proverb would have had before it was incorporated into Q. Had Thomas read the final phrase in his text, he would certainly have incorporated it (cf. the rejection of worldly possessions in *Gos. Thom.* 110).

While the sayings in this section of Q are mostly sayings of secular wisdom, another Q section contains a larger number of prophetic sayings and community rules: Q/Luke 11:27–12:56. Here the parallels in the *Gospel of Thomas* are even more complete with sayings corresponding to Q = Luke 11:27–28, 33, 34–35a, 39–40, 52; 12:2, 3, 10,

---

[1] Bultmann (*Synoptic Tradition,* 87): "The concluding sentence in particular, with its application in the second person, gives the impression of being an edifying addition."

13–14, 16–21, 22–31, 33, 35, 39, 49, 51–53, 56. Perhaps also Luke 17:20–21, 34 belonged to the same part of Q. With these sayings of Q, the parallels in the *Gospel of Thomas* share the prophetic perspective and emphasize the eschatological presence of the salvation in Jesus and his words.

For this section of Q/Luke it is also instructive to ask which materials are not represented among the sayings of the *Gospel of Thomas*. They are mostly materials which must be assigned to the final redaction of Q:[1] The Sign of Jonah (Matt 12:38–42 = Luke 11:29–32); most of the material from the speech against the Pharisees (Luke 11:39–52);[2] only two isolated sayings appear, and only one of these is directed against the Pharisees (see below) while there is no trace in Thomas of the other materials which Matthew has assembled in his much more inclusive speech against the Pharisees (Matthew 23). There are no parallels in Thomas to the persecution sayings of Matt 10:17–20, 28–33 (= Luke 12:2–9, 11–12), nor to the allegory of the master of the house returning late from a wedding (Luke 12:36–38)—a secondary Lukan composition without a parallel in Matthew.[3] There is also no trace of the admonitions to watch for the coming of the Son of man (Matt 24:44 = Luke 12:40), of the parable of the Faithful and the Unfaithful Servant (Luke 12:41–46 = Matt 24:45–50)—both are elements of the secondary apocalyptic redaction of Q—and of the parable of the Servant's Wages (Luke 12:47–48) which was added by Luke from his special source. Finally the sayings about the coming of the Son of man in Q/Luke 17 do not appear in Thomas.

A number of observations on some of the sayings of this section confirm the thesis that the parallels of the *Gospel of Thomas* to this Q section are probably related to the very earliest stage of the composition of the Synoptic Sayings Source.

Gos. Thom. 89	Q/Luke 11:39–40
Jesus said, "Why do you wash the outside of the cup?	And the Lord said to him, "Now you Pharisees cleanse the outside of the cup and the dish, but inside you are full of extortion and wickedness? You fools!

---

[1] See Lührmann (*Redaktion,* passim) and Kloppenborg (*Formation of Q,* passim).

[2] The composition of the Q speech against the Pharisees belongs to the final stage of the development of this document; see Kloppenborg, *Formation of Q,* 139–47.

[3] Unless one wants to refer to the parable of the Ten Virgins of Matt 25:1–13.

Do you not realize that he who made the inside is the same one who made the outside?"	Did not he who made the outside make the inside also?"

This is the first of the two sayings which Thomas shares with the synoptic speech against the Pharisees. However, it can be understood as a community rule rather than a polemical saying. There is no reference to the Pharisees; the accusation that those who practice such purification "are full of extortion and wickedness" is missing, as is the slanderous "You fools!" That *Gos. Thom.* 89 reverses the order "outside/inside" in the second part of the saying is of no consequence because there is no polemical intent.

Gos. Thom. 39	Q/Luke 11:52
The Pharisees and the scribes have taken the keys of knowledge. You yourselves did not enter, and you prevented those who were trying to enter.	Woe to you lawyers (Matt: scribes and Pharisees, hypocrites)! for you have taken away the keys of knowledge and hidden them. They themselves have not entered, nor have they allowed to enter those who wish to.

In this saying, Thomas mentions explicitly the Pharisees and scribes. "Scribes and Pharisees" (Matt 23:13) is most likely the designation used in Q, rather than the typically Lukan "lawyers."[1] On the other hand, the notorious Matthean addition "hypocrites" (fourteen times in Matthew) is missing in *Gos. Thom.* 39.[2] Thomas preserves the original form of this saying.[3]

Gos. Thom. 44	Q/Luke 12:10[4]
Whoever blasphemes against the Father, will be forgiven,	And everyone who says a word against the Son of man will be forgiven,

---

[1] Cf. Luke 7:30; 10:25; 11:45, 46, 53; 14:3.

[2] It is rare in the other Synoptic Gospels; in Mark only 7:6; in Luke only three times in 6:42; 12:56; 13:15.

[3] There is, however, another saying about the Pharisees, formulated as a curse, which has no synoptic parallel, *Gos. Thom.* 102: "Woe to the Pharisees, for they are like a dog sleeping in a manger of oxen, for neither does he eat nor does he [let] the oxen eat."

[4] A variant of this Q saying has been preserved in Mark 3:28–29. This version may have influenced the text of Matthew.

and whoever blasphemes against the Son will be forgiven, but whoever blasphemes against the Holy Spirit will not be forgiven, either on earth or in heaven.

but the one who blasphemes against the Holy Spirit will not be forgiven. (Matt adds: either in this age or the coming one.)

The transmission of this saying in the Synoptic Gospels is complex. There are five different elements which appear in different combinations in the several variants (Luke 12:10; Mark 3:28–29; Matt 12:31–32; *Gos. Thom.* 44):

(1) Any kind of blasphemy (forgiven): Mark and Matthew.
(2) Blasphemy against the Father (forgiven): *Gospel of Thomas*.
(3) "Word" against the Son of man (forgiven): Luke and Matthew.
(4) Blasphemy against the Son (forgiven): *Gospel of Thomas*.
(5) Blasphemy against the Holy Spirit (unforgivable): all versions (Matthew twice).

Luke 12:10 is considered to be closest to the original Q version by most scholars; however, "Son of man" as a title of Jesus would have to be assigned to the later stage of Q. But even here it remains extremely awkward.[1] The best solution is to assume that Q, like Mark, was originally speaking about the blasphemy against the Holy Spirit,[2] uttered by "a son of man" = any human being, and that "son of man" was later misunderstood as a title of Jesus.[3] In the collection of sayings used by the *Gospel of Thomas* this saying probably was formulated like Mark 3:28–29; the elaboration in *Gos. Thom.* 44 is then best explained as an independent development. The final phrase which *Gos. Thom.* 44 and Matt 12:32 share may have been an original part of Q.

Q/Luke 12:16–21 = *Gos. Thom.* 63, the parable of the Rich Fool is presented in Thomas in a form that is clearly superior to the Lukan version (see the discussion below in the section on parables).

---

[1] See the detailed discussion in Kloppenborg, *Formation of Q*, 208–14.

[2] See the rule in *Did.* 11.7: "Do not test or examine any prophet who is speaking in the spirit; for every sin shall be forgiven, but this sin shall not be forgiven." This is most likely the earliest form of this community rule.

[3] "Mark has the relatively most original form: everything can be forgiven the sons of men (originally the son of man, i.e., men) save the blasphemy against the Spirit . . . (The form in Q) arose from a misunderstanding: any word spoken against the Son of man (i.e. against Jesus) can be forgiven . . ." (Bultmann, *Synoptic Tradition*, 131).

Gos. Thom. 10	Q/Luke 12:49
I have cast fire upon the world, and see, I am guarding it until it blazes.	I came to cast fire upon the earth; and would that it were already kindled.

Luke 12:50

I have a baptism to be baptized with; and how I am in anguish until it is over.

Gos. Thom. 16	Q/Luke 12:51–53
People think, perhaps, that it is peace which I have come to cast upon the world. They do not know that it is dissension which I have come to cast upon the earth: fire, sword, and war. For there will be five in a house: three will be against two, and two against three,	Do you think that I have come to give peace on earth? No, I tell you, but rather division. For henceforth in a house there will be five divided, three against two and two against three; they will be divided,
the father against the son, and the son against the father.	father against son, and son against father, mother against her daughter, mother-in-law against her daughter-in-law and daughter-in-law against her mother-in-law.

Thomas's version of these sayings lacks Luke 12:50, certainly an addition by the author of the Gospel.[1] Also missing in the *Gospel of Thomas* is the pedantic, and certainly secondary, enlargement of the family relationships at the end of Luke 12:53. Instead of Luke's "division" (vs. 51), *Gos. Thom.* 16 has "fire, sword, and war," probably an expansion of the original reading of Q, "sword," which is preserved in Matt 10:14.

Gos. Thom. 91	Q/Luke 12:56
You read the face of the sky and of the earth, but you have not recognized the one who is before you, and you do not know how to read this moment?	Hypocrites! You know how to interpret the appearance of the earth and the sky; but why do you not know how to interpret the present time?

There is no trace in Thomas of the first part of this saying (Q/Luke 12:54–55). The secondary address "hypocrites" of Luke 12:56 (no

---

[1] Cf. Bultmann (*Synoptic Tradition,* 153–54) on Luke 12:50 as a secondary development of Luke 12:49.

parallel in Matt 16:3b) is missing in Thomas as is Matthew's expansion *"the signs* of the time."

There are fewer parallels in the *Gospel of Thomas* to other sections of Q. Parallels to the Q sections about the preaching of repentance of John the Baptist, the baptism of Jesus, and the temptation story (Luke 3:22–4:13) are missing completely, though John the Baptist is mentioned (*Gos. Thom.* 46 = Q/Luke 7:28).[1] Only occasionally does Thomas bring an isolated saying paralleling any of the Q materials in Luke 8–10 and 13–16.[2] It is remarkable that there are no Thomas parallels to any of the materials which Luke draws from his special source.[3] Only once does Thomas include a saying that Luke did not draw from either Mark or Q: "No one drinks old wine and immediately desires to drink new wine" (*Gos. Thom.* 47c = Luke 5:39)—evidently a free proverb.

The materials which the *Gospel of Thomas* and Q share must belong to a very early stage of the transmission of Jesus' sayings. All of them fit well in the first composition of the Synoptic Sayings Source.[4] In a few instances, a saying reflects Matthew's rather than Luke's wording; in these instances, there are good reasons to believe that Matthew has preserved the original wording of Q. Thus, the *Gospel of Thomas* is either dependent upon the earliest version of Q or, more likely, shares with the author of Q one or several very early collections of Jesus' sayings. However, these collections are of a different character than the one used in Corinth which emphasized the mediation of secret revelation through the words of Jesus. Yet neither do they reflect a purely proverbial wisdom orientation; rather, prophetic sayings are included which incorporate the wisdom material into the perspective of a realized eschatology, centered upon the presence of revelation in the words of Jesus.

---

[1] This is the only Thomas parallel to the discussion of John the Baptist in Q/Luke 7:18–35 in which John is actually mentioned. The saying Q/Luke 7:24–25 ("What did you go out into the desert to see?") has a parallel in *Gos. Thom.* 78, but the introduction relating this saying to John is missing.

[2] The Q parables of Luke 13:18–19, 20–21; 14:16–24; 15:4–7 will be discussed in the following section.

[3] The only exceptions could be Luke 12:13–14 and 16–21, if they are assigned to Luke's special source rather than to Q.

[4] Kloppenborg (*Formation of Q,* passim) and Lührmann (*Redaktion,* passim) occasionally assign a saying of Q that has a parallel in the *Gospel of Thomas* to the later stage in the redaction of this document. However, in no instance does such a saying reflect the tendencies of the redactor.

2.2.4.3 Thomas and the Parables of Jesus

(1) Thomas's Parables and the Synoptic Sayings Source

There are total of twelve similitudes and parables in the Synoptic Sayings Source. The *Gospel of Thomas* includes parallels to half of these parables.

Parable	Q/Luke	Gos. Thom.
The Builders	Q 6:47–49	———
Children at Play	Q 7:31–32	———
Rich Fool	Q 12:16–21[1]	# 63
Watchful Servants	Q 12:35–38[2]	———
Thief in the Night	Q 12:39	# 21b, 103
Faithful & Unfaithful Servant	Q 12:42–46	———
Mustard Seed	Q 13:18–19[3]	# 20
Leaven	Q 13:20–21	# 96
Great Banquet	Q 14:16–24	# 64
Lost Sheep	Q 15:3–7	# 107
Lost Coin	Q 15:8–10[4]	———
Talents	Q 19:12–27	———

It cannot be determined with certainty whether the Q parables which are missing in Thomas belong to the earlier stage of Q or to its later redaction. The Builders (Q 6:47–49) is assigned to the first stage of Q.[5] Children at Play is connected with the Q pericope about John the Baptist and, in this context, would belong to the second stage of Q.[6] The section Q/Luke 7:18–25 is certainly dominated by redactional perspectives, and several layers of views of the relationship between Jesus and John are combined into a complex unit.[7] The parable itself, without the application to John the Baptist,[8] could have been part of

---

[1] It is transmitted only in Luke without a parallel in Matthew, but is most likely a Q parable; see above the discussion of Thomas and Q.

[2] A Matthean parallel is missing, unless one considers the parable of the Ten Virgins (Matt 25:1–13) to be Matthew's replacement for this Q section. For a survey of opinions see Kloppenborg, *Q Parallels,* 136.

[3] This parable is also transmitted in Mark 4:30–32. Thomas's form of the parable is more closely related to Mark than to Q and will be discussed in the next section.

[4] There is no parallel in Matthew for this Lukan parable. The close connection with the preceding parable of the Lost Sheep could indicate that the two parables were already joined in Luke's source. For a brief survey of the divided opinion of scholars, see Kloppenborg, *Q Parallels,* 176.

[5] Kloppenborg, *Formation of Q,* 185–90. It fits well into the sapiential speech character of Q 6:20–49.

[6] Kloppenborg, *Formation of Q,* 115–17.

[7] Lührmann, *Redaktion,* 24–31.

[8] For the original form of the parable see Bultmann, *Synoptic Tradition,* 172.

an earlier stage of Q, but it is difficult to assign it to a particular context.[1] The Watchful Servants (Luke 12:35–38) is not a true parable, but a secondary composition of metaphors.[2] If it was a part of Q, it certainly comes from the hand of the redactor who introduced the apocalyptic orientation. That same redactor is also responsible for the parable of the Faithful and Unfaithful Servant (Q/Luke 12:42–46), which expresses clearly the unexpected coming of the parousia.[3] Whether the Lost Coin (Luke 15:8–10) was part of Q remains uncertain at best. The last of the Q parables (19:12–27) which is missing in Thomas expresses the redactor's theme of judgment and thus belongs to the later stage of Q.[4]

All of the parables which certainly belong to the later stage of Q, and one parable which cannot be assigned to Q with certainty (Luke 15:8–10), are missing in the *Gospel of Thomas*. Of the parables included in the early composition of Q, only one does not have a parallel in Thomas (Luke 6:47–49). To be sure, it can be argued that the author of this gospel would not have chosen clearly apocalyptic materials in any case. Even so, those who argue for a dependence of the *Gospel of Thomas* upon the canonical gospels must assume that its author was quite capable of using materials whenever they suited his purposes. It seems more likely, however, that Thomas not only had direct access to the traditions which formed the basis of Q's earliest composition, but that he also preserved forms of such materials which are more original than the forms in which they are extant in the common sayings source of Matthew and Luke. The following examples will demonstrate this.

Gos. Thom. 63	Q/Luke 12:16–21
There was a rich man who had much money. He said, "I shall put my money to use so that I may sow, reap, plant and fill my storehouse with produce, with the result that I shall lack nothing.	The land of a rich man brought forth plentifully. And he thought to himself, "What shall I do, for I have nowhere to store my crops?" And he said, "I will do this: I will pull down my granaries, and build larger ones; and there I will store all my grain and my goods. And I will say to myself,

---

[1] Luke 7:31–35 "could have been combined with the two preceding sections only after the secondary interpretation had been added to the parable, because a thematic connection (with John the Baptist) is established only through this addition" (Lührmann, *Redaktion*, 30).

[2] Bultmann, *Synoptic Tradition*, 118.

[3] "The master of the servant will come on a day when he does not expect him and at an hour he does not know" (Luke 12:46); see Kloppenborg, *Formation of Q*, 150–51.

[4] Lührmann, *Redaktion*, 70–71; Kloppenborg, *Formation of Q*, 164–65.

'Soul, you have many goods laid up for many years; rest, eat, drink, be merry.'"

Such were his intentions, but the same night he died.

Let him who has ears hear.

But God said to him, "Fool! this night your soul is required of you; and the things you have prepared, whose will they be?" So is whoever lays up treasure for himself, and is not rich in the sight of God.

There are two secondary features in the narrative of Luke: the conclusion[1] and the moralizing discourse. Both are missing in Thomas's version which presents this story in the more original form of a reversal parable. On the other hand, Thomas has also transferred the parable into a different milieu. The rich man is no longer a wealthy farmer but a decurion from the city who wants to invest his money successfully. The maxim at the end of *Gos. Thom.* 63 is of course secondary, but it does not reveal any knowledge of Luke's conclusion.

Gos. Thom. 21b[2]	Q/Luke 12:39–40
Therefore I say, "If the owner of a house knows that the thief is coming, he will begin his vigil before he comes and will not let him dig through into his house of his domain to carry away his goods.	But know this, if the owner of the house had known what hour the thief was coming, he would not have left his house to be dug into.
	You also must be ready; for the Son of man is coming at an hour you do not expect.

The Q version has shortened the parable, leaving out the purpose of the coming of the thief, i.e., to steal the goods of the owner of the house. That Q's parable presupposed such a continuation of the parable and was not simply an expansion of the metaphor of the "day of the Lord coming like the thief in the night" (1 Thess 5:2; Rev 3:3), is evident in the phrase "to be dug into." Thomas's version suggests that the parable was cut short in Q in order to add the reference to the coming of the Son of man.

---

[1] See Bultmann, *Synoptic Tradition,* 178, who also suggests that this conclusion may not have been a part of Luke's original text because it is missing in D and in two Vetus *Latina* manuscripts.

[2] A similar version of this parable is preserved in *Gos. Thom.* 103:

Fortunate is the man who knows where the brigands will enter, so that [he] may get up, muster his domain, and arm himself before they invade.

The absence of secondary apocalyptic motifs is also evident in Thomas's version of the parable of the Great Banquet (Q/Luke 14:16–23 = *Gos. Thom.* 64).[1] Matt 25:2–10 has allegorized this parable.[2] Luke also added some allegorical features when he appended the second invitation to those "on the roads and hedges" of the countryside (Luke 14:23), apparently a reference to the Gentile mission.[3] At the end of his parable Thomas reports only the invitation to those on the streets of the city, and there are no traces of any allegorization in his version. This version is based unquestionably upon the original form of the parable and not on either Matthew or Luke. On the other hand, Thomas has changed the excuses of the first invited guests so that they reflect more closely the milieu of the city. There are four invitations, instead of three, and the excuses are "I have claims against some merchants," "I have bought a house," "My friend is to be married," and "I am on my way to collect rent from a farm." At the end Thomas adds, "Businessmen and merchants [will] not enter the places of my Father." No doubt, this is a secondary application.

Similar observations could be made with respect to the parables of the Leaven and the Lost Sheep. In the case of the latter parable, *Gos. Thom.* 107 lacks the secondary applications found in Matt 18:14 ("So it is not the will of my father who is in heaven that one of these little ones should perish") and Luke 16:7 ("There will be more joy in heaven over one sinner repenting than over ninety-nine righteous persons who need no repentance").[4] The parable of the Mustard Seed, which belongs with the parables that Thomas shares with Mark, will be discussed in the next section.

In the case of the five parables common to Q and Thomas, it is evident that they derive either from an early stage of Q or from an earlier collection which the compiler of Q also used. Such a collection was still very close to the telling of stories in the oral tradition, not a source dominated by the redactional activity of a writer who wanted to impress his theology upon the materials he used. Thus the parables of the *Gospel of Thomas* are to be read as stories in their own right, not as artificial expressions of some hidden Gnostic truth.[5]

---

[1] A detailed and helpful discussion of this Thomas parable in relation to its Synoptic parallels has been presented by Crossan, *Four Other Gospels*, 39–52.

[2] Bultmann, *Synoptic Tradition*, 175. Matthew "has allegorized the parable into an image of the history of salvation" (John Dominic Crossan, *In Parables: The Challenge of the Historical Jesus* [New York: Harper & Row, 1973] 71). See also the detailed comparison of the several versions in James Breech, *The Silence of Jesus: The Authentic Voice of the Historical Man* (Toronto: Doubleday, 1982) 114–23.

[3] Bultmann, *Synoptic Tradition*, 175; Crossan, *In Parables*, 71–72.

[4] Bultmann, *Synoptic Tradition*, 171.

[5] On this problem see my essay, "Three Thomas Parables," in A. H. B. Logan and

(2) Thomas and Mark

What is missing in the Synoptic Sayings Source are most of the parables which appear in the parable chapters of Mark (chapter 4) and Matthew (chapter 13).[1] In addition to the parables shared with Q, the *Gospel of Thomas* knows at least two of the parables of Mark 4: the Sower (Mark 4:3–9 = *Gos. Thom.* 9) and the Mustard Seed (Mark 4:30–32 = *Gos. Thom.* 20).[2] It is also possible that the parable of the Seed Growing Secretly (Mark 4:26–29) is reflected in *Gos. Thom.* 21 ("Let there be among you a man of understanding. When the grain ripened, he came quickly with his sickle in his hand and reaped it"). However, this latter parable may not have been part of the original Markan text (it is not reproduced by Matthew and Luke)[3] and may, therefore, not be related to the source of Mark 4.

The theory that the parables of Jesus are "secrets" (μυστήρια) is completely alien to Q. However, this theory may have served very early as a theme for the collection of some of Jesus' parables. The respective statement in Mark 4:11–12 is not attributable to Mark's redactorial work,[4] but must have been part of the source used by Mark 4. What is strange in the text of Mark is the use of the term "secret" (μυστήριον), and especially its use in the singular as a characterization of the entire parable-teaching of Jesus as a "mystery." The term does not occur anywhere else in the canonical gospels except for the two synoptic parallels of Mark 4:11 (Matt 13:11; Luke 8:10) which both read the plural "secrets" or "mysteries" (μυστήρια). In any case, it is not a typically Markan term at all. However, if Mark inherited the term together with the parables of chapter 4, the plural would have been appropriate. Matthew and Luke may have preserved the original

---

A. J. M. Wedderburn, eds., *The New Testament and Gnosis: Essays in Honor of Robert McL. Wilson* (Edinburgh: Clark, 1983) 195–203.

[1] The only overlap of Mark and Q is the parable of the Mustard Seed (Mark 4:20–32 and Q/Luke 13:18–19).

[2] Both emphasize the smallness of the mustard seed—a feature which is missing in the Q form of the parable (Luke 13:18–19).

[3] See below on the relationship of the original text of Mark to the canonical Gospel of Mark, # 4.1.2.1.

[4] Most scholars consider Mark 4:11–12 as an editorial insertion by the author of the Gospel, especially because of the introductory phrase καὶ ἔλεγεν αὐτοῖς, cf. Joachim Jeremias, *The Parables of Jesus* (rev. ed.; London: SCM, New York: Scribner's, 1963) 13–18 (however, Jeremias's view is that the saying of vss. 11–12 is an older Palestinian tradition); Heinz-Wolfgang Kuhn, *Ältere Sammlungen im Markusevangelium* (StUNT 8; Göttingen: Vandenhoeck & Ruprecht, 1971) 130–32; Dieter Lührmann, *Das Markusevangelium* (HNT 3; Tübingen: Mohr/Siebeck, 1987) 85–88.

text of Mark 4:11 and thus also of Mark's source.[1] In that case, each of the parables is designated as a "secret" which requires interpretation.[2]

That the term "secrets" belongs to an older tradition of the parables is confirmed by the *Gospel of Thomas* where the same designation appears in the plural in the introduction to a collection of three parables:

> It is to those [who are worthy of my] mysteries that I tell my mysteries. Do not let your left hand know what your right hand is doing. (# 62)

It is possible that the three following parables, Rich Fool (# 63), Great Banquet (# 64), and Wicked Tenants (# 65), may have formed a unit, introduced by the word about the "mysteries," before they were included into the present text of the *Gospel of Thomas*. The author of this Gospel does not make any attempt to spell out this theory of the secret with respect to the parables which follow; he also cites parables elsewhere in the gospel without ever indicating their esoteric character. All three parables of this small collection have Synoptic parallels. The Rich Fool appears in Luke only, but most likely came to Luke from the Synoptic Sayings Source (see above). The Great Banquet also belongs to Q (Matt 21:1–10 = Luke 14:16–24). However, the third parable, the Wicked Husbandmen, came to Matthew (21:33–41) and Luke (10:9–17) from the Gospel of Mark (12:1–9).

In Mark 12 as well as in *Gos. Thom.* 65, the parable of the Wicked Husbandmen is connected with the saying about the rejection of the cornerstone (Mark 12:10–11 = *Gos. Thom.* 66). This is not a Markan addition to the parable; Mark's own redactional connection, leading back into the previous context that was interrupted by the insertion of the parable, appears in 12:12–13 with an explicit reference to the parable ("they understood that he said this parable about them"). Thus the saying about the rejected cornerstone was already connected with the parable in Mark's source. However, Thomas does not reflect Mark's editorial connection of parable and saying but cites the saying as an independent unit.[3] Mark's source may have contained more

---

[1] The question of the preservation of Mark's original text in the extant manuscripts of this Gospel will be discussed below in more detail (# 4.1.2.2).

[2] Jeremias (*Parables,* 14–16) rightly argues for the traditional character of Mark 4:11–12 and also connects the meaning of "parable" with Hebrew מָשָׁל = "riddle," "saying." But he fails to relate this observation to the Pauline usage where "mystery" is always a single saying or piece of tradition that requires interpretation.

[3] In Thomas the saying about the stone rejected by the builders (# 66) has its own introduction ("Jesus said"). "If one had only *Thomas,* therefore, one would not imagine any special connection between *Gos. Thom.* 65 and 66" (Crossan, *Four Other Gospels,* 54).

than one parable. The introduction (Mark 12:1) says: "And he began to speak to them in parables" but only one parable follows.[1] Whether or not this parable of Mark 12 derives from the same collection as the parables of Mark 4, it is evident that the sources of Mark and the *Gospel of Thomas* were closely related.

It has been debated, whether Thomas's version of the parable of the Wicked Tenants exhibits more original features than the allegorical version of Mark 12. *Gos. Thom.* 65 lacks the allusions to the parable of the Vineyard of Isaiah 5, and it fits very well the economic situation in Palestine of that period.[2] That this non-allegorical version still does not qualify as an original parable of Jesus[3] is no argument against the existence of such a version in a source that was used by Mark 12.[4]

That Thomas preserves a more original stage of that source of Mark is strikingly demonstrated by a comparison of the two versions of the parable of the Sower (Mark 4:3–9 = *Gos. Thom.* 9). Crossan[5] and Cameron[6] have shown that the text of the Markan parable is influenced by the allegorical interpretation which follows in Mark 4:13–20. The following synopsis will show that (secondary Markan additions in italics):

Gos. Thom. 9	Mark 4:3–9
Now the sower went out, took a handful (of seeds), and scattered them.	Behold, the sower went out to sow.
Some fell on the road; the birds came and gathered them.	And it happened in the sowing that some fell on the road; and the birds came and ate them.

---

[1] Matthew (22:33) and Luke (20:9) correct the introduction accordingly.

[2] This has been demonstrated by Martin Hengel, "Das Gleichnis von den Weingärtnern Mc 12,1–12 im Lichte der Zenopapyri und der rabbinischen Gleichnisse," *ZNW* 59 (1968) 1–39.

[3] Against Lührmann (*Markusevangelium,* 199–200) who uses this argument in order to maintain his claim that the Thomas version is "a reduction of the version of Mark."

[4] See also my essay, "Three Thomas Parables," in A. H. B. Logan and A. J. M. Wedderburn, eds., *The New Testament and Gnosis: Essays in Honor of Robert McL. Wilson* (Edinburgh: Clark, 1983) 199–200.

[5] Crossan, *In Parables,* 39–44.

[6] Ron Cameron, *Parable and Interpretation in the Gospel of Thomas* (F&F 2.2; Sonoma, CA: Polebridge Press, 1986) 20–21.

Others fell on rock, did not take root in the soil	And others fell on rock where it did not have enough soil, *and immediately it sprouted because it did not have depths of soil, and when the sun came up it was scorched*
(did not take root in the soil) and did not produce ears. And others fell on thorns, they choked the seeds and worms ate them.	because it did not have roots, and it withered. And others fell in the thorns and it sprouted and the thorns choked it, *and it did not produce grain.*
And others fell on good soil and it produced good fruit: it bore sixty per measure and a hundred and twenty per measure.	And others fell on good soil and it produced fruit, *growing up and increasing,* and it bore thirty and sixty and hundredfold.

(3) *Thomas and Matthew*

There are four parables in the *Gospel of Thomas* which have parallels only among Matthew's additions to his reproduction of the Markan parable chapter. The first of these is the parable of the Tares (*Gos. Thom.* 57 = Matt 13:24–30). Thomas tells this parable in a somewhat shorter version but, like Matthew, ends with the reference to the burning of the weeds at harvest time, possibly a reference to the last judgment. But there is no trace of the allegorical interpretation which Matthew (13:36–43) has appended. The other three parallels to Matthew 13 are found in *Gos. Thom.* 109, 76, and 8:

Gos. Thom. 109	Matt 13:44
The kingdom is like a man who had a hidden treasure in his field without knowing it. And [after] he died, he left it to his [son]. The son [did] not know (about the treasure). He inherited the field and sold [it]. And the one who bought it went plowing and [found] the treasure. He began to lend money at interest to whomever he wished.	The kingdom of heaven is like treasure hidden in a field which a man found and covered up; then in his joy he goes and sells all that he has and buys that field.

Gos. Thom. 76	Matt 13:45–46
The kingdom of the Father is like a merchant who had a consignment of merchandise and who discovered a pearl. That merchant was shrewd. He sold the merchandise and bought the pearl alone for himself.	Again the kingdom of heaven is like a merchant in search of fine pearls, who, on finding one pearl of great value, went and sold all that he had and bought that pearl.

| You too seek his unfailing and enduring treasure where no moth comes near to devour and no worm destroys. | = Matt 6:19–20; Luke 12:33 |

Gos. Thom. 8	Matt 13:47–50
The man is like a wise fisherman who cast his net into the sea and drew it up from the sea full of small fish. Among them the wise fisherman found a fine large fish. He threw all the small fish back into the sea and chose the large fish without difficulty. Whoever has ears to hear, let him hear.	The kingdom of heaven is like a net which was thrown into the sea and gathered fish of every kind; when it was full, men drew it ashore and sat down and sorted the good into a vessel, but threw away the bad.
	So it will be at the close of the age. The angels will come out and separate the evil from the righteous and throw them into the furnace of fire; there men will weep and gnash their teeth.

The comparison of these three parables with their Matthean counterparts is particularly instructive. In the third of these parables, the Fisherman, Thomas has preserved the intent of the wisdom parable better than Matthew: it is a wisdom parable, "told about the discovery of one's own destiny," one of the stories "about a person who finds, discards, and chooses the one fine thing."[1] Matthew, changing the parable of the Fisherman into a parable of the Fishnet, has produced an allegory for the last judgment—a secondary development.

The relationship of the other two parables in the *Gospel of Thomas* to the original form of these parables is complex.[2] In the Pearl, the Thomas version has been contaminated by elements from the parable of the Treasure: the merchant is not in search of fine pearls, but finds one by accident, like the man who "finds" a treasure in the field, and a treasure saying is added at the end (= Matt 6:19–20; Luke 12:33). Thus the author is quite aware of the traditional association of the two parables.

The original parable of the Hidden Treasure, however, is not actually quoted by Thomas. If one considers *Gos. Thom.* 109 as a quotation of that parable, one arrives at a judgment like Jeremias's, who called it "utterly confused." But Jeremias already recognized that *Gos. Thom.*

---

[1] Cameron, *Parable and Interpretation,* 29.

[2] For a most instructive and elaborate analysis and interpretation see John Dominic Crossan, *Finding is the First Act: Trove Folktales and Jesus' Treasure Parable* (Philadelphia: Fortress, 1979).

109 is actually a reproduction of a rabbinic parable where the story describes how angry one can get if one misses such an opportunity.[1] This story, otherwise widespread in folklore and in the complex legal Talmudic discussion about ownership of treasures found,[2] has been deliberately changed by the *Gospel of Thomas*. It says nothing about the angry reaction of the first owner of the field (who is actually dead when the treasure is discovered!), but emphasizes that the two original owners of the field "did not know about the treasure." The contrast in the parable is, therefore, between not knowing and finding, that is, "knowing."[3] Since "treasure" has at this point in the story clearly become a metaphor, the following "lending money at interest to whomever he wished" must be understood metaphorically as the communication of knowledge.[4]

In Matthew all four parables are introduced as parables of the kingdom of heaven. Thomas introduces two of these parables with "The kingdom of the Father is like. . ." (## 57 and 76) and one of them with "The kingdom is like. . ." (# 109). Moreover, many scholars have argued that in # 8 (Fishnet) the peculiar introduction "The man is like a wise fisherman" has replaced a reference to the kingdom.[5] Similar introductory phrases are used elsewhere in Thomas for parables, but they are relatively rare: "kingdom of the Father" also in ## 96, 97, and 98 (the latter two do not have synoptic parallels), "kingdom" also in # 107, and "kingdom of heaven" in # 20. *Gos. Thom.* ## 8, 9, 21a, 21b, 21d, 60, 63, 64, 65 are reproduced without a special introduction. That all four parables which Thomas shares with Matthew's special material were introduced with a reference to the kingdom could indicate that both used a common source. The parable introductions— "the kingdom is like . . ."—do not belong to the original wording of any of the parables, especially not to parables introducing the behavior or

---

[1] Jeremias, *Parables,* 32–33.

[2] See the monograph of Crossan quoted above.

[3] Crossan (ibid., 106) says: "The Gnostic story is not interested in indolence as against industry but in ignorance as against knowledge."

[4] Andreas Lindemann ("Zur Gleichnisinterpretation im Thomasevangelium," *ZNW* 71 [1980] 233–34) suggests as the (Gnostic?) interpretation that the hearer is requested to work hard with whatever he has in order to find the kingdom of God. However, in the present context the parable has a negative meaning, because what the finder does with his treasure is rejected in the following saying (# 110: "Whoever finds the world and becomes rich, let him renounce the world"). The problem with this interpretation is that the context of the sayings in the *Gospel of Thomas* is a notoriously poor guide to their interpretation, although it may well have preserved traditional associations of materials.

[5] For references to other literature see Cameron, *Parable and Interpretation,* 26–27, especially nn. 67 and 68.

action of a particular person, like the Pearl and the Treasure. In any case, Thomas draws on a tradition that contained the secondary introduction "the kingdom is like . . . ," which is also reproduced in the parables of Matthew 13.

Of the four parables of the *Gospel of Thomas* without synoptic parallels, three occur in the last part of this gospel. Two are introduced as parables of the kingdom, as are three of the parables which Thomas shares with Matthew and which are quoted in the same section of the *Gospel of Thomas*.

57	Tares	Matt 13:24–30	Kingdom of the Father
60	Samaritan with Lamb		
76	Pearl	Matt 13:45–46	Kingdom of the Father
97	Woman with Jar		Kingdom of the Father
98	Assassin		Kingdom of the Father
109	Treasure	(Matt 13:44)	Kingdom

This introduction to the parables, not often used elsewhere in Thomas, might indicate that at least some of the special parables of the *Gospel of Thomas* were drawn from the same source from which also the parables shared with Matthew were derived. They may well be older materials.[1] At least one of them expresses the same single-minded determination, e.g., *Gos. Thom.* 98:

> Jesus said, "The kingdom of the Father is like a certain man who wanted to kill a powerful man. In his own house he drew his sword and stuck it into the wall in order to find out whether his hand could carry through. Then he slew the powerful man."

The interpretation of the other special parables of Thomas is difficult and cannot be discussed here in detail. But at least one correction in the translation of the parable of the Samaritan Carrying a Lamb, suggested by Hans-Martin Schenke, needs to be emphasized: *Gos. Thom.* 60 is usually translated "*They* saw a Samaritan carrying a lamb on *his* (i.e., *the Samaritan's*) way to Judaea." But the text should certainly be restored to provide the following translation: "*He* (i.e., *Jesus*) saw a Samaritan carrying a lamb, when *he* (i.e., *Jesus*) was on his way to Judaea." The conclusion in the extant text of the *Gospel of Thomas* ("You too look for a place for yourselves within repose, lest you become a corpse and be eaten") is probably secondary. But what the interpre-

---

[1] Klaus-Hunno Hunzinger ("Unbekannte Gleichnisse Jesu aus dem Thomas-Evangelium," in Walther Eltester, ed., *Judentum, Urchristentum, Kirche: Festschrift für Joachim Jeremias* [BZNW 26; Berlin: Töpelmann, 1960] 209–20) was the first to argue for the presence of early traditions in these parables.

tation of this parable and of the parable of the Woman Carrying a Jar (*Gos. Thom.* 97) could have been remains an open question.

The parables which the *Gospel of Thomas* shares with the Synoptic Sayings Source have to be viewed together with other materials shared by the two documents. These common materials account for the majority of the synoptic sayings and parables in Thomas. Of the seventy-nine units in the *Gospel of Thomas* which have parallels in the Synoptic Gospels, a total of forty-six are Q materials,[1] compared to only twenty-seven sayings and parables shared with Mark (including those which Matthew and Luke drew from Mark).[2] Only twelve are shared with special materials of the Gospel of Matthew, while special Lukan material occurs only once in Thomas.

Thomas materials shared with Matthew only, apart from the parables, are relatively few and do not warrant the hypothesis of a special source shared by the two writings:

Q/Matt 5:8,10	# 69a	prophetic saying	Blessed the persecuted
Matt 5:14	# 32	wisdom saying	City on a mountain
Matt 6:1–18	# 6a,14a	community rule	On Fasting and prayer
Matt 6:3	# 62b	proverb	Right and left hand
Matt 10:16	# 39b	proverb	Wise as serpents
Matt 11:28–30	# 90	wisdom saying	Invitation to heavy-laden
Matt 15:14	# 40	community rule	Plant not by the Father
Matt 18:20	# 30	community rule	Where there are two . . .

Some of these may have been Q materials, and others isolated sayings which circulated independently of any written sources. The relationship of Thomas with Mark, however, is much more striking and requires special consideration.

2.2.4.4 Thomas and the Gospel of Mark

The *Gospel of Thomas* shares a total of twenty-seven sayings and parables with the Gospel of Mark. Of these as many as seven also have parallels in Q (marked with *).

---

[1] See the listing above.

[2] *Gos. Thom.* 4b, 5, 6b, 9, 13(?), 14c, 20,, 21d, 21e, 22a, 25, 31, 33b, 35, 41, 44, 46b, 47d, 47e, 48, 55b, 62a, 65, 66, 67, 71, 99, 100, 104, 106.

Mark and Thomas

Mark	Thom.	Type	Topic
2:18–20	# 104	community rule	Fast without the bridegroom
2:21	# 47e	wisdom saying	New wine in old skins
2:22	# 47d	wisdom saying	Old patch on new garment
3:27	# 35	wisdom metaphor	House of a strong man
*3:28–29	# 44	community rule	Blasphemy against the Spirit
3:32, 34	# 99	community rule	Jesus' true relatives
4:3–8	# 9	parable	Sower
4:9	# 21e	wisdom saying	Whoever has ears to hear
4:11	# 62a	esoteric rule	Mystery of the parables
*4:21	# 33b	wisdom saying	Lamp not under a bushel
*4:22	# 5, 6	wisdom saying	Hidden and revealed
*4:25	# 41	prophetic saying	Who has will be given
4:26–29	# 21d	parable	Seed Growing Secretly
*4:30–32	# 20	parable	Mustard Seed
*6:4–5	# 31	proverb	Prophet in fatherland
7:15	# 14c	community rule	Clean and unclean
(8:27–30	# 13	(christological)	"Tell whom I am like")[1]
*8:34	# 55b	community rule	. . . take up his cross
?8:36	# 67	proverb	Gain the whole world . . .
10:13–16	# 22	community rule	Enter as children
10:31	# 4b	prophetic saying	First will be last
*11:23	# 71	community rule	Mountain move away
12:1–8	# 65	parable	Wicked Tenants
12:10	# 66	prophetic saying	Rejected cornerstone
12:14–16	# 100	community rule	Tax to Caesar
12:31	# 25	community rule	Love your brother
?13:17	# 79b	prophetic saying	Womb not conceiving[2]
14:58	# 71	prophetic saying	Destroy this temple

Only in the case of the parable of the Mustard Seed is it possible to say whether or not Thomas is closer to Mark or Q:

Gos. Thom. 20	Mark 4:30–32
The disciples said to Jesus, "Tell us what the kingdom of heaven is like." He said to them, "It is like a mustard seed. It is the smallest of all seeds.	He said, "With what shall we compare the kingdom of God, or what parable shall we use for it? It is like a mustard seed which, when it is sown

[1] This passage can hardly be counted as a true parallel. There is certainly no direct dependence upon a common tradition.

[2] Mark 13:17 is formulated as a woe over those who are pregnant or nursing. Thomas, however, is formulated as a beatitude for those who have not conceived and the breasts which have not given milk.

But when it falls on tilled soil, it produces a great plant and becomes a shelter for birds of the sky."

on the earth, is the smallest of all seeds on the earth. But when it is sown, it grows up and becomes larger than all plants and it puts forth large branches so that under its shadow the birds of the sky can dwell."

The emphasis upon the contrast of the small seed and the large plant is missing in the Q form of this parable (Luke 13:18–19), which differs from the Markan version also in other respects: it speaks of the "garden" into which the seed is thrown, and it says that it becomes a "tree" (δένδρον) and that "the birds are nesting in its branches." Mark and Thomas use the appropriate term "vegetable" (λάχανον), and they correctly describe birds as nesting under the branches. One could also argue that the contrast "small seed/large plant" is a structural element of the original parable that is lost in Q/Luke's version. In any case, Thomas's parallels with Mark do not require the assumption of a literary dependence; what both have in common are original features of the parable.[1]

It is typical in the parallels of the *Gospel of Thomas* to Markan sayings that the narrative frameworks of the Markan setting for the sayings are absent. In several cases Thomas presents a brief chria, introduced by a question of the disciples, where Mark writes an extended apophthegma.

<table>
<tr><td align="center">*Gos. Thom.* 104</td><td align="center">Mark 2:18–20</td></tr>
<tr><td></td><td>And the disciples of John and the disciples of the Pharisees were fasting;</td></tr>
<tr><td>They said to Jesus, "Come, let us pray today and let us fast."</td><td>and they came and said to him, "Why do the disciples of John and the disciples of the Pharisees fast, but your disciples do not fast?"</td></tr>
<tr><td>Jesus said, "What is the sin that I have committed, or wherein have I been defeated?</td><td>And Jesus said to them, "Can the sons of the bridegroom fast as long as the bridegroom is with them? As long as they have the bridegroom with them, they cannot fast. But days are coming, when the</td></tr>
</table>

---

[1] One could argue that Thomas's version does not seem to reflect the technical eschatological term "dwell" (κατασκηνοῦν, cf. Jeremias, *Parables,* 147: "actually an eschatological technical term for the incorporation of the Gentiles into the people").

But when the bridegroom leaves the   bridegroom will be taken from them,
bridal chamber, then let them fast   and then they will fast on that day."
and pray."

The first part of Jesus' answer in *Gos. Thom.* 104 is evidently a later
expansion. The second part corresponds to the last sentence of this
pericope in Mark, albeit without the explicit reference to "that day"
with which Mark points to the day of Jesus' death.[1] There is no reference in Thomas to the disciples of John and the Pharisees. At least
with respect to the latter, there would have been no reason for Thomas
to delete it, had it been a part of his text or tradition.

Gos. Thom. 99	Mark 3:31–34
	And his mother and his brothers came, and standing outside they sent to him, calling him. And a crowd was seated around him,
The disciples said to him, "Your brothers and your mother	and they said to him, "Behold, your mother and your brothers and your sisters are
are standing outside." He said to them,	outside, looking for you." And Jesus answered and said to them, "Who are my mother and my brothers?" And looking around at those sitting about him, he said, "Behold, my mother and
"Those here who do the will of my Father are my brothers and my mother. It is they who will enter the kingdom of my Father."	my brothers! Whoever does the will of God is my brother and my sister and my mother."

As in the previous example, Thomas's text is a brief chria, lacking any
of Mark's elaborate introductory setting of the stage and discourse.
Thomas also does not share Mark's peculiarity of stating the answer
first in the form of a rhetorical question. Thus Thomas's version of this
pericope, except for the secondary conclusion, corresponds to its more
original form.

---

[1] Lührmann (*Markusevangelium,* 63) explains the singular "on that day" after the
preceding plural ("days will be coming") as a reference to the Christian practice of fasting on Fridays (the day of Jesus' death). See also Kuhn, *Ältere Sammlungen,* 69–72.

Gos. Thom. 31[1]	Mark 6:4–5
Jesus said, "A prophet is not accepted in his fatherland, nor does a physician perform healings among those who know him."	And Jesus said to them, "A prophet is not without honor except in his fatherland." And he could not do any mighty work there, except that he laid his hands on a few sick people and healed them.

This is a particularly instructive parallel. When the Greek text of *Gos. Thom.* 31 (*Pap. Oxy.* 1.6) was discovered, Emil Wendling[2] demonstrated that Mark 6:4–5 was constructed on the basis of this saying. While Mark quoted the first part of the saying at the end of his apophthegma about Jesus' rejection in Nazareth, he changed the second part into narrative. Rudolf Bultmann[3] confirmed this observation through form-critical analysis.[4] This saying, in the form in which it is preserved by Thomas, was the nucleus of the later development of the apophthegma that appears now in Mark's text.[5]

Gos. Thom. 14c	Mark 7:15
For what goes into your mouth will not defile you, but that which issues from your mouth—it is that which will defile you.	There is nothing outside a human which by going into him can defile him. But the things coming out of a human being are what defile him.

The basic difference between Thomas and Mark is that Mark states the second half in general terms ("what comes out of a human being"), while Thomas specifies "what comes out of your mouth." In this respect Thomas agrees with the form of this saying in Matt 15:11 ("but what comes out of the mouth defiles a human being"). This might argue for a dependence of Thomas upon Matthew. However, the Matthew/Thomas form of this saying is most likely original: the first half of the saying requires that the second half speak about words which the mouth utters, not excrements (see Mark 7:19). Moreover, what the *Gospel of Thomas* quotes here is the one single saying from the entire pericope that can be considered as a traditional piece and that formed the basis for the original apophthegma—consisting of

---

[1] The text offered here is a translation of the Greek text of *Pap. Oxy.* 1.6.

[2] *Die Entstehung des Marcus-Evangelium* (Tübingen: Mohr/Siebeck, 1908) 53–56.

[3] *Synoptic Tradition,* 31–32.

[4] See my discussion in "ΓΝΩΜΑΙ ΔΙΑΦΟΡΟΙ : The Origin and Nature of Diversification in the History of Early Christianity," in Robinson-Koester, *Trajectories,* 129–32.

[5] The first part of this saying, as it is quoted in Mark 6:4, is preserved independently in John 4:44.

vss. 1–2, 5, and 15—out of which the present complex text of Mark 7:1–23 has been developed.[1]

Gos. Thom. 100	Mark 12:14–16
They showed Jesus a gold coin and said to him,	And they (some of the Pharisees and the Herodians) came to Jesus and said, "Teacher, we know that you are true and do not care for anyone; for you do not regard the position of people, but truly teach the way of God.
"Caesar's men demand taxes from us."	Is it permitted to give taxes to Caesar or not? Should we pay them or should we not?" But knowing their hypocrisy, he said to them, "Why do you tempt me? Bring me a denarius that I may see it." They brought one. And he said to them, "To whom belongs the image and the inscription?" They said, "To Caesar."
He said to them, "Give Caesar what belongs to Caesar, give to God what belongs to God, give me what is mine."	But Jesus said to them, "Give Caesar what belongs to Caesar, and (give) to God what belongs to God." And they were amazed at him.

In this brief chria of the *Gospel of Thomas* all of the narrative and discourse sections are missing which tie the Markan parallel to the context of Mark 12 where various people come to Jesus in order to trap him. Thomas preserves what must have been the basis of the elaborate exchange in Mark's extended apophthegma. The last phrase in Thomas ("and give me what is mine"), on the other hand, is a later expansion emphasizing the commitment to Jesus.

All these examples demonstrate that the Thomas versions of the Markan materials are closely related to the earliest stages of the transmission and development of the respective traditions. If one also considers Thomas parallels to Markan texts which have been discussed in the context of Q parallels and parables, there is no evidence that Thomas knew any of the further redactions of the Markan passages by Matthew and/or Luke.

More difficult is the question of a possible common source of the sayings materials shared by Mark and Thomas. In the case of Thomas' parallels to Q (including the shared parables), it was possible to isolate certain clusters of sayings which pointed in this direction. Except perhaps for the parables, no such clusters can be identified with respect to the numerous units shared by Mark and Thomas. There is a relatively higher number of community rules shared by both: nine out

[1] Cf. Lührmann, *Markusevangelium*, 125–26.

of twenty-seven units belong to this category (thirty-three percent), compared with only eight out of a total of forty-eight units in the case of Thomas and Q (sixteen percent). Was one of the common collections a small catechism? The answer to this question, as with any discussion of the sayings in Mark, is difficult as long as there is no clarity about the origin and sources of the sayings and apophthegmata in Mark's Gospel. There is general agreement that Mark did not know the Synoptic Sayings Source, but relied on various smaller collections, probably in written form, though it is difficult to define such collections with certainty.[1] If scholarship investigates further the possible contribution of the *Gospel of Thomas* to the identification of such early collections of sayings, more clarity may also be gained with respect to the sources of Mark's Gospel.

2.2.5 THE GOSPEL OF THOMAS AND THE JOHANNINE TRADITION

The first investigation of the relationship of the *Gospel of Thomas* to the Fourth Gospel of the New Testament was presented by Raymond E. Brown in 1963.[2] It was guided by the explicit question of "how much use, if any, *Gos. Thom.* makes ... of St. John's Gospel,"[3] and it ended with the conclusion that there was probably no direct use of St. John's Gospel, but that "traces of Johannine influence could be attributed to the second general source of *Gos. Thom.*," that is, a source which contained tendentious modifications of synoptic sayings and sayings "that are alien to the spirit of Jesus and without parallel in the thought of the canonical Gospels."[4] Not the author of the *Gospel of Thomas* but the compiler of that second source may have known John's Gospel.[5]

This position has prevailed among most scholars, and very little use has been made of parallels from the *Gospel of Thomas* for the interpre-

---

[1] See the helpful discussion in Lührmann, *Markusevangelium,* 12–15 (with a listing of relevant literature).

[2] "The Gospel of Thomas and St. John's Gospel," *NTS* 9 (1962/63) 155–77.

[3] Ibid., 158.

[4] Ibid., 177.

[5] Ibid. It should be noted that Brown states explicitly at the end "that this is only one possible interpretation of the evidence we have presented" (p. 177). However, in his commentary on the Gospel of John (Raymond E. Brown, *The Gospel according to John* (2 vols; AB 29–30; Garden City, NJ: Doubleday, 1966–70]), Brown essentially repeats this statement: "... if there is any dependence of one on the other, it is quite indirect, and the direction of the dependence would be Thomas on John" (p. liii). "Wherever these gospels (i.e., the *Gospel of Truth* and the *Gospel of Thomas*) have developed a common theme, the Gnostic documents stand at much greater distance from the primitive gospel message than does John" (p. lxxxii).

tation of the Fourth Gospel and in the investigation of its religious milieu. It is necessary to reopen the question from a different perspective: one must begin with an assessment of the life situation and purpose of the *Gospel of Thomas's* sayings, especially its "Johannine" sayings, and compare this with the role and functions of parallel materials in the Fourth Gospel and in the formation of the tradition of the Johannine community. This quest will be continued later in the treatment of the Gospel of John. It is the purpose of this chapter to investigate the tradition and collection of the sayings of Jesus insofar as this relates to these two gospels, Thomas and John.

The discourses of the Gospel of John have been developed on the basis of traditions which consisted primarily of sayings.[1] The purpose of the discourses is to explore and discuss critically the meaning and interpretation of such sayings. This is accomplished through changes of the wording of such sayings as well as by placing sayings into a particular context in the composition of a discourse so that the context becomes a critical commentary. On the other hand, the author of the *Gospel of Thomas* achieves his interpretation of traditional sayings by creating variants which thus illuminate particular aspects of understanding. In several instances, John and Thomas interpret the same traditional saying, albeit with the use of quite different hermeneutic principles. Sayings about the life-giving power of the word(s) of Jesus appear in both gospels several times:

Gos. Thom.	John
# 1: Whoever finds the interpretation of these sayings will not taste death (θανάτου οὐ μὴ γεύσηται).[2]	8:51: Whoever keeps my word will not see death (θάνατον μὴ θεωρήσῃ) in eternity.
# 111: And the one who lives from the Living One will not see death.	8:52: Whoever keeps my words will not taste death (θανάτου μὴ γεύσηται) in eternity.[3]

---

[1] We shall return to this later in the discussion of the Fourth Gospel. I have argued this case in several articles: "Dialog und Spruchüberlieferung in den gnostischen Texten von Nag Hammadi," *EvTh* 39 (1979) 532–56; "The History-of-Religions School, Gnosis, and the Gospel of John," *StTh* 40 (1986) 115–36; "Gnostic Sayings and Controversy Traditions in John 8:12–59," in Charles W. Hedrick and Robert Hodgson, Jr., eds., *Nag Hammadi, Gnosticism, and Early Christianity* (Peabody, MA: Hendrickson, 1986) 97–110.

[2] Greek version of *Pap. Oxy.* 654,1.

[3] The second quote is the repetition of the statement of Jesus by the Jews. Brown ("Thomas and John," 159) remarks that "the only difficulty is that *Gos. Thom.* has its parallel in the Jewish rephrasing of Jesus' own statement." But since this is a literary composition anyway, this does not constitute a problem.

18b: Blessed is he who will take his place in the beginning; he will know the end and will not taste death.

6:63: It is the spirit that gives life, the flesh is of no avail. The words I have spoken to you are spirit and are life.

19c: For there are five trees for you in paradise. . . . Whoever becomes acquainted with them will not taste death.

6:68–69: Simon Peter answered him, "Lord, to whom shall we go? You have words of eternal life, and we have come to believe and to know that you are the Holy One of God."

Thomas's hermeneutical procedure is evident. Not Jesus' words themselves, but their interpretation gives life, that is, the finding of their hidden truth. This truth is hinted at by different pointers: the finding of Jesus (the Living One), the knowledge of the trees of paradise, the knowledge of one's beginnings.

John, on the other hand, does not hesitate to quote the traditional saying about the life-giving power of Jesus' words unaltered: "The words I have spoken are spirit and are life," and "you have words of eternal life."[1] However, in the context in which these quotes appear they are immediately followed by a qualification. "But there are some of you who do not believe" (John 6:64); and (after Peter's confession) "Jesus answered them and said, 'Did I not select the twelve of you, and one of you is a traitor.'" In the other instances of the quote of this saying, John introduces a subtle change in the wording (analogous to Thomas's hermeneutic method): "Whoever keeps (τηρήσῃ) my word . . ." which is elsewhere explained as "keeping my commandments" (John 14:13, 21; 15:10). Moreover, the discussion about Jesus' claim that he is the giver of life-giving words in John 8 ends with the report that they took up stones in order to throw them at Jesus (8:59).

In a closely related saying, which connects the hearing of the words of Jesus with discipleship, John has introduced a significant change in the wording of a saying that Thomas seems to have preserved in a more original form:

Gos. Thom. # 19b	John 8:31–32
If you become my disciples and listen to my words, these stones will minister to you . . .	If you abide in (μένετε ἐν) my word, you will truly be my disciples, and you will know the truth, and the truth will set you free.

For Thomas the saying implies that listening to Jesus' words will con-

---

[1] Note that the adjective "eternal" or the phrase "in eternity" occurs repeatedly in these materials common to Thomas and John. It is, however, a Johannine trait that is never repeated in any of Thomas's parallels.

vey mysterious powers to the disciples. John substitutes the term "abide in"—a typical Johannine concept which emphasizes the faithfulness of Jesus' disciples.[1] He then adds "the truth will make you free"—a Stoic maxim[2] which has no parallel in the sayings tradition. Variations of a metaphorical saying which describes the revelation as a (bubbling) spring of water occur twice in Thomas and twice in John:

Gos. Thom.	John
# 13: Because you have drunk, you have become intoxicated from the bubbling spring which I have measured out.	4:14: Whoever drinks from the water that I shall give him, will not thirst in eternity, but the water that I shall give him will become in him a spring of bubbling water unto eternal life.
# 108: He who will drink from my mouth will become like me. I myself shall become he, and the things that are hidden will be revealed to him.	7:37–38: If anyone thirsts, let him come [to me]; and let him drink who believes in me. As the Scripture said, "From within him shall flow streams of living water."[3]

The metaphor of drinking was widespread in various religious contexts in antiquity.[4] But there are no occurrences among the sayings of Jesus except for the four passages quoted above, which are all variations of the same saying. In John 4:14, the Johannine reformulation of the saying is visible in the phrase "unto eternal life."[5] But the interpretation is achieved by the placement of the saying in the context of a discourse. The woman's request for this water is cut short by Jesus' command to go and get her husband. The following discourse clarifies that the establishment of faith in Jesus is a more complex process, while the two passages of the *Gospel of Thomas* presuppose that drinking from this spring results immediately in inspiration (here called metaphorically "intoxication"); even more, it establishes a reciprocal identity with the revealer and the communication of secret knowledge (# 108). It is especially this latter understanding that the complex reformulation of the saying in John 7:37–38 wants to avoid. Although

---

[1] "Abide in" occurs frequently in the Fourth Gospel; cf. especially John 15:4–10; also 1 John 2:6, 10, 24; 3:6, 24; 4:13, 16. On the concept see Bultmann, *Gospel of John,* on John 5:38 and 16:4.

[2] C. H. Dodd, *Historical Tradition in the Fourth Gospel* (Cambridge: Cambridge University Press, 1963) 380, cf. 330.

[3] This translation follows Brown (*Gospel of John,* 1. 319); cf. his discussion of the translation ibid., 320–22.

[4] For a survey of the evidence see Bultmann, *Gospel of John,* on John 4:11.

[5] It is used twelve times in the Gospel of John and clearly reveals the style of the author.

no particular scriptural passage can be identified as the source of the quotation,[1] the purpose of the saying's alteration is evident: Scripture confirms that Jesus remains the source of living water. The believer does not achieve mystical identity with the revealer.

Both in John and in Thomas, the synoptic sayings about the light[2] are further developed into mythological metaphors in which the revealer's and the revelation's designation as "light" describes their true nature.

Gos. Thom.	John
# 24b: There is light within a man of light and he lights up the whole world. If he does not shine, he is darkness.	11:9–10: If someone walks in the day, he does not stumble, because he sees the light of this world. But if someone walks in the night, he stumbles because the light is not in him.
	12:35–36: Walk as you have the light, that darkness may not overcome you. . . As you have the light, believe in the light so that you become sons of the light.
# 77a: It is I who am[3] the light which is above them all. It is I who am the all.	8:12: I am the light of the world. He who follows after me will not walk in the darkness, but will have the light of life.

In *Gos. Thom.* 24b, this light also describes the true identity of the believer. That the same saying is used in John 11:9–10 is evident in the final phrase ("because the light is not him"). However, John hesitates to describe the believer's metaphysical identity as "light." He prefers formulations like "having the light" (8:12) and "sons of light" (12:36). On the other hand, the revealer is repeatedly identified with the light, especially in the "I am" saying (8:12; cf. 9:5; 12:46).[4] To be sure, the *Gospel of Thomas* also uses the "I am" formulation in # 77. One may doubt, however, whether John 8:12 is dependent upon such a saying. John 8:12 formulates the "I am" saying on the basis of an older saying that emphasized the contrast "light/darkness," while *Gos. Thom.* 77 is a divine self-predication contrasting divine supremacy

---

[1] See the discussion in Brown, *Gospel of John,* 321–23.

[2] Matt 6:14–16, 23; Luke 8:16; 11:33–35.

[3] This saying and # 61 are the only two passages of the *Gospel of Thomas* where the typically Johannine "I am" or "It is I" appears (ἐγώ εἰμι, Coptic: ᴀɴoκ πe).

[4] See also the description of the revelation as "light" in John 1:4, 5, 7, 8–9; 3:19–21.

and the existing universe.[1] There are parallels to such statements in John:

Gos. Thom. # 77a	John 3:31
It is I who am the light which is above them all. It is I who am the all.	He who comes from above is above all things.

However, the reformulation of the traditional saying about the light in the Gospel of John ties "belief in the light" directly with belief in Jesus who suffered and was crucified; cf. John 8:28: "When you see the Son of man being raised up (i.e., on the cross), you will recognize that I am."

Perhaps the following parallel belongs in this context:

Gos. Thom. #19a	John 8:58
Blessed is he who came into being before he came into being.	Truly, truly, I say to you, before Abraham was, I am.

For the Gnostic understanding it is crucial to know that one's own origin lies before the beginning of earthly existence. John consciously avoids this application of divine origin to all believers and restricts it to Jesus as the revealer.

This is confirmed in several sayings and statements in which John and Thomas use closely related terminology about coming from and returning to the kingdom, the light, or the Father. In each instance, John restricts these statements to Jesus whereas Thomas brings them as general statements about the believer.

Gos. Thom.	John
# 49: Blessed are the solitary and elect, for you will find the kingdom. For you are from it, and to it you will return.	16:28: I have come out from the Father and I have come into the world. I am again leaving the world and return to the Father.

---

[1] The problem of the origin of the "I am" sayings cannot be discussed in this context; see Brown, *Gospel of John*, 1. 535–38. In this as well as in other instances it seems that traditional sayings used by John are not formulated in this style; furthermore, "I am" sayings are relatively rare, or even completely absent, in such writings as the *Gospel of Thomas*, the *Dialogue of the Savior*, and the *Apocryphon of James*. This would tend to' support the thesis that the Johannine "I am" sayings were created by the author of the Fourth Gospel.

50a: If they say to you, "Where did you come from?", say to them, "We came from the light, the place where the light came into being on its own accord . . ."

8:14b: . . . because I know whence I came and where I am going, but you do not know whence I came and where I am going.

1:9: The true light that enlightens every human being was coming into the world . . .

13:3: Jesus knowing that the Father had given all things into his hands and that he had come from God and was returning to God, . . .

Both John and Thomas use the same traditions, perhaps the same sayings. Is there is any dependence of one upon the other, or are both using the same older materials? If Thomas is dependent upon John, one must conclude that he deliberately generalized John's statements about the heavenly origin of Jesus and transformed them into the announcement that everyone who gains true knowledge can claim divine origin and return to it. However, there are indications that John already presupposed this generalized belief and rejected it deliberately. The believers do not arrive at salvation through knowledge about themselves, but through knowledge of Jesus. At the same time, John does not accept the alternative concept which sees Jesus as the paradigm for the Gnostic. How then do the disciples obtain salvation through Jesus in whom is present the Father and whose children they are destined to become?[1] The answer to this question is the topic of the farewell discourses in John 13–17.

In these discourses, John uses sayings which also occur in the *Gospel of Thomas*. He alludes to them repeatedly:

Gos. Thom.	John
# 38b: There will be days when you seek me and will not find me.	13:33: Only a little while I am with you. You will seek me and, as I said to the Jews so I now say to you, where I am going you cannot come.

---

[1] For the presence of the Father in Jesus see John 14:7–11; for "children of God" see John 1:12; 20:17. On this theological problem of the Fourth Gospel in its critical discussion of Gnostic alternatives see the excellent brief characterization by George W. MacRae, "Gnosticism and the Church of St. John's Gospel," in Charles W. Hedrick and Robert Hodgson, Jr., eds., *Nag Hammadi, Gnosticism, and Early Christianity* (Peabody, MA: Hendrickson, 1986), especially pp. 92–94.

7:34: I am going away and you will seek me, and where I am going you cannot come.

8:21: I am going away and you will seek me, and you will die in your sins, and where am going you cannot come.

24a: His disciples said, "Show us the place where you are, since it is necessary for us to seek it."

14:3: I am going to prepare a place for you . . . and where I am going you know the way. Thomas said, "Lord we do not know where you are going. How do we know the way?"

69a: Blessed are they who have been persecuted within themselves. It is they who have truly come to know the Father.

14:7: If you had known me, you would also know the Father; from now on you have known him and have seen him.

8:19: You have neither known me nor the Father; if you had known me, you would also have known my Father.

37a: His disciples said, "When will you become revealed (ἐμφανὴς εἶναι) to us and when shall we see you?"

14:22: Judas[1] . . . said to him, "How is it that you will reveal (ἐμφανίζειν) yourself to us and not to the world?"

That "Jesus knew that he had come from God and was returning to God" (John 13:3, see above) has been placed at the beginning of the farewell discourses. The saying about "seeking me and not finding me" (John 13:33) is then used to reject both the notion of Jesus as the paradigm for the Gnostic believer and the concept of the discovery of one's own divine origin. The disciples are not united with Jesus by following him, but by keeping his new commandment of loving each other as Jesus has loved them (13:34); in this "loving each other" their belonging to Jesus will become manifest (13:35). Following Jesus to "the place to which he goes" (14:2–3) is answered by the statement about the presence of the Father in Jesus (14:7–11) and doing the works of Jesus (14:12). This is the only way the Father can be known. Finally, Jesus' revelation to the disciples (14:22) is the event of his and the Father's return into the believer (14:23) which is, in turn, interpreted as the coming of the Paraclete, the Spirit of Truth (14:26). This latter statement is in sharp contrast to the saying of *Gos. Thom.* 38 where

---

[1] The Old Syriac translations read here "(Judas) Thomas."

Jesus says that he will become revealed to the disciples:

> When you disrobe without being ashamed and take up your garments and place them under your feet like little children and tread on them, then [will you see] the son of the living one, and you will not be afraid.[1]

Comments on sayings preserved in the *Gospel of Thomas* are notably present also in John 16,[2] while there are no parallels to John 17—the most "Gnostic" chapter of the farewell discourse to which Thomas might have been expected to have the greatest affinity:

Gos. Thom.	John
[# 49: Blessed are the solitary and elect, for you will find the kingdom. For you are from it, and to it you will return.]	[16:28: I have come out from the Father and I have come into the world. I am again leaving the world and return to the Father.]
# 92: Seek and you will find.	16:23b–24: Whatever you ask the Father, he shall give to you in my name . . . Ask and you will receive that your joy may be full.
Yet, what you asked me about in former times and which I did not tell you then, now I desire to tell, but you do not inquire after it.	16:4b–5: Those things I did not tell you from the beginning when I was with you. Now I am going to the one who sent me, and none of you asks me, 'Where are you going?'
	16:12: Yet many things I have to say to you, but you cannot bear them now.
	16:23a: And on that day you will not ask me anything.
	16:30: Now we know that you know all things, and you have no need that someone asks you. By that we believe that you came from God.

The last sentence in the final statement of the disciples (16:30) deliberately uses the term "to believe" (πιστεύειν) instead of "to know"

---

[1] One might also consider, whether other statements in the farewell discourses consciously refer to the question of "not being afraid," e.g., John 14:27 ("Peace I leave with you . . . let your heart not be shaken . . .").

[2] The first of these sayings has already been quoted above.

(εἰδέναι); the latter term is more often used about Jesus' own knowledge of his origin and in negative statements which characterize unbelief, cf. John 8: "for I know (οἶδα) whence I have come and where I am going, but you do not know (οὐκ οἴδατε) whence I come and where I am going."[1] For the disciples that knowledge about Jesus, and indeed also their knowledge of the Father, is faith. However, because it is faith and not knowledge, it has to face the paradox of Jesus' crucifixion and death and is therefore immediately challenged by Jesus' statement, "Do you now believe? The hour is coming, indeed it has come, when you will be scattered . . ." (John 16:31–32).

Several discourses of the Gospel of John can be understood as interpretations of a tradition of sayings which has been preserved in the *Gospel of Thomas*. Brown[2] had observed that parallels to the *Gospel of Thomas* are concentrated in the farewell discourses and in the discourse of John 7:37–8:56. But the reason for this concentration of parallels is that John is here discussing a tradition of sayings which proclaim a salvation that is based upon the knowledge of one's origin.

Whether such sayings are also present in other instances is more difficult to decide. There are some similarities in wording and phrasing which I shall list in the following without comment.

Gos. Thom.	John
# 43: His disciples said to him, "Who are you that you should say these things to us?"	8:25–26a: They said to him, "Who are you?"
[Jesus said to them,] "You do not realize who I am from what I say to you, for you have become like the Jews . . ."	Jesus said to them, "First of all, what I say to you. I have many things to say and to judge about you."
# 61: I am he who exists from the undivided. I was given some of the things of my Father.	5:18: . . . but because he called God his father, making himself equal to God.
	3:35: The Father loves the Son and has given everything into his hand. Cf. 13:3 (see above); 10:29.

---

[1] John never says that the disciples "know" whence they are coming and where they are going. But the author is familiar with the language which describes destiny by origin, cf. 8:23: "You are from below, but I am from above; you are from this world, I am not from this world." See further, Bultmann, *Gospel of John,* on John 3:1–4.

[2] "Thomas and John," 175–76.

# 11: The heavens will pass away, and the one above it will pass away. The dead are not alive, and the living will not die.	11:26: He who believes in me will live, even if he dies, and everyone who lives and believes in me will not die in eternity.

# 13: I am not your master.	15:15: No longer do I call you servants.

# 29: If the flesh came into being because of the spirit, it is a wonder. But if the spirit came into being because of the body, it is a wonder of wonders.	3:6: What is born of the flesh is flesh, and what is born of the spirit is spirit.

In the theological terminology the most striking parallel between Thomas and John is the use of the term "Father" for God. The term occurs in the *Gospel of Thomas* thirty times and is certainly part of the tradition of Thomas's sayings. It cannot be explained as the result of a casual borrowing from the Gospel of John, but characterizes the tradition of sayings that is common to both gospels. "Living Father" also appears in both documents: *Gos. Thom.* 3: ὁ πατὴρ ὁ ζῶν, John 6:57: ὁ ζῶν πατήρ.

The Gospel of John is the end product of a long development of the tradition about Jesus in the Johannine church.[1] In the beginning of this tradition the Johannine community certainly knew and interpreted sayings of Jesus which were only later expanded into lengthy speeches. One collection of such sayings also made its way into the *Gospel of Thomas* which preserved the theological perspective that must have dominated its initial stage. Like Paul's opponents in 1 Corinthians, also the Johannine Christians knew sayings of Jesus which gave life and salvation.

Connections between Thomas's sayings and those used by Paul's Corinthian opponents have already been discussed. There is no overlap between those sayings and the group of sayings which Thomas shares with John. However, there is some commonality with sayings from the Synoptic Sayings Source, notably with Q/Luke 10:22:

---

[1] A good account of some aspects of this history and development is given by Raymond E. Brown, *The Community of the Beloved Disciple: The Life, Love, and Hates of an Individual Church in New Testament Times* (New York: Paulist Press, 1979).

> All things have been handed over to me by my Father, and no one knows who the Son is except the Father, or who the Father is except the Son and anyone to whom the Son wishes to reveal him.

This "Johannine" saying has always been recognized as a somewhat alien element which was probably added to Q at a later stage of its redaction,[1] though the saying is certainly older. Its presence in Q does not indicate a close relationship between the sayings common to Thomas and John on the one hand, and the Synoptic Sayings Source on the other.

2.2.6 ESOTERIC THEOLOGY[2]

"Wisdom" is the theme of this writing. As in the *Wisdom of Solomon*, wisdom sayings express the truth about God and about the essence of the human self. They speak about human nature and destiny and, by extension, about the nature of the world and of the proper relationship to the world in which people dwell. The wisdom sayings of the *Gospel of Thomas,* like other Jewish and Christian sayings collections of this type, contain sayings that reveal what is fundamental about people and their behavior. Still other sayings discuss the comportment proper to the tenuous nature of a human being's sojourn in the world. Such sayings and the orientation they reveal are by no means unique to Thomas. They are typical of the early Christian sayings tradition to which Thomas, together with Matthew, Mark, and Luke, was heir.

A number of wisdom sayings speak of divine Wisdom who invites human beings to follow her in order to find the true life here in this world and in the hereafter. It is necessary, therefore, to recognize the present moment in which the words of Jesus are heard; at this point the sayings include a prophetic element, sometimes in sayings paralleled by synoptic sayings, at other times in sayings only found in Thomas:

> His disciples said to him, "When will the repose of the dead come about, and when will the new world come?" He said to them, "What you look forward to has already come, but you do not recognize it." (*Gos. Thom.* 51)

---

[1] Lührmann, *Redaktion,* 97–98; Kloppenborg, *Formation of Q,* 197–203.

[2] The following paragraphs owe much to the contributions of Steven Patterson to our jointly authored essay, "The Gospel of Thomas," in *Bible Review* 6/2 (1990) 28–39, although little of this final section of our manuscript was included in the published version.

His disciples said to him. "Twenty-four prophets spoke in Israel, and all of them spoke of you." He said to them, "You have omitted the one living in your presence, and have spoken (only) of the dead." (*Gos. Thom.* 52)

Thomas sees this coming of the kingdom primarily as an event that takes place as the disciples gain a new understanding of themselves:

Jesus said, "If those who lead you say to you, 'See, the kingdom is in the sky,' then the birds of the sky will precede you. If they say to you, 'It is in the sea,' then the fish will precede you. Rather the kingdom is inside of you, and it is outside of you. When you come to know yourselves, then you will be known, and you will realize that it is you who are the sons of the living Father. But if you will not know yourselves, you dwell in poverty and it is you who are that poverty." (*Gos. Thom.* 3)

Thomas contains a number of sayings whose meaning is not as transparent as the common wisdom forms cited thus far. But there are indications that this is by design. These sayings reveal a more radical concept of secret knowledge. They speak of hidden truths about human existence, heavenly origins, separation from the world, and liberation of the soul from the body. It is particularly this understanding of salvation that is critically interpreted in the Gospel of John. The Thomas Christians are told the truth about their divine origins, and given the secret passwords that will prove effective in the return journey to their heavenly home:

Jesus said, "Blessed are the solitary and the elect, for you will find the kingdom. For you are from it, and to it you will return" (*Gos. Thom.* 49).

Jesus said, "If they say to you, 'Where did you come from?', say to them, 'We came from the light, the place where the light came into being on its own accord and established [itself] and became manifest through their image.' If they say to you, 'Is it you?', say, 'We are its children and we are the elect of the living Father.' If they ask you, 'What is the sign of your Father in you?' say to them, 'It is movement and repose.'" (*Gos. Thom.* 50)

The religious perspective represented in such Thomas sayings as these has often been associated with Gnosticism. Gnostics believed that both their origin and their destiny lay in the supreme deity who dwells in a heavenly place removed from the evil world, the creation of a rebellious angel or demiurge. Though this demiurge seeks to hold humans in ignorance of their true identity, in sleepiness and intoxication, a divine messenger will come and awake them and relieve them from the bonds of ignorance by bringing true knowledge about themselves. In saying # 28 of the *Gospel of Thomas*, Jesus speaks with the voice of this heavenly messenger:

> Jesus said, "I took my place in the midst of the world, and I appeared to them in the flesh. I found all of them intoxicated; I found none of them thirsty. And my soul became afflicted for the human beings, because they are blind in their hearts and do not have sight; for empty they came into the world, and empty too they seek to leave the world. But for the moment they are intoxicated. When they shake off their wine, then they will repent."

However, this moment of return to which the Thomas Christians aspire requires preparation beyond the simple memorization of passwords, about which *Gos. Thom.* 50 speaks. One must also cultivate the proper understanding of the world in order to be ready to leave its confines when the time comes:

> Jesus said, "Whoever has come to understand the world, has found (only) a corpse, and whoever has found a corpse is superior to the world." (*Gos. Thom.* 56)

> Jesus said, "He who has recognized the world has found the body, but he who has found the body is superior to the world." (*Gos. Thom.* 80)

Understanding the world—a thing that is really dead—leads inevitably to a proper understanding of the body and corporeal existence. Becoming superior to the world involves deprecation of the flesh in favor of the spirit. Jesus even marvels over how it is that something so glorious as the spirit has become mired in the flesh:

> Jesus said, "If the flesh came into being because of the spirit, it is a wonder. But if spirit came into being because of the body, it is a wonder of wonders. Indeed, I am amazed at how this great wealth has made its home in this poverty." (*Gos. Thom.* 29)

Flesh and spirit, body and soul, are two different components in a human being, joined in an unholy mix which spells doom for both:

> Jesus said, "Woe to the flesh that depends upon the soul; woe to the soul that depends upon the flesh." (*Gos. Thom.* 112)

Separating the soul from corporeal existence does not mean that the soul would henceforth exist as a disembodied spirit, wandering abstractly through the cosmos without form and identity; rather, the soul freed from its prison would enter into a new kind of corporeal existence which awaits her in the heavenly realm. This new "body" is often spoken of as one's heavenly "image," which awaits the soul, but remains guarded and enclosed in the safety of the godhead until it can be properly claimed. Thus Thomas speaks of "images," for the present concealed in the Father, but waiting for the moment when their splendor will be revealed to the utter astonishment of those by whom they will be claimed:

> Jesus said, "The images are manifest to man, but the light in them remains concealed in the image of the light of the Father. He will become manifest, but his image will remain concealed by his light." (*Gos. Thom.* 83)

> Jesus said, "When you see your likeness, you rejoice. But when you see your images which came into being before you, and which neither die nor become manifest, how much will you have to bear!" (*Gos. Thom.* 84)

This understanding of human existence also involves a radical social ethos. "Knowing" is the key for the right understanding of the believers' existence in the world. But this does not mean that Thomas Christianity was a conclave of an isolated meditating elite. There are many sayings in Thomas (a number of these shared with the canonical Gospels) which specify the kind of behavior and mode of living in the world that is appropriate for those who are truly "children of the Father." At the heart of this life style is a social radicalism that rejects commonly held values. The sayings speak of rejecting the ideal of a settled life in house and home, and they require itinerancy:

> Jesus said, "Become passers-by." (*Gos. Thom.* 42)

In the rejection of popular piety, Thomas's sayings are more radical than Matthew's (chapter 6) criticism of the practice of fasting, praying, and almsgiving:

> His disciples questioned him and said to him, "Do you want us to fast? How shall we pray? Shall we give alms? What diet shall we observe?" Jesus said, "Do not tell lies, and do not do what you hate, for all things are plain in the sight of heaven." (*Gos. Thom.* 6)

> Jesus said to them, "If you fast, you will give rise to sin for yourselves; and if you pray, you will be condemned; and if you give alms, you will do harm to your spirits." (*Gos. Thom.* 14a)

Shrewd business sense is rejected, in keeping with the canonical gospels (cf. Matt 5:42; Lk 6:34; 12:13–15):

> [Jesus said], "If you have money, do not lend it at interest, but give [it] to one from whom you will not get it back." (*Gos. Thom.* 95)

At the end of the parable of the Great Banquet (Matt 22:1–10; Lk 14:15–24) the *Gospel of Thomas* adds a characteristic sentence:

Businessmen and merchants [will] not enter the places of my father. (*Gos. Thom.* 64)

To be "children of the living Father" is to be free from the society and not to be bound to the world and its values. "Blessedness" does not depend upon the marks of success in this world. One's identity should not be determined by whatever is valuable for personal status in the social fabric of the world: householder, family member, religious leader, successful business person:

> Jesus said: "Whoever finds the world and becomes rich, let him renounce the world." (*Gos. Thom.* 110)

But the ideal of the itinerant man, who is independent of all social and family bonds, also seems to imply that women engaged in the pursuit of common values and social conventions likewise are not fit for this role unless they accept the ideal of the ascetic man:

> Simon Peter said to them, "Let Mary leave us, for women are not worthy of life." Jesus said, "I myself shall lead her in order to make her male, so that she too may become a living spirit resembling you males. For every woman who will make herself male will enter the kingdom of heaven." (*Gos. Thom.* 114)

2.3 The Synoptic Sayings Source

2.3.1 Q AND THE TWO-SOURCE HYPOTHESIS

According to the two-source hypothesis, the Gospel of Mark is the oldest of the three so-called Synoptic Gospels. It was used by the other two Synoptic Gospels, Matthew and Luke, who in addition to Mark, both used a second common source, the so-called Synoptic Sayings Source.

Markan priority was first recognized by Karl Lachmann (1835) and Gottlob Wilke (1838). Christian Hermann Weiße was the first who recognized that Matthew must have employed, in addition to Mark, a second source which consisted of a collection of sayings of Jesus (1838).[1] The architect of the two-source hypothesis and classic advocate of Markan priority is Heinrich-Julius Holtzmann.[2] The most

---

[1] On the history of the development of this hypothesis see Werner Georg Kümmel, *Das Neue Testament: Geschichte der Erforschung seiner Probleme* (Orbis 3.1; Freiburg/München: Alber, 1958) 177–91.

[2] See his *Die synoptischen Evangelien: Ihr Ursprung und ihr geschichtlicher Charac-ter* (Leipzig: Engelmann, 1863); cf. idem, *Lehrbuch der historisch-kritischen Einleitung in das Neue Testament* (Freiburg: Mohr, 1892) 342–61.

detailed elaboration of the two-source hypothesis—augmenting it by the thesis that Matthew and Luke used two other sources in addition to Mark and the Synoptic Sayings Source —was presented by B. H. Streeter.[1] In one form or another, this hypothesis has been accepted by most scholars.[2] Nevertheless, arguments against the existence of a Synoptic Sayings Source, often coupled with arguments against the priority of Mark, have been brought forward frequently.[3] The most recent challenges try to revive the so-called "Griesbach hypothesis." In 1789/90, decades before the formulation of the two-source hypothesis, Johann Jakob Griesbach had criticized the traditional view which had been generally accepted for centuries, namely, that Matthew was the oldest of the four canonical gospels, that Mark had used Matthew, and that Luke had used both Matthew and Mark. Griesbach still maintained the priority of Matthew but modified this traditional position by arguing that it was Luke who had used Matthew first, and that Mark had used both Matthew and Luke.[4] The most outspoken advocate for the more recent revival of this hypothesis, William Farmer,[5] has welcomed in particular the critique of the Markan priority by Hans-Herbert Stoldt and supported the publication of its English translation.[6]

Some of the arguments in favor of the Griesbach hypothesis rest on the observation that Matthew and Luke agree in several instances against the extant text of Mark's Gospel, the so-called minor agreements of Matthew and Luke.[7] I shall argue below in the treatment of

---

[1] *The Four Gospels: A Study of Origins* (London: Macmillan, 1924).

[2] Presentations of the arguments in favor of the two-source hypothesis and of its more recent challenges can be found in Vielhauer, *Geschichte,* 268–80, and in more detail in Schmithals, *Einleitung in die drei ersten Evangelien* (GLB; Berlin: De Gruyter, 1985) 182–233. A very helpful discussion of the Q hypothesis was published by Frans Neirynck, "Recent Developments in the Study of Q," in Delobel, ed., *LOGIA,* 29–75; see also Neirynck, "L'édition du texte du Q," in idem, *Evangelica: Gospel Studies—Études d'Évangile (Collected Essays)* (BEThL 60; Leuven: Peeters, 1982) 925–33.

[3] An excellent survey of the arguments for and against the Synoptic Sayings Source with extensive documentations of the opinions of the individual scholars in question can be found in Arthur J. Bellinzoni, Jr, *The Two-Source Hypothesis: A Critical Appraisal* (Macon, GA: Mercer University Press, 1985) 219–434.

[4] Cf. Kümmel, *Das Neue Testament,* 88–89; Schmithals, *Einleitung,* 142–45.

[5] *The Synoptic Problem* (New York: Macmillan, 1964; 2d edition Macon, GA: Mercer University Press, 1976). For Farmer's other publications see the listing in Bellinzoni, *The Two-Source Hypothesis,* 459.

[6] *History and Criticism of the Marcan Hypothesis* (Macon, GA: Mercer University Press, 1980).

[7] For a critical discussion of these arguments of Farmer (and Stoldt) in support of the Griesbach hypothesis see Frans Neirynck, *The Minor Agreements of Matthew and Luke against Mark* (BEThL 37; Louvain: Leuven University Press, 1974); furthermore several articles by the same author in his *Evangelica: Gospel Studies—Études*

the Gospel of Mark[1] that many of the minor agreements between Matthew and Luke result from the fact that both Matthew and Luke used a text of Mark that was different from the text which is preserved in the manuscript tradition of the canonical Gospel of Mark.

All attempts to disprove the two-source hypothesis favor the priority of Matthew or of some earlier form of Matthew which was possibly written in Aramaic. This is a very problematic position, burdened with great difficulties, especially with regard to the sayings materials of Matthew's Gospel. In most instances, very good arguments can be brought forward to show that the Gospel of Luke has preserved more original forms of the sayings shared by Matthew and Luke; thus Matthew cannot have been the source of these Lukan sayings. Moreover, if there was no common sayings source shared by Matthew and Luke, an explanation of the source, or sources, of Matthew's sayings must still work with the assumption of some earlier document(s) through which these sayings came to the author of the First Gospel. Scholars who deny the existence of a Synoptic Sayings Source, still have to find a theory by which the transmission of the sayings to the author of Matthew's Gospel can be explained. In other words, the rejection of the two-source hypothesis solves nothing and creates new riddles for which even more complex and more improbable hypotheses have to be proposed.

The two-source hypothesis maintains that Matthew and Luke both used Mark, or at least some form of the Gospel of Mark, as their primary source and, in addition, employed a second common source which consisted mostly of sayings of Jesus.[2] More recent research has not only made the existence of this source more probable, it has also demonstrated that one can reconstruct its formation, development, and redaction as a literary document. The observations which argue strongly for the existence of a Synoptic Sayings Source and its use by Matthew and Luke are the following:

(1) What Matthew and Luke share in addition to their common Markan pericopes consists almost exclusively of sayings. The only exceptions are: one miracle story (Matt 8:5–13 = Luke 7:1–10), materi-

---

d'Évangile (BEThL 60; Leuven: Peeters, 1982) 769–810; also C. M. Tuckett, The Revival of the Griesbach Hypothesis (NTSMS 44; Cambridge, Cambridge University Press, 1983); Schmithals, Einleitung, 150–52.

[1] See below # 4.1.

[2] For this source, the siglum "Q"—the first letter of the German word for "Source" = Quelle—has been commonly used since the beginning of this century. This designation and siglum was chosen as a neutral term that does not imply any prejudice with respect to its literary character and historical value; cf. Martin Dibelius, Botschaft und Geschichte (2 vols.; Tübingen: Mohr/Siebeck, 1953–1956) 1. 97–98.

als about John the Baptist and Jesus' baptism (parts of Matt 3:1–17 = Luke 3:2–9, 16–17, 21–22), and the story of Jesus' temptation (Matt 4:1–11 = Luke 4:1–13). This requires the assumption of a common source which consisted mostly of sayings of Jesus and probably of some other shared non-Markan materials.

(2) The numerous verbal agreements of these parallel passages cannot be explained as dependence of either Matthew upon Luke or dependence of Luke upon Matthew because, in numerous instances, Luke's version is evidently the more original one. But there are also passages in which Matthew rather than Luke has preserved words and phrases which cannot be explained as the product of Matthew's editorial work. Indeed, in some instances what is certainly original in a particular saying may occur partially in Luke and partially in Matthew. A striking example is the following passage (words from the original version of the saying are underlined):[1]

Matt 7:23	Luke 13:27	Psalm 6:9
καὶ τότε	καὶ ἐρεῖ λέγων	
ὁμολογήσω	ὑμῖν·	
αὐτοῖς ὅτι		
οὐδέποτε ἔγνων	οὐκ οἶδα	
ὑμᾶς,	πόθεν ἐστέ·	
ἀποχωρεῖτε ἀπ᾽	ἀπόστητε ἀπ᾽	ἀπόστητε ἀπ᾽
ἐμοῦ	ἐμοῦ πάντες	ἐμοῦ πάντες
οἱ ἐργαζόμενοι	ἐργάται	οἱ ἐργαζόμενοι
τὴν ἀνομίαν.	ἀδικίας.	τὴν ἀνομίαν.

The second half of this saying is a quotation of Ps 6:9. But while the first words of the sentence derived from this psalm are accurately preserved only in Luke, the last words of the quotation have an exact parallel only in Matthew. One must assume that there was a common source used by both authors and that this common source quoted the sentence exactly as it occurred in Ps 6:9.

(3) The sequence in which certain groups of sayings occur in the Gospel of Luke often reveals an association and composition of sayings that is more directly related to the process of the collection of oral materials, while Matthew interrupts or disturbs such sequences whenever his motivations as an author of literature are evident. In his ver-

---

[1] I have not given an English translation because a translation would not reflect well enough the subtle differences between the two texts.

sion of Jesus' speech for the "sending of the disciples" (Matt 9:37–11:1), Matthew parallels Luke in the reproduction of a series of sayings which instruct missionaries with respect to their conduct. But he repeatedly interpolates materials which belong to other contexts and often do not fit the genre of an older collection of originally oral sayings:

Matthew	Material	Older Q collection	Other Sources
9:37–38	Saying	Q 10:2	
10:1	Introduction		Mark 6:7
10:2–4	List of the twelve disciples		Mark 3:16–19
10:5–6	... not to the Samaritans		?
10:7	Instruction to preach	Q 10:9	
10:8	Matthean redaction		
10:9–10	Instruction about equipment	Q 10:4	Mark 6:8–9
10:11a	... entering a house/city	Q 10:5a	
10:11b	Expansion of command		Mark 6:10
10:12–13	Rule about stay in a house	Q 10:5b–6	
10:14	Rule about leaving	Q 10:10–11	Mark 6:11
10:15–16	Saying	Q 10:12, 3	
10:17–22	Persecution sayings		Mark 13:9–13
10:23	Matthean redaction		
10:24	Saying: master and disciple		Q 6:40
10:25	Matthean redaction		
10:26–33	Group of sayings		Q 12:2–9
10:34–35	Sayings about divisions		Q 12:51–53
10:37–38	Sayings about discipleship		Q 14:26–27
10:39	Saying about one's life		Q 17:33
10:40	Saying about acceptance		Mark 9:37
10:41	Matthean redaction		
10:42	Saying about disciple's aid		Mark 9:41
11:1	Matthean redaction		

Q/Luke 10:2–12 exhibits all the features of an early collection of rules for the conduct of the missionary. Its composition most likely took place in the oral transmission of such regulations, and Q still reflects the loose connection of such a unit of tradition. That Matthew's text is the result of a secondary redaction, revealing the use of written sources, is evident in the manner of his composition. He employed one primary source, i.e., Q, still intact in Luke's version, in order to compose a literary speech in which he included additional materials which were mostly drawn from his other major source, i.e., Mark (6:7; 3:16–19; 6:8–9; 6:10; 6:11; 13:9–13), then adding materials drawn from other contexts of both sources (Mark 13:9–13; Q 6:40; 12:2–9; 12:51–53; 14:26–27; 17:33; Mark 9:37; 9:41). In the case of Mark, the materials which Matthew used from his collection of rules about missionaries appear in the same sequence. But in the case of Q, Matthew changed their original order.

To prove the thesis that both Matthew and Luke used, in addition to Mark, such a source of sayings is not identical with the reconstruction of this source, either with respect to the sequence of its materials or with respect to the exact wording of its sayings. Moreover, although Matthew and Luke sometimes agree in their reproduction of the wording of a Q saying, there are also considerable differences, so that one wonders whether there were not two different editions of Q, one used by Matthew, the other by Luke. This is most likely with respect to the Q materials which appear in Matthew's Sermon on the Mount. Here Matthew does not appear to have used Q directly, i.e., the inaugural sermon of Jesus of Q 6:20–49, but rather a "sermon" into which a predecessor of Matthew had already incorporated sayings from other sections of Q.[1] However, such considerations do not invalidate the fundamental hypothesis of the existence of Q as a document *sui generis,* a literary composition in its own right, which can be largely reconstructed and which can be described and analyzed with respect to the stages of its development.

2.3.2 THE COMPOSITION AND REDACTION OF Q

2.3.2.1 *Some General Considerations*

The question of the composition and redaction of Q has been discussed ever since the hypothesis of its existence was proposed. Various attempts have been made to reconstruct the document and to establish its original wording.[2] In the course of the scholarly discussion a consensus has emerged with respect to several basic assumptions about Q: (1) Although there are some instances in which individual sayings reveal an Aramaic substratum, the first composition of Q was in Greek and not in Aramaic.[3] (2) The order of the sayings in Q is, in general, more faithfully preserved in Luke than in Matthew;[4] how-

---

[1] On this question see below in the chapter on the redaction of Q (# 2.3.4).

[2] See the discussion in Schmithals, *Einleitung,* 216–223; Frans Neirynck, "Recent Developments in the Study of Q," in Delobel, ed., *LOGIA,* 35–41; Kloppenborg, *Formation of Q,* 219–26. From 1984 to 1988, a seminar of the Society of Biblical Literature under the direction of James M. Robinson, now continued in regular annual working sessions as "International Q Project," is attempting to achieve a consensus in the reconstruction of this document, considering carefully all earlier attempts.

[3] Schmithals, *Einleitung,* 222–23.

[4] The relevant literature is listed in Kloppenborg, *Formation of Q,* 64–65; Schmithals, *Einleitung,* 217–19.

ever, although Matthew often moved groups of Q sayings to a different context, he often parallels Luke in the sequence of the individual sayings within such groups. (3) Luke preserves the original wording of the sayings more faithfully than Matthew, although even Luke occasionally edited his Q materials and Matthew cannot be ruled out as the document in which the original wording of its source is still extant. (4) As a rule no narrative materials but only sayings shared by Matthew and Luke should be assigned to Q—exceptions are materials concerning John the Baptist and the story of the healing of the centurion's son. (5) Convincing arguments are necessary in order to establish that sayings derive from Q whenever they are preserved only in one of the two Gospels; but the possibility cannot be excluded *a priori*. (6) The document Q must have undergone at least one substantial redaction in its development until it circulated in the form in which Matthew and Luke used it for the composition of their Gospels. (7) Q probably underwent one additional redaction before it was used by Matthew, though this latest redaction already exhibits some features, which are generally judged to be typically Matthean.

If Luke's order of the pericopae of Q can be taken as following most closely the original order of Q itself, it appears that the author of Q grouped the sayings under certain thematic headings. This observation permits the inclusion into Q of some sayings appearing in these units although they are preserved only by Luke, as well as of sayings appearing only in Matthew if they are closely connected with topics and with parallels in Q/Luke. That a saying attested only once in the parallel tradition may have been present in Q can be confirmed in numerous instances by a parallel in the *Gospel of Thomas*.[1] According to these criteria of inclusion, it is possible to determine the content and order of Q in its major subsections with a great degree of certainty.[2]

The result of this reconstruction gives us the document Q as it was used by Luke and Matthew (or a pre-Matthean redactor of Q). But this document is apparently the result of at least one major redaction of a still older document.[3] Tensions and inconsistencies which can be observed within this common source of Matthew and Luke can hardly be explained as resulting from shifts in the history of different units of oral traditions that were used in the community of Q prior to their

---

[1] On the parallels of the *Gospel of Thomas* and Q see above # 2.2.4.2.

[2] In the following I am especially indebted to Kloppenborg, *Formation of Q*, 64–80.

[3] On the several attempts of a redactional analysis of Q and the problems of such analyses see Kloppenborg, *Formation of Q*, 95–101. In the following I shall base my arguments primarily on Kloppenborg's work and refer to earlier authors only occasionally.

collection and composition into a literary document.[1] The most obvious signs of a secondary redaction of Q can be found in the apocalyptic announcement of judgment and of the coming of the Son of man which conflicts with the emphasis upon the presence of the kingdom in wisdom sayings and prophetic announcements.[2] In the following presentation of the several sections of Q, special attention will be paid to the distinction between sayings belonging to the original document and materials added by the redactor.

2.3.2.2 John the Baptist and the Temptation of Jesus

Pericope or saying	Q / Luke	Matthew	Other
Appearance of John [a]	3:2b–4	3:1–3, 5	Mark 1:3–5
Preaching of repentance[3]	3:7–9	3:7–10	
Eschatological preaching [b]	3:16–17	3:11–12	Mark 1:7–8
Baptism of Jesus [c]	3:21–22	3:13–17	Mark 1:9–11
Temptation of Jesus	4:1–13	4:1–11	(Mark 1:12–13)

[a] Matthew and Luke agree in the omission of the quotation from Mal 3:1 (= Mark 1:2), and both use the phrase ἡ περίχωρος τοῦ Ἰορδάνου (Matt 3:5; Luke 3:3). This justifies the inclusion of these verses into Q. It is reasonable to assume that Q must have introduced the appearance of John in some fashion.

[b] Matthew and Luke agree with Mark only in the announcement of the coming of the "Stronger One," but do not include the phrase ἐγὼ ἐβάπτισα ὑμᾶς ὕδατι, and read αὐτὸς ὑμᾶς βαπτίσει ἐν πνεύματι ἁγίῳ καὶ πυρί instead of Mark's ἐν πνεύματι ἁγίῳ. The judgment metaphor Q 3:17 has no Markan parallel.

[c] The agreements of Matthew and Luke are very slight[4] and do not justify the inclusion of this pericope.

The announcement of judgment characterizes this opening section of Q in which John the Baptist calls for repentance and announces the

---

[1] This is essentially the solution of the problems presented by Siegfried Schulz, *Q: Die Spruchquelle der Evangelisten* (Zürich: Theologischer Verlag, 1972).

[2] That these apocalyptic materials belong to the redaction of Q was first argued convincingly by Lührmann (*Redaktion*). Kloppenborg (*Formation of Q*) has presented an analysis of Q in which he characterizes the original formation of this document as a composition of sapiential speeches and, following Lührmann, its redaction as characterized by the announcement of judgment over this generation. My own view is primarily based on the observations and arguments of these two scholars.

[3] In Luke, this saying is followed by the so-called "social preaching of John" (Luke 3:10–14) which only very few scholars derive from Q; see Kloppenborg, *Q Parallels*, 10.

[4] See Kloppenborg, *Q Parallels*, 16.

coming of God ("the stronger one who is coming after me") for judgment with fire and spirit (Q 3:7–9, 16–17). Only these sayings can be assigned to Q with some degree of certainty. The temptation story in Matt 4:1–11 and Luke 4:1–13 requires a common source for these two Gospels, but it is difficult to prove that this source was Q.[1] In any case, the entire opening section must be assigned to the redaction of this document.

2.3.2.3 Inaugural Sermon to the Disciples

Pericope or Saying	Q / Luke	Matthew	Other
Introductory phrase[a]	6:12, 20a	5:1–2	
Blessing of the poor	6:20b	5:3	Gos. Thom. 54
Blessing of the hungry	6:21a	5:6	Gos. Thom. 69b
Blessing of those who weep	6:21b	5:4	Rom 12:15
Blessing of hated, persecuted[b]	6:22–23	5:10–12	Gos. Thom. 68–69a
Love your enemies	6:27–29	5:44	Rom 12:14
Give to the one who asks	6:30	5:42a	Acts 20:35
Lending money	(6:34)	5:42b	Gos. Thom. 95
Be children of your Father	6:35b	5:48	
Golden rule	6:31	7:12	Gos. Thom. 6b[2] ?
Serving two masters[c]	16:13	6:24	Gos. Thom. 47a-b
On judging	6:37–38	7:1–2	1 Clem. 13.2[3]
Plants of the Father[d]		15:13	Gos. Thom. 40
Blind leading the blind	6:39	15:14	Gos. Thom. 34[4]
Disciple not over his master	6:40	10:24–25	John 13:16[5]
Splinter in the brother's eye	6:41–42	7:3–5	
Tree and fruit	6:43	7:16–18	Gos. Thom. 43
No figs from thistles	6:44	12:33	Gos. Thom. 45a
Good things from the heart	6:45	12:34–35	Gos. Thom. 45b
"Those who say, 'Lord, Lord'"	6:46	7:21	2 Clem. 4.2
Response of the Lord[e]	13:26–27	7:22–23	2 Clem. 4.5

[a] Luke's mention of the "mountain" in 6:12 and of the disciples in 6:20, both paralleled in Matt 5:1, indicates that the "sermon" in Q was

---

[1] Lührmann (Redaktion, 56) argues against inclusion of this pericope in Q. But see the detailed discussion in Kloppenborg, Formation of Q, 246–62. Kloppenborg (ibid., 262) comes to the conclusion that it was a late addition to Q which signifies the movement of Q "toward a narrative or biographical cast."

[2] It is not certain that this saying of the Gospel of Thomas is a real parallel; see above # 2.2.4.2.

[3] Further parallels appear in Rom 2:1 (". . . you who are judging; for in judging another you condemn yourself") and Mark 4:24.

[4] Cf. also Rom 2:19.

[5] A further parallel appears in Dial. Sav. 53 (139,11): "The disciple resembles his teacher."

introduced by a phrase that identified setting and audience.

ᵇ Those who are persecuted are mentioned only in Matt 5:10–11, and most scholars exclude the entire section Matt 5:5–10 from Q. But because *Gos. Thom.* 68 and 69a also blesses the disciples when they are persecuted, the persecuted were most likely also mentioned in the blessings of Q.

ᶜ οἰκέτης appears only in Luke and is usually considered to be secondary. However, the *Gospel of Thomas* also presupposes this word.[1]

ᵈ The parallel to this saying (Matt 15:13) in *Gos. Thom.* 40, and its close connection with Matt 15:14 = Q/Luke 6:39 may justify its inclusion in Q in this context.[2]

ᵉ Matt 7:21 and 7:22–23 belong together and may have stood together in Q.[3] That the parallel to Matt 7:22–23 appears in Luke 13:26–27 is probably due to Lukan redaction.[4] Luke 13:22–27 is a Lukan composition for which Luke has used various materials; see below the note to Q/Luke13:24.

The large number of parallels in the *Gospel of Thomas* and in other early Christian writings is striking. This section of Q has not only preserved many sayings which circulated widely at a very early date, it was most likely a cluster of sayings that existed independently in a number of variants in oral or written form before it was used by the author of Q, and it was apparently also known to Paul (Romans 12) and to the *First Epistle of Clement* (chapter 13).[5] A mixture of wisdom sayings and prophetic sayings of Jesus (to the latter category I would especially assign the beatitudes, but also the prediction of exclusion of those who only say "Lord, Lord") characterizes this portion of Q. This

---

[1] See above # 2.2.4.2.

[2] Almost all scholars exclude this saying from Q; see Kloppenborg, *Q Parallels*, 38.

[3] This, however, does not imply that the Matthean formulation of this Q saying is to be preferred over the text preserved in Luke. On the contrary, Matt 7:21–23 exhibits features which show the redaction of the pre-Matthean author of the Sermon on the Mount; see Betz, "An Episode in the Last Judgment (Matt. 7:21–23)," in idem, *Essays,* 125–57. It is difficult to determine, whether the parallel in *2 Clem.* 4 is dependent upon Matthew and Luke or upon the pre-Matthean Sermon on the Mount or at least upon the milieu in which this sermon was written (so Betz, ibid., 143–46). There are also Lukan features in *2 Clem.* 4, and the mixture of Matthean and Lukan elements in this quotation is paralleled in Justin, *1 Apol.* 16.9–12 and *Dial.* 76.5; see Koester, *Synoptische Überlieferung,* 75–91; see also below ## 5.1.2 and 5.2.1.4.

[4] Kloppenborg (*Formation of Q,* 235–36) argues for inclusion into the context of Q 13:24–14:35 and understands the saying not as directed against disciples, but "at unresponsive recipients of Christian preaching."

[5] See above, ## 2.1.2 and 2.1.4.3.

is not simply a "sapiential speech,"[1] but a prophetic, and thus eschatological, announcement of the presence of the rule of God. However, there is no trace of an apocalyptic perspective which predicts judgment and condemnation.

2.3.2.4 John, Jesus, and This Generation [2]

Saying or Pericope	Q / Luke	Matthew	Other
The centurion's son [a]	7:1–10	8:5–13	John 4:46–54
Answer to John's inquiry [b]	7:18–23	11:2–6	
Why did you go to the desert? [c]	7:24b–26	11:7–9	Gos. Thom. 78
Reference to Mal 3:1 LXX	7:27	11:10	
The smallest in the kingdom [d]	7:28	11:11	Gos. Thom. 46
The kingdom and John [e]	16:16	11:12–14	
The publicans and John	7:29–30	21:31–32	
The children of this age	7:31–35	11:16–19	

[a] This is one of only two miracle narratives in Q. In favor of its inclusion[3] is the fact that it appears right after the inaugural sermon of Jesus in both Matthew and Luke.[4] The predominance of dialogue in this story makes it an apophthegma rather than a miracle narrative.[5] It is debated whether Luke 7:3a, 4–6a should be included in the Q version (parallels are missing in Matthew). The vocabulary of these verses is Lukan, and the duplication of the sending of emissaries is awkward.[6]

[b] Most scholars consider Luke 7:21 as a Lukan addition; some would also see 7:20 as Lukan.[7]

[c] It is remarkable that, like Q 7:24b–25, the parallel in the *Gospel of Thomas* also does not contain a reference to John the Baptist. The relationship to John the Baptist is established in Q through the placement of the originally independent saying into this context and in Luke by the addition of 7:24a, which is clearly redactional.

---

[1] Kloppenborg (*Formation of Q*) uses this designation for the units of the original composition of Q.

[2] The heading is taken from Kloppenborg (*Q Parallels,* p. xxxi). It is difficult to find an appropriate heading for this section of Q. The materials collected in this section, or at least their application to John the Baptist, may derive from Q's later redactor. But in the final form, Q 7:1–35 is a section that is distinct from the preceding "Speech to the Disciples" and the following "Instruction for the Mission."

[3] Most authors include this pericope (Kloppenborg, *Q Parallels,* 50).

[4] See Bovon, *Evangelium nach Lukas,* 346.

[5] Bultmann, *Synoptic Tradition,* 38–39.

[6] Bovon (*Evangelium nach Lukas,* 346) suggests that at least the second sending in vs. 6 be eliminated.

[7] See Kloppenborg, *Q Parallels,* 52; Bovon, *Evangelium nach Lukas,* 370.

ᵈ Q 7:28 is a saying that praises the greatness of John (7:28a), with a secondary Christian addition which diminishes John's status (7:28b).[1] However, the form of this saying that appears in *Gos. Thom.* 46 does not contain a polemic against John the Baptist. The saying merely emphasizes the contrast between the old (from Adam to John) and the new (the kingdom). The polemical formulation ("[even] the smallest in the kingdom is greater than he") instead of "whoever becomes a child will know the kingdom and will become greater than [even] John" is thus due to the redactor of Q who inserted the saying into this context.[2]

ᵉ The placement of this saying is problematic, though most scholars agree that it appeared in Q. Matt 11:12–14 argues for a placement in this context.

Like the initial section of Q—the preaching of John the Baptist—this section points to the redactor of Q as its author. Except for two sayings (Q 7:24b-26 and 7:28) there are no parallels in the *Gospel of Thomas*. Both of these sayings are originally free sayings which do not contain any polemic against John. In its present form, with the concluding threat against "this generation" (Q 7:31–35), the composition of this entire Q section must be assigned to the redactor. However, some of the sayings used here may have stood in the earlier version of Q, although it is no longer possible to determine the context in which they originally appeared.

2.3.2.5 The Followers of Jesus and Their Mission

Pericope or saying	Q / Luke	Matthew	Other
No home for the human being ᵃ	9:57–58	8:19–20	Gos. Thom. 86
Let the dead bury the dead	9:59–60	8:21–22	
Who puts his hand to the plow ᵇ	9:61–62		
The harvest is great	10:2	9:37	Gos. Thom. 73
Like sheep among wolves	10:3	10:16a	
Clever like serpents ᶜ		10:16b	Gos. Thom. 39b
Instructions for the road ᵈ	10:4–7	10:9–11	Mark 6:8–13
Instruction for entering a place	10:9–12	10:7,14f	Gos. Thom. 14b
Woe over Chorazin etc. ᵉ	10:13–15	11:21–23a	
Those who receive me … ᶠ	10:16	10:40	John 13:20
Hidden from the wise … ᵍ	10:21	11:25–26	1 Cor 1:20

[1] Cf. Bultmann, *Synoptic Tradition*, 164.
[2] On the relationship of this saying to the present context see Lührmann, *Redaktion*, 27–29.

| Authority given to the Son | 10:22 | 11:27 | John 3:35 |
| Blessedness of the witnesses | 10:23–24 | 13:16–17 | 1 Cor 2:9 |

a In the Q version of this saying, "Son of man" was probably understood as title of Jesus. But the *Gospel of Thomas* never uses this title for Jesus. Thus its form of the saying has preserved the original meaning which compares the animals with the situation of human beings.[1]

b This third saying of a group of three about following Jesus has no parallel in Matthew, but its language is not Lukan; it agrees in style and content with the two preceding units, and there are good reasons why Matthew would have omitted it.[2]

c The close connection between Matt 10:16a and 10:16b and the appearance of a parallel in the *Gospel of Thomas* argues for an inclusion of Matt 10:16b into Q.[3]

d Some of the instructions here parallel Mark quite closely. Matthew 10 has combined Mark's mission speech with the mission instructions found in Q and with other materials from a special source and from Mark 13. But Luke 10:2–16 follows Q without Markan intrusions, while Luke reproduces the Markan mission speech elsewhere (Luke 9:1–6).

e The woe against Chorazin and Bethsaida is evidently an intrusion into an older collection of sayings concerning the mission of the disciples. It is an originally independent saying, and it is difficult to judge at which stage of the development of Q it was interpolated. Matt 11:23b–24 has no Lukan parallel, but may have been a part of this prophetic tradition.[4]

f This saying is attested frequently elsewhere; cf. Mark 9:47; 1 Thess. 4:8; *Did.* 11.4; Ignatius *Eph.* 6.1. It concludes the mission speech quite appropriately. The following sayings in Luke (10:17–20), which have no parallel in Matthew, have been considered by some authors for inclusion in Q, but there are no convincing arguments for this assumption.[5]

g This saying and the following two sayings differ markedly from other Q materials, while their parallels in 1 Corinthians 1–4 and in the *Gospel of Thomas* and the Gospel of John are striking because of their

---

[1] "Man, homeless in this world, is contrasted with the wild beasts." (Bultmann, *Synoptic Tradition,* 28); cf. Kloppenborg, *Formation of Q,* 191–92.

[2] See Kloppenborg, *Q Parallels,* 64; idem, *Formation of Q,* 190–91.

[3] Most authors would not include Matt 16:16b in Q; see Kloppenborg, *Q Parallels,* 72.

[4] See Kloppenborg, *Q Parallels,* 74.

[5] See Kloppenborg, *Q Parallels,* 76.

emphasis upon the presence of revelation in Jesus' words.[1] They are certainly very old sayings and may have been added here by the author of Q (not by the redactor, whose theological orientation is quite different) in order to emphasize the authority of the disciples.

Almost all materials in this section of Q are widely attested, both in the *Gospel of Thomas* and elsewhere. However, while the hand of the Q redactor is not visible in the composition of these sayings, they do not reflect a unified theme. The section seems to be composed of three different older clusters: (1) sayings about discipleship which imply the rejection of all normal social conditions (Q 9:57–62), (2) a collection of sayings about the mission of the disciples (Q 10:2–12,16)[2] to which a prophetic saying pronouncing the doom of the Galilean cities has been added by Q's redactor (Q 10:13–15), and (3) sayings about the presence of the revelation in Jesus' words (Q 10:21–24) which belong to an old tradition of revelation sayings that is attested as early a 1 Corinthians 1–4 and is also preserved in the Gospel of Thomas. All three clusters must have existed independently, in oral or written form, prior to the composition of Q. With respect to the cluster of sayings about the mission of the disciples, this is evident by its appearance in Mark 6.[3] The independent existence of the cluster of revelation sayings is evident because of the parallels in 1 Corinthians 1–4, the *Gospel of Thomas,* and the Gospel of John.[4]

2.3.2.6 The Community in Conflict

Pericope or Saying	Q / Luke	Matthew	Other
The Lord's Prayer [a]	11:2–4	6:9–13	*Did.* 8.2
Request to ask and to seek [b]	11:9–13	7:7–11	*Gos. Thom.* 92, 94
Beelzebul accusation [c]	11:14–20	12:22–28	Mark 3:22–26
The house of the strong one [d]	11:21–22	12:29	*Gos. Thom.* 35
"He who is not with me . . ."	11:23	12:30	Mark 9:40
Return of the evil spirit	11:24–26	12:43–45	
True blessedness [e]	11:27–28		*Gos. Thom.* 79
The sign of Jonah [5]	11:29–32	12:38–42	

[1] See the parallel in *Gos. Thom.* 17 and possibly *Gos. Thom.* 4; cf. the discussion above in # 2.1.3.

[2] A variant of this collection is preserved in Mark 6; see below.

[3] See Philip Sellew, *Dominical Discourses: Oral Clusters in the Jesus Sayings Tradition* (to be published by Fortress Press).

[4] See above, # 2.1.3.

[5] Luke 11:16 ("Others, in order to test him, were requesting a sign from heaven") also belongs to this pericope. Its parallel in Matthew (12:38) appears in the original context.

Light not under a bushel[f]	11:33	5:15	*Gos. Thom.* 33b
The light of the body[g]	11:34–36	6:22–23	*Gos. Thom.* 24
Pharisees wash outside only[h]	11:39–41	23:25–26	*Gos. Thom.* 89
Pharisees tithe mint and rue	11:42	23:23	
Pharisees take the first seats	11:43	23:6	Mark 12:39
They are like hidden tombs	11:44	23:27	
The Pharisees' heavy burdens	11:46	23:4	
They built tombs of prophets	11:47–48	23:29–30	
The oracle of Wisdom	11:49–51	23:34–36	
They took key of knowledge[i]	11:52	23:13	*Gos. Thom.* 39
Lament over Jerusalem[j]	13:34–35	23:37–39	

[a] While Matthew and Luke exhibit marked differences in their versions of the Lord's Prayer, its quotation in *Did.* 8.2 is almost identical with Matthew's version. It is debated whether the Didache version is dependent upon the text of the Gospel of Matthew or derives from the same liturgical tradition.[1] An author would be more likely to write down the wording of this prayer as it was used liturgically rather than copy it from a written source. This does not necessarily raise doubts with respect to the presence of the Lord's prayer in this context of Q.[2] But it is questionable whether either Matthew or Luke copied its text from their common source.[3]

[b] Apart from the parallels in the *Gospel of Thomas* cited above (see also *Gos. Thom.* 2), there are numerous statements in the Gospel of John which are based on this saying (14:13–14; 15:7, 16; 16:23–26). Variants of this saying also appear in Mark 11:24; *Dial. Sav.* 20 (129,14–16), *Apocr. Jas.* (NHC I, 2) 10,34–34; 10,39–11,1.[4]

[c] This is the second of two miracle stories in Q. Almost all authors believe that the close agreements of Matthew and Luke against Mark—who does not report an exorcism by Jesus at the beginning of the Beelzebul controversy—justify its inclusion in Q. Because of the influence upon Matthew and Luke of the parallel collection of sayings on exorcism in Mark 3:23–30, it is difficult to determine the exact extent of Q in this pericope. But most scholars agree that Luke 11:15, 17–20 (without vs. 18b) and 23 belong to Q.[5] On the inclusion of Luke 11:21–22, see the following note.

[d] Many scholars doubt that this metaphor was included in Q, because the parallels in Matthew are too slight; both Matthew and

---

[1] See above, # 1.4.3.

[2] See Kloppenborg, *Q Parallels*, 84; idem, *Formation of Q*, 203–6.

[3] Whether either wording of the Lord's Prayer is more original is a different question, which cannot be answered by any hypothesis regarding its exact wording in Q.

[4] See also my documentation in "Gnostic Writings," 238–44.

[5] See the detailed discussion in Kloppenborg, *Formation of Q*, 121–27.

Luke may be dependent upon Mark. But the presence of this metaphor in the *Gospel of Thomas* supports the arguments in favor of its inclusion.[1]

e The inclusion of this saying is suggested by the parallel in the *Gospel of Thomas*; there are cogent reasons to explain its omission in Matthew: he reports the Markan apophthegma of Jesus' true relatives in 12:46–50 (= Mark 3:31–35), that is, immediately after the preceding Q pericope Matt 12:43–45 = Luke 11:24–26. Thus, the Markan pericope substitutes for Q/Luke 11:27–28.

f A variant of this saying is quoted in Mark 4:21. The text of this saying in *Gos. Thom.* 33b resembles most closely Luke 11:33: both versions contain the phrases "under a basket"[2] and "in a hidden place." The latter phrase does not appear in either Matt 5:15 or Mark 4:21 (= Luke 8:16). *Gos. Thom.* 33b also confirms the concluding phrase of Luke 11:33 ("that those who enter may see the light") as the original wording of Q (Matt 5:15 concludes the saying with the phrase, "and it gives light to all in the house").

g A further variant of this saying appears in *Dial. Sav.* 8.

h The parallel in *Gos. Thom.* 89 lacks the address of the saying to the Pharisees.

i In *Gos. Thom.* 39 this saying is addressed to the Pharisees and scribes (= Matt 23:13; Luke 11:52 is addressed to the lawyers), but the first phrase of the saying itself agrees with Luke 11:52 (". . . have taken the keys of knowledge"). The term "lawyer" (νομικός) is specifically Lukan;[3] it never appears in Mark, and only once in Matthew (22:35).[4]

j Only Matthew places this pericope at the end of the speech against the Pharisees; but he may have preserved the original order of Q.[5] Both, the lament about the killing of the prophets (Matt 23:34–36 = Luke 11:49–51) and the lament about Jerusalem (Matt 23:37–39 = Luke 13:34–35) are oracles of Wisdom and may have stood together in Q at the end of the woes against the Pharisees.[6] That this section in

---

[1] See Kloppenborg, *Q Parallels*, 92; idem, *Formation of Q*, 125.

[2] The words οὐδὲ ὑπὸ τὸν μόδιον are missing in 𝔭45.78 A L Γ Ξ 0124 etc.; but they are attested in ℵ B C D W Q F etc. Older editions of the NT usually included the phrase; Nestle-Aland, *NT Graece*, encloses the phrase in brackets.

[3] It is used in Luke 7:30; 10:25; 11:45, 46, 52, 53; 14:3.

[4] This occurrence of νομικός may be caused by Matthew's source Mark, because the Lukan parallel (10:25) also uses the term. Matt 22:35 and Luke 10:25 also agree in the use of the verb "to test" (Matt: πειράζων, Luke: ἐκπειράζων), and in the address διδάσκαλε. The extant text of Mark 12:28 does not seem to preserve the Markan text that Matthew and Luke read; see below, # 4.1.2.2.

[5] See the discussion in Kloppenborg, *Q Parallels*, 158; idem, *Formation of Q*, 227–28. Kloppenborg includes Luke 13:34–35 in the sapiential speech of Q/Luke 13–14; see below.

[6] Bultmann, *Synoptic Tradition*, 114–15; Lührmann, *Redaktion*, 48.

the present text of Luke concludes with a final "woe" (against those who have hidden the keys of knowledge, Luke 11:52) is due to Lukan redaction.

This section of Q includes diverse materials, but is dominated by the Q redactor's announcement of judgment over "this generation," which is especially evident in the "woes against the Pharisees." Unfortunately, it is very difficult to determine with any certainty the original Q sequence of these seven "woes," because both Matthew and Luke seem to have disturbed this original sequence.[1] However, not all materials included in this section are therefore introduced into Q by this redactor. Apart from the three major units of controversy—the debate about the exorcism of demons and the speech against the Pharisees and the saying about the sign of Jonah—there are a number of wisdom sayings which, in themselves, have no polemical intent (Q 11:27–28, 33, 34–36 = *Gos. Thom.* 79, 33b, 24). They may have been part of the original version of Q. The same can be assumed for the Lord's Prayer and for the community rule about asking and praying (Q 11:2–4, 9–13). But even the two controversy units may have incorporated older Q materials such as the metaphor about the house of the strong one (Q 11:21–22 = *Gos. Thom.* 35) and the sayings about washing the outside of the cup (Q 11:39–41 = *Gos. Thom.* 89) and about the Pharisees' taking the keys of knowledge (Q 11:52 = *Gos. Thom.* 39). It is worth noting that the parallels to this section in the *Gospel of Thomas* do not reveal any of the tendencies of controversy and of judgment over this generation.[2] The wisdom oracles concluding this section of Q are not paralleled elsewhere in Christian traditions, although Thomas presents formal parallels of such wisdom sayings.[3] But the sayings which are used in the Beelzebul controversy represent an older cluster which the redactor took over as a whole and which was used independently by the Gospel of Mark.[4]

---

[1] Kloppenborg (*Formation of Q,* 140) reconstructs the following sequence: Luke 11:42, 39–41, 43, 44, 46, 47–48, 52. However, he makes the unlikely suggestion that the oracle of wisdom (Luke 11: 49–51) was placed in Q before the last woe (Luke 11:52).

[2] To be sure, the Pharisees and scribes are mentioned in *Gos. Thom.* 39, but there is no "woe" pronounced against them.

[3] On the character and origin of these wisdom oracles and on their parallels in the *Gospel of Thomas* see Robinson, "LOGOI SOPHON," 103–5.

[4] See Philip Sellew, *Dominical Discourses: Oral Clusters in the Jesus Sayings Tradition* (to be published by Fortress Press); idem, "Beelzebul in Mark 3: Dialogue, Story, or Sayings Cluster?" F&F *Forum* 4 (1988) 93–108.

2.3.2.7 The Community Between This World and the Other World

Pericope or Saying	Q / Luke	Matthew	Other
Hidden and revealed [a]	12:2	10:26	*Gos. Thom.* 5, 6b
"Preach from the rooftops"	12:3	10:27	*Gos. Thom.* 33
Fear of those who kill the body	12:4–7	10:28–31	
Fearless confession	12:8–9	10:32–33	Mark 8:38
The blasphemy not forgiven [b]	12:10	12:32	*Gos. Thom.* 44
The spirit's assistance [c]	12:11–12	10:19	Mark 13:9–11
Dividing the inheritance [d]	12:13–15		*Gos. Thom.* 72
The parable of the Rich Fool	12:16–21		*Gos. Thom.* 63
On cares [e]	12:22–32	6:25–34	*Gos. Thom.* 36
Heavenly treasure	12:33–34	6:19–21	*Gos. Thom.* 76b

[a] The contrast between hidden and revealed is also expressed in the saying Mark 4:22. It is likely that Paul in 1 Cor 2:7–10 comments on this saying; see above # 2.1.3.

[b] Further parallels appear in *Did.* 11:7 and Mark 3:28–30 (= Matt 12:31); see the discussion about the relationship of the several versions of this community rule, above # 2.2.4.2.

[c] Mark 13:9–11 has been combined with Q 12:11–12 in Matt 10:17–20. The original text of the Q version is preserved by Luke.

[d] This apophthegma as well as the following parable have no parallels in Matthew. But both also occur in the *Gospel of Thomas* and otherwise fit the criteria of inclusion.[1]

[e] *Gos. Thom.* 36 parallels only Q 12:22. A longer parallel is preserved in the Greek version of the *Gospel of Thomas, Pap. Oxy. 655,* which contains parallels also to Q 12:25, 27a.

The materials of this section, of which most are paralleled in the *Gospel of Thomas,* belong to the category of "rules of the community" and they exhibit features similar to those sayings in the preceding section which do not belong to the judgment speeches of the redactor. In the original version of Q, they could have belonged to a section of rules of the community which began with the Lord's Prayer. The only exceptions are Q 12:4–7 and 12:8–9, both without parallels in the Gospel of Thomas; the latter introduces Jesus as the future Son of man—here as elsewhere a sign of the hand of the redactor of Q.[2] Q 12:10, in its

---

[1] For a discussion of the incorporation into Q of this and the following pericope see Kloppenborg, *Q Parallels,* 128, and above # 2.2.4.2.

[2] On the redactional character of the introduction of this saying see Lührmann, *Redaktion,* 51–52. Lührmann (p. 51) also argues that the correspondence of a positive and a negative formulation in this saying is more original than the purely negative form of Mark 8:38.

present form, also contains a reference to the Son of man. But "Son of man" is understood as a title of Jesus only in the context of the final form of Q. Originally the contrast in this community rule must have been between the forgivable blasphemy against human beings and the unforgivable blasphemy against the Holy Spirit.[1]

2.3.2.8 The Coming Judgment

Pericope or Saying[2]	Q / Luke	Matthew	Other
Parable of the Thief[a]	12:39–40	24:43–44	Gos. Thom. 103
Faithful and Unfaithful Servant[b]	12:42–46	24:45–51	
Fire on earth[c]	12:49		Gos. Thom. 10
Not peace, but the sword	12:51–53	10:34–35	Gos. Thom. 16
Signs of the time[d]	12:54–56	16:2–3	Gos. Thom. 91
Agreement with adversary	12:57–59	5:25–26	
Parable of the Mustard Seed[e]	13:18–19	13:31–32	Gos. Thom. 20
Parable of the Leaven	13:20–21	13:33	Gos. Thom. 96

[a] The parable of the Thief occurs twice in the Gospel of Thomas: # 103 formulated as a beatitude ("Blessed is the man who knows where the brigands will enter . . .") and # 21 incorporated into a composite saying, followed by an admonition ("You then, be on guard against the world . . ."). In neither case do the Thomas parallels emphasize the time (Matt: ποίᾳ φυλακῇ, Luke: ποίᾳ ὥρᾳ) of the coming of the thief, nor is there an application regarding the time of the coming of the Son of man (cf. Q: ὅτι ᾗ ὥρᾳ οὐ δοκεῖτε ὁ υἱὸς τοῦ ἀνθρώπου ἔρχεται).

[b] Luke 12:41–42a and 47–48, both without a parallel in Matthew, are not to be included in Q.[3] The parable of the Faithful and Unfaithful Servant (Q 12:42b–46) cannot be understood as an older tradition, but is an allegorizing admonition which is wholly dominated by the expectation of the coming of the Son of man. In the context of Q, it explains the preceding emphasis upon the uncertainty of the hour of his coming.[4]

---

[1] See above, # 2.2.4.2, the discussion of this saying in the Gospel of Thomas.

[2] The preceding section about the watchful servants, Luke 12:35–38, is assigned to Q by some scholars because of their assumption that the parable of the Ten Virgins (Matt 25:1–13) derives from the same Q tradition (Kloppenborg, Q Parallels, 136). However, the resemblances are too slight and the admonition to be watchful is so widespread (1 Cor 16:13; 1 Thess 5:6; 1 Pet 5:8; Rev 3:2, 3; 16:15; Did. 16.1) that a special written source for Matt 25:1–13 need not be presupposed.

[3] See Kloppenborg, Q Parallels, 140; idem, Formation of Q, 151, n. 212: both insertions belong together and are Lukan.

[4] For the interpretation of this "parable" see especially Lührmann, Redaktion, 69–70.

ᶜ Although a Matthean parallel is missing for Luke 12:49, it does not contain Lukan features and should be assigned to Q; see also the parallel in *Gos. Thom.* 10. However, the following saying, Luke 12:50 ("I must be baptized with a baptism . . ."), is a Lukan addition.[1]

ᵈ The much shorter version of the *Gospel of Thomas* agrees with Luke 12:56 in the emphasis upon recognizing "this moment" (Luke: τὸν καιρὸν τοῦτον, Matt: τὰ σημεῖα τῶν καιρῶν).

ᵉ An independent variant appears in Mark 4:30–32. *Gos. Thom.* 20 resembles Mark insofar as his version also emphasizes the smallness of the seed.

The sayings in this section must all be understood as warnings regarding the uncertainty of the coming of the Son of man. They emphasize that this uncertainty means "soon." This allowed the redactor to include sayings which actually speak about the presence of the eschatological moment in Jesus and his words. That this was the original meaning of such sayings is not only evident in the parallels of the *Gospel of Thomas,* but also in the introduction "I have come" of Q 12:49, 51, 53, and in the formulation "this moment" (Q/Luke 12:56). It is quite likely that these latter sayings had a place in the original version of Q.

2.3.2.9 *Eschatological Didache*[2]

Pericope or Saying	Q / Luke	Matthew	Other
The narrow gate ᵃ	13:24	7:13–14	
Gentiles in the kingdom ᵇ	13:28–30	8:11–12	
[Ox in a well][3]	14:5	12:11	
[Whoever exalts himself][4]	14:11	23:12	
Parable of the Great Banquet	14:16–24	22:1–10	*Gos. Thom.* 64
Whoever does not hate father	14:26	10:37	*Gos. Thom.* 55,101

[1] See Kloppenborg, *Q Parallels,* 142; idem, *Formation of Q,* 151, n. 213.

[2] This section of Q contains diverse materials concerned with the status and conduct of the disciples in the eschatological division, including admonitions. Kloppenborg (*Q Parallels,* p. xxxii) calls the Q materials in Luke 13 and 14 "The Two Ways." But also most of the Q materials of Luke 15:1–17:6 are parenetic in character and may have belonged to the same Q unit.

[3] That this saying belonged to Q is extremely doubtful. Matthew attached this saying in 12:11–12 to his version of the healing of the man with the withered hand (Matt 12:9–14 = Mark 3:1–6). It is more likely that this was a favorite and well-known argument against Sabbath observation which circulated in the oral tradition.

[4] This saying that Luke attaches to one of his favored meal scenes (Luke 14:7–11) and again to the story of the Pharisee and the Publican (18:14) does not require a written source but may have come from the oral tradition.

Whoever carries his cross	14:27	10:38	Mark 8:34
Whoever seeks his life[1]	17:33	10:39	Mark 8:35
About salt	14:34–35	5:13	Mark 9:50
Parable of the Lost Sheep	15:4–7	18:12–14	Gos. Thom. 107
Parable of the Lost Coin[2]	15:8–10		
Serving two masters	16:13	6:24	Gos. Thom. 47a
Validity of the Law[3]	16:17	5:18	Gos. Thom. 11[4]
On divorce	16:18	5:32	Mark 10:11–12
About scandals	17:1–2	18:6–7	Mark 9:42[5]
About forgiveness	17:3–4	18:15, 21	
About faith	17:6	17:20	Mark 11:22–23

[a] It seems that only Luke 13:24 belongs to this section of Q. The following verse, Luke 13:25, is a Lukan redaction[6] by which the Q saying of Luke 13:24 is connected to another Q passage, Luke 13:26–27 = Matt 7:22–23, that originally may have belonged to Q's inaugural sermon.[7]

[b] The conclusion of this saying ("The last will be first . . . ," Luke 13:30) appears in Matt 20:16 at the end of the parable of the Laborers in the Vineyard (Matt 20:1–15). Since it is a gnomic saying from the oral tradition that was added at random in other contexts as well (cf. Mark 10:31; Matt 19:30; Gos. Thom. 4b), it is impossible to be certain about its original place in Q. The next Q saying in this Lukan context, the lament over Jerusalem (Luke 13:34–35), is better placed after Q 11:49–51; see above.

---

[1] Since this saying belongs together with the two preceding sayings and Matthew preserved all three sayings in the same unit (Matt 10:37–39), one can assume that they also formed a unit in Q.

[2] There is no parallel either in Matthew or in the Gospel of Thomas. But the close connection between the two parables in Luke 15:1–10 and their parallel structure may indicate that Luke found both together in his source; cf. Kloppenborg, Q Parallels, 176.

[3] Luke 16:16 has been listed above because it probably belonged to the Q section about John the Baptist.

[4] The saying in the Gospel of Thomas parallels the first half of the Q saying, but contains no statement about the law. It probably should not be considered as a variant of Q 16:17.

[5] A variant of this saying is quoted in 1 Clem. 46.8; see above # 2.1.4.3.

[6] Kloppenborg, Q Parallels, 154.

[7] See above note on Matt 7:22–23. Kloppenborg (Formation of Q, 224–25) includes Luke 13:26–27 in Q 13–14, but rightly excludes Luke 13:25 (ibid., p. 224–25, n. 217).

2.3.2.10 The Coming of the Son of Man

Pericope or Saying	Q / Luke	Matthew	Other
Desiring and not finding[1]	17:22		Gos. Thom. 38
The suddenness of the coming	17:23–24	24:26–27	Gos. Thom. 113
"Where the corpse is . . ."	17:37	24:28	
The days of Noah	17:26–30	24:37–38	
"Two will be on a couch . . ."	17:34–35	24:40–41	Gos. Thom. 61a
Parable of the Talents	19:12–25	25:14–28	
"Whoever has, shall be given"	19:26	25:29	Gos. Thom. 41[2]
Judging the tribes of Israel	22:28–30	19:28	

In its final form, this section of Q with its emphasis upon the sudden appearance of the Son of man is most characteristic of the theology of the redactor of Q. Although there are some parallels to this section in the *Gospel of Thomas,* none of them mentions the Son of man. These sayings paralleled in Thomas may indeed have been included in the original composition of Q; but it is difficult to be certain about their place and context in that first version of the Synoptic Sayings Source.

2.3.3 PURPOSE AND CONTEXT OF THE COMPOSITION OF Q

John Kloppenborg[3] has made an important contribution by defining the genre of the original composition of Q as a collection of sapiential speeches. This identifies the literary genre which served as the catalyst for the composition of this document and made it more than just a random collection of sayings. This genre-critical approach to the reconstruction of Q's history and redaction supersedes older attempts which tried to determine the stages of the development of Q on the basis of certain theological assumptions.[4] The demonstration of this

---

[1] This saying is generally considered not to have been part of Q. However, the parallel in the *Gospel of Thomas* and its usage in the Gospel of John (8:21–22; cf. 7:33–34; 13:33) demonstrate that this is indeed a variant of an older saying. The unusual and most likely secondary feature of the Q/Luke version is the introduction of the title "Son of man."

[2] A parallel is preserved in the small collection of sayings in Mark 4:21–25 (4:25 = Luke 8:18b).

[3] *The Formation of Q,* passim.

[4] For the older literature see Kloppenborg, *Formation of Q,* passim. Most evident is the failure of the "theological-history" approach in Siegfried Schulz, *Q: Die Spruchquelle der Evangelisten* (Zürich: Theologischer Verlag, 1972). Schulz assigns to the older Jewish-Christian community of Q all materials related to an assumed post-Easter enthusiasm and a prophetic radicalization of Torah. Schulz (and others) have rightly emphasized that the earliest composition of Q must have contained eschatological-prophetic elements. But the type of the eschatology which characterized this early stage of Q must be determined by form- and redaction-critiical analysis.

hypothesis necessarily implied the argument that the basic parts of this wisdom book were structured as wisdom discourses. Moreover, Dieter Lührmann[1] had already identified the apocalyptic tendency of a later redaction of Q—a radical departure from the orientation of an earlier stage of Q.[2] Kloppenborg further clarified how this apocalypticizing tendency of the redactor interfered with the original structure of the sapiential discourses, because the redactor created several sections which are characterized by the apocalyptic theme of the announcement of a future judgment over "this generation." Furthermore, the redactor revised several of the eschatological sayings of the original version of Q in such a way that they could serve as predictions of the coming judgment and of the appearance of the Son of man.

The original version of Q must have included wisdom sayings as well as eschatological sayings. It cannot be argued that Q originally presented Jesus simply as a teacher of wisdom without an eschatological message. The close relationships of the *Gospel of Thomas* to Q cannot be accidental.[3] Since the typical Son of man sayings and announcements of judgments which are characteristic of the redaction of Q are never paralleled in the *Gospel of Thomas,* it is evident that its author had no knowledge of the final version of Q, nor of the secondary apocalyptic interpretation that the redactor of Q superimposed upon earlier eschatological sayings. The *Gospel of Thomas* is either dependent upon Q's earlier version or upon clusters of sayings employed in its composition.

The eschatological orientation of the original composition of Q is distinctly different from the apocalyptic perspective of the redactor. This is striking with respect to the "announcement of judgment" section which discusses the role of John the Baptist. Two sayings of the original version of Q, paralleled in the *Gospel of Thomas,* were used in its composition:

---

[1] *Die Redaktion der Logienquelle,* passim.

[2] Paul Hoffmann (*Studien zur Theologie der Logienquelle* [NTA, NF 8; 3d ed.; Münster: Aschendorff, 1982]) has presented perhaps the most impressive theological interpretation of Q that rejects the attempt of a redaction-critical analysis. Lührmann's (*Redaktion,* 8) brief criticism of this approach is still valid.

[3] It has been argued in the preceding chapter that this has implications for the reconstruction of Q: parallels in Thomas to sayings which are attested only in either Matthew or Luke may well have been Q sayings.

Q/Luke 7:24–26	Gos. Thom. 78
When the messengers of John had departed, he began to speak to the crowds concerning John: "What did you go out to the wilderness to see? A reed shaken by the wind? But what did you go out to see? A man clothed in luxurious clothing? Behold, those who are richly clothed and live in luxury are in royal palaces. But what did you go out to see? A prophet? Yes I tell you, and more than a prophet."	Jesus said: "Why have you come out to the countryside? To see a reed shaken by the wind? And to see a person dressed in rich clothing like your rulers and your powerful ones? They are dressed in rich clothing, but they cannot understand the truth."

The Q saying is forced to refer to John through the addition of a secondary introduction (7:24a: "When the messengers of John had departed . . .") and indirectly through its conclusion (7:26: "A prophet? Yes, I tell you, and more than a prophet."); but even with this conclusion the saying would not necessarily refer to John the Baptist were it not placed into this context by the redactor of Q. It would be more natural to understand it as a saying pointing to Jesus himself and to his prophetic message to the poor in contrast to the claims of the rulers of the world. This is confirmed by the absence of any reference to John the Baptist in the Thomas version of the saying. On the other hand, the reference to the rich who cannot understand the truth is in keeping with the theology of the *Gospel of Thomas*. It appears to have replaced the more original reference to Jesus' prophetic ministry. In its original understanding and place in the first composition of Q, this saying is closely related to the "blessing of the poor" (Q/Luke 6:20), the opening phrase of Jesus' "inaugural sermon."

The second older saying used in the same context is Q 7:28:

Q 7:28	Gos. Thom. 46
I tell you, among those born of women no one is greater than John; yet the least in the kingdom of God is greater than he.	Among those born of women from Adam until John the Baptist, there is no one superior to John the Baptist that his eyes should not be lowered before him. Yet I have said, whichever one of you comes to be a child will be acquainted with the kingdom and will become superior to John.

Q 7:28 has been understood as a saying that praises the greatness of John (7:28a) with, as it seems, a secondary polemical Christian addition which in turn diminishes John's status (7:28b). However, the saying as it appears in *Gos. Thom.* 46 consists of two antithetical parts which form an original unity.[1] It does not contain a polemic against John the Baptist, nor does it assign the eschatological role of a precursor to him. The saying merely emphasizes the contrast between the old (from Adam to John) and the new (the kingdom). The polemical formulation ("[even] the smallest in the kingdom is greater than he") instead of "whoever becomes a child will know the kingdom and will become greater than [even] John" is probably due to the redactor of Q who inserted the saying into this context of the "announcement of judgment" section. The more original form of the saying would have been closer to the form preserved in the *Gospel of Thomas*. It was a saying which emphasized the eschatological moment of the kingdom's presence.

Q/Luke 10:23–24 is certainly a saying that circulated very early, since it can be presupposed for the discussion of Paul with Corinthians:[2]

> Blessed are the eyes that see what you see [and the ears that hear what you hear]. For I tell you that many prophets and kings wanted to see what you are seeing and did not see it, and to hear what you are hearing and did not hear it.

The closest parallel to this saying appears in *Gos. Thom.* 17 (cf. 1 Cor 2:9):[3]

> I shall give you what no eye has seen and what no ear has heard and what no hand has touched and what has never occurred to the human mind.

The same eschatological emphasis is found in several Q sayings which now appear in the "announcement of judgment" sections of Q/Luke 11, 12 and 17 but should be assigned to the original composition of Q. Most of these have parallels in the *Gospel of Thomas*. The eschatological presence of salvation is emphasized in Q/Luke

---

[1] See the discussion in Kloppenborg, *Formation of Q*, 109, n. 30.

[2] See above, # 2.1.3.

[3] Cf. also *Gos. Thom.* 38: "Many times have you desired to hear these words which I am saying to you, and you have no one else to hear them from. There will be days when you look for me and will not find me." This may be a variant of the same saying, but it is more closely related to sayings which are used in the Gospel of John about the coming and going of the revealer; see above, # 2.2.5.

11:27–28[1] which may have followed the preceding saying in the original version of Q:[2]

> As he was saying these things, a woman from the crowd raised her voice and said to him, "Blessed is the womb that bore you and the breasts that you sucked." And he said, "Rather, blessed are those who hear the word of God and keep it."

In Q/Luke 12 there are seven units of sayings which constitute the "announcement of judgment" section of Q 12:39–59. Of these as many as five have parallels in the *Gospel of Thomas,* and in every instance an apocalyptic orientation has not yet been introduced into the sayings of Thomas' version.

Q/Luke 12:39–40	Gos. Thom. 21b, 103[3]
But recognize this, that if the householder had known what hour (Matt: in what part of the night) the thief was coming he would not have left his house to be dug into.	Therefore I say: if the owner of a house knows that a thief is coming, he will be on guard before he comes and will not let him dig through into his house of his domain to carry away his goods. You then be on guard against the world. Arm yourself with great strength, lest the robbers find a way to come to you.
You also must be ready, for the Son of Man will come at an hour you do not expect.	

In both citations of this saying in the *Gospel of Thomas* the emphasis lies on preparedness in general, not on the uncertainty with respect to the hour or the time of night at which the thief is coming. The latter perspective is the result of a secondary interpretation by the redactor of Q who also added the reference to the coming of the Son of man.[4] That the eschatological presence of the salvation which is emphasized in the original version of Q implies danger, controversy, and division is

---

[1] There is no parallel to this saying in the Gospel of Matthew. But the saying also appears in *Gos. Thom.* 79 where it is expanded by a negative statement of a more apocalyptic flavor: "For there will be days when you will say, 'Blessed are the womb which has not conceived and the breasts which have not given milk.'"

[2] According to Kloppenborg (*Formation of Q,* 121) this saying now appears in an "announcement of judgment" section that is obviously composed by the redactor: Q 11:14–52. But Kloppenborg does not think that Luke 11:27–28 was an original part of this section.

[3] The same metaphor is quoted in *Gos. Thom.* 103: "Fortunate is the man who knows where the brigands will enter, so that he may get up, muster his domain, and arm himself before they invade."

[4] On the composite character of Q 12:39–40 see Schulz, *Spruchquelle,* 268–71; Kloppenborg, *Formation of Q,* 149.

also emphasized in the three following sayings in this section which
have parallels in the *Gospel of Thomas* :

Q/Luke 12:49 (cf. *Gos. Thom.* 10):
I have come to cast fire upon the earth, and how I wish that it were
already ablaze!

Q/Luke 12:51 (cf. *Gos. Thom.* 16a):
Do you think that I have come to give peace upon the earth? No, I tell
you, but rather division (Matt: but the sword).

Q/Luke 12:52–53 (cf. *Gos. Thom.* 16b):
For from now on there will be five in one house divided, three against
two and two against three; they will be divided father against son and
son against father, mother against daughter and daughter against her
mother . . .

In the present context these sayings, especially Q 12:52–53, speak of
the apocalyptic divisions which are expected to come in the future.[1]
But Q 12:49 and 51 still reveal in their formulation that they originally
announced the eschatological events directly related to Jesus' coming
and his message, not to an expected apocalyptic event of the future.
Since also the blessing of those who are persecuted (Q 6:22–23) belongs
to the original stage of Q, the saying of Q 12:52–53 "might have been
understood concretely with reference to the rejection and violence
experienced by members of the community itself."[2]

The final saying in this section, Q/Luke 12:54–56 (cf. *Gos. Thom.*
91), even in the form in which it is preserved by Luke,[3] emphasizes the
eschatological moment and does not reveal any redactional changes
which would make this saying conform more with the future-oriented
eschatology of the redactor of Q:[4]

Q/Luke 12:54–56	*Gos. Thom.* 91

When you see a cloud rising in the
west, you say immediately, "Rain is
coming," and so it happens. And

---

[1] For an analysis of this latter saying and its traditional apocalyptic connotations,
see Schulz, *Spruchquelle,* 258–60.

[2] Kloppenborg, *Formation of Q,* 152, with reference to Hoffmann, *Studien,* 72–73.

[3] Luke 12:56 reads τὸν καιρὸν δὲ τοῦτον πῶς οὐκ οἴδατε δοκιμάζειν; Matt 16:3 has
changed this to τὰ δὲ σημεῖα τῶν καιρῶν.

[4] Even Kloppenborg (*Formation of Q,* 152) admits: "Even though it does not spell out
a specific apocalyptic timetable . . ." But he continues to relate the saying to an
impending apocalyptic catastrophe.

when a south wind is blowing, you
say, "it will be hot," and it happens.
Hypocrites, you know how to
interpret the face of the earth and the   You read the face of the sky and the
sky; but   earth, but you have not recognized
                                            the one who is before you, and you do
why do you not know how to interpret   not know how to interpret this
the present moment?   moment.

John Kloppenborg has called "the threat of apocalyptic judgment . . .
the formative literary and theological motif in this cluster of Q sayings."[1] As these sayings appear now in the final redaction of Q, this is
undoubtedly correct. But the older Q materials used for the composition of this section did not speak about the threat of apocalyptic judgment. Rather, this theme has found expression only by means of
editorial changes in the older sayings and through the insertion of
additional apocalyptic materials. The unit that most strongly fits this
redactional tendency is the so-called parable of the Faithful and
Unfaithful Servants (Q/Luke 12:42b–46). Parallels to this unit are
missing in the *Gospel of Thomas*—no surprise, because it cannot be
understood as an older traditional saying at all. Rather, it is an
allegorizing redactional creation which is wholly dominated by the
expectation of reward and punishment in the coming judgment.

The Q apocalypse of Luke 17:20–37, in its present form the product
of the redactor, may also contain some older eschatological sayings.
There are no parallels in the *Gospel of Thomas* to the coming of the
Son of man like lightning (Q/Luke 17:23–24), nor to the expansion of
this saying by the comparison with the days of Noah (and the Sodom-
ites, Q 17:26–32). Thomas provides a parallel only to two sayings from
this apocalypse: Q/Luke 17:20–21 = *Gos. Thom.* 113 (cf. also # 3) and
Q/Luke 17:34 = *Gos. Thom.* 61a. While the latter saying, speaking
about the divisions which occur in the eschatological moment, is a
variant of the saying Q 12:51–52 = *Gos. Thom.* 16 (see above), the first
of these sayings (which has no parallel in Matthew) emphasizes the
mysterious presence of the kingdom:

Q/Luke 17:20–21	*Gos. Thom.* 113
When he was asked by the Pharisees when the kingdom of God would be coming, he answered them, and said,	His disciples said to him, "When will the kingdom come?"

---

[1] *Formation of Q,* 148.

| "The kingdom of God does not come by observation, nor will they say, 'Lo, it is here,' or 'There.' For behold, the kingdom of God is among you." | Jesus said, "It will not come by waiting for it. It will not be a matter of saying, 'Here,' or 'There it is.' Rather the kingdom of the Father is spread out upon the earth, and human beings do not see it." |

The phrase of Luke 17:21, which is translated here with "the kingdom of God is among you" (ἡ βασιλεία τοῦ θεοῦ ἐντὸς ὑμῶν ἐστιν), should not be interpreted either psychologically ("the kingdom of God is in your hearts") or in terms of future eschatology ("the kingdom of God will be there suddenly"),[1] although the latter interpretation may have been intended by the redactor of Q. The parallel in the *Gospel of Thomas* demonstrates that the kingdom is understood to be mysteriously present in the understanding and in the actions of the disciples. The author of the *Gospel of Thomas* may have intended a spiritualized (possibly "Gnostic") interpretation. But in the context of the original version of Q, this saying referred to the disciples' ability to grasp the significance of the eschatological moment in which their response to Jesus' words creates new dimensions of human existence.

It is in this light that one must read the wisdom discourses of the original composition of the Synoptic Sayings Source. The inaugural sermon of Jesus, Q/Luke 6:20–49, is a wisdom discourse, and even the blessings at the beginning of the inaugural sermon have their parallels in wisdom literature. However, while Wisdom calls blessed the wise who follow her precepts and do what is demanded,[2] Jesus blesses the situation in which those to whom his message comes happen to be: the poor, the hungry, those who weep, those who are persecuted. Such beatitudes are not sapiential, but prophetic.[3] The first sentences of the original version of Q introduce Jesus as a prophet, not as a teacher of wisdom.[4] His message fulfills the expectation that is, in a different context and tradition, expressed in the eschatological psalms of

---

[1] For a discussion of the various alternatives in understanding this phrase, see the commentaries.

[2] For examples of this typical wisdom makarism, see Prov 8:32, 34; Sir 14:1, 2, 20; 50:28. There are also numerous parallels in wisdom psalms: Ps 1:1; 106:3; 112:1; 119:1–2; 128:1–2. In early-Christian literature, such makarisms appear typically in writings which are dependent upon Jewish wisdom traditions: James 1:12, 25; *Did.* 1.5. See also Koester, *Synoptische Überlieferung*, 234–35.

[3] Kloppenborg (*Formation of Q*, 188–89) realizes that these beatitudes do not fit the normal pattern of sapiential blessings, but maintains that "the contents of Q 6:20b–49 are overwhelmingly sapiential."

[4] Schulz (*Spruchquelle*, 79–81) is correct in his claim for a prophetic understanding of the beatitudes. However, they should not be called "prophetic-apocalyptic," referring to the future enthronement of God.

Luke 1.[1] These eschatological makarisms are resumed in Q in the "blessedness of the witnesses" (Q 10:23–24) and the "blessedness of those hear his word" (Q 11:28).[2]

The admonitions which follow upon the beatitudes of the inaugural sermon formally correspond to the genre of the wisdom discourse.[3] However, with respect to their content, they depart radically from admonitions normally found in this genre of literature. The traditional wisdom discourse advises the followers of wisdom either with respect to prudent and merciful behavior in the existing society,[4] or it encourages them to remain faithful to the precepts of wisdom (and of the law) even in face of the rejection by the world, promising a heavenly reward and vindication. The admonitions of Q 6:27–36 are fundamentally different. To love one's enemies, to turn the other cheek, to lend to those from whom no return can be expected—these are neither admonitions to prudent and merciful behavior nor do they encourage the faithful fulfillment of wisdom's precepts in an otherwise hostile society. On the contrary, they send the disciples into the midst of the society in which their deeds will announce the eschatological moment in which new criteria for human action and interaction will change the world. Only the following admonitions on judging, blind guides, teacher and student, hypocrisy, good fruit from good trees, and building the house on firm ground (Q 6:37–45) rehearse traditional wisdom themes, albeit sometimes radicalized.[5] The conclusion, Q 6:46–49, is a typical peroration of a wisdom discourse.[6] Thus in its structure and organization, the inaugural sermon is, no doubt, sapiential.[7] The wisdom discourse is the genre which guided its literary composition. However, it incorporates a message of

---

[1] The so-called Magnificat (Luke 1:46–55) and Benedictus (Luke 1:68–79).

[2] On the different character of the beatitudes in the Sermon on the Mount (Matt 5:3–12) see Betz, *Essays*, 22–32.

[3] This, however, cannot be decided on the basis of the introduction λεγὼ ὑμῖν (Schulz, *Spruchquelle*, 79); see Kloppenborg, *Formation of Q*, 176.

[4] The examples for such wisdom admonitions which are adduced by Kloppenborg (*Formation of Q*, 177) as parallels to the command to love one's enemy (Sir 4:10; Seneca *De beneficiis* 4.26.1) prove the point: they simply recommend that one be kind to widows and orphans and bestow benefits on the ungrateful.

[5] See the references in Kloppenborg, *Formation of Q*, 178–85.

[6] Kloppenborg, *Formation of Q*, 185–87. Hoffmann (*Studien*, 155) sees the parable of the Builders in the context of the expectation of Jesus' coming as the Son of man; this view of the parable neglects the results of the redaction-critical analysis of Q. In the context of the discourse Q 6:20–49, any reference to a future eschatological figure is uncalled for.

[7] Kloppenborg, *Formation of Q*, 189.

a realized eschatology which determined the self-understanding of the early Q community.

The discourse on discipleship and mission (Q 9:57–62; 10:2–12 [13–15],[1] 16, 21–24) is introduced by radical eschatological demands. To follow Jesus means to follow the human being ("son of man") who has no place to lay his head (Q 9:57–58) and to leave it to the "dead" to bury the dead (Q 9:59–60). The mission discourse itself may indeed contain rules which resemble those given to a Cynic teacher (Q 10:4–7), but the purpose of the mission is once again the proclamation of the eschatological moment: "Heal those who are sick and say, 'the kingdom of God has come upon you'" (Q 10:9). If Q 10:13–15 belongs to the redactor, the original discourse did not speak about a future judgment awaiting those who do not repent, but assured the disciples that the rejection they experience is, in fact, a rejection of Jesus himself (Q 10:12). The thanksgiving for revelation and the blessedness of the witnesses (Q 10:21–24) demonstrate that the urgency of the mission is not dictated by the nearness of the coming judgment but by the knowledge of the present eschatological fulfillment.

More traditional wisdom and "two ways" materials appear in the Q discourse preserved in Luke 11–12. These include instructions on prayer (Q 11:2–4, 9–13),[2] the admonition not to fear those who can kill the body (Q 12:4–7), the warning not to blaspheme the spirit, and the assurance of the support of the spirit (Q 12:10–12). Perhaps also the rule against dividing inherited worldly goods and the parable of the Rich Fool (Q 12:13–21), and finally the sayings against worldly cares (Q 12:22–34) fit well into an eschatologically-oriented collection of wisdom sayings and community rules.

The final major block of materials from the original sapiential speeches is preserved in some of the Q materials of Luke 13–14. Kloppenborg[3] assigns the following materials to this section: Luke 13:24–30, 34–35; 14:16–24, 26–27; 17:33;[4] 14:34–35. However, Q/Luke

---

[1] Whether this saying, with its "woe" against Chorazin and Bethsaida, belongs to the original discourse, seems questionable. Lührmann (*Redaktion*, 60–61) assigns it to a later stage because of its close connection to Q 10:21–22, together with Q 10:2, which in his judgment presupposes the Gentile mission. Neither argument is convincing. The Gentile mission began during the very first years of the Jesus movement, and the heightened wisdom christology expressed in 10:21–22 must already be presupposed for 1 Corinthians 1–4. On the other hand, 10:13–15 reveals an apocalyptic orientation which is more characteristic of the redaction of Q.

[2] Perhaps also the instruction about clean and unclean, Q 11:39–40, which the redactor incorporated into the discourse against the Pharisees was part of this section in the non-polemical version in which it is preserved in the *Gospel of Thomas*.

[3] *Formation of Q*, 223–37.

[4] Luke 17:33 = Matt 10:39 must have followed originally upon Luke 14:26–27 = Matt 10:37–38.

13:34–35, the lament over Jerusalem, seems to be out of place and could be assigned to the "announcement of judgment" redaction of Q.[1] On the other hand, one might add Q 15:4–7 (Lost Sheep), 16:13, 17–18 (serving two masters, on the law, and on marriage and divorce) and Q 17:1–6 (on scandals, forgiveness, and faith). They fit well into a section that has been correctly characterized as the "two ways."[2] The metaphor of the "narrow gate" (Q 13:24) explicitly designates this section as "instruction" (διδαχή). However, this is not teaching for an isolated Jewish-Christian community. The following sayings in this section, Q 13:26–27 (rejection of the false teachers) and 28–30 (Gentiles in the kingdom), imply that the Q community has gone into the Gentile mission. Since 13:26 speaks of those "who have taught," it should not be construed as a rejection of unbelieving Jews, but of those who have refused to participate in the mission to the Gentiles or have hindered it.[3] The parable of the Great Supper (Q 14:16–21a, 23) continues this emphasis upon the invitation of the Gentiles.[4] Most of the community rules that follow are not typical for a Jewish-Christian community, but could be found anywhere in community regulations which are dependent upon "two ways" materials.

For the followers of Jesus whose tradition is represented in the original composition of Q, the turning point of the ages is the proclamation of Jesus. In the sayings of Jesus, his followers find the continuation of this announcement. These sayings are not only reassurance of the eschatological moment, they are also the rule of life for the community of the new age insofar as Jesus continues to speak in sayings of wisdom and in rules for the community. Jesus may indeed have been viewed as the heavenly Wisdom. This is especially evident in Q 10:21–22 which defines the relationship of Jesus to the Father in terms of the established sapiential concept of Wisdom and God.[5] If Q 13:34–35, the lament over Jerusalem, should belong to the original composition of Q, Jesus is also the one who sends Wisdom's envoys.

---

[1] Most likely, Matt 23:37–39 has preserved its original location in Q, i.e., at the end of the speech against the Pharisees. See Lührmann, *Redaktion,* 48.

[2] Kloppenborg, *Q Parallels,* p. xxxii.

[3] Luke's text is to be preferred here. Matt 7:22–23 has changed the Q text into a condemnation of Hellenistic charismatics; see below on the Sermon on the Mount, # 2.3.4.

[4] Luke 14:21b–22 is a secondary Lukan addition which expresses a special interest in the invitation of the poor to the kingdom. It seems that Luke 14:24 also is a Lukan addition; the original Q parable did not especially emphasize the rejection of those who were invited first (= Israel).

[5] Kloppenborg, *Formation of Q,* 319–20.

Just as the departure of Wisdom or of her envoy does not constitute a change in the urgency of the message, so too Jesus' death would not be seen as a crisis of his proclamation. The disciples are already called to follow in the steps of Jesus, in their discipleship (Q 9:57–62) as well as in their task to carry on his proclamation (Q 10:2–12). Jesus' departure would make this call even more urgent. The ages have already begun to turn through Jesus' announcement. Any emphasis upon Jesus' suffering, death, and resurrection would be meaningless in this context. Thus Q can not be seen as a teaching supplement for a community whose theology is represented by the Pauline kerygma. Q's theology and soteriology are fundamentally different.

If these formative concepts for the tradition and composition of Q can be explained as a continuation of wisdom teaching, a departure from these concepts is evident in two respects: (1) the ethical demands of Q are far more radical than those of traditional wisdom teaching; (2) Q's wisdom is addressed to a community in whose life the kingdom of God is present, not to an individual who follows the advice of a father or teacher. Kloppenborg[1] has emphasized that "in contrast to the generally conservative comportment of the (traditional wisdom) instruction, Q represents an ethic of radical discipleship which reverses many of the conventions which allow a society to operate, such as principles of retaliation, the orderly borrowing and lending of capital, appropriate treatment of the dead, responsible self-provision, self-defense and honor of parents."[2] Instead, the behavior which Jesus requests is a demonstration of the kingdom's presence, i.e., of a society which is governed by new principles of ethics. This not only ascribes a kerygmatic quality to the ethical demands of Jesus, it presents Jesus as a prophet rather than a teacher of wisdom. Although formal claims of Jesus to prophetic authorization, such as a vision of a calling or the introductory formula "thus says the Lord," are missing, the prophetic role of Jesus is evident in the address of these ethical demands to a community, not just to individual followers. To be sure, there are no such terms as "New Israel" in Q; these people called by Jesus are not just a sectarian group, but represent the community of the new ages, the people of God. They are the ones who will sit at table with Abraham in the banquet of the kingdom (Q 13:28–30).

It may seem surprising that a community which claims in such a radical form the presence of a new society does not reflect, in its tradition, more vestiges of a controversy with Judaism, i.e., the religious

---

[1] Ibid., 318–21.
[2] Ibid., 318.

and social world from which it presumably emerged and which continued to form its cultural and religious matrix. There is certainly a strongly emphasized awareness of persecution (Q 6:22–23), rejection (Q 10:16), and division (Q 12:49–53); but these experiences are not understood as a rejection by "the Jews" or by "Israel." The woes against the Pharisees (Q 11:37–52) belong—except for one or two sayings—to the secondary redaction of Q, as do other polemical texts. The question encountered here is not so much a difficulty in defining the setting of the Q community, as it is a problem of the traditional understanding of what is commonly called "Judaism" and of the relationship of "Jews" and "Christians" at the beginnings of the Jesus movement. Both terms are as inappropriate as the notion that Jesus was rejected by the "Jews" and that they killed him. The context of Jesus' proclamation and of the mission of his followers after his execution (by the Roman authorities!) was one of great diversity within Israel, characterized by the not always peaceful coexistence of various groups and sects in Palestine as well as in the diaspora. Hostility and persecution that one sectarian group experienced at the hand of others was not necessarily understood as a rejection by "Israel."

Unfortunately, the texts belonging to the original composition of Q are completely silent with respect to the question of Israel's temple and law.[1] The saying about washing the outside of the cup (Q 11:39–40), originally probably not a saying against the Pharisees, gives voice to a lack of concern with respect to the technical questions of law observance. If Q 11:52,[2] accusing the Pharisees that they have taken the keys of knowledge, belongs to Q's original composition, it does not criticize the Pharisees' praxis of observing the law, but their claim to exclusive teaching authority.[3] A special problem is presented by Q 16:16, a saying which contrasts the law and the prophets "until John" with the kingdom of God. However, the original wording and meaning of the saying is so uncertain that it would be unwise to base any hypothesis upon its interpretation.[4] Moreover, it is quite unlikely

---

[1] The case would, of course, be different if one ascribed *Toraverschärfung* and polemic against the Pharisees to the seminal texts of Q (Schulz, *Spruchquelle*, 94–141).

[2] = *Gos. Thom.* 39.

[3] This is also expressed in the second saying against the Pharisees in the *Gospel of Thomas* (#102): "Woe to the Pharisees, for they are like a dog sleeping in a manger of oxen, for neither does he eat nor does he [let] the oxen eat."

[4] "The pericope is a notorious *crux interpretum* and virtually every detail is disputed: its position in the order of Q, the original order of its two component statements (Matt 11:12–13 || Luke 16:16a, b), the reconstruction of the original saying and its meaning" (Kloppenborg, *Formation of Q*, 113). For further discussion and literature see ibid., 112–115.

that this saying can be assigned to the original composition of Q; it fits better into the redactor's interest "in the opposition between Jesus (and John) on one side, and 'this generation' on the other."[1] Q 16:17 ("It is easier for heaven and earth to pass away than for one dot of the law to be dropped") should be assigned to the redactor of Q because of its apocalyptic perspective.[2] But it certainly indicates that the law is considered as binding for the community.

As a whole the sapiential speeches of Q are not concerned with the question of law and tradition. Their message transcends the limitations of Israel and of its religious tradition; the mission of the disciples is to everyone. Jesus' command not to go to the streets of the Gentiles and to the cities of the Samaritans (Matt 10:5–6) was added later to Q's mission speech by Matthew.[3] It has no place in the older version of that speech. That the Gentiles are invited is evident in Q 13:28–30: "They will come from the East and the West ..." But this does not imply that the community placed itself outside of Israel. Q was composed at a time when the controversy of the law had not yet emerged, and when the question of observance of the Law had not yet been used as a criterion in order to decide whether or not the followers of Jesus were within or outside of Israel. Such a situation can be assumed to have existed during the first years after the death of Jesus anywhere in Palestine or anywhere in the diaspora where the question of the law, triggered by the Pauline mission, was not yet a concern. A Greek-speaking environment is more likely than an area of towns and villages in which the predominant language was Aramaic.

2.3.4 THE REDACTION OF Q AND ITS PLACE IN ISRAEL

The redaction of Q presents a different picture. There are three new elements: (1) the announcement of judgment over "this generation"; (2) the apocalyptic expectation of Jesus' return as the Son of man; (3) the demarcation of the line that both relates and separates Jesus and John the Baptist. The third element may constitute the last stage of the redaction of Q prior to its use by Luke.

Those who do not accept the message of Jesus and oppose the community are generally called "this generation." The term occurs for the first time at the end of the discourse about John the Baptist in the

---

[1] Kloppenborg, *Formation of Q*, 114.

[2] This saying is assigned by Schulz (*Spruchquelle*, 114–16) to the oldest stratum of Q. However, Schulz correctly describes its apocalyptic orientation.

[3] It is possible that these verses had their origin in the Jewish-Christian redaction of Q that also produced the version of the Sermon on the Mount used by Matthew. On this Jewish-Christian redaction of Q see below # 2.3.4.

introduction to the parable of the Children in the Market (Q 7:31). The opponents are characterized as those who refused to listen; John and Jesus belong together insofar as they are two representatives of the divine envoys whose message was ignored. In the "announcement of judgment" section Q 11:14–52, the polemic is more explicit. In the Beelzebul Controversy (Q 11:14–23), the opponents[1] question the divine authorization of the work of Jesus and thus the legitimacy of the message of the community. Q 11:19 (". . . through whom do your sons drive out demons?") may indicate that Israel as a whole is implicated.[2] But this is not stated explicitly. Even in the pericope concerning the sign of Jonah (Q 11:16,[3] 29–32), the opponents remain anonymous: "Others, in order to test him, were seeking from him a sign from heaven" (Q 11:16).[4]

A more specific identification of the opponents appears in the woes against the Pharisees (Q 11:47–52). But because of the differences in the address in Matthew and Luke, the text of Q cannot always be reconstructed with certainty. Luke's identification of those who are addressed in the woes changes from "Pharisees" (Φαρισαῖοι, 11:39, 42, 43) to "lawyers" (νομικοί, 11:46, 52), while Matthew addresses the woes which derive from Q to the "scribes and Pharisees, hypocrites" (Γραμματεῖς καὶ Φαρισαῖοι ὑποκριταί, 23:13, 23, 25, 27, 29; cf. 23:2). It is usually held that the latter address is due to Matthew's redaction.[5] But while there can be no doubt that the addition of "hypocrites" must be ascribed to Matthew,[6] the address to the "scribes and Pharisees" appears in Matthew 23 consistently in the introduction to materials which derive from Q.[7] In instances of other materials and of redactional additions, Matthew uses this phrase only once (23:15); else-

---

[1] The text of Q simply introduced them as τινές ("some"); Matt 12:24 has changed this to "the Pharisees"; cf. Mark 3:22: "The scribes who had come down from Jerusalem."

[2] Kloppenborg, *Formation of Q*, 127.

[3] Q 11:16 has been placed into the Beelzebul controversy by Luke; its original position in Q as the introduction to the sign of Jonah pericope is beyond doubt; cf. Matt 12:38 where this sentence properly introduces that pericope (Matt 12:39–41 = Luke 11:29–32).

[4] It is again Matthew (12:38; cf. 16:1) who introduced the scribes and Pharisees as the opponents.

[5] See, e.g., Schulz, *Spruchquelle*, 95–96; Kloppenborg, *Formation of Q*, 142 (n. 175: "The phrase 'scribes and Pharisees' is almost certainly Matthean").

[6] Matthew adds this word also in other contexts of controversy with the Pharisees; compare Matt 15:7 with Mark 7:6, and Matt 24:51 (μετὰ τῶν ὑποκριτῶν) with Luke 12:46 (μετὰ τῶν ἀπίστων).

[7] The mention of the "scribes and Pharisees" in Matt 23:2 also belongs to these Q passages because it appears in the general Matthean introduction to the speech in which Q 11:46 = Matt 23:4 is the first of the Q sayings used by Matthew.

where he prefers different addresses.[1] On the other hand, Luke's address "lawyers" is so typically Lukan that it cannot derive from Q, and Luke's assignment of the first woes to the Pharisees and the rest of the woes to the lawyers is artificial. That the woes were addressed in Q to the "scribes and Pharisees" finds a confirmation in the parallel to Q 11:52 in *Gos. Thom.* 39 ("Pharisees and scribes").[2] This would suggest that "scribes and Pharisees" are the opponents of the Q community throughout its history, from the composition of the sapiential speeches—polemic against those who took away the key of knowledge would be quite appropriate here—even to the reformulation of the Q material in the Sermon on the Mount (see below) and ultimately to the Gospel of Matthew itself. Important for the understanding of Q's polemic against the scribes and Pharisees is Q 16:17: the law will retain its validity until this world will come to an end. The redactor of Q does not place the new community outside of Israel and of its law.

Q 10:13–15 announces the coming judgment explicitly with the view to two Galilean towns, Chorazin and Bethsaida: even Tyre and Sidon will be better off in the coming judgment. And the same saying threatens that Capernaum will be condemned to Hades. Except for the lament over Jerusalem (Q 13:34–35) and the localization of John the Baptist's activity in the area of the Jordan (Q 3:3), these are the only names of places which occur in Q. It is, therefore, tempting to assume that the redaction of Q took place somewhere in Galilee and that the document as a whole reflects the experience of a Galilean community of followers of Jesus. But some caution with respect to such conclusion seems advisable for several reasons. One single saying provides a very narrow base. Polemic against the Pharisees cannot confirm Galilean provenience—Greek-speaking Pharisees could be found elsewhere in the diaspora, viz., Paul who persecuted the church in Greek-speaking synagogues, probably in Syria or Cilicia. Even the sayings used for the original composition of Q were known and used elsewhere at an early date: they were known to Paul, were used in Corinth by his opponents, employed perhaps in eastern Syria for the composition of the *Gospel of Thomas,* and quoted by *1 Clement* in Rome at the end of the 1st century. The document itself, in its final redacted form, was used for the composition of two gospel writings, Matthew and Luke, which both originated in the Greek-speaking church outside of Palestine.

---

[1] "Blind guides" (ὁδηγοὶ τυφλοί, 23:16, 24), "blind Pharisee" (Φαρισαῖε τυφλέ, 23:26), "serpents, brood of vipers" (ὄφεις, γεννήματα ἐχιδνῶν, 23:33).

[2] For the appearance of "Pharisees" in traditional sayings, cf. *Gos. Thom.* 102; for "scribes" cf. Mark 12:38.

On the other hand, the Synoptic Sayings Source is an important piece of evidence for the continuation of a theology of followers of Jesus that had no relationship to the kerygma of the cross and resurrection. It is evident now that this was not an isolated phenomenon. The opponents of Paul in 1 Corinthians 1–4, the *Gospel of Thomas,* the *Dialogue of the Savior,* and the opponents of the Gospel of John in the Johannine community[1] all shared this understanding of the significance of Jesus' coming. This in itself does not establish a date for the redaction of Q. There is, however, one feature in the redaction of Q which ties this document to a particular geographical area, namely, the expectation of the coming Son of man and the use of this term as a christological title. The redactor of Q shares this title of Jesus with apocalyptic traditions used by the Gospels of Mark and John. It occurs nowhere else in early Christian literature, and it is most probable that there is only one common origin for its emergence.

As long as one assumes that the Gospel of Mark was composed in Rome and John's Gospel in Ephesus, the explanation of their common dependence upon traditions using this title is difficult to explain. It is much more likely that all three documents—Mark, John, and Q in its final redaction—originated in the same geographical area, namely, western Syria or Palestine.[2] More important than the precise geographical location is the question of the religious ferment that triggered this novel interpretation of the role of Jesus as a coming figure of the apocalyptic drama. The Judaic War of 66–73 CE is usually the event which one associates with such ferment. But there may have been other events during the decades before the Judaic War that could have triggered a more intense apocalyptic expectation.[3]

Mark 13:14 and 14:62 (cf. 13:26) point to the Book of Daniel[4] as the scriptural text which was seminal for the development of the apocalyptic expectation of Jesus as the coming Son of man. But it is difficult to be more precise with respect to geographical origin and exact date because a literary relationship between Mark and Q cannot be demonstrated.[5] However, an organized community in which the apocalyptic

---

[1] See below, ## 3.1.1 and 3.4.4.4.

[2] With respect to Mark and John, this will be discussed further below (## 3.4 and 4.1).

[3] Schmithals (*Einleitung,* 400) dates the Markan apocalypse in the year 40 CE, when Caligula ordered his statue to be erected in the temple of Jerusalem.

[4] Explicit quotations and deliberate allusions to Dan 7:13 and 9:27 are evident in these passages.

[5] Some scholars have claimed that the redaction of Q presupposes the Gospel of Mark (see Schmithals, *Einleitung,* 398–99) because of the reference to Jesus' miracle-working in the answer to John the Baptist's disciples (Q 7:18–23). Even the Q story of the temptation of Jesus (Q 4:1–13) has been understood as a direct development of

interpretation of scripture was an ongoing activity must be presupposed.[1] The scriptural texts used are those of the Greek translation. A Greek-speaking environment is once again more likely than an area like Galilee where Aramaic would have been the more common language. On the other hand, for the redactor of Q "this generation" is represented by the (scribes and) Pharisees, the teachers of Israel. The question of unbelief in Israel weighs more heavily than rejection by the Gentile world.

The Synoptic Sayings Source was used in this revised form by the author of the Gospel of Luke, perhaps in Antioch or in Ephesus. Was it also known to Papias of Hierapolis, and should his reference to "Matthew who composed the sayings" be understood as a testimony to Q, circulating as a document under the authority of Matthew? In spite of major and weighty objections,[2] this hypothesis has merits. While Papias talks about Mark as composing the "things said and done by the Lord,"[3] he ascribes to Matthew only the composition of "the sayings" (τὰ λόγια).[4] The *Gospel of Thomas* gives conclusive evidence that the apostle Thomas was considered in the tradition as the author of a work that contained mostly sayings of Jesus. It may be more than accidental that Matthew and Thomas are mentioned side by side in the Synoptic Gospels' lists of the apostles: Mark 3:18; Matt 10:3; Luke 6:15.[5] In the *Dialogue of the Savior,* Judas (Thomas) and Matthew, together with Mary, are the disciples who question Jesus about the interpretation of his sayings. In the *Gospel of Thomas,* Peter, Matthew, and Thomas are the three disciples who respond to Jesus' question, "compare me to someone and tell me who I am like" (# 13). Matthew's answer is, "You are like a wise philosopher." Thomas's answer, which follows, is evidently a reference to this apostle as the possessor of the secret tradition and thus as the author of a writing of secret sayings: Jesus draws Thomas aside and tells him three things which he cannot divulge. Does this imply that Matthew was known as

---

Mark 1:21–22. But these Q sayings do not presuppose the Gospel of Mark itself; they are dependent upon traditions also used by Mark. It is certainly absurd to see the lament over Jerusalem (Q 13:34–35) as a proleptic reference to Mark's story of Jesus' entry to Jerusalem; cf. Q 13:35b, ". . . you will not see until it happens that you say 'Blessed is the one who comes in the name of the Lord.'" This final clause of the Q saying refers to the eschatological coming of the Son of man.

[1] This is also evident in the explicit references to Genesis 7, 18, and 19 in the Q apocalypse, Luke 17:27–32.

[2] For a summary of this discussion see Cameron, *Apocryphon of James,* 108–12.

[3] Eusebius *Hist. eccl.* 3.39.15.

[4] Eusebius *Hist. eccl.* 3.39.16.

[5] In Acts 1:13, Thomas is listed together with Philip and separated from Matthew by Bartholomew.

the authority for a book of sayings of wisdom, sapiential discourses? This questions could perhaps be answered in the affirmative.

The Gospel of Matthew may have taken over the name of its author from the source of sayings that was used in its composition. But it is not likely that Matthew used Q in the same form in which it was known to Luke. While general differences in the use of Q sayings by Matthew and Luke do not necessarily require a complex hypothesis of two different redactions of Q, the Sermon on the Mount of Matthew 5–7, in which one finds almost all the sayings from Q's inaugural discourse and many other Q materials, raises the question of a further pre-Matthean redaction of Q. The past scholarly consensus was, of course, that the author of the Gospel of Matthew composed the Sermon on the Mount. In that case, one could assume that Matthew knew Q in the same form as it was used by Luke. However, this consensus has recently been questioned by Hans Dieter Betz in several articles which are now conveniently collected in one volume in English translation.[1] Betz's observations are significant for the understanding of the further development of the community of Q. He distinguishes between the concerns of the Sermon on the Mount and those of Matthew with regard to the relationship of the followers of Jesus to Judaism. The former is committed to defining the theology of the followers of Jesus in such a way that they can justify their continued legitimate existence within Judaism. Matthew, on the other hand, presupposes the situation "of the universal church which has already incorporated Jewish-Christian traditions as well as Gentile-Christian communities."[2]

The author of the Sermon on the Mount faces and solves a problem that was not yet explicit in the original composition of Q, namely, the relationship of the followers of Jesus to the law-abiding community of Israel. The controversies with "this generation" and the polemic against the Pharisees in the redaction of Q reflects, as we saw, rejection by other groups within Israel; but they did not yet raise clearly the challenge for the followers of Jesus to define in which way they could justify their claim to be counted as truly law-abiding Israelites, in whatever form they understood and interpreted the law. The urgency of an answer to this question, Betz argues,[3] was ultimately dictated by

[1] *Essays on the Sermon on the Mount* (Philadelphia: Fortress, 1985). Hans Dieter Betz intends to put forward a conclusive presentation of his arguments in a forthcoming commentary on the Sermon on the Mount, to be published by Fortress Press in the Hermeneia series.

[2] Hans Dieter Betz, "The Beatitudes of the Sermon on the Mount," in idem, *Essays*, 22.

[3] Ibid., 19–22.

the Pauline Gentile Christianity which had declared and propagated its freedom from the law. The author of the Sermon on the Mount, who was at the same time the pre-Matthean redactor of Q, gives an answer that firmly places the Q community within Judaism and thus transforms this group of followers of Jesus into a Jewish-Christian sect.

The primary accomplishment of this redaction was a programmatic expansion of the inaugural sermon (Q 6:20–49) into an epitome[1] of the teachings of Jesus. Quite a few Q sayings which appeared elsewhere in the earlier document were transferred into this new work.[2] The theological theme for this epitome was developed on the basis of the older saying Q 16:17 ("It is easier for heaven and earth to pass away than for one dot of the law to be dropped"), which was transferred to a central position in the first part of the Sermon on the Mount and completely reformulated (Matt 5:17–20) in order to reject explicitly the claim or accusation that Jesus had come to abolish the law and the prophets.[3] The abstract of Jesus' teaching, well-known as the "antitheses" of the Sermon on the Mount, demonstrates that Jesus is the authoritative interpreter of the law, with the implication that those who follow this interpretation in their actions will thus have heeded the request for a righteousness, i.e., a fulfillment of the law, that is better than that of the scribes and Pharisees.

The following survey demonstrates how sayings in the Sermon on the Mount from other contexts of Q are interwoven with those which come from the inaugural sermon of Q 6:20–49:

Saying or Unit	Matt	from Q 6:20–49	other Q texts
Beatitudes	5:3–12	6:20–23	
About the salt	5:13		14:34–35
About the light	5:15		11:33
About the law	5:18		16:17
Reconciliation w. opponent	5:25–26		12:58–59
On divorce	5:32		16:18

[1] This designation of the genre of the Sermon on the Mount has been suggested by Hans Dieter Betz, "The Sermon on the Mount (Matt 5:3–7:27): Its Literary Genre and Function," in idem, *Essays*, 1–16.

[2] One or the other of the Q sayings which now appear in the Sermon on the Mount may have stood already in the original inaugural sermon of Q and were transferred to another context by Luke. But on the whole, the judgment stands that Luke preserved the original order of Q more often than Matthew; cf. Kloppenborg, *Formation of Q*, 79–80.

[3] On the analysis and interpretation of this saying in its new formulation see Hans Dieter Betz, "The Hermeneutical Principles of the Sermon on the Mount (Matt. 5:17–20)," in idem, *Essays*, 37–53.

On retaliation	5:39–42	6:29–30	
Love your enemies	5:43–48	6:27–28, 32–36	
Lord's Prayer	6:9–13		11:2–4
Treasure in heaven	6:19–21		12:33–34
Metaphor of the eye	6:22–23		11:34–35
Serving two masters	6:24		16:13
On cares	6:25–34		12:22–31
On judging	7:1–5	6:37, 41–42	
Answer to prayer	7:7–12		11:9–13
Golden Rule	7:12	6:31	
The narrow gate	7:13–14		13:23–24
Tree and fruit	7:16–20	6:43–45	
Saying "Lord, Lord"	7:21	6:46	
Rejection of evil workers	7:22–23		13:26–27
Parable of the Builders	7:24–27	6:47–49	

The incorporation of these sayings from other contexts of Q indicates the purpose of the composition of the Sermon on the Mount. Among these sayings are especially materials from traditional "instructions" (διδαχή) so that the continuation of the Sermon on the Mount (Matthew 6–7) appears as cultic and moral teaching along the theme of the "two ways." Hans Dieter Betz has called Matt 6:1–18 "A Jewish-Christian Cultic *Didache*."[1] It presents the rules for the cultic life, almsgiving, prayer, and fasting, and emphasizes that the fulfillment in righteousness, which can expect a reward from God, requires secrecy—otherwise the reward is already received and thus wasted. The anti-Pharisaic polemic of Q is visible also here;[2] but in spite of the fact that the temple and its cult are never mentioned, these rules for cultic piety are quite in keeping with Judaism; Christian elements are nowhere visible.[3] The last section of the Sermon on the Mount consistently follows the "two ways," cf. the transfer of the "two ways" materials from other sections of Q, especially the saying of the narrow gate (Q 13:24). In keeping with the genre of "instruction" (διδαχή), the last verses are sayings of eschatological warning. They do not primarily serve as general admonitions to all believers; rather, they have a polemical intent. Those whose appeal against the eschatological verdict will be rejected are the pseudo-prophets who are "wolves in sheep's clothing" (Matt 7:15), who have not brought good fruit (Matt 7:16–20). They have said "Lord, Lord," but did not do the will of the Father in heaven (Matt 7:21). What is meant by "the will of the Father" is made explicit in the rejection of those who have pro-

---

[1] *Essays,* 55–69.

[2] Cf. the use of "hypocrites" in Matt 6:2, 5, 16.

[3] Betz, *Essays,* 62, 65.

phesied in the name of Jesus, driven out demons in the name of Jesus, and performed miracles in the name of Jesus (Matt 7:22): they are "the workers of lawlessness" (οἱ ἐργαζόμενοι τὴν ἀνομίαν), that is, they are Christian missionaries who have not fulfilled the law.[1]

If the pre-Matthean redaction of Q which produced the Sermon on the Mount reveals the final establishment of the community of Q as a law-abiding Jewish-Christian group, conclusions can be drawn with respect to the dating of Q and its redactions. The decision to remain within the limits of law-abiding Israel must be dated quite early. The Pharisees who are the opponents of this group are not yet, as in the Gospel of Matthew, the Pharisees who represent the beginnings of rabbinic Judaism after the Judaic War. They are a rival group within a framework of the religion of Israel in which the interpretation of the law that the Sermon on the Mount presents would have been quite thinkable and in keeping with Jewish tradition. The Sermon on the Mount is anti-Pharisaic, but this is a phenomenon contained completely within the community of Judaism. The polemic against the Gentile-Christian mission belongs to the time of Paul rather than to a later period. Therefore, the entire development of Q, from the first collection of the sayings of Jesus and their assembly into sapiential discourses to the apocalyptic redaction and, finally, the pre-Matthean redaction, must be dated within the first three decades after the death of Jesus. The history reflected in the development of this source is analogous to the history of the first Greek-speaking Christian communities in the diaspora of Syria, like that of Antioch. Antioch's church was founded by Greek-speaking Jewish missionaries who proclaimed a new Israel into which Gentiles were invited. These missionaries were then attacked by Pharisees like Paul. But even after Paul had joined this new effort of Gentile mission, the conflict reemerged within the circles of the followers of Jesus. Antioch's Christians where now forced to debate the question of the fulfillment of the law with their brothers and sisters in Jerusalem (the controversy known as the "Apostles' Council"), and they finally decided that the Gentile church should not be obliged to abide by the law. The Q community reflects the same stages of development. It apparently begins with an openness to the invitation to Gentiles, experiences attacks by the Pharisees, but then makes a different decision, namely, to stay

---

[1] Ibid., 19–21. Betz (Ibid., 19–20) also asks: "Can it be a coincidence that the wise disciple, whose life is represented in the parable of Matt. 7:24–27, builds his house 'upon the rock' (τεθεμελίωτο ... ἐπὶ τὴν πέτραν)? Can this 'rock' be anything other than an allusion to Peter and his church, against which Paul may be polemicizing, in concealed form, in 1 Cor 3:11 ('For no other foundation can one lay than that which is laid, which is Jesus Christ')?"

within the confines of the law. According to the Sermon on the Mount, the decision for the law did not include an explicit defense of circumcision and dietary laws. This defines a position that resembles that of Peter. He took the side of the law-abiding Jewish followers of Jesus at the Jerusalem Council, but later did not hesitate to eat with the Gentiles when he visited Antioch.[1] The author of the Gospel of Matthew demonstrates dependence upon such Jewish-Christian traditions under the authority of Peter.[2] It is not unlikely that the Jewish-Christian redaction of Q used by Matthew belonged to these Peter traditions.

One final note regarding the Epistle of James can be added. It was evident in the discussion of the gospel tradition of the Epistle of James[3] that the sayings and parenetic materials used in that writing were closely related specifically to Matthew 5, and in general to a Jewish-Christian perspective that advocated adherence to the law without demanding observance of circumcision and dietary legislation. The Epistle of James also shares with the Sermon on the Mount the rejection of the Pauline thesis which claims that Christ is the end of the law. The author of this epistle and the redactor of Q who produced the Sermon on the Mount belong to the same Jewish-Christian milieu; both share the decision that the followers of Jesus belong to law-abiding Israel and that fulfillment of the law, though without any emphasis upon circumcision and ritual law, is the appropriate interpretation of the teachings of Jesus.

---

[1] Gal 2:11–14; see Hans Dieter Betz, *Galatians: A Commentary on Paul's Letter to the Churches in Galatia* (Hermeneia; Philadelphia: Fortress, 1979) on Galatians 2, especially the excursus on "The Conflict at Antioch," pp. 103–4.

[2] Cf. Matthew 16:17–19; see below # 4.3.4.

[3] See above, # 2.1.4.4.

3

From Dialogues and Narratives to the Gospel of John

3.1 Dialogue Gospels

3.1.1 THE DIALOGUE OF THE SAVIOR

3.1.1.1 The Document and its Dialogue Source

The fifth writing in Codex III of the Nag Hammadi Library, occupying pp. 120,1–147,23, is entitled by incipit and explicit "The Dialogue of the Savior."[1] This copy of the Coptic translation of the originally Greek text of the document is the only extant text of the work. The text is fragmentary; on pp. 120–32 the first or the last two to ten letters of each line are missing; pp. 137–38 and 143–46 have substantial lacunae at the top of each page; on p. 147 only a few letters of line 9 to 23 have survived.[2]

In its preserved form, this writing is a compilation of various sources and traditions; its several sections exhibit great differences in style and content. The primary source used by the author seems to have been an older dialogue gospel which can be isolated with some degree of certainty because the dialogue form appears only here, while other materials as well as the lengthy introduction of the author are written as monologues of the Savior. The title "Savior" is used for the

---

[1] The writing has been published with translation and notes by Stephen Emmel, ed., with an introduction by Helmut Koester and Elaine Pagels, *Nag Hammadi Codex III,5: The Dialogue of the Savior* (NHS 26; Leiden: Brill, 1984). For English translations with brief introductions see Stephen Emmel, Helmut Koester, and Elaine Pagels, "The Dialogue of the Savior," in Robinson, ed., *Nag Hammadi Library*, 244–5; Cameron, *Other Gospels*, 38–48. For a German translation see Beate Blatz, "Der Dialog des Erlösers," in Hennecke-Schneemelcher, *NT Apokryphen I*, 245–53. There is no translation of this document in Hennecke-Schneemelcher-Wilson, *NT Apocrypha I*.

[2] See the description of the manuscript by Stephen Emmel, *Nag Hammadi Codex III,5*, pp. 19–36.

speaker primarily in the secondary monologue sections, while the older dialogue gospel usually employs the title "Lord" (only twice is he called "Savior" here[1]) for Jesus in conversation with Judas, Matthew, and Mary. The four extant sections of the dialogue gospel are combined with other materials as follows:[2]

Incipit 120,1	Title
1–3[3] (120,2–124,22)	Introduction
4–14 (124,23–127,19)	Dialogue, part 1
15–18 (127,19–128,23)	Creation myth
19–20 (128,23–129,16)	Dialogue, part 2
21–24 (129,16–131,18)	Creation myth, continued
25–34a (131,19–133,21[?])	Dialogue, part 3
34b–35 (133,21[?]–134,24)	Wisdom list
36–40 (134,24–137,3)	Apocalyptic vision
41–104a (137,3–146,20)	Dialogue, part 4
104b (146,20–147,22)	Concluding instructions
Explicit (147,23)	Title

It is very difficult to ascertain the date of the composition of the document. Since it is not mentioned by any Church Father, nor is there evident use of the work in any of the other works from the Nag Hammadi Library, the *terminus ad quem* for the composition must remain the date of the extant Coptic manuscript, that is, some time in the 4th century. A *terminus a quo* cannot be established with certainty, because there is no evidence for the use of either the canonical gospels or the Pauline epistles or of any other known writing, with the possible exception of the *Gospel of Thomas*. The terms and phrases used in the author's language resemble those of the deutero-Pauline and catholic epistles.[4] This could suggest a date for the composition of the extant

---

[1] See below; the names Jesus or Jesus Christ never occur.

[2] For a more detailed argument concerning the character of the various sections see Emmel, Koester, and Pagels, *Nag Hammadi Codex III,5*, pp. 2–15; Elaine Pagels and Helmut Koester, "Report on the *Dialogue of the Savior* (CG III,5)" in R. McL. Wilson, ed., *Nag Hammadi and Gnosis: Papers Read at the First International Congress of Coptology (Cairo, December 1976)* (NHS 14; Leiden: Brill, 1987) 66–74.

[3] The first numbers refer to the units in Stephen Emmel's translation of the text. They are also used in the translation published in Robinson, ed., *Nag Hammadi Library*, and in the German translation by Beate Blatz quoted above. In the following they will be used with a paragraph sign (#) in order to distinguish them from the references to page and line(s).

[4] See the references in Koester and Pagels, *Nag Hammadi Codex III,5*, p. 10.

document in the first half of the 2d century.[1] The repeated use of the title Savior would also point to this time.

The dates to be assigned to the sources used by the author represent a different question. The dialogue sections are elaborations of sayings of Jesus which show no sign of the use of any known gospel, though some sayings as well as the arrangement of the dialogue may point to a knowledge of the *Gospel of Thomas*. Other sources used by the author do not show any specifically Christian influence; the wisdom list used in ## 34b–35, as a whole a pre-Christian product, has been expanded by a references to baptism (134,6–8) and perhaps to the knowledge of the Father and the Son (134,14–15),[2] thus suggesting a relationship to the saying used in Q/Luke 10:21–22 and John 14:7–9.[3] The dialogical elaborations of sayings of Jesus in the dialogue sections resemble those of the Gospel of John and of the *Apocryphon of James*. Thus the date for the composition of the dialogue gospel that was used by the author depends upon a determination of its relationship to the corresponding sections in these writings, specifically in the Gospel of John.

Apart from the sections which the author took from this dialogue source, the *Dialogue of the Savior* does not share any characteristics of a gospel writing. Our investigation will therefore be limited to these particular sections of the document, which comprise about sixty-five percent of the text.

Questions and answers in the dialogue[4] are usually quite brief, some units comprising only one question by one of the three disciples (sometimes by "all" the disciples) and an answer of the Lord in form of a saying. These units resemble many "sayings" in the *Gospel of Thomas* which are often introduced by a question of the disciples. In other instances, a sequence of questions and answers discusses a particular topic. A traditional saying may constitute the final answer; but sayings are also used in the formulation of a disciple's question, while the answer given by the Lord is actually a secondary interpretation of the problem posed by the understanding of the saying that was quoted at the beginning of such a dialogue unit. Several of these units of the

---

[1] This date was suggested by Koester and Pagels (*Nag Hammadi Codex III,5*, pp. 15–16). Beate Blatz (Hennecke-Schneemelcher, *NT Apokryphen I*, 247) suggests the 2d century.

[2] But the text is uncertain at this point. See Emmel, *Nag Hammadi Codex III,5*, pp. 68–69.

[3] See Koester and Pagels, *Nag Hammadi Codex III,5*, p. 8.

[4] For the following see the description of the dialogues by Koester and Pagels, *Nag Hammadi Codex III,5*, pp. 2–8.

dialogue can be compared with respective traditional sayings or passages from other gospels.

3.1.1.2 The Use of Sayings in Dialogues

Dial. Sav. ## 4–8

The text of the initial question of Matthew (# 4) is not preserved. Only fragments remain of the answer of the "Savior" (# 5), a question of Judas (# 6), and a statement by the "Lord" (# 7). But a second statement, introduced by "The Savior[1] said," is well preserved in its first part (# 8).

Dial. Sav. # 8 (125,18–126,5)	Parallels Matt 6:22–23[2]
The lamp [of the body] is the mind. As long as [the things inside] you are set in order, that is, [. . .] . . ., your bodies are [luminous]. As long as your hearts are [dark], the luminosity you anticipate [? will not come]. I have . . .	The lamp of the body is the eye. If your eye is single, your whole body will be luminous. But if your eye is evil, your body will also be dark. If now the light within you is darkness, how great is the darkness!

Other variations of the same saying appear in the *Gospel of Thomas* and in the Gospel of John:

Gos. Thom. 24b: There is light within a man of light and he lights up the whole world. If he does not shine, he is darkness.

John 11:9–10: If someone walks in the day, he will not stumble, because he sees the light of the world; but if someone walks in the night, he stumbles, because the light is not in him (cf. John 12:35).

The basis of this saying is identical with that of the Q saying recorded by both Matthew and Luke. In the interpretation, the word "eye" from the metaphor has been replaced by its allegorical equivalent "mind." In the subsequent passages, the contrasting pairs of enlightened heart/luminous bodies and dark heart/lack of the coming luminosity, replace the metaphors of the original saying in order to emphasize the correlation of inner enlightenment to the expected salvation into midst of the light.

---

[1] ## 5 and 8 are the only two instances in which Jesus is called "Savior."

[2] Cf. Luke 11:34–35.

Dial. Sav. ## 9–12

Dial. Sav. ## 9–12 (126,6–17)	Matt 7:7/Luke 11:9
His [disciples said, "Lord], who is it who seeks [and finds] and[1] reveals?"	Ask, and it will be given to you; seek and you will find.
[The Lord said to them], "[It is] the one who seeks [who also] reveals . . . [. . .]."	*Gos. Thom.* 94 (cf. 92) He who seeks will find, and he who knocks will be let in.
[Matthew said, "Lord, when] I [listen . . .] and [when] I speak, who is it who [speaks and who is it] who listens?"	*Gos. Thom.* 33a Preach from your housetops that which you will hear in your ear.
[The Lord] said, "It is the one who speaks who also [listens], and it is the one who can see who also reveals."	John 16:13 (The spirit of truth) will not speak from himself, but what he hears he will speak and announce to you what is coming.

This section is an elaboration of the traditional saying about seeking and finding which is quoted in the initial question. Already there, it has been expanded to include the notion of "revealing." Sayings like *Gos. Thom.* 33a and John 16:13 may have been used in order to establish the conclusion, formulated as a new saying of the Lord, that the authority for speaking and revealing presupposes that one has not only found but also listened and seen.

Dial. Sav. ## 13–14

Dial. Sav. ## 13–14 (126,17–127,19)	Luke 6:21b
[Mary] said. "Lord, behold! Whence [do I] bear the body [while I] weep, and whence while I [laugh]?"	Blessed are those who weep now, for you shall laugh.
The Lord said, "[. . .] weep on account of its works [. . .] remain and the mind laughs [. . .] . . . [. . .] . . . spirit. If one does not [stand] in darkness, he	John 16:20 . . . you will weep and lament, but the world will rejoice. You will be full of sorrow, but your sorrow will be turned into joy.

---

[1] Instead of "[and finds] and," Emmel reconstructs "who is it who also."

will [not] be able to see [the light]. So I tell you [. . .] light is the darkness. [And if one does not] stand in [the darkness, he will] not [be able] to see the light.

[lines 7–13 are unintelligible]

John 12:35

Only a short time the light is among you. Walk as you have the light, so that darkness will not overcome you. And he who walks in the darkness does not know where he goes. As you have the light, believe in the light, so that you become children of the light.[1]

then the powers [. . .] . . . which are above as well as those [below] will [. . .] you. In that place [there will] be weeping and [gnashing] of teeth over the end of [all] these things."

Matt 8:12

But the sons of the kingdom will be thrown out into the outer darkness, and there will be weeping and gnashing of teeth.

The use of several traditional sayings in this section is evident. But because of the poor preservation of the text it is not possible to be certain about the interpretation. The term "weeping" forms an inclusio: at the beginning, weeping is connected to existence in the body; at the conclusion, it is the powers above and below who are weeping over the end of the world. The central part seems to interpret the "laughing of the mind" as the seeing of the light. A comparison with John 16:20 shows that, in both texts, weeping is related to the existence in the world; but in John 16, it is existence in the world while Jesus has departed, and joy is to come at his return as the spirit of truth, while in the Dialogue of the Savior the liberation of the mind who has seen the light is the cause of joy.

Dial. Sav. #19–20

This section (128,23–129,16) is a brief dialogue that has been inserted into the narrative of the creation myth (127:19–128,23 and 129,16–131,18). It consists of a question of Matthew and a somewhat lengthy answer of the Lord. But the text is so poorly preserved that neither the question nor the answer are quite intelligible. In the answer, the Lord speaks about "the means to overcome the powers above as well as those below." This indicates that this section originally continued the dialogue of the preceding section ## 13–14. But

---

[1] See also *Gos. Thom.* 33b ". . . but rather he sets (the lamp) on a lampstand, so that everyone who enters and leaves will see its light." Cf. Matt 5:15; Luke 11:33.

the conclusion of the Lord's statement clearly reflects the use of a traditional saying:

Dial. Sav. 129,14–16	John 16:24
And [let] him who [knows] seek and find and [rejoice].	Until now you have not asked anything in my name; ask and you will receive so that your joy may be full.[1]

3.1.1.3 Dial. Sav. ## 25–30 and John 14

Dial. Sav. ## 25–30 (131,19–132,19)	John 14:2–12
[Mary] hailed her brothers [. . .] . . . "you ask the son . . . [. . .] . . . them, where are you going to put them?"	2: In my father's house are many dwellings; if not, I would have told you,
[The Lord said] to her, "Sister, [. . .] will be able to inquire about these things . . . [. . .] . . . he has somewhere to put them in his [heart . . .] . . . to come [forth . . .] and enter . . . [. . .] . . . [. . .] so that they might not hold back . . . [. . .] this impoverished cosmos."	because I go to prepare a place for you. 3: . . . And I come again and take you to myself, so that where I am you also you will be. 4: And where I go, you know the way.
[Matthew] said, "Lord I want to [see] that place of life, [this place] where there is no wickedness, [but rather] there is pure [light]." The Lord [said], "Brother [Matthew], you will not be able to see it [as long as you are] carrying flesh around." [Matthew] said, "Lord, [even if I will] not [be able] see it, let me [know it]."	5: Thomas said to him, "Lord, we do not know where you are going; how can we know the way?" 6: Jesus said to him, "I am the way and the truth and the life; no one comes to the Father except through me." 8: Philip said to him, "Show us the father and it will be sufficient for us."
The Lord [said], "[Everyone] who has known himself has seen [it . . .]	9: Jesus said to him, ". . . Who has seen me has seen the Father. How do

---

[1] See also the sayings about seeking/finding in Matt 7:7; Luke 11:9; *Gos. Thom.* ## 2, 92, 94.

	you say, 'Show us the Father?'
	10: Do you not know that I am in the Father and the Father in me? ... The Father who dwells in me does his works.
everything given to him [alone] to do [. . .] . . . and has come to [? do / ? resemble] it in his [goodness]."	12: . . . He who believes in me will also do the works that I do, and will do greater ones than these.

Mary's initial question apparently raises the question of the "place of life" to which the disciples will go. The topic is formulated on the basis of a traditional saying, cf. *Gos. Thom.* 24:

> His disciples said to him, "Show us the place where you are, since it is necessary for us to seek it." He said to them, "He who has ears, let him hear. There is light within a man of light, and he lights up the whole world. If he does not shine, he is darkness."

The same question, the place of life, also introduces the dialogue of John 14:2–12. In both instances, the request is repeated in modified forms. In the *Dialogue of the Savior* the question moves from "seeing" the place to "knowing" it. In John 14 it moves from knowing the way to showing the Father. The *Dialogue of the Savior* concludes with the typical reference to knowledge of oneself as the goal of the search, once more on the basis of a traditional saying, cf. *Gos. Thom.* 3b:

> When you come to know yourselves, then you will become known, and you will realize that it is you who are the sons of the living Father. But if you will not know yourselves, you dwell in poverty, and it is you who are that poverty.

In both *Dial. Sav.* ## 25–30 and in John 14 the final stage is doing the appropriate works. As a whole, both are variants of the same composition of a brief revelation dialogue, not independently constructed on the basis of the same traditional sayings. This makes the differences even more striking. In John 14, there is no reference to self-knowledge; rather, this familiar notion is replaced quite surprisingly by a reference to knowledge of Jesus. Accordingly, the works which the believer does are not the result of one's own goodness, but they emerge from faith in Jesus and imitate the works of Jesus. John 14:2–12 appears to be a deliberate christological reinterpretation of the more traditional Gnostic dialogue, which the *Dialogue of the Savior* has preserved in its more original form. That the discourses

and dialogues of John's Gospel present such reinterpretations of
Gnostic dialogues in other instances will be discussed below.[1]

Dial. Sav. ## 31–34

The parable of the stone and its interpretation (132,19–134,1) could
be based on older traditions and seems to employ apocalyptic materials (cf. Isa 24:18–20). In its second half, Jesus' answer alludes to
several sayings that are closely related to the preceding dialogue section:

Dial. Sav. ## 34b (133,14–24)	Gos. Thom. 50
[. . .] . . . you, all the sons of [men. For] you are from [that] place. [In] the hearts of those who speak out of [joy] and truth you exist. Even if it (or he) comes forth in the body of the Father among men and is not received, still it (or he) [does (not?)] return to its (or his) place.	We came from the light, the place where the light came into being of its own accord. . . .
	John 1:9–11
	He was the true light that enlightens every human being coming into the world, . . . and the world did not know him. He came to his own, and his own did not receive him.[2]
Whoever [does not] know [the work] of perfection [knows] nothing. If one does not stand in the darkness, he will not be able to see the light.	See above on *Dial. Sav.* # 8 (125,18–126,5)

3.1.1.4 Sayings in Dial. Sav. ## 41–104

Most of the last and most extensive portion of the dialogue,
41–104a (137,3–146,20), consists of smaller units, sometimes tied
together by catchword association. It is not possible to recognize major
units of sustained dialogue on a particular topic. In the following I
shall present those portions of the dialogue which are well preserved
and have evident parallels in sayings elsewhere.

Dial. Sav. ## 49–50 (138,11–20)

Judas said, "Behold, the rulers dwell
above us, so it is they who will rule

---

[1] See below # 3.4.4.3.
[2] Cf. also *Gos. Thom.* 28.

over us." The Lord said, "It is you who will rule over them. But when you rid yourselves of jealousy, then you will clothe yourselves in light and enter the bridal chamber."

Gos. Thom. 75

Jesus said, "Many are standing at the door, but it is the solitary who will enter the bridal chamber.

Dial. Sav. ## 51–52
(138,20–139,7)

Judas said, "How will [our] garments be brought to us?
The Lord said, "There are some who will provide for you, and there are others who will receive [. . .]. For [it is] they [who will give you] your garments. [For] who [will] be able to reach that place [which] is [the] reward? But the garments of life were given to man

Gos. Thom. 36–37
(*P. Oxy. 655,* frag. 1b)

"Who could add anything to your age? He himself will give you your garment." His disciples said, "When will you become revealed to us, and when shall we see you?" Jesus said. "When you disrobe without being ashamed and take up your garments and place them under your feet like little children and tread on them, then [you will see] the son of the living one and you will not be afraid."[1]

John 14:4–5

because he knows the path by which he will leave. And it is difficult for me even to reach it."

"And where I am going, you know the way." Thomas said to him, "Lord, we do not know where you are going. How do we know the way?"

Dial. Sav. # 53 (139,8–13)

Mary said, "Thus with respect to 'the wickedness of each day,'

Matt 6:34b

Its own wickedness is sufficient for each day.[2]

Matt 10:10

and 'the laborer is worthy of his food,'

The laborer is worthy of his food.[3]

---

[1] A parallel to this saying appears in the *Gospel of the Egyptians,* see below the discussion of *2 Clem.* 12, # 5.1.3.

[2] This is the second of two free proverbs which Matthew has added to the Q collection of sayings "On cares" (Matt 6:25–33 = Luke 12:22–31).

[3] The Matthean version is quoted here. Cf. Luke 10:7: "The laborer is worthy of his wages." It is debated which of the two versions stood in Q. However, this is a free saying that is quoted frequently in both versions; cf. 1 Tim 5:18; *Did.* 13.2.

and 'the disciple resembles his teacher.'" She uttered this as a woman who had understood completely.

Matt 10:24 = Luke 6:40

A disciple is not over (his) master.[1]

Dial. Sav. ## 56–59 (139,20–140,14)

[Matthew] said, "Tell me, Lord, how the dead die [and] how the living live." The [Lord] said, "[You have] asked me about a saying [. . .] which eye has not seen, [nor] have I heard it except from you. But I say to you that when what invigorates a man is removed, he will be called 'dead.' And when what is alive leaves what is dead, what is alive will be called upon." Judas said, "Why else, for the sake of truth, do they kill and live?" The Lord said. "Whatever is born of truth does not die.
Whatever is born of woman dies."

Gos. Thom. 11

Jesus said, ". . . The dead are not alive, and the living will not die. In the days when you consumed what is dead, you made it what is alive. . . "

Gos. Thom. 17

Jesus said, "I shall give you what no eye has seen and what no ear has heard and what no hand has touched and what has never occurred to the human mind."[2]

John 11:25

He who believes in me will live even if he dies, and everyone who lives and believes in me will not die in eternity.

Dial. Sav. ## 65–68 (141,2–11)

Matthew said, "[Why] do we not rest [at once]?" The Lord said, "When you lay down these burdens." Matthew said, "How does the small join itself to the big?" The Lord said, "When you abandon the works which will not be able to follow you, then you will rest."

Gos. Thom. 90

Come unto to me, for my yoke is easy, . . . and you will find rest for yourselves.[3]

Gos. Thom. 37

His disciples said, "When will you become revealed to us and will we see you?" Jesus said, " When you disrobe without being ashamed and take up your garments and place them under your feet like little children and tread on them, then [will you see] the son of

---

[1] Cf. John 13:16: "A servant is not greater than his master, nor is an apostle greater than the one who sent him."

[2] Cf. 1 Cor 2:9; see the discussion of this saying above, # 2.1.3.

[3] Cf. Matt 11:28–30; Gos. Thom. (P. Oxy. 654, 2) ". . . and once he has ruled, he will attain rest."

the living one, and you will not be
afraid.

Dial. Sav. ## 73–74 (142,4–9)

[Judas] said, "Tell me, Lord, what the
beginning of the path is." He said,
"Love and goodness. For if one of
these existed among the rulers,
wickedness would not have come into
existence."

John 14:5–6

Thomas said to him, "Lord, we do not
know where you are going; how do we
know the way?" Jesus said to him, "I
am the way and the truth and the
life. No one comes to the father
except through me."

Dial. Sav. ## 75–76 (142,9–15)

Matthew said, "Lord, you have
spoken about the end of everything
without concern." The Lord said,
"You have understood all things I
have said to you and you have
accepted them on faith. If you have
known them, then they are [yours]. If
not, then they are not yours."

Gos. Thom. 51

His disciples said to him, "When will
the repose of the dead come about,
and when will the new world come?"
He said to them, "What you look
forward to has already come, but you
do not recognize it."

Dial. Sav. ## 77–78 (142,16–19)

They said to him, "What is the place
to which we are going?" The [Lord]
said, "Stand in the place which you
can reach."

(See above the parallels to # 25 and
60–63)

Dial. Sav. ## 84–85
(143,11–144,1)

Judas said Matthew, "We [want] to
understand the sort of garments we
are to be [clothed] with, [when] we
depart the decay of the [flesh]. The
Lord said. "The rulers [and] the
administraters possess garments
granted [only for a time], which do
not last. [But] you, as children of
truth, not with these transitory
garments are you to clothe
yourselves. Rather, I say [to] you that
you will become [blessed] when you
strip [yourselves]. For it is no great
thing . . . [. . .] outside."

Gos. Thom. 37

His disciples said, "When will you
become revealed to us and will we see
you?" Jesus said, " When you disrobe
without being ashamed and take up
your garments and place them under
your feet like little children and tread
on them, then [will you see] the son of
the living one, and you will not be
afraid."

Dial. Sav. ## 90–95
(144,12–145,7)[1]

Judas said, "You have told us this out of the mind of truth. When we pray, how should we pray?" The Lord said, "Pray in the place where there is no woman." Matthew said, "'Pray in the place where there is no woman,' meaning, 'Destroy the works of womanhood,' not because there is any other [manner of birth], but because they will cease [giving birth]. Mary said, "Will they never be obliterated?" The Lord said, "[Who] knows that they will [not] dissolve and . . . (the remainder and # 95 are very fragmentary)

Gos. Thom. 6

His disciples questioned him and said to him, "Do you want us to fast? How should we pray? What diet shall we observe?"

Gos. Thom. 114

Simon Peter said to them, "Let Mary leave us, for women are not worthy of life." Jesus said, "I myself shall lead her in order to make her male, so that she too may become a living spirit resembling you males. For every woman who will make herself male will enter the kingdom of heaven."

Gospel of the Egyptians [2]

Salome said, "How long will human beings die?" The Lord said, "As long as women will give birth."

Dial. Sav. # 104b (147,14–22)

For I say [you . . .] . . . you take . . . [. . .] . . . you . . . [. . .] who have sought, having [understood] . . . this, will [rest . . .] he will live [forever. And] I say to [you . . .] . . . so that you will not lead [your] spirits and your souls into error.

John 6:63

It is the spirit that gives life, the flesh is of no avail; the words that I have spoken to you are spirit and life.

John 8:51

Truly, truly, I say to you, if anyone keeps my word, he will never see death.

Gos. Thom. 1

Whoever finds the interpretation of these sayings will not experience death.

An examination of the sequence of the topics which are discussed in the dialogue sections of this document as well as a comparison of the individual statements with parallels elsewhere reveals a surprising familiarity with the sayings of the *Gospel of Thomas*. The saying about seeking and finding is discussed in the first part of the dialogue (cf. *Gos. Thom.* 2), and the dialogue seems to conclude with an elabora-

---

[1] See also above, *Dial. Sav.* ## 56–59.
[2] Clement of Alexandria *Strom.* 3.9, 63–64; cf. ibid., 3.9, 45.

tion of the introduction to the *Gospel of Thomas* (#1) which speaks about the finding of life through the interpretation of the sayings. The saying of *Gos. Thom.* 2 may also have influenced the order in which several topics are discussed in the dialogue portions of the *Dialogue of the Savior*. In *Gos. Thom.* 2, seeking, finding, amazement, ruling, and resting are described as the steps of the order of salvation. *Dial. Sav.* #8 speaks about seeking and finding; #25 raises the question of "the place of life"; ##47–50 discuss "who will rule over us"; #65 raises the question of resting. If the apocalyptic vision (*Dial. Sav.* 36–40) was part of the original dialogue, it could be understood as a commentary on the topic of "amazement."

This dialogue as a whole would then be a commentary on the eschatological time table which is implied in *Gos. Thom.* 2. The disciples have sought and have found; but their rule and their rest will only appear in the future. At the present time, the "rulers" of the cosmos still exercise their authority, and the time at which the disciples will rule over them, has not yet come (*Dial. Sav.* ##47–50). The rest can only be obtained when they can rid themselves of the burden of their bodies (*Dial. Sav.* #28). Mary, who recognizes this, is praised as a disciple who has understood the all (*Dial. Sav.* #53).

The question of the "works of womanhood" (*Dial. Sav.* ##91–95) occupies a prominent place in the dialogue. It is a topic that belongs to the overarching concern of wearing the body, that is, these works are understood as the continuation of existence in the body through childbearing—possibly a commentary on the final saying of the *Gospel of Thomas* (114) about Mary, the woman who is not worthy of the kingdom unless she is made male. A saying that is elsewhere preserved in the *Gospel of the Egyptians* provides the answer: rejection of the works of womanhood does not imply a degradation of women as such. "Becoming male" (*Gos. Thom.* 114) would imply, in the understanding of the *Dialogue of the Savior,* that women will stop bearing children and, in this respect, resemble the male. This document is thus taking a position that is diametrically opposed to the Pastoral Epistles of the New Testament: 1 Tim 2:13–15 asserts that women will be saved by bearing children. Moreover, the *Dialogue of the Savior* features Mary as the most prominent of the disciples of Jesus in the discussion with the Lord, while 1 Tim 2:11–12 demands explicitly that women should be silent in the assembly of the church.

The dialogue gospel that the author of the extant document used has been incorporated into a framework that can no longer be called a "gospel" in the proper sense of the word.[1] The extant document is a

---

[1] For a more detailed discussion of the relationship of the older dialogue gospel to the extant document, see Koester and Pagels, *Nag Hammadi Codex III,5,* pp. 9–15.

theological treatise which is concerned with the relationship of realized and future eschatology. It is probably a baptismal instruction
which interprets baptism as the moment in which the time of the
abandonment of labor and the attainment of rest is celebrated in an
anticipatory fashion: "Already the time has come, brothers, for us to
abandon our labor and stand at rest" (120,3–6). But passing through
the spheres for the final attainment of rest presupposes the "time of
dissolution" (122,2–3). What has already been experienced in baptism
will have its consequences only once the soul passes through the
powers and rulers on its way to the heavenly abode.[1] This theology is
closely related to early Christian documents which come from the time
of about 100 CE. Thus the date of the document in its preserved form is
most likely the beginning of the 2d century CE; the dialogue gospel
used by its author may have been composed during the last decades of
the 1st century CE.[2]

3.1.2 THE APOCRYPHON OF JAMES

3.1.2.1 The Document

The *Apocryphon of James* (NHC I,2), often also referred to as the
Epistula Iacobi, occupies the first pages of Codex I (1,1–16,30) of the
Nag Hammadi Library.[3] The manuscript is quite well preserved
except for a few lacunae at the top of the first three pages. No title
appears in the manuscript. The document begins with an epistolary
prescript: "[James] writes to [. . .].[4] Peace [be with you from] peace,

---

[1] The closest parallels to this anticipatory eschatology, related to the understanding
of baptism, can be found in Eph. 2:1–6; Col 3:1–4; Clement of Alexandria *Exc. Theod.,*
77.1–2; *On Baptism A* (NHC XI,2b; 41,23–38); *On Baptism B* (NHC XI,2c; 42,16–19).

[2] For a discussion of the date of composition, see Koester and Pagels, *Nag Hammadi
Codex III,5,* pp. 15–16.

[3] It was first published by Michel Malinine, Henri-Charles Puech, Gilles Quispel,
Rudolphe Kasser, R. McL. Wilson, and Jan Zandee, eds., *Epistula Iacobi Apocrypha*
(Zürich: Rascher, 1968). A new edition has been published by Francis E. Williams, ed.,
"The Apocryphon of James," in Harold W. Attridge, ed., *Nag Hammadi Codex I (The
Jung Codex): Introductions, Texts, Translations, Notes* (2 vols.; NHS 22–23; Leiden:
Brill, 1985) 1. 13–53; 2. 7–37. For English translations see Francis E. Williams, "The
Apocryphon of James," in Robinson, ed., *Nag Hammadi Library,* 29–37; Cameron,
Other Gospels, 55–64. A new German translation by Dankwart Kirchner, "Brief des
Jakobus," appears in Hennecke-Schneemelcher, *NT Apokryphen I,* 234–44. There is
no English translation of this document in Hennecke-Schneemelcher-Wilson, *NT
Apocrypha.*

[4] Neither the name of the sender nor the name of the addressee are preserved.
While it is quite clear from the following sentences that the sender must be James (the
brother of Jesus?), the addressee remains uncertain. Hans-Martin Schenke ("Der
Jacobusbrief aus dem Codex Jung," *OLZ* 66 [1971] 117–130) has suggested Cerinthus

[love from] love, [grace from] grace, [faith] from faith, life from holy life" (1,1–7). But the next section shows that this is only a secondary framework for the transmission of a "secret book"[1] that was revealed to James and Peter by the Lord and written by James[2] "in the Hebrew alphabet" (1,10–17). Notwithstanding this claim, there is no question that the Coptic text is a translation from a Greek original.

The first scholarly assessment of the *Apocryphon of James* saw the document as a speculative Gnostic writing, tried to locate its thought within the known framework of types of Gnostic theology, and assigned its literary genre to that of the later Gnostic dialogues.[3] A new approach for the investigation of the document was initiated by Ron Cameron.[4] He begins with the observation that the *Apocryphon of James* "states explicitly that it is providing a written record of those sayings which Jesus revealed to James and Peter."[5] As there are frequent quotations of traditional sayings in this document,[6] Cameron proposes "to analyze the *Apocryphon of James* form-critically in order to clarify the ways in which sayings of Jesus were used and transformed . . . ," including "a formal isolation of individual sayings, an identification of their traditional and redactional elements, and a reconstruction of the compositional history of the document."[7]

---

as the person to whom the letter was addressed; see also Kirchner, "Brief des Jakobus," 236–37.

[1] The Coptic transcription of the Greek word ἀπόκρυφον appears in 1,10.

[2] Because of the association of James with Peter, common in Jewish-Christian documents, it is tempting to identify James with the brother of Jesus. However, no such identification is indicated in the document. Rather, James appears, like Peter, as one of the twelve disciples. See the discussion of the name of the author in B. Dehandschutter, "L'Epistula Jacobi apocrypha de Nag Hammadi (CG I,2) comme apocryphe néotestamentaire," *ANRW* 2.25/6 (1988) 4536–39.

[3] See for this hypothesis, with a comprehensive discussion of earlier views, Dehandschutter, ibid., 4520–50. For a brief report and literature see Ron Cameron, *Sayings Traditions in the Apocryphon of James* (HTS 34; Philadelphia: Fortress, 1984). Dehandschutter does not refer to the work of Ron Cameron, which was published in 1985.

[4] Cameron, *Apocryphon of James*.

[5] Ibid., 3.

[6] See also Kirchner, "Brief des Jakobus," 237.

[7] Cameron, *Apocryphon of James*, 3. The following analysis of the sayings and dialogues of this writing is based upon the results of Cameron's investigation. Dehandschutter ("L'Epistula Jacobi apocrypha," 4540–47) presents a thorough discussion of the problem of the literary genre of this document, albeit with quite different results.

3.1.2.2 Opening Scene and Hermeneutics of the Dialogue

The opening scene of the writing (*Apocr. Jas.* 2,8–21) is important for the understanding of the hermeneutical situation in which dialogues are developed on the basis of traditional sayings:

> ... the twelve disciples [were] all sitting together and remembering what the Savior had said to each one of them, whether in secret or openly, and [putting it] in books—[But I] was writing that which was in [my book]—lo, the Savior appeared, [after] departing from [us while we] gazed after him. And after five hundred and fifty days since he had risen from the dead, ...

"Remembering" what Jesus had said, is a key term for the oral tradition.[1] In Papias of Hierapolis, it also marks the transition from this tradition to the collection and written exposition of the sayings. The setting described in the opening section of the *Apocryphon of James* corresponds to that of Papias.[2] Whether or not the sayings are taken from a written document, the hermeneutical situation described here implies that sayings of Jesus, or collections of sayings, are transmitted in the free tradition and that the process of their interpretation is identical with the production of written documents. According to the witness of Eusebius,[3] in the case of Papias of Hierapolis the resulting books are called "Interpretation of the Sayings of the Lord" (Λογίων κυριακῶν ἐξήγησις). In the *Apocryphon of James* the writing which results is a dialogue of Jesus with two of his disciples, James and Peter, into which a few longer discourses of Jesus have been interpolated.[4] Although the setting for the writing of the document is a dialogue with Jesus after his resurrection, the basis of the work is an interpretation of traditional sayings of Jesus.[5] That is evident at the

---

[1] For the use of this term and for the following discussion and relevant literature see above, # 2.1.4.3.

[2] This has been demonstrated convincingly by Cameron, *Apocryphon of James*, especially pp. 122–23: "... the term 'remembering' is understood here as an introduction to a collection of 'secret sayings' of Jesus, and is used to refer to the composition of these sayings in 'secret books.'"

[3] *Hist. eccl.* 3.39.1.

[4] Several suggestions have been made with respect to possible secondary interpolations into the original dialogue; cf. Williams, "Apocryphon of James," 17–18. Williams himself (ibid., 18–19) suggests that the two longer discourses on martyrdom (4,24–6,20) and about prophecy (6,21–7,10) were inserted into an earlier work.

[5] Cameron (*Apocryphon of James,* passim) has argued convincingly for the independence of the sayings tradition of this writing. Arguments for dependence upon the canonical Gospels, especially upon the Gospel of John, are summarized and discussed by Dehandschutter, "L'Epistula Jacobi apocrypha," 4547–50; see ibid. (p. 4585) for earlier studies of this question.

very beginning of the dialogue. The first statement of Jesus which initiates the dialogue, responding to a question of the disciples ("Have you departed and removed yourself from us?"), is based on a traditional saying:

> No, but I shall go to the place whence I came. If you wish to come with me, come! (2,23–27).

This statement is a variant of an often-repeated phrase in which the one who has his or her origin in the divine world announces the return to that world.[1] It ultimately derives from the myth of Wisdom, and it made its way into the tradition of sayings of Jesus at an early date, both as a description of the disciples' return to the place of their origin and as a statement about Jesus' coming and going.[2] The former appears in the tradition of sayings in the small catechism *Gos. Thom.* 50:

> Jesus said, "If they say to you, 'Where did you come from?' say to them, 'We came from the light, the place where the light came into being . . .' If they say to you, 'Is it you?' say, 'We are its children, and we are the elect of the living Father.' If they ask you, 'What is the sign of your Father in you?' say to them, 'It is movement and repose.'"

This basic catechism is elaborated in other Gnostic texts.[3] In all these instances, the return of the disciples to the place of their origin is not dependent upon Jesus' or the revealer's own coming and returning. The disciples themselves have come to know who they are and, therefore, possess the power to return to their origin.

The saying at the beginning of the first dialogue in the *Apocryphon of James,* however, is a statement about Jesus' coming and going. This saying establishes the point of departure for an exploration of the question of the disciples' situation in view of Jesus' return.[4] An addition to the quotation of the saying initiates the dialogue: "If you wish to come with me, come!" (2,25–26). The response of the disciples is also a compositional device for the construction of the dialogue: "They all answered and said to him, 'If you bid us, we come'" (2,26–28). Jesus' answer is again formulated on the basis of another traditional saying:

> Truly, I say unto you, no one will ever enter the kingdom of heaven at

---

[1] See the discussion of parallels in Cameron, *Apocryphon of James,* 58–62.

[2] For the latter, parallels occur most frequently in the Gospel of John; cf., e.g., "I have gone out from the Father and have come into the world; I am leaving the world again and I am going to the Father" (John 16:28).

[3] Cf. especially *1 Apocalypse of James* (NHC V,3) 33,11–34,20.

[4] This is a major topic in the dialogues of the Gospel of John, see below # 3.4.4.3.

my bidding, but (only) because you yourselves are full. (2,29–33)

The saying which is presupposed here is attested in the synoptic tradition as well as in the Gospel of John:[1]

> Truly, I say to you, whoever does not receive the kingdom of God as a child, will never enter into it. (Mark 10:15)

> Truly, truly, I say to you, unless someone is born anew (or: from above = γεννηθῇ ἄνωθεν), he can not enter the kingdom of God. (John 3:3, 5)[2]

This portion of the dialogue of *Apocr. Jas.* 2,22–33 is analogous in its formal structure to the beginning of the dialogue of John 14:2–6 which has already been quoted as a parallel to *Dial. Sav.* 25–30:[3]

Apocr. Jas.	John 14
We said to him, "Have you departed and removed yourself from us?" But Jesus said, "No, but I shall go to the place from whence I came. I you wish to come with me, come!"	2: In my father's house are many dwellings; if not, I would have told you, because I go to prepare a place for you. 3: . . . And I come again and take you to myself, so that where I am you also you will be. 4: And where I go, you know the way.
They all answered and said, "If you bid us, we come."	5: Thomas said to him, "Lord, we do not know where you are going; how can we know the way?"
He said, "Truly, I say unto you, no one will ever enter the kingdom of heaven at my bidding, but (only) because you yourselves are full."	6: Jesus said to him, "I am the way and the truth and the life; no one comes to the Father except through me."

In the *Apocryphon of James* as well as in the *Dialogue of the Savior*, the believers have to find the qualification in themselves. This agrees with the traditional saying about entering the kingdom of God that is used here; it always emphasizes that one must be reborn or become like a little child. John 14, however, connects the believers' "way"

---

[1] On the analysis of these parallels and the underlying original saying see Cameron, *Apocryphon of James*, 66–68.

[2] The more original form of the saying's Johannine version may be preserved in Justin, *1 Apol.* 61.4: "Unless you are reborn (ἀναγεννηθῆτε) you will not enter the kingdom of heaven." On the use of this saying in other contexts see Cameron, *Apocryphon of James*, 69–70.

[3] See above, # 3.1.1.

closely with the person of Jesus.

In the immediate continuation of the dialogue James and Peter are taken aside for secret instruction (2,33–39), but the beginning of this instruction is lost because the first lines of p. 3 consist of untranslatable fragments. In the following (*Apocr. Jas.* 3,8–14), the appeal to the disciples that they should be filled, which is frequently repeated in this writing,[1] is expanded by an admonition which recalls the lament of the revealer of *Gos. Thom.* 28. Moreover this lament includes the remark that human beings came into the world "empty" and seek to leave it "empty."

Apocr. Jas. 3,8–11	*Gos. Thom.* 28
Do you not, then, desire to be filled? And your heart is drunken; do you not, then, desire to be sober? Therefore, be ashamed!	I found all of them intoxicated; I found none of them thirsty; and my soul became afflicted for the sons of men, because they are blind in their hearts and do not have sight; for empty they came into the world, and empty too they seek to leave the world. But for the moment, they are intoxicated.

Without a further question of the disciples, a transitional statement explores another dimension of the theme of "remembering":

> Henceforth, waking or sleeping, remember that you have seen the Son of man, and spoken with him in person and listened to him in person (3,11–17).

This is followed by an elaborate series of woes and blessings based on a saying that the Fourth Gospel has added to the appearance of Jesus to Thomas:

Apocr. Jas. 3,17–26	John 20:29
Woe to those who have seen the Son [of] man; blessed will they be who have not seen the man, and they who have not consorted with him, and they who have not spoken with him, and they who have not listened to anything from him; yours is life.	Because you have seen me, you believe? Blessed are those who have not seen and yet believe.

This saying is used again in the discourse of *Apocr. Jas.* 12,31–13,1, which contains several additional Johannine sayings (see below). The

---

[1] *Apocr. Jas.* 2,33–35; 3,35–36; thirteen times in the section 4,1–22.

remainder of this first section of the dialogue (3,38–4,22) is an interpretation of the concept of "being full."

3.1.2.3 The Apocryphon of James and the Synoptic Tradition

A new segment of the dialogue begins with a quite different saying of Jesus:

Apocr. Jas. 4,23–30	Mark 10:28–30
But I (James) answered and said to him, "Lord, we can obey you, if you wish, for we have forsaken our fathers and our mothers and our villages and followed you.	Peter began to say to him, "Lo, we have left everything and followed you." Jesus said, "Truly, I say to you, there is no one who has left house or brothers or sisters or mother or father or children or lands, for my sake and the gospel who will not receive . . ."

	Matt 6:13
Grant us, therefore, not to be tempted by the devil, the evil one."	And lead us not into temptation, but deliver us from evil.

In Mark 10:28–30 the beginning of the saying has already been used for the formulation of the question of Peter ("Lo, we have left everything and followed you").[1] In Apocr. Jas. 4,25–28 the entire saying has been transferred into the statement of James.[2] It is further combined with a request that is formulated on the basis of the last petition of the Lord's Prayer (Matt 6:13b).[3] The Apocryphon of James uses these two sayings as an introduction to a longer statement of Jesus which interprets the sayings by emphasizing obedience in spite of persecution: ". . . but if you are oppressed by Satan and persecuted, and you do his (i.e., the Father's) will, I [say] that he will love you and make you equal with me . . ." (4,38–5,3). The discourse continues to announce that the disciples will also have to suffer the fate of Jesus:

---

[1] See the discussion of the formulation of secondary introductions from sayings in Cameron, *Apocryphon of James,* 75–78.

[2] The text of *Apocr. Jas.* 4,25–28 could derive from either Mark or Matthew (19:29) or an older version of the saying. No trace of the peculiar Lukan reformulation ("wife," "parents") appears.

[3] This petition is missing in the Lukan version of the Lord's Prayer, Luke 11:2–4. But it is found in Matt 6:13 and *Did.* 8.2, and it may have been an original part of that prayer. Dependence of the *Apocryphon of James* upon the Gospel of Matthew cannot be argued on this basis.

Or do you not know that you have yet to be abused and to be accused unjustly; and have yet to be shut up in prison, and condemned unlawfully, and crucified <without> reason, and buried <shamefully>, as (was) I myself, by the evil one. (5,9–20)

The conclusion of the discourse gives occasion for another statement of James and a response by Jesus:

"Scorn death, therefore, and take thought for life! Remember my cross and my death, and you will live."
But I answered and said to him, "Lord, do not mention to us the cross and death, for they are far from you."
The Lord answered and said, "Truly, I say unto you, none will be saved unless they believe in my cross. But those who have believed in my cross, theirs is the kingdom of God." (5,31–6,7)

The prediction of the suffering of the disciples goes further than analogous predictions of the Synoptic Gospels[1] because it uses a credal formula about Jesus' condemnation, crucifixion, death, and burial.[2] The use of credal formulae for the creation of sayings of Jesus is most clearly evident in the "predictions of the passion" in Mark 8:31; 9:30–32; 10:32–34. The dialogue in the *Apocryphon of James* takes this development one step further by applying such a formula to the prediction not only of the suffering of Jesus, but also of the suffering of the disciples. The concluding double saying of Jesus, introduced by "Truly, I say unto you," imitates the form of traditional sayings, but is in reality a new formulation which draws the conclusion from the preceding dialogue.[3]

3.1.2.4 *The* Apocryphon of James *and Johannine Sayings*

Another dialogue section of this writing that is based on several sayings appears in *Apocr. Jas.* 12,31–13,1. In this instance, parallels to these sayings appear in the Gospel of John.

---

[1] Cf., e.g., Mark 13:9; Matt 10:17–25.

[2] The context requires that the resurrection is not mentioned.

[3] Jesus' reference to his death, James's protest, and Jesus' rejection of this protest and subsequent call to the disciples to believe in his cross seems analogous to the dialogue between Jesus and Peter following the first prediction of the passion in Mark 8:30–34. In both instances, a credal formula is used in the construction of the dialogue. But there is no indication of a direct dependence. See on this passage Cameron, *Apocryphon of James*, 85–90.

Apocr. Jas. 12,31–13,1	John 12:35–36
As long as I am with you, give heed to me and obey me; but when I depart from you, remember me.	The light is with you for a little longer. Walk while you have the light. . . . While you have the light, believe in the light. . . .

	John 14:9
And remember me because when I was with you, you did not know me. Blessed will they be who have known me; woe to those who have heard and have not believed.	Have I been with you so long, and yet you do not know me?

	John 20:29
Blessed will they be who have not seen, [yet have believed]!	Because you have seen me, you believe? Blessed are those who have not seen and yet believe.

The last saying had been used already in a different context (3,17–21). The first sentences in this passage of the *Apocryphon of James* are modelled on the myth of Wisdom who appears among human beings, but remains unknown.[1] Many elements of this myth are used also in the Gospel of John, especially in the farewell discourses. It is not accidental, therefore, that more parallels to the Johannine farewell discourses can be found in the *Apocryphon of James:*

Apocr. Jas. 7,1–6	John 16:29
At first I spoke to you in parables and you did not understand; now I speak to you openly, and you (still) do not perceive.	The disciples said to him, "Behold, now you speak openly and you say no parable (παροιμία)."

Apocr. Jas. 10,32–34	John 16:23b
Invoke the Father, implore God often, and he will give to you.	Truly, truly, I say to you, whatever you ask the Father in my name, he will give to you.

Apocr. Jas. 9,4–6	John 16:26
I intercede on your behalf with the Father, and he will forgive you much.	On that day you will ask in my name, and I do not say that I will request the Father in your behalf.

There is no sign of a dependence of the *Apocryphon of James* upon the Gospel of John. On the contrary, John 14:9 is a specific application of

---

[1] Cameron (*Apocryphon of James*, 47) calls it "a fragment of a farewell speech of Wisdom." See ibid. for parallels from wisdom literature.

the more general statement that the *Apocryphon of James* has preserved. The blessedness of those who have believed without seeing, coupled with other blessing and woes, does not reveal any trace of the specific context and use of the saying at the end of the appearance of Jesus before Thomas in John 20:29. When Jesus emphasizes in John 16:26 that he will not intercede with the Father on behalf of the disciples, it is evidently a polemical formulation that rejects the more common belief in Jesus as the mediator, which is expressed in the parallel of the *Apocryphon of James*.

The tradition of sayings with which the *Apocryphon of James* is familiar also includes sayings from the *Gospel of Thomas* (see above the parallel to *Apocr. Jas.* 3,9–11). Also *Apocr. Jas.* 9,18–24 may recall a saying from this gospel:

Apocr. Jas. 9,18–24	*Gos. Thom.* 69a	[Q]Matt 5:11
Hearken to the word; understand knowledge, love, life, and no one will persecute you, nor will anyone oppress you, other than you yourselves.	Blessed are they who have been persecuted within themselves. It is they who have truly come to know the Father.	Blessed are you when men revile you and persecute you . . .

In *Gos. Thom.* 69a, the concept of persecution has been spiritualized. *Apocr. Jas.* 9,18–24 presupposes this secondary spiritualizing of the blessing of those who are persecuted rather than the form of the saying preserved from Q in the Gospel of Matthew.[1]

3.1.2.5 The Parables

Of special interest are the parables of the *Apocryphon of James*. There are interpretations of two parables in *Apocr. Jas.* 7,22–8,27. A list of parables has been inserted between these two parables in 8,4–10; the list is introduced (8,1–4) by Jesus saying, ". . . you have compelled me to stay with you another eighteen days for the sake of the parables. It was enough for some <to listen> to the teaching and understand:"

The Shepherds	Luke 16:4–6
and the Seed	Mark 4:3–9 parr
and the Building	Matt 7:24–27; Luke 6:47–49

---

[1] See above, # 2.3.2.

and the Lamps of the Virgins	Matt 25:1–12
and the Wage of the Workmen	Matt 20:1–15
and the Didrachmae	Luke 16:8–9
and the Woman	Luke 18:2–8

The identification of the Synoptic Gospels' parallels is not always certain. Luke 16:4–6 talks only about one shepherd; the Seed could refer to either Mark 4:3–9 or Mark 4:26–29, even to the parable of the Mustard Seed (Mark 4:30–32 || Q 13:18–19); the identification of the Didrachmae with the parable of the Lost Coin, and that of the Woman with the parable of the Unjust Judge is tentative at best. In any case, reference seems to be made to parables of all three Synoptic Gospels, because the parables of the Laborers in the Vineyard and the Ten Virgins appear only in Matthew, the Seed growing Secretly only in Mark, and the the Lost Coin and the Unjust Judge only in Luke. This list of parables in the *Apocryphon of James* is the only strong indication for a use of canonical gospels in this writing. Since the list is not related to either the preceding or the following parables, it is probably an interpolation.[1]

The parables which are actually quoted and interpreted in the *Apocryphon of James* do not depend upon any canonical source. The one that comes closest possibly to being derived from a canonical gospel is the parable of the Grain of Wheat which follows upon the list of parables. It is prefaced by a special introduction ("Become earnest about the word! For as to the word, its first part is faith; its second, love; the third, works; for from these comes life," 8,10–15):

Apocr. Jas. 8,16–23	Mark 4:26–29
For the word is like a grain of wheat; when someone had sown it, he had faith in it; and when it had sprouted, he loved it because he had seen many grains in place of one. And when he had worked, he was saved because he had prepared it for food, (and) again	The kingdom of God is as if a man should scatter seed upon the ground, and should sleep and rise night and day, and the seed should sprout and grow, he knows not how. The earth produces of itself, first the blade, then the ear, then the full grain in the ear.

[1] This is confirmed by a reference to Jesus' stay for "eighteen days" with the disciples in the introduction to the list (8,3), while the setting given at the beginning of the writing speaks of Jesus' appearance "after five hundred and fifty days after he had risen from the dead" (2,19–21). Cf. Williams, "Apocryphon of James," 19: "The difficulty at 8.1–4, where James and Peter are reproached for delaying the Savior a mysterious "eighteen days more for the sake of parables," might be solved by assuming that this passage originated in a separate source."

he left (some) to sow.   But when the grain is ripe, at once he
                                          puts in the sickle, because the
                                          harvest has come.

To be sure, both parables talk about the same, indeed rather common-place, agricultural phenomenon. What is emphasized in each story, however, is very different. In one instance, it is the loving and work-ing attention that is given to the growing fruit; in the other instance, it is exactly the opposite. It is quite difficult to explain one of the parables as the interpretation of the other. The introduction to the parable in the *Apocryphon of James* makes the parable an allegory that illustrates "believing," "loving," "working," and "being saved" as the path of salvation. Whatever its original form may have been,[1] it has been reformulated in order to fit the theme of its introduction. But it is evident that the topic indicated in the introduction to the parable differs from the secondary interpretation by the author of this writing in 8,23–27; it was part of the traditional form of the parable. The author's interpretation appears at the end of the parable: "So also can you yourselves receive the kingdom of heaven; unless you receive this through knowledge, you will not be able to find it" (8,23–27).

The parable in *Apocr. Jas.* 12,20–30 uses the same imagery:

For this cause I tell you this, that you may know yourselves.
    For the kingdom of heaven is like an ear of grain after it had sprouted in a field. And when it had ripened, it scattered its fruit and again filled the field with ears for another year.
    You also, hasten to reap an ear of life for yourselves that you may be filled with the kingdom.

Again the interpretation appended by the author of the writing is obvi-ously secondary because its most important point is the "reaping of an ear" (= to be filled with the kingdom) which is not even mentioned in the parable itself.[2] Thus the parable must have been an independent piece of tradition which originally spoke about the spread of the king-dom through the fruit which it produced.

The third parable of the *Apocryphon of James* is the parable of the Palm Shoot (7,22–35). Ron Cameron has analyzed this parable in

---

[1] "The original form of this parable may be irrecoverable" (Cameron, *Parable and Interpretation*, 8; idem, *Apocryphon of James*, 8–11).
[2] Cameron, *Parable and Interpretation*, 7; idem, *Apocryphon of James*, 12–16.

detail and has been able to explain its strange imagery.[1] I am here quoting this parable in Cameron's translation together with his analysis:[2]

(1) Introduction (7,22–23)

"Let not the kingdom of heaven wither away."

(2) Parable (7,24–28)

"For it is like a date palm (shoot) whose fruits dropped down around it. It put forth buds and, when they blossomed, they (i.e., the fruits) caused the productivity (of the date palm, literally: "the womb") to dry up."

(3) Application (7,28–32)

"Thus is it also with the fruit which comes from the single root: when it (i.e., the fruit) was (picked) fruits were collected by many."

(4) Expansion (7,33–35)

"It was really good. Is it (not) possible now to produce the plants anew for you, (and) to find it (i.e., the kingdom of heaven)?"

To understand this parable is so difficult because of the peculiar way in which date palms produce fruit. They are dioecious plants; the female tree can produce fruit only if a male tree stands nearby or if it is artificially fertilized by male pollen. Otherwise the immature fruits will drop to the ground and perish.[3] The introduction ("Let not the kingdom of heaven wither away") was written for a parable that told of the dying of the immature fruits of the female palm tree and thus of the withering of its productivity. This original parable must have been told as a warning, like the parable of the Fig Tree (Luke 13:6–9). The problems of the extant text are due to several layers of secondary interpretations which misunderstand the nature of the fruit production of the date palm. An interpolation in the parable itself ("It put forth buds and when they blossomed") and the application ("fruits were collected by many") seem to understand the story as a parable of growth, analogous to the parable of the Ear of Grain. A later (Gnostic) interpretation which emphasized the "single root" and added the "Expansion" ("find the kingdom," 7,33–35) represents the final stage of the interpretation. In all three parables, an obviously secondary Gnos-

---

[1] Cameron, *Parable and Interpretation*, 9–13; idem, *Apocryphon of James*, 17–30.

[2] *Parable and Interpretation*, 9.

[3] This was well known in antiquity, and it is frequently described. The relevant passages are quoted by Cameron, *Parable and Interpretation*, 10–11; idem, *Apocryphon of James*, 19–21.

tic interpretation appears at the end, while earlier interpretations are preserved in the introductory phrases.

3.1.2.6 Conclusions

It is still too early to draw final conclusions concerning the character and date of the *Apocryphon of James*. Further scholarly analysis is needed. Its final form may have resulted from one or several redactions. This is already evident in the dual setting and description of the document at the beginning, first as a letter from James to an unknown addressee, then as a secret book revealed by the Lord to James and Peter. The first and external frame, written as a first-person singular report by James (1,1–35; 16,2–30), is certainly the latest frame that the document has received. But even the second, and most likely more original introduction, as well as the conclusion in which James and Peter return to the other disciples and announce that they had been witnesses of Jesus' return to heaven (15,5–16,2), must be part of a secondary framework for an older dialogue gospel. The dialogues themselves do not presuppose a setting after Jesus' resurrection and ascension (2,17–21). As in the Gospel of John, they are farewell discourses in which Jesus explains what he has said before his departure, but neither resurrection nor ascension are presupposed in these discourses. There also seems to be a difference in the use of the titles for Jesus. Only in the secondary frames is Jesus called Savior (1,23; 1,32; 2,11; 16,25). In the dialogue itself, the title appears only once at the beginning (2,40);[1] otherwise the title Lord prevails.[2] This older dialogue seems to be composed on the basis of the free tradition of sayings of Jesus. Its sayings are not drawn from several written gospels (including the *Gospel of Thomas*) but represent an earlier stage of the development of the sayings tradition in which the collection of sayings coincides with their interpretation in the form of dialogues between Jesus and his disciples, analogous to the dialogue that formed the basis for the *Dialogue of the Savior*. Both documents are thus witnesses for a development of the tradition of Jesus' sayings which must be presupposed for the composition and writing of the dialogues and discourses of the Gospel of John.

---

[1] Some editors supply the title Savior also in the lacuna of 4,2; see Williams, "Apocryphon of James," note to p. 32.

[2] 4,23; 4,31; 5,36; 6,1; 6,22; 6,28; 6,32; 6,35; 13,31; 13,36. See also Cameron, *Apocryphon of James*, 4.

3.2 The Collection of Narratives about Jesus

3.2.1 MIRACLE CATENAE

It is most probable that miracle stories of Jesus were told at the very earliest stage of the Christian mission. The telling of these stories probably went hand in hand with the performance of miracles by the apostles. Such miracles are reported in the Acts of the Apostles.[1] There remains, of course, the question of the sources used by the author and of the reliability of such reports. However, Paul himself refers to his own activity of performing miracles, cf. 1 Thess 1:5:

For our gospel came to you not only in word, but also in mighty work (δυνάμει) and in the Holy Spirit and in full conviction.

The Book of Acts also refers regularly to Jesus' miracles as part of his ministry, sometimes in standard formulae, cf. Acts 2:22:

Jesus of Nazareth, a man attested to you by God with mighty works and wonders and signs (δυνάμεσι καὶ τέρασι καὶ σημείοις) which God did through him in your midst.

The earliest composition of stories of miracles must be located in the Christian propaganda in the Hellenistic world as Christian missionaries were confronted with competing claims of other prophets, missionaries, and miracles workers. The presence of divine and supernatural power was not only attested by the performance of a miracle or through a story told about a great miracle worker, it was also effective when it was published as a record of the superhuman accomplishments of a god or of a divine man. Records published in stone and exhibited in Asklepios sanctuaries told of the healing powers of the god.[2] Written collections of reports about the great deeds of leaders, heroes, and lawgivers are known from the realm of philosophical and religious propaganda of the Hellenistic world.[3] These must have served as models for the composition of writings, properly called aretalogies,[4] reporting the miracle stories of the apostles and of Jesus.

---

[1] Cf., e.g., Acts 3:1–10; 5:12; 6:8; 13:6–12; 14:8–18.

[2] E. and J. Edelstein, *Asklepios: A Collection and Interpretation of the Testimonies* (2 vols.; Baltimore: Johns Hopkins University Press, 1945).

[3] Ludwig Bieler, ΘΕΙΟΣ ΑΝΗΡ: *Das Bild des "göttlichen Menschen" in Spätantike und Frühchristentum* (Darmstadt: Wissenschaftliche Buchgesellschaft, 1967); Moses Hadas and Morton Smith, *Heroes and Gods: Spiritual Biography in Antiquity* (Religious Perspectives 13; New York: Harper & Row, 1965).

[4] Morton Smith, "Prolegomena to a Discussion of Aretalogies, Divine Men, the Gospels, and Jesus," *JBL* 90 (1971) 174–99.

The first evidence of such written collections comes, as Dieter Georgi has demonstrated,[1] from Paul's Second Letter to the Corinthians. The "letters of recommendation," which Paul's opponents brought to Corinth and which they solicited from the Corinthians,[2] were documents in which the great deeds were listed which these foreign missionaries had performed. These miracle reports would have contained not only stories of healings and exorcisms, but also reports of ecstasies (cf. 2 Cor 5:13), visions (cf. 2 Cor 12:1–7), and successful prayers (cf. 2 Cor 12:7–9). In the same letter Paul explicitly rejects the image of a "Christ according to the flesh" (2 Cor 5:16). This possibly refers to reports of the miracles of Christ which the opposing apostles had told.

Direct evidence for the existence of written documents recording the miracles of Jesus comes from some of the sources that were used in the Gospels of Mark and of John. It is not unlikely that such writings were originally composed as handbooks for Christian faith healers. But soon they must have been intended to communicate the powerful message of Jesus the "divine man." Stories about Jesus' power over nature, about the heavenly voice at his baptism, and eventually, about his miraculous birth, were added to these collections of healing stories.

The Gospel of Mark used one or several such collections.[3] A source of aretalogical stories seems most clearly present in Mark 4:35–6:52. It contained the following stories:

4:35–41	Stilling of the tempest
5:1–20	Gerasene demoniac[4]
5:22–24, 35–43	Raising of the daughter of Jairus
5:25–34	Healing of the woman with an issue of blood[5]
6:30–44	Feeding of the five thousand[6]

[1] Dieter Georgi, *The Opponents of Paul in 2 Corinthians: A Study in Religious Propaganda in Late Antiquity* (Philadelphia: Fortress, 1985).

[2] Cf. 2 Cor 3:1: "Or do we need, as some do, letters of recommendation (συστατικαὶ ἐπιστολαί) to you or from you?"

[3] Paul J. Achtemeier, "The Origin and Function of the pre-Markan Miracle Catenae," *JBL* 90 (1971) 198–221.

[4] Its length alone distinguishes this exorcism from the other exorcisms reported in Mark. Moreover, the satirical motif of this story—the demons are driven into the pigs who then drown themselves in the sea—is quite alien to the other Markan exorcisms.

[5] These two stories seem to have been artfully connected already in Mark's source.

[6] It would seem natural to include also the following story about the Walking on the Sea (6:45–52). However, the two stories are separated by the mention of Bethsaida, which apparently introduces a new cycle; see below.

Mark 6:45 mentions that Jesus and his disciples intended to go to Bethsaida. The same town is mentioned again in Mark 8:22. These two references to Bethsaida, the only two in the entire gospel literature, enclose another cycle of stories which is to some extent parallel to the cycle of Mark 5:35–6:44:[1]

	First Cycle		Second Cycle
4:35–41	Stilling of the tempest	6:45–52	Walking on the sea
5:1–20	Gerasene demoniac		
5:22–43	Daughter of Jairus		
5:25–34	Women with issue of blood	7:24–30	Canaanite woman
		7:32–36	Healing of a deaf mute
6:30–44	Feeding the five thousand	8:1–10	Feeding the four thousand
		8:22–26	Healing of a blind man

It is doubtful whether other miracles stories of the Gospel of Mark were also drawn from one or several written sources. Some of these may have belonged to written collections of a different character. The healing of the man with the withered hand (Mark 3:1–6) was apparently part of a collection of apophthegmata, short controversy stories, which Mark used in chapters 1–3. Other miracle stories, such as the healing of the leper (1:40–45), the healing of the man sick of the palsy (2:1–12), the so-called healing of the epileptic child (9:14–29), and the healing of the blind man (Bartimaeus) on the road to Jerusalem (10:46–52), could have circulated independently.

The Gospel of John permits us to discern with more certainty the source of miracle stories used in that writing. There is no question that a written source of miracles of Jesus underlies chapters 2–11 of the Gospel of John. It was a writing containing miracle stories of Jesus which may have been used in the mission and propaganda of the Johannine community. The beginning of this source is clearly marked at the end of the story of the wine miracle at Cana (2:1–11) by the remark:

> This was the first of the signs (ἀρχὴν τῶν σημείων) which Jesus did in Cana of Galilee, and he revealed his glory, and his disciples believed in him. (2:11)

After the story of the healing of the son of the royal official (4:46–54) follows a similar remark:

---

[1] The entire "Bethsaida section," Mark 6:45–8:26, is not reproduced by the Gospel of Luke. This has resulted in the hypothesis that it represents a later interpolation into the Gospel of Mark; see below, # 4.1.2.

This is the second sign (δεύτερον σημεῖον) when he came from Judea into Galilee. (4:54)

It has also been suggested that the original ending of the Semeia Source has been preserved in John 20:30–31:[1]

Jesus did many other signs (σημεῖα) before his disciples which are not written in this book; but these are written in order that you believe that Jesus is Christ, the Son of God, and that believing in him you may have life in his name.

The name σημεῖα = "signs," "miracles" does not fit the Gospel as whole; it would be very appropriate, however, for a collection of miracle stories. Moreover, this concluding remark of the Fourth Gospel emphasizes the belief in Jesus on the basis of his miracles; similar remarks occur in the context of some other miracle stories (cf. 2:11, quoted above; 5:44; 6:2; 11:45). Because of the use of the term "signs" (σημεῖα) as a designation for miracles in the context of these stories (John 2:11; 4:45; 6:2, 14), the name Semeia Source or Source of Signs has become established among scholars as a label for this source.[2]

The following stories derive from this Semeia Source:

2:1–11	Wine miracle at the wedding feast of Cana
4:46–54	Healing of the son of a royal official
5:2–9	Healing of a lame man at the Pool of Bethzatha
6:5–14	Feeding of the six thousand
6:16–25	Tempest and walking on the sea
9:1–7	Healing of a blind man
11:1–45	Raising of Lazarus

It is evident that the Semeia Source drew its stories from the same traditions which also provided the materials for the miracle catenae of the Gospel of Mark. The story of the Feeding of the Multitudes and a miracle story connected with the Sea of Galilee appear in all three collections. The character of the Semeia Source, however, is quite different. The stories of the Markan cycles describe Jesus as a man with extraordinary powers who is not above using magical techniques; he

---

[1] On this passage see Bultmann, *Gospel of John*, 697–99; Brown, *Gospel of John*, 2.1055–58.

[2] Bultmann, *Gospel of John*, 113 and passim. A variant of this source hypothesis was suggested by Robert Thomson Fortna, *The Gospel of Signs* (Cambridge: Cambridge University Press, 1970). Fortna assumes that miracle stories and the passion narrative were both derived from one and the same narrative source. A modification of Bultmann's source hypothesis has been presented by Ernst Haenchen, *The Gospel of John* (Hermeneia; Philadelphia: Fortress, 1984) 1. 67–90.

employs magical words,[1] uses magical manipulations,[2] and holds a long discourse with a demon.[3] All of these features are absent from the stories of the Semeia Source. Here Jesus documents his power in a different way, not as magician but as a god. He changes water into wine like the Greek god Dionysos (John 2:1–10), his powerful word heals even from a distance (4:46–54), at the Pool at Bethzatha Jesus accomplishes what an angel from heaven was expected to do (5:2–9), the multitudes' expectations are not just fed by a skilled miracle worker but by a god who can walk across the Sea of Galilee and move a ship miraculously to the other shore (6:1–21), the man who receives sight has been blind from birth (9:1–7), and the raising of Lazarus who has been in his tomb for four days, presents Jesus as a god who commands power over the realm of Hades (chapter 11). The miracles of Jesus are more than miracles, they are epiphanies.

In the form in which the author of the Fourth Gospel used the Semeia Source, it was composed in Greek, though it is not impossible that it was originally written in Aramaic. In any case, it originated most likely in Syria/Palestine, like the Gospel of John itself. The inclusion of a story that once belonged to the circle of the wine god Dionysos gives clear evidence for the Hellenistic-syncretistic milieu which determined the forms of Christian propaganda in this eastern region of the Roman empire.

3.2.2 THE UNKNOWN GOSPEL OF PAPYRUS EGERTON 2

3.2.2.1 The Papyrus and the Problem of its Interpretation

In the year 1935 fragments of a papyrus from Egypt were published as *Papyrus Egerton 2*. Two damaged pages, a fragment of a third page, and a scrap of a fourth with only one readable letter contained passages from a gospel that was otherwise unknown.[4] More recently,

---

[1] Mark 5:41: ταλιθὰ κοῦμ = Greek transcription of Aramaic for "maiden rise." Mark 7:34" ἐφφαθά = Aramaic for "be open." Also the words spoken to the sea in Mark 4:39 (σιώπα, πεφίμωσο) must be understood as magical formulae.

[2] Spittle is used for the opening of the eyes of the blind man (Mark 8:23).

[3] Mark 5:7–10.

[4] H. Idris Bell and T. C. Skeat, *Fragments of an Unknown Gospel and Other Early Christian Papyri* (London: British Museum, 1935); a corrected text was published by the same authors shortly thereafter: *The New Gospel Fragments* (London: British Museum, 1935). English translations can be found in J. Jeremias, "An Unknown Gospel with Johannine Elements (Papyrus Egerton 2)," in Hennecke-Schneemelcher-Wilson, *NT Apocrypha*, 1. 94–97; Ron Cameron, *Other Gospels*, 72–75. For a recent German translation with introduction see Joachim Jeremias and Wilhelm Schneemelcher, "Papyrus Egerton 2," in Hennecke-Schneemelcher, *NT Apokryphen I*, 82–85. The English translation in Hennecke-Schneemelcher-Wilson, *NT Apocrypha*, 1. 96–97, does not yet reflect the discovery of an additional portion of *Papyrus Egerton*

another small fragment, *Pap. Köln Nr. 255*,[1] containing 5 lines, has been identified as part of *Papyrus Egerton 2*. According to the judgment of the original editors, the hand of the papyrus resembled the hands of datable papyri from the period of the late 1st and early 2d centuries.[2] However, the editor of the new fragment, Michael Gronewald, cites convincing arguments for a date of the style of the handwriting rather closer to *Papyrus Bodmer II* (= NT 𝔭[66]), i.e., to about the year 200 CE.[3]

The Greek text of this papyrus preserves debates of Jesus with the Pharisees, the story of the healing of a leper, and a few fragmentary lines which probably belong to another miracle story. Thus the preserved fragments show that they came from a writing which contained, like the canonical Gospels, both sayings and narratives of Jesus. At the time, the discovery of such a gospel aroused considerable interest and scholarly controversy about the question of the dependence of this gospel upon the Gospels of the New Testament canon.[4] However, this debate was cut short by of the outbreak of World War II. In 1946, Goro Mayeda published his dissertation on *Papyrus Egerton 2*[5] in which he came to the conclusion that the text of this gospel was not dependent upon any of the canonical gospels.[6] This result has been debated ever since,[7] although few major investigations of the papyrus have been published since Mayeda's dissertation appeared.[8]

---

2. I acknowledge gratefully the generosity of the author who gave me access to his still unpublished dissertation and permitted me to use his new and revised English translation: Jon B. Daniels, *The Egerton Gospel: Its Place in Early Christianity* (Dissertation Claremont Graduate School, Claremont, CA: 1990).

¹ Michael Gronewald, "Unbekanntes Evangelium oder Evangelienharmonie (Fragment aus dem Evangelium Egerton)," in *Kölner Papyri (P. Köln)* vol. 6 (Abh.RWA, Sonderreihe Papyrologica Coloniensia 7; Cologne: 1987) 136–45.

² Bell and Skeat, *Unknown Gospel*, 1–7.

³ See also E. G. Turner, *Greek Manuscripts of the Ancient World* (Oxford: Clarendon Press, 1971) 13.

⁴ This debate is reported in Goro Mayeda, *Das Leben-Jesu-Fragment Papyrus Egerton 2 und seine Stellung in der urchristlichen Literaturgeschichte* (Bern: Haupt, 1946) 94–95. See also the literature listed in Joachim Jeremias and Wilhelm Schneemelcher, "Papyrus Egerton 2," in Hennecke-Schneemelcher, *NT Apokryphen I*, 84; cf. Joachim Jeremias, "An Unknown Gospel with Johannine Elements," in Hennecke-Schneemelcher-Wilson, *NT Apocrypha*, 1. 96.

⁵ This dissertation was inspired by Martin Dibelius at the University of Heidelberg, but accepted for a degree by Rudolf Bultmann at the University of Marburg.

⁶ Mayeda, *Leben-Jesu-Fragment*, passim.

⁷ See Hennecke-Schneemelcher, *NT Apokryphen I*, 83; Vielhauer, *Geschichte*, 638; Brown, *Gospel of John*, 229–30.

⁸ Exceptions are F.-M. Braun, *Jean le Théologien* (3 vols.; Paris: Gabalda, 1959–1966) 1. 87–94; Jeremias, *Unknown Sayings*, 18–20.

Jeremias, in his introduction to the translation of the fragments,[1] has formulated the problem of this gospel text and, at the same time, the most commonly accepted solution as follows:

> The juxtaposition of Johannine and Synoptic material and the fact that the Johannine material is shot through with Synoptic phrases and the Synoptic with Johannine usage, permits the conjecture that the author knew all and every one of the canonical gospels.

If this conclusion were true, *Papyrus Egerton 2* would appear to be, even with a date of ca. 200 CE, a spectacularly early piece of evidence for the establishment of the four-gospel canon of the New Testament. Jeremias's observation, however, is not quite accurate. To be sure, both Johannine and synoptic features occur in the gospel texts of *Papyrus Egerton 2*. The problem is that this judgment, which finds a thorough mixture of synoptic and Johannine language, relies on criteria which are derived from the observation of the often strikingly different languages of the Synoptic Gospels on the one hand, and the Gospel of John on the other hand. These features, however, characterize the end-product of a long development. The presence of "synoptic" language in any "Johannine" context, and of "Johannine" language in any "synoptic" context, may well attest an earlier stage of the development in which pre-Johannine and pre-synoptic characteristics of language still existed side by side.

Most recently, Jon B. Daniels, in his learned and very detailed Claremont Graduate School dissertation,[2] has presented strong arguments for the independence of the gospel fragment preserved in *Papyrus Egerton 2*. With respect to the synoptic parallels, Daniels says, "Egerton's account of Jesus' healing a leper plausibly represents a separate tradition which did not undergo Markan redaction." With respect to the Johannine parallels, he concludes that the author's "compositional choices suggest that he or she did not make use of the Gospel of John in canonical form."[3] The following discussion of the text will demonstrate my agreement with Jon Daniels's assessment.

---

[1] In Hennecke Schneemelcher-Wilson, *NT Apocrypha*, 1. 95.

[2] See above.

[3] Quoted from the "Abstract" of the dissertation. This chapter of my book was essentially finished before I had access to Jon Daniel's dissertation, although I had learned much from discussions with the author while he was engaged in his research for the thesis. I am delighted to find almost complete confirmation of the arguments set forth in what follows.

3.2.2.2 About Scripture and Moses

The papyrus begins with a fragmentary sentence in which Jesus seems to say to the "lawyers" (νομικοί) that they may punish everyone transgressing the law. The term "lawyer" is typical for the Gospel of Luke.[1] But here as elsewhere in the papyrus, there is very little else that would suggest dependence upon Luke.

The first preserved pericope of the fragment has a close parallel in the Gospel of John, but its language sometimes is not yet as "Johannine" as that of the author of the Gospel of John.

Pap. Eg. 2, 1 verso, 7–20[2]	John 5:39–40
To the rulers of the people he said this word, "Search (ἐραυνᾶτε)[3] the scriptures in which you think you have life (ζωήν).	You search (ἐραυνᾶτε) the scriptures, because you think that in them you have eternal life (ζωὴν αἰώνιον).
These are they which bear witness of me.	These are they which bear witness of me. Yet you refuse to come to me that you may have life.
	John 5:45
Do not think that I have come to accuse you before my Father; there is one who accuses you, Moses, in whom you have set your hope."	Do not think that I shall accuse you before the Father; there is one who accuses you: Moses, in whom you have set your hope.
	John 9:28–29
And when they said (to Jesus),	. . . and they said (to the man who was blind), "You are his disciple, but we are disciples of Moses.
"We know that God has spoken to Moses; but as for you, we do not know [whence you are]."[4]	We know that God has spoken to Moses; but this one, we do not know whence he is."

---

[1] See above in the discussion of Q (# 2.3.3) on Luke 11:52.

[2] I have compared my translations of *Papyrus Egerton 2* with Jon Daniels's new reconstruction of the Greek text and have followed his translation in many instances.

[3] The Greek ἐραυνᾶτε can be translated as either an imperative ("Search!") or as in indicative ("You search"). The former translation is preferable for *Pap. Eg. 2*, the latter for John 5:39.

[4] The bracketed words translate the Greek text πόθεν εἶ which has been restored on the basis of John 9:29. With respect to arguments for this restoration, see Daniels, *Egerton Gospel*, 24, n. 1.

Jesus answered and said to them,
"Now already accusation is made
against your unbelief (ἀπιστία) with
respect to those to whom he bore
witness.[1]

Because if you had believed Moses,
you would believe me; because it is
about me that he wrote to your
fathers."

John 5:46

Because if you had believed Moses,
you would believe me; because it is
about me that he wrote.

The only "synoptic" element in this passage is the address to the "rulers of the people." This term is not used in John for the opponents of Jesus; rather, here as elsewhere, Jesus' speech is addressed to "the Jews" (cf. John 5:15–16, 19), the stereotypical opponents of the Johannine Jesus. A minor difference is that *Pap. Eg. 2* uses the simple "life," whereas John 5:39 has "eternal life," which is more typical for the language of this Gospel. The phrase "Jesus answered and said" (ἀποκριθεὶς καὶ εἶπεν) is also never used in the Gospel of John, but is frequent in the Synoptic Gospels. The term "unbelief" (ἀπιστία) never occurs in the Gospel of John, but has synoptic parallels.[2] Otherwise, the language is "Johannine" throughout. But because some typical Johannine terms are missing in the parallel of *Papyrus Egerton 2,* it is possible that its text represents a pre-Johannine version of this controversy of Jesus with his opponents.

The comparison of the vocabulary cannot be conclusive. The real problem lies elsewhere. Is it possible to understand the rationale of the composition of the papyrus on the basis of the assumption that it used the Gospel of John? In that case, the author of *Papyrus Egerton 2* had taken a passage from John 5:39–47, eliminated the section 5:41–44 and the two parallel conclusions 5:40 and 5:47, but interpolated a sentence from John 9:20 between 5:45 and 5:46. It is, therefore, easier to explain John 5:39–47 as a secondary expansion of the debate between Jesus and his opponents which *Papyrus Egerton 2* has preserved in its more original form. The relationship between the original text and the Johannine redaction is presented in the following table:

5:39   "You search the scriptures in   = *Papyrus Egerton 2*
        which you think you have life."

---

[1] Daniels (ibid., 24) translates, "In those who have been commended by him." See ibid., n. 2.

[2] For a detailed presentation of the evidence see Mayeda, *Leben-Jesus-Fragment,* 15–27.

5:40	"But you do not want to come to me in order to have eternal life."	Johannine conclusion
5:41–44	"I do not take honor from human beings, . . . How can you believe, who receive glory from one another, and do not seek the glory that comes from the one and only God?"	Johannine interpolation
5:45	"Do not think that I have come to accuse you before my Father; there is one who accuses you: Moses in whom you have set your hope."	= *Papyrus Egerton 2*
	And when they said (to Jesus), "We know that God has spoken to Moses; but as for you, we do not know whence you are."	= *Papyrus Egerton 2* transferred by John to 9:29, addressed to the man who was blind.
	"Now already accusation is made against your unbelief with respect to those to whom he bore witness.	Omitted by John
5:46	Because if you had believed Moses, you would believe me; because it is about me that he wrote to your fathers."	= *Papyrus Egerton 2*
5:47	"But if you do not believe his writings, how will you believe my words?"	Johannine conclusion

3.2.2.3 The Attempt to Arrest Jesus

The priority of *Papyrus Egerton 2* is the best explanation also in the case of the report about hostility against Jesus which appears after a lacuna of several missing lines.

Pap. Eg. 2 (1 recto, 22–31)	John 7:30	John 10:31, 39
[. . . to gather] stones together [to stone] him. And the rulers laid their hands on	So they sought to arrest him.	The Jews took up stones to stone him. Again they tried to arrest him.

him to [deliver] him to
the crowd. But they
were not able to arrest
him since the hour of
his being handed over
had not yet come. But
the Lord himself
escaped from their
hands and turned
away from them.

But no one laid hands
on him,
because his hour

had not yet come.

But he escaped from
their hands.

Similar attempts to arrest Jesus are also mentioned in John 7:44
("Some of them tried to arrest him, but no one laid his hands on him")
and 8:20 ("and no one laid hands on him, because his hour had not yet
come"). The parallels are once more very close.[1] An explanation of this
segment of *Papyrus Egerton 2* as a secondary patchwork of several
Johannine passages does not seem very appealing. The phrase "his
hour had not yet come" might be considered to have been created by
the author of the Gospel of John. In that case argumants for a dependence of *Papyrus Egerton 2* upon the Fourth Gospel would be persuasive. However, though references to the "hour" occur several times
in John,[2] the use of the term "hour" in reference to the suffering and
death of Jesus also appears in the Gethsemane pericope of Mark 14:35:
". . . and he prayed that, if it were possible, the hour might pass from
him."[3] Thus it would seem quite possible that the reference to the
"hour" of Jesus' betrayal appeared in a source of the Fourth Gospel. It
is, then, preferable to explain John's multiple reference to failed
attempts to arrest Jesus as reflections and usages of only one traditional report, such as the one which is preserved by *Papyrus Egerton 2*.

3.2.2.4 *The Healing of a Leper*

Less problematic is the third pericope of *Papyrus Egerton 2*, the
story of the healing of a leper.

[1] On the slight difference in vocabulary see Mayeda, *Leben-Jesu-Fragment*, 27–31.
[2] See also John 2:4 (". . . my hour has not yet come"); 5:25 ("Truly, truly, the hour is
coming and is now that the dead will hear the voice of the Son of God . . ."); 12:23 ("The
hour has come that the Son of man be glorified").
[3] The belief in the importance of the "hour," be it for the performance of a miracle, or
for the determination (sometimes astrologically) of any action determined by God or by
fate, is widespread in antiquity; see Bultmann, *Gospel of John*, 117, n. 1.

Pap. Eg. 2 (1 recto 34–41)	Mark 1:40–44[1]
And behold, a leper came to him and said,	[40] And a leper came to him beseeching him and kneeling said to him,
"Master Jesus, wandering with lepers and eating with them in the inn, I myself became a leper. If therefore [you will], I shall be clean."	"(Master)[2]
	if you will, you can make me clean."
	[41] And[3] he stretched out his hand and touched him and
Accordingly the Lord said to him, "I will, be clean!" [And immediately] the leprosy left him.	said to him, "I will, be clean!" [42] And immediately the leprosy left him.
	[43] And he sternly charged him and sent him away immediately.[4]
Jesus said to him,	[44] And said to him,
	"See that you say nothing to anyone;
"Go and show yourself to the [priests], and offer for the purification as Moses has commanded,	but go, show yourself to the priest and offer for your purification what Moses commanded for a proof to the people."

John 5:14

"Behold you have become healthy.
Sin no more that nothing worse may befall you."

and sin no more . . ."

This miracle story is evidently identical with the one that is told by Mark. The only element that seems to presuppose Matthew or Luke is the address "Master" which, however, may have been an original part of the Markan text and of the tradition that he used. That the redactional additions Mark 1:43 and 44a are missing and that no other redactional elements of either Mark's or Matthew's or Luke's text appear in *Papyrus Egerton 2* argues for independence of its version of

[1] Synoptic parallels appear in Matt 8:1–4 and Luke 5:12–14, a variant appears in Luke 17: 11–19 (the healing of the ten lepers). However, *Papyrus Egerton 2* does not share any special features with that account.

[2] The address "Master" (κύριε) appears only in the text of the two synoptic parallels, Matt 8:2 and Luke 5:12. This agreement of Matthew and Luke demonstrates that the same address stood originally also in the text of Mark. On the problem of the "common agreements" of Matthew and Luke which may have preserved Mark's original text see below # 4.1.2.1–3.

[3] The following phrase "moved by pity" (σπλαγχνισθείς) and the variant ὀργισθείς (D) do not seem to have belonged to the original text of Mark. The parallel synoptic versions do not show any trace of either reading.

[4] The verse Mark 1:43 has no parallels in either Matthew or Luke. It certainly does not belong to the original story and is probably a later interpolation into the Markan text.

the story. The absence of a gesture of worship and the simple healing through the word of Jesus alone, may also be signs of an earlier version of the story. The expansion at the beginning which tells how the sick man contracted his leprosy—it shows unfamiliarity with the actual practice in Israel—is certainly a secondary feature. But that is no compelling reason for the assumption that the story is dependent upon any of the Synoptic Gospels.[1] As strange as the last sentence is (resembling Jesus' admonition to the invalid from the pool of Bethzatha), it is hardly enough to argue for literary dependence. There is no question anyway that the author of this gospel knew traditions and sources which were used in the Gospel of John.

3.2.2.5 Paying Taxes to the Kings

The last of the pericopes of *Papyrus Egerton 2* (2 recto, 43–59) presents a very puzzling picture. The pericope is an apophthegma that exhibits all normal features of this form:

Introduction:	. . . and they came to him testing him with questions saying, "Teacher Jesus, . . . "
Question of the opponents:	"Is it permitted to give to the kings . . . "
Jesus reaction:	But Jesus, knowing their intention, became angry.
Jesus answer:	"Why do you call me teacher with your mouth and do not do what I say?"
Expansion with a quotation from Scripture:	"Well did Isaiah prophesy concerning you . . ."

But the comparison with analogous passages from other gospels reveals that these parallels appear in quite different contexts of three or four different writings:

Pap. Eg. 2 (2 recto, 43–59)	Mark 12:13–15	John 3:2
. . . and they came to him testing him with questions saying:	And they sent to him . . . to entrap him in his talk. And they came and said to	
"Teacher Jesus, we know that you have come [from God],[2]	him, "Teacher, we know that you are true and you care for no	"Rabbi, we know that you are a teacher come from God."

---

[1] I am, therefore, not convinced by the arguments in favor of the hypothesis that the author knew all three Synoptic Gospels, which have been put forward by Frans Neirynck, "Papyrus Egerton and the Healing of the Leper," *EThL* 61 (1985) 153–60.

[2] Restoration on the basis of the parallel passage John 3:2.

for what you do bears
witness beyond all the
prophets.[1]

Tell us, is it permitted
to give to the kings
what pertains to their
rule? Shall we give it
or not?"
But Jesus, knowing
their intention,
became angry[2] and
said,

"Why do you call me
teacher with your
mouth and do not do
what I say?

Well did Isaiah
prophesy concerning
you when he said,

'This people honor me
with their lips, but
their heart is far away
from me. In vain do
they worship me,
[teaching] precepts of
human beings.'"

men; for you do not
regard the position of
men, but truly teach
the way of God.
Is it permitted to pay
taxes to Caesar or not?
Should we pay them or
should we not?"
But knowing their
hypocrisy, he said to
them, "Why do you put
me to the test? Show
me a coin."

Luke 6:46

Why do you call me
"Lord, Lord," and do
not do what I say?

Mark 7:6–7
(= Matt 15:7–9)

Well did Isaiah
prophesy of you
hypocrites, as it is
written,[3]
"this people honor me
with their lips, but
their heart is far away
from me. In vain do
they worship me,
teaching as doctrines
the precepts of human
beings."

This text from *Papyrus Egerton 2* indeed looks like a quilt of pieces
from at least four different New Testament passages: Mark 12:13–15;
John 3:2; Luke 6:46; and Mark 7:6–7. The problem is that there are
two solutions which are equally improbable: it is unlikely that the per-

---

[1] No convincing parallel can be cited for the second half of this sentence. John 10:25
(and other Johannine passages) speak about "bearing witness," but prophets are not
mentioned in such contexts. Cf. also *Gos. Thom.* 52: "His disciples said to him,
'Twenty-four prophets spoke in Israel and all of them spoke in you.'"

[2] Mark 1:43 has been quoted as a parallel to "(he) became angry." However, Mark
1:43 may not even be a part of the original Markan text; see above.

[3] "As it is written" is missing in Matthew.

icope of *Papyrus Egerton 2* is an independent older tradition, and it is equally hard to imagine that anyone would have deliberately composed this apophthegma by selecting sentences from three different gospel writings. There are no analogies to this kind of gospel composition, because this pericope is neither a harmony of parallels from different gospels, nor is it a florilegium. If one wants to uphold the hypothesis of dependence upon written gospels, one would have to assume that the pericope was written from memory.[1] But in this case, one must also ask whether the author was informed by memory of written gospels or of oral traditions. The latter seemed to be the case with respect to the story of the healing of the leper. Also concerning the pericope about paying dues to the kings, it is possible that it rests on memory of the oral tradition of the apophthegma about paying tax to Caesar (Mark 12:13–15) and of the saying about those who say "Lord, Lord" (Luke 6:46). That the parallel to Mark 12:14 has such a "Johannine" ring (cf. John 3:2) is not as strange as it may seem; the gospel of which this papyrus has preserved a fragment apparently contained other materials which were used by the author of the Fourth Gospel. What appears here is a language that is pre-johannine and pre-synoptic at the same time. The quote from Isa 29:13 (Mark 7:6–7) is, of course, not part of the oral gospel tradition; but it was known and used elsewhere in early Christian literature.[2] What is decisive is the fact that there is nothing in this pericope that clearly reveals redactional features of any of the gospels in which parallels appear. The author of *Papyrus Egerton 2* here uses individual building blocks of sayings for the composition of this dialogue;[3] none of the individual blocks has been formed by the literary activity of a previous gospel writer.[4]

If *Papyrus Egerton 2* is indeed not dependent upon the Gospel of John, it is an important witness to an earlier stage of the development of the dialogues of the Fourth Gospel. The piece of dialogue about Moses and the Scripture that is preserved here reveals controversies with (Jewish) opponents about the interpretation of Scripture which the Fourth Gospel has used and expanded also in other instances, especially in chapters 7 and 8. There they were combined with a

---

[1] Proposed by Joachim Jeremias and repeated in Hennecke-Schneemelcher, *NT Apokryphen I*, 83.

[2] It is alluded to in Col. 2:22; *1 Clem.* 15.2

[3] See the cogent arguments of Daniels, *Egerton Gospel*, 156–73.

[4] Crossan (*Four Other Gospels*, 78–87) goes one step further, and he is possibly right. He argues (ibid., 86) that Mark's source was *Pap. Eg. 2* (". . . directly dependent on the papyrus text. It might be possible that Mark is dependent on some other version exactly similar to" it).

polemic against Gnosticizing interpretations of sayings of Jesus.[1] That *Papyrus Egerton 2* shows no traces of the latter polemic would also speak against its dependence upon John.

3.2.3 THE PASSION NARRATIVE AND THE GOSPEL OF PETER

3.2.3.1 The Discovery and Interpretation of the Gospel of Peter

In the year 1892, a fragment of a *Gospel of Peter* was published that had been found in Akhmim in Upper Egypt in 1886/1887.[2] The Greek text and translations have been published a number of times,[3] and several monographs have appeared,[4] especially in recent years, which deal in detail with the text and the problems of its interpretation.[5]

The Akhmim fragment of this writing, an amulet found in a tomb, has been dated to the 8th or 9th centuries. No other manuscript or fragment was known until Dieter Lührmann discovered that two small papyrus fragments from Oxyrhynchus, written ca. 200 CE, which had been published in 1972,[6] actually belonged to the Gospel of Peter.[7] This confirms a *terminus ad quem* for the composition of the *Gospel of*

---

[1] See below, # 3.4.4.3.

[2] U. Bouriant, "Fragments du texte grec du livre d'Énoch et de quelques écrits attribué à saint Pierre," in: *Mémoires publiées par les membres de la mission archéologique francaise au Caire* 9 (Paris: 1892). For a brief survey of the status of the text and its evaluation see Stephen Gero, "Apocryphal Gospels: A Survey of Textual and Literary Problems," *ANRW* 2.25/5 (1988) 3985–86.

[3] H. B. Swete, *The Apocryphal Gospel of Peter: The Greek Text of the Newly Discovered Fragment* (London:1893); Klostermann, *Apocrypha I;* most recently M. G. Mara, *Évangile de Pierre: Introduction, texte critique, traduction, commentaire et index* (SC 201; Paris: Gabalda, 1973). For English translations, see Christian Maurer, "The Gospel of Peter," in *NT Apocrypha*, 1. 180–88 (but without consideration of the new fragments); Cameron, *Other Gospels,* 76–82. A new German translation (with introduction) was published by Christian Maurer and Wilhelm Schneemelcher, "Petrusevangelium," in Hennecke-Schneemelcher, *NT Apocryphen I,* 180–88.

[4] The only somewhat older detailed study is that of Léon Vaganay, *L'Évangile de Pierre* (EtB; 2d ed.; Paris: Gabalda, 1930).

[5] See Mara, *Évangile de Pierre,* quoted in note 2 above; Jürgen Denker, *Die theologiegeschichtliche Stellung des Petrusevangeliums: Ein Beitrag zur Frühgeschichte des Doketismus* (EHS.T 36; Bern and Frankfurt: Lang, 1975); John Dominic Crossan, *The Cross that Spoke: The Origins of the Passion Narrative* (San Francisco: Harper & Row, 1988); see also idem, *Four Other Gospels,* 125–181 (all subsequent references will be to the more detailed later publication of Crossan [*The Cross that Spoke*]; cf. also Benjamin A. Johnson, "The Empty Tomb Tradition in the Gospel of Peter" (Diss. Harvard University, 1965).

[6] R. A. Coles, ed., "Pap. Oxy. 2949," in G. M. Browne et al., *The Oxyrhynchus Papyri,* Vol. 41 (Cambridge: Cambridge University Press, 1972) 15–16 and plate II.

[7] Dieter Lührmann, "POx 2949: EvPt 3–5 in einer Handschrift des 2./3. Jahrhunderts," *ZNW* 72 (1981) 216–26. On this discovery see Crossan, *The Cross that Spoke,* 6–9.

Peter of 200 CE. A date before the year 200 CE had already been assumed for this document on the basis of a description of a "Gospel put forward in the name of Peter" by Bishop Serapion of Antioch, which has been preserved by Eusebius in his *Ecclesiastical History*. Eusebius dates Bishop Serapion in the reign of Commodus (180–192 CE).[1] Eusebius's quotation from Serapion's book "Concerning what is known of the Gospel of Peter," written to the church in Rhossus,[2] is as follows:[3]

> For our part, brethren, we receive both Peter and the other apostles as Christ, but the writings which falsely bear their names we reject, as men of experience, knowing that such were not handed down to us. For I myself, when I came among you, imagined that all of you clung to the true faith; and without going through the Gospel put forward by them in the name of Peter, I said: If this is the only thing that seemingly causes captious feelings among you, let it be read. But since I have now learnt, from what has been told me, that their mind was lurking in some hole of heresy, I shall give diligence to come again to you: wherefore, brethren, expect me quickly. But we, brethren, gathering to what kind of heresy Marcianus belonged ..., were enabled by others who saw this very Gospel, that is, by the successors of those who began it, whom we call Docetae (for most of the ideas belong to their teaching)—using [the material supplied] by them, were enabled to go through it and discover that most part indeed was in accordance with the true teaching of the Savior, but that some things were added, which also we place below for your benefit. Such are the writings of Serapion.

What is preserved of the *Gospel of Peter* in the Akhmim fragment[4] is a report of the trial of Jesus, his crucifixion, death, and burial, and three epiphany accounts: in the first, the guards at the tomb are the witnesses of the resurrection; in the second, Mary Magdalene and the women are witnesses of the empty tomb; in the third, Peter and Andrew and some other disciples are witnesses of Jesus' appearance at the lake—however, the fragment ends just after a few lines introducing the third epiphany story. Peter, in the first person singular, is the narrator.

There are numerous features in these accounts which are obviously secondary: Jesus is condemned and crucified by Herod, while Pilate is completely exonerated; the anti-Jewish polemic seems intensified; the story of Jesus' resurrection from the tomb is told elaborately, introduc-

---

[1] *Hist. eccl.* 5.22.1.

[2] Rhossus is a city in Cilicia, ca. thirty miles northwest of Antioch.

[3] *Hist. eccl.* 6.12.2–6; translation from LCL.

[4] The Oxyrhynchus Papyrus fragment parallels a few lines of the first part.

ing also the cross that follows Jesus out of the tomb and speaks; a good deal of direct discourse enhances the narrative throughout. Parallels with the passion and resurrection accounts of all four canonical gospels are numerous. Therefore, the first assessment of the newly discovered document almost unanimously favored dependence of the *Gospel of Peter* upon all four Gospels of the New Testament canon and argued for a relatively late date in order to explain the uncontrolled growth of legendary features.[1] Other scholars, however, doubted that the *Gospel of Peter* could simply be understood as a patchwork of pieces and snippets from the canonical gospels. Following suggestions by Martin Dibelius, Philipp Vielhauer notices, on the one hand, an exaggeration of the fantastic and miraculous features, but also states: "The way in which the suffering of Jesus is described by the use of passages from the Old Testament without quotation formulae is, in terms of the history of the tradition, older than the explicit scriptural proof; it represents the oldest form of the description of the passion (of Jesus)."[2] Jürgen Denker[3] has used this observation as the basis for his thesis: the *Gospel of Peter* is dependent upon the traditions of interpreting Old Testament materials for the description of Jesus' suffering and death; it shares such traditions with the canonical gospels, but is not dependent upon the canonical writings. The question remains whether the close agreements with the canonical gospels are not too numerous for the hypothesis of an independent presence of such traditions in the *Gospel of Peter*.[4]

Dominic Crossan[5] has gone further. Utilizing Denker's observations about the interpretation of Scripture as the nucleus for the formation of the passion narrative, he argues that this activity resulted in the composition of a literary document at a very early date, i.e., in the middle of the 1st century CE. On the basis of a comparison of the *Gospel of Peter* with the canonical gospels and with other extracanonical traditions about Jesus' passion, he reconstructs an entire text, the *Cross Gospel*, and tries to demonstrate that this earliest of all written passion narratives was used not only by Mark, but also by Matthew and Luke (in addition to their use of Mark) and by John (in addition to

---

[1] See, e.g., J. Armitage Robinson, "The Gospel according to Peter," in idem and M. R. James, *The Gospel According to Peter, and the Revelation of Peter: Two Lectures on the Newly-Dicovered Fragments together with the Greek Text* (London: Clay, 1892) 11–36 (published in the very year of the first publication of the Akhmim Fragment); Theodor Zahn, *Das Evangelium des Petrus* (Erlangen und Leipzig: Deichert, 1893).

[2] Vielhauer, *Geschichte,* 646 (translation mine).

[3] *Petrusevangelium,* passim.

[4] Schneemelcher in Hennecke-Schneemelcher, *NT Apokryphen I,* 183.

[5] *The Cross that Spoke,* passim.

John's usage of Matthew, Mark, and Luke).[1] The *Gospel of Peter* then becomes a fifth, but very important, witness for this *Cross Gospel*. It was the basis for its earliest stratum to which texts from the intracanonical tradition were added at a later stage of its literary development.[2]

There are three major problems regarding this hypothesis. The first relates to the reliability of the extant text. It is important to remember that almost all of the Greek text of the *Gospel of Peter* is known exclusively through a single late manuscript. During the process of its transmission, copyists of its text could have been influenced by the texts of the canonical gospels. What the Akhmim fragment presents may not be identical with the original text of that writing. The question is, therefore, whether this fragment still indicates that its original—not necessarily the entire extant text—was independent of the canonical gospels, even if the extant text occasionally includes a phrase which demonstrates influence of the canonical gospels. During the first period of their transmission, all gospel texts were very unstable.[3] The text of the canonical gospels later enjoyed a certain degree of protection, beginning with the process of canonization in the 3d and 4th centuries CE. Apocryphal gospels, however, never shared that privilege.

The second problem regarding Crossan's ingenious hypothesis is his confidence in major literary compositions of a very early date as the well spring for, and almost exclusive source of, all later gospel literature.[4] In our discussion of the process of the formation of the gospel tradition, two observations applied to all relevant materials: (1) the oral tradition continued for many decades and remained an important factor, influencing even later stages of the written records; (2) the earliest written materials were relatively small compositions of special materials which paralleled the oral use of traditional materials, such as collections of wisdom sayings or of miracles stories, which were assembled for very practical purposes.

---

[1] Crossan (*The Cross that Spoke,* 17) says: "My first major proposition is that the original Cross Gospel is the one passion and resurrection narrative from which all four of the intracanonical versions derive."

[2] "My second major proposition, then, is that an intracanonical stratum was combined with that original *Cross Gospel* in the *Gospel of Peter*" (Crossan, ibid., 20).

[3] More evidence for this instability of the text of even the canonical gospels will be discussed below in the chapters on John, Mark, Matthew, and Luke.

[4] This is also evident in Crossan's view of the Synoptic Sayings Source. In view of the numerous minor agreements of Matthew and Luke in instances in which both use Mark, Crossan prefers "the theory of Mark *and* Q as twin sources for the *narratives* of Matthew and Luke" (ibid., 19; italics mine). See also his *Four Other Gospels: Shadows on the Contours of Canon* (Minneapolis: Seabury-Winston, 1985).

A third problem regarding Crossan's hypothesis is related specifically to the formation of reports about Jesus' trial, suffering, death, burial, and resurrection. The account of the passion of Jesus must have developed quite early because it is one and the same account that was used by Mark (and subsequently by Matthew and Luke) and John, and as will be argued below, by the Gospel of Peter.[1] However, except for the story of the discovery of the empty tomb, the different stories of the appearances of Jesus after his resurrection in the various gospels cannot derive from one single source. They are independent of one another. Each of the authors of the extant gospels and of their secondary endings drew these epiphany stories from their own particular tradition, not from a common source.[2]

3.2.3.2 The Passion Narrative

It is neither possible nor necessary to present here a detailed comparison of the entire passion narrative of the *Gospel of Peter* with the corresponding texts of the canonical gospels.[3] Both Denker and Crossan have contributed substantially to a better understanding of the passion narrative by demonstrating how it was developed through scriptural interpretation. The relationship of the Gospel of Peter and of the canonical Gospels to these exegetical traditions not only determines the judgment about literary dependence; it also provides insights into the growth of the narrative traditions which ultimately formed the account of Jesus' suffering and death. A few examples must suffice here.

The passion narrative of the *Gospel of Peter* parallels the canonical accounts. The fragment begins with the remark that no one among the Jews, neither Herod nor the judges, was washing his hands. Most probably, accounts of Jesus' arrest, of his trial before Pilate, and of Pilate washing his hands preceded this remark. The handwashing scene is otherwise known only from Matt 27:24–25, and on the surface

---

[1] In this respect, Crossan's reconstruction of one single source for all passion narratives seems justified. However, it is doubtful whether this account was as comprehensive and as fixed a literary document as Crossan assumes.

[2] At this point, Crossan's thesis is seriously flawed. He assigns the story of Jesus epiphany at the lake, the last partially preserved episode of the *Gospel of Peter,* to the "intracanonical stratum" (*The Cross that Spoke,* 291–93, 413). However, its "canonical" equivalent, John 21:1–14, has made it into the canon, to be sure, but is certainly not an original part of the Gospel of John. John 21 is a later addition, made to the Fourth Gospel some time after its composition at a date that can no longer be determined with any certainty. The "intracanonical tradition" of Dominic Crossan is a fiction as far as the stories of Jesus' appearances to his disciples are concerned.

[3] I refer to the detailed and expert discussions in Denker (*Petrusevangelium*) and Crossan (*The Cross that Spoke*).

it seems evident that this was the source for *Gos. Pet.* 1.1 (and whatever preceded). But the relationship of the parallels is more complex. The episode of the handwashing is one of the many features of the passion narrative that is based on the interpretation of scriptural passages, but the references to such passages are somewhat different in both instances.

The ritual on which the handwashing scene is based is described in Deut 21:6–8 (LXX):

> If someone is slain and the murderer cannot be found, the elders and judges (κριταί) shall measure the distance to the nearest city and the elders of that city shall bring a heifer, and the priests shall break its neck. "And all the elders of that city ... shall wash their hands over the heifer ... and they shall testify, 'Our hands did not shed this blood, neither did our eyes see it shed.'"

The text continues (vs. 8) with a declaration of innocence which contains the phrase, "Set not the guilt of innocent blood in the midst of your people Israel, but let the guilt of blood be forgiven them." Several passages in the psalms refer to this ritual and combine with it a declaration of innocence. The scene as described by Matthew is based on Dtn 21:6–8 as well as on the psalms:

Matt 27:24–25	Ps 26 (LXX 25): 5–6
So when Pilate saw that he was gaining nothing ... he took water and washed his hands (λαβὼν ὕδωρ ἀπενίψατο τὰς χεῖρας) before the crowd saying, "I am innocent (ἀθῷός εἰμι) of this man's blood; see to it yourselves."	I hate the company of evildoers, and I will not sit with the wicked. I wash my hands in innocence (νίψομαι ἐν ἀθῴοις τὰς χεῖρας) and go about thy altar, O Lord.[1]
	Deut 21:8
And all the people answered, "His blood be on us and on our children."	Set not the guilt of innocent blood in the midst of thy people Israel.

The formula used by Pilate corresponds to that used in the psalms. The final declaration of the people is formulated on the basis of Deut 21:8. The guilt of the people is expressed in this last phrase in a declaration that mocks the prayer described in the ritual.

Gos. Pet. 1.1 gives the account as far as it is based on Dtn 21:6–7, but the reference to Dtn 21:8, the mockery of the prayer, is missing. Instead the guilt of Herod and of the judges (κριταί) is established

---

[1] Cf. Ps 73:13 (LXX 72:13): "All in vain have I kept my heart clean and washed my hands in innocence (ἐνίψαμεν ἐν ἀθῴοις τὰς χεῖράς μου)." The formula appears also in 2 Sam (= 2 Reg) 3:28–29.

because they do not follow the ritual of washing their hands. A formal declaration of innocence also appears in the *Gospel of Peter,* but only later in 11:46 where Pilate says: "I am clean (ἐγὼ καθαρεύω) from the blood of the Son of God." However, this declaration is not based on the psalm passages reflected in Matthew, but on a different wording of the declaration of innocence which appears in Dan 13:46 (= Sus 46): "I am clean (καθαρός) from the blood of this woman." It is evident that the accounts in the *Gospel of Peter* and in the Gospel of Matthew both derive from the same exegetical tradition, but each gospel writer has developed the nuclear tradition which was based on Deut 21:6–8 in a different way. One cannot assume literary dependence of one gospel upon the other, nor literary dependence of both upon some more original written source; rather both accounts testify to a still fluid development of an exegetical tradition within the framework of the passion narrative.

The scene of mocking and abusing Jesus appears twice in the synoptic tradition, once before the synedrion, and a second time as the mocking by the soldiers after the trial before Pilate,[1] but there is only one scene in the *Gospel of Peter*.

Gos. Pet. 3.6–9[2]	Canonical Gospels
6 So they took the Lord and pushed him in great haste (ὤθουν αὐτὸν τρέχοντες) and said, "Let us drag (σύρωμεν) the Son of God, now that we have gotten power over him."	
7 And they put upon him a purple robe (πορφύραν)	Mark 15:17: And they dressed him with a purple robe (πορφύραν). Matt 27:28: And they stripped him and put a scarlet robe upon him (χλαμύδα κοκκίνην).[3] Luke 23:11: and they put a shining garment (ἐσθῆτα λαμπράν) on him. John 19:2: and arrayed him in a purple robe (ἱμάτιον πόρφυρον), cf. John 19:5.

---

[1] Luke also reports a mocking before Herod (Luke 23:11); but he omits the mocking by the soldiers (Mark 15:16–20), i.e., he transferred the motif of this latter scene to the pericope of Jesus before Herod.

[2] Translation by Crossan (modified).

[3] Some witnesses (D it) of the text of Matt 27:28 combine the readings of Mark and Matthew: καὶ ἐνδύσαντες αὐτὸν ἱμάτιον πορφυροῦν καὶ χλαμύδα κοκκίνην περιέθηκαν αὐτῷ.

and sat him on the judgment seat (ἐκάθισαν αὐτὸν ἐπὶ καθέδραν κρίσεως) and said, "Judge righteously, O King of Israel!"

John 19:13: and he sat down on the judgment seat (καὶ ἐκάθισεν ἐπὶ βήματος)[1]

8 And one of them brought a crown of thorns and put it on the Lord's head.

Mark 15:17 = Matt 27:29: and plaiting a crown of thorns, they put it on him (Matt: on his head). John 19:2: and the soldiers plaited a crown of thorns and put it on his head, cf. John 19:5.

9 And others who stood by spat on his face (ἐνέπτυον αὐτοῦ ταῖς ὄψεσι),

Mark 14:65: And they began to spit at him (ἐμπτύειν αὐτῷ) = Matt 26:67: And they spat in his face (ἐνέπτυσαν τὸ πρόσωπον αὐτῷ). Mark 15:19: and they spat at him (καὶ ἐνέπτυον αὐτῷ) = Matt 27:30 (καὶ ἐμπτύσαντες εἰς αὐτόν).

and others struck him on the cheeks (τὰς σιαγόνας αὐτοῦ ἐράπισαν),

John 18:22: one of the servants standing by struck (ἔδωκεν ῥάπισμα) Jesus with his hand. John 19:3: and struck him (ἐδίδοσαν αὐτῷ ῥαπίσματα)

others pierced him with a reed (καλάμῳ ἔνυσσον),

Mark 15:19: and they struck his head with a reed (ἔτυπτον καλάμῳ). Matt 27:29: and they put a reed (κάλαμον) into his right hand . . . 30: and they took the reed (κάλαμον) and struck (ἔτυπτον) him on his head.

and some scourged (ἐμάστιζον) him saying,

John 19:1: Then Pilate took Jesus and scourged him (ἐμαστίγωσεν). Mark 15:15 = Matt 27:26: . . . and having scourged (φραγελλώσας) Jesus, he handed him over to be crucified.

"With such honor let us honor the Son of God (τιμήσωμεν τὸν υἱὸν τοῦ θεοῦ)."

Matt 27:40: save yourself, if you are the Son of God (εἰ υἱὸς εἶ τοῦ θεοῦ), and come down from the cross.[2]

---

[1] The extant text probably means that Pilate sat down on the judgment seat. But it is possible that the tradition used by the Gospel of John spoke about Jesus being seated on the judgment seat.
[2] This sentence belongs to the mocking of the Crucified. In the scene of the mocking before the soldiers Jesus is addressed as "King of the Jews."

One can assume that the only historical information about Jesus' suffering, crucifixion, and death was that he was condemned to death by Pilate and crucified. The details and individual scenes of the narrative do not rest on historical memory, but were developed on the basis of allegorical interpretation of Scripture.[1] The earliest stage and, at the same time, the best example of such scriptural interpretation is preserved in the *Epistle of Barnabas*.[2]

One of the important seminal scriptural passages in this process was Isa 50:6: "I have given my back to scourges (εἰς μάστιγας), and my cheeks to strokes (εἰς ῥαπίσματα). I hid my face (τὸ πρόσωπόν μου) from shame and spitting (ἐμπτυσμάτων)." Of this passage, the first half is quoted in *Barn.* 5:14 in a context in which Barnabas develops various elements of the suffering of Jesus without any reference to traditional narrative materials.

Other features of the scenes of the mocking of Jesus arose from a further expansion of the interpretation of Isa 50:6 with the help of Zach 12:10 and of the scapegoat ritual. *Barn.* 7.7–11 demonstrates this exegetical process. *Barnabas* is not only dependent upon the description of the scapegoat ritual of Leviticus 16, but also uses Jewish traditions which are later attested in Mishnah and Talmud.[3] The following elements of the ritual are important:

(1) There are two identical goats, one that is sacrificed, the other driven into the wilderness.

(2) The scapegoat is crowned with red wool on its head (τὸ ἔριον τὸ κόκκινον περὶ τὴν κεφαλὴν αὐτοῦ).

(3) The scapegoat is put among the thorns (εἰς μέσον τῶν ἀκανθῶν τιθέασιν).

(4) The scapegoat is spat upon (ἐμπτύσατε); this establishes a bridge to Isa 50:6.

(5) The scapegoat is pierced (κατακεντήσατε); this establishes a link with Zach 12:10: "Then they shall look upon the one they have pierced" (τότε ὄψονται εἰς ὃν ἐξεκήντησαν).[4]

(6) Possibly the scapegoat was also "nudged with a reed," though this is not included in *Barnabas*; but a parallel passage of the *Sibyl-*

---

[1] A detailed discussion of the development of the scene of the mocking of Jesus on the basis of scriptural interpretation can be found in Crossan, *The Cross That Spoke*, 114–59; cf. also my *Synoptische Überlieferung*, 152–54.

[2] On the date of the composition of this writing see my *Introduction*, 2. 276–77; Crossan, *The Cross That Spoke*, 120–21.

[3] See the references in Koester, *Synoptische Überlieferung*, 152–53; Crossan, *The Cross That Spoke*, 117–20

[4] This text, as quoted also by Justin *1 Apol.* 52.12, represents the text of Lucian and Aquila, Symmachus, and Theodotion.

line Oracles (1.373–74) mentions the reed: "they shall pierce his sides with a reed (νύξουσιν καλάμῳ) because of their law."[1] Thus, *Barn.* 7.9 can conclude:

> They will see (ὄψονται) him then on that day (i.e., of the parousia) wearing the red robe (τὸν ποδήρη τὸν κόκκινον) and they will say, "Is not this the one whom we had once crucified, reviling and piercing (κατακεντή-σαντες) and spitting (ἐμπτύσαντες); truly this was the one who once said that he was the Son of God (ἑαυτὸν υἱὸν Θεοῦ εἶναι).

In the scene of the mocking of Jesus, the crown of thorns and the red robe are derived from this exegesis of the scapegoat ritual. Possibly also the reed (κάλαμος) that is given into Jesus' hands (in Mark, Matthew, and the *Gospel of Peter*) has its origin in this ritual. Furthermore, *Barn.* 7.9 indicates that Jesus' address as the "Son of God" was part of the traditional interpretation.

On the other hand, the reports of the mocking of Jesus cannot fully be explained on this basis. There seem to be elements which derive from a different traditional topos, the "royal mocking." As an important example of this topos, Crossan[2] has drawn attention to the story of the mocking of Carabas during the Jewish pogroms under the Egyptian governor Flaccus, which Philo reported.[3] The influence of this topos on the various accounts of the mocking of Jesus is evident: the red (κόκκινος) robe, derived from the scapegoat ritual, is replaced by the royal purple (πορφύρα), Jesus is seated on a throne, the reed becomes a scepter, the eschatological acclamation of Jesus as "Son of God" is turned into the mocking of the "King of the Jews."

All these developments must be presupposed for the scenes of the mocking of Jesus in the extant gospel literature. But both the elements of the exegetical tradition and of the topos of the royal mocking are present in these accounts in such a way that simple literary dependence alone cannot explain the development. That is even evident in the case of the Synoptic Gospels. One example must suffice: in Mark 15:17, Jesus is dressed with a royal purple (πορφύρα); Matt 27:28, reproducing this Markan passage, substitutes the garment that was developed in the exegetical/scapegoat tradition and replaces Mark's royal robe with the scarlet garment (χλαμὺς κοκκίνη).

The *Gospel of Peter* reveals a very close relationship especially to

---

[1] Crossan (*The Cross That Spoke*, 151–52) proposes "that the (scapegoat) ritual included the people's hurrying the poor animal on its departure from city to desert by prodding its sides by sharpened reeds."

[2] *The Cross That Spoke*, 139–41.

[3] *In Flaccum*, 32–39.

the exegetical/scapegoat tradition, often closer than that of the canonical parallels:

Exeg. Trad.	Gos. Pet.	John	Synoptic Gospels
scarlet (κόκκινος) robe	purple robe (πορφύρα)	ἱμάτιον πόρφυρον.	Mark: πορφύρα Matt: χλαμὺς κοκκίνη
crown of thorns	crown of thorns	crown of thorns	crown of thorns
spitting in the face (πρόσωπον ... ἐμπτυσμάτων)	spat on his face (ἐνέπτυον αὐτοῦ ταῖς ὄψεσι)		And they spat in his face[1] (ἐνέπτυσαν τὸ πρόσωπον αὐτῷ)
cheeks for strikes (τὰς σιαγόνας εἰς ῥαπίσματα)	struck him on the cheeks (τὰς σιαγόνας αὐτοῦ ἐράπισαν)	struck him (ἐδίδοσαν αὐτῷ ῥαπίσματα)	
pierced with a reed (νύξουσιν καλάμῳ)	pierced with a reed (καλάμῳ ἔνυσσον),	19:34: pierced with a spear (λόγχῃ ἔνυξεν)[2]	struck with a reed (ἔτυπτον καλάμῳ)
scourges (εἰς μάστιγας)	scourged (ἐμάστιζον)	scourged him (ἐμαστίγωσεν)	scourged (φραγελλώσας)
He said he was the Son of God (λέγων ἑαυτὸν υἱὸν θεοῦ εἶναι)	let us honor the Son of God (τιμήσωμεν τὸν υἱὸν τοῦ θεοῦ)		save yourself, if you are the Son of God (εἰ υἱὸς εἶ τοῦ θεοῦ)[3]

It is evident that alone in the *Gospel of Peter* all three items from the Isaiah passage appear together, while John only includes the first and the second (scourges and strikes) and Mark and Matthew only the first and the third (scourges and spitting). Moreover, only the *Gospel of Peter* and John use the same Greek terminology for "scourging" (μαστιγοῦν), in agreement with Isaiah, while Mark and Matthew substitute the more common Roman term for this punishment (φραγελλοῦν), and only Isaiah and the *Gospel of Peter* mention the cheeks (τὰς σιαγόνας) explicitly with respect to the strikes. The piercing with a reed from the scapegoat allegory is preserved only in the *Gospel of Peter*, while John has used this item for the piercing of Jesus' side after his death; Mark and Matthew misread the tradition and changed it to

---

[1] The term "face" (πρόσωπον) appears in Matthew only.

[2] This episode, which happens after Jesus' crucifixion is also dependent upon this exegetical tradition, but has been secondarily moved to Jesus' death.

[3] This parallel, which does belong to the scene of the mocking before the synedrion or by the soldiers, has been transferred by Matthew to the mocking of the crucified Jesus (27:40).

"strikes with a reed"; Matt 27:29 has changed this further into a royal mockery feature: the reed is given into Jesus' hand for a scepter. The reference to Jesus as the Son of God is present only in the mocking scene of the Gospel of Peter; Matthew must have known this item from the exegetical tradition but inserted it into the mocking of the crucified, where it does not appear in the Markan parallel (Mark 15:30).

The relationship of the *Gospel of Peter* to the parallel accounts of the canonical gospels cannot be explained as a random compilation of canonical passages. It is evident that the mocking scene in this gospel is a narrative version that is directly dependent upon the exegetical tradition which is visible in *Barnabas*. The narrative version of this tradition as it is preserved in the *Gospel of Peter* has not yet split the mocking account into several scenes. This is an argument for the thesis that this account is older than its various usages in the canonical gospels.

On the other hand, only Matthew has preserved the Isaiah term for "face" (πρόσωπον), while the *Gospel of Peter* has substituted a different Greek word (ὄψεις); Matthew also preserves the reference to Jesus as the Son of God. Although he is otherwise dependent upon Mark, Matthew still had access to the exegetical tradition of Isaiah interpretation which was used by the *Gospel of Peter*. This is also evident in the Gospel of John which has preserved various elements either directly from the same exegetical tradition or from an independent narrative account based upon this same tradition.[1]

Another example of the direct dependence of the *Gospel of Peter's* passion narrative upon exegetical traditions is the reference to gall and vinegar in the drink given to Jesus. *Gos. Pet.* 5.16 reports this incident after the crucifixion of Jesus:

And one of them said, "Give him to drink gall with vinegar (χολὴν μετὰ ὄξους)." And they mixed (it) and gave him to drink.

---

[1] Luke has rarely been mentioned or quoted in the discussion. Evidently Luke is much farther removed from the original exegetical tradition. Furthermore, he has eliminated completely the scene of mocking by the soldiers (Mark 15:16–20) and transferred some features to the appearance of Jesus before Herod (Luke 23:6–12). D. R. Catchpole (*The Trial of Jesus* [Studia Postbiblica 18; Leiden: Brill] 174–83) has argued that the respective passages in Luke are altogether dependent upon a very different early account of the passion. However that may be, there is little in Luke to indicate that he was acquainted with the particular tradition of scriptural intepretation that was used by the other canonical Gospels and by the *Gospel of Peter*. See also Crossan, *The Cross That Spoke*, 147–49.

It has, of course, long been recognized that this incident has been developed on the basis of Ps 69:21 (LXX 68:22):[1]

And they gave me gall (χολήν) in my food, and for my thirst they gave me vinegar (ὄξος) to drink.

The exegetical tradition which applied this scriptural passage to the crucifixion of Jesus is, once more, visible in *Barnabas*. In 7.3a the author makes the statement that Jesus, when he had been crucified, received vinegar and gall for a drink (ἐποτίζετο ὄξει καὶ χολῇ), and in 7.5a he introduces a repetition of this statement in the first person singular:

... when I am about to sacrifice my flesh on behalf of my new people, you shall give me to drink gall with vinegar (χολὴν μετὰ ὄξους).

Surprisingly, *Barnabas* does not explicitly mention or quote the psalm passages in this context nor anywhere else in his writing, although there can be little doubt that the passage *Barn.* 7.3–5 is framed by references to it. Between the two references he presents a quote and interpretation of Lev 23:29 (*Barn.* 7.3b) and a quotation of unknown origin which is introduced by "What then does he say in the prophet?" (7.4). The content of the quote is a command that, on the Day of Atonement, the priests alone shall eat the entrails of the sacrificed goat unwashed and with vinegar (μετὰ ὄξους). This quote from "the prophet," in fact, includes the reference to the fulfillment of the psalm which was quoted above (7.5a) and continues with a reference to the people's fasting while the priests eat (7.5b). It has not been possible to identify with certainty the origin of this reference to the eating of the entrails of the sacrificed goat, though there may have been a Jewish tradition about such instruction, as is indicated by a later Talmudic passage.[2]

The procedure is analogous to the one we have observed above with respect to the mocking scene. A scriptural passage forms the basis, even if it is not quoted explicitly in this case. An explanation of a sacrificial ritual on the basis of Jewish traditions follows. The result is a new insight into a detail of the circumstances of the suffering of Jesus that would eventually be developed into a narrative account.

---

[1] On the interpretation of this passage from Barnabas see my *Synoptische Überlieferung*, 148–52; Crossan, *The Cross That Spoke*, 209–12.

[2] See Hans Windisch, *Der Barnabasbrief* (HNT.EB 3; Tübingen: Mohr/Siebeck, 1920) 344; Koester, *Synoptische Überlieferung*, 150; Crossan, *The Cross That Spoke*, 210–11.

The brief narrative that appears in *Gos. Pet.* 5.16 has several parallels in the canonical gospels:

Gos. Pet.	Mark 15:23	Matt 27:34	John
	(before the crucifixion) And they gave him wine mixed with myrrh (ἐσμυρνισμένον οἶνον)	(before the crucifixion) And they gave him to drink wine mixed with gall (οἶνον μετὰ χολῆς μεμιγμένον)	

After Jesus has been crucified:

Gos. Pet.	Mark 15:36 = Matt 27:48	Luke 23:36	John 19:29–30
And one of them said, "Give him to drink gall with vinegar (χολὴν μετὰ ὄξους)." And they mixed (it) and gave him to drink.	And one of them ran and, filling a sponge full of vinegar (ὄξους), put it on a reed and gave it to him to drink.	The soldiers also mocked him, coming up and offering him vinegar (ὄξος).	A bowl full of vinegar (ὄξους μέσον) stood there; so they put a sponge full of the vinegar on a hyssop and held it to his mouth. When Jesus had received the vinegar, he said, "It is completed (τετέλεσται)."
And they fulfilled everything and completed (ἐτελείωσαν) the measure of their sins . . .			

Among the references to something to drink that is offered to Jesus, Mark 15:23 has apparently nothing to do with Ps 69:21. To offer wine mixed with myrrh to someone who was about to be crucified seems to have been a custom which was sometimes observed. It was a sedative that would diminish the pain.[1] The second incident of giving something to drink to Jesus in Mark and Matthew, at the same time the only one in the *Gospel of Peter* and in the Gospels of Luke and of John, is entirely dependent upon the interpretation of Ps 69:21. In all five reports, this incident involves vinegar. However, all four canonical gospels report that the drink was only vinegar in this case; none of

---

[1] Erich Klostermann, *Das Markusevangelium* (HNT 3; 4th ed.; Tübingen: Mohr/Siebeck, 1950) 163.

them mentions gall. Matthew, however, occupies a special position: he mentioned gall also, but he used that reference in a modification of his source, Mark 15:23, replacing the "wine mixed with myrrh" given to Jesus before the crucifixion by "wine mixed with gall" (Matt 27:34). Thus, Matthew has been able to find a place for both, the gall and the vinegar of Ps 69:21, in his Gospel.

The tradition of scriptural interpretation of the psalm which is evident in *Barnabas* originally created one single event of giving something to drink to Jesus, a drink of (poisonous) gall mixed with vinegar. *Barn.* 7.5 already indicates that this is the fulfillment of prophecy regarding the sacrifice of Jesus. The oldest narrative account which developed on this basis reported such an incident as it is preserved in the *Gospel of Peter;* this report would have appropriately added the remark "and they fulfilled everything." In the subsequent transmission of this report, the original narrative was split up into two different incidents. Mark 15:36 preserves only the second, the drink of vinegar, and so does John 19:29. But John 19:28 retains, at the same time, the reference to the fulfillment of Scripture (Jesus . . . , that the Scripture be completed, said, "I thirst," cf.: when Jesus had received the vinegar, he said, "It is completed," John 19:30).[1] Luke is simply dependent upon this curtailed tradition of scriptural interpretation which he has drawn from the Gospel of Mark, but he omitted the Markan reference to the drinking of wine mixed with myrrh for theological reasons.[2] Matthew must have had independent access to this exegetical tradition which originally mentioned both gall and vinegar.[3] Thus he replaced the Markan description of the first incident by a formulation which more appropriately described the fulfillment of Scripture. No question, the *Gospel of Peter* has preserved the most original narrative version of the tradition of scriptural interpretation. In this instance, a dependence of the *Gospel of Peter* upon any of the canonical gospels is excluded. It is unlikely that such a dependence exists with respect to any other features of the passion narrative of this gospel.[4]

---

[1] In the extant text of John, this remark has a much more pregnant significance: Jesus has completed all the works he was sent to do (cf. Bultmann, *Gospel of John,* 675). But the tradition or source of the Gospel of John probably expressed by this phrase is that the fulfillment of the scripture had been accomplished.

[2] The perfect martyr, Jesus, does not need drugs in order to suffer his fate heroically.

[3] It is not very likely that "gall" was introduced by Matthew because of some misunderstanding of the Markan text; see Koester, *Synoptische Überlieferung,* 151.

[4] For further discussion of this question see Denker, *Petrusevangelium,* and Crossan, *The Cross That Spoke,* passim.

3.2.3.3 Epiphany Stories

In the passion narrative that was used by the Gospels of Mark and John and that also formed the basis for the *Gospel of Peter's* passion narrative, the story of the discovery of the empty tomb[1] must have followed immediately upon the story of the burial of Jesus.[2] Studies of the passion narrative have shown that all gospels were dependent upon one and the same basic account of the suffering, crucifixion, death, and burial of Jesus. But this account ended with the discovery of the empty tomb. With respect to the stories of Jesus' appearances, each of the extant gospels of the canon used different traditions of epiphany stories which they appended to the one common passion account. This also applies to the *Gospel of Peter*. There is no reason to believe that any of the epiphany stories at the end of this gospel derive from the same source on which the account of the passion is based.[3]

For the stories of Jesus' burial and the discovery of the empty tomb, the *Gospel of Peter* used the source that also underlies Mark and John, which ended with the discovery of the empty tomb. Also here, the story of Jesus' burial (*Gos. Pet.* 6.23–24) is connected with Joseph (of Arimathea)[4] and with his tomb that was located in a nearby garden (cf. John 19:41). The episode of Joseph requesting the body from Pilate was relocated in the *Gospel of Peter* to a position before the scene of the mocking of Jesus (2.3–5).[5]

---

[1] Mark 16:1–6; John 20:1–10.

[2] Mark 15:42–47; John 19:38–42. Luke (23:50–56; 24:1–11) follows Mark's order. Matthew interpolated the account of the securing of the tomb (Matt 27:62–66) between the story of the burial (Matt 27:57–61) and the empty tomb pericope (Matt 28:1–10). On this interpolated account see below.

[3] In this respect, my analysis differs fundamentally with that of Crossan whose very ingenious hypothesis assumes the existence of an older "Cross Gospel" which included the epiphany story at the tomb, and into which a later redactor inserted accounts drawn from the canonical gospels, such as the account of the burial of Jesus (6.23–24), the discovery of the empty tomb (12.50–13.57), and the appearance of Jesus at the lake (14.60). Crossan's observations regarding redactional features are very astute. But, as will be seen, these redactional elements reveal the hand of the original author of the *Gospel of Peter*, who tries to connect several originally independent resurrection accounts.

[4] He is simply called "Joseph" in *Gos. Pet.* 2.3 and 6.23.

[5] Crossan (*The Cross That Spoke*, 20–23) considers the story of the burial of Jesus as one of the later interpolations from the canonical gospels (Crossan speaks of "the intracanonical tradition") into the original "Cross Gospel," and Joseph's request for the body in *Gos. Pet.* 2.3–5 as a preparatory redactional link for this interpolation. This complicates the matter unnecessarily. There is no evidence to support the hypothesis that the report of Jesus' burial by Joseph of Arimathea in John 19:38–42 is dependent upon Mark 15:42–47; see the discussion of this question in Bultmann, *Gospel of John*, 667–68. Thus the story of the burial belongs to the source used by Mark and John and also by the *Gospel of Peter*.

However, in the *Gospel of Peter* the story of the discovery of the empty tomb does not immediately follow upon the story of the burial. Rather an elaborate story of the resurrection of Jesus from his tomb has been interpolated after the account of the burial (*Gos. Pet.* 7.25–11:49). It is a narrative full of miraculous events, but its structure reveals the basic formal features of an epiphany story. It consists of (1) an introduction which sets the scene for the epiphany, (2) the appearance of heavenly figures, (3) a miracle, (4) the epiphany of the risen Lord, and (5) the reaction of the witnesses.

Novelistic features have expanded several sections of this story, and redactional remarks have been inserted in order to connect this story with its context. But the basic elements of the older story are still evident.

(1) Introduction

This is the most novelistic part because it reports the people's unrest in view of the signs that occurred at the death of Jesus and uses this as the reason for the request for a guard at the tomb (7.25–28).[1] The older epiphany story must have featured an introduction that began with 8.29 and concluded with 9:34.

> The elders came to Pilate and said. "Give us soldiers so that we can guard his tomb for three days, lest his disciples come and steal him and the people think that he rose from the dead, and do evil to us."
> And Pilate gave them the centurion Petronius with soldiers to guard the tomb.
> [And with them, the elders and scribes went to the tomb.]
> And with the centurion and the soldiers [all who were][2] there rolled a big stone and placed it before the door of the tomb. And after they had affixed seven seals and pitched a tent they kept guard.

(2) The appearance of two heavenly figures (9.35–36)

> Now in the night in which the Lord's day dawned, when the soldiers, two by two in every watch, were keeping guard, there rang a loud voice in heaven and they saw the heavens opened and two men came down from there in great brightness and drew near to the tomb.

---

[1] Crossan (*The Cross That Spoke,* 23) has rightly identified 7.26–27 as a secondary intrusion into the introduction for the epiphany. This section describes the disciples' fear which drives them into hiding in order to prepare for the later story of Jesus' appearance before the disciples. However, 7.26–27 does not come from the hand of a later redactor who inserted canonical materials into an older "Cross Gospel."

[2] The bracketed phrases are secondary expansions in order to increase the number of people present. The elders and scribes are forgotten later in the story.

(3) A miracle (9.37–38a)

That stone which had been laid against the entrance to the tomb started of itself to roll and gave way to the side, and the tomb was opened, and both the young men entered in. When now the soldiers saw this, they awakened the centurion [and the elders—for they also were there to assist at the watch].[1]

(4) The epiphany of the risen Lord (10.39b–40)

They saw again three men coming out from the tomb, and two of them sustaining the other, and a cross following them, and the heads of the two reaching to heaven, but that of him who was lead by them by the hand overpassing the heavens.[2]

(5) The reaction of the witnesses (11:45)

When the centurion and his company saw this, . . .[3] they said, "In truth, he was the Son of God."[4]

The epiphany story, as reconstructed here, does not reveal any signs of a later time or tradition. What is secondary here is due to the attempt of the author of the gospel who wanted to connect the older epiphany story to the literary context of his writing and to continue his apologetics in behalf of an exoneration of Pilate.[5] If the story itself belongs to the older oral tradition of epiphany stories related to Jesus' resurrection, are there any traces of this story elsewhere in the extant gospel literature? There are indeed several indications that parts or

---

[1] That the centurion is awakened is necessary, since he is the primary witness. The bracketed words are a secondary expansion that wants to involve other witnesses.

[2] Two secondary insertions follow. The first (10.41–42) has been interpolated in the interest of the doctrine of the descent into Hades and the preaching to the dead: "And they heard a voice from the heavens, 'Have you preached to those who sleep?' And from the cross was heard the answer, 'Yes!'" The second insertion—the appearance of another young man from the heavens who enters the tomb (11.44)—is redactional: this angelic person is needed in the tomb for the following story of the discovery of the empty tomb (12.50–13.57). It is not a later interpolation, but belongs to the redactor who connected the different stories of the resurrection appearances (*pace* Crossan).

[3] This section has been partially changed in order to make the confession a part of the report to Pilate, which had already been prepared in the insertion of 11:43 and is continued in 11.46–49. This report to Pilate, as it stands now, is apparently due to the author of the *Gospel of Peter*. It is clearly an apologetic motif that exonerates Pilate, and it is closely connected with the description of Pilate in the passion narrative (cf. 1.1; 2.3–4).

[4] Most likely the original story continued with a report of the events to the authorities who had ordered the guard at the tomb and the command to the soldiers to keep silence; cf. *Gos. Pet.* 11.47–49 with Matt 28:11–15. For further discussion of the relationship of these two passages, see below.

[5] See the identification of the redactional materials in the preceding notes.

fragments of this story have been used in different contexts in Mark as well as in Matthew.

The conclusion of the story with the reaction of the witnesses ends in the statement, "In truth he was the Son of God." The same statement is also reported in the Gospel of Mark after the death of Jesus (Mark 15:39):

> And when the centurion who stood facing him saw that he (Jesus) thus expired, he said, "Truly, this man was a Son of God."

In the context of Mark, this statement seems quite unmotivated. There was no spectacular event that the centurion could have witnessed.[1] Matthew has noticed this and inserted an account of miraculous occurrences (earthquake, opening of the tombs, Matt 27:51b–53) before the centurion's confession. Moreover, in Mark's account a centurion had not been mentioned before (only "soldiers" had been named). However, in the epiphany story of the *Gospel of Peter* a centurion had been introduced at the beginning of the story (8.31), and the confession at the end comes from the centurion and his company.

Three fragments of this epiphany story appear in the Gospel of Matthew: the guard at the tomb (27:62–66); the appearance of an angel from heaven (28:2–4); and the bribing of the soldiers (28:11–15). All three have very close parallels to the epiphany story of the *Gospel of Peter*.

The Guard at the Tomb

Gos. Pet. 8.28–33	Matt 27:62–66
Scribes, Pharisees and elders . . .	High priests and Pharisees . . .
Go to Pilate (immediately).	Go to Pilate on the next morning after the day of Preparation.
Ask for a guard for three days so that his disciples would not come and steal the body and the people would say that he rose from the dead.	Tell Pilate that Jesus had said that he would rise after three days. ask for a guard so that his disciples would not come and steal the body and tell the people that he rose from the dead, so that the last fraud would be worse than the first.

---

[1] Mark 15:38 reports that the curtain of the temple was torn in two; but that would be a strange motivation for a statement of someone standing at the cross of Jesus.

Pilate gives them the centurion Petronius.	Pilate gives them a guard.
They go, roll a stone before the tomb's door and seal it with seven seals and keep guard.	They go and secure the tomb and seal the stone and keep guard.

It is evident that we are dealing here with the same story. Although some features in the *Gospel of Peter* seem more exaggerated than in Matthew, e.g., the seven seals placed on the stone, there are no elements that reflect peculiarities of Matthew's version of the story. Crossan[1] thinks that the Pharisees are a secondary intrusion into the *Gospel of Peter* because they are soon forgotten; only the elders go to Pilate. But the Pharisees are also forgotten in Matt 28:11–15 where only the high priests and the elders are mentioned. The best solution is to assume that the original story mentioned only the elders. While Matthew explicitly connects the request with Jesus' predictions that he would rise "after three days,"[2] the request for guards for a three-day period in *Gos. Pet.* 8.30 may simply mean that the tomb must be secured "until the people have seen for themselves that Jesus is simply and irrevocably buried."[3] In this case the "three days" reflect the Jewish belief that the soul of a dead person remains in the neighborhood of the tomb for three days.[4] It is unclear in Matt 27:65 whether the guard is composed of Roman soldiers or is the high priests' own Jewish guard.[5] In Matt 28:11–15 it is clearly a Jewish guard which is bribed by the elders to keep silent so that the governor (Pilate) would not hear about the miraculous opening of the tomb and would think that the disciples stole the body. The ambiguity in Matt 28:11 is apparently caused by the fact that Matthew's source, like the *Gospel of Peter*, presented the guard as a cohort of Roman soldiers.[6]

Matt 27:62–66 (and 28:11–15) is usually called an apologetic legend.[7] But what Matthew reports here is not a complete story at all. It requires a continuation for which Matt 28:11–15 is not quite sufficient. What is missing is the presence of the guards as witnesses. Matthew was quite aware of that and inserted a reference to the

---

[1] *The Cross That Spoke*, 270.

[2] Matt 12:38–40; 16:21; 17:22–23; 20:18–19.

[3] Crossan, *The Cross That Spoke*, 270.

[4] See the story of the raising of Lazarus, John 11:17, 39, and Bultmann, *Gospel of John*, 400, n. 8.

[5] Pilate said to them ἔχετε κουστωδίαν. It is a much discussed problem whether ἔχετε is an imperative (= "take a guard!") or an indicative (= "you have a guard [yourselves]").

[6] Crossan, *The Cross That Spoke*, 397.

[7] Bultmann, *Synoptic Tradition*, 287.

guards into the story of the discovery of the empty tomb (Matt 28:2–4). However, this insertion not only has all the signs of the clumsiness of such a secondary interpolation; it also reveals that Matthew knew more of the the older epiphany story which the *Gospel of Peter* preserves.

Gos. Pet. 9.35–10.38	Matt 28:1–4
Now in the night in which the Lord's day dawned,	Now late on the Sabbath when the first day of the week was dawning, Mary Magdalene and the other Mary went to see the tomb.[1]
when the soldiers, two by two in every watch, were keeping guard, there rang a loud voice in heaven and they saw the heavens opened and two men came down from there in great brightness and drew near to the tomb. That stone which had been laid against the entrance to the	And behold, there was a great earthquake; for an angel of the Lord descended from heaven (see below)
tomb started of itself to roll and gave way to the side, and the tomb was opened,	and came and rolled back the stone and sat upon it.
(see above)	His appearance was like lightning, and his raiment white as snow.
and both the young men entered in. When now the soldiers saw this, they awakened the centurion.	And for fear of him, the guards trembled and became like dead men.

I completely agree with Crossan's statement that "Matthew is ... conflating two sources in his account of the angel and the guards."[2] That is especially evident with respect to the statement about the time at the beginning of the account.[3] These statements are perfectly clear in Mark 16:1–2 and in *Gos. Pet.* 9.35. Mark first recounts that the women buy the ointments as soon as the Sabbath is over (διαγενομένου τοῦ σαββάτου), i.e., in the evening after sunset. They go to the tomb early the next morning (λίαν πρωὶ τῇ μιᾷ τῶν σαββάτων). Matt 28:1 has combined some of that information with the time given by the epiphany story of the *Gospel of Peter*: "In the night in which the Lord's

---

[1] This verse (Matt 28:1) is taken from the Markan version of the story of the discovery of the empty tomb (Mark 16:1), but it has suffered some major alterations; see below.

[2] *The Cross That Spoke*, 352.

[3] See the detailed documentation for the following in Crossan, *The Cross That Spoke*, 352–55.

day dawned" (τῆ δὲ νυκτὶ ἦ ἐπέφωσκεν ἡ κυριακή). This, however, indicates something like the hour of midnight, certainly still the dark of the night before sunrise. The combination of both times in Matthew results in the strange statement that the women come to the tomb "late on the Sabbath" (ὄψε τῶν σαββάτων), "when the first of the week was dawning" (τῆ ἐπιφωσκούσῃ εἰς μίαν σαββάτων). This awkwardness alone is sufficient to prove the dependence of Matthew upon the epiphany story. The verses 28:2–4 are then explained without difficulty. Matthew replaces the two figures of the epiphany story with the one figure that is needed to greet the women, and he turns the guards at the tomb into people who were "like dead," so that the angel can talk with the women without witnesses.

This is sufficient for Matthew to enable the guards to return to the high priests and report all the things that had happened (Matt 28:11). Matthew's conclusion of the account of the guard at the tomb (28:11–15) differs from *Gos. Pet.* 11:46–49. In the latter, the soldiers report directly to Pilate;[1] then a group of persons designated as "all" (πάντες) comes to Pilate and requests him to swear the centurion and the soldiers to silence. Matthew, on the other hand, had already indicated that it was a guard that reported to the Jewish authorities. Thus he changes the conclusion to have the high priests and elders bribe the guard with money so they would say that his disciples had stolen the body while they were asleep. The elimination of Pilate and the bribery to the effect that the soldiers should tell a lie, thereby even incriminating themselves (they were not supposed to fall asleep!), are evidently secondary. What Matthew has presented here is no longer a plausible story but a piece of fiction that wants to explain why "this rumor is told among the Jews until today" (28:16). The *Gospel of Peter* wants to exonerate Pilate at the expense of the Jewish authorities; the Gospel of Matthew wants to shift the entire responsibility to "the Jews."

There is a good chance that also the epiphany section of the resurrection story of the *Gospel of Peter* has survived in the Synoptic Gospels. The story of the transfiguration of Jesus (Mark 9:2–8) has been designated as a displaced resurrection account.[2] There are several features which the account of the transfiguration shares with *Gos. Pet.* 9.36–10.40 and also with Matt 28:2–4.[3] Jesus appears "in

---

[1] The author of the gospel takes this occasion to insert another declaration of innocence by Pilate: "I am clean of the blood of the Son of God; you have made this decision." See the discussion above, # 3.2.3.2.

[2] Bultmann, *Synoptic Tradition*, 259.

[3] Matt 17:1–8 has introduced some additional features drawn from the resurrection account that he used in 28:2–4: the disciples fall on their face, terrified; Jesus turns to

garments glistening, intensely white" (Mark 9:3). Two angelic figures are standing with Jesus, who are then identified as Moses and Elijah. The epiphany story, which is generally known as the "transfiguration," may indeed be nothing else but a faint echo of the account which the *Gospel of Peter* has preserved in full.[1]

The next section of the *Gospel of Peter* is the account of the discovery of the empty tomb (12.50–13.57). If the *Gospel of Peter* used a source for his passion narrative that was related to the sources of Mark and John, the story of the discovery of the empty tomb would have concluded that source. Can it be shown that *Gos. Pet.* 12.50–13.57 is indeed not dependent upon any of the accounts of the canonical gospels?[2] It must at once be recognized that this portion of the writing has been heavily edited by the redactor. It was already prepared by the redactional insertion at the end of the epiphany story, which told of another figure descending from heaven and entering into the tomb (11:44). The story of the discovery of the tomb itself has been interrupted by repeated comments referring to the fear of the Jews which are always coupled with reflections about the question of pious duty with respect to one who has died (12.50, 52, 54).[3] But apart from these secondary comments, the basic story agrees with fundamental features of its canonical parallels.

Gos. Pet. 12.50–13.57	Mark 16:1–8
	And when the Sabbath had passed,
Mary Magdalene took with her	Mary Magdalene, and Mary the
female friends	mother of James, and Salome bought
	spices so that they might go and
early in the morning of the Lord's day	anoint him. And very early on the
and went to the tomb where he had	first day of the week they went to the
been laid.	tomb when the sun had risen.
And they said,	And they were saying to one another,
". . . Who will roll away the stone for	"Who will roll away the stone for us
us that is set on the entrance of the	from the door of the tomb?"
tomb [that we may go in	

---

them saying, "Rise up, fear not" (Matt 17:6–7). See Crossan, *The Cross That Spoke*, 358.

[1] Denker, *Theologiegeschichtliche Stellung*, 99–101. I am not convinced, however, that it is possible to explain special Lukan features in the story of the transfiguration (Luke 9:30–32) as due to literary dependence upon the same source (Crossan, *The Cross That Spoke*, 359–60).

[2] Crossan (*The Cross That Spoke*, 15–30) assigns this story to the "intracanonical stratum" of the gospel.

[3] These motifs are closely related to other redactional insertions elsewhere in the writing; see *Gos. Pet.* 7.26–27; 14.59.

and sit beside him and do what is
necessary] because the stone is large
. . ." So they went and found the tomb
open.

And looking up they saw that the
stone was rolled back; for it was very
large.

And they came near, stooped down,
and saw there a young man sitting in
the midst of the tomb, beautiful and
dressed with a bright shining robe,

And they saw a young man sitting to
the right, dressed with a white robe,

and they were amazed.
who said to them,

But he said to them,
"Do not be amazed!

"Why have you come? Whom do you
seek? Not the one who was crucified?
He rose and went away. But if you do
not believe, stoop and see the place
where he lay, for he is not there. He
rose and went to the place whence he
was sent."

You seek Jesus of Nazareth who was
crucified.
He was raised; he is not here.
See the place where they laid him.

But go and tell his disciples and Peter
that he is going before you to Galilee;
there you will see him as he told you."
Then the women fled in fear.
And they went out and fled from the
tomb, for trembling and
astonishment had come upon them.
And they said nothing to anyone, for
they were afraid.

There is nothing in this account that could not have been derived from
Mark or from the source that Mark used. Special features of the parallels in Matt 28:1–10, Luke 24:1–11, and John 20:1–10 are absent. But
what is also missing in the *Gospel of Peter* are the typical Markan
redactional elements: the command to tell the disciples to go to Galilee
(Mark 16:7) and the exaggerated emphasis upon fear and astonishment (Mark 16:5, 8), perhaps also the reference to the purchase of
spices (Mark 16:1)—there is no reference to this in the parallel story in
John 20. But in agreement with John 20, Mary Magdalene is the only
woman who is explicitly named, while not one of the other names
(Mary mother of James, Salome, the other Mary) appears.

The third resurrection story in the *Gospel of Peter* is the appearance
of Jesus at the lake (14.60), but only the beginning is preserved. What
remains is the list of the disciples who were present. But this list does
not agree with the parallel account in John 21:1–14. John 21:2 names
Simon Peter, Thomas called the Twin, Nathaniel of Cana, the sons of
Zebedee, and two other disciples. *Gos. Pet.* 14.60 names Simon Peter,

his brother Andrew, and Levi the son of Alphaeus. It is not known whether any additional disciples were introduced here, because the preserved text ends at this point. Already the discrepancies in the list of names argues against any dependence of this last epiphany story upon the supplemental chapter of the Gospel of John.

The *Gospel of Peter*, as a whole, is not dependent upon any of the canonical gospels. It is a composition which is analogous to the Gospels of Mark and John. All three writings, independently of each other, use an older passion narrative which is based upon an exegetical tradition that was still alive when these gospels were composed, and to which the Gospel of Matthew also had access. All five gospels under consideration, Mark, John, and Peter, as well as Matthew and Luke, concluded their gospels with narratives of the appearances of Jesus on the basis of different epiphany stories that were told in different contexts. However, fragments of the epiphany story of Jesus being raised from the tomb, which the *Gospel of Peter* has preserved in its entirety, were employed in different literary contexts in the Gospels of Mark and Matthew.

3.3 The Transmission of the Four Canonical Gospels

3.3.1 THE MANUSCRIPTS

Four gospels from the period of early Christianity have been admitted into the canon of the New Testament writings. They are known under the names of their assumed authors Matthew, Mark, Luke, and John.[1] Because of their canonical status, these four gospels have been preserved in a very large number of manuscripts.[2]

---

[1] Editions of the Greek text of the individual gospels: Eberhard Nestle and Erwin Nestle, *Novum Testamentum Graece* (26th ed. by Kurt Aland et al.; Stuttgart: Deutsche Bibelstiftung, 1979 and later reprints); Kurt Aland et al., *The Greek New Testament* (New York: United Bible Societies, 1966 and later reprints). Synoptic edition with the text of all four gospels: Kurt Aland, *Synopsis Quattuor Evangeliorum* (Stuttgart: Württembergische Bibelanstalt, 1963 and reprints, also with English text on facing pages). Synoptic edition of Matthew, Mark, and Luke (with passages from John wherever relevant): Albert Huck, *Synopsis of the First Three Gospels* (13th ed. fundamentally revised by Heinrich Greeven; Tübingen: Mohr/Siebeck, 1981); M.-E. Boismard & A. Lamouille, *Synopsis Graeca Quattuor Evangeliorum* (Leuven: Peeters, 1986). English translation (text of the RSV) of the earlier edition of Huck, *Synopsis*: Burton H. Throckmorton, *Gospel Parallels: A Synopsis of the First Three Gospels* (4th ed.; Nashville and New York: Nelson, 1979); Kurt Aland, *Synopsis of the Four Gospels: Greek-English Edition* (6th ed.; Stuttgart: United Bible Societies, 1983).

[2] Bruce Metzger, *The Text of the New Testament* (Oxford: Clarendon, 1964); Kurt Aland, *Kurzgefaßte Liste der griechischen Handschriften des Neuen Testaments* (ANTF 1; Berlin: De Gruyter, 1963); Nestle-Aland, *NT Graece*, 684–716.

The oldest of the manuscripts transmitting all four gospels in one single codex[1] is the New Testament Papyrus $\mathfrak{p}^{45}$,[2] written in the beginning or the middle of the 3d century CE. However, this manuscript is very fragmentary. Only chapters 20, 21, 25–26 of the Gospel of Matthew, chapters 4–13 of the Gospel of Mark, chapters 6–13 of the Gospel of Luke, and chapter 10 of the Gospel of John have been preserved. The complete text of all four Gospels of the New Testament occurs for the first time in the two oldest manuscripts which comprise the entire text of the Greek Bible: Codex Sinaiticus (א/01)[3] and Codex Vaticanus (B/03); both are uncial codices written in the middle of the 4th century CE. From the 5th century, four such codices with the text of all four gospels are preserved: Codex Alexandrinus (A/02) Codex Claromontanus (C/04), Codex Bezae Cantabrigiensis (D/05),[4] and Codex Washingtonianus (W/032).[5] A larger number of uncial manuscripts with the text of all four gospels date from the 6th,[6] 8th,[7] 9th,[8] and 10th[9] centuries. From the 9th and the following centuries an extremely large number of minuscule manuscripts with the text of the

---

[1] It also included the Acts of the Apostles.

[2] The major part of this manuscript is the *Chester-Beatty Papyrus I*; a small section, containing Matt 25:41–26:39, is preserved as *Pap. Graec. 31974* of the Österreichische Nationalbibliothek in Vienna. The papyrus was first published in 1933; see Metzger, *Text*, 251–52; Kurt Aland, *Repetitorium der griechischen christlichen Papyri I: Biblische Papyri* (PTS 18; Berlin: De Gruyter, 1976) 269–72.

[3] The custom to designate the uncial manuscripts of the NT with capital letters began with Wettstein's edition of 1751–52. As more and more uncial manuscript became known, Greek capital letters were also used and, in one instance—Codex Sinaiticus—a Hebrew letter was introduced. In the year 1908, Caspar René Gregory devised a new system which is now generally recognized. In this system, uncials are designated by Arabic numbers beginning with the numeral 0 (though the older designations with a capital letter are still used together with the number for the first 45 manuscripts of the list), minuscules are designated with regular numbers (not beginning with 0), lectionaries with the letter "l" followed by a number. See Kurt Aland, *Der Text des Neuen Testaments* (Stuttgart: Deutsche Bibelstiftung, 1982) 82–84.

[4] This codex, already known at the time of the Reformation, is a bilingual, containing both the Greek text and—on facing pages—the text of the Old Latin translation.

[5] This is the only major four-gospel manuscript now kept in the United States: Washington, DC, Smithsonian Institution/Freer Gallery of Art # 06.274. It has become famous because it is the only known manuscript which presents an expansion of the secondary ending of the Gospel of Mark (16:9–20) after Mark 16:14, the so-called Freer Logion.

[6] N/022, O/023, 087. Here and in the following notes, I am listing only those manuscripts which are regularly used in Nestle-Aland, *NT Graece*.

[7] E/07, L/019, Y/044, 047, 0233, 0250.

[8] F/09, G/011, H/013, K/017, M/021, U/030, V/031, X/033, Δ/037, Θ/038, Π/041, Ω/045, 0133, 0135.

[9] S/028, Γ/036, 0141.

four Gospels of the New Testament are preserved—several thousand are recorded— as well as many gospel lectionaries, i.e., manuscripts which contain only the pericopes for the gospel readings of the ecclesiastical year.[1]

3.3.2 THE TRANSLATIONS

Additional witnesses for the text of the canonical gospels are translations into other ancient languages. The oldest of these are the Old Latin translation from the end of the 2d century,[2] the Syriac translation from the 3d century,[3] and the Coptic translations of which the oldest, the translation into the Sahidic dialect, also dates from the 3d century.[4]

3.3.3 TRANSMISSION AND ATTESTATION OF THE
FOUR-GOSPEL CANON

Evidence for the transmission of the four-gospel canon in one single codex appears for the first time in the middle of the 3d century. In the earliest period of the transmission of the canonical gospels their text circulated in manuscripts which contained only the text of one gospel or, in some instances, of two gospels.[5] Some of these manuscripts of individual gospels are the oldest extant witnesses of Christian writings. The custom to copy only one individual gospel continued into the later period. However, it is often not possible to determine whether a fragment with the text of only one gospel comes from a codex containing all four gospels or even the entire New Testament.

It had long been assumed that the oldest witnesses to the four-gospel canon were the *Muratorian Canon* and the *Anti-Marcionite Gospel Prologues*. The *Muratorian Canon*,[6] a list of the canonical books translated from a Greek original into a rather clumsy Latin,[7] is

---

[1] On the text of the Synoptic Gospels in the new (26th) edition of Nestle-Aland see Neirynck, "The Synoptic Gospels according to the New Textus Receptus," in idem, *Evangelica*, 883–98.

[2] On the Old Latin translation, also called *Vetus Latina*, see Metzger, *Text*, 72–79.

[3] Although the Syrian church generally used the four-gospel harmony of Tatian (the *Diatessaron*), an old translation of the four separate gospels has been preserved in two manuscripts (sy^c and sy^s). On the old Syriac translation see Metzger, *Text*, 68–71.

[4] On the several translations into Coptic dialects see Metzger, *Text*, 79–81.

[5] These manuscripts will be discussed later in the individual treatment of the canonical gospels.

[6] Latin Text in Aland, *Synopsis*, 538; English translation in Hennecke-Schneemelcher-Wilson, *NT Apocrypha*, 1. 42–45; see also Lee Martin McDonald, *The Formation of the Christian Biblical Canon* (Nashville: Abingdon, 1988) 135–37.

[7] This has been disputed; but see von Campenhausen, *Formation*, 245.

still widely believed to have been composed in Rome or Italy before the end of the 2d century.[1] It is fragmentary at the beginning: the mention of the Gospels of Matthew and Mark is not preserved. But the Gospel of Luke is discussed as "the third Gospel book," the Gospel of John follows as the fourth. If the early date of this canon list were established, its information about the four-gospel canon and the authors of two of these gospels would indeed be very valuable. However, serious doubts with respect to a 2d-century date have been raised by Albert Sundberg.[2] It is, therefore, difficult to maintain this date; the document is more likely to have been composed in the Eastern Church after the middle of the 4th century.

Also with respect to the so-called *Anti-Marcionite Gospel Prologues*[3] serious questions have been raised concerning an early date.[4] These *Prologues*, originally composed in Greek, appear in several dozen Latin Bible manuscripts. Only *Prologues* for Mark, Luke, and John are extant; the *Prologue* for Luke is also preserved in Greek. It is very doubtful whether these *Prologues* can be considered as a unit. They may have been composed separately, and it is not possible to assign the same date to all three *Prologues*. While a date in the second half of the 4th century is likely for the *Prologues* for Mark and John and the second part of the *Prologue* for Luke, the first part of the latter may have been written much earlier.[5]

Therefore, the earliest witness for the four canonical gospels as a unit remains Irenaeus, ca. 180–200:

> Matthew brought forth a written gospel among the Hebrews in their own language, while Peter and Paul in Rome were preaching the gospel and founding the church. But after their death Mark, the disciple and inter-

---

[1] Von Campenhausen, *Formation*, 243–46.

[2] "Canon Muratori: A Fourth-Century List," *HTR* 66 (1973) 1–41; see also idem, "Canon of the NT," *IDBSup* 136–40. More recently, Sundberg's arguments have been accepted and cogently supported by McDonald, *Formation*, 135–39.

[3] Critical edition: Dom Donatien De Bruyne, "Les plus anciens prologues latins des évangiles," *Revue Bénédictine* 40 (1928) 193–214. Texts in Albert Huck, *Synopse der drei ersten Evangelien* (9th ed. by Hans Lietzmann; Tübingen: Mohr/Siebeck, 1936) p. VII; Aland, *Synopsis Quattuor Evangeliorum*, 532–33.

[4] It had been widely assumed that these Prologues to the Gospels were written between 160 and 180 CE. On the problems of their interpretation and dating see J. Regul, *Die antimarcionitischen Evangelienprologe* (Vetus Latina: Die Reste der altlateinischen Bibel; Aus der Geschichte der lateinischen Bibel 6; Freiburg: Herder, 1969). Regul argues for a 4th-century date for these *Prologues*.

[5] See R. G. Heard, "The Old Gospel Prologues," *JTS* n.s. 6 (1955) 1–16. Heard argues against De Bruyne's widely accepted view (see the literature cited ibidem, p. 1, n. 1) that the Prologues were composed as a single unit. About the Lukan Prologue, see below, # 4.4.2.

preter of Peter, also himself transmitted to us in writing the things which were preached by Peter; Luke also, the follower of Paul, set down in a book the gospel which was preached by Paul. Thereafter John, the disciple of the Lord who had even rested his head on his breast, gave forth the gospel while he was staying at Ephesus.[1]

This tradition about the origin of the four canonical gospels appears, with some variations, in other Church Fathers.[2] It was a firmly established and widely used tradition by the end of the 2d century.

3.4 The Story of the Johannine Gospel [3]

3.4.1 THE TRANSMISSION

The oldest fragment of a gospel manuscript that has come to light is a small piece of a papyrus containing a few verses of the Gospel of John (18:31–33, 37–38), the New Testament $\mathfrak{p}^{52}$.[4] It was written in the first half of the 2d century and is, with the possible exception of a fragment of an extracanonical gospel (*Papyrus Egerton* 2)[5] the oldest fragment of any Christian writing that has been found to date. But it is probably not surprising that the Gospel of John is attested in Egypt at such an early date. There are more papyrological witnesses to the use of this Gospel which have come from the Egyptian deserts. $\mathfrak{p}^{66}$, written ca. 200 CE,[6] contains almost the entire text of John's Gospel.

---

[1] *Adv. haer.* 3.1.1 in Eusebius *Hist. eccl.* 5.8.2–4. Further references of Irenaeus to the four canonical gospels have been collected by Aland, *Synopsis,* 534–38.

[2] Clement of Alexandria in Eusebius *Hist. eccl.* 6.14.5–7; Origen in Eusebius *Hist. eccl.* 6.25.3–6; 6.15.1–2. For the text of these references and quotations of the relevant passages see Aland, *Synopsis,* 539–48.

[3] For a general review of recent scholarship on John see Robert Kysar, "The Fourth Gospel: A Report on Recent Research," *ANRW* 2.25/3 (1985) 2389–2480. The question of the literary genre in the scholarly debate has been reviewed by Johannes Beutler, "Literarische Gattungen im Johannesevangelium: Ein Forschungsbericht 1919–1980," *ANRW* 2.25/3 (1985) 2506–68. A representative collection of essays was published by Karl Heinrich Rengstorf, *Johannes und sein Evangelium* (WdF 82; Darmstadt: Wissenschaftliche Buchgesellschaft, 1973). Some important monographs are C. H. Dodd, *The Interpretation of the Fourth Gospel* (Cambidge: Cambridge University Press, 1953); Robert T. Fortna, *The Fourth Gospel and its Predecessor: From Narrative to Present Gospel* (Philadelphia: Fortress, 1988). Major Commentaries: Bultmann, *Gospel of John*; C. K. Barrett, *The Gospel according to St John* (London: S.P.C.K., 1958); Rudolph Schnackenburg, *The Gospel according to John* ((Herder's Theological Commentary on the NT; New York: Herder, 1968 and following years); Brown, *Gospel of John*.

[4] John Rylands Library, Manchester, *Pap. Graec. 457*; cf. Aland, *Repetitorium,* 286.

[5] See above, # 3.2.2.

[6] Cologny, Bibliotheca Bodmeriana, *Pap. Bodmer II*; cf. Aland, *Repetitorium,* 296–98.

$\mathfrak{p}^{75}$ from the 3d century[1] preserves large portion of John 1–15,[2] and five other papyri from the same century are smaller fragments from manuscripts of the same Gospel.[3] Since all papyri of the New Testament from this early period have been found in Egypt, it is impossible to draw conclusions from such finds with respect to the usage and distribution of the Gospel of John in general; but there can be little doubt that this Gospel was widely known in Egypt at a very early time.[4]

However, it is very unlikely that it was written in that country; the close relationship of John's Gospel to syncretistic Judaism and to the Gnosticizing interpretation of the sayings of Jesus (see below), the ties of the Gospel with Palestinian geography (Samaria, Jordan), and the history-of-religions milieu in general point to a Syro-Palestinian origin.[5]

3.4.2 EXTERNAL ATTESTATION

The early distribution and usage of the Gospel of John in Egypt is confirmed by external evidence. Several Gnostic writings from Egypt used it,[6] and the first commentaries ever written on any gospel are

---

[1] Cologny, Bibliotheca Bodmeriana, *Pap. Bodmer XIV and XV*; cf. Aland, *Repetitorium,* 309–11.

[2] This same Papyrus also contains portions of the Gospel of Luke; see below # 4.4.1.

[3] $\mathfrak{p}^5$ (vss. from chaps. 1, 16, and 20), $\mathfrak{p}^{22}$ (John 15:25–16:2; 16:21–32), $\mathfrak{p}^{28}$ (John 6:8–12, 17–22), $\mathfrak{p}^{39}$ (John 8:14–21), $\mathfrak{p}^{80}$ (John 3:34).

[4] The later attestation for the text of this Gospel from Egypt is also very rich: one papyrus from the 4th century ($\mathfrak{p}^6$, fragments from John 10–13 in Greek and in Coptic), nine papyri from later centuries, and a total of about 30 uncial manuscripts on parchment which contain at least portions of the Fourth Gospel; the oldest of these (0162, containing John 2:11–22) was written in the 3d or 4th century.

[5] The evidence of papyrus finds should not be overestimated in the determination of the country of origin of a particular writing, since only the climatic conditions of Egypt permitted the survival of manuscripts from this early period. Scholars are divided with respect to the origin of John's Gospel. Some argue for Syrian origin (cf. Vielhauer, *Geschichte,* 445–60), others defend the ecclesiastical tradition about the disciple John of Ephesus as the author of this gospel (cf. Brown, *John,* pp. ciii-iv). On the problem concerning this ecclesiastical tradition see below.

[6] E.g., the Valentinian texts cited in Clement of Alexandria *Excerpta ex Theodotou* (Greek text in Walther Völker, *Quellen zur Geschichte der christlichen Gnosis* [SAQ 5; Tübingen: Mohr/Siebeck, 1932] 63–86; English translation in Werner Foerster, *Gnosis,* 1.222–33) and the Naassene Fragment quoted by Hippolytus *Ref.* 5.7.2–9 (Greek Text in Völker, *Quellen,* 11–26). Cf. W. von Loewenich, *Das Johannesverständnis im zweiten Jahrhundert* (BZNW 13; Gießen: Töpelmann, 1932). Some of the earlier writings from Nag Hammadi also display usage of the Fourth Gospel, e.g., the *Gospel of Philip* (NHC II,3), cf. Jacques E. Ménard, *L'Evangile selon Philip* (Paris: Letouzey & Ané, 1967)29–32; the *Testimony of Truth* (NHC IX,3), cf. Birger Pearson, *Nag Hammadi Codices IX and X* (NHS 15; Leiden: Brill, 1981) 112 and notes to the translation. In other instances, dependence upon the Gospel of John is not clear (*Gospel of Truth*) or

commentaries on the Gospel of John which derive from Egypt.[1] On the other hand, John's Gospel is not well known elsewhere. Ignatius of Antioch, although his theological language is closely related to that of John, does not seem to know this writing.[2] Nor is the Gospel of John known in Asia Minor before the middle of the 2d century: Polycarp of Smyrna, Papias of Hierapolis, and the Pastoral Epistles (written in Ephesus after the year 100) never refer to it. In Rome, neither 1 Peter nor *1 Clement* nor Justin Martyr reveal any knowledge of the Fourth Gospel. However, later in the 2d century, this Gospel begins to be used also in Asia Minor and Rome. Justin's student Tatian includes it in his four-gospel harmony, the *Diatessaron*; Irenaeus knows a tradition about the disciple John, a tradition according to which this disciple became established in Ephesus;[3] and the Montanist movement, which arose in Phrygia of Asia Minor after the middle of the 2d century, understands its prophecy as the return of the Johannine Paraclete.[4]

3.4.3 INTEGRITY OF THE TEXT

It does not appear that the text of the Gospel of John as it is extant in the oldest manuscripts has preserved the text of the autograph without changes. John 21, though belonging to the older stages of the transmission of the text, is certainly a later appendix.[5] After the story of Jesus' appearance before the disciples and Jesus' word to Thomas

---

unlikely (*Apocryphon of James, Dialogue of the Savior, Gospel of Thomas*; see the chapters on these writings).

[1] A Valentinian Exposition to the Prologue of the Gospel of John (Irenaeus *Adv. haer.* 1.8.5–6; Greek text in Völker, *Quellen*, 93–95; English translation in Foerster, *Gnosis*, 1.144–45); the commentary of Heracleon on the Gospel of John (Origen *Comm. in Joh.*, passim; Greek Texts in Völker, *Quellen*, 63–86; English translation in Foerster, *Gnosis*, 1.162–83). See Elaine H. Pagels, *The Johannine Gospel in Gnostic Exegesis: Heracleon's Commentary on John* (SBLMS 17; Nashville: Abingdon 1973).

[2] Henning Paulsen, *Studien zur Theologie des Ignatius von Antiochien* (FKDG 29; Göttingen: Vandenhoeck & Ruprecht, 1978) 36–37; Schoedel, *Ignatius,* 9.

[3] Irenaeus, the bishop of Lyon (ca. 180 CE) who came from Asia Minor, is the first author who ascribes this Gospel to "John the disciple of the Lord . . . when he was living in Ephesus" (*Adv. haer.* 3.11 = Eusebius *Hist. eccl.* 5.8.4). Older traditions also know of a presbyter (elder) John of Ephesus who may have been the author of the Book of Revelation. The best discussion of this question can be found in Vielhauer, *Geschichte,* 456–60.

[4] Materials and discussions in Adolf Hilgenfeld, *Die Ketzergeschichte des Urchristentums* (Leipzig, 1884; reprint Darmstadt: Wissenschaftliche Buchgesellschaft, 1966) 560–601. On the question of the Montanists' reliance on the Fourth Gospel see ibid., 563–64, 599–601.

[5] See the discussion in Brown, *Gospel of John,* 2.1077–85; literature on this question ibid., pp. 1143–44.

("Blessed are those who have not seen and yet believe," 20:29), John 20:30–31 gives the proper original conclusion of the gospel:[1]

> Now Jesus did many other signs in the presence of his disciples which are not written in this book; but these are written that you may believe that Jesus is the Christ, the Son of God, and that believing you may have life in his name.

John 21 adds the story of an appearance of Jesus before his disciples at the lake (21:1–14) of which at least the beginning is independently transmitted in the *Gospel of Peter*.[2] This story serves to introduce a discussion about the relationship of the tradition of the Johannine church to the authority of Peter. The leading authority for the church of the tradition under the name of Peter is confirmed through the threefold question of Jesus, "Simon, do you love me?" and the following requests, "Feed my sheep!" (21:15–17). But what about the authority of the Johannine tradition? It is represented by the "disciple whom Jesus loved," who also follows Jesus and about whom Peter asks, "Lord, what about this man?" (21:20–21) Jesus' mysterious answer, "If it is my will that he remain until I come, what is that to you?" confirms the right of the special tradition of the Beloved Disciple. It does not mean that he will not die; this is explicitly rejected (21:22–23). It means that the Johannine tradition, and specifically this written Gospel, has lasting validity.[3] That is said explicitly when the allegorical framework is finally discarded in the statement of John 21:24:

> This is the disciple who is bearing witness to these things, and who has written these things; and we know that his testimony is true.

John 21:25, once more referring to the many other things which Jesus did but could not be written in this book, imitates the original conclusion of the Gospel.

The redactor who added chapter 21 may also have been responsible for some minor additions in the text of chapters 1–20. One of these redactional passages is apparently John 6:51b–59.[4] The original

---

[1] Because it speaks of the "signs" (σημεῖα) that Jesus did, this conclusion may already have served as the ending of the Source of Signs (Semeia Source) from which John drew his miracle stories; see below # 3.4.4.1, and above # 3.2.1.

[2] See above, # 3.2.3.3.

[3] This juxtaposition of Peter and the Beloved Disciple is comparable to the one of James and Thomas in *Gos. Thom.* 12–13.

[4] Most convincing arguments for the secondary character of this disputed passage have been brought forward by Günther Bornkamm, "Die eucharistische Rede im Johannesevangelium," *ZNW* 47 (1956) 161–69. For an assessment of the discussion about these verses and bibliography see Brown, *Gospel of John*, 1. 281–94, 303–4.

discourse on the bread that has come down from heaven ended in John 6:51a with Jesus' statement, "I am the living bread which came down from heaven; those who eat of this bread will live forever." The continuation of this claim follows in John 6:60–62: the disciples find this a "hard saying," to which Jesus responds, "Then what if you were to see the Son of man ascending where he was before?" The "hard saying," thus, is Jesus' claim that he has come down from heaven, but not the content of the interpolated verses which emphasize the physical eating of Jesus' flesh and the drinking of his blood. The interpolation was made in order to emphasize the sacramental eating and drinking of Jesus' flesh and blood.

The verses John 5:27b–29; 6:39b, 40b, 44b, which present a realistic view of the resurrection on the last day, also belong to these redactional passages.[1] John 5:24–27a has stated unequivocally that those who believe in Jesus have eternal life and will not come into the judgment, and that now is the hour "that the dead will hear the voice of the Son of God, and those who hear will live." John 5:28–29 qualifies this statement through the introduction of a more traditional view of eschatology:[2]

> Do not marvel at this. For the hour is coming when all who are in the tombs will hear his voice and come forth, those who have done good, to the resurrection of life, and those who have done evil, to the resurrection of judgment.

The brief clause, "but I shall raise him on the last day," interpolated in John 6:39, 40, and 44, reveals the same traditional eschatological orientation.

That the pericope about Jesus and the adulteress, John 7:53– 8:11, did not belong to the early text of the Gospel of John is clearly shown by the manuscript tradition: it is missing in the older papyri ($\mathfrak{p}^{66}$ and $\mathfrak{p}^{75}$) and in the oldest uncial codices (ℵ, B, A) as well as in the oldest translations (sy^{s,c}, sa),[3] and appears for the first time in the 5th-century, Greek-Latin bilingual Codex D, and subsequently in most of the later manuscripts and the younger translations.[4]

---

[1] Bultmann, *Gospel of John*, 261.

[2] 5:27b, "because he is Son of man" (ὅτι υἱὸς ἀνθρώπου ἐστίν) is odd in this context. Elsewhere John always uses articles with this title. Moreover, the authority to give life and to judge was just assigned to Jesus as the Son of God. "Son of man," however, occurs in the Synoptic Gospels as the typical title for the one who is coming on the clouds for the final judgment; cf. Mark 13:26; 14:62; Luke 17:22–24.

[3] For the discussion of the manuscript evidence for this pericope see Bruce Metzger, *A Textual Commentary on the Greek New Testament* (New York: United Bible Society, 1971) 219–22; Brown, *Gospel of John*, 1. 332–38.

[4] Several later manuscripts place this pericope into the Gospel of Luke after Luke

Another aspect of the question of the integrity of the extant text of this Gospel concerns the order of its chapters and sections. Major disorder exists in two instances. The first concerns the sequence of chapters 4–7. At the end of chapter 4, Jesus is in Galilee, at the beginning of chapter 5 he goes to Jerusalem, chapter 6:1 says, "And after this Jesus went to the other side of the Sea of Galilee," and 7:1 reports that Jesus left Jerusalem and went about in Galilee, because the Jews were seeking to kill him. Moreover, John 7 continues the discussion of the theme of judgment which had been initiated in chapter 5. If the order were chapters 4, 6, 5, 7, all these difficulties would be removed.[1]

The second major disorder is apparent in John 14:30–31. At the conclusion of this first part of the farewell discourses Jesus says:

> I will no longer talk much with you, for the ruler of this world is coming. He has no power over me, but I do as the Father has commanded me, so that the world may know that I love the Father. Rise, let us go hence.

But it is only in 18:1 that this command is followed by an appropriate action:

> When Jesus had spoken these words, he went forth with his disciples across the Kidron valley where there was a garden, . . .

In spite of the clear "Rise, let us go hence" in John 14:31, chapters 15–17 continue the farewell discourses. It has been suggested that chapters 15–17 are a later interpolation. But in language, style, and content these three chapters belong with 13–14. It is clear, therefore, that they are not in the right place. Chapters 15–16 may have followed John 13:34–35, because 15:1–17 is a commentary on the commandment to love each other, and 13:36–38 seems a good continuation of 16:31.[2] This leaves John 17, the fare-well prayer of Jesus. No satisfactory solution has been found for the placement of this chapter.[3] That John 17 was added after the displacement of chapters 15–16 had already occurred, is also possible because chapter 17 is characterized by a theological interpretation of Jesus' departure that differs markedly from the farewell discourses in chapters 13–16; its orientation is more explicitly Gnostic.

21:38; see Metzger, *Textual Commentary*, 173.

[1] See Bultmann, *Gospel of John*, 209–10, following older suggestions. More recent commentators are hesitant to engage in such reordering of the chapters.

[2] Bultmann, *Gospel of John*, 459–60.

[3] Bultmann (*Gospel of John*, 460–61) suggests to place it after 13:31a, i.e., after the designation and departure of Judas and before the statement "Now is the Son of man glorified."

Rudolf Bultmann, in his landmark commentary on the Gospel of John, suggested in numerous instances the relocation of smaller units, often consisting of just a few verses.[1] The result is convincing insofar as it establishes several discourses which make much more sense than some of these chapters of the Gospel in their extant form, especially regarding chapters 7–8, 10, and 12. However, it is extremely difficult to explain what caused the disorder of the extant text. The relocation of major sections can be justified by assuming that pages in a papyrus codex became displaced. But the reconstitution of the original by relocating both some large and many very small units requires the analogy of an ancient piece of pottery that broke into several larger and many smaller pieces—unfortunately an analogy which does not fit the material transmission of ancient literature.

3.4.4 SOURCES AND COMPOSITION

3.4.4.1 The Problem of the Sources of John

The question of the sources used by the author of the Fourth Gospel is debated, but written sources were no doubt used. Various theories have been proposed.[2] The text of the Gospel shows a number of seams at which the author inserted new materials or his own comments into an older document; in many instances, it is evident that the author is adding secondary interpretations to older written or oral materials.[3] But the style of the writing is uniform throughout (even including the secondary appendix chapter 21) so that it is very difficult to determine the exact extent of the source in each single instance. Moreover, it is not possible to understand this work as the product of a single author who artfully brought together several sources, composing them into a new literary work. Whatever older written documents served as sources for this composition had already gone through a process of interpretation and commentary in the preaching, liturgy, teaching, and internal debates of the Johannine community—a process that must have been part of the community's life over a period of several

---

[1] E.g., for a chapter which he entitles "The Light of the World" he reconstructs the following original order: John 9:1–41; 8:12; 12:44–50; 8:21–29; 12:34–36; 10:19–21.

[2] Cf. the discussion and literature in Brown, *Gospel of John*, 1. pp. xxiv-xl. The most influential source hypothesis was proposed by Bultmann, *Gospel of John*. An extensive evaluation of this hypothesis has been presented by Dwight Moody Smith, *The Composition and Order of the Fourth Gospel* (New Haven: Yale University Press 1965); cf. also idem, "The Sources of the Gospel of John: an Assessment of the Present State of the Problem," *NTS* 10 (1963/64) 336–51.

[3] James M. Robinson, "The Johannine Trajectory," in Robinson-Koester, *Trajectories*, 232–68.

decades, probably of more than half a century. Several layers of interpretation that reflect the history of this community and the development of its theology had already been added to the more original materials when the author of the Gospel began to collect them in order to compose the document that we now call the Gospel of John. Moreover, the author of the Fourth Gospel is not likely to have been a stranger to the Johannine community; he must have participated himself in the effort of interpreting and shaping older traditions, ordering the community's life, and debating opponents within and without its circles. Nowhere are we told that the author produced his work in one piece in a brief period. Several earlier drafts of parts of the work may have been written and may have been used in the ongoing life of the community before the work finally reached the form in which it is preserved by the oldest manuscripts.[1]

In spite of the problems which are encountered in the attempt to define sharply the sources used in the work and distinguish them from the author's redaction, one can still point to several types of sources or traditions that provided the materials for the composition.

3.4.4.2 The Semeia Source

The character of the miracle stories used in the Gospel of John and the very fact that the miracles were apparently numbered in a way that does not always agree with the actual sequence of their occurrence in the work leaves no doubt that they were derived from a written source. This has been discussed above.[2] What is of interest here is the use of this source by the author of the Gospel. The Semeia Source was not just a random collection of sundry miracle stories, but a composition that had a message: Jesus is the divine man who strides upon the face of the earth displaying supernatural power, beginning with the miraculous change of water into wine like the god Dionysus (John 2:1–11) and ending his mission by raising the dead (John 11). The author of the Fourth Gospel has adopted this source as the basis of the first half of his writing, John 2–11, the "Book of Signs," as it has been called.

Two contradictory elements characterize the use of the Semeia Source, as it has been incorporated into the Gospel: on the one hand, nothing is taken away from the powerful effect of the miracles. On the other hand, it is repeatedly emphasized that belief in the miracles is not only insufficient; it falsifies what true belief in Jesus ought to be.

---

[1] See the theory adopted by Brown, *Gospel of John*, 1. pp. xxxiv-xxxix.
[2] See # 3.2.1.

Repeated references to the problem of the belief propagated by the Semeia Source accompany the reproduction of its stories:

> At the end of the wine miracle at Cana:
> This is the first of his signs Jesus did at Cana in Galilee, and manifested his glory; and his disciples believed in him. (2:11)

> When Jesus thereafter appeared in Jerusalem:
> Many believed (ἐπίστευσαν) in his name when they saw the signs which he did; but Jesus did not entrust himself (οὐκ ἐπίστευεν ἑαυτόν [1]) to them. (2:23–24)

> In answer to the royal official whose son was ill:
> "Unless you see signs and wonders (σημεῖα καὶ τέρατα) you do not believe (οὐ μὴ πιστεύσητε)." (4:48)

> After the miracle of the feeding of the multitudes:
> When the people saw the sign which he had done, they said, "This is indeed the prophet who has come into the world." Perceiving then that they were about to come and take him by force to make him king, Jesus withdrew again to the hills by himself. (6:14–15)

> After the trials of the man who was blind, when Jesus finds him, he said, "Do you believe in the Son of man?" He answered, "Sir, who is he that I may believe in him?" Jesus said to him, "You have seen him, and it is he who speaks to you." He said, "Lord, I believe." (9:35–38)

All of these comments are due to the redactional work of the author of the gospel. Miracles call forth belief in Jesus, among the disciples, in the man who was blind, among the people. But that Jesus does not "entrust himself" to this belief, that he escapes from those who want to make him king, is confirmed in the description of the effect of the greatest miracle, the raising of Lazarus.

> After the raising of Lazarus:
> Many of the Jews, therefore, who had come with Mary and had seen what he did, believed in him ... So the chief priests and the Pharisees gathered the council and said, "What are we to do, for this man performs many signs. If we let him go, every one will believe in him, ..." But Caiaphas ... said, "You know nothing at all; you do not understand that it is expedient for you that one man should die for the people...." (11:45–50)

Many of the people now believe in Jesus, but the Jerusalem authori-

---

[1] The reading ἑαυτόν is found in p[66] and in the majority of manuscripts. But the alternate reading αὐτόν (ℵ A B L) can also be read as αὑτόν = "himself."

ties decide that this is cause enough to put Jesus to death. That Jesus is a divine man who displays his miraculous powers is the cause of his condemnation.

This interpretation of the Semeia Source goes hand in hand with another use of its materials: they become the basis of, and provide the topics for, the composition of some of the discourses and dialogues of the Fourth Gospel. The materials for these discourses, however, were prepared by a different type of source materials from the Johannine tradition. This will be discussed below. There is another narrative source which has been used by the author, namly, the passion narrative.

3.4.4.3 The Passion Narrative

The similarities of the Johannine and the Markan passion narratives suggest that the author of the Fourth Gospel used a written narrative source also for the second part of his writing. This assumption is confirmed by several agreements between John and the *Gospel of Peter,* the third independent witness of this passion narrative and its development on the basis of scriptural exegesis.[1]

Pericope	John	Other gospels
Conspiracy of the hierarchs	11:45–53	Mark 14:1–2 parr.
Anointing at Bethany	12:1–8	Mark 14:3–9; Matt 26:6–13
Entry into Jerusalem	12:9–19	Mark 11: 1–10 parr.
Betrayal of Judas		Mark 14:10–11 parr.
Preparation for Passover		Mark 14:12–16 parr.
Last Supper	13:1–2	Mark 14:17 parr.
Words of Institution		Mark 14:22–25 parr.
Foot Washing	13:3–11	
Designation of the traitor	13:18–30	Mark 14:18–21 parr.
Prediction of Peter's denial	13:36–38	Mark 14:26–31 parr.
Christ in Gethsemane	(18:1)	Mark 14:32–42 parr.
Jesus' arrest	18:2–12	Mark 14:43–52 parr.
Jesus before the synedrion	18:13–24	Mark 14:53–65 parr.
Denial of Peter	18:15–27	Mark 14:66–72 parr.
Mocking before the synedrion		Mark 14:65 parr.
Jesus brought before Pilate	18:28–32	Mark 15:1 parr.
The end of Judas		Matt 27:3–10
Trial before Pilate	18:33–38	Mark 15:2–5
Jesus before Herod		Luke 23:6–16
Jesus or Barabbas	18:39–40	Mark 15:6–15a parr.
Pilate's wife & handwashing		Matt 27:19, 24–25

[1] See above, # 3.2.3.2.

Jesus scourged	19:1	Mark 15:15b parr.
Mocking by the soldiers	19:2–3	Mark 15:16–20; Matt 27:27–31
Trial before Pilate continued	19:4–16	
Simon of Cyrene crossbearer		Mark 15:21 parr.
Woe to women of Jerusalem		Luke 23:27–32
Crucifixion	19:17–22	Mark 15:22–24a, 25–27
Dividing of the garment	19:23–24	Mark 15:24b parr.
Mocking of the Crucified		Mark 15:29–32 parr.
Jesus and the two criminals		Luke 23:39–43
Women at the cross	19:25–27	(Mark 15:40–41 parr)
Vinegar for a drink	19:28–29	Mark 15:34–36 parr.
Jesus' death	19:30	Mark 15:37 parr.
Prodigies at the death		Mark 15:38 parr.
The tombs of Saints open		Matt 27:51–53
Soldier pierces Jesus' corpse	19:31–37	
Burial of Jesus	19:38–42	Mark 15:42–47 parr.
Discovery of the empty tomb	20:1–10	Mark 16:1–8 parr.

The passion narrative source of John began, like Mark's source, with the stories of the anointing of Jesus in Bethany, John 12:1–8, and of the entry into Jerusalem, John 12:9–19,[1] and it ended with the story of the discovery of the empty tomb, John 20:1–10. As the table shows, almost all pericopes appear in the same order in which they are preserved in Mark. But dependence of John upon Mark or any of the other Synoptic Gospels is not possible for the following reasons: (1) Nowhere does John reveal a knowledge of the vocabulary and style of Mark.[2] (2) Markan expansions of his passion narrative source have no parallels in John: the preparation for the Passover (Mark 14:13–16), clearly a secondary expansion which upsets the original passion chronology; the mocking before the synedrion (Mark 14:65), a secondary variant of the scene of the mocking by the soldiers; the novelistic expansion of the Barabbas incident (Mark 15:6–15a); the episode of Simon of Cyrene who is forced to bear the cross (Mark 15:21); the mocking of the crucified Jesus (Mark 15:29–32). There are

---

[1] The sequence of the two stories is reversed in the Gospel of Mark. John may have preserved the original order. It would be natural that Jesus went to Bethany before entering Jerusalem. Mark had an obvious interest in using the story of the entry into Jerusalem first, in order to introduce the Jerusalem ministry of Jesus; he also wanted to tie the story of Jesus' anointing more closely with the death and burial of Jesus (cf. Mark 14:8 which has no parallel in the Johannine account).

[2] There may be a few phrases which have been added to the text of John through marginal glosses at a later date. This is most obvious with respect to the sentence, "The poor you have always with you, but you do not have always me" (John 12:8 = Matt 26:11 [Mark 14:7]). The sentence is missing in several witnesses (D sy^s) of the text of John; cf. Bultmann, *Gospel of John,* 415–16.

no parallels to any of these secondary features of Mark in the *Gospel of Peter* either. (3) There is no trace in John of any of Matthew's and Luke's additions to the Markan passion narrative (see the table above). (4) John's chronology of the last meal and the death of Jesus agrees with the chronology of Mark's source and with that of the *Gospel of Peter*. According to John 18:28 and 19:14 Jesus was crucified on the Day of Preparation, that is, in the afternoon before the First Day of Passover, which began in the evening after sunset with the eating of the Passover lamb.[1] Mark 14:1 actually presupposes the same chronology: "It was now *two* days before the Passover and the Feast of the Unleavened Bread."[2] But the interpolated story of the preparation for the Passover Meal (Mark 14:12–16) confuses this chronology. John has preserved the more original and historically accurate date.[3]

There are, on the other hand, numerous secondary features in the Johannine passion narrative. In the last meal of Jesus with his disciples (John 13:1–30; cf. Mark 14:17–25), John does not describe this meal as the institution of the Lord's Supper. At this point, John leaves the passion narrative source and inserts the farewell discourses of Jesus (John 13–17). The narrative of the source is resumed in John 18:1 with the arrest of Jesus (cf. Mark 14:43–52) and continues in the trial of Jesus before the synedrion, the betrayal of Peter, the trial before Pilate (including the Barabbas scene), the mocking by the soldiers, crucifixion, dividing of the garment, inscription on the cross, drinking of vinegar, Jesus' death and burial, and the discovery of the empty tomb. All of these are paralleled in Mark 15–16. But rarely does John follow his source verbatim. The most remarkable expansion appears in the trial before Pilate which John has rewritten in the form of various dialogues between Jesus and Pilate, and between Pilate and the accusers and the people.

The stories of the appearances of Jesus after his resurrection (John 20:11–29) have no parallels in Mark or in the other gospels;[4] they belong to the special traditions of the Johannine community.[5]

---

[1] See Bultmann, *Gospel of John*, 651.

[2] The hierarchs conspire to have Jesus executed *before* the feast in order to avoid a a tumult among the people (Mark 14:2).

[3] John is also interested in the implied symbolism: Jesus dies at the hour at which the Passover lambs are slaughtered. See Bultmann, *Gospel of John*, 664. But that does not prove that he invented that dating.

[4] The only exception is the story of Jesus' appearance at the lake in the supplement chap. 21 which is paralleled in the *Gospel of Peter*; see above, # 3.2.3.3.

[5] The remarkable differences between the stories of Jesus' appearances after the resurrection in all four canonical gospels make it certain that the passion narrative employed by John and Mark did not include any of these stories, but ended with the account of the finding of the empty tomb. Cf. Bultmann, *Synoptic Tradition*, 288–91.

3.4.4.4 Dialogue Sources

In the employment of the Semeia Source and of the Passion Narrative Source the Gospel of John shares important traditional materials with the three other Gospels of the New Testament. But the large sections of the Fourth Gospel which consist of extensive discourses of Jesus and dialogues with his disciples have no parallels in the three other Gospels of the canon. Even the major complexes of speeches of Jesus in the Gospel of Matthew (e.g., the Sermon on the Mount, Matthew 5–7, see below) cannot be cited as parallels or analogies. They are primarily the result of a compilation of traditional sayings of Jesus, while the Johannine discourses seem to contain comparatively little traditional materials and resemble more closely the revelation discourses of Gnostic writings.

Rudolf Bultmann had, therefore, presented the hypothesis that these Johannine discourses were the result of an interpretation of a pre-Christian Gnostic source containing revelation discourses which were then edited and expanded by the author of the Fourth Gospel.[1] However, it has not been possible to provide evidence for the existence of such Gnostic revelation discourses and dialogues in pre-Christian Gnosticism. Bultmann's hypothesis has, therefore, been rejected almost unanimously by subsequent scholarship. More recent commentators are normally concerned only with the description and analysis of the style and structure of the Johannine discourses and dialogues and interpret them as if they were literary products of the author of the Gospel.[2] C. H. Dodd[3] has tried to identify traditional materials which were utilized in the composition of the Johannine discourses, but with limited results because he used the Synoptic Gospels as the primary criterion in this search.

Recent discoveries of dialogues in Gnostic gospels have been more instructive in order to illuminate the origin of the Johannine dialogues and discourses.[4] They show that dialogues were initially developed in

---

However, the appearances of the Risen Lord are still showing similar formal characteristics; see Lyder Brun, *Die Auferstehung Christi in der urchristlichen Ueberlieferung* (Oslo: Aschehoug [Nygaard], 1925).

[1] Bultmann, *Gospel of John,* passim; cf. Heinz Becker, *Die Reden des Johannesevangeliums und der Stil der gnostischen Offenbarungsrede* (FRLANT 68; Göttingen: Vandenhoeck & Ruprecht, 1956). A detailed analysis of Bultmann's method and a reconstruction of the Greek text of his Redenquelle can be found in D. M. Smith, *Composition and Order,* 15–34.

[2] See Brown, *Gospel of John,* 1. pp. cxxxii–cxxxvii (with literature).

[3] *Historical Tradition in the Fourth Gospel* (Cambridge: Cambridge University Press, 1963) 335–420.

[4] See my essays "Dialog und Spruchüberlieferung in den gnostischen Texten von

the process of the interpretation of sayings of Jesus.[1] If the Johannine discourses and dialogues belong to this trajectory of the development of Jesus' sayings, they emerge as genuine gospel materials which belong to the further development of the tradition of sayings. This has become especially evident as hitherto unknown sayings were discovered in the Nag Hammadi Library, especially in the *Gospel of Thomas*.[2] In addition to these sayings, proverbs, kerygmatic formulae, and theological traditions seem to have been used. In many instances, the author of the Fourth Gospel did not compose these discourses *de novo*, but utilized and expanded older existing discourses. To demonstrate this for the entire text of the extensive discourses and dialogues of the Gospel of John is a task that still waits to be done. A few examples must suffice here.[3]

John 3:3 and 5 begin the dialogue with Nicodemus with a saying quoted by Jesus which is also attested in Justin *1 Apol.* 61.4:

John 3:3	John 3:5	Justin *1 Apol.* 61.4
Truly, truly, I say to you, unless someone is born again (or: anew), he cannot see the kingdom of God.	Truly, truly, I say to you, unless someone is born from water and spirit, he cannot enter into the kingdom of God.	Unless you are reborn, you cannot enter into the kingdom of heaven.
ἐὰν μή τις γεννηθῇ ἄνωθεν, οὐ δύναται ἰδεῖν τὴν βασιλείαν τοῦ θεοῦ.	ἐὰν μή τις γεννηθῇ ἐξ ὕδατος καὶ πνεύματος, οὐ δύναται εἰσελθεῖν εἰς τὴν βασιλείαν τοῦ θεοῦ.	ἂν μὴ ἀναγεννηθῆτε, οὐ μὴ εἰσέλθητε εἰς τὴν βασιλείαν τῶν οὐρανῶν.

The saying used by John belongs to the baptismal tradition, as Justin

---

Nag Hammadi," *EvTh* 39 (1979), 532–56; "Gnostic Sayings and Controversy Traditions in John 8:12–59," in Charles W. Hedrick and Robert Hodgson, Jr., eds., *Nag Hammadi, Gnosticism, & Early Christianity* (Peabody, MA: Hendrickson, 1986) 97–110.

[1] See above the discussions of the development of dialogues and discourses, # 3.1.1–3.

[2] The first collection of the relevant parallels to the Gospel of John was published by R. E. Brown, "Thomas and John," but he assigned these parallels in the *Gospel of Thomas* to Johannine influence upon what he deemed to be a 2d-century Gnostic writing and unfortunately did not utilize them for his analysis of the Johannine discourses.

[3] It also not possible to list all traditional sayings used in this Gospel. Parallels to sayings of the Synoptic Gospels are well known and can be easily identified; see the commentaries and Dodd, *Historical Tradition,* passim. I will, therefore, try to include as much as possible of the parallels from apocryphal gospels. But see also the above discussion of the *Gospel of Thomas* (# 2.2.5), the *Dialogue of the Savior* (# 3.1.1), and the *Apocryphon of James* (# 3.1.2).

attests.[1] The original form of the saying is better preserved in Justin than in John. The term "to be reborn" (ἀναγεννηθῆναι) belongs to baptismal language,[2] while John changes this to γεννηθῆναι ἄνωθεν, which can be understood as either "to be born again" or "to be born from above," in order to create the misunderstanding of Nicodemus (3:4) that provides the occasion for a dialogical exploration of the saying in the following verses. The second change introduced by John appears in the second part of the saying: he says "you cannot see" instead of "you cannot enter," because "to see" must be understood as equivalent to "to experience";[3] it points to present participation rather than to a future eschatological event. That John is quite aware of the baptismal setting of the saying becomes clear in 3:5 ("from water and spirit").[4] It is baptism that is explained in the following verses as being born "by the spirit," that is, "from above" (3:6–8). A traditional theological maxim, also attested by Ignatius and perhaps deriving from a liturgical context, is used to illustrate the contrast between spirit and flesh:

John 3:6, 8	Ign. *Phld.* 7.1
What is born by the flesh is flesh and what is born by the spirit is spirit. . . . the wind/spirit (πνεῦμα) blows where it wills . . . but you do not know whence it comes and where it goes.	If some want me to err according to the flesh, but the spirit does not err because it is from God, because it knows whence it comes and where it goes.

Nicodemus's repetition of the question (3:9) is answered by a communal confessional statement, quite unexpectedly given in the first-person plural by Jesus (3:11):

Truly, truly, I say to you, We speak what we know and we give witness to what we have seen.

The style is similar to the introduction of 1 John ("What we have seen

---

[1] Dependence of Justin upon the Gospel of John cannot be assumed neither here nor in any other instance. There are no quotations of narrative materials from the Fourth Gospel in Justin Martyr, and typically Johannine formulations of sayings never appear; cf. Arthur Bellinzoni, *The Sayings of Jesus in the Writings of Justin Martyr* (NovT.Sup 17; Leiden: Brill, 1967) 134–38. See also below # 5.2.

[2] Cf. such passages as 1 Pet 1:3, 23.

[3] Cf. Bultmann, *Gospel of John*, 135, n.2.

[4] ὕδατος καί should not be eliminated as a later gloss, *pace* Bultmann. The manuscript evidence for the deletion consists of only a few vulgate manuscripts; a conjecture is not justified.

and what we have heard, we also proclaim to you . . ." 1:3).[1] Traditional material is also evident in the verses that follow. These include:
a reference to the descent and ascent of the revealer (3:13); an
interpretation of Nu 21:8–9 (Moses raising the snake in the wilderness, John 3:14a) which is interpreted as an oblique reference to the
crucifixion ("so the Son of man must be raised up," that is, on the cross,
3:14b); and a theological sentence about God giving his Son which is
added (3:16)[2] and interpreted.

The discourse in John 5:19–47—possibly continued in John 7—
reveals not only the use of isolated sayings and maxims, but of a
source which presented a small dialogue of Jesus with his opponents
that the author subsequently expanded into a major discourse. If the
assessment of the relationship of *Pap. Egerton 2* to the Gospel of John
given above[3] is correct, the discussion about the scriptures and Moses
in John 5:39–40 and 45–47 are drawn from a written source. That
John interrupted this source—which spoke about the witness given by
the scriptures and by Moses—with a discussion about "taking
honor/glory" (δόξα, 5:41–44), can be explained on the basis of the
author's understanding of the parallelism between "witness" and
"honor." For the evangelist, these are parallel concepts: Jesus does
not bear witness to himself (5:31), and he does not seek his own glory
(7:18).[4] While the source for this dialogue, represented by *Pap. Egerton 2*, wants to affirm Jesus' claim to be the legitimate heir of Moses,
John's elaboration of this source discusses the paradox that the claim
of the revelation can be demonstrated neither by external testimony
nor by the performance of glorious deeds by the messenger (such a
messenger would be the one who comes "in his own name," 5:43).

The continuation of this discourse in John 7 employs several sayings. John 7:33–34 utilizes traditional statements about the revealer
leaving the world again, which appear also in other contexts of the
Gospel of John:

> John 7:33–34: Still a short time I shall be with you, and I am going to
> the one who sent me. You will seek me and not find me, and where I am
> you cannot come.

> John 8:21–22: I am going away and you will seek me, . . . Where I go you
> cannot come.

---

[1] See also *Dial. Sav.* 12 (126,15–17): "It is the one who speaks who also listens, and
it is the one can see who also reveals." For the first person plural, cf. John 1:14.
[2] Rom 5:8.
[3] See above # 3.2.2.
[4] Cf. Bultmann, *Gospel of John*, 262–63.

John 13:33: Only a short time I shall be with you; you will seek me, and as I said to the Jews so I am saying now to you, "where I am going you cannot come."

Gos. Thom. 38: There will be days when you look for me and not find me.

Apocr. Jas. 2,23–27: "Have you departed and removed yourself from us?" But Jesus said. "No, but I shall go to the place whence I came. If you wish to come with me, come!"

Another saying appearing in this context has already been used before in the story of the encounter of Jesus with the Samaritan woman:

John 4:14: He who drinks from the water I give him, will never thirst into eternity. But the water that I will give him will become in him a spring of bubbling water for eternal life.

John 7:37–38: If anyone thirst, let him come to me and let the one who believes in me drink. As the Scripture has said,[1] from within him shall flow streams of living water.

John 8:12–59 occupies a special position with respect to the use of sayings and the development of dialogues. Traditionally, this unit has been viewed as completely disjointed.[2] But if one considers the relationship of traditional sayings to dialogue that evolves in the process of their interpretation, John 8 may represent a stage in this development that is more original than the well-organized dialogues and discourses in other sections of the Gospel. It is instructive to consider one portion of John 8—verses 12–36—in order to observe the relationship between sayings, sources, or references to scripture on the one hand, and the development of the dialogue, on the other (the secondary dialogue portions are given in italics):

Saying or Source	John 8
"There is light within a man of light, and he lights up the whole world. If	12: "I am the light of the world. He who follows after me will not walk in

---

[1] For this debated reference to Scripture see Bultmann, *Gospel of John,* 303–4, n. 5.

[2] Bultmann (*Gospel of John,* passim) split this section into several smaller units and assigned them to contexts as follows: 7:19–24; *8:13–20;* 7:1–14; 7:25–29; *8:48–50; 8:54–55;* 7:37–44; 7:31–36; 7:45–52; *8:41–47; 8:51–53; 8:56–59;* 9:1–41; *8:12;* 12:44–50; *8:21–29;* 12:34–36; 10:40–12:32; *8:30–40;* 6:60–71. R. E. Brown (*Gospel of John,* 1. 342) says: "An analysis of the structure of ch. viii (12ff.) is perhaps more difficult than that of any other chapter or discourse in the first part of the Gospel."

he does not shine, he is darkness."
(*Gos. Thom.* 24).[1]

"Blessed are the solitary and elect for
you will find the kingdom. For you
are from it and to it you will return."
(*Gos. Thom.* 49)[2]

"Only on the evidence of two
witnesses, or three witnesses, shall a
charge be sustained." (Deut. 19:15b)

"No one knows the Son except the
Father, and no one knows the Father
except the Son and anyone to whom
the Son chooses to reveal him."
(Q/Luke 10:22)[3]
And the rulers laid their hands on
him that they might arrest him and
deliver him to the crowds; but they
were not able to arrest him, because
the hour of his being handed over had
not yet come. (*Pap. Eg. 2*)
"Have you departed and removed
yourself from us?" But Jesus said,
"No, but I shall go to the place
whence I came. If you wish to come,
come with me." (*Apocr. Jas.* 2,23–27)

the darkness, but will have the light
of life."
13: *The Pharisees then said to him,
"You are bearing witness to yourself,
your testimony is not true."*
14: *Jesus answered, "Even if I bear
witness to myself, my testimony is
true,*
because I know whence I came and
where I am going. But you do not
know whence I come and whither I
am going.
15: *You judge according to the flesh, I
judge no one. . . .*
17: *In your law it is written* that the
testimony of two men is true.
18: *I bear witness to myself, and the
Father who sent me bears witness to
me."*
19: *They said to him, therefore,
"Where is your Father?" Jesus
answered,* "You do not know me or
the Father; if you knew me, you
would also know the Father."[4]
20: *These words he spoke in the
treasury, as he taught in the temple,*
but no one arrested him, because his
hour had not yet come.

21: *Again he said to them,* "I am
going away and you will seek me, *and
die in your sin;* where I am going you
cannot come."[5]

---

[1] There are numerous other attestations of this saying; cf. *Dial. Sav.* 127,1–6; John
11:9–10; 12:35–36.
[2] See also *Gos. Thom.* 50: "If they say to you, "Where did you come from?" say to
them, "We came from the light . . .""
[3] See also *Gos. Thom.* 69; *Dial. Sav.* 134,14–15.
[4] This saying is quoted a number of times in the Gospel of John; cf. especially John
14:7–10.
[5] The same saying is used in John 7:34, 36 and 13:33.

"There will be days when you will look for me and not find me." (*Gos. Thom.* 38).

22: *Then said the Jews, "Will he kill himself, since he says, 'Where I am going you cannot come?'"* 23: *He said to them, "You are from below, I am from above; you are of this world, I am not of this world.* 24: *I told you that you would die in your sins, for you will die in your sins unless you believe that I am he."*

His disciples said to him, "Who are you that you should say these things to us?" [Jesus said to them,] "You do not realize who I am from what I say to you, but you are like the Jews, . . ." (*Gos. Thom.* 43).

25: They said to him, "Who are you?" Jesus said to them, "First of all, what I say to you.[1] 26: *I have many things to say and to judge about you. But he who sent me is true, and I declare to the world what I have heard from him." They did not understand that he spoke to them of the Father.* 28: *So Jesus said, "When you have lifted up the Son of man, then you will know that I am he. . . ." As he spoke thus, many believed in him.

"If you become my disciples and listen to my words, these stones will minister to you. There are five trees in paradise . . . Whoever becomes acquainted with them, will not experience death." (*Gos. Thom.* 19) [A Stoic maxim][2]

31: *Jesus then said to the Jews who had believed in him,* "If you remain in my words, you will truly be my disciples, and you will know the truth,

and the truth will make you free." 33: *They answered him, "We are descendents of Abraham and have never been in bondage to anyone. How is it that you say, 'You will be made free'?"*

---

[1] This sentence, τὴν ἀρχὴν ὅ τι καὶ λαλῶ ὑμῖν, presents notorious difficulties for the translator (see R. E. Brown, *Gospel of John*, note on 8:25). It is the first part of a two-fold answer (τὴν ἀρχήν = "first of all"); the first answer is the same as in the saying *Gos. Thom.* 43: whatever Jesus says represents his identity. The second answer follows in John 8:28: "When you have lifted up the Son of man, then you will know that I am he." See also below on the christology expressed in the "I am" formula.

[2] For the argument that the sentence, "The truth will make you free," is a Stoic sentence see C. H. Dodd, *Historical Tradition*, 380, cf. 330.

"Therefore no one who sins is free."
(Epictetus, *Diss.* 4.1.3)[1]

[a traditional legal or parabolic
saying][3]

34: *Jesus answered them, "Truly
truly, I say to you,* Everyone who
commits sin is a slave.[2]
The slave does not continue in the
house forever; the son continues
forever. 36: *So if the Son makes you
free, you will be free indeed."*

Many of the sayings used in this dialogue have parallels in the *Gospel
of Thomas.* These are all sayings which speak about the presence of
light and knowledge in the human beings who are saved: they have the
light in themselves, and they know that they have come from the kingdom and will return to it. Thus these sayings reveal a typically Gnostic understanding of salvation. It is characteristic for the composition
of the Johannine discourses that such claims as "having the light" or
"having come from above" are exclusively made by Jesus.

The Gnosticizing understanding of salvation that is presented by
the pre-Johannine interpretation of the sayings is refuted by the
author of the Gospel by lodging the claim to divine descent with Jesus
alone. The "I am" formula, so typical of John's Gospel, serves primarily this purpose. At the very beginning of the dialogue (in John
8:12), a traditional saying has been reformulated in this way: "I am the
light of the world." Here as elsewhere, the "I am" formulae are anti-
Gnostic devices, and they must be seen as products of the author of the
Gospel. In fact, the special type of "I am" formulae employed here[4] are
not often found in Gnostic literature.[5] They are an important
ingredient of John's anti-Gnostic christology because they assert that
it is only through belief in Jesus who is the life that salvation can be
gained, not through the discovery of light in oneself.

[1] C. H. Dodd, ibid.; Bultmann, *Gospel of John,* 438.

[2] Most manuscripts (except D b sy[s]) read "to sin" (τῆς ἁμαρτίας) after "a slave." But
it is certainly a later addition; see Bultmann, *Gospel of John,* 438.

[3] C. H. Dodd, *Historical Tradition,* 379–82; Bultmann, *Gospel of John,* 440.

[4] This does not deny the fact that "I am" statements are frequent in various contexts
of Hellenistic-Roman religion. Bultmann (*Gospel of John,* 225, n. 3) has analyzed the
several forms of the "I am" formula. He distinguishes four types: (1) the presentation
formula answering to the question "who are you?" (2) the qualificatory formula answering to "what are you?" (3) the identification formula in which someone identifies
him/herself with a special god or power, e.g., in magic; (4) the recognition formula
which answers the question "who is the one whom we expect?" Most of the Johannine
formulae belong to this latter group. With "I am" Jesus answers the question "who is
the bread of life, the light of the world, etc.?"

[5] The formula is rare, e.g., in the *Gospel of Thomas,* cf. # 77: "I am the light that is
above the All." However, this represents the identification formula (see the preceding
note), not the typically Johannine recognition formula. See further on the "I am" formula, R. E. Brown, *Gospel of John,* 1. 535–38.

Another use of the "I am" formula in John is closely connected with this anti-Gnostic christology. In John 8:28 Jesus says, "When you have lifted up (ὅταν ὑψώσητε) the Son of man, then you will know that I am he (ὅτι ἐγώ εἰμι)." The "lifting up" is a reference to Jesus' crucifixion.[1] This is underlined in Jesus' threefold answer "I am he" (ἐγώ εἰμι) to the the guard who comes to arrest him, who says that they are seeking Jesus of Nazareth (John 18:5, 6, 8). As John binds salvation closely to belief in Jesus, he binds this belief to Jesus as the one who is to be glorified as he is lifted up on the cross.

The farewell discourses of the Gospel of John are also largely developed on the basis of such sayings. In particular the saying about seeking and finding, and its interpretation, has played a dominant role here. This saying is, of course, well known in the tradition of sayings, in which it occurs in numerous variations.[2] It is frequently used as a challenge to seek and find life and salvation.[3] The author of the Fourth Gospel has introduced the topic of seeking early in his writing, and it occurs again at the very end. The first encounter of Jesus with another person begins with Jesus' question to two disciples of the Baptist who are following him, "What do you *seek*?" (1:38). Then Andrew comes to his brother Simon and says, "We have *found* the Messiah" (1:41). And when Philip tells Nathaniel about Jesus, he says, "We have *found* him of whom Moses and the law and also the prophets wrote" (1:45). As the encounters with Jesus begin with this question, so at the end of the Gospel, when Judas arrives with the soldiers, Jesus asks three times, "Whom do you *seek*?" And after the discovery of the empty tomb, Mary Magdalene meets Jesus and Jesus says to her, "Woman, why are you weeping? Whom do you *seek*?" (20:15).

It is evident that, for the Gospel of John, seeking Jesus—not seeking for the meaning of his words—is the central theme. For both the crowds and for the disciples, the mystery of the seeking after Jesus is captured in the statement of John 7:34 and 36:

You will seek me and not find me, and where I am you cannot come.

In John 13:33, the disciples are confronted with the same mystery:

Yet a little while I am with you. You will seek me, and as I said to the Jews so I am saying now to you, "Where I am going, you cannot come."

---

[1] See John 3:14; 8:58.
[2] Q/Luke 11:9–10 ("Ask and it will be given to you; seek and you will find; knock and it will be opened to you") is the most familiar form, and is traditionally understood as an encouragement to prayer. Cf. *Gos. Thom.* 92 and 94.
[3] See *Gos. Thom.* 1 and 2.

As far as the hostile crowds are concerned, their inability to find Jesus could simply be explained as the result of their unbelief. However, for the disciples too, the question of being with Jesus after his departure, and reaching the place to which he is going, is central for continuing belief in him. The farewell discourses of the Gospel of John are concerned with this question, because a Gnostic answer was already at hand: those who are prepared spiritually can follow the redeemer to the heavenly realms.

The farewell discourses of the Gospel of John reject this Gnostic solution explicitly. Like the parallel dialogues in the *Apocryphon of James* (1,22–33) and the *Dialogue of the Savior* (## 25–30, p. 132,5–19),[1] John 14 begins with Jesus' statement of a place to which he is going:

> "In my father's house are many rooms. If it were not so, would I have told you that I go to prepare a place for you? . . . And you know the way where I am going." Thomas said to him, "Lord, we do not know where you are going. How can we know the way?" Jesus said to him, "I am the way and the truth and the life; no one comes to the Father but by me." (John 14:2–6)

This pronouncement of Jesus sounds like a direct refutation of the statement in the *Apocryphon of James,* "No one will enter the kingdom of heaven at my bidding" (2,29–34). In John 14, the believers are fully dependent upon Jesus in their quest for the way to the kingdom. As in the *Dialogue of the Savior,* the request for a visionary experience as an alternative is rejected in John 14:

> Philip said, "Lord, show us the Father and we shall be satisfied." Jesus said to him, "Have I been with you so long, and yet you do not know me, Philip? He who has seen me has seen the Father . . . I am in the Father and the Father in me." (John 14:8–9)

However, in contrast to the *Dialogue of the Savior,* John 14 does not reject the vision in order to request the finding of the true knowledge of oneself in self-recognition; rather, John points to Jesus as the presence of the Father. Thus faith in Jesus is identical with the finding of eternal life. However, the works done by those who have found life in Jesus are not the works of their own goodness, but the works of Jesus:

---

[1] See above, ## 3.1.1 and 3.1.2.

> Truly, truly, I say to you, he who believes in me will also do the works
> that I do, and greater works than these he will do, because I go to the
> Father. (John 14:12)

Once more the theme of seeking and asking is resumed in the following statement of Jesus:

> Whatever you ask in my name, I will do. (John 14:14)

The disciples are still the ones who seek and who ask. But the
emphasis is no longer on the *receiving* of what they ask for, but on
Jesus' *doing* on their behalf what they have asked for.

These sentences of the Johannine farewell discourses are formulated in a direct controversy with the alternatives set forth in the
Gnostic interpretation of the same sayings. John wants to show that
there can be no answer except one: faith in Jesus. In Gnostic
discourse, the disciples will go away to find their true home in the
divine world. In John (14:18–24), Jesus will come again to the disciples; he and the Father will make their home in those who love him.
Thus the emphasis is no longer on Jesus' coming and returning to the
Father, but on Jesus' going to the Father and once more returning to
the disciples who are not taken out of the world, but remain in the
world. The Gnostic order of the descent/ascent pattern is reversed.
Jesus will return and be with the disciples forever as the Paraclete,
the Spirit of Truth, who will remind them of everything that Jesus has
said.

The theme of seeking and finding appears once more at this point.
In the *Dialogue of the Savior* (# 20; p. 129,14–15) the following variant
of this saying occurs:

> Let him who [knows] seek and find and [rejoice].

The *Apocryphon of James* (10,22–11,1) also uses this saying in a
discourse that parallels very closely themes of the Johannine farewell
discourses:

> Behold I shall depart from you and go away and do not wish to remain
> with you any longer, just as you yourselves have not wished it. Now
> therefore follow me quickly. This is why I say unto you, "for your sakes I
> came down." ... Invoke the Father and implore God often, and he will
> give to you. Blessed is he who has seen you with him, when he was pro-
> claimed among the angels and glorified among the saints; yours is life.
> Rejoice and be glad as sons of God. Keep his will that you may be saved
> ... I intercede on your behalf with the Father.

One may be tempted to view this passage as a Gnostic commentary upon John 16. However, Ron Cameron[1] has demonstrated that it is very unlikely that the discourses of this writing were based upon John's Gospel. One must assume that both writings are dependent upon a common source in which sayings of Jesus were interpreted according to Gnostic hermeneutical principles: Jesus came down for the disciples' sake; at his return the disciples are asked to follow him; they are requested to ask the Father and have the assurance that Jesus will intercede in their behalf; a reference to the vision of God as the source of life follows, to which the disciples respond rejoicing.

The author of the Fourth Gospel has reinterpreted this source once more in a reversal of the Gnostic pattern. The disciples will rejoice at the return of Jesus; the disciples will pray to the Father, but Jesus will no longer intercede with the Father on their behalf:

> Hitherto you have asked nothing in my name; ask and you will receive, that your joy may be full . . . On that day you will ask in my name, and I do not say that I shall pray to the Father for you, because the Father himself loves you, because you have loved me and have believed that I came from the Father. (16:24–27)

It is no longer the religious experience of the vision of God which gives the assurance of salvation. Rather, the love of the Father and the love of Jesus and the disciples' loving each other describe the realm in which the salvation is present.

3.4.5 THE COMPOSITION

Seen as a whole, the Gospel of John is a complex literary composition employing a variety of sources and materials which themselves are already the product of a still continuing history of interpretation. It is also possible that the Fourth Gospel was written in several stages, as its sources were continuously reinterpreted during their use in the Johannine community. While an early draft of the Gospel may have come into existence soon after the middle of the 1st century, it was probably not composed in its present form until the very end of the century, and later redactional comments were added even during the 2d century, perhaps in the context of the production of the Johannine Epistles, especially 1 John.[2]

---

[1] *Apocryphon of James,* see especially pp. 116–120. See the discussion above, # 3.1.2.

[2] Raymond E. Brown, *The Community of the Beloved Disciple* (New York: Paulist Press, 1979) 93–144.

Nevertheless, the Gospel of John is not a random composition or haphazard compilation of various materials and sources. Several of its chapters are masterfully composed literary pieces. The two most striking examples are perhaps chapters 9 and 11.

John 9:1–41 begins with the reproduction of the miracle story which the author derived from the Semeia Source (9:1–7). But the usual final feature of the miracle story, the acclamation of the bystanders, has been deleted, or better, replaced by a series of encounters. These are described in a sequence of scenes with different actors: the blind man, the crowd, the parents, the Pharisees, and finally Jesus himself. Each scene discusses two questions: how is it possible that the formerly blind man can see? and, who is the one who healed him? In these encounters, the faith of the man who was blind grows into ever more certain recognition of Jesus:

Scene 1 (9:8–12)
   The neighbors,
   the man who was blind.

Are you the man who was blind?
   "I am he."
Who healed you?
   "I do not know."

Scene 2 (9:13–18)
   The Pharisees,
   the man who was blind.

How could someone who heals on the Sabbath come from God?
What do you say about him?
   "He is a prophet."

Scene 3 (9:19–23)
   The Pharisees,
   the parents.

Is this your son who was born blind?
   "Yes."
How does he see now?
   "We do not know."

Scene 4 (9:24–34)
   The Pharisees,
   the man who was blind.

Accusation: you are his disciple.
But we know that God spoke to Moses.
The man who was blind:
   "Jesus must come from God"
Pharisees: You are a sinner,
   because you were born blind.

Scene 5 (9:35–38)
   Jesus,
   the man who was blind.

Do you believe in the Son of man?
You have seen him.
The man who was blind:
   "I believe, Lord."

Scene 6 (9:39–41)	Pharisees: Are we also blind?
Jesus,	Jesus:
the Pharisees.	Because you say that you see, your sin remains.

John 10:40–11:54 is also developed on the basis of a traditional miracle story from the Semeia Source. In this case, the miracle story has been utilized to provide the external frame for the entire unit, while the discourses have been set in between the various segments of the traditional story. The arrangement of the sections is symmetric so that the subsections correspond to each other:

Location: Jesus is away on the other side of the Jordan (10:40–42).
  Miracle story: the encounter, through messengers (11:1–7).
  Jesus loved Martha and her sister and Lazarus (11:4–7).
  Miracle story: Jesus and the disciples on the way to Bethany (11:7–16).
    First discussion with disciples (11:8–10):
    Jesus' time is limited, because he must die.
    Second discussion with disciples (11:11–16):
    Disciples may have to face death also.
  Miracle story: arrival in Bethany (11:17–19).
    Encounter with Martha who confesses her faith (11:20–27).
    (begins with, "Lord, had you been here, my brother would not have died").
    Encounter with Mary who weeps (11:28–32).
    (ends with, "Lord, had you been here, my brother would not have died").
  Miracle story: Jesus raises Lazarus (11:33–44).
  Jesus weeps: How he did love Lazarus! (11:34–35)
  Miracle story: reaction of the crowd (11:45–53);
    results in the decision to put Jesus to death.
Location: Jesus goes away near the desert (11:54).

The Gospel of John as a whole is composed very carefully in such a way that the several sections reveal a strict correspondence to each other. The Gospel is framed by a tripartite introduction, consisting of the prologue, the preaching of John the Baptist, and the call of the disciples (1:1–51), and a three-part conclusion presenting three appearances of the risen Lord to Mary Magdalene, the disciples, and the disciples with Thomas (20:1–31). In this framework two main sections are clearly delineated: the public activity of Jesus (2:1–11:54) and the passion narrative which, in turn, frames the farewell discourses (11:55–19:42). The link between the two sections is provided by the story of the raising of Lazarus, which triggers the decision to put Jesus to death.

It is difficult, however, to construct a rationale for the arrangement of the materials within each of these two parts of the Gospel. In the first part, the author follows the sequence of the Semieia Source; but the dialogues and discourses are connected with the stories from this source in very different ways, and sometimes (chapters 7, 8, 10) not at all, while one miracle story from the source of signs (the healing of the official's son, 4:46–54) stands without an accompanying dialogue. In the second part, the author follows the sequence of events in his source for the passion narrative; but it is extremely difficult to find a principle of organization for the farewell discourses which have been inserted into this source (chapters 13–17).

Internal links between the two main parts are provided in several ways. There are pointers to the eventual raising up, or glorification, of Jesus on the cross in the first part of the Gospel;[1] a number of traditional sayings used in the dialogues of the first part reappear in the farewell discourses;[2] and the Gospel reports in its first part several unsuccessful attempts to arrest Jesus,[3] while the hour for the glorification is determined by Jesus' own decision that it is "now" (John 12:31–32).

These links between the two parts of the Gospel of John are crucial for the successful accomplishment of the impossible task that the author has set for himself: to write a biography of "Wisdom Incarnate." Jesus is the Logos, like heavenly Wisdom the mediator of creation, divine, uncreated. In traditional wisdom theology, her presence in the world remains hidden. It is present in the life of those who follow her whose true identity the world does not know. But the Gospel of John does not depict the hidden presence of Wisdom in her followers, like the Wisdom of Solomon. The author tells the story of the life of Wisdom herself, of the Logos himself, in the form of a biography of Jesus, the Wisdom/Logos incarnate. This biography, therefore, becomes a paradox. Jesus is a human being from Nazareth, and everybody knows that he comes from Galilee (7:27, 41–42), and he says, "The bread from heaven, the light of the world—it is I." Like a divine human being, the man from Nazareth does many miracles and rejects the belief which responds to these miracles, and is condemned to death because too many people believe in his miracles. Like Wisdom herself, Jesus has come from the Father and is returning to the Father, but neither the Jews nor the disciples will follow;[4] they remain in the

[1] E.g., John 3:14–15; 8:28.

[2] See especially the saying about Jesus going away to a place where the Jews cannot follow him (7:33–35; 8:21–22) which is repeated in 13:33.

[3] 7:30, 32, 44–45; 8:20, 59; 10:31, 39.

[4] Whoever added chap. 17 to the Gospel of John knew that this paradox required an answer, telling the disciples that they would certainly follow later. However, this answer is Gnostic.

world in which they will experience tribulations because the heavenly messenger who called them is a human being who dies on the cross which the disciples are requested to understand as the "overcoming of the world" (16:33).

The author of the Fourth Gospel knows quite well that the myth of Wisdom is always docetic, because she is never really human. Accordingly, her followers' ultimate identity is not human but divine. John's "the Word became flesh" (1:14) is pointedly anti-docetic. Biography is the vehicle of this polemical thesis, because heavenly Wisdom cannot have a true biography, though her being on earth, hidden and rejected, can be imitated by those who recognize that they themselves are a hidden divine presence on earth. Jesus' biography, as presented in the Gospel of John, cannot be imitated in the story of the life of the disciples. But the Paraclete, the Spirit of Truth, in whom Jesus returns, will remind the disciples of the new commandment that he gave to them, namely, to love each other (13:34–35). By this love they are not imitating the life of the human being Jesus, but they are imitating God who so loved the world that he gave his Son (3:16). This anti-docetic paradox is the principle of composition for the Fourth Gospel.

4

The Synoptic Gospels

4.1 The Story of the Gospel of Mark[1]

4.1.1 TRANSMISSION AND ATTESTATION

Although a rather early date must be assigned to the Gospel of Mark, its earliest attestation in extant manuscripts is markedly poorer than the attestation for Matthew and Luke—not to speak of the early appearance of the Gospel of John in papyrus finds from Egypt. Mark's Gospel appears for the first time in the oldest extant manuscript containing all four canonical gospels ($\mathfrak{p}^{45}$) which was written in the middle of the 3d century CE. No other manuscript evidence for Mark exists before the 4th century, where Mark is included in the oldest uncial manuscript of the entire Greek Bible (ℵ and B), in one papyrus ($\mathfrak{p}^{88}$), and in two uncial fragments (059, 0188). About twenty-five more fragments from uncial manuscripts, written between the 5th and 10th centuries present texts from Mark's Gospel. Many of these may be fragments from manuscripts containing all four canonical gospels.[2]

There are also no certain quotations from the Gospel of Mark before Clement of Alexandria and Irenaeus (last two decades of the 2d century). The only earlier passage that possibly points to a passage from

---

[1] A general review of scholarship on Mark has been presented by Petr Pokorny, "Das Markus-Evangelium: Literarische und theologische Einleitung mit Forschungsbericht," *ANRW* 2.25/3 (1985) 1969–2035; see also Gottfried Rau, "Das Markusevangelium: Komposition und Intention der ersten Darstellung christlicher Mission," *ANRW* 2.25/3 (1985) 2036–2257. A collection of representative essays was published by Rudolf Pesch, *Das Markusevangelium* (WdF 411; Darmstadt: Wissenschaftliche Buchgesellschaft, 1979). The most controversial recent monograph on Mark is Burton L. Mack, *A Myth of Innocence: Mark and Christian Origins* (Philadelphia: Fortress, 1988).

[2] On the text of Mark in the new edition (26th) of Nestle-Aland, *NT Graece*, see Frans Neirynck, "The Nestle Aland: The Text of Mark in N 26," in idem, *Evangelica*, 899–924.

the Gospel of Mark is found in the writings of Justin Martyr, *Dial.*
106.2–3:

> ... and when it says that he (Christ) had given the name Peter to one of
> his apostles, and when it is also written in his Memoirs that it happened
> (καὶ γεγράφθαι ἐν τοῖς ἀπομνημονεύμασιν αὐτοῦ γεγενημένον καὶ τοῦτο) after
> he had given to two other apostles, the sons of Zebedee, the name Boan-
> erges, that is Sons of Thunder.

"His Memoirs" in this text must mean "Peter's Memoirs" (not "Christ's
Memoirs"). This can only be a reference to the Gospel of Mark which
was connected with Peter in the presbyter tradition that is also quoted
by Papias of Hierapolis and by Clement of Alexandria.[1] Moreover, the
remark that follows in *Dial.* 106.3 about the sons of Zebedee demonstrates a knowledge of the text of Mark 3:17, the only passage in the
New Testament where the designation "Boanerges" of the sons of
Zebedee appears. Otherwise, there is no instance in Justin's writings
where the use of Mark can be ascertained.

But there is a noteworthy reference to this Gospel with an explicit
mention of its author in the fragments of the writings of bishop Papias
of Hierapolis (before the middle of the 2d century) which are preserved
by Eusebius (*Hist. eccl.* 3.39.15). It is reported by Papias as a statement of one of the "presbyters" (καὶ αὐτὸ ὁ πρεσβύτερος ἔλεγεν):

> Mark became the interpreter of Peter and wrote down accurately all that
> he remembered of the things said and done by the Lord (ὅσα ἐμνημόνευ-
> σεν ... τὰ ὑπὸ τοῦ κυρίου ἢ λεχθέντα ἢ πραχθέντα), not indeed in the (right)
> order, because he had not heard the Lord nor had he followed him, but
> later on, as I said, he had followed Peter who used to give his teachings
> as demanded by necessity, not, however, in order to make a composition
> of the words of the Lord (τῶν κυριακῶν λόγων). Thus Mark did nothing
> wrong in writing down individual pieces just as he remembered them.
> For only to one thing he gave his attention, to leave out nothing of what
> he had heard and to make no false statements in them.[2]

Thus, Mark's Gospel was known by the name of its author no later
than the middle of the 2d century. This is noteworthy when one considers Justin Martyr, who makes extensive use of the Gospels of

---

[1] See below on Papias and Mark and on Clement's reference to the *Secret Gospel of
Mark*. See alo the following note.

[2] This presbyter tradition is repeated in a slightly different form by Irenaeus (*Adv.
haer.* 3.1.1 = Eusebius *Hist. eccl.* 5.8.2–4) and by Clement of Alexandria *Hypotyposeis*
(in Eusebius *Hist. eccl.* 6.14.5–7). However, the letter of Clement of Alexandria which
preserves quotations from the *Secret Gospel of Mark* (see below # 4.1.5) makes a different statement about the composition of Mark, though it also connects Mark with
Peter.

Matthew and Luke without ever mentioning their assumed authors by name. That the Gospel of Mark was not quoted, referred to, or copied more frequently may be due to the fact that it was overshadowed by the other two Synoptic Gospels, Matthew and Luke, who had incorporated most of the Markan materials into their own more comprehensive compositions.

4.1.2 THE INTEGRITY OF THE TEXT

Neither Justin's nor Papias's references to the Gospel of Mark allow a judgment about the integrity of the text of this writing. There are, however, two earlier witnesses to the text of Mark: according to the two-source hypothesis[1] both Matthew and Luke, written just before or shortly after the year 100 CE, have used Mark's Gospel and have copied large portions of its text, albeit with numerous editorial alterations. A comparison of Mark's extant manuscript text with the Markan portions of Matthew and Luke raises an intriguing and difficult problem: has the text of the Gospel of Mark which Matthew and Luke used survived intact in the tradition of the manuscripts, or was the original version actually lost just as was the other major source of these two gospels, the Synoptic Sayings Source? Most important is the observation that Matthew and Luke agree in a number of instances in their reproduction of Markan passages, while differing from the extant texts of Markan manuscripts. Only a few examples can be mentioned here.[2] It is hardly possible to argue that all these minor agreements can be explained by the assumption that Matthew and Luke used a Markan text that differed from the one preserved in the canonical manuscript tradition. A large number of the minor agreements are due to common stylistic and grammatical corrections of the sometimes awkward Markan text or are caused by accidental common omissions.[3] There is also the possibility that later scribes altered the text of Luke under the influence of the better-known text of Matthew, thus creating secondary agreements of Matthew and Luke against Mark.[4] In this context I am rather concerned with those instances of agreements in which a recognizable editorial purpose could be the reason for a later

[1] See the discussion above in # 2.3.2.

[2] A complete list of the relevant texts of Matthew, Mark, and Luke demonstrating these agreements of the two later Gospels against their source has been published in Neirynck, *Minor Agreements,* 55–195.

[3] Neirynck (ibid., 199–288) presents a thorough classification of these agreement of Matthew and Luke against Mark.

[4] This possibility is repeatedly discussed by Francois Bovon, *Das Evangelium nach Lukas. 1. Teilband: Lk 1,1–9,50* (EKK 3/1; Zürich: Benziger Verlag, and Neukirchen: Neukirchener Verlag, 1989).

change of the Markan original text, that is, of the text that Matthew
and Luke knew.[1]

4.1.2.1 "Common Omissions" of Passages from Mark

The apophthegma about plucking grain on the Sabbath, Mark
2:23–28, concludes with two sayings of Jesus, Mark 2:27, "The Sabbath was made for people, and not the people for the Sabbath," and
2:28, "The Son of man (or: every human being = ὁ υἱὸς τοῦ ἀνθρώπου) is
master over the Sabbath." Matthew and Luke reproduce only the
second of these two sayings. It is usually argued that the first saying,
"The Sabbath was made for people . . .," was too bold for the later
understanding of the church and thus deleted by Matthew and Luke,
although it was the more original saying of Jesus.[2] However, criticism
of the Sabbath observation was pervasive at that time, as is shown by
passages like Col 2:16; Ign. *Mg.* 9.1; *Barn.* 15. Thus it is more likely
that the original text of Mark was later expanded by the addition of
this saying. Only the saying preserved in Matthew and Luke belonged
to the original text of Mark.

The parable of the Seed Growing Secretly, Mark 4:26–29, is not
reproduced by either Matthew or Luke. If Matthew found the parable
in his copy of Mark, one must resort to the explanation that he
replaced it with the parable of the Tares (Matt 13:24–30). However,
the multiple additions to the Markan parable chapter in Matthew 13
show that Matthew was eager to expand this chapter.[3] Since Luke
also does not reproduce this parable in his version of the parable
chapter (Luke 8:4–18) nor anywhere else in his Gospel, it is more
likely that the original text of Mark did not include it.[4]

The story of the encounter of Jesus with the rich man, Mark
10:17–31, is reproduced quite faithfully and often verbatim by
Matthew (20:16–30) and Luke (18:18–30). But Mark's canonical text
includes two passages which are missing in the other two Synoptic
Gospels and appear to be secondary expansions of a more original
Markan text that Matthew and Luke still read. Mark 10:21 introduces
Jesus' final answer to the rich man with the remark, "And Jesus
looked at him and loved him" (ὁ δὲ Ἰησοῦς ἐμβλέψας αὐτῷ ἠγάπησεν

[1] See the more detailed discussion in my essay, "From Mark to Secret Mark," 35–57.

[2] Cf. Bultmann, *Synoptic Tradition,* 16–17. Bovon (*Evangelium nach Lukas,*
267–68) recognizes that Mark 2:27 does not originally belong in this context, but
wonders whether Matthew and Luke still knew this saying from the oral tradition and
therefore omitted it in their reproduction of Mark.

[3] Cf. Matt 13:33, 44–46, 47–50, 51–52.

[4] Vielhauer (*Geschichte,* 273–75) considers this the only certain evidence for the
thesis that the original text of Mark differed from the canonical text.

αὐτόν), and Mark, after Jesus' general statement about those who have wealth (10:23), cites a repetition of Jesus' answer which is introduced by a report about the amazement of the disciples (ἐθαμβοῦντο, 10:24).[1] In the following repetition of the statement about the difficulty of entering the rule of God, the reference to wealth as an obstacle no longer appears. Not one of these Markan features of the pericope is paralleled in either Matthew or Luke.

In Mark 12:28–31 (= Matt 22:34–40 and Luke 10:25–28) the pericope about the Great Commandment is introduced by a reference to Dtn 6:4 ("Hear, O Israel . . .") and has received an appendix about "the scribe who is not far from the rule of God" (Mark 12:32–34). Neither feature has a parallel in Matthew and Luke. In a brilliant analysis, Günther Bornkamm[2] has demonstrated that this appendix is a later addition to Mark's text, written from the perspective of Hellenistic propaganda. The scribe acknowledges that Jesus "in truth" (ἐπ' ἀληθείας, 12:32) put forward first of all the confession of Hellenistic Jewish and Christian propaganda that "God is one"—thus the quote of Dtn 6:4, which appears only in Mark (12:29), is a secondary expansion. He then adds, in his repetition of the commandment to love God (Dtn 6:5), the phrase "out of your whole understanding" (ἐξ ὅλης τῆς συνέσεως, 12:33), and contrasts the love of one's neighbor with "burnt offerings and sacrifices" (a typical commonplace of Jewish and Christian propaganda). Finally, Jesus answers that the scribe has spoken "with understanding" (νουνεχῶς, Mark 12:34).

When Jesus is arrested, Mark 14:51–52 reports that a young man who is following Jesus, "wearing a linen cloth over his naked body" (περιβεβλημένος σινδόνα ἐπὶ γυμνοῦ), is grabbed by the armed men but lets go of the linen cloth and flees naked. Neither Matthew nor Luke show any trace of the report of this strange incidence in the texts of their Gospels.

One other passage which is completely missing in Luke but reproduced in Matthew, must be added here, though it is not a "common omission" in the strict sense: the request of the sons of Zebedee, Mark 10:35–39:

---

[1] This term appears in several other Markan passages without parallels in Matthew and Luke. It will be discussed further below.

[2] "Das Doppelgebot der Liebe," in: Walther Eltester, ed., *Neutestamentliche Studien für Rudolf Bultmann* (BZNW 21; Berlin: Töpelmann, 1954) 85–93.

Matt 20:22–23	Mark 10:38–40a
Jesus answered them and said,	But Jesus answered them,
"You do not know what you are asking.	"You do not know what you are asking.
Can you drink the cup that I shall drink?	Can you drink the cup which I drink;
	or can you be baptized with the baptism
	with which I am baptized?"
They said to him, "We can."	And they said to him, "We can."
He said to them, "The cup	He said to them, "The cup that I drink
you will drink.	you will drink;
	and with the baptism with which I am
	baptized you will be baptized.
But to sit at my right hand . . ."	But to sit at my right hand . . . "
ἀποκριθεὶς δὲ ὁ Ἰησοῦς εἶπεν·	ὁ δὲ Ἰησοῦς εἶπεν αὐτοῖς·
οὐκ οἴδατε τί αἰτεῖσθε.	οὐκ οἴδατε τί αἰτεῖσθε.
δύνασθε πιεῖν τὸ ποτήριον ὃ ἐγὼ μέλλω	δύνασθε πιεῖν τὸ ποτήριον ὃ ἐγὼ πίνω,
πίνειν;	ἢ τὸ βάπτισμα ὃ ἐγὼ βαπτίζομαι
	βατισθῆναι;
λέγουσιν αὐτῷ· δυνάμεθα.	οἱ δὲ εἶπαν αὐτῷ· δυνάμεθα.
λέγει αὐτοῖς·	ὁ δὲ Ἰησοῦς εἶπεν αὐτοῖς·
τὸ μὲν ποτήριόν μου πίεσθε,	τὸ ποτήριον ὃ ἐγὼ πίνω πίεσθε, καὶ τὸ
	βάπτισμα ὃ ἐγὼ βαπτίζομαι
	βαπτισθήσετε.
τὸ δὲ καθίσαι . . .	τὸ δὲ καθίσαι . . .

In Mark 10:38, Jesus answers the request of the sons of Zebedee with two questions, "can you drink the cup that I drink?" and "can you be baptized with the baptism with which I will be baptized?" After their affirmative response, Jesus confirms that they will indeed drink this cup and be baptized with this baptism (Mark 10:39). In the Matthean parallel (20:22–23) only the first of these double questions and confirmations appears. The reference here is certainly to martyrdom for which the image of drinking the chalice seems appropriate.[1] However, baptism as a metaphor for death or martyrdom reflects a later usage of language in Christian literature.[2] That the metaphor was used in this way in Mark's original text, written some time in the second half of the 1st century, is highly improbable. Matthew seems to have preserved the original text of Mark, while the expansions in the present text of Mark may have resulted from a secondary redaction,

[1] That "drinking the cup" appeared as a metaphor for the death of Jesus very early is confirmed by its occurrence in both Mark 14:36 parr. and John 18:11.

[2] Cf. Hans von Campenhausen, *Die Idee des Martyriums in der alten Kirche* (2d ed.; Göttingen: Vandenhoeck & Ruprecht, 1953) 60–61. Baptism is interpreted by Paul as a symbol for dying and rising with Christ in Rom 6:3–11; but the concept of martyrdom is not implied in such an interpretation.

most likely a homiletic reference to the Christian sacraments, eucharist (drinking the cup) and baptism.[1]

4.1.2.2 Original Wording Preserved in Matthew and Luke

The parables as mystery:

Matt 13:11	Mark 4:11	Luke 8:10
To you is given to know the mysteries of the kingdom of heaven.	To you is given the mystery of the kingdom of God.	To you is given to know the mysteries of the kingdom of God.
ὑμῖν δέδοται γνῶναι τὰ μυστήρια τῆς βασιλείας τῶν οὐρανῶν	ὑμῖν τὸ μυστήριον δέδοται τῆς βασιλείας τοῦ θεοῦ	ὑμῖν δέδοται γνῶναι τὰ μυστήρια τῆς βασιλείας τοῦ θεοῦ

According to the overwhelming majority of textual witnesses, the text of Mark 4:11, "To you is given the mystery of the rule of God," differs from the parallel passages in Matthew (13:11) and Luke (8:10), which agree in reading "to know" (γνῶναι) after "is given" (δέδοται) and the plural "mysteries" (μυστήρια) instead of the singular "mystery" (μυστήριον) of Mark 4:11. Thus Matthew and Luke agree in their formulations: "To you is given to know the mysteries of the rule of God" (Matthew: "of the heavens"). As far as the context is concerned, both Matthew and Luke drew everything surrounding this discourse of Jesus with the disciples (the parable of the Sower and its allegorical interpretation) from the Gospel of Mark, not from any different common source. It is difficult to avoid the conclusion that they preserved the original Markan text in the statement of Jesus to the disciples in Mark 4:11. Moreover, the plural "mysteries" is appropriate here: each of the parables is "a mystery," i.e., a mysterious saying or a riddle that must be explained.[2] This is the more original usage of the term,[3] while

---

[1] Morton Smith, *Clement of Alexandria and a Secret Gospel of Mark* (Cambridge, MA: Harvard University Press, 1973) 186–87.

[2] Jeremias (Parables, 13–18) has demonstrated that Mark 4:11–12 is an older saying that was originally independent. He points to the antithetical parallelism of the phrases, "to you the mystery is given" and "to those outside it comes in parables." However, Jeremias fails to explain why Mark 4:11 reads the singular "mystery" as antithesis to the plural "parables" (cf. also the plural in Mark 4:34: "to his disciples he explained all these things"). The problem is resolved if one assumes that the plural formulation in the first half of the antithesis, as it is preserved in Matt 13:11 and Luke 8:10 ("to you it is given to know the mysteries"), was also the original reading of Mark 4:11. See also the discussion above in # 2.2.4.3.

[3] As was pointed out above (# 2.2.4.3) the *Gospel of Thomas* uses the term in the plural in a saying that introduces several parables: "It is to those who are worthy of my mysteries that I give my mysteries" (# 62). Furthermore, Paul confirms the analogous

the use of the singular "mystery" as a designation of the entire preaching of Jesus or of the entire Gospel occurs only in later Christian literature.[1]

The predictions of the passion:

Matt 16:21	Mark 8:31	Luke 9:22
. . . and to be killed, and on the third day to be raised.	. . . and to be killed and to rise after three days.	. . . and to be killed, and on the third day to be raised.
. . . καὶ ἀποκτανθῆναι καὶ τῇ τρίτῃ ἡμέρᾳ ἐγερθῆναι.	. . . καὶ ἀποκτανθῆναι καὶ μετὰ τρεῖς ἡμέρας ἀναστήσεται.	. . . καὶ ἀποκτανθῆναι καὶ τῇ τρίτῃ ἡμέρᾳ ἐγερθῆναι.

Matt 16:21 and Luke 9:22 agree in their reading "and on the third day to be raised" while their common source, Mark 8:31, says: "and to *rise after* three days."[2] In his reproduction of the second and third prediction of the passion (Mark 9:31; 10:34), Matthew (17:23; 20:19) also uses the formula "and on the third day to be raised" (καὶ τῇ τρίτῃ ἡμέρᾳ ἐγερθῆναι), instead of Mark's "he will rise" (ἀναστήσεται). In these two instances, the evidence is less conclusive with respect to the original reading of Mark because a Lukan parallel to the second prediction of the passion (Mark 9:31) is missing and in the parallel to Mark 10:34, Luke (18:33) agrees with Mark's "he will rise" (ἀναστήσεται). Luke uses the formula "and he shall rise on the third day" also in 24:7, 46, though he never uses the Markan formulation "after three days." "To be raised" (ἐγερθῆναι) is more common in the oldest Christian

---

usage; when referring to an individual saying, he uses the singular (Rom 11:25; 1 Cor 15:51), otherwise the plural; cf. 1 Cor 13:2: "and if I knew all the mysteries" (see also 1 Cor 4:1; 14:2). See Günther Bornkamm, "μυστήριον," *TDNT* 4 (1967) 822–23.

[1] Typical for this later usage is the identification of "mystery" and "gospel," or the close association of the two terms; cf. Eph 6:19: "to make known the mystery of the gospel" (γνωρίσαι τὸ μυστήριον τοῦ εὐαγγελίου, see also Eph 3:1–7).

[2] Mark's "after three days" instead of "on the third day" is peculiar. It contradicts Mark's own dating of the resurrection: the empty tomb is found in the morning of the third day. Morton Smith (*Clement of Alexandria,* 163–64) points out that "after three days" actually means "on the fourth day" and that there is an interesting parallel in John 11:17 and 39, i.e., in the Johannine parallel to the story of the raising of the young man which is reported in the *Secret Gospel of Mark* : Lazarus was raised on the fourth day after his death. This will be discussed further in the treatment of the *Secret Gospel of Mark,* see below, # 4.1.5.

usage (see also 1 Cor 15:4) and is, therefore, most likely the term that appeared in Mark's original text.[1]

The story of the healing of the epileptic child, Mark 9:14–29, is the most complex miracle narrative in Mark and presents the most difficult problems for the explanation of its relationship to the parallels in Matthew (17:14–21) and Luke (9:38–43a).[2] Mark's version of the story is more than twice as long as the parallel versions in Matthew and Luke. Mark 9:14b–16, 21, 22b–24, parts of 25–27, and 28 have no parallels in either Matthew or Luke. The comparison of the three versions of the final part of the story is especially revealing:

Matt 17:18–20a	Mark 9:25–29	Luke 9:42–43
And Jesus	And when Jesus saw that a crowd came running together	And Jesus
rebuked it,	he rebuked the unclean spirit and said, "You dumb and deaf spirit, I command you, come out of him and never enter into him again."	rebuked the unclean spirit
and the demon came out of him, and the boy was healed from that hour.	And after crying aloud and shaking him much it came out. And he (the boy) became like dead, so that many said, "He died." But Jesus grasped his hand and raised him up, and he rose.	and he healed the child and returned him to his father.
		And all were astonished at the majesty of God.

---

[1] See also the use of ἐγείρειν in other formulaic passages in the letters of Paul (Rom 4:24; 1 Thess 1:10).

[2] Commentaries try to explain the complexity of the Markan story as the result of an inept redaction by the author of the Gospel who may have tried to conflate two older stories. However, they do not use the much simpler forms of the story in Matthew and Luke as a guide for the reconstruction of the original story in Mark. For discussion and literature, see Schmithals, *Markus*, 407–24.

| And his disciples came to him privately and said, "Why could we not cast it out?" | And when he had entered the house, his disciples asked him privately, "Why could we not cast it out?" |

It seems that Matthew and Luke read a version of this story in their copy of Mark which did not contain the verses of Mark to which they have no parallel. Especially the phrases and sentences of Mark 9:25–27 which are missing in the other two Synoptic Gospels have the appearance of secondary alterations or additions. Matt 17:18 and Luke 9:42b must have read a common source which reported briefly that Jesus exorcised the unclean spirit (ἐπετίμησεν κτλ.), that the child was healed (Matt: ἐθηραπεύθη, Luke: ἰάσατο), and perhaps that the crowd reacted (preserved only in Luke 9:43). The extant text of Mark, however, quotes in full the wording of an exorcistic formula, indeed the longest such formula in the Synoptic Gospels (τὸ ἄλαλον καὶ κωφὸν πνεῦμα, ἐγὼ ἐπιτάσσω σοι, ἔξελθε ἀπ᾽ αὐτοῦ καὶ μηκέτι εἰσέλθῃς εἰς αὐτόν).[1] Surprisingly, this is an exorcism for a deaf-mute person, not for an epileptic child.[2] The redactor shows little interest in the healing of the disease. Rather, he wants to describe the effect of a powerful exorcism in order to introduce the subsequent action of Jesus, which has no parallel in Matthew and Luke: the demon departs with appropriate demonstration (κράξας καὶ πολλὰ σπαράξας), the boy is left "as if dead" (ὡσεὶ νεκρός), and the bystanders say "he died" (ἀπέθανεν). This prepares for an action of Jesus which is described as the raising of a dead person: Jesus takes him by the hand (κρατήσας τῆς χειρός), raises him, and he rises (ἤγειρεν αὐτόν, καὶ ἀνέστη). The story, as it is preserved in the extant text of Mark, appears to be a deliberate redaction of an older exorcism story which Matthew and Luke still read in their text of Mark. The redactor revised the story in such a way that it resembled a story of the raising of someone who died as a victim of demonic action.[3]

---

[1] All other exorcistic formulae cited in the Synoptic Gospels are very brief; cf. Mark 1:41; 2:11; 3:5; 10:52; Luke 8:54; 13:12; 17:14.

[2] Mark's later redactor has changed the introduction of the story (9:17) accordingly (ἔχοντα πνεῦμα ἄλαλον); the original description of the disease, epilepsy, is still visible in Mark 9:18, 20, 22.

[3] The close resemblance of this scene and its wording with the description of the raising of the young man in the *Secret Gospel of Mark* will be discussed later (see # 4.1.5).

4.1.2.3 Peculiar Terminology in the Canonical Markan Text

That a number of special terms of the Gospel of Mark are not reproduced by either Matthew or Luke is to be expected. This does not necessarily imply that they were introduced by a later redactor. Nevertheless, the absence of certain terms in passages which Matthew and Luke took from Mark's Gospel is surprising. That the word "gospel" (εὐαγγέλιον) is missing in several Matthean parallels, although Matthew uses this term in other contexts, has already been discussed.[1]

The words "to teach" (διδάσκειν) and "teaching" (διδαχή) certainly occurred in the oldest text of the Gospel of Mark, because Matthew or Luke or both reproduce them in their usage of the following Markan passages: 1:21, 22; 6:2, 6; (7:7;) 11:18; 12:14; 14:49. However, there are a number of Markan passages in which the term occurs without parallels in the corresponding passages of Matthew and Luke. In Mark 1:27, the witnesses of Jesus' exorcism (1:23–26) remark about "a new teaching with authority" (διδαχὴ καινὴ κατ᾽ ἐξουσίαν). The phrase "new teaching" appears only in one other New Testament passage, Acts 17:19: "What is this new teaching that is proclaimed by you?" (τίς ἡ καινὴ αὕτη ἡ ὑπὸ σοῦ λαλουμένη διδαχή;). As Acts 17:32 reveals, this new teaching is "the resurrection from the dead" (ἀκούσαντες δὲ ἀνάστασιν νεκρῶν . . .). Another important parallel occurs in the gospel fragment *Pap. Oxy. 1224*, 2 v. col. I: "Which new teaching do they say you teach, and which new baptism do you proclaim?" (π[ο]ίαν σέ [φασιν διδα]χὴν καιν[ὴν διδάσκειν ἢ τί β]ά[πτισμ]α καινὸν [κηρύσσειν;]).[2]

In Mark 6:7 the Twelve are sent out "with power over the unclean spirits"; when they return (Mark 6:30) they announce all they have done "and what they had taught" (καὶ ὅσα ἐδίδαξεν). No such phrase appears in the parallels of either Matthew or Luke. In the following introduction to the story of the feeding of the five thousand, Mark 6:34 says, "and Jesus began to teach (διδάσκειν) them many things." Matt 14:14 reports instead that Jesus healed the sick; Luke 9:11 contains a similar remark (καὶ τοὺς χρείαν ἔχοντες ἰάσατο) after a reference to Jesus' "speaking" (ἐλάλει) about the rule of God. Mark 8:31 and 9:31 introduce the first and second predictions of the passion with the words "he began to teach" and "he taught" (Matthew uses the verb δεικνύειν, Luke has εἰπών). In addition to these passages, Mark 2:13; 4:1–2; 10:1; 11:17; 12:35, 37, 38 also use the word "to teach" in the

---

[1] See above # 1.3.3–4; Luke avoids the term altogether in his Gospel and can, therefore, not serve as witness to its occurrence or absence in his copy of Mark.

[2] Erich Klostermann, *Apocrypha II: Evangelien* (KlT 8; 3d ed.; Berlin: De Gruyter, 1929) 26.

description of Jesus' activity, while Matthew and Luke use different verbs in their parallel passages.

Most striking is the use of the verbs θαμβεῖσθαι and ἐκθαμβεῖσθαι in Mark. Both verbs express the amazement that befalls people when they witness extraordinary events.[1] The Gospel of Mark is the only writing in the New Testament employing these verbs; the noun also occurs in the Lukan writings. In Mark, these verbs describe the reaction of people to the exorcism in the synagogue (Mark 1:27),[2] the amazement of the people who meet Jesus as he comes down from the mountain of the transfiguration (Mark 9:15), the reaction of the disciples to Jesus' word about the difficulty of wealthy people entering the rule of God (Mark 10:24), the mood of the disciples as they follow Jesus to Jerusalem (Mark 10:32), Jesus' own mood in Gethsemane (Mark 14:33), and finally the reaction of the women as they meet the youth, dressed in a white robe, in the empty tomb (Mark 16:5; cf. 16:6).

All these features point to a redaction of the Gospel of Mark *after* its usage by Matthew and Luke. The origin and purpose of this redaction can be assessed only after the discussion of the *Secret Gospel of Mark* with which it seems closely associated (see below # 4.1.5).

4.1.2.4 The Urmarkus Hypothesis

Quite different from the question of a later redaction of Mark's text after its circulation in the form in which Matthew and Luke knew and used it, is the attempt to reconstruct a more original draft of the Gospel of Mark, known as the *Urmarkus* hypothesis.[3] External evidence for two different versions of Mark circulating at an early date can be derived only from the observation that Luke does not reproduce the section Mark 6:45–8:26. Luke 9:19 = Mark 8:27 follows directly upon Luke 9:17 = Mark 6:44. Luke may have used a copy of Mark that had accidentally lost a few pages.[4] However, there are some special features which differentiate this particular section from the rest of

---

[1] In Hellenistic religious language, these terms are employed in the context of magic performances: cf. G. Bertram, "θάμβος, κτλ.," *TDNT* 3 (1965) 4–7. Plutarch describes θάμβος as the typical result of superstition (Bertram, ibid., 4).

[2] Luke seems to have read the verb here in his copy of Mark because Luke 4:36 uses the noun θάμβος in his concluding remark about the people's reaction. The noun is also used in Luke to describe Peter's reaction to the miraculous draught of fishes in 5:9. It also occurs once in Acts (3:10).

[3] Most characteristic is the attempt of Emil Wendling, *Die Entstehung des Marcus-Evangeliums* (Tübingen: Mohr/Siebeck, 1908). On the *Urmarkus* question in general see Schmithals, *Einleitung,* 201–8.

[4] This was argued most recently by Ernst Haenchen, *Der Weg Jesu* (Berlin: Töpelmann, 1966) 303–4.

Mark's Gospel. It begins with the report of Jesus' going to Bethsaida (Mark 6:45) and ends with the story of the healing of a blind man from Bethsaida (Mark 8:22–26). Thereafter Jesus goes to the town of Caesarea Philippi, and the town of Bethsaida never occurs again in the Gospel.[1] This section of Mark is also characterized by the appearance of a number of doublets of other Markan pericopes: 6:45–54, the walking on the water, is a variant of the stilling of the tempest (Mark 4:35–41); 8:1–10, the feeding of the four thousand, is evidently a secondary elaboration of the story of the feeding of the five thousand (Mark 6:30–44); 8:22–26 is one of two stories reporting the healing of a blind man in this Gospel (cf. Mark 10:46–52). Two of the healing stories in this section, Mark 7:32–36 and 8:22–26 (both also missing in Matthew), are the only two narratives in the Synoptic Gospels in which the healing is accomplished through elaborate manipulations; all other healings are accomplished through Jesus' word, simple gesture, or touching with or taking by the hand. Mark 6:45–8:26 exhibits some peculiar features also in its general vocabulary. E.g., the term "to understand" (συνίημι) occurs four times (6:52; 7:14; 8:17, 21), but elsewhere in Mark only once in an illusion to Isa 6:9–10 (Mark 4:12). The synonymous verb νοεῖν is found twice here (7:18; 8:17), elsewhere in Mark only in 13:14. The adjective "without insight" (ἀσύνετος) is used in Mark only in this section (8:17).[2]

The cumulative evidence of these peculiarities may allow the conclusion that an earlier version of Mark, which was used by Luke did not yet contain the "Bethsaida section" (Mark 6:45–8:26), whereas Matthew knew the expanded version which, therefore, must have come into existence very soon after the original composition of the original gospel. An *Urmarkus* hypothesis, however, cannot be established on this basis because those searching for the *Urmarkus* wanted to discover a gospel that was "more primitive" than any text that can be reconstructed on the basis of external evidence. It seems wise to limit the reconstruction of the history of Mark's text to instances that can be controlled by external evidence: the earliest version used by Luke; a text of Mark amplified by the "Bethsaida section" (Mark 6:45–8:26) which was available to Matthew; a new edition,

---

[1] Elsewhere in the canonical gospels, Bethsaida is mentioned only in Luke 9:10, in the woe over Bethsaida and Chorazin Matt 11:21 = Luke 10:13, and in John 1:45; 12:21 as the town from which Philip came. In John 5:2, the correct reading is Βηθζαθά, not Βηθσαϊδά.

[2] On the relationship of Mark and Matthew with respect to the use of this term see Gerhard Barth, "Matthew's Understanding of the Law," in Günther Bornkamm, Gerhard Barth, and Heinz-Joachim Held, *Tradition and Interpretation in Matthew* (Phildalphia: Westminster, 1963) 105–11.

characterized by various redactional features not paralleled in either Matthew or Luke—as will be seen later, this edition is closely related to the *Secret Gospel of Mark* ; a new edition which was admitted to the canon of the New Testament; and, finally, a further expansion occurring in the manuscript tradition of the four canonical gospels which is evident in the adding of appearances of the risen Lord in Mark 16:9–20.[1]

4.1.3 SOURCES AND TRADITIONAL MATERIALS

The development of the tradition which preceded the composition of Mark cannot be discovered in the futile pursuit of an *Urmarkus,* but only through the identification of sources used by the original author of this Gospel. Some of these sources can be recognized with a high degree of certainty, because Mark was more of a collector than an author.[2] At the same time, it is not possible to determine the exact extent and wording of such sources and traditions with certainty, because Mark neither copied his sources slavishly nor did he make them always subject to extensive redaction.[3]

4.1.3.1 The Miracle Stories

Among other narrative materials used by Mark were one or two catenae of miracle stories, probably in written form.[4] They exhibit certain similarities to the material that was collected in the Semeia Source of the Gospel of John; compare the stilling of the tempest (Mark 4:35–41; also Mark 6:45–52) with John 6:16–21, the feeding of the multitudes (Mark 6:30–44; also Mark 8:1–10) with John 6:1–13,

---

[1] These verses are never attested in any early papyri and are missing in the 4th-century uncial manuscripts ℵ and B and in some manuscripts of the Syriac, Sahidic, and Armenian translations. A further expansion of Mark 16:14, the so-called Freer Logion, appears in the 5th-century Codex Washingtonianus (W).

[2] "Phenomena in the text of the Gospel of Mark and the comparison with Q, with John, and with the extra-canonical tradition can support the assumption that Mark, to a large extent, reproduces traditions which he received and can, therefore, not be viewed as an author who has formulated everything himself for the first time" (Lührmann, *Markusevangelium,* 13).

[3] See on this question the perceptive review article of Frans Neirynck, "L'évangile de Marc. A propos de R. Pesch, *Das Markusevangelium,*" in idem, *Evangelica,* 491–561.

[4] Paul J. Achtemeier, "Toward the Isolation of Pre-Markan Miracle Catenae," *JBL* 89 (1970) 265–91; idem, "The Origin and Function of Pre-Markan Miracle Catenae," *JBL* 91 (1972) 198–221.

the healing of the blind man (Mark 8:22–26; also Mark 10:46–52) with John 9:1–7.[1]

The stories of Jesus' exorcisms, however, have no parallels in the Fourth Gospel and must have been derived from a different collection which could have comprised Mark 1:21–28; 5:1–20; 7:24–30; 9:14–29.[2] That such collections existed in written form prior to the composition of Mark is fairly certain. But it is not possible to determine either the exact extent of these sources or their precise wording.[3] The author of the Gospel certainly also had access to miracle stories which were freely circulating in oral form as they were used in the propaganda and mission of the church, for example the story of the healing of a leper (Mark 1:40–45).[4]

4.1.3.2 Collections of Sayings and Controversy Stories

With respect to the sources for sayings materials, two written documents used by Mark are clearly recognizable: a collection of parables (4:1–34)[5] and a composition of apocalyptic materials (13:1–37).[6] Furthermore, certain groups of apophthegmata—short stories which conclude with a saying of Jesus—can be identified which must have been collected before they were incorporated into the Gospel of Mark. The first group comprises apophthegmata which deal with controversies between the Christian community and their Jewish opponents about fasting (Mark 2:18–22), observation of the Sabbath (2:23–28; 3:1–6), the authority to exorcise demons (3:20–30), the question of clean and unclean (7:1–23), and the question of marriage and divorce (10:1–12). The last of these apophthegmata could also have come from a second collection dealing with questions of church discipline, that is, resulting from debates among Christians in which the authority of Jesus was invoked. In this second group the disciples sometimes appear as the questioners: about the validity of exorcism in the name of Jesus outside of the Christian community (9:38–41); offenses

---

[1] See above, ## 3.2.1; 3.4.4.1.

[2] The latter in its more original form, i.e., like most of the other exorcisms of Mark a comparatively brief story as it is preserved by Matthew and Luke; see above.

[3] It is, e.g., quite possible that the collection of exorcisms also contained such stories as Mark 1:29–31; 2:1–12; 3:1–6 and others.

[4] On the parallel in *Papyrus Egerton 2* see above # 3.2.2.4.

[5] Heinz-Wolfgang Kuhn, *Ältere Sammlungen.*

[6] Marxsen, *Markus,* 101–40; Lars Hartman, *Prophecy Interpreted: The Formation of some Jewish Apocalyptic Texts and of the Eschatological Discourse Mark 13 Par.* (CB.NT 1; Uppsala: Almquist & Wiksells, 1966); most important, including a detailed reconstruction of the source of Mark 13, is Egon Brandenburger, *Markus 13 und die Apokalyptik* (Göttingen: Vandenhoeck & Ruprecht, 1984).

against believers (9:42); the right to excommunicate (9:43–47);[1] acceptance of children into the Christian community (10:13–16); acceptance
of wealthy people (10:17–31); ranks of honor in the community
(10:35–45). A third group comprised four or five apophthegmata which
discuss the rights and the legitimacy of the followers of Jesus as a special group within the confines of the Jewish community. These may
have their origin in the early Jerusalem community—all of these are
deliberately placed in the Jerusalem ministry of Jesus, and in each of
them a special Jewish group or its representative appears as the inter-
rogator: the followers of Jesus as a baptizing prophetic movement compared to that of John the Baptist (11:27–33); the question whether
Jesus' followers belong to those Jewish sects which are loyal to the
Roman government (12:13–17); theological identification with either
Pharisees or Sadducees (12:18–27); adherence to the Great Commandment of Judaism (12:28–34); and the significance of Jewish messianic
expectations (12:35–37).[2]

4.1.3.3 The Passion Narrative

Most evident is the use of a written source in the last section of the
Gospel, the passion narrative. Mark's source began with Jesus' entry
into Jerusalem (11:1–10),[3] continued with the anointing in Bethany
(14:3–9), the arrest of Jesus, his trial before the synedrion and before
Pilate, the mocking by the soldiers, the Barabbas incident, crucifixion,
death, and burial, and concluded with the story of the women's
discovery of the empty tomb. This source is clearly a variant of the
written report of the passion which was used by the Gospel of John.[4]
The comparison with the passion narrative of the *Gospel of Peter*[5] has
demonstrated that also this Gospel's version must be dependent upon
the same source. But Mark's version contains a number of secondary
features, e.g., the splitting up of the scene of the mocking of Jesus into
several episodes; Jesus is mocked before the synedrion (Mark 14:65),
by the soldiers (15:16–20), and by the bystanders at the cross
(15:29–32). Also secondary is Mark's insertion of the preparation for

---

[1] Helmut Koester, "Mark 9:43–47 and Quintilian 8.3.75," *HTR* 71 (1978) 151–53.

[2] That the fourfold scheme of questions in Mark 12 corresponds to a Rabbinic pattern has been shown by David Daube, *The New Testament and Rabbinic Judaism* (New
York: Arno, 1956) 158–69.

[3] Or perhaps with the story of the anointing in Bethany (Mark 14:3–9). In that case,
John has preserved the more original order of the stories in this source in which the
entry into Jerusalem was the second story; see above # 3.4.4.2.

[4] See above on the Johannine passion narrative source, # 3.4.4.2.

[5] See above, # 3.2.3.2.

Passover (14:12–16), which interferes with the original date of Jesus' crucifixion before the Passover that was indicated in Mark's source.[1]

4.1.4 MARK'S WORLD AND THE COMPOSITION OF HIS GOSPEL

Mark is primarily a faithful collector. Insofar as he is also an author he has created an overriding general framework for the incorporation of traditional materials, but he has still left most of his sources and materials fairly intact. His Gospel is therefore a most important witness for an early stage of the formative development of the traditions about Jesus. The world which these traditions describe rarely goes beyond the circle of Galilee, Judea, and Jerusalem,[2] which is not the world of the author nor of the readers for whom the book was written. Mark's information about Palestine and about its people is fairly accurate wherever he leaves his sources intact. But from his redaction of the sources it is clear that the author is not a Jewish-Christian and that he does not live in Palestine. Except for the importance of Jerusalem and of Jesus' journey there, geographical data have little effect upon the organization and composition of Mark's traditions and sources.

Mark composes his materials according to a theological schema which is directly related to the religious significance of the various traditions about Jesus in his own mostly Gentile-Christian environment.[3] The Gospel is characterized by a strong emphasis upon the proclamation of Jesus' death as a saving sacrifice (Mark 10:45). In concrete terms, this event is present in Mark's church in the celebration of the eucharist which remembered Jesus' death as the pouring out of the blood of the covenant and looked forward to the eschatological moment of the messianic banquet (14:22–25). But it is equally present in the telling and reading of the narrative of Jesus' suffering and death as it has been developed on the basis of exegetical traditions in which Scripture provided the answer to the why and how of Jesus suffering.

There is a strong connection between the development of the passion tradition and the apostolic authority of Peter and traditions under

---

[1] Lührmann, *Markusevangelium*, 229. I agree with Lührmann that Mark 14:1–2 belongs to Mark's source; it was not created by the author of the Gospel and it agrees with the dating of the crucifixion in John, i.e., before the first day of Passover.

[2] The area of Caesarea Philippi, the capital of the tetrarch Philip near the sources of the Jordan river, where Mark locates the confession of Peter (8:27), does not belong to Galilee and would be understood as Gentile country.

[3] It will become evident that my view of this environment of Mark differs fundamentally from that of the fascinating recent book of Burton L. Mack, *A Myth of Innocence: Mark and Christian Origins* (Philadelphia: Fortress, 1988).

his name. (Simon) Peter appears repeatedly in Mark's Gospel,[1] and
he is singled out as the one who confesses Jesus to be the Christ (8:29),
though he is never appealed to as the authority behind Mark's Gospel.[2] However, Peter is attested early in Syria as an important apostolic authority:[3] as the one who confesses Jesus as a "righteous angel"
in *Gos. Thom.* 13; in the tradition about the "rock" on which Jesus will
build his church, which Matt 16:17–19 has added to the Markan pericope of the confession of Peter; as the author of the *Gospel of Peter*; and
finally as the author of two other writings, the *Apocalypse of Peter* and
the *Kerygma of Peter*.[4] The latter is of special interest because it
describes how the disciples discovered the meaning of Jesus' fate by
studying the Scripture: the disciples opened the books of the prophets
and found there predicted, partly in parables and partly literally, "his
coming, his death, his cross, and all the other torments which the Jews
inflicted on him, his resurrection and assumption . . ." All these writings and traditions belong to Syria, not to Rome.[5]

As Mark's version of the words of institution for the eucharist indicates, his community's belief in Jesus' suffering and death as saving
sacrifice is closely connected with the apocalyptic expectation of his
return. The motif itself is not new. It characterized Paul's understanding of the eucharist: "As often as you eat this bread and drink the
cup, you proclaim the Lord's death until he comes" (1 Cor 11:26).[6] But
in Mark's community it has found a specific expression as the belief in
the coming Son of man, a concept that the redactor of the Synoptic
Sayings Source shares.[7] The urgency of this expectation may have
been reinforced by the recent destruction of Jerusalem. This would
allow a date for the composition of Mark shortly after 70 CE.

Another important component of early Christian missionary
activity in Syria must have been the proclamation of Jesus as the
"divine man," which was reinforced by the apostles' performance of

---

[1] Together with his brother Andrew, he is one of the first two disciples called (1:16);
Jesus heals his mother-in-law (1:29–31); Peter is one of three witness of the
transfiguration (9:2–9) as well as being the speaker in this pericope (9:5); he also plays
a role in the passion narrative (14:29–31; 53–72; 16:7).

[2] The later tradition which describes Mark as Peter's amanuensis (see above,
4.1.1) is not expressed in the Gospel itself.

[3] It may not be accidental that Paul (Gal 2:11) is a witness for his presence in
Antioch.

[4] Fragments are preserved in Clement of Alexandria *Strom.* 6.5.39–41, 43, 48;
6.15.128.

[5] The location of Peter, and subsequently of the Gospel of Mark, in Rome is a secondary development. See Lührmann, *Markusevangelium*, 5.

[6] See also the eschatological orientation of the eucharistic prayers in *Didache* 9–10.

[7] See above # 2.3.4.

powerful miracles. The tradition of these communities about Jesus most likely consisted of aretalogies, that is, collections of miracle stories of Jesus which eventually found their way into the Semeia Source used by John and also into the miracle catenae employed by Mark. But Mark does not use these sources as just some other pieces of information about Jesus. On the the contrary, he is very aware of the religious threat that this understanding of Jesus' ministry poses to the belief in the saving sacrifice of the crucified Christ. In his Gospel he explicitly rejects the kerygmatic claims of the aretalogical tradition and, by incorporating stories of Jesus' miracles into a writing that is dominated by the passion narrative, establishes the story of Jesus' suffering as the criterion for the determination of the religious significance of the aretalogical tradition.

All of these materials, written sources as well as collections of traditions in written or oral form, have been welded together by the author of the Gospel of Mark into a work in which all of the activities of Jesus are overshadowed by the account of his suffering and death. All arrangements of the sources and traditional materials serve the theological intention of the author to present, in the form of a written document, the "messianic secret" of Jesus that God's revelation in history is not fulfilled in the demonstration of divine greatness, but in the humiliation of the divine human being in his death on the cross.[1] Jesus' opponents, Pharisees and Herodians, decide as early as Mark 3:6 that they want to destroy him. In the first part of the Gospel, the disciples who witness all of Jesus' powerful deeds exhibit a marked lack of understanding; this is expressed several times by redactional remarks at the end of miracle stories (cf. 6:52; 8:14–21). The turning point in the understanding of the disciples comes with the confession of Peter (8:27–30), whose designation of Jesus as "the Christ"[2] sums up the insight into Jesus' dignity that corresponds to the demonstration of his power in the miracles he performed. But this confession is immediately countered by Jesus' prediction that the "Son of man" must suffer and be rejected by the elders, high priests and scribes, be killed, and rise after three days (8:31)—the first of three predictions[3] of the suffering of the Son of man which from this point on determine

---

[1] William Wrede, *The Messianic Secret* (Library of Theological Translation; London: Clarke, 1971): English translation of a classical monograph which was first published in German in 1901; James M. Robinson, "The Messianic Secret and the Gospels Genre," in idem, *The Problem of History in Mark and other Marcan Studies* (Philadelphia: Fortress, 1982) 11–53.

[2] This is most likely the original reading. The manuscripts which add "the Son of God," or "the Son of the Living God" are influenced by the expanded text of Matt 16:16.

[3] The other two appear in 9:31–32 and 10:32–34.

the character of the narrative: Jesus is on his way to Jerusalem. The reader learns that the powerful deeds of the Christ cannot be the key to the understanding of the mission of Jesus. On the contrary, the miracles of the Christ provoked the reactions which resulted in his condemnation. As the disciples are going with Jesus to Jerusalem (8:34–10:45), they learn discipleship under the perspective of the Son of man who has come to give his life as ransom for many (10:45). It is in this section of the Gospel that the author has placed most of his church order materials. But the Son of man is also the one who will come on the clouds of heaven. Thus Mark inserted a speech of Jesus composed of apocalyptic predictions into the instructions of Jesus given before his arrest. The final juxtaposition of the titles "Christ" and "Son of man" marks the high climax of Jesus' trial before the synedrion: the high priest's question, whether he is the Christ the Son of the Blessed One, is answered positively; but the title which conveys true insight into Jesus' dignity is added immediately: "And you will see the Son of man sitting at the right hand of the Power and coming with the clouds of heaven." The Gospel of Mark is thus written as a guide to christology in narrative form. Christology is the ordering principle according to which the materials are arranged.

By combining aretalogical materials with the passion narrative, Mark produced for the first time what can be called a "biography of Jesus." This, however, is not an accidental creation. The model was the biography of the prophet. Characteristically, Mark's Gospel begins with the appointment of Jesus through the heavenly voice, "You are my beloved Son in whom I am well pleased" (Mark 1:11), directed to Jesus (not to the crowds as in Matt 3:17). Like Elijah, Jesus spends forty days in the wilderness (Mark 1:12–13). The prophetic call for repentance opens the preaching of Jesus (Mark 1:15). The hostility that Jesus experiences is the result of his conduct of office. Jesus' interpretation of Israel's law and ritual is "prophetic Torah."[1] He suffers the fate of the prophet in his death and is vindicated. This is not all that the Gospel of Mark has to say, but it is the biographical framework which provides the literary model for the writing of this "gospel."[2]

---

[1] Mark 7:1–23; 10:1–12; 12:29–31.
[2] See above the discussion of the genre of the gospel, # 1.6.

4.1.5 THE SECRET GOSPEL OF MARK[1]

4.1.5.1 Discovery, Publication, and Evaluation

The only known fragment of the *Secret Gospel of Mark* is a quotation in a letter of Clement of Alexandria. This letter was discovered 1958 by Morton Smith in the Mar Saba Monastery, twelve miles southeast of Jerusalem.[2] A learned monk had copied the letter into the back of an edition of the letters of Ignatius of Antioch by Isaac Voss that had been published in 1646.[3] The monk's handwriting can be dated to about 1750.[4] The Greek text was published 1973 by Morton Smith with extensive notes, appendices, and indices.[5] It was reprinted in a revised edition of the index volume of the publication of the works of Clement of Alexandria in the series "Die griechischen christlichen Schriftsteller" of the Berlin Academy.[6] English translations have been published by Morton Smith and by Ron Cameron.[7]

It is known that Clement of Alexandria wrote letters. But not one of these letters had survived, although quotations from Clement's letters appear in the *Sacra Parallela* attributed to John of Damascus who stayed at the Mar Saba Monastery from the beginning of the 8th century to his death (ca. 750 CE). The first question was, therefore, whether this letter was indeed the copy of a genuine letter of the Alexandrian Father. There are a number of scholars who have expressed doubts with respect to its authenticity.[8] However, vocabulary, style,

---

[1] Some of the following paragraphs are an adaptation of my introduction to the translation of the *Secret Gospel of Mark*, which is scheduled to be published by Polebridge Press in a new edition of the New Testament Apocrypha.

[2] Morton Smith, *Clement of Alexandria and a Secret Gospel of Mark* (Cambridge, MA: Harvard University Press, 1973 [transcription, plates, and translation: pp. 445–54]); idem, *The Secret Gospel: The Discovery and Interpretation of the Secret Gospel According to Mark* (New York: Harper & Row, 1973). See also Crossan, *Four Other Gospels*, 91–98.

[3] *Epistulae genuinae S. Ignatii Martyris* (Amsterdam: J. Blaeu, 1646).

[4] For information about the hand of the writer see Morton Smith, *Clement of Alexandria*, 1–4; idem, "Ἑλληνικὰ Χειρογραφία ἐν τῇ μονῇ τοῦ Ἁγίου Σάββα," *Nea Sion* 52 (1960) 110ff, 245ff.

[5] *Clement of Alexandria*, 445–54.

[6] Otto Stählin and Ursula Treu, *Clemens Alexandrinus*, vol. *4.1: Register* (2d ed.; Berlin: Akademie-Verlag, 1980) pp. XVII–XVIII.

[7] M. Smith, *Clement of Alexandria*, 446–47; idem, *The Secret Gospel: The Discovery and Interpretation of the Secret Gospel According to Mark* (New York: Harper & Row, 1973) 14–17; Ron Cameron, *Other Gospels*, 67–71. For a German translation, see H. Merkel, "Das 'geheime Evangelium' nach Markus," in Hennecke-Schneemelcher, *NT Apokryphen I*, 89–92.

[8] On the heated debate about the authenticity of the letter see Wilhelm Wuellner, ed., *Longer Mark: Forgery, Interpolation, or Old Tradition?* (Colloquy 18; Berkeley, CA: The Center for Hermeneutical Studies, 1976); Morton Smith, "Clement of Alexandria

syntax, and manner of quotation in the letter are either identical with, or similar to, that of Clement's genuine writings.[1] Skepticism is hard to justify.[2]

It is not possible to identify the addressee, a certain Theodorus. The Karpokratians who are attacked in the letter as those who had contaminated the *Secret Gospel of Mark* with their falsifications are discussed critically by Clement and in other Church Fathers.[3] Since the letter refers to an Egyptian sect, it is not unlikely that it was written during Clement's Alexandrian period, i.e., between 175 and 200 CE. But a date between 200 and 215 is also possible.[4]

The letter responds to a request from Theodorus for information about a "secret gospel" used by the Karpokratians. Clement calls their secret gospel a falsification of the genuine *Secret Gospel of Mark* which was composed by Mark himself in Alexandria[5] and was still used in the Alexandrian church in Clement's day. Following the presbyter tradition that is also used by Papias of Hierapolis and elsewhere by Clement himself, he ascribes authorship to Mark who was the amanuensis of Peter in Rome.[6] However, the ascription of a "secret gospel" to the same Mark is not attested anywhere else.

It is evident in Clement's letter that this *Secret Gospel of Mark* was an expanded edition of what Clement considers to be the first Gospel that Mark wrote. Mark, Clement says, produced the second writing to be communicated only to those who where "initiated into the great mysteries."[7] Yet a third version of a gospel written by Mark was used

---

and Secret Mark: The Score at the End of the First Decade," *HTR* 75 (1982) 449–61. For further discussion and literature see Saul Levin, "The Early History of Christianity in the Light of the 'Secret Gospel' of Mark," *ANRW* 2.25/6 (1988) 4270–92.

[1] Comparisons with parallels in Clement's writings are presented and discussed in great detail by Morton Smith, *Clement of Alexandria,* 6–85.

[2] For a general assessment and survey see Gero, "Apocryphal Gospels," 3976–78.

[3] Irenaeus, Tertullian, Hippolytus, Epiphanius, and others. For full documentation see Morton Smith, *Clement of Alexandria,* Appendix B.

[4] After leaving Alexandria at the outbreak of the persecution, Clement probably died ca. 215 CE.

[5] For a discussion of the tradition about Mark as the founder of the church in Alexandria see Birger A. Pearson, "Earliest Christianity in Egypt: Some Observations," in idem and James E. Goehring, eds., *The Roots of Egyptian Christianity* (Studies in Antiquity and Christianity; Philadelphia: Fortress, 1986) 137–45.

[6] A full presentation of these passages can be found in Morton Smith, *Clement of Alexandria,* 19–22. Two of these come from quotes from Clement's works in Eusebius (*Hist. eccl.* 2.15 and 6.14.5–7), the third from a fragment of Clement's *Hypotyposeis* (in the Latin *Adumbrationes Clementis Alexandrini in epistolas canonicas*).

[7] This may be a somewhat fancy expression, designating those Christians who were advancing to a higher degree of knowledge (γνῶσις), or it may point to another rite,

by the sect of the Karpokratians.[1] Clement calls this a "copy" (ἀπόγρα-φον)[2] of the genuine secret gospel. At the time at which Karpokrates flourished in Alexandria, in the first half of the 2d century, no firmly organized church with bishop and presbyters existed there, and it must be assumed that anybody could obtain copies of any writing used by Christians in Alexandria.[3] This also establishes a terminus ad quem for this gospel early in the 2d century.

4.1.5.2 The Relationship of Secret Mark to Mark's Gospel

Clement notes two differences between *Secret Mark* and the Gospel of Mark that was read publicly: (1) the former contained a story of the raising of a young man, which was added to Mark's text after Mark 10:34; (2) it reported an encounter of Jesus with this young man's sister, mother and Salome, added after Mark 10:46a. On the basis of the information that is provided by Clement, it is not possible to say whether there were any other differences between these two gospels as Clement knew them. Both additions are quoted in Clement's letter. Vocabulary and style of the additions are fully compatible with the Gospel of Mark.[4] *Secret Mark,* therefore, must belong to the same "school" or community which had produced the canonical Gospel. Both gospels are related to each other as closely as the Gospel of John and its later redaction, which interpolated John 6:52b–59 and added chapter 21 to the book.[5] This also implies that the date of composition of *Secret Mark* should not be too far removed from the date for the writing of the Gospel of Mark.

The story of the raising of the young man is told as follows:[6]

---

perhaps a second baptism for more mature Christians (see Morton Smith, *Clement of Alexandria,* 168).

[1] A full treatment of Karpokrates and his sect, including a discussion of all relevant literature, can be found in Morton Smith, *Clement of Alexandria,* 266–78 (all ancient sources are quoted in full in Appendix B of this book, pp. 295–350).

[2] The term ἀπόγραφον may have pejorative connotations (Morton Smith, *Clement of Alexandria,* 49).

[3] Pearson ("Earliest Christianity in Egypt," 149–151) lists a number of writings that must have been current in Alexandria early in the 2d century.

[4] That, however, is also the case in the longer ending of Mark (16:9–20), which is certainly secondary. It does not prove that the additions were made by the same author.

[5] See above # 3.4.3.

[6] All translations from the *Secret Gospel of Mark* are my own. They will also appear in the new edition of the New Testament Apocrypha to be published by Polebridge Press. I have, of course, consulted the translation of Morton Smith in his *Clement of Alexandria.*

And they came to Bethany, and there was a certain woman whose brother had died. And she prostrated herself before Jesus and said to him, "Son of David, have mercy on me." But the disciples rebuked her. And Jesus, being angered, went with her into the garden where the tomb was. And immediately a great voice was heard from the tomb. And Jesus, drawing near, rolled away the stone from the entrance to the tomb. And immediately, going in where the young man was, he stretched out (his) hand and raised him, grasping his hand. And the young man, looking at Jesus, loved him and began to beseech him that he might be with him. And as they came out of the tomb, they went into the house of the young man, for he was rich.

It is immediately evident that this story shows many similarities with the story of the raising of Lazarus in John 11.[1] That it is, in fact, the same story is evident in the emphasis upon the love between Jesus and the man who was raised by him (cf. John 11:3, 5, 35–36), expressed twice in the additions of *Secret Mark*.[2] Both stories are also located in Bethany. But it is impossible that *Secret Mark* is dependent upon John 11. In its version of the story, there are no traces of the rather extensive Johannine redaction (proper names, motif of the delay of Jesus' travel, measurement of space and time, discourses of Jesus with his disciples and with Martha and Mary). As to its form, *Secret Mark* represents a stage of development of the story that corresponds to the source used by John.[3] The author evidently still had access to the free tradition of stories about Jesus, or perhaps to some older written collection of miracle stories. But the story of the raising of the young man in Secret Mark has an appendix for which parallels in the Fourth Gospel's version are missing, except for the motif of love between Jesus and the man who was raised:

And the young man (νεανίσκος), looking at Jesus, loved him (ἐμβλέψας αὐτῷ ἠγάπησεν αὐτόν) and began to beseech him that he might be with him. . . . And after six days Jesus gave him an order; and when the evening had come, the young man (νεανίσκος) went to him, dressed with a linen cloth over his naked body (περιβεβλημένος σινδόνα ἐπὶ γυμνοῦ). And he remained with him that night, because Jesus taught him the mystery of the kingdom of God (ἐδίδασκε γὰρ αὐτὸν ὁ Ἰησοῦς τὸ μυστήριον τῆς βασιλείας τοῦ θεοῦ).

---

[1] For an analysis of this story of *Secret Mark* in relation to John 11, see Crossan, *Four Other Gospels*, 111–18.

[2] The only other canonical parallel is Mark 10:21, which will be discussed below.

[3] Morton Smith, *Clement of Alexandria*, 148–158; Koester, "From Mark to Secret Mark," 41–42.

This is evidently an addition to an older story of the raising of the young man and it could be dismissed as completely secondary were it not for the fact that exactly in these sentences a number of remarkable parallels to the preserved text of the Gospel of Mark appear. However, all Markan parallels appear in the extant manuscript text of Mark only; they are missing in Matthew's and Luke's parallel versions and do not seem to have been parts of the text of Mark that they knew.

Secret Mark	Mark
The young man, looking at Jesus, loved him (ἐμβλέψας αὐτῷ ἠγάπησεν αὐτόν).	10:21: Jesus looked at him (i.e., the rich man) and loved him (ἐμβλέψας αὐτῷ ἠγάπησεν αὐτόν).
the young man (νεανίσκος) went to him,	14:51–52: (after the arrest of Jesus) A young man (νεανίσκος) had followed him who was
dressed with a linen cloth over his naked body (περιβεβλημένος σινδόνα ἐπὶ γυμνοῦ).	dressed with a linen cloth over his naked body (περιβεβλημένος σινδόνα ἐπὶ γυμνοῦ), and they grabbed him. But he let the cloth go and fled naked.

Secret Mark	Mark 4:11	Matt 13:11; Luke 8:10
Jesus taught him the mystery of the kingdom of God	To you is given the mystery of the kingdom of God.	To you is given to know the mysteries of the kingdom of heaven/of God.
(ἐδίδασκε γὰρ αὐτὸν ὁ Ἰησοῦς τὸ μυστήριον τῆς βασιλείας τοῦ θεοῦ).	(ὑμῖν τὸ μυστήριον δέδοται τῆς βασιλείας τοῦ θεοῦ)	(ὑμῖν δέδοται γνῶναι τὰ μυστήρια τῆς βασιλείας τῶν οὐρανῶν / τοῦ θεοῦ

It has already been argued above that the remark "Jesus loved him" in the story of the rich man, does not seem to have been part of the original text of Mark that Matthew and Luke read.[1] It occurs nowhere else in the canonical gospels except for the story of the raising of Lazarus in John (11:5, 36). In the preserved manuscripts of the text of Mark, however, this remark appears in the story that just precedes (10:17–31) the point in Mark's text at which Clement found the story of the raising of the young man (10:34). Mark 14:51 is the only passage in all the canonical gospels in which a young man dressed in a linen cloth over his naked body appears.[2] The singular "mystery,"

---

[1] On this passage and on Mark 14:51–52 see above, # 4.1.2.1.

[2] There is, of course, also the "young man dressed in a white robe" (νεανίσκον ... περιβεβλημένον στολὴν λευκήν) whom the women see in the tomb of Jesus (Mark 16:5; Gos. Pet. 13.55); but there the brightness of the robe underlines the angelic presence

employed in *Secret Mark,* is used in the canonical gospels only in Mark 4:11, and Matthew and Luke apparently read the plural "mysteries" in their text of Mark.[1] And the extant text of the Gospel of Mark contains numerous instances in which the terms "to teach" and "teaching" appear without a parallel in either Matthew or Luke.[2] It seems that the change in the text of Mark 4:11 and the additions of Mark 10:21 and 14:51–52 are due to the same redactor who inserted the story of the raising of the young man after Mark 10:34.

This raises some questions with respect to other passages in the text of Mark, especially in chapters 8–10, in which Matthew and Luke have preserved the original text, while the extant text of Mark appears to have resulted from a secondary redaction. If one assumes that *Secret Mark* included these passages in the form in which they have been preserved in the text of canonical Mark, while Matthew and Luke represent the original Markan text, a very interesting relationship to the story of the raising of the young man emerges:

Matt/Luke = original Mark	Revised Mark and *Secret Mark*
First prediction of the Passion	
Matt 16:21 = Luke 9:21	Mark 8:31
. . . and be raised on the third day . . . καὶ τῇ τρίτῃ ἡμέρᾳ ἐγερθῆναι.	. . . and after three days he will rise . . . καὶ μετὰ τρεῖς ἡμέρας ἀναστήσεται.
After the Transfiguration	
Matt 17:14 = Luke 9:37–38a	Mark 9:15
And when they came to the crowd, a man came to him and kneeling before him, he said . . .	And immediately all the crowd, when they saw him, were amazed (ἐθαμβήθησαν), and they ran up to him and greeted him.
Exorcism of the Epileptic Child	*Raising the Afflicted Child*
Matt 17:18 = Luke 9:42	Mark 9:26–27
. . . and the demon departed	. . . the demon departed and the boy is left "as if dead" (ὡσεὶ νεκρός), and the bystanders say "he died" (ἀπέθανεν).

(in *Gos. Pet.* 13.55 the robe is characterized as shining most brightly [λαμπροτάτη]). It is hard to imagine that Mark wants the reader to understand that this is the same young man who fled naked.

[1] See above, # 4.1.2.2.

[2] Mark 1:27; 2:13; 4:1–2; 6:30, 34; 8:31; 9:31; 10:1; 11:17; 12:35, 37–38; see also above, # 4.1.2.2.

and he was healed (Matt: ἐθηραπεύθη,
Luke: ἰάσατο)

But Jesus took him by the hand
(κρατήσας τῆς χειρός),
raised him, and he rose (ἤγειρεν
αὐτόν, καὶ ἀνέστη).

Second Prediction of the Passion

Matt 17:23 (Luke —)   Mark 9:31

... and be raised on the third day.   ... and after three days he will rise.
... καὶ τῇ τρίτῃ ἡμέρᾳ ἐγερθῆναι.   ... καὶ μετὰ τρεῖς ἡμέρας ἀναστήσεται.

The Rich Man

Matt 19:21 = Luke 18:22   Mark 10:21

But Jesus   But Jesus looking at him loved him (ὁ
                                              δὲ Ἰησοῦς ἐμβλέψας αὐτῷ ἠγάπησεν
                                              αὐτόν)
said to him, ...   and said to him, ...

Matt 19:23–24 = Luke 18:24–25   Mark 10:23–24

"... it will be hard for a rich man to   "How hard it is for those who have
enter the kingdom of heaven."   riches to enter the kingdom of God."
                                              And the disciples were amazed
                                              (ἐθαμβοῦντο) at his words, but
Again I tell you,   Jesus answered and said to them
                                              again, "Children, how hard it is to
                                              enter the kingdom of God!
"It is easier for a camel to go through   It is easier for a camel to go through
the eye of a needle..."   the eye of a needle ..."

Third Prediction of the Passion

Matt 20:17–19 = Luke 18:31–33   Mark 10:32–34

(Matt only: And when they were   And they were on the road going up to
about to go to Jerusalem).   Jerusalem, and Jesus was going
                                              ahead of them, and they were amazed
                                              (ἐθαμβοῦντο) and those who followed
                                              were afraid (ἐφοβοῦντο).
And he took the Twelve (Matt: in   And taking the Twelve again, he
private on the road) and said to them   began to tell them ...
"... and on the third day he will be   "... and after three days he will rise."
raised" (Luke: "rise").
καὶ τῇ τρίτῃ ἡμέρᾳ ἐγερθήσεται (Luke: καὶ μετὰ τρεῖς ἡμέρας ἀναστήσεται.
ἀναστήσεται).

The Young Man Raised
Secret Mark after Mark 10:34

There was a certain woman whose
brother had died (ἀπέθανεν) . . .
(Jesus) stretched out (his) hand and
raised him, (ἤγειρεν αὐτόν, κρατήσας
τῆς χειρός) grasping his hand. And
the young man, looking at Jesus,
loved him (ὁ δὲ νεανίσκος ἐμβλέψας
αὐτῷ αὐτῷ ἠγάπησεν αὐτόν). . . . they
went into the house of the young
man, for he was rich (ἦν γὰρ
πλούσιος).

The Sons of Zebedee [1]

Matt 20:22–23

Jesus answered them and said, "You
do not know what you are asking.
Can you drink the cup that I shall
drink?"

They said to him, "We can." He said
to them, "The cup you will drink.

But to sit at my right hand . . . "

Mark 10:38–40a

But Jesus answered them, "You do
not know what you are asking. Can
you drink the cup which I drink; or
can you be baptized with the baptism
with which I am baptized?"
And they said to him, "We can." He
said to them, "The cup that I drink
you will drink; and with the baptism
with which I am baptized you will be
baptized.
But to sit at my right hand . . ."

In Jericho

Mark 10:46

And they came into Jericho.

And he[2] came into Jericho, And there
were the sister of the young man
whom Jesus loved (τοῦ νεανίσκου ὃν
ἠγάπα αὐτὸν ὁ Ἰησοῦς) and his mother
and Salome, and Jesus did not
receive them.

---

[1] For the Greek texts see above # 4.1.2.1

[2] Crossan (*Four Other Gospels,* 109–10) rightly calls attention to the fact that the
Secret Gospel, as quoted by Clement, read the singular, while the manuscripts of Mark
have the plural. But this does not necessarily imply that Clement's copy of the canonical Markan text also read the singular.

And when he was leaving Jericho with his disciples and a great crowd, Bartimaeus, a blind beggar, ...	And when he was leaving Jericho with his disciples and a great crowd, Bartimaeus, a blind beggar, ...

Secret Mark has arranged the original text of Mark in such a way that chapters 8–10 would have presented two stories of the raising of a dead person by Jesus, each placed after a prediction of the passion. These predictions themselves were altered so that they would speak of the "resurrection" (ἀναστῆναι) of Jesus, instead of Jesus "being raised" (ἐγερθῆναι). If these changes came from the hand of the redactor who produced the *Secret Gospel of Mark,* one would also ascribe to him the following changes in these chapters: the emphasis upon the "amazement" in the introduction to the story of the raising of the epileptic child: "All the crowd, when they saw him were greatly amazed" (ἐξεθαμβήθησαν, Mark 9:15); the statement of the amazement (ἐθαμβοῦντο) of the disciples after Jesus' saying about riches (Mark 10:24); the description of the amazement and fear of those who followed Jesus just before the insertion of the story of the raising of the young man: "and they were amazed (ἐθαμβοῦντο) and those who followed were afraid" (ἐφοβοῦντο, Mark 10:32); the expression of Jesus' love for the rich man (Mark 10:21) which creates a connection to the following story in *Secret Mark* ;[1] the addition of the baptism with which Jesus and the disciples must be baptized (Mark 10:38–39), which changes the prediction of martyrdom into a cryptic reference to baptism and eucharist; and the encounter in Jericho, which explains why the extant text of Mark 10:46 describes Jesus' entering and leaving Jericho without telling what happened there.[2]

It is difficult to be certain whether all or some of the other features in the preserved text of Mark which are not reflected in Matthew and Luke also reveal the hand of the *Secret Mark* redactor. One should certainly ascribe to him the change of the plural "mysteries" into the singular in Mark 4:11 and the insertion of the episode of the young man fleeing naked in Mark 14:51–52,[3] and perhaps also the increased

---

[1] Riddles remain here. Only Matt (19:20, 22) calls the rich man a νεανίσκος, the same term that is used in the *Secret Gospel* for the man raised by Jesus. Mark does not use this term (10: 17, 31). Only Luke, in agreement with the *Secret Gospel's* characterization of the youth who was raised, says of the rich man ἦν γὰρ πλούσιος σφόδρα (18:23), while Mark 10:22 and Matt 19:22 describes his wealth with the words ἦν γὰρ ἔχων χρήματα πολλά.

[2] Matthew's and Luke's parallels give little evidence for Mark's original text. In Matt 20:29 Jesus meets the blind man "coming out of Jericho"; in Luke 18:35 Jesus and his disciples "are approaching Jericho."

[3] For an attempt at a Gnostic interpretation of the significance of this addition see Hans-Martin Schenke,"The Mystery of the Gospel of Mark," *Second Century* 4 (1984) 65–82.

emphasis upon the "teaching" activity of Jesus.[1] In any case, the canonical Gospel of Mark shows evidence of the redaction which was also responsible for the insertion of the story of the raising of the young man in *Secret Mark*. In other words, the text of canonical Mark—it is the same text as the one known to Clement of Alexandria as Mark's public Gospel[2]—is not the original Mark used by Matthew and Luke, but an abbreviated version of the *Secret Gospel of Mark*.[3] It was only the latter that had survived, and in order to make this text suitable for public reading, the story of the raising of the young man and his subsequent private initiation by Jesus as well as the reference to this young man's sister and mother and Salome after Mark 10:46b were removed.

According to Clement of Alexandria, another version of the *Secret Gospel of Mark* was used by the Karpokratians. He explicitly quotes only one example for the difference between the legitimate Alexandrian and the falsified Karpokratian version: after the story of the raising of the young man, added in *Secret Mark* following Mark 10:34, the latter contained the words, "Naked man with naked man." This phrase, as well as some other things about which Clement's correspondent wrote, were not found in the Alexandrian church's version. A second difference between the two gospels is indicated by Clement's remark with respect to Secret Mark's addition at Mark 10:46 where he says that "the Secret Gospel adds *only*, 'And there were the sister of the young man . . .' But the many other things about which you wrote appear to be and are falsifications." These scanty remarks do not allow any conclusions with respect to the character of the Karpokratian *Secret Gospel of Mark*. It is true that the Karpokratians have been accused of sexual license even by Clement himself.[4] However, in this letter Clement does not indicate that the phrase "Naked man with naked man" has any such implications. Nakedness was widely practiced in early Christian baptism,[5] and this is most likely expressed in

---

[1] See for a full discussion Koester, "From Mark to Secret Mark," 44–47.

[2] Checking the quotations from the Gospel of Mark in Clement's writings demonstrates that there is no instance in which he quotes the more original text of Mark that Matthew and Luke used.

[3] Crossan (*Four Other Gospels*, 107–110) assumes that the *Secret Gospel of Mark* was the most original version of this Gospel. That, however, does not excplain the fact that Matthew and Luke used a copy of Mark which contained none of the features that are characteristic of the *Secret Gospel*.

[4] *Strom.* 3.2, 10.1. For other evidence see Morton Smith, *Clement of Alexandria*, Appendix B.

[5] Hippolytus (*Apostolic Tradition* 21.11) specifies that both the catechumen and the presbyter shall stand in the water naked.

this phrase of the Karpokratian version of this new edition of Mark's Gospel.

4.2 Stories about Jesus' Birth and Childhood

4.2.1 EARLIEST INFANCY NARRATIVES[1]

Stories about Jesus' birth must have circulated long before the writing of the Gospels of Matthew and Luke, whose infancy narratives are the earliest written records of such stories. But it is very difficult to be certain about the origin and development of these narratives. Their basic genre is that of the popular "personal legend," which was well known in the world of Israel, as well as in the world of Greece and Rome. In all these legends, some kind of divine agency at the conception or the birth of a great hero, king, or religious leader is a constitutive element.

Israel's scripture itself knew of the story of Sarah and the miraculous birth of her offspring Isaac who was born, as Paul (Gal 4:23) says, "through the promise" (in contrast to the birth of Ishmael who was born "according to the flesh"). Exod 2:1–11 tells the story of the divine protection of the infant Moses. Most of all, Hannah, the mother of Samuel, whose story is told in 1 Samuel 1, became the prototype of the barren woman who, because of her prayer and piety, conceives the child that should become the new leader of the people. Against this background, one can well understand the origin of the story that tells of the wondrously announced birth of John the Baptist (Luke 1:5–25). In fact, many details in this story recall the ancient narratives of Sarah and Hannah.[2] It is the story of the birth of the new prophet of Israel in the power of Elijah who will receive the holy spirit already in his mother's womb, will bring the nation back to its God, and reconstitute Israel as God's people (Luke 1:15–17). The entire story and the announcement of the mission of John remain entirely within the

---

[1] The most comprehensive recent investigation of the infancy narratives of the canonical gospels is Raymond E. Brown, *The Birth of the Messiah: A Commentary on the Infancy Narratives of Matthew and Luke* (New York: Doubleday, 1977). For recent scholarship see idem, "Gospel Infancy Narrative Research 1976–1986," *CBQ* 48 (1986) 468–83, 660–680. A most important and seminal essay was published by Martin Dibelius in 1932 "Jungfrauensohn und Krippenkind: Untersuchungen zur Geburtsgeschichte Jesu im Lukasevangelium," and reprinted in idem, *Botschaft und Geschichte: Gesammelte Aufsätze*, vol. 1 (Tübingen: Mohr/Siebeck, 1953) 1–78. For bibliography, see also Bovon, *Evangelium nach Lukas*, 43–45; Ulrich Lutz, *Matthew 1–7: A Commentary* (Minneapolis: Augsburg, 1989) 101–2.

[2] See Bovon, *Evangelium nach Lukas*, 52–62, 94–103.

confines of Israel's tradition and expectation. There are no Hellenistic or Christian elements in this narrative. There can be little doubt that it was formed and transmitted by the community of John the Baptist which, in this story, proclaimed the memory and heritage of their great prophetic leader.

With the stories surrounding Jesus' birth in both Matthew and Luke, the reader is introduced to a similar, yet also quite different world. There is still traditional Jewish messianic language, and the Lukan stories of the annunciation (1:26–38) and of the birth of Jesus (2:1–20) formally parallel the corresponding stories about John. Even with respect to a fundamental distinction between John and Jesus, namely the attribution of royal titles to the latter, they appear to remain within the confines of Israel's traditional terminology: the child to be born will be given the throne of David, his father (Luke 1:32), and the Magi from the East come to seek the newborn king of the Jews (Matt 2:2). But the horizon is no longer that of the prophetic tradition of Israel; nor do the stories about Jesus' birth simply tell of some divine intervention at the birth of another prophet or, for that matter, of another great man like some Hellenistic legends. Rather, they speak of the birth of the divine child that marks the beginning of the new age of the history of the world. All that is old is passing away with his birth; the new age of "peace on earth for all humankind" has come (Luke 2:14). These stories utilize the genre of "personal legend" and cast it into the language of scripture, but they transcend the traditional frame of this genre. They are, first of all, eschatological proclamation. Inasmuch as nothing less than the new age of the world begins with the birth of the child, the story of God's miraculous intervention into the natural processes of birth and death[1] requires a recourse to a mythic language that is unheard of in the traditional vocabulary of Israel and has few parallels in the language of the world of Greece and Rome.

Perhaps the only true parallel to these stories can be found in the *Fourth Eclogue* of Vergil that also speaks of the turning point of the ages in the birth of the child. The boldness of Vergil's poetic language is inspired by the same eschatological tension as the vision of the narratives about the birth of Jesus and of its announcement. In spite of a multitude of publications about the birth stories of Jesus during the last six decades no modern author has been able to grasp the dimensions and the depth of spirit of these gospel stories as well as did the great scholar of classical philology and history-of-religions Eduard

---

[1] There is a correspondence between the stories of Jesus' birth and of his resurrection.

Norden in his monograph about "The Birth of the Child."[1] He has demonstrated that the roots of the concept of the birth of the divine child, who will usher in the new age, lie in Egyptian mythology and mystery language. Not that one could trace either Vergil's eclogue or any of the gospel stories directly to one or several Egyptian legends or myths. But Egyptian lore about the birth of the god Aion (= Eternity, New Age) and about the birth of Horus/Harpokrates from Isis, as well as the statuettes of Isis with her child on her lap, had become widely known in the Greco-Roman world, beginning even before the Hellenistic period.

The identification of the form and language of the legends about Jesus' birth as "scriptural"[2] is not sufficient. Of course, they were told by people who knew Isaiah's prophecies that announced the coming of the divine child.[3] But even these ancient prophecies themselves belong to the same larger world from which Vergil learned the language and the concepts of his prophetic poems. The titles of the child of Isaiah 9:6, born to rule in the new age, "Wonderful Counselor, Mighty God, Everlasting Father, Prince of Peace," are the same as those which were given to Pharaoh at his enthronement.[4] The theme of peace among the animals, which appears in Isaiah's prophecy (Isa 11:6–8) as well as in Vergil's 4th Eclogue, has a firm place in ancient Egyptian enthronement language.[5] The message of peace on earth to all people of divine pleasure may remind us of Isaiah's "prince of peace," but it also recalls the propaganda for Rome and its ruler as the guarantor of peace for the entire inhabited world, which could claim Vergil as its prophet.

It is generally agreed that the infancy narratives belong into a rela-

---

[1] Eduard Norden, *Die Geburt des Kindes: Die Geschichte einer religiösen Idee* (Leipzig: Teubner, 1924; reprint: Darmstadt: Wissenschaftliche Buchgesellschaft, 1958).

[2] It is the primary merit of the commentary on the infancy narratives of Matthew and Luke by Brown (*Birth of the Messiah*) that it presents in detail the relevant stories and prophecies of scripture which have provided, to some degree, forms, themes, and language for these narratives. Unfortunately, Brown does not place these narratives into the wider context of the continuing influence of the Egyptian throne language and its resurgence in the language of political and religious expectation in the Hellenistic and Roman world.

[3] All of Isaiah 7–11 has been very influential, not only Isa 7:14 ("behold a virgin shall conceive and bear a son and shall call his name Immanuel") and 9:6–7 ("For to us a child is born, to us a son is given, and the government shall be on his shoulder"), but also Isa 11 (the prophecy of the coming of the shoot from the root of Jesse).

[4] See Hans Wildberger, *Jesaja 1–12* (Biblischer Kommentar, Altes Testament 10/1; Neukirchen-Vluyn: Neukirchener Verlag, 1972) 376–80.

[5] Wildberger, ibid., 456–57.

tively late phase of the development of the gospel tradition. For Paul, the sonship of Jesus dates from his resurrection from the dead (Rom 1:3–4). This is reflected in the Gospel of Mark where the confession of the centurion at the cross of Jesus constitutes the first time that a human being applies the title "Son of God" to Jesus.[1] That the two later Synoptic Gospels, Matthew and Luke, date the divine sonship of Jesus from his birth is not only related to a christological development which eventually resulted in the formulation of a christology that assumed Christ's preexistence as God's Son from before the beginning of the world. It is also related to the full realization of Christianity's entrance into the world of Hellenism and Rome. Paul's message announced the salvation for Jews and Gentiles before the coming of Christ in glory. Paul knew that his message had political implications. But it was left to the next generation to spell out the Christian antithesis to the eschatological claims of Roman imperial rule. The Book of Revelation is the best known testimony, and it is no accident that this book includes a story of the birth of the messiah that borrowed heavily from Hellenistic mythology (Revelation 12). The stories of Jesus' divine conception and miraculous birth belong into the same context.

The most striking feature revealing the non-Jewish origin of the story of the birth of Jesus is the divine conception of the child. "The idea of divine generation from a virgin is not only foreign to the Old Testament and to Judaism, but it is completely impossible."[2] This statement of Rudolf Bultmann is still valid insofar as the origin of this concept is concerned, and it cannot be moderated by theological or historical reflections.[3] This concept is Hellenistic and, ultimately, Egyptian. No other religious or political tradition of antiquity can be identified as its generator. However, though Jewish circles did not create this concept, it may well have found a cautious acceptance in certain circles of Hellenistic Judaism.

The most striking example of this Hellenistic-Jewish understanding of the stories of miraculous conception and birth is indirectly preserved by Philo of Alexandria in his *De Cherubim*.[4] In this treatise, Philo speaks of four women of Israel's history (Sarah, Leah, Rebecca, and Zipporah) as examples of virtues. In doing so, he clearly draws on

---

[1] Elsewhere in Mark, only the heavenly voice (Mark 1:11; 9:7) and the demons (3:11; 5:7) address Jesus with this title.

[2] Bultmann, *Synoptic Tradition*, 291.

[3] See especially the two excursus "Virginal Conception" and "The Charge of Illegitimacy" in Brown, *Birth of the Messiah*, 517–542.

[4] Dibelius ("Jungfrauensohn und Krippenkind," 30–33) has drawn attention to the importance of this treatise for the understanding of the Christian infancy narratives.

older legends about the miraculous ways in which these women conceived and gave birth. According to Gen 21:1, Sarah conceives when
God visits her, while she is alone (μονοθεῖσαν),[1] although the son to
whom she gives birth is born to Abraham (De Cherub. 45). The
account about Leah (De Cherub. 46) is even more explicit: she conceives "when God opens her womb" (Gen 29:31). Philo remarks that
normally "opening the womb of a woman" is done by the husband, that
is, through intercourse. Rebecca became pregnant through the one to
whom Isaac sent his prayers (De Cherub. 47), and Zipporah became
pregnant "completely without any mortal agency" (κύουσαν ἐξ οὐδενὸς
θνητοῦ τὸ παράπαν, De Cherub. 47). If it was possible, albeit allegori-
cally, for the Hellenistic Jew Philo to accept the concept of divine generation,[2] it must have been even less offensive to the traditional stories
used by authors of the Gospels of Matthew and Luke to tell of the
divine conception of the Savior whose message would challenge the
political claims of the divine Augustus and his heirs.

The Synoptic Gospels record several different older stories about
the birth of Jesus. All these stories are politically motivated. They
share only one of these stories, namely the announcement of the conception without human (male) agency: the dream of Joseph (Matt
1:18–25) and its variant, the story of the annunciation (Luke 1:26–38).
The other Synoptic stories were developed independently of each other
and they do not presuppose the narrative of the miraculous conception. Matthew's account of the visit of the magi and the murder of the
babes of Bethlehem (Matt 2:1–23) possibly combines two different
traditional stories, namely the story of the visit of the magi and
another story of the plot of Herod.[3] The last of these older stories
appears in Luke 2:1–20; it records the visit of the shepherds to the cra-
dle of the new-born child.

The two Matthean stories were formed in a very Biblical environment. The story of the coming of the magi from the East to worship
the new-born king (2:1–12) exhibits features of the story of Balaam
(Numbers 22–24).[4] The story of the plot of Herod (2:13–23) certainly
retains a historical memory of the murderous cruelty of Herod the

---

[1] The text of Gen 21:1 does not stress explicitly that Sarah was alone at her visitation by God. But that the tradition of the interpretation had emphasized this feature
is also evident in Paul, when he connects the story of Sarah's miraculous conception
with Isa 54:1 (= Gal 4:27): ". . . for the desolate has more children than she who has a
husband" (ὅτι πολλὰ τὰ τέκνα τῆς ἐρήμου μᾶλλον ἢ τῆς ἐχούσης τὸν ἄνδρα).

[2] See Bultmann's (Synoptic Tradition, 438) comment on Dibelius' article: "the
abstinence of the bridegroom until birth is specifically pagan."

[3] See Brown, Birth of the Messiah, 188–206, 225–29.

[4] Ibid., 193–96.

Great. At the same time, it is colored also by the Biblical accounts of
the Patriarch Joseph in Egypt, the birth of Moses, and the murder of
the children of the Israelites by Pharaoh.[1] The Biblical and Palestinian setting of these stories is evident. However, the intention of
both stories differs sharply from the parochial interests of a Jewish
environment. With the "East" as the homeland of the magi and with
the flight to Egypt, the horizon of the rule of the new king has become
universal. It must be added that the reconstruction of the pre-
Matthean stories remains extremely difficult, because Matthew not
only combined elements of two stories into a new unit, he also added
his own perspective by the repeated formula quotations which point to
the fulfillment of scripture—not necessarily the same scriptural passages which contributed to the formation of the original stories.

The Lukan story of Jesus' birth and the proclamation to the
shepherds (Luke 2:1–20) reveals a different milieu. Although the setting at Bethlehem and the shepherds may recall the city of the
shepherd boy David, there is no attempt to model the story on any
Biblical precedent, nor does it show any specific Palestinian coloring.
There is no reason to believe that the story originated in Palestine.
The introduction (2:1–5) which relates the birth of Jesus to Augustus
may have been added by Luke in order to create a parallel between
Jesus, the bringer of peace for the people of the earth, and Augustus
who could boast that he had established peace after decades of civil
war. But even the proclamation to the shepherds about the child in
the manger appeals to general beliefs of the Greco-Roman world. In
the Jewish tradition at the time of Jesus, shepherds are not generally
seen in a very positive light.[2] But in Greco-Roman mythology, legend,
and poetry the shepherd represents the golden age at which gods and
human beings live in harmony and nature is at peace.[3] Like the
bucolic poems of Vergil, Luke's story appeals to this romantic element
of the eschatology of the Roman world.

4.2.2 THE PROTO-GOSPEL OF JAMES

The Gospels of Matthew and Luke provide the only access to the
earliest stories about Jesus' birth and infancy. There seems to be no
older story in any apocryphal gospel that has survived independently,
although there may have been some isolated pieces of information,
such as the localization of the birth of Jesus in a cave which appears in

---

[1] Ibid., 225–29 and Table VII, p. 109.

[2] See Dibelius, "Jungfrauensohn und Krippenkind," 64–65.

[3] Ibid., 72–73. The attempt to demonstrate a special relationship to the cult of
Mithras has not been successful; see Dibelius, ibid., 67–73.

Justin Martyr[1] and also in the *Proto-Gospel of James*. On the other hand, the apocryphal birth and infancy gospels contain a wealth of legendary material that continues to grow throughout the following centuries.[2] Only two of the infancy gospels can be dated with some certainty into the 2nd century, the *Proto-Gospel of James* and the *Infancy Gospel of Thomas*.

The *Proto-Gospel of James*[3] is preserved in many Greek manuscripts and numerous translations of which those into Syriac, Arabic, Armenian, Coptic, and Slavonic are the most prominent.[4] None of these translations can claim to be a direct rendering of an older Greek text of this gospel. But with the exception of a few earlier fragments, even all Greek manuscripts which were known until a few years ago were written after the 10th century and show great variations in many details. A somewhat better access to the original Greek text was opened up more recently through the discovery and publication in 1958 of the *Papyrus Bodmer 5*,[5] a manuscript of the 3rd or 4th century. A fuller study of the transmission of the text of the *Proto-Gospel of James* and a new critical edition has been possible through this discovery.[6]

The discovery of *Papyrus Bodmer 5* makes clear that several parts of the later Greek manuscripts and of the translations into other ancient languages did not belong to the original story. The description, by Joseph in the first person, of the sudden cessation of nature at the moment of Jesus' birth (chapter 18.2) and the prayer of Salome (chapter 20.2) are missing in this papyrus. But even this relatively

---

[1] *Dial.* 78.5; see below # 5.2.2.2.

[2] See Oscar Cullmann on the younger infancy gospels in his "Kindheitsevangelien," in Hennecke-Schneemelcher, *NT Apokryphen*, 1. 363–72. This section is essentially the same as that in the English translation of the previous German edition (Hennecke-Schneemelcher-Wilson, *NT Apocrypha*, 1. 404–17).

[3] For a general discussion of this document see Edouard Cothenet, "Le Protévangile de Jaque: origine, genre et signification d'un premier midrash chrétien sur la Nativité de Marie," *ANRW* 2.25/6 (1988) 4245–69; Gero, "Apocryphal Gospels," 3978–79.

[4] See Oscar Cullmann on the "Protevangelium des Jakobus" in his "Kindheits-evangelien," in Hennecke-Schneemelcher, *NT Apocrypha*, 1. 335–36. A Latin translation did exist in ancient times; but the book was banned in the Western church. Only one fragmentary Latin manuscript of the 9th century has been discovered.

[5] M. Testuz, *Papyrus Bodmer V: Nativité de Marie* (Cologny: Bibliotheca Bodmeriana, 1958).

[6] E. de Strycker, *La forme la plus ancienne du Protévangile de Jacques: Recherches sur le Papyrus Bodmer 5 avec une édition du texte grec et une traduction annotée* (SHG 33; Brussels: 1961). The German translation in Hennecke-Schneemelcher, *NT Apo-kryphen*, 1. 338–49, is based upon this new edition, as is also the English translation of the previous German edition (Hennecke-Schneemelcher-Wilson, *NT Apocrypha*, 1. 374–88) which was reprinted in Cameron, *Other Gospels*, 109–21.

early papyrus includes portions that did not belong to the original work, especially the concluding chapters (22–24) which report about the death of Zacharias, the father of John the Baptist.[1] The work is entitled "The Birth of Mary, Revelation[2] of James." This has raised the question whether the entire report about the birth of Jesus (chapters 17–21) also should be viewed as a secondary expansion of the original writing, that is, whether the original writing was confined to the account of Mary's birth and virginity. But that cannot be proven.

It is evident that the author of the *Proto-Gospel of James* used the canonical gospels of Matthew and Luke. But it was certainly known to Origen, perhaps even to Clement of Alexandria. This establishes a date for its composition some time during the 2nd century CE. The pseudepigraphical author of the work is most likely "James, the brother of Jesus." However, it is not a Jewish-Christian writing like most of the other pseudepigrapha under the name of James, the brother of the Lord. The writing reveals no sectarian bias and it cannot be assigned to a particular Christian group or sect of the 2nd century. Its character differs fundamentally from any of the literature that characterized the nascent sectarian and anti-heretical writings of this period, because it is pure hagiography, perhaps the earliest hagiographical book of Christianity.

The topic of the *Proto-Gospel of James* is not the birth of Jesus, but the birth and virginity of Mary. It was written for the glorification of Mary and is, thus, a surprisingly early witness for the rapid expansion of biographical legends, not only about Jesus—that is already evident in the infancy narratives of Matthew and Luke—but also about Jesus' mother and her parents. But while the stories about the birth of Jesus still reveal the eschatological message of the proclamation of a new age with all its political implications, the *Proto-Gospel of James* exclusively caters to the interests of personal piety and, possibly, to an incipient cult of the mother of Jesus, analogous to the cult of a hero or heroine of the Hellenistic-Roman world.

The author has no real knowledge of the Temple of Jerusalem and its cult, no matter how often reference is made to Jewish ritual and purity rules. There are numerous allusions to, and borrowings from, the Biblical stories of Sarah and Hannah as well as from the canonical Gospels' story of Mary. But rarely does the author copy slavishly. Rather, the author's piety is wholly shaped by the language of the Bible. In this respect the analogy to the canonical gospel's infancy nar-

---

[1] See Cullmann in Hennecke-Schneemelcher, *NT Apokryphen*, 1. 337.

[2] This term is used in *Papyrus Bodmer 5*. Later manuscripts use "Narrative" or similar terms.

ratives is very close. However, the heroines of the story, Anna and her daughter Mary, are not Jewish women but examples of Hellenistic piety. Female sterility, the sorrow of Anna, could be a theme in any culture, Jewish, Greek, or Roman. But pregnancy of the "widow"—as is said of Anna—and virginity, combined with divine conception, here even extended to the "virgin birth," are presented in this writing as the mystery of the female that demands worship. That Mary remains a virgin even after she has given birth introduces the ascetic ideal of a life-long commitment to virginity. One is encountering a dimension of piety, in the form of a personal legend in the Hellenistic style, that is especially concerned with the role of the female in the process of the revelation's appearance in the flesh. The miraculous signs of the Synoptic Gospels' story that signify the arrival of the divine are here replaced by the wondrous virtues of virginity and ascetic dedication.

4.2.3 THE INFANCY GOSPEL OF THOMAS

While the *Proto-Gospel of James* is primarily concerned with hagiographical material and persons of the period before the birth of Jesus, the *Infancy Gospel of Thomas* focuses upon stories dealing with the childhood of Jesus. That this writing existed in some form in the 2nd century is not certain but also not improbable, although it does not seem likely that the *Epistula Apostolorum* quoted the *Infancy Gospel of Thomas*. But a reference in Irenaeus (*Adv. haer.* 1.13.1) suggests that this writing was used by the Marcosians. The title of the writing in most Greek manuscripts, "Report of the Israelite philosopher Thomas about the Childhood of the Lord"[1] claims an apostle as the author, but there is no relationship of this writing to any of the known Gnostic literature in the tradition of "Judas Thomas the Twin."[2]

No final judgment about the original form and content is possible. The variety of the available evidence in Greek manuscripts and in numerous translations is hopelessly confusing.[3] The traditions about

[1] Oscar Cullmann on the "Kindheitserzählung des Thomas" in his "Kindheitsevangelien," in Hennecke-Schneemelcher, *NT Apokryphen I*, 353. Cullmann, following A. de Santos Otero (see below), suggests that the Slavonic translation may have preserved the more original title "The Childhood of our Lord Jesus Christ." Thus, the name of the apostle Thomas would not have been connected with this writing in the earliest period of its transmission.

[2] See above, # 2.2.2.

[3] Cullmann in Hennecke-Schneemelcher, *NT Apokryphen*, 1. 349–360; see also idem, "The Infancy Story of Thomas" in his "Infancy Gospels," in Hennecke-Schneemelcher-Wilson, *NT Apocrypha*, 1. 388–401 (however, much of the introduction of this earlier edition must now be considered out of date). The best discussion of the problems of the transmitted texts and translations has been presented by Stephen Gero, "The Infancy

the childhood of Jesus constantly grew, were altered, and attracted new materials during a history of many centuries of transmission; later manuscripts of the *Infancy Gospel of Thomas* also include parts of the *Proto-Gospel of James*. None of the extant Greek manuscripts can be dated before the 14th century.[1] The Latin and Syriac versions are attested by manuscripts from an earlier period, but some of them remain unpublished. Arabic, Armenian, and Georgian versions seem to be secondary translations. Most important is probably the rich attestation of the *Infancy Gospel of Thomas* in the Slavonic tradition;[2] however, a satisfactory critical evaluation of the available evidence has not yet been achieved.[3]

Even if the earliest version of this gospel remains uncertain, there can be little doubt that stories about the childhood of Jesus were circulating during the 2nd century. The *Epistula Apostolorum*, written in the second half of that century, attests to one of the stories that is also contained in the various versions of the *Infancy Gospel of Thomas*, namely, the story that Jesus was sent to school where the teacher asked him to say "Alpha," whereupon Jesus responded with the request that the teacher explain to him first the meaning of "Beta" (*Epist. Apost.* 4 [15]).[4] But similar older stories may already have circulated at the time of the writing of the Gospel of Luke. To be sure, wherever the various versions of the *Infancy Gospel of Thomas* narrate the story of Jesus at twelve years in the Temple, they are clearly dependent upon the text of Luke 2:41–52. But this Lukan text itself exhibits features which suggest that the author has used an older story that told about the presence of Jesus' divine power even before his public appearance.[5] The primary interest that prompted the production of such stories is biographical.[6] The development of such stories is a comparatively late phenomenon in the formation of the

---

Gospel of Thomas: A Study of the Textual and Literary Problems," *NovT* 13 (1971) 46–80; see also idem, "Apocryphal Gospels," 3981–84.

[1] On the dates of the Greek manuscripts and of the manuscripts of all extant versions, see Gero, "The Infancy Gospel of Thomas," 49–55.

[2] All extant manuscripts derive from one or several translations made in the 10th–11th century; see Gero, ibid., 55.

[3] See Gero, ibid., 53–54, especially p. 53, n. 6 with respect to the important work of A. de Santos Otero (*Das kirchenslavische Evangelium des Thomas* [PTS 6; Berlin: De Gruyter, 1967]).

[4] For the full text of this passage, see C. Detlef G. Müller, "Epistula Apostolorum" in Hennecke-Schneemelcher, *NT Apokryphen*, 1. 208; H. Duensing, "Epistula Apostolorum," in Hennecke-Schneemelcher-Wilson, *NT Apocrypha*, 1. 193.

[5] Brown, *Birth of the Messiah*, 480–83. Brown designates such narratives as "hidden life stories."

[6] See Bovon, *Evangelium nach Lukas*, 154.

Synoptic tradition, but Luke shows that this development had begun as early as the end of the 1st century.[1]

Some of the narratives of the *Infancy Gospel of Thomas* make it evident that the childhood stories mirror the miracles of the later ministry of Jesus.[2] In the first story (chapter 2) Jesus makes twelve sparrows from clay, and a Jew complains to his father Joseph that he had violated the Sabbath; the story is modelled on gospel stories in which Jesus, during his ministry, violates the Sabbath.[3] He heals the foot of a worker who had accidentally split it with an axe (chapter 10), and saves his brother James who had been bitten by a viper. He raises a child who had fallen from the upper story of a house (chapter 9), the little child of a neighbor who had died (chapter 17),[4] and resuscitates a man who died during the building of a house. Of the several variants of the story of Jesus in school (chapters 6–7; 14 and 15), the story in chapter 15 tells of Jesus finding a book, taking it, and, without reading, by the power of the holy spirit expounding the law for all who were present; influence of the Jesus' first preaching in Nazareth (Luke 4:16–22) is evident. The parable of the sower (Mark 4:3–9 parr.) apparently provides the motif for the story of the miraculous harvest of hundred measures of wheat from a single seed that Jesus had planted (chapter 12).

But other miracle stories do not mirror any of the narratives of Jesus' ministry. They resemble more the narratives of the apocryphal Acts of the Apostles, especially the punishment miracles that tell of the death of other children who have made the boy Jesus angry (chapters 3–4) and of the death of the teacher who struck Jesus on the head (chapter 14).[5] Some stories seem to be borrowed from general popular lore.[6] The stories about the superiority of Jesus over his teachers have a parallel in stories about Buddha as child, and the

---

[1] Brown (*Birth of the Messiah,* 487–88) suggests that also the story of the wine miracle at Cana (John 2:1–12) was originally such a "hidden life" tradition.

[2] "'Hidden life' stories show that he was God's Son even as a boy by having him work miracles just as he does in the ministry" (Brown, ibid., 481).

[3] See, e.g., Mark 3:1–6; John 5:2–16.

[4] See Mark 5:35–43; Luke 7:11–17; both stories have clearly influenced the story of the raising of the neighbor's child. See also John 11.

[5] See the punishment miracles *Acts of Peter* 32; *Acts of Thomas* 8–9.

[6] This is most likely the case with respect to the story of the carrying of water in the garment (chap. 11), the miraculous stretching of a piece of wood in order to make two beams of equal length (chap. 13), and the story of Jesus and the dyer from the Arabic version of the Infancy Gospel (see Cullmann, "Infancy Gospel of Thomas" in Hennecke-Schneemelcher-Wilson, *NT Apocrypha,* 1. 400–401).

story of the clay sparrows that receive life through Jesus clapping his hands recalls the motif of an Egyptian fairy tale.[1]

It is evident that the majority of these stories are either based on the older traditions about Jesus' public ministry, especially as they are already enshrined in the canonical gospels, or are drawn from the wider store of various narratives of the ancient world. The tendency to incorporate an increasing amount of such materials into the hagiographical exploration of Jesus' childhood is richly attested in the later infancy gospels.[2]

4.3 The Gospel of Matthew [3]

4.3.1 MANUSCRIPTS

In contrast to the Gospel of Mark, the Gospel of Matthew is quite well attested in the earliest tradition of Christian communities. There are two early papyri, written about 200 CE, containing at least the fragmentary text of the Gospel of Matthew.[4] Six more papyri were written in the 3d century.[5] Rich attestation comes from the 4th century: six papyri,[6] five uncial manuscripts,[7] and of course, the two oldest manuscripts which present the entire text of the Bible ($\aleph$ and B, i.e., Codices Sinaiticus and Vaticanus). About three dozen uncials and two papyri from the following centuries can be added to these

---

[1] Relevant parallels are listed and discussed in Bauer, *Leben Jesu*, 95–97.

[2] Examples from these later narratives are translated by Cullmann, "Later Infancy Gospels," in Hennecke-Schneemelcher-Wilson, *NT Apocrypha*, 1. 404–17; see also Bauer, *Leben Jesu*, 97–100.

[3] For a general review of recent scholarship on the Gospel of Matthew see Graham Stanton, "The Origin and Purpose of Matthew's Gospel: Matthean Scholarship from 1945–1980," *ANRW* 2.25/3 (1985) 1889–1951. Some of the important monographs are Bornkamm-Barth-Held, *Tradition and Interpretation*; Jack Dean Kingsbury, *Matthew: Structure, Christology, Kingdom* (Philadelphia: Fortress, 1975); idem, *Matthew as Story* (2d ed.; Philadelphia: Fortress, 1988). A representative collection of important essays has been published by Joachim Lange, *Das Matthäusevangelium* (WdF 525; Darmstadt: Wissenschaftliche Buchgesellschaft, 1980).

[4] $\mathfrak{p}^{64}$ and $\mathfrak{p}^{67}$, both fragments of the same manuscript, with a few verses from Matthew 3, 5, and 26; $\mathfrak{p}^{77}$ with the text of Matt 23:30–39.

[5] $\mathfrak{p}^1$, $\mathfrak{p}^{35}$, $\mathfrak{p}^{37}$, $\mathfrak{p}^{53}$, $\mathfrak{p}^{70}$. All of these are only small fragments, containing but a few verses. $\mathfrak{p}^{45}$, presenting the text of all four canonical gospels, also preserves only a few verses of Matthew 20 and 21, and Matt 25:41–26:39. Thus there is no early attestation of the entire text of Matthew that is comparable to that for the text of the Fourth Gospel, where $\mathfrak{p}^{66}$ and $\mathfrak{p}^{75}$ have preserved considerable portions of the text; see above # 3.4.1.

[6] $\mathfrak{p}^{19}$, $\mathfrak{p}^{21}$ (both 4th or 5th century), $\mathfrak{p}^{25}$, $\mathfrak{p}^{62}$, $\mathfrak{p}^{71}$, $\mathfrak{p}^{86}$.

[7] 058, 0160, 0171, 0231, and 0242.

witnesses.[1] There can be no doubt that this Gospel was most widely used and most frequently copied in the early Byzantine period.

4.3.2 ATTESTATION

References to texts from the Gospel of Matthew and quotations from this writing appear frequently in ancient Christian literature.[2] However, the sayings quoted in *1 Clem.* 13.2 and 46.8, and the various parallels in the *Epistles of Ignatius* and the *Epistle of Barnabas* cannot be taken as evidence for the use of the Gospel of Matthew.[3] More difficult to evaluate are the quotations of sayings in *Did.* 1.3–5,[4] but this small collection of sayings of Jesus, composed from various sources, is most likely an interpolation which was made after the middle of the 2d century.[5] No use of the First Gospel can be demonstrated in any other section of the *Didache*.[6]

In the middle of the 2d century, quotations from the text of Matthew's Gospel are clearly in evidence. The sayings collection used by the author of *2 Clement* is based on the text of Matthew (and Luke, and probably an apocryphal source);[7] the Valentinian author Ptolemy, in his *Letter to Flora*,[8] uses the Gospel of Matthew frequently, and Jus-

---

[1] Among these are 𝔭[44] (6th or 7th century), 𝔭[83] (6th century); uncials from the 5th century A (02), C (04), D (05), W (032), and 0170; from the 6th century N (022), P (024), Z (035), Σ (042), Φ (043), 0164, and 0237; from the 7th century 0102, 0104, 0106, 0107, 0200, and 0204; from the 8th century E (07), L (019), 047, 064, 067, 071, 073, 078, 085, 087/092b, 089, 094, 0116, 0118, 0148, 0161, 0234, and 0250; from the 9th century F (09), G (011), H (013), K (017), M (021), U (030), V (031), 0128, 0135, 0136, 0196, 0197, 0255, and 0271; from the 10th century S (028), X (033), and 0249.

[2] The most comprehensive collection of materials can be found in Massaux, *Influence de l'Évangile de Saint Matthieu*. However, Massaux ascribes to the use of the Gospel of Matthew numerous instances in which quotations from the free oral tradition are more likely. See also the more balanced judgments in Köhler, *Rezeption des Matthäusevangeliums*.

[3] Koester, *Synoptische Überlieferung*, 4–61, 124–53. For the use of Matthew in the Apostolic Fathers see also *The New Testament in the Apostolic Fathers* by a Committee of the Oxford Society of Historical Theology (Oxford: 1905); Leon E. Wright, *Alterations of the Words of Jesus as quoted in the Literature of the Second Century* (Cambridge, MA: Harvard University Press, 1952). See also above ## 2.1.4.3 and 3.2.3.2.

[4] Koester, *Synoptische Überlieferung*, 220–37.

[5] Bentley Layton, "The Sources, Date and Transmission of *Didache* 1.3b–2.1," *HTR* 61 (1968) 343–83. For the discussion see also W. Rordorf, "Le Probléme de la transmission textuelle de *Didachè* 1,3b.–2,1," in: Franz Paschke, ed., *Überlieferungsgeschichtliche Untersuchungen* (TU 125; Berlin: Akademie-Verlag, 1981) 499–513; Niederwimmer, *Didache*, on *Did.* 1.3–5.

[6] Koester, *Synoptische Überlieferung*, 160–223. See above # 1.4.3.

[7] Koester, *Synoptische Überlieferung*, 70–105.

[8] In Epiphanius, *Adv. haer.* 33.3.1–7.10. The Greek text has been edited by Gilles Qispel, *Ptolémée, Lettre à Flora: Analyse, texte critique, traduction, commentaire et*

tin Martyr quotes large sections from a gospel harmony which was composed from the Gospels of Matthew and Luke, possibly also Mark.[1]

The name of Matthew, however, never appears in the context of these quotations, which is probably due to the fact that at least 2 *Clement* and Justin do not use one or several separate gospels but a harmony they know as "the gospel,"[2] and not as the work of a particular author.[3]

4.3.3 AUTHOR AND INTEGRITY

Matthew as the name of an author of a writing appears for the first time in a fragment of bishop Papias of Hierapolis who lived in the first half of the 2d century:

> Matthew composed the sayings (τὰ λόγια) in the Hebrew language, and each translated them (ἡρμήνευσεν) as best he could. (Eusebius, *Hist. eccl.* 3.39.16)

This remark has been variously interpreted, and the scholarly debate has not produced a definitive and generally accepted explanation.[4] In Eusebius's report, this quote from Papias's writings follows immediately upon his quote from the same author about the Gospel of Mark.[5] Thus the reference to Matthew as the author of "the sayings" is widely understood as a reference to the canonical Gospel of Matthew, and there can be no question that this is what Eusebius thought when he copied Papias's information. But the difficulties are evident. First of all, Papias speaks only about "the sayings" of Jesus. As a reference to the Gospel of Matthew, this must seem very strange, especially in view of the fact that Papias states, with respect to the Gospel of Mark, that Mark wrote "the things said *and done* by the Lord." Second, Papias's reference to a "Hebrew" composition by Matthew is extraordinary because it is certain that there never was a Semitic (Hebrew or

---

index grec (2d ed.; SC 24; Paris: Cerf, 1966); see also Völker, *Quellen,* 87–93; English translation in Layton, *Gnostic Scriptures,* 306–15; see also Foerster, *Gnosis,* 1. 154–61.

[1] See below, # 5.2.

[2] However, Justin uses both the plural (*1 Apol.* 66.3) and the singular (*Dial.* 10.2).

[3] The only exception may be Justin, *Dial.* 106.3, where a reference to information about Peter that can come only from the Gospel of Mark (3:16–17) is said be be written in "his," i.e., Peter's memoirs. See above # 4.1.1.

[4] The most recent comprehensive discussion can be found in Ron Cameron, *Apocryphon of James,* 108–12.

[5] See above, # 4.1.2.

Aramaic) original of the Gospel of Matthew.[1] Third, there is no evidence for the existence of various differing translations into Greek in which the Gospel of Matthew could have been circulating in its earliest period, as is claimed in Papias's statement.[2] To be sure, that Matthew was the oldest Gospel and that it was originally written in Aramaic (or Hebrew) is the traditional view, which was held from the time of the ancient church. The oldest statement comes from Irenaeus:

> Now Matthew published among the Hebrews in their own tongue also a written Gospel, while Peter and Paul were preaching in Rome and founding the church (quoted in Eusebius *Hist. eccl.* 5.8.2).

Origen's *Commentary on Matthew* refers to something that he claims to have "learned from the traditions":

> ... that first was written (the Gospel) according to Matthew, who was once a tax collector and afterwards an apostle of Christ, who published it for those who from Judaism came to believe, composed as it was in the Hebrew language (quoted in Eusebius *Hist. eccl.* 6.25.4; LCL).

Eusebius made a similar statement—without indicating a particular source—when he described the time of Domitian:

> Matthew had first preached to the Hebrews, and when he was at the point of going to others he transmitted in writing in his native language the Gospel according to himself, and thus supplied by writing the lack of his own presence to those from whom he was sent (*Hist. eccl.* 3.24.6; LCL).

It is quite probable that all these statements are ultimately inspired by Papias's tradition about "Matthew who composed the sayings in Hebrew." Through the claims of Jerome, this assumption of the originally Hebrew Gospel of Matthew was connected with the theory of its fragmentary preservation in the so-called *Gospel according to the Hebrews*.[3] The priority of a Hebrew (or Aramaic) Matthew is still held

---

[1] The Greek literary style of the Gospel of Matthew and its use of Greek sources (Mark and Q) and materials exclude this.

[2] Unless one wants to assume that Papias's information is wrong on all counts, with respect to the character of this Gospel, with respect to its original language, and with respect to the translation into Greek, Papias' remark is better understood as a reference to an altogether different writing. The writing he describes would have been a collection of sayings, composed in Hebrew (i.e., Aramaic), and translated into Greek several times. This characterization fits the Synoptic Sayings Source quite well: it was probably composed originally in Greek, but some of its part may have been translated from Aramaic into Greek more than once, and it consisted primarily of sayings of Jesus. See above # 2.3.1.

[3] For a discussion of the Jewish-Christian Gospels and the problems caused by

by some today. But hypotheses in favor of this assumption usually propose that some earlier form or part of Matthew was composed in Hebrew, and that it was this earlier version on which some of the other gospels were dependent.[1] What is actually at stake here is the integrity of the Gospel of Matthew itself. Theories developed about a more original Matthew, whether first written in Hebrew or not, always assume that there was an earlier version of this Gospel of a character that differed clearly from the Gospel of Mark and from the Synoptic Sayings Source, i.e., from the two sources used by Matthew according to the two-source hypothesis, and from the preserved Greek text of Matthew.[2] Over against such speculations, it still seems to be the most plausible assumption that the manuscript tradition of Matthew's Gospel has preserved its text more or less in its oldest form. To be sure, there are variations in the manuscript transmission. But unlike the Gospels of John and Mark, there are no indications, internal or external, that an originally Hebrew or Greek text of the Gospel of Matthew underwent substantial alteration before the emergence of the archetype(s) of the text upon which the extant manuscript tradition depends.

We do not know the author of this Gospel. That the original composition of the Matthew's Gospel was in Greek and that it depended upon earlier Greek gospel sources, makes it highly unlikely that Jesus' disciple Levi/Matthew wrote the Gospel which bears his name. However, the name Matthew may have been connected with the tradition of sayings and their written composition which the author used, i.e., with the Synoptic Sayings Source.

Jerome's ambiguous statements about the Hebrew Matthew see Philipp Vielhauer, "Jewish-Christian Gospels," in Hennecke-Schneemelcher-Wilson, *NT Apocrypha*, 1. 117–39.

[1] This was first proposed by Ferdinand Christian Baur, *Kritische Untersuchungen über die kanonischen Evangelien, ihr Verhältniß zueinander, ihren Charakter und Ursprung* (Tübingen: Fues, 1847) 572–82. On the controversies about Baur's view in the Tübingen school see R. H. Fuller, "Baur versus Hilgenfeld: A Forgotten Chapter in the Debate on the Synoptic Problem," *NTS* 24 (1977–78) 355–70. For a more recent theory of a Hebrew Proto-Matthew see Malcom Lowe and David Flusser, "Evidence Corroborating a Modified Proto-Matthean Synoptic Theory," *NTS* 29 (1983) 25–47.

[2] The most cogent, albeit it very complex, synoptic source theory recently developed, which assumes that an earlier version of Matthew existed, which functioned as a source also for the other Synoptic Gospels, was proposed by Boismard, see P. Benoit and M.-É. Boismard, *Synopse des quatres Evangiles en français*, vol. II: *Commentaire* (Paris: Cerf, 1972). Cf. also M.-É. Boismard, "The Two-Source Theory at an Impasse," *NTS* 26 (1979–80) 1–17. For criticism see F. W. Beare, "On the Synoptic Problem: A New Documentary Theory," *ATR* SS 3 (1974) 15–28.

4.3.4 SOURCES

The two-source hypothesis remains the most probable basis for a more accurate definition of the sources used by Matthew. This hypothesis says: (1) Mark is the oldest extant gospel and was used both by Matthew and Luke. (2) In addition, Matthew and Luke used a second common source, containing mostly sayings of Jesus (thus called the Synoptic Sayings Source, or "Q"), that is no longer extant but can be reconstructed with a fair degree of certainty.[1] An additional problem arises from the observation that Matthew gives evidence for having used a different edition of the document Q, especially concerning the Q materials now incorporated in the Sermon on the Mount (Matthew 5–7). This "sermon" may be the result of a special redaction of Q, as has been discussed above.[2]

The two-source hypothesis cannot fully explain the source problem of the Gospel of Matthew. The reasons are manifold: (1) as has been pointed out in the treatment of Mark,[3] the extant copies of Mark seem to derive from a revised version of that Gospel and not from the earlier version used by Matthew (and Luke); (2) the reconstruction of the Synoptic Sayings Source must necessarily remain hypothetical; (3) there are numerous sayings materials in Matthew which are not paralleled in Q and obviously derive from a special source used only by Matthew, often called "M";[4] (4) the narratives about the birth of Jesus in Matthew (chapters 1–2) have no relationship to any of these sources, nor are they in any way connected with the traditions of Luke's birth narrative[5]—thus a fourth source or tradition must be posited for these materials.

---

[1] On the recent debate about the renewal of the so-called Griesbach hypothesis see above # 2.3.1.

[2] See # 2.3.4 on the consequences of the hypothesis developed by Hans Dieter Betz, *Essays on the Sermon on the Mount*.

[3] See above # 4.1.

[4] The hypothesis that one must assume the existence of a special source for Matthew (M) and a special source for Luke (L), in addition to Mark and Q (four-source hypothesis), was most elaborately developed by B. H. Streeter, *The Four Gospels: A Study of Origins* (London: Macmillan, 1924). However, it is not necessary to assign all the special Matthean sayings of Jesus to "M" because they may already have been incorporated into the Jewish-Christian redaction of Q that Matthew used; see above # 2.3.4.

[5] Brown, *Birth of the Messiah*; see above # 4.2.1.

4.3.5 MATTHEW'S USE OF SOURCES

The basic framework of the narrative in Matthew's Gospel is derived from Mark. In the first part of his Gospel, Matthew has somewhat rearranged the Markan order, primarily for the composition of the chapters describing Jesus' healing ministry (Matthew 8–9). Matthew at first followed Mark's narrative (with some omissions) up to Mark 1:39 = Matt 4:23–25, then left this context for the insertion of the Sermon on the Mount (Matthew 5–7), and afterwards (Matt 8:1) returned to the Markan context for two healing miracles which he uses to introduce two chapters he composed himself about Jesus' healing ministry. Mark 1:40–45 (healing of the leper) and Mark 2:1–12 (healing of the man sick with palsy) each constitute the first story of the two parts of this composition (= Matt 8:1–4; 9:1–8). Most of the other healing narratives in these two chapters are drawn from different contexts of Mark's Gospel[1] (one comes from another source, apparently Q,[2] and one may be a Matthean composition[3]). At the same time, Matthew included materials found in the same Markan context, although they did not describe Jesus' healing ministry.[4] It is also important to observe that the stories which Matthew drew from other Markan contexts in the composition of these chapters appear exactly in the same order in which they are reported in Mark. The following chart illustrates Matthew's compositional procedure:

[1] Mark 1:21–39; 4:35–41; 5:1–20, 21–43; 8:22–26(?). The latter, a story of the healing of two blind men, also contains elements of Matt 20:29–34 = Mark 10:46–52; it was perhaps composed by Matthew, as was the following story, Matt 9:32–33; see Bultmann, *Synoptic Tradition,* 212, and the next footnotes.

[2] Matt 8:5–13 = Luke 7:1–10. On the problem of the presence of this miracle narrative in Q, a writing that contained mostly sayings, see Robinson, "Kerygma and History," 56–57; Lührmann, *Redaktion,* 57–58: the story as it appeared in Q contained mostly dialogue and only very little narrative material; the narrative elements of the Matthean and Lukan versions have almost nothing in common; thus they were added by the two authors independently of each other.

[3] Matt 9:32–33 (healing of a dumb demoniac) seems to be composed by Matthew on the basis of the brief story of the exorcism of a dumb demon (Matt 12:22–23 = Luke 11:14) which Q had used as introduction for the Beelzebul controversy (Q/Luke 11:15, 17–20, 23). With regard to the possible Matthean authorship of Matt 9:32–33 see Bultmann, *Synoptic Tradition,* 212.

[4] Call of Levi (Matt 9:9–13 = Mark 2:13–17), question about fasting (Matt 9:14–17 = Mark 2:18–22).

	Matthew	Mark same context	Mark other context	Other source
Summary account	4:23–25	1:39		
Sermon on the Mount	5:1–7:29			Q and M
Leper	8:1–4	1:40–45		
Centurio's servant	8:5–13			Q/Luke 7:1–10
Peter's mother	8:14–15		1:29–31	
Healing summary	8:16–17		1:32–34	
Discipleship	8:18–22			Q/Luke 9:57–60
Stilling a tempest	8:23–27		4:35–41	
Gadarene demoniacs	8:28–34		5:1–20	
Man sick with palsy	9:1–8	2:1–12		
Call of Levi	9:9–13	2:13–17		
Question of fasting	9:14–17	2:18–22		
Jairus' daughter	9:18–26		5:21–43	
Two blind men	9:27–31		8:22–26[1]	
Dumb demoniac	9:32–33			Q/Luke 11:14

Apart from these changes in the Markan order in the first part of the Gospel, other deviations are few. The pericope of the call of the Twelve (disciples) from Mark 3:13–19 and the instruction for the sending of the Twelve from Mark 6:7–13 have been used to form the introduction and part of the material in Matthew's sending of the twelve disciples and mission discourse (Matt 9:35; 10:1–4, 9–11, 14). Mark 1:22 (reaction to Jesus' teaching) has been used as the conclusion of the Sermon on the Mount (Matt 7:28–29), while the healing of the demoniac in the synagogue, introduced by the remark about Jesus' teaching (Mark 1:23–28), has been omitted. Also missing is the parable of the Seed Growing Secretly (Mark 4:26–29).[2]

Pericope Title	Mark	Matthew
Reaction to Jesus' teaching	1:22	7:28
Demoniac in synagogue	1:23–27	———
Report of Jesus' exorcism	1:28	4:24
Call of the Twelve	3:13	5:1
	3:14–15	———
	3:16–19	10:2–4

---

[1] Unless Matthew is using Mark 10:46–52 for this story; see above.

[2] However, this pericope may not have been part of the Markan text used by Matthew; see above # 4.1.2.1.

Sending of the Twelve   6:6–7   9:35–10:1
                                         6:8   10:5, 8, 9
                                         6:9–11   10:10–11, 14
                                         6:12–13   ─────────

Otherwise all Markan sections are reproduced by Matthew in their exact Markan order.

The use of the Gospel of Mark is even more obvious in the second half of Matthew. From 14:1 (= Mark 6:14) to the end of the work, Matthew reproduced almost all Markan pericopes in the same order in which they appear in Mark. The only sections which are omitted are the healing stories of the deaf-mute (Mark 7:32–36) and of the blind man of Bethsaida (Mark 8:22–26),[1] and the apophthegmata about the strange exorcist (Mark 9:38–41) and of the widow's mite (Mark 12:41–44). In the Synoptic Apocalypse, Matthew passes over the Markan conclusion of the discourse (13:33–37).

It is more difficult to determine the changes made by Matthew in his use of the Synoptic Sayings Source, because this source can be reconstructed only by detailed comparison with the corresponding sections reproduced by Luke. The use of Mark reveals two literary procedures. On the one hand, Matthew tends to leave the order of materials in his sources intact. On the other hand, the desire to construct larger thematic units is evidenced in the description of Jesus' healing ministry in Matthew 8 and 9; for such purposes Matthew rearranges the order of his sources. Thus it would not be out of character for the large speeches in the Gospel of Matthew to be the result of eclectic collection and redaction of sources and materials available to the author.

However, in several of his speeches, Matthew follows a set procedure. Except for the first of the five major speeches, the Sermon on the Mount (Matthew 5–7), he begins a speech with the reproduction of some Markan materials, then adds sayings from Q, and concludes with materials drawn from his special source or other contexts and traditions.

The second major discourse, recorded at the occasion of the sending of the twelve disciples (Matt 9:37–10:42), combines three smaller discourses, beginning with one from Mark (6:6–11), then adding materials from one or two discourses from Q (= Luke 10:2–16; 12:2–9), but also supplying material from other Markan contexts:

─────────

[1] However, this Markan story may have influenced Matt 9:27–31; see above.

Pericope or Saying	Matthew	Mark	Other Sources
Description of situation	9:35a	6:7	
Summary account	9:35b[1]		
Sheep without a shepherd	9:36	6:34	
The harvest is great	9:37		Q 10:2
Authority for the disciples	10:1	6:7	
Names of the Twelve	10:2–4	3:16–19	
"He commanded them . . ."	10:5	6:8a	
Not to the Gentiles . . .	10:5b–6		"M" source[2]
Proclamation and healing	10:7–8		Q? (Luke 9:2)
Mission instructions	10:9–11	6:8b–10	
". . . no shoes . . ."	10:10b		Q 10:4
Worker's wages	10:10c		Q 10:7
Entering a house	10:12–13		Q 10:6–10a
Leaving a place	10:14	6:11	(Q 10:10a–11)
Punishment for rejection	10:15		Q 10:12
"Like sheep among wolves"	10:16		Q 10:3
Persecution of the disciples	10:17–23[3]	13:9–13	
Disciple not over the master	10:24–25		Q 6:40
Fearless confession	10:26–33		Q 12:2–9
Division in households	10:34–36		Q 12:51–53
Conditions of discipleship	10:37–39		Q 14:26f; 17:33
Acceptance of the disciples	10:40–42	9:37, 41	

The procedure is similar in the composition of the parable speech, Matthew 13. Here as well as in the eschatological speech (Matthew 24), the Gospel of Mark already presented to Matthew materials in the form of a speech of Jesus. Thus Matthew essentially reproduces parts of the parable chapter from the Gospel of Mark (4:1–20, 25, 30–32 = Matt 13:1–13, 18–23, 31–32) and adds materials from Q (= Luke 10:32–34; 13:20–21) as well as four parables from his special source (Matt 13:24–30 and 36–43, 44, 45–46, 47–50).[4]

Parable	Matthew	Mark	Other Sources
Introduction	13:1–2	4:1–2	
The Sower	13:3–9	4:3–9	

[1] This is a Matthean composition based on Mark 1:39; 3:7–10. Matthew uses the same materials for the summary account in 4:23–25, which introduces thé Sermon on the Mount; see also Luke 8:1.

[2] These instructions have no parallel either in Q or in Mark. They may be due to the Jewish-Christian redactor of Q who also composed the Sermon on the Mount; see below.

[3] Matt 10:23 seems to be a Matthean composition.

[4] About this special Matthean source for the parables and its possible relationship to a source used by the *Gospel of Thomas* see above # 2.2.4.3.

Reason for parables	13:10–12	4:10–12	
Logion	13:13	4:25	
Scriptural formula quotation	13:14–15		Isa 6:9–10
Blessed witnesses	13:16–17		Q 10:23–24
Interpretation of the Sower	13:18–23	4:13–20	
The Tares	13:24–30		Special Source
The Mustard Seed	13:31–32	4:30–32	Q 13:18–19[1]
The Leaven	13:33		Q 13:20–21
Use of parables	13:34	4:33–34	
Scriptural formula quotation	13:35		Ps 77:2(?)[2]
Interpretation of the Tares	13:36–43		Special source
The Hidden Treasure	13:44		Special source
The Pearl	13:45–46		Special source
The Fishnet	13:47–50		Special source

Some of the church order materials in Matthew's catechism (18:1–35) were already assembled by Mark, and the discourse begins at the point at which Matthew, in the reproduction of his source, has reached Mark 9:33–37, that is, the pericope which he uses as the opening for the discourse. What has been added by Matthew has been drawn from various contexts of Q and from Matthew's special source. Again, we can observe the peculiar method of the redactor: Mark is used at the beginning of the discourse, then materials from Q are added, and special source materials dominate in the final portion of the discourse:

Pericope	Matthew	Mark	Other Sources
Dispute about greatness	18:1–5[3]	9:33–37	
About offences	18:6–9	9:42–48	
Parable of the Lost Sheep	18:12–14[4]		Q 15:3–7
About forgiveness	18:15		Q 17:3
Reproving a brother	18:16–17		Special source
Power of binding & losing	18:18		Special source
Prayer and fulfillment	18:19		Special source

[1] In this parable, Matthew follows the order of Mark 4, but has also used Q in the editing of his version of the parable: λαβὼν ἄνθρωπος in vs. 31, and the verb αὐξάνω in vs. 32 have no parallels in Mark but only in Luke 13:18–19.

[2] This passage from the Psalms, in its Greek form, is remotely related to Matt 13:35. About more closely related sayings see above # 2.1.3.

[3] Matthew has revised this Markan pericope radically, omitting the saying of Mark 9:35 about being first (it appears later in Matt 20:27), and inserting another saying about entering the kingdom as children (Matt 18:3), which he drew from a different Markan context (Mark 10:15).

[4] Matt 18:10 is a saying of unknown origin; Matt 18:11 does not belong to the original text of Matthew but is an intrusion from Luke 19:10, which is missing in the most reliable manuscripts (ℵ B etc.).

Presence of Jesus	18:20	Special source[1]
Forgive seven times seventy	18:21–22	Q 17:4
Parable: Unmerciful Servant	18:23–35	Special source

The eschatological discourse in Matthew 24–25 is an expanded version of Mark's apocalypse (Mark 13:1–37). All verses from Mark 13 which are used by Matthew appear in the same order in which they are found in Mark. Matthew uses the same procedure that he employed in his composition of the parable speech, Matthew 13: he begins with a large section of Mark in which he maintains the Markan order of the materials; he then inserts sections from Q,[2] and he relies on special sources in the final part of the discourse:

Pericope	Matthew	Mark	Other Sources
Destruction of Jerusalem	24:1–3	13:1–4	
Signs of the parousia	24:4–8	13:5–8	
Tribulations of the disciples	24:9a–b	13:9a, 13a[3]	
	24:10–12		Special source[4]
	24:13	13:13b	
	24:14		Source?[5]
The final tribulations	24:15–25	13:14–23	
How the Son of man comes	24:26–27		Q 17:23–24
Saying about the corpse	24:28		Q 17:37
Parousia of the Son of man	24:29–31	13:24–27	
Parable of the Fig Tree	24:32–33	13:28–29	
Time of the parousia	24:34–36	13:30–32	
About watchfulness	24:37–39		Q 17:26–27
Saying about divisions	24:40–41		Q 17:35
Admonition: watchfulness	24:42	13:35	
Parable of the Thief	24:43–44		Q 12:39–40
The two servants	24:45–51		Q 12:42–46
Parable of the Ten Virgins	25:1–12		Special source[6]
Admonition: watchfulness	25:13	13:35	

---

[1] A parallel to this saying appears in *Gos. Thom.* 30.

[2] Matthew uses the Q materials here and elsewhere more freely. However, almost all of the Q materials used here have parallels in Luke 12 and 17. The eschatological prophecies of these two Lukan chapters may have formed a single unit in Q; see above, # 2.3.3–4.

[3] Mark 13:9b–12 had already been used in Matt 10:17–21.

[4] That these verses (and possibly other materials of Matthew 25) are drawn from a particular source is evident in the close parallels in *Did.* 16; see Koester, *Synoptische Überlieferung,* 173–90; John S. Kloppenborg, "Didache 16,6–8 and Special Matthaean Tradition," *ZNW* 70 (1979) 54–67; Niederwimmer, *Didache,* 250–56.

[5] This verse is probably a formulation of Matthew for which he may have used Mark 13:9–10.

[6] Matt 25:10–12 has a parallel in a passage that appears in Luke 13:25. It is debated whether this is a Q saying or a secondary formulation by the author of Luke's Gospel; see Kloppenborg, *Q Parallels,* 154. In any case, it is highly unlikely that Luke

| Parable of the Talents | 25:14–30 | Q 19:11–27 |
| The Last Judgment | 25:31–46 | Special source |

Some of the smaller discourses of Matthew are also expansions of Markan discourse sections. The discourse on clean and unclean, Matt 15:1–20, reproduces Mark 7:1–23, adding special materials in Matt 15:12–14.[1] The speech against the Pharisees is based on Mark 12:38–40 (= Matt 23:1, 6). However, almost all the materials of this discourse reproduce a collection of sayings from Q (Matt 23:4, 13, 23, 25–27, 29–30, 34–36 = Luke 11:46, 52, 42, 39–40, 44, 47–48, 49–51) to which Matthew adds special materials (Matt 23:2–3, 5, 8–10, 15–22, 24, 28). As in the case of the Sermon on the Mount (see below) one may doubt that the author of the First Gospel composed this discourse himself. Rather he may have used an already expanded version of the collection of sayings against the Pharisees from Q.

That the Sermon on the Mount was not a fresh creation by the author of the First Gospel is evident from a comparison with Luke's Sermon on the Plain (Luke 6:20–49); almost all the materials appearing in that discourse have parallels in Matthew 5–7.[2] Thus Q presented a discourse which was the ultimate basis for Matthew's Sermon on the Mount. Hans Dieter Betz has persuasively argued that Matthew was not directly dependent on Q/Luke 6:20–49, but upon a further expansion of this Q section, a written Jewish-Christian teaching manual which had already assembled most of the materials now incorporated in Matthew 5–7.[3] Thus with respect to the first major discourse in Matthew, the contribution of the author of the First Gos-

---

13:25 (or an older saying used here) was the basis for the formulation of the parable Matt 25:1–13.

[1] Matt 15:13 is a saying about the "Plants not planted by the Father," which Matthew probably drew from the free tradition of sayings; however, it is also attested in *Gos. Thom.* 40. Matt 15:14, the saying about the blind leading the blind, has a parallel in Luke 6:39 and *Gos. Thom.* 34. Whether or not any of these two sayings stood in Q is difficult to determine. On Matt 15:14 = Luke 6:39 see Kloppenborg, *Q Parallels,* 38.

[2] The only exceptions are Luke 6:24–26, which has no parallel at all in Matthew, and Luke 6:39–40, which Matthew has used in 15:14; 10:24–25.

[3] Hans Dieter Betz, "Die Makarismen der Bergpredigt (Matthäus 5,3–12): Beobachtungen zur literarischen Form und theologischen Bedeutung," *ZThK* 75 (1987) 3–19. Cf. also idem, "Eine judenchristliche Kult-Didache in Matthäus 6, 1–18," in Georg Strecker, ed., *Jesus Christus in Historie und Theologie: Neutestamentliche Festschrift für Hans Conzelmann zum 60. Geburtstag* (Tübingen: Mohr-Siebeck, 1975) 446–57; idem, "The Sermon on the Mount: Its Literary Genre and Function," *JR* 59 (1979) 285–97; idem, "Kosmogonie und Ethik in der Bergpredigt," *ZThK* 81 (1984) 139–71. These essays are now collected in idem, *Studien zur Bergpredigt* (Tübingen: Mohr-Siebeck, 1986); ET idem, *Essays on the Sermon on the Mount.* See above, # 2.3.4.

pel should not be overestimated. Still, it is evident that the section of Q which appears in Luke's Sermon on the Plain provided the basic structure for this speech, while Markan parallels appear only occasionally.

Pericope or Saying	Matthew	Q	Other Sources
The situation	4:25		Mark 3:7–8
The mountain setting	5:1	6:12	Mark 3:13
Beatitudes	5:3–12	**6:20–23**	
Metaphor of the salt	5:13		Mark 9:50
Metaphor of the light	5:13–16	11:33	
Relevance of the law	5:17–20		Special source
1st antithesis: murder	5:21–24		Special source
Parable about reconciliation	5:25–26	12:57–59	
2d antithesis: adultery	5:27–28		
The offending eye	5:29–30		Mark 9:43, 47f
3d antithesis: divorce	5:31–32	16:18	Mark 10:11–12
4th antithesis: swearing	5:33–37		Special source[1]
5th antithesis: retaliation	5:38–42	**6:29–30**	
6th antithesis: love & hate	5:43–45	**6:27–28**	
Sayings on loving others	5:46–47	**6:32–33**	
Conclusion	5:48	**6:36**	
On almsgiving	6:1–4		
On prayer	6:5–8		Special source[2]
Lord's Prayer	6:9–13	11:2–4	Special source
Prayer and forgiveness	6:14–15		Mark 11:25–26
On fasting	6:16–18		Special source
On treasures	6:19–21	12:33–34	
Saying on the eye	6:22–23	11:34–36	
Serving two masters	6:24	16:13	
On cares	6:25–34	12:22–31	
On judging	7:1–5	**6:37f, 41f**	
No pearls before the swine	7:6		Special source
Answer to prayer	7:7–11	11:9–13	
Golden Rule	7:12	**6:31**	
The narrow gate	7:13–14	13:23–24	
Wolves in sheep's clothing	7:15		Special source
Tree and fruit	7:16–20	**6:43–45**	
Those who say "Lord. Lord"	7:21	**6:46**	
Judgment on the lawless	7:22–23	13:26–27	
Parable of House Building	7:24–27	**6:47–49**	
Reaction to Jesus' words	7:28b–29		Mark 1:22

[1] See above on James 5:12, # 2.1.4.
[2] For this section and the following on prayer and fasting see the sayings in the *Gospel of Thomas*, # 6a, 14a.

I have highlighted the materials of the Sermon on the Mount which have parallels in Luke 6. Most of them occur in Matthew 5–7 in the same order as in Luke's Sermon on the Plain. This Q speech was certainly the basis for the composition. Other materials which have been added at numerous points are drawn mostly from other contexts of Q, while Markan sayings appear only occasionally. Thus the manner of composition differs markedly from the other major speeches in Matthew in which a Markan context and Markan materials always provide the basis for the speech. This observation would confirm the hypothesis that Matthew was not the author of the Sermon on the Mount. Rather, it was composed by an author who did not know Mark and was primarily dependent upon the Synoptic Sayings Source.

Matthew opens his Gospel with a genealogy of Jesus and narratives about Jesus' birth (Matthew 1–2). Only in 3:1 does he begin to follow his major source, the Gospel of Mark. The infancy narratives (Matt 1:18–2:23) derive from a special source which had collected popular legends about miraculous events accompanying Jesus' birth. But these narratives are dominated by an unusual motif which is a striking feature of Matthew's redaction of this source. The principle of this redaction is evident in the transformation of the narrative to a record that confirms the fulfillment of prophecy. The prophecies are explicitly quoted, introduced by the repeated elaborate formula "(this happened) in order to fulfill what had been said (by the Lord) through the prophets" (τοῦτο δὲ γέγονεν ἵνα πληρωθῇ τὸ ῥηθὲν ὑπὸ κυρίου διὰ τοῦ προφήτου λέγοντος). This formula appears four times in Matt 1:18–2:23 (1:22; 2:15, 18, 23); a differently formulated fifth reference, "thus it is written through the prophet" (οὕτως γὰρ γέγραπται διὰ τοῦ προφήτου), forms the centerpiece of the story of the visit of the Magi (2:5). This method of using narrative for the confirmation of prophecy is a characteristic editing feature of the author of this Gospel.[1] It is, therefore, likely that these first chapters of the Gospel, as they now appear in the text, have been composed by Matthew on the basis of older legends. In the process of such composition, the traditional materials lost the beauty of their legendary narrative structure and became fragmentary records confirming the theological theory of scriptural fulfillment in historical events.[2]

The tendency to use traditional materials for the proof of fulfillment of prophecy has also determined Matthew's redaction of other narra-

---

[1] This formula also appears in Matt 4:14–16; 8:17; 12:17–21; 13:14–15, 35; 21:4–5; 27:9. Cf. Krister Stendahl, *The School of St. Matthew and Its Use of the Old Testament* (2d ed.; Philadelphia: Fortress, 1968).

[2] Compare the legends used in the infancy narrative of Luke; see below, # 4.4.3.2.

tive sources used in his Gospel. Jesus' first preaching in Capernaum "in the regions of Zebulon and Naphtali" is a fulfillment of Isa 9:1–2 (Matt 4:13–16); his healing ministry fulfills Isa 53:4 (Matt 8:16–17) and Isa 42:1–2 (Matt 5:17); his preaching in parables fulfills Ps 77:2; his riding into Jerusalem is a fulfillment of Zech 9:9. This motif is also evident in the passion narrative: Jesus' suffering is necessary in order to fulfill the "scriptures of the prophets" (Matt 26:56), and the piece of land that the high priests buy with Judas's money is named in order to fulfill Jer 39:6–15 (Matt 27:9–10). In this way, Matthew changes radically the narrative impact of the stories he uses. He is not capable of just telling a story. All traditional narratives become theological proofs and are deprived of their ability to communicate "story." This apologetic feature places Matthew in the context of early Christian apologetics. His method of the interpretation of scripture in relation to fulfillment of historical record is paralleled in the apologetic procedures of Justin Martyr.

4.3.6 THE COMPOSITION OF THE GOSPEL OF MATTHEW

Whereas for the Gospel of Mark the narrative structure essentially determined the presentation of the ministry of Jesus, Matthew, though following for the most part Mark's narrative, highlights the discourses of Jesus. They become the center of Jesus' ministry. While almost all the healing activity of Jesus is described in a curtailed form in chapters 8–9, into which Matthew has assembled the Markan healing and miracle narratives, the speeches constitute the focus of Jesus' ministry. The miracles and other narratives from Mark have been drastically shortened in Matthew's text[1] and sometimes are mere skeletons. Only the appearance of Jesus as an almost superhuman being who is worshiped by those he encounters is important for Matthew; the narrative details, on the other hand, would only distract from this focus upon Jesus' dignity.

The speeches in Matthew's Gospel, however, are always more comprehensive and contain more materials than their counterparts in Mark and Q. By composing these speeches out of all the available materials from his sources and probably also from the still-fluid oral tradition of Jesus' sayings, Matthew has created five large discourses:

---

[1] Cf., e.g., the Gerasene demoniac (Mark 5:1–20 = Matt 8:28–34) is divided into 20 verses in Mark, but only 7 verses in Matthew. The story of the death of John the Baptist has 176 words in Mark 6:17–29, only 137 words in Matt 14:3–12. On the redaction of the narrative materials in Matthew, see Heinz Joachim Held, "Matthew as Interpreter of the Miracle Stories," in Bornkamm-Barth-Held, *Tradition and Interpretation*, 165–299, especially 168–92.

the Sermon on the Mount (Matt 5:1–7:29), the missionary instruction
(9:35–11:1), the parable discourse (13:1–53), the discourse on the
order of the church (18:1–19:1), and the eschatological discourse
(24:1–26:1). Each of the first four discourses concludes with the sentence "and it happened, when Jesus had finished these words . . ."; the
last discourse ends with "and it happened, when Jesus had finished
all these words . . ." Immediately following upon this last sentence
Matthew reports the hierarchs' council of death (26:1–2).

With respect to the passion narrative, Matthew follows Mark faithfully with relatively few redactions. Narrative sections are occasionally shortened. Some new materials, however, are added. The first of
these is the report of the death of Judas (Matt 27:3–10); here the last of
the formula quotations occurs (27:9–10, quoting a combination of
verses from Zechariah and Jeremiah). As in the stories of the infancy
narrative, this legendary report is entirely dominated by the desire to
demonstrate the fulfillment of scripture. In these cases, Matthew is
still able to draw on the exegetical tradition that was responsible for
the development of the passion narrative, and he used it for apologetic
purposes. In the trial scene, Matthew adds the episode with Pilate's
wife (27:19) and the handwashing scene of Pilate (27:24–25).[1] After
the report of the death of Jesus, Matthew inserts a description of miraculous phenomena, prodigia occurring at the death of a great human
being (27:51–53); and after the story of the burial he utilizes fragments
of an older epiphany story for the construction of an apologetic legend
of the guard at the tomb.[2] Finally, the story of the discovery of the
empty tomb is expanded by the report of the appearance of an angel
who rolls away the stone from the tomb (28:2–4)—another fragment of
the epiphany story preserved in the *Gospel of Peter*.

The source for the final story of the appearance of Jesus to his disciples (Matt 28:16–20) is an independent tradition. It may rest on an
older epiphany account (cf. John 20:19–22), but it has been heavily
redacted by the author of the First Gospel. Jesus' command to "make
disciples of all nations" testifies to Matthew's unqualified endorsement
of the mission to the Gentiles, while the emphasis upon "teaching
them everything that I have commanded you" is a confirmation of his
belief that neither the great deeds of Jesus nor his suffering and death

---

[1] The motif for these additions is clearly apologetic, but it should not be read as a
polemic against "Judaism." Rather, the polemic corresponds to the established Jewish
tradition of prophetic polemic against the political establishment in Jerusalem and the
people who had been misled by their leaders. With respect to the scriptural basis of
the handwashing scene see the discussion above on the parallel scene in the *Gospel of
Peter*, # 3.2.3.2.

[2] See above, # 3.2.3.3.

are meant to be the guiding principle of that mission. Rather, the teachings of Jesus, primarily represented in the speeches of Jesus which Matthew composed, should serve as the foundation of the church.

Nevertheless, these speeches—instruction for the churches—are not presented in the literary form of a manual of discipline. They are set forth as part of a biographical writing. The biographical framework, to be sure, has been inherited from the Gospel of Mark. But Matthew did not simply use the Markan framework as a purely external vehicle for the presentation of a church manual. The changes that he introduced reveal also his understanding of the "life of Jesus," which differs from that of Mark in two respects. First, Jesus' life, from the very beginning, is fulfillment; already his very birth fulfills what was promised. Second, the divine dignity of the person of Jesus is more strongly emphasized, although there is no single title that would summarize the entire dignity of Jesus that is pictured in the story of his birth, life, and death. Titles of Jesus may become more elaborate. The Markan formulation of the confession of Peter, "You are the Christ" (Mark 8:29) becomes, "You are the Christ, the Son of the Living God" (Matt 16:16). People approaching Jesus or witnessing his miracles "worship" him.[1] The story of the stilling of the tempest has become an allegory for the appearance of the Lord at the height of the eschatological tribulation[2] and the same risen Lord promises his disciples that he will be with them to the end of the days (Matt 28:20). But Jesus is also Wisdom who offers her mild yoke to all who wish to come (Matt 11:28–30). As Wisdom incarnate, Jesus is also the one who suffers and dies, rejected like the suffering righteous ones. The Gospel of Matthew can be called the biography of Wisdom, but Jesus as Wisdom is, at the same time, the eschatological Lord whose dignity is already visible in his earthly life and whose cross, the symbol of his suffering and death, will appear as the sign of his eschatological return.[3]

---

[1] Compare, e.g., Matt 9:18 with Mark 5:22; Matt 14:33 with Mark 6:51.

[2] Compare Matt 8:23–27 with Mark 4:35–41. See Günther Bornkamm, "The Stilling of the Storm in Matthew," in Bornkamm-Barth-Held, *Tradition and Interpretation,* 52–57.

[3] The "sign (σημεῖον) of the Son of man" (Matt 24:30) which will precede Jesus as he comes on the clouds of heaven very probably was the sign of the cross.

4.4 The Gospel of Luke [1]

4.4.1 MANUSCRIPTS

Luke's text is not as well attested as the text of John's and Matthew's Gospels, but better attested than the text of Mark. In addition to the four-gospel papyrus from the 3d century ($\mathfrak{p}^{45}$)—the only attestation of Mark before the 4th century—there are three papyri with parts of Luke's text from the 3d century.[2] Since $\mathfrak{p}^4$ preserves considerable portions of the Third Gospel, there is at least some direct evidence for the text circulating in this early period. In addition to the uncials from the 4th and the following centuries containing the text of all four canonical Gospels,[3] one papyrus and three uncial manuscripts with the text of Luke come from the 4th century,[4] and there are three papyri[5] and about two dozen uncial manuscripts containing at least portions of Luke's text from later centuries.

No manuscript preserves the work of Luke in its original form, i.e., the Gospel of Luke and the Acts of the Apostles together. They were originally two volumes of *one* work. In even the earliest extant manuscripts from ca. 200, the work had already been split into two sections of which the former was soon assigned to a collection of gospels. Thus Luke's work has not been preserved in the form in which it was published by its author.[6] The text-critical problems of Luke's text are essentially the same as those of the other canonical gospels, with one exception: the so-called Western Text[7] presents a number of interesting and controversial alternative readings.

---

[1] For literature on the Gospel of Luke in general and for the present status of scholarship see Martin Rese, "Das Lukasevangelium: Ein Forschungsbericht," *ANRW* 2.25/3 (1985) 2260–2335.

[2] $\mathfrak{p}^4$ with portions of Luke 1–6; $\mathfrak{p}^{69}$, preserving a few verses from Luke 22, and $\mathfrak{p}^{75}$ with parts of Luke 3–9; 17; and 22 (and presenting also the text of the Gospel of John; see above # 3.4.1).

[3] See above # 3.3.

[4] $\mathfrak{p}^{82}$ (Luke 7:32–34, 37–38); 0171 (verses from Luke 22 and Matt 10); 0181 (Luke 9:59–10:14). The first of these uncials may have been written ca. 300 CE.

[5] $\mathfrak{p}^3$ (6th/7th century: Luke 7:36–45; 10:38–42); $\mathfrak{p}^7$ (4th–6th century: Luke 4:1–2); $\mathfrak{p}^{42}$ (7th/8th century: Luke 1:54–55; 2:29–32).

[6] See Bovon, *Evangelium nach Lukas*, 13–14.

[7] Represented by D, some Vetus Latina manuscripts, the old Syrian translation, and quotations in several Church Fathers as early as Justin Martyr. It is therefore not possible to assign these readings to the 4th century. See Bovon (*Evangelium nach Lukas*, 14): the Western Text is about as old as the Egyptian Text which originated in the 2nd century and is represented by $\mathfrak{p}^{75}$, $\aleph$, B, and C.

Western Text	*Egyptian and / or Majority Text*

Luke 3:22

You are my Son, today I have begotten you (ἐγὼ σήμερον γεγέννηκά σε) = Ps 2:7	You are my beloved Son, in you I am well pleased (ἐν σοὶ εὐδόκησα) = Isa 42:1

Luke 6:5

The same day he saw someone working on the Sabbath and said to him, "Man, if you know what you are doing, you are blessed, but if you don't know, you are cursed and a transgressor of the law."[1]	And he said to them, "The Son of man is Lord of the Sabbath."

Luke 22:17–20

And he took the cup and when he had given thanks he said, "Take this and divide it among yourselves. For I tell you, from now on I shall not drink of the fruit of the wine until the kingdom of God comes." And he took bread, and when he had given thanks he broke it and gave it to them, saying, "This is my body."	And he took a cup and when he had given thanks he said, "Take this and divide it among yourselves. For I tell you, that from now on I shall not drink of the fruit of the wine until the kingdom of God comes." And he took bread, and when he had given thanks he broke it and gave it to them, saying, "This is my body which is given for you. Do this in my remembrance." And in the same way he took the cup after the meal, saying, "This cup is the new covenant in my blood that has been poured out for you."

Another interesting variant appears in two minuscules (162, 700) and Gregory of Nyssa in the second petition of the Lord's Prayer:

Luke 11:2

Manuscript 700	*Majority Text*
Your Holy Spirit come over us and cleanse us. (ἐλθέτω τὸ ἅγιον πνεῦμά σου ἐφ᾽ ἡμᾶς καὶ καθαρισάτω ἡμᾶς).	Your kingdom come. (ἐλθέτω ἡ βασιλεία σου).

Scholarly opinion in textual criticism has tended to prefer the readings of the Egyptian text (represented by 𝔭[75], ℵ, B, and C) over the

---

[1] This saying occurs in Codex D after Luke 6:10.

Text, and there are good reasons for not accepting the variants offered to Luke 6:5 and 11:2. However, there is evidence for the existence of some Western Text readings as early as the middle of the 2d century.[1] For the question of the original text of Luke, it is necessary to reconsider the weight of this text as perhaps the earliest available witness.[2]

4.4.2 ATTESTATION

Nothing is said about the Gospel of Luke in the fragments of Papias of Hierapolis which are preserved in Eusebius' *Ecclesiastical History.* But it is widely attested that just before the middle of the 2d century Marcion used this Gospel as the basis for his edition of Christian Scriptures.[3] The report about Marcion's use of Luke appears for the first time in Irenaeus (ca. 180 CE):

> He mutilates the Gospel which is according to Luke, removes all that is written respecting the generation of the Lord, and sets aside a great deal of the teaching of the Lord's discourses in which the Lord is recorded as most clearly confessing that the creator of this universe is his Father. (*Adv. haer.* 1.25.1)

Thus the Gospel of Luke, perhaps written as late as the first decades of the 2d century, became the first Gospel ever to be elevated to something that could be called "canonical status," albeit in its revised Marcionite edition.

Apart from the use of Luke by Marcion, there is no certain evidence for its usage and its text before the middle of the 2d century. While Marcion apparently also knew the Gospel of Matthew but rejected it, the first early catholic writers who use the text of written gospels, Justin Martyr and *2 Clement,* use the text of Matthew as well as the text of Luke (and, in the case of Justin, also the text of Mark). In fact, apart from Marcion, a harmony of Matthew and Luke was apparently the earliest form through which the text of the Gospel Luke came to be used. This harmony is not only in evidence in Justin and *2 Clement* but also in the *Gospel of the Ebionites.*[4] The name of the author of the

---

[1] They appear in Justin *Dial.* 88 and 103.6.

[2] There are several references and discussions of this question in the recent volume of published contributions to a University of Notre Dame conference, April 15–17, 1988 on the text of the gospels in the 2d century: William L. Petersen, ed., *Gospel Traditions in the Second Century: Origins, Recensions, Text, and Transmission* (Notre Dame, IN: University of Notre Dame Press, 1989). See also Bovon, *Lukasevangelium,* 13–14.

[3] See above, # 1.7.

[4] For the Greek texts see Klostermann, *Apocrypha II,* 13–15; ET in Hennecke-Schneemelcher-Wilson, *NT Apocrypha,* 1. 156–58.

Third Gospel of the New Testament canon never appears in such contexts. Evidence for this Gospel as a separate writing under the name of Luke appears for the first time in Irenaeus in his discussion of the origin of the four canonical Gospels:

> ... and Luke also who was a follower of Paul put down in a book the gospel that was preached by him (sc. Paul).[1]

It is interesting to note that Irenaeus agrees with Marcion in assuming that Luke's Gospel is the gospel that Paul had preached. The so-called *Anti-Marcionite Prologue* has also been referred to as a testimony from the second half of the 2d century to the Gospel of Luke and to its author:[2]

> Luke is a Syrian of Antioch, a Syrian by race, a physician by profession. He had become a disciple of the apostles and later followed Paul until his (Paul's) martyrdom, having served the Lord continuously, unmarried, without children, filled with the Holy Spirit he died at the age of eighty-four years in Boeotia.[3]
>
> [Since there were already other gospels, that According to Matthew written in Judea, that According to Mark (written in) Italy, he was urged by the Holy Spirit to write his whole gospel among those in the regions of Achaea, as he indicates this in the preface that there were already other writings before him ...][4]

While the *Canon Muratori* and the *Prologues* to the Gospels of Mark and John are most likely products of the second half of the 4th century,[5] the first part of the *Prologue* to the Gospel of Luke, the only one of these prologues that is preserved in its original Greek, may have been composed in the last decades of the 2d century.[6] The former, as well as the second part of the *Prologue to Luke,* merely reflect what came to be the accepted opinion about the origin of the gospels in the ancient church. However, the first part of the *Prologue to Luke* provides information that is not reflected elsewhere: that Luke was

---

[1] Eusebius *Hist. eccl.* 5.8.3.

[2] Greek text, English translation, and critical notes in Heard, "Old Gospel Prologues," 7–9.

[3] Manuscript A reads "in Thebes, the capital of Boeotia" (Θήβαις τῇ μητροπόλει τῆς Βοιωτίας).

[4] Since the second part of the Lukan *Prologue,* bracketed above, also makes reference to the Gospels of Matthew and Mark, later also to Acts and to Revelation, it is unlikely that it was composed as an introduction for the Gospel of Luke; cf. Heard, "Old Gospel Prologues," 4.

[5] See above # 3.3.3, on the *Anti-Marcionite Prologues* to the canonical Gospels.

[6] Heard, "Old Gospel Prologues," 7–11.

unmarried and had no children, and that he died in Boeotia.[1] The historical value of this information, including the name of the author, is of dubious value. Ever since Marcion (who never mentions the name of an author for the gospel that he included in his canon), the desire to connect the author to Paul, as well as the evident information about Paul in the second half of the work, the Acts of the Apostles, would make Luke a natural choice because he was mentioned in Phlm 24, Col 4:14, and 2 Tim 4:11.

4.4.3 SOURCES AND SPECIAL MATERIALS

4.4.3.1 Luke's Sources

According to the two-source hypothesis, Luke's primary sources are the same as those of Matthew, i.e., the Gospel of Mark and the Synoptic Sayings Source. Insofar as this is the case, Luke closely resembles Matthew in form and content. In the first and third parts of his writing, Luke uses the Gospel of Mark for the outline of the events of the ministry of Jesus and inserts at certain points materials drawn from Q. In the use of both these sources, Luke is normally more conservative than Matthew because he usually leaves the sequence and wording of his sources more or less intact, and he does not try to compose major units, such as Matthew's speeches.

4.4.3.2 Luke's Special Materials

Like Matthew, Luke employs additional materials which are not drawn from either of these two sources. However, in the case of Luke, these materials are more extensive and more diversified. Most of them are usually assigned to a third source used by Luke ("L"), which differs fundamentally from both the Synoptic Sayings Source and the special source used in the Gospel of Matthew. While the latter consisted mostly of sayings, Luke's special source, or sources, also included a number of narratives as well as some example stories and parables which are attested nowhere else in the gospel traditions. Some of these materials were inserted by Luke into the Markan narrative framework; but most appear in a separate section which Luke has created as the central piece of his composition, the Lukan travel narrative (9:51–18:14). Because of the variety of the special materials in Luke, it is difficult to argue for one single source as the wellspring of

---

[1] Joseph A. Fitzmyer, S.J., *The Gospel According to Luke: Introduction, Translation, and Notes* (2 vols.; AB 28/28A; Garden City, NY: Doubleday, 1981–85) 1. 39. Bovon (*Evangelium nach Lukas*, 23–24) is more doubtful with respect to an early date for this prologue or parts of it.

all his special materials. Luke probably used several smaller collections of sayings in this section, most prominent among these a collection of parables, and also a collection of miracle stories, which Luke used in this section and elsewhere.[1] The diversity of the special materials included in Luke's Gospel warns against the assumption of just one major special source for Luke.[2] It is more likely that an educated and widely traveled author like Luke had access to a variety of written documents as well as orally circulating materials. Luke wrote at a comparatively late date, several decades after Matthew, that is, after the turn of the 1st century, when more of the gospel materials had been collected in written form. In fact, in the proem (1:1–4) Luke refers to a variety of earlier attempts to write down the traditions about Jesus. On the other hand, Luke's church does not seem to have lost the connection to the continuing and still developing free (oral) tradition of sayings of Jesus and stories about him.[3] Luke is therefore a remarkable witness for the continuing free circulation of oral or written collections of sayings of Jesus and of narratives about him as late as three generations after his death.

The most important special materials incorporated into the Gospel of Luke are the following:

Healing Miracles:

The raising of the widow's son	7:7–17
The healing of a woman with a spirit of infirmity	13:10–17
The healing of a man with dropsy	14:1–6
The healing of the ten lepers	17:11–19

Apophthegmata:

The woman that was a sinner	7:36–50
The serving women	8:1–3
Mary and Martha	10:38–42
The blessedness of the mother of Jesus	11:24–26
Dividing the inheritance	12:13–14
Call for repentance	13:1–5

[1] Luke 7:11–17 ("the widow's son"), 13:10–17 ("the women with a spirit of infirmity"), 14:1–6 ("the man with the dropsy"), 17:11–19 ("the ten lepers"—a variant of Mark 1:40–45).

[2] Several other hypotheses have been advanced to explain Luke's relationship to his special materials. Prominent among these is the suggestion that Q and the special materials were first combined to a "Proto-Luke" (Vincent Taylor, *Behind the Third Gospel: A Study of the Proto-Luke Hypothesis* [Oxford: Oxford University Press, 1926]). For a critique see Conzelmann and Lindemann, *Interpreting the NT,* 231–32.

[3] Bishop Papias of Hierapolis, who may have been a younger contemporary of Luke, was still able to draw on the oral traditions for the composition of his "Interpretations of the Oracles of the Lord." Cf. Eusebius *Hist. eccl.* 3.39.

| Answer to Herod | 13:31–33 |
| Zacchaeus | 19:1–10 |

Sayings (a selection):

The social teaching of John the Baptist	3:10–14
The woes against the rich	6:24–26
"I saw Satan fall like lightning . . ."	10:18–20
Punishment according to responsibility	12:47–48
"I have come to throw a fire on earth . . ."[1]	12:49
"I have to be baptized with a baptism . . ."	12:50
Order of dignity at a meal	14:7–14
Friends with the unjust mammon	16:9
Coming of the rule of God[2]	17:20–21
The destruction of Jerusalem	19:39–44
The two swords	22:35–38

Parables and Example Stories:

The Good Samaritan	10:29–37
The Friend at Midnight	11:5–8
The Rich Fool[3]	12:16–21
The Barren Figtree	13:6–9
Building a House and Waging a War	14:28–33
The Lost Coin	15:7–10
The Father who Had Two Sons (Prodigal Son)	15:11–32
The Unjust Steward	16:1–8
Dives and Lazarus	16:19–31
The Servant's Wages	17:7–10
The Unjust Judge	18:1–8
The Pharisee and the Tax Collector	18:9–14

Insertions into the Passion Narrative:

The eating of the Passover	22:15–18
The words to Peter	22:31–32
Jesus before Herod	23:6–16
The women of Jerusalem	23:27–31
Jesus and the two crucified criminals	23:32,39–43

Legends:

| The promise of the Baptist's birth | 1:5–25 |
| The annunciation | 1:26–38 |

[1] This saying, paralleled in *Gos. Thom.* 10, may be a Q saying that Matthew omitted; see above # 2.2.4.2 and 2.3.2.

[2] The parallel in *Gos. Thom.* 113 could be an indication that this saying was derived from Q; see above # 2.2.4.2. and 2.3.2.

[3] Most likely this example story came from Q and not from L; see Kloppenborg, *Q Parallels*, 128.

The birth of John the Baptist	1:57–66, 80
Mary's visit with Elizabeth	1:39–45, 56
The nativity of Jesus	2:1–20
The circumcision of Jesus	2:21–40
Jesus at twelve years in the temple	2:41–52

Epiphany Stories:	
The miraculous draught of fishes	5:1–11
The road to Emmaeus	24:13–35
The appearances of the risen Christ	24:36–49
The ascension	24:50–53

Hymnic materials:	
The Magnificat	1:46–55
The Benedictus	1:68–79
The Song of Simon	2:29–32

4.4.4 THE COMPOSITION OF THE GOSPEL OF LUKE

It must be remembered that the so-called Gospel of Luke is only the first part of a much larger work which includes the Book of the Acts of the Apostles and, in fact, describes the entire period from the birth of John the Baptist and Jesus to the arrival of the Christian message in Rome. The work was published in two volumes as a matter of convenience: as the work was first written and published in the form of scrolls, the maximum capacity of a scroll required two "volumes."[1] Thus the placing of the first volume of this work among the four Gospels of the New Testament does not correspond to its original purpose. The intention of the author is not understood at all if the Gospel of Luke is seen as a parallel to the Gospel of Matthew, although both documents have two sources in common. The author never intended to write something that would eventually be called a "gospel," and he certainly did not understand the first sentence of the Gospel of Mark ("The beginning of the gospel of Jesus Christ," Mark 1:1) as designating a literary genre.

But since the first part of Luke's work deals with Jesus and shares sources about Jesus with Matthew, some comparisons of Matthew and what we now call the "Gospel of Luke" are helpful. Like Matthew, Luke does not begin his Gospel with the appearance of John the

[1] The "prologue" to the Book of Acts is not the introduction of an entirely new and different work, but a resumption of the prologue of Luke 1:1–4. Thus Acts 1:1–2 functions primarily as a dedication—a Greek custom which designates the work as a piece of monographic literature.

Baptist and the baptism of Jesus, but with birth narratives (Luke 1:5–2:52). With these he also includes the story of the birth of John the Baptist (1:5–25, 57–66). The stories themselves derive from different traditions and they belong to the latest stage of the novelistic development of Synoptic narrative materials. The character of the stories relating to John the Baptist differs markedly from those about Jesus' birth. There is good reason to believe that the former came from the tradition of the followers of John. As these traditional legends appear here in the first two chapters of the Third Gospel, they owe their form and composition to the author of the work.[1] Luke has achieved the presentation of this narrative cycle not by adding occasional redactional comments, but by skillful literary arrangement which results in an introduction to his Gospel of extraordinary beauty.

The two stories of the announcement of the births (1:5–25 and 1:26–38) open the cycle; the meeting of the two mothers (1:39–56) provides a double link, on the one hand between John and Jesus, on the other hand between the announcement stories and the birth stories. Each of the birth stories (1:57–80 and 2:1–40) includes a second part in which the newly born child is greeted in the form of a kerygmatic hymn (the Benedictus of Zachariah, 1:67–79, and the Nunc Dimittis of Simeon, 2:29–32). Both birth narratives end with statements about the growth of the child that begin with exactly the same words ("And the child grew and became strong . . . ," 1:80; 2:40). The story of Jesus at twelve in the temple (2:41–52) provides the link to the following narrative about Jesus.

Announcement of John's birth		Announcement of Jesus' birth
	Visit of the two mothers	
John's birth		Jesus' birth
	Jesus at twelve years in the temple	

Here, as elsewhere in this Gospel, Luke expresses theological significance by the relative position of certain traditional units in the narrative. Theological purpose does not violate the fact that John the Baptist and Jesus belong together; but they meet only once, namely, in their mothers' womb. When Jesus comes to his baptism (3:21), John is already imprisoned (3:19–20). There is no longer any parallelism between the two figures.

After the infancy narratives, Luke picks up the thread of the narrative of the Gospel of Mark which he will follow for the entire first part of his writing (Mark 1:2–9:50 = Luke 3:1–9:50) and again for the third

---

[1] Bovon (*Evangelium nach Lukas*, 46–47) has shown that the composition is analogous to that of the Cornelius story in Acts 10:1–11:18).

part of the Gospel (Mark 10:13–16:8 = Luke 18:15–24:12).[1] In this use
of Mark, Luke occasionally and quite purposefully moves a pericope to
another context, and he frequently inserts materials from Q and occasionally also from a special source. The following table, comparing
Mark and Luke up to the beginning of the passion narrative, will illustrate Luke's method of composition.[2]

Pericope	Luke	Mark	Other Sources
Synchronism	3:1–2		redactional
The Baptist	3:3–6	1:2–6	
Preaching of repentance	3:7–9		from Q
Social teaching	3:10–14		from L
Messianic preaching	3:15–16	1:7–8	
Conclusion	3:17–18		from Q
John's imprisonment	3:19–20	*6:17–18*	
Baptism of Jesus	3:21–22	1:9–11	
Genealogy of Christ	3:23–38		from L (cf. Matt)
Temptation of Jesus	4:1–2	1:12–13a	
Dialogue with Satan	4:3–12		from Q
Conclusion	4:13	1:13b	
Preaching in Galilee	4:14–15	(1:14–16)	redactional
Jesus in Nazareth	4:16	*6:1–2*	
Jesus' scripture reading	4:17–21		redactional
Peoples' reaction	4:22–24	*6:3–4*	
Jesus' preaching	4:25–27		from L
Rejection	4:28–30	*6:5–6*	
Healing in the synagogue	4:31–37	1:21–28	
Peter's mother-in-law	4:38–39	1:29–31	
Healing summary	4:40–41	1:32–34	
Departure from Capernaum	4:42–44	1:35–39	
Peter's draught of fishes	5:1–11		from L
Healing of a leper	5:12–16	1:40–45	
Healing of paralytic	5:17–26	2:1–12	
Call of Levi	5:27–32	2:13–17	
Question about fasting	5:33–38	2:18–22	
Saying about old wine	5:39		oral tradition
Plucking grain on a Sabbath	6:1–5	2:23–28	
Healing of a withered hand	6:6–11	3:1–6	

[1] For a detailed analysis of the use of Mark in the Gospel of Luke see Tim Schramm,
*Der Markus-Stoff bei Lukas: Eine literarkritische und redaktionsgeschichtliche Unter-
suchung* (SNTS.MS 14; Cambridge: Cambridge University Press, 1971).

[2] "From L" points to all special materials, without prejudice regarding the source
from which Luke derived such materials. The passages from Mark are italicized whenever Luke has inserted them into a different context. I have not noted all redactional
additions of Luke within the units referred to.

Call of twelve disciples	6:12–16	*3:13–19*	
Healing summary	6:17–19	*3:7–12*[1]	
Sermon on the Plain	6:20–49		from Q
Centurio's servant healed	7:1–10		from Q
Widow's son raised	7:11–17		from L
Sayings about the Baptist	7:18–35		from Q
The women who was a sinner	7:36–50	*14:3–9*[2]	(from L?)
The ministering women	8:1–3		from L
Parable of the Sower	8:4–15	4:1–20	
Sayings about parables	8:16–18	4:21–25[3]	
Jesus' true relatives	8:19–21	*3:31–35*	
Stilling of the tempest	8:22–25	4:35–41	
Gerasene demoniac	8:26–39	5:1–20	
Jairus' daughter	8:40–56	5:21–43	
Sending of the Twelve	9:1–6	6:6–13	
Herod about Christ	9:7–9	6:14–16	
Feeding of five thousand	9:10–17	6:30–44[4]	
Confession of Peter	9:18–21	8:27–30	
First passion prediction	9:22	8:31[5]	
Sayings about discipleship	9:23–27	8:34–9:1	
Transfiguration	9:28–36	9:2–8[6]	
Healing of epileptic child	9:37–43a	9:14–29	
Second passion prediction	9:43b–45	9:30–32	
Dispute about greatness	9:46–48	9:33–37	
The strange exorcist	9:49–50	9:38–41[7]	
Blessing of the children	18:15–17	10:13–16[8]	
The rich young man	18:18–30	10:17–31	

[1] Mark 3 is the only Markan chapter in which Luke has made some major changes: Mark 3:7–12 and 3:13–19 have been reversed; the apophthegma about Christ's true relatives (Mark 3:31–35) has been moved to Luke 8:19–21; the Beelzebub controversy (Mark 3:20–30) has been combined with parallel Q material and moved into the travel narrative (Luke 11:18–23).

[2] This story may be a Lukan composition on the basis of Mark 14:3–9, which Luke skips in his reproduction of Mark 14.

[3] Missing from Mark's parable chapter are the parable of the Seed Growing Secretly (Mark 4:26–29)—perhaps not a part of the original version of Mark—and the parable of the Mustard Seed (Mark 4:30–32); Luke 13:18–19 cites a variant of this parable in a context dependent upon Q.

[4] The entire so-called Bethsaida section of Mark 6:45–8:26 is missing in Luke's Gospel.

[5] The rebuke of Peter, Mark 8:32–33, is missing in Luke.

[6] Luke leaves out Mark 9:9–13, the discussion about Elijah's coming.

[7] The sayings about offenses (Mark 9:42–48) have been omitted by Luke; but a variant (from Q) appears in Luke 17:1–2. A variant of the saying about the salt (Mark 9:50) appears in Luke 14:34–35, perhaps from Q = Matt 5:13.

[8] Luke omits the instructions about divorce (Mark 10:1–12).

Third passion prediction	18:31–34	10:32–34[1]
Healing of a blind man	18:35–43	10:46–52
Zacchaeus	19:1–10	from L
Parable of the Talents	19:11–27	from Q
Entry into Jerusalem	19:28–38	11:1–10
Prediction of its destruction	19:39–44	from L
Christ in the temple	19:45a	11:11a[2]
Cleansing of the temple	19:45b–48	11:15–19
Question about authority	20:1–8	11:27–33
Parable: wicked husbandmen	20:9–19	12:1–12
Question of tribute to Caesar	20:20–26	12:13–17
Question about resurrection	20:27–40	12:18–27[3]
Question of David's son	20:41–44	12:35–37a
Speech against Pharisees	20:45–47	12:37b–40
The widow's mite	21:1–4	12:41–44
Synoptic apocalypse	21:5–36	13:1–37
Teaching in the temple	21:37–38	redactional
The council of death	22:1–2	14:1–2
Betrayal of Judas	22:3–6	14:10–11[4]

In the central part of Luke, the travel narrative (9:51 to 18:14), almost everything comes from Q and L. Only a few pericopes from the Gospel of Mark are used in this section of Luke. Materials from Mark 3:20–30 (Beelzebub controversy) were combined with a variant from Q in Luke 11:14–23; a Q variant of Mark 3:28–29 (the unforgivable sin) appears in Luke 12:10. The parallel to Mark 9:42–48 (about offenses) in Luke 17:1–2 is drawn from Q, not from Mark. For the introduction to the story of the Good Samaritan (10:25–28), Luke has used Mark 12:29–31. It can be assumed that the sequence of materials in the travel narrative was primarily determined by Q, if the thesis is indeed correct that Luke reproduced the sayings of Q in about the same order in which they stood in his source. Although Luke in general follows Mark's order quite faithfully, he occasionally moves a pericope to

[1] The apophthegma of Christ and the sons of Zebedee (Mark 10:35–40) was omitted by Luke and the following sayings about serving (Mark 10:41–45) have been moved into the context of the last supper (Luke 22:24–27).

[2] Mark 11:11b, Jesus' return to Bethany, is omitted by Luke, as is the following episode of the cursing of the fig tree (Mark 11:12–14) together with the discussion of this episode (Mark 11:20–25).

[3] The following question about the Great Commandment (Mark 12:28–31) has been moved to Luke 10:25–28 as an introduction to the story of the Good Samaritan. Its Markan appendix (12:29–34) is missing in both Matthew and Luke and was probably not part of Mark's original text; see above # 4.1.2.1.

[4] The material from the story of the anointing in Bethany (Mark 14:3–9) seems to have been used by Luke for his story of Jesus and the woman who was a sinner, Luke 7:36–50; see above.

another context. Therefore, he may also have moved one or the other Q saying.

It is obvious that Luke follows the Markan outline and sequence much more faithfully than Matthew. Unlike Matthew's use of Mark, there are no major rearrangements like the collecting of almost all miracle stories from Mark into one major section describing Jesus' healing ministry in Matt 8–9. Not all Lukan changes can be discussed here.[1] However, some are significant for the understanding of Luke's view of Jesus' ministry.[2]

Luke has marked the special character of the time of Jesus' ministry by a number of significant changes at the beginning of his story. These changes strongly designate Jesus' ministry as a new beginning, and they point forward to events still to come in this ministry and even subsequently in the second part of Luke's work, the Acts of the Apostles. Most remarkable is the transposition of the story of the Baptist's death. The long narrative of Mark 6:17–29 is reduced to a short note in the context of the Baptist's ministry, just before the baptism of Jesus (Mark 3:9–11 = Luke 3:21–22). The result, in Luke's text, is that John is no longer mentioned when Jesus is baptized. John is preacher and prophet rather than baptizer.[3] Jesus' ministry is thus characterized as a period no longer intertwined with that of Israel, which is represented in John the Baptist, who is Israel's last prophet (not Elijah redivivus: Luke omits the Elijah reference of Mark 9:9–13). Jesus is not the continuation of the revelation to Israel, but its fulfillment.

The story which follows, that of Jesus' temptation (Luke 4:1–13), is derived from Q, begins in the desert, but does not end with the temptation on the mountain where Satan shows Jesus all the kingdoms of the world.[4] Rather, in the last temptation, Jesus is on the pinnacle of the temple in Jerusalem. The reader will learn that the last part of Jesus'

---

[1] For further discussion see the relevant commentaries, especially Fitzmyer, *Luke,* passim; and Bovon, *Evangelium nach Lukas,* 19–22 and passim.

[2] On these Lukan redactions of Mark see Hans Conzelmann, *The Theology of St Luke* (London: Faber, 1960) passim. Conzelmann's work, which appeared in its German original first in 1953 (*Die Mitte der Zeit: Studien zur Theologie des Lukas* [BHTh 17; 3d ed.; Tübingen: Mohr/Siebeck, 1960]), has been the seminal beginning of a fresh assessment of Luke's redactional activity in his use of sources. See also Conzelmann and Lindemann, *Interpreting the NT,* 229–36. A thorough critical evaluation of the subsequent research has been published by François Bovon, *Luke the Theologian: Thirty-three Years of Research (1950–1983)* (Princeton Theological Monograph Series; Allison Park, PA: Pickwick, 1987). An anthology of this author's articles on Luke-Acts has appeared in German translation: François Bovon, *Biblisch-theologische Studien: Gesammelte Aufsätze* (BThSt 8; Neukirchen-Vluyn, Neukirchener Verlag, 1985).

[3] Bovon, *Evangelium nach Lukas,* 179.

[4] This was probably the original order of Q which Matthew preserved.

ministry took place in the temple, and that he died in Jerusalem. The sentence with which Luke describes the departure of Satan is also characteristically formulated. Mark 1:13 ends the episode of Jesus' temptation in the wilderness with the statement, "and the angels came and served him." Matt 4:11a has probably preserved the original ending from Q's story: "Then Satan left him." Luke 4:13 says: "When he had completed all temptation, the devil left him until a certain moment." This moment is most likely Luke 22:3 where Luke begins the story of Judas's betrayal with the remark, "And Satan went into Judas." The return of Satan marks the end of the time of revelation.[1] Luke 4:13 and 22:3 form a parenthesis[2] that includes the time in which Jesus' ministry is not endangered by the interference of Satan. Corresponding to this is a geographical schema designating the special character of the places of Jesus' ministry and its three periods: (1) Jesus' activity in Galilee and Judea (Luke 4:1–9:50); (2) Jesus' travel to Jerusalem (9:51–19:27); (3) Jesus' ministry in the temple (19:28–21:38).

The activity in Galilee and Judea opens with the first preaching of Jesus in Nazareth (Luke 4:16–30). The framework is taken from Mark 6:1–6, "Jesus' rejection in Nazareth," but the story has been moved to a position at the beginning of the description of Jesus' ministry and thoroughly revised. The Lukan redaction[3] presents Jesus quoting Isa 61:1–2 and announcing the fulfillment of this prophecy "today." The time of salvation begins in Jesus' home town in Galilee. The reader will know that this marks the beginning of the space in which the salvation will be at work. This designation of the locality of the beginning looks forward not only to Galilee, Judea, and Jerusalem, but ultimately to the conclusion of the Lukan work, i.e., the arrival of the Christian proclamation in Rome.

During the entire period of the first part of Jesus' ministry, he never leaves Galilee and Judea, and these two countries are treated as if they were one, and as if Jerusalem lay outside of this area.[4] This is properly the Holy Land where everything has special significance: the mountain as the place of prayer (even at the scene of the transfiguration; cf. Luke 9:28), the sea as the place for revelations to the disciples (Luke 5:1–11; 8:22–25). Thus there is no "Sermon on the

---

[1] Conzelmann, *Theology of St Luke,* 28–29 and passim.

[2] Conzelmann and Lindemann, *Interpreting the NT,* 233–34.

[3] Apparently no other source than Mark has been used here; cf. Bovon, *Evangelium nach Lukas,* 207–8.

[4] Luke's knowledge of the geography of Palestine was probably limited and inaccurate. But the primary purpose of this geographical construction is the presentation of a theological schema.

Mount"[1] or parable instruction from a boat on the lake.[2] In this Holy
Land, Jesus preaches the coming of the kingdom. Here he is the
divine man who performs miraculous deeds and raises the dead
(7:11–17). In this land he is victorious over those who question him,
and here he is not threatened by any hostility.[3]

The character of Jesus' ministry changes during the long travel to
Jerusalem (9:51–19:27). There is a different urgency in Jesus' instruction to the disciples. As the travel begins, would-be followers are
warned that compromises are not possible for the disciple (9:57–62).
Two eschatological speeches dominate this part of Luke's Gospel
(12:2–59 and 17:20–37). The nearness of the kingdom of God becomes
the repeatedly emphasized single content of the message entrusted to
the disciples (9:60b; 10:11b).[4] But Luke has also placed most of the
church order materials and all the major parables into this section.

To understand the third part of Jesus' ministry, it is important to
observe the changes which Luke has made in his use of Mark's story of
the entrance into Jerusalem (Mark 11:1–11).

Mark 11	*Luke 19*
	28: And when he had said this, he went on ahead, going up to Jerusalem.
1: And when they drew near to Jerusalem to Bethphage and the Mount of Olives, he sent two of his disciples . . .	When he drew near to Bethphage and Bethany at the mount that is called "Of Olives," he sent two of the disciples . . .
8: And many spread their garments on the road and others leafy branches which they had cut from the fields.	36: And as he rode along, they spread their garments on the road.
	37: As he was now drawing near, at the descent of the Mount of Olives, the whole multitude began to rejoice . . .
	41: And as he was drawing near, he saw the city and wept over it.
11: And he entered Jerusalem and went into the temple, and when he had looked round at everything, he went out to Bethany with the Twelve.	45: And he went into the temple.

[1] Luke deletes this localization of the sermon in Q which Matthew has preserved
(Matt 5:1) and lets Jesus preach it "on a plain" (Luke 6:17).

[2] Compare Luke 8:4 with Mark 4:1–2.

[3] Compare, e.g., Luke 6:11 with Mark 3:6.

[4] In both instances, Luke has added these sentences to the sayings from his source.

Luke deletes the mention of "Jerusalem" in Mark 11:11a so that Jesus enters directly into the temple (Luke 19:45). At the same time, he deletes the reference to Jesus' return to Bethany at night (Mark 11:11b). In this way, the entire last portion of Jesus' ministry according to Luke (19:45–21:36) is presented as ministry in the temple,[1] while Jesus goes to the Mount of Olives during the night (Luke 21:37). The pattern is taken from Ezekiel: Jesus represents the divine "glory"; as long as he resides in the temple, the temple functions as the house of Yahweh, but as he finally leaves and moves to the Mount of Olives, the destruction of the temple is imminent.[2]

Luke's redaction of the Markan text seems slight in these instances. Nevertheless, Luke has created an entirely new view of the ministry of Jesus. It begins with the fulfillment in Nazareth of the prophecy of Isaiah and ends with the last presence and final departure of the divine glory from the temple. Conzelmann has rightly called this period of Jesus' ministry "the center of time."[3] It is preceded by the time of Israel and the prophets which comes to an end with John the Baptist, and it is followed by the time of the church which begins with the passion and death of Jesus, who thus becomes the first of the martyrs of the church.

While Matthew has left the Markan passion narrative more or less intact,[4] Luke has made several changes and also inserted special material.[5] A clearly secondary feature is the explicit emphasis upon the last meal as a Passover meal (Luke 22:15). Several sayings are added to the scene of the last meal of Jesus (Luke 22:28–38). The trial before Pilate (Luke 23:2–5) differs sharply from the Markan account (Mark 15:2–5), and Luke has added an appearance of Jesus before Herod (Luke 23:6–16). The narrative of the crucifixion is enlarged by the addition of novelistic episodes: the women of Jerusalem on the road to Calvary (Luke 23:27–32); a discourse of Jesus with the two criminals (Luke 23:39–43). On the other hand, features of Luke's

---

[1] Conzelmann (*Theology of St Luke*, 75–78) has shown that this is the result of deliberate redaction by Luke of the Markan text.

[2] Klaus Baltzer, "The Meaning of the Temple in the Lukan Writings," *HTR* 58 (1965) 263–77.

[3] This is the exact translation of the title of the German original of *The Theology of St Luke: Die Mitte der Zeit.*

[4] See above, # 4.3.5–6, on Matthew's use of sources and composition.

[5] The deviations from Mark, especially in the passion narrative but also in other parts of the Gospel, have resulted in the hypothesis of an altogether different source used by Luke, at least in the passion narrative. Cf. Friedrich Rehkopf, *Die lukanische Sonderquelle: Ihr Umfang und Sprachgebrauch* (WUNT 5; Tübingen: Mohr/Siebeck, 1959); other literature in Bovon, *Evangelium nach Lukas*, 19.

source (Mark) pointing to the agonies suffered by Jesus have been left out. Instead, Jesus dies piously like a perfect martyr (23:46).

Like Matthew, Luke retains the story of the discovery of the empty tomb from the Gospel of Mark. Matthew added only one relatively brief account of the appearance of the risen Lord at the conclusion of his Gospel (Matt 28:16–20). Luke has expanded the conclusion of his Gospel by incorporating three narratives of the appearances of Jesus: the road to Emmaeus (Luke 24:13–35), the appearance in Jerusalem (Luke 24:36–49), and the ascension (Luke 24:50–53). These stories form the link to the second part of the work which begins with the repetition of the story of the ascension (Acts 1:6–11).

The story of the church begins where the story of Jesus ended, in Jerusalem. But that second part of the narrative soon goes beyond Jerusalem. As the message of Jesus began in Nazareth and was first proclaimed publicly in Galilee and Judea, so the apostles' activity begins in Jerusalem and with the public proclamation in Samaria and Syria. As Jesus traveled during the second part of his ministry, the apostles, especially Paul, travel in the Book of Acts throughout the Greek world. The goal is no longer Jerusalem but Rome, though Paul's presence in the temple paradoxically provides the cause for the Christian message to arrive in Rome. The Gospel of Luke is not only the foundation for the Christian mission; it is also its paradigm.[1] "Gospel" as a "biography" of Jesus has been incorporated into a story of the beginnings of a religious movement.

---

[1] To do justice to the Gospel of Luke would require a full treatment of the Book of Acts. This, however, would go beyond the limits of this investigation.

5

The Harmonization of the Canonical Gospels

5.1 Quotations in the Second Epistle of Clement

The *Second Epistle of Clement* contains a number of quotations of sayings of Jesus. In one instance, such a saying is introduced with the formula, "For the Lord says in the Gospel" (λέγει γὰρ ὁ κύριος ἐν τῷ εὐαγγελίῳ, *2 Clem.* 8.5). As has been argued above,[1] this quotation formula as well as the repeated use of the present tense "he says" (λέγει)[2] instead of the aorist "he said" (εἶπεν)[3] and the quotation of one saying with the formula "another scripture says" (ἑτέρα δὲ γραφὴ λέγει, *2 Clem.* 2.4), may prove that *2 Clement* is quoting from a written source that he calls "the gospel." The character of that source, however, can only be determined on the basis of the investigation of the materials which are quoted and the determination of their relationship to known written gospels.

5.1.1 DEPENDENCE UPON EITHER MATTHEW OR LUKE

Dependence upon the redactional work of the Gospel of Matthew is evident in the quotation of Matt 10:32 (Q/Luke 12:8) in *2 Clem.* 3.2:

2 Clem. 3.2	Matt 10:32	Q/Luke 12:8
The one who confesses me before human beings,	Everyone who confesses me before human beings,	Everyone who confesses me before human beings,

---

[1] On this quotation formula, see above # 1.4.4.

[2] *2 Clem.* 3.2; 4.2; 5.2; 6.1; 13.4.

[3] The quotation formula "The Lord said" (εἶπεν ὁ κύριος) is used only in *2 Clem.* 4.5 and 9.11. In 5.4 and 12.2 it appears within the context of a traditional apophthegma. In 12.6, φησίν introduces the final clause of a longer pericope.

| I shall confess him before my father. | also I shall confess him before my father who is in heaven. | the Son of man will confess him before the angels of God. |

It is most likely that the reference to the Son of man in the third person in Luke 12:8 and the mention of the heavenly court as the "angels of God" represent the original wording of Q.[1] Matthew changed this to the first person statement "I shall confess ..."[2] Thus, "my father" is also due to Matthew's redaction. The wording of this saying as it is quoted in 2 Clem. 3.2 is dependent upon the Gospel of Matthew.[3]

2 Clem. 6.2 contains a quotation of the saying about gaining the world but losing one's soul (Mark 8:36 || Matt 16:26 and Luke 9:25). The version presented in the Matthean synoptic parallel is certainly the basis of the citation. Matt 16:26 had changed Mark's infinitive construction (κερδῆσαι ... ζημιωθῆναι) into a conditional clause (ἐὰν κερδήσῃ ... ζημιωθῇ).[4] It is exactly this conditional clause that is reproduced in 2 Clem. 6.2.[5]

However, these are the only two quotations of 2 Clement that can be explained by recourse to dependence upon Matthew alone. The quotation of the saying about "serving two masters" in 2 Clem. 6.1 points to Luke 16:13 rather than to Matt 6:24, for 2 Clement says "No servant" (Οὐδεὶς οἰκέτης = Luke) instead of Matthew's simple "No one" (Οὐδεὶς). Yet, in this case Luke may present an older form of the saying, because the same formulation also appears in the Gospel of Thomas (# 47a). The citation of the command to love one's enemies in 2 Clem. 13.4, introduced by the unique quotation formula "because God says" (ὅτι λέγει ὁ θεός), contains two phrases which are paralleled only in Luke: Οὐ χάρις ὑμῖν ... ἀλλὰ χάρις ὑμῖν (Luke 6:32: ποία ὑμῖν χάρις) and τοὺς μισοῦντας ὑμᾶς (Luke 6:27: τοῖς μισοῦσιν ὑμᾶς), while special features of the Matthean parallels (5:46, 44) do not appear.[6]

---

[1] Cf. also the negative formulation in Luke 12:9 and the variant of this saying in Mark 8:38. Both refer to the Son of man in the third person and describe the heavenly court as "the angels of God."

[2] Bultmann, Synoptic Tradition, 150–52.

[3] For further discussion, see Koester, Synoptische Überlieferung, 71–73.

[4] Luke 9:25 has changed Mark's infinitive construction into participial clauses and expanded the second part of the saying (κερδήσας ... ἀπολέσας ἢ ζημιωθείς).

[5] Koester, Synoptische Überlieferung, 73–74. The introductory clause of 2 Clem. 6.2, τί γὰρ τὸ ὄφελος, differs from the introductory formulation of all three Synoptic parallels, but is also found in the quotation of this saying in Clement of Alexandria, Strom. 6.14, 112.3. It is unlikely that this reflects an independent non-canonical tradition.

[6] Cf. Koester, Synoptische Überlieferung, 75–76.

5.1.2 HARMONIZATIONS OF MATTHEW AND LUKE

The remaining quotations of sayings in *2 Clement* reveal that the relationship of their texts to the Synoptic Gospels is much more complex. The hypothesis of dependence upon Matthew in some instances, and upon Luke in others, cannot account for their peculiar forms.

Several of the sayings quoted in *2 Clement* are harmonized versions of the Matthean and Lukan texts. This is most clearly evident in the quotation of sayings which Matthew and Luke have derived from Mark.

2 Clem. 9.11	Matt 12:50	Mark 3:35	Luke 8:21
My brothers			My mother and my
are those	Everyone	He	brothers are those
who do the will of	who does the will of	who does the will of	who hear the word
my father.	my father in heaven,	God,	of God and do it.
	he is my brother …	he is my brother …	
			μήτηρ μου καὶ
Ἀδελφοί μου			ἀδελφοί μου
οὗτοί εἰσιν	ὅστις γὰρ ἂν	ὃς ἂν	οὗτοί εἰσιν
οἱ ποιοῦντες	ποιήσῃ	ποιήσῃ τὸ	οἱ
τὸ θέλημα	τὸ θέλημα	θέλημα	τὸν λόγον
⸀τοῦ πατρός μου.	τοῦ πατρός μου	τοῦ θεοῦ,	τοῦ θεοῦ
	τοῦ ἐν οὐρανοῖς,		ἀκούοντες καὶ
	αὐτός μου ἀδελφός	οὗτος ἀδελφός μου	ποιοῦντες.
	… ἐστίν.	… ἐστίν.	

2 Clem. 9:11 combines the Lukan participial formulation of the saying (οἱ ποιοῦντες) with the Matthean change of "will of God" into "will of my father." This, however, is not simply an accidental mixture of Synoptic parallels. The same harmonization of Matthean and Lukan redactional changes of Mark's text of this saying appears in its quotation in Clement of Alexandria[1] and in the *Gospel of the Ebionites*.[2] *2 Clem.* 9.11 thus presupposes a more widely known document or a tradition in which this saying already appeared in a harmonized version.

2 Clem. 5.2–4 quotes a brief dialogue which reflects Lukan vocabulary of a saying in its first part, but again exhibits harmonizations of the Matthean and Lukan version in its second part; the dialogue that connects the two sayings has no parallel in the Synoptic Gospels:

---

[1] Ἀδελφοί μου γὰρ … καὶ συγκληρονόμοι οἱ ποιοῦντες τὸ θέλημα τοῦ πατρός μου (*Ecl. proph.* 20.3).

[2] οὗτοί εἰσιν οἱ ἀδελφοί μου καὶ ἡ μήτηρ καὶ ἀδελφαὶ οἱ ποιοῦντες τὰ θελήματα τοῦ πατρός μου (quoted in Epiphanius *Haer.* 30.14.5). See my *Synoptische Überlieferung*, 77–79, for more detailed documentation.

2 Clem. 5.2–4	Matt 10:16	Luke 10:3
The Lord says (λέγει), "You will be like lambs (ἀρνία) in the midst of wolves." Answering, Peter says to him, "What if the wolves scatter the lambs?" Jesus said to Peter, "The lambs should not fear the wolves after they have died;	Behold, I am sending you like sheep (πρόβατα) in the midst of wolves.	Behold, I am sending you like lambs (ἄρνας) in the midst of wolves.

	Matt 10:28	Luke 12:4–5
and also you do not fear those who kill you and are not able to do anything to you.	and do not fear those who kill the body but are not able to kill the soul.	Do not fear those who kill the body and afterwards have no more that they can do. I will show you whom to fear:
But fear the one who after your having died has authority over soul and body to throw into the hell of fire.	But fear more the one who is able to destroy body and soul in hell.	Fear the one who after he has killed has the authority to throw into hell.

μὴ φοβεῖσθε τοὺς ἀποκτεννόντας ὑμᾶς καὶ μηδὲν ὑμῖν δυναμένους ποιεῖν, ἀλλὰ φοβεῖσθε τὸν μετὰ τὸ ἀποθανεῖν ὑμᾶς ἔχοντα ἐξουσίαν ψυχῆς καὶ σώματος τοῦ βαλεῖν εἰς γέενναν πυρός.	μὴ φοβεῖσθε ἀπὸ τῶν ἀποκτεννόντων τὸ σῶμα, τὴν δὲ ψυχὴν μὴ δυναμένων ἀποκτεῖναι. φοβεῖσθε δὲ μᾶλλον τὸν δυνάμενον καὶ ψυχὴν καὶ σῶμα ἀπολέσαι ἐν γεέννῃ.	μὴ φοβηθῆτε ἀπὸ τῶν ἀποκτεννόντων τὸ σῶμα, καὶ μετὰ ταῦτα μὴ ἐχόντων περισσότερόν τι ποιεῖν . . . φοβήθητε τὸν μετὰ τὸ ἀποκτεῖναι ἔχοντα ἐξουσίαν ἐμβαλεῖν εἰς τὴν γέενναν.

The mixture of readings drawn from Matthew and from Luke is evident.[1] Two arguments speak against a direct dependence upon

---

[1] See the analysis ibid., 94–99.

Matthew and Luke for *2 Clement's* quotation. (1) It is unlikely that the author of *2 Clement* was responsible for the composition of the entire dialogue between Jesus and Peter. The first part, Jesus' initial statement about the sending of the disciples like lambs into the midst of wolves, is entirely gratuitous in the context of *2 Clement* 5. The author's argument is not based on the experience of adversities and threats of death in this world; it rather contrasts the brevity of the earthly sojourn with the great and wonderful promise of eternal life (cf. *2 Clem.* 5.5). (2) Similar harmonizations of Matt 10:28 and Luke 12:4–5 also appear in two other quotations of the passage: Justin, *1 Apol.* 19.7; *Ps-Clem. Hom.* 17.5.2.[1]

If these harmonizations must be ascribed to the source that *2 Clement* used, it is also evident that this source cannot have been been a complete gospel harmony. The source must have contained only such harmonized sayings that were connected with each other through a secondary framework of questions and answers, but without any narrative materials. *2 Clem.* 5.2–4 exhibits the typical features of a secondary development of dialogical units which were formed within the tradition of sayings. The *Gospel of Thomas* and especially the *Dialogue of the Savior* provided examples for this development of the sayings tradition.[2] What is remarkable here is the fact that the sayings appearing in *2 Clement* are drawn from gospels which also contain narrative materials such as Matthew and Luke. However, the Synoptic Gospels were not the exclusive source for the sayings collection used in *2 Clement*.

5.1.3 NON-CANONICAL SAYINGS IN 2 CLEMENT

The quotation of a saying in *2 Clem.* 8.5 appears at first glance to be taken from Luke 16:10–12. Moreover, this is the only saying in *2 Clement* that is explicitly introduced with a quotation formula that refers to "the gospel." However, non-canonical parallels call for a different explanation:

		Irenaeus
2 Clem. 8.5	Luke 16:11, 12, 10	*Adv. haer.* 2.34.3
For the		And therefore
Lord says in the gospel,		the Lord said ...

---

[1] There are a few minor differences which can easily be explained as further developments in a harmonized tradition of sayings; cf. Koester, *Synoptische Überlieferung*, 97. For further discussion of the harmonizations of sayings in Justin Martyr, see below # 5.2.1.4.

[2] See above ## 2.2.4; 3.1.1.

"If you have not preserved the small thing, the great things, who will give them to you?" . . .

"He who is faithful in very little, is faithful also in much."

---

[11] If you have not been faithful in the unjust mammon, that which is true, who will entrust it to you? [12] And if you have not been faithful in that which is another's, that which is your own, who will give it you? [10] He who is faithful in very little, is faithful also in much; and he who is dishonest in a very little, is dishonest also in much.

"If you have not been faithful in a small thing, that which is great, who will give it to you?"

λέγει γὰρ ὁ κύριος ἐν τῷ εὐαγγελίῳ· εἰ τὸ μικρὸν οὐκ ἐτηρήσατε, τὸ μέγα τίς ὑμῖν δώσει;

ὁ πιστὸς ἐν ἐλαχίστῳ καὶ ἐν πολλῷ πιστός ἐστιν.

---

[11] εἰ ἐν τῷ ἀδίκῳ μαμώνᾳ πιστοὶ οὐκ ἐγένεσθε, τὸ ἀληθινὸν τίς ὑμῖν δώσει; [12] καὶ εἰ ἐν τῷ ἀλλοτρίῳ πιστοὶ οὐκ ἐγένεσθε, τὸ ἡμέτερον τίς δώσει ὑμῖν; [10] ὁ πιστὸς ἐν ἐλαχίστῳ καὶ ἐν πολλῷ πιστός ἐστιν, καὶ ὁ ἐν ἐλαχίστῳ ἄδικος καὶ ἐν πολλῷ ἄδικός ἐστιν.

Et ideo dominus dicebat . . . , "Si in modico fideles non fuistis, quod magnum est, quis dabit vobis?"[1]

The second half of the saying quoted in 2 Clem. 8.5 agrees verbatim with Luke 16:10a. But it is unlikely that it is excerpted from the cluster of sayings in Luke 16:9–13 which are secondary additions to the parable of the Unjust Steward (Luke 16:1–8). The first half of 2 Clem. 8.5 may reveal an alteration by the author of 2 Clement. "If you have not preserved . . ." (εἰ οὐκ ἐτηρήσατε) reflects the interests of the author who adds to the quotation of the saying the admonition, "Preserve your flesh pure" (τηρήσατε τὴν σάρκα ἁγνήν).[2] Its original wording most likely agreed with that of the quotations in Irenaeus and Hilarius (εἰ πιστοὶ οὐκ ἐγένεσθε). But this saying cannnot be derived from Luke 16. Rather, it must be assumed that it is the original form of the saying

---

[1] The same saying is quoted in Hilarius, Epistula seu libellus, chap. 1 (MPL 10.753b): Si in modico fideles non fuistis, quod maius est, quis dabit vobis?

[2] The verb τηρεῖν is frequently used in 2 Clement, cf. 6.9; 7.6; 8.4.

that has been modified in Luke 16:11 and 12 in order to provide a commentary for the preceding parable.[1] While the original form is not preserved in Luke, it has survived in the free tradition of sayings and was incorporated into the collection which *2 Clement* used. It is very interesting that exactly in this instance *2 Clement* refers to his source as "the gospel"—possibly the earliest evidence for the designation of a sayings collection as "gospel."

In the quotation of *2 Clem.* 4.2, 5, a saying from the free tradition is combined with sayings drawn from the Synoptic Gospels . The first saying is introduced by "for he says" (λέγει γάρ), the second (4.5) by "the Lord said" (εἶπεν ὁ κύριος):

2 Clem. 4.2, 5	Matt 7:21–23	Luke 6:46; 13:26–27
[2] Not everyone who says "Lord, Lord," will be saved (σωθήσεται),	[21] Not everyone who says "Lord, Lord," will enter the kingdom of heaven,	[6:46] Why do you call me, "Lord, Lord,"
but he who does	but he who does	but do not do what I say?
the righteousness.	the will of my father in heaven.	
	[22] Many will say to me on that day, "Lord, Lord, did we not prophecy in your name, and did we not cast out demons in your name, and did we not do many powerful deeds in your name?"	[13:26] Then you will begin to say to me, "We ate and drank before you, and you taught in our streets.
[5a] If you were assembled in my bosom, but would not do my commandments, I would expel you.		
[5b] And I shall say to you, "Depart from me, I do not know you whence you	[23] And then I shall testify to them, "I never knew you;	[27] And he will say to you, "I do not know (you)[2] whence you are;

---

[1] Luke 16:10b–12 are secondary formulations. For further discussion see Koester, *Synoptische Überlieferung,* 101. That εἰ πιστοὶ οὐκ ἐγένεσθε belongs to the original form of the saying is still visible in Luke 16:11 and 12. But it is not possible to consider *2 Clem.* 8.5a as a further secondary development on the basis of Luke (*pace* Koester, ibid.).

[2] The word ὑμᾶς is missing in 𝔭[75] B L R 070 1241 *pc* it.

are,	go away from me, those	you are; stay away from me,
workers of	who are doing	all workers of
lawlessness."	lawlessness."	injustice.

| καὶ ἐρῶ ὑμῖν· Ὑπάγετε ἀπ' ἐμοῦ, οὐκ οἶδα ὑμᾶς, πόθεν ἐστέ, | καὶ τότε ὁμολογήσω αὐτοῖς ὅτι οὐδέποτε ἔγνων ὑμᾶς, ἀποχωρεῖτε ἀπ' ἐμοῦ οἱ | καὶ ἐρεῖ λέγων ὑμῖν· οὐκ οἶδα (ὑμᾶς), πόθεν ἐστέ, ἀπόστητε ἀπ' ἐμοῦ |
| ἐργάται ἀνομίας. | ἐργαζόμενοι τὴν ἀνομίαν. | πάντες ἐργάται ἀδικίας. |

The parallels in Matthew belong to the same unit. But one cannot be certain whether this reflects the order of Q and the two parts of the unit were separated by Luke, or whether Matthew combined two Q sayings which were originally unconnected. Regardless of this question, both Matthean and Lukan redactional elements are evident in the quotation of 2 Clement. Luke 6:46 apparently preserved the more original form of the saying about those who say "Lord, Lord." The construction of the sentence (οὐ πᾶς ὁ λέγων ... ἀλλ' ὁ ποιῶν) in 2 Clement reflects Matthew's redaction.[1] Elements of Lukan redaction, however, prevail in the last part of the quotation.[2] Most evident is the mixture of Matthean and Lukan elements in the final phrase. From the quotation of Ps 6:9 (ἀπόστητε ἀπ' ἐμοῦ, πάντες οἱ ἐργαζόμενοι τὴν ἀνομίαν) which forms the basis of this phrase,[3] the citation in 2 Clem. 4.5 preserves the term "lawlessness" in agreement with Matthew, but renders it in the genitive, while combining it with the Lukan change of οἱ ἐργαζόμενοι into ἐργάται. This mixture of Matthean and Lukan redactional elements appears once more in the quotation of the same saying in Justin, 1 Apol. 16:11, which agrees with 2 Clement in the reading ἐργάται τῆς ἀνομίας.[4]

Although the influence of both the texts of Matthew and of Luke is evident, 2 Clement has replaced the central section of the saying with an altogether different description of the claim of those who want to be accepted by the Lord, "If you were assembled in my bosom ..." A

---

[1] The changes in 2 Clement, "to do righteousness" (δικαιοσύνην) and "to be saved" (σωθήσεται) reflect the typical vocabulary of the author of this letter; see the discussion in Koester, Synoptische Überlieferung, 81–82.

[2] The formulation of the sentence οὐκ οἶδα ὑμᾶς, πόθεν ἐστέ in Luke 13:27 is apparently a Lukan change under the influence of the tradition quoted in Luke 13:25.

[3] The phrase must have stood in Q as an exact quote from the Psalm; see above, # 2.3.1.

[4] This is, in part, confirmed by another quotation of this passage in Dial. 76.5; see the further discussion of these harmonizations below, # 5.1.2.1.

parallel is preserved in a manuscript of the so-called Zion Gospel Edition. The manuscripts belonging to this group are characterized by a number of marginal notations which offer alternative readings of certain passages of Matthew, introduced by "The Jewish gospel (Τὸ Ἰουδαϊκόν) reads here the following . . ." Minuscule 1424, which belongs to this group of manuscripts, notes in the margin to Matt 7:5 a saying that is a close variant of the central section of the quotation in *2 Clem.* 4.2, 5:

"The Jewish Gospel"[1]	*2 Clem.* 4.5a
The Jewish gospel reads here the following:	
If you were	If you were with me assembled
in my bosom and would not do	in my bosom and would not do
the will of my father in heaven,	my commandments,
I will cast you out of my bosom.	I would expel you.
Τὸ Ἰουδαϊκὸν ἐνταῦθα οὕτως ἔχει·	εἶπεν ὁ κύριος·
ἐὰν ἦτε	ἐὰν ἦτε μετ' ἐμοῦ συνηγμένοι
ἐν τῷ κόλπῳ μου καὶ	ἐν τῷ κόλπῳ μου καὶ μὴ ποιῆτε
τὸ θέλημα τοῦ πατρός μου τοῦ ἐν	τὰς ἐντολάς μου,
τοῖς οὐρανοῖς μὴ ποιῆτε,	
ἐκ τοῦ κόλπῳ μου ἀρρίψω ὑμᾶς.	ἀποβαλῶ ὑμᾶς.

The marginal notations of this group of manuscripts are usually assigned to the Jewish-Christian Gospels, specifically to the *Gospel of the Nazoreans*.[2] This gospel was essentially an expanded edition of the Gospel of Matthew. It is, therefore, not surprising to find in the manuscript of the Gospel Edition Zion a form of this non-canonical saying which reflects the language of Matthew; cf. the phrase "the will of my father in heaven." *2 Clem.* 4.5a, however, does not exhibit any signs of the influence of Matthean language. It is, therefore, unlikely that the author drew the saying from an expanded version of the Gospel of Matthew. Rather, the source of *2 Clem.* 4.2, 5 was probably the same collection of sayings that is used elsewhere in this writing, that is, a collection based on Matthew and Luke that also incorporated sayings from the free tradition.

The inclusion of such non-canonical sayings into *2 Clement's* source is also evident in the quotation of *2 Clem.* 12.2, 6.[3] Parallels to this

---

[1] Text in Klostermann, *Apocrypha II*, 7.

[2] See Vielhauer, "Jewish-Christian Gospels," in Hennecke-Schneemelcher-Wilson, *NT Apocrypha*, 1. 136, 139–46.

[3] *2 Clem.* 12.3–5 interrupts the quotation by presenting a seriatim interpretation of the three phrases of the first part of the saying.

saying are found in the *Gospel of the Egyptians*[1] and the *Gospel of Thomas*[2]:

2 Clem. 12.2, 6	Gos. Thom. 22	Gos. Egypt.
[2] When the Lord himself was asked by someone, when the kingdom of God would come,	Jesus saw infants being suckled. He said to his disciples, "These infants being suckled are like those who enter the kingdom." They said to him, "Shall we then, as children, enter the kingdom?"	When Salome inquired, when she would know the things about which she had asked,
he said (εἶπεν),	Jesus said to them,	the Lord said, "When you tread upon the garment of shame,[3]
"When the two will be one,	"When you make the two one, and when you make the inside like the outside,	and when the two become one,
and the outside like the inside,	and the outside like the inside, and the above like the below, and when you	
and the male with the female	make the male and the female	and when the male with the female

---

[1] This fragment of the *Gospel according to the Egyptians* is preserved in a quotation in Clement of Alexandria, *Strom.* 3.13, 92.2, introduced by, "What is said here, we do not have in the four gospels transmitted to us, but in the Gospel according to the Egyptians ..." (... ἐν τῷ κατ᾽ Αἰγυπτίους εὐαγγελίῳ). On the fragments of the *Gospel of the Egyptians,* see W. Schneemelcher, "The Gospel of the Egyptians," in Hennecke-Schneemelcher-Wilson, *NT Apocrypha,* 1. 166–78.

[2] A detailed discussion of *2 Clem.* 12.2, 6 with its parallels has been presented by Tjitze Baarda, "2 Clement 12 and the Sayings of Jesus," in Delobel, ed., *LOGIA,* 529–56.

[3] A parallel to this sentence appears in *Gos. Thom.* 37: "His disciples said, 'When will you become revealed to us, and when shall we see you?' Jesus said, 'When you disrobe without being ashamed, and take up your garments and place them under your feet like little children and tread on them, then [will you see] the Son of the Living One, and you will not be afraid."

neither male nor female.	one and the same, so that the male not be male nor the female female,[1]	is neither male nor female.
When you do these things, he said (φησίν),[2] the kingdom of my father will come.	then will you enter the kingdom."	

It is impossible to argue for any kind of literary dependence of one of these reproductions of this saying upon an other. In the text of the saying that is preserved in the quotation of *2 Clem.* 12, there are no secondary elaborations, and the questioner remains unnamed. *Gos. Thom.* 22 is a more complex composition.[3] The introduction which describes the situation ("Jesus saw infants being suckled") belongs to a different traditional saying about entering the kingdom of God like children; cf. Mark 10:15. The saying itself in the *Gospel of Thomas* is characterized by the addition of a series of analogous phrases. None of these secondary features is paralleled in the quotation of *2 Clem.* 12. The version of the saying from the *Gospel of the Egyptians*[4] leaves out the second of the three phrases ("and the outside like the inside"), and it combines this saying with a second saying about "treading upon the garment of shame" that is independently preserved in *Gos. Thom.* 37.[5] This, as well as the naming of the person who asks the question (Salome), argues for the secondary character of the reproduction of this traditional saying in the *Gospel of the Egyptians*.[6] The form of this saying as it is quoted in *2 Clem.* 12 is, therefore, its oldest and most original form. It must have been circulating in the free tradition

---

[1] The *Gospel of Thomas* inserts here: "and when you fashion eyes in the place of an eye, and a hand in the place of a hand, and a foot in place of a foot, and a likeness in the place of a likeness . . ."

[2] The word φησίν here must be understood as an introduction of a quote; cf. Baarda, "2 Clement 12," 548–49.

[3] See the detailed comparison of *2 Clem.* 12 and *Gos. Thom.* 22 by Baarda ("2 Clement 12," 544–47).

[4] It is quoted by Clement of Alexandria in the context of a refutation of the encratite teachings of Cassian, who had based his arguments on this quote; see Baarda, "2 Clement 12," 537–39.

[5] Baarda ("2 Clement 12," 542–43) suggests that either the *Gospel according to the Egyptians* or Cassian, whom Clement of Alexandria quotes, had combined the two sayings, which the *Gospel of Thomas* still preserves as two independent units.

[6] For further discussion of the relationship of *2 Clem.* 12 to the *Gospel of the Egyptians*, see Koester, *Synoptische Überlieferung*, 102–4 (note that those pages were written before the publication of the *Gospel of Thomas*).

of sayings from which the author of the sayings collection that *2 Clement* knew and used obtained also other non-canonical materials.

Several conclusions can be drawn from the observations we have made regarding the quotations of sayings in *2 Clement*. The author of this mid-2d-century work quotes from a collection of sayings of Jesus. Insofar as these sayings have parallels in the Synoptic Gospels, their text reveals a harmonization of Matthean and Lukan elements which occasionally are paralleled elsewhere, especially in Justin Martyr. In addition to these harmonized sayings from Matthew and Luke, *2 Clement's* sayings collection included sayings from the free tradition, that is, non-canonical sayings which have also found their way into so-called apocryphal gospels. However, nowhere is a direct dependence of *2 Clement* upon such apocryphal gospels indicated. Although features of the Matthean and Lukan redaction of sayings are evident, there is no trace of any narrative materials from these canonical gospels. On the other hand, the sayings in the collection that *2 Clement* used seem to have been set into a framework of brief dialogues. The possible reference to this written collection of sayings as "the gospel" argues for a date of composition after the middle of the 2d century.

5.2 The Gospel Quotations of Justin Martyr

5.2.1 SAYINGS IN JUSTIN'S WRITINGS

Justin Martyr, who wrote his Apologies for the Christians and his Dialogue with the Jew Trypho during the last decade of the rule of Antoninus Pius (138–161), is the first of the Christian writers to cite materials from written gospels extensively. He knew and quoted especially the Gospels of Matthew and Luke; he must have known the Gospel of Mark as well, though there is only one explicit reference to this Gospel;[1] he apparently had no knowledge of the Gospel of John.[2] In addition to extensive quotations of sayings in Justin's writings, his scriptural proof for the truth of the Christian message makes ample use of narrative materials from the Synoptic Gospels.

Many of the sayings quoted by Justin are grouped together under special headings in *1 Apol.* 15–17. Smaller clusters are cited in *Dial.* 17.3–4; 35.3; 51.2–3; and 76.4–7. Individual sayings appear occasionally throughout Justin's writings, and some are quoted in the context of Justin's interpretation of Psalm 22 in *Dial.* 99–107.

---

[1] *Dial.* 106.3; see above # 4.1.1.

[2] The only possible reference to the Gospel of John is the quotation of a saying in *1 Apol.* 61.4; see the discussion below.

The relationship of Justin's quotations to the tradition of sayings and to written gospels is complex, and various solutions have been proposed in order to explain the peculiar forms of his sayings.[1] The most striking feature is that these sayings exhibit many harmonizations of the texts of Matthew and Luke.[2] However, the simple assumption of a harmonized gospel source alone cannot explain all peculiarities of the quotations. It is best to consider each feature by itself; but because of the large number of sayings quoted in Justin only some characteristic passages can be discussed.

5.2.1.1 Quotations from the Free Tradition

Justin is not always dependent upon the text of a written gospel; he had access to sayings from the free tradition. This is most obvious in *1 Apol.* 61.4. The saying "Unless you are reborn, you cannot enter into the kingdom of heaven" is quoted in the context of a description of the Christian ceremony of baptism. Justin must have obtained this saying through the tradition of the baptismal liturgy, and is not dependent upon a written gospel. It has been shown above[3] that Justin's version is more original than the forms of the saying that appear in John 3:3 ("Truly, truly, I say to you, unless someone is born again [or: anew], he cannot see the kingdom of God") and John 3:5 ("Truly, truly, I say to you, unless someone is born from water and spirit, he cannot enter into the kingdom of God").[4]

In *Dial.* 35.3 Justin quotes the saying "There will be divisions and factions" (Ἔσονται σχίσματα καὶ αἱρέσεις)." It has no parallel in any known written gospel[5] but is quoted elsewhere in ancient Christian literature.[6] In 1 Cor 11:18–19, Paul says: ". . . I hear that there are

---

[1] Adolf Hilgenfeld (*Kritische Untersuchungen über die Evangelien Justins, der Clementinischen Homilien und Marcions* [Halle, 1850]) argued for the use of an apocryphal gospel. Wilhelm Bousset (*Die Evangeliencitate Justins des Märtyrers in ihrem Wert für die Evangelienkritik* [Göttingen: Vandenhoeck & Ruprecht, 1891) believed that he had found evidence for the use of the Synoptic Sayings Source. Edouard Massaux ("Le texte du Sermon sur la Montagne de Matthieu utilizé par Saint Justin," *EThL* 28 [1952] 411–48) argued for exclusive use of the Synoptic Gospels.

[2] This has been argued convincingly first by Ernestus Lippelt, *Quae fuerint Justini Martyris* ΑΠΟΜΝΕΜΟΝΕΥΜΑΤΑ (Dissertationes Philologicae Halensis 15.1: 1901); see also Arthur Bellinzoni, *Sayings in Justin Martyr.*

[3] See above # 3.4.4.3.

[4] See especially the detailed arguments in Bellinzoni, *Sayings in Justin Martyr,* 134–38. Bellinzoni also discusses related quotations of this saying in Patristic literature.

[5] The origin of this saying is debated. The only saying in the Synoptic tradition that could be compared is Luke 12:51, "Do you think that I have come to give peace on earth? no, I tell you, but rather division (διαμερισμόν)"; cf. *Gos. Thom.* 16.

[6] It is also quoted in the *Didascalia* (see below), in Didymus, *De trinitate* 3.22, and

divisions (σχίσματα) among you ... For indeed there must be factions
(αἱρέσεις) among you." Justin is hardly dependent upon Paul; he never
refers to any of Paul's writings. But the possibility that Paul formulated his criticism of the Corinthians on the basis of this saying should
not be excluded. In *Dial.* 35.3 it appears as the second in a cluster of
four sayings into which it was apparently incorporated before it was
quoted by Justin; see the discussion below.

It is difficult to determine the origin of the saying in *Dial.* 47.5:
"Therefore, our Lord Jesus Christ said, 'In the things in which I shall
overcome you, I shall also judge you' ('Εν οἷς ἂν ὑμᾶς καταλάβω, ἐν
τούτοις καὶ κρινῶ)." There are parallels to this saying in ancient Christian writers,[1] but nowhere is it quoted as a saying of Jesus. Rather, it
is either identified as a pronouncement of God or as a prophecy of
Ezekiel. Justin may have misunderstood a reference to "the Lord" in
the introductory formula of his source (a pseudepigraphical book attributed to Ezekiel?) and thus ascribed the saying to Jesus,[2] or he may
have known this saying from an oral tradition.

5.2.1.2 Quotations that Could be Derived from Matthew

1 Apol. 15.1 quotes Matt 5:28 ("Whoever looks at a woman in order
to desire her ...."). There are no parallels to this saying in other gospels, and it is most likely a Matthean composition. The introductory
formulation in Justin ('Ὃς ἂν ἐμβλέψῃ) differs from Matthew (πᾶς ὁ
βλέπων), but is paralleled in numerous Patristic quotations.[3] Thus,
Justin may not be quoting Matthew directly, but some catechetical collection of sayings derived from Matthew.

1 Apol. 15.4 quotes Matt 19:11–12 ("There are some made eunuchs
by human beings ...."). There is again no parallel to this saying in any
other gospel. Modifications in Justin's quotation[4] can be ascribed to
his editorial work.

---

in Lactantius, *Div. Inst.* 4.30. In the latter case, it is not identified as a saying of
Jesus. Dependence upon this saying is possible also in *Ps.-Clem. Hom.* 16.21.4: "There
will be," as the Lord said, "false apostles, false prophets, factions (αἱρέσεις), lust for
power."

[1] The texts of the quotations in Clement of Alexandria, *Quis dives salvetur* 40.1–2;
Ps.-Athanasius, *Quaest. ad Antiochum* 36; *Vita S. Iohannici;* and Johannes Climacus,
Scala Paradisi 7, can be found in Bellinzoni, *Sayings in Justin Martyr,* 132–33.

[2] Bellinzoni, *Sayings in Justin Martyr,* 134.

[3] See ibid., 57–58.

[4] Justin abbreviates the saying and reverses the order of the first two categories of
eunuches.

1 Apol. 16.5 (On Swearing) has a gospel parallel only in Matt 5:34–37, but Justin's quote also shares some features with the quotation of this saying in Jas 5:12:[1]

Just. *1 Apol.* 16.5	Jas 5:12	Matt 5:34–37
	. . . my brothers and sisters,	[34] But I say to you
Do not swear at all (μὴ ὀμόσητε ὅλως)	do not swear (μὴ ὀμνύετε), either by heaven	not to swear at all (μὴ ὀμόσαι ὅλως), either by heaven, because it is the throne of God,
	or by earth,	[35] or by earth, because it is the footstool of his feet, or by Jerusalem, . . .
	nor with any other oath.	[36] nor shall you swear by your head, . . .
Let your Yes be Yes and your No be No (ἔστω δὲ ὑμῶν τὸ ναὶ ναὶ καὶ τὸ οὒ οὔ), Everything beyond these is from evil.	Let your Yes be Yes and your No be No (ἤτω δὲ ὑμῶν τὸ ναὶ ναὶ καὶ το οὒ οὔ), so that you may not fall under condemnation.	[37] Let what you say be "Yes, yes" and "No, no." (ἔστω δὲ ὁ λόγος ὑμῶν ναὶ ναί, οὒ οὔ) Everything beyond these is from evil.

That Justin is quoting Matthew and not James is evident in the first and the last clause. The absence of Matt 5:34b–36 is probably due to omission on the part of Justin. But the phrase "Let your Yes be Yes and your No be No" is identical with the corresponding sentence in Jas 5:12. Surprisingly, this phrase from Jas 5:12 also appears in a large number of Patristic quotations of Matt 5:37,[2] and a combination of this phrase with Matt 5:37b, that is, a text that is identical with that of Justin's reference, can be found twice in the *Pseudo-Clementine Homilies,* in both instances understood as a saying of Jesus.[3] Thus, also in this instance it is not likely that Justin is quoting directly from the text of Matthew, but from a catechism, whose text was influenced by the formulation preserved in Jas 5:12 but not necessarily directly dependent upon the the Epistle of James.

---

[1] See the comparison of Matt 5:34–37 and Jas 5:12 above in # 2.1.4.4.

[2] All relevant material is presented in Bellinzoni, *Sayings in Justin Martyr,* 66.

[3] Ἔστω δὲ ὑμῶν τὸ ναὶ ναὶ καὶ τὸ οὒ οὔ, τὸ γὰρ (δὲ) περισσὸν τούτων ἐκ τοῦ πονηροῦ ἐστιν (3.55.1 and 19.2.4; ed. Rehm, GCS pp. 77 and 253).

In *1 Apol.* 15.17 Justin concludes a cluster of sayings with a citation of Matt 6:1 (". . . do not do this in order to be seen by people"). Again, there is no parallel in any other gospel. The quotations of Matt 6:19–20 in *1 Apol.* 15.11 and of Matt 7:21 in *1 Apol.* 16.9 appear in a series of sayings in which harmonizations of the texts of Matthew and Luke are otherwise evident.[1] It is significant that dependence on Matthew alone is restricted to sayings of Matthew that have no Synoptic parallel, and that even in these instances it is most probable that Justin is quoting from a catechism.

5.2.1.3 Sayings that Could be Derived from Luke

There are very few instances in which exclusive dependence upon Luke's Gospel is likely.[2] The only clear instance is the quotation of Luke 17:48 ("Everyone to whom much is given, of him much is required") in *1 Apol.* 17.4. There is no parallel to this saying in either Matthew or Mark; Luke has added this originally independent saying to the parable of the Servant's Wages (Luke 17:47–48a). However, in the manuscripts of Luke, this saying appears in two different versions, one in the Majority Text of the manuscripts (𝕸), the other in the so-called Western Text (D):

Justin *1 Apol.* 17.4	Luke 17:48 𝕸	Luke 17:48 D
Whom God has given more,	From everyone to whom much has been given much will be required, and from the one to whom much has been entrusted,	From everyone to whom much has been given even much more will be required, and from the one to whom much more has been entrusted,
even more will be demanded from him.	even much more will be demanded.	even more will be demanded.

---

[1] It is, therefore, misleading to classify these and similar passages as sayings which are dependent upon Matthew only (*pace* Bellinzoni, *Sayings in Justin Martyr,* 61–62, 67–69).

[2] Bellinzoni (*Sayings in Justin Martyr,* 70–73, cf. 20–22) lists *1 Apol.* 15.3; 16.1; and 16.10. But the first of these sayings (On marrying a divorced woman) actually combines elements of Luke 16:18 and Matt 5:32b (19:9). All three appear in an otherwise harmonized cluster of sayings. It would be natural that in such compositions some phrases or sentences are reflecting exclusively the version of either Matthew or Luke.

ᾧ πλέον ἔδωκεν ὁ θεός,	παντὶ δὲ ᾧ ἐδόθη πολύ,	παντὶ δὲ ᾧ ἔδωκαν πολύ,
	πολὺ ζητηθήσεται παρ'	ζητήσουσιν ἀπ' αὐτοῦ
	αὐτοῦ, καὶ ᾧ παρέθεντο	περισσότερον, καὶ ᾧ
	πολύ,	παρέθεντο πολύ,
πλέον	περισσότερον	πλέον
ἀπαιτηθήσεται παρ'	αἰτήσουσιν αὐτόν.	ἀπαιτήσουσιν αὐτόν.
αὐτοῦ.		

To be sure, Justin quotes this saying in an abbreviated form. But there can be no doubt that the basis of his quotation is the Western Text, as preserved in Codex D, and not the Majority Text of the Lukan manuscripts.[1] The abbreviated form of the quotation of this saying, however, does not seem to be accidental. There are several instances in Patristic literature in which a similar abbreviated form of the saying appears and, moreover, the use of the composite verb ἀπειτεῖν (Codex D) instead of the Majority Text's αἰτεῖν is pervasive in such quotes.[2] This would argue for Justin's dependence upon a special catechetical tradition also in this instance.

5.2.1.4 Harmonizations of the texts of Matthew and Luke

The vast majority of the sayings quoted in Justin's writings are harmonizations of the texts of Matthew and Luke. These harmonizations are not casual or accidental, but systematic and consistent,[3] and they involve the composition of longer sections of parallel sayings from both gospels. The consistency of the harmonizations is evident in the quotation of Matt 7:22–23 = Luke 13:26–27 which is cited by Justin twice, in *1 Apol.* 16.11 and *Dial.* 76.5:[4]

1 Apol. 16.11	Dial. 76.5	Matt 7:22–23	Luke 13:26–27
Many will say to me,	Many will say to me on that day	Many will say to me on that day	Then you will start to say,

---

[1] Special affinities of Justin's quotations with the Western text are well known and are a very strong argument for the existence of this text type in the early 2nd century; see also below.

[2] See the examples listed in Bellinzoni, *Sayings in Justin Martyr*, 73.

[3] This certainly excludes the reference to careless quotation from memory as an explanation for Justin's harmonizations.

[4] There are a total of twelve sayings that Justin quotes more than once, and not all of these can be discussed here. Bellinzoni (*Sayings in Justin Martyr*, 8–48) has demonstrated that the harmonizations of several gospel texts are consistent in most instances.

Lord, Lord, did we not in your name eat and drink	"Lord, Lord, did we not in your name eat and drink	Lord, Lord, did we not in your name	"we ate and drank before you and you have taught in our streets."
	and prophesy and drive out demons,	prophesy, and in your name drive out demons, and in your name	
do powerful deeds?"		do many powerful deeds?"	
And then I shall say to them,	And I shall say to them,	Then I shall testify to them, "I never knew you,	And he will say to you, "I do not know you whence you are.
go away from me, workers of unrighteousness."	go away from me.	go away from me, those who are working lawlessness."	Stay away from me all workers of unrighteousness."
1 Apol. 16.11	*Dial.* 76.5	Matt 7:22–23	Luke 13:26–27

πολλοὶ δὲ ἐροῦσί μοι	πολλοὶ ἐροῦσί μοι τῇ ἡμέρᾳ ἐκείνῃ ·	πολλοὶ ἐροῦσί μοι τῇ ἐκείνῃ τῇ ἡμέρᾳ ·	τότε ἄρξεσθε λέγειν ·
κύριε κύριε, οὐ τῷ σῷ ὀνόματι	κύριε κύριε, οὐ τῷ σῷ ὀνόματι	κύριε κύριε, οὐ τῷ σῷ ὀνόματι	
ἐφάγομεν καὶ ἐπίομεν	ἐφάγομεν καὶ ἐπίομεν		ἐφάγομεν ἐνώπιόν σου καὶ ἐπίομεν καὶ ἐν ταῖς πλατείας ἡμῶν ἐδίδαξας ·
	καὶ προεφητεύσαμεν καὶ	ἐπροφητεύσαμεν καὶ τῷ σῷ ὀνόματι	
	δαιμόνια ἐξεβάλομεν;	δαιμόνια ἐξεβάλομεν καὶ τῷ σῷ ὀνόματι	
καὶ δυνάμεις ἐποιήσαμεν;		δυνάμεις πολλὰς ἐποιήσαμεν;	
καὶ τότε ἐρῶ αὐτοῖς ·	καὶ ἐρῶ αὐτοῖς ·	καὶ τότε ὁμολογήσω αὐτοῖς ·	καὶ ἐρεῖ λέγων ὑμῖν · οὐκ οἶδα ὑμᾶς πόθεν ἐστέ ·
ἀποχωρεῖτε ἀπ᾽ ἐμοῦ ἐργάται τῆς ἀνομίας.	ἀναχωρεῖτε ἀπ᾽ ἐμοῦ	ἀποχωρεῖτε ἀπ᾽ ἐμοῦ οἱ ἐργαζόμενοι τὴν ἀνομίαν.	ἀπόστητε ἀπ᾽ ἐμοῦ πάντες ἐργάται ἀδικίας.

The basis of both quotations in Justin is obviously the same harmonized text of Matthew and Luke. To be sure, each of the two quotations does not represent the entire text. But insofar as they do quote the

same words, they agree almost completely.[1] One may even assume
that the text, from which Justin quotes each time, included at least
one additional phrase which appears in neither one of his two quotations: οὐκ οἶδα ὑμᾶς πόθεν ἐστέ = Luke 13:27 (instead of Matthew's οὐδέ-
ποτε ἔγνων ὑμᾶς), because this phrase is paralleled in the harmonized
quotation of the same saying in 2 Clem. 4.5 where one also finds the
harmonized version of the last phrase, ἐργάται (τῆς) ἀνομίας.[2] The
method of harmonization includes two different procedures: (1) whenever the texts of Matthew and Luke are closely parallel, either the
Matthean or the Lukan phrase or a conflation of both is chosen;
(2) Whenever the texts of Matthew and Luke differ considerably, as in
Matt 7:22 and Luke 13:26, major portions of the two texts are combined; thus, one finds Luke's "we were eating and drinking" as well as
Matthew's "we prophesied etc."—albeit the former is now introduced
by the Matthean "in your name" instead of Luke's "before you."

More important even than the observation of consistent harmonizations of the Matthean and Lukan parallels of individual sayings is the
question of the system of composition of sayings in this harmonized
gospel. The context of 1 Apol. 16:9–13, in which the above quotation of
Matt 7:22–23 = Luke 12:26–27 appears, provides some insight into the
procedure of composition.[3]

1 Apol. 16.9–13	Matthew	Luke
Not everyone who says to me, "Lord, Lord" will enter into the kingdom of heaven, but the one who does the will of my father in heaven.	7:21 Not everyone who says to me, "Lord, Lord" will enter into the kingdom of heaven, but the one who does the will of my father in heaven.	6:46 Why do you call me, "Lord, Lord," and do not do what I say.
He who hears me and does what I say, hears	7:24 Everyone who hears these my words and does them . . .	6:47 Everyone who comes to me and hears my words and does them . . .

[1] Minor differences like ἀποχωρεῖτε for ἀναχωρεῖτε are of no concern.

[2] See above, # 5.1.3.

[3] This passage is also discussed in Bellinzoni, Sayings in Justin Martyr, 98–100; see
especially his diagram, p. 99; cf. Helmut Koester, "The Text of the Synoptic Gospels in
the Second Century," in: William L. Petersen, ed., Gospel Traditions in the Second Century: Origins, Recensions, Text, and Transmission (Christianity and Judaism in Antiquity 3; Notre Dame: Notre Dame University Press, 1989) 30.

^{10:16} He who hears you, hears me; he who rejects you, rejects me; and he who rejects me, rejects the one who sent me.

the one who sent me.

Many will say to me on that day, "Lord, Lord, did we not in your name eat and drink [and prophesy and cast out demons][1] and do many powerful works?"	^{7:22} Many will say to me on that day, "Lord, Lord, did we not in your name prophesy and in your name cast out demons and in your name do many powerful works?"	^{13:26} Then you will begin to say, "We ate and drank before you, and you taught in our streets."
And then I shall say to them, "[I do not know you whence you are.][2] Go away from me, you workers of lawlessness." There will be wailing and gnashing of teeth,	And then I shall testify to them, "I have never known you, go away from me, those who are doing lawlessness," ^{13:42b-43,42a} There will be wailing and gnashing of teeth.	^{13:27} But he will say to you, "I do not know you whence you are. Stay away from me all workers of unrighteousness." ^{13:28} There will be wailing and gnashing of teeth, when you see Abraham . . .
when the righteous will shine like the sun,	Then the righteous will shine like the sun in the kingdom of their father.	
but the unrighteous will be sent into the eternal fire. Many will come in my name	And they will throw them into the furnace of fire. ^{24:5a} Many will come in my name, saying "I am the Christ," and they will lead many astray.[3]	

---

[1] The bracketed words occur only in the parallel quotation of this saying in *Dial.* 76.5, see above.

[2] The bracketed words are missing in Justin's citation, but are quoted in *2 Clem.* 4.5, see above # 5.1.1.3.

[3] This saying from the Synoptic apocalypse relies on Mark 13:5 and is also reproduced by Luke (21:8). This may be an accidental parallel, but it could also indicate that Justin omitted something from his source; see below.

	7:15 Beware of the false prophets who come to you	
on the outside dressed in skins of sheep, but	in sheep's clothing, but	
inwardly they are ravenous wolves.	inwardly they are ravenous wolves.	
From their works you will know them.	**7:16a** From their fruit you will know them.	
Every tree that does not produce good fruit is cut down and thrown into the fire.	**7:19** Every tree that does not produce good fruit is cut down and thrown into the fire.	**3:9** Every tree that does not produce good fruit is cut down and thrown into the fire.[1]

This section of Justin's quotation of Jesus' sayings rests on a deliberate and careful composition of the parallel texts of Matthew and Luke, but is also disrupted by interpolations from different contexts. The author begins with Matt 7:21 (= Luke 6:46); he then moves to the following verse in Luke (6:47), but combines it with part of a saying that opens with a similar phrase and appears elsewhere in Luke (10:16), instead of citing the parable of the builders which is introduced by Luke 6:47. After this disruption, the cluster continues with Matt 7:22–23 and harmonizes this passage with its Lukan parallel 13:26–27. The Lukan context of this saying determines the choice of the next saying, Luke 13:28, but its continuation is taken from Matthew's parallel (13:42–43) to that Lukan passage.[2] The following saying, however, returns to the context of Matthew 7, quoting Matt 7:15–16a,[3] 19, though the introductory phrase to Matt 7:15 is perhaps drawn from Matt 24:5. Clearly, a text that was produced as a harmony of Matthew and Luke served as the basis for the composition of this cluster of sayings. However, this assumption does not solve all problems of Justin's quotation of these sayings in *1 Apol.* 16.9–13.

The intrusion of a phrase from Luke 10:16 and the opening of Matt 7:15 with a phrase from Matt 24:5 are strange. If both Luke 10:16 and

---

[1] Luke 3:9 = Matt 3:10 is a saying that belongs to the preaching of John the Baptist. Matthew has transferred the saying into the context of the Sermon on the Mount (7:19)—clear evidence that Justin is directly or indirectly dependent upon Matthew and not on a pre-Matthean collection of sayings.

[2] This is one of the sayings that might be dependent upon the text of Matthew only (see above). However, its incorporation into the present context is due to the process of harmonization, since it is chosen because its Lukan parallel follows upon a saying from Luke that had just been quoted.

[3] Matt 7:15–16a is introduced by a phrase taken from Matt 24:5. That is not accidental: the quotation of Matt 7:15–16a in *Dial.* 35.3 is also introduced in this way; see below.

Matt 24:5 were quoted in full, the character of the collection of sayings that Justin used would be become clear—it would be evident that all the sayings deal with the problem of legitimacy of the missionary and of false prophets and teachers. But Justin has deliberately omitted from his source not only most of Luke 10:16 and the continuation of Matt 24:5 ("saying 'I am the Christ,' and they will lead many astray"), but also the reference to false prophets in Matt 7:22 ("and prophesy and cast out demons"),[1] and the introduction to the quote of Matt 7:15 ("Beware of the false prophets"). The reason for these omissions is formulated by Justin himself in his introduction to the quotation of these sayings (*1 Apol.* 16.8):

> Those who are not found to live as he has taught, are recognized as not being Christians, even if they say with their mouth the teachings of Christ; because he said that not those who only say, but those who do the works will be saved.

Thus, Justin himself did not compose this cluster of sayings for this particular context. He used an already existing collection. But sayings that warned against false prophets would not have served his purpose. He wanted to quote sayings speaking about hearing and doing. Thus, he removed the respective references to false prophets. Moreover, the cluster he used probably followed a different order: it must have begun with Matt 7:15. Justin instead started with Matt 7:21 and moved Matt 7:15–16, 19 to the end which allowed him to begin and to conclude the section with an emphasis upon good works. This also explains Justin's change of "From their *fruit* you will know them" (Matt 7:16) into "From their works you will know them."

Justin's use of these sayings presupposes three stages of development: (1) a systematic harmonization of the texts of Matthew and Luke, (2) the composition of a cluster of sayings which warn against false prophets, (3) Justin's editing of this collection in order to show that Christ's teaching speaks about the contrast between words and works. It is necessary to distinguish the first two stages. They were not just two different concerns in one and the same stage of composition, namely a composition of a sayings cluster that at the same time harmonized sayings from Matthew and Luke.[2]

---

[1] That these phrases were part of Justin's source is evident from the citation of the same passage in *Dial.* 76.5.

[2] Bellinzoni (*Sayings in Justin Martyr,* 100) collapses stage (1) and (2) of this process. He assumes that the harmonizations were made specifically for the composition of a catechism. This assumption, however, cannot explain why also the narrative materials quoted by Justin were drawn from a harmonized gospel text.

The existence of similar material, or even a portion of the same cluster of sayings composed of warnings against false prophets, is evident in the quotation of four sayings appearing in *Dial.* 35.3.[1] This strongly suggests that the composition of clusters was not identical with the production of a harmonized gospel text. The quotation in *Dial.* 35.3 shows that this cluster contained further sayings which were not reproduced in *1 Apol.* 16. A parallel in the *Apostolic Constitutions* (6.13) has been used to explain the reference of *Dial.* 35.3. However, it will become evident that this parallel is misleading:

Dial. 35.3	Matthew	*Apost. Const.* 6.13[2]
Many will come (ἐλεύσονται) in my name	24:5 Many will come (ἐλεύσονται) in my name	Many will come (ἐλεύσονται) to you
	7:15 Beware of the false prophets who come (ἔρχονται) to you	
on the outside dressed in skins of sheep (ἐνδεδυμένοι δέρματα προβάτων),[3] but inwardly they are ravenous wolves.	in the dress of sheep (ἐν ἐνδύμασι προβάτων) but inwardly they are ravenous wolves.	in the dress of sheep (ἐν ἐνδύμασι προβάτων) but inwardly they are ravenous wolves.
	7:16 From their fruits you shall recognize them.	From their fruits you shall recognize them.
And: There will be divisions and factions.		[There will be factions and divisions.][4]
And: Beware of the false prophets who will come (ἐλεύσονται) to you on the outside dressed in skins of sheep (ἔξωθεν ἐνδεδυμένοι δέρματα προβάτων) but inwardly they are ravenous wolves.	7:15 Beware of the false prophets who come (ἔρχονται) to you in the dress of sheep (ἐν ἐνδύμασι προβάτων) but inwardly they are ravenous wolves.	Beware of them.

---

[1] For a detailed comparison, see Bellinzoni, *Sayings in Justin Martyr,* 102–6.

[2] This passage is a reproduction of the *Didascalia* where it is preserved both in its Syriac and Latin version (Chap. 25, Connolly, pp. 210–211): "Venient ad vos in indumentis ovium, ab intus autem sunt lupi rapaces, et fructibus eorum cognoscitis eos. Adtendite vobis: exsurgent enim pseudochristi et pseudoprofetae et seducent multos."

[3] Justin uses the same formulation in the quote of *1 Apol.* 16.13.

[4] This saying appears in a different context in the *Syriac Didascalia* (Chap. 23, Connolly, p. 198), but is missing in the corresponding text of the *Apostolic Constitutions*.

And:

| Many false christs and | 24:24 False christs and false prophets will arise (ἐγερθήσονται) and give great signs and wonders so that, if possible, they will lead astray even the elect. | False christs and |
| false apostles will arise (ἀναστήσονται) and will lead astray many of the believers. | 24:11 Many false prophets will arise (ἐγερθήσονται) and will lead astray many. | false prophets will arise (ἀναστήσονται) and will lead astray many. |

There are several problems in the text of these four sayings. The first saying agrees verbatim with the quotation in *1 Apol.* 16.13. In both instances the reference to Matt 7:15–16a is introduced by a phrase borrowed from Matt 24:5 ("Many will come in my name"),[1] in both cases the reference to false prophets is omitted and the phrase "on the outside dressed in skins of sheep" replaces Matthew's "in the dress of sheep." The quote of this saying in *Apost. Const.* 6.13 also begins with "Many will come" and omits the reference to false prophets, but the phrase "in my name" does not appear, and the remainder of the text is an exact quotation of Matt 7:15. Thus, this is not a true parallel. What Justin is quoting here is his own edited text of the saying from *1 Apol.* 16.13.

The second saying cited by Justin, "There will be divisions and factions" (ἔσονται σχίσματα καὶ αἱρέσεις), has no parallel in the canonical gospels, but is attested elsewhere.[2] It is tempting to assume that this saying belongs to the traditional cluster of sayings quoted in *Apost. Const.* 6.13;[3] but it appears in a different context in the *Didascalia*.

A parallel to the third saying of *Dial.* 35.3 is missing in the *Didascalia* and the *Apostolic Constitutions*. What Justin is quoting here is a form of the saying that must have been the basis for the text of *1 Apol.* 16.13 and the first saying of *Dial.* 35.3. Like that quotation, the text departs from that of Matt 7:15 in the formulation "on the outside dressed in skins of sheep."

The fourth saying is a variant of Matt 24:11, and it is closely paralleled by the quotation in the *Didascalia* and the *Apostolic Constitutions*. Justin's quotation shares with Matt 24:11 the term "many" (πολλοί) before "false christs" (Matt 24:11 has "many false prophets") and

---

[1] The only difference is that *1 Apol.* 16.13 uses ἥξουσαι, *Dial.* 35.5 has ἐλεύσονται.

[2] See above.

[3] Bellinzoni, *Sayings in Justin Martyr,* 104–5.

the final phrase "they will lead astray many." But the reference to false christs does not appear in Matt 24:11; it is drawn from Matt 24:24. "False apostles" in Justin, instead of "false prophets" in Matt 24:11 (24:24) and *Apost. Const.* 6.13, seems to be a change introduced by Justin.[1] He and the *Apostolic Constitutions* both insert "false christs" from Matt 24:24 into the text of the quotation of Matt 24:11. Since Justin quotes the same conflation of these two Matthean passages also in *Dial.* 82.2,[2] it must have been a feature of his source which could have influenced later quotations of this saying. But this common feature of the quotations of Justin and of the *Didascalia* and *Apostolic Constitutions* is too small a base for the hypothesis of a common source or tradition for the entire unit. Rather, the author of the *Didascalia,* upon which the *Apostolic Constitutions* depends, is simply using Matthew, because the citation of Matt 24:11 is continued in a straightforward fashion with Matt 24:12–13. Evidence for a direct dependence upon Matthew in the *Didascalia* is so strong that it is hard to argue for the use of another kind of source that this writing shared with Justin.[3]

While the exact wording of Matthew's text occurs almost consistently in the *Didascalia,* this is not the case in Justin's sayings of *Dial.* 35.3. Rather, the wording of the variants from a special source predominates. Moreover, not only does Justin reflect this special wording in other quotations of some of these sayings, it is also evident that he has the entire cluster in front of him whenever he quotes one of its sayings. In *Dial.* 51.2, Justin says, "he (Jesus) indicated beforehand that in the time until his parousia there would be, as I said before, factions[4] and false prophets in his name." This reference combines elements from three different sayings of the cluster about false prophets.[5]

What is hard to explain in Justin's quotation of *Dial.* 35.3 is the repetition of the variants of Matt 7:15 in the first and the third saying of this cluster. If Justin used a collection of sayings here, one must

---

[1] See Bellinzoni, *Sayings in Justin Martyr,* 103.

[2] "He said that many false prophets and false christs would come in his name and lead many astray."

[3] I disagree with the statement, "both authors used a single source or tradition that had already combined these features" (Bellinzoni, *Sayings in Justin Martyr,* 106).

[4] The manuscript text of Justin's writings reads here ἱερεῖς. Editors of Justin's text have correctly emended this to αἱρέσεις.

[5] The quote of Matt 24:11 in *Dial.* 82.2 contains the reference to the coming of the false prophets and christs "in his name," which does not appear in the quotation of Matt 24:11 in *Dial.* 35.4, but is part of other sayings of the same cluster; cf. *1 Apol.* 16.11,13 and the first saying of *Dial.* 35.4.

assume that it began with the second saying, while the first saying
was added by Justin. In *Dial.* 35.2–3 he states that there are indeed
people who confess the crucified Jesus as Lord and Christ but do not
teach his commandments, and that Christ had predicted beforehand
that this would happen in his name. A series of sayings beginning
with "There will be divisions and factions" would not have served
Justin's purpose too well. Therefore he prefixed to these sayings a
variant of Matt 7:15 that he had formulated himself.

5.2.1.5 The character of Justin's source

Harmonizations of Matthew and Luke are evident in most of these
sayings. They occur also in other clusters of sayings quoted by Justin
in *1 Apol.* 15–17.[1] Whenever Justin cites a saying more than once, the
same harmonizations are repeated, and in several instances quotations in other ancient Christian writings concur with Justin's harmonizations.[2] In none of these instances are narrative materials quoted in
the context of the sayings. Usually, however, Justin does not seem to
quote sayings directly from a harmonized gospel text. As in *2 Clement,*
he is apparently relying upon collections of sayings which were composed on the basis of harmonized gospel texts and which incorporated
additional sayings from the non-canonical tradition.

Justin cites clusters under special headings. These headings are
Justin's own formulations, but the sayings quoted in each instance
must have been grouped together thematically before their use by Justin in his writings. This was already evident in the sayings about false
teachers and prophets which Justin used and revised in order to
demonstrate the contrast between words and works (*1 Apol.* 16.9–13).
That the sayings were originally composed into clusters for a purpose
different from Justin's interpretation is evident also in other parts of
these sayings clusters. *1 Apol.* 15.10–17 is a striking example. The
sayings are here introduced by the statement:

> That one should share with the needy and should do nothing in order to
> obtain praise, he said this (εἰς δὲ τὸ κοινωνεῖν τοῖς δεομένοις καὶ μηδὲν πρὸς
> δόξαν ποιεῖν ταῦτα ἔφη, *1 Apol.* 15.10).

The following sayings are quoted:

---

[1] See Bellinzoni, *Sayings in Justin Martyr,* especially 76–86. Bellinzoni also argues
for harmonizations of Matthew and Mark in two instances (ibid., 87–88); however, this
is less convincing.

[2] Ibid., 8–48. See also the parallel between *2 Clement* and Justin discussed in the
previous chapter.

1 Apol. 15.10–17	Matthew	Luke[1]
[10] Give to everyone who asks you . . .	5:42	6:30
If you lend to those from whom you hope to receive . . .	5:47a	6:34a
Even the publicans do this.	5:46b	(6:32b)
[11] Do not collect treasures for yourselves on earth.	6:19–20a	(12:33)
[12] What will it profit a human being to gain . . .	16:26	9:25
Therefore collect treasures in heaven . . .	6:20a	(12:33)
[13] Be generous and merciful like your father . . .	5:45 (48)	6:36
[14] Do not be anxious what you will eat . . .	6:25–26	12:22–24
[15] Do not be anxious . . . your father . . . knows . . .	6:31–32	12:30
[16] Seek first the kingdom of heaven . . .	6:33	12:31
Where your treasure is, . . .	6:21	12:34
[17] Do not do this in order to be seen before people	6:1	—

Only the first and the last of these sayings (16:10 and 17) are directly related to the topic mentioned by Justin in his introduction. The other sayings deal with the question of worldly treasure and are framed by Matt 6:19–21. Several of the sayings are harmonizations of the texts of Matthew and Luke.[2] But what Justin quotes is not the text of a harmonized gospel. Rather, he cites a cluster of sayings which were brought together under a particular theme. It is possible that Justin himself edited this collection so that it would serve more adequately the purpose of his citation. The addition of Matt 6:1 as a concluding sentence in particular may be due to Justin's editing.

The catechetical character of these clusters of sayings is evident in their usage in Justin, although Justin himself has sometimes provided headings which do not agree with the topic that governed their original composition. It is difficult to determine in each instance the degree to which Justin has supplemented and rearranged these collections. But it appears that the catechetical collections already existed and that Justin himself did not compose them. This does not exclude Justin's own personal knowledge of, and access to, the underlying harmonized gospel. On the contrary, in quoting narrative materials Justin certainly deals first-hand with such a gospel, and he occasionally also quotes sayings with reference to the narratives in which they are embedded.

---

[1] Texts given in parenthesis have not influenced the wording of the saying quoted by Justin.

[2] Bellinzoni (*Sayings in Justin Martyr,* passim) has discussed these sayings in detail and demonstrated the presence of harmonizations in *1 Apol.* 15:10 and 14.

5.2.2 THE GOSPEL NARRATIVES IN JUSTIN'S WRITINGS

5.2.2.1 Scriptural Proof and Gospel Narrative

Justin Martyr is the first Christian writer who makes extensive use of narrative materials from written gospels. The context is the proof of the truth of the Christian proclamation from scripture. Christ's suffering and death, understood in terms of the description of the suffering righteous, became the primary motivation for the development of the passion narrative. Study of the scriptures answered the question of the "why" of Jesus' passion and crucifixion. Luke 24:26–27 presents this question and its answer in a classic form when Jesus, still not recognized, asks the disciples on their way to Emmaus. "Was it not necessary that the Christ should suffer these things and enter into his glory?" And then Luke reports, "And beginning with Moses and all the prophets, he interpreted to them in all the scriptures the things concerning himself." But Luke already stands at the end of this phase of the development of the narrative tradition.

For Justin, the question of the "why" is no longer determinative. Rather, he now lays claim to the developed narrative and uses its agreement with scriptural prophecy as a proof for the revelatory truth of the events. Justin agrees that the story that is told about Jesus might be nothing more than the story of an ordinary human being who accomplished miracles through magical art and was therefore believed to be a Son of God (*1 Apol.* 30). Therefore, he defines the principles of his demonstration in this way:

> We shall set forth our demonstration not just believing those who tell the story, but of necessity persuaded by those who prophesy before it happens because of seeing with one's own eyes that it happened and is happening as it was prophesied. (*1 Apol.* 30)

> Because what is considered among human beings unbelievable and impossible to happen, that God has indicated beforehand through the prophetic spirit that it would happen so that, when it happened, it would not be disbelieved but believed on the basis of its being prophesied beforehand. (*1 Apol.* 33.2)

The foundation of the proof for the truth of Christian faith is, therefore, the Bible of Israel—a book of venerable ancient prophecy. But the proof for the historical fulfillment of prophecy cannot be convincing as long as the correspondence between prophecy and historical fulfillment is only approximate. Justin is concerned that the evil demons already knew about such prophecy and used it for the creation of the pagan cults and their myths, falsely claiming that these cults were the institutions in which the prophecies had been fulfilled. In this way they wanted to deceive the people, but since they misunderstood some of the prophecies, it is possible to detect the mistakes they made in their fabrications of pagan myths.[1]

The Christian proclamation about Jesus as the Son of God, however, is true, because the Christians possess trustworthy historical documents—"Remembrances of the Apostles"—from which it can be shown that everything in Christ's appearance and work happened in complete agreement with prophecy. What is demonstrated to be true is the Christian kerygma, not the story of the gospels. The reports contained in the gospels are used to show that the facts about Christ which the kerygma proclaims happened in complete agreement with the prophecy that announced them.

Before beginning his proof from scripture in his First Apology, Justin quotes an expanded version of the Christian kerygma (31.7), and the following chapters then demonstrate that in each instance prophecy and fulfillment agree:

> In the books of the prophets we find it announced beforehand that he would appear, born through a virgin, grow up, heal every disease and sickness and raise the dead, and be despised and unrecognized and crucified and die and be raised and ascend to the heavens and be and be called the Son of God, and that some would be sent by him to every nation, and that the Gentiles would believe.

In his demonstration in the following chapters, Justin does not always precisely follow this order, but he begins with arguments for the time of Christ's coming (chapter 32), the miraculous nature of Jesus' birth (chapter 33), and the place of birth in Bethlehem (chapter 34). Chapter 35 discusses his growing up unrecognized, events of Jesus' passion, and the entry into Jerusalem; chapter 45 brings a prophecy about Christ's inthronization; chapter 48.1–3 speaks about his healing and raising the dead, 48.4–5 about his suffering. Finally, chapters 50–53 discuss the crucifixion, resurrection, sending of the disciples, parousia of Christ, and the faith of the nations.

Relatively little actual narrative material is quoted in the *First Apology*. The only extensive demonstration with quotations from written gospels appears in chapters 33–34 in the discussion of the announcement of Jesus' birth and of its place, Bethlehem. More extensive quotations of narrative materials appear in the *Dialogue with Trypho*, especially in the interpretation of Psalm 22 in *Dialogue* 99–107. In all instances the quotations are abbreviated, because Jus-

---

[1] See especially *1 Apology* 54.

tin wants to quote primarily those passages and phrases which correspond to the words of the prophecy. The gospel texts quoted by Justin have parallels in all three Synoptic Gospels, and sentences from Matthew and Luke (rarely if ever from Mark) are often mixed or harmonized in these quotations. In several instances, additional phrases that have no support in extant gospel texts are inserted in order to create an even more thorough correspondence between prophecy and fulfillment. The question is whether Justin composed these harmonizations and inserted additional phrases just for the purpose of his demonstration of scriptural proof or whether he drew on a written gospel text that was already harmonized and expanded.

It seems to me that we are not witnessing the work of an apologist who randomly selects pieces from various gospels and invents additional phrases for the purpose of a tight argument of literal fulfillment of scripture; nor can one solve the complex problems of Justin's quotations of gospel narrative materials by the hypothesis of a ready-made, established text of a harmonized gospel as his source. Rather, his writings permit insights into the work of a school of scriptural exegesis in which careful comparison of written gospels with the prophecies of scripture endeavored to produce an even more comprehensive new gospel text.

The materials with which Justin worked consisted of (1) traditional collections of scriptural prophetic passages related to the story of Jesus that had already been used by earlier Christian writers such as the authors of the *Epistle of Barnabas,* the *Gospel of Peter,* and the Gospel of Matthew; (2) improved texts of the Greek translation of at least some books of the Hebrew Bible; (3) several gospel writings among which Matthew and Luke predominate; (4) a harmony of the Synoptic Gospels. In this context, it is possible to discuss only the last two sets of materials in some detail, although the question of the scriptural texts used by Justin must also be considered insofar as they belong to the context of the gospel narrative.[1]

---

[1] For the traditional collections of prophecies, see Stendahl, *School of St. Matthew*; Wilhelm Bousset, *Jüdisch-christlicher Schulbetrieb in Alexandria und Rom: Literarische Untersuchungen zu Philo und Clemens Alexandrinus, Justin und Irenäus* (FRLANT N.F. 6; Göttingen: Vandenhoeck & Ruprecht, 1915); see also above # 3.2.3. For the improved Greek translation of the Hebrew Bible, see Dominique Barthélemy, O.P., "Redécouverte d'un chainon manquant de l'histoire de la Septante," *RB* 60 (1953) 18–29; idem, *Les devanciers d'Aquila: Première publication intégrale du texte des fragments du Dodécaprophéton* (Supplements to Vetus Testamentum 10; Leiden: Brill, 1963), especially pp. 203–12.

5.2.2.2 The Narrative of Jesus' Birth

1 Apol. 33 gives as proof concerning Jesus' birth the prophecy of Isa 7:14. The text of this scriptural passage is presented in a form that is influenced by its quotation in Matt 1:23:

Isa 7:14	Matt 1:23	1 Apol. 33.1
Behold, the virgin will conceive in the womb and bear a son, and you shall call his name Emmanuel.	Behold, the virgin will conceive in the womb and bear a son, and they will call his name Emmanuel, which is translated, "God is with us."	Behold, the virgin will conceive in the womb and bear a son, and they will say in his name, "God is with us."
ἰδοὺ ἡ παρθένος ἐν γαστρὶ λήψεται¹ καὶ τέξεται υἱόν, καὶ καλέσεις τὸ ὄνομα αὐτοῦ Ἐμμανουήλ.	ἰδοὺ ἡ παρθένος ἐν γαστρὶ ἕξει καὶ τέξεται υἱόν, καὶ καλέσουσιν² τὸ ὄνομα αὐτοῦ Ἐμμανουήλ, ὅ ἐστιν μεθερμηνευόμενον μεθ' ἡμῶν ὁ θεός.	ἰδοὺ ἡ παρθένος ἐν γαστρὶ ἕξει καὶ τέξεται υἱόν, καὶ ἐροῦσιν³ ἐπὶ τῷ ὀνόματι αὐτοῦ Μεθ' ἡμῶν ὁ θεός.

Justin shares with Matthew's quotation the plural form of the verb in the second half of the sentence, although he is using a different verb (ἐροῦσιν instead of καλέσουσιν), and he repeats Matthew's translation of Ἐμμανουήλ. The focus of Justin's attention is not, strictly speaking, the Matthean form of the Isaiah quotation, for he shows no interest in the name "God with us." His primary concern is with the first part of this prophetic text that is quoted by Matthew. But in the following proof for the fulfillment of this prophecy, he turns first to the text of Luke; only later does he add elements from Matthew.

---

¹ This is the reading of the LXX manuscript B and the minuscules belonging to the so-called Lucianic recension, while LXX A reads ἕξει (= Matt 1:23). The former is the LXX text with which Justin was familiar, because it appears in his other quotations of this passage (*Dial.* 43.5; 66.2; 67.1; 68.6; 71.3).

² The change to the 3rd person plural instead of the 2nd person singular is deliberately introduced by Matthew, because the child's actual name is not "Emmanuel"; Matthew wants to point to the fact that he will also be called symbolically with this messianic name. See Stendahl, *School of St. Matthew,* 98.

³ Though Justin chooses a different word, its 3rd person plural is dependent upon Matthew's text. In other quotations of the passage (*Dial.* 43.5; 66.3) Justin follows the text of the LXX (καλέσεις), and he also cites the Greek transcription of the Hebrew name (Ἐμμανουήλ), omitting the translation of the name (μεθ' ἡμῶν ὁ θεός).

Matt 1:20–21	Luke 1:31–32	1 Apol. 33.5
		... and the angel of God proclaimed to her and said
What is conceived (γεννηθέν) in her, is from the Holy Spirit. She will bear a son.	And behold, you will conceive (συλλήψη) in the womb and bear a son, and you shall call his name Jesus. He will be great and be called Son of the Most High.	"Behold you will conceive (συλλήψη) in the womb from the Holy Spirit and bear a son and he will be called Son of the Most High.
And you shall call his name Jesus, because he will save his people from their sins.		And you shall call his name Jesus, because he will save his people from their sins.

The text of *1 Apol.* 33.5 is a harmonization of the two angelic announcements, the one from Matthew in which the angel calls Joseph in a dream, the other from Luke's narrative of the annunciation. While the passage begins with a sentence from Luke, "from the Holy Spirit" is interpolated from Matt 1:20.[1] The naming of Jesus and the reason for this name is given according to Matt 1:21. To be sure, Justin has a special interest in this explanation of the name "Jesus," for he comments later that this Hebrew name means "savior" in Greek, and then quotes Matt 1:21 once more (*1 Apol.* 33.7–8). But in order to argue for the fulfillment of Isa 7:14 in *1 Apol.* 33.3–6, the report of the command to name the child "Jesus" did not need to refer to the Matthean form. Moreover, the quotation of Matt 1:21, that is, the angel's command to Joseph to name the child, is introduced in *1 Apol.* 33.8 by: "Therefore the angel said to the virgin." It is evident, therefore, that Justin is quoting a harmonized gospel text in which part of the angel's command to Joseph (Matt 1:21) as well as the quotation of Isa 7:14 from Matt 1:23 had already been combined with the angel's words to Mary in Luke's story of the annunciation.[2] At the same time, although quoting the text of Isa 7:14 from Matthew, Justin is quite aware of the origin of this reference. He introduces it as prophesied

---

[1] Luke mentions the Holy Spirit only in the later response of the angel to Mary's question; see below.

[2] This does not imply that this harmonized gospel narrative deleted the angel's command to Joseph entirely. *Dial.* 78.3 reports that an angel had commanded Joseph not to expel his wife, because "what is in her womb is from the holy spirit." See further below.

through Isaiah, while Matthew 1:22 only refers to "what has been said by the Lord through the prophet."

Justin's gospel text must have continued with the remainder of the Lukan pericope of the annunciation. In the introduction to the harmonization of Luke 1:31–32 and Matt 1:20–21, Justin had already alluded to the Lukan continuation of the story: *1 Apol.* 33.4 ("The power of God, coming down upon the virgin, overshadowed her and made her pregnant, although she was a virgin") recalls Luke 1:35 ("The Holy Spirit will come upon you and the power of the Most High will overshadow you"). A fuller reproduction of this passage is given in *Dial.* 100.5 in the context of an Eve/Mary typology that is reminiscent of the Adam/Christ typology of Romans 5:[1]

> Although Eve was an uncorrupted virgin, having received (συλλαβοῦσα) the word from the serpent she gave birth to disobedience and death; but the virgin Mary received faith and joy when the angel Gabriel proclaimed to her . . .

This sentence introduces a quotation of Luke 1:35 and 38 (vss. 36–37, the reference to the pregnancy of Elizabeth, is omitted):

Luke 1:35, 38	*Dial.* 100.5
"The Holy Spirit will come upon you and the power of the Most High will overshadow you; therefore the holy one that is born (from you)[2] shall be called Son of God."	. . . that the spirit of the Lord would come upon her and the power of the Most High would overshadow her; therefore the holy one that is born from her should be called Son of God,
Mary said, "Behold, I am the servant of the Lord; let it be to me according to your word."	she answered, "let it be to me according to your word."

Justin agrees with Luke's text almost completely, but has changed "Holy Spirit" to "spirit of the Lord." This is a change that was not

---

[1] This typology appears in narrative form in the *Proto-Gospel of James* (13.1) where Joseph, having discovered the pregnancy of Mary, complains (translation from Hennecke-Schneemelcher-Wilson, *NT Apocrypha*, 1. 381):

> Has the story of Adam been repeated in me? For as Adam was absent in the hour of his prayer and the serpent found Eve alone and deceived her and defiled her, so also has it happened to me.

[2] The words ἐκ σοῦ appear only in some manuscripts (C Θ *f*¹ 33 *pc* a c e [r¹] vg^cl sy^p; Ir^lat Tert Ad Epiph). This addition, however, must be presupposed for Justin. Justin should, therefore, also be listed as a witness in the text-critical apparatus of Nestle-Aland.

made *ad hoc* by Justin for the citation in *Dialogue* 100, but must have been part of his harmonized gospel text, because in that text a reference to the holy spirit had already been made in the harmonization of Luke 1:31 with Matt 1:20 ("Behold you will conceive in the womb from the Holy Spirit").

In the discussion of the prophecy for the place of Jesus' birth (*1 Apology* 34), Justin only quotes the prophecy of Micah 5:1 and then remarks that Jesus was born in this "village in the land of Judah which is 35 stades from Jerusalem" (*1 Apol.* 34.2). No actual narrative material from a gospel is quoted. But one finds here the remark that such information can be found in the "records which have been made under Cyrenius (Quirinius), the first (Roman) governor (ἐπίτροπος) of Judea." Since Cyrenius is mentioned only in Luke 2:2, a knowledge of Luke's birth narrative of Jesus is indicated.[1] However, the quotation of the text of Micah 5:1 is not given in the text of the LXX; rather, Justin follows the form of the text quoted in Matt 2:6:

Micah 5:1(2)	Matt 2:6	*1 Apol.* 34.1
And you Bethlehem, house of Ephratha, you are the smallest among the thousands of Judah. From you shall come who is to be the leader in Israel.	And you Bethlehem, land of Judah, you are by no means the smallest among the rulers of Judah, for from you shall come a ruler who is to shepherd my people Israel.	And you Bethlehem, land of Judah, you are by no means the smallest among the rulers of Judah, for from you shall come a ruler who is to shepherd my people.
Καὶ σύ, Βηθλέεμ οἶκος τοῦ Ἐφραθα, ὀλιγοστὸς εἶ τοῦ εἶναι ἐν χιλιάσιν Ἰούδα· ἐκ σοῦ μοι ἐξελεύσεται τοῦ εἶναι εἰς ἄρχοντα ἐν τῷ Ἰσραήλ.	Καὶ σὺ Βηθλέεμ, γῆ Ἰούδα, οὐδαμῶς ἐλαχίστη εἶ ἐν τοῖς ἡγεμόσιν Ἰούδα· ἐκ σοῦ γὰρ ἐξελεύσεται ἡγούμενος, ὅστις ποιμαίνει τὸν λαόν μου Ἰσραήλ.	Καὶ σὺ Βηθλέεμ, γῆ Ἰούδα, οὐδαμῶς ἐλαχίστη εἶ ἐν τοῖς ἡγεμόσιν Ἰούδα· ἐκ σοῦ γὰρ ἐξελεύσεται ἡγούμενος, ὅστις ποιμαίνει τὸν λαόν μου.

---

[1] Justin does not seem to have any independent knowledge of Cyrenius, nor of any other data of the Roman administration in Palestine. That he calls Cyrenius the *first* Roman administrator of Judea is a result of his theory of salvation history because, according to Gen 49:10 ("Not will a ruler be missing from Judah, until he comes to whom it is assigned"), Justin assumes that Jewish rulers continued in Judea until the coming of Jesus (*1 Apol.* 32.1–3).

The form of the quotation that appears in Matt 2:6 departs considerably from both the LXX and the Hebrew text. It is, in fact, a combination of Micah 5:1 and 2 Sam 5:2; only the latter speaks of the prince's function as a shepherd of Israel.[1] This conflated quotation was wholly the work of Matthew.[2] There can be no question that Justin is quoting this Matthean text.[3] On the other hand, he explicitly identifies Micah as the author of this prophecy, while Matthew 2:5 only says, "Thus it is written through the prophet." But Justin is not aware that the citation in Matthew is actually a conflation of Micah 5:1 with 2 Sam 5:2; therefore, he quotes also the clause from 2 Sam 5:2 as part of a Micah prophecy, but omits the mention of Israel at the end which comes from the text of Micah.[4]

But in references of Justin to the appearance of the star at the birth of Jesus and to the coming of the "wise men" to worship the new-born child, the absence in *1 Apol.* 34 of explicit quotations from the Matthean story of "The Visit of the Magi" (Matt 2:1–12) is striking. All of the respective statements are scriptural quotations accompanied by more general references to the fulfillment. However, even these references reveal a knowledge of gospel texts and perhaps also deliberate changes of such texts on the basis of additional exploration of scripture. Such changes become more clearly evident in his discussion of the birth narrative in *Dialogue* 77–78 (see below).

Justin speaks about the appearance of the star at the birth of Jesus for the first time in *1 Apol.* 32.13 (ἄστρον δὲ φωτεινὸν ἀνέτειλε, καὶ ἄνθος ἀνέβη ἀπὸ τῆς ῥίζης Ἰεσσαί). This statement indicates the fulfillment of a prophecy that is a conflation of three different scriptural passages:

Nu 24:17	Isa 11:1, 10	*1 Apol.* 32.12
And a star will rise from Jacob and a man will stand up from Israel		And a star will rise from Jacob
	[1] And a branch will come forth from the root of Jesse and a flower will rise up from the root.	and a flower will rise up from the root of Jesse,

---

[1] The people say to David, "And the Lord said to you, 'You shall be shepherd of my people Israel, and you shall be prince over Israel.'"

[2] See Stendahl, *School of St. Matthew*, 99–101.

[3] See also Massaux, *Influence de l'Évangile de Saint Matthieu*, 496.

[4] "Israel" is also omitted in the quotation of this passage in *Dial.* 78.1.

[10] And on that day the root of Jesse shall stand to lead the nations, and upon him the nations will set their hope.

Isa 51:5

... and upon his arm the nations will set their hope.

... and upon his arm the nations will set their hope.

Nu 24:17

ἀνατελεῖ ἄστρον ἐξ
Ἰακὼβ καὶ ἀναστήσεται
ἄνθρωπος ἐξ Ἰσραήλ

Isa 11:1, 10

[1] Καὶ ἐξελεύσεται ῥάβδος
ἐκ τῆς ῥίζης Ἰεσσαί,
καὶ ἄνθος ἐκ τῆς ῥίζης
ἀναβήσεται
[10] καὶ ἔσται ἐν τῇ ἡμέρᾳ
ἐκείνῃ ἡ ῥίζα τοῦ Ἰεσσαὶ
καὶ ὁ ἀνιστάμενος
ἄρχειν ἐθνῶν, ἐπ᾽ αὐτῷ
ἔθνη ἐλπιοῦσιν.

1 Apol. 32.12

ἀνατελεῖ ἄστρον ἐξ
Ἰακώβ,

καὶ ἄνθος ἀναβήσεται
ἐκ τῆς ῥίζης Ἰεσσαί,

Isa 51:5

... καὶ εἰς τὸν βραχιόνα
μου ἔθνη ἐλπιοῦσιν.

καὶ ἐπὶ τὸν βραχιόνα
αὐτοῦ ἔθνη ἐλπιοῦσιν.

This combined quote was not created by Justin, who introduces it as a quotation from Isaiah (καὶ Ἡσαίας δέ,[1] ἄλλος προφήτης, ... οὕτως εἶπεν). Nu 24:17 and Isa 11:1 together were already known to Matthew who refers to the latter at the end of his birth narrative (2:23): "In order to fulfill what was said through the prophets, that he should be called a Nazarene" (ὅτι Ναζωραῖος κληθήσεται). Matthew here refers to the Hebrew text of Isa 11:1 which contains the term נצר, translated in the LXX with ἄνθος. Matthew was aware of this Hebrew equivalent,[2] but Justin only knew the combined quote in its Greek text and can, therefore, only make the general remark: "And a flower arose from the root of Jesse which is Christ." He does not refer to Matt 2:23 in that context.

Dial. 106.4 also connects the mention of the rising of the star at Jesus' birth with a quotation of Nu 24:17 and adds that "this is written in the memoirs of his apostles." At the same time, Justin remarks

---

[1] In his first edition of Justin's writings, Otto had emended the text to read καί instead of δέ. Thus, the impression was created that Justin was conscious of the conflated character of this quote. But Otto corrected this in later editions and explicitly rejected this misunderstanding.

[2] See Stendahl, *School of St. Matthew*, 103–4. The combination of these scriptural passages is apparently also presupposed in the *Testaments of the Twelve Patriarchs*, *Test. Judah* 24.1, 5–6.

that, at the time of the rising (ἀνατολή) of the star, "the magi of Arabia who had learned from it (i.e., from the star about the birth) came and worshiped him." Whereas Matthew (2:1) derives from Nu 24:17 (ἀνατελεῖ ἄστρον) that the Magi came from the East (ἀπὸ ἀνατολῶν), Justin relates the term directly to Jesus by adding Zech 6:12: "Behold a man, 'Rising' is his name" ('Ιδοὺ ἀνήρ, 'Ανατολὴ ὄνομα αὐτοῦ).[1] For the designation of the place from which the Magi came, Arabia, Justin relies on another scriptural passage. That is not evident in *Dialogue* 106, because in this reference to the coming of the Magi it has already become part of a revised gospel story.

But in *Dialogue* 77–78 Justin identifies Isa 8:4 as the prophecy which indicated the place from which the Magi would come: "Before the child will learn to cry 'father' or 'mother,' he will take the power of Damascus and the spoils of Samaria before the king of Assyria" (*Dial.* 77.2–3). Damascus, Justin explains, was then a city of Arabia (*Dial.* 78.10).[2] The "king of Assyria" refers to Herod "because of his godless and lawless character" (*Dial.* 77.4). This sets the stage for the rewriting of the Synoptic birth narratives (*Dialogue* 78), for which Justin uses both Matthew 2 and Luke 2. All new elements are derived from the interpretation of scriptural prophecy. The Magi are always referred to as coming from Arabia.[3] Because of Micah 5:1, Bethlehem is referred to as a city of Judah, and Joseph goes to Bethlehem with Mary "because he is from the tribe of Judah" (78.4; cf. Luke 2:4: "because he was from the house and lineage of David"). The time of the coming of the Magi is fixed "right at the time of his birth" (ἅμα τῷ γεννηθῆναι αὐτόν, 77.4).[4]

Whether the reference to the birth of the child in a cave (ἐν σπηλαίῳ τινὶ σύνεγγυς τῆς κώμης) is also a narrative element that was added on the basis of the interpretation of scripture, is less certain. Justin relates the remark explicitly to a prophecy from Isaiah (*Dial.* 78.7–8)

---

[1] In *Dial.* 106.4 this passage is introduced with "and another scripture says." But in *Dial.* 126.1 Justin says that Jesus was called "Rising (ἀνατολή) by Zechariah."

[2] That is historically correct, because Damascus then belonged to the realm of the Arabian Nabateans, although Justin knows, and states explicitly, that at his time Damascus belonged to Syro-Phoenecia.

[3] *Dial.* 78.1, 2, 5, 7; 102.2; 103.3; 106.4. Only in *Dial.* 78.9 does Justin call them simply "the Magi."

[4] The reason for this timing is evident in *Dial.* 77: Justin wants to make sure that the prophecy Isa 8:4 cannot refer to the king Hezekiah, because what is said in the prophecy has happened "before the child will learn to cry 'father' or 'mother.'" But the phrase "right at the time of his birth" also introduces the reference to the coming of the Magi in *Dial.* 88.1; 102.2, although there is no argument about the interpretation of Isa 8:4 in those contexts. Cf. also *Dial.* 106.4 where the appearance of the star is said to have happened "right at the time of his birth."

and adds that he had already referred to this prophecy earlier, namely in *Dial.* 70.1–2 where he discusses the falsification of a prophecy from Isaiah among the worshipers of Mithras who call their place of initiation "a cave." He then proceeds to quote Isa 33:13–19 where the Greek text of vs. 16b says: οὗτος οἰκήσει ἐν ὑψηλῷ σπηλαίῳ πέτρας ἰσχυρᾶς ("he shall dwell in a high cave of a strong rock").[1] Following his report about the birth in a cave in *Dial.* 78.5–6, Justin once more refers to the falsification of this prophecy in the cult of Mithras and the inspiration of this cult by the devil. Did Justin invent the reference to the birth in a cave on the basis of Isa 33:16? That seems very unlikely, because there is no evidence that Isa 33:16 or any part of its context ever played a role in the scriptural interpretation of the story of Jesus.[2] Does Justin follow an established tradition which identified Jesus' birthplace as a cave near Bethlehem? The *Proto-Gospel of James* (18.1) relates that Joseph, realizing that they are in a desert when Mary's hour of giving birth arrives, "found a cave there and brought her into it."[3] It is not likely that Justin's gospel text presented such a report,[4] because he never repeats it anywhere else in his writings. It has been suggested that Justin, coming from Palestine himself, personally knew of a place of worship in a cave near Bethlehem.[5] That there was such a place is evident in a remark of Origen in his *Contra Celsum* (1.51).[6] But Origen wrote this two or three generations later, and one cannot be sure that a cave cult that remembered the birth of Jesus existed near Bethlehem at the time of Justin. Perhaps the knowledge of the story of Mithras' birth in a cave and the designation of Mithras sanctuaries as "caves" prompted Justin to discuss the question of the falsification of prophecy with respect to Jesus' birth. The reference to the scriptural prophecy mentioning the cave would then be an afterthought and not the source of a new piece of information about the story of Jesus.

In *Dial.* 78.7–8 Justin finally reports about the murder of the innocents by Herod and the flight to Egypt. In the details of his report as

---

[1] The words σπηλαίῳ πέτρας ἰσχυρᾶς translate the Hebrew text סלעים מצדות = סלעים משׂגבו מצדוח "his defense will be the fortress of rocks." The reason the Greek translates the first of these Hebrew terms with σπήλαιον is unclear.

[2] Dibelius, "Jungfrauensohn," 76.

[3] For other early Christian reports about Jesus' birth in a cave, see Dibelius, ibid., 75–77; Bauer, *Leben Jesu,* 61–68. Neither in the *Proto-Gospel of James* nor anywhere else is the reference to Isa 33:16 repeated.

[4] That he is dependent upon the *Proto-Gospel of James* is highly unlikely.

[5] Joachim Jeremias, *Golgotha* (Leipzig: 1926) 14–16; see also Dibelius, "Jungfrauensohn," 76–77.

[6] Dibelius, "Jungfrauensohn," 75.

well as in the quotation of the respective scripture (Jer 31:15), Justin is simply dependent upon Matt 2:13–18. He quotes Jeremiah exactly like Matthew, whose citation "comes the nearest to giving an abbreviated translation of the M.T. (Massoretic Hebrew text), possibly with some influence from the LXX."[1]

Perhaps what is visible in this treatment of the Synoptic birth narratives is not the finished product of a harmony of Matthew and Luke, but the process of the production of such a harmony by an author who seeks to update the narrative information of the two gospel writings with additional exploration of scriptural prophecy. Justin introduces some new passages from scripture, from which he derives more details of the narrative; but he also uses and reapplies prophecies that are already recorded in the gospel story. The purpose of the harmonizations is not to achieve a richer unified narrative, but to produce a more complete record of the fulfillment of scripture. Matthew had begun this process in his own gospel because speaking about the birth of Jesus is for him a demonstration of its legitimacy: it fulfills scripture. Justin continues this process. If one attempted to reconstruct Justin's harmonized gospel—or the one that was in the process of being produced in his school—one would probably find that it was more a record of incidents of fulfillment of prophecy than the story of a wonderful arrival of the divine savior in this world.

5.2.2.3 John the Baptist and the Narrative of Jesus' Baptism

Gospel materials about John the Baptist in Justin's *Dialogue with Trypho*[2] are used in two different contexts. In *Dialogue* 49–51 Justin wants to show that the prophecy of the coming of Elijah before the appearance of the Messiah has been fulfilled in the coming of John the Baptist. In *Dialogue* 88 the demonstration is concerned with the question of Christ's full preexistent possession of divine power and spirit (*Dialogue* 87); the narrative of Jesus' baptism is discussed in order to reject the idea that he received the spirit only at that moment. In both instances, Justin emphasizes that the presence of the divine spirit, and thus also of prophecy, had ceased with the coming of Jesus and that all spiritual gifts are now at work among the Christians. In each instance the selections of gospel narratives that are quoted or summarized are influenced by the purpose of the discussion. But they also share some peculiar features that differ from the narrative of any particular gospel.

---

[1] Stendahl, *School of St. Matthew,* 102.
[2] Justin does not discuss the Baptist in his *First Apology.*

About the appearance of John the Baptist, Justin always says that he "was stationed at the Jordan":

Dial. 49.3 ... who sat at the Jordan crying out.
Dial. 51.2 ... when he was still sitting at the Jordan river.
Dial. 51.2 ... when John was still sitting at the Jordan.

Dial. 49.3 ὅστις ἐπὶ τὸν Ἰορδάνην καθεζόμενος ἐβόα.
Dial. 51.2 ἔτι αὐτοῦ καθεζομένου ἐπὶ τοῦ Ἰορδάνου ποταμοῦ.
Dial. 51.2 Ἰωάννου γὰρ καθεζομένου ἐπὶ τοῦ Ἰορδάνου.

The description of the locality of his activity as stationary[1] at the Jordan is peculiar. In Mark 1:4 John appears "in the desert," in Matt 3:1 "in the desert of Judea." Only Luke 3:3 deliberately restricts the area of John's activity to "all the districts of the Jordan" (ἦλθεν εἰς πᾶσαν τὴν περίχωρον τοῦ Ἰορδάνου), but Luke still allows John to walk around like an itinerant preacher, rather than making him stationary.[2] In most later traditions, the only locale with which John is connected is "the Jordan."[3] Justin here shows that his gospel text is influenced by this tendency of the tradition rather than by any specific passages from the canonical gospels.

The two terms "to cry out" (βοᾶν) and "to proclaim" (κηρύσσειν) are always used to describe the character of his message:

Dial. 49.3 ... who sat at the Jordan crying out.
Dial. 51.2 John went before him and cried out to the people to repent.
Dial. 88.2 John went before him as the herald of his coming.
Dial. 88.7a John ... proclaiming a baptism of repentance.
Dial. 88.7b ... and he cried out.

Dial. 49.3 ἐπὶ τὸν Ἰορδάνην καθεζόμενος ἐβόα.
Dial. 51.2 Ἰωάννης προελήλυθε βοῶν τοῖς ἀνθρώποις μετανοεῖν.
Dial. 88.2 προελήλυθεν Ἰωάννης κῆρυξ αὐτοῦ τῆς παρουσίας.
Dial. 88.7a Ἰωάννου ... κηρύσσοντος βάπτισμα μετανοίας.
Dial. 88.7b ... καὶ αὐτὸς ἐβόα.

The term "to proclaim" (κηρύσσειν) also occurs in Mark 1:7 and Luke 3:3; but while Justin is using exclusively these two verbs for the description of John's preaching, all canonical gospels also employ other

---

[1] καθίζομαι has the meaning of being (permanently) resident in one particular place; cf. Bauer, *Leben Jesu,* 103.

[2] The Gospel of John attempts to define more specifically various places of John's activity: "in Bethany beyond the Jordan, where John was baptizing" (John 1:28), "at Aenon near Salim, because there was much water there" (3:23).

[3] Bauer, *Leben Jesu,* 103.

terms.[1] The description of John as "herald" (κῆρυξ) is missing altogether in the canonical Gospels. The verb "to cry out" (βοᾶν) appears in the Synoptic Gospels only in the quotation of Isa 40:3 (φωνὴ βοῶντος);[2] it is not used in the description of John's preaching. Justin (*Dial.* 50.3–5) quotes the entire passage Isa 39:8–40:17, including verse 6: "A voice saying, 'Cry out!' and I said, 'What shall I cry?'" (φωνὴ λέγοντος· Βόησον. καὶ εἶπον· Τί βοήσω;). Throughout the *Dialogue with Trypho*, he prefers the verb "to cry" for the introduction of prophetic speech,[3] while it is used only rarely for a saying of Jesus.[4] The use of this verb for the proclamation of John the Baptist clearly marks his speech as prophetic announcement. He is the "prophet" (προφήτης, *Dial.* 49.3, 4; cf. 51.2) and the "proclaimer" ("herald" = κῆρυξ, *Dial.* 88.2) of the coming of Christ. Although the Synoptic Gospels also designate John as a "prophet,"[5] the term is never used in the story of his ministry.[6] Since all of Justin's alterations of the description of John are consistent and appear repeatedly, it is probable that they were already incorporated into the text of his gospel.

That this gospel text was a harmony is evident in many details of Justin's description of John's appearance and preaching:

Dial. 88.7	Matt 3:1	Mark 1:4	Luke 3:3
When John was sitting at the Jordan.	in the wilderness of Judea	in the wilderness	into all the region around the Jordan
Ἰωάννου γὰρ καθεζομένου ἐπὶ τοῦ Ἰορδάνου	ἐν τῇ ἐρήμῳ τῆς Ἰουδαίας	ἐν τῇ ἐρήμῳ	εἰς πᾶσαν τὴν περίχωρον τοῦ Ἰορδάνου

---

[1] λέγων Matt 3:1; Mark 1:7; John 1:26; λέγει John 1:21, 29; εἶπεν Matt 3:7; John 1:22; ἔλεγεν Luke 3:7; ἀπεκρίνατο λέγων Luke 3:11; ὡμολόγησεν John 1:20.

[2] Matt 3:3 and Mark 1:2 quote only this verse (Mark combines it with Mal 3:1); Luke 3:4–6 expands the citation to include also Isa 40:4–5.

[3] *Dial.* 12.1; 14.1; 17.2; 20.4; 24.3; 25.1; 27.2, 3; etc.

[4] *Dial.* 17.3, 4; 76.7. For sayings of Jesus, Justin prefers εἶπεν (*1 Apol.* 15.1, 8; 16.9; 19.6; etc.; *Dial.* 35.3; 47.5; 49.3, etc.), διδάσκειν (*1 Apol.* 15.9; 17.1) and other verbs.

[5] The term occurs occasionally, e.g., Mark 6:15 par; Matt 14:5; Q/Luke 7:26.

[6] John 1:21–25 explicitly rejects the identification of John the Baptist as a prophet. That appears even more clearly, if vss. 22–23 (the quote of Isa 40:3) have been interpolated by a later redactor; cf. Bultmann, *Gospel of John*, on 1:22–23.

Dial. 88.7	Matt 3:1	Mark 1:4	Luke 3:3
proclaiming a baptism of repentance	proclaiming	proclaiming a baptism of repentance for the forgiveness of sins	proclaiming a baptism of repentance for the forgiveness of sins
κηρύσσοντος βάπτισμα μετανοίας	κηρύσσων	κηρύσσων βάπτισμα μετανοίας εἰς ἄφεσιν ἁμαρτιῶν	κηρύσσων βάπτισμα μετανοίας εἰς ἄφεσιν ἁμαρτιῶν

As has been stated above with respect to the location of John's activity, Justin is closest to Luke's text. The description of the content of his proclamation, "baptism of repentance," could have been derived from Luke, but also from Mark, while there is no equivalent in Matthew.

Dial. 88.7: καὶ ζώνην δερματίνην καὶ ἔνδυμα ἀπὸ τριχῶν καμήλου μόνον φοροῦντος καὶ μηδὲν ἐσθίοντος πλὴν ἀκρίδας καὶ μέλι ἄγριον.	Matt 3:4: εἶχον τὸ ἔνδυμα αὐτοῦ ἀπὸ τριχῶν καμήλου καὶ ζώνην δερματίνην περὶ τὴν ὀσφὺν αὐτοῦ· ἡ δὲ τροφὴ αὐτοῦ ἀκρίδες καὶ μέλι ἄγριον. Mark 1:6: καὶ ἦν ... ἐνδεδυμένος τρίχας καμήλου καὶ ζώνην δερματίνην περὶ τὴν ὀσφὺν αὐτοῦ, καὶ ἐσθίων ἀκρίδας καὶ μέλι ἄγριον.

For a description of John's dress and nourishment, either Matthew or Mark could have been Justin's source; in the use of the verb ἐσθίειν Justin agrees with Mark. There is no equivalent in Luke's Gospel to this description.

Dial. 88.7	Luke 3:15–16a	John 1:19–20
The people assumed	As the people were filled with expectation and all were questioning in their hearts, whether John might	When they sent ... to ask him, "Who are you?"
that he was the Christ; to them he cried out,	be the Christ, John answered all of them by saying,	... and he confessed,
"I am not the Christ,	"I baptize you with water ..."	"I am not the Christ."
but the voice of one crying ..."		cf. vs. 23: "I am the voice of one crying out in the wilderness..."

Dial. 88.7	Luke 3:15–16a	John 1:19–20
οἱ ἄνθρωποι	Προσδοκοῦντος δὲ τοῦ	ὅτε ἀπέστειλαν … ἵνα
ὑπελάμβανον αὐτὸν	λαοῦ καὶ	ἐρωτήσωσιν αὐτόν· σὺ
	διαλογιζομένων πάντων	τίς εἶ; …
	ἐν ταῖς καρδίαις αὐτῶν	
	περὶ τοῦ Ἰωάννου,	
	μήποτε αὐτὸς	
εἶναι τὸν Χριστόν·	εἴη ὁ Χριστός,	
πρὸς οὓς καὶ αὐτὸς ἐβόα·	ἀπεκρίνατο λέγων πᾶσιν	καὶ ὡμολόγησεν ὅτι
	ὁ Ἰωάννης·	
Οὐκ εἰμὶ ὁ Χριστός,	ἐγὼ μὲν βαπτίζω …[1]	ἐγὼ οὐκ εἰμὶ ὁ Χριστός,
ἀλλὰ φωνὴ βοῶντος.		cf. vs. 23: ἐγὼ φωνὴ
		βοῶντος ἐν τῇ ἐρήμῳ …

Only Luke formulates the thoughts of the people, concerning whether John might be the Christ, in such a way that his text could have served as the basis of Justin's formulation. However, the answer "I am not the Christ" has a parallel only in the Gospel of John; the continuation of the Baptist's answer in Justin ("but the voice of a crier") also recalls the text of the Fourth Gospel. That Justin knew the Gospel of John, or the tradition about John the Baptist that was used in this Gospel, cannot be categorically excluded. But this singular similarity with John's text is too weak to be a basis for the argument of Justin's acquaintance with the Fourth Gospel. It is possible that Justin developed the answer of the Baptist on the basis of Luke's text[2] and the Isaiah prophecy.[3]

The proclamation of John the Baptist about the one who is coming after him presupposes both Matthew's and Luke's text:[4]

Dial. 49.3 (88.7)[5]	Matt 3:11–12	Luke 3:16b–17
I baptize you with water for repentance, but the one who is stronger than I is coming;	I baptize you with water for repentance, but one who is stronger than I is coming after me;	I baptize you with water, but the one who is stronger than I is coming;

[1] John's answer in Luke 3:16b–17 is the saying about the stronger one who is coming after him; see below.

[2] See also Acts 13:25, where Luke quotes the same passage from his Gospel, but notes that John answered, "I am not he" (οὐκ εἰμὶ ἐγώ).

[3] See the discussion in Wilhelm Bousset, Die Evangelienzitate Justins des Märtyrers in ihrem Wert für die Evangelienkritik (Göttingen: Vandenhoeck & Ruprecht, 1891) 66–68; cf. also Massaux, Influence de l'Évangile de Saint Matthieu, 517–18, 547–48.

[4] No peculiar features of Mark's text are reflected in Justin's quotations.

[5] The quotation in Dial. 88.7 contains only the second sentence, beginning with ἥξει.

I am not worthy to carry his sandals. He will baptize you with the Holy Spirit and fire. His winnowing fork is in his hand and he will clear his thrashing floor and to gather the wheat into the grannary; and the chaff he will burn with unquenchable fire.	I am not worthy to carry his sandals. He will baptize you with the Holy Spirit and fire. The winnowing fork is in his hand and he will clear his thrashing floor and to gather his wheat into the grannary; and the chaff he will burn with unquenchable fire.	I am not worthy to untie the thong of his sandals. He will baptize you with the Holy Spirit and fire. His winnowing fork is in his hand in order to clear his thrashing floor and to gather the wheat into his grannary; but the chaff he will burn with unquenchable fire.
Dial. 49.3 (88.7)	Matt 3:11–12	Luke 3:16b–17
Ἐγὼ μὲν ὑμᾶς βαπτίζω ἐν ὕδατι εἰς μετάνοιαν· ἥξει δὲ ὁ ἰσχυρότερός μου οὗ οὐκ εἰμὶ ἱκανὸς τὰ ὑποδήματα βαστάσαι· αὐτὸς ὑμᾶς βαπτίσει ἐν πνεύματι ἁγίῳ καὶ πυρί. οὗ τὸ πτύον αὐτοῦ ἐν τῇ χειρὶ αὐτοῦ, καὶ διακαθαριεῖ τὴν ἅλωνα αὐτοῦ καὶ τὸν σῖτον συνάξει εἰς τὴν ἀποθήκην, καὶ τὸ ἄχυρον κατακαύσει πυρὶ ἀσβέστῳ.	Ἐγὼ μὲν ὑμᾶς βαπτίζω ἐν ὕδατι εἰς μετάνοιαν· ὁ δὲ ὀπίσω μου ἐρχόμενος ἰσχυρότερός μού ἐστιν, οὗ οὐκ εἰμὶ ἱκανὸς τὰ ὑποδήματα βαστάσαι· αὐτὸς ὑμᾶς βαπτίσει ἐν πνεύματι ἁγίῳ καὶ πυρί. οὗ τὸ πτύον αὐτοῦ ἐν τῇ χειρὶ αὐτοῦ, καὶ διακαθαριεῖ τὴν ἅλωνα αὐτοῦ καὶ τὸν σῖτον συνάξει εἰς τὴν ἀποθήκην, καὶ τὸ ἄχυρον κατακαύσει πυρὶ ἀσβέστῳ.	Ἐγὼ μὲν ὕδατι βαπτίζω ὑμᾶς· ἔρχεται δὲ ὁ ἰσχυρότερός μου, οὗ οὐκ εἰμὶ ἱκανὸς λῦσαι τὸν ἱμάντα τῶν ὑποδημάτων αὐτοῦ· αὐτὸς ὑμᾶς βαπτίσει ἐν πνεύματι ἁγίῳ καὶ πυρί. οὗ τὸ πτύον αὐτοῦ ἐν τῇ χειρὶ αὐτοῦ, διακαθαριεῖ τὴν ἅλωνα αὐτοῦ καὶ τὸν σῖτον συνάξει εἰς τὴν ἀποθήκην, καὶ τὸ ἄχυρον κατακαύσει πυρὶ ἀσβέστῳ.

On the whole, there is considerable agreement between the versions of Justin, Matthew and Luke.[1] As Justin reflects special formulations of both Matthew and Luke, there can be no question that his quote harmonizes the text of these two Synoptic Gospels.

Similar harmonizations of special features of the texts of these two Gospels are also present in Justin's report about the baptism of Jesus. In *Dial.* 88, Justin twice reports the coming of the holy spirit upon Jesus at his baptism. He gives this report in order to demonstrate the fulfillment of the prophecies of Isa 11:1–3 and Joel 2:28–29 about the coming of the spirit which he had quoted in *Dial.* 87.2 and 6.

---

[1] There are no special features of Mark 1:7–8 in Justin's quotation. Moreover the saying of Matt 3:12 = Luke 3:17 is missing in Mark altogether.

Dial. 88.3	Dial. 88.8	Matt 3:13–17	Luke 3:21–22
			But it
And then, when	And when	Then	happened when
Jesus came	Jesus came	Jesus came from	all the people were
to the Jordan river,	to the Jordan	Galilee to the Jordan	baptized,
where John was		to John to be	
baptizing,		baptized by him . . .	
and when Jesus			
came down into the			
water, and a fire			
was kindled in the		when Jesus had	and when Jesus had
Jordan, and when		been baptized, just	been baptized
Jesus emerged		as he came up	and was praying,
from the water,		from the water, and	
		behold, the heavens	the heaven
		were opened	was opened
		and he saw	
the Holy Spirit flew	the Holy Spirit flew	the spirit of	and the Holy Spirit
down upon . . .	down upon him in the	God descending like a	descended upon him in
	form of a dove, and	dove and alighting	bodily form like a
	with it a	upon him. And a	dove. And a
	voice came	voice	voice
	down from heaven,	from heaven said,	came from heaven,
	"You are my Son,	"This is my beloved	"You are my Son,
	today I have begotten	Son with whom I am	today I have begotten
	you."	well pleased."	you."

Dial. 88.3	Dial. 88.8	Matt 3:13–17	Luke 3:21–22
καὶ τότε ἐλθόντος	καὶ ἐλθόντος	Τότε παραγίνεται	Ἐγένετο ἐν τῷ
τοῦ Ἰησοῦ	τοῦ Ἰησοῦ	ὁ Ἰησοῦς ἀπὸ τῆς	βαπτισθῆναι
ἐπὶ τὸν	ἐπὶ τὸν	Γαλιλαίας ἐπὶ τὸν	ἅπαντα τὸν λαὸν
Ἰορδάνην ποταμόν,	Ἰορδάνην	Ἰορδάνην	
ἔνθα ὁ Ἰωάννης		πρὸς τὸν Ἰωάννην	
ἐβάπτιζε,		τοῦ βαπτισθῆναι	
		ὑπ' αὐτοῦ . . .	
κατελθόντος τοῦ			
Ἰησοῦ ἐπὶ τὸ			
ὕδωρ καὶ πῦρ			
ἀνήφθη ἐν τῷ			
Ἰορδάνῃ,			
		βαπτισθεὶς δὲ ὁ	καὶ Ἰησοῦ
καὶ ἀναδύντος		Ἰησοῦς εὐθὺς	βαπτισθέντος καὶ
αὐτοῦ ἀπὸ τοῦ		ἀνέβη ἀπὸ τοῦ	προσευχομένου
ὕδατος		ὕδατος· καὶ ἰδοὺ	
		ἠνεῴχθησαν οἱ	ἀνεῳχθῆναι τὸν
		οὐρανοί,	οὐρανόν,

ὡς περιστερὰν τὸ	τὸ	καὶ εἶδεν πνεῦμα	καὶ καταβῆναι τὸ
ἅγιον πνεῦμα	πνεῦμα τὸ ἅγιον	θεοῦ καταβαῖνον	πνεῦμα τὸ ἅγιον
	ἐν εἴδει	ὡσεὶ	σωματικῷ εἴδει
	περιστερᾶς	περιστεράν,	ὡς περιστερὰν
ἐπιπτῆναι ἐπ'	ἐπέπτη	ἐρχόμενον ἐπ'	ἐπ'
αὐτόν,...	αὐτῷ, καὶ	αὐτόν· καὶ ἰδοὺ	αὐτόν, καὶ
	φωνὴ ἐκ τῶν	φωνὴ ἐκ τῶν	φωνὴ ἐξ
	οὐρανῶν ἅμα	οὐρανῶν	οὐρανοῦ
	ἐληλύθει·	λέγουσα·	γενέσθαι·
	υἱός μου εἶ σύ·	οὗτός ἐστιν ὁ υἱός	υἱός μου εἶ σύ,
	ἐγὼ σήμερον	μου ὁ ἀγαπητός,	ἐγὼ σήμερον
	γεγέννηκά σε.	ἐν ᾧ εὐδόκησα.	γεγέννηκά σε.[1]

Justin's reports are based upon the Synoptic accounts. But they again demonstrate a harmonization of the texts of Matthew and Luke.[2] That John was baptizing at the Jordan when Jesus came is reported in Matthew (and Mark), but not in Luke, where neither John nor the Jordan are mentioned.[3] Also the report of Jesus' baptism requires Matthew's Gospel rather than Luke's terse remark "when Jesus was baptized." But the "Holy Spirit" (Matthew: "spirit of God," Mark: "spirit") is clearly Lukan. This term must have been given in Justin's text, because the quote of Isa 11:1–3 actually contains the phrase "spirit of God" (= Matthew). "In the form (ἐν εἴδει) of a dove" also presupposes Luke's "in bodily form (σωματικῷ εἴδει), as a dove." Finally, the heavenly voice is given by Justin in a citations of Ps 2:7, while Mark and Matthew present a wording of the heavenly voice which is a conflation of Isa 42:1 and 44:2. Only the Western text of Luke 3:22 presents the heavenly voice in the form that must be presupposed for Justin's source.[4] Justin cannot have been the author of this form of the heavenly voice; he had no special interest in proving

---

[1] This text of Luke 3:22 appears only in the so-called Western Text (D it; Meth Hil Aug). This is the accepted text in Huck-Greeven, *Synopsis,* but is rejected by Aland (*Synopsis*) and Nestle-Aland (*NT Graece*) in favor of the majority reading σὺ εἶ ὁ υἱός μου ὁ ἀγαπητός, ἐν σοὶ εὐδόκησα = Mark 1:11.

[2] Mark 1:9–11 also could have been the basis of some elements of Justin's report; but there are no peculiar Markan features in his text.

[3] Luke reports the imprisonment of John the Baptist before the baptism of Jesus (Luke 3:19–20) in order to create a clear, albeit superficial, separation of John and Jesus. "The reference to the imprisonment in iii, 19f. divides the section concerning John from the section concerning Jesus in the sense of drawing a distinction between the epochs of salvation . . ." (Conzelmann, *Theology of St Luke,* 21).

[4] The question of the original text of Luke 3:22 is not up for debate here; on this problem see Bovon, *Evangelium nach Lukas,* on Luke 3:22. That Justin quotes Luke in this form indicates that readings of the Western Text existed as early as the middle of the 2nd century.

the fulfillment of this scriptural text, although he is quite aware of its appearance in scripture as a word of David, i..e, a psalm that David wrote.[1] That Justin's source already contained this form of the heavenly voice is confirmed in *Dial.* 103.6, where he refers to it once more in passing; introducing a remark about Jesus temptation, he again quotes the exact text of Luke 2:22 D = Ps 2:7.

In order to prove the fulfillment of the prophecies of Isa 11:1–3 and Joel 2:28–29, Justin only had to report the coming of the spirit upon Jesus. But not only does he add the report about the heavenly voice, he also mentions "that a fire was lit in the Jordan." Nothing in the context of Justin's discussion requires a mention of this phenomenon. It must have been part of the text Justin is quoting. It is difficult to determine the origin of this new element in the account of Jesus' baptism.[2] The *Gospel of the Ebionites*[3] tells of an appearance of light after Jesus' baptism. However, it is doubtful whether *fire* and *light* can simply be identified.[4] A discussion of the complex history-of-religions problem of the appearance of fire at the event of an epiphany may not be necessary at this point. In the Synoptic Sayings Source, John the Baptist announces the one who comes after him who will baptize "with the Holy Spirit and with fire" (Q/Luke 3:16). Once this prophecy, originally referring to the coming of God for the final judgment, is applied to Jesus' coming, it seems natural that the report of Jesus' baptism would contain not only an account of the coming of the Holy Spirit upon Jesus, but also an account of the appearance of fire at the event of his baptism. Thus, Justin is using a report about the baptism of Jesus that reveals a further consistent development which goes beyond the account of the Synoptic Gospels but finds its natural explanation in the inherent dynamics of the evolving text itself. The baptism of Jesus is seen as the complete fulfillment of John the Baptist's prophecy.

5.2.2.4 The Passion Narrative

Materials from the passion narrative appear in Justin's writings in two different settings: (1) in the context of various traditional scrip-

[1] Only a portion of the manuscripts of the LXX designates this psalm as a "Psalm of David." This designation is missing in the Massoretic tradition of the Hebrew text of Psalm 2.

[2] On the apocryphal reports about the appearance of light or fire in the reports about Jesus' baptism see Bauer, *Leben Jesu*, 134–39.

[3] Epiphanius, *Haer.* 30.13; see also below on the *Diatessaron* # 5.3.5.2.

[4] For the Pseudo-Clementines (*Hom.* 11.26.4; *Rec.* 6.9; 9.7.10) fire and light are clearly two different elements: it is the water that quenches the fire.

ture quotations that have played a role in the development of the passion narrative, (2) in Justin's detailed interpretation of Psalm 21 [22] (*Dial.* 99–106).

Clusters of traditional scriptural prophecies are quoted three times: *1 Apol.* 35; 38; and *Dial.* 97. In most instances, the same scriptural passages have been used elsewhere in the formation of the narrative of Jesus passion and death.

Scripture	*1 Apol.* 35	*1 Apol.* 38	*Dial.* 97	Use in other literature
Exod 17:12			×	(*Barn.* 12.2)[1]
Isa 50:6–8		×		*Barn.* 5.1; 6.1–2; Matt 26:67; 27:30
Isa 53:9			×	1 Pet 2:22
Isa 57:1–2			×	
Isa 58:2	×			*Gos. Pet.* 3.6–7; John 19:13
Isa 65:2	×	×	×	*Barn.* 12.4
Ps 3:5–6		×	×	1 Clem. 26.2
Ps 21:8–9[2]		×		Matt 27:39
Ps 21:17, 19[3]	×	×	×	*Barn.* 6.6; 5.13; Matt 27:35; *Gos. Pet.* 4.12

These citations are drawn from traditional collections of prophecies, and the accounts of the fulfillment of these scriptures reflect traditional narratives. In *1 Apol.* 35.6–8 Justin adds a brief narrative that cites four details of a narrative about Jesus' passion and crucifixion, and he adds that all of these are recorded in the "Acts of Pilate."[4] As fulfillment of Isa 65:2 ("I have stretched out my hands . . ."), Justin reports that "Jesus Christ stretched out his hands when he was crucified by the Jews who contradicted him and said that he was not the Christ." There is no such detail in the narratives about the crucifixion in any known gospel.[5]

As fulfillment of Isa 58:2 ("They now request judgment from me"), he gives a brief reference to the fulfillment which has parallels in the *Gospel of Peter*[6] and perhaps in the Gospel of John.

---

[1] *Barnabas* does not quote the exact verse that appears in *Dial.* 97.1, but gives a general abstract of Exod 17:8–11 with the report about Moses holding up his arms.

[2] According to the counting of the LXX, = Ps 22: 6–7 of the Hebrew Text.

[3] = Ps 22:16, 18 in the Hebrew text.

[4] On these references to the "Acts of Pilate" in Justin and elsewhere, see above, # 1.7.

[5] On Isa 65:2 in the passion narrative, see Crossan, *The Cross that Spoke*, 229–231.

[6] See also above, # 3.2.3.2.

1 Apol. 35.6	*Gos. Pet.* 3.6, 8	John 19:13
. . . ridiculing (διασύροντες) him,	. . . they said, "Let us drag (σύρωμεν) the Son of God . . ."	
they sat him on a judgment seat (ἐκάθισαν ἐπὶ βήματος)	. . . and sat him on the judgment seat (ἐκάθισαν αὐτὸν ἐπὶ καθέδραν κρίσεως) and	. . . and he sat down on the judgment seat (καὶ ἐκάθισεν ἐπὶ βήματος).
and said, "Judge us!"	said, "Judge righteously, O King of Israel!"	

The parallel in the *Gospel of Peter* requires a common source for this Gospel and Justin. The origin of the report about "dragging" (σύρειν) or "ridiculing" (διασύρειν) is obscure, but the parallel cannot be accidental. Nonetheless, the *Gospel of Peter* cannot have been Justin's source, because he uses the word βῆμα for "judgment seat," like John 19:13. Thus, all three parallels must derive from the same piece of information about Jesus' passion, whatever its character.

The fulfillment of Ps 21:17 [22:16] ("They pierced [ὤρυξαν] my hands and my feet") is said to point to the nails (ἥλοι) which were fixed through Jesus' hands and feet when he was crucified. There is no corresponding account in known gospel texts. Neither "nails" (ἥλοι) nor "fixing with nails" (καθηλοῦν) are mentioned in accounts of the crucifixion,[1] not is there a reference to "nails" in Ps 21:17 quoted by Justin. But *Barn.* 5.14 quotes Ps 118 [119]:120: "Nail my flesh" (Καθή-λωσόν μου τὰς σάρκας) in the context of prophecies referring to the crucifixion, and Ignatius, *Sm.* 1.1–2, addresses the Smyrneans as those who are established in faith "as if nailed (καθηλωμένοι) to the cross of the Lord Jesus Christ" and then refers to Christ as "being nailed for us in the flesh" (καθηλωμένος ὑπὲρ ἡμῶν τῇ σαρκί). It is, therefore, quite likely that Justin knew of an account of Jesus' crucifixion in which this detail was emphasized. That he did not develop this information independently is evident, for the passage from the Psalms quoted by him (Ps 21:17) does not contain a reference to piercing with nails.[2]

[1] However, *Gos. Pet.* 6.21 says that "they drew out the nails from the hands of the Lord" when they took him down from the cross for burial.

[2] See also the discussion in Crossan, *The Cross that Spoke*, 228–29. The mention of the marks of the nails in Jesus' hands at the appearance of his resurrection (John 20:25) would be a secondary reflection of this narrative detail. However, Crossan (ibid., 230) would rather connect this feature with Isa 65:2 (the stretching out of the hands).

The last of the details mentioned by Justin relates to the casting of lots and the dividing of the garments according to Ps 21:19. Only here does Justin reproduce a narrative detail that is also recorded in all the canonical Gospels: Mark 15:24 parr and John 19:23–24, in the latter instance with an explicit quotation of Ps 21:8, as well as in *Gos. Pet.* 4.12. However, dependence upon any of these canonical accounts is not very likely. Mark 15:24 (and, following Mark, also Matt 27:35 and Luke 23:34) first report the dividing of the garments (διαμερί-ζονται τὰ ἱμάτια αὐτοῦ) according to Ps 21:19a, then speak about distributing them by lot (βάλλοντες κλῆρον) according to Ps 21:19b. *Gos. Pet.* 4.12, though using different terminology, agrees with this Synoptic account. John 19:23–24 presents a more elaborate interpretation of Ps 21:19a/b: the garments (ἱμάτια) of Jesus are divided into four parts for the four soldiers, but then they decide not to divide the tunic (χιτών) but rather to cast lots about it. Justin first speaks about the casting of lots about the garment (ἱματισμός); this narrates the fulfillment of Ps 21:19b, that is, the part of this verse of the psalm that he had actually quoted. Then Justin adds that they divided it among them; this is the fulfillment of Ps 21:19a which Justin had not quoted before. Justin's narrative, thus, rests directly upon an interpretation of both halves of Ps 21:19, as does John 19:23–24, but without revealing any influence from the Johannine passage. However, Justin's account was not invented for this context on the basis of the scriptural passage, because the first half of the verse is not even quoted here. Therefore, Justin must have quoted selectively both a cluster of scriptural prophecies and a narrative account that was independent of the respective passages in the canonical Gospels as well as of the *Gospel of Peter*.

In the cluster of prophecies quoted in *Dial.* 97, Ps 21:17, 19 is the last scripture that is quoted and the only one to which an account of the fulfillment is added. It begins with the piercing of Jesus' hands and feet with nails, in words very similar to those used in *1 Apol.* 35.7. Then follows the report about the dividing of the garments. But this time, both Ps 21:19a and 19b are quoted, and the dividing of the garments is told before the mention of the casting of lots.[1] In the context of the systematic interpretation of all the verses of Psalm 21, Justin once more quotes Ps 21:17 and 19 (*Dial.* 104.1), but does not mention the piercing of the hands and feet; he only remarks that he had men-

---

[1] Justin expands the latter by saying "they cast lots (λαχμός), each leaving the selection of what he wanted to the decision of the lot (κλῆρος)." This formulation does not necessarily require recourse to a different tradition; cf. *Gos. Pet.* 4.12: λαχμός, John 19:24: λάχωμεν αὐτῷ τίνος ἔσται.

tioned already that the soldiers divided the garments among themselves (*Dial.* 104.2).

In *1 Apology* 38, the last prophecy quoted is Ps 21:8–9, and Justin adds a few remarks which are drawn from the context of the mocking of the crucified Jesus. It is worth noting that the selection of sentences from the psalm quoted in *1 Apol.* 38.6 corresponds exactly to the sentences which describe the fulfillment (38.8):

Ps 21:8–9	Quote from the Psalm	Narrative of mocking
All who look at me mock at me,		When he was crucified,
they speak with lips, they shake the head.	they speak with lips, they shake the head saying,	they turned out the lips and shook the heads saying,
"He hoped for the Lord,		He who raised the dead,
he may rescue him, if he delights in him.	he may rescue him,	may he rescue himself.

πάντες οἱ θεωροῦντές με ἐξεμυκτέρισάν με, ἐλάλησαν ἐν χείλεσιν, ἐκίνησαν κεφαλήν·		σταυρωθέντος γὰρ αὐτοῦ
Ἤλπισεν ἐπὶ κύριον, ῥυσάσθω αὐτόν, εἰ θέλει αὐτόν.	Ἐλάλησαν ἐν χείλεσιν, ἐκίνησαν κεφαλήν λέγοντες· Ῥυσάσθω ἑαυτόν.	ἐξέστρεφον τὰ χείλη καὶ ἐκίνουν τὰς κεφαλὰς λέγοντες· Ὁ νεκροὺς ἀνεγείρας ῥυσάσθω ἑαυτόν.

Whatever the relationship of this description of the mocking to the corresponding accounts of the Synoptic Gospels, it is clear that Justin quotes neither a full text of the Psalm 21 nor a full account of any written gospel. Rather, he copies a piece of scriptural proof that was developed in the school tradition of the early church.

All the citations of narrative materials about the passion and crucifixion of Jesus sofar discussed reveal Justin's indebtedness to the school tradition of scriptural proof. There is very little, if any, new contribution of Justin himself. However, Justin was not just a passive heir of this school tradition; he was an active participant. This becomes clear whenever Justin himself creatively constructs scriptural proof. The clearest evidence for this is his interpretation of

Psalm 21 [22] in *Dialogue* 99–107. In that context, Justin has once more presented the mocking of the crucified on the basis of Ps 21:8–9:

Ps 21:8–9[1]	1 Apol. 38.8	Dial. 101.3	Synoptic Gospels
			Luke 23:35a:
All those who look at me,		Those who looked at him	The people stood looking
			Matt 27:39
they	they	they	those who passed by
speak with lips,	turned out the lips	turned the lips.	blasphemed him,
they shake the head.	and shook the heads	each shook heads,	shaking their heads and saying . . .
			Luke 23:35b
They scoffed at me		and they scoffed together[2]	and the leaders scoffed at him
	saying, He who raised the dead,	and said sarcastically,	
			Matt 27:40
[may he save him]		"[He has called himself the Son of God;] may he come down and walk about.	"Save yourself, if you are the Son of God, come down from the cross."
[may he save him]		Let God save him."	**Matt 27:43**
	may he rescue himself.		"He trusts in God,
He hoped upon the Lord; may he rescue him, may he save him, if he delights in him.			(let God) rescue him now, if he delights in him;
		He has called himself the Son of God.	for he said, 'I am the Son of God.'"

Ps 21:8–9	1 Apol. 38.8	Dial. 101.3	Synoptic Gospels
			Luke 23:35a:
Πάντες οἱ θεωροῦντές με		οἱ θεωροῦντες αὐτὸν	εἱστήκει ὁ λαὸς θεωρῶν
			Matt 27:39 [3]
καὶ ἐλάλησαν ἐν χείλεσιν, ἐκίνησαν κεφαλήν·	ἐξέστρεφον τὰ χείλη καὶ ἐκίνουν τὰς κεφαλὰς	καὶ τὰ χείλη διέστρεφον, τὰς κεφαλὰς ἕκαστος ἐκίνουν,	παραπορευόμενοι ἐβλασφήμουν αὐτὸν κινοῦντες τὰς κεφαλὰς αὐτῶν

[1] The text of Ps 21:8–9 is given here exactly as it is quoted in *Dial.* 103.3.
[2] Literally: "They crinkled their noses at each other."
[3] Cf. Mark 15:29.

Luke 23:35b

	τὰς μυξωτῆρσιν ἐν	ἐξεμυκτήριζον δὲ
ἐξεμυκτέρισάν με.	ἀλλήλοις	καὶ ὁ ἄρχοντες.
	διαρρινοῦντες.	

λέγοντες· Ὁ   ἔλεγον
νεκροὺς ἀνεγείρας εἰρωνευόμενοι·   **Matt 27:40** [1]

[σωσάτω αὐτόν]   σῶσον σεαυτόν, εἰ
                  [Υἱὸν θεοῦ ἑαυτὸν   υἱὸς εἶ τοῦ θεοῦ,
                  ἔλεγε] καταβὰς   καὶ κατάβητι ἀπὸ
                  περιπατεῖτο·   τοῦ σταυροῦ.

[σωσάτω αὐτόν]   σωσάτω αὐτὸν ὁ
                  θεός.   **Matt 27:43** [2]

Ἤλπισεν ἐπὶ   πέποιθεν ἐπὶ
κύριον,   τὸν θεόν,
ῥυσάσθω αὐτόν,   ῥυσάσθω ἑαυτόν.   ῥυσάσθω νῦν,
σωσάτω αὐτόν,[3]
ὅτι θέλει αὐτόν.
                                       εἰ θέλει αὐτόν· εἶπεν
                  Υἱὸν θεοῦ ἑαυτὸν   γὰρ ὅτι θεοῦ εἰμι υἱός.
                  ἔλεγε.

What becomes apparent here is typical of Justin's treatment of traditional materials about scripture and fulfillment. One could say that Justin is updating the traditional scriptural proof. First, he goes back to the entire and full text of the Greek Bible and quotes the complete text of Psalm 21, rather than only the excerpt that has been used in the traditional proof of scripture and fulfillment. Second, he makes recourse to the actual text of written gospels and uses relevant passages from Matthew and Luke that would demonstrate a more complete fulfillment of prophecy. In that process, sentences which do not fit the prophecy are omitted, for example, the narrative phrase "he who has raised the dead" (*1 Apol.* 38.8) is now left out, because it has no equivalent either in the prophecy of Psalm 21 or in the record of the written gospels. On the other hand, a phrase that is supported by the text of a gospel, like "let him come down from the cross," is preserved although there is no support for it in the text of the psalm. But Justin takes a third step: he updates the narrative itself. "They twist their lips" (καὶ τὰ χείλη διέστρεφον) is a sentence of Justin's narrative that has no equivalent in any written gospel; it is added by Justin, because there is a phrase in the psalm which requires a corresponding

---

[1] Cf. Mark 15:30; Luke 23:35b.

[2] There are no Synoptic parallels to this Matthean verse.

[3] This phrase is missing in Justin's quote of Ps 21:9 in *Dial* 101.3, but it appears in the quotation of the entire psalm in *Dial.* 98.3 as well as in the manuscripts of the LXX.

sentence in the story of the passion in order to make the fulfillment perfect.

In the narrative that tells the fulfillment of the prophecy of Ps 21:8–9, a convincingly complete account would not have been possible, unless Justin had drawn on all available evidence from written gospels. Thus, more than one Gospel, certainly Matthew and Luke, possibly also Mark, are required to serve. The result is a harmony of these Gospels. But it must have been a harmony that was not simply composed for the purpose of scriptural proof. In that case, only those sentences would have been quoted, which have a direct correspondence in the text of scripture. However, Justin's gospel quotations also contain sentences and phrases, which are not required for the demonstration, and to which there are no corresponding scriptural prophecies. One of these sentences without direct scriptural equivalent appears in the scene of the mocking of the crucified Jesus, in which he is challenged to descend from the cross.

Justin Martyr is the first Christian writer who is aware of the fact that the written gospels have become a "text." However, he may not have been the first to set down, side by side, texts from "scripture" and texts from written records of Jesus. That honor must be given to Marcion who, in his "Antitheses," juxtaposed gospel quotations with passages from scripture—albeit in order to emphasize the contrast. Justin is intent upon demonstrating the identity of scripture and fulfillment. The gospels become a historical record that proves this identity. However, many gospels would not do, either for Marcion or for Justin. While Marcion reduces the record to one single purified gospel, Justin includes as much of the tradition as is possible. A gospel harmony is the answer, and Justin reveals the process of its composition. Marcion rejects the traditions which he felt were falsified. Justin includes as much as was possible—and the criterion for inclusion is the scriptural prophecy. Had Justin prevailed, and not Irenaeus, a harmony of the available gospel literature would have been the answer. His student Tatian fulfilled that task, but, as will be seen in the next chapter, his work was accepted only in the Eastern church.

5.3 Tatian's Diatessaron

by William L. Petersen

5.3.1 THE DIATESSARON'S SIGNIFICANCE

The *Diatessaron* (Greek: διὰ τεσσάρων = "through [the] four [gospels]") is a gospel harmony, created about the year 172. Its putative composer, Tatian, combined the four canonical Gospels with one or more extra-canonical sources, and wove them into a single continuous account. Duplications were removed, contradictions were reconciled, and parallel passages were harmonized.

The importance of the *Diatessaron* rests upon four points. First, the *Diatessaron* is the most extensive, earliest collection of 2d-century gospel texts extant. Since it incorporated virtually the entire text of the four canonical Gospels, as well as some material from extra-canonical gospels, its comprehensiveness far outstrips the scattered parallels of other early sources. And as a creation of the mid-second century, its antiquity surpasses all other sources, save Justin, Marcion, Clement of Alexandria, the Jewish-Christian Gospel fragments, and, perhaps, some of the Nag Hammadi texts. "Pour retrouver les plus anciennes leçons évangeliques, la connaissance de l'oeuvre de Tatien est d'une importance primordiale."[1] Second, since the *Diatessaron* is the earliest specimen of a gospel harmony yet recovered *in extenso,* it affords us a unique opportunity to examine the techniques and concerns of a 2d-century harmonist. We know that numerous other 2d-century harmonies existed (Justin's harmony is one example); yet only the *Diatessaron* survives in blocks big enough to afford a panoramic view of the endeavor. Third, like any document created in a particular time and place, the *Diatessaron* reflects the theology and praxis of its locale. Consequently, the *Diatessaron* "offers extraordinary insights into the patterns of cultural transmission from the earliest Christian to the medieval world."[2] Fourth, it is not by chance that both Arthur Vööbus and Bruce Metzger begin their respective *Early Versions of the New Testament*[3] with chapters on the *Diatessaron*, for the *Diatessaron* is usually considered to be the most ancient of the versions. Furthermore, the *Diatessaron* is quite probably the form in which the gospels first appeared in Syriac, Latin, Armenian, and Georgian. As such, it

---

[1] Louis Leloir, "Le *Diatessaron* de Tatien," *OrSyr* 1 (1956), 209.

[2] Robert Murray, "The Gospel in the Medieval Netherlands," *HeyJ* 14 (1973) 309.

[3] Arthur Vööbus, *Early Versions of the New Testament* (PETSE 6; Stockholm: 1954); Bruce Metzger, *The Early Versions of the New Testament* (Oxford: Clarendon, 1977).

occupies a position unique in the history of the dissemination of the gospels, for it served as the foundation of four of the major New Testament versions, each of which bears the *Diatessaron*'s imprint.

5.3.2 AUTHORSHIP

Although we know that there were other early harmonies, and that a work called a Διὰ Τεσσάρων was composed by the otherwise obscure Ammonius of Alexandria,[1] tradition links only one name with the *Diatessaron*, that of Tatian. The citations upon which that statement rests are given below, in section 5.3.3; here we present the items in Tatian's biography to which we will refer (in section 5.3.7) when dating the *Diatessaron* and locating its place of composition.

Tatian's only other extant work, the *Oratio ad Graecos*,[2] provides some biographical details. He says he was born in the land of the Assyrians (*Or.* 42), which, technically, would mean east of the Euphrates, but which, taken colloquially, could mean Syria in general.[3] He appears to have had a disdain for power, wealth, adventure and sex (*Or.* 11). Leaving his home in the East, Tatian wandered westward, passing through various philosophic schools, until one day he read some "barbarian writings, older than the doctrines of the Greeks, more divine than their errors" (*Or.* 29). This was the Septuagint. Tatian converted to Christianity, and, in the one firm chronological fix we possess, became a student of Justin Martyr's in Rome. Irenaeus tells us that after Justin's death Tatian was expelled from the primitive Roman community for being an Encratite and a follower of the Gnostic Valentinus.[4] Epiphanius says that he left Rome and returned to the East, where his teachings had great influence.[5]

---

[1] *Ep. ad Carpianum* 1 (most readily available in Nestle-Aland, *NT Graece*, 73*).

[2] Molly Whittaker, ed., *Oratio ad Graecos and Fragments* (Oxford Early Christian Texts; Oxford: Clarendon, 1982); Whittaker's Introduction contains a good brief biography of Tatian.

[3] Lucian, whose home was Samosata, calls himself an "Assyrian," and calls Hierapolis an Assyrian city (*De Dea Syra* 1); cf. the treatment of Theodor Zahn, *Tatians Diatessaron* (FGNK 1/1; Erlangen: Deichert, 1881) 268–70. Also noteworthy is the fact that Tatian is called ὁ Σύρος by Clement of Alexandria (*Strom.* 3.12, 81.1) and Theodoret of Cyrrhus (*Haer. fab. comp.* 1.20; MPG 83, 372), while Epiphanius calls him τὸ γένος Σύρος (*Haer.* 46.1.6; eds. Holl and Dummer, 204).

[4] Irenaeus *Adv. haer.* 1.28.1 (eds. Rousseau and Doutreleau 354); on Encratism, see Henry Chadwick, "Enkrateia," *RAC* 5. 343–65, esp. 352–54.

[5] *Haer.* 46.1.8 (edd. Holl and Dummer 204).

5.3.3 ATTESTATION

Given the early and wide dissemination of the *Diatessaron* throughout the entire Christian world, it is convenient to divide our analysis into Western and Eastern attestation.

In the West, the first mention of the *Diatessaron* is in Eusebius *Hist. eccl.* 4.29.6:

> Tatian, their (the Encratites') first head, brought together a combination and collection—I do not know how—of the gospels. He called this the *Diatessaron*, which is still in circulation among some people.

Epiphanius, a later 4th-century writer, also speaks of the *Diatessaron* (*Haer.* 46.1.8–9[1]):

> It is said the gospel *Diatessaron* was created by him (Tatian), which some call according to the Hebrews.

In the 5th century, Theodoret, who from 423 to 457 was bishop of Cyrrhus, a small Syrian town two days' journey from Antioch, reports (*Haer. fab. comp.* 1. 20[2]):

> He (Tatian) composed the so-called *Diatessaron* by cutting out the genealogies and whatever goes to prove the Lord to have been born of the seed of David according to the flesh. And this work was in use not only among his own party but even among those who follow the tradition of the Apostles, who used it somewhat too innocently as a compendium of the Gospels, without recognizing the craftiness of its compositions. I myself found more than two hundred copies in reverential use in the churches of my diocese, all of which I removed, replacing them by the Gospels of the four Evangelists.

Finally, in the sixth century, Victor, bishop of Capua in Italy from 541 to 554, came across a manuscript of a harmonized gospel, but lacking a title or author's name. Victor directed that a copy of the manuscript be made and, in his preface to the new copy (which is our present Codex Fuldensis), he relates how, after much difficult research, he came to the conclusion that the work must be the harmony of Tatian. Inexplicably, however, Victor does not call Tatian's work a *Diatessaron*, but a *Diapente* (= "Through five [gospels]").

Before leaving the West, two points bear mention. First, it is notable that Irenaeus never mentions that *Diatessaron*, although he knows Tatian. Similarly, the silence of Clement of Alexandria, who

---

[1] Epiphanius *Haer.* 34–64, eds. Holl and Dummer (GCS 66; 2d ed.; Berlin: Akademie-Verlag, 1980) 204–5.

[2] *MPG* 83. 372.

also mentions Tatian and may, in fact, have been one of Tatian's pupils,[1] remains puzzling—unless the *Diatessaron* was composed in the East, after Tatian left the West. Second, although the first mention of the *Diatessaron* is by Eusebius in the early 4th century, the *textual* imprint of the *Diatessaron* is found in many earlier western works, such as the writings of Novatian (d. 258),[2] the Roman Antiphonary,[3] and the Vetus Latina manuscripts.[4] We must conclude that the *Diatessaron* saw circulation in the West long before Eusebius's remark.

In the East, there is also abundant evidence of early circulation of the *Diatessaron*. Indeed, even the most casual reading of the Old Syriac Gospels (extant in two manuscripts: Codex Sinaiticus [sy^s, 4th century] and Codex Curetonianus [sy^c: 5th century]), shows that they have already been influenced by the textual variants and harmonistic readings of the *Diatessaron*.[5] And in the 4th century, many of the gospel quotations of the Syrian writers Aphrahat and Ephrem are in the form of the *Diatessaron*. Ephrem even wrote a commentary on "The Gospel of the Mixed," as the *Diatessaron* was known in Syria, but he fails to name Tatian or use the word *Diatessaron*.

The word *Diatessaron* first appears in Syriac in the 4th century, in the Syriac translation of Eusebius's *Church History,* where the Syriac translator not only translates Eusebius's words (4.29.6), but makes clear his firsthand knowledge of the harmony:

> Now this same Tatianus their former chief collected and mixed up and composed a gospel and called it *Diatessaron*; now this is (the Gospel) of the Mixed, the same that is in the hands of many unto this day.[6]

---

[1] Clement's remark about having studied Christianity with "an Assyrian" (*Strom.* 1.1, 11.2) is often interpreted as referencing Tatian.

[2] Anton Baumstark, "Die Evangelienzitate Novatians und das Diatessaron," *OrChr* 27 [3d series 5] (1930) 1–14.

[3] Idem, "Tatianismus im römischen Antiphonar," *OrChr* 27 [3d series 5] (1930) 165–74.

[4] Heinrich Joseph Vogels, *Beiträge zur Geschichte des Diatessaron im Abendland* (NTA 8/1; Münster: Aschendorff, 1919).

[5] See, e.g., the work of Friedrich Baethgen, *Evangelienfragmente: Der griechische Text des Cureton'schen Syrers* (Leipzig: Hinrichs, 1885), later supported by Vogels, Plooij, and Burkitt. This view holds the field today: cf. the *Early Versions of the New Testament* by either Bruce Metzger or by Arthur Vööbus; see also Matthew Black, "The Syriac Versional Tradition," in Aland, ed., *Die alten Übersetzungen,* 130–32.

[6] *The Ecclesiastical History of Eusebius in Syriac,* eds. William Wright and Norman McLean (Cambridge: Cambridge University Press, 1898) 243; the text is also given in F. C. Burkitt, ed., *Evangelion da-Mepharreshe: The Curetonian Version of the Four Gospels* (2 vols.; Cambridge: Cambridge University Press, 1904) 2. 175.

Notice how the translator deleted Eusebius's "I do not know how," and modified the last phrase, so that it emphasizes even more strongly the *Diatessaron*'s continuing use. Although the Greek διὰ τεσσάρων is transliterated into Syriac, the name must not have meant anything to a Syriac reader, for the translator felt obliged to supply the *Diatessaron*'s common Syriac name, "of the Mixed."

In a 5th-century Syrian work, the *Doctrina Addai*, the *Diatessaron* is also named, but in an awkward way:

> Moreover, much people day by day assembled and came together for prayer and for the reading of the Old Testament and the New, the *Diatessaron*.[1]

The word "*Diatessaron*" in the *Doctrina Addai* is probably a later interpolation,[2] if for no other reason than that it is so anachronistic. After this, the word "Diatessaron" remains unused in Syriac literature until the late 8th century, when the Nestorian scholar Theodore bar Konai names the work and attributes it to Tatian.[3] In the 9th century, Ishocdad of Merv tells us that Ephrem wrote a commentary on it, and then proceeds to cite the *Diatessaron* as an authority.[4] After this period, both Tatian and the *Diatessaron* are referenced in Syriac literature.

In order to have influenced the gospel citations of Aphrahat, Ephrem, and the oldest separated Syriac gospel manuscripts (sy^sc), the *Diatessaron* must have been in circulation in Syria from the beginnings of Syrian Christianity, where it appears to have been known as "the Gospel of the Mixed" (*da-Mehallete*). Only later—perhaps as late as the 8th or 9th century—did the name "*Diatessaron*" become the work's common designation in Syriac. This explains why the first use

---

[1] George Phillips, ed., *The Doctrine of Addai, the Apostle* (London: Truebner, 1876) 34 (folio 23a); a more recent edition is that of George Howard, ed., *The Teaching of Addai* (SBLTT 16; Chico, CA: Scholars Press, 1981) 73.

[2] The competition between the designations "New" and "*Diatessaron*" led Burkitt (*Evangelion da-Mepharreshe*, 2.174) to conclude that we have an interpolated text before us. However, Burkitt felt "New" was the intruder. This seems unlikely, once one realizes how anachronistic the use of the word "*Diatessaron*" is at this point in Syriac literature.

[3] *Theodorus bar Konai. Liber Scholiorum II*, ed. Addai Scher (CSCO 69; Louvain: Peeters, 1912) 305. Elze (*Tatian und seine Theologie*, 120–24) gives a review of the Syrian testimonies concerning Tatian.

[4] *The Commentaries of Ishocdad of Merv*, ed. M. D. Gibson (HSem 5–7; 3 vols.; Cambridge: Cambridge University Press, 1911), e.g., vol. 2 (HSem 6), 45 (text); vol. 1 (HSem 5), 27 (translation). Ishocdad's report that Ephrem wrote a commentary on the *Diatessaron* appears in 2. 204 (text); vol. 1. 123 (translation).

of the word in Syriac, by the 4th-century translator of Eusebius's *Church History* appears to be a transliteration, which obliges the translator to append its standard Syriac name "of the Mixed." The use of *"Diatessaron"* in the *Doctrina Addai* is probably a later interpolation, since it is so anachronistic: one must wait four centuries before the word will again be used in Syriac.

5.3.4 WITNESSES TO THE DIATESSARON

No direct copy of Tatian's *Diatessaron* exists. Instead, the scholar must be content with a wide array of sources, and attempt to reconstruct the *Diatessaron*'s text from them. These sources, called "witnesses" to the *Diatessaron*, range in genre from poems to commentaries, in language from Middle Dutch to Middle Persian, in extent from fragments to codices, in date from 3d to 19th century, in provenance from England to China. Mastering these sources is the key to Diatessaronic scholarship.

The most convenient way to classify the Diatessaronic witnesses is geographically, commencing with the most valuable (i.e., what scholarship views as the most reliable). Below is a partial list which begins with the Eastern witnesses

5.3.4.1 *Eastern Witnesses*

Ephrem's *Commentary*

The greatest Father of the Syrian church, Ephrem Syrus (obit 373), composed a *Commentary on the Gospel of the Mixed*. It survives in an Armenian recension[1] (two manuscripts: Venice: Bib. Mechitarist, nos. 312 and 452, both dating from 1195), as well as in the original Syriac[2] (Dublin: Chester Beatty Library, no. 709; late 5th or early 6th century). This lone Syriac manuscript was missing forty-one folios, which were recently discovered in 1987.[3] The editor of both recensions, Louis Leloir, suggests that neither is inherently superior, for sometimes one, then the other, seems to preserve the best text.[4] Ephrem's *Commentary* is the most important Eastern witness because of its early date,

---

[1] Louis Leloir, ed., *Saint Éphrem, Commentaire de l'Évangile concordant, version arménienne* (CSCO 137 [text] and 145; Louvain: Peeters, 1953 & 1954).

[2] Idem, ed., *Saint Éphrem, Commentaire de l'Évangile concordant, texte syriaque* (CBM 8; Dublin: Hodges Figgis, 1963).

[3] Idem, "Le Commentaire d'Éphrem sur le Diatessaron, Quarante et un folios retrouvés," *RB* 94 (1987) 481–518.

[4] See Louis Leloir's comments in his *Éphrem de Nisibe, Commentaire de l'Évangile concordant ou Diatessaron* (SC 121; Paris: Edition du Cerf, 1966) 28–29. This volume is a French translation of the Commentary, with a helpful introduction.

and the fact that Syriac is the language in which Tatian composed his harmony (see section 5.3.7). Consequently, the *Commentary* stands closest to Tatian not only in date, but also in diction.

The Arabic Harmony

This Arabic translation of the *Diatessaron* survives in six manuscripts, dating from the 12th to the 19th century.[1] Colophons in several of the manuscripts state that the text was translated from the Syriac by the Nestorian exegete Ibn at-Tayyib (obit 1043). Like most Diatessaronic witnesses, the Arabic Harmony has been "Vulgatized"; that is, the genuine Diatessaronic variants have often been removed and replaced with the "standard" gospel reading of a particular time and place. In the case of the Arabic Harmony, it appears that Peshitta readings were frequently substituted for the Diatessaronic reading. This suggests that the Harmony was translated from a Syriac exemplar which had already been Vulgatized. Although the text of the Arabic is not without value for recovering Diatessaronic readings, its chief importance is its witness to the *Diatessaron*'s sequence of the harmonization.

The Persian Harmony

This fascinating document survives in a single manuscript (Florence: Bibl. Laurent., Cod. Orient. 81; dated to 1547).[2] Syriasms in the text show that it was translated from a Syriac *Vorlage*. First edited in 1951, the sequence of the Persian Harmony diverges from the other Diatessaronic witnesses. Because of this, Tjitze Baarda has questioned whether one can really speak of it as a witness to the *Diatessaron*, suggesting instead that it is a harmony which is independent of the *Diatessaron*.[3] Nevertheless, the text of the Persian Harmony contains numerous Diatessaronic readings—according to some stu-

---

[1] The standard edition is that of A.-S. Marmardji, *Diatessaron de Tatien* (Beyrouth: Imprimerie Catholique, 1935). The earlier edition of Agostino Ciasca, *Tatiani Evangeliorum Harmoniae Arabice* (Rome: Bibliographia Polyglotta, 1888), upon which the English translations of H. Hogg ("Tatian's *Diatessaron*," in *The Ante-Nicene Fathers*, Vol. 10 [additional volume], ed. A. Menzies [5th ed.; Grand Rapids, 1969], 63–129) and J. Hamlyn Hill (*The Earliest Life of Christ ever Compiled from the Four Gospels being the Diatessaron of Tatian* ... [Edinburgh: Clark, 1894]) were based, is out-dated.

[2] Edition: *Diatessaron Persiano*, ed. Guiseppe Messina (BibOr 14; Rome: Pontificio Instituto Biblico, 1951).

[3] Tjitze Baarda, "In Search of the *Diatessaron* Text," *Vox Theologica* 17 (1963) 111; also in idem, *Early Transmission of the Words of Jesus: Thomas, Tatian and the Text of the New Testament* (Amsterdam: Uitgeverij, 1983) 69.

dies, far more, in fact, than the Arabic Harmony. Baarda suggests, probably correctly, that the gospel text used by the creator of the Persian Harmony contained Diatessaronic readings. In this manner, the Persian Harmony, composed in a sequence independent of Tatian's *Diatessaron*, acquired numerous Diatessaronic readings.

The Syriac Versions (sy^s sy^c sy^p sy^pal)

The two manuscripts of the Old Syriac Gospels (Sinaiticus and Curetonianus) contain harmonizations and variant readings paralleled in the *Diatessaron*, as do the later Syriac versions, such as the Peshitta (sy^p)[1] and the Palestinian Syriac Lectionary (sy^pal).[2] Harmonizations distinctive of the *Diatessaron* show that it preceded and influenced the oldest separated Syriac gospels known to us. This fact has led some scholars to argue that the *Diatessaron* was the form in which the gospels first appeared in Syriac.

The Gospel Quotations of Aphrahat, Ephrem, Rabbula of Edessa, Isho^cdad of Merv, and the Liber Graduum

Given that a Syriac *Diatessaron* appears to antedate the oldest Syriac separated gospels, it is not surprising to find that virtually all of later Syriac literature is shot through with Diatessaronic readings. Among those works which have received scholarly scrutiny are the *Demonstrations* of Aphrahat (obit c. 367), one of the earliest Christian Syriac writers.[3] He frequently quotes the gospels in the form of the *Diatessaron*. Similarly, Ephrem Syrus (obit 373), who composed the *Commentary* on the *Diatessaron*, also cites the gospels in this form in his many hymns and sermons.[4] Coming from this same fourth-century period, the Syriac *Liber Graduum*, or "Book of Steps," fre-

---

[1] See the evidence in my *The Diatessaron and Ephrem Syrus as Sources of Romanos the Melodist* (CSCO 475; Leuven: Peeters 1985) 156–58.

[2] See my remarks ibid., as well as the study of Matthew Black, "The Palestinian Syriac Gospels and the Diatessaron," *OrChr* 36 [3d series 14] (1939) 101–11. The second part of Black's study never appeared.

[3] The presence of Diatessaronic readings was first noted by Theodor Zahn, in a review of George Phillips, *The Doctrine of Addai, the Apostle . . .*, in GGA 1877 (lacks vol. no.) 183–84. Aphrahat's citations from the Gospel of John have been studied by Tjitze Baarda, *The Gospel Quotations of Aphrahat, the Persian Sage,* vol. 1: *Aphraat's Text of the Fourth Gospel* (2 vols.; Meppel: Kripps, 1975).

[4] These are available in an excellent edition, which spans more than eighteen volumes in CSCO, edited by Edmund Beck. Ephrem's gospel text has been studied by Louis Leloir, *Le Évangile d'Éphrem d'après les oeuvres éditées. Recueil des textes* (CSCO 180; Louvain: Peeters, 1958). Earlier, F. C. Burkitt (*Ephraim's Quotations from the Gospel* [TaS 7,2; Cambridge, 1901]) embarked upon a similar task.

quently offers quotations from the *Diatessaron*.[1] In the 5th century, the famous bishop of Edessa, Rabbula, who in his *Canons* insists on the use of the "separated gospels" in his churches (a canon undoubtedly directed against the *Diatessaron*, the gospel "of the mixed"), nevertheless sometimes cites the gospel in a form which contains Diatessaronic readings.[2] It is unclear whether this is a result of his gradual transition from use of a *Diatessaron* to the separated gospels, or of a lapse of memory, or of the above-mentioned imprint which the *Diatessaron* left upon the later separated gospels. Later, the 9th-century Syrian writer Isho‘dad of Merv quotes from the *Diatessaron* in his commentaries on the Four Gospels, and identifies it as the source of these quotations.[3]

The Old Armenian and Old Georgian Versions of the Gospels

Stanislaus Lyonnet scrutinized the gospel citations of the oldest extant Armenian liturgical and Patristic writers, and found that they often offer Diatessaronic readings.[4] Since Armenian Christianity was introduced from Syria, this discovery is not surprising. A parallel situation exists in the case of the oldest Georgian gospel citations, which also betray Diatessaronic influence.[5] Since Georgian Christianity was imported from Armenia, the route by which these texts arrived in Georgia is manifest. In both of these ancient churches, it appears that the gospels first circulated in the form of a *Diatessaron*.

Manichaean Documents

We know that the Manichaeans used the *Diatessaron*, for its readings have been found in the *Kephalaia*, the *Homilies* and the *Psalms*,

---

[1] Cf. A. Rücker, "Die Zitate aus dem Matthäusevangelium im syrischen 'Buche der Stufen'," *BZ* 20 (1932) 342–54; see also the unpublished dissertation of Fiona J. Parsons, *The Nature of the Gospel Quotations in the Syriac Liber Graduum* (Birmingham, 1969).

[2] Cf. Arthur Vööbus, "Investigations into the Text of the New Testament used by Rabbula," *Contributions of the Baltic University (Pinneberg)* 59 (1947). See also idem, *Studies in the History of the Gospel Text in Syriac* (CSCO 128; Louvain: Peeters 1951) 179–86; and the study of Tjitze Baarda, "The Gospel Text in the Biography of Rabbula," *VigChr* 14 (1960) 102–27; also idem, *Early Transmission*, 11–36.

[3] Edition: Gibson, ed., *The Commentaries of Isho‘dad*.

[4] *Les origines de la version arménienne et le Diatessaron* (BibOr 13; Rome, 1950).

[5] Cf. Anton Baumstark, "Zum georgischen Evangelientext," *OrChr* 26 [3d series 4] (1929) 117–21. See also the more recent remarks of Joseph Molitor, "Das Neue Testament in georgischer Sprache. Der gegenwärtige Stand seiner Erforschung und seine Bedeutung für die Gewinnung des griechischen Urtextes," in Aland, ed., *Die alten Übersetzungen*, 314–44.

as well as in such miscellaneous Manichaean works as the Turfan Fragments.[1] That Mani, who was raised in a Judaic-Christian community in the 3d century, should have known the *Diatessaron* is not surprising, for Tatian's creation seems to have incorporated Judaic-Christian elements.[2]

Romanos the Melodist

This 6th-century Syrian-born hymnographer quotes the *Diatessaron* in his Greek hymns, composed in Constantinople in the court of Justinian I. His use of the *Diatessaron*[3] in his *Kontakia* is significant, for not only are these hymns considered masterpieces of world literature, but they were also sung in the Imperial Court.

Arabic and Karsuni Gospel Manuscripts

Curt Peters logged thirteen Arabic and two Karsuni (a type of script used by Nestorian and Jacobite Christians when writing Arabic) gospel manuscripts which contain Diatessaronic readings.[4] Since they rest upon a Syriac *Vorlage,* the presence of Tatianisms is only to be expected.

The Dura Fragment

One of the earliest Christian parchments known to us is the so-called Dura Fragment, discovered at Dura-Europos in Syria in 1933. The *terminus ad quem* is set by the destruction of the town in the winter of 256–257 CE. The fragment (New Haven: Yale University,

---

[1] On the Manichaean Diatessaronic readings, see: Anton Baumstark, "Ein 'Evangelium'-Zitat der Manichäischen Kephalaia," *OrChr* 34 [3rd series 12] (1938) 169–91; idem, review of H. J. Polotsky, *Manichäische Homilien (Manichäische Handschriften der Sammlung A. Chester Beatty. Band I)*, in *OrChr* 32 [3rd series 10] (1935) 257–68; Gilles Quispel, *Tatian and the Gospel of Thomas* (Leiden: Brill, 1975) 68; idem, "St. Augustin et l'Évangile selon Thomas," in *Mélanges d'histoire des religions offerts à Henri-Charles Puech* (Paris: Presses universitaires de France, 1974) 379–92; William L. Petersen, "An Important Unnoticed Diatessaronic Reading in Turfan Fragment M-18," in Tjitze Baarda, A. Hilhorst, G. P. Luttikhuizen, and A. S. van der Woude, eds., *Text and Testimony: Festschrift A. F. J. Klijn* (Kampen: Kok, 1988) 187–92.

[2] The Jewish-Christian *Gospel of the Hebrews* is the prime candidate for the extra-canonical source employed by Tatian alongside the four canonical gospels.

[3] See my *The Diatessaron and Ephrem Syrus.*

[4] Curt Peters, *Das Diatessaron Tatians* (OrChrA 123; Roma: Pontificium institutum orientalium studiorum, 1939), 48–62; see also Anton Baumstark, "Das Problem eines vorislamischen christlich-kirchlichen Schrifttums in arabischer Sprache," *Islamica* 5 (1931) 562–75; idem, "Arabische Übersetzung eines altsyrischen Evangelientextes," in *OrChr* 31 [3rd series 9] (1934) 165–88.

Dura Parchment 24) contains fourteen legible lines of Greek text, from the passion narrative.[1] The text is harmonized. At first considered decisive evidence for a Greek original of the *Diatessaron*,[2] later studies were more cautious, and found signs of translation from Syriac.[3] Daniël Plooij also noted the existence of harmonized Syriac passion narrative collections, independent of the *Diatessaron*, and suggested that the fragment, whose sequence has some agreement with the *Diatessaron* but also some differences, might be from one of these unrelated passion narrative collections.[4] At present, our best evidence seems to indicate that the fragment is from a *Diatessaron* and translated from Syriac. It establishes an extremely early date for circulation of a Greek *Diatessaron*. Ironically enough, we have no other evidence of a Greek *Diatessaron* save this fragment, found deep in Syria.

5.3.4.2 Western Witnesses

Codex Fuldensis and the Latin Harmonies

Copied in 546 CE at the request of bishop Victor of Capua, this Latin codex (Fulda: Landesbib., Bonif. 1) is a harmonized life of Jesus, composed from the gospels.[5] Although its text is a very pure Vulgate, its sequence is distinctly Diatessaronic. That the document was Vulgatized at some point in its transmission is a demonstrable fact, for while the *text* of Fuldensis is Vulgate, the readings in the *capitularia* (the "table of contents," as it were) have *not* been revised accordingly; they preserve the original Diatessaronic readings.[6] This is irrefutable evi-

---

[1] Edition: Carl H. Kraeling, *A Greek Fragment of Tatian's Diatessaron from Dura* (StD 3; London: Christophers, 1935). A corrected edition is found in Charles B. Welles, et al., eds., *The Parchments and Papyri: The Excavations at Dura-Europos . . . , Final Report*, vol. 5, pt. 1 (New Haven: Yale University Press, 1959) 73–74.

[2] So the fragment's editor, Carl H. Kraeling, also F. C. Burkitt, "The Dura Fragment of Tatian," *JTS* 36 (1935) 255–59, who, while arguing for Latin, saw the Fragment as precluding a Syriac original.

[3] So Daniël Plooij, "A Fragment of Tatian's *Diatessaron* in Greek," *ET* 46 (1934–35) 471–76; and Anton Baumstark, "Das griechische 'Diatessaron'-Fragment von Dura-Europos," *OrChr* 32 [3rd series 10] (1935) 244–52.

[4] Plooij, ibid., 476.

[5] Edition: *Codex Fuldensis*, ed. Ernst Ranke (Marburgi/Lipsiae: Elwert, 1868).

[6] This phenomenon was first noted by Johann Christian Zahn, "Ist Ammon oder Tatian Verfasser der ins Lateinische, Altfränkische und Arabische übersetzten Evangelien-Harmonie? und was hat Tatian bei seinem bekannten Diatessaron oder Diapente vor sich gehabt und zum Grunde gelegt?" in C. A. G. Keil and H. G. Tzschirner, *Analekten für das Studium der exegetischen und systematischen Theologie*, vol. 2, pt. 1 (Leipzig, 1814) 183–88. It was later investigated in more detail by Theodor Zahn, *Tatian's Diatessaron* (FGNK 1; Erlangen: Deichert, 1881) 300–3; and Heinrich

dence that at some earlier date there existed in the West an unvulgatized (or "Old Latin," in the sense of the Vetus Latina, i.e., pre-Vulgate) Latin *Diatessaron*. While obviously impoverished as a source of Diatessaronic readings, Codex Fuldensis has the same sequence of harmonization as the Arabic Harmony, and as Ephrem's *Commentary*. Hence, it is an important witness for fixing the order of the *Diatessaron*'s text. It is also our oldest Western Diatessaronic witness.

In addition to Codex Fuldensis, no fewer than seventeen other Latin gospel harmonies, all related to the Diatessaronic tradition, have been noted by scholars. Only two have been edited: Codex Sangallensis (a Latin-Old High German bilingual: Stiftsbib. no. 56; dated ca. 830),[1] and Codex Cassellanus (Landesbib., Ms. theol. fol. 31; 9th century).[2] Some of these manuscripts descend from Codex Fuldensis and its Vulgatized Latin text. Others, however, have escaped much of the Vulgatization to which Fuldensis was subjected, and preserve many more Diatessaronic readings and sequential harmonizations. The fact that Codex Cassellanus, for example, interpolates the Diatessaronic reading *occurrit, ut tangeret eum* between John 20:16 and 17, a reading which is absent from Fuldensis, confirms the conclusion drawn on the basis of the disagreement between the *capitularia* and the text of Codex Fuldensis: at one time there existed an unvulgatized, "Old Latin" *Diatessaron*. This Old Latin *Diatessaron*, now lost, has not vanished without a trace, for its textual imprint is still to be found in many of these other Latin gospel harmonies.

The Old High German Harmonies

The oldest Old High German harmony is a bilingual manuscript, Codex Sangallensis (Stiftsbib. no. 56; dated ca. 830).[3] Each side of each folio contains two columns, with Latin on the left, and the Old High German (in the East Frankish dialect) on the right. The Latin is pure Vulgate, agreeing almost perfectly with Codex Fuldensis. Quite

---

Joseph Vogels, *Beiträge zur Geschichte des Diatessaron im Abendland* (NTA 8/1; Münster: Aschendorff, 1919).

[1] Edition: Eduard Sievers, *Tatian, lateinisch und altdeutsch* (Bibliothek der ältesten deutschen Literatur-Denkmäler 5; 2d ed.; Paderborn: Schöningh, 1892); studies: Anton Baumstark, *Die Vorlage des althochdeutschen Tatian, herausgegeben von Johannes Rathofer* (Niederdeutsche Studien 12; Köln: Böhlau, 1964); Gilles Quispel, *Tatian and the Gospel of Thomas: Studies in the History of the Western Diatessaron* (Leiden: Brill 1975).

[2] Edited and studied by: C. W. M. Grein, *Die Quellen des Heliand. Nebst einem Anhang: Tatians Evangelienharmonie herausgegeben nach dem Codex Cassellanus* (Cassel: Kay, 1869).

[3] Edition: Eduard Sievers, *Tatian, lateinisch und altdeutsch* (Bibliothek der ältesten deutschen Literatur-Denkmäler 5; 2d ed.; Paderborn: Schöningh, 1892).

naturally, scholars assumed that the Old High German column had been translated from its neighboring Latin column; and since the Latin was without significant variant readings, what variants there were in the Old High German column must be "geringfügig und fast bedeutungslos."[1] But in 1872 the Germanist O. Schade noticed agreements between the Old High German column and Vetus Latina (not Vulgate!) manuscripts—agreements which were lacking in the neighboring Latin column of Sangallensis.[2] The meaning of these agreements was clear: the Old High German column was *not* slavishly dependent upon its Vulgate neighbor, but had its own, independent textual tradition. Later investigations confirmed Schade's observation: Codex Sangallensis' Old High German column has suffered less Vulgatization than its Latin column.[3]

Today, in addition to Codex Sangallensis, two other manuscripts offer readings from the Old High German Tatian: Oxford, Bodleian, Junius 13 (17th century, but a copy of an older, now lost manuscript),[4] and Paris, Bib. Nat., Ms. lat. 7641 (10th century).[5] Reports survive of three other Old High German Tatian manuscripts, but all of them have been lost.

The Vetus Latina, Novatian, and the Roman Antiphonary[6]

The Vetus Latina group of manuscripts, which preserve a pre-Vulgate text, contains variants which find parallels in the *Diatessaron*. Since these reflect the oldest known separated gospel text in Latin, and since they too have been influenced by the *Diatessaron*, scholars conclude that the situation is analogous to the one in Syria, where the Vetus Syra manuscripts showed Diatessaronic influence. Therefore,

---

[1] So Sievers, ibid., p. xviii.

[2] Oskar Schade, *Altdeutsches Wörterbuch*, vol. 1 (Halle: Buchhandlung des Waisenhauses, 1872) pp. xviii–xix.

[3] See the extensive examples offered by Anton Baumstark, *Die Vorlage des althochdeutschen Tatian, herausgegeben von Johannes Rathofer* (Niederdeutsche Studien 12; Köln: Böhlau, 1964), and by Rathofer, "MS Junius 13 und die verschollene Tatian HS-B," *Beiträge zur Geschichte der deutschen Sprache und Literatur* (Ausgabe Tübingen) 95 (1973) 13–125. More recently, however, Rathofer has assumed a more skeptical position: "Die Einwirkung des Fuldischen Evangelientextes auf den althochdeutschen 'Tatian.' Abkehr von der Methode der Diatessaronforschung," in A. Oennerfors, *et al.*, eds., *Literatur und Sprache im europäischen Mittelalter: Festschrift Karl Langosch* (Darmstadt, 1973) 256–308.

[4] See P. Ganz, "Ms. Junius 13 und die althochdeutsche Tatianübersetzung," *Beiträge zur Geschichte der deutschen Sprache und Literatur* 91 (1969) 28–76.

[5] See D. Haacke, "Evangelienharmonie," in W. Kohlschmidt and W. Mohr, eds., *Reallexikon der Deutschen Literaturgeschichte* (2d ed.; Berlin: De Gruyter, 1958) 1. 410–413.

[6] See the references above p. 406 nn. 3–5.

in Latin, just as in Syriac, the *Diatessaron* must have seen circulation before the separated gospels were translated into the vernacular.

Parallel investigation into the text of the oldest Roman Father whose Latin writings are preserved, Novatian, and into the oldest Roman *Antiphonary,* show that the gospel citations of both reflect the readings of the *Diatessaron.* This led scholars to the conclusion that the gospels first saw circulation in Latin in the form of a Latin *Diatessaron.*

The Liège Harmony and its Middle Dutch and Middle High German Allies

The most important Western source of Diatessaronic readings is the Liège Harmony. Now in the Universiteitsbibliotheek in Liège (Manuscript no. 437), the work is composed in Limburgs (a dialect of Middle Dutch) and dates from about 1280 CE. First edited in 1835,[1] its connection with the Diatessaronic tradition was made public by J. A. Robinson in 1894.[2] The scholarly edition of Daniël Plooij set new standards for presenting the text of a Diatessaronic witness.[3] His edition contains an apparatus full of parallels from other Diatessaronic witnesses, and is an indispensable research tool. In the manuscript's Preface the Dutch scribe says he composed the harmony himself, working from Latin gospel texts; but the Liège Harmony's sequence is Diatessaronic, and its text is full of Vetus Latina and Diatessaronic readings—hardly the result if a 13th-century scribe were working from the by-then-standard Vulgate and creating a harmony *de novo.* Rather, in the Liège Harmony we possess a copy—albeit, several times removed and in Dutch—of the unvulgatized Latin *Diatessaron* which lies behind Codex Fuldensis. Consequently, the manuscript is a gold mine of Diatessaronic readings, some of which find their only parallel in Ephrem's *Commentary* or the Old Syriac Gospels. Together with a few Syriasms in the Dutch text, this fact led Plooij to conclude that the lost, unvulgatized Latin ancestor of the Liège Harmony had been translated directly from Syriac into Latin, without a Greek intermediary.[4] The presence of these Syriasms in a Western Harmony, and the manuscript's sometimes singular parallels with the Vetus Syra and

---

[1] G. J. Meijer, *Het Leven van Jezus, een Nederlandsch handschrift uit de dertiende eeuw* (Groningen: Oomkens, 1835).

[2] "Tatian's *Diatessaron* and a Dutch Harmony," *The Academy* 45 (1894) 249–50.

[3] Daniël Plooij, C. A. Phillips and A. H. A. Bakker, eds., *The Liège Diatessaron,* Parts 1–8 (VNAW 19/21; Amsterdam, 1929–1970).

[4] Cf. Plooij's two studies: *A Primitive Text of the Diatessaron* (Leiden: Sijthoff, 1923), and idem, *A Further Study of the Liège Diatessaron* (Leiden: Brill, 1925).

Ephrem support the conclusion that the original language of the *Diatessaron* was indeed Syriac and not Greek.

The Liège Harmony (or a similar manuscript) was the archetype for a series of harmonies in Middle Dutch. No fewer than seven manuscripts exist, the most famous of which are the Stuttgart Harmony (Landesbib., 140, 8°; dated 1332),[1] the Hague Harmony (Koninklijk Bib., M 421; dated 1473),[2] the Cambridge Harmony (Univ. Library, Dd. 12.25; dated to the 13th or 14th century),[3] and the Haaren Harmony (Groot-Seminarie; dated c. 1400).[4] Additionally, there are at least ten manuscripts or fragments of harmonies in Middle High German, which derive from the same Middle Dutch tradition transmitted in the Liège Harmony. Only one of the complete manuscripts has been edited, the Zürich Harmony (Zentralbib. G 170 App. 56; dated to the 13th or 14th century).[5] Generally speaking, these Middle High German harmonies, along with the Middle Dutch harmonies, are all secondary witnesses to the type of a text best preserved in the Liège Harmony, although there appear to be exceptions.[6]

The Medieval Italian Harmonies

Two recensions of the *Diatessaron* survive in Medieval Italian. The one, the Venetian recension, so-named because of its dialect, survives in a lone manuscript (Venice: Marciano, no. 4975; 13th or 14th century). The other recension, the Tuscan, survives in twenty-six manuscripts, dating from the 14th and 15th century.[7] Both recensions come from a Latin *Diatessaron* other than Codex Fuldensis, for the

---

[1] Edition: *De Levens van Jezus in het Middelnederlandsch*, ed. J. Bergsma (De Bibliotheek van Mittelnederlandsche Letterkunde 54, 55, 61; Groningen: Wolters, 1895–98).

[2] The variant readings of the Hague (or Haagse) Harmony, as this MS is known, are found in the apparatus of J. Bergsma's edition of the Stuttgart Harmony (see previous note). Since the Hague Harmony is closely related to the Stuttgart Harmony, reconstructing the text of the former is an easy task.

[3] Edition: *Het Diatessaron van Cambridge*, ed. C. C. de Bruin (CSSN series minor, tome 1, vol. 3; Leiden: Brill, 1970).

[4] Edition: *Het Haarense Diatessaron*, ed. C. C. de Bruin (CSSN series minor, tome 1, vol. 2; Leiden: Brill, 1970).

[5] *Das Leben Jhesu*, ed. Christoph Gerhardt (CSSN series minor, tome 1, vol. 4; Leiden: Brill, 1970).

[6] For example, Anton Baumstark felt that two of the collections of fragments which have seen editions, the so-called "Himmelgarten" and "Schönbach" Fragments, reflected two different, older, less-Vulgatized Diatessaronic traditions than the rest of the Middle High German tradition: see Anton Baumstark, "Die Himmelgarten Bruchstücke eines niederdeutschen 'Diatessaron'-Textes des 13. Jahrhunderts," *OrChr* 33 [3rd series 11] (1936) 80–96; idem, "Die Schönbach'schen Bruchstücke einer Evangelienharmonie in bayrisch-österreichischer Mundart des 14. Jahrhunderts," *OrChr* 34 [3rd series 12] (1937) 103–26.

[7] Both are printed in the same volume: V. Todesco, A. Vaccari, and M. Vattasso, eds.,

development. And, indeed, the *Diatessaron* is thought either to have influenced the Western Text, or to have been created from gospels which were full of Western readings; but it is still unclear which scenario is correct.[1] Therefore, scholarship today sifts the individual Diatessaronic witnesses, searching for agreements among them, which, after screening for extraneous influences, may justly be called "Diatessaronic." One point of Vogels' rule, however, remains: by a quirk of logic, we can only be sure we have recovered the text of the *Diatessaron* in readings which *differ* from the standard canonical text. Since large portions of the Diatessaron's text agree with the current canonical text, there is no way to tell whether readings in Diatessaronic witnesses which *now* agree with the canonical text are the result of Vulgatization or part of the harmony's original text. Only in those passages where the harmony's text *diverges* from the canonical text, can a judgement be made. Consequently, all modern Diatessaronic research is a search for deviations from the canonical text.

Three rules aid in this search.[2] First, to be considered genuinely Diatessaronic, a reading should be found in both Eastern *and* Western witnesses. The rationale is that while a "local" reading might have found its way into, say, the Vetus Syra and Ephrem, in the East, this same "local" reading could not have found its way into a Western witness, like the Liège Harmony, save via the medium of the *Diatessaron*. Second, the reading should be absent from all non-Diatessaronic sources whence our Diatessaronic witnesses might have acquired it. For example, if a reading found in the Liège Harmony also occurs in the Vulgate, then one must search for other Diatessaronic support, for the Liège reading may have come from no more exotic a source than the Vulgate. Similarly, even if a reading is widespread in Diatessaronic sources, both East and West, but is also found in numerous Patristic sources not connected with the *Diatessaron*, then caution must be exercised, for these Patristic sources create "interference," and prevent one from drawing a direct line from the prospective

---

[1] The fundamental studies are by Frederick Henry Chase, *The Old Syriac Element in the Text of Codex Bezae* (London: Macmillan, 1893); idem, *The Syro-Latin Text of the Gospels* (London: Macmillan, 1895). The dissertation of A. F. J. Klijn, *A Survey of the Researches into the Western Text of the Gospels and Acts*, vol. 1 (Utrecht 1949), offers an excellent survey of researches since Chase and discussion of the problems involved. See also the more recent study of Walter Henss, *Das Verhältnis zwischen Diatessaron, christlicher Gnosis und "Western Text"* (BZNW 33; Berlin: De Gruyter, 1967).

[2] These were originally put forward in my article, "Romanos and the Diatessaron: Readings and Method," *NTS* 29 (1983) 484–507. A fuller discussion is found in my *The Diatessaron and Ephrem Syrus*, 55–57. This study also contains numerous readings derived using the three rules.

witnesses back to Tatian's harmony. Third, the genre of all of the sources with the reading should be that of a gospel harmony, or, if different, the source should have come under the influence of the harmonized "Life of Jesus" genre. For example, the Liège Harmony and *The Heliand* are both harmonized lives of Jesus; they are clearly within the circle of harmonized texts. The Vetus Latina, Peshitta and the hymns of Romanos are not gospel harmonies. Yet, each has, in its history, been exposed to or been influenced by the harmonized "Life of Jesus" tradition. In the case of the Vetus Latina and the Peshitta, this contact appears to have been indirect, since the earliest gospel in these languages was almost certainly a *Diatessaron*; hence, Diatessaronic readings were in the eye, ear, and textual tradition of these languages when the separated gospels were translated. In the case of the hymns of Romanos, the influence appears to have been direct, for Romanos was, in fact, retelling Jesus' life in a harmonized form, drawing from all of the gospels and extra-canonical material. The fact that his gospel citations often agree with those of the *Diatessaron* means that he must have been using the *Diatessaron* directly, as one of his literary sources.

Before considering some examples, the caveats must also be given. First, since we are dealing with texts which span more than a millennium, and whose languages are exceptionally diverse, we must be alert for apparent agreements which are nothing more than the result of the grammatical requirements or syntactic conventions of a language. For example, at Luke 7:42, five Western witnesses give a variant to the standard Greek text. While the Greek reads "Which of *them* will love him more?" the Liège Harmony (and its related allies, the Stuttgart, Hague and Zürich Harmonies) and the Venetian Harmony read, "Which of *these two* will love him more?" The identical variant occurs in the Arabic and Persian Harmonies. Although the variant appears Diatessaronic, it must be discounted, for the Eastern witnesses are suspect. The reason: although the Western languages do not have the dual, it is standard in such a construction in Arabic and Persian. Second, one must be alert to ambiguous translations in the many vernacular languages. For example, at John 20:17, Ephrem, Aphrahat, Romanos and the Venetian Harmony all have Jesus' words as "I *go* to my Father and your Father," against the canonical "I *ascend* to my Father and your Father." The reading of the Liège Harmony, "Ik *vare* te minen vader . . ." is ambiguous, for in Middle Dutch, *vare* may mean either "to fly" or "to go." The evidence of Liège is, therefore, a *non liquet,* despite the fact that it might well be in agreement with

other Diatessaronic witnesses give the standard canonical reading is easily explicable: they have all been Vulgatized, that is, the deviant Diatessaronic reading—so obvious in this case—was removed and was replaced with the canonical reading.

5.3.5.4 Reading 3

Sometimes we stumble across readings which are arguably earlier than the present canonical text. One is in Matt 8:4 (and parallels), where the canonical text runs: "Go, show yourself to the priest and offer the gift *which Moses commanded,* in a testimony to them." No fewer than six Diatessaronic witnesses, four in the East (both recensions of Ephrem's *Commentary,* Isho°dad's *Commentary,* Romanos), and two in the West (the Liège and the Venetian Harmonies), give the following (with minor variants): "Go, show yourself to the priest(s) and fulfill the Law."[1] With Eastern and Western support, and no other known sources from which these Diatessaronic witnesses might have acquired the reading, we must conclude that it is the reading of Tatian. And in it, Jesus required that someone "fulfill the Law."

In the early church, the *Diatessaron* seems to have seen currency not in Gentile-Christian circles, but in Judaic-Christian communities. The reading of the *Diatessaron* is certainly more congenial to Judaic Christianity than to the group which later came to dominate the church, and which edited its canonical texts: Gentile Christians. We must hold open the possibility that the present canonical reading might be a later revision of an earlier, stricter, more explicit and more Judaic-Christian text, here preserved only in the *Diatessaron.*

5.3.5.5 Reading 4

A similar circumstance may be at work in the *Diatessaron* at Matt 27:52–53, where, the canonical text reads: "(52) And the graves were opened, and many bodies of the saints who had fallen asleep were raised. (53) And coming out of the tombs after his resurrection, they entered into the holy city and appeared to many." In the next verse, 54, the centurion offers his confession upon seeing the wonders sur-

---

[1] The evidence is: (1) Ephrem (Syriac): Leloir, ed., *Saint Éphrem,* 98; (2) Ephrem (Armenian): *Commentaire,* ed. Louis Leloir (CSCO 145; Louvain: Peeters, 1954), 126; (3) Isho°dad: *Commentary,* ed. Gibson, 2. 70; (4) Romanos: *Romanos le Mélode. Hymnes II,* ed. J. Grosdidier de Matons (SC 110; Paris: Editions du Cerf, 1965) 376; (5) Liège: *The Liège Diatessaron,* eds. Daniël Plooij, C. A. Phillips and A. Bakker, parts 1–8 (VNAW 19/21; Amsterdam 1929–70) 104; (6) Venetian: *Il Diatessaron Veneto,* ed. V. Todesco, pt. 1 of *Il Diatessaron in Volgare Italiano,* StT 81 (Città del Vaticano 1938) 50.

rounding Jesus' death: "When the centurion and those who were with him, keeping watch over Jesus saw the earthquake and what took place, they were filled with awe, and said, 'Truly, this was the Son of God!'"

Source-critically, vss. 52 and 53 are from some special source of Matthew; they are missing from the other Synoptic Gospels. When we turn to the Diatessaronic witnesses, we discover an interesting fact: three of our Eastern sources (Ephrem, in his *Commentary* and in no fewer than three of his hymns, Ishoᶜdad, in his *Commentary,* and Romanos in two of his hymns), and three Western sources (twice in the Pepysian Harmony, the Venetian Harmony and *The Heliand*) speak only of "the dead" coming out of their tombs. The greater detail of the canonical account—all of which is theologically loaded: "bodies" (more specific and agreeing with Paul at 1 Cor 15:35–44), "of saints" (certainly superior to the mere "dead" of the *Diatessaron,* and therefore more developed, and also Pauline), "who had fallen asleep" (again a more elegant description, and again used by Paul in 1 Cor 15:20 and 1 Thess 4:14)—suggests that the *Diatessaron's* reading is earlier.

Supporting this conclusion is another apparent Diatessaronic reading in the same passage. It is an omission, and therefore one must be careful in arguing from it, for the argument is *e silentio.* But in this case, the omission is an active omission, that is, it changes the meaning of the text. Therefore, it elicits greater credence than a passive omission, that is, one which does not alter the meaning of the text. In numerous Diatessaronic witnesses, both East (Ephrem, twice in his *Commentary,* and in three of his hymns; twice in the *Commentary* of Ishoᶜdad; and twice in the hymns of Romanos) and West (twice in the Pepysian Harmony; *The Heliand*), the resurrection *and appearance* of the risen "dead" occur *simultaneously* with Jesus' death on the cross. In other words, the *Diatessaron* omitted the canonical "after his resurrection," which—most bizarrely—delays the appearance of those resurrected *for three days!* Rather, according to the *Diatessaron,* the "dead" were raised *and revealed there and then* as one more sign of the gravity of Jesus' death. The reading of the Pepysian Harmony gives some idea of the scene, according to Tatian:

> And with that, the veil that hung in the temple before the high alter burst in two pieces, the earth quaked, and the stones burst, and the dead men arose out of their graves. And so said the centurion . . .[1]

---

[1] The evidence for this reading is too complex to give here; it is presented in my *The Diatessaron and Ephrem Syrus,* 95–112. The citation from the Pepysian Harmony is from Goates' edition, 100.

(Readings 1 and 5) that Tatian drew upon the harmonized gospel traditions used by his teacher, Justin.[1] Justin's harmony did not incorporate John; the *Diatessaron* does. This means that Tatian could not have simply "annotated" Justin's harmony; at the minimum, he had to do a rather thorough revision. Second, as seen in Reading 1, the *Diatessaron* has agreements with extra-canonical sources, most notably with the Jewish-Christian gospel tradition.[2] This suggests that Tatian used not just the four canonical Gospels, but at least one extra-canonical source. Third, Tatian appears to have used a redaction of the canonical Gospels which was very old—sometimes, perhaps, revealing a textual tradition that was *more* ancient than our present canonical text (Reading 3 and 4)—and which had a Jewish-Christian flavor. Into this mix, Tatian seems to have introduced his own distinctive Encratite views. The result was the *Diatessaron*.

There are readings in the *Diatessaron* which find parallel in the *Gospel of Thomas,* and the Diatessaron has an exceptional number of Western Text readings.[3] How this puzzle is to be resolved remains a mystery. It is the best working hypothesis to assume dependence by *Thomas* and the *Diatessaron* on a common tradition, which was "Western."

5.3.7 ORIGINAL LANGUAGE, DATE, AND PROVENANCE

Although Latin, Greek, and Syriac have been suggested as the language in which Tatian composed his harmony, experts today conclude that the deed was done in Syriac.[4] Only in this manner can one account for the Syriasms and Semitisms present in the Western witnesses. The hypothesis that the *Diatessaron* was composed in Greek or Latin, based on the Greek Gospels, makes it impossible to

---

[1] See my article, "Textual Evidence of Tatian's Dependence Upon Justin's ΑΠΟΜΝΗ-ΜΟΝΕΥΜΑΤΑ," *NTS* 36 (1990) 512–34. See also above # 5.2.

[2] On this see especially C. A. Phillips, "Diatessaron—Diapente," *BBC* 9 (February 1931) 6–8; J. H. Charlesworth, "Tatian's Dependence upon Apocryphal Traditions," *HeyJ* 15 (1974) 5–17; and my *The Diatessaron and Ephrem Syrus,* 47–51.

[3] See Gilles Quispel, "L'Évangile selon Thomas et le Diatessaron," *VigChr* 13 (1959) 87–117; idem, "L'Évangile selon Thomas et le 'Texte Occidental' du nouveau Testament," *VigChr* 14 (1960) 204– 215; idem, *Tatian and the Gospel of Thomas: Studies in the History of the Western Diatessaron* (Leiden: Brill, 1975). See also the references above # 5.3.5.1.

[4] For a review of the arguments and the evidence for Syriac, see my "New Evidence for the Question of the Original Language of the Diatessaron," in: Wolfgang Schrage, ed., *Studien zum Text und zur Ethik des Neuen Testaments zum 80. Geburtstag Heinrich Greeven* (BZNW 47; Berlin: De Gruyter, 1986) 325–43.

account for the parataxis (where subordination is found in the Gospels) and variants which are paralleled only in the Old Syriac.

The date of the *Diatessaron's* composition can be fixed to between 163 (the earliest date of Justin's death) and the time of Tatian's own death (probably about 185). If Eusebius's report that Tatian was expelled from the Roman church in 172 is correct, and if, as is often surmised, the *Diatessaron* was composed after this date, then the range is narrowed to the time from 172 to ca. 185.

The matter of provenance is more difficult to determine, since there was a significant Syriac-speaking community in Rome about this time.[1] Therefore, although one might think that having determined the original language as Syriac would mean composition in the East, it is also possible that Tatian composed his harmony in Rome in Syriac. The early influence of the *Diatessaron* on the Latin gospel tradition, on Novatian, and on the Roman Antiphonary is more difficult to account for if composition is placed in the East. F. C. Burkitt, who suggested that Latin was the original language, opined that Tatian created his harmony in Rome, and then produced a second, revised edition once back in the East.[2] Burkitt's suggestion of Latin is unanimously rejected today, but the possibility of two *Diatessarons*, one Roman in origin, and one Syrian in origin, would go some way towards accounting for the early presence of Diatessaronic influence in both the East and the West, and also for some significant differences between the Eastern and Western witnesses in their sequence of harmonization. The matter remains *sub judice*, but composition in the East is difficult to reconcile with the empirical evidence of Diatessaronic readings in Rome in the second and third century.

A complicating factor in all this is the harmony of Justin, about which we know so little.[3] If it, and not Tatian's creation, accounted for what we "mistakenly" take for Diatessaronic influence in the early Latin texts, then a major obstacle to Eastern provenance is removed. Then the *Diatessaron* would almost certainly have been composed in the East. However, our meager knowledge of the influence of Justin's harmony makes this suggestion only informed speculation. Until further evidence can be assembled, Rome appears the most likely place of composition.

---

[1] The *Liber pontificalis* (ed. L. Duchesne [Paris 1886] 1. 134) states that Anicet, bishop of Rome from 154 to 165, was a Syrian; cf. the remarks of Arthur Vööbus, *Early Versions of the New Testament* (PETSE 6; Stockholm 1954) 4 and 6.

[2] F. C. Burkitt, "Tatian's Diatessaron and the Dutch Harmonies," *JTS* 25 (1924), 128–130.

[3] But see the discussion of Justin's harmony above # 5.2.